More praise for *Th*

"Exhaustively researched, infused with issues of a nation and the small quirk *Full Measure* is fiction that brings histo

"*The Last Full Measure* primarily follows three men—Lee, Ulysses S. Grant and Joshua Lawrence Chamberlain, a Union hero at Gettysburg—through the last two years of war. Shaara picked them because 'each, in his way, rose to a higher level, not just as a war hero, but as a man of character and dignity and honor.' Shaara's work similarly rises. His achievement in *The Last Full Measure* is showing us through these three characters how a nation was forever changed."

—*Detroit Free Press*

"After reading *The Last Full Measure*, I know Michael Shaara is smiling in Heaven."

—Gabor Borritt
Director, the Civil War Institute
Gettysburg, PA

"Jeff Shaara's prose is clear and even vivid . . . executed robustly, with [an] expert command of detail and compassionate eye for emotion and disillusionment. . . . He is at his best in showing the near unraveling of Lee's religiosity, a stubborn faith that God was on his side, contrasting it with the flinty doggedness of Grant, who trusted in his cigars and his unbroken lines of supply more than he did a Supreme Being."

—*Chicago Sun-Times*

"Ideally, the Homeric Civil War Epic that Americans have longed for depicts both sides even-handedly and compassionately, encompasses major battles led by major leaders, and appeals to all readers, North and South, young and old, men and women—the trilogy begun by the father and finished by the son is that epic, and Jeff Shaara's *The Last Full Measure* brings the monumental trilogy to a triumphant conclusion. The Shaara vision of its origins in blood and courage illuminates America's future on the threshold of the new millennium."

—David Madden
Director, The United States Civil War Center

"*The Last Full Measure* brings a unique and monumental father-son trilogy to a triumphant conclusion. . . . Shaara sustains a major achievement that distinguishes this trilogy from most other Civil War novels: He gives a balanced experience of the temperament, sensibility, and character of generals on both sides of the battle lines. Shaara also proves once and for all that, though influenced by his father, he has a voice and talent all his own."

—*BookPage*

Please turn the page for more reviews. . . .

"A STIRRING EPIGRAPH TO HIS FATHER'S REMARKABLE NOVEL."
—Publishers Weekly

"Shaara captures the humanity of the men involved and the raw power and sorrow of hand-to-hand combat."

—Memphis Commercial Appeal

"This volume marks the first time Ulysses S. Grant has appeared as a character, and among the book's achievements is Shaara's compelling, persuasive, and sympathetic portrait of this unusual and somewhat enigmatic general whose reputation has, for some reason, never quite matched his accomplishments."

—American Way

"Shaara is at his best and the novel at its strongest in the vivid descriptions of the horrific battles that took place as Grant and Lee struggled for superiority in the field. Attention to detail and superb research make these passages poignant and memorable and bring new respect to the men who fought for both sides."

—The Chattanooga Times

"If you enjoyed *Gods and Generals*, Jeff Shaara's first novel about the Civil War, you'll like *The Last Full Measure* even more. . . . *The Last Full Measure* belongs on the bookshelf of anyone with an interest in the Civil War. Unlike history texts, it injects life into the war and the men who fought it."

—Lancaster Intelligencer Journal

"Writing good historical fiction is a delicate balancing act. The author must stay true enough to actual events to satisfy those who really know their history, yet also serve those who hunger for a compelling story. Jeff Shaara does both in his new novel, *The Last Full Measure*. . . . A superb, exciting, thought-provoking book. . . . Rich in detail and stunning in emotional impact."

—Stewart News (Florida)

"[A] monumental novel of the closing battles of the Civil War . . . If your idea of a grand vacation from the real world is sharing epic adventures with noble companions, dashing through heroic action, braving danger, brooking tragedy—and all without breaking a sweat—few books are better suited to head your summer reading list than *The Last Full Measure*. . . . This novel is a paean to the virtues of honor and decency, an old-fashioned, gratifying and sublime vision of history."

—America West

THE LAST FULL MEASURE

JEFF SHAARA

BALLANTINE BOOKS
NEW YORK

A Ballantine Book
Published by The Random House Ballantine Publishing Group

Published in the United States by The Random House Ballantine Publishing Group, a division of Random House, Inc., New York, and simultaneously in Canada by Random House of Canada Limited, Toronto.

www.ballantinebooks.com

Library of Congress Catalog Card Number: 99-90092

ISBN: 0-345-42548-0

Manufactured in the United States of America

First Hardcover Edition: June 1998
First Trade Paperback Edition: May 1999

10

To my friend Ron Maxwell,
who has taught me to never lose sight of the dream

TO THE READER

THIS STORY IS THE THIRD PART OF A TRILOGY, FOLLOWING THE lives of key characters of the Civil War, from the aftermath of the Battle of Gettysburg, through the surrender at Appomattox, and beyond. While the cast of characters of that momentous event was huge, this story follows primarily three men: Robert E. Lee, Joshua Lawrence Chamberlain, and Ulysses S. Grant.

This is neither a history book nor a biography, but a story told from the points of view of the characters themselves, through their own eyes and their own experiences. In many ways these are ordinary people caught up in extraordinary times. These particular characters stand apart because each, in his own way, rose to a higher level, not just as a war hero, but as a man of character and dignity and honor. To some these characteristics are quaint and out of date. To many others they are qualities that our modern world is sorely missing.

In some ways this is a very different story from the first two parts of the trilogy. After Gettysburg there is a change in the way men see the war, and in the way they fight it. There is little enthusiasm now for the traditional assault, sending dense lines of men across open ground into the massed guns of a heavily fortified enemy. Gettysburg has badly wounded both sides, and though it is clearly a defeat for Lee's army, neither side is quick to pursue another fight on such a huge scale. In the West—Tennessee and Mississippi—the war still rages, but in Virginia there is now a lull, a time for both armies to heal their wounds and plan the next great strategy to bring the awful war to an end. What no one can know is that Gettysburg is not the final battle, and that for nearly two more years there will be no peace.

It is the job of the historian to tell us *what* happened, to provide the dates and places and numbers, all the necessary ingredients of textbooks. It is the job of the storyteller to bring out the thoughts, the words, the souls of these fascinating characters, to tell us *why* they should be remembered and respected and even enjoyed. While this is a novel, it is not false history. The time line, the events, and the language are as accurate as I could make them.

It has been my great privilege to become close enough to these marvelous characters to tell their story, and so, to bring them to you.

Jeff Shaara

ACKNOWLEDGMENTS

FOR THE CONSIDERABLE ASSISTANCE I HAVE RECEIVED IN THE writing of this book I must thank the following:

Gabor Boritt, The Civil War Institute, Gettysburg, Pennsylvania, for generously providing information and materials and insight on the character of Abraham Lincoln.

Chris Calkins, Chief Historian, Petersburg National Battlefield, Petersburg, Virginia, for the generous gift of his time, his singular knowledge of those special hidden places and his enthusiasm for sharing them.

Dr. John Elrod, President, Washington and Lee University, for his extraordinary graciousness and hospitality, making available the Lee and Junkin residences, occupied still by the university president and dean, thus allowing prying eyes into the privacy of his own home.

Patrick Falci, of the Civil War Round Table of New York, who is a tireless source of information and research material, and who sacrificed a large chunk of his vacation time to serve as guide for much of the field research.

Beth Ford, Cincinnati, Ohio, who generously provided a marvelous collection of original published works from the postwar era, including the published battle reports of every Confederate general.

Keith Gibson, Director of the VMI Museum, Lexington, Virginia, and his wife, **Pat Gibson,** whose hospitality and friendship continue to provide insight and direction, and whose talent and enthusiasm for the music of the period always remind us that there is more to our history than the written word.

Cory Hudgins, and all the staff of the Museum of the Confederacy, in Richmond, Virginia, for their enthusiastic cooperation, and knowledge of details otherwise lost to history.

Joan McDonough, President, the Civil War Round Table of New York, for her own suggestions of source materials; her tireless energy and assistance in fact-checking are always appreciated.

Len Reidel, the Blue and Gray Educational Society, Danville, Virginia, for providing difficult to locate documents and material on several of the characters.

Gordon Rhea, Charleston, South Carolina, author of *The Battle of the Wilderness* and *The Battle of Spotsylvania Courthouse and the Road to Yellow Tavern*, for not only having produced the two finest accounts of these events that I have come across, but for his generosity and support of this project by providing additional research materials.

Diane Smith, East Holden, Maine, whose own research into the lives of Joshua and Fannie Chamberlain provided insights into and discussion of aspects of their personal relationship not readily available.

Michael Wicklein and **Susan Saum-Wicklein,** of the Association for the Preservation of Civil War Sites, Hagerstown, Maryland, for their generous assistance with biographical material I simply couldn't find.

It is also my privilege to acknowledge the continuing friendship and support of **Clare Ferraro**, the former publisher of Ballantine Books in New York, without whose faith and confidence I would not now be nor probably ever have been a writer.

Every writer needs guidance, and for that I must thank **Doug Grad**, editor, Ballantine Books, who has been a patient sounding-board, and has always supported my ideas. He is one of the few who seem to understand the magic of this amazing process, how the story flows from the mind to the page, a process that is baffling to me yet.

This process never could have been completed without the constant support and tolerance of my wife **Lynne**. She reads every word, offers welcome insight into what I am doing right, and what I am doing wrong, but more, she has endured my journey through stress, euphoria, aggravation, fear, exhaustion, and, when the work allows, laughter.

The positive attention that *Gods and Generals* received was a wonderful surprise, and something that has pointed me in a direction I will follow for the rest of my life. My brief writing career has already provided me many positives, and a great deal of fulfillment. I did not start this journey, I merely continue it, and I am following enormous footprints. I will never stand before an audience, or dedicate a book, without acknowledging the man who opened the door. Thanks, Dad.

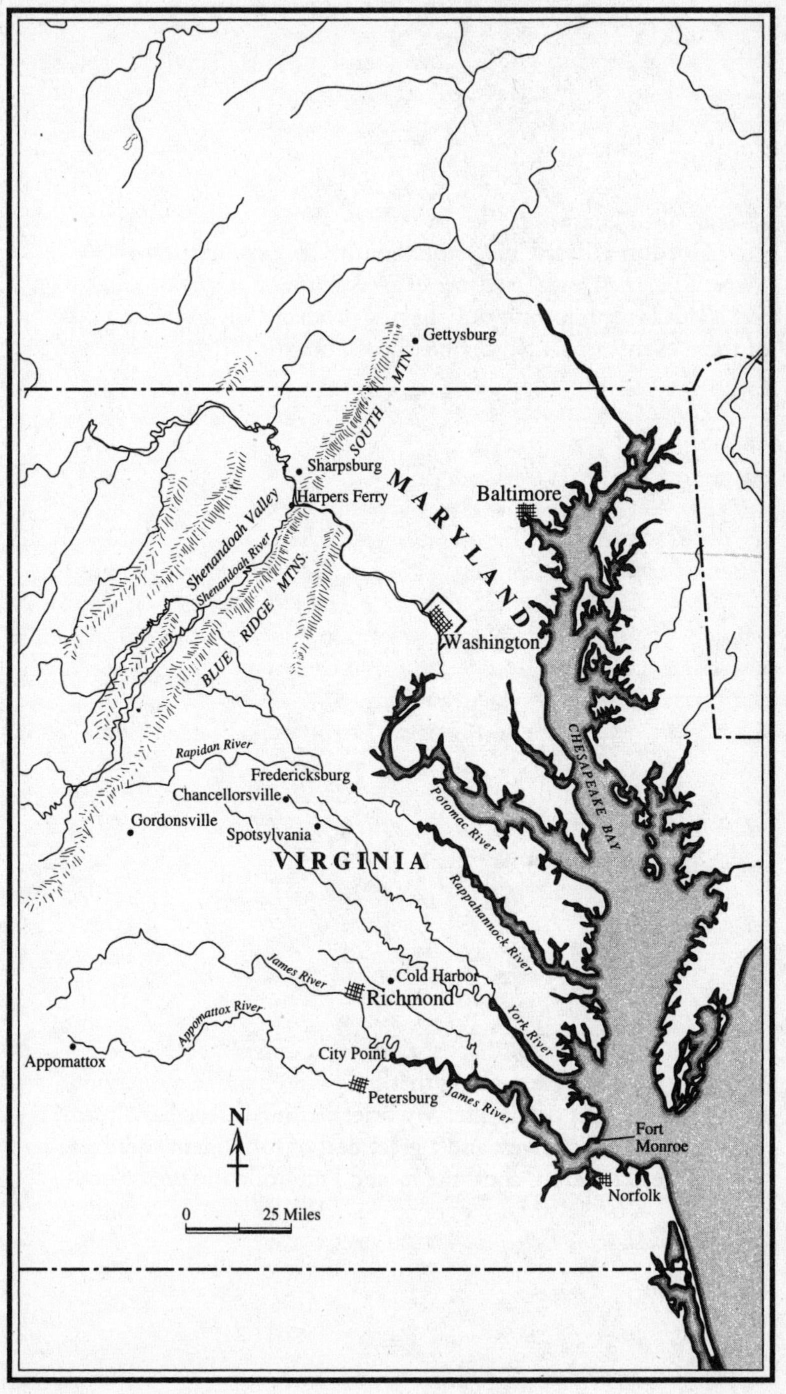

Gettysburg
SOUTH MTN.
Sharpsburg
Harpers Ferry
MARYLAND
Baltimore
Shenandoah Valley
Shenandoah River
BLUE RIDGE MTNS.
Washington
CHESAPEAKE BAY
Rapidan River
Fredericksburg
Chancellorsville
Gordonsville
Spotsylvania
VIRGINIA
Potomac River
Rappahannock River
Cold Harbor
James River
Richmond
Appomattox River
York River
Appomattox
City Point
Petersburg
James River
Fort Monroe
Norfolk
N
0
25 Miles

INTRODUCTION

BY JULY 1863 THE CIVIL WAR HAS BEEN FOUGHT OVER THE FARMlands and seacoasts of the South for better than two years, and is already one of the bloodiest wars in human history. It is a war that most believed would be decided by one quick fight, one great show of strength by the power of the North. The first major battle, called Bull Run in the North, Manassas in the South, is witnessed by a carefree audience of Washington's elite. Their brightly decorated carriages carry men in fine suits and society matrons in colorful dresses. They perch on a hillside, enjoying their picnics, anticipating a great show with bands playing merrily while the young men in blue march in glorious parade and sweep aside the ragged band of rebels. What they see is the first great horror, the stunning reality that this is in fact a *war*, and that men will die. What they still cannot understand is how far this will go, and *how many* men will die.

In the North, President Lincoln maintains a fragile grip on forces pulling the government in all directions. On one extreme is the pacifist movement, those who believe that the South has made its point, and so, to avoid bloodshed, Washington must simply let them go, that nothing so inconsequential as the Constitution is as important as the loss of life. On the other extreme are the radical abolitionists, who demand the South be brought down entirely, punished for its way of life, its culture, and that anyone who supports the southern cause should be purged from the land. There is also a great middle ground, men of reason and intellect, who now understand that there is more to this war than the inflammatory issue of slavery, or the argument over the sovereign rights of the individual states. As men continue to volunteer, larger and larger numbers of troops take to the fields, and other causes emerge, each man fighting for his own reason. Some fight for honor and duty, some for money and glory, but nearly all are driven by an amazing courage, and will carry their muskets across the deadly space because they feel it is the right thing to do.

From the North come farmers and fishermen, lumberjacks and shopkeepers, old veterans and young idealists. Some are barely Americans at all, expatriates and immigrants from Europe, led by officers who do not speak English. Some are freedmen, Negroes who volunteer to fight for the preservation of the limited freedoms they have been given, and to spread that freedom into the South.

In the South they are also farmers and fishermen, as well as ranchers, laborers, aristocrats, and young men seeking adventure. They are inspired first by the political rhetoric, the fire-breathing oratory of the radical secessionists. They are told that Lincoln is in league with the devil, and that his election ensures that the South will be held down, oppressed by the powerful interests in the North, that their very way of life is under siege. When the sound of the big guns echo across Charleston harbor, when the first flashes of smoke and fire swallow Fort Sumter, Lincoln orders an army to go south, to put down the rebellion by force. With the invasion comes a new inspiration, and in the South, even men of reason are drawn into the fight, men who were not seduced by mindless rhetoric, who have shunned the self-serving motives of the politicians. There is outrage, and no matter the issues or the politics, many take up arms in response to what they see as the threat to their homes. Even the men who understand and promote the inevitable failure of slavery cannot stand by while their land is invaded. The issue is not to be decided after all by talk or rhetoric, but by the gun.

On both sides are the career soldiers, West Pointers, men with experience from the Mexican War, or the Indian wars of the 1850s. In the North the officers are infected and abused by the disease of politics, and promotion is not always granted by performance or ability. The Federal armies endure a parade of inept or unlucky commanders who cannot fight the rebels until they first master the fight with Washington. Few succeed.

In the South, Jefferson Davis maintains an iron hand, controlling even the smallest details of governing the Confederacy. It is not an effective system, and as in the North, men of political influence are awarded positions of great authority, men who have no business leading soldiers into combat. In mid-1862, through an act of fate, or as he would interpret it, an act of God, Robert Edward Lee is given command of the Army of Northern Virginia. What follows in the East is a clear pattern, a series of great and bloody fights in which the South prevails and the North is beaten back. If the pattern continues, the war will end and the Confederacy will triumph. Many of the fights are won by Lee, or by his generals—the Shenandoah Valley, Second Manassas. Many of the fights are simply lost by the blunders of Federal commanders, the most horrifying example at Fredericksburg. Most, like the catastrophic Federal defeat at Chancellorsville or the tactical stalemate at Antietam, are a combination of both.

By 1863 two monumental events provide an insight into what lies ahead. The first is the success of the Federal blockade of southern seaports, which prevents the South from receiving critical supplies from allies abroad, and also prevents the export of raw materials, notably cotton and tobacco, which provide the currency necessary to pay for the war effort. The result is understood on both sides. Without outside help, the Confederacy will slowly starve.

The second is the great bloody fight at Gettysburg. While a tragic defeat for Lee's army, there is a greater significance to the way that defeat occurs. Until now, the war has been fought mostly from the old traditions, the Napoleonic method, the massed frontal assault against fortified positions. It has been apparent from the beginning of the war that the new weaponry has made such attacks dangerous and costly, but old ways die slowly, and commanders on both sides have been reluctant to change. After Gettysburg, the changes become a matter of survival. If the commanders do not yet understand, the men in the field do, and the use of the shovels becomes as important as the use of muskets. The new methods—strong fortifications, trench warfare—are clear signs to all that the war has changed, that there will be no quick and decisive fight to end all fights.

As the Civil War enters its third year, the bloody reports continue to fill the newspapers, and the bodies of young men continue to fill the cemeteries. To the eager patriots, the idealists and adventurers who joined the fight at the beginning, there is a new reality, in which honor and glory are becoming hollow words. The great causes are slowly pushed aside, and men now fight with the grim determination to take this fight to its end; after so much destruction and horrible loss, the senses are dulled, the unspeakable sights no longer shock. All the energy is forward, toward those men across that deadly space who have simply become the enemy.

ROBERT EDWARD LEE

Born in 1807, he graduates West Point in 1829, second in his class. Though he is the son of "Light-Horse" Harry Lee, a great hero of the American Revolution, late in his father's life Lee must endure the burden of his father's business and personal failures more than the aura of heroism. Lee is devoutly religious, believing with absolute clarity that the events of his life are determined by the will of God. On his return from West Point, his mother dies in his arms. The haunting sadness of her death stays hard inside him for the rest of his life, and places him more firmly than ever into the hands of his God.

He marries the aristocratic Mary Anne Randolph Custis, whose father is the grandson of Martha Washington, and whose home is the grand mansion of Arlington, overlooking the Potomac River. The Lees have seven children, and Lee suffers the guilt of a career that rarely brings him home to watch his children grow, a source of great regret for him, and simmering bitterness in his wife Mary.

Lee is a brilliant engineer, and his army career moves him to a variety of posts where his expertise and skill contribute much to the construction of the military installations and forts along the Atlantic coast. He goes to St. Louis and confronts a crisis for the port there by rerouting the flow of the Mississippi River. In 1846 he is sent to Mexico, and his reputation lands him on the staff of General-in-Chief Winfield Scott. Lee performs with efficiency and heroism, both as an engineer, a scout, and a staff officer, and leaves Mexico a lieutenant colonel.

He accepts command of the cadet corps at West Point in 1851, considered by many as the great reward for good service, the respectable job in which to spend the autumn of his career. But though his family is now close, he misses the action of Mexico, finds himself stifled by administrative duties. In 1855 he stuns all who know him by seizing an opportunity to return to the field, volunteering to go to Texas, to command a new regiment of cavalry. But even that command is mundane and frustrating, and there is for him nothing in the duty that recalls the vitality and adventure of the fighting in Mexico. Throughout the 1850s Lee settles into a deep gloom, resigns himself that no duty will be as fulfilling as life under fire and that his career will carry him into old age in bored obscurity.

As the conflict over Lincoln's election boils over in the South, his command in Texas begins to collapse, and he is recalled to Washington in early 1861, where he receives the startling request to command Lincoln's new volunteer army, with a promotion to Major General. He shocks Washington and deeply disappoints Winfield Scott by declining the appointment. Lee chooses the only course left to an officer and a man of honor and resigns from his thirty-year career. He believes that even though Virginia has not yet joined the secessionist states, by organizing an army to invade the South, Lincoln has united his opponents and the southern states, which must eventually include Virginia. Lee will not take up arms against his home.

In late April 1861 he accepts the governor's invitation to command the Virginia Militia, a defensive force assembled to defend the state. When Jefferson Davis moves the Confederate government to Richmond, the Virginia forces, as well as those of the other ten secessionist states, are absorbed into the Confederate army. Lee is invited to serve as military consultant to Davis, another stifling job with little actual authority. In July 1861, during the first great battle of the war, Lee sits alone in his office, while most of official Richmond travels to Manassas, to the excitement of the front lines.

In June 1862, while accompanied by Davis near the fighting on the Virginia peninsula, commander Joe Johnston is wounded in action and Davis offers command of the Army of Northern Virginia to Lee. Lee accepts, understands that he is, after all, a soldier, and justifies the decision with the fact that his theater of war is still Virginia. Defending his home takes on a more poignant significance when Lee's grand estate at Arlington is occupied and ransacked by Federal troops.

Lee reorganizes the army, removes many of the inept political generals, and begins to understand the enormous value of his two best commanders, James Longstreet and Thomas Jackson, who at Manassas was given the nickname "Stonewall." Using the greatest talents of both men, Lee leads the Army of Northern Virginia through a series of momentous victories against a Federal army that is weighed down by its own failures, and by its continuing struggle to find an effective commander. Much of Lee's war is fought in northern Virginia, and the land is suffering under the strain of feeding the army. The burden of war and of the Federal blockade spreads through the entire Confederacy and inspires Lee and Davis to consider a bold and decisive strategy.

In September 1862, Lee moves his army north, hoping to gather support and new recruits from the neutral state of Maryland. The advance results in the battle of Sharpsburg—known as Antietam in the North—and though Lee does not admit defeat, the outrageous carnage and loss of life force him to order a retreat back into Virginia. But his army is not pursued by the Federal forces, and with new commanders now confronting him, Lee begins a great tactical chess game, and accomplishes the greatest victories of the war.

In December 1862, at Fredericksburg, Virginia, his army maintains the defensive and completely crushes poorly planned Federal assaults. In May 1863, at Chancellorsville, Lee is outnumbered nearly three to one, and only by the utter audacity of Stonewall Jackson does the huge Federal army retire from the field with great loss. But the battle is costly for Lee as well. Jackson is accidentally shot by his own men, and dies after a weeklong struggle with pneumonia.

Lee and Davis continue to believe that a move northward is essential, that with weakened confidence and inept commanders, the Federal army need only be pushed into one great battle that will likely end the war. In June 1863, Lee's army marches into Pennsylvania. He believes that a great fight might not even be necessary, that just the threat of spilling blood on northern soil will put great pressure on Washington, and the war might be brought to an end by the voice of the northern people. The invasion of the North will serve another purpose: to take the fight into fertile farmlands where Lee might feed his increasingly desperate army.

Some in Lee's army question the strategy, raising the moral question of how to justify an invasion versus defending their homes. Others question the military judgment of moving into unfamiliar territory, against an enemy that has never been inspired by fighting on its own ground. There are other factors that Lee must confront. Though he is personally devastated by the death of Jackson, Jackson's loss means more to his army than Lee fully understands.

As the invasion moves north, Lee is left blind by his cavalry, under the flamboyant command of Jeb Stuart. Stuart fails to provide Lee with critical information about the enemy and is cut off from Lee beyond the march of the Federal army, an army that is moving to confront Lee with uncharacteristic speed. The Federal Army of the Potomac has yet another new commander, George Gordon Meade, and if Lee knows Meade to be a careful man, cautious in his new command, he also knows that there are many other Federal officers now rising to the top, men who are not political pawns but in fact hard and effective fighters.

The two armies collide at a small crossroads called Gettysburg, a fight for which Lee is not yet prepared, and the fight becomes the three bloodiest days in American history. As costly as it is to both armies, it is a clear defeat for Lee. He had believed his army could not be stopped, and begins now to understand what Jackson's loss might mean—that as the fight goes on, and the good men continue to fall away, the war will settle heavily on his own shoulders.

Joshua Lawrence Chamberlain

Born in 1828 near Brewer, Maine, he is the oldest of five children. He graduates Bowdoin College in 1852, and impresses all who know him with his intellect, his gift for words and talent for languages. He is raised by a deeply religious mother, whose greatest wish is that he become a man of the cloth, and for a short while Chamberlain attends the Bangor Theological Seminary, but it is not a commitment he can make. His father's ancestry is military. Chamberlain's great-grandfather fought in the Revolution, his grandfather in the War of 1812. His father serves during peacetime years in the Maine Militia and never sees combat. It is family tradition that his son will follow the military path, and he pressures Chamberlain to apply to West Point. When Chamberlain returns to the academic community, a career for which his father has little respect, the disappointment becomes a hard barrier between them.

He marries Frances Caroline (Fannie) Adams, and they have four children, two of whom survive infancy. Fannie pushes him toward the career in academics, and his love for her is so complete and consuming that he likely would have pursued any path she had chosen.

Considered the rising star in the academic community, Chamberlain accepts a prestigious Chair at Bowdoin, formerly held by the renowned Calvin Stowe, husband of Harriet Beecher Stowe. Her controversial book, *Uncle Tom's Cabin*, inspires Chamberlain, and the issues that explode in the South, so far removed from the classrooms in Maine, reach him deeply. He begins to feel a calling of a different kind.

As the war begins in earnest, and Chamberlain's distraction is evident to the school administration, he is offered a leave of absence—a trip to Europe, to take him away from the growing turmoil. Chamberlain uses the opportunity in a way that astounds and distresses everyone. He goes to the governor of Maine without telling anyone, including Fannie, and volunteers for service in the newly forming Maine regiments. Though he has no military experience, his intellect and zeal for the job open the door, and he is appointed Lieutenant Colonel, second-in-command of the Twentieth Maine Regiment of Volunteers.

After a difficult farewell to his family, Chamberlain and his regiment join the Army of the Potomac in Washington, and in September 1862 they march toward western Maryland, to confront Lee's army at

Antietam Creek. The Twentieth Maine does not see action, but Chamberlain observes the carnage of the fight and, for the first time, experiences what the war might mean for the men around him. Three months later he leads his men into the guns at Fredericksburg and witnesses firsthand what the war has become. He spends an amazing night on the battlefield, yards from the lines of the enemy, and protects himself with the corpses of his own men.

In June 1863 he is promoted to full colonel, and now commands the regiment. He marches north with the army in pursuit of Lee's invasion. By chance, his regiment is the lead unit of the Fifth Corps, and when they reach the growing sounds of the fight at Gettysburg, the Twentieth Maine marches to the left flank, climbing a long rise to the far face of a rocky hill known later as Little Round Top. His is now the last unit, the far left flank of the Federal line, and he is ordered to hold the position at all cost. The regiment fights off a desperate series of attacks from Longstreet's corps, which, if successful, would likely turn the entire Federal flank, exposing the supply train and the rear of the rest of the army. Low on ammunition, his line weakening from the loss of so many men, he impulsively orders his men to charge the advancing rebels with bayonets, surprising the weary attackers so completely that they retreat in disorder or are captured en masse. The attacks end and the flank is secured.

During the fight, he is struck by a small piece of shrapnel, and carries a small but painful wound in his foot. As the army marches in slow pursuit of Lee's retreat, the foul weather and Chamberlain's own exhaustion take their toll, and he begins to suffer symptoms of malaria.

Though he is unknown outside of his immediate command, this college professor turned soldier now attracts the attention of the commanders above him, and it becomes apparent that his is a name that will be heard again.

ULYSSES SIMPSON GRANT

Born in 1822 in Point Pleasant, Ohio, he graduates West Point in 1843. Small, undistinguished as a cadet, it is his initials which first attract attention. The U.S. becomes a nickname, "Uncle Sam," and soon he is known by his friends as simply "Sam." He achieves one other notable reputation at the Point, that of a master horseman, seemingly able to tame and ride any animal.

His first duty is near St. Louis, and he maintains a strong friendship with many of the former cadets, including "Pete" Longstreet.

Grant meets and falls madly in love with Julia Dent, whose father's inflated notion of his own aristocratic standing produces strong objection to his daughter's relationship with a soldier. Longstreet suffers a similar fate, and in 1846, when the orders come to march to Mexico, both men leave behind young girls with wounded hearts.

Grant is assigned to the Fourth Infantry and serves under Zachary Taylor during the first conflicts in south Texas. He makes the great march inland with Winfield Scott and arrives at the gates of Mexico City to lead his men into the costly fighting that eventually breaks down the defenses of the city and gives Scott's army the victory. Grant leads his infantry with great skill, and is recognized for heroism, but is not impressed with the straight-ahead tactics used by Scott. He believes that much loss of life could have been avoided by better strategy.

He returns home with a strong sense of despair for the condition of the Mexican peasantry, which he sees as victims of both the war and their own ruling class. It is an experience that helps strengthen his own feelings about the abominable inhumanity of slavery.

Returning to St. Louis, Grant receives reluctant consent to marry Julia, and eventually they have four children. He receives a pleasant assignment to Detroit, but in 1852 he is ordered to the coast of California, an expensive and hazardous post, and so he must leave his family behind. The following two years are the worst in his life, and despite a brief and enjoyable tour at Fort Vancouver, he succumbs both to the outrageous temptations of gold-rush San Francisco and the desperate loneliness of life without his young family. Shy and withdrawn, he does not enjoy the raucous social circles of many of his friends, and the painful isolation leads him to a dependency on alcohol. His bouts of drunkenness are severe enough to interfere with his duty, and his behavior warrants disciplinary action. Because of the generosity of his commanding officer, Grant is afforded the opportunity to resign rather than face a court-martial. He leaves the army in May 1854 and believes his career in the military is at a painful conclusion.

He returns to his family unemployed and penniless, and attempts to farm a piece of land given him by Julia's father. With no money to provide the beginnings of a crop, Grant attempts the lumber business, cutting trees from the land himself. He eventually builds his own house, which he calls, appropriately, "Hardscrabble."

He is generous to a fault, often loaning money to those who will never repay the debts, and despite a constant struggle financially, he is always willing to help anyone who confronts him in need.

In 1859 he is offered a position as a collection agent for a real estate firm in St. Louis, and trades the small farm for a modest home in the city, but the business is not profitable. Though he is qualified for positions that become available in the local government, the political turmoil that spreads through the Midwest requires great skill at intrigue and political connections, and Grant has neither. He finally accepts an offer from his own father, moves to Galena, Illinois, in 1860, and clerks in a leather and tanned goods store with his brothers, who understand that Grant's military experience and West Point training in mathematics will make for both a trustworthy and useful employee. But the politics of the day begin to affect even those who try to avoid the great discussions and town meetings, and Grant meets John Rawlins and Elihu Washburne, whose political influence begins to pave the way for an opportunity Grant would never have sought on his own.

As the presidential election draws closer, Grant awakens to the political passions around him, involves himself with the issues and the candidates, and finally decides to support the candidate Abraham Lincoln. When Lincoln is elected, Grant tells his friend John Rawlins that with passions igniting around the country, "the South will fight."

Persuaded by Washburne, Grant organizes a regiment of troops from Galena and petitions the governor of Illinois for a Colonel's commission, which he receives. After seven years of struggle as a civilian, Grant reenters the army.

Serving first under Henry Halleck, he eventually commands troops through fights on the Mississippi River at Forts Henry and Donelson, each fight growing in importance as the war spreads. Promoted eventually to Major General, Grant is named commander of the Federal Army of Tennessee, but still must endure Halleck's fragile ego and disagreeable hostility. On the Tennessee River at a place called Shiloh, facing a powerful enemy under the command of Albert Sidney Johnston, Grant wins one of the bloodiest fights of the war, in which Johnston himself is killed. Here, Grant's command includes an old acquaintance from his days in California, William Tecumseh Sherman.

In July 1862, when Halleck is promoted to General-in-Chief of the army and leaves for Washington, the army of the western theater is a confused mishmash of commands under Grant, Don Carlos Buell, and William Rosecrans. While the focus of the nation is on the great battles in Virginia, Grant gradually establishes himself as the most consistent and reliable commander in the West. He finally unites much of the Federal forces for an assault and eventually a long siege on the critical river port of Vicksburg, Mississippi. In July 1863, the same week Lee's army confronts the great Federal forces at Gettysburg, Grant succeeds in capturing both Vicksburg and the Confederate force that had occupied it.

Now, Lincoln begins to focus not just on the great turmoil of Virginia, but toward the West as well, and it is Grant's name that rises through the jumble of poor commanders and the political gloom of Washington. After the disasters of leadership that have plagued the army, Lincoln's patience for the politics of command is at an end. He begins to speak of this quiet and unassuming man out West, a general who seems to know how to win.

PART ONE

Four score and seven years ago our fathers brought forth, upon this continent, a new nation, conceived in liberty, and dedicated to the proposition that all men are created equal. Now we are engaged in a great civil war . . .

1. LEE

July 13, 1863

It was a high bluff, overlooking the dark violence of the swollen river. He sat alone, watched as the men fell into line and the columns began moving slowly through the steady rain. He felt the coolness run down his neck, the water soaking every part of him, his hat, his clothes. A vast sea of mud surrounded them all. The Potomac was rising again, was well beyond their ability to ford, as they might have done before the rains. Now, it was angry and swirling. In the darkness, the motion was accented by the small fires that lined the riverbank, a flickering protest to the misery of the weather, the only guiding light the men would have to reach the crossing.

Lee straightened his back, stretched, pulled at the miserable wetness in his clothes. He reached down, patted Traveller gently, said quietly to the horse, "He has given us one more night . . . he has not come."

He was thinking now of George Meade, the commander of the vast Federal army he knew was encamped out there, somewhere, deep in the thick darkness. He had expected them to come at him well before now. It had been ten days, and Lee's army had been strung out for miles, moving southwest away from Gettysburg. The army had begun the march away from the bloody fields in a terrible downpour, led away by the wagons of the wounded, and Meade had not pursued. But they reached the Potomac to find the river swollen nearly out of its banks, their one good bridge swept away, and so they would have to try to build another, or wait longer for the river to drop.

When Meade had finally moved, he pushed his army in a more roundabout way, to come at them from downriver. But there was too much time, Lee's men had fortified into a strong defensive line, and so Meade waited again. Lee had known the risk was enormous, and he feared the attack at any time. There was some skirmishing, small outbreaks of musket fire, the feeling out of two great armies close together. The only real assaults had been with cavalry, all along the march, the Federal horsemen thrusting and jabbing, while Stuart held them away from the main lines. When the skies finally cleared and the roads began to dry, Meade moved his army close, and Lee was backed hard against the high water. Now they had dug in, the quick work of men with shovels, because even the foot soldiers knew that they were trapped and a strong push from a healthy enemy could crush them. But Meade did not come.

It was Major Harman, the foul-tempered and foul-mouthed quartermaster of Jackson's old Second Corps, who saved the day. Lee smiled now, remembered Jackson's embarrassment as Harman would ride by, screaming profanities at a line of slow moving wagons. Jackson would glance at Lee like a small boy expecting an angry response from a stern parent, and Lee would look away, would make no issue of it, knew well that Jackson would tolerate the man's harsh outbursts because he was very good at his job. Now Harman was serving new commanders, and still did his job. He'd scouted the countryside, found the abandoned houses and barns, the people far away from this invading army. Harman ordered the houses dismantled and the wood planking thrown into the river, swept downstream to where the engineers waited. The wood was collected and strung together into a snaking mass of ragged timber. They had laid tree branches across the planks, muffling the sounds of the wagons' wheels, and now the ambulances and the guns and the weary soldiers were finally crossing the river.

Lee still watched them, the glow from the fires throwing light and shadows on the faces, some looking up toward him, seeing him on the high knoll. But most stared straight ahead, looked silently at the back of the man in front, or down at the slow rhythm of bare feet, moving slowly, carefully, and they all knew they were marching south.

He thought of Jackson again, closed his eyes and saw the sharp face, the brightness in the clear blue eyes. We miss you, General. No, do not think on that. He opened his eyes, looked around to his staff, saw Taylor, sitting with the others, a cluster of black raincoats.

"Major, have we heard from General Ewell?"

Taylor moved up, pushed his horse through the mud close to Lee. "Yes, sir. He reports his men are crossing well. They should be south of the river by daylight."

Lee nodded, wanted to say more, to break away from the thoughts of Jackson, but the image was still there, would not go. Lee turned back toward the march of the men, felt the wetness again. Taylor waited, watched Lee, could sense his mood through the darkness, backed his horse away.

Below, along the river, a group of horsemen moved out of the woods, and Lee saw the flag of the First Corps. They rode slowly toward the knoll, then one man moved out in front and spurred his horse up the hill, broad thick shoulders slumped against the rain. The wind suddenly began to blow, the rain slicing across them, and the big man leaned into it, held his hat in place with a gloved hand.

"General Longstreet . . ."

Longstreet looked up, peered from under the wide wet hat, nodded, saluted. "General Lee. We're moving pretty quick, considering the conditions. The bridge may not hold. We're watching it pretty close . . . both sides of the river."

"It is a blessing, General." Lee looked to the water again, the slow march of the troops. "Major Harman may have saved this army."

Longstreet followed Lee's look, and for a moment the wind stopped and there was just the quiet sound of the rain. Suddenly, beyond the trees, there was a rumble, one sharp blast from a big gun. They waited for more, but the silence flowed back around them. Longstreet looked that way, said, "Damned fools . . . save your ammunition."

He looked toward Lee, lowered his head, did not like to swear in front of Lee, but Lee did not seem to notice, was again staring at the marching troops. Longstreet saw now that Lee was counting, nodding to the regimental flags as they caught the brief flickers from the fires.

"We'll make it all right, sir. If Meade hasn't hit us by now, he isn't coming at all. Ewell is making good time down below, and the First Corps is nearly all across. Hill's corps is right behind us."

Lee nodded, looked now out in the darkness, to the far trees. "He should have hit us here. We gave him an opportunity. God . . . gave him an opportunity. The rains slowed us, kept us here. Now, God has taken his opportunity away."

Lee paused, and Longstreet waited.

Lee said, "I don't understand His ways. . . . I thought it would never be like this. The Almighty was with us, the fight was ours . . . we should have won the day. But it was not to be. I thought . . . I understood. But now, He is allowing us to go back home."

Longstreet looked at Lee for a long moment, said, "I thought Meade would end it. He is making a mistake letting us escape. I suppose . . . there will be another day."

Now there was the sharp sound of another gun, a brief flash of light in the trees far downriver, then another gun, closer, the reply. Lee watched, sat up straight.

Longstreet said, "No musket fire. They're just playing . . . probably firing at the wind. Meade's cavalry is moving around, but no infantry. They're still in place."

Lee shook his head. "He dug trenches. He came right at us, and then dug trenches."

Longstreet said, "The scouts have been bringing in some numbers. . . . Word is, he's pretty beat up. Maybe worse than us. They lost some good people. . . . John Reynolds is dead, that's for certain. I heard Hancock was down, and Dan Sickles. Meade's still new to command, doesn't want to make any mistakes. He won the fight, he knows it. Let those folks in Washington absorb that. They haven't had much to cheer about."

Lee looked at Longstreet, ran the names through his mind. "General, he has not lost what we have lost. We cannot replace what has been taken from us, and this fight has taken too much. I do not understand why we have been . . . punished so. We could have ended the war, right over there, if we had prevailed on that ground. The pressure on Washington . . . we took the fight to *them*, it was the only way. And we have paid a terrible price." He paused, said quietly, to himself, "I would have thought . . . surely God does not want this to go on."

Longstreet watched the troops again, said, "There were many mistakes."

Lee did not answer, thought again of Jackson, closed his eyes, fought the image. But it would not go away. The image stared hard at him, and Lee knew that Jackson *was* there, had *seen* the great fight, the great bloody disaster. Lee thought, If you had been here . . . if you had led them . . . it would have been very different.

From down below, one of Longstreet's staff moved up the hill, said, "General, excuse me. The last of the corps is on the bridge, sir. General Hill's column is forming on the road, behind those woods."

Longstreet turned, nodded. "Thank you, Major. We'll move across in a minute." He turned to Lee, paused, saw Lee's eyes closed, said quietly, "General Lee? With your permission, sir, I will take my staff across the river. I expect General Hill should report to you soon. I'm sure he wants to get across this river as much as we do."

Lee looked at him now, and Longstreet suddenly felt foolish, knew it was the wrong thing to say.

Lee looked into the shadow of Longstreet's face. He felt a small tug of anger, but he would not say anything of it, would not lay blame on anyone. "General Longstreet, you may accompany your corps."

Longstreet bowed slightly, saluted, pulled the horse away. Lee watched him, the staff gathering together, the horses moving in slippery steps down to the bridge head.

Longstreet was right, there were many mistakes. But he would not think on that now, would not see the faces, the commanders who had not done the job, would not think on troop movements and poor cooperation, could not even recall his own orders, the horrors of what he had seen, what they had all seen in those three days. He had tried to understand it, to sort it out, but it was too soon, and he knew the memories would come back in time, and the images would be as sharp and painful as so many of the memories he carried from the fights long before.

Even the great victories held vast horror, but he could not even recall those, the days when you knew you had beaten those people, had driven them from the field, commanders like Pope and Hooker, who by their bluster and profane arrogance invited nothing less than total defeat. And the incompetence of Burnside, who threw his very good army against an impossibly strong position, and so sent his own men to a senseless slaughter. Lee tried to recall the feeling, standing on his hill behind Fredericksburg, hearing the bright yells and joyous shouts from below, his men looking out at the bloody fields in front of them, understanding how utterly complete their victory had been. He tried to remember the chaos at Chancellorsville, the complete destruction of the Federal flank, how Jackson had nearly crushed the Federal army in a panic so complete that had the daylight not run out . . . it could have ended the war right there. But Jackson would not be stopped by nightfall, kept moving forward, even when his men could not, and in a dark and terrifying night his own men had panicked at the sound of horses, had fired at silhouettes in the moonlight.

Lee saw the face again. He had not been to see Jackson after he was wounded, but the reports from the doctors, from the staff, were optimistic, just an arm, he would recover. Then suddenly the bright blue light was gone, and not from the wounds, but from pneumonia. And it was only . . . He tried to think. Two months ago. Or an eternity.

Already now there were letters, reports beginning to move through the army, commanders deflecting the blame they knew was yet to come. There would be the newspapers, of course, and the letters from home, questioning. Some of the officers had already made protests, angry challenges, hot criticisms of the generals Lee trusted so much, men he *had* to trust. But those men had not performed, and in the maze of faces and names and mistakes, he knew that ultimately no one could be held responsible but him.

Now there was fresh motion on the road, reflections from a new line of troops. It was the Third Corps, A. P. Hill's men. They moved out of the woods, marched down toward the angry water, and again Lee watched, sat quietly on Traveller as his army moved silently through the wet misery of the retreat, knowing once again the war would roll on in a bloody wash of men and machines back into Virginia.

AUGUST 1863

HE HALTED THE ARMY SOUTH OF THE RAPIDAN RIVER, NEAR Orange Court House, and as they slowly gathered together, many of the stragglers and men with light wounds began to return. In the weeks since the start of the retreat, it was the first time Lee could see his army for what it had now become, how badly the impact of Gettysburg had changed the strength, how deep were the wounds.

The fields around the Rapidan were bare now. No farmers worked the land, the homes and barns were empty, most of the big trees were gone. The war had long since claimed this part of Virginia, and Lee hardly recognized this countryside. He stood at the edge of a wide field of dried mud, knew that this land, this fertile and beautiful ground, had once borne the bounty, the tall corn, the vast green oceans of grain. Now it was gray and barren, wagon tracks cutting through in all directions, the former campsites of both armies, and for now it was his again.

The men were spread out around him, secure in the new camp, and Lee rode along the hard road, away from his own tents, where the staff worked with the papers, sorting out the problems in the regiments, the brigades, the endless fight for supplies.

Taylor had encouraged him to slip away, and Lee was grateful, knew this young man with the boundless energy could handle the business of headquarters, the vast clutter of details. He rode slowly away, did not look back, did not see Taylor watching him, peering past the lengthening line of soldiers, officers, men with complaints or "urgent" business.

He moved down the hard road, past the troops who now stopped to watch him. There were shouts, calls of greeting, and even now, even with the hard wounds of the great defeat, the men still rose up and gathered, still called his name. He reined the horse, lifted his hat, a small salute, looked at the faces and then beyond, saw the numbers, the wide field spread with the men who were still there, still with him. They did not look to him for comfort or pity, and he did not see pain or defeat. They still made the cheerful calls, faces bright with the look that says, We are still your army, and we will fight again.

There had been desertions, many stragglers who were captured or simply disappeared. The muddy roads out of Pennsylvania had swallowed up many who had lost the strength, the energy, for the fight. The casualties were staggering, over twenty thousand men, nearly a quarter of his army gone. But as much as he mourned the loss of the fighting men, it was their commanders, the brigade and regimental officers, who would have to be replaced. As the war flowed into its third year, the men who knew how to lead, the capable commanders with an instinct for battle, were becoming more and more scarce.

He thought of the names, saw the faces: Lew Armistead, Barksdale, Pender, Garnett, Pettigrew. They were gone, and there were none better. He thought of young John Bell Hood, the huge blond-haired man from Texas whom he had known so well in the old cavalry, the man who loved chasing Comanches all through the misery of the frontier. Lee had always thought Hood was indestructible, but he was down too, a severe wound, might still lose an arm. And old Isaac Trimble, the man who brought him the news of Ewell's failure to take Cemetery Hill, a catastrophic mistake in a fight with many mistakes. Trimble was a fierce and disagreeable man whom Lee knew he could trust absolutely, but Trimble had been wounded as well, had to be left behind, and so was captured.

You could not train new leaders, you could not replace what a man had brought with him from the battlefields in Mexico. There was no fresh class from West Point or VMI. The new officers were young, very young, and if a man did not have the gut instinct, could not take his men forward with absolute command of himself and his situation, there was no time to teach him, to show him his mistakes. Now, when mistakes were made, the men did not come back.

He spurred the horse again, moved beyond the camp, saw the road turning through a small grove of thick trees. It was hot, growing hotter, and he looked to the shade, moved that way. He heard the sound of water, saw a small stream snaking its way in the dark coolness, flowing close to the road. He reined the horse, watched the thin stream of water rolling over polished rocks, was suddenly very thirsty. He climbed down, and Traveller moved to the water with him. Lee bent low, cupped his hand and took a deep cold drink. He stood, wiped at his face with a wet hand, watched the horse now nosing the edge of the stream. He could still hear the men, the sounds of the camp carrying beyond the fields, and there was even music, a banjo, and he smiled at that, felt a sudden pride. Yes, he thought, they are not beaten. I should take a lesson from that.

He reached into his pocket, felt for the letter, pulled it out. It was the reply, the inevitable response from Jefferson Davis. Lee understood that in this army, in any army, it was the commander who must bear the responsibility. If he did not dwell on that, the newspapers did, great ponderous prose from the fat men in their clean offices in Richmond, Charleston, Atlanta, the men who had built up the expectations of their nation with the move northward. They gave their readers the first reports of the glorious invasion of the North, reported outrageous rumors as fact, the defeat of Meade's army, the imminent capture of Washington.

Lee had not seen the papers until after the battle, then read the absurd reports with deep dread, because he knew that when the truth came out, when the reports of the fighting became real, the impact would be far worse. So with the first major accounts from Pennsylvania, the papers that had given the people grand headlines of their mythic victory, the victory that would surely end the war, now gave them the story of crushing defeat. The papers had provided the power behind the myth, and many had come to believe that his army was invincible. Now they had to accept that it was not always so, and many would not accept it. Even the reasonable, moderate voices could not temper what many were saying. Lee had lost the fight. As he absorbed the anger, the reckless calls from the papers, the voices of those quick to place blame, to seek the simple explanation, he responded in the only way he could. In early August his letter of resignation had gone to the president.

The letter had been as much a response to the papers as to the president personally, an effort to relieve any criticism of the army, the men who had done the fighting. And if Lee accepted responsibility for the failure, he also began to accept that his health was becoming an issue, and for the first time he had wondered if his heart problems might have clouded his judgment. So, at least he had provided Davis with an excuse, a reason for accepting his resignation, which would preserve his honor.

Now, as Lee stood beside the big horse in the cool shade, he held Davis's reply in his hand. He opened the letter, read it again. If Davis had become fragile, even suspicious and secretive in his dealings with his other commanders, he could still show Lee the warmth that many never saw, that Lee had often forgotten. He scanned the page, paused at the words "my dear friend," smiled, then read silently.

> To ask me to substitute you by one in my judgment more fit to command, or who could possess more of the confidences of the army, or of the reflecting men of the country, is to demand an impossibility.

He looked back toward the sounds from the field, thought, The confidences of the army. He knew Davis was right, he had just seen it again in the faces of the men. He put his hand out, touched Traveller's neck, said aloud, "Well, if they want me to lead them still, then I will lead them. After all, my friend, what else can I do?"

He climbed up, considered moving farther away, exploring the road deeper into the shade of the trees, but before he could tug at the reins, the big gray horse turned its head and began to carry him back to his men.

2. CHAMBERLAIN

Brunswick, Maine, August 1863

He had seen her from the window of the train, moved toward the doorway, and when the train slowed enough he jumped down to the platform. The pain from the wound in his foot shocked him, and he staggered, fell forward, caught himself with one hand, then stood again, and the twist in his expression told her he was hurting.

Fannie moved toward him now, and he reached for her, and the pain was gone. She lifted her hands to him, and he saw the look, that same dark sadness, the look she had when he'd left her a year ago. He hugged her, and they stood for a long moment, said nothing. He could feel her arms pulling hard at him, and he did nothing to end it, would feel her pressing against him as long as she would have it go on. As people moved from the train, filling the platform, there were glances, discreet stares, a few children began to point, hushed by embarrassed mothers. As she kept him tight to her, he began to sag, to feel the weakness, leaned against her more, and still she held him, said quietly, "Oh God . . . oh God . . ."

She was crying now, and he moved slowly, lifted her away and saw the tears. She smiled then, said, "How do you feel?"

"Not very well. It was a rough trip. I feel like . . . bed."

They began to walk. She held his arm as they moved away from the train. He still leaned against her, and they climbed down the short steps. As she guided him toward the carriage, people began to recognize him, saw more than just the blue uniform, saw the familiar face of the professor, the man many of them had known before. People began to move closer, there were greetings, hands came toward him. He tried to smile, to be gracious, but the weakness was overwhelming, and the smile faded and he could only nod. He climbed slowly up into the carriage, and Fannie moved around, sat beside him.

Chamberlain saw now the young man sitting up in front, watching them, holding the reins, and he looked at the smiling face, thought, Yes, it's . . . He tried to clear his head, staggered through names, said, "Yes, Mister . . . Silas. The rhetoric class."

The boy was beaming now, flattered at the recognition. "Yes, sir, *Colonel* Chamberlain. Welcome home."

Chamberlain remembered he was in uniform, had forgotten all about that, how the people here saw him, what it was like for him to come back home from such a different place. And he knew now what they all knew. He was not a professor anymore.

Chamberlain looked at Fannie now, who was watching him, questioning him silently with hard concern.

"We should get you home. Mr. Silas asked if he could drive me to the station. Many of your . . . the students have been calling on me every day. The word did get out, I'm afraid . . . that you were coming home."

He glanced out toward the small crowd, saw the people staring at him with a look of sorrow, dread. She waved a hand and said, "Thank you, he's all right. We're taking him home now."

Chamberlain looked at the faces, the sadness, did not understand. He saw a man, familiar, and the man removed his hat, gave a small bow, said, "God bless you, Colonel. We pray for you, sir."

Chamberlain looked at the man, the others, suddenly wondered if they expected a speech. He said, "Thank you. I'm only here for a while . . . please, do not be concerned for me." He looked up at the boy, who was staring at him intently, and he suddenly felt confused, embarrassed.

Fannie said, "Mr. Silas, we should proceed."

The boy slapped at the horse, and the carriage rolled into the wide street, the boy holding the horse to a slow walk. People were still gathering, pointing, but Chamberlain began to sag again, leaned weakly against Fannie, closed his eyes, heard his name in small faint voices. He was suddenly very sleepy, and the gentle lurch of the carriage rocked him against her side, his head resting against her shoulder. Fannie put her hand softly against his face and felt the hot sweat of the fever.

The malaria had been coming on slowly, during the weariness of the long marches, the summer heat beating him down. What the marches had not taken from him, the battlefield had—the small wound in his foot, the shock of the fight on Little Round Top. But it was afterward, the slow and miserable march, the sluggish pursuit of Lee's army, the mud and the wet chills, that had weakened him, left him prone to the sickness. And since there had been no fight, with Lee escaping across the Potomac, he'd been granted leave, two short weeks, much of it in a long train ride home to Maine.

He heard a child's voice, and then Fannie, a stern whisper, and he looked toward the door. He saw her gently guiding the small boy out of the room, but the child saw Chamberlain looking at him over the thick bed covering, called out, "Daddy!" spun free of Fannie's grasp, ran to the bed and jumped up.

Chamberlain wanted to reach out, catch him, but the weight of the covers and his own weakness would not let him move. He did not fight it, smiled weakly, said, "Good morning, Wyllys. Are you helping your mother this morning?"

With a small groan, Fannie lifted the boy, and Chamberlain saw now how much bigger he was, tried to remember, fought through the fog in his mind, thought, He is *four*. The boy protested, but Fannie carried him out of the room, and Chamberlain heard her in the hallway, scolding him.

Now she was back, moving quietly to the bed. "I'm sorry. I've tried to keep them quiet. Daisy was in here earlier. She just wanted to look at you, but Wyllys . . . he doesn't understand why you're not up playing with him."

"Neither do I." Chamberlain tried to sit, to slide up from under the blanket, but there was no strength, no energy. He closed his eyes, frowned, then looked up at her. "This is ridiculous. I'm supposed to be a soldier, a man of action." He tried to laugh, watched her eyes, and she smiled, could not help it.

She sat on the bed, put a hand on his forehead. "Well, my soldier, you still have some fever. So, you will not be seeing much action of any kind for a while."

He reached up for her hand, held it for a brief moment. She stood, and he tried to hold on to her, to keep her from leaving, but she was away now, at the door. "I'll bring you something cool to drink. And, you should eat something. I have some breakfast."

She was gone, and now he let himself relax, felt the weight of the blanket again. He stared up at the ceiling, then over toward the window, but there was no sunlight, the curtain was down. He flexed his foot, felt the small stab of pain, but knew it was improving. He'd been walking with less of a limp before he stopped walking at all.

He had always been a miserable patient, had no tolerance for being ill, fought it angrily, thought of the disease, went through this every time he was sick: What right do you have to invade me? It was a rhetorical question, it never seemed to make the sickness go away. He never did understand why he got sick in the first place. Punishment? Was this the hand of God, slowing you down from your own work, telling you, "Stop, you're not doing it right"? But what if your work was good, of benefit to others? Even doctors got sick. He thought of the bizarre illogic of that. How can You punish a doctor when he is helping cure the illnesses of others?

He thought of his mother: This was a question for her. He smiled, pictured the stern devout face, the faith of the pious optimist. She would say the malaria is a sign from God, a message: give up this foolishness, this soldiering, and come home and accept the life she had always insisted was his destiny; take up the cloth, preach the word of God. And here he was, at home. Maybe she was right. He felt the impatience again. Maybe this was *her* doing, maybe she had talked God into giving him this disease. But I won't take this lying down, Chamberlain thought. It won't work. Now he relaxed again, felt guilty. No, his mother just wanted what was best. That's what mothers did. She had never seen him as anything but her gift from God, and the gift had to be repaid. But there were other ways. God did not need everyone to be a preacher.

He smelled food, was suddenly very hungry. Yes, I am better, he thought. I will fight this thing. He suddenly felt Shakespearean. Plague, be gone! Out, damned spot! He tried to focus, sort out the smells, an exercise. What food is that? Bread, yes, and something burnt; when Fannie cooks, there is always something burnt. He wanted to get up, push away the covers, but his body did not respond, and he suddenly felt depressed, his mind slowed, quieted. I cannot stay here, he thought. And he knew he would not stay here, that this was only a short break, the inconvenience of illness, that when his strength came back, the uniform would be there.

He closed his eyes. I should rest, sleep, he thought. But there was no sleep, because now he began to think of his men. He thought of the mud, the deep mire of the roads. Still, they had moved eagerly through the rains, always believing they would catch Lee's army, that there would be another fight, possibly the last fight. Each man had moved as quickly as the man in front of him would allow, and they did not take the time to see the numbers, what was left of the regiment, how many were no longer there. There were no official reports yet, the men did not know how badly their army had been bled. They only saw the men beside them and the man who led them. They looked at him differently now; every one of them carried the memory of the colonel who had stood out in front of them on that bloody rocky hill, and they all had written of it, letters home, had remembered that place, Little Round Top. They would never forget that he'd ordered them to do the unbelievable, the wild bayonet charge through those men from Alabama, the shock so complete that the rebels had simply stopped fighting. Those who could not run had given up, had nothing left inside to resist the small wave of screaming blue troops that suddenly rolled down into their lines.

For a moment he was there again, running wildly through the rocks and trees. His heart was racing, and seeing the raw shock in the faces of the enemy, he opened his eyes, stared up at the ceiling of his room, clenched his fists under the covers of the bed.

To do it again . . . another fight. He thought, How can there be another fight like that? Was it not enough? It should have been, we should have hit them again, and on the march, finally, there had been hope, maybe Lee would just . . . surrender? Surely, with his back to the river . . . but then it became familiar, and the veterans understood, had been through this before. There would be no attack, they had waited too long, and Lee had prepared, was ready for it. And so they were brought to a halt from behind, from their own commanders, the men under the great tents who alone knew how badly hurt this army had been.

They had seen bits of Lee's lines, small skirmishes, often at night, firing only at brief flashes of musket fire, firing back at the brief glimpses of them. Chamberlain stayed close to his men, and they spoke of it, that even if the fight was not to happen then, they realized what Gettysburg had meant, that Lee's invasion was stopped, that the Army of the Potomac had finally put the right people in the right place. The hard power of the good guns and the good soldiers had been put to the test, and they had prevailed. It was the test they'd always wanted, especially the veterans, the men who had been there from the beginning, from the early disasters at Bull Run, at Fredericksburg, men who carried the fight as well as any soldier could. They never felt they had been beaten by the enemy, by that man over there who pointed his musket at your heart. Their aim was as sharp and as clear as his. Chamberlain knew his own men well, knew they all shared something new, the feeling that this time they had been led by men who knew how to command, the men who let the soldiers decide the battle. On Little Round Top they'd seen the faces of those other fellows, those men in the ragged clothes, faces the generals never saw, and they learned that when the fight came to the bayonet, when there were no trenches and no lines and the enemy looked you in the eye, the uniform made no difference. It was the heart of these men, his men, that had won the fight. And they were ready to do it again.

HE PULLED THE BELT TIGHTER, KNEW HE'D LOST SOME WEIGHT. But at least he was out of bed, had even gone outside, taken a short walk with the children. He was still weak, and had considered asking for a longer leave. The two weeks had expired, but the army was moving again, and so he would go back and join his men in Virginia.

He stood in front of the long mirror, looked at the navy blue of the jacket, the light blue pants, saw no dirt. Fannie had cleaned the uniform, and except for the small frayed areas along the cuffs, it looked nearly new. He frowned at that, thought, This is not quite right. He had gotten used to the dirt. It was good dirt, the dirt of the fields, the muddy ground, the spray from the impact of the incoming shell, the close shudder of death. He stared at clean knees, elbows, wondered, What will the men say?

She came into the room, carrying a stack of bed linens, saw him staring at himself, smiled. "There, now isn't that better? You were quite a mess, you know."

He had not asked her to clean the uniform, but nodded, tried not to show his disappointment. "Yes . . . much better. Thank you." There was no enthusiasm in his voice.

She put the linens on the bed, moved beside him, looked at the both of them in the mirror, said, "I have actually . . . gotten used to this. I never thought I would. My husband, the soldier."

He put his arm around her waist, stood tall, posing. "We are a respectable couple." He coughed, let her go, moved away and sat on the bed.

"And you, my dear colonel, are still sick."

He did not look at her, knew she was right, the weakness was still there. He had tried to make a good show, playing with the children, making preparations for the trip south.

"They need me. The orders . . . I have no choice."

She folded her arms, said sternly, "I don't recall hearing the war had stopped because you were ill. My guess is they will go on fighting whether you are there or not."

He did not want the argument, felt the energy draining out of him. "They do need me. I've been called back. I tried to extend the leave. . . ."

"Oh, yes, I know. But Mr. Lincoln's army cannot stand for one of their heroes to be idle."

He knew this was coming. She had nursed him with joyous energy, had truly enjoyed his being home, even if he was mostly in bed. They had not argued, she did not show the anger of a year ago.

He never knew he would be a soldier, had never thought much about causes and patriotism. There had always been the expectations, the pressure from his father. Chamberlain always resisted, had always believed that his greatest gift was his mind, that teaching was his destiny. But the war had changed that, the causes, the talk of politicians became bloody action, the men with powerful ideas and the force of will and guns that this country had never seen before.

When it all began, he tried to understand the dangers, felt the new frustration of being far from the loud voices, and then from the fight. Then the young people, the quiet faces he spoke to every day, began to speak back, and soon many of them were gone, had put on the uniform and taken the trains south. That shocked him most of all, the passion of the students, the young men who many of the faculty at Bowdoin considered to be but children. But they had become educated, were listening, hearing all the talk, the rhetoric, the voices of reason and the voices of outrage.

Chamberlain found himself speaking of it as well, his prepared lessons fading from his mind, losing their importance in the face of the spreading violence. He had never been political, did not understand much about what drove men to become politicians. The politicians were dangerous; the strength and the passion of their voices had pulled the people on both sides toward this brutal fight. The other professors had accused him of undermining the school, encouraging these boys to join the army, would not see beyond the dark halls of Bowdoin. His anxieties were seen as contagious, and so he had been offered a leave of absence, two years, a trip to Europe perhaps, a tonic for his stress. Instead he had gone to the governor and volunteered to join the army, because he knew it was the most important thing he would ever do. But he hadn't discussed it with anyone, didn't tell them he was going. And he had not discussed it with Fannie.

She left the room now. He heard her moving down the stairs, and he let out a breath, thankful. He knew she was still angry about that, and he would always regret that he did not trust her to support his decision. He had been certain she would object, would not allow him to enlist, and when he finally told her what he'd done, she *was* angry, but it was the anger of love, of fear. Now he would leave her again, and he knew the emotions would be the same.

He heard voices now, from the front of the house, the unmistakable cries of the children for their "Grampa." Chamberlain stood, felt his way along the bed, straightened, took a deep breath, tried to find the energy. He heard his father's voice now, the booming sound he only seemed to make around the small children. Chamberlain glanced in the mirror, checked the uniform, then moved toward the stairway.

He heard the sounds moving into the parlor, the children still bouncing around their grandfather, and the subdued voices of the women.

He paused, listened, heard his father ask, "So, when is he leaving?"

Fannie hushed the children, said, "Tomorrow morning, the first train."

"Oh my dear. So soon . . ." It was his mother, and Chamberlain smiled, had mouthed the words exactly as she spoke them. He moved down the last step, went to the parlor, and his father rose, had a child on either side of him, holding tight.

Fannie reached for them, said quietly, "Not now . . . let Grampa be for now." There were mild protests, and then his father was free of the small hands, and Chamberlain looked into the old face, and his father moved beside him, past, went into the hall. Chamberlain knew what this meant, knew to follow, that the men would be alone now. He followed his father out to the front porch, and there were no words.

They sat in the creaking chairs, and Chamberlain waited, would let his father have the first word. There was a long minute, and his father rocked the old chair slowly, then said, "Tomorrow morning?"

"Yes. The leave's up. They called me back."

"I hear there might be a fight . . . Lee's on the move."

Chamberlain nodded, had not heard anything that specific, wondered, How does he always seem to know what is happening?

"The regiment holding up? The boys doing all right?"

Chamberlain said, "None finer in the army. Just . . . not as many of us now."

"Part *of* it. Always has been." The old man stilled the chair, stood, walked to the porch railing and stared out across the green yard.

There was a pause, and Chamberlain said, "Tom's fine. He's a good officer. He'll command his company soon."

The old man said nothing, and Chamberlain could not see his face, knew he would not say much about his youngest son, had never expected Tom to volunteer.

Chamberlain stood now, moved to the railing, waited, sorted the words, then said, "In the last fight . . . we were in a bit of a jam. I had to use him." He paused, had been thinking of this moment for weeks. "There were men going down, the line was weakening. I sent him in, ordered him to fill a gap in the line. Didn't even think about it . . . until later. If something had happened to him—"

"You won the fight." The old man did not look at him, and Chamberlain wanted to say more, to explain.

"I'm sorry . . . it would have been hard to tell you that, if he had—"

"You won the fight." The old man looked at him now, a sharp hard stare. "You did what officers are supposed to do. You would have learned that at the Point."

Chamberlain sagged. He'd heard this before. That he had not gone to West Point, but stayed in Maine to finish his schooling, was something his father had never understood, had never seen the value in. Even when he was young Chamberlain had heard this, great stories of his ancestors. His father believed the military was the only way a man could measure himself, could find the respect, something to carry with you all your life. They did not argue; his father's disappointment was subtle, quiet. But Chamberlain had always known it was there, and after his graduation, when the first teaching appointments came, when Chamberlain accepted the position at Bowdoin, there was little pride from his father.

His mother had dreamed of the glorious day her oldest son would serve God, seek the ministry, and she still hoped. But his father never spoke of that, the ministry would not bring honor to the family, no matter how devoutly his wife disagreed. When Chamberlain had volunteered for the army, there had been few words between them, but he could feel the quiet attention, that his father was suddenly interested.

By now the people had learned of Gettysburg. Word had spread all over Maine, through letters and newspaper stories, that Chamberlain had done something truly extraordinary. Fannie had written him that his father had begun to take long walks through Brewer, even went across the river, to Bangor, the town he never cared to visit, because now he could talk of his boy the soldier, and the people would come to him to hear all they could of this man's son, the hero of Little Round Top.

The old man stared out again across the yard, said, "This Meade fellow . . . you expect he's ready to wrap this up?"

"General Meade is a good commander. He's finding his way, learning what his army can do. He'll be fine."

"Damned well better be. Gone on long enough. Lee's given all he's got. Time to finish the job."

Chamberlain said nothing, thought, Lee is not whipped, not yet. The old man glanced at Chamberlain's shoulder strap, the silver eagle. "Full colonel. What do you hafta do to be a general?"

Chamberlain smiled, said, "Not sure . . . it would take a few more good fights, I suppose."

The old man said nothing, and Chamberlain watched him, waited. After a minute the old man turned, looked past him toward the front door, moved that way, said, "I better check on those youngsters. . . ." He moved past Chamberlain, then stopped, and Chamberlain waited, felt the old man struggling silently. The old man stared down at the floor, then reached out his hand, touched Chamberlain's arm, still did not look at him, but wrapped his hard fingers around the blue cloth, a tight sharp squeeze. He held it for a brief moment, then moved away, to the door and into the house.

Chamberlain still felt his father's grasp, smiled, felt something move inside of him, knew it was the first time; that if the words were not there, if the old man did not know how to tell him, Chamberlain knew now the barriers were behind them, that finally he had made his father proud.

3. CHAMBERLAIN

AUGUST 1863

HE WOUND HIS WAY AMONG THE CAMPSITES, PAST GROWING fires, the end of a peaceful day, the men relaxing from a slow, easy march. The smells were drifting by him, coffee and bacon, and he felt a rush, the excitement. He was back with the army, back in northern Virginia.

The return trip had not been too rough, but he felt the weariness, a dull throb in his head. As he moved through the camps, he already felt stronger, the remnants of the illness fading away. Officers noticed him as he passed their units, men Chamberlain had never seen. Some spoke to him, nods, casual greetings. The soldiers ignored him, it was their own private time, and unfamiliar officers did not attract attention. The daylight was nearly gone, but he could see the red Maltese cross in the distance, the flags of the Fifth Corps, and then the flag of the First Division. Near the flag were the larger headquarters tents, and he saw many officers now, sitting in a circle, some standing behind. There was laughter, a brief glimpse, the passing of a bottle. Beyond the big tents he saw the brigade colors, saw finally the Third, moved that way. Now some men began to call out, he was recognized, and he saw a few familiar faces, the cordial greetings, then heard a voice behind him.

"Colonel Chamberlain . . ."

He turned, saw a tall man, lanky, long strides, moving from the cluster of officers, and he stood straight, saluted.

"General Griffin. I have returned, sir. I was going to report as soon as I found my men, sir."

Griffin returned the salute, briefly patted Chamberlain on the shoulder. "No matter, Colonel, no urgency. Might I walk with you?"

It was an unusual request, generals walked wherever they pleased.

"Certainly, sir. I was headed toward the Third Brigade over that way, unless you want to go . . . elsewhere." He felt awkward, self-conscious, waited for Griffin to move, fell into step beside him.

"Colonel, I don't believe we've spent much time together. Not since Gettysburg. The men . . . my staff tells me they hear your name every day."

"Thank you, sir."

"You back for duty? You . . . fit?"

"Oh yes, sir. It was a touch of malaria." He made a face. Don't explain, he thought. Never give the generals a reason to doubt you. He looked toward the flags, began to move a bit faster. Where was the regiment? He was beginning to feel the familiar rumble in his gut, thought, Generals do that, they make you think too much.

Griffin stayed close to him, and men were now standing as they moved past. There were salutes from low-ranking officers, a few voices. Griffin was not often among the men, was rarely sociable, except around his staff and other officers of high rank. Chamberlain had first met him at Fredericksburg, after the long and horrible night on the cold ground, the night spent close to the enemy. Chamberlain would always recall that meeting, Griffin holding out his hand to him, a ragged, exhausted man who had slept behind the cover of the bodies of his own men. Griffin had simply told him, "Good work."

Chamberlain had not understood that, had not thought there was any good work in that horrible assault, the pure stupidity of marching up against the stone wall, straight into the massed fire of Lee's strength. It had been his first real fight, leading his men forward into the smoke, the first time he heard the screams and the sickening sound of the lead ball cracking the skull of the man beside you. All of that was a fog, a cold blur. He did not try to remember, did not pick out the details. But he did remember Griffin, and his words.

Chamberlain had always heard that Charles Griffin was not anyone's friend, but a man of great temper, quick to bring down his wrath on the man, private or colonel, who did not do his job. And Griffin demanded more than a good job. Chamberlain did not mind that, had been taught and trained by another manic disciplinarian, Adelbert Ames, knew that no matter how much the men grumbled, the low curses behind the commander's back, the training would save their lives. The men knew it too, were veterans now, had marched into the deafening roar of the fire, felt the lightning flash of fear, that small edge of panic, and they understood that it was that cursed discipline, inside each of them now, that kept the panic away.

Chamberlain saw his own regimental colors, changed course slightly, pointed. "The Twentieth Maine . . . my unit."

They walked closer to the fires, and now more men rose, and the salutes gave way to shouts, the men gathering, emerging from tents, all moving toward Chamberlain. Chamberlain smiled at the familiar faces, then saw Tom.

The young man jumped up, ran forward. "Lawrence . . . Colonel! You're back!" Tom moved close, put his hands on Chamberlain's arms, a wide boyish grin on his face. "We been waiting for you . . . we knew we weren't going nowhere till you got back!"

Chamberlain had shut off his own smile, stared at his brother with a silent scolding, motioned with his eyes toward Griffin and said stiffly, "Lieutenant Chamberlain, thank you. General Griffin, this is Lieutenant Tom Chamberlain . . . my brother, sir."

Tom's smile vanished and his mouth opened as he looked at Griffin with wide startled eyes. He remembered to salute now, stepped back, snapped his arm in place. "Sir!"

Griffin returned the salute, did not focus on Tom, said aloud, to the gathering crowd, "Gentlemen, I share your enthusiasm for the return of your colonel. And I am sure he is equally anxious to see you. However, if you will excuse us, we have a matter to discuss. He won't be long."

There were small murmurs from the men, quiet questions. They rarely saw the division commander, knew something was up. Even the officers traded glances. Chamberlain looked at Griffin, surprised, and suddenly nervous, said, "Certainly, General. Always at your disposal, sir."

Griffin turned, moved away from the light of the fires, and Chamberlain followed. They moved down a long hill, a clearing between short pines. Griffin stopped, stared out into the darkening woods. "Did you hear about Colonel Rice?"

Chamberlain had a sudden dark dread; his stomach turned. Jim Rice had replaced Strong Vincent as brigade commander, Chamberlain's immediate superior. Vincent was a popular commander and a very good soldier, the man who had seen the value of the ground and so placed the Twentieth Maine on Little Round Top. Vincent had been badly wounded on that same day, and died a few days later, and it had deeply affected the men. Chamberlain thought, What has happened now, to Rice? "Is he . . . all right?"

Griffin heard the hesitation, looked at Chamberlain, laughed. "Oh, yes, Colonel, he's quite all right. He's been promoted to brigadier general, they moved him to the First Corps."

Chamberlain let out a breath. "Thank God. That's wonderful . . . well deserved."

"Well deserved." Griffin shook his head. "The ways of the army . . . promote a man after you arrest him."

Chamberlain was confused, did not know what Griffin was talking about. "Sir . . . I had not heard . . ."

"Right, you were on leave. When we were on the march chasing after Lee, Rice allowed his men to make camp bedding from a farmer's haystack, let them sleep above the mud instead of in it. Probably saved half the brigade from drowning. But the corps heard about it, some staff officer dusted off the regulations, and General Sykes had him arrested . . . 'molesting private property.' "

Griffin put his foot up on a stump, leaned on his knee, stared out into the trees. "It got straightened out pretty quick. Somebody at Meade's headquarters heard about it, knew the newspapers would have a carnival. We let Lee escape, so we make up for it by arresting our best officers."

Chamberlain stood, watched Griffin, the nervousness now replaced by something else—curiosity. "Well, sir . . . General Rice will surely make us proud." He felt awkward again, did not enjoy formal small talk.

Griffin said, "There's quite a few fellows who think they're the one to fill his vacancy, some of 'em deserving. Tough choice. I picked you." Chamberlain stared, waited for more. Griffin turned toward him, said, "You, Colonel. I want you to command the Third Brigade."

Chamberlain smiled, tried to suppress it but could not, looked away, embarrassed.

Griffin did not seem to notice, said, "It's not permanent, there's no promotion in rank, not yet. I did send in my recommendation. That's an issue for Washington. Doesn't really matter anyway. You might run into a bit of resistance from your regimental commanders. Some of them been around a bit longer than you. I've made it clear . . . they do understand who's in command. It's your brigade, Colonel."

Chamberlain saluted, still smiled. "Thank you, sir!"

Griffin was not smiling, returned the salute. "You earned it, Colonel. We still have a job to do, and we need the best men to do it." Griffin looked up the hill, began to move away, glanced back at Chamberlain. "You need to pick a successor to take over the regiment. Make a recommendation pretty quick. You know your men. We'll go with anybody you say, most likely. Enjoy your evening, Colonel."

Griffin climbed the rise, and Chamberlain watched him crest the hill but did not follow. He felt like laughing, remembered a year ago, standing in front of the governor, hearing the words "lieutenant colonel," the same feeling, like a small boy receiving a great Christmas present. Now he was to lead the brigade, the whole brigade. He thought of the men, above him on the hill, the men from Maine. I will have to tell them . . . something, he thought. He felt a sudden dread, choosing someone else to command them. Who? How would the men respond? It should be someone from within the regiment, of course. But he could not focus, the names did not come, it was too soon. He began to climb the hill, moved in long quick steps back to the fires, to the wonderful smells of the food.

SINCE THE LOSSES AT GETTYSBURG, WASHINGTON HAD MADE great efforts to rebuild the army, and reinforcements were coming in daily. But not all the new troops were men eager for a fight. With the draft now in full force, many of these recruits were men who had avoided the first calls for volunteers; some had even been a part of the violence, the draft riots. But now they faced the reality that they would serve whether they wanted to or not. Others were substitutes, men paid to take the place of those who could afford to buy their way out of the process. Often these men were motivated only by the gold they received, and when they first experienced the constraints of discipline, or the first brush with the horror of what a fight with the rebels might bring, many simply disappeared. To the fighting units who had won the great glory and honor on the field, these new numbers added little, except for new problems, problems this army did not need. Meade and his commanders could not afford to be tolerant of this threat to the morale of the men who were still willing to carry the fight, and so, when deserters were caught, the punishment was swift and certain.

HE STOOD IN A LINE, SURROUNDED BY THE ENTIRE FIFTH CORPS. They were lined up by division across a wide field, the men facing each other on three sides of a square. On the fourth side, the open end, he could see the short row of freshly dug graves, and beside each one a simple wooden coffin. Once the troops had completed the formation, the drums began, a slow steady roll, and finally there was motion, across the field. He could see the prisoners being brought forward, the men moving in slow, jerking motions, held to small steps by the chains around their legs. Now each man was placed into position, standing beside his own grave, and then they were sat down, each on the front of his own coffin.

Around Chamberlain, men began to make small sounds, nervous, faces turning away, some looking down. Chamberlain did not turn away, stared at the five men, felt a low hot sickness in his gut.

Suddenly the drums were silent, and for a small moment there was no other sound. Now an officer began to read something, the orders, words Chamberlain could not hear. The man finished his duty, moved away, another officer shouted something, and from one side a row of riflemen stepped sharply into position. The officer shouted again, and Chamberlain could hear the metallic sound, the guns snapped to the chests. Then he heard the single word, the hard voice of the officer again: *"Aim!"* More of the men around Chamberlain turned away now, a small groan flowing through the lines. He blinked hard, felt the sickness again, rising slowly, and he clenched his fists, said to himself, No, do not turn away. Watch this. See it.

Now the officer raised his sword, and Chamberlain heard the word clearly, the only sound breaking through the deathly calm. *"Fire!"*

The sound startled them all, a sharp hard rattle, and all around him men shuddered, jumped. He had jumped as well, blind reflex, but he did not turn away, could see the impact of the lead balls in the men, the punch in their clothes, each man collapsing, falling into a grotesque heap. There was a long quiet moment, and he stared at the bodies, could see the blood now, a dark stain spreading out on the dusty ground. All around him the men began to look at the scene, the horror, and suddenly the drums began, startling them all again. There were new orders, close by, and Chamberlain focused, heard the call to march. The great example was over.

FEW OF THE MEN, EVEN THE VETERANS FROM THE OLD ARMY, HAD ever watched a firing squad, but today they had seen one, the shocking spectacle of five men shot down by their own.

Chamberlain drank a cup of coffee, poured it from reflex, did not taste the awful burn of a pot that had sat on the fire all day, left behind in the haste to fall into line. He put the cup down, looked around the camp, saw men moving slowly, some sitting now, many just standing alone. It was late in the day, and the food would come soon, but no one spoke of it, no one gathered at the fires. He thought of Ames, of Griffin, the discipline. That was what today was about, of course. They all know that, he thought. But this was something new. Occasionally this had happened before, men were shot or hanged, usually for some hateful crime, murder, the rape of a citizen. But today men were killed because they would not fight. And it had never been made into something so . . . public. He thought of the pronouncement, the Official Word, read before the executions. Of course, it was official. The army, he knew, was not like any other organization, any business. If you are here, he thought, you fight for your country, and possibly die for your country, and you are not allowed to change your mind. How odd . . . We are fighting—some of us, anyway—for . . . freedom? And soldiers are not free.

He watched his men, thought, Stop this, you're thinking too much again. Those five men . . . ran away. If they did that in a fight, it could cause a disaster. If the man standing right next to you ran away, it could cost you your own life. I just didn't think . . . we would have to be reminded of that.

He was still with the regiment, it had been just three days since Griffin had given him the change of command. He'd given much thought to who would replace him, had made a choice in his mind only this morning, and then the news had come to the camp, Ellis Spear had received a promotion to major. Before the war, Spear had been a schoolteacher, and it was rare for anyone to have something in common with Chamberlain. From the beginning there had been friendship, and Chamberlain discovered that Spear was not only there for good conversation, but had proven himself a good soldier, and a good commander as well. That made it simpler still, for Spear was to be his recommendation to General Griffin.

The men began to relax now, more were moving about. He heard small voices, conversations. A few were looking at him, and he saw sadness in some, sharp anger in others. He was suddenly very weary, thought, Maybe a short nap, turned for his tent. Then he saw Spear walking toward him and said, "This was not a pleasant day, Major."

Spear clenched down hard on a small pipe, seemed deep in thought. "Colonel, if you don't mind? A word?"

Chamberlain pointed toward his tent, moved that way, and Spear followed. They ducked inside. Chamberlain sat on the cot, pointed at the small wooden stool. Spear sat down slowly, held the pipe in his hand, stared at it.

"What is it, Ellis?"

Spear thought, looked at the ground. "Colonel . . . I'm not sure. This was a difficult day."

"You're not sure of what?"

"I'm not sure I could do that to my own men. If that's what it takes to command . . . I have to tell you that, Colonel." He paused. "I don't know if I could order a man to stand there and shoot one of his own. How do you do that?"

"We have done it before, Ellis. We do it every time we fight."

"But that's the enemy . . . it's different."

"Is it? I was raised to believe that men aren't supposed to kill each other at all. Yet, somehow, we have accepted doing exactly that. We have learned to kill men who we have been taught are our enemy. Men are dying around us in greater numbers and in ways more horrible than anything mankind has ever experienced. This war has inspired the creative minds of brilliant men to invent extraordinary weapons, new and incredibly efficient killing machines, canister, torpedoes, mines. It's a part of everything around us. The disturbing thing about today . . . what shocks us is not that we killed men in blue uniforms, but that it was so . . . *easy*. The order is given, the muskets are fired, and the army has made its point. If we do not do our duty, it could happen to us."

"Is that how you saw this today? Was it our duty to shoot those men?"

Chamberlain looked up, glanced at the dull light of the sunset reflecting through the walls of the tent. "Yes, Major. And God help us."

4. CHAMBERLAIN

October 1863

THEY MARCHED IN THE DARK, THROUGH THE SAME FAMILIAR mud, the thick glue of the Virginia roads, the brown sludge that had paralyzed this army once before, nine months earlier. It had been late January, and General Burnside, tempted by a brief taste of spring weather, quickly moved the army up along the Rappahannock, away from the great bloody disaster of Fredericksburg. It was a good plan, move up and around Lee's flank, and even Washington had approved. But it had still been winter, and the weather turned, the hard and angry howl of wind and rain softening the roads, swallowing the wagons and the guns. The miserable army had finally been halted, then returned to the camps they never should have left. They now called it the "Mud March," and it had been the last command decision for Ambrose Burnside.

Chamberlain felt the horse lifting its legs, the effort of each step on the thickness of the road. He shifted in the saddle, straightened his back. There was no rhythm, no gentle rocking of the horse; instead, each step was deliberate and tiring. Behind him he heard low curses, small jokes about generals and mud, one man trying to start a song, drowned out by jeers. He stared out ahead, saw the light of a lantern, men pulling at a wagon, one man with a long pole, prying at a buried wheel, lifting it from the thick ooze. His men began to call out, teasing, and he heard one man say, close behind him, "Just shoot it and put it out of its misery."

He smiled, turned, could not see the man in the darkness, thought, Yes, even tonight . . . they are in good spirits, the morale is as high as it has ever been. They want a fight. We *need* a fight.

There had not been much fighting since Gettysburg, at least not for these men. The action was in the West, at a place Chamberlain had never heard of. He rolled the word around in his mind: *Chickamauga*. The Federal army was being commanded there by William Rosecrans, and all Chamberlain knew was that the rebels had driven "Old Rosy" from the field, the papers calling it a bloody disaster, a panicked rout. That Rosecrans's army was not totally destroyed was credited to General George Thomas, who held his ground while the rest of the Federal army escaped into the city of Chattanooga. Now Washington had pulled two corps away from Meade's army, sending them to strengthen Rosecrans.

Chamberlain began to think about numbers: How many are we now? Eighty thousand? Does it matter? Does it mean we are not as strong? He thought of all the fights, the reports he'd seen. The numbers were always on their side, Lee was always outnumbered. And until Gettysburg, Lee nearly always won. So, it wasn't just numbers. Then . . . what? Luck? No, he thought, we needed more than luck at Fredericksburg. It was something else, intangible. Commanders. . . . He pictured Meade in his mind, had seen him several times, mostly before Gettysburg. The army respected him; no one ever said he wasn't a good soldier. But whether he was the right commander . . .

Some had said the job should have gone to Reynolds, but Reynolds was dead. Many wanted Hancock, some wanted Sickles, but both had taken bad wounds at Gettysburg, and neither had yet returned to the army. No, he thought, we will follow George Meade until he either wins the war or makes some awful mistake.

He moved closer to a cluster of lanterns, saw a row of cannon and men gathered around one broken gun, the barrel pointing up between two crooked wheels. Men were pulling it aside, and there was an officer. Chamberlain moved to the side of the road, halted the horse, said, "May we lend a hand?"

The man did not look at him, and Chamberlain waited, watched the men straining in silence, lifting and pushing. Suddenly, there was a loud crack, the groan of splitting wood, and the gun carriage collapsed completely, the wheels folding in, the cannon barrel now pointing straight up at Chamberlain. He flinched, stared at the hole, the small round blackness in the dull lamplight, and ducked away, leaned back in the saddle, felt a cold twist in his stomach. The gun was pulled off the roadway, the men still silent, the officer now moving away.

Chamberlain pulled his horse around, alongside the column, glanced back at the barrel of the big gun, felt embarrassed, thought, Well now, that wasn't such bravery, was it? He still felt the jolt, wondered,

How many men get that close, stare right into that hole before ... Can you see it? Do you see the blast, the split-second image of death before it takes you away? He moved the horse to the head of the column, fell in alongside the color bearer, a quiet sergeant with a full black beard. Chamberlain nodded, was always polite, and the sergeant glanced at him, said nothing, had ridden beside many commanders. Chamberlain stared ahead, thought of the cannon: Maybe that's the best way; if you have to go, go out in pieces, one big blast. He'd seen too many who went the other way, the men who cried and screamed, who felt every horrible moment of their own death, who fought to hang on.

He shook his head, brushed away the image, scolded himself: Stop that.

Focusing ahead, he saw more lanterns, the dark roadway speckled in dull spots of light. He was suddenly hungry. The march had begun before they could eat, and he felt his pockets, pulled out one old piece of hardtack, put it into his mouth without looking at it. It was always better that way. He knew not to chew, let the thing get soft first, but he was really hungry now, and so he bit down, felt his mouth fill with dry crumbs. He grabbed at his canteen, put it to his mouth, felt the blessed wetness, swallowed. Now his mouth felt like wet dough, and he drank some more, washed it down. He put the canteen aside, ran his tongue around the stale taste in his mouth, thought, Wonderful, that may be all for tonight. Remember it with a smile.

It had been this way since Gettysburg, the orders coming down at odd times, a short march or a longer one. Then they would stop, there would be no orders for a while, and they'd spread out into barren fields. Always they expected to see the enemy, and there might be a small skirmish, or nothing at all, and then more orders, and they would march back again, on the same roads. Sometimes the orders were more specific, a hint of urgency from headquarters, and so they would march at night, hurried along by the commanders, the men who knew ... *something*. Tonight they were marching north, so were they being chased? He thought of the numbers again, the missing troops, the men sent to Tennessee. Lee must know ... maybe it was a mistake, we are too weak.

They knew Lee had sent troops to the West as well, Longstreet's corps. Of course it was a secret, but around these armies there were few well-kept secrets. The spies had brought in the Richmond newspapers, and they were amazed to see a full written account of Longstreet's troop movements, even his route of travel. And so headquarters understood that sending Federal troops west would be no secret either.

Meade was always being pushed by Washington, the impatience of a government that had expected Gettysburg to bring greater results, a quick conclusion. But Meade was still wary, knew that Lee was as dangerous as he had ever been, that Lee's army would wait for him, try to outmaneuver him. When Washington pushed Meade forward, he would only go far enough to probe, seek an opportunity. If the opportunity was not there, if Lee did not leave himself open to attack, Meade would draw away again. For two months the armies stalked each other like two cats, and now Meade was backing away again. By morning the army would reach a small river, Broad Run, and cross to the safety beyond, at the fords around Bristoe Station.

HE WAS ON THE NORTH SIDE OF THE STREAM, AND WATCHED from his horse as the last of the brigade moved across. Below Broad Run he saw a squad of blue cavalry come up out of the far woods, riding hard, moving closer to the rows of troops crossing the stream. Now he saw more cavalry, emerging from the woods farther to the right, and there were scattered shots, musket fire in the woods. His column began to break up, men falling out, trying to see behind them, the sounds rolling across the stream, and the officers began to shout, moving the men back into line.

Chamberlain watched the distant woods, could see nothing, and he yelled toward his men, "Keep moving, clear away from the water, let the column across!"

His men pushed forward, and Chamberlain felt a sudden rush of energy, thought, Yes, they *are* chasing us. Below the stream the cavalry began to dismount, officers yelling orders to form a skirmish line. Chamberlain saw that his men were well above the stream now, saw the last of the First Division crossing, and he rode back to the bank, where Griffin was splashing his horse through the shallow water, coming toward him.

Griffin pointed back to the line of cavalry, yelled, "Colonel, prepare to receive an attack! Move your column to that rise above the creek. Lee's right on our tail!"

Chamberlain turned, saw his men moving up on the ridge, said, "Right away, sir! We're there already. I'll turn them this way." He saluted, spurred the horse, climbed the short rise. The men were turned, the regiments forming a line of battle facing the stream. Chamberlain watched Griffin direct more troops into line toward his flank, and he rode forward, climbed a small knoll and saw them. Below the stream, across a wide field, two thick lines of rebels came out of the woods, advancing toward the last of the men still waiting to cross. Then Griffin was beside him, and Chamberlain watched him staring hard across the field. Griffin said, "It's A. P. Hill . . . they got up around us. They're trying to cut us off. But it's too late."

Chamberlain could see the rebel lines moving closer, and now there was a solid line of gray smoke and the sound of the volley. The cavalry line was being overwhelmed, and they rushed back toward the stream, closer to the mass of blue infantry. Then the rebels moved forward again, pressing the attack.

Griffin said, "Only a division . . . maybe two brigades. They don't have the strength! What the hell is going on? Where's the rest of them?"

The rebels moved closer, there was another volley, and along the stream shells began to explode, the booming of rebel guns from far across the field. Chamberlain's chest was pounding now; he heard the

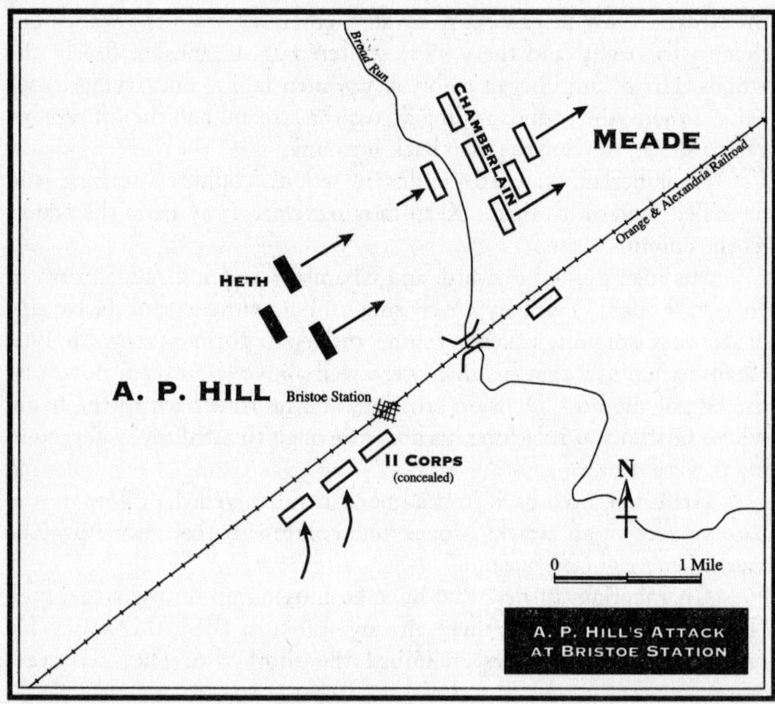

A. P. HILL'S ATTACK AT BRISTOE STATION

whiz of a musket ball over his head, then another, closer. He looked down along the lines of the brigade, saw the faces staring out at the enemy. The musket fire was steady now, and Griffin was saying something, pointing. Chamberlain tried to hear, followed Griffin's gesture. Off to the left, beyond the stream, he saw a bright flash, but it was not cannon, there was no smoke. He leaned forward, tried to see through a row of small trees, realized it was a reflection, the sun glancing off the massed bayonets of many, many men. Griffin was still pointing, said, "It's . . . the Second Corps . . ."

Chamberlain saw it all now, the smoke from the fight in front of them clearing away in the breeze. On the far side of the stream there was a railroad cut, and the Second Corps had moved up, twelve thousand men hidden by a high embankment, unseen by the rebels. Now a mass of muskets pointed out over the embankment, and suddenly there was a sharp cracking volley, a flaming blast into the flank of the rebel assault. The smoke flowed across the field, and Chamberlain felt an odd turn in his gut, the shock of the mass of fire, of watching a whole battle line collapse at once. The rebels began to turn what was left of their line, to face the railroad cut, and some moved forward, to charge this new enemy, but there was another volley, and those lines collapsed as well. Then the big Federal guns above the stream began to fire, and Chamberlain felt the ground shake, and Griffin stood up in his stirrups, yelled, "A trap! A perfect trap!"

Abruptly, Griffin spurred his horse and rode forward, followed by his staff. Chamberlain turned, saw the sergeant behind him, holding the flag, and the man was staring grimly, silently, toward the field. Chamberlain followed the man's eyes, could see the last of the rebels moving away. The musket fire faded, the big guns quieted, and in minutes it was over. Now came the shouts, the wild yells. He looked down the lines of his brigade, and the men were cheering, waving hats, muskets held high. Then the loud voices rang out to the left, across the stream, the men behind the railroad cut. Chamberlain watched the last of the rebels fade back into the far trees, and he thought, This was more than a skirmish. We won . . . we beat them. It was over so quickly. He tried to feel the excitement of the men around him, but it was held away by his own surprise at what had happened, at how clearly he'd seen it. He looked across the field at the men left behind, a horrifying mass of rebel dead. It was a foolish attack, he thought. There was no strength. And they didn't know the railroad cut was full of infantry. Griffin was right. They walked right into a trap.

He moved his horse forward, close to the edge of the stream, saw men in blue moving out into the field, tending the wounded rebels. There were men with canteens, men with stretchers. The cheering had stopped, and now the sounds came from the field, faint and high and terrible, and more soldiers moved out to help the men they had shot down. In the distance some of the wounded were still crawling back toward the woods, pulling themselves away from a perfect disaster.

5. LEE

October 1863

He reached the edge of the woods, stopped the horse, stared out beyond the wide field. He could see the stream, the small wood buildings. He looked to the low hills beyond, closed his eyes, waited, then forced himself to look at the ground close by, the wide sweep of open grass covered with the bodies of his men.

Along the stream he saw cavalry, a squad of Stuart's men. Stuart was already following Meade's trail, the roads north, and the messages came back to Lee in a steady flow: Meade was moving away. Lee knew Meade would not stop until he reached the next good ground, would protect himself from any surprises. For a while, at least, there would be no more fighting on this field, along this stream, this place called Bristoe Station.

Troops began to move up around him, skirmishers, sent into the field to make sure there were no enemy stragglers and no lingering sharpshooters. The men began to look to the bodies, to prod and poke, to search for some sign of life, but the wounded were gone. Those who had not been able to retreat were now carried by the Yankees.

Hill was beside him, sat quietly, watching Lee, waiting. Lee spurred the horse, moved out into the field. The soldiers moved with him, spread out farther to the front, watching, focused on the far hills across the stream, the tops of trees. There was no calling out, no cheers, nothing to reveal to hidden eyes who this might be, the white-bearded officer on the tall gray horse.

The horse stepped between the bodies of the dead, and Lee looked out across to the railroad cut, saw bodies spread all along the embankment. He removed his hat, held it by his side, rubbed his hand through the white hair, thought, If there had been more strength . . . we might have pushed them out of the cut, routed them across the stream. He tried to see it in his mind, the flags and the swarm of men pushing up and over the embankment, but the image was not there. This was not a field where victory had been turned away by brilliant strategy or a crucial piece of luck. It had not been close, a decision forced by the gallant heroics of one man rising up to turn the flow. It had been a simple bloody mistake.

Lee looked back at Hill, and Hill moved his horse forward, close beside Lee. The staff stayed back. Only Taylor rode out, stayed a few feet away, on the other side. Taylor stared at the dead, made an angry sound, a low discreet grunt. Lee did not acknowledge it, knew that Taylor did not respect Hill, did not regard him as a good commander. But Taylor could never say that to Lee.

Lee had not done this often—ridden out onto the bloody fields, fields where there were so many of his men, and so very few of the men in blue. There had not been many defeats like this, one-sided tragedies. Now it was up to Hill himself to explain; not to make excuses, but to understand what he'd done, the incredible disastrous mistake.

Lee still stared ahead, heard Hill clear his throat, a small cough, heard him shift himself in the saddle. Lee knew Hill was not well, had great discomfort riding, seemed to be in pain all of the time. The pain was on his face, and in the shape of his body, a great hard weight on his shoulders, pushing him down. Hill cleared his throat again.

"General Lee, there was a lack of . . . good reconnaissance."

Lee said nothing, waited for more.

"We did not know the Yankees were in force on this side of the run. I ordered . . . I believed that speed was the priority. He was spread out . . . I thought I could catch his rear unprotected."

Lee nodded quietly, still said nothing. He understood now how this could have happened.

A. P. Hill was a difficult man to command, sensitive and easy to provoke. He carried with him a dark stain from a past that he could not escape. At West Point he had missed graduating with his class in 1846, had to wait one more year, and the reason was scandalous and embarrassing: He had built a reputation as a young man who enjoyed the parties and the houses of ill-repute, the rowdy temptations of New York, and he'd suffered from what was described discreetly as a "social affliction." The late graduation meant he'd barely made it to the fight in Mexico, a fight won by the heroism of many of his classmates, Jackson, McClellan. And even in Lee's army he had never found a comfortable command. There was the great feud with Longstreet, a dispute begun by a newspaper report in Richmond, giving Hill more credit than Longstreet felt he deserved for the good fights on the Virginia peninsula, the Seven Days battles. Their arguments and hostility grew so intense that Hill challenged Longstreet to a duel, something Lee could not tolerate. Lee had only defused the situation by transferring Hill to Jackson's command. But Hill did not perform to Stonewall's rigid and inflexible standards, and so he found himself the focus of Jackson's hot temper as well. There were more charges, threats of arrest and court-martial, a controversy that ended only with Jackson's death.

But on the field, Hill had made his reputation. At Second Manassas, his battered line held their ground against Pope's overwhelming strength, and saved Jackson's flank until the great crushing blow from Longstreet swept the Federals from the field. At Sharpsburg, Hill pushed his men on a hard forced march, arriving on the field when Lee's entire position was near collapse. His division had driven Burnside's surprised troops back across Antietam Creek, and from that moment the cry among the men was "up came Hill." He bathed himself in that, the pride of his men, and most had considered him then the best division commander in the army. Since Jackson's death, Hill commanded a much larger force, many of Jackson's troops; but since Gettysburg, and through the small nameless fights of autumn, he'd shown none of the fire that had given him his reputation. It was a crushing disappointment to Lee, and he was beginning to see how it could be a great danger to the army. Here, on this one open field, in a fight that lasted less than one hour, because Hill was in a hurry, they had lost nearly two thousand men.

"Sir, I will prepare my report."

Lee nodded, put his hat on. The sun was dropping into the tops of the trees behind them, and he knew nothing would happen for a while. He understood Meade now, as he had understood the others before him, and he could anticipate the jabs, the deep probes, Meade's way of looking for an advantage. Lee knew if there was to be a fight soon, he would have to press it. But the rolling country out in front of him, across Broad Run, was too familiar. The roads ran across more fields, up toward another stream called Bull Run, where the two great battles of Manassas had been fought. The land was stripped by the war, desolate and barren, and Lee's army could not support itself there. Where else could they go now but back, southward, to the protection of the big river behind them, the Rappahannock?

Lee glanced at Taylor, still said nothing, but Taylor knew the look, pulled his horse away and moved back toward the waiting staff. Lee took a deep breath, looked down at the bodies close around them, and Hill motioned, cleared his throat.

"Sir . . . General Lee . . . I am sorry . . . sir."

Lee looked at Hill, saw the shame, the grief in the face of this small sickly man. He felt a sudden dark anger, impatience. He looked away toward the darkening sky, gripped his anger, clamped it down, would not show it, would not lecture him. He thought, There is nothing I can say that will change this. This was a lesson from God, and General Hill must learn from this, must take this with him, and it will not happen again.

Hill waited, peered up at Lee from under the brim of the battered hat. After a quiet moment Lee said, "Well, General, let's bury these poor men, and say no more about it."

THE ARMY MOVED SOUTH ALONG THE RAILROAD, THE GREAT steel link with the north, the Orange and Alexandria. He sat on Traveller, watched a detail of men with sledgehammers, some with long steel pry bars. They knew he was watching them, and so the work was fast and without complaint, and the officers did not have to tell the men how to do their job.

They pulled and twisted, and gradually a long piece of track pulled free of the rail bed. Now more men dragged the rail to a neatly stacked pile of logs, and with one great groan they laid it on top, balancing it carefully so that each end of the rail stuck far out in each direction. There were already several more rails on the stack, and now an officer moved up, carried a small tuft of burning straw, knelt beside the woodpile, spread the flame slowly around the edges. The fire began to climb, and in a few short minutes it engulfed the woodpile completely. Lee pulled at the horse, moved away from the tracks, heard the men whooping, knew that when the fire was at its hottest, the weight of the heavy steel would begin to tell, that as the steel heated and softened, the ends of the rails would begin to sag. Then the men would lift them off the fire and push them hard against a fat tree trunk, twisting them more, so when they cooled and the steel hardened again, they could never be used for rails.

He rode toward his camp, thought of the railroad, the shipments moving south from Washington, supplying Meade's army. He felt a black anger, gripped the reins tightly, did not hear the men he passed, the bright salutes, the small cheers. He did not look at them because he knew he'd see gaunt faces, rags, bare feet. From the south, the railcars did not bring the supplies that Meade received so easily from the great factories and farms of the North. The supplies were simply not there to send, the farms depleted, the citizens of the small towns and the larger cities, choked by the naval blockade, fighting their own war of survival.

Always when he moved north, he repaired the railroads as he went, fixing what a retreating Federal army had destroyed. But now, instead of repairing the damage, Lee was creating it, destroying the tracks himself. He did not share the enthusiasm for the job that his men had shown. They did not understand, not yet, that the war had changed. The defeat at Gettysburg had cost them too much, and there would be no more invasions north. With Meade in pursuit, even a hesitant pursuit, Lee knew he could not simply make a stand or drive forward into the enemy. He had to rely on maneuver now, draw Meade into a vulnerable place, allow Meade to make a careless mistake. The only way to do that was to bring Meade south with them.

It was nearly dark, and he saw his campfire, saw Taylor signing a paper, handing it to a courier. The man moved away quickly, efficiently, and Lee climbed down from the horse, handed the reins to an orderly, moved to the fire.

There were other men waiting to see Taylor, the daily routine of the headquarters, but when they saw Lee, staring quietly, alone, into the fire, they did not approach. He watched the flames, heard nothing but the soft sound of the burning wood, did not hear Taylor send aides toward the soldiers, telling them: later. Taylor moved into the firelight, and Lee looked into the boyish face, saw the major's uniform, knew Taylor would not be self-conscious; the promotion had just been announced, and the new coat would be slow in coming, the insignia of Lieutenant Colonel.

Lee said, "Colonel, we have destroyed our own railroad."

Taylor nodded, said quietly, "Yes, sir."

Lee looked back into the fire. "We are backing away from an enemy we could have beaten. We must wait for him to come to us. We do not have the means . . . to press the attack. The men . . . we are not providing for the men."

"Sir, it is a disgrace. Richmond must be made to understand. . . ."

Lee saw the anger in Taylor's face, knew that his aide shared his frustrations. He is so young, Lee thought. He does not understand . . .

you must find the control, you must not let the darker emotions surface. Lee raised his hand in a calming gesture. "No, Colonel. Richmond cannot help us. It has been clear for some time . . . we must do with what we have. The president has assured me that all that can be done is being done. But the men do not receive shoes, the rations are disgraceful. I have begun to fear . . . it seems there is treachery. Someone in the quartermaster's office does not want us to prevail." He paused, thought, No, I should not . . . we must not be a party to rumor.

Taylor was watching him, wide-eyed, and Lee said, "Colonel, this is in confidence . . . do not speak of this to anyone. I must depend on you, as my chief of staff. You must understand the importance in not allowing the business of this army to reach beyond this headquarters. It seems that principle is not being followed elsewhere. There are those in the government who find it necessary to discuss our strategy with the newspapers. I have learned more about our troop movements in Tennessee from the Richmond papers than I have from the president." He looked up, above the fire, toward the shadows, men moving through the camp. Taylor said nothing, still watched him. Lee now looked at the young man, and Taylor stood upright, a reflex to Lee's quiet anger.

Lee said, "Colonel, from this point on I must examine any dispatch that goes to Richmond. We will have to be more . . . discreet about what we tell the president, the secretary of war. And, especially, the quartermaster general." Taylor nodded slowly, absorbing Lee's words, and there was a silence. Lee thought, He is so young . . . he may not understand the importance . . .

He suddenly felt the absence of Longstreet. Lee could talk about any subject, the politics of Richmond, the dark troubling doubts, and Longstreet would always listen, patient, watching him with sad dark eyes. Then Longstreet would always offer something of his own, might even make an argument, but always respectful, only enough to make a point. Lee knew that lately, since Gettysburg, the disagreements between them had been deeper, less was said face-to-face, that Longstreet's dark moods had taken him further away. With Longstreet now in Tennessee, Lee did not think on that, on the disagreements, the controversies about Longstreet's sluggishness. Lee had seen the newspapers, knew that many were now blaming Longstreet for the defeat at Gettysburg, but Lee would not hear that, would not support anyone who spoke out, offered an indiscreet opinion. That kind of talk was not good for the army, and he knew that Longstreet was still his best soldier, the man he would have to depend on as the war went on. The bloody fields at Bristoe Station, the image of Hill's careless attack, had driven deep into Lee. He knew he would have to rely on Longstreet more than ever now, that even if Longstreet moved a bit slower than Hill might, he would not make that kind of mistake.

Lee did not know when Longstreet might return. In Tennessee, Longstreet had taken his men into the fight with as much fury and skill as the fight had needed, had driven the Federals hard at Chickamauga. But now Longstreet was under the command of Braxton Bragg, and Lee had heard only bad reports from that command, disgruntled officers, an angry Longstreet most of all.

Bragg's only support came from the president, and so when calls began to flow in from the field for Bragg's replacement, incredible reports of incompetence and friction with his commanders, nothing changed, because Davis would not remove a man he liked. Lee thought, How can Bragg . . . manage? What must that be like, the constant grumbling in headquarters, intrigue and protests? How can any man run an army if he does not have the respect . . . if he is so far removed from his command? Good fighting generals did not have to be popular generals, but it was clear now from the reports, from Longstreet's own letters to Lee, that Bragg was neither.

Taylor was still watching him, was shifting back and forth with idle energy. There is none of that here, Lee thought, the harsh words, the jealousies of great egos. And I have this young man . . .

Walter Taylor was the most valuable officer Lee had, a fiercely loyal and protective chief of staff who alone could do what Lee did not have the strength to do. Lee's staff, among the very best, had always been small. There were many who had sought the prestigious positions, but they learned they could not bear the strain, the quantity of work nearly impossible. Taylor never complained, was clearly in charge, was always where Lee needed him to be.

Taylor was still moving, rubbed his hands together, seemed nervous. Lee knew the young man had something to say, that it would come out in a burst of indiscretion, the impatience of youth.

"Sir! Surely they must know the harm . . . we must make them understand. If the quartermaster . . . if General Northrop is responsible, sir . . . we must do something!"

Lee thought, Do something? Do . . . what? He'd grown weary of asking, of explaining the army's great needs, of calling for new troops. As each request went south, he had only felt a greater sadness. Richmond could not even send them shoes.

"What we will do, Colonel, is limit the flow of information, limit the correspondence. We will reveal what is necessary to reveal, and nothing more."

"I understand, sir. We will limit the correspondence. It is . . . most regrettable, sir."

Lee took a long breath, stared deep into the fire, felt the heat now, felt it move through him, ball up in a tightness in his chest, a dull hard pain.

"Yes, Colonel. It is most regrettable."

6. LEE

December 1863

He was close to Richmond now, could see people along the dirt roads, wagons moving slowly, some stopping briefly to watch the train. They were used to the trains now, but a few spotted him, saw the white hair and the uniform, the old familiar face gazing at them through the window, and they would wave. A few hats would go up, cheers and shouts, and later they would tell their friends that he'd been there, that they had seen him with their own eyes.

He did not respond, saw patches of snow, the mud on the roads, thought now about the winter, and the men with bare feet.

There had been one more push from Meade. Once more he'd come south, across the river, crossing at a place where Lee had made preparations. Lee had thought the place defended, but the defense did not work. Meade moved quickly and with power, surprised Lee's troops, moved across the bridge that should have been protected. It was another mistake.

Lee pulled back to the west then, beyond the edge of the Wilderness, the place where Jackson had nearly destroyed the Federal army that past spring. Lee did not think of those days, of missed opportunities, of the pain of that night, when the courier brought him the news, the unbearable image of Jackson falling from his saddle, shot down by his own men. Lee had learned that in this war there were many strokes of what some called luck, but he did not believe that, thought: God has His reasons, and sometimes the tide turns against you, but there will be a balance. If we were victorious that day, we would pay a price another day. He saw Jackson's face again, the sharp blue eyes, and he could not help it, thought, *Why*? Was it necessary to take *him*? He had asked that question often, prayed long for an answer, for some understanding, but it had not come.

Now when Meade pushed toward him, Lee ordered them to put up defenses through the deep woods, a place called Mine Run, and the dirt had flown and trees were felled. It was a great change from the earliest days of the war. When he'd first suggested the digging of trenches around Richmond, he received hoots of derision in the newspapers, was called "Granny Lee," or the "Queen of Spades." Wars should be fought by men standing straight, facing the enemy, and no honor would ever be won by men who hid behind cover. But the soldiers themselves did not care what the papers said. They had seen the horrors, the bloody reality of what that kind of honor could do to the men around them, and they welcomed the trenches. When the order came, every man sought to put his hands on a shovel.

Meade had come up close, but there was only scattered fighting, no great attack. A freezing rain had soaked them all, and for several days the two armies crouched low in the brush. Then word came from Stuart that Meade's flank was exposed, vulnerable. So it was Lee who made the decisive move, pushed his army quietly around Meade's flank. But in the dawn, when the orders came to advance, Lee's troops swept forward and found no one waiting. Meade had pulled away again, a long head start for the protection of the big river, and Lee knew he'd let Meade escape, that Mine Run had been another lost opportunity.

With Meade safely away, Jefferson Davis asked him to come to Richmond, and Lee agreed. He did not like to leave his troops in the field, but there would be no more fighting now; the winter had come hard into Virginia, and the men began to build the huts and shelters that would be their winter quarters. There was another reason Lee agreed to make the trip. Mary was there, the family had rented a small house, and Lee hoped there would be an opportunity to share the Christmas holidays with at least part of his family.

He could see the church spires, the tops of the taller houses, and the train lurched around a curve, rattled on worn tracks. The railroads were in ragged condition, overused, and there was little time or manpower to make repairs. He felt the train slow, saw more buildings and more people. Sitting back, he laid his head against the seat, thought of Mary, of the children, of the tall Christmas trees, those times long ago when he could leave his post and share the warmth of the celebration, of the church services and fireplaces, snowfalls and great feasts. He closed his eyes, felt a hard weariness come over him, and the images began to fade. But he wouldn't let them go, not yet, still tried to feel the warmth, the soft love of home.

LEE LOOKED AT THE EMPTY WHEELCHAIR, PUSHED INTO THE CORner of the room, facing the wall. Mary would not use it, would still try to get around the small house with the crutch, and he knew not to argue. The arthritis had gotten worse, a slow deterioration that the doctors could not stop, one arm now curled and useless.

Hearing voices, he moved into the small parlor, saw his son Custis helping Mary slowly down onto the couch.

Custis glanced up at him, smiled, said, "There now, here's Father . . . perhaps you would prefer if *he* read to you."

"No, Custis, please. I love the sound of your voice." She smiled at the young man, and Lee saw the two of them as one, so much of her in his face, the gentleness.

Lee said, "I see you are in good hands. I thought . . . maybe some tea." She looked at him now, and he waited, could not predict how she would respond to him, what her mood would be.

"That would be fine, Robert. Is there anyone else home this morning?"

"No, it's just us. A bit peaceful this morning."

Custis said, "Father, sit here on the couch. I'll get the tea."

Mary began to protest, raised her hand, but Custis was quickly out of the room, and Lee smiled, knew what his son had done. He moved to the couch, said, "Might I sit? We have not had much time alone."

She nodded, smiled now, said, "Sit down, Robert. You treat me like I'm your schoolmistress. Is this how you act around your generals?"

There was humor in her voice, something he had not heard in a long time. He sat, gently, stayed apart from her, was always careful about hurting her, knew how frail she'd become, how often the pains came. She turned to face him, and he saw the effort, leaned forward to help, put a hand on her arm.

"Thank you, Robert. It's all right."

She looked at him closely, the white hair, the lines around his eyes. He understood the changes, the absence, that when so much time had passed, the effects of the war would show in his face, and it had depressed her. He'd always held the image of her from those times when she was the Belle of Arlington, cared for by her father, spoiled certainly, and it was the memories of youth, before her pains came, that Lee carried with him.

He was the same with the children, saw them as small, scurrying about the old mansion with noisy glee. He had to make himself see them, each of them as they were now, and it was difficult. Annie had died over a year ago, suddenly and without warning, and Lee had never recovered from the shock of that, of the impact of disease. It was a reminder that God was still watching over them, that no matter how much death was brought by the hands of men, the tools of war, God would decide when each would be called away.

His son Rooney was in a Federal prison, captured while recuperating from wounds, hauled away by blue soldiers while his pleading wife looked helplessly on. Robert Jr. was still on the line, manning an artillery battery. The girls would stay away in school or with friends over the holidays, and Lee was sad to hear they would not be home, but he did not speak of it, could not complain of his children's absence when for most of their lives his own absence had been felt so deeply. Lee heard Custis in the kitchen, heard the rattle of teacups, spoons.

Mary looked away, was gazing toward the small window that faced the street, said, "He is . . . wonderful to me. It is good that he can be here."

"I am grateful for that. We are fortunate his position . . . his duty is here."

She looked at him, and he knew what was coming. "Have you heard from Rooney? Is there any word?"

He shook his head. "No . . . they won't release him. I have tried . . . it is a difficult situation. He is considered a . . . prize."

"Of course. He is a Lee."

"I will keep at it. There might still be some negotiating, we do have several important prisoners. Perhaps there will be a trade."

"Charlotte is not taking it well. She is very ill. Even the baths, the springs, have done her no good. To watch him carried off like that . . . the cruelty. I am worried about her."

Lee looked down, did not want to think of his son that way; saw the beaming face, the huge young man, always a bright smile. His eyes followed the dark pattern in the rug, the deep purple of a rose. "I will do what I can."

There was a silence, and Mary said, "So, where are you off to today?"

"The president . . . I have been asked to meet with him."

"The president . . ." She made a small frown. "Well, we must not allow the president to get lonely. He cannot seem to run this country without a Lee beside him. At least he permitted Custis to have this day at home, to spend some time with his mother."

There was another rattle of china from the hallway, and Custis entered, carefully holding a tray and teacups. "So, you are talking about me when I'm not in the room?" He set the tray down on the small table, carefully handed a china teacup to his mother.

Lee reached down, stirred at his own cup, said, "Your mother is grateful the president has allowed you to spend some time . . . with your family." He paused, knew those words held great irony for Mary, for all of them.

Custis moved toward the window, looked out into the dull gray of the morning, shook his head. "He is . . . a complicated man."

Lee waited for more, knew Custis was careful with his words. Lee said, "He carries the weight of this war, the weight of the country on his shoulders. It may be too much for one man."

Custis began to pace in the small room, and Lee could see a dark anger in the handsome face. "Father, he will not listen . . . he will not accept any help. He busies himself with trivial details, spends half the day arguing with cabinet people, legislators, even generals, about . . . personalities. He wants to fill every position, every post, by himself. It is most frustrating. I don't know what my job is, what it is he expects me to do. He says just . . . *be* there."

Lee watched him, nodded, thought, Yes, I know. He recalled the early months of the war, when Virginia first joined the Confederacy. He had been Davis's first real adviser then, understood that Davis would allow nothing to pass through his offices without his personal inspection. Davis still yearned for the fight, still kept the fond memories of the great adventure in Mexico, memories they all had. He would put himself in command of troops if he did not think it would cripple the government. Lee thought of Davis sitting in his office, hidden behind piles of papers, and he suddenly remembered, pulled out his pocket watch.

"I'm sorry . . . I must leave. The president is expecting me." He stood up, saw Mary turn awkwardly, tilting her head, trying to look up at him, and he reached out his hand, put it softly on her shoulder. "I will be home for dinner. . . ."

She nodded stiffly, put her hand on his for a brief moment, said to Custis, "Please help me up, will you. I've changed my mind . . . I don't feel like a reading right now. Maybe later . . ."

Lee stood back, let his son move close, and he helped her stand. She held herself against Custis's arm, looked at Lee, and he saw a coldness in her eyes, the change in her mood. She said, "Tell Mr. Davis . . . tell him we have lost our home, we have lost children. The longer this goes on, the more we will lose. Tell him there are too many widows . . . too many mothers missing their sons. There are enough gravestones! Tell him that!"

Lee stared at her, was shocked, had rarely heard her say anything about the war. She moved toward the hallway, and Custis moved with her. Then she stopped, looked at him again, and he saw the hard anger in her face.

"Go! Tell him!"

Lee said nothing, watched her move out of the room, stood alone for a moment. He knew he could not do as she wanted, that there would be more fighting, and more soldiers would die, and he could not think about the widows and the families. He could only carry out his duty and lead his men forward until God had seen enough, until God decided this bloody war would end.

THEY CALLED IT THE WHITE HOUSE, AND NO ONE GAVE MUCH thought to the irony of that. This was the home of President Davis and his family, and it did not compare to the grand sweeping mansion in Washington. The name was a simple description of the home.

Since the beginning of the war, Davis had been prone to illness, some real, some imagined. As his army had absorbed the defeats of the past months, his health had worsened, the illness affecting his mind as well. He became suspicious, protective, more likely to distrust his subordinates. He began to conduct more and more of the business of the government from his own home, converted one room into an office, would often not leave the home for days at a time.

Lee approached the steps, looked up to the front door, saw it open. There were hushed voices, and three men emerged, talking quietly among themselves. Lee stopped, waited, and the men came down the steps toward him. He noticed the fine suits, silk shirts, gold watch chains, the finery of official visitors. They saw him now, and for a brief moment they stared, recognizing him. He removed his hat, and they seemed to recover their formality, moved down the steps, came past him. He nodded as they passed, and they glanced at him discreetly, but there were no smiles, no one spoke. The men moved to a carriage, and Lee watched them climb inside. There was a slap of leather, and the carriage quickly pulled away. He turned, moved up the steps, thought, *Europeans.*

He saw now that the door was still open, a soldier inside standing at attention, waiting for him to enter. Lee moved into the house, and the soldier closed the door, stiff and formal. Lee looked toward the small secretary's office, what had once been a closet, a large square hole cut in the wall so the front door could be seen. He heard commotion, saw movement in the small office, the sound of a chair pushed back, and he waited. A man came out quickly, adjusting his coat, thrust a hand toward him. It was Davis's secretary, Burton Harrison.

Harrison was a neat, dapper man. He shook Lee's hand warmly, said, "General Lee, how wonderful! How are you, sir?"

Lee smiled, had always been amused by the secretary's energy, his manic protection of Davis. "I am quite well, Mr. Harrison." He noticed Harrison glancing around the small space, self-conscious.

Harrison said, "Forgive . . . my office, General. The president insists, and so we must make do with what we have. It can be difficult—" He stopped, and Lee saw a pained look, Harrison showing displeasure at his own indiscretion. "I . . . didn't mean to suggest I am not happy here. This is the president's home. We must make do—"

There was a high squeal from Davis's office, behind Harrison. The secretary jumped, startled, and the pained look returned. "I should tell the president you are here," he said. "Excuse me . . ."

Lee nodded. There were more squeals, the laughter of children, then he heard an older voice, and the sound of heavy steps. Harrison was gone, had fled back into the small office when the door opened. Lee backed against the wall as two children burst into the hallway, squealing with laughter. Davis was behind them, bent over, the pursuer, growling like some deranged beast.

The children rushed past Lee, and Davis straightened, looked at Lee with surprise, then smiled and put a hand on Lee's shoulder, supporting himself, breathing heavily. "Well, hello General . . . excuse me . . ." Lee felt the weight of the hand, was suddenly uncomfortable, as though he'd intruded on something very private. Davis took a deep breath, and the children waited in a far doorway. Davis said, "Not now, you two . . . stay put for a while . . . the general and I have some work to do." Davis glanced into the small room, said, "Mr. Harrison, please see we are not disturbed."

Lee looked at Harrison, who nodded nervously, then jumped, startled again by the sudden cries of the children, protesting the interruption of their play. Now a maid appeared, a large round woman with deep black skin. She pulled the children quickly into their room, and Davis looked at Lee, smiled, took a deep breath. Now the smile began to fade, and Lee saw the sadness return, the dark eyes filled with sickness, the weight and gloom of the war coming over him again. Davis turned, moved into his office, said, "Come in, General."

There was no one else in the office, and Lee was not surprised, knew that by now these meetings were often private, that Davis had become unwilling to let his staff handle the affairs of running the government. Lee moved in, sat in a small wooden chair, and Davis went to the far corner of the room and closed another door, the door to the children's room and their small sweet sounds.

Davis moved to his own chair, sat behind a small desk, looked at Lee. "It's difficult . . . not spending all day with them. This is perhaps . . . not the best way to run a government."

Lee said nothing, could now hear small muffled sounds from the next room.

Davis said, "All morning long . . . the meeting lasted for hours, and nothing . . . no commitment, no encouragement. I am afraid . . . we cannot expect much help after all."

Lee sat straight in the chair, said, "The . . . French?"

"Yes . . . you saw them?" Davis leaned forward, rested his hands on the desk. "There is no chance now. Not since the summer, since Vicksburg . . ." He paused, looked down, said, "Since Gettysburg . . ."

Lee could see the word was awkward for Davis, but Lee nodded, knew the mention of the place carried no blame.

Davis looked at Lee now, said, "And there was still a chance, even the English could see that we were still in control, still held on. We just had to show them . . . one victory, one real smashing blow. I am certain of it . . . they would still have come in, would have broken the blockade. But . . . events have changed that."

Lee knew that Davis was talking about the enormous and stunning defeat of Braxton Bragg. Bragg had penned the Federals up tightly in Chattanooga, and the official reports as well as northern papers said the Federals were starving, it would be Vicksburg in reverse. It should not have taken much longer; the shroud of winter would force Rosecrans to surrender, and they all knew the pendulum would swing, the momentum lost at Vicksburg would turn their way in the West. But Bragg had grown careless, weakened his army by sending Longstreet's corps up toward Knoxville, to relieve the occupation there by Burnside's forces. And little attention had been paid when Lincoln, weary of Rosecrans, sent a new commander to Chattanooga, a name that was vaguely familiar to Lee, the man known mostly for engineering the strangle of Vicksburg. His name was Ulysses Grant.

Quickly, Grant punched through Bragg's choke hold, found a way to bring supplies into Chattanooga, and his men were not starving anymore. But Bragg was still in control, the Federal army still held tightly inside Chattanooga. Suddenly, and with complete efficiency, Grant surprised Bragg by advancing across the entire front, the blue soldiers climbing straight up the hills, first the invincible position of Lookout Mountain, not invincible after all. Then, incredibly, while Bragg's army looked down from Missionary Ridge, Grant formed his lines in the wide-open fields beside the city. The rebels had admired and applauded the parade ground pageantry, until Grant sent his massed battle lines forward, straight into the hill, the men climbing up rock by rock, protected by the ravines and cracks in the earth. Bragg had the high ground, but never counted on a direct assault, had not put his men into proper position, and so when the rebels tried to shoot straight down the hill, they had to expose themselves to the fire from the flat ground below. As Grant's men climbed the hill in greater and greater numbers, most of Bragg's army simply dissolved, pulling away from the crest of the hill. The retreat became an utter panic, a complete disaster. Now, Grant's army was in pursuit, and Bragg was withdrawing into Georgia. Davis had been forced to accept that it was time to replace him, that his friend was, after all, not the man for the job.

Davis looked at Lee, who had known this moment would come. There had been rumors, even mention in the Richmond papers that Lee would go west, take command of Bragg's shattered army. There was something ominous about Grant, something new, a deadly efficiency that the southern commanders had not faced before. To many, it was only logical that Lee be the one to confront him, the best man to face what was beginning to be the most dangerous threat. But it was not a duty Lee wanted.

Davis sat back in the chair again, rubbed his head with his hand, said, "We are not . . . in a position of strength. The Europeans know that . . . the people know that. Certainly the enemy knows that."

Lee nodded, said, "Yes, I imagine he does."

Davis still rubbed his head, and Lee saw his face twisting, feeling the pain of the headache. "General, are you the man we need? Are you willing . . . to replace General Bragg?"

Lee settled into the chair, took a deep breath and said, "I am willing to serve wherever you assign me." He watched Davis's face, the deep eyes now looking at him. Davis nodded, said nothing. "But, I believe there are others who are more suited for that command. It is not likely that the Army of Tennessee would perform well for a commander they did not know."

Davis put his hands on the desk, did not show surprise at Lee's response.

Lee said, "General Meade is still in Virginia. I believe that he is still the greater threat, certainly to Richmond. And we are still the greatest threat to Washington. The war, ultimately, must be won . . . here. The Army of Northern Virginia is familiar with my command. I do not believe they would respond well to a major change in command. They are accustomed to . . . things as they are now."

Davis smiled, said, "I should have had you here to talk to those Frenchmen. You have always been a fine diplomat."

Lee let out a breath, felt great relief. He had thought Davis might order him west no matter what he said.

Davis looked at the clutter of paper on his desk, shuffled through it, read. Lee had seen this before, knew the matter had passed, that they would now move on. Davis read from a page, rubbed one hard finger idly against his temple, said, "Well, now, General, if your army requires that you stay in Virginia, we must provide someone equally inspiring to the Army of Tennessee. . . ."

THE HOUSE WAS FILLED WITH CHRISTMAS, BRIGHT RIBBONS streaming around the windows, candles casting small shadows. He heard the voices in back, happy sounds flowing through the dark hallways, and he stopped in the dim light of the parlor, looked at the wheelchair still sitting in the corner of the room. He smelled the pine branches, sharp and familiar. He looked at the dark needles, and the smell was of the woods . . . the camps. He was suddenly very sad, still listened to the voices, stood quietly in the dim light of the room, tried to feel what they were feeling, the joy in the sounds, the holiday. But there was no holiday in the camps of the army. It was just a pause in time, the wait for the weather. They would not fight because it was impossible to move, the guns and wagons could not travel the icy, muddy roads, the men could not march through freezing nights. But it would not be long, it had never been long enough, and the roads would dry, the sun would warm them enough to move again, and there would be new fights, and new ground to cover, and places they had never heard of, villages and crossroads and small quiet rivers that would become the new horrible names they would always remember.

He moved to the small couch, sat down, felt stiff, cold, thought, I am not well. He put his hand on his chest, slid it up to his left shoulder, massaged. I do not understand . . . is it just that I am . . . old? He felt the tightness in his chest, always there now, and when it did not hurt, on those mornings when he would wake without the pain, he was grateful, gave a thankful prayer.

He thought of the past few days, the drudgery of the meetings, the arguments, men with great opinions and little understanding. He had known it would be this way, that by coming to Richmond he would be pulled into it, hear it firsthand, that men with oil in their voices would take him aside, greet him with fat handshakes, take him into their confidence, seek his valuable approval, the influence of a powerful, respected man.

There had been great debate about Bragg's replacement, and finally Davis reluctantly agreed that the best man for the job, the one the troops themselves had always followed, was Joe Johnston. It had been a bitter pill for Davis, because Johnston had never cooperated with him, had never cooperated with anyone, and they all knew that Johnston would begin it all again, would run his own show, respond selectively to orders, regard Davis's instructions as inconvenient suggestions. On the Virginia peninsula, when McClellan had come at Richmond from the sea, Johnston cut off all communication with Davis, fought the Federal invasion exactly as he saw fit. When Johnston had been wounded, Davis was forced to make a painful decision, to give up Lee, his most trusted adviser, to send him from the capital to command the army. It had been Lee who organized and equipped the new army, Lee who designed the defensive lines of Virginia, the lines that proved so crucial to the first big fight at Manassas. But Davis had still wanted him nearby, and so Lee suffered quietly in the stifling air of a Richmond office while others led the fighting. But with Johnston down, Davis had to concede that the army's well-being was as important as his own, and finally Lee was given the opportunity to command the army in the field.

When Johnston's wounds healed, he'd gone west, but his command was separate from Bragg's, one of the great flaws in the organization of the army. Johnston had not been there when Bragg needed the strength, had kept himself secure and well defended in Mississippi, against an enemy that was making the fight somewhere else. Despite all of this, Davis had been made to understand, and Lee agreed, that when it came to putting troops in the field, when there were decisions to be made that could decide where and how the battle would be fought, Joe Johnston was the best man they had left.

Lee stared at a candle flickering on the windowsill, still heard the voices, heard Mary, clearly in command, thought, I should let them know I'm home. They will be concerned, ask stern questions: Have I eaten? Is my coat warm enough? He smiled. They worry too much about me. Everyone worries too much. . . .

He tried to stand up and a sharp pain stung him, a sudden hard pinch in his throat. He sat again, stared at the candle, and the pain flowed slowly out of him, then was gone. He heard himself breathing, sat back on the couch, thought, Easy, let it go. *Thank God.*

All during the autumn the pains had come, and he'd spent many days alone in his tent. He would not discuss the ailment, not even with Taylor, and he did not tell anyone that the trip to Richmond would be for that as well, to rest, the soft comfort of home. He could never admit that to anyone, not even to Mary, and for the first few days it had helped, he'd slept well, felt stronger. But now, knowing he would return to his men, that Davis would not send him out of Virginia, the pains surprised him, coming back again. The last few nights he had lain awake staring up into the dark, talking quietly to God, feeling the motion in his chest. But even the prayers did not comfort him, and he could not stop thinking about what they still must do, how the war would go on until *he* did something, that it was *his* responsibility.

It was only a few days until Christmas, and he knew they were glad he was home, that it should be a joyous time. He stood again, slow, careful, moved toward the sounds from the kitchen. He steadied himself in the doorway, saw motion in the dark hall. Mary came out of the kitchen, leaning on the small crutch, saw him standing in the shadow of the candle. She stopped, surprised, said only, "Oh . . ." and looked at him, but they did not speak. Suddenly he could not look at her, stared down at the floor. He wanted to say something, give her something. It was always so hard.

After a quiet moment she said, "I don't need the explanation, Robert. Go . . . go on back to your army. You won't ever really be here, this won't ever be your home . . . until the war is over. We have had Christmas without you before. We will manage."

He still said nothing, felt her eyes digging deep inside him, seeing all of him, and he thought, Of course, she always knows. But there was no bitterness in her voice, not this time. He did not hear the dark anger, just the sadness, the calm acceptance of all they had missed, the family gatherings, the children growing up under the eye of their father. She had, after all, married a soldier.

She began to move away, then stopped, said, "You don't have to explain . . . not to me . . . not to any of us. If they need you to end the war, then end the war. We will still be here. We are still your family. Now, go on. They're waiting for you, you know."

She moved away, hobbled slowly down the hall, back toward their room. He watched her, waited until she was gone, then stared at the dark space, closed his eyes, saw the vast cold camp, shelters and fires, great fields of guns and wagons and horses. And then he saw the faces, the men of his ragged army, waiting for him to return, the army that waited for the command to send them forward once again, maybe for the last time.

He opened his eyes, looked into the dark, saw his faint shadow from the dim light of the candle, said quietly, "Yes . . . I know . . ."

PART TWO

... testing whether that nation, or any nation, so conceived, so dedicated, can long endure. We are met here on a great battlefield of that war. We have come to dedicate a portion of it as a final resting place for those who here gave their lives that that nation might live. It is altogether fitting and proper that we should do this.

But in a larger sense we can not dedicate—we can not consecrate—we can not hallow this ground. The brave men, living and dead, who struggled here, have consecrated it, far above our poor power to add or detract ...

7. GRANT

March 1864

THE LINE MOVED SLOWLY, THERE WAS MUCH TALKING, NERVOUS anticipation. He could feel the motion, the energy of the crowd, held back by the people in front, moving only with small short steps. Gradually they drew closer to the wide doorway. Now he could see into the next room, saw the pale blue walls, lit by one small chandelier. The sounds of the people began to quiet; those who had passed through the doorway were now nearly silent. He held the boy's hand, looked down, saw his son trying to see past the line of people, the glorious dresses of the women, the fine suits of the men. But the boy was too short and the crowd pressed together too closely, and so they just eased along slowly, until it was their time to enter the blue room.

He had not changed his uniform, had lost the key to his trunk, and so, had thought it might not be proper . . . and he didn't want to embarrass the boy. Frederick was only twelve, had become used to traveling with his father through the army camps, even on the march. But neither of them had ever been to see the President. He smiled at the boy, who still strained to see the adventure that lay in front of them, thought, He is used to the attention, he loves it, the son of the commander, all the officers, their wives, frittering and making a to-do around him, since the commander himself will have none of it. He thought, now, of the boy's mother: Yes, this would be for you, you enjoy this much more than I do, the receptions in great halls, shaking hands with well-dressed folks, the stifling dignity of meeting Important People. He glanced down at his uniform, saw the smudges, the worn cloth. If she were here . . . I would *not* be here. I should have taken my pistol and shot my way into the trunk, broken the lock. He smiled again, thought of her sulking, the pursed lower lip. She would definitely not approve of *these* clothes, not here, not tonight. The boy looked up at him, and he could see that part of her, the excitement in the boy's face, as they moved ever closer to the Big Moment.

He could hear small comments, realized now that people were pointing at him. Most did not know who he was, and he heard names, guesses, none of them correct. He did feel embarrassed now, began to think this was a bad idea. I should have waited until tomorrow, when the official ceremony would take place. But he had arrived early, and when the boy had heard there was a reception at the White House, the issue was settled. He frowned, thought at least he could have found a way to clean up the uniform.

Now he was in the blue room, and suddenly he could see the President, tall above the crowd, made more so by the slight bows of the people as they passed by, small greetings, careful handshakes. He was stunned by the face, the deep gray eyes, the hard lines, the sadness of a man who felt all the weight of this great bloody war, who must answer to the widows and the children, must find some way of explaining why he did this, why this war had to go on until the rebels were brought down. The tall man was smiling, saying a few words, then a brief nod and another smile. Then the eyes were caught by the blue of the uniform, and suddenly Lincoln stepped forward, moved through the startled row of silk and satin, pearls and lace, reached out a great heavy hand and beamed a wide smile.

"Why, here is General Grant! This is a great pleasure, I assure you!"

Grant took the hand, felt Lincoln's strong grip. Grant felt the warmth, the smile that seemed to spread out over him, over the room. He felt himself pulled away from the crowd, did not see them gather around now, did not feel the boy move close to his side, the attention now focused fully on this small man in the rumpled blue uniform. He stared up into the eyes, felt a sudden weight shifting onto him, more than just the eyes of the President. He felt himself smile, said, "Thank you, sir. Mr. President, sir. It is a pleasure to meet you."

He felt foolish, thought, He is the President of the United States . . . think of something to say. It had not occurred to him that he might actually *speak* to Lincoln, not tonight, had expected maybe to see him, catch a glimpse of the big man through a crowd.

Lincoln still had him by the hand, pulled Grant through the throng of people, and now they were seeing the uniform, the obvious lack of formal preparation. There were amused comments, nods of

"Yes, now here is a *real* soldier . . ." He heard his name flowing out, carried along in a small wave, "General Grant," and in the hallway beyond, the wave grew into shouts, someone began a cheer. He looked around the room, saw the faces watching him, staring.

Lincoln released him, said, "General Grant, allow me to introduce Secretary Seward."

Grant looked at the long thin face of the Secretary of State, smiling at him with the charm of the diplomat. He took the hand that Seward offered, but Seward's words slipped by, the polite formality, and Grant could only hear the rhythm of his name, a slowly rising chorus in the gathering crowd. Now Lincoln was moving him along, and Grant saw a woman, standing alone, watching him with hard quiet eyes. He was led closer, and she did not speak, watched him carefully, appraising him, and he heard someone say, "Mrs. Lincoln . . . this is General Grant . . ."

She was wearing a small hat, a strange cluster of fresh flowers, her long straight hair pulled back tightly. There was a wide-open space around her, the people did not approach her, no one stood close. He made a short bow, thought again of his uniform, felt completely awkward, thought, I should apologize.

But she spoke, and near them there were suddenly no voices, only quiet. "General Grant . . . how nice to meet you. I hear that you bring a bit less refinement and a bit more bulldog to this war."

There was laughter, and Grant tried to smile, bowed again, had no idea what to say. He glanced at Frederick, said, "Mrs. Lincoln, allow me to introduce my son, Frederick Dent Grant."

She reached out a hand, touched the boy's cheek, and the boy flinched slightly. She said, "Yes, how nice. My sons are often with their father as well. Teach them . . . show them how to be men."

Grant smiled, nodded, was not sure what she meant, wondered if it was sarcasm. There was a brief silence, and he thought, Say something . . . words, something appropriate. She was smiling at Frederick still, and suddenly she began to move away, a wide path opening in the crowd. The voices behind him began to grow again, and he turned, saw that the room was filling rapidly, the neat order of the reception line was gone, the crowd mobbing into the room. Grant felt for Federick's hand, and the boy gripped him hard, pulled close beside him.

Suddenly there was a hand on his shoulder, and he was turned, pulled, saw now it was Seward. He followed, pushed through the noise, the hands reaching out to him, saw the tall figure of Lincoln move on in front of them. Seward moved up behind Lincoln, and

Grant followed to another room, saw it was larger, the walls light green, high white ceilings, an extraordinary chandelier. Seward led him to one side, the crowd following close behind, pushing through the wide doorway. Lincoln stopped beside a small couch, and Seward pointed, said, "General, it might be best . . . climb up here, stand on the couch."

Grant looked at Seward, said, "On the couch . . . my boots?"

"Please, General, it's all right. They seem to want to get a good look at you. It might be the only way to calm them down." Grant looked at the elaborate lace, the silk brocade, looked at Lincoln, and Lincoln was smiling, obviously enjoying the moment. Grant looked again at the couch, then took one step up, steadied himself with one hand on Seward's shoulder.

The room was larger, began to fill as well, and Grant saw other uniforms, the marine guard, the men now moving into the crowd, trying to ease them into lines. Hands were raised toward him now, and he watched the faces, saw the smiles, heard his name again. He looked down, saw Frederick beside the couch, and the boy was smiling now, was beginning to absorb the excitement and the attention from the crowd. Grant watched the marines guiding the people along, silently, gently, but the numbers and the energy were too great, and the people surged up close to him, and his name was now a single chant, the crowd calling out, "*Grant . . . Grant . . . Grant . . .*"

Beside him, Lincoln said something to Seward, and Seward leaned close to him, said, "General, when you have had enough of your adoring crowd, the President requests you join him in the drawing room."

The two men moved away, and Grant was now alone, the hands reaching up to him, a sea of silk and flowers, perfume and cigars, politicians and diplomats and reporters. He began to reach for the hands, a brief grasp for those who came close. They began to file by, but did not leave, and so the room grew more crowded, the marines began to ease away, could do nothing but stand out of the way, moved back against the far wall, watching him as well. Now the chant began again, his name, and he stared in amazement, tried to smile, thought, I am no hero . . .

There was no escape, they would not let him leave, and he shook the hands, nodded politely at the kind comments, the friendly greetings. He looked out over the faces, began to feel now what this was about, the raw enthusiasm for this one soldier. He understood the look now, something he had not noticed before, had not seen in the face of soldiers. He was giving them . . . *hope*.

THERE HAD NOT BEEN A POSITION OF LIEUTENANT GENERAL IN the army for years. Winfield Scott had been the only man since George Washington to hold that rank, and certainly no one since the start of the war had shown himself particularly worthy. After three years now, after the disastrous incompetence of some commanders, the political intrigue that surrounded others, the infighting in Washington, and the morale problems in the field, and as the casualty numbers grew more horrifying, Lincoln understood that something profound and meaningful was fading away from the people. The rebellion was bleeding more from the country than its young men. If it was to turn around, if something was to be saved out of this great war, it would fall on one man who did not speak to crowds, who did not enjoy the raw attention of an admiring public, who did not perform on the field with one eye on the newspapers.

Grant was no one's political favorite, he had not accumulated debts from men of power. He did not get along with General Halleck at all, but Lincoln had learned through bitter experience that it was not Halleck who would win the war from his comfortable office in Washington.

Grant had shown Lincoln something that the others had not. He could win . . . and he did not need to tell you he had won. If he did not win, he did not send a steady stream of explanations, excuses, he did not lay blame. And, he did not make the incessant calls to Washington for reinforcements. Lincoln had become so accustomed to hearing from his commanders how the enemy was always superior, that from the earliest days of McClellan's command, the Federal army would never be strong enough to whip their enemy. Even when there were successes, when the Federal soldiers showed their commanders that they could in fact whip those other fellows, the success was never complete, the opportunity for complete victory had never been followed up. The commanders did not seem to believe it, did not have the fire of confidence, did not appear to understand that with just a little more—another quick strike, another strong blow—those tough boys in the ragged clothes just might do as the blue army had done so often: back away. And if the blow was strong enough, and deliberate enough, it just might end the war. If Grant had his success far from the capital, far from the attention of the eastern newspapers, it was the *people* who were beginning to hear about him from the soldiers, from the men who fought under his command. He did not ride the grandest horse, he did not wear the fanciest uniform. But he had understood his army, had given the right orders, put his men in the right places. At first the names did not cause excitement in the east: Fort Donelson, Shiloh. But then came his triumph at Vicksburg, a complete and utter victory, a mass surrender of a major rebel army, and with that came Federal control of the entire Mississippi River. *Now* the papers picked up the name. When he broke out of Chattanooga, a violent clubbing of Bragg's army that swept them out of Tennessee, Grant had suddenly reversed the tide in the West. He had pulled his army together like one massive fist, cocked and ready to strike directly into the heart of the deep South. When word of this extraordinary breakthrough reached Washington, Lincoln made up his mind. If there was to be one man to control the flow of the war, he wanted Ulysses Grant.

THE MARINE HELD THE DOOR OPEN, AND HE PASSED BY, RE-turned a crisp salute. The door closed behind him, and the sounds of the crowd faded away. He had left Frederick behind, the boy now the center of attention, surrounded by the ladies. The boy had begun to charm them with the innocence and guile only a twelve-year-old knows, and Grant knew he would be fine on his own.

Lincoln sat alone at a small table, and Grant glanced around the room, saw portraits, a mantel covered with flowers, a huge silver tray lying flat on a dark table in the corner. Lincoln held out a hand, motioned to a chair, was smiling, seemed energetic, enthusiastic.

"Please, General, have a chair. I am delighted . . . truly delighted to have you here. Allow me to make good use of this opportunity . . . I have wanted to talk to you."

Grant sat, still looked around the room, felt Lincoln watching him, said, "Thank you, sir. I could have waited until tomorrow. . . ."

"Nonsense, I'm glad you came tonight. You caused quite a stir. The crowds don't respond much anymore . . . not to me, anyway. These weekly receptions have become pretty routine. This was a delight."

There was a pause, and Grant waited, did not know what else to say. Lincoln leaned forward, across the small table, and Grant felt the energy, the mind working. Lincoln stared at him, and Grant felt himself pulled forward, drawn to Lincoln's stare.

"General, there was no one else. I heard all the names, people politicking for the favorite general . . . but when it came down to it, when Congress approved the position, I considered no one else for the job. No one, not one of the men who staked their claim . . . was as deserving as you. The army gains nothing by blessing its commanders with meaningless titles. The rank of Lieutenant General *has* meaning. It belongs to only one man, and that man must understand the job he faces. I have no doubt that my choice is the right one."

Lincoln still stared at him, waited patiently for a response.

Grant said, "Thank you, sir. I hope the Secretary . . . and General Halleck agree. There are many who presently outrank me as major generals."

"Not anymore! And that is the point. Stanton, Halleck . . . you should see them scramble around here, trying to keep the details from my prying eyes. They don't feel I have any business trying to run this war. They see me as a leaking bucket, that if I am informed of anything resembling a secret, I will crow about it from the roof of the White House. There have been times, though, I admit . . . there were times when I was naive enough to have done just that. I have always made the mistake of trusting too much . . . of believing in the sincere intentions of those who profess to be my friends. It has, on occasion, been a problem."

Grant nodded, felt a smile, said, "Yes . . . I understand, sir. I may have done some of the same. It has cost me . . . I don't have much of a talent for business."

"Fortunately, it is not business that concerns us, Mr. Grant. And I *do* believe you have other talents, specifically, a talent for making a fight. And, there's the lesson, perhaps for both of us. *Make* the fight, don't talk about it. You cannot imagine . . . the volume of talk that flows around this place. Washington is like a barnyard full of braying mules . . . and that includes most of my cabinet. I'll make you a deal, Mr. Grant. You don't tell me how you plan to run this army, and I won't tell you how to run it either."

Grant sat back in the chair, looked for the smile, the joke. But Lincoln still stared at him, and he realized suddenly that Lincoln was serious.

"Mr. Grant, I have tried sometimes . . . to figure out what the army needs. I have tried to help where it seemed a great deal of help was needed. I have even made it official, sent out presidential decrees, written up special orders. Most of them have come out of frustration. And, likely, most of them have been wrong. But you cannot imagine what it is like to have all the authority to issue orders, and no power to see them carried out. But that will change now. I am giving you my word, Mr. Grant. If you take this army out and *use* it, I will give you whatever you ask for. And no one in this town will interfere. If they do, *that* is something I can control." Lincoln sat back in his chair, smiled now. "You were correct, Mr. Grant, there are a few ruffled feathers around here. Actually, there are times when I rather enjoy that . . . give some of these fine fat fellows a little indigestion. But make no mistake. There's nothing I have said to you, nothing implied in any of this, that does not carry the full power of the United States government. Tomorrow, there will be a ceremony. You will stand there and listen to me make a fool speech. . . ."

He paused, reached into his coat pocket, brought out a folded piece of paper, handed it to Grant.

"Here, that's my speech, that's what I'm going to say. I thought you should have some warning. My guess is, you don't dwell long and hard on grand public pronouncements. Neither do I. But you know they'll all be waiting for your profound thanks, how undeserving you are, all that. Especially those folks with the ruffled feathers, they'll look for you to toss them a fat piece of humble pie."

Grant opened the paper, scanned the words, was relieved to see only a few lines.

"I understand, sir. Thank you. I'll think of something . . . appropriate."

"Don't give it any more effort than you feel comfortable doing. It's not the words that mean anything. The Secretary of War will hand you a piece of paper that says you are a lieutenant general. There is a great deal of power in that . . . beyond the ceremony, beyond my speech, beyond what the newspapers make of it. How you use that power will likely determine if this nation survives. I am a great believer . . . no, let me put it another way. I have a great *love* for the Constitution. It is the thing I live for, it is the reason I sit here in this chair." He paused, then said, "The wisdom in *those* words, the power of an *idea*, how man should govern his affairs, how humanity should respect itself . . . it is what separates us from the caveman, from thousands of years of the select few making all the decisions for the rest of us. If we allow this rebellion to succeed—if we do not hold those ideas together for our children—then we sink back to the Dark Ages. We might as well send the Queen of England an apology for all the trouble we caused, ask if they will take us back. And we will deserve no better."

Lincoln leaned forward in his chair, and Grant felt the dark eyes pressing into him. He absorbed the words, felt the great weight, the enormous sadness.

Lincoln said in a low voice, "This is all so . . . new, the idea of one nation treating all of its citizens the same, that we do not divide ourselves into classes. I made a speech . . . last November, you may have read about it, the dedication of the National Cemetery at Gettysburg. It bedeviled me for the longest time . . . the first words . . . how to begin that, how to express that very thought, our *youth*. Europeans measure their history in centuries. The Chinese, my God, their system has been around for thousands of years. It is no wonder that this union, this precocious child of a country, is having such problems. There is so little to guide us, no example we can follow, we have no one to turn to except ourselves. The Constitution . . . this new idea . . . has been around for less than a century."

He paused, shook his head. "*Four score* . . . I don't usually go for the poetic."

Grant nodded, had heard of the speech, the few short minutes that so many were now quoting, had been surprised at the controversy in the newspapers, the opinions and politics swirling around that little speech like a hurricane. He thought of Washington. No, this is not where I want to be.

Lincoln looked at his hands, turned them over, flexed his long fingers, said in a low voice, "Perhaps we are simply arrogant, perhaps we have not earned the respect . . . perhaps the rest of the world should not take us seriously. But if we succeed, if we can end this rebellion and bring ourselves back together again, if we prove that this system works . . . we become a threat. What then will stop others, anywhere people allow themselves to *think*, people who do not wish to suffer under someone else's domination, who can use us for inspiration? What will stop this system from spreading all over the world? Can you imagine that, Mr. Grant? Can you imagine the power of that? I'm guessing there are many—call them what you will, kings, monarchs, despots—listening to reports of our war, staring out the windows of their enormous palaces, wondering if there is not some John Adams or Ben Franklin or George Washington somewhere out there, someone who will rise up out of muddy fields or the oppression of some small village and sweep them away." He looked at Grant, sat back in the chair, shook his head again.

"Forgive me, Mr. Grant. I am somewhat of an idealist. Some around here think I'm something of a lunatic. Comes with the job, I expect."

Grant said, "Quite all right, sir. I do understand the value . . . what we are fighting to keep. It's more than just the oath I took, or the rally around the flag."

Lincoln sat up straight, and Grant saw the flash of fire. Lincoln pounded a heavy hand on the table. "*Yes,* Mr. Grant. I have no doubt of that. I also have no doubt that you are aware that if we do not win this war—if we do not show the world that this system can *work*, that we can build a nation and manage our affairs from the power of an idea written on a piece of paper—then that idea will die out. And it must not die out. If we lose this war, something of great value will be lost with it. History will record that the idea did not work, that our piece of paper did not carry the power of a monarchy, the Constitution was not as efficient as the power of an elite ruling class, that it is acceptable for one class of human being to possess and dominate another. There is a significance to this that goes far beyond our borders, and far beyond our time."

Lincoln pushed back the chair, stood up, held out a hand, and Grant saw the hard glare in the eyes giving way to something softer, the warmth returning. Grant stood, took the hand, and Lincoln said, "And now, the matter is in *your* hands. Take good care, Mr. Grant."

THE TENTS WERE IN THE DISTANCE, UP A LONG RISE. SPREAD around were the smaller tents of the army, a vast sea of white. Beyond, in the wide fields, the regiments were at drill, neat blue squares, flags, and the bright reflection from raised muskets. He rode with his staff now, a long cigar clamped in his mouth, the gray smoke swirling up and around the neat beard. Beside him was John Rawlins, a thin anxious man who never stopped moving, seemed to search the countryside, each turn of the road, each small rise, always alert. Grant smiled, thought, He's always waiting for something bad to happen. Grant had known Rawlins from the beginning of the war, the first organization of the regiments in Illinois. To the rest of the staff, the two men were a perfect blend—they were complete opposites.

Grant stared ahead, saw now the headquarters flag. Out in front, his security guard, a small squad of cavalry, reached the picket outpost, a small hut with no windows. A man in blue moved out into the road, then two more men emerged from the hut, watching the riders approach. The cavalry captain leaned over, said something Grant could not hear. Now several more of the guards appeared, moved into the road, all staring at Grant. There was a hushed shout, and quickly they jumped to attention, muskets hard on their shoulders. The cavalrymen moved aside, lined the edge of the road, and their captain saluted as Grant moved close. Grant saw the stripes on one sleeve, the sergeant of the guard, the man stiff and straight, and Grant reined the horse to a halt, said nothing, waited for Rawlins.

Rawlins said, "Sergeant, might we find General Meade on this road?"

The man stepped forward, still at attention, tried to keep his eyes to the front, but turned just slightly, stared up at Grant with his mouth open.

Rawlins said, "I say, Sergeant! Might we find—"

"Yes sir! Straight ahead, sir! The large flagpole . . . follow that, sir!"

They moved on, and Grant could hear the whispers now, the cavalrymen dismounting, the guards questioning, curious.

Rawlins said, "General, I will have a word with that sergeant. He should have kept his eyes to the front. We are not here to provide for their amusement."

Grant saw the large flag, a slow quiet slap against the tall wood pole, said, "This is a different army, Colonel. They are entitled to be curious about their new commander."

Rawlins slumped, said, "They think we are all backwoodsmen. That's all I hear. They think just because we come from the West, we have no . . . refinement."

Grant smiled, said nothing, thought of Mary Lincoln's strange compliment, *a bit less refinement*. "And what have we heard about them, Colonel? City boys with soft hands. It's natural, a bit of rivalry. Up to now it's been two wars, two armies, two different personalities."

"But we're not ruffians and heathens, sir!"

Grant smiled, still watched the flag. "Not all of us."

He saw the larger tents now, and men began to gather, snapping to attention. Grant stopped the horse, and an orderly stepped forward, a young private with no right arm. The man saluted with his left hand, held it, stared silently ahead.

Grant returned the salute, and the young man said, "If you will permit me, sir . . . I will take your horse."

Grant looked at the man's uniform, felt suddenly awkward, and he climbed down, stared at the boy's empty sleeve, thought, They are not *all* soft.

He looked around, realized now that many men had quietly moved closer, watching him, and no one spoke.

Rawlins stepped forward, scanned the uniforms for rank, said, "You . . . Major, this is General Grant. We are seeking General Meade."

The man was looking at Grant now, said, "Yes, sir. Welcome, sir. General Meade is back here, in his tent—"

"I'm right behind you, Major."

Grant saw Meade emerge from the tent, his wide black hat clamped down on his head. Meade stepped through the men, moved up to Grant, saluted. Grant returned the salute, saw Meade quickly scan him up and down with the look of a man whose stomach hurts. Meade said, "Welcome to the Army of the Potomac, General."

Grant nodded, glanced at the men watching him. "Thank you, General. This is Colonel Rawlins, my chief of staff." He turned to Rawlins, said, "Colonel, I wish to speak to General Meade. Introduce yourself and the rest of the staff to General Meade's people. Get acquainted."

Rawlins snapped his boots together, exaggerated formality, and said, "Yes sir! Right away, sir!"

Grant looked at him for a brief moment, thought, This may be more difficult than I thought. We have no need for posturing. He looked at Meade again, saw the same sour expression, and a small hint of impatience. Grant said, "General, might we have a word?"

Meade turned, held out an arm toward his tent, said flatly, "At your convenience, General. After you."

Grant moved to the tent, Meade followed him, and Grant stopped, looked back at Rawlins, who was still standing stiffly. "Colonel . . . at ease."

He moved into the tent, saw two chairs, a small desk. He sat in the smaller chair, leaned back, removed his hat, laid it on his knee, pointed to the larger chair, said, "General, please, take a seat. It isn't necessary for us to be . . . so formal. The air in this camp is thick enough as it is."

Meade sat, kept his hat on, said, "General Grant, this army is quite familiar with your successes in the West. Your promotion was applauded, by this command as much as anyone's. I hope you are able to do what Washington expects you to do. We all hope for that."

There was no enthusiasm in Meade's voice, and there was a silent moment. Grant said, "I assure you . . . there will be a fundamental change in the way we operate. Washington . . . the President is aware of the failure of the policy of allowing each army to operate independent of the others. There has been no coordination, no plan that involves all theaters of activity. That will change."

There was another silent moment, and Meade said, "I welcome . . . any changes the commanding general may wish to make. We have already made many changes here. I have tried to put the best men where they need to be. We have some good men in this army, the best . . . the best in the East. I am certain the general has his own strong feelings about his commanders in the West."

Grant felt suddenly annoyed. "General Meade, may we dispense with the rehearsed speeches? I don't care to be referred to in the third person."

Meade seemed surprised, glanced at Grant's hat, removed his own, put it on the desk, ran his fingers around the rim, and Grant saw something new in his face, relief. Meade said, "Then sir, if I may say—"

"Yes, General, you may say whatever you please."

"Thank you, sir. Washington has made it clear that they place little value on the ability of the Army of the Potomac to hold its own with your people in the West. There is the feeling in this camp that the Secretary, even the President, has sent you here to teach us how to fight. If my people seem a bit testy . . . it's because they don't care to be judged against your . . . against the army in the West. These men have fought some pretty hard fights. We haven't always done as well as we might have, but it is not the men. Washington must pass judgment on *my* leadership. I am prepared for that. But there has been a great deal of reorganization since Gettysburg. It has been my priority to put the best commanders where they can do the most good. We *do* have good people in this army. Good commanders are good commanders no matter where they happen to be fighting. This army sits under the shadow of Washington, and Washington can be . . . impatient. Most of what they know of your command is what they see on paper. Here, a week doesn't pass without some bloated dignitary parading through the camp asking my people how long it will take us to end this war. They go back to Washington and tell the newspapers we are sitting around doing nothing while our enemies boast of their great victories." Meade stood now, put his hat on his head, and Grant sat back, waited.

"Forgive me, sir. But if I don't . . . if you don't hear this now, you may never hear it. You may find out the hard way. The enemy here is not the enemy out West. I know something of command. Robert E. Lee is not Pemberton, he is not Bragg. No disrespect . . . your success out West is to be commended. But what flows through here from Washington, all we have been hearing is that we only need General Grant, and old Bobby Lee will turn tail. Well, sir, now you are here. Now you will find out what this army has known for a long time. It will take more than a few new corps commanders to march us into Richmond!" Meade was red-faced, breathing heavily.

Grant pointed to the chair, said, "Thank you, General. Please sit down."

Meade seemed surprised, looked at the chair and sat. Grant reached into his coat pocket, pulled out a cigar, then another pocket, moved deliberately, pulled out a small metal box, and Meade could see a piece of flint, Grant now striking it against a piece of steel. The sparks began to ignite a twist of cloth, and there was a plume of black smoke, the cloth began to burn, and Grant slowly lit the cigar. Meade watched him intently, seemed to calm down, and Grant held out the cigar, looked at it, said, "I don't know many of your people, but that will change. Some of the names are familiar, I knew some of them at the Point, some in Mexico. What I am depending on is coordination, that your army will work *with* the forces in the West. General Sherman has succeeded me in command of those forces, and I will be informing both of you what our new campaign will involve."

He stopped, saw Meade's expression change, saw surprise. "What is it, General?"

Meade removed his hat again, looked down. "Forgive me, sir, but it was my assumption that this command . . . that *I* would not be a part of your plans. It is no secret that the President has been impatient with my efforts."

"General Meade, you were in Mexico. Do you recall how rumors affected the army then?"

Meade looked at Grant now, and Grant could see the memories, Meade's own experiences in Mexico, coming back to him. Meade said, "We were cut off from the coast, from Washington, from everybody. General Scott's decision . . . to move the army inland on its own . . . we went through a different panic every night." Meade smiled now, the first change in his expression. "There were supposed to be ten thousand Mexicans waiting for us around every turn."

Grant nodded, smiled as well. "And behind us, and above us . . . Santa Anna was on top of every mountain, every water hole was poisoned, they moved like ghosts in the night."

They sat in silence for a moment, absorbed the sudden rush of memories. But Grant focused, pushed the thoughts of Mexico away, looked at Meade, and Meade was serious again, said, "I had thought the reports were reliable . . . that General Sherman would be assuming command of *this* army."

Grant was surprised, said, "Really? And where are you going? Tennessee?" Grant felt a sudden twinge of impatience.

Meade said, "I assumed . . . because of Washington's lack of enthusiasm for my performance . . . I would be relieved. I would only request . . . that you inform me without delay. Washington has always had a policy of dragging these things out, letting the commanders . . . sweat a bit. There seems to be some delight on the part of the Secretary to maintain suspense, and General Halleck has a habit of launching surprise attacks on his subordinates."

Grant felt a surge of anger, thought of Halleck, took a deep breath. "There is no surprise attack here. I have no intention of replacing you. We cannot run this army by trial and error. I know your record, I know how you command. I have no doubt you will continue to serve this army well. I have experienced the impatience of the Secretary. He makes grand judgments based on what he reads, not what he sees. And General Halleck is now . . ." He paused, had not thought of this before, of all the implications of his promotion. "General Halleck is now *my* subordinate. What pleases Washington is no longer to be your concern. What pleases *me* . . ." He paused, thought of his own words, felt the anger slip away, was suddenly embarrassed, surprised at himself. "Perhaps I should say that differently. . . ."

Meade slapped his hand hard on the desk. "No sir! You have made yourself quite clear. I am greatly relieved to hear that. We heard . . . the word was that your promotion might be . . . political. Something . . . for the newspapers to play with. I had thought, if you moved to Washington, you would probably . . ." He paused. "You would probably become one of *them*."

Grant looked at the cigar again, said, "I have been advised to maintain my headquarters in Washington. I have no intention of doing so. I had thought . . . perhaps I would go back out West, Nashville. But General Sherman knows me well, he knows what I expect of him, and he knows his opponent there. Here . . . it is different. I believe you are correct about General Lee. How we deal with *your* opponent will determine the outcome of the war."

Meade nodded, and Grant saw the enthusiasm building. Meade said, "Yes, Lee is all that stands between us and Richmond. If we can maneuver him away, move on Richmond again—"

Grant abruptly stood up, and Meade stopped, watched him. Grant tapped his hat against his leg, freeing a cloud of dust. His mind began to move, rethinking the plan he had sketched, hammered, and picked at for weeks. He paced for a moment, then stopped and looked at Meade.

"No. Our objective has *always* been Richmond. That is *not* our objective now. They are not beaten until *he* is beaten. If we seize Richmond, they will just move their government somewhere else. We will tie up our army occupying a place of small value and this war will go on for years. Richmond is a symbol, and three years ago this war was all about symbols. Symbols are for politicians and newspapers, something emotional to rally around. But if we have learned anything, it is that war is about fighting, about armies and guns and the death of men. As long as there are armies, there will be a war. I don't care about symbols. Our objective is *Lee*."

As the spring moved into Virginia and the roads hardened, Grant began to put his plan into words. In the West, Sherman would press Joe Johnston, and as in Virginia, the goal was Johnston's army, to draw him out into battle where Sherman's numbers could prevail. If Johnston were defeated, Atlanta would fall, and the Confederacy would be divided even further, the great railroad connections cut. But Grant understood that merely confronting Lee would not make Lee fight on anyone else's terms but his own, and so the plans in Virginia were more complicated. On the Virginia peninsula, a large force was assembled under the command of Ben Butler. Butler was no one's friend, had not distinguished himself as a great leader of troops, but he was a powerful political force in Washington, a man Lincoln could not afford to antagonize. If Grant did not place much value on Butler's abilities, Butler himself did, and so his influence and his ability to intimidate Washington meant that Grant had no choice but to put him in charge of a sizable command. Butler's objective was to move up the James River, pressuring Richmond from the east. If Richmond was too heavily defended, then Butler could move south of the James and assault the valuable railroad junction at Petersburg.

To the west of Lee's army, in the Shenandoah Valley, Grant assigned Franz Sigel to command a smaller force that would move south, up the valley, confronting whatever forces Lee had there. Early in the war Sigel had led the Eleventh Corps, made up mainly of New Yorkers and Pennsylvanians of German ancestry. He was a graduate of the German Military Academy, an experienced fighter who had emigrated himself because he happened to pick the wrong side in a brief revolution. He had seemed to be a natural choice to lead his former countrymen in the Eleventh, was an inspiration to the many Germans who had now taken up the Union cause. But he was undistinguished as a field commander, and he was replaced early in 1863 by Oliver Howard. It was Howard who would then carry the stain of the Eleventh, the men who would panic at Chancellorsville, collapsing from the surprise flank attack from Jackson, a failure that would always be theirs.

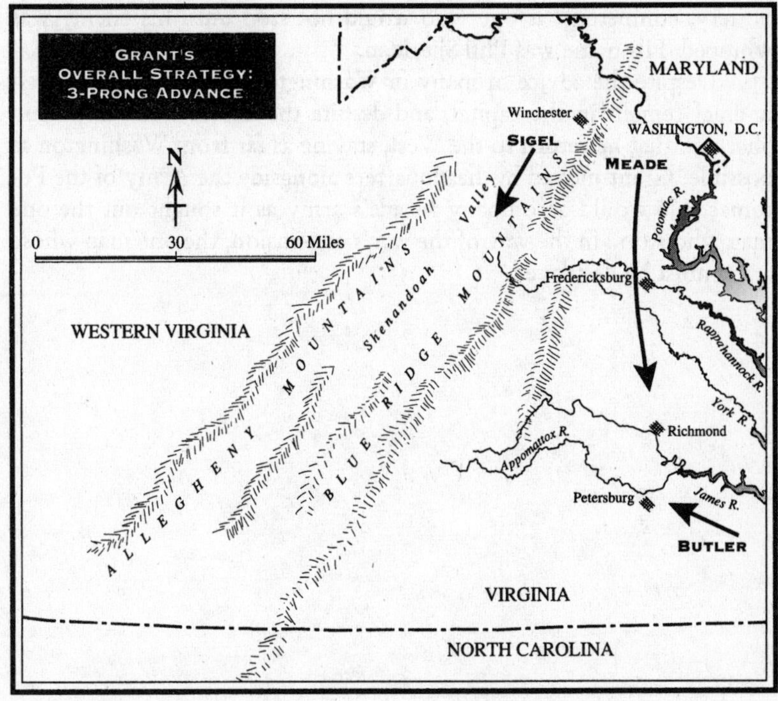

Since Howard had performed no better than Sigel, Sigel's removal had angered many of the immigrants even more, and Grant understood that Sigel's presence had value in drawing immigrants into the army. If he was undistinguished, at least he was already in place, in western Virginia. Sigel's assignment in the valley would be to prevent Lee from reinforcing himself from the Confederate troops there. If Sigel moved hard into Virginia's most fertile and productive farmland, it was a threat Lee could not ignore.

Grant made one more major change. The Federal army had never made the best use of its cavalry, and Jeb Stuart had embarrassed his blue counterparts consistently. As the war had gone on, the blue horsemen learned more about their enemy and his successes, and gradually they changed the way they fought. But the high command had still not understood fully the value of cavalry, and often they were held in the rear, guarding wagon trains or sent far off on useless raids. Grant intended to change that. In the West there was one division commander, a man who led infantry, who Grant believed could be given the new responsibility of commanding horsemen. The man had built a reputation as fiery, competent, as one who would not stop until his enemy was whipped. His name was Phil Sheridan.

Despite the advice of many in Washington that the new general-in-chief remain in the capital, and despite the advice from his friend Sherman that he return to the West, staying as far from Washington as possible, Grant moved his headquarters alongside the Army of the Potomac. He would accompany Meade's army as it sought out the one man who stood in the way of the war's conclusion, the one man whose army must be destroyed.

8. LEE

May 1864

THE COURIERS CAME NOW AT REGULAR INTERVALS, STUART'S messengers bringing a steady stream of information. The hard words for Stuart's failure at Gettysburg had long faded from the newspapers, and if they mentioned Gettysburg at all now, if the papers still had a bitter need to find fault, the focus was shifting more in Longstreet's direction. Stuart was the great and gallant hero, the mention of the name always painting an inspiring picture in the minds of the people, the dashing cavalryman, the plumed hat, mocking and humiliating the enemy's inept horsemen. What had flickered through the newspapers, the hint of improper behavior, a brief public scolding for the playful ride around the enemy, was forgotten now by the reality of what the new year would bring.

The papers now gave more energy to new outrage against Lincoln, whose call for seven hundred thousand *new* troops demonstrated the aggressiveness of this unrelenting man who would still send his armies into their country. There was growing frustration with the length of the war, the casual confidence of a quick victory long erased. If blame had to be placed for that, then the angry headlines and political speeches were growing openly hostile toward Jefferson Davis as well, as though Davis himself was responsible for the great disparity in strength, the increasing void between the vast power and fertility of the North and the creeping starvation and emptiness of the South.

But there were some who did not pay much attention to the rants in the papers, who knew something of tactics and strategy, who remembered Gettysburg as more than some vague and horrible disaster. The conversations were brief and private, and even in Stuart's camp the men understood that this brash and self-assured cavalier had for once let his commander down.

Stuart never spoke of it, but his staff knew something was different, noted something more serious, that he was more sober, his playful moods less prevalent. It had been nearly a year, but Stuart kept the memories fresh in his mind. His cavalry had finally returned to Lee's army late in the fight at Gettysburg, but the damage had been done, the ground chosen for them by an enemy Lee was not ready to fight, the tide already turned against them. Had Stuart been where Lee needed him to be, the fight around Gettysburg might not have happened at all; they could have kept Meade at bay, moved farther into the enemy's country, into the rich farmlands where the army could have sustained itself as long as it had to. Then, they could have struck in any direction, Philadelphia, Baltimore, and the panic in the northern cities, the reality that the bloody fields would be their own, could have put enough pressure on Washington to make the peace.

Stuart did not dwell on politics, but he had heard the talk, the bruises on his reputation. His anger at the "insults" had quickly faded. It was that one night that stayed with him, and he would lie awake staring up at bright stars, would focus on that, riding into Lee's headquarters with all the boisterous pageantry that always swept along with him. He'd expected the face of a relieved parent, the fatherly warmth Lee had shared with him since he was a cadet at West Point, the enthusiasm for the return of the favorite son, but he saw instead a hard red-faced anger, a look he'd never seen before, Lee fighting himself to hold it down. The warmth was replaced by the deep chill of disappointment. It was something Stuart would never forget.

Now, the couriers went out toward headquarters at all hours with the smallest bit of new information. Lee would never be blind again.

LEE SAT AT HIS SMALL DESK, READ THE REPORTS. IT WAS CONfirmed now, the Federal Ninth Corps, Burnside's troops, had moved east, had left their position around Knoxville and were on the trains, and very soon would add to the strength of Meade's army. He put the paper down, realizing it would be in Virginia after all. He stood, walked to the opening in the tent, stared out down the wide hill, saw his men milling through their camps, some at drill, some gathered at the fires.

Taylor, sitting at a small table out in the open, saw him, and Lee saw the line of officers and a few privates waiting patiently, the daily complaints and requests. The look on Taylor's face was a silent question: Do you need me? Lee shook his head, stepped into the open, suddenly felt the urge for coffee, moved toward the mess wagon. He saw Marshall now, the young man moving toward him, and Lee smiled as he walked; there was always something about Marshall that made him smile. He was young, nearly as young as Taylor, wore small round glasses that made him resemble a schoolboy, studious and efficient.

Marshall stopped, saw Lee focused on the wagon, said, "General, may I get you something?"

Lee said, "No, Major, quite all right. Just taking a bit of a break."

Lee reached the wagon, and the mess sergeant had a cup ready, poured a thick black liquid from a tin pot, handed it slowly to Lee and said quietly, so as not to disturb his thoughts, "Sir."

Lee took the cup and drew it up, caught the rising steam, breathed it in. The man held out a small metal box, and Lee took a spoon from it, scooped it full of the brown crystals, stirred the hard sugar into the cup. He stared at the thick swirl, slowly took a sip, felt his tongue curl at the bitterness, then glanced up at the sergeant, who was smiling, proud of his brew. Lee nodded, tried to smile, thought, Maybe . . . more sugar. The sergeant still held the box out, and Lee thought, No, we must make do . . . even the little things. He put the spoon back in the box, turned toward his tent, looked again into the cup. The men do not have the luxury of coffee, he thought, not real coffee anyway. He recalled seeing men grinding up straw and corn husks, peanut shells and tree bark, anything that could be boiled into a hot black liquid. He knew they were trading with the Yankees, that when the armies were close, the men along the picket lines would make their own quiet armistice, swapping their tobacco for coffee, newspapers for hardtack. He did not approve, but would not give the order to stop. The pickets know more than the rest of us, he thought. They are so close, and so they see it clearly.

It had taken him a long time to understand what the men on the front lines had accepted long ago. But Lee still saw the faces, knew the names, had served with so many of them, fought with them in Mexico, chased Comanches with them in Texas, had watched many of them work their way through West Point. The foot soldiers had no guilt, no difficulty killing the men in blue, no confusion about whether the Yankees were indeed the enemy. It is our sad duty, but I cannot think of them that way, Lee reflected. They are simply . . . those people.

He had believed from the beginning that there was a difference, something superior in his men that went beyond what they brought to the battlefield. But despite the poor commanders, the blue soldier had proven he would fight, and that if God gave him the chance, he would *win* the fight. Lee had finally begun to understand that the hand of God might cover more than just his army. Those boys, those other fellows, were not that different from them after all.

He thought, But God is still with us, He still watches over us, and He is still guiding us. If He is guiding them as well, if He puts the good fight in them, it is to test us, test our resolve. In the end, He will judge us for that, for our heart, for how we do our duty.

The wave of religious spirit had again swept through the winter camps. Just as the year before, the revival tents had spread out all through the army, the men gathering in great numbers before the renewed enthusiasm of the chaplains. There had been civilian visitors as well, preachers, men of great fiery oration. It was the perfect way for the men to spend the bleak winter, to relieve the boredom by the strengthening of their faith.

He looked northward, over the wide bleak fields, over distant rolling hills. It was not the same over there . . . across the river. They are such a mix of people, so little in common with us . . . even with each other. But even before Gettysburg he had been surprised, began to see something new in the spirit of the blue soldiers, the men who charged hard into his guns. He thought of the vast horror of the stone wall at Fredericksburg, how they still came, wave after wave. They do not fight for the same cause, he thought, they are not defending against an invader, they do not fight to protect their homes, but still . . . *they fight.*

He had not thought it possible that this would still go on. He'd assumed that after all the bloody fights, and so many utter defeats, those fellows would not have the stomach for this, they would simply go home. He'd thought it would come from the soldiers themselves, the men who saw the horrors, knew the fear, the panic, the sickening loss. He thought they would finally say, "*Enough*, there is no good reason for this, we are dying for fat men in silk suits who hide in clean white buildings." The blue lines would thin, the enthusiasm for the fight draining away, and with that, the Federal army would cease to be.

He had not often seen them up close, but he understood who they were. He'd seen many prisoners, thought of the faces, the bitter sadness of men who were out of the fight. Yet they do not make the fight, he thought. It is not the foot soldier who brings this war against us. They are farmers and laborers and clerks, and surely they feel just as we do, that we all have the right to be left alone. We do not threaten their cities, we do not seek to destroy their homes, we do not blockade their ports or starve their families. Yet they are still inspired . . . by what? It is not the inspiration that comes from great leadership. There has never been great leadership. It was not Meade who turned us away in Pennsylvania. We were beaten by our own mistakes, and the fight of their soldiers. Now, Washington has given them a new commander, and like all the rest, he must bring them into our guns again. But this time, they will be different . . . they will know what it feels like to *win*.

He drank from the cup again, ignored the bitterness, stared out at the camps of his men, thought, We are fighting for our independence, and that is the greatest fight there can be. Throughout the winter he had thought of his men as akin to the men at Valley Forge, the small shivering army of George Washington, praying and enduring through the misery of the elements, surviving, somehow, so they could take the fight to the enemy again. Washington had prevailed against great odds, against the better equipped army of a great empire. It had always inspired him, the great fight against long odds, the success against a powerful enemy. There is not much difference between Washington's army and ours, he mused. We are fighting, after all, for the same reasons, for the same cause. And, we *can* succeed. With the weather warming, the roads drying out, the army is rested, morale is high, and they are ready again.

He knew the First Corps was coming back, that Longstreet was already bringing them out of Tennessee, would be close very soon. That would bring the numbers back up, make Lee as strong as he would ever be. Now the reports from Stuart confirmed he was right, the fight would be *here*. But this time it could be very different, this time the Federals would be led by someone who did not put his picture in the newspapers, who did not make grand speeches. He tried to remember the face, the name a vague memory from long ago, a brief meeting in Mexico, but there was nothing that brought that back to him, nothing to separate the name "Grant" from so many others. He knew only that this man had risen to the top, that something had so inspired Lincoln that he'd given this man complete control.

He walked to his tent, saw Taylor signing papers, heard his name called, soldiers trying for some piece of personal attention, but he did not respond, moved into the tent. He looked at the latest message from Stuart, saw several more scattered on the table. Understanding what Stuart was doing, the overefficiency, he smiled, thought, General, don't wear out your horses.

He sat, moved the papers into a single pile, set the cup down, stared away at nothing. He began to think of moving the army, the new defense, the new commanders, felt relief that Longstreet was coming back. Yes, you are still my warhorse. And I will need you, and I will need General Stuart. He looked out through the opening in the tent, could see across the far fields, saw the large dark mound of Clark Mountain rising in the distance, a dull intrusion into the blue sky, thought, I should go up there, speak to the lookouts. Grant's army will not sit still for long. And we must be prepared.

He emptied the cup, felt the bitterness filling him, felt the familiar twist in his gut, the surge of energy for the new fight. He stood then, moved out of the tent, thought, If Grant is in Virginia, then he is here because *I* am here. . . .

THEY WAITED FOR HIM ON THE WIDE HILL, WATCHED HIM QUIetly as he rode toward them, Traveller carrying him through the small trees, the trail winding between large flat rocks. He had a fresh energy, felt better than he had in weeks, had pushed the horse hard up the hill, felt the thrill of the hard ride. His staff, whom he'd left behind, were just now coming into view. He gazed across the summit of the hill, felt the coolness, saw the flowers, God's hand draped across the land in rich green patches, the new growth of spring. The horse was breathing hard, and he leaned over, patted the animal's neck, gave a small laugh.

Clark Mountain was really a large flat hill, but it loomed high above the Rapidan River and was ideal for an observation post. The lookouts themselves began to gather now, staying back behind the small group of commanders, and Lee halted the horse, dismounted, instinctively looked at the larger man, standing in front of the others.

"General Longstreet, you are looking well this morning."

Longstreet made a short bow, held a short pipe in one hand, smiled briefly. He knew Lee's moods, had not seen this one for a long while, said only, "General Lee."

Behind Longstreet, Lee saw the others watching him still, and no one would speak until he'd acknowledged them. He was used to this courtesy now, understood the formality of rank, looked to the tall thin man behind Longstreet who was moving forward gingerly on the wooden leg, stepping awkwardly across the uneven rock.

"General Ewell—"

"Sir!" Ewell snapped to attention, saluted, and Lee returned it.

Then Lee saw a smaller man, the red beard neatly trimmed, the old hat propped slightly askew. "General Hill . . ." He paused, hesitated to use the words that seemed to come naturally when greeting Hill. "Are you well today, General?"

Hill glanced at Longstreet, who did not look at him, and Lee knew this was a sensitive point, that Hill was aware of the talk in the camps of the other commanders, the longstanding feud with Longstreet never really resolved. Hill's frequent illnesses had become well-known, and many were saying it was only when the big fight was coming that he would withdraw to his cot. Hill stood straight, said, "Yes, General. I am quite well."

Lee made small greetings to the others, saw the sour expression of Jubal Early, Ewell's division commander, an outspoken and unpopular man, and more recently the man who was seen as the true commander of Ewell's Second Corps, the strength behind the weakening control of Ewell.

Ewell understood that his reputation had diminished. Under Jackson, early in the war, he'd led his division with great fire, had built affection from his men by often putting himself where a commander had no business going, right on the line, moving into the fight beside his men. The bravado had cost him a leg, and with that loss something else had gone out of him as well, something unexpected. After Jackson's death, when Ewell and Hill were promoted to inherit the divided command, Ewell had seen his first great opportunity at Gettysburg, staring down at him from the top of Cemetery Hill. Lee knew, as did the others, that Ewell had not performed, had stared up at the weak Federal defenses on the hill and done nothing. Even when his commanders had offered to assault the key position on their own responsibility, Ewell held them back, suddenly lost the great fire Jackson had always relied on. More recently, Ewell had married, moved his wife into his headquarters, and, if his strength had seemed to drain away with the loss of the leg, whatever control he still held over his staff now came from his wife. It was an odd and uncomfortable experience for his men to realize that Ewell was no longer in command, that he had served Jackson so well because he was best suited to be under the domination of someone else. With Jackson gone, many in the field knew it was now Early. In camp, the staff knew it was his wife.

Lee walked a few steps toward the north face of the hill, raised his field glasses. Hill moved closer, and Lee could feel him there, silent, trying to absorb something from him. It was painful and obvious that Hill's confidence was still badly bruised by the disaster at Bristoe Station, and at every opportunity now he seemed to hover close to Lee, seeking . . . Lee wasn't sure what, but he felt the neediness, the pull at him. Lee gazed through the glasses, thought, You will have your chance, General. There will be time for amends.

The others raised field glasses as well, an exercise of respect since they had already seen what Lee was now viewing. Across the river, a vast sea of white specks, the tents of Grant's enormous army, spread out over the bare fields. It had been a familiar scene for weeks now, but there was something new, the reason the corps commanders were here, why they would meet on this tall hill. There was a swarm of activity all through the neat squares of white; slowly the neat checkerboard was distorting, the tents disappearing. Grant was preparing to move.

Lee had read reports, some from the northern papers, some from Stuart, that the Federal army was set to begin its campaign. Ewell's corps was along the river below them, guarding against a crossing that could bring Grant straight at Lee's army, but Lee knew it would not be like that, Grant would not expose himself to his army's strength. Grant had two choices. If he moved out to the left, to the west, and came across the Rapidan upstream, he could threaten to move on the Shenandoah, or cut the rail lines that fed the Confederate army. But that would take Grant far from his own supply lines, from the security of the big rivers in the east. The only other route south would be downstream, at the fords that had been used by Hooker's army a year ago, Germanna and Ely, the routes that led straight down into the Wilderness.

Lee said nothing, and the others were watching him again, already knew what the activity across the river would mean. Lee turned, gradually scanned the open ground to the northeast, then down across the river and across the thickets and dense growth of the Wilderness. He put the glasses down, stared out, thought, Yes, it will have to happen there. He did not feel an instinct about Grant as he had about so many of the others, but everything he had read, every piece of information he could find, told him that this man would not use trickery and deceit. His army was too large and too cumbersome, and so they would advance by the shortest route, the straight line. The straight line toward Richmond was down through the Wilderness. There were other reasons as well. As Grant moved south, he would be between the Confederate army and Fredericksburg, and at Fredericksburg the good roads and the Rappahannock could still provide a good supply line for the Federal troops. And if they move quickly and get below us, Lee thought, we will have a serious problem.

Lee knew he would not receive help from Davis, that the president was as concerned as he had ever been with administering the army, about promotions and transfers of officers. Davis had even moved his friend Braxton Bragg to Richmond, put the despised Bragg in the only place where those who so disliked him could not have an effect—right beside Davis as his principal adviser. The defenses of Richmond were now manned by troops that belonged to Lee's army, including what was left of Pickett's division, the force that had been so decimated at Gettysburg.

More of Lee's troops were tied up in North Carolina, even though Lee himself had information that the Federals there had already moved north, to reinforce Grant's forces on the peninsula east of Richmond. Davis's response to Lee's warnings about the new threat to Richmond was to create a new military department, with jurisdiction south of the James River. The command of all the territory below Richmond was given to the one man who had repeatedly shown a clear envy of Lee's prominence and popularity, and so could not be relied on to lend support to Lee's effort. The job was given to the man whose greatest notoriety came from commanding the firing on Fort Sumter: P.G.T. Beauregard.

Lee still stared out across the Wilderness, did not search for detail, for any landmark, because even from this vantage point, there was none. It was the same dense mass that had swallowed up Joe Hooker's army, and somewhere in those vast green thickets, along some dim trail, was the spot where Jackson had fallen. Jackson had taken one risk too many, had ridden too far forward on a night when both exhausted armies held tight to their guns, would respond with sudden manic violence to any sound. One sound had been the thundering hoofbeats of Jackson and his staff.

Lee turned his head to the north again, did not look down toward Grant's army, just out to the open sky, thought, There is no resting place . . . no sacred ground. We must do it all again, here. If Grant has the numbers, the strength, we have the advantage of knowing the ground, of knowing how that terrible bloody place can paralyze an army, the unseen enemy, the sounds of the fight echoing across the creeks and hollows, no point of reference, no way to know who is in front of you, or beside you . . . or behind you.

He still said nothing, and they began to move closer to him, expecting him to discuss the plan, what he would ask them to do. He felt a sudden lightness, felt his mind open up, stared out into the clear blue and felt like he could step out, off the hill, away from it all. He felt drawn by God, that familiar sense that God was close to them. He had felt like this before, at Manassas, when he could see the panorama of Pope's army swept from the field by his men, and at Fredericksburg, his invincible line destroying the enemy's continuing assaults. But there was also the last day at Gettysburg, when he sat on the big horse and watched his men march in those beautiful strong lines across that wide field, moving ever closer to that one clump of trees, a mile of wide-open glory, and he'd felt God beside him as he waved them forward through the smoke and brilliant flashes of light, and waited for the smoke to clear knowing they were up and over the Federal lines. But when the smoke cleared it was not like that at all, and those who had survived came slowly back across the field, shattered and beaten, and God was not beside him.

He felt a sudden shock, blinked hard, sensed the men around him again. He felt his breath choke in his throat and put his hand on his chest, focused, brought himself back to this place. He turned, saw Longstreet beside him, watching him, concern in the blue eyes. But Longstreet said nothing. Lee thought, He does not believe God was with us that day. They were his men, and he did not want them to go. But I believed they would prevail, they could do anything. It had to be something in us . . . in our will. We cannot lose that, it is what God wants from us. We must not lose faith. Grant is just another test. God is watching us to see if the will is still there. It *is* still there.

He took another deep breath, said, "General, you know this man. Will he do what we suppose him to do?"

Longstreet took the pipe from his mouth, seemed surprised at the question. "Grant? Well, yes, I don't believe Sam Grant is a very complicated man." Longstreet stared out toward the north, thought for a moment, said, "I believe there is one thing we may depend on. Once he begins to move, once he is in front of us, we had better be prepared to stay there awhile. He will not go away until we *make* him go away."

Lee said nothing, looking out to the north again, thought, If Grant is not complicated, then our job will be easier. We do not have the strength to strike him where he sits, so we must let him come to us, commit himself, at a time and place of his own choosing. But there has always been a mistake, sooner or later, with all of them. It does not matter if Grant is different from McClellan, or Burnside, or Hooker. He will make a mistake. God will provide. . . .

Lee raised his arm, pointed out to the east, toward the Wilderness. "He will cross there . . . at Ely's or Germanna. We must focus our attention there."

There were nods, low comments, and they waited, expected him to say more. But he did not feel like making plans, issuing the orders, the small details that these men would need. He felt something much larger was already in motion around them, the plan already in place, inevitable and certain. Abruptly, he turned, moved to the horse, mounted. They watched him, silent, curious, and he looked away, out toward the place where Jackson had fallen, and he felt the glare of the sharp blue eyes, knew Jackson was still there, would still help them. Yes, slow them down, General, he thought, hold them there and it will not matter if he has the numbers and the guns. It will not be a fair fight. The advantage will be ours.

9. GRANT

May 4, 1864

There was motion everywhere, horses and wagons, guns and men. He rode past a row of supply wagons, each marked with the insignia of their corps, the three-leaf clover of Hancock's Second, the Maltese cross of Warren's Fifth, Sedgwick's Sixth with the St. Andrew's cross.

He passed the wagon train now, the wagons moving farther to the east, the route that would take them out of harm's way, down across the river closer to Fredericksburg. He could see the river now, the thick columns of blue soldiers crossing on pontoon bridges. He pulled the horse off the road, moved to a small rise. The staff followed, settled behind him, with only Rawlins close by.

He glanced up, saw the stark bright sky, the blazing sun. It was a perfect day, and he looked again at the river, could even see the reflection on the water, the line of troops magnified, the river sparkling with the reflections from the rows of muskets.

He was between the Fifth and Sixth Corps, watching them cross Germanna Ford. He knew that to the east Hancock was crossing at Ely's, and it was just like this, quiet and efficient, the men moving at a good pace, that they would soon be south of the river. Even Burnside was in position above them. The Ninth Corps, waiting for the order, would guard the north side of the river until the rest of them were across. Then Burnside too would move down, strengthening the army, which was already very strong. Grant thought of the numbers, nearly 140,000, the same number Joe Hooker had a year ago, but Hooker had spread them out, an elaborate plan that relied on coordination and communication, and the result was a disaster.

No, he thought, we will pass by Chancellorsville, and it will

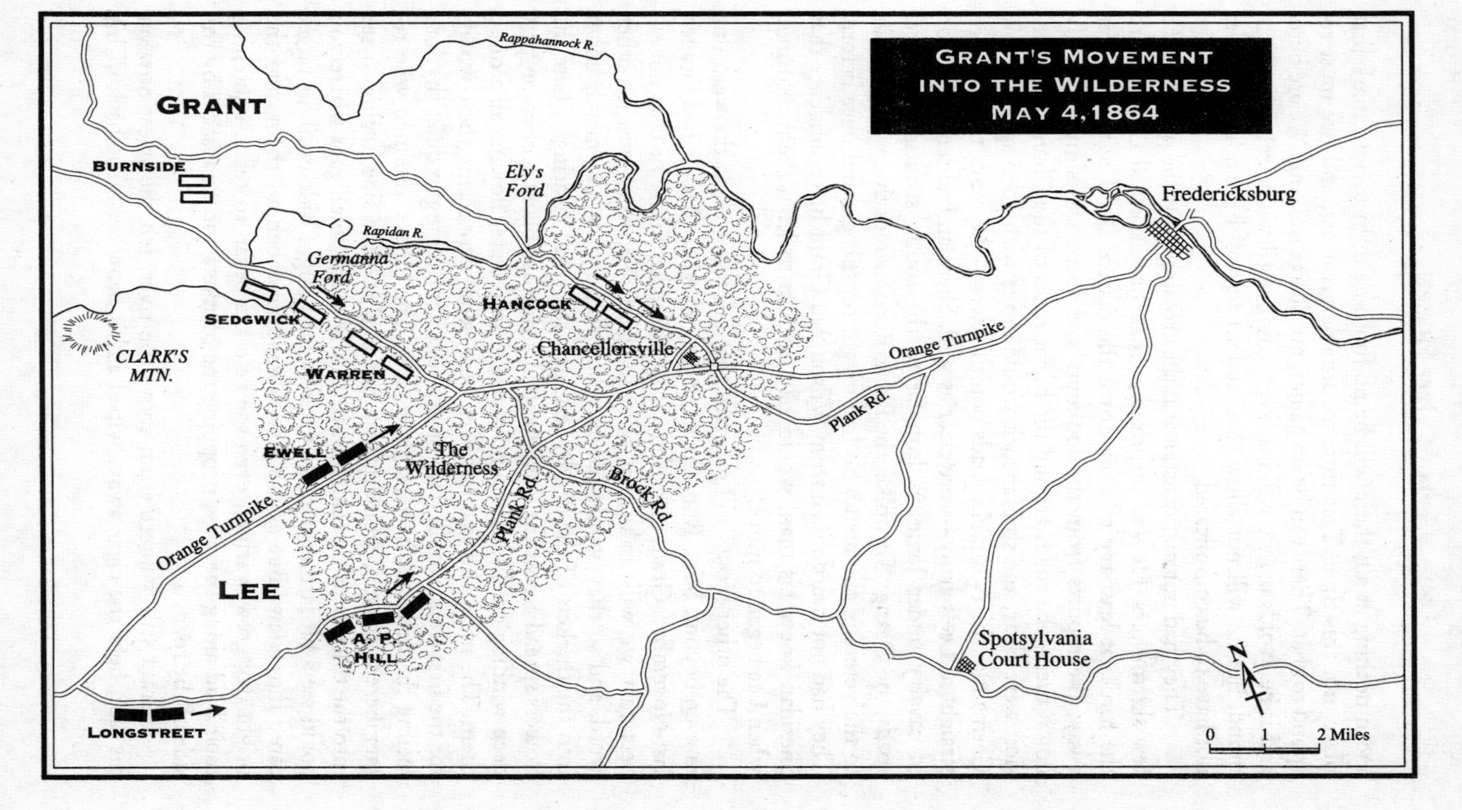
Grant's Movement
into the Wilderness
May 4,1864
Grant
Rappahannock R.
Burnside
Ely's
Ford
Rapidan R.
Germanna
Ford
Hancock
Sedgwick
Clark's
Mtn.
Warren
Chancellorsville
Orange Turnpike
Fredericksburg
Plank Rd.
Ewell
The
Wilderness
Brock Rd.
Plank Rd.
Orange Turnpike
Lee
A. P.
Hill
Spotsylvania
Court House
Longstreet
N
0
1
2 Miles

mean nothing at all, there will be no footnote in history to mark that place, not this time. This time we are one great fist, and Lee must respond to that. There can be no games, no elusive stalking. We are here, and if he avoids us, we will just keep going until we march into Richmond. But he will not allow that, and so we will have a fight. It does not have to be complicated.

They had not met resistance at the crossings, just the potshots of a few skirmishers. He was surprised at that, had expected Lee to guard the fords, at least try to slow down the march. But Lee was still far away, the reports from the lookouts said there was simply nobody down there, the roads around the burnt ruins of the Chancellor mansion were clear, and so Hancock would move with good speed. Below Germanna, the two main roads pointing west—the roads that pointed straight at Lee's army—were clear as well. Sheridan had sent a division of cavalry under James Wilson far to the south, scouting the vital roads, the Orange Turnpike, the Plank Road, names that were familiar to the veterans, the men who had fought on this ground once before. They had not heard much from Wilson, but Grant had confidence that Sheridan knew his man, would rely on him to keep them informed when Lee began to move.

The other scouts still reported that Lee was well to the west, dug in even beyond Mine Run, the same ground where Meade had escaped last November. Grant marveled at that, thought, Surely he does not expect that we will make that mistake again? Yet there was no other word, and so they would see no rebels this day, would march down into the thickets of the Wilderness, past the small clearings where the flowers spread across the deep green in a glorious blanket of color, past deep winding creeks, the sound of the unseen water flowing all around them. The men who had not been here, who were seeing these woods for the first time, would stare up at the sky, marching in quiet rhythm, feeling the delicious heat on their faces. The others, the men who remembered Jackson, would glance nervously to the side, trying to see into the thick brush, peeking instinctively at the small gaps where you could see a bit farther, a place where a man might hide until his target came into view. But as the river disappeared behind them, and the bright day grew warmer, even the veterans began to relax, lightening their load along the way, dropping the blankets and knapsacks by the side of the road.

Grant still watched from above the river, felt the sweat now on his face, held the cigar away, wiped at his brow with the back of his gloved hand. He did not like the gloves, the dull yellow cotton, preferred the feel of the leather straps in his bare hands. They were a gift, and Rawlins had insisted they would make the necessary impression. He wore a gold braid on his hat, another change, never thought much about the uniform, but that was Rawlins again, the concern for appearances. Grant had to tell himself it mattered, that the men would look to see the dashing figure of the commanding general, and they would expect some pomp, some excess of finery. The gold braid was his only grudging concession to that. He tasted the cigar again, also a gift, the dark aroma filling him, the wonderful smoke drifting to his eyes, his nose, and he thought, Yes, there is one good thing about being the commanding general, beyond the pageantry, the ridiculous vanity, something few of them would ever understand. You *can* get the best cigars.

There was motion in the water, a row of horsemen splashing across the river, the soldiers on the bridges calling out, wet protests, some laughing. Grant watched them come, saw now it was Sheridan.

There had been comments about the appointment, this small man with the small round face. He wore a strange box hat and looked more often like an Italian street vendor than a commander of troops, but Grant knew his habits well, had seen him take his division up the hill at Chattanooga, climbing the ragged face of Missionary Ridge, and they did not stop until they were at the top, Bragg's army melting away in front of them. There had even been a question about following orders, whether Sheridan had ignored his instructions, should never have pushed his men that far up the hill; but Sheridan made no excuses, no explanations. The question quickly faded away, because Grant understood that when the fight is in front of you, and the enemy is handing you the high ground, there is great value in a commander who does not halt his men to clarify his orders. Grant never doubted that Sheridan could handle command of the cavalry corps, that nothing would be lost by the new assignment. He was a superb horseman, and was grateful to be brought east to confront Jeb Stuart.

Sheridan rode toward Grant, his men filing out neatly on either side of him. Sheridan saluted, and Grant could see he was furious. "Sir! We have been ordered . . . General Meade has ordered . . ." He was red-faced and looked down for a moment.

Grant said, "General, please proceed. Is there a problem?"

Sheridan closed his eyes, clamped down, seemed to be fighting for control. "Sir, General Meade has ordered most of my men to the east, toward Fredericksburg. There are reports that some of the enemy's horsemen have been located in that area. General Meade seems to believe that the wagon trains may be in jeopardy." Sheridan took a deep breath.

Grant motioned at him with the cigar. "Yes, so . . . what is your concern, General?"

"Sir! General Meade has us guarding the wagon trains! Surely the commanding general understands that we can better serve the army by spreading out farther to the south, protecting the roads. We have yet to locate any sizable force of the enemy, and we aren't likely to if we are sitting at Fredericksburg."

Grant glanced at Rawlins, could feel his chief of staff shifting nervously on the horse, impatiently waiting for an opening, the appropriate time for comment. Grant said, "You have something to say, Colonel?"

Rawlins tried to look surprised, said, "Oh . . . well, sir, if I may offer. A sizable portion of General Sheridan's men are already in position down below us. General Wilson is protecting our right flank. I had thought General Sheridan would be pleased that his men are, in fact, being used in valuable service."

Grant waited, wondered if the flow of words from Rawlins had ended.

Sheridan jumped in and said, "Sir, General Wilson is new to command. If it had been my decision, *his* division would guard the wagons. It is the smallest division in the corps. Now, that is not possible. General Meade insists, sir, that the bulk of my command stay to the east. He has . . . pardon me, sir, but General Meade is giving great credibility to the threat from Stuart. I have seen nothing to indicate this threat exists."

There was a silent pause, and Grant said, "General, has General Wilson located the enemy's cavalry?"

Sheridan looked down, seemed suddenly embarrassed. "I . . . don't know, sir. I have not received word from General Wilson in . . . some time."

"Well, then, until you do, I would tend to go with General Meade's instincts. He has been here before, he has dealt with Stuart before. Unless you can determine with certainty that his orders are a mistake . . . I would suggest you obey them."

Sheridan nodded, said, "Yes, you are correct of course, sir. I will send word to General Wilson to inform us of any contact with Stuart. I am convinced we will not find him at Fredericksburg. If you will excuse me, sir." Sheridan saluted, turned the horse, and the troops followed after him, thundering down to the river, splashing across.

Grant saw a row of guns now, moving onto the bridge.

Rawlins smiled, said, "General Sheridan is a might small for a job this big, wouldn't you say, sir?"

Grant did not smile at the joke, looked briefly at Rawlins, then watched the bridges again, the swaying motion of the pontoons under the great weight of the big guns.

"Colonel, General Sheridan will be big enough for all of us before this is through."

THERE WERE FEW CLEARINGS, BUT THEY HAD FOUND ONE OPEN mound, rising above the level of the trees that spread out all around them, and he had chosen the spot for his headquarters. Meade had set up his tents nearby, and by midday the three corps were completely across the river, spread far along the roads that cut through the Wilderness.

There was a small house, long abandoned, a few pieces of furniture remaining, and Grant would use it only for meetings, was more comfortable in the tent. He leaned against a tall fat tree stump, pulled a fresh cigar from his coat. Meade's camp was slightly below him, and Grant smiled at that. Meade had clearly given thought to the elevation of the headquarters tents, and made sure he was not higher up the rise than Grant.

But it was the flag that caught Grant's attention. Meade had been given a new one, a field of deep lavender, with the stark likeness of a golden eagle in the center, circled with silver. Grant stared at it, shook his head, saw Meade now coming up the hill toward him. He thought, Let it go. Meade was never predictable, you never knew how he would react to anything. The breeze picked up, and the flag stood out straight, grand and regal. Grant couldn't resist the urge, pointed with the cigar, said to Meade, "What's this . . . are we in the presence of Imperial Caesar?"

Meade turned, looked up at the flag, and Grant saw him frown, a look Grant was becoming familiar with now. Meade carried a small folding chair, sat down, settled the chair into the soft ground. "If it is offensive . . . I can remove it."

"Not at all, it lends an air of . . . the majestic. Not sure Secretary

Stanton would approve. If he pays us a visit, I would suggest you stow it away. He would likely take it home with him." Grant put the cigar in his mouth, hid a smile.

There was activity below them, couriers beginning to arrive, breathless horsemen, the staff moving to meet them. Grant saw one officer bringing a man up the hill toward him, and the staff officer said, "General, excuse me, sir, this man has information about the enemy's position."

Grant looked at the man, had expected to see a cavalry uniform, but saw infantry, a captain. The man looked at Grant, then Meade, seemed to gulp. Meade leaned back in the chair, said, "What do you have for us, son?"

"From General Warren, sir . . . I'm to tell you that his men are halting per orders, sir, and are on the Orange Turnpike. There is no sign of the enemy in our front, sir." There was a pause. Grant saw other staff officers moving closer, the anticipation of hearing some piece of real news.

Meade said, "That's it? That's Warren's report? What about the cavalry . . . they're supposed to be on his flank."

"Uh, no sir, we haven't seen any cavalry, not since early this morning. There's nobody, sir. No horses, no rebs."

Meade looked at Grant, and Grant turned, moved toward his tent, said quietly, "General, a moment, if you please . . ."

Meade stood, said, "Well, Captain, go on back to General Warren and tell him to keep an eye out. Lee's not just going to watch us walk all the way to Richmond."

Meade moved behind Grant and they ducked into the tent. Grant sat on a small chair, pointed at another, and Meade sat down. Grant held the cigar in his hand, looked at Meade, said, "Where is he?"

Meade thought, then said, "Lee?"

"Well, Lee too. I'm talking about Wilson. The cavalry. Where are the reports?"

Meade was suddenly nervous, wrapped his fingers around his knees, gripped hard. "I will send someone down there. It is possible—in this infernal place—he is lost."

Grant watched him quietly, said slowly, "It is also possible that he has his hands full of a fight. Lee knows where we are, this is his ground. Wilson's not that good of a horseman to sneak up on him. And he sure isn't going to sneak up on Stuart."

Meade nodded, said, "We should bring the army together, tighten up. Is Burnside expected tonight?"

"He's supposed to be across the river by dark. We'll see about that, but I'm not concerned about General Burnside right now. I'm much more concerned with how far Lee will let us go before he does something."

"Mine Run . . . he must be waiting for us there."

Grant thought, Yes, General, he would like us to make your mistake again, and you would like to have a second chance. He leaned back in the chair, said, "No. He cannot afford to just wait for us. If we move on to the south, we will have slipped by him and have a clear shot at Richmond, and he will not allow that. He has to *move*, to come at us. The only question is . . . when."

Meade seemed puzzled, said, "You want us to wait for him? *Here?* Shouldn't we keep going? He *wants* us to stay here. This is the best place for him to attack."

Grant nodded. "Yes. And so we will let him. General Meade, we cannot defeat him if we cannot find him. He knows where we are, and he has three choices. He can retreat, move himself closer to Richmond and wait for us again; he can sit still and watch us go by; or he can attack. He has not built this tiresome godlike reputation by retreating or sitting still. He will come. And every time he comes, he loses more and more of his army. It is a simple case of mathematics."

Meade stared at Grant, nodded slowly and said, "But I would feel better if I knew where . . . I do not like surprises."

Grant thought now of Sheridan, but would not ask; there was no real danger yet, the numbers were too strong, the lines too compact. Lee would have to come in face-to-face, line against line, and Grant saw the faces of the commanders, Hancock, Sedgwick, Warren. This time, he thought, we have the right people, and we are ready for you. He pulled at the cigar, felt the smoke wash around his face, watched as Meade wrestled with his caution, wondered if Meade would ever understand the value of cavalry.

MAY 5, 1864

THE ORANGE TURNPIKE RAN DUE WEST, DISAPPEARED INTO THE deep woods of the Wilderness, and on both sides of the road the picket line had spread out on the edge of a wide field. They were mostly veterans, and along the tree line there was one regiment from New York, from the north country, the rugged mountains that gave their men willingly to this great army.

They could hear the birds, the first sounds of the land coming awake. One man rolled over, felt the musket, lifted it up and laid it against the stump beside him. He was young, had the smooth face of a boy, and they called him Chuckie, short for Charles. No one called him Charles but his mother. He didn't like the nickname, but he knew these men were his friends, that they trusted him, they had shared some awful bloody times. There were other nicknames as well, old Bugeye, Redleg, Hawknose. No one seemed to mind, it was all good-natured, and he knew that "Chuckie" was better than most.

Beneath him the blanket was rumpled and wet. He had kept it wrapped around him through a warm night, and so the blanket and his clothes were soaked in the raw smell of sweat. He always used the blanket, had relied on it for survival through the winter, and now as the nights gave hint of the coming summer, he would still use it. It was his shield, his protection against the drone of the mosquitoes, the small whining sounds that darted and hovered over his face. He'd spent his life in the cold mountains, and hadn't known about these strange little creatures and the misery they caused. He remembered the first one, setting down on his hand, and he had watched it, curious, not really feeling any bite, nothing like the bites of the black flies he had endured as a child. And then he'd forgotten it, and it was a day later when the bite appeared, the intense itch, the swollen redness. But there was another greater terror, a threat from below, from the soft damp ground. Months before, when his unit was in pursuit of Lee, crossing the Potomac in the steaming rain, he'd spent one hot night with his arms bare, had ignored the blanket and slept on a cool bed of damp leaves. He did not feel the slow advance of the tiny creatures from the ground beneath him, but suffered for days with the bites, a massive assault he would never forget. He had tried to see them, wondered what they looked like, always now swept the dirt with his bare hands. But they did not appear, and so he lay only on the blanket now, wide-awake, would never make that mistake again. Now he slept during the day, the brief rest stops, those days when they didn't move at all, when it seemed the generals didn't know which way they wanted to go.

He was used to the picket duty; it seemed nearly every night that he found himself out in front of the army, spread out into the woods, the first line against any movement by the enemy. It had been a while since they'd actually seen any rebs, and now most of the others had no trouble sleeping. They would use their bayonets, burrow down into a shallow pit in the ground, and the veterans joked and laughed at the new boys who slept with their muskets in their hands. He smiled, thought of that older fellow, Buchman, the woodsman, the thick black beard, the man who said he could smell the enemy. He wouldn't dig in at all, would just prop himself up against a fallen tree, seemed to fall asleep at will and wake only when the bugle sounded, the call that meant breakfast.

If they spoke at all, quiet voices in the black night, they always talked about the grouchy lieutenant. Chuckie thought about him a lot, wondered if it was just his nature to be so angry. He thought, Maybe it's something at home, a letter . . . maybe his wife has taken up with a neighbor. He did not like to think of that, none of them did; they fought to keep those thoughts far away. Chuckie rarely got letters anymore. His wife had given up asking him to leave all this, to come home. She did not understand what this meant to him, why it was important. He'd tried to explain, but he was not good with words, she would not understand, and when she stopped answering his letters, it scared him worse than anything he'd seen from the rebels. He thought about the lieutenant again, wondered, Maybe that's why he seems to be so mad all the time, and he takes it out on us, on this unit.

The unit was still in good shape, but the new faces did not erase the memory of the ones who were gone. He still recalled the early days, the excitement, the adventure of riding the long trains, the men who became friends, who learned about marching and formations and bugle calls. He made an effort to remember them, especially the ones with no families, believed they needed to be remembered. He would try to keep the faces in his mind, see them in the night sky, but it hadn't worked, because when he saw the faces, he also saw the wounds, the shattering of bones, could not keep the horrors away, the reasons why so many of them were gone.

Now, while some in the line would sneak a quick nap, and others would stare into the darkness toward the invisible enemy, he would lie on the blanket and search the dark for the little creatures that flickered invisibly above his face. He'd focus on the small high whine of the mosquito, wait for it to stop, knew now that silence meant the attack had truly begun. He would swat at his face, his ears, beating off the assault, and then the whine would begin again. He tried putting the blanket over his face, but they would still get through, no defense would work. Then he would feel a slight tickle somewhere on bare skin, the return of the strange little creatures that crawled and probed up through the leaves, moving silently onto the blanket until they found some tender place—and he'd explode into motion, scratching frantically, the counterattack.

There was a damp mist this morning, and he peeked up over the tree trunk, could see the road in the distance, disappearing up a long rise into the woods. He lay on the edge of a field, had not really known how big it was, if there were woods across the way. They had been sent out after dark, the grouchy lieutenant again ordering them into the woods. The order had come in a wave of cursing, harsh words, and angry shouts which he hadn't understood.

He used to think of the mountains, of the cool streams and fishing in the deep ponds near his home. But that had faded away with the faces of his friends. He'd begun to believe he might never leave Virginia, that it was his destiny to spend the rest of his life enduring the torture, the torment from the nightly assault of the tiny insects. He wondered if it was punishment, that he or someone in his family must have done something terrible, some unspeakable offense to God. He could not tell the others, could not talk about it at all. They teased him about his fear of the creatures, laughed that if the rebels just sent their bugs into battle, Chuckie would be the first to run away.

He could hear the others stirring now, low talk, and some were standing, arms high, the long stretch. The sky began to glow far behind him; he could see the silhouettes of the trees where the rest of the army was coming to life. He looked out again to the front, could see clearly a thick line of trees across the field, the tall grass in the field standing breathlessly still. He thought of coffee now, sniffed the air for the smell of bacon. He shifted around, felt the soreness in his feet, wondered if they would march like they had yesterday, the river crossing, then the blessed halt in the afternoon. He'd wanted to jump right into the river, they all had, but the officers pushed them hard, the march fast and urgent, and they hadn't expected to stop suddenly, surrounded by the thick woods.

Down the line, one man was pointing something out, and the voices stopped. Across the field, where the road disappeared into the trees, there was a muffled, low sound. He stared into the mist, focused, saw a horse, then more, a man with a flag. They came out of the woods, were moving straight down the road into the clearing. He felt a twist in his gut, grabbed for the musket, then thought, *Cavalry.* He remembered the lieutenant saying something . . . their horsemen were supposed to be out to the west, between them and the rebs. He felt a wave of relief, his hand shaking, and he stood, wondered about riding a horse all day, if he would ever get the chance. . . .

The horsemen kept coming forward, and behind them there was a flash, a glint of steel. He could not see clearly, heard now another sound, behind him, officers riding up fast. Men were beginning to shout, there was motion all through the trees behind him. He stared out across the field again, and now he could see beyond the horses, a heavy column of infantry coming out on the road, emerging in a thick line from the trees. Now there were shouts from across the field, and the infantry began to move off the road, the column dividing, a long line flowing out in both directions on the far side of the field. Men were beginning to move around him, the men of his unit, and someone called his name, and he still stood, watched the incredible sight of hundreds of men flowing out of the woods, the lines across the field growing longer by the second, more motion behind him, more shouts.

He turned, saw the men of his unit backing away, saw the lieutenant, ducking low, moving along the edge of the field toward him, waving at him, motioning him back, out of the field. He did not want to leave, not yet, had never been this close, had never seen the rebels so clearly. He watched the horsemen, could see them clearly now, saw uniforms that were not blue, and he felt the excitement, the moment building inside of him, and he wanted to yell, to shout, to say something to them: *I see you.*

The horsemen began to turn away, backing toward the flow of infantry, and he looked around, down the line, sought the familiar faces, but there was no one there. He could still hear the sounds behind him, thought of the lieutenant, the orders to pull back. He turned, began to step away from the stump, and something stung him, punched him down hard. He tried to lift himself up, but he could not move his arms, could not move at all. The grass was sticking to his face, and he tried to rise, to turn his head. Now he felt hands, and he was rolled over, could see the treetops, the sky, and a face above him. It was the lieutenant, holding him by the shoulders. There was no anger in the man's face, but something different, softer, and the lieutenant was saying something, but the words were faint, far away. The hands let him go now, and the face was gone. He felt himself sink slowly down into the tall grass, thought of the blanket, his shield, but this time he was not afraid, felt the soft wet ground under his back, where the tiny creatures waited.

10. LEE

May 5, 1864

He had risen early, well before the first light. He tried to see the campfires where Grant had stopped for the night, and rode out late to catch some glimpse, some flicker of light. But he knew the Wilderness, knew he could see very little in any direction, not even the camps of his own men, spread behind him beyond the trees. He thought of Grant, thought, You have made a mistake, you have surrendered your advantage, you have penned yourself up in the one place I would have chosen, and now I will find a way to hurt you.

He rode Traveller through the dark, thought of coffee, but could not go back to the small fire and wait for the daylight. He was more excited than he could remember, felt the twist in his gut, felt himself breathing heavily. You knew what it felt like, when there would certainly be a fight, when the armies were very close, like two waves rolling in opposite directions, a force no one could stop. Always he'd thought of God, had prayed that not too many would die, and he rarely asked for more than that; asking for victory or the death of your enemies was not appropriate somehow. He would quote the verse, silently to himself, *Blessed be the Lord my strength, which teacheth my hands to war and my fingers to fight . . . touch the mountains and they shall smoke . . .*

He had memorized that verse years before, Psalm 144, knew somehow, strangely, that it was for *him*, that God had put those words there as a sign, words to guide him to his duty. For nearly two years now, since that rainy night on the peninsula when Davis had given him command of this army, he'd led them knowing that God was there, truly, and those few words had so much meaning. If anyone doubted that, they had only to recall the great victories, the men marching into the horror with the calm, the absolute confidence, they shared with him. It did not matter who led those other boys, or how many more there might be across the fields. God had set this all in motion, and the outcome was already determined.

He thought now of that awful day at Gettysburg. He could not escape that, knew God was there as well, and he would never understand why it had happened, had never believed it would end like that. It was still fresh in his mind, would come to him at times like this, when the new fight was coming fast, reminding him that on that one field, God had turned against them. He struggled to understand, could only guess: We were not on our own land. The invasion north had been a difficult decision, and always there was something uncomfortable, a small voice in his mind that he tried to avoid. When we fight in Virginia, we are defending our own land, and we are victorious. But we invade their land, and God takes that away. The verse came again: *Cast forth lightning and scatter them: shoot out thine arrows and destroy them . . . deliver me out of great waters, from the hand of strange children . . .*

He rode back down the Plank Road, toward his staff, could hear the motion of men in the woods around him. He stopped, listened hard, turned to the north, thought, Maybe . . . I should ride up there, see what Ewell is doing. But no, I must let them command. He knows my orders. He saw the face in the dark, the strange high-strung man, so excitable, quick to anger, and he thought, Something has been taken from him. It was something inside Ewell himself, some personal defeat that Lee did not understand. It could be the missing leg, of course, but around the camps the staff was making unkind comments about Ewell's wife, her domination of her new husband. Lee had met her briefly, and knew she was always close to Ewell now; the jokes rippled through the staff about the petticoat command. Lee tried not to judge, and his staff did not make their jokes in his presence. He did not spend much time in Ewell's camp, still preferred to be closer to Longstreet, as it had always been, even when Jackson was alive.

He knew there was another reason he stayed away from Ewell's camp. The staff consisted of many of the same people who had served with Jackson, and he knew the faces well, Sandie Pendleton, James Power Smith, the foul-mouthed quartermaster Harman. It was Pendleton in particular who affected Lee, something in the young man's face that was clear and unmistakable, the loss, the sadness that Lee had tried so hard to put aside. Pendleton had been Jackson's chief of staff, had been at the bedside when Jackson had breathed the last painful breath, and Lee knew he would carry that with him the rest of his life. Now Pendleton served Ewell, and Ewell had shown nothing of the influence of Jackson, of the fire, the instinct for moving *forward*. Pendleton knew it, they all knew it.

Lee still stared through the dark, past the small sounds close by, to the broad silence from the north. He did not like being that far away from Ewell's corps. The two parallel roads moved apart nearly three miles at this point, something he hadn't realized from the maps until this morning. Lee knew the turnpike was a good road and that Ewell was marching his men east. Lee had stayed close to Hill, down below on the Plank Road. The two roads eventually merged near Chancellorsville, then split again as they broke out of the Wilderness closer to Fredericksburg, but first they would pass right through the heart of Grant's army.

He did not know how Grant's lines were spread, only that the Federal Fifth Corps had come the closest, was somewhere near where Ewell was now marching. He did not want the fight yet, had hoped the

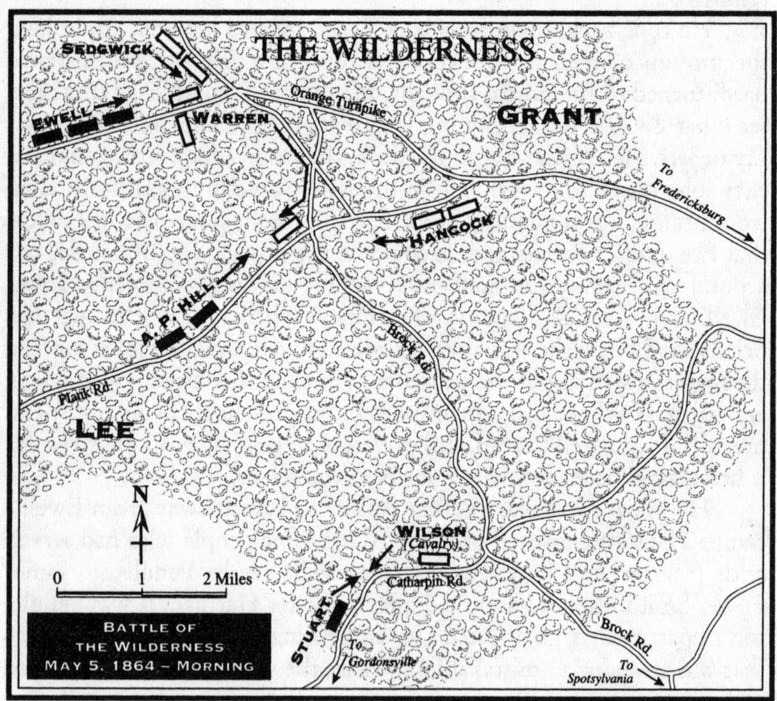

day would dawn without a major confrontation, because they were not yet strong. Longstreet was still well back, a good day's march from the place where Lee now sat, but he was coming. He'd been ordered to move out quickly, and Lee thought, This time he must not be slow.

It had been necessary to keep Longstreet farther west, since there had still been the chance that Grant might move out that way, try to cut Lee off from the valley. It would have been the wrong move, and though Lee did not believe Grant would make that kind of mistake, he could not take the risk and leave his own left flank unprotected. Once Grant had crossed the river and moved straight into the Wilderness, Lee immediately sent for Longstreet.

It was not by chance that Lee was close to Hill this morning. Hill was sick again, could barely ride a horse. The illness was more and more severe, and Lee had accepted that Hill might not be fit at all, might have to be relieved. But then Hill appeared, pained and weak, and declared himself ready for duty. Lee would not remove him if Hill said he could lead his men. And when Lee studied the lists of commanders, there was no name that rose above the rest, no one whom he felt comfortable with in that position. If Hill's corps needed a commander, Lee began to realize that he might move one step closer to the line, might have to take command himself.

The men were moving into the road now. The darkness was just beginning to break, and when they passed by him, there were small noises. Only a few men cheered or raised a hat. The woods around him were now strangely silent; there was no music, none of the jovial cursing of an army pulled out of slumber. He watched the faces, saw deadly calm, men who had done this before.

He saw Hill coming up the road, the horse brought him closer, and Hill looked very bad, the eyes deep and dark, the face drawn. Even Hill's uniform was bleak and plain, no insignia of rank, the black hat slumped down around Hill's ears. Hill said, "Good morning, sir. Fine day for a fight."

Lee nodded, said, "Good morning, General Hill. We should ride forward, if you please."

Lee nudged the horse gently and moved alongside the column of men. They rode for several minutes, the daylight growing stronger, but off the road, in the woods, the daylight did not matter, there was nothing to be seen. The road curved slightly, and suddenly there was a break off to the left, a wide field. Lee saw a small house on the far side, turned the horse. Hill followed, and the staff stayed behind, spread out in the field. They moved close to the house, and Lee reined the horse, listened hard. He stared up to the north, toward the turnpike, heard a roll of musket fire, a dull rattle muffled by the dense growth. Now there was more fire, to the west, in front of Hill's column.

Hill looked to his staff, said, "Send some people up there . . . I want to know who we are facing. Get me some idea of strength!" There were salutes, and men rode out toward the road, moving quickly away.

Lee said, "Your lead division . . . is General Heth, is it not?"

"Yes, sir. We should have heard something by now."

Hill was sweating, and Lee could hear the pain in his voice. Now Lee heard another sound, familiar, heavy hoofbeats, and a small group of horsemen came out of the trees in front. Lee saw it was Stuart.

Lee could not help a smile, saw the cape, the fresh uniform, his hat spouting a black peacock feather, one side of the brim pinned to the top, and he could not look at Hill now, would not subject himself to the amazing contrast between these two men.

"General Stuart, your appearance suggests something of a celebration."

Stuart was beaming at Lee's reception, swept the hat down in a low sweeping bow. "*Mon general,* I am at your service."

Lee dismounted, and the others followed, and Lee moved closer to the old house. Stuart bounded forward, and Lee knew the sign, knew there would be a burst of words.

"General Stuart, please report."

"Sir! You will find that the enemy has performed an admirable service. He is at this moment spread out all over the countryside. I have observed only a small force in front of this column, skirmishers mostly, but they are reinforcing. General Hill should expect to meet no more than a division at the crossroads to the east. Haste would be advisable, sir."

Lee looked at Hill, and Hill said, "We are moving to meet them. I am aware of the importance of the Brock Road intersection. I have instructed General Heth to advance as quickly as he can."

There was little enthusiasm in his voice. Hill did not have any of Stuart's energy, the tight bursts of emotion, the anger and the fire for what was coming toward them. Lee said, "General Stuart, there is musket fire in the north. Have you been in contact with General Ewell?"

Stuart turned that way, and they all listened. The firing had slowed to a small scattering of faint pops.

"No, sir. I have not been able to ride up that way. The ground between the roads is quite dense, sir. I believe the maps do not account . . ." Stuart reached into his coat, pulled out a small piece of paper, unrolled it, studied it a brief moment, then held it out to Lee. "Here, sir. The turnpike is well north of us at this position, sir. The maps show us closer together than we really are."

Lee listened for the guns again, but the sounds had faded into silence. He said, "Yes, I am aware that the maps are somewhat in error, and so we have a problem. There is a wide gap between us and General Ewell. He must not bring on an engagement before we have filled that gap. If General Grant discovers we are in two separate positions, he will cut us in two. General Hill, you must move a brigade off to the left, spread them into the woods to the north. We cannot allow any of Grant's people to cut between—" He stopped, frozen. The others were watching him, and now began to turn, following his gaze.

A hundred yards away, at the far edge of the woods, a single line of blue soldiers was moving slowly forward, had stepped clear of the thick brush. Lee felt a hard cold fist in his chest, and for a moment no one moved at all. Then, across the field, one hand went up, there was a small quick shout. The blue troops stopped, facing Lee, and there was complete silence. Lee could see their faces, saw them looking straight at him, at Stuart's striking uniform, in stunned amazement. He thought, Surely, they must know . . . they must know who we are . . . who *I* am. Lee turned his head slowly toward Traveller, thought about the saddlebag, the pistol he never wore, and he began to move slowly, heard his footsteps in the grass, looked again at the line of blue, the muskets slowly coming up, pointing toward them. He looked at the one man who had spoken, the man in charge, the hand still in the air, hanging there, could see the man's fingers balling slowly into a fist. Lee reached behind him, felt for the flap of the saddlebag, reached inside, felt the steel of the pistol, wrapped his fingers around the handle, began to pull it free of the bag, still watched the one man, the fist in the air. The hand began to move, came slowly down. The man said something, a quiet voice, and the line of men suddenly backed away, merged back into the thickness of the trees and were gone.

Now Stuart moved by him, was quickly up on his horse, and Taylor had climbed onto his horse too, moved forward, put the horse between Lee and the woods. Stuart said, "They're gone! We scared 'em away!" He began to spin the horse, yelling out, waving the hat, and now the others were all on their horses.

Lee said, "General Stuart, we should move out of this field. General Hill, I would suggest you bring your people out this way with some haste. Those men could be in advance of a much larger force. We cannot allow them to reach this place. . . ."

He saw a column of Hill's men coming forward, already moving into the field, officers shouting. One man rode up close to Hill, saluted, said something Lee could not hear. Hill pointed to the far trees, and the men began to run forward, streaming past Lee. He looked at Stuart again, and Stuart was smiling, red-faced. He said, "General Lee, the enemy has missed another opportunity! They had no idea . . . they were so close!"

Lee looked again to the trees, saw Hill's men forming a wide straight line, moving forward into the woods, and he began to let down, felt the cold shake in his hands, smiled, nodded at Stuart's excitement. Yes, they had been very close. It had been up to one man, perhaps a sergeant, one man who could have given the order to fire, but instead he'd seen the situation very differently. He may have thought his small command had made a dangerous mistake, lost in the brush perhaps, seeking out some landmark, some direction, and stumbled into the lines of the enemy. Instead of making an aggressive move, of capturing or assaulting this small group of men and horses, they had been wary, cautious. Lee glanced at the sky, said a small prayer. *You had a hand in this, it was not yet my time, thank You.*

Stuart was still watching the trees, his horse jerking about in small jumps, and Lee could feel Stuart's hot energy, the flare for the fight, the enemy so close to them, thought, No, General, we did not scare them away, it was this place . . . this infernal thicket that made them cautious. But they will go back and find their commander, and then they will return.

THEY WERE OUT IN FRONT OF HIM NOW, HAD FILED INTO THE woods, spreading into thick lines, pressing forward. There had been some musket fire, but it was not concentrated. Hill's men had not yet found the strong lines of the enemy. Lee stared to the north, to the wide gap that still yawned between Hill and Ewell, tried to hear the sounds of a fight above them, if Ewell had gone too far forward. It was still small and scattered, and Lee thought, Wait . . . not yet. He had sent word back to Longstreet again, move up *now*, and the reply had come that Longstreet was on the move, would be there by dawn the next day.

The staff was moving all around him, couriers bringing in pieces of information. Stuart was doing what he could to protect Hill's flanks, but the woods were no place for cavalry. There was nothing to be seen until you burst right into the faces of the enemy, then suddenly found yourself within a few yards of surprised infantry—men waiting for the sounds in front of them to become motion, something to shoot at.

He paced near the old house, knew what was happening, that both armies were groping blindly, thought, Grant is not moving away, or trying to get past us to the south, but is spread out in the tangle to our front. And that is where we need him to be.

There was a shout behind him, and Lee heard Taylor, turned, saw Pendleton coming out of the woods. Lee was suddenly anxious, the first word from Ewell since the distant sounds had reached them.

Pendleton saw him, drove the horse close, dismounted. "Sir . . . General Ewell sends his compliments. The general wishes to report that he has done as you instructed, sir. He has deployed across the turnpike and is now strengthening those lines, sir. The left flank is secure up toward the river, we are trying to extend the right flank in this direction. It is difficult ground, but General Early's division is in place." Pendleton was breathing heavily, and Lee waited, let him catch his breath.

"Thank you, Colonel. What can you tell me about the position of the enemy?"

Pendleton said, "Sir, the enemy is right in front of us. We have observed heavy columns moving from left to right. General Ewell . . . General Ewell will not advance unless you order him to, sir."

Lee saw the look in Pendleton's face, understood the young man would say no more than that, did not have to. Lee looked up toward the north, thought, I cannot make all your decisions, General.

He looked at Pendleton, said, "We must not bring on a general engagement until we are at full strength. But if General Ewell sees the opportunity, if the enemy is vulnerable, he must not allow those people to get past him."

Pendleton was watching him, and Lee saw something in his face: silent frustration.

"Colonel, I do not know what strength is in front of him. *He* must make that decision. Tell him he must do what the conditions suggest."

Pendleton stiffened, said, "Yes, sir, I understand."

Pendleton climbed the horse, and there was a new sound, and they all looked to the north, stared across the field past the house, felt the wave of sound roll across them, the steady high rattle of muskets, and this time it did not fade, but grew, deep and steady. Lee looked at Pendleton, said, "I believe General Ewell's decision has been made for him."

11. GRANT

Morning, May 5, 1864

THERE WAS NO CAVALRY BETWEEN THE GREAT MASSES OF INfantry. Wilson's division had moved too far south, well below Lee's position, had lost themselves in the vast tangles, and finally had run straight into a heavy fight with Stuart. The sounds were hidden by the dense mass of woods, and so no one at Grant's headquarters knew that they had no screen at all, that down both roads to the west there was nothing but Lee's army, moving toward them like two hard spikes, driving straight for the exposed flanks of blue.

Meade had moved away from Grant's headquarters, the camp wagons loaded early and rolled south near a place called the Lacy house. Grant waited up near the river for the approach of Burnside's corps, still had no reason to expect Lee to be so close.

THE COFFEE WAS GONE, THE TABLES BEING CLEARED, AND GRANT moved into the tent. He had heard nothing from Meade, could now hear the low rattle of distant muskets, the occasional sharp thunder of a single cannon. He picked up his coat, the plain dark jacket, did not look at the only bit of color, the shoulder straps that carried his three small gold stars. He reached down through his camp chest, felt for the wooden box, pulled it up, opened it, saw the mass of black cigars, more gifts from the people. He grabbed a handful, stuffed them into his coat, put the box down, then paused, reached down again, grabbed the rest, stuffed them into another pocket, thought, This could be a long day.

He moved back into the sharp daylight, pulled his coat around his shoulders, pulled on his dull cotton gloves, saw the headquarters wagons moving out into the road, waiting for his order to move. Around him staff officers moved in unhurried calm, no one concerned about the sounds of the guns. One man sat at a table, writing on a thick brown pad of paper, and Grant saw it was Horace Porter. He moved that way, and the young man stood, saluted, waited for Grant to speak.

Porter was a tall, thin man, handsome, with a small goatee. He had been with McClellan early in the war, was later sent at his own request to the West, where he served with Rosecrans. When Grant replaced Rosecrans at Chattanooga, Porter had built a reputation for organizing artillery, and was ordered to Washington to sit in an office close to Halleck. But Grant remembered the bright young man with affection. Porter had recognized something in Grant that was profoundly different from the sluggishness of his other commanders, and so when Grant was given command of the army, Porter requested to join Grant's staff. Now he was the most popular man in camp, a clear contrast to the annoying perfection of Rawlins, who pecked and hovered over the whole staff.

"Colonel, have we heard anything from General Burnside?"

Porter shook his head. "No, sir, not since early this morning. He should be at the river crossings by now."

Grant looked out toward the river. "Yes, he *should* be." Grant pulled out a cigar, lit it.

Porter said, "Sir, should we send someone . . . ?"

Grant stared again toward the river. "Yes, Colonel, send another message. Tell General Burnside we are *still* waiting for him to arrive." He turned, the low roar of guns still rolling out of the trees far below. "You hear that, Colonel? The party has begun. We are in the wrong place. I do not intend to spend my day sitting here waiting for General Burnside." He puffed several times on the cigar. Smoke rolled around him, drifting away in a gray cloud. He gripped the cigar hard in his mouth, said in a low voice to himself, "This is ridiculous."

Porter leaned forward, said, "Sir?"

Grant looked at him now, said, "I have discovered something, Mr. Porter. The general-in-chief apparently is supposed to sit back and wait for people to tell him what is going on. I don't know what is going on."

He looked around, saw his horse, held by a groom, began to move that way, stopped, said to Porter, "Colonel, send word to General Burnside that I expect him to join this army at his earliest opportunity. *We* . . . are going to see just what General Meade is up to."

The staff had moved closer, heard his words, and men began to climb horses. Grant took the leather straps from the groom, climbed up as well, moved the horse into the road. The flags appeared, moved into line behind him, and he turned, saw Rawlins now, scrambling to his horse, and Rawlins seemed annoyed, always seemed annoyed, pulled away from some important task.

Grant said, "Colonel Rawlins, give the order. Advance . . ."

There were hoofbeats, and down the road a man came up fast. Grant saw a courier, tried to recall the man's name, thought, Sedgwick's man . . . Hyde . . . Colonel Hyde.

Hyde saluted, pulled out a paper, said, "General Grant, General Meade wishes me to report, sir. . . ." Hyde paused, read from the paper, "The enemy is advancing on the turnpike, and I have ordered General Warren to advance the Fifth Corps and meet him. General Sedgwick has dispatched Getty's division down to the Plank Road to confront another column of the enemy's advance. General Hancock is expected to support General Getty." Hyde stopped, looked at Grant, said, "Sir, we have a fight. The enemy is not at Mine Run as we supposed."

Grant moved the cigar in his mouth, and there was a silent moment. The musket fire was flowing up toward them now in one steady mass. Grant said, "No, Colonel, it seems General Lee was not content to watch us parade by. But if he wants a fight, then we will give him one."

HE SAW MEADE, THE WIDE HAT FLOATING ABOVE THE HEADS OF the staff, men moving in all directions, Meade's sharp voice blowing across the open yard of the Lacy house.

Grant climbed down from the horse, and Meade saw him, moved quickly, said, "General Grant, it seems certain that despite anything we may have been told, the enemy wishes us to fight on this ground!"

Grant tossed the spent nub of a cigar aside, reached into his pocket, felt for another, thought, We have not been told much of anything. He moved past Meade, looked around the open field, looked to Rawlins, said, "Right here, Colonel. I will make headquarters close to General Meade."

The staff began to move, the wagons coming forward into the yard. Meade said nothing, stared grimly at Grant as Grant moved by him. Grant moved to a freshly cut tree stump, sat down, lit the cigar. Meade motioned to an aide, and a chair was brought forward. Now a man came forward with a map, and Meade opened it, spread it on the ground, sat heavily in the chair, said, "Sir, we are engaged on two fronts. Up here, the turnpike, Warren has been ordered to press the attack. He is pushing the enemy back to his entrenchments . . . as best as we can tell." Grant looked up at Meade, but Meade did not look at him, pointed again at the map. "Down below, the Plank Road, Hancock's corps is being brought back up to reinforce Getty. . . ."

Grant said, "Brought back up? From where?"

Meade looked at him now, took a deep breath. "We felt—General Hancock felt—we were led to believe there was a considerable force of the enemy south of our flank. There was some fighting below the Plank Road. It seems . . . it was only the cavalry. General Hancock has been ordered back up to the Brock Road intersection. We did not believe the enemy was advancing there in force . . . until Getty was attacked."

Grant said nothing, thought, *The cavalry.* That's what the cavalry is for, to find the enemy, to tell us where he is moving. He felt his hands clench, was beginning to see it now. Lee had waited for him to extend on the roads in the Wilderness, had never intended to wait behind cover. Now they were spread out in a long line, fighting on two fronts. He looked again at the map, at the wide space between the two roads, said in a quiet hiss, "General Meade, how many men do we suppose Lee is sending at us?"

Meade blinked. "I don't know . . . we have heard . . . best guess is about sixty thousand. We have met Ewell's corps on the turnpike, Hill's corps on the Plank Road. We had thought Longstreet was further south, down the Brock Road . . . but he's not shown himself. Wilson's cavalry didn't find anyone but Stuart. It seems . . . our information may have been wrong about Stuart being at Fredericksburg."

Grant leaned back, looked across the open ground toward the sound of the fighting, felt the anger growing, thought, Is all our information wrong? Grant looked down to the map, said, "You haven't found all of Lee's army, General. Where's Longstreet?"

Meade looked down at the map, said quietly, "We . . . actually don't know, sir."

"Then you have not accounted for sixty thousand men. We are not facing an enemy that strong. He has to be spread out pretty thin."

"There's no one, as far as we can tell, here." Meade pointed to the space between the two roads. "We've sent some people in there, but the ground is awful. Swamps, gullies, visibility less than fifty yards."

Grant clamped the cigar tightly in his teeth, said, "If we can't see through that ground, neither can Lee. We need to punch through there. If he's on the two roads in strength, we can split his army in two."

Meade nodded, said, "Well, yes, but I thought . . . Burnside could move into that gap, protect our flanks. We're spread pretty thin too."

Grant stared at Meade, felt the man's hesitation, the caution flowing across him like a disease. "General, I would suggest you press the enemy's position. Advance your men on both roads. Order Warren to extend southward, Hancock to extend northward, until they link up in the center. Even without Burnside, we have twice the enemy's strength. If that means we are spread thin, then he is in much more serious trouble than we are. Is that not plain to you, sir?"

Meade looked at the map, stood suddenly, moved away quickly. Grant watched him, heard the sharp bite in Meade's voice, orders going out, aides writing furiously, horses beginning to move.

Grant looked down at the map again, pushed it aside with his foot, saw a fat chunk of wood, picked it up, rolled it over in his hand. He reached into his pocket, pulled out a pocketknife, began to slice slowly at the wood, small shavings curling away, floating to the ground around his feet. He stared hard at the wood, felt his anger flowing out through his hands, thought, Why can they not understand? Is it that we are too big, there is too much of this army? Are we so cumbersome that it is not possible to move effectively? He was beginning to see the flaw in the army's organization, that Meade was hesitant to act with his commander so close, and the hesitation was magnified when the enemy was watching you, waiting for it. He thought of chess, a game he had played a few times. But he was impatient, did not enjoy the game, waiting for an opponent to make a move. It was a game he could not control, could not use enough energy, could not press an attack to any advantage. He had thought, Maybe I just don't understand it. He had a mind for mathematics, but there was more to chess than simply solving a problem, and the frustration of that was too much. Now he had the feeling of being back at the board, facing an opponent who understood the game better than he did, and if the opponent did not have as many pieces, if he was missing, say, his knights, or his queen, then this should be easy. We *have* the pieces, he thought, with more in reserve. All we have to do is press him, confront him. Is this not, after all, a question of power? His hands worked the knife, the block of wood slowly getting smaller, and he thought of playing that game, of how the game *should* be played, the extra pieces you could add. . . .

Porter stood to one side, watched him quietly, saw Grant working the pocketknife furiously, saw the knife now shredding the fingers of Grant's glove, the dull yellow thread falling around Grant's feet, his eyes focused far away, staring at an imaginary chessboard.

ACROSS THE THICK MASS OF GREEN AND BROWN, OVER THE DEEP ravines and sloping hillsides, through the dense mass of trees and brush and muddy swamps, the sounds of the growing battle swelled and poured up toward the Lacy house. Along the roads that led west, the commanders sent their men into a fight against an enemy they could not see, the troops feeling their way along the rugged ground, the big guns behind them silent and useless. If the flanks were unprotected, if no coordination could be possible in the thick wood, it did not seem to give either side an advantage.

Throughout the afternoon both sides clawed carefully at each other, blasts of musket fire ripping through small trees. The men who stood and peered out, frustrated by blindness, aiming for some glimpse, for anything that moved, were the first ones cut down, never seeing their enemy. As the lines of battle fell into confusion, the men who survived the deadly whisper of the musket ball were the ones who lay flat, patient and still while leaves and small limbs rained down on their heads, clipped and sliced from the growth above them. If their officers tried to move them, prod them forward, screaming and cursing through the horrible din of the firing, it was the officers who became the best targets, their shiny gold buttons the only part of a man the enemy might see.

All day the two sides had pressed forward and pulled away, men scampering across small rises and down through sharp gullies, only to race back to where they had begun. By late in the afternoon even the officers understood that no one would win this day, that no lines would be carried, no enemy overrun. When the darkness spread over the field, both sides still lay flat, sometimes only yards apart, still firing at small sounds, at the flashes from the men firing back.

Now, between the lines, the wounded began to call out, the screams and the praying echoed through the darkness. The horror of the sounds grew in each man because there could be no help, no one could move forward. Those who could not accept that, who tried to crawl, to reach the voices, if only to take a canteen or pull a man back to the safety of a rock, found a deadly response, that someone was watching, waiting. There would come the brief terrible flash of the musket, the sharp whine of the ball, the smack of lead against tree, against rock, against bone. In the growing darkness each man began to feel that the enemy was all around him, not just the man waiting with the musket, as blind as you, but this horrible ground, the small black spaces around each man, and each man wondered why those men *back there*—with the fine horses and the hot food, polished brass and white tents—why they would send their soldiers into this terrible place.

12. LEE

Late Evening, May 5, 1864

It had been two great fights, the momentum shifting back and forth between the turnpike and the Plank Road. Ewell's men had absorbed the first major push, but held their ground, the men digging in quickly in the thick woods, a crude line of cut trees, mounds of dirt piled as fast as bayonets or tin cups could dig. The Federals had hit them hard, but could not move Ewell away. Soon the Federal forces on the turnpike were scattered and groping with the confusion of men who have lost their officers, all sense of direction swallowed by the woods around them.

Then the great roar of the fight had shifted down to the Plank Road, where Hill's advance eastward toward the intersection of the Brock Road suddenly and completely reversed, a hard thrust by the Federal Second Corps. Hancock's troops had reached the key point first, with far greater strength, and pushed out hard against the only enemy that came close to him, Harry Heth's division. With Hancock's forces outnumbering Heth by nearly five-to-one, it did not take long for Heth to find himself in serious trouble, his men clinging to whatever cover they could find. By late in the day Heth had been reinforced by Hill's other division, under Cadmus Wilcox, and Hancock's great strength had been neutralized by the ground, as all of Grant's numbers had been. The assault, which had outflanked Heth on both sides, now ground down, and as to the north, Hancock's men found themselves in utter confusion, the momentum of their attack blunted and turned away by the thickets and the steady response of Heth's muskets.

Late in the afternoon, Ewell had pushed out again, striking at the jumbled mass of blue troops in front of him, but the order had to come from Lee. Ewell was still tightly behind his makeshift wall, but Lee could not allow the fight to swing southward with all the power Grant could bring, and so he prodded Ewell to do . . . *something*, create some opportunity. Grant had shown no willingness to move away, to leave the Wilderness, and the long lines of march were now tightened into thick lines of battle. The dangerous gap between Lee's two corps had already invited Grant to push through, and it was only the ground itself that kept the blue troops from splitting Lee's forces in half.

If Lee were to turn the tide in his favor, he would have to take every chance to strike at confusion, at disorganized regiments, at the chaos that the attacking troops had stumbled into. But Ewell had hesitated, and asked for clarification, the couriers moving back and forth between the two parts of the army in a mad rush, often passing each other on the rugged trails. Lee was seeing it more clearly than ever, that if Ewell were to do anything at all, make any decision that would show the old spirit, the orders would have to come from him. But even then Ewell pressed forward only as far as his own men could make a coordinated attack, and soon the coordination collapsed in the dense woods. Finally Ewell pulled his men back to their entrenchments, content to let the night darken the bloody ground where so many had fallen.

THERE HAD BEEN NO PAUSE, NO BREAK FOR FOOD OR REST. LEE had been on Traveller for most of the day, and he could feel the wet hide of the tired animal, his pants soaked by thick foam. He had kept close to the steady fight in front of Hill's men, but there would be nothing to see, no sign of the enemy's strength except for the sounds of their muskets, and there had been many muskets. Lee counted seven separate assaults, each one a vast wave rolling toward them from the east, and each time there were more blue troops, new units, the prisoners coming now from every division, every brigade of Hancock's enormous corps. Lee had watched Hill carefully, saw clearly that if Hill had never shown the talent for commanding an entire corps, he was still the best man the army had at leading a division. In this place, where there was no coordination and no way to even know where a corps would begin and end, where the placement of a single regiment could turn the tide of the attack, Hill had been brilliant. Lee tried to stay with him, but in the chaos, Hill had never stopped moving, guiding the smaller units back and forth through the brush, down the small trails, shifting the troops into place against the blind heavy punches of Hancock's great numbers. With Wilcox's help, Heth had held his ground, and as the light began to fade, the darkness filling the small spaces in the gloomy woods, Hancock finally pulled away, his men now flowing back behind his own fortifications, thrown up quickly along the Brock Road.

Lee was still focused toward the front, could hear the shouts of men, the sounds echoing on all sides, the same sounds that had filled these woods all day. There was a rhythm to it, the voices rolling into one long sound just before each new assault, another wave of Hancock's men striking hard at Hill's weakening lines. Only then would the voices be pushed away, drowned out by the roar of the guns, the steady chatter of musket fire. Lee expected it again, waited for it, moved the horse onto the road itself, a dangerous place, listened hard, thought, Hancock will come again, he will not stop. He's the best they have.

He felt himself shaking, gripping the leather straps hard, his chest pounding. There were scattered sharp cracks, single shots, and he strained to see, stared out toward the wide path through the trees. The smoke was clearing away, and the road was filling with blessed darkness. Now the sound of the muskets was gone, and he heard cheering, faint and hollow, but it was not a celebration of victory, but of relief, and there was no strength behind the voices, no energy, and now they began to fade away as well.

Men were moving down the road toward him, slowly, many wounded, and he saw the stretcher bearers now, and slowly the road began to fill with new sounds, faint cries, the rattle of ambulance wagons. A wagon rolled by him, moving forward, and he stared at it, breathing heavily. Looking behind him, he saw more wagons, more wounded. He tried to focus, took one long breath, let it out slowly, tried to calm the hard thumps in his chest, thought, It's . . . *over.*

There were more horses now, and he heard a voice, turned, saw Taylor, covered with dirt, his horse soaked with muddy sweat. Taylor said, "General Hill is over this way, sir. He is ill. He asked me to . . . inform you, sir."

Lee said nothing, pulled at the horse, moved slowly into the field, looked across through the last faint daylight, glanced at the far edge of the woods, where the blue soldiers had appeared that morning. Now he saw Hill's staff gathering, saw the headquarters flag. There was a tent, the dirty white canvas straightening as the tent poles were pulled tight. Hill was sitting on the ground, leaning back against a log. He was bareheaded, his dark red hair matted flat, his face black with dirt. Lee dismounted, touched the ground with stiff legs and was suddenly light-headed, unbalanced. He held the saddle for a moment, steadied himself. He felt a hand under his arm, was startled at the touch, saw it was Taylor.

"You . . . all right, sir?"

There was something tender in Taylor's voice, and Lee felt himself suddenly giving way, touched by the young man's care. He wanted to say something, to thank him. He felt his legs now, pulled himself up straight, and Taylor backed away, and Lee saw embarrassment.

Taylor said, under his breath, "I'm sorry, sir. Please excuse me."

Lee tried to smile, made a small nod. Taylor had responded with instinct, a helpful hand, and it was an awkward moment. There was no one in the army closer to Lee, and still there was a distance, a boundary clearly understood by both of them. Of course, he thought, we must not show weakness, not in front of the men. Lee turned slightly, away from Hill and the staffs, said quietly, "It's all right, Colonel. I have been in the saddle . . . my legs were a bit stiff. Do not be troubled by it. This has been a long day for all of us."

He looked at Hill now, who did not try to stand, but looked up at him with black eyes, the thin face drawn and hollow.

"General Hill, are you well enough to speak with me?" Lee moved close, leaned over. Behind him, Taylor motioned to the others, and the staffs backed away.

Hill looked at Lee, said, "General Lee, my men . . . have honored themselves. This was a day for all of them to remember."

Lee looked at the pale sickness in the man's face, thought, It has been a long time . . . there has not been much to be proud of in this command. He said, "General Hill, *you* have honored your men."

Hill sat up straight, shifted his legs, his face showing a sharp twist of pain. "Sir, I regret I am not well tonight. I am surprised . . . all day there was no problem, nothing kept me from my men. But when the fighting began to slow, it came all at once . . . like . . . a wave."

Lee straightened, said, "General Hill, you will again be of good service to this army. Rest now." He turned, said aloud, "We should all rest now. Those people will be back tomorrow, I am certain of it. We must make preparations."

He looked down at Hill again, and Hill said, "Sir, my men . . . they must be relieved. I do not see how they can hold out for another day like today."

Lee lowered his voice. "Don't worry, General. They *will* be relieved. General Longstreet will be here by morning. We will face General Grant with a fresh corps, fresh guns." He looked around, motioned to Taylor, and Traveller was led forward. Lee moved to the big horse, climbed up slowly, made a small groan as he sat, shifted his weight.

He turned the horse, his staff gathered behind, and he looked at Hill again, said, "General Hill, this army has many things to be thankful for. But we must make preparations. When General Longstreet arrives, your men will shift to the north, locate and anchor against General Ewell's flank. I will prepare the orders. We will close that open space, and we will meet those people as one solid line. Rest now, General. The Almighty has shown us we are not to be beaten, not here, not on our own ground."

Hill saluted weakly, and Lee spurred the horse, moved back to the road, past the wagons, the sounds of the wounded, past rows of big guns, crews watching him move by, hats in the air. He stared out down the road, away to the west, thought, Godspeed, General Longstreet.

THEY SLEPT WHERE THEY HAD FOUGHT, LYING FLAT ON WET leaves, on soft mud, behind a cover of old logs or the bodies of the dead. There were few shots now, most of the Yankees were gone, back to their camps, their fires, their food. But there were still skirmishers, stragglers, men who had not yet found their units, had not heard the orders to pull back. They held their muskets at the ready, would shoot at anything that moved, any sign of the enemy, and so you did not raise your head, you did not make a sound. Now, all along the lines, or what was left of lines, the blanket of darkness brought safety, and the men began to sleep, most still gripping their muskets, some holding to a new musket, taken from the man beside him who would not need it in the morning. Some crawled slowly, moving from body to body, searching for unused cartridges, maybe a piece of hardtack, a full canteen.

There were no orders. Many of the men had already found the bodies of the officers who led them, and many other officers crouched low beside these men who had done the fighting. Word had come when the shooting had stopped, passed slowly to the men who could be found: "We held the ground, we are *done*, and in the morning, they will pull us out." For now they were to stay put, stay in place, and if there was no order to dig in, to throw up a heavy defense, it would not matter because they would be replaced.

The commanders did not share the tired confidence of the men. Heth had gone to Hill, had told him the lines were in no shape for a new fight, there was no organization, but Hill was deep into the illness, sent Heth back to his camp with a sharp reminder that it was Lee himself who had told them that by dawn Longstreet would be there, and Heth's men would not have to fight. As much as Heth worried about his defenses, he understood what kind of fight his men had given this day, and so, if his commanders were confident, he would let his men rest where they were.

In front of the scattered groups of men, brushfires had begun to spread, small flickers set off by the flashes of so many muskets, and then, pushed by a small breeze, the rising crackle of the flames. Some men called it the Devil's laughter, but worse than the sounds came the thick black smoke, carrying the smells, wet cloth and burning bodies.

It had been like this before, a year ago, almost to the day, that horrible day Jackson went down. The brush and leaves had caught fire then too, and many of these men could still hear the terrible cries of the wounded, the men trapped out front, where there could be no help.

The darkness was lit now by the fires rolling through the brush in front of them, and many did not sleep, had seen this before and so could not keep their eyes away. The veterans did not fear death from the quick deadly stab of the lead ball as much as what they now saw. They prayed they would not be caught watching the slow hand, the fiery beast moving toward them, clawing along the floor of this awful ground until it swept past, burning the breath out of the men whose wounds would not let them escape.

Down the lines, one man saw motion, the shape of a head, heard the cry, crept out behind his small piece of cover, crawled slowly down a low rise, could see the boy clearly now, the face familiar, maybe a friend. Beyond the low wall of flame there was a sharp crack, but the enemy's aim was poor, the man heard the ball strike beside him, a dull punch in the soft dirt. He pulled himself around quickly, slid back to his shelter. He peeked over the rise, cursed the enemy he could not see, but the boy's face was looking back at him, and the face was reflecting the hard light of the fire, the eyes staring wildly at him, filled with the terror. The man tried not to see, lowered his head, knew it would not take long, soon would come the last sound, the boy's scream. He tried to put himself far away, think of other days, then the boy's name came to him, a sudden nightmare of memories, of marching and fighting, sharing the bad food, and now he could not look away. He eased his head up over the cover, and the boy was still looking at him, the eyes saying all he could say. There were more shots, thudding against the small mound in front of him, one ball whizzing close to his ear. He dropped down, his face in the dirt, then slowly eased his head up again, saw now the flames were jumping ahead, began to reach the boy's clothes, and the man stared with horror, could see the wounds now, the blood on the boy's pant leg. Suddenly the boy waved, yelled something. His eyes were darting around, a madness lit by the flames now beginning to swallow him, and once more he looked back at the man, begged him one last time. The man slowly slid his musket forward, lowered the barrel, sighted the small metal bead to the eyes of the boy. The boy closed his eyes, waited, and the man steadied a shaking hand, blinked away a hard tear, and pulled the trigger.

EARLY MORNING, MAY 6, 1864

LEE HAD NOT BEEN TOLD ABOUT THE CONDITION OF HILL'S DEFENSES. Heth and Wilcox both knew that if Longstreet did not come, that if the morning broke over these woods, Hancock was stronger yet, and there would be no way to hold back another strong assault. But Hill would not allow them to adjust the lines, sort through the tangle of units, the confusion of command. He was insistent that these men not be disturbed, that there would be no fight for them in the morning. Frustrated, Wilcox had even gone to Lee directly, but Lee had put him at ease, shown him the latest message from Anderson, Longstreet's first division already very close now, and the rest of the corps was not far behind. Lee's confidence was contagious, and Wilcox had not pressed the point of the sad condition of their defenses, had gone back to his camp to finally get some sleep of his own.

LEE WAS AWAKE EARLY, LAY ON THE SMALL COT AND TRIED TO hear the sounds, and there was only the quiet. He sat up, put his feet out on the floor of the tent, felt the sharp jab in his knee, the stiffness of the day before. He stood, pushed his shoulders back, took a deep breath, felt his chest, put his hand on the slow rhythmic thump. The pains had not come back, not since the weather had warmed, and he was grateful for that, said a short prayer, *One more day . . . Thank You . . .*

He buttoned his coat, moved out into soft mist. There was a small fire, a coffeepot, and he was surprised to see Stuart, standing alone, staring down into the fire. Lee smiled, moved closer to the fire, and Stuart did not see him, still stared into the flames. Lee glanced around, saw no one moving, looked toward the staff tents, knew Taylor would be up soon, was always up early. Lee said quietly, "Good morning, General."

Stuart turned his head, nodded, said nothing. Lee waited, expected something more, the enthusiasm, the bright greeting. Lee was suddenly concerned, said, "General Stuart, are you well?"

Stuart seemed to focus, suddenly came alive, abruptly saluted, said, "Oh, General Lee, yes, quite well, sir. Forgive me . . . I was . . . sleeping. The fire . . . there is something in the fire. . . ." He paused, looking back down into the low flames. "Something peaceful, as though God is holding something open to you, some small bit of Himself. It is comforting."

Lee nodded, did not know what to say. He had heard that Stuart could sleep anywhere, anyplace at all, but had not thought it possible to sleep standing up.

"Yes, General, the Almighty is all around us. In everything that touches us . . ."

Stuart shook his head. "No . . . well, yes, of course, sir. But lately I have had the feeling that something has changed. It is difficult to explain."

Lee nodded, said, "Perhaps, General, since Gettysburg . . . I have seen it in some of the men, I have seen it in myself. We must not expect God to win our fight for us. This is not His struggle. He will comfort us as long as we do what is right. And everything we do cannot be right. We must remember that."

Stuart looked at him, and Lee saw something in the eyes he had never seen, a dark concern. Stuart nodded, did not seem to hear what he'd said. Stuart looked out into the deep darkness, then up at the clear sky, flecked with stars.

"They have gotten better." He looked at Lee again. "The horsemen, the enemy is getting better. There was never any doubt. We were superior, we had better riders, better commanders. If we met them head on, there was no doubt we would take the field. Something has changed."

Lee saw motion from the staff tents, the aides beginning to emerge. He leaned closer to Stuart, said, "General, you are still the finest . . ." He paused, was beginning to feel embarrassed. "You have grown better as well. You are of great service to this army, and will continue to be. Did you not confront those people yesterday, and did they not leave you the ground?"

Stuart nodded, a small smile, said, "Yes, it was tough for a while.

Wilson's division. I heard Sheridan himself was there for a while. I hear he's quite a horseman."

Taylor moved up behind Lee, and Lee turned, saw coffee cups, and Taylor hesitated, would not interrupt. Lee waved him forward, was feeling awake now, cheerful, said, "Good morning, Colonel. We're all up a little early this morning."

Taylor saluted Lee, then Stuart, and said, "Yes, good morning, sir. Allow me to pour some coffee, sir."

Lee moved aside and Taylor leaned toward the coffeepot. Stuart moved away from the fire, stared out into the dark again, said, "General Lee, if you will excuse me, I should get my men into the saddle. They may try our flank again."

Taylor held a cup of coffee out to Lee, and Lee said, "General Stuart, some coffee before you go?"

Stuart moved to his horse, climbed up, said, "Thank you, but no, sir. I suspect General Sheridan is waiting for us somewhere out there." He grinned now, suddenly reached for the gray hat, swept it down in a low bow.

"Mon general," and he spurred the horse, made a quick yelp, and moved away toward the road. Lee watched him until he disappeared in the dark, could still hear the hoofbeats on the hard road, fading away.

Taylor still held the cup, and Lee took it, held the steam up to his face, breathed it in.

"Colonel Taylor, we should be hearing from General Longstreet soon. Send someone out on the road, to guide him into position. I wish us to be ready when those people make their move."

Taylor moved away, and Lee walked out into the tall grass, stared out over the open field, looked up at the great mass of stars, the small blinking eyes of God. It will be a good day, he thought. He turned, could see the dark shapes of the row of big guns, Poague's batteries, their crews beginning to gather, one man wiping at a brass barrel with a rag, sweeping away the wet mist. Lee walked toward the road, could hear more sounds, the army stirring in the woods around him. Riders were beginning to move quickly now, the first dispatches of the day.

He reached the road, looked off to the west, the black space in the woods, pictured it, the sounds, the beat of the horses, the sharp flutter of the flags, maybe a band, drums, the cheerful sound of the great advance of his strong army, and in front, the big man, the wide shoulders, and the grim expression that said only, "We are here for a fight." Lee stepped into the road, the first glow of the dawn behind him, and he could see a bit farther down the road, expected to see it even now, the great scene as he pictured it in his mind. But there was nothing there, the road still yawned wide and empty through the trees. Behind him, far into the dense woods, Hill's men lay quietly, still filled with the sleepy exhaustion of their good fight. The stars were beginning to fade away, the first glow of daylight spread out above the trees, and now there was a sound. Lee turned, felt a cold thump in his chest, and the sound grew, a great wave of shouts and cheers. It was not the sound he was used to hearing, the high scream of the rebel yell. He stared at the gray light, thought, No, they cannot come . . . not yet.

Around him men began to shout. The rest of the gun crews ran up, moving around the cannon with quick motion. He stared at the sounds, heard someone calling to him, saw Taylor, the staff, Traveller. He climbed the horse, pushed forward, moved down the road toward the sound. Now the sounds changed, a rising wave of muskets, and the hail of lead began to fly around him. He felt the horse move, pulled off the road, saw Taylor, Marshall, their faces watching him. He stood now, looked for Hill, for the commanders, and the wave of musket fire grew, volleys blending together. There were new shouts, the voices of

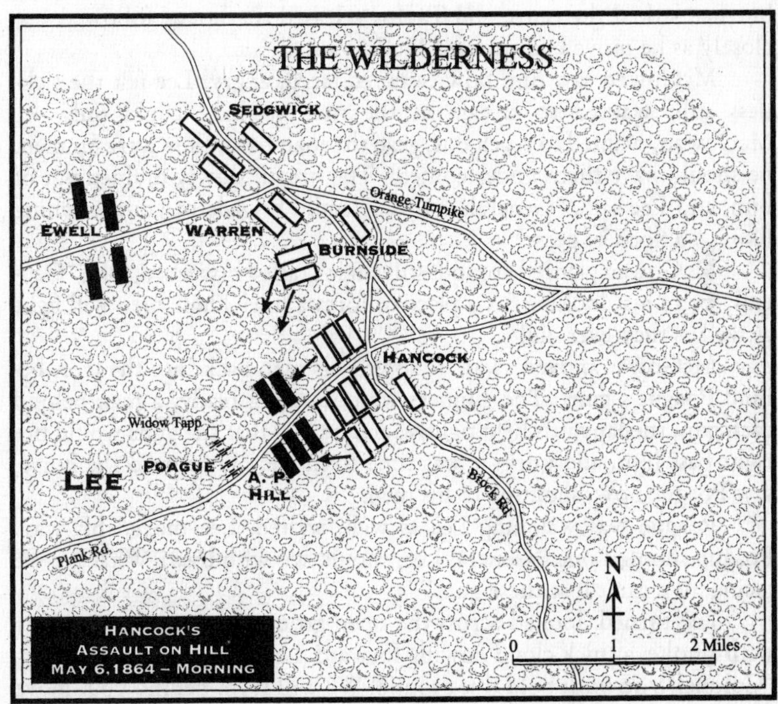

his own men, and they were coming out of the woods, moving back, away from the great blue wave that was flowing through the thick woods. He could see more troops now, on both sides of the road, no order, no lines, men running back toward him, pouring into the open field. They began to run past him, and he saw the faces, the animal fear, the unstoppable panic.

He began to shout, yelling at them to stop, saw an officer, a man on a horse, and the man looked at him, stunned. Lee yelled out, "Halt these men! Turn them around! What unit is this?"

The man hesitated, then was suddenly gone, carried in the wave of panic. There were more men on horses, more officers, and Lee saw them waving swords, some striking hard on the men who ran by them, yelling at them to stop, to fight. Lee saw a familiar face, rode forward onto the road, saw Sam McGowan, from South Carolina, older, a man Lee had always liked. McGowan was waving to the side of the road, yelling something Lee could not hear. But the men were not slowing, there was no fight in them. Lee began to feel sick, his stomach twisting.

Taylor still held the bridle, was pulling Lee off the road again, but Lee jerked the reins, and Taylor released the horse, followed Lee closely as he moved out toward McGowan.

McGowan saw him now, was red-faced, angry. Lee felt the sickness still, wanted to scream at the men to halt, could only see McGowan, wanted to reach out, grab the man hard, they were *his* men, he should have them under control. The breath slowly drained out of him, and Lee said, "General, is this splendid brigade of yours running like . . . a flock of geese?"

McGowan glanced around, still angry, raised his sword, said, "General, we're just looking for a place to form a line! These men will fight as well as they ever did!"

McGowan moved away, followed his men back into the trees behind Poague's guns. The gunners were standing ready, a man behind each gun, the lanyards held tightly, and he saw that the guns would fire right past him, and knew it was time to move. He spurred the horse, saw Poague now, shouting to his men.

Poague was watching Lee as well, waited. Lee moved his way. Poague shouted out, "General Lee, should we withdraw? What are we facing? We can't lose these guns!"

Lee turned, looked across the open ground, the trees now heavy with smoke, a thick cloud flowing forward. Lee turned to Poague, said, "Colonel, you *must* hold this ground! We will form behind you, move the men back up in support. You must not let those people come across that field!"

Poague looked out at the open ground, said, "We're ready for 'em sir. Sixteen guns. Double canister. We'll be here when the sun goes down, sir!"

Lee watched the far trees, and more volleys ripped through the air, the deadly sounds flying close to him. He heard the sharp crack of lead hitting a brass cannon, saw men beginning to fall along the guns, and then he heard shouting down the line, saw Poague pointing, could see down the road now, a thick mass of blue crowding out of the woods.

Suddenly, the guns opened up, one massive line of fire. The horse jumped, and Lee felt his heart leap in his chest. The smoke washed over him, and Taylor had the bridle again, steadied the big horse, pulled him back. Now Lee was out of the smoke, behind the guns. Across the field, all across the road, the woods came alive with the shattering impact of the hot metal. Trees flew into pieces, and now he could see the men on the road, and the great blue wave was a mass of twisted men, the wave halted, but now there were new sounds in the woods, more men coming forward, and Lee could see them on the road as well, pushing forward, over their own dead, another solid line. The guns exploded again, and again the smoke covered the field. He spurred the horse, moved farther back, saw his men gathering, a weary, ragged army, some attempt at a line, men picking up muskets dropped by the men who were far to the rear now.

Lee rode along the thin line, called out, "Form here, move up to the guns! Form here!"

The officers were gathering as well, and Lee heard the orders coming fast and clear, the orders he would have given, and now the voices were strong, the men were beginning to listen. He rode farther back, past small groups, men still dazed, breathless, men trying to find the soldier inside themselves, recovering from the shock of the massive blue wave. He saw the numbers, thought, We do not have the strength. If Hancock has sent in his entire corps . . . Poague cannot hold them back . . . we will lose the guns.

The men around him began to move back toward the fight, but the crushing wave of blue troops was closer still, the sharp sounds of lead still flew past him, men were falling all around.

Taylor yelled out, "General, please! This is not the place for you!"

Lee raised his hand toward Taylor, said nothing, was watching the guns again, the crews working with efficient speed, firing steadily,

Poague moving in and out of the smoke, directing the fire. More soldiers were coming up from the rear. Another thin line formed behind him, began to move forward, but Lee saw the first line coming back again, men still going down, and he wanted to yell again, no, do not run, but they could not stand up before the tide rolling toward them.

He saw an officer, riding hard from below the road, and the man saw him, moved quickly up, said, "General, we are being flanked . . . below the road! The enemy is extending below our right. General Wilcox is ordering the men to withdraw, but there is no order, sir. I cannot find General Heth. We don't know where his flanks are!" The man was out of breath, lowered his head, and Lee heard a slap, a dull crack of bone, and the man slumped, slid slowly off the horse. There was blood on the man's shirt, and Lee looked at it, saw the red stain spreading, the man's face looking at him, past him, the eyes not seeing.

Lee looked out past the guns again, closed his eyes, a short prayer, *Bless this man,* thought, I do not know his name. He heard Taylor again, calling to him, but thought, No, I will not move, we will fight it out right here, we have chosen the ground, God has given us this ground . . . if it must end, it will end on this ground.

The gun crews were dropping quickly now, the officers manning the pieces, the firing beginning to slow, the efficiency dropping with the loss of the men. He saw a break in the smoke, saw across the field, the road still swarming with the blue mass. He closed his eyes, said quietly, *"Thy will be done . . ."*

Behind him there were new shouts, and Taylor was yelling, manic, waving his hat. Lee turned, looked back along the road, saw the battered and beaten soldiers moving aside, lining the edge of the woods, and beyond he could see the flags, horses, a heavy column of soldiers, moving forward at a trot, the double quick. Now the men were beside him, moving past, a steady rush toward the thick smoke. He tried to see them, an officer, see who they were, what unit, and suddenly he felt Traveller jerk to the side. He looked down, saw an older man, a sergeant, and the man was pulling Traveller to the side. Lee felt an explosion of anger, yelled at the man, "Stop! What are you doing?"

Now there were more men around him, and the old sergeant looked at him, a hard grim face, said, "General Lee to the rear!"

He was still angry, thought, Who are you to suggest . . . and now all around him the men began to shout, *"Lee to the rear! Lee to the rear!"*

He glanced around, and the men had formed a tight arc around the horse, were moving him back, away from the road, from the big guns. The anger began to slip away, and he could see there was no use, no order would sway these men. He raised his hand, waved them away, saw now these were not Hill's men, did not carry the black grime of the fight. He yelled to the sergeant, "What is your unit?"

The man still pulled the horse, moved to the side of the road, said, "We're from Texas, sir. General Hood's division. Now, you just make yourself at home right here, and let us do the work. And I don't want to see you out that-aways again, you understand? I'll be back, and I expect you to be a-settin' right here."

Lee felt a sudden jolt, turned, looked away, down the road, thought, Texans . . . No, these are not Hill's men.

There were flags now, moving with the fast rush of more troops, fresh troops, and one man rode tall alongside the advance, the wide shoulders, the brim of the hat low across his face. Longstreet had arrived.

13. LONGSTREET

MID-MORNING, MAY 6, 1864

THEY HAD MARCHED THIRTY MILES IN LESS THAN TWO DAYS, and when Lee's final order came, they began the last leg at one o'clock that morning. The plan had been for them to come up from the southwest, reaching the Brock Road below Hancock's defenses, pushing northward to contain Grant in the Wilderness. But Grant had chosen the fight, had contained himself, and with Hill's corps badly outnumbered, Lee had changed Longstreet's advance, moved him up through the woods, to come in behind Hill on the Plank Road.

The men did not need to be told what lay in front of them. From first light they had heard the assault as Lee had heard it, a rolling tide of musket fire, and so their step had quickened. Now, with the smoke hanging low over the road in front of them, they began to move faster yet, the officers keeping them together. Hill's men were moving back still, and the heavy columns let the worn and beaten soldiers pass through, and there were jeers and insults, but no one believed that Hill's men were not good soldiers. If Hill was badly beaten, it meant the fight in front of them would be a test many of them had never experienced.

Longstreet reached the clearing, could see Lee now, close behind Poague's guns. The guns were still firing, the heavy thunder shaking the ground. Through brief clearings in the smoke Longstreet could see the flashes of musket fire across the field, the strong lines of the enemy, partially hidden, firing from behind the cover of the brush. Down below the road, deep into the woods, he could hear more firing, the enemy pushing forward on the flank.

He had not fought on this ground before, was staring out into the horror of the thick brush for the first time. He had not been here when they fought around the small intersection to the east, the crossroads at the Chancellor mansion, had not been here when Jackson had gone down. Lee had sent him south, to southern Virginia, a mission to send much needed supplies to the army, and at the same time Longstreet had hoped to rid the coast there of Federal troops. All that spring he had punched and struck in futile assaults on the Federal stronghold at Suffolk, and nothing had come of it but more casualties they could not afford. Lee had finally ordered him back, but the rails had been slow, and he did not arrive in time to help win the fight at Chancellorsville. Lee had prevailed with a weakened army, but the enemy then had been Joe Hooker. Now it was Longstreet's old friend, and Longstreet knew that Lee would need every piece of his strength at hand if Grant was ever to be pushed away.

His mind began to work, there was very little time. His men were advancing now close behind the big guns, the officers spreading them out into thick battle lines, and Longstreet turned, shouted to his staff, to Moxley Sorrel, said, "Major, we must not move into those woods in heavy lines. This is not the place."

Sorrel nodded, but did not understand, and Longstreet looked past him, saw Joe Kershaw, waving his sword in a high arc, spreading his men out into the woods.

Longstreet spurred the horse, moved close to Kershaw, said, "General, advance your men in a strong skirmish line, let them find their own way."

Kershaw seemed puzzled, said, "Sir, a skirmish line? The enemy will pick them apart piecemeal. Are you sure, sir?"

It was not like Kershaw to question orders, and Longstreet glared at him, had no patience, there was no time for discussion. "General, advance your men in a strong skirmish line. Follow them up with more of the same. Send them in slowly, let them make their own way. Tell them to fight on their own, not to worry about straight lines. Use the ground, the cover. The enemy will not pick them off if they cannot see them! Look at this place!"

Kershaw nodded. "Yes, sir. I will order the lines . . . regiment strength."

Longstreet looked back at Sorrel, shouted above the sounds of the guns, "Where is General Field? I want him to do the same thing, press the enemy slowly. There will be no massed charge! We must press slowly, steadily. The enemy is far outside his own defenses. Do you understand, Major?"

Sorrel saluted, stared at him, began to nod, said, "Yes . . . yes, sir. I understand."

Sorrel moved away, and Longstreet pounded a fist against his saddle. Good, he sees it too. We cannot just go by the manual here. If the enemy is firing blind, a massed assault just gives him targets. If we move carefully, move up where we can see him, then *we* will *not* be firing blind . . . and we can make them very uncomfortable.

Longstreet spurred the horse, moved closer to the big guns, looked down the road, empty now of the blue troops. The fire from Poague's guns had cleared them away from the deadly open space, but the musket fire was still heavy on both sides of the road. To the right, below the road, a bugle sounded, and Longstreet could see his men moving forward, a single line disappearing into the thickets. There was still heavy firing, some of Hill's men, the ones who did not run, still holding a shaky front below the road.

Behind Longstreet more troops were coming up, and now he saw Micah Jenkins at the front of his brigade, the young man from South Carolina, pointing his sword toward the enemy. Longstreet watched him, nodded, saw the troops moving with speed, no hesitation. Longstreet shouted, "General, over that way, follow those men into line below the road!"

Jenkins saluted, tipped his hat, moved past him. Longstreet had always thought Jenkins would rise quickly, knew he was brilliant, had led a brigade in nearly every fight Longstreet had been in. He had not been to West Point, knew only what he had experienced on the bloody fields, and Longstreet knew it was simply a matter of time before Jenkins commanded a division, or even a corps.

In the open ground above the road the rest of Field's division had begun to spread out in front of Poague's guns, and the big guns had slowed their fire. Poague would not fire over the heads of the men so close to his front. The roar of the fight came only from the muskets, and the gray line began to move forward. Longstreet could hear the deadly sounds of the minié balls all around him, and now he could see Lee again, beside the road, not far from Poague's guns.

He spurred the horse forward. The guns began to fire again, slowly, down the line, the gray troops far out in the field, Poague sending the shot and shell safely over their heads. Lee was standing up in the stirrups, and Longstreet reined up beside him, watched him, saw a look he had never seen. Lee was wide-eyed, his hair blown and wild, and now Lee reached over, put a hand on Longstreet's shoulder, gripped the gray cloth, and Longstreet saw the damp reflection in Lee's eyes. They did not speak. The sounds of the big guns rolled over them, the horses began to move about, and Lee let the hand drop, looked at Longstreet, said, "I thought . . . it was my time. I was ready to lead them, to take them across myself."

Longstreet said, "No, General, these men know what to do. They will not likely permit you to take them into *this* fight."

Lee smiled, put the hat back on, adjusted it slowly. "No, they were rather insistent. I believe, actually, I am under arrest. Some fellow from Texas ordered me . . . to stay back. He was . . . persuasive."

Longstreet laughed, looked across the field, saw the Texas flag reaching the far woods. "John Gregg's brigade . . . Hood would be proud of them. They're leading the attack."

The musket fire began to slow in front of them, the gray lines had reached the far trees. Below the road there was new firing, scattered out, but farther away, to the east.

Lee said, "The flank . . . we held the flank. We're pushing them back. . . ." He looked at Longstreet, and Longstreet nodded, knew that Lee would not say more, that it would come out later, in the reports, formal and specific.

Longstreet knew there had been disappointments before, that Lee would rarely say anything, the reproaches would be subtle, that the commanders who knew Lee well knew he would find a way to tell them silently: You did not perform . . . you will do better next time. With Longstreet, Lee had been more patient than with many of the others. Longstreet was important to Lee in ways that even Longstreet did not understand. Lee almost always stayed near him, on the field, in camp.

But at Gettysburg something changed in their relationship, the closeness strained. Of Longstreet's division commanders, Lee had always been closest to John Bell Hood, their friendship dating back to the old army, in Texas, the cavalry. But Pickett had been Longstreet's favorite, there was always humor, the good-natured insults of the man who had been last in his class at West Point. George Pickett had been Longstreet's friend since Mexico, and now Pickett was a shattered man, would never get over that horrible day, the disastrous assault that would forever carry his name. Pickett knew, as they all knew, that it was Lee's order that sent so many men across that bloody open ground, so many men who did not come back. Pickett was in Richmond now, in command of the Home Guard, and he was an angry, bitter man, who blamed Lee. Longstreet knew that somewhere inside himself, there was a small angry voice that told him Pickett was right.

Longstreet had received the reports of the fight yesterday, the couriers bringing him Lee's information, that it was Hancock again, through these woods, the same Hancock who had held the heights at Gettysburg, the strong center of the line where Pickett's division had been crushed. Pickett should be here, he thought, there would be justice in that.

Men were still coming forward, from the road behind them, and Longstreet could see the signs of men who had already been in a fight. They were Hill's men, moving back to the fight they had escaped from that morning. There were officers, leading men they had never seen. Some of the men had found familiar faces, their own units, and pieces of regiments were coming into line. They were moving past, looking now at Lee and Longstreet, and they began to cheer, exhausted and hoarse, but the muskets were held high, the hats rose up, and they moved forward to the fight.

Lee began to move his horse, rode alongside the men, and they cheered louder. Longstreet pushed the horse ahead, said, "General, if *you* would like to place these men, I believe I will retire to some safer place."

Lee looked at him, the eyes dark, the fury of the battle had filled him again, but he softened, absorbed what Longstreet had said. "Yes, General, this is your fight now."

Longstreet saluted, said, "General, with your permission . . ."

Lee returned the salute, and Longstreet spurred the horse, moved across the road, the staff following him down into the deadly brush.

HANCOCK'S FORWARD THRUST HAD BEEN BOGGED DOWN NOT just by Poague's guns, or the thin defense of Hill's unprepared men, but by the ground, by the men's own motion. As the lines went forward, they lost their connection to units beside them, there was little they could do but fire their muskets at what they believed to be the enemy in front of them. Some were able to advance faster than others, some ground was better, some had to climb down and wade through muddy swamps, and others moved around the small fires that still swept through the brush.

By the time Longstreet's men picked their way forward, Hancock's momentum had been lost. But there was no time for the Federal lines to re-form, for the officers to pull their men together. Longstreet's riflemen began to punch small holes in the confused blue masses, the men fighting on their own, one at a time, slipping carefully through the blindness to find the thick mass of blue targets. As more of Longstreet's troops found their targets, Hancock's lines began to pull back, finding their own cover, picking out targets as well. Longstreet's troops began to mass together, and the blind thickets and uncertain ground to their front slowed them as well. As the midday sun warmed the ground around them, both sides slowed their fire, dug in and kept a careful watch on the woods to their front, satisfied now to wait for something to shoot at.

HIS NAME WAS MARTIN LUTHER SMITH, AND LONGSTREET REmembered him well from West Point. They had graduated the same year, 1842, but Smith had ranked far ahead in the class, and so while Longstreet had little to say about his choice of assignments, the men at the head of the class could choose the more prestigious posts. Smith had gone on to become a fine engineer, had eventually designed the great works around Vicksburg, the works that had kept Grant's army away for so long.

Lee had spent most of his career in the old army as an engineer as well, had performed in that role as well as anyone ever had, both in peacetime and in Mexico. There, it was Winfield Scott who had recognized the value of Lee's skills and brought him to the general staff. It was a lesson Lee remembered, and so, as Smith's reputation grew, Lee would understand his value as well, and bring this man close to him.

Smith's horse was small and dark, and Smith slumped in the saddle. Longstreet rode beside him, towered above him. The men moved aside, some began to cheer, but Longstreet did not notice. He was focused on the small man beside him.

"Right through here, General. There . . ." Smith said.

Longstreet moved forward, saw the ground suddenly drop away, clearing in both directions. He moved the horse carefully, dropped down into the cut, saw out in both directions.

Smith stayed up above, said, "There you are, General. This runs all the way . . . well I expect they intended eventually to run it all the way to Fredericksburg. For our purposes, it runs east far enough."

There was no boast in Smith's voice, and Longstreet stared east, down the long straight ditch, an unfinished railroad cut. He moved the horse back up the rise, and his staff was watching him, knew the look, waited for what would come. He looked at Moxley Sorrel, said, "Major, you see what we have here? This is an opportunity . . . a bloody fine opportunity. Send word . . . pull the three closest brigades. We will move through this railroad cut until we are directly south of the enemy's flank. Then . . ." He paused, rubbed his beard, looked hard at Sorrel. "Then, Major, *you* will lead them. When they are in place, you will advance them out of the cut and attack the flank."

Sorrel's eyes were wide. "Me? You want me . . . ?" He smiled now, a wide beaming smile, looked around, saw the stunned faces of the others, looked back at Longstreet, who did not smile.

Longstreet said, "You have earned this, Major. Now, speed is critical. *Move!*"

Sorrel pointed to two of the couriers, and with a quick shout was gone into the brush.

Longstreet looked at Smith, said, "General Lee would say this is a gift from God. I would never disagree with the commanding general." He looked back toward the cut, shook his head, looked again at Smith, said, "Allow me, sir . . . to thank *you*."

The three brigades, under Wofford, Mahone, and Tige Anderson, had slipped along the cut exactly as Longstreet had foreseen. The firing along the front lines was scattered, neither side making a serious push

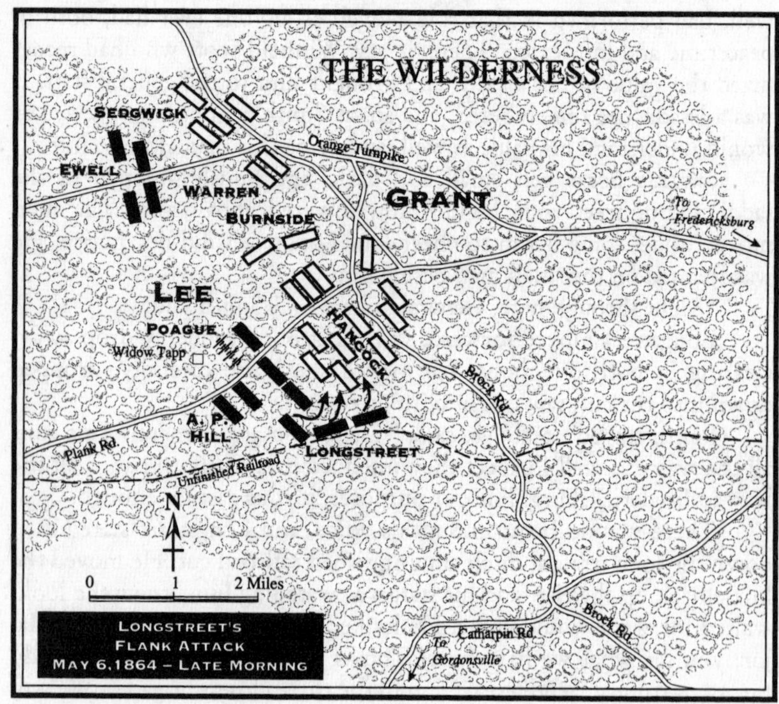

LONGSTREET'S
FLANK ATTACK
MAY 6,1864 – LATE MORNING

toward the other. Longstreet waited in the woods below the Plank Road, slapped one hand against the saddle, a slow nervous rhythm. The woods around him were mostly quiet, a few sharp cracks of musket fire echoing far in front. He began to move the horse forward, slowly stepping through a thick tangle of vines, then farther, across a thick carpet of small trees, cut down by the fight that had roared through these woods. He looked up at the sun, now nearly overhead, thought, We have the time, we have plenty of time. But he was not patient, did not know what was happening, if Sorrel was close, if they had been found out. He listened hard, thought, No, the enemy does not know, there would be firing, we would hear it.

The staff stayed back, and no one spoke, and he pounded his fist into the saddle again, said, "Let's go . . . !" and suddenly he heard it, the high screams, the rebel yell rolling through the woods in front of him in a terrible wave, and he spurred the horse hard, jumped it through the brush, could hear the guns now, the first wave of firing. To the left, near the road, there was another yell, and the men there began to move forward as well, clawing their way up and out of their low cover into the solid lines of blue. The attack was growing now, the woods alive with the new sounds.

Hancock's solid line was now caught in a trap, a deep V, Longstreet's men coming at him hard from two directions. Longstreet moved forward again, closer, the fire of the Yankees now cutting the leaves and brush around him. But there were not many, the musket fire was his own. Hancock's men were running, the flank collapsing completely, the panic of the surprise assault spreading along their lines. The blue troops began to flow in one great wave toward the road, each company, each regiment, carried along by the ones alongside.

Longstreet still moved forward, tried to see, thought, The road, I should send word . . . if Sorrel keeps advancing, he will cross in front of the troops along the road. He pushed the horse through the thickets, rode down suddenly into deep mud, the horse pulling itself free slowly. The staff was behind him now, and all around him men were moving toward the sound of the firing, *his* firing. The horse climbed out of the mire, and he could hear the sounds of Sorrel's advance now, closer to the road, and the firing began to slow. There were more horses, officers.

Micah Jenkins waved, rode toward him, yelled, "Did you see it, sir? Did you see it? They're gone, we pushed 'em clean out of the woods!"

Longstreet said nothing, was listening to the fading battle. He turned to Jenkins, said, "We have a problem, General! We must get these men into line, keep the assault moving forward. We're tripping all over ourselves out there!"

Jenkins stared at him, began to understand. One flank had overrun the other, the attack might have been *too* successful.

There were more horses, and Longstreet saw Smith. The engineer was breathing heavily, had lost his hat, said to Longstreet, "Sir, we can still push east . . . all the way past the Brock Road! The enemy's flank is exposed."

Longstreet said, "Push with what, Mr. Smith? Our people are crowding all over themselves. It will take too much time to sort them out."

Jenkins said, "Sir, my brigade is close by, we're in good shape . . . it won't take long. Let me pull them together, sir!"

Longstreet nodded, said, "Yes, go! General Smith, guide us to the best route. Waste no time! Let's move!"

Smith pointed, said, "This way, there's a road, a trail. We can put the troops in column up ahead, it's a short distance. . . ."

Smith moved the small horse, Longstreet followed, and now Jenkins moved up beside him. The orders had gone out, and Jenkins's men began to appear out of the woods. They formed quickly, the orders were clear. From below, more troops came forward.

Longstreet saw Joe Kershaw, shouted, "General, bring your people in line here! Whatever strength you can! Support General Jenkins!"

Kershaw saluted, shouted orders back to his aides, then turned, moved up beside Longstreet. He looked behind them, saw Jenkins's troops filling the open space, moving forward, a strong column, strong enough to turn anyone's open flank. Kershaw said, "General . . . these are Jenkins's troops? They're wearing . . . black."

Jenkins laughed, said, "Makes 'em hard to see in this place. They fade right into the shadows."

Kershaw shook his head. "Not sure about that . . . makes 'em look like Yankees."

Longstreet was moving ahead, ignored the talk behind him. He thought again of Pickett, the laughing face, thought, You would have enjoyed this, George. This is not like Gettysburg.

He thought of Grant now, had kept that away as long as he could. It had been a sickening surprise that Grant came east. Longstreet had made his move on Knoxville when Grant took command at Chattanooga, and so they had never faced each other. He had not spoken of that, how he had hoped they would not meet, not like this. They were close in the old days, and Longstreet thought often of Grant's wedding, Julia the radiant bride.

Longstreet laughed suddenly, and faces turned toward him. He ignored the men around him, thought now of Grant putting on the dress, grumbling. At Jefferson Barracks, back in St. Louis, the soldiers would perform plays, usually Shakespeare. Grant's shortness made him a natural for the female roles, and it was a distinction Grant hated. Grant as Desdemona, Grant as Ophelia. He laughed again, thought, There was always great humor at Sam's expense. And no one there would ever have believed he would command an army.

We were very young, and we didn't know much about anything. We sure didn't know much about war. Now . . . we know a great deal.

He looked back, saw the line was moving well, quickly advancing. He stopped the horse, the others rode up close beside him, the faces watched him, waiting. He said, "Gentlemen, we have upset General Hancock once today, let's see if we can do it again."

They moved forward, broke into the clear. He saw the opening, a wide trail, led the column that way. The shooting had nearly stopped, the woods suddenly quiet around him. The only sound came from the rear, the sounds of cracking brush, of men moving with deliberate steps, the grim silence of soldiers who know they are part of something important.

In front of them Longstreet saw motion, a small opening in thick brush, a glimpse of a flag, and he thought, Yes, good, more troops, saw the flag clearly now, held high by a man in gray. Suddenly the troops turned, there were shouts, and he saw flashes, small puffs of smoke. The sounds whizzed by, and he heard grunts, the cry of a horse, and then he felt the sharp pull, felt himself in the air, pulled up off the horse, then set down hard in the saddle. He heard a voice.

Kershaw was yelling frantically, "Friends! We are *friends*!"

There were more shouts, and men began to fill the road in front of them. He tried to see, but felt his head rock forward, saw the blood now, stared at the flow of red down his shirt, felt the wetness, the warmth, watched it spread slowly down his chest, thought, It does not . . . hurt.

The horse was moving still, and Longstreet began to rock in the saddle, and now there were hands on the horse, someone grabbed the reins, and he felt himself slide down, hands holding him. He was turned to one side, saw bodies, one face, saw it was Jenkins, sprawled flat on the ground, a bloody stain spreading out under his head, the face staring out at him with lifeless eyes. He tried to yell, but there was no sound, and he thought, *No . . . God no.*

They set him down on his back, and he was looking into the bright sun, closed his eyes, tried to breathe. The air would not come, and he fought for it, felt himself choking, the blood filling his throat, and he coughed, took a small breath, thought of the men behind him, the great opportunity, thought, Do not stop . . . keep them moving . . . tell General Lee . . . *keep them moving. . . .*

14. HANCOCK

Late Afternoon, May 6, 1864

THE ATTACK ON HIS FLANK HAD EXHAUSTED ITSELF, AS ALL THE attacks had done in the thickets of the woods. Now his men were moving back to the Brock Road, to the safety of the strong defenses. He sat on the big horse, watched them come, saw not panic, but the slow dragging movements of men punched by a hard defeat. They were climbing up and over the great walls of logs, and all down the Brock Road his troops were pulling themselves together, recovering from the shocking assault. The defenses grew stronger.

It had been hours now, and there had been no attack, not even a strong skirmish. He kept his eyes to the woods to the front, thought, They will come. It's as hard for them as it is for us . . . moving in that damned place. But they surprised us, rolled us back completely. They will not just let us sit now, licking our wounds. They will come.

He had secured the flank, and back behind his left, a mass of artillery waited for targets, guns that had been silent all day. Out in front there was nothing to shoot at but the sounds, and the sounds could be your own men. Down on the left, the big guns were now in position, and if the rebels came that way, tried to make the sweep far around the flank, they would have to cross in front of the guns. No, he thought, they will see that as clearly as we do. Out in the brush, our flank was vulnerable. Back here, the flank is secure.

To the right, the woods were a mass of sounds, but they were not the sounds he'd expected to hear. Burnside had been ordered to move into the gap between the roads, to push hard into Hill's left, but there had been nothing from Burnside, no word, no sign of his men. There were sounds of a fight, but it was not strength, no massed assaults. Burnside was out there, he thought, somewhere, half his men looking for the other half, probably shooting at each other. But the woods will keep Lee from moving that way as well. Damn this place!

He moved the horse slowly along the road, still peered out toward the woods. He thought of ordering his own men forward, but no, even headquarters understood that little would be gained. He had done that already, at dawn, driven the enemy back in complete chaos, but the chaos spread to his own advance, commanders losing their own men in the thickets. By the time Longstreet suddenly appeared in front of them, the chaos was complete. Hancock's assault had become a stalemate, then a retreat, men fighting their way backward. He looked down the road, saw more men filing up and over the logs, the defense stronger still. Our advantage is here, he thought. Now it is time to wait.

Two days before, he had marched the Second Corps right past the ruins of the Chancellor mansion, the place where he'd held the rebels away a year ago. It was a memory he carried into every fight, the collapse of command, Joe Hooker suddenly losing his nerve. Hancock had been the rear guard, had held Lee at bay while the rest of the army backed away, northward, to the safety of the river. The Battle of Chancellorsville had been a complete disaster, but the defeat was not inflicted by Lee or by the rebels. Hancock's men, and the others, the great power and spirit of the Federal army, had been beaten by their own commander.

He had tried not to dwell on that, moved quickly past the ruins of the mansion, stared to the front, toward the dense woods, but those sights brought a different horror. In the small clearings, patches of burned brush, he could see the bones, men and horses, the sickening remains of the fight a year ago. The men saw it too, and many remembered this awful place, marched quietly, no one hoping for another fight on this ground. Many others, the replacements, stared at the bones and the wreckage in stunned silence, some only now understanding that the next fight could do the same to them.

The wound still bothered him, nearly every day. It had come the third day at Gettysburg, facing the last great assault from Lee's army. The musket ball struck his saddle, shattered the wood and exploded it underneath him, punching splinters and fragments up inside of him. The doctors thought they had removed all the fragments, but the pains were still there, and the wound still festered and burned, and if the doctors didn't know, he did. There were more fragments inside of him yet. He would need surgery again.

There was not much about that day he could recall. He had watched them come, a great wave of men, Pickett and Pettigrew, nearly fifteen thousand soldiers, pushing straight at his defenses. When he saw it was Pickett, he also knew it was Armistead.

Lewis Armistead commanded one of Pickett's brigades, and Armistead had been as close to Hancock as anyone before the war, a friendship that grew from the early days, Mexico, Kansas, the Seminole Wars in Florida. They had parted ways in Los Angeles, when news of Fort Sumter reached the West Coast. Much of the army simply dissolved, so many resigning, going south. He knew they would meet eventually, that there were too many in this war who were facing their friends, their brothers, across the deadly space. He had not allowed himself to feel the sadness of that. It was, after all, Armistead's choice.

He still didn't understand that, how the good men, the honorable men, could betray their oath as officers, betray their country. He had asked himself, tormented himself with the question: When this is over, will we still be friends? Will I be able to look him in the eye and not see a traitor?

Pickett's great assault had brought Armistead and his men straight into Hancock's guns, and unlike most of the shattered gray wave, Armistead's men reached the Federal lines, actually broke through, pushed across the low stone wall in one last desperate surge. But they were too few, and the men in blue too many, and Armistead fell just inside Hancock's own lines.

Hancock never saw him that day, had already gone down with his own wound. Now there would be no answers. He would never know if Armistead could still have been his friend. It all seemed so very long ago.

He moved the horse again, heard more scattered musket fire from the right, thought, *Burnside.* You're in there, somewhere. It would be nice if you would tell me where, or what the hell you're doing.

The field across the road was quiet now, the last of his men safely behind the log wall. There was a steady flow of black smoke down to the left, a brushfire moving with the breeze, rolling slowly toward the road, toward the pine of the wall. He moved that way, saw the smoke drifting across his men, a thick cloud. Men began to move out of the way, waving their arms. Some were laughing, and he heard a man say, "You boys keep a lookout. Them rebs could be hidin' in the smoke!"

He looked across the field, toward the trees, and suddenly there was a new sound, a ripple of musket fire, the high shriek of lead, dull smacks in the wall. Then the rebels were there, moving forward, and now there came the sound, the awful scream he had heard before. It was the rebel yell.

His men began to fire at the gray line, and he watched, thought, How many . . . how strong? The rebels moved closer, but the charge didn't come. They simply stopped, knelt, were trading volleys with his men behind the wall. Now the fire from his own men began to take effect, and the rebel line was falling apart. He stared, thought, This is insane. They can't just . . . stand there. It will be a slaughter.

He saw a staff officer moving along the road, coming toward him. The man reined up his horse, saluted, said, "General Hancock, we have word from General Burnside. He is moving into position on our right front. General Burnside reports he will try to assault the rebel flank, if we can only hold them in place, sir!"

Hancock stared at the man, felt a burst of anger. "If we can hold them . . . why? So he can watch? Where the hell has he been all day? Now, we don't need him, we are behind a big damned wall. The enemy is coming right at us!"

Suddenly there was a great burst of sound, across the field in the far trees. Hancock turned, saw a new wave, a heavier line of infantry emerging from the trees. The sounds of the muskets rolled all around him, the road filling with gray smoke, the hot smell of powder. Now it was a fight.

The staff was gathering behind him now, and he could hear the shouts, the men yelling at him. He jerked the horse, moved away from the wall, behind the road, thought, No, this is not the place for you to be. He moved back into tall trees, followed by the staff, saw more officers waiting for him, looks of pained relief. Well, hell, he thought. If I can't see it for myself, how am I to know what's going on?

Now a man rode quickly up behind him, a staff officer, the man ducking low. Hancock turned the horse, and the man yelled, "Sir . . . we have a gap in the lines! General Ward reports the enemy is advancing into our center, sir!"

Hancock stared at the man, watched him wilt under the hot gaze. "Yes, Captain, I can see where the enemy is assaulting! A gap? Where? Where is General Ward?"

"Uh . . . I don't know sir. When I left him, he was moving to the rear . . . with his men."

Hancock looked toward the road, thought, His men? Ward has broken? He's the center of the line. How could they have given way? He spun the horse, and now the black smoke was boiling past him. It wasn't a brushfire anymore. It had reached the sticks and timbers of the wall, and now a great roaring bonfire began to spread out on both sides, sheets of flame towering above the road. Blue troops with blackened faces were streaming toward him, men with burnt clothes, a new panic from an enemy you could not hold away.

He saw officers now, yelled, "Dammit! Get these men back in line!" They were moving in a rush all around him, shouts and curses, and now he could hear the sounds of the muskets, the hot lead cutting the air around him.

He turned, yelled to his staff, "Get word to all units . . . send support to the center! Order up the reserves, to the middle of the line! Tell the officers . . . follow the smoke! Go toward the smoke!"

Now there was a new burst of musket fire, all along the wall, and he tried to see, thought, Yes, hold them back. Suddenly there was a great chorus of screams, and he saw a burst of men leaping through the flames. The rebels had reached the logs, were rushing forward through the wall of flames. They began to flow out from the wall, and he could see them pointing, quick aim, scattered shots. They were looking for

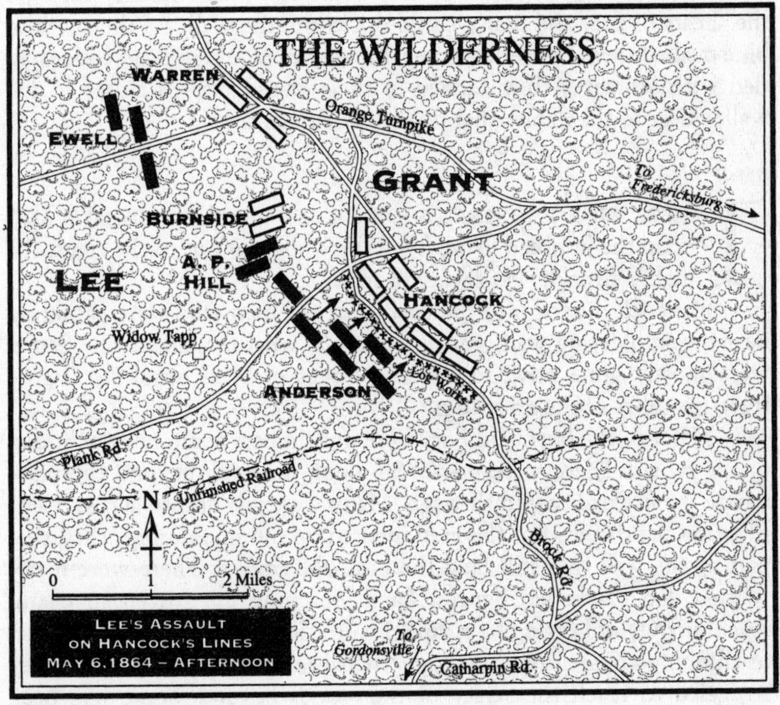

LEE'S ASSAULT ON HANCOCK'S LINES MAY 6.1864 – AFTERNOON

targets, began now to fire up and down the road, where the men in blue still huddled at the wall, where the flames had not yet spread.

Hancock could see the faces now, men with singed hair, blackened clothes. He spurred the horse, and the staff followed, moved farther back into the trees. The smoke was everywhere, from the fight, from the growing fire. He moved into an open clearing, took a deep breath of blessed air. On the trails behind him a column of his men was moving forward, the reserve, and he pointed, yelled to an officer, "There, double quick! They have broken through!"

The fresh troops moved toward the fire, the great crackling roar now blending with the sounds of the fight. From both directions, the Federal troops were moving toward the breakthrough, a tightening arc, containing the surge of rebels. The fight became hand-to-hand, the men in blue growing in number, too many for the rebels to push through. The break in the lines was shrinking, the rebels pushed back to the wall, to the great horror of the flames. Many gave up the fight, began to run, to climb through the fire, and those who escaped had to make the deadly retreat across the open ground. Many of the wounded tried to pull away as well, but they could not move quickly through the sheets of fire, and many could not climb the wall. As the surge of blue pushed them tighter together, those who would not surrender battled with whatever they carried in their hands, backed closer to the wall, closer to the flames that finally consumed them.

THERE WERE SCATTERED SHOTS, A FEW REBEL SKIRMISHERS, AND then the jumbled firing from the woods far out to the right, the fight Burnside was trying to make.

Hancock moved into the road, past the men who were gathering near the smoldering wall, staring quietly at what remained. The flames were mostly gone now, but small plumes of black smoke still rose from the ashes of the great logs.

Many of the burnt timbers were not timbers at all, but the bodies of the rebels. There were bodies all along the wall, beyond the place where the fire had roared through. Many were just draped across, some in grotesque shapes. But the men focused on the smoldering ashes, that part of the wall that still held the heat, the smoke. There were many twisted and blackened figures, hands reaching up, frozen in death, reaching out, still trying to escape the fire. Some were caught in the act of climbing up, seeking the escape, their breath swept away while they struggled to reach the safety of the woods beyond. Some had been wounded, men who crawled toward the wall, only to have the flames roll over them. The clothes were mostly gone, burned away, and the men in blue stayed back, did not yet have the stomach for pulling the dead away, not like this, not when there was nothing to hold, to touch, but the burnt flesh, the charred bones.

There was a gentle shift in the breeze, and Hancock caught the awful smell, could see some of his men backing away now, some beginning to be sick. Hancock pulled his mind away, turned the horse off the road, thought, No, not here, you cannot let them see you . . . you cannot be affected by this. He pushed the horrible sights from his mind, moved the horse past more men who were gathering on the road. He turned, saw staff officers moving to catch up with him, and he thought, Tell them, keep them ready, pass the word. But he said nothing, realized the rebels were through here. This fight was over. No one over there would ask them to do this again, to charge this line. We are too strong, he thought. Nothing can be gained. He reined the horse, looked back to the road. No, they will not come again, not here. The soldiers have seen something new, a new horror, a new way to die. They have seen the face of hell.

15. LEE

LATE AFTERNOON, MAY 6, 1864

THEY WERE SPREAD OUT ON BOTH SIDES OF THE ROAD, A LONG line of trenches and piled debris, the men sitting low behind their cover. Lee saw motion down along the line, the red battle flags of each regiment, a slight wave in the fading breeze. The sun was beginning to set and long shadows spread across the road. He dismounted, still looked eastward, saw the dark smoke from the Brock Road, from that awful place where his men lay scattered, the smoke from the breastworks still rising, and Hancock's people safely behind their wall.

Faces were watching him, men were turning about, pointing at him. There were some shouts, but the men were brutally tired, and many were already sleeping. He walked off the edge of the road, into the darker shade, but there was no cool relief.

The staff waited out on the road, and Taylor followed him, moved quietly. Now even the affectionate salutes of the men faded out, and the woods were quiet. Taylor stayed a few steps back, and Lee sat on a long dead tree, punctured by many holes, colored by blood. Lee looked at the stain on the soft wood, put his hand on it, felt the wood crumble, slid his hand along, felt the rotting wood roll into small pieces under his fingers. He looked down beside the tree, to the thick mat of old leaves, saw another stain and, half buried, a man's shoe, old black leather. He reached down, freed it from the dirt, held it up in his hand, saw a hole, the sole worn through, the heel long gone. He thought, There are not many shoes in this army. This one . . . was lucky.

He did not often think of that, did not even use the word. What was luck, after all, but the will of God? He tossed the shoe aside, then looked at it again, thought, No, I should find him, he will want it. It was an odd feeling, that he must have known this man, must find him. . . .

He looked at the dark stain again, realized there might be no need. He tried to clear his mind, pull himself away, thought, You cannot do this, you cannot see them like this . . . one at a time. He stood, brushed the dead wood from his pants, thought, You can never be this close. You cannot be absorbed in the fate of each man. But you *are* closer. This terrible fight has done that, the war has done that, slowly, over time, taken the good men, the good leaders. There is something in this . . . a lesson, God has shown you that you must not forget that each of these men has his own pain, dies in his own blood, has his own soul. The line is so thin, the strong line between the commander and these men, the men who lead the charge, the men who face the guns.

He had kept Longstreet's image away until now, his mind holding instead to the faces of the men he did not know, the men who left their shoes behind. But if he did not show it to his staff, he could not keep it away from himself for very long, and so the image came to him. Longstreet's wound was thought to be fatal, but the doctors reached him quickly and the bleeding was stopped. I was not there, Lee thought, I don't know how I could have endured that. He had not seen Jackson after the arm was amputated, had been grateful for that, would not remember him as anything but the magnificent fighter, would see the man as he'd always been, not as he'd died. And now he thought of Longstreet, fought the image of the big man choking on his own blood. The staff had put Longstreet's hat over his face, to shield him from the sun, and so the men who gathered around thought he was already dead. Longstreet had heard the talk, heard them crying, lifted the hat off his face himself, and waved it at them. Taylor had been there and seen it, heard what the soldiers were saying, that it was a miracle, Longstreet back from the dead. Lee shook his head. No, he will die in his own time, in his own way. He is too stubborn to leave it in God's hands.

He looked around, the shadows filling the spaces, thought again of Jackson, and now Longstreet, both shot by their own men. He was so pleased that the fight would be *here*, this awful place, and he remembered he'd felt the same way a year ago, when Hooker had drawn himself up into these woods. But there was a difference now. Lee knew that Jackson had gone down as a price to be paid, a balance, that God would not give Lee such a great victory without something in return. This time the victory was not complete. Grant was not rushing away toward the river, as Hooker had. And so Longstreet would not die, not yet. Lee felt certain of that, the justice . . . God would be fair.

Taylor was watching him, and Lee saw him now, saw a sadness in the young man's face. He appeared pale, weakened.

"Colonel, have you any word? Anything I have not already been told?"

Taylor said, "You mean about General Longstreet, sir? No, sir, just what the surgeons said. He should survive. It is a terrible wound. When I left him about an hour ago, he was awake, but . . . his neck. I cannot think of it without feeling sick. I'm sorry, sir."

Lee nodded, said, "It is a ghastly thing . . . that we do here, that we do to each other. We are not supposed to think on that . . . it is part of the duty, of the tragedy. And there are so many . . ."

Taylor moved closer, said, "At least, sir, the general will survive. He will be back. He told me that himself."

Lee looked out past the distant line of men, looked to the gray light, fading in the small dark spaces, felt the anger rise, said, "That is what we were told about General Jackson." He pushed it away. No . . . do not question, there must be no bitterness. *Forgive me, Lord. I am weakened . . . I will not question Your will.*

He turned now, began to walk back toward the road. Taylor moved out in front, went to the horse, took the reins from an aide, held them out. Lee stopped, looked up at the others, saw Marshall, the young man staring at him through small wire glasses.

"Colonel Marshall, have we received anything yet from General Ewell?"

Marshall sat up straight in the saddle, always responded to Lee with nervousness, something Lee did not understand.

"Um . . . no sir. Just that he expects his attack to begin about . . . now, sir." Marshall looked at a small pocket watch. "Yes . . . about now."

Lee climbed the horse, moved to the center of the road, looked to the north, stared at the spreading darkness. There was no sound.

The meeting had come at Lee's request, early that afternoon, to find out exactly what was happening in Ewell's front. He thought of Ewell's explanations, still felt the small fury that had swirled inside of him, an anger he would never reveal. Ewell had done little all day, except hold the Federals in front of him tight in their lines. Both sides were aware of the other's strength, and so, as Hancock's flank was being rolled up by Sorrel's surprise from the railroad cut, and later, as the attack against the Federal defenses on the Brock Road had threatened Hancock's position, neither Warren nor Sedgwick could risk weakening their defenses in front of Ewell. But if there had been no Federal advance there, nothing to lend support to Hancock's hard thrust early that morning, Ewell had done nothing as well, content to enjoy his strong defensive lines, while Hill, and then Longstreet, made the fight to the south.

Lee could understand a stalemate, both sides wary of making a mistake against strong defenses of the enemy, but what had stirred his anger was the final detail of Ewell's report. He had mentioned a possible plan, an idea that had come from John Gordon.

Gordon's brigade lay now on Ewell's far north flank, the left flank of Lee's entire position. Gordon had scouted out around the Federals in front of him and found that Sedgwick's lines simply . . . ended. There was no protection beyond the Federal right, no great mass of cavalry, no skirmish line extending up toward the river. Sedgwick's people had not even dug trenches. The night before, Gordon had seen it for himself, slipped quietly east, well behind Sedgwick's lines, and watched men in blue preparing their evening meal, with no preparation against anything that might come at them from above, from the direction of the river.

Gordon's brigade belonged to Jubal Early's division, and Early would hear none of Gordon's plan, did not believe that a quick sweep up and around the Federal flank would accomplish anything, and might in fact be disastrous. There had still been the question of Burnside's whereabouts, and Lee's cavalry had no answers to that. Stuart was focused well below, far beyond the right flank. But now, with Burnside suddenly appearing down near the Plank Road, that mystery had been solved.

Lee had stared at Ewell in disbelief. All day long they had known of an extraordinary opportunity, and nothing was done about it. He thought of Ewell, standing in front of him like some awkward flapping bird, explaining all sides of the issue. The staff often joked about that, but Lee had no use for it, would not judge. He tried hard, would see only a man who had given up a piece of himself to this service, had lost a leg on the battlefield, had earned the respect. But . . . he is not the same man, he thought. He will not take the initiative. The order approving Gordon's attack had come directly from Lee.

He did not know John Gordon well, except that he was not a professional soldier. He had come to the army from Georgia, an educated man who advanced through the ranks by leading infantry with solid, quiet competence. Lee thought of Jubal Early and Early's distrust of the plan. Early would distrust any plan that he did not conceive, could intimidate everyone around him, and since Gettysburg, Lee had known that Ewell was capable of allowing Early to influence him more than was appropriate. Lee was growing weary of that. Early was vocal and openly hostile about so many things, had even made a point of protesting the presence of Gordon's wife, who had been close to her husband through many of the fights. Lee did not object to the wives being near, as long as their husbands performed their duty. Gordon had shown no sign of a problem in that area, certainly had shown nothing of the oppressive influence that Ewell's wife had brought to *his* headquarters.

He hadn't noticed the small clouds in the west, painted with the red glow from a setting sun; there was no time for the small moment of beauty, the quiet serenity. The sharp colors faded away now, the sun well below the distant trees, and what light remained was fading quickly into a gray haze. He tried to feel some optimism, that this could still work, it might be an excellent plan. If Sedgwick could be panicked, Grant might have no choice but to pull back to the east, toward Fredericksburg. With the river behind him, there might be no escape. The risk, of course, was that Gordon was wrong, that there were more blue troops behind Sedgwick, and that Gordon might be flanked himself.

Lee stared out through the dull light, thought, It has to be in our favor. Men will panic quickly in a night assault, when they cannot see their attackers. The problem is that it would be very difficult to follow up any breakthrough, to move Ewell's other forces forward in the dark. But we must take every chance. Lee clenched his fist, still stared at the silence, waiting, thought, I wish General Ewell understood that. If Gordon is wrong, at least let him be wrong moving *forward*. . . .

16. GRANT

EVENING, MAY 6, 1864

HE STILL WORKED THE KNIFE, SLOWLY, SHORT DELIBERATE strokes, the wood shavings scattered into a thick pile around his feet. The fires were growing around him now. He glanced up, saw the staff lining up with small cups, a fresh pot of coffee. He saw Porter looking at him, holding two cups, and Grant shook his head, no.

He carved the last stick into a sharp point, sharp enough for a toothpick, tossed it aside, heard a sound, a small laugh, looked beyond his tent and saw a cluster of bright colors, brass buttons, and gold braid. He was used to foreign visitors. There was always some prince or dignitary, some old soldier from the great European wars. One old Frenchman told stories of his close friendship with Napoleon, another had fought against him in some frozen field in Russia. They were usually the guests of some congressman, someone looking to show off his influence.

Their first impression of headquarters was often disappointing. Many expected their presence to be the most significant event of the day, as though there should be some elaborate ceremony. Then they would hear the guns, a sound like nothing heard in Europe, not even in the days of Napoleon, and then the wounded would flow past, wagons and ambulances filled with the screams and faint cries of the men who endured the horror of this most *modern* war. When that experience had passed, the visitors did not venture far from the tents, there was not quite as much boasting of their own heroics and how much more civilized war had once been. Even those from the most remote lands knew they were seeing the new face of war, and when they left, there was something different about them, something subdued.

Grant had no objection to the visits, but was not as cordial or open as many expected. He had little time for the ceremony of it, and often he would offend them by his lack of attention. He tried to be polite, but many spoke very little English, and if they did, and the accents were strong, he had a hard time understanding them, and it embarrassed them. Even when they were direct, a formal request for information, he'd seen their attraction to the reporters, and so there was very little he would tell them about what was happening. To them, he was just this odd quiet man, and none thought he had the flare, the great ceremonial *presence*, of the real commander. They would speak among themselves, talking about Lincoln, and smile knowingly, of course, the two men so similar, so symbolic of this young, crude country.

The group began to move away, stifled the smiles, and Grant looked down at his hands, the small knife, the dirty gloves with the fingers torn away.

Rawlins said, "They have no graciousness! They should be grateful we allow them here."

Grant looked up, saw Rawlins sipping the hot coffee from his tin cup, and said, "They don't hurt anything. As long as they stay out of the way, they add a little color to the place."

Rawlins sniffed. "But, they're so . . . *rude*! Talking about you that way, I overheard them, I know what they're talking about. It's the . . . the knife. Your habit."

Grant rolled the knife over in his hand, said, "You mean the whittling?"

"They think all of us . . . their papers describe Americans as some kind of savages, as though we have no culture, no dignity. I saw a cartoon, you, the President, and a caricature of Uncle Sam, sitting around a campfire with whittling sticks!"

Grant thought, So, that's why the laughter. I fit the image.

The Europeans had moved away, down the hill toward Meade's camp. Rawlins said, "I had better . . . keep an eye on them. They're heading toward General Meade's tent. You know how *he* is. He seems to offend them every time he speaks." Rawlins hustled away, and Grant watched him move down the hill, catching up to the bright uniforms, the elegant caped suits, Rawlins all smiles and short bows. Grant shook his head, smiled, thought, Old friend, you have a great future after this war. You're a natural diplomat.

He reached down, felt for another piece of wood, but his hand touched only the bare ground. He'd worked his way through the small pile. He folded the knife, put it in a pocket, stood, stretched, saw an officer, recognized him, one of Hancock's men. The man was running up the hill from Meade's tent, held a piece of paper, and Grant waited.

The man saluted, said, "General, sir, Major Garrett. Sir, General Meade requested I pass this along to you."

Grant nodded, felt in his pocket for a cigar. Garrett waited for a sign, some permission to speak. Grant slowly lit the cigar, said nothing.

Garrett said, "Um . . . with your permission, sir, General Hancock wishes to inform you that there is no activity in his front. The enemy has pulled back to his entrenchments. General Hancock has made contact with General Burnside's flank. But it is General Hancock's opinion that the enemy has no intentions of renewing his attack."

Grant tasted the smoke, held the cigar out, looked at it, said, "Fine. Congratulate General Hancock on a fine day's work. You are dismissed."

Garrett saluted, then smiled, said, "Oh, sir . . . I don't know if you have heard. The enemy prisoners are talking about General Longstreet. Some say he is dead. We can't be sure of that. But there is no doubt he is down, out of the fight."

Grant felt a cold stab, stared at the man with his mouth open, the cigar suddenly motionless, and Garrett's smile faded. Grant said, "No, Major, I had not heard. I want to know . . . tell General Hancock I want to know if he is alive . . . how it happened. Go!"

Garrett saluted again, moved quickly down the hill. Grant walked over to his tent, stared at the dark space inside, thought, Old Pete, you damned fool. Can't stay out of range . . . always too close. He remembered Mexico, Longstreet's wound at Chapultepec, missing the final assault because he insisted on carrying his own flag, the perfect target. Now . . . what? Someplace he ought not have been. Well, then, good, go home. Stay with Louise, have more children. He thought of St. Louis, of Jefferson Barracks. We were young and stupid, strutting and prancing in those uniforms like we were all heroes. Or would be. And the women . . . surely they saw more to us than that, the ridiculous boasting of our great military careers, of how we would all be generals someday. Did we really believe that? We surely must have convinced the women, because all of us married, right there, fought the greatest battle of our lives, fought against the will of their fathers, none of them wanted soldiers for their daughters. But it was a fight the fathers would lose, and usually it was because of the mothers. Grant smiled now, thought of his own wedding, Longstreet towering above the others, but perfect, the glory of the dress blues, young soldiers home from the great war with Mexico. But . . . if we all believed in our own glory, if we had the same dreams, if we really thought we would all be generals one day, it never should have been like this. We should not be killing each other.

He turned, saw more riders, men moving in all directions. It was near full dark, and the fires were drawing in circles of men, like blue moths around a lamplight.

He heard his name, men looking for him, messengers from the front. He still stared into the dark, saw the big man's face, the deep blue eyes, thought, I will not bear this, the fault is not mine. You made a decision old friend, a very bad decision. All of you . . . He thought of the others, the young men from the Point, all the old friends. Die for your cause, if you have to. I will do what *I* have to do.

He squinted at the firelight, saw the gathering couriers, the faces all watching him, and he clamped down hard on the cigar, moved closer to the fire. He nodded to Porter, the silent signal, and Porter motioned toward one man.

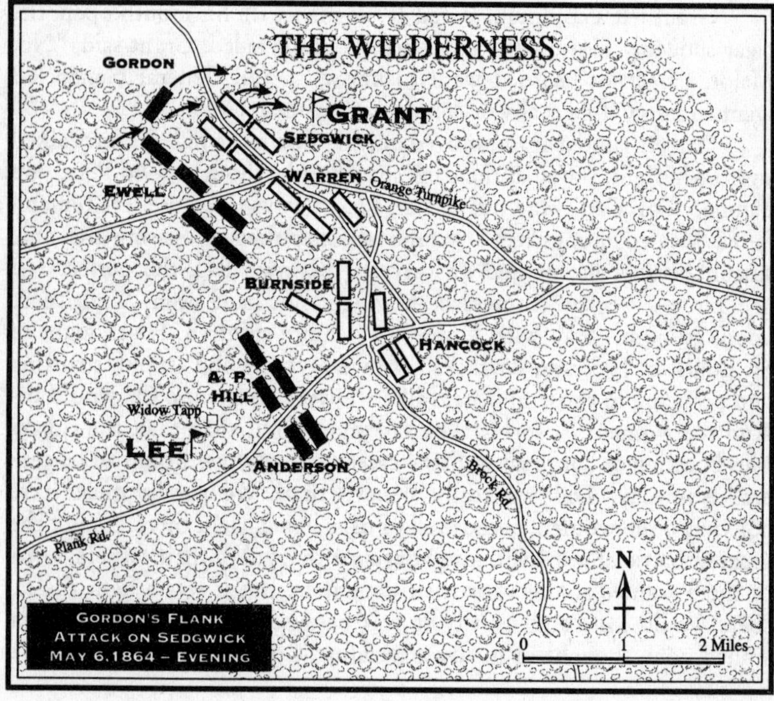

The man saluted, said, "Sir, General Sedgwick sends his compliments, and wishes you to know, sir, that the enemy is firmly in his barricades, and the general expects no more activity tonight."

There was a sudden noise from the right of the line, a roar of sound rolled up the hill, a sudden burst of musket fire, the high wailing scream of men. The officers all turned, looked out into the dark. Some began to move to their horses. Grant heard the shrill whine of a shell. Behind the camp there was a sharp blast and a wagon shattered into pieces. Now the scattered sounds of the lead balls began to zip by them, one punching the side of Grant's tent.

Grant said, "I believe General Sedgwick is mistaken."

IT HAD LASTED ABOUT AN HOUR, AND SEDGWICK'S RIGHT FLANK had collapsed. The enemy could have no grand success, the great surprise had been dulled by the darkness and the thick brush, and so the curtain was brought down on yet another assault. Grant had not seen Sedgwick, but the messages came in quick order, hundreds of blue troops captured, one brigade shattered. The panic had spread down the line, men had poured back through the headquarters, wild-eyed, running from demons screaming after them in the dark. Troops had quickly been pulled from the left, sent to stop the tide, but in the tangle of woods, men were still scattered, some were still running, and there was little anyone would do now in the pitch-darkness.

Grant was furious. Sedgwick had assured headquarters that the flank had been secured, his line re-fused, the end turned back on itself at a ninety-degree angle. But the order was never given to the right commanders, and now those commanders, Shaler and Seymour, were in the hands of the rebels. He would say nothing to Sedgwick, that would be Meade's job, to find out what bloody mistake had let the rebels get around the flank.

Meade had come up to his camp, and the couriers were still coming, most of them directed to Meade. Grant sat on the stump, listened to the reports, kept his anger tight in a thick column of cigar smoke.

He watched Meade, listened quietly. It was a younger officer, one of Meade's staff, a man Grant did not know, and he could see that the young man was clearly infected with the panic. His voice rolled through the camp, and those not moving past were stopping to listen. "Sir! The reports are that Lee is moving between us and the river. The cavalry is in Fredericksburg already! By morning we will be completely cut off!"

Meade waved his arms, yelled out, "Well, who is in charge up there? Have we no troops who can be sent? How did this happen?" Meade leaned close to the man's face, raised his voice to a full yell, "Captain, we need some answers!"

The young man paused, tried to swallow, pointed out toward the darkness, said weakly, "The reports . . . I will try to get more reports . . . sir. . . ."

Grant stood, moved close to Meade, said quietly, "The attack on our flank was small. They cannot move a large army in this country any better than we can. It has not been dark for very long, and if I recall, before the sun went down, we still had Ewell in *front* of us. I believe, if your young man here walks in a straight line down the Orange Turnpike, he will still find Ewell's troops. If he doesn't, then come back and tell me. If he does, then we will know for certain whether or not the enemy is in our rear."

There was another rider, a colonel, and the man jumped from his horse, an obvious show of urgency. He had lost his hat, his coat was torn. He stumbled toward them, said, "General Grant . . . General Meade, forgive me, sirs, but I have just come from the shooting. The enemy is moving into our flank with a large force, sir. The entire line is rolling up. Lee is circling behind the army, right back here, sir. The headquarters should be moved. You are in great danger, sir. Lee is—"

Grant held up his hand and the man froze. He turned his head, listened, thought, The shooting has stopped. He glanced at the only sound, the winded breathing of the colonel, and the man slowly straightened, also hearing the silence. Grant moved out into the light, glanced again at the winded officer, the man staring at him with wide wounded eyes. Grant said, "Colonel, you are a bit late. Your great battle has already ended. Your timeliness is noted."

He moved toward the fire, felt the anger again, said aloud, "Gentlemen . . . a word, please. General Meade, if I may speak to your staff?"

Meade said nothing, nodded dumbly.

"Gentlemen, I am growing tired of hearing about all these terrible injuries that General Lee is going to inflict on this army. If I take all your reports into account, we have the rebel army running over both flanks, in our rear, and probably surrounding Washington. I will say this once. I do not wish to hear any more speculation on what General Lee is about to do to *us*. I would encourage you to consider another point of view . . . *my* point of view. You will speculate more on what *I* intend to do, on what *this* army intends to do. Am I clear?"

There was a silent moment, firelight reflecting on the quiet faces.

He put the cigar in his mouth, moved back to his stump and sat down. The faces still watched him, and there was still no sound. He was suddenly exhausted, thought, I do not like making speeches.

The silence was broken by Meade, his voice echoing over the camp. "Anyone who does not have business here is dismissed!"

Men began to move away. Grant could see the fires clearly now, saw Meade looking at him, and Meade nodded grimly, lifted the hat slightly, moved away to his own camp.

Grant looked down, kicked through the wood shavings, saw nothing large enough to attack with the knife. He stood, moved to his tent, thought of Longstreet, said to himself, I hope you are alive, Pete. But we're coming after you again.

MAY 7, 1864

BREAKFAST WAS OVER, AND HE HAD BEEN THE FIRST TO FINISH, walking away from the tents into bright morning sun, the mist already burning away. He still enjoyed the sour taste in his mouth, rolled his tongue around, the first cigar of the day would wait a few more minutes. He had secured a box of cucumbers, and no one gave much thought to the request. The staff was always alert for the possibility of eggs, or even white flour, and the quartermasters would do what they could to accommodate them, would furnish whatever could be had for the commanding general, but the staff never revealed that the luxuries were not for Grant, but for them. He was quite happy with the cucumbers.

They had watched him in silence, slicing it into a mound of neat green circles, then pouring the vinegar over the top. Quickly, he would eat the small feast, and while the others enjoyed the smells, the roasting of bacon, the hot bread, his breakfast was done.

There had been no sounds from the front. No assault came from Ewell, and below there was no faint thunder from in front of Hancock. He knew the skirmish lines were strong, had moved out as far as they could, and the enemy was hard behind his works. To the north, Sedgwick's lines had been adjusted, pulled back slightly, turned to the right. Now a squad of cavalry patrolled up toward the river. There would be no more surprises from that part of the field.

He moved down the hill, could see a long line of wagons behind the camp, the wagons that many had said were captured, Lee's phantom success from the night before.

He was feeling restless, but better than he had since the fight began. He had actually slept, deep and long, dreams of Julia, the children. He'd woken with the bugle, jarred out of some wonderful memory, childhood, very small, riding a horse down the long narrow roads of home. It was the most comforting memory he had, being so very alone, except for the horse. He did not have many friends, had always been shy around the other boys, but after a time, when he'd learned to ride, the people in the small town had come to know him. He had an instinct, a skill for breaking the wild horses, a small boy on a great dangerous animal, holding tight and letting the horse lash out with all its anger. He would feel the horse testing him, would speak to it, and soon the animal would change. The boy could hand the reins to its astonished owner, but the boy would know the horse had no owner, and he always believed the horse knew that as well.

When he was older, at the Point, it was not his quick wit, dry humor, or skill with the lessons that made him friends, but his ability to ride. They had always thought of him as a natural for the dragoons, the cavalry, but he did not have the grades, could not choose where he would serve. The system did not reward the skill of the cadet, just the standing in the class, and his was of no distinction.

He kicked down the hill, through thick grass, and there was a sudden violent flutter, an explosion of small wings. A covey of quail blew up around him, flew away into the trees below. He felt his heart beating, laughed, heard a voice behind him.

"Where's your shotgun, General?"

He turned, still smiled, saw the bulky figure of Elihu Washburne stepping carefully down toward him, the dark formal suit out of place on a grassy hillside.

"It wouldn't matter. I wouldn't hit them anyway."

Washburne reached him, was breathing heavily. He was a large round man with long white hair streaming back from a high, broad forehead. He put a hand on Grant's shoulder, laughed through the heavy breaths, said, "No, I never knew you to show much inclination to hunt. However, your secret is safe with me."

Grant was puzzled. "Secret . . . ?"

"Your dismal marksmanship. If the men knew, might not be good for morale." Washburne laughed again, and Grant smiled.

He had asked Washburne to come along, to travel with the army on the move south and leave behind the dusty walls of the capitol. Washburne had been a congressman from Illinois for years, and it was Washburne who had seen something in this young man that the state of Illinois had sorely needed. When the regiments were organized, the first response to Lincoln's call for volunteers, there had been no one else around Galena qualified to command, to put the regiments together.

Washburne had only known him from those weeks before the real fighting began, had met him the same time as Rawlins met him. Grant's only importance to the people of Galena was that he had been in the Mexican War, but there was celebrity in that. Rawlins was consumed by the romance of it, had come to Grant with boyish enthusiasm, wanting to hear the stories, the exploits, but Washburne had seen much more. He had an instinct for character, saw beyond the shy seriousness, believed that Grant was a man who could give something to his country beyond service in a war that had long faded in importance.

When Washburne took Grant to Governor Yates, Grant had made no great impression, had left the meeting feeling there was no place for him in the *new* army. But there were sharp words behind closed doors, and the strength of Washburne's influence gave Grant his first regimental command.

It was unusual for Grant to warm up to a politician, but there was a connection between them that Grant still did not understand. Washburne was so very different from Grant's father, had seen the world, understood the great complexities of government, of power. Around Washburne, Grant spoke openly, something he did with no one else. He was the one man Grant could feel comfortable letting down the barriers that held away the old enemies, the frailties, the personal failures that no one in that camp could ever be aware of.

As the war spread, and Grant was far removed from the eyes of Washington, it was Washburne who kept his name on the desks of the important, and when the time finally came, when Lincoln made the choice of a commander for the luckless army, Congressman Washburne was given the honor of officially nominating his friend Grant for the new rank of Lieutenant General.

Washburne glanced up at the sun rising above the trees, said, "Anything going to happen today? People seem pretty relaxed."

"Not likely. Lee is back where he can do the most good, behind his works. He *wants* us to come at him now. He's been bloodied pretty bad. He doesn't want many more days like yesterday."

Washburne crossed his arms, glanced up toward the tents, said, "Do we? I hear . . . they hurt us pretty badly too."

Grant said nothing, looked at the ground. He pulled a cigar out, lit it, felt the heat swirl around his face, said, "We can afford it. Lee can't. He knows that."

"I'm not sure of that, my friend. The newspapers want numbers, and we can't give them these kind of numbers. The people won't stand for it. Mr. Lincoln wants to be reelected."

Grant looked at Washburne, seemed surprised. "Reelected . . ." The word struck him. He thought about that, had not considered . . . November. "I suppose that's true."

He stepped through the grass, slowly, felt his way along the side of the hill. Washburne moved beside him, shaky, uncertain steps.

Grant looked at Washburne's shoes. "Need to get you some boots."

Washburne laughed, said, "Boots today, then a uniform tomorrow?" Grant smiled, and Washburne said, "No, I suppose not. One thing you don't need is another politician."

There was a brief rumble, from over the hill. Washburne stopped, looked that way. "Something? Artillery?"

Grant did not look up, said, "One gun, somebody saw a ghost."

Washburne nodded. "A lot of ghosts out there. Some people say Lee's a ghost, everywhere at once, sees everything you do."

Grant looked at the cigar, tossed it aside. "Not anymore. Right now . . . he's expecting us to run away. We have always run away like a whipped colt, run until we're too tired to run anymore."

Washburne was serious now, glanced again at the camp, saw a few faces watching them from a distance, lowered his voice. "Did we lose this fight? Forgive me, General, but the word is Hancock got pretty badly hurt. . . ."

Grant nodded. "Hancock hurt them first, drove Hill's corps right out of these woods. This ground . . . you can't push out so far when you can't see. Lee was lucky, hit us with Longstreet when we were the most vulnerable. Hancock understood how it happened, said he was rolled up like a wet blanket. But Lee couldn't finish the job, didn't have the strength. Like last night—a good plan, they hit Sedgwick where he was vulnerable. But they didn't have the power to hurt us, to *really* hurt us. If Lee does not understand that now, he will very soon. Everywhere we go, he has to follow. Anytime we stop, he will either fight or lose more ground. But it will not happen here. We have done all we can do here. He is in command of the ground. If that means he won this fight, fine. It doesn't really matter. We'll make another fight. He'll have to win that one too. I don't think . . . he can keep winning with what he has left."

Washburne nodded, said, "Just remember the newspapers, the politicians. You see this fight differently than they do. If you admit you lost here, that is all that will matter. Another victory for Lee. You have to anticipate that, face the consequences."

Grant reached for another cigar, stopped, looked at Washburne. "The President told me I would be left alone."

"*He* will leave you alone. But after November . . ."

Grant thought of the politicians, all the reasons why he would never stay in Washington. He felt a sudden anger, said, "There will be no retreat, we will keep this army moving, we will force Lee to come to *us*. We already control the Mississippi, the seaports. If he does not fight us, we will capture his cities, burn his supplies, and destroy his railroads."

Washburne looked down, said, "But . . . what about Davis, and Richmond? If we focus on Lee, that is just one part of the whole. The Confederacy, the rebellion, starts with Jefferson Davis."

Grant looked at Washburne, slowly shook his head. "No, sir. Those men over there, those so-called soldiers of the rebellion, they are not dying for a government in Richmond. They do not charge into our guns screaming the name of Jefferson Davis. They are fighting for *Lee*. Lee *is* the rebellion. If he is defeated, if his army surrenders, then make no mistake, this war is over."

There was another thunderous sound, above the camp, another big gun. Grant looked that way, said, "Richmond serves one purpose. Lee must defend it. If we threaten the city, he will have to confront us. Lee will soon learn . . . we are not going away. If the newspapers and all those people in Washington must hear that, fine, I will write it down, send a letter to Stanton. You can deliver it yourself, read it to him, to all of them, make them understand what we are going to do. If it takes all summer . . . if it takes all year . . . it is only a matter of time before *General Lee* must face the consequences."

EVENING, MAY 7, 1864

ALL DAY LONG THE SKIRMISHERS AND SHARPSHOOTERS FROM both sides prodded and punched the nervous lines of their enemy. Observers were sent out, the deadly job of moving forward until they could actually see them, count the numbers, make sure the strong lines still lay in place.

By late afternoon the Federal wounded had been sent east, a long line of wagons rocking painfully toward Fredericksburg. Now the rest of the wagons, the food and ammunition, began to move, and for a time they moved east as well, but then, once the sounds of creaking wheels and bouncing timbers were beyond the hearing of Lee's lookouts, the wagons began to turn south.

The soldiers lined up as they always had, filled the road with quiet curses, the units smaller now, the lines shorter from the casualties they would leave behind. The officers tried to keep them quiet, but the grumbling was always there, rolled along the column like a dull wave. Much of it was about Grant. They were still not convinced, the great reputation had not shown them much in this place. Lee was still over there, the war was no different yet. But when the orders came to move, and the column began to ease ahead, some of the men did not need the sun to tell them direction. The word began to filter down the lines, and the grumbling stopped, there was something new about this march, something these men had never been a part of before. If the fight in the Wilderness had not gone their way—the most optimistic called it a draw—they were not doing what this army had always done before, they were not going back above the river. If they had never said much about Grant, had never thought him any different from the ones who had come before, if they had become so used to the steady parade of failure, this time there was a difference. Some wanted to cheer, but were hushed by nervous officers. So along the dusty roads hats went up and muskets were held high, a silent salute to this new commander. This time, they were marching *south*.

Well after dark, Sedgwick had pulled away from Ewell, moved back to Chancellorsville, then turned southward. Burnside followed him, taking the same route. Behind Hancock's wary troops, on the Brock Road, Warren's Fifth Corps marched quietly, and only when Warren was safely past did Hancock order his men to fall into column, away from the safety of their log wall. They would march all night, keeping tight and in line, because on the march they would be vulnerable.

Meade had given orders to the cavalry to clear the roads south, and Sheridan had sent the horsemen forward as though the job was already accomplished. But Stuart was waiting, and below the marching columns of infantry, the cavalry ran into a hard stiff wall of gray. By morning the roads were still not clear, the infantry had to slow, began bunching up, the commanders impatient with the unexplainable delay. When Stuart began finally to give way, Sheridan's troopers found themselves confronted not by a reserve force of cavalry, but by infantry. Lee had marched south as well, and if the Federals even knew they were in a race, by the next morning they knew they had lost.

The ground was much better here, the dense brush of the Wilderness fading into farm country, cut by small rivers and patches of heavy woods. Grant's objective had been to move well into the open ground. The maps showed a key intersection, convenient roads spreading to the east and south. But when the infantry could finally advance, they found what the cavalry already knew. Along the wide ridges, behind the heavy fence rows, the men in gray were preparing again, shovels and axes and bayonets throwing and pushing the dirt, cut trees piled high to their front. They formed their lines in an arc, just north of the intersection, a small village known mainly for the one landmark, the courthouse. It was called Spotsylvania.

17. LEE

May 9, 1864

He was up at three, had begun to make that his routine. He'd been awake even before that, staring up at the dark and thinking of Jackson. He had never understood how Jackson could come so completely awake after only a short rest, rising with perfect energy. Jackson would often call his men awake hours before the first light, order them up and into the roads before anyone could see what was in front of him. It had worked, of course, even the commanders did not need to know where they were going, something Dick Ewell had found maddening. Jackson never felt the need to tell anyone of his plans, just point them in the right direction, and soon a surprised enemy would find an unstoppable force bearing down on them from someplace where no one had ever thought the enemy would be. But Jackson himself, Lee thought, how could *he* do this, how could *he* go without sleep? Now the image was there, the sharp blue eyes, the image Lee tried not to see. God bless him, he thought. I really do miss him.

He had dressed quietly, and now walked out past the tents, would not even disturb Traveller. He stepped through a small patch of woods, could hear the sounds in front of him, the shovels. The men were working in shifts, and when one group would rest, the shovels would pass to another, and with each hour the entrenchments were stronger.

Jackson would not have done this, he thought. He would not have stopped, dug in to these long lines. The idea had come from Longstreet, and it was the fundamental difference between the two men. Jackson would have them on the road now, or be pressing them through a faint trail in the woods to strike the enemy with deadly surprise. No, Lee thought, something is very different now. The commanders, certainly, on both sides. Jackson had never faced Grant. Lee had wondered about that, especially since Gordon's flank attack on the Federal right, too weak, had begun too late. Jackson would have seen the opportunity immediately, would have stripped his lines bare, sent a great smashing blow around Sedgwick. Lee was certain of that, felt it rise up from some dark hole inside of him.

Ewell could not see that, would not act, would wait for orders. How much longer can Ewell command? he wondered. He is collapsing, not in battle, not in one great disaster, but slowly, a bit each day, becoming weaker in his mind, his resolve crumbling, falling away.

There was another kind of collapse with Hill, but the decay of that command was different. Hill could still perform with the old energy, move his troops with precision, with instinct, but then he would be gone, the sickness would simply swallow him up, and he would sit in his camp completely out of touch, no sense of a plan, his mind completely empty. Lee did not yet understand that, but had seen it with perfect clarity in the Wilderness. The first day, Hill had been perfection, but by the desperate fight on the second day, he was not even on the field. Now the sickness had grown, and Hill was out again, and Lee thought, Will he ever be back?

It was a possibility he could not afford to ignore, and so he had given command of Hill's Third Corps to Jubal Early. He knew how the men felt about Early, especially the officers, but Early was a fighter, and if his personality made quick enemies, he at least knew how to move troops. Hill accepted the change with dignity. Even he knew Lee had no choice. Early's removal from Ewell had created an opening in the Second Corps. Lee quickly promoted John Gordon to command of Early's division.

It had been an easy decision. Lee had felt some of the old enthusiasm, the confidence a commander has when he knows the army is in good hands, that the job will be done. Even though Gordon was not a West Pointer, he had already shown a talent for command and an instinct for strategy. Lee had not felt that way about anyone in a long time, except Stuart. And Longstreet.

The doctors had assured him the wounds were not fatal. Longstreet was far away now, and it would be a long time before he could return to the army, an army that could not afford to be without him. Even with all the criticism of Longstreet, the newspapers, talk of controversy and blame, there was no one Lee would rather confide in, no one with whom he felt comfortable sharing the quiet thoughts, the quiet moments. Now there was no one else.

Dick Anderson now commanded the First Corps, and if the choice had inspired no one, not even Lee, Anderson at least was dependable. Though he'd never shown anything like Jackson's fire or the rugged stubbornness of Longstreet, he had performed with the best skills of both men the day before. It was Anderson who had won the race for Spotsylvania.

Lee moved out of the patch of trees, could see the men outlined against the night sky. The dirt was flying, around him the sound of axes echoing in the woods. He saw logs, carried forward on the shoulders of tired men. The works were becoming a vast long wall, a deep trench behind, a wide ditch in front, sharpened poles and branches pointing out toward the enemy.

He walked down to the left, passed behind long lines of laboring men, and no one saw him, there were no calls, no cheers. He began to climb, a long rise, a wide hill, paused, thought of the name. They called it Laurel Hill, and now it was a great stronghold. Porter Alexander's big guns were dug in facing north and west, the crews moving slowly in the dark, the quiet work of good men, men who know how deadly

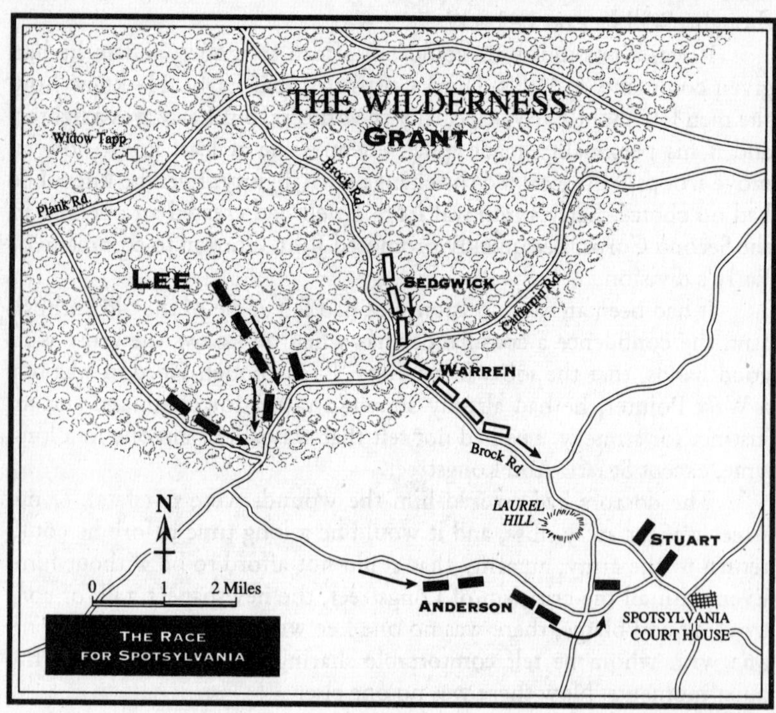

their work could be. There were deep entrenchments here as well; Anderson had the gun positions well protected by infantry. Lee nodded, thought, Nothing will move us from *this* ground.

He began to walk back toward his camp, stopped, looked back up the rise, thought of the words again. *Nothing will move us from this ground.* There was no change greater than that, he thought. Something tugged in his gut, and he was suddenly anxious, angry. Longstreet had always believed in trenches, in hiding behind strong works. But when we won the great battles, he thought, it was because we *attacked.* Longstreet had always argued against that, and there had been Jackson to show him he was wrong. But the men . . . it was the men who began to understand. Lee thought of West Point. We learned how to fight the old way, the books were all about Napoleon, the textbooks translated from the French. But Napoleon did not have these guns. It has taken us too long to learn the lesson. Too many times we have ridden across the bloody fields, spread with the incredible horror of what these guns can do. Longstreet gave them shovels, at Fredericksburg, on the heights, and they laughed, the men thought it was not . . . *manly.* We would stand up and face the guns. Lee shook his head. Now we do not have enough shovels. No one believes in standing up in front of certain death. There is no honor in foolishness.

He could see the tents now, daylight slowly spreading over the rolling ground toward his right flank, where Early was digging his trenches as well. He thought of Grant: We gave him no reason to retreat. Some had said Grant would move away, to Fredericksburg, toward the Rappahannock, running away from his first bloody fight with Lee's army. The rumors spread from the lookouts, excited men who came to Lee with the first reports of troop movement, clouds of dust rising from long lines of black cannon. But Lee had seen the maps, knew that the roads to Richmond came right through . . . *here.* If Grant wants Richmond, he must fight his way through these works, he thought. We must sit and wait. And if he does not come at us here, then we must find his weakness, again, we must strike out at opportunity and we must not be late or make any mistakes. He thought of the commanders again, and the tight tug in his gut returned.

None of them would talk about it, there was no hint of it even from the trenches, from the men on the front line, the men who could *see* the strength of the blue lines in front of them. But it was inside of *him* now, stirring deep in some very small place. *It is only a matter of time.* He had sent that to Davis, a response to the threat from Butler, moving up the peninsula now. The message had been clear and blunt:

Make preparations to protect Richmond, bring troops to protect the rail center at Petersburg. Davis was still seeing the army as some great organizational puzzle, departments to be moved about and manipulated. There were good defenses around Richmond, but Davis was still convinced there must be a presence at all the major points, and even minor ones, anyplace the enemy was a threat. Troops were still scattered down through the Carolinas, a weak attempt at containing a Federal threat that was as much in Davis's mind as it was in the field. But Lee's message did stir something in Richmond, because, finally, Beauregard was moving troops north, from his base in North Carolina. The movement was slow, and the troops very few. Lee had been amazed at that, felt the gut-twisting frustration that no one else seemed to share his concern for the value of Petersburg.

He knew, of course, that Davis would send few reinforcements to him. He had accepted for weeks that he would have to make the fight against Grant with whatever he had. That made the trenches, the defensive tactics, an absolute necessity, because there was nothing he could do about Grant's vastly greater numbers. But it is more than numbers, he thought. It has *always* been more than numbers. Every victory had come against superior forces. The advantage was strategy, tactics, the willingness to do what must be done to win the fight. The Federal commanders had never brought that to the field. And so he had always felt he had the edge, knew that Jackson would devour an enemy many times his size by sheer audacity.

Longstreet could be as stubborn and as vigilant as anyone those other fellows put in line against him. Even Longstreet's "slows," his seemingly sluggish movement, had been positive. Lee had thought Longstreet dangerously slow at Second Manassas, but he had not ordered Longstreet to advance, had relied on Longstreet's judgment, and when the First Corps finally moved, they drove Pope's army into complete chaos. Now, in the fight just past, Lee had to believe that if Longstreet had been in place when he wanted him, if he'd been in line against Hancock's attack, it might have been disastrous. He knew Hancock was the best they had, and his strength might have driven Longstreet back as it had Hill. Longstreet's "delay" in reaching the field might have been the one reason why Hancock collapsed. The timing, ultimately, had been perfect.

He felt the tug in his gut again, thought, If it is that, the intangible, something inside of us, something *they* do not have, then what have we lost? Who is it that I can trust to take a fight to the great numbers, and who will prevail? The name burned in his mind, the laughing face, the red beard, the ridiculous hat. Of course, he thought . . . Stuart. He smiled, nodded to himself. Yes, we still have that, *his* spirit is still in these men, and they will still look to him. He has learned along with the rest of us, he has made mistakes and gained the experience, and with that comes our ability to win this fight, *still* win this fight. But the others . . . there must still be time, they must learn. They may all rise to it, men like Gordon, Anderson, Early, but we may not have much time. And so I must do *this*, check the lines, I must be closer. I must watch over them all. I must make sure there are *no* mistakes.

He could see the staff now, moving around the small fire, and he moved toward the wagons where the food would be, felt himself sweating, his breathing short and hard. He glanced at his tent, thought of the small bed, felt the weariness crawling over him, settling down into the turmoil of his gut. He took a deep breath, tried to hold himself together, tightened the grip inside, said aloud, "No."

Faces turned toward him, but he did not see them, was staring out toward the gray light rising over the far trees, thought of Grant. Now there is *another* change. So now there will not be much sleep.

18. GRANT

May 9, 1864

THEY CALLED HIM "UNCLE JOHN," AND THERE WERE FEW IN THIS army who had earned as much respect from their troops as Sedgwick. If he had not shown the kind of heroism that made newspapermen happy, he had always been a solid commander, had led troops since the beginning of the war, and commanded the Sixth Corps since Chancellorsville. He was older than most, had come out of the Point in 1837, the same year as Jubal Early. A New Englander by birth, he carried none of the trappings of the "easterner," and many could not believe this rugged man was from New England. There was too much of the western frontier in him, the sharp eye of a man who has fought the Indian, the rugged exterior of a man who understands trickery, who understands his enemy.

He had served in Mexico, after winning a fighter's reputation in the first Seminole Wars. Afterward, in an army that lost many of its best men to the tedium of the frontier, Sedgwick had thrived, fought Indians wherever the action was hot, served in Utah and then Bloody Kansas, when the army found itself in the center of the worst kind of violence, citizens fighting each other over the question of slavery.

He could be gruff and profane, but the men loved him because he was efficient, because he knew how to place his troops where they would do the most good, with the least harm. He'd been up front again this morning, correcting one officer's mistake, adjusting lines of infantry that had dug in too close to the mouths of their own big guns. The men on the front lines had become wary of the rebel sharpshooters, stayed low, flinching from the small bits of lead whistling overhead, sent at them from a hidden enemy very far away. Sedgwick had laughed at them, teased one man in particular, a sergeant, who was curled into a ball on the ground. Sedgwick had stood straight, gazing out across the open ground to far trees, the cover of those men with the long rifles, was still laughing when the bullet struck him, below the eye, spun him around and dropped him onto the sergeant who still crouched low beside him.

PORTER WAS SHAKING, AND GRANT WAITED, COULD SEE IT IN THE man's face, stung with the terrible news.

"Sir, yes, General Sedgwick was killed . . . just a few minutes ago. They're bringing the body back now."

Grant stared at the young man, said nothing. He held the cigar in his hand, looked at it, watched the ash fall to the ground, looked at Porter again, said, "Are you certain? Is he really . . . dead?" He stood, walked toward the tent, felt himself weaken, draining of energy. This is a disaster, he thought, worse than the loss of a division. He pictured Sedgwick's face, the large heavy man, handsome, graying beard. How does that happen, one man . . . just taken away? He looked back at Porter again, said, "Is he really dead, Colonel? Are you *certain*?"

Porter nodded quietly.

Grant moved into the tent, sat down on the hard bed, stared at nothing. He thought, We should tell Meade . . . but of course, Meade would know. And Meade would have to choose someone to replace him, someone to command a very good corps. There were not many good commanders to choose from.

He had hoped to hit Lee hard this morning, but the army was still moving in slow steps, cautious and clumsy. Meade wanted to assault the flanks, had sent Hancock to the west, into a ragged terrain of woods and water, while Burnside would try to move east and attack what should be an exposed flank. But nothing was happening, there was no coordination, and Grant was understanding finally why for three years this army had not won its fights.

He had watched Meade carefully, knew that Meade was still edgy about his job, still carried the insecurity that it would take only one sharp moment, one episode when Grant lost his temper, and he would be gone. Grant knew Meade was not very happy being so close to the eye of his commander, but he had not wanted Meade removed for he knew that Meade still knew his own army better than he did. If Grant had once thought that unimportant, now, at this moment, realizing the Sixth Corps needed a new commander, he understood why Meade had to remain. But there was still frustration, and he thought, I cannot get him to understand, if we are to make a mistake, let it be because we moved too quickly, not too slowly. He thought of Sheridan, and knew the two men had not gotten along, not at all, two men with strong egos and very different ways of thinking. The staff had told him this morning that Sheridan was meeting with Meade, that the staffs had gathered at a respectful distance while a violent argument boiled out of Meade's tent. He knew that if they did not come to some agreement, if Meade was stubborn enough to stick to his old ways and did not share Sheridan's understanding of cavalry tactics, he would hear about it, would have to settle it himself. He felt suddenly anxious, frustrated, tossed the stump of a cigar out through the tent flaps. Lee is right out there, waiting for us, he thought. He can move faster, because he has fewer troops to move, fewer wagons, fewer guns. All the things that give us the advantage also slow us down. And he has fewer commanders, he has control of his army. It seems . . . that I do not.

Burnside had still not moved into position, the assault on Lee's right flank delayed, the only sounds the small rattle of skirmishing. I cannot just . . . relieve everyone who doesn't perform to my standards, he thought. I cannot put colonels into command of divisions, and I cannot command the corps myself.

He moved back outside, saw Porter still standing by his small table, waiting for him, waiting for instructions. Along the road he could see wagons moving in both directions, some filled with wounded men from the fights exploding along the front lines, the uncoordinated bursts of activity. He saw one flag, the St. Andrew's cross, the flag of the Sixth, men gathered around, some hearing the awful news for the first time. He could see the looks on the faces, the shock, could hear the sounds now, one man sobbing out loud. This will take something away from them, he thought. For a while, at least, they will not fight the same way.

Lee lost Jackson, and then lost Gettysburg. But we will not lose here, not on this ground, not with these men. Every time we go at him, every good fight, even on those days when it is very bad, we bring something away, we add that to who we are, and we become better, stronger. There is something in the men who are veterans . . . they *know* they are veterans, they have seen the worst of it, some have seen the worst of themselves. Even if they have endured bad commanders, have endured defeat by an enemy none thought would be so strong or so well commanded, we are still better equipped, and by now we are better prepared.

He thought of the chessboard again. If Lee is faster, more compact, we still have the power, and we will just keep at him. If he keeps moving south, we will follow him south, and very soon he will run out of places to go. But for now he is right out there, and maybe today, or tomorrow . . . he glanced at the sky, the bright sun. The weather is ours, but the longer we delay . . .

He moved toward Porter, said, "Colonel, go to General Meade. Ask him if he has chosen a replacement for General Sedgwick."

HE HEARD MEADE FIRST, THE BOOMING ANGRY VOICE, HAD grown used to it, the voice that seemed to carry over the entire field. Usually it was aimed at a staff officer, often an innocent man who happened to bring the wrong piece of information, something Meade might not want to hear. But the voice was coming closer, and Grant sat up on his bed, wiped his face with his hand, heard another voice now, a high pitch, clear anger. It was Sheridan.

He tried to clear his head, had told Rawlins he would take a short rest, had not expected to fall asleep. He still sat on the bed, waited, listened, and the voices were close, grew quiet, small low comments, like two angry children coming to Papa, both of them right, both of them wrong.

It was Rawlins, the face appearing between the tent flaps. "Sir, forgive the interruption to your rest. We have visitors."

Grant motioned with his hand, a small wave. "Be right out. Tell them not to kill each other before I get there."

Rawlins looked at him with wide eyes, said, "I don't think it has come to that. . . ." He glanced back, then looked inside again, whispered, "But it would be advisable, sir, if you were to make haste."

Grant pulled on his boots, and Rawlins held the flap back, stood stiffly as Grant moved past. He squinted at the sunlight, saw the two men standing formally at attention, waiting for him. He reached into his pocket, felt for a cigar, but the pocket was empty. He sagged, thought, Worse yet, I am unarmed. He said, "Well, gentlemen, are we feeling the full effects of this awful day?"

Neither man spoke, glanced at each other, then Meade nodded, said, "Yes, sir. It is an awful day indeed. John Sedgwick was much loved. There is a gloom throughout the Sixth Corps, if not the whole army."

Grant nodded, and Sheridan said, "Yes, gloom. Now, sir, allow me to address you directly, if that is permissible. I do not wish to offend the chain of command." There was sarcasm in Sheridan's voice.

Grant took a deep breath, said, "You may proceed, General."

Sheridan stepped forward, his face began to flash fire, and he removed his hat, held it tightly, said, "General Grant, it is my contention that this army has been habitually misusing its cavalry. General Meade and I have quite different viewpoints with regard to the function of the horsemen. I have tried to convince General Meade that we should not be assigned such mundane tasks as guarding wagons and scouting the countryside for the general's dinner!"

Grant looked at Meade, saw the eyes expand, waited for the coming explosion.

"Dinner! I have never suggested . . . ! General, this is outrageous!" Meade puffed, removed his hat, his fist curling the brim hard in his hand. Grant raised his hand, calming, thought, No, General, don't hit him with the hat.

"Gentlemen, I have no time for this. I would like to hear something more specific, from both of you. General Sheridan, if you don't feel the cavalry is being used properly, then give me an alternative. What would be *your* strategy?"

Sheridan nodded, was clearly prepared for this moment, said in a quiet voice, "Sir, from everything I have heard, this army's cavalry has, more often than not, been turned about, confused and left highly embarrassed by the skill of the enemy in general, and Stuart in particular. From what I understand of your overall plan, sir, we are to pursue General Lee's army until we can draw him into a fight. If you will allow, I would like the same opportunity. I propose to take this army's cavalry and, instead of raiding supply depots and vandalizing railroad tracks, I would like to pursue General Stuart. If given a free hand . . ." He glanced at Meade. "If given a free hand, I will *whip* General Stuart." Sheridan put his hat on, a final punctuation mark.

Grant looked at Meade, said, "General?"

Meade glanced at Sheridan, put his hat on as well, said, "He will leave us blind. We cannot maneuver this army in the enemy's country without the use of cavalry."

Sheridan turned, said, "General, you have not allowed me to maneuver at all! You counter my orders, you place my men without consulting me . . ."

Grant felt a small headache blooming, reached again, felt the inside of the empty pocket, said, "That's it, gentlemen. General Meade, if General Sheridan says he can whip Stuart, then we should let him. If we destroy the enemy's cavalry, we will have gained an advantage that may hasten the end of the war."

Sheridan beamed a smile, saluted Grant, said, "Sir, we will move immediately! I will send regular reports."

"Send them to General Meade. You are dismissed."

Sheridan spun, moved away, began to shout instructions to his staff. Grant looked at Meade, who stared down at the ground like a scolded puppy. Grant said, "General, we must take risks. We *know* where Lee is, and for now, the cavalry's eyes are not as important as what he may be able to accomplish." He paused. "Do we have a replacement for General Sedgwick?"

Meade looked up, nodded. "Yes, sir. It was a bit of a problem . . . General Ricketts was next in line by rank. But it was always Sedgwick's preference that Horatio Wright succeed him, in the event . . . He will be adequate to the task. The men will accept him, I believe."

Grant nodded, thought of Wright, had known him in the West, a good engineer, had commanded in Ohio briefly. "Fine. I will send his name to Washington. Is that all for now, General?"

Meade nodded, saluted. Grant returned it, and Meade moved away. Grant watched him, felt the headache again, moved toward the tent, and Rawlins appeared, rushed in front, lifted the flap. Grant looked at him, said, "Colonel, you will do me a great service if in the future, before we deal with these people, you remind me not to forget my cigars."

MAY 10, 1864

HE HAD BELIEVED THE ARMY WAS READY, HAD THOUGHT THEY would begin a general assault all along Lee's lines. Burnside was on the left, and if Lee had strengthened his flank, Grant knew Burnside had the numbers. The ground was not difficult, there was no anchor to protect the rebels from being swept away by the three large divisions that Burnside could push forward. On the right, Hancock was still finding rough going, his forces spread over a deep creek, movement hampered by woods and the guns of Lee's left. Grant knew that Lee was responding to the threats to both his flanks, and so it was likely Lee's center had been weakened. There was still Laurel Hill of course, with the mass of big guns that commanded much of the field, but a quick strike, a hard cutting blow to the center, could break Lee's army in half. Both the Fifth and Sixth Corps were in position, and even some of Hancock's people could shift to the left and add to the strength. All they would require was a first wave, one spearhead, to make a quick thrust at Lee's position, break through, and then the vast numbers from the two corps could rush up support. By dark it could be over. The two halves of Lee's army could be rolled up in two neat packages, or at worst, Lee would be gone, a headlong rush southward toward safer ground, a confused and panicked retreat.

The plan came from one young man, Emory Upton, ambitious, egotistical, with a good eye for tactics and a good eye on his own reputation. He was not popular with his troops, commanded a brigade with his focus clearly on a greater responsibility. But if his men had no particular regard for their colonel, the commanders above had great respect for his plan.

The attack would be Upton's brigade, reinforced by four additional regiments from the Sixth Corps. Upton was explicit in his orders: there would be no firing, no stopping to shoot at the strong log works of the rebels. They would move quickly across the open ground, a tight spearhead, punching across the rebel line in one small break. Once beyond, the break would be widened, and Upton would be reinforced. Support would come first from another brigade to his left, and then, all along the front, a general assault that would prevent Lee from shifting troops to the damaged center.

The attack began with the same hopeful optimism this army had seen too many times before, and it was a failure from the first command. The troops assigned to support Upton's men were not in place. Farther along the line, the Fifth Corps faced Laurel Hill, and the men there had no enthusiasm for assaulting a nearly impossible position. Hancock's Second Corps was divided, still fumbling through the confusion on the right. Burnside was in the best position on the field, could have moved at any time toward a weak defense, a defense that was weaker still because Lee had pulled troops away, strengthening the rest of the line, something no one on the Federal side knew.

Upton's men did exactly as he had planned, ran across the deadly open field, leaping up and over the rebel trenches. The fight lasted an hour. Behind him, Upton saw the open field empty of the vast support he was to have received, empty except for the scattered bodies of his own men.

GRANT LOOKED AT THE MAP AGAIN, RAN HIS FINGER ALONG THE curving arc of Lee's lines. He made a fist, wanted to pound the table, shatter it into pieces, held his hand tight above the map, took a deep breath, let it go. He stood straight, looked at the faces watching him. No one spoke. He caught the eyes of each man, slowly, moved his stare through the group. Some returned the look, some looked away, and he thought, Yes, they know . . . the ones who will not look me in the eye, they know who carries the blame.

Most of them were there, the commanders who had failed their men. He still stared at them, and the silence lasted for a full minute, then two. He saw fidgeting now, saw Rawlins, standing to one side, nervous, shifting his weight.

"What is it, Colonel? You have something to say?"

Rawlins turned pale, hesitated, then said, "Uh . . . sir, do you have any orders?"

Grant looked back toward the assembled group, the firelight now reflecting off the polished brass, the gold braid decorating the sagging shoulders. He glanced at Rawlins, thought, They should stand here all night. He looked briefly at Horatio Wright, his first day in corps command, saw Meade, moving slowly forward, preparing for Grant's verbal assault. There were others, men who had come to headquarters with their commanders, a few Grant did not know. He glanced at the faces, said, "Any of you . . . Colonel Upton?"

There was a silent pause, and Wright stepped forward. "General, Colonel Upton was wounded in the assault. He will survive, but he is at the corps hospital."

"Keep me advised, General. He's the only one of . . . *us* who did his job today." He reached for a cigar, the last one in his pocket, rolled it over in his hand, then lit it slowly.

Meade cleared his throat, said, "General, I will forward to you General Wright's official request for Colonel Upton's promotion to brigadier general. We all are aware, sir, that he performed an extraordinary task today."

Grant held the cigar tightly in his teeth, looked at Meade, said, "Fine." He stepped toward the fire, flicked an ash out into the flames. The others began to move closer behind him, still quiet. He looked at them again, said, "Gentlemen, what do we have to do? Is it . . . too many men? Do we simply have too many men to coordinate an attack? Is it the reports, our intelligence? I was told Lee was weak in his center, only his flanks were strong. I am safe in saying, gentlemen, that Lee was most definitely *not* weak in his center." He glanced around, knew already who was not there.

"I do not see General Burnside. Smart man." He thought, No, no personalities, don't single anyone out. No one is more at fault than I am.

Warren moved up to the fire now, a small, handsome man, always dapper, a wide gold sash across his waist. He said, "General Grant, perhaps we should have . . . discussed today's plan in detail . . . a council of war perhaps."

Grant pulled the cigar from his mouth, looked at Warren, was not surprised that this would come from him, the man whose attention to detail exceeded anyone's in the army.

"General Warren, councils of war do not *fight*. They allow disagreements of opinion to affect judgment. The council of war you should be concerned with is *this* one." He tapped the side of his head. "That seems to be a problem. My decisions do not seem to be reaching all of you with enough . . . authority. I had thought we had a plan today. If we had made a general assault, struck the flanks hard, then Colonel Upton's strike at the center could have been supported. Am I correct that Upton was successful?"

Meade said, "Yes, sir. Quite successful, sir. His men broke through the enemy's line, held a gap open for nearly an hour. There was . . . failure to exploit the success."

Wright glanced at Meade, said, "General, there was not time . . . there was poor communication. Colonel Upton's plan was precisely correct, sir. We . . . did not follow it up."

Grant moved through the men, a path opening in the gathering of blue coats. He moved toward his tent, felt the frustration building, muttered to himself, "No, we did not follow it up . . . not at all."

He stopped, turned, said, "What would you have me do about that? I could court-martial all of you, but someone would insist I be on that list as well. Fine. So we will move forward, move past this. This was a terrible day. I do not want to hear how much better we may have performed if John Sedgwick was here. He is not here, and I have confidence that General Wright can handle the job. *Learn* from this, gentlemen. If Colonel Upton's plan worked, then we will use that. If those damned fortifications over there can be broken, if one colonel can take one brigade across that field, then we should consider what an entire corps could do. I have no doubt that the enemy is still where we left him today. We have given him no reason whatsoever to change that. We *gave* him a victory today. If there was ever a day an army was not served by its command, this was it. Think about nothing else . . . think about the men we left out on that ground today. The opportunity is still there . . . *Lee* is still there, waiting for us. Next time, gentlemen, we will do it right!"

19. STUART

MAY 11, 1864

THE SCOUTS HAD REPORTED THAT SHERIDAN WAS MOVING south with nearly thirteen thousand horse soldiers, three times what Stuart could bring to the field. They were spread along the roads that led straight at the heart of Richmond, in a column over ten miles long.

He had ridden all night, rested now on the side of a wide hill. He lay flat in the thick grass, stared up at a cloudy sky, the clouds growing darker, rolling in from the west. He tried to focus, to concentrate on what would happen now, the fight with Sheridan's cavalry swelling up in front of him. But he stared far away into the dark sky and saw only the sad face of his wife, Flora's eyes still digging into him, a gloom from her that he had not expected.

He had seen her that morning, could not help himself. Flora and the children were close by, guests of an estate where they all had felt safe, far behind the lines, far from the threat of Grant's army. But Sheridan's advance had changed that, and Stuart would not let duty keep him away from his family. It had been inside of him for a while now, since the first fight at Spotsylvania. He would not talk about it, but everyone close to him knew the laughter, the swagger, was gone. The staff saw it as a new sense of danger, the focus on the new enemy, that Stuart, for all his arrogance and strut, would prove he was still the best cavalry officer of the war. Now the war was changing, and the men believed Stuart was changing with it, getting down to the serious business of dealing with a serious enemy.

He didn't know what the men were seeing, had thought he was the same. But if they saw the change, it was because he was feeling it deep inside, a small black hole spreading inside of him. He had thought, it is her, it is the children, I have not seen them in so long. But it was deeper than even that, of missing his children, of holding his wife tenderly against him. He only knew it was important to see them, to leave the men and the pursuit of the enemy for just a brief time. The staff understood, of course, no one would find fault with that.

The ride had been fast and short, and he rode hard into the lush green yard of the grand house, had called out, saw the children first, the yard filling with all the children in the house, joyous cries, rushing toward this grand soldier on the fine horse, gathering around him, touching the animal. Then he saw Flora, rushing onto the porch, down into the green of the rich yard, and the tears came from both of them. It was painfully quick, he did not even dismount the horse, something holding him away, pulling him back. They touched hands, he had leaned down and kissed her, looked for a long moment into her eyes, through the tears, then rode quickly away.

He had not looked back, now wished he had, wished he'd said more to the two children. Staring at the dark gray sky, he tried to see them. We should have time, he thought, the time to sit, talk with them, smile at the playful stories. He had never let that bother him before, the war was *his* playground. He'd always thought the time would come later, gathering around the great fireplace, the marvelous stories of his great and glorious battles. He always saw a future bright with the promise of a life for his children, a life in a new South, independent, prosperous. It had never occurred to him that they could lose the war, that God would allow him to go home in defeat. He stared at the motion, the rolling wave of thick clouds, thought, No, it will never be like that. I would rather be dead. . . .

His men were in dismal condition, had ridden hard and long to catch up to Sheridan's head start. The horses had not fared well through the winter, and every man had the responsibility to do the best he could with his mount, but the grain was scarce, and the horses had to subsist on worse than what the soldiers had. If the men accepted that there was not enough to eat, the horses showed the effects, the thin weakness of slow starvation. The spring had brought new growth to the open fields, and when the men rested now, the horses at least could graze, but it hadn't been enough, the stamina was not there, there was no time. During the night, they pushed the horses hard, there was no choice, and so today neither the mounts nor the men were in shape for a hard fight.

They had thought it obvious that Sheridan was making a strong raid into Richmond—it was the largest Federal cavalry force ever assembled in one column. Stuart divided his smaller forces, sent one thrust at Sheridan's rear guard again and again. But the attacks had no power, were only a minor annoyance, and they did not stop the great mass of blue from pushing south. Stuart had taken the bulk of his force on a parallel route, shorter, to strike at Sheridan's exposed flanks, to hit him from the side, hurt him enough to slow the column, make them turn back to confront the danger from Stuart's hard blow. It would keep Sheridan occupied so Richmond could prepare, give the defenders there the time to make ready.

They were north of Sheridan's path, above a crossroads named for a long-abandoned stage stop, Yellow Tavern, only six miles from the streets of Richmond. He had sent word to Davis, asking for help from the small infantry force that crouched in the defenses around the city. But there hadn't been time, and the defenders were watching the greater danger, to the east, where Butler's advancing army was plodding forward.

Sheridan was coming from the northwest, and Stuart spread his men along the best ground, along the crest of the rolling hillsides above the intersection. The men were in a strong line, along the ridges, waiting for the long blue column to pass below them on their way down to the city. If Davis had sent the infantry, they could have slowed Sheridan enough for Stuart to hit him hard, trapping Sheridan from two directions. It might have been the only way the smaller number could turn back the great blue force. But now he understood there would be no help, there would be no infantry, that what forces he had above Yellow Tavern would be all he could throw into the fight.

He could hear the musket fire now, the feeling out, scouts from both sides pressing into the other. He sat up, saw his staff watching him, following his lead, and quickly the men were moving to the horses, the short rest over.

He had never believed it would happen this way, that the glory of all he had done, the reputation and the victories, would be overshadowed, slowly erased by an evolution he could not predict. As badly as his horses had suffered, the Federal horses had grown fatter. As his men were beaten down by the lack of supplies, by the poor food, the enemy was stronger, their equipment better. He knew about the Spencer carbines, of course, the seven-shot short-barreled rifles the bluecoats were using. It was a sad joke, the men complaining that the Yankees could load on Monday and shoot at you every day of the week. His men still used single-shot carbines, and even when they captured the new weapons, there was no way to load them. The arms makers in the South did not have the ability to produce the new-sized cartridges. But he did not see the new weapons as a turning point, as something that would turn the fight against him.

The Federal commanders had never understood the tactics, never used their cavalry to any advantage, the greater numbers, the better horses. He thought of Sheridan again, had wondered if there was anything about this man that was different, if he would bring something new, any kind of challenge, something to bring the excitement back to the glorious fight. At Spotsylvania his men had endured the repeating rifles, the stronger horses, but still they kept the enemy away, held Sheridan back long enough for the infantry to hold the important ground. Now there was no infantry, no piece of ground to hold. This would be a fight between men, one man pressing forward, one man doing everything he could to turn him away.

He climbed the horse, patted the neck, and the staff waited for him to give the order. He stared out to the west, then to the south, could see small wisps of smoke rising from the woods, from the small skirmishes. He knew his men would be falling back, the feeling out would be over very soon, and Sheridan would resume the march, push his men forward in a clear open dash down the open roads to Richmond.

He thought of Sheridan, knew only what he'd heard, the small fiery man, full of hot words and reckless tactics. There *was* a difference in this man, something Stuart had not expected. He had become so used to the rest, Averill, Stoneman, Kilpatrick, men you never saw, who did not understand momentum, the value of quickness, control of the field. Stuart was used to having a fight go his way, as though he had orchestrated it, both sides, guiding the men into line, riding through the fight itself, feeling the rhythm of the battle, the momentum, the glorious action. Even if the fight was not perfect, if his men took the worst of it, there was something to be had from the fight itself, of pushing the horses across the dangerous ground, the screams, the thunderous sounds of the battle. It was the thing he lived for, the one thing about this war that made sense of the horror, of the loss of the men around him. That they would win, that his men would ultimately destroy the enemy, was never in doubt. If his men were ever unsure, all they would have to do was watch their commander, the wide cape, the plumed hat, riding through them with the sword high, yelling at them with all the fire in his soul. They would see it in his face, in his eyes, and would share the same fire, the spirit for the fight. It was *fun*.

He knew the change had come to him at Spotsylvania. The fight with Sheridan had been grim and desperate. The enemy had not run away, had been merely *held* away, a brutal fight for every foot of ground. He could not make the glorious rides, could not spend time in the rallying of his men, the playful shouts at the enemy. There had been no time for anything but the hard and deadly fight.

He knew how well that fight had gone, what an extraordinary day it had been. He'd seen it in Lee's face, the softness, the glint in the old man's eyes. He had learned that about Lee, long ago. You would not hear the words, Lee would not tell you if you did well, but there was no mistaking the look, the small quiet nod. Only once, the disastrous day at Gettysburg, had there been something else, the anger. Even then there was no scolding reproach, none of the loss of temper, the profane violence so common from men like Ewell. But Lee's words had been very clear. Stuart had taken that with him, carried it now always, had *never* felt anything like the shock of that, the horrible aching image of Lee's disappointment. It had brought him closer to the old man than even Lee had understood, and Stuart had made a vow to himself—there would never be any reason for Lee to be disappointed; he would never see that look on the old man's face again.

Far down the rise he could see men coming out of the far trees, his own men, moving back up to the strong lines. They had been on foot mostly, hidden in the thickness of the creek bottoms, picking at Sheridan's skirmishers through heavy trees. They'd done all they could, and now it would be up to the main body if Sheridan would be stopped here. He looked to the side, along the crest of the ridge, saw long lines of horsemen disappearing into a thick wood. He thought, Yes, we can move the flank down close to the road without being seen.

The staff was behind him now, and he turned, saw Venable, said, "Go . . . to the trees . . . tell them to watch their right. They should advance in the trees as far as they cannot be seen. Tell Wickham to move at his discretion." He knew those men well, his first command, the first Virginia regiments. He nodded, thought, Yes, they will know what to do.

He glanced at the sky, saw gray clouds turning darker still, heard a distant rumble. Along the line men began to talk, the tension slipping out of them, horses moving, the violent sound familiar. But he stared to the west, above the trees, saw the brief flash. It was not cannon, but lightning, thunder, a solid black wall moving toward them, a sharp wind whipping through the trees, blowing up and over the crest of the hill. He watched the swirling of the black clouds, saw shapes, like long dark fingers, a fist curling tightly, then dissolving, then another. He stared, had a sudden rush of energy. Yes, it is the hand of God. He is here!

From below, in the direction of the tavern, his men were still moving up the ridge, and now horsemen appeared, rode up toward him. He was still watching the violence of the storm above him, and the men came close and reined the horses, watching him.

One man saluted, said, "Sir, the enemy is stopping. They're forming on this side of the road. They are not moving past."

He looked past the man, down the wide hill, and now beyond a row of trees he saw movement, a heavy column of blue. They were forming into thick lines, facing the ridge where he sat. He heard thunder again, the wind whipped around him, nearly took his hat off, and he grabbed the hat, wanted to wave it high, to shout, the glorious call to the fight, the cheer that always filled his men with the bloody fire. But the sound did not come. He looked up again, to the solid black wall blowing over the trees, the rain now soaking his men down the line. Now he saw the enemy flags held stiffly by the wind, and behind, coming up the rise slowly, a vast line of blue crawling forward, moving straight at the crest of the ridge.

"Sir, they aren't moving south anymore. They are coming right at us!" Stuart glanced at the man, said nothing, still held the hat in his hand. The rain began to blow around them now, and he felt a sudden chill, as if pulled very far away, watching this unfold from some great distance.

The blue mass began to move up the rise, and now there was new thunder, the sound of big guns.

Down the hill the high screams began to streak overhead, whistling shot hurtling past him. He heard the voices of his men now, the rebel yell rising, spreading in a wave over the ridge. His men began to return the fire, the sharp rattle of the carbines mixed with the sound of the cannon, hard bursts behind him, all along the line.

He lifted his field glasses, scanned the blue lines, stared through the wetness, searched among the flags, the long rows of horsemen, looked for *him*, thought, Sheridan is there, I should be able to see him. He should make himself seen, face me. He grabbed his sword, yelled a violent sound, felt the cold rising in his chest, looked up, his eyes blinded by the rain. Now he knew what was happening, why the raid had begun in the first place. He felt like God had opened something inside of him, a window into some perfect place, and suddenly he could see with absolute clarity.

Yes, there *was* a difference. Sheridan was doing what none of them had done before. The blue horsemen were not moving on Richmond, the prize was not railroad cars and supply lines. He put the glasses down, stared out to the heavy wave of blue, thought, You are coming after . . . *me*.

THROUGH THE SMOKE AND THE RAIN, THEY PUSHED THE LINES back and forth through the muddy fields. When there were no lines, men fought in small bunches, the horses bringing them together, hand-to-hand struggles, sword against sword, pistols blazing into the faces of men you could touch.

Many of them were on foot, the horses shot away, moving desperately to stay together, some kneeling to shoot, others lying flat in the shallow depressions, trying to load wet powder, their carbines useless in the downpour.

Stuart kept the horse in motion, directed men into line, whatever men he could rally, kept them moving to the front, to the awful confusion of the fight. He had counted the enemy flags, knew it had been only one division, Merritt's, the tough brigades of Custer, Devin, and Gibbs. Stuart held the good ground, kept the fight from pushing them too far in disorder. But there was no pause, Sheridan kept coming, moving Wilson's division into the fight, and slowly, order broke down, and over every rise, in every small depression, men found themselves in the face of the enemy, and then, short yards away, a blessed line of friends.

It lasted all morning, then into the afternoon. Stuart rode along a fence line, stopped, saw a group of his men trying to form a line, and he pointed out over a low rise, yelled, "There, advance there!"

The men saw him, one officer waving a sword, and they moved up and over the rise. On the far side a small cluster of blue soldiers were turning that way, to meet the new threat, and now smoke flowed up toward Stuart, the sounds of the volley mixed with the steady hiss of the rain.

He held the horse against the fence line, saw men moving up beside him, using the fence for protection, firing now at glimpses of blue. He glanced down, saw bodies along the far side of the fence, faces staring up, washed clean by the rain. All around him, bodies of both sides were scattered along every fence, at the edge of every rise, against every tree. But he would not look at that, yelled to the men around him, "Give it to them . . . there, over there! For your country . . . ! For the glory of God . . . !"

The men were looking toward him, more now moving up along the fence, and the wind howled around him, the cape billowing out, the red lining flashing at the enemy, a red shadow wrapping around him. He saw blue now, men stopping to aim, and around him, his men answered with a blast of fire.

He looked across the field, saw another fence, small trees, could see his men lining up behind, scattered pops of firing, small flashes in the dark rain, the men who could keep their powder dry. He saw a scattering of blue, soldiers caught in a small trap, men falling, then more blue, moving toward the fence. There was a burst of smoke, the blue mass dissolving, and Stuart raised the hat, let out a yell. Around him, faces looked up, and he saw the fire, the victory. He kept the hat high, and the men began to yell with him.

In the field before them, down a wide slope, men were streaming back toward the road, men in blue, scattered and broken, and Stuart pointed, yelled again, and there was musket fire from the fence beside him. Farther up the fence line a new wave of blue came over the rise, but it was not a line of battle. The men were running, the faces staring straight ahead, looking for the safety of their own lines. He raised his pistol, pointed it at a group of blue, only yards away, fired the pistol, fired until it was empty, felt the rage building, felt the horse move beneath him, thought, Yes, we will charge them . . . God is with us . . . God has seen the glory of our fight!

He glanced to each side, looked for officers, looked again to the front, saw men in blue moving past in a wave of blind retreat. Now one man turned, and Stuart saw the man's face, older, a face that did not have the panic of the men around him. The man's eyes focused on him now, and the man stopped moving, stared at Stuart with a black calm, the eyes cold and hard. Stuart felt a chill, could not turn away from the man's stare, the noise around him quieting, fading into the hard whisper of the rain, and it was just the two of them, alone in the swirling black of the storm.

The man slowly raised his arm, held a pistol, pointed it with a steady hand, and Stuart sat up straight in the saddle, now saw the bright flash, felt the hard punch in his stomach, his breath sucked away. The man lowered the pistol, still looked at him with the cold eyes, then turned, walked away, disappeared into the black rain.

20. LEE

MAY 11, 1864

THE RAIN FELL ALL THROUGH THE AFTERNOON, THE MEN HUDdled in the deepening mud of the trenches. The high mound of dirt and timber in front of them was a solid wall of protection, and the enemy had not come back. Many were beginning to believe that he would not come back at all, that this ground, the massive strength of these entrenchments, would push Grant into motion. The fight would be somewhere else.

The engineers had designed the line, spread along the high brow of ridges that wound through the swamps and open fields. The line extended forward in the center, pushed out around a ridge, formed an inverted U, and the engineers knew it was not the best way to design a defense, that the U itself was vulnerable. But if the line had been straight, the high ground would have been out front, in the enemy's hands, and artillery could have used the hill to cause serious problems for Lee's entire position. The soldiers called it the "mule shoe," and the men who settled into the works in front kept a careful eye toward the gentle roll of the open ground in front of them and to the solid line of woods beyond. But the day had passed with only the scattered firing of the skirmishers, the occasional glimpse of the enemy by the vigilance of the sharpshooter. The great mass of men just sat in place, wet and chilled and miserable.

The dark came early, flowed across the woods and fields under the heavy weight of the clouds. They had seen this before, knew by now that when the rain settled upon them like this, there would be no relief. This was a Virginia spring, and the streams and swamps fed off the storm, and the men knew the left flank was safe for now. Where Hancock had tried to press around them, it was nearly impassable, the creek beds roaring, pouring new water into the boggy lowlands, which now became muddy lakes.

There had been one piece of bright light, the word passed all through the men in the field. Even the men farthest from the dry tents of the commander took it with a smile, had made their own quiet salute toward Lee's camp. His son, Rooney, had come back to the army, released from the Federal hands, recovered now from the wounds. In the camp itself there had been cheering, the glad hugs and enthusiastic handshakes, but Lee had greeted his son more with relief than happiness. The homecoming was not all joy, and Rooney had brought that as well, the sadness, the grief. Charlotte had not survived the winter, could not regain her frail health, consumed by the worry for her husband. But there was no time for consolation, for the comfort of father to son, something Lee had always had difficulty showing. They all knew, with Stuart off toward Richmond, in pursuit of Sheridan's raid, Rooney would have to take command of what cavalry Lee still had close to the army.

Now word was coming to headquarters, Grant might be moving, pulling to the east. Wagons were moving on the roads to Fredericksburg, and Lee could not know if it was just a flow of wounded or the beginning of a full-scale withdrawal.

The word had gone out to the right flank, to Early's command: keep a sharp eye. If Grant was indeed moving away, retreating toward Fredericksburg, Early would be in line to pursue, could possibly strike a vulnerable Federal march. But the weather kept the scouts blinded. Little good information could be had when the men could not see through the rain and heavy mist that blew in solid sheets across the low hills.

Lee would not order any movement, not yet, not until he was certain Grant was moving more than wagons. But speed would be essential, and so he had ordered the slowest part of the army, the cannon that lined the mule shoe, to pull back and make ready to move east at the first confirmation that Grant was on the march. Along the great curving line, the men closest to the enemy, who still huddled behind the tall works, were bent low under dripping shelters made from anything they could find, choking on the thick smoke from sputtering fires. They watched in nervous disbelief as the great power of their artillery limbered up, the horses pulling the guns through the thick mud of the faint trails, taking them away, to the roads far behind the lines.

There would be little to eat, the fires could not stay lit long enough to cook the raw bacon, and so the men gnawed and chewed on what they had. There was one blessing: the rain could soften the hardtack, wash down the taste of the stale flour. As the dark had spread over them, heads would peek over the wall, staring quietly into the blackness, at the strange noises from the far woods. As the night wore on, the noises continued, the sound of music.

Their own bands had no enthusiasm for joining in, the playful competition across the lines, each side trying to outdo the other. And so the men listened curiously, could even make out the tunes drifting across the field. Some laughed, joked about the Yankee commanders, ordering their men to play lullabies so the Yankees could sleep, some wondering about the cruelty of making the bands play in the driving rain. But the men farther out, the pickets, began to send word back to their officers, there were other sounds as well. The music would pause, small silent gaps between songs, and the new sounds would emerge, the sound of men talking, of movement, the occasional clinking of a tin cup, the stacking of muskets, a hushed order, a curse. The sounds were growing, spreading, a great mass of men marching close, gathering together. Now the music was not enough to disguise what was happening in the woods, and the men began to understand why the music had played, why it continued to play, late into the miserable night.

MAY 12, 1864

LEE HAD STAYED CLOSE TO HIS OWN CAMP, FEELING THE WEATHER in his bones, the stiffness, a dull ache in every step. He had waited for the old illness to return, almost expected it, knew he was very tired. But the pains had not come that way, the hot pinch in his throat, the cold stab in his chest. He had prayed for that, *Please* . . . and now he made a new prayer, thankful, blessed relief from the problems with his heart.

He sat alone, shuffled through damp papers. It is certainly this dismal weather, and nothing more, he thought. God has given us a rest, will cleanse the fields, and neither side will do much until it clears away. He stared out through the opening in the tent, saw water pouring in a stream off one side of a raised tent flap, had a sudden flash of memory, the first autumn of the war.

He'd been sent into the field for the first time, before Davis had given him command of this army. McClellan had pushed a Federal army south through the rugged mountains of western Virginia, and Davis sent Lee out to manage a bad situation, two southern commanders, Wise and Floyd, fighting for turf, for authority, and neither one able to stop squabbling long enough to fight McClellan. The place was called Cheat Mountain, Lee's first fight of the war, and it had been a failure. There was poor coordination, miserable communications, a plan that was washed away by days of weather like this, the already poor roads pulling the men down into a deep sea of mud. Lee had no experience in the difficult terrain, had devised a plan of surprise that simply didn't work, falling apart in the hands of inexperienced men in terrible conditions. There had been harsh judgment in the papers. Lee's first campaign could have condemned him to a post firmly behind the doors of his Richmond office. He did not search for excuses, kept the experience alive, would always remember the lesson: *Know* the ground, *know* the men in your command. But he had forgotten about the weather, how a good army could be held down, the morale of the men, the fighting spirit, chilled by the cold wet hand of God.

He saw movement, a horseman, heard the man calling out. He stood, felt the stiffness in his knees, saw Taylor moving toward the man, heard the voice, unfamiliar. He waited, saw Taylor turn, look at him, and Lee stepped out under the tent flap. Now more horsemen began to ride in, mud splattering on the gathering staff, and Taylor moved close, water running off his hat.

"Sir, we have reports from the Second Corps, from the mule shoe . . . the picket line reports the enemy is gathering in force to their front."

Lee saw Marshall now, speaking to another courier, and Marshall moved quickly toward him, wiping at his glasses.

"Sir, we have word from General Ewell. He requests with some urgency, sir, that the artillery be returned to his front. He says the command there reports the enemy is massing for an assault!"

Lee absorbed the words, thought of the reports earlier, Grant's wagons moving east. He felt a cold turn in his gut, looked at Taylor, said, "You see what this weather can do? I have reports Grant is moving away, now he is coming right at our center."

He stepped back into the tent, found a blank piece of paper, thought, All right, the guns should be moved back. He wrote the order, handed it to Taylor, and the young man rushed out, tripped over the tent stake, the flap shutting closed, dumping water down in a mass. Lee stood in the dark, heard the commotion, horses moving, quick shouts. It will be light soon, he thought, and we will see what General Grant has done. He felt angry, shook his head. I wanted to believe . . . he would be gone. It made sense, the strong defenses. They came at us all down the line, couldn't make us move, could only leave their dead in front of our guns. He would not do it again . . . not with the weather so bad.

He thought of the men out front, huddled in shallow pits, the skirmishers, thought, They are uncomfortable, they are hearing the sounds of the enemy in motion, and they fear the worst. It makes sense. But surely, Grant has had enough . . . those people have had enough. What more must we do?

The flap opened and Taylor leaned in, water dripping from his face, his hand. "Sir . . . sorry, sir. I'll fix the tent."

Lee could see past him, a faint gray light, the trees around the camp thick with fog. "No, Colonel, it's time to begin the day. I'll be along in a moment."

Taylor backed away, and the flap dropped back down. Lee reached for his coat, stretched his back, felt a pain surge through his stomach, a small wave of nausea. Maybe, he thought, another day of rest, another break. If the rain lasts, nothing will happen. . . .

The flap jerked open and Taylor was wide-eyed, pointing, and now Lee could hear it, beyond the trees, toward the front of the line, a

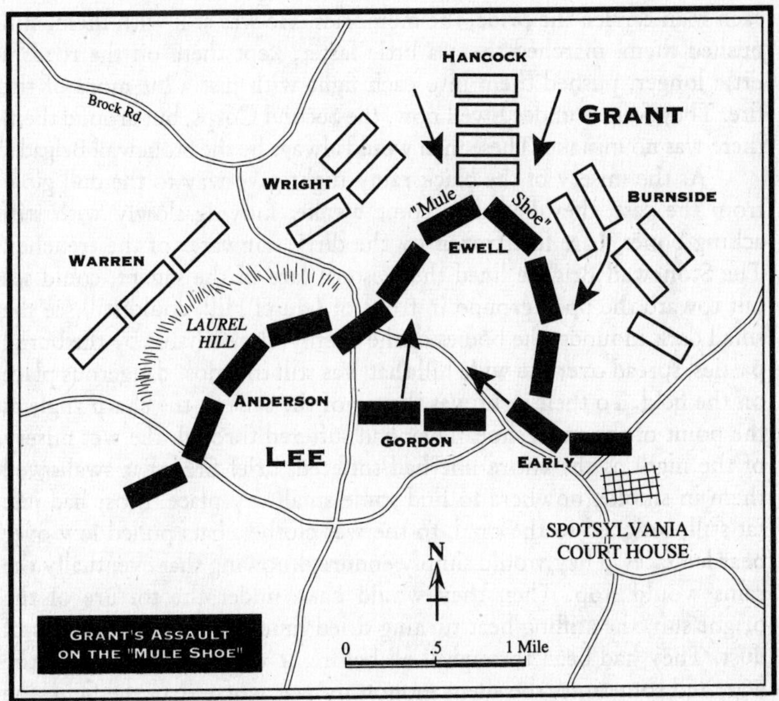

GRANT'S ASSAULT ON THE "MULE SHOE"

solid wave of sound, rolling through the fog and the rain. He stepped out into the gray mist, and the sound was louder, the low hard growl of some great beast, growing now, into a violent roar. He felt his chest pound, saw the quick motion of men around him, horses and shouts. He stared blindly at the sound, the center of the line, beyond the small trees, toward the curving rise they called the mule shoe.

THEY WERE THE FIRST VIRGINIA BRIGADE, HAD FORMED IN THE first weeks of the war, the first call for volunteers. Most came from the rich farmlands of the Shenandoah, and they learned how to march, to fight, to become a small piece of this great army, under the grim command of a strange professor from VMI. From the beginning, Thomas Jackson showed them something about themselves, that they could do the impossible, the outrageous, and that it was already there, inside each of them. They began to believe that, after the hard fight at First Manassas, the fight that gave Jackson the name all would know him by, but he would not keep that to himself, had always insisted the name belonged to the men. Now, with Jackson gone, each man carried the pride, the memories. He was still with them, still pushed them, marched them a little faster, kept them on the roads a little longer, pushed them into each fight with just a bit more of the fire. They fought under Ewell now, the Second Corps, but around them there was no mistake. These men would always be the Stonewall Brigade.

As the misery of the black rainy night gave way to the dull glow from the east, they began to come awake, moving slowly with stiff aching bones, bare feet frozen by the dirty rainwater of the trenches. The Stonewall Brigade lined the western face of the salient, could see out toward the open ground in front of Laurel Hill, could still see the small dark mounds, the bodies of the enemy, unreachable by the burial parties, spread over the wide hill that was still the most dangerous place on the field. To their right was the tip of the salient, the sharp angle at the point of the mule shoe. They had suffered through the wet misery of the night as the entire line had suffered, brief fires that swallowed them in smoke, nowhere to find some small dry place. Most had just sat still, resigned to the mud, to the wet clothes, hats pulled low over bearded faces. They would simply endure, knowing that eventually the rains would stop. Then they would bake under the torture of the bright sun, the stifling heat turning dried mud into choking clouds of dust. They had been through it all before, it was the *quiet* part of the war, and sometimes the silent monotony was worse than the fight, the weather showing no mercy, and these men would sit quietly, dreaming about the cool green hills of the Shenandoah Valley.

They could see the first light now, but the trees beyond the open ground were hidden, a thick fog flowed past them, a light breeze, and any man who stood, who tried to stretch the pain out of his back and legs, would feel the sudden chill, drop back down into a shivering mass.

They had heard the noises across the way, the invisible sounds of motion, of men talking, even the whispers carried across the black space. As the light began to find them, there were some who braved the cold rain, tried to see out into the field, to find some gap in the fog. Along the line there were voices now, and the men who sat huddled behind the wall heard new sounds, and they began to stand as well. There were small sharp cracks, the musket fire from the pickets out front. There was nothing unusual about that, the skirmishers always waited for the first piece of daylight, always looked for the small blue motion across the way, each wanting to fire the first shot of the day. But there was another sound, and suddenly the pickets were at the wall, climbing over in a rush, and now the officers began to shout, men grabbed their muskets, lay them along the top of the wall, pointed out through the openings in the wooden barricade, still not knowing what was happening.

Now there were hard shouts, some could see into the fog, and the sounds flowed down the line, the eyes sharp now, awake, staring through the rain. They still could not see the far trees, but they did not have to. Across the open ground a dark mass rolled toward them, a solid line, coming slowly, silent and ghostly. There were no shouts, no bands played, and no guns fired. The wave rolled steadily, closer to the barricade. They could begin to see faces now, small pieces of color, the brass of the officers, the small flutter of flags. Pieces of the wave dropped out of sight, moving down into the small depressions in front of the wall, then appeared again, closer, climbing the low hills, and finally there was sound, the orders screamed out along the line. The muskets all pointed out from the wall now, and the order echoed in the trenches: *"Fire!"*

There were scattered sounds, small pieces of gunfire. Heads began to turn, men staring in shock, most of the sounds from the vast rows of guns coming as small pops, the light crack of the percussion cap. Frantically, men put new caps on their guns, a quick aim, and again the guns did not fire. Even the most careful man had not been able to keep his musket completely dry. The thick wetness of the night had found its way into even the most secure place, and so the guns would not fire. The powder was wet.

Now the great dark wave began to make its own sounds, the neat blue mass coming apart, men running toward the wide ditch and the barriers that lay out in front of the wall. They clawed their way past the pointed sticks, others jumped up, pushed the brush down with the weight of their bodies. Men stepped on the shoulders of their friends, and now the shooting finally began, a hot rush of sound all along the line, and it came from the men in blue, men standing high on top of the wall, pointing the muskets down into the faces of the enemy. There were new shouts, a vast chorus rising along the wall, the blue wave beginning to pour over in one surge of motion. When the first volley had been fired, they did not stop to reload, but used the bayonet, and when the enemy was too close even for that, the guns became clubs, and the men stood face-to-face, punched and grabbed, wrestled and grappled. The officers emptied their pistols close to the chests of the men in front of them, the swords flew, flashes of steel cut through the damp mist all along the line. Now the shouts, the manic screaming of the attackers blended in with the new sound, the pain and panic of the wounded. The wave kept coming, and the men in gray, who had thought the wall invincible, now began to pull away, crawling and leaping through trenches, the works that spread out in all directions behind the wall. Some still tried to fight, to hold back the crushing wave, but far out beyond the wall the wave was long and deep, still moving forward, and when the rebel guns finally began to fire, and the men in blue began to fall across the bodies of their enemy, the wave did not stop, and soon the trenches behind the wall were a solid mass of blue. The gray defenders began pulling back farther, many of them no longer in the fight, men screaming in utter panic, stumbling past the men who still tried to stop the tide. But the brave were soon swallowed, surrounded. Men dropped their muskets, hands in the air, staring at the muzzles pointing at their chests, feeling the sharp point of the bayonet, staring into the black eyes of their enemy.

LEE HAD TRIED TO REACH THE FRONT, BUT THE SALIENT WAS IN Federal hands. He knew it had been Hancock, and it was not some weak thrust, a poorly coordinated attack like the one from Upton, but well timed, focused, nearly twenty thousand men pouring into the mule shoe like a great unstoppable tide. The surprise had been complete and deadly, and Lee's men, those who survived, had no choice but to pull back.

He had looked for the big guns, the great firepower he'd ordered away. Out behind the trenches he saw a few of them, but they were not there in time, could not be unlimbered fast enough. Some had even been captured, and Lee thought, It was a mistake . . . an awful mistake.

He moved the horse behind a small clump of trees, saw many men now, some still running away, some slowing, gathering, finding the strength. Hancock's men were still moving forward, deep into Lee's center, but it was disorganized. Hancock's assault had been *too* successful, the men moving farther and faster than their officers could control.

Lee moved up into the trees, tried to see, guided by the hard sounds, stared into the mist, the low wet fog. He could see small flashes of light, the musket fire, could hear the sounds, men shouting, the wounded, the panic. He clenched his fists, thought, It is the Wilderness again . . . we cannot see.

There was a new burst of firing to the right, and he looked that way, stared into the rain, could see nothing. But the new sounds were not in front, and he thought, They are still advancing . . . they are cutting us in half.

He felt a twist of cold in his gut, pulled the horse around, and now saw Marshall, wiping at his glasses, and Lee motioned to the rear, said, "Let's move, Colonel! We must do something about this!"

They splashed through deep mud, dropped down into a small trench, then up, and suddenly they were surrounded by a scattered mass of men, some running, some with the stagger of the wounded or men who have lost the fight. He stopped the horse, saw one man running, without a musket, coming straight toward him. Lee shouted, "Stop! Turn around! What unit are you? Who is in command?"

He saw the man's face, and it was not a man, but very young, a boy. The boy would not stop, ran right past him, never looked at him, and Lee could only watch him go, thought, He is so young. God help us. We are fighting with *children*.

The sounds echoed all around, there was no front line anymore, no one place where help could be sent. More men ran past him, and he fought the anger, felt the raw fury rising, and he raised the hat, shouted, screamed, "Stop! Turn and fight!"

Even the men who saw him, who heard him, did not stop. Lee felt his voice fade, held his hat in his hand, watched the men move by, chased by the terror, and he felt the rage ball up inside him, felt the helpless frustration. He shouted again, and some men slowed, heard the force in his voice, but then the terror would return, brought by others moving by, or the sound of the musket ball. They would not look at him then, would run again, and there was nothing he could say, they ran from demons he could not control.

He spurred Traveller past a small clump of trees, could see out to the open ground now, up toward the salient, could see the long wall, the fog now thick with the smoke of the guns. He saw a small block of men, a dull gray line moving forward from the left, rushing into the fight, and he yelled again, "Yes! Push them . . . !" But the line dissolved into the smoke, and now there was only a cluster of blue, emerging, dropping down into a low trench, then coming up, moving right toward him. He jerked the horse to the side, moved back through the trees. There was a wide field, an old house, and now he saw men behind him, officers in tattered gray, advancing, fresh troops. He felt a stab in his chest, saw it was a brigade, maybe more, a line of men stretching far into the trees, neat lines slowly stepping forward.

He shouted again, "Forward, move forward!" and this time there were cheers, the men hearing him. He turned the horse, moved out in front of them, pulled Traveller around, faced the sounds of the fight, began to move slowly forward, joining the line.

Now there were men on horses, a flag, and he saw the sharp uniform, a young man moving close, ramrod straight, and the man saluted, said, "General Lee, do you intend to lead my men into battle?"

Lee saw the young face, the man watching him with a curious grin. It was John Gordon. Lee said nothing, looked at the troops again, felt his chest pound, small ripples of pain, the tightness spreading all through him.

Gordon eased his horse in front of him, blocking his way, said, "General Lee, forgive me, sir, but you will not lead my men in this charge. That, sir, is my job. These men have never failed you, and they will not fail you now. This is not the place for you, sir."

Lee stared at the handsome face, and Gordon was not smiling now. He looked at the others, the staff, officers watching him, the line of men stepping past him. Now the men began to shout, waving hats, he could see the faces watching him, the voices surrounding him in one chorus:

"Lee to the rear . . . Lee to the rear . . . !"

A man moved his horse close to Gordon, and Lee felt Traveller turn, the man holding the bridle. He looked at the man, a quick burst of anger, *How dare you* . . . but the eyes were hard, the man's face grim and determined. Lee felt the breathing slow, felt suddenly deflated, empty, said to Gordon, "You are quite correct, General. The duty is yours." He pointed toward the salient, to the sounds of the fight. "We must push those people away, General."

The men were cheering again, and he pulled Traveller around, moved through Gordon's men, then turned, watched the lines move forward, the smoke now flowing across, the muskets coming off the shoulders, bayonets pointing forward. Now the sounds of the fight, the scattered bursts, began to grow, spreading out in front of him into one long chorus, the musket fire blending with the high terrifying scream of the rebel yell.

THE MORNING PASSED, AND THE HEAVY MIST AND FOG AGAIN gave way to steady rain. Gordon's men had sealed the breach, and with their momentum taken away, Hancock's men withdrew back to the high wall, the thick protection of the dirt and logs. Early had kept Burnside back, strengthened the right of the salient, and as the afternoon wore on, the two armies faced each other only a few feet apart, face-to-face on either side of the great long barricade.

THEY WERE SOAKED WITH THE RAIN, WITH THE SWEAT OF THE fight, and now they were back up to the wall. The numbers were very small, but they could see that, did not take time to look for familiar faces, to ask who was in command. Those who had returned, who had stayed close to the fight, knew what they had done, that the enemy had broken through, poured over their strong defense, but now they'd come back, had cleared the mule shoe of Yankees. But the enemy was not gone, was still very close, *right there,* on the other side of the wall.

What was left of the Stonewall Brigade blended together with men from other units, and the officers did not know the men around them, had given up trying to sort the companies, to find familiar faces. When they reached the barricade, they had seen the blue coats scrambling away, climbing back over the wall, and the sounds of the fight had become a roar of voices, deafening shouts. Some climbed up onto the wall, thought they would see the enemy flooding away, pouring across the field, back to the far trees. But the men in blue were still there, and if the curious man stared too long, he would be pulled over, and if he survived, he was a prisoner. As the men realized they were so close, the voices, the shouts, had risen to a frenzy. Some heard the voices from inside themselves, the boiling panic that tells you, *Run,* move from this deadly place. The sounds came from beyond the wall as well, screaming confusion. Some did run, backed away, left their muskets, splashed out of the trenches, had never been so close to the enemy, and did not have it in them to be that close now. Others responded with rage, climbed the wall, would strike out, could not stand to huddle low in the face of the men they had hated for so long. Some just crouched low, could hear the voices of the enemy, began to hear men like themselves, curious. Some yelled to the man on the other side of the logs, would call out to him, taunts, curses. But the sounds were still flowing over them, and it did not matter if that man was like you, if he was as afraid as you. If he showed himself, you would try to kill him with every part of your being. If the musket was empty, you would put the bayonet through his heart, or smash in his skull with the butt of the gun. And you knew, if you gave him the chance, if you were careless, he would do the same to you. Instinct took over, and there was only survival, the mindless anger.

There were holes in the log wall, small gaps, and men were loading muskets, passing them up to others, to the men who would wait calmly, patiently sighting down the long barrel into the opening, waiting for some flash of blue, a piece of the enemy. The musket would fire, and a fist would punch the air, *success,* the men below cheering. Some believed the enemy was beaten, hugged the other side of the wall in helpless panic, and if a man thought himself a hero, he would lead a new charge, would jump up on the wall, shoot into the faces of the men on the other side, throw the musket down, reach back for another, screaming in mindless rage, expecting the enemy to flee from the show of bravado. But the enemy was waiting as well, some chance to strike out at the rebels who had taken their success away, and so the man who would be heroic would be swept from the wall in a hail of lead.

The gaps in the logs held another danger. A man would lean too close, get careless, distracted perhaps, reaching for a new musket, and suddenly there would be the dull grunt, and the man would stare down, the red stain would spread, and the bayonet would be pulled back, disappear through the gap in the logs.

The bodies were spread everywhere, but in the trenches it was worse, because beneath your feet, in the mud that had now come over your knees, you did not feel them, you did not know what you were standing on. Some were only wounded, men who could still have been saved, would have survived if they had escaped the mud, had not been trampled, pressed down by the feet of the men who still fought.

As the night finally came over them, the men began to collapse with exhaustion, and when they finally sat, staring at the dark, they would make the sickening discovery, would feel something in the deep mud, would catch a glimpse, a small piece of uniform, or might touch something, a hand, a cold face. But there was no shock, no turning away, the emotions, the compassion, had been taken away, was drained from them. The fight had never let up, and when the darkness came, few noticed. The fight did not change because the *sounds* were still there, and the men were fighting something larger than the enemy they could see. On both sides of the wall the mass of men became something different, something beyond human. Even the hate began to fade, as did the duty, the need to fight that came from reason, from command, from intelligence. The sounds and the violence drove them further, soldiers possessed by something automatic, the darkest side of man. Those who saw it, who kept some piece of sanity, of conscience, tried to pray, to beg that this horror, this unspeakable slaughter, be stopped. But even the most devout began to feel the raw emptiness, the presence of the Beast, that God had done this, had brought these armies to this awful place, had let these men create their own hell, while He closed His eyes and turned away.

THERE WERE MEN NOW WORKING, DIGGING IN ALL ALONG THE new line, cutting straight across the base of the mule shoe. The ground was not as high, but it was a better position, more compact, defensible, easier to move troops to a new threat anywhere along the line. Lee had put them to work himself, had gathered up stragglers, men stumbling about in the confusion of the fight, some who had panicked earlier, some with small wounds, now slowly moving forward again. With the blue troops cleared out of the salient, these men became soldiers again, and Lee had guided them, put them to work with the shovel, the ax. He could still hear the fight up at the angle of the salient, but the sounds were not moving, the battle was hard in one place, and so for now the danger was past.

He would wait until late, midnight perhaps, then pull the men back from the salient, disengage from the fight and bring them into the new trenches, strengthen this new shorter line. There were horrible losses. Ewell's corps had been shattered, two generals captured, thousands of men lost as prisoners. Thousands more were flowing into the hospitals, or lay spread in a thick mass on the bloody ground. It would take days to get the units regrouped, sort out the commands. He had seen one quick report, one message to Ewell that had been sent on to him. He had stared at the paper, and when he read the words, he saw the face again, the sharp blue eyes, knew the news would spread through the army like a dark wind. The Stonewall Brigade had ceased to exist.

It was dark when he reached the camp, and he saw no one moving. The rain was still falling, and so there was no fire. He dismounted, looked around, tried to see someone, an aide to take Traveller's reins. Finally a man came forward, a shadow in the gloom, his face hidden under a dripping hat. The man saluted Lee silently, and Lee handed him the leather straps, and the man backed away, led the horse to the small makeshift corral. The rain became harder now. A gust of wind drove through Lee's clothes. He felt the chill, the shiver, could see the violent pulsing of the tents. He pulled his coat tighter, but it was soaked through, and there would be no warmth until the clothes were dry, and so he moved to his tent, still did not see anyone, knew the staff was scattered, men moving from Ewell to Gordon, from the fight in front to the hospitals behind. Still, he thought, this is . . . strange. This does not feel like headquarters.

He reached the tent, and the wind slowed, the flaps calmed, and he opened the tent, stared into the black space, moved slowly inside. He peeled the coat off his shoulders, tried to feel for the small chair, would lay it across the back, and now he heard a sound. It was a man crying. "Hello . . . who is there . . . ?"

The voice started low, and the man cleared his throat. It was Taylor. "Sir, forgive me . . . I had to wait for you. I wasn't sure where you were."

Lee began to see, caught the motion, Taylor standing up. Now Taylor flicked a match, a small glow filled the tent, and Taylor lit the oil lamp. Lee watched him, saw Taylor's hand shaking, said, "What is it, Colonel? What has happened?"

Taylor looked at him, then glanced down, put his hand on a piece of paper. "Message, sir . . . from Richmond." He slid the paper toward Lee, and Lee waited, knew Taylor would tell him more. "General Stuart has died, sir."

Lee stared at the paper, let it lie. Taylor's words were enough. He nodded, felt suddenly very heavy, his legs weak, weighed down by the wetness in his clothes. Taylor backed away from the chair, and Lee moved forward, sat slowly, his hands on the table. There was a silent moment, the whisper of rain on the tent, and Lee felt something filling him, dark and cold, felt frozen, motionless. He forced a breath, glanced up at Taylor.

The young man moved toward the opening in the tent, stopped, composed himself, pulled at his coat and said, "He will be terribly missed, sir."

Lee looked at the young man, searched for words, something to say. He thought of the stream of messages, Stuart wearing out the horses of his staff so that he would never again make the mistake he had made at Gettysburg. Even the mistakes, he thought, even when Stuart had one eye on the headlines, on his reputation, he was still the eyes of the army.

Taylor began to move, reached to push the tent flaps open, paused, said quietly, "Are you all right, sir? May I bring you something?"

Lee wanted to speak, felt the wave rising in him, fought it, pushed it away, wrapped himself hard around the emotion, said, "He . . . never brought me a piece of false information."

Taylor shook his head, and Lee saw him weaken again. The words did not help, there was no comfort. "No, sir." Taylor backed out of the tent, still watching Lee. "I am . . . terribly sorry, sir."

Lee nodded, turned, was losing the control now, the weariness taking over. The flaps closed and he was alone, stared into the dull yellow of the oil lamp. I must say something, he thought, write it down, a message to the army. They will look to me for comfort. His mind stumbled through the words, the speeches, all the letters, but there was no sense, nothing came to him. He thought of his children, the relief of seeing Rooney come back, the loss of Annie. He would always feel the guilt for not being there, not watching them grow up.

From the beginning of the war, the first time the troops looked to him as a leader, he had eased the guilt by embracing all of them, had quietly realized that he loved them all, they were all like his own children. It had come from Jackson first, the strange urgency behind the bright blue eyes, the anxious need to please, the frantic devotion to duty. Stuart had been the charmer, the boy everyone would love, who always knew the eyes were on him. Longstreet was older, serious, perhaps too serious since the fever had taken his own children away. And Longstreet had little use for Stuart's theatrics, the grand show of the uniform, the red-lined cape, the gaudy plume in the hat. But Lee knew it was all of it, all that Stuart was, the show, the spectacle, the headlines. And the cavalryman.

He still stared into the light, thought, *The army*. That is the important thing . . . we do not have the luxury of personal loss, of missing our comrades. There are too many, and I do not have the right . . . to grieve for anyone. I must plan . . . find some way to replace him. There is no time. . . .

He could not fight it. The strength slipped further away, his head began to drop down, and he put his arms on the table, rested, still looking at the light. The army, he thought, we must have eyes, we must know where Grant is going. . . .

He heard a horse outside, voices, and knew it would wait, Taylor would not disturb him now. The rain slowed, and the sounds of the battle were fading. He forced himself to think of the duty, pushed the words through his mind: I must replace him. He thought of his nephew, Fitz Lee, and Hampton, the big man from South Carolina, but his mind would not work, the names slipped away, the faces blank, unreal. He was suddenly anxious, his heart waking in his chest. He stared down at the piece of paper, the message he had still not read. He cannot be replaced. None of them . . .

He laid his head down on his arms, turned his face down, closed his eyes, and he could not keep it away any longer, the control was gone, and he began to cry.

21. CHAMBERLAIN

May 14, 1864

He had come by way of Fredericksburg, moving slowly south, kept off the road by the wagons moving north. He had often been forced to wait, could not move the horse at all, the road narrowing, only room for the endless line of wagons, winding through dense woods or crossing a stream. When he stopped and waited, he heard the sounds, the voices of the wounded. He had tried to see them at first, easing the horse up close, looking into some of the ambulances, and the sights were always the same, the sounds and the smells began to overwhelm him, and so, as he worked his way closer to the army, he kept the horse to the side, let the wagons pass.

The malaria had come back, worse this time, and he'd been too sick to even make the trip back to Maine. He was confined to a hospital in Washington, surrounded by the screaming of the wounded, and the horror and the loneliness had been unbearable. Through the fever he sent word to Fannie, and this time she came to him, made the rail trip southward. It was Fannie's healing hand that finally brought the strength back to him. If weeks in a bed began to drive him insane, what followed was worse. Washington was swirling with official business, the paperwork of war. The need for discipline, for policing the huge army, had created a massive backlog of court-martial cases. Chamberlain's presence was too convenient to be overlooked, and so for nearly two months he had endured a new confinement: court-martial duty.

Finally, after a vigorous stream of letters to the War Department, he was allowed to return to the Fifth Corps.

He reached the camp above the bloody field at midday, and the rain still came down, the roads flowing with thick mud. He had reported to Griffin, saw something in the man's face he had not seen before, something dark and angry, and they did not talk, just the formality, reporting for duty.

Lee had pulled back, straightened his lines farther south. In front of the Fifth, the rebel line still included the strength of Laurel Hill, and no one in the corps believed there would be another attack here. If the army would try Lee again, it would surely be somewhere else.

His brigade, the entire army, had endured a solid week of bloody action, and Chamberlain could not just parade into the camp, announce his return as though nothing had happened, as though these men were not different now, changed by what they'd been through. It had been clear that Griffin was not the same man, and Chamberlain was curious about that, what it was, what was new. It was more than just another battle, more guns, more blood. It was something Chamberlain had missed, and the frustration of that ate at him, the selfish luxury of being sick when your own men were dying at the hand of the enemy. He walked through the camp, looked at the men, saw them one at a time, unusual. This is not like Gettysburg, he thought, or even the disaster at Fredericksburg. The men were not talking, even the music was subdued. He walked past a group of men from Pennsylvania, one man writing a letter, one reading a Bible. The faces were empty, blank, the others staring into some faraway place. He heard a low conversation, the words again, "the angle," thought, This is something I have missed, something I have to learn.

He rode toward the lines of the Twentieth Maine, felt a sudden urgency, unexpected, a small cold panic rising from all the talk of how many were gone, how bad the fight had been. Once he left Griffin, he had only one thought: *Find Tom.*

The regiment was assigned to a position along a deep trench, facing a long rise, a wide hill where the enemy's guns watched their every move. Griffin had told him about Laurel Hill, that they'd tried it, driven forward four times in all, each time leaving more men behind, spread across the terrible open ground. The last time was not as bad, the attack having not really gotten close. Warren had resisted moving out at all, but the word was that Grant had ordered them forward, to support Hancock's great burst at the salient. Warren still hesitated, had nearly been relieved of command, and the men believed it was because of them, that he would not order his men to march into certain slaughter.

He eased the horse through the boggy ground, ducked under dripping trees. He saw the flag now, the men rising, watching him, voices coming toward him. "Colonel! Colonel Chamberlain!"

He waved, felt embarrassed, did not ride into the lines of the Twentieth Maine to be applauded.

He accepted the kindness, the greetings, searched the faces, then saw the young man emerging from a large muddy hole. Tom stared at him for a moment, not believing, then ran forward, the dignity of the young officer erased by the pure glee of seeing his older brother. Chamberlain stayed on the horse, was still embarrassed, felt he was not a part of them now, as though they had moved on, left him with something still to prove.

Tom reached up to him, said, "Lawrence, you're back! I wondered if we'd ever see you again!"

Chamberlain leaned over, could not hide a smile, took his brother's hand, said, "They can't keep me away. I have better uses to this army than court-martial duty."

More men were moving closer, happy greetings, and he waved to them, still smiled. He looked at his brother, the beaming smile, and said, "Can you ride with me? Is it all right?"

Tom looked back toward the trees, and now Chamberlain heard a familiar voice. It was Ellis Spear.

"By all means, Colonel. Welcome back to Virginia. Lieutenant Chamberlain, please return by dark. We may have to move."

Tom saluted Spear, and Chamberlain smiled again, "Thank you, Colonel Spear. I'll have him home in time for supper."

There was laughter, and Chamberlain glanced at Tom's horror and was instantly sorry. The boy, red-faced now, moved toward the horses. Chamberlain thought, He will never forgive me. They will remind him to be home for supper . . . forever.

THE VAST PILES OF LOGS AND DIRT WERE STILL IN PLACE, A FEW gaping holes, fat logs smashed into pieces, the places where Hancock's big guns had rolled up close, throwing solid shot right into the line, blowing holes in the rebel defense. All across the field there were burial parties, grim men with shovels, men with stretchers. Some were carving names, initials, into anything they could find, stabbing them into the ground beside the small mounds of fresh earth.

Tom followed him up to the wall itself. The rain had slowed to a heavy mist, the only sound the shovels of the workers. Chamberlain reined his horse, climbed up on the wall, sat high on a piece of wood, a short log, saw it had been shot to pieces, small holes all along what was left. Behind the wall there was one fat tree, lying on its side, the branches ripped away, and he looked at the base of the tree, where it had been cut down. The tree, nearly two feet thick, had been sliced through by the hail of musket balls. He stared at the white wood, could see small black spots, the lead balls that had not passed through, thought, My God . . . no one . . . how many could survive this?

Tom said nothing, stayed on the horse, stared at the grisly scene. Farther behind the wall they saw patches of dirty white, the wet shirts of coatless men who did not notice the rain, more burial parties, many more stretchers. Some carried stretchers toward the gaps in the wall, and Chamberlain saw movement on the stretchers, men in black bloody rags who had survived, pulled out alive from under mounds of corpses, men who had been thrown into the muddy bottom of trenches, stepped on and fallen on, but somehow stayed alive.

He saw a line of men alongside a deep trench, and one blue coat, an officer. The man said something, a quiet order, and the shovels began to throw dirt into the trench. Chamberlain looked down where the dirt fell, felt his stomach turn, looked away, felt himself grab at the air, a sharp breath. He had seen too much of what they were burying, a thick mass of what once were men, a mass grave of the enemy, or of friends no one could identify.

There were small pops of musket fire, to the south. Lee was still down there, skirmishers still playing the game, patiently waiting for some glimpse, picking off the careless, the men behind another strong line. The workers paid no attention, went about their gruesome business with slow deliberate steps.

On the north side of the wall, where Hancock's men had made the assault, the field was mostly empty now, the graves filled, and he saw horses, a staff, moving under a flag.

He glanced at Tom, said, "I had better get back, find out what is happening, what might happen next. General Griffin probably needs me."

He dropped down off the wall, climbed up on the horse, gazed over the long wall one more time, said, "I never believed this . . . I had thought Gettysburg was the last fight."

Tom looked down, said, "I heard that a lot, Lawrence. But this was . . . something different. I heard that these men here just wouldn't stop. The officers lost control, couldn't pull them away."

Chamberlain looked out over the field. "How could we do this again, after what we did at Gettysburg?" he asked. "How many times do we do this to each other before someone says, 'All right, that's enough'? Is there a greater meaning here, some will of God that we destroy ourselves, some divine punishment?"

Tom shook his head. "Don't know, Lawrence. Buster would say . . . it's just war."

Chamberlain thought of Buster Kilrain, the old Irishman, so different from him, and so much his friend. Kilrain was buried now on that hill in Gettysburg, the place where Lincoln himself had made that speech. Kilrain was a crusty and cynical man who carried his own reasons for fighting the war, saw this as the struggle against the "gentlemen." Chamberlain looked along the shattered timbers of the wall, the deep red stains, thought, What do gentlemen have to do with what happened here? This was not about causes or class struggle, this was about killing, about facing an enemy and tearing his heart out. Kilrain did not believe in the godliness of man, did not believe that inside of us we hold a piece of the angel. Chamberlain saw the gruff old face, could still hear the thick brogue, and said, "Yes, Buster, you would have understood this. So what happens now?"

Tom shrugged, said, "We go on till it ends, I reckon."

Chamberlain shook his head. "No, there's something more," he said. "The men who survived this have learned something new, that slaughter is acceptable, that mass killing is now routine. What does that do to us? If God is watching us, what judgment does He make now?"

He moved the horse in a slow walk, and Tom was beside him.

Chamberlain said, "You remember when Mother would read to us from the Bible? That wonderful fireplace . . . She held our attention with every word. Maybe you don't remember . . . you were pretty small."

Tom smiled, said, "No, I remember it, Lawrence. I still hear her sometimes. She loved to tell us the stories."

Chamberlain looked at Tom with surprise, said, "I wish I could . . . hear her." He paused. "Things did not turn out as she had hoped."

They rode on, did not talk, did not share the private memories now.

Chamberlain remembered her pure joy the first time he could recite the Ten Commandments, something even his father had enjoyed. Of course, he thought, there was something military about that. It was a list of rules. How important they were to her . . . how little meaning they had now. *Thou shalt not kill.* Yes, we shall kill. And before this is over, we shall kill again.

He rarely prayed anymore, had let his mother's devout hand slip away from him, had left it somewhere in his childhood. Now he closed his eyes, tried to think of some prayer, some question, some plea for divine intervention. His mind worked, words tumbling in a mass of nonsense. He opened his eyes, stared up, thought, Maybe that is how it must be. There can be no prayers, not now, not while this goes on. We have not earned the right.

He focused, told himself, All right, enough. Your brain causes you too much trouble. You are back, you are with the army again. Your brother is safe.

There were more horsemen now, men moving off to the east, more flags. He said, "Something's happening . . . too much brass moving around. I think it's time to go."

They stopped the horses, and Tom suddenly reached over, touched him, held him by the shoulder. He looked at his brother then, saw a difference in Tom's face, a sadness in his eyes.

Tom said, "Lawrence, you be careful. It would kill Mama if you didn't come home."

Chamberlain felt the emotion rising, tried to hold it away, looked down for a moment, thought, There is nothing to say. We will both do what we have to do. He could not look at Tom, no words of caution. We are different now, both of us. We are soldiers. He looked at the ground, at the dark mud, said, "Come on. It's time to go."

They spurred the horses, moved along the wall, felt the rain coming again, black clouds rolling low over the far trees. The horses splashed through deep mud, and Chamberlain glanced up at the angry sky, heard low thunder, and behind him the steady sound of the shovels.

22. LEE

May 24, 1864

There would be no more assaults against the strength of Lee's trenches. The cavalry commanders now reported directly to Lee, and it was clear from all they could see that Grant was pulling away from Spotsylvania, and again it was not to retreat. The Federals were moving south, another looping line that would take them closer to Richmond and, once again, around the rear of Lee's right flank. Since his best defense against the massed assaults came from waiting behind entrenchments, Lee had to wait, could not anticipate, could not commit his army to move into open ground to intercept Grant's movement. It was only when he knew Grant was on the march that he could leave the trenches behind.

It was much as before, since the fight in the Wilderness. Grant's march was slow, encumbered by a much larger force, many wagons, long lines of guns. Lee suffered from fewer numbers, but the one advantage still remained: he could move faster. He had one other advantage: Grant was moving on a roundabout course, while he had the straighter roads, and if he did not know exactly what Grant's objective was, he could at least plant his army in the best place to interrupt him, dig in again, the shovel and the ax now as valuable as the musket. This time the defense was formed below the North Anna River. It was strong, a difficult river to ford, made worse by the many days of rain. And it cut through the ravines and wooded land like a great brown snake, with sharp bends and high banks. By the time Grant could reach the few places where his army might push across, Lee was already in place, waiting for him.

He had hoped to keep Grant north of the river, keep him from coming across at all, but on the left, where the Third Corps had dug their lines, the woods between the troops and the river was already swarming with blue coats, a growing mass of the enemy.

The march to the river had been long and tense. Grant's people were to the east, and all along the way, care had to be taken that Lee was not suddenly confronted on the flank, whether by design or by accident. Hill was back in command of the Third Corps, the illness improving. Lee had welcomed his return, but it meant Early would return to Ewell's command, back to his division, and John Gordon would step down further, to command his brigade. It was a situation that required change.

He had risen early again, and it was a routine that was wearing him down. He could not eat, felt no stomach for the breakfast. He had watched the staff pick at the hard stale biscuits, scraping off the light blue mold, heard low comments, mild curses. His gut was still bothering him, and the sight of the biscuits had driven him from the table. He would wait, try to find something later, maybe a blessed gift, a local farmer offering some precious piece of his dwindling pantry.

The sun was up now, and the rain was gone; the sharp blue of the sky warmed them all. He tried to take a walk, to feel the dry air, fill himself with healing, but the churning in his gut would not go away, had driven him back to his tent.

He was on his back, staring at the blank canvas, the flaps open, the breeze billowing into the tent. He took a deep breath, then another. For a moment the cramp under his belt loosened, and he sat up, saw Taylor outside the tent, watching him.

Taylor stepped forward now, said, "General, excuse me, I have some coffee here, if it will help, sir."

Taylor held out the cup, and Lee caught the smell, strong and awful. He said, "Coffee? Are you certain, Colonel?"

Taylor looked into the cup, made a small frown. "Well, sir, it's what we've been using for coffee."

"Thank you, but I'll do without for now."

Taylor seemed relieved, backed out of the tent, tossed the contents of the cup out behind him, then turned to Lee, said, "Sorry, sir. I didn't know what else to do."

Lee smiled, nodded, then felt a small cramp return, and he took another long breath, waited for it to pass. "Colonel, we must not let word of this . . . of my condition, to reach the men. There can be no weakness now, none at all. Do you understand?"

Taylor moved closer, lowered his voice. "Of course, sir. 'The general is resting in his tent.' Anyone who has asked for you is being told that, sir."

"Very well, Colonel. Have we sent word to General Gordon?"

Taylor stood, nodded, "Yes, sir. Major Venable conveyed your request." He turned, peered out of the tent. "I will escort him here as soon as he arrives, sir."

Taylor was gone now, and Lee lay back on the cot again, slowly began to shake, wrapped his arms tightly around his waist, tried to hold the shaking away, but the chill came from deep inside him. He waited for it to pass, but the shivering filled him inside, his arms clamped hard across his chest. His mind fought it, a silent prayer, *God, please* . . . and slowly the shivering stopped, the deep knot in his gut let go. He was breathing heavily, felt the sweat now on his face, soaking his shirt. He closed his eyes, but there was no rest, his heart pounding. He thought, This is very bad, I must not allow this to interfere . . . we have much work to do.

There were voices, and he opened his eyes, pulled himself up painfully, sat up again, and Taylor was at the opening of the tent. "Sir, General Gordon, at your request."

Taylor backed away, and now Gordon stepped up, looked at Lee with concern, said, "General . . . you sent for me, sir?" He lowered his head, leaned in, tried to see Lee's face. "Are you all right, sir?"

Lee pointed to the small chair, said, "Sit, please, General. I am fine, yes. A bit of a stomach problem, nothing to be concerned about."

Gordon moved to the chair, nodded. "Yes, sir. I am sure it's just a minor ailment, sir."

Lee pulled out a handkerchief, wiped at his forehead, said, "It is of no concern, General. What is of concern is your command. I have already conferred with General Ewell, and it has been decided that your services to this army are of great value. I have prepared papers to send to the Secretary, recommending your promotion to Major General."

Gordon stood, stiff and formal, tried to hide the smile. "Thank you, sir. I have merely done my duty, sir."

Lee shifted his weight on the cot, wrestled with another cramp. "Please, General, sit down. There is more. It is not appropriate, given your service, and given your new rank, for you to return to brigade command. General Ewell also agrees that your handling of division strength forces in the last affair was admirable. We have reorganized somewhat . . . you will now command a division, consisting of three brigades, including your own. General Ewell will provide details. The Second Corps will now consist of your division and General Early's." He paused, watched Gordon slowly sit, his back straight, staring straight ahead. Lee suddenly thought of Jackson, the same posture, the man who never touched the back of a chair. But Gordon is young, he thought. He is not a professional . . . and he is not Jackson.

"General Gordon, this army needs all of its good commanders. We have lost too many. I would consider it a personal favor if you did not expose yourself to the fire of the enemy. This army must depend on your service."

Gordon said, "Yes, sir. I understand, sir. You will not be disappointed."

"No, I do not expect I will. You are dismissed, General."

Gordon stood, snapped a quick salute, moved quickly out of the tent. Lee sagged, was drained, felt weaker now than before. Gordon has the strength, he thought, the energy. So many of them had that . . . all of them, even . . . me. Now we will depend on the youth, the few men like Gordon who have not yet failed. He felt a wave of depression, told himself, No, have faith. One good man . . . can make a difference, can turn the direction of the war. He has already shown the fire, he knows how to face the enemy. I just wish . . . there were more like him.

HE RODE IN A WAGON, TOWARD THE LEFT FLANK, WHERE HILL was waiting. His gut was full of fire. The ailment that had punched and prodded him for days was now a full storm, and he could not even ride the horse. It could not be helped, the word had spread, and as the troops along the road watched the wagon pass, small cheers surrounded him. He felt the wagon slow, heard voices, familiar, Hill's staff. Now there were faces, helping hands, and he emerged from the wagon, his feet finding the hard ground, and he saw Hill.

Hill had come back with a flourish, had told Lee, told everyone, that his illness was gone, behind him; he was prepared for whatever faced the army. But Lee saw beyond the words, the bravado, looked briefly at the sunken eyes, the thin face. Hill was still not a well man. He felt a sudden impatient anger, turned his head, walked slowly away from the staffs. The pain in his gut was twisting into a hard knot again, and he stopped, clamped his eyes shut, thought, *Please*. Hill was beside him now, looked carefully at Lee, silent, seeing the sweat on Lee's face.

To the north, along the river, there was a small wave of musket fire, scattered thunder from big guns. Lee looked that way, knew that Grant's men had filled the woods between Hill and the river, thought, They should not be there, they should be on the other side of the river. He felt the anger again, stared hard at the sounds. Some dark place inside of him was suddenly boiling up, the control slipping away. He looked at Hill, the weakness, the frailty, one more failure, and he felt his voice rise, bursting out of him.

"General Hill, why did you not do as Jackson would have done? Those people should not be there, they should never have been allowed to cross the river. You should have thrown your whole force on those people and driven them back!" His voice cracked, the breath gone. His fists were clenched, and the sweat soaked him again.

Hill stared at him, seemed to sink down, feeling the weight of Lee's anger. Hill looked down then, said, "Sir, we did not . . . we did not learn of the enemy's crossing—"

Lee turned, was not listening to what Hill was saying, the explanation, heard only the fight within himself, the struggle for control. He held up a hand, stopped Hill in mid-sentence. "It is done. Prepare your defense, General. I must return to my headquarters."

Hill saluted, and Lee turned, saw the staff behind him, saw the faces, knew they had heard the anger, the harsh words. He moved toward the wagon, thought, I do not have time for explanation . . . this is not a time for comfort. He glanced at Hill, said, "General, we must be vigilant. General Grant is coming again."

IT WAS A PERFECT PLAN, THE ONLY KIND OF MANEUVER AGAINST THE numbers Grant was pushing toward them. The roads that led to Richmond crossed the North Anna in a place where Lee had fortified on a high knoll, a place called Ox Ford. On both sides of Ox Ford, the river curved up and away, like a wide U, and so, if Grant could not cross where Lee had his greatest strength, he would have to cross on either side. It was exactly what Lee hoped he would do, because Lee had pulled his defenses into an inverted V, both flanks pointing back away from the river. If Grant continued his advance, his army would come across the river in two separate pieces, far removed from each other. It was the kind of opportunity Lee had watched for, prayed for, and Grant kept coming.

On the left flank, where Hill's lines threw up a powerfully compact defense, the Federal Fifth Corps was advancing below the river

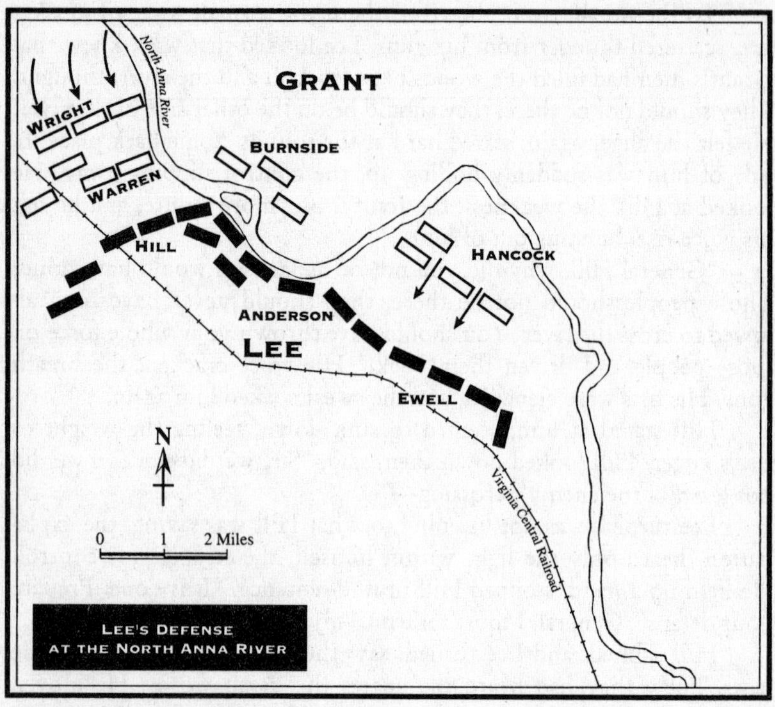

toward them. Behind, above the river, the Sixth waited to cross as well. But the key to Lee's plan was on his right flank, downstream. Burnside was straight across Ox Ford, facing Lee's strongest position, and could do nothing but watch Porter Alexander's mass of cannon staring at them from the heights below the river. Farther downstream, Hancock's Second Corps was pushing across the river into an open area, behind which Lee had drawn half his army into a tightly coiled spring, waiting for the most vulnerable moment when Hancock's troops were spread out, a line of march led by men who stared curiously at the empty roads in front of them, a pathway south that seemed to be wide open.

HE HAD NOT RISEN FROM THE BED, THE BLANKET HOLDING HIM down in the sea of cold sweat. He could hear the sounds, outside, the horsemen moving in and out of the camp, the reports from the cavalry. Taylor would let no one see him, but he knew from the sound of the voices that something was very wrong.

His eyes were closed and he felt a small breath of air on his face. Lee looked up, blinked into focus, saw Taylor leaning over him. He tried to smile, the young man's soft concern drifting over him.

Taylor whispered, "Sir, if it is all right, I must tell you, sir. We have word from the right flank."

Lee nodded, felt the stab of pain growing in his gut again, clenched his teeth, fought it, said in a low voice, "Yes, Colonel, what is it?"

Taylor watched him, waited, saw Lee's face relax, said, "Sir, General Ewell did not advance per your instructions, sir. The attack was not made. The enemy has now entrenched. General Ewell reports that it is unlikely his attack would succeed now."

Lee stared past Taylor's face, up into the dull blankness of the tent. He closed his eyes, nodded, made a small motion with his hand, a silent command to Taylor: dismissed.

The fire tore through his mind, but there was no strength, and he could not respond to it, could not feel anger. We have let them go . . . *again*. If I had been there . . . He thought of Ewell, understood now that it was definite, as though the sentence had been passed down to him from God. Ewell is not fit. He cannot command. I don't understand, but I cannot just let him be, hope that he grows stronger, that whatever is missing in him returns.

There were more voices, Taylor still managing the couriers, and now the young man was back in the tent, crept closer, and Lee opened his eyes, looked up at him.

Taylor said, "Sir, the enemy is still across from General Hill. The troops in front of General Ewell are not withdrawing. The cavalry reports the enemy is still divided. The opportunity is still there, sir."

Lee saw the excitement in the Taylor's face, the show of enthusiasm. He said, "What time is it, Colonel?"

Taylor pulled out a small watch, and his face fell, the excitement faded. "Um . . . a bit after seven, sir."

Lee said, "It's too late. Tomorrow . . . we must try again tomorrow."

Lee felt the weakness pulling at him now, closed his eyes again. Taylor stayed close to him, waited, watching, then slowly backed away, moved out into the fading daylight.

Lee was not sleeping, felt his mind still working, and he thought of Ewell, of Hill, the two flanks of his army, both men staring out at their enemy waiting for *him* to guide them. Something about Napoleon came into his mind, odd, something he had not thought about in years, a quote from an old textbook: *To command is to wear out.* No, I am not worn-out, not yet. The army is not worn-out. He felt the fog rolling across his brain, saw the face of Napoleon. No, you are wrong. There will be tomorrow . . . *tomorrow* we will have another chance. . . .

23. GRANT

MAY 25, 1864

HE HAD MOVED FROM SPOTSYLVANIA, THROUGH THE BUSY RAILroad stop of Guiney's Station. The headquarters would be near there, at least for one night, the tents spread across the open lawn of a plantation house. The house, the land, belonged to a family named Chandler, and the women in the house had been cordial, polite to the commander of their enemy. He did not learn until that evening that the small wooden building beside the grand mansion had been the place where Stonewall Jackson had died.

As the army moved farther south he had moved the headquarters closer to the North Anna, the tents now spread out along the hard road. The rains had stopped, the wood at last was dry, and the troops built huge fires, tall and roaring with great stacks of logs and brush. The fires were not for warmth; the late spring heat had already brought the steam up from the swamps and thick woodlands around the rivers. The fires were a message to Lee's army, to the scouts, to the lookouts who watched them from the tops of tall trees, who stared into the dark night for the signs of motion, some sign of which way the blue army was moving. The fires were their answer, a symbol of the spirit of these men, and the message to the enemy was plain. This army was still moving south, was still coming after them.

The maps were spread across a large table, and Grant leaned low, scanned the dark pencil lines, the positions of the troops. The reports were all in, the staff was confident that the troop positions were accurate. He followed the curving line of the North Anna, tugged hard at the cigar, the smoke rolling around him. He moved now, around the table, looked at the maps from the south, from Lee's point of view. He thought, We are in serious trouble, we have been in serious trouble all day.

He looked up at Porter, said, "Are you certain of this? Lee's right flank is . . . here?"

Porter stepped forward, Meade easing up beside him, looking over Porter's shoulder. Porter said, "Yes, sir. We scouted all through those woods. The enemy has a strong line, has dug in down to the southeast. General Hancock's corps is directly in line to attack them, sir."

Grant nodded, thought, Yes, and that's what Lee would like us to do. He moved his hand along the map, out to the west. "How far is this? What is the distance over to the right flank?"

Porter was nervous now, sensed Grant's mood, and Meade stepped up in front of him, said, "Too far. Six miles. Too damned far. We would have to cross the river twice to support Hancock. *Twice.*"

Grant looked up at Meade, saw the agitation in the man's face, Meade now rocking back and forth. Grant looked at the map again, shook his head, thought, We gave Lee a chance . . . we made a mistake, trying to spread out on both his flanks. He had an opportunity today, a very good opportunity, and he did nothing.

He thought of the numbers, the reports from the staff. The casualties have been horrific, for us and for them, he thought. But Lee cannot absorb that, fight after fight. He is weakening, with every fight he is weakening. He has no choice but to dig a deep hole and wait for us.

He glanced up at Meade, thought, You *know* better than this, to weaken us like this, spread all over creation, facing a compact enemy. Now you want us to back away. This time you may be right. He said, "General Meade, I believe it is time for us to leave this place. Would you agree?"

Meade nodded, said quietly, hiding his words from the staff, "I thought it was not a good place . . . we should pull the army together. We can still put up a good defense. . . ." He ran his hand over the map, searching.

Grant said, "We do not need a good defense. Lee is in no position to attack us. We will pull the army together in the morning, and move on these roads to the southeast. We will be closer still to Richmond, and Lee will have to come out from behind those fat trenches and stop us." He waited for Meade's reaction, and Meade stared at the map, his face showing nothing.

Meade looked at Grant, said, "To the southeast . . . I will prepare the orders." He began to move away, stopped, and said, "Sir."

Grant moved away from the table, the meeting over. He felt a blossoming headache, thought, We are like some big stupid beast, blind to everything that does not hit us in the face. We have an enemy in front of us who is already beaten, may be beaten more than he realizes himself. Meade, Burnside . . . don't they see that?

He walked to the edge of the trees, heard music now, a tuneless mishmash of banjos and harmonicas. The fires spread all along the road, far along the wide shallow hills. *They* know, he thought, the *men* know. If I could just convince the people who give them the orders.

He walked out into the road, looked up, saw a vast sea of bright stars, a cloudless perfect night, and now he thought of Sherman. You should be here, my friend, you would know how to make this fight. But he knew that would not happen, that Sherman's war was in the West. He'd received word, Sherman had pushed Joe Johnston back toward Atlanta, was advancing slowly, deliberately, following Johnston's gradual retreat. He smiled, thought of Sherman's impatience. He is driving you mad, isn't he, General? Johnston won't fight you, he won't come out and play your game. You press him and he gives ground. But Johnston will run out of ground too, just like Lee. They cannot just keep backing away, digging more trenches. We are strangling them, slowly, and with perfect certainty. It would already be over, if . . .

He dropped his head, stared into the dark. The word had come from below Richmond, below the James River. Ben Butler's great thrust toward Richmond, toward the valuable rail center at Petersburg, had been choked to a halt. Butler had overwhelming numbers, but had allowed himself to be hemmed in by the geography of the land, by the great sweeping curves of the James River. Now his vastly superior army was trapped in a place called Bermuda Hundred, held there by a narrow stretch of land that Beauregard could seal with a small force.

He had no use for Butler, didn't know anyone in the army who did, but Butler brought great political influence to his position. To suggest Butler was not fit to command an army in the field was a subject that even Lincoln avoided. Grant thought of the great plan, the good strategy; Butler should have been such a threat to Richmond, to Lee's supply lines, that by now either Lee should have pulled back into the Richmond defenses or Butler should be right in his rear. Instead Butler had bottled up his army into an impossible place, and a few thousand of Beauregard's soldiers were the cork.

The great plan had another weak point as well. In the Shenandoah, Franz Sigel's forces had moved south with another great show of bluster and talk, had finally met the enemy, a strange mix of scattered rebel units, under the command of John Breckinridge. Breckinridge had even called out the cadet corps from VMI, throwing them straight into the fight at a small town called New Market. The boys in their new uniforms became men, leaving ten of their young comrades on the field, and Breckinridge and this strange mix of commands routed Sigel completely. The capture of the Shenandoah, the plan to deprive Lee of the crucial supplies, the one part of Grant's plan that seemed the least hazardous, was now thoroughly erased.

He looked up at the stars again. Does all that matter, after all? The war is still *here*, the enemy is still Lee. Sherman is moving on Atlanta, and he *will* succeed, there is no doubt of that. Once Johnston has been defeated, Sherman will have cut Lee off from all support from the deep South, all the rail junctions. And if *we* move closer to Richmond, Lee will have to come after us. It may take only one good fight, one more chance, get Lee out in the open. We are *so* close. . . .

THE LAND WAS SWAMPY, CUT BY SMALL STREAMS AND LARGER rivers, patches of thick woods and small open fields. It was the same land McClellan had moved through two years before, the huge Federal army having pushed hard up the peninsula, the first thrust at Richmond. McClellan had moved through this ground cautiously, had always believed the rebel army was far larger, stronger, than his, and with his caution he gave away every opportunity. The defense of Richmond had been given to Lee, the failure of the western Virginia campaign forgotten, and during the Seven Days battles, Lee had used the land, the swamps and creeks, to his best advantage. McClellan finally pulled his great army away, back down the peninsula, chased by Lee's tactics, and more, by the lost opportunities and ghosts he could not defeat.

Now Grant came into the same land, but from the opposite direction, and he had no illusions about the strength of the enemy that scrambled to intercept him, at every bridge, every crossing of the swampy rivers. The Federal army continued to push along the tree-lined roads, through the open lands that rose above the swamps, where farmers still planted and Lee's army could still find food. Here, the roads began to come together, merging into the routes that led south, straight into the heart of Richmond.

The marches had been quick and efficient, and Lee had confronted them in small skirmishes, with cavalry and whatever strength he could press hard into their path. But Sheridan's horsemen had won the race for a vital crossroads, a place where Grant had a choice, to move on toward the city itself or slide farther to the southeast, around the city, directly to the banks of the James River. Lee's priorities were given to him by Davis, and he had responded in the only way that could save Richmond. The rebels now faced Grant's numbers in a north-south line, Grant now on the eastern side, facing west. But Grant had captured the crossroads he'd wanted, and Lee would have to guess where he might move next. But first there was an opportunity, this time for the men in blue. Lee had finally come out to meet them, extended in a line that spread out along a deep ravine, a winding stretch of open ground and patches of woods, west of the roadways Grant had captured. The intersection carried an English name, a type of traveler's rest where one could find sparse shelter but no fire, no hot food. It was called Cold Harbor.

MORNING, JUNE 3, 1864

THE RAINS HAD COME AGAIN, THE DAY BEFORE, AND THE ground had swollen into soft mud. By dawn the rains had stopped, but the small creeks were again strong and deep, and the men who took their place in line were still wet and cold from the march the night before.

They were called Heavy Artillery, had spent most of the war in the comforts of the big forts, the strong fortifications around Washington, Norfolk, Fort Monroe. It had been a plum assignment, and most of these men had come into the army with some influence, the power of a family name, the favor of a politician, the means of securing the safe posts. But Grant changed that, had not seen the need for a powerful force of troops guarding the cities from an enemy that was far away. So the Heavy Artillery came south, marched in the footsteps of the men of both armies, the men who had always, up to now, done the real fighting. There was grumbling, desertion, the men who had grown soft in the comfort of the forts now beaten down by the heat and hardship of the march. But Grant wanted all the strength he could bring to the fight, and these men would replace many of those who were lost, the vast numbers of casualties from the vicious fights of May.

Many of the veterans gathered along the roads, whistled and hooted at the clean uniforms, pointed and joked at the slow march of the men whose belt line was still soft. No one welcomed these new units to the fighting strength of the army, saw only raw numbers, not men who would hold the line, who could be counted on to lead the charge.

When the first order came at four-thirty in the morning, many of the men who stepped into the open ground had never seen the face of the enemy, never heard the steady roar of the great lines of muskets, the sharp whiz and dull slap of the musket ball. With the first light, the orders came down, and the men moved out in wide solid lines, flowing across a flat clear space, some slowed by the ravine, some climbing up toward a vast dense line of fire, a strong line of the enemy, protected by the quick work of the shovel. The rebel lines had been dug with the skill of men who have learned the bloody lesson, who understand with perfect clarity the value of a deep trench and a heavy dirt wall.

When the full glow of daylight had spread across the flat open ground, had lit the bottom of the winding ravine, many of the dead of the Heavy Artillery would lie beside the veterans, men who had faced the guns in every fight, the broken remains of hard men who would never flinch at the flashes from the guns to their front.

The Federal assaults were halted, and those who survived sought whatever protection they could find, moving through the vicious storm of the enemy's fire. They slid across the bodies of their friends, huddled together in small depressions in the ground, behind the shattered trunks of trees, anywhere there was blessed cover. When the orders came again, advance, resume the attack . . . the men who had marched into the slaughter and survived would not do it again. Many simply fired their muskets in the air, a show of noise for the commanders behind the lines, an angry protest at the needless disaster. They had moved across the small piece of ground into their worst nightmare of the war, a complete and utter failure, thousands of men shot down in a fight that lasted only a few minutes.

THE HORSEMEN MOVED THROUGH THE CAMP, ORDERS FLOWING out to all parts of the long line. Grant had listened to the hard wave of the first assault, the sun finally breaking through the clouds, and he had believed, from the first rattle of the muskets, this might truly be the final blow.

The reports began to come back to headquarters, and the mood began to change. By mid-morning the sounds of the fight were gone, just the occasional crack from the single musket, a small assault far to one end of the line, meaningless.

He climbed the horse now, had to see it, could not understand what had happened. In the trees to one side, beyond the tents of the headquarters, he had seen Meade, screaming like some great mad beast, a blistering tirade to some nameless officer. Grant did not ride that way, turned, moved straight toward the front, where the great burst of sounds had come, the center of the long line. He had stayed at the headquarters, would wait for it, the joyous word, the breakthrough. But after the first great wave, the musket fire had slowed. Now only faint scattered shots were heard, mostly to the north, where the fight had not been heavy, was not supposed to be heavy. But in front of him, where they should have punched through, swarmed up the shallow rise to divide and crush Lee's army, there was only silence.

He had not said anything to the staff, saw Rawlins busy with some couriers, but he would not wait, thought, Something is wrong, *again,* and this time I will see, I will be there before it is over. The anger had swelled inside of him, and he gripped the reins of the horse, stared straight toward the front line, kicked the horse hard, began to move forward.

He heard a voice, turned, saw Meade riding hard after him, thought, *Not now,* felt the anger building toward Meade, but the look on Meade's face was not what he expected.

Meade reached him, halted the horse, said, "Sir . . . it is no good. The brigade commanders report they are pinned down, cannot even pull away. The enemy has the ground, the position. Sir . . ." Meade paused, and Grant waited, had prepared himself for another tirade, listening with grinding patience while Meade puffed out in red-faced anger.

But Meade's face was drained of color, a look Grant had not seen before, shock, the look of defeat. Meade lowered his head, said, "Sir, it has been a tragedy. We lost . . . a great number. The ground is . . . it is worse than anything I have seen, sir. Begging your pardon, General. I don't know how else to say it."

Grant stared at Meade, felt a hot sickness rising, thought, If this is your caution . . . if we have stopped because you ran out of nerve . . . He fought the anger, clenched his fists, took a deep breath, said, "Can they not advance? They should have carried the fight! Lee is not that strong. What happened?"

Meade still looked down, shook his head. "They will not advance. I ordered support, but the men would not move forward. It was—forgive me sir—it was a perfect slaughter."

Grant waited for more, and Meade abruptly pulled the horse away, moved back toward the headquarters. Grant turned, looked out toward the lines, thought, This is . . . *madness.* It cannot be.

He spurred the horse, moved down a narrow ravine, heard shouts, the staff behind him. He felt the anger rising, thought of Meade's caution, the face of a man who had lost the fire. I will see this, he thought, I will know what has happened. They cannot tell me there is no fight left in these men. He spurred the horse, pushed hard through a thicket of briars, reached a trail, turned the horse, moved toward the sounds that now emerged from the woods, from the ground in front of him. He moved forward along the trail, saw now the woods were thick with soldiers. Some were walking, moving slowly away from the lines, blank faces, bloody stains on ragged uniforms. Now he saw officers, men on horses, some on foot, and one man saluted him, but most did not notice him. He slowed the horse, and now the staff hurried up behind him.

Rawlins was suddenly there, said, "Sir, what are you doing? Where are we going? Do you have orders, sir?"

He looked at Rawlins, felt his anger boiling in his brain, felt his jaw clench, said, "What has happened to this army, Mr. Rawlins?"

Rawlins stared at him, said nothing, and Grant spurred the horse again, rode down into a shallow depression, saw a vast line of blue, huddled together in a solid mass, spread out on both sides of him. Now the sounds flowed out all around him, and he could hear shouts, the voices of his men, the cries and screams of the wounded. The sounds began to grow, and he pushed the horse up a small rise, saw vast blue clusters, men crouched together, hatless, bloody shapes, faces staring up into the sky. He stopped the horse, saw a row of big guns, the crews sitting on the ground, the officers staring at him quietly. He pushed the horse past the guns, climbed a small rise, and now he could see it, spread out in front of him. The ground was like a wide flat table, a few large trees, the bark splintered, the trees stripped bare. All across the rich green of the grass lay the bodies in blue, a thick carpet, reaching across the open ground. To the far side he saw the long tall mound, the fresh dirt facing him like a dark brown wave, motionless, frozen in time. The mound spread out in both directions, hidden behind brush, snaked and curved out across a wide field, then farther, disappearing into a patch of woods. He saw a glimmer of motion, a reflection behind the mound, the morning sun now reflecting off the thick rows of bayonets. There were small gaps in the mound, and he saw movement, and across the horrible field of blue it was the only motion he saw. It was the face of the enemy.

Rawlins was beside him, and the horse was jerked to the side. He felt them pulling him back down the rise. He heard the new sounds, a burst of firing, the musket balls flying over his head. He still tried to see over the rise, wanted to turn the horse, but the reins were not in his hand. He turned, thought, This is not real, a nightmare . . . But he saw Rawlins looking at him, the reins of his horse in Rawlins's hand, and he knew Rawlins was real, that all of it was real.

Rawlins leaned close to him, held the reins out, said in a whisper, "Sir . . . we must leave here. We will move to the rear in good order. The men must not see you like this, sir."

Grant took the reins, looked at Rawlins, saw the embarrassment, Rawlins glancing about at the faces now watching them. Grant said nothing, looked at the faces himself, and there was no cheering, no salutes. The men huddled behind low mounds of dirt, crouched low behind trees. The faces stared, eyes deep and dark, and he spurred the horse, prodded gently, began to move along the trail, the eyes moving with him as he passed by. He began to see each of them now, looked at them one at a time, the men who made his fight, who stood up to the guns. He saw officers, more eyes watching him, thought, Pull them together, form your lines. But the words did not come, there were no orders. There was no fight left in these men.

They moved back behind the trees, past the brush, away from the sounds. Men were moving now, horsemen rushing with dispatches, the business of headquarters. The staff began to scatter, the tents now in view, and Grant halted the horse, saw a small piece of color, motion, against a fallen tree. He leaned forward in the saddle, saw now it was a man. The face was looking up at him, reflected the bright sun, the man's lips a light blue. Grant moved the horse, was suddenly jostled, the horse jumping, startled by a passing courier, an officer riding quickly along the trail. The man's horse was kicking up a spray of mud as he passed, and Grant felt his own horse calming, the grip of the reins hard in his hand. He looked at the soldier again, saw a splatter of mud on the man's face. He felt a twist in his gut, felt his throat tighten, climbed down from the horse. Now there was a hand on his shoulder, and a soft voice.

"Allow me . . . sir."

It was Porter, and the young man moved past him, eased down over the upturned face of the soldier, wiped the mud from the man's face. The man's eyes blinked, and he looked now at Grant, stared with cold silence. Porter stood up, looked at Grant, said, "He's not going to make it, sir."

Grant could not look away, stared at the man's black eyes, thought, There must be something. How do we just . . . walk away?

Porter was beside him now, said, "He's done for, sir. We should go. . . ."

Porter moved to his horse, and Grant still watched the man, the eyes still held him. He had never done this before, had always stayed back, away from where the men fell, where the blood stained the ground. He could never admit that, never talked about it, but now he was facing it, could not leave this man, not yet. He wanted to say something, to ask the man . . . what? There were no words, no questions, and he moved toward the man, a step closer, saw that the eyes were not looking at him anymore, were staring ahead now into the sun, far away into some other place.

Evening, June 3, 1864

THROUGHOUT THE DAY THERE HAD BEEN SMALL SKIRMISHES ALL along the line, but there would be no great assault now.

Grant was far behind the awful place, sat alone in the dark, could still see it in his mind, could still see Meade's shock, the words "a perfect slaughter," and he could not escape the image of the one soldier, one man, the eyes that had watched him. He tried to think of his wife, of church, of Heaven. Is that where he is now? He felt angry, scolded himself, You should know about this. What is it like? He could have told you, if you had reached him sooner. You were the last thing he saw . . . in this life. Did he take that with him? Are the wounds healed now?

He stood, stared into the dark, away from the small fires. Is this what madness is, coming so close to death that it holds on to you, obsesses you? He began to walk, nervous steps, moved behind the tents, then stopped, clenched his fists. One man . . . how can you be so affected by one man? Is it because . . . you watched him die? You saw the face? How many faces lay on that field today? Is it any different because you weren't there to see it?

He closed his eyes, thought again of Julia, thought, You would know what to say, you would have the Lesson, God's comforting words for this. There are no comforting words here. Here, it is all about duty, and making the right decisions. And men must die . . . even when the decisions are the very best ones. If today was a bad decision . . . we can do no better than to make a good decision tomorrow.

The anger stayed with him all day, and the commanders had come around, bringing the explanations. He listened, said very little, absorbed just how bad it had been. This was a disaster, and after all the talk, the excuses, the maps, the numbers, it had come to him, the anger slowly replaced by something else, something much worse. He understood now, thought, You cannot blame them. It is not Meade's caution, or the inexperience of Wright, the ridiculous attention to detail that curses Warren. This is not Burnside's inept slowness or Hancock's overaggressiveness. We cannot blame this on poor coordination, or bad timing, or the curse of bad weather.

He began to move again, walked further into the dark, stared at nothing. There is no one to blame but me. This was my fight, my opportunity. He thought of Lee. He is not some demon, he made no grand strategy, no brilliant countermove. I sent them . . . I ordered them across this ground. Lee lined his men up in a straight line behind a big pile of dirt and cut this army to pieces. And I did not see it . . . I did not know it was going to happen.

He moved toward a small fire, saw men sitting in a circle. The voices were low, the faces still, eyes staring into the flame. He moved closer, saw Rawlins, Porter, others, men from Meade's staff. The tents spread out beyond, flaps open and still, for there was no breeze. There were more men sitting near a wagon, men leaning up against the spoked wheels. There was motion, a bottle, one man handing it to another, the bottle upturned, then passed along. He moved that way, and the faces turned toward him, one man holding the bottle carefully, cradling it like a small child. There were nods, small casual greetings, too casual, but he did not notice, turned, moved toward the tents. Now he saw a group of men moving slowly away from him, men disappearing into tents, staff officers, staggering slowly out of the firelight. There was a small table, a deck of cards scattered loosely, and in the center of the table, another bottle.

He stopped beside the table, stared at the cards, the colorful depictions of royalty, and knew his mind was playing with him, would not let him look at it, but slowly he saw it, fixed his eyes on the label, focused on the faint lettering. He reached out, felt his fingers tighten around the neck of the bottle, lifted it up slowly, saw the light pass through. It was nearly empty, but there was still the last good drink, enough to warm a man all the way down, the delicious burn.

It had been a long time ago, and it had been a fight he had to win. The gold rush did something to the men in California, took something away, all the lessons of home, all the rules about decency, dignity. The army was not immune, and in a place where every temptation was bold and colorful, few had been able to keep themselves away from the crude pleasures.

Julia stayed in Missouri with her family, had not made the journey, had not joined him in that amazing place, San Francisco. The loneliness had eaten at him like a disease, and the disease exposed something in him he did not understand, a weakness, and he had been consumed by it, by the numbing comfort of the bottle. He did not frequent the gambling halls, the clubs, where women offered company to a man whose family was so far away. He avoided the sounds and the lights, and so he was faced with long quiet nights, would listen to the sounds of wild streets from a dark room, trying with every piece of himself to see her face, keep her name in his mind. When it became harder, and her face faded, there was only sadness, and with the sadness came the bottle.

Julia would never know how far down he had gone, that it had been the drinking that finally cost him his job. He had resigned from the army, a choice provided by a generous commander, saving him from the humiliation of a court-martial. He always carried the weight of that—that it mattered little if he had been a good soldier, he also had a dangerous weakness. When he went back east, to his family, to life as a civilian, he made a silent vow, to her, to his children, the most important decision of his life. The weakness would never come back, would be kept away. He would always remember how his career, his life, had nearly been shattered by the bottle.

Now he moved the bottle in a small circle, swirling the brown liquid, thought of the word: *shattered*. How many men had their lives shattered today . . . how many families? He thought of the newspapers, the reporters. The numbers were already flying through the camp, thousands of casualties, and they will report that. Many men died here today because . . . I made a horrible mistake. Many men have died since this campaign began, and we have not yet brought this to a close. What right do I have to take so much from these men, without giving them something in return? I had thought . . . it would be over by now.

There was a hand on his arm, and he jumped, startled, saw it was Rawlins.

"Sir, please . . . allow me." Rawlins took the bottle slowly from Grant's hand. Grant saw Porter now, the others, men gathering slowly behind him. Rawlins tossed the bottle to another man, said, "General, if we may be of service, sir?"

Grant looked at the others, the man with the bottle, then focused on Rawlins. "Your service is noted, Colonel." Grant saw the look in Rawlins's face, the look of the one man in the camp who knew of the disease. There was a silent moment, and Grant nodded, said, "Colonel, the men may be excused."

Rawlins motioned with his hand, and the others moved off.

Grant did not watch them. He walked away from the fires, into the darkness. He heard footsteps, the crunch of leaves, a voice. "General . . . if you don't mind, sir, may I walk with you?"

Grant knew the voice, did not look at the face. It was Porter. "You have something to say, Colonel?"

"Oh . . . uh, no, sir, I just thought . . . well, sir, you look like you need some company."

Grant looked at him now, the firelight reflecting on the young man's face. He nodded, said, "All right, Colonel, suit yourself."

Grant moved further into the dark, Porter moving beside him. Grant stopped, looked at the stars, stared silently into the deep black space.

Porter said, "We lost . . . a good many men today. We haven't given out the official casualty count. Not yet. It is frightful, sir."

Grant said nothing, felt deep into his pocket, pulled out a cigar, lit it slowly, felt the smoke swirl around his face. He still watched the stars, said, "I have underestimated him."

Porter leaned forward, tried to see Grant's face in the dark. "Sir? Who, sir?"

Grant lowered the cigar, crossed his arms. "Lee. I have underestimated General Lee. That should be pleasing to some in this army. I've heard the comments from General Meade's people. I don't know anything about fighting a war until I've fought Bobby Lee. Didn't pay much attention to all that. Just talk. Now . . . maybe . . . they're right."

"I don't believe that, sir. No one does . . . not the ones who matter."

"The ones who matter, Colonel, are a long way from here. It's the people up North who matter. We can't keep sending troops home in boxes. Mr. Lincoln has an election coming up. If he can't give the people a victory, then someone else will get the chance. Likely, it will be someone who knows how to play on the people's unhappiness. Do you know what that will mean, Colonel?"

Porter shook his head, said, "No, sir."

"It means the war will end. Quickly. And if the victory is not in our hands, there is only one other way it can end. We will have to back away, withdraw the troops, and the rebels will have their country. The Union will cease to exist."

Porter said nothing, followed the small glow of Grant's cigar moving in the dark.

"There is only one way to make war, Colonel. You have to *hurt* somebody. Maybe you have to hurt *everybody.* Make them feel it, understand what it is we are doing out here. If this war is worth fighting in the first place, then it is worth winning. We cannot win unless we fight. If we fight, men will die. If more of *them* die, then we will win. It has nothing to do with cities, or government, or what is barbaric and what is civilized. We are *here*, and the enemy is over there, and if we must give the newspapers the horrifying truth, then the people will know. If Mr. Lincoln does not want me to win this war, then he can make that decision. But there is no other way to see it. If these men do not fight and bleed and die, if we do not make the rebels quit by destroying their will to fight, by destroying their army, then the only other choice is to walk away."

Porter rubbed his hand through his hair, took a deep breath, said, "I don't know, sir. The enemy is still over there. It seems like no matter what we do, we have to face those boys behind those works. It seems like . . . nothing changes."

Grant drew at the cigar, flicked the ash away. "I made a serious mistake today. We cannot just throw strength at strength and prevail. There is another way, there has to be. Lee has outmaneuvered us, outfought us. He has been a better commander than I have. Maybe he's smarter, maybe he's just luckier."

He turned, looked back toward the fires. "If we have made one great mistake, all of us, it has been that we have failed to understand *our* strength. He has guns, we have guns. He can dig trenches, we can dig trenches. So, if we cannot crush him . . . if it costs us too much to smash him with one blow . . . then we will strangle him. We will stretch his supplies until he cannot eat, we will stretch his manpower until he cannot defend. We will make them hurt, until they cannot fight."

Porter stared, wide-eyed, said, "Um . . . forgive me, sir . . . how?"

Grant looked at the cigar, tossed it down, stepped on it, the faint glow of the ash buried in the soft dirt. "South . . . cross the James. We will cut him off, from his food, his supplies. We will isolate Richmond. We will start by doing what Butler was supposed to do. We will take this army where it will hurt him the most. We will capture Petersburg. We will squeeze him and stretch him until there is no fight left in that damned bunch of rebels."

He turned, moved toward the glow of the fires, Porter following behind. He tried to think of the plan, the troops, the commanders, but in the dark, staring up into the small pieces of starlight, he saw the lone soldier again, the black eyes, staring at him. He stopped, looked to the ground, closed his eyes, pushed the face from his mind, thought, No, it cannot be like that. There is only one way . . . the only way we can succeed. We cannot allow that . . . we *cannot* see the *faces*.

JUNE 15, 1864

THEY LEFT THE CAVALRY TO SCREEN THE MOVEMENT, SLIPPED away from the disaster of Cold Harbor with the measured steps of an army that knows the enemy is still strong. They moved quickly, made their way down to the shores of the wide James River, marched calmly past grand plantations, great white mansions spread along the water, so many monuments to the glory of old Virginia. One in particular was their destination, an enormous estate called "Berkeley Hundred," the ancestral home of President William Henry Harrison. Here, there was a wharf, long boat docks that had once received royal yachts and flotillas of brightly dressed aristocracy. Now, the men of Grant's army gathered along the wide banks, waited in turn for the ferries and transports of the navy to move them across the river.

On the march, the veterans noticed something else about the sounds, the distinct tramp of marching feet, the quiet rhythm that says the wagons, the supplies, the big guns are not with us. Many had seen the great noisy columns moving away on other roads, and if they knew that Grant had slipped them quietly away from the enemy, there was still the nervous glance, the bad joke, unprotected infantry, the supplies and guns leaving them vulnerable. The foot soldiers did not know that upriver, the great columns of horses and wagons had reached another point on the wide river, Wyannoke Landing. The drivers and teamsters had stared in amazement as a pontoon bridge waited for them, a bridge nearly half a mile long, held in place in midstream by anchored ships. The wagons, guns, and nervous drivers began to cross a bridge longer than many had ever seen, the longest pontoon bridge ever built. The James was not calm, and stiff waves rolled against the bridge, bouncing the wagons, rocking the guns, but in less than a day the long columns of men and machine were across. It was an efficient march, inspired by the deep water beneath their feet.

By late in the day most of the great army, a hundred thousand men, was on the south side of the James River. The men were formed into their units, companies and regiments, brigades and divisions, and a

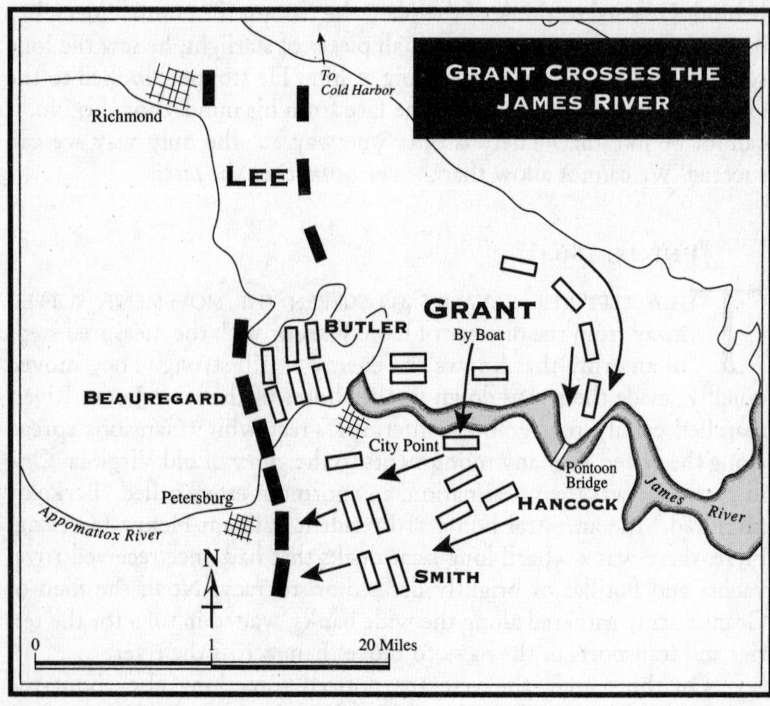

vast sea of blue spread out away from the river. As the camps began to form, the tents and fires filling the wide fields, the sounds were still muted, low conversation, a calm that surprised even the veterans. They all knew now what had happened at Cold Harbor, what had been happening to them since the first days in May, when the great campaign had begun. The massive assault that would end the war had cost this army nearly forty percent of its strength, nearly fifty thousand casualties. The reinforcements had come, rebuilt the army, brought the numbers back up, but the veterans had little respect for raw numbers, for the soft men who had never faced the guns. The veterans had seen what great numbers could mean, that when the enemy waited for you behind strong defenses, the great numbers meant a greater loss, and the hard strength of the blue army had been slowly drained away. There was quiet talk about Grant, but the veterans remembered McClellan and Hooker, Pope and Burnside, and their officers still told them Grant was the best man they could turn to, and they were coming to understand that the cost in numbers was the cost of waging war. But the blind optimism from the days before the Wilderness was gone. There was little of the excited talk of victory, of finally going home. Even the music had changed; when the army was in the camps, you did not hear the noisy clash of patriotic fever. The air echoed now with a sweeter sound, soft sad songs, songs of home and family, of God and the souls of the men who were no longer there. Even the commanders understood, you cannot force good morale, and the music reflected the mood of the army. No one gave the order, no one tried to change the spirit of the men with mindless calls for boisterous flag waving.

As the march reached the shores, when the vast winding river appeared before them, some wondered if it would be as before, two years ago with McClellan, when that huge army had reached these same shores, to load onto the boats that would take them away from the enemy, moving downriver, out of Virginia and back to Washington. Grant's boats were not taking them away, but on a short ride straight across the river. The talk stopped, and they all understood that Grant was not McClellan after all. They were still moving south, deeper into the heart of the enemy. The officers, the men who saw the maps, knew they were moving even beyond Richmond, the great prize that the politicians and newspapers seemed to value above all else. If they did not know what Grant had in mind, they knew now it was not to be Richmond, that once across the wide James, they would push on until they found the ragged army of those tough rebels. They did not yet know where the fight would be, but to the west, men were moving to meet them, filling a vast line of trenches, more deep earthworks, artillery officers gathering their men beside the big guns that had waited since the beginning of the war, guns that had never been fired, the guns defending the crucial rail center of Petersburg.

PART THREE

. . . The world will little note, nor long remember what we say here, but can never forget what they did here. It is for us, the living, rather to be dedicated to the great task remaining before us—that from these honored dead we take increased devotion to that cause for which they here gave the last full measure of devotion . . .

24. LEE

JUNE 15, 1864

THERE WAS AN ARROGANCE TO THE MAN, AN ANNOYING POSture of superiority. Lee had heard his words, listened patiently while the young captain pleaded his case, alternating humble requests with sudden boisterous demands, and Lee knew through it all that the young man was only repeating what had been so carefully drilled into him. Lee understood that, after all, he was hearing the voice of this man's commander, General Beauregard.

"General Lee, if we do not receive the troops from your command, if we do not have your support, the general is not responsible . . . he cannot be held responsible for what will occur. The numbers are all . . . right there, plain as day, sir. What else can be done?"

The young man was pointing to the pile of papers, the neat stack he had placed on Lee's desk. Lee glanced down, did not touch the papers, leaned back in his chair, said, "Captain Paul, does General Beauregard know exactly who it is that threatens his position?"

Paul hesitated, then said, "Certainly, sir. We are facing the troops of General Grant."

"Captain, there are no Federal troops on this continent who are *not* the troops of General Grant. Does General Beauregard know *which* troops? Do we know which Federal corps?"

Lee saw the man's eyes staring at him in a dull glaze. No, he thought, he doesn't know.

Lee stood, the quiet signal. Taylor moved up, had Paul's hat in his hands, held it out to the surprised young man. Paul looked at Lee, then at the pile of paper, still had more of his presentation to make.

Lee said, "Captain, you may return to General Beauregard. Tell him we are well aware what General Grant is doing, and we are making dispositions accordingly. You are dismissed."

Paul took the hat, saluted, straightened his back, regained the arrogance, turned, brushed against Taylor as he left the tent, and was gone.

Lee sat again, looked at the papers, said to Taylor, "Colonel, we should keep General Beauregard's paperwork in a secure location. It would not be prudent to allow this valuable information to fall into enemy hands." He could not hide the sarcasm, the weariness from days of frustration.

The illness had passed, and he was actually feeling the old energy, could ride the horse now for long stretches. But there was a new illness, an old affliction that was coming back to haunt him, to infect the entire army. It was the politics of Richmond, the administrative hand of Jefferson Davis.

The James River was Davis's dividing line, where Lee's authority stopped and Beauregard's began. Beauregard had finally moved his headquarters up from the Carolinas to Petersburg, responding to the threat from Ben Butler. Butler was still tightly contained, but now the threat was much greater. Lee knew Grant was moving south, knew of the great river crossings. The word passed quietly from loyal civilians and careful scouts. It was no surprise.

North of the James, Lee had brought Grant's great numbers to a bloody halt. If Grant tried to move toward Richmond, Lee was now in his path, and Lee knew that Grant would not make another mistake like that. There would be no more opportunities like the bloodbath at Cold Harbor. Grant had only two choices: to retreat, or to move south, cross the James and isolate Richmond from below. Lee never considered that Grant would retreat, had long accepted what the papers were calling the "hammering tactics." Now he was beginning to understand something else: that Richmond might not be the target. Davis was sending Lee a stream of correspondence, needless reminders of the value of the capital, the urgency of a strong defense. The same cries were coming from Beauregard in Petersburg. He thought about the pleas, begging him to respond to an enemy that he had been facing across miles of bloody fields, an enemy he'd come to know, an army that was always there, shifting and maneuvering, moving slowly, then a quick blow, striking out and pulling away. But the indignant messages still came, and he held the anger tight inside. They called to him with outrage, as though he had no idea who this enemy was, how serious the threat. The messages were filled with predictions for Lee's benefit, as though he knew nothing about Grant and what he would likely do next.

He walked outside the tent, felt the bright sun, moved toward the horses. Yes, he thought, I will send what I can, we must move quickly. This time Beauregard is right, he is not seeing ghosts.

Beyond the command tents, faces turned toward him, and he paused beside the horse, saw the men watching him, saw the ragged clothes, the thin faces, the bones of his army. There were a few cheers, hats waved, and Lee nodded to them, reached for the reins, climbed up on the big horse.

He heard Taylor shout something, knew there would be an aide moving up behind him, that Taylor would never let him ride off alone, not anymore, not since the illness. Lee smiled at that, thought, He is like a father, stern, overprotective. And I am the son. I had thought . . . it was the other way around. He turned, saw Taylor standing by the tent, hands on his hips, watching until the aide was up on the horse. Lee moved Traveller away on the hard road, still smiled.

He did not take great pleasure in the victory at Cold Harbor. He began to think on that, on the horror of that ground, of the enemy's loss. And what did we gain? He is still there, and he will come again. Our defenses, our strong trenches . . . keep us from moving like we used to. We are slowed down by the only thing that saves us. He thought of Jackson, spoke to him: You would not have understood trenches. You would not sit still in the face of the enemy. You would press forward, mobile, fast. Lee was struck by an odd thought: that Jackson's way could have been a terrible mistake, the hard fight, pressing forward, always forward. Grant has been inviting us to come out in the open, to fight him on his terms. Jackson might have done exactly that.

He felt guilty then, never believed Jackson could have been anything but the commander this army needed. But the war had changed, the ways of fighting, gentlemen on bloody fields. He thought of the great river itself, the James. Early in the war it had been suggested the river be mined for protection against Federal gunboats moving on Richmond. The idea was cast aside with indignation, dismissed entirely for its barbarism. It was not the way wars were fought, not the way gentlemen conducted themselves on the field. That was only three years ago, but Lee knew those ideas were from another time. Now the James *was* mined, torpedoes filled with black powder. Honor had been replaced by efficiency.

He still wondered about Grant, if it was the man himself who had done this. No, he thought, there is no blame, there is only the will of God. Jackson was taken from us because it was his time. Now the war is fought by different men, many different faces. Lee knew the numbers, knew he had lost a third of his generals since Grant's offensive began. Longstreet would not return for many months. Ewell was finally sent to Richmond, given command of the city's guard, a face-saving position for a man who had once given the army so much. Hill was fit, at least for the time being, but if Lee did not think on it, the others all knew that when the next great fight came, Hill's sickness would return. No one had stepped forward, none of the names seemed to matter. Anderson was still merely competent; his greatest day would still be remembered as the race to Spotsylvania. At Cold Harbor no one stepped forward, there was no bright stroke of command. They won because the enemy had made their own mistakes, had beaten themselves to death.

He would not think of Stuart, could still not accept that; there had been no answer, no comfort. So many are gone, he thought, except . . . me. I am still here because God is not yet through with me. Lee forced himself not to ponder that, to ask why. There is only the duty. I need not understand it any better than that. When the duty has passed, there will be no mistaking it. Then God will take me as well.

He rode past the sound of running water. The thick trees around him smelled of dark spaces, rotting wood. He felt the sweat on his face, but it was not the sweat of sickness, of the fever. He still felt for it, probed for the horrible twist in the gut, but it was gone completely, and even his appetite had returned. As they had come closer to Richmond, the gifts flowed into camp again, many citizens sending the last bounty the land had given them. The packages of food were welcomed now, and he was eating regularly. He was grateful for the generosity of the people who kept their suffering to themselves, who did not have much to give, but he knew that the army was suffering more. Vegetables were almost nonexistent, and what passed for meat was either rancid or pure fat. The men were surviving on crackers and moldy flour.

Lee was beginning to understand what this meant to the fighting strength of the army. The marches were much slower now, and the work details accomplished little before the men simply fell out, exhausted, hollow eyes staring ahead at nothing.

He stopped the horse, looked back at the aide who was behind him at a discreet distance. He could hear the sounds of the army, a low echo through the woods, and he tried to hear more, was suddenly swarmed by mosquitoes, a thin cloud singing around his head, picking at his ears, his face. He waved his arm, spurred the horse again, thought, Keep moving.

He knew that Beauregard was right, after all. Petersburg was the target. If the rail center there was captured, the supplies would stop, and the symbolic buildings of Richmond would mean nothing to the starving men of this army. But Beauregard had done himself no favors, had always requested more men than the army could ever provide, was always issuing grand proclamations, great involved schemes to invade unimpeded into the North, grand impossible conquests which he would of course always lead. Now that he was facing a serious threat, the calls for troops were as frantic as ever, but Davis had heard too much of that, and Beauregard would not get his way.

The frustration came over Lee now in a wave. With Grant south of the James, he thought, Beauregard is in command. It becomes his war. That will not sit well in Richmond, and so Davis will change the departments again, shift responsibility to suit his moment, creating more confusion, more chaos.

And all the while, Grant presses forward.

LEE HAD LEARNED QUICKLY THAT GRANT HAD NOT FORGOTTEN the Shenandoah Valley. The inept Franz Sigel had been replaced, and the new threat to the South's most fertile breadbasket came from David Hunter. Lee had known Hunter from the old army, had seen a side of the man in Mexico that had not impressed anyone's sense of decency. Hunter carried a barbaric viciousness into the fight, and now into the farmlands of the valley. Moving south, his forces swept into Lexington, burned the buildings of VMI, burned the home of Virginia's Governor Letcher. The outrage was loud and direct, one more reminder that this war was no longer fought by gentlemen, but Lee knew that beyond the mindless destruction, the threat to the supply line was very real, and so he weakened his army again, sent Jubal Early with the Second Corps to push Hunter away. When Early crossed the Blue Ridge Mountains, Hunter's bravado collapsed, and the Federal troops pulled away without a fight, withdrew to the west, across the Alleghenies, the Federal commander satisfied with the damage he had inflicted on the civilians.

With Hunter no longer a threat, Early's men began to look northward, and Lee now saw an opportunity. Early would march toward Washington, repeating on a smaller scale what Lee had tried to accomplish twice before. If Early's numbers were not great enough to actually occupy the city, the threat would still shake Lincoln's chances for reelection, and certainly cause Grant to respond by sending troops, weakening his army as well.

Lee's plan was sound, but the strength was not enough. Grant sent Wright's Sixth Corps, who moved quickly, filling the great heavy defenses around Washington with veteran troops. Early reached the outskirts of Washington too late to cause any real harm.

Lee continued to support Beauregard's calls for troops to the defenses of Petersburg, and Beauregard accomplished an amazing feat, defending the city itself with a handful of troops while Grant's Eighteenth Corps, commanded by "Baldy" Smith, hesitated in front of the nearly defenseless city. Smith was to be supported by Hancock's Second Corps, who arrived on the field under a fog of confused orders. The attack never came, an attack that would have seen the Federal troops marching into Petersburg virtually unopposed. The delay cost Baldy Smith his command.

Beauregard finally strengthened the lines around Petersburg with whatever troops he could put in place, but his skill at defending the city did not save him from the wrath of Davis. Making a tactical mistake, Beauregard removed the line of troops that were holding Ben Butler's blue forces in place, allowing Butler's men to strike out at the one line of communication between Petersburg and Richmond. It was all the excuse Davis needed. Beauregard was removed, and Lee's authority to defend Petersburg was made clear. With Grant's intentions now beyond doubt, Lee moved his men south, wrapping a hard line around the city, filling the trenches and earthworks with the men who understood their duty: that no matter how much strength the enemy brought against them, they could not leave this ground. They were defending the last great lifeline of their country.

25. CHAMBERLAIN

JUNE 18, 1864

THERE WERE SIX REGIMENTS, ALL MEN FROM PENNSYLVANIA, BUT they all knew his name, this college professor from Maine, knew he would lead them as well as any one of their own. They had moved far below the James by now, marching behind the rest of the army, the men of the Second Corps, the Eighteenth. Word was already spreading, another opportunity lost, bad coordination, bad communication. Some of the staff officers had seen a furious Meade, a fiery torrent of temper launched at the unfortunate officer whose duty happened to take him to headquarters. Rumors were flying that Hancock had failed, Smith was relieved. Chamberlain had heard all of it and finally had gone to Griffin to find out the truth. Now he was back with the men, riding beside the marching column. He kept the image of Griffin with him, the anger, red-faced, explosive. Yes, the opportunity had been there, there was virtually no defense at Petersburg. But there had been confusion, hesitation—the curse of the army—commanders who could not see what lay in front of them, men who would not take the responsibility. If there was no initiative, no risk, there was no victory.

Now they were moving south, the Fifth Corps to be the left flank of the army. There had been another attack, Meade sending the center of the line against the lightly held rebel works. But the rebel lines were empty, the defenders now back to the outskirts of Petersburg, a tighter line. Meade ordered them to press on, still believing the rebel numbers were very few, but the foot soldiers saw the guns, the fresh cannon and heavy lines of muskets. The rebel works were now filling with Lee's men, the numbers rising rapidly. If headquarters did not understand what was happening across from them, then they would learn of it from the men on the front lines. There would be no mindless rush to make up for the indecision of before. This would not be another Cold Harbor.

Chamberlain heard the bugles in front, the men beginning to slow the march, moving into the deep brown grass of the fields. There were guns, distant rumbling, from the north, up where Burnside had halted, and Chamberlain reined the horse, listened, thought, No, no attack, not yet. We just got here.

The men of the brigade were nearly all sitting now, faces covered with the grime of the march, the blue of the uniforms dulled by layers of dirt. At the look of men who had absorbed the road beneath them, Chamberlain felt a smile, could not hide it. When they had crossed the James, there was a brief pause, and the men were close to the water. They did not have to be told that this might be the only opportunity they would have, and so they'd swarmed into the water, clothes and all, splashing the thick layers of dirt away, the memories of the hard marches and the bloody fights flowing away downriver. He'd sat on the big horse, watching them, heard the laughing, the pure joy, had ached to join them. It would not do, of course. The officers had to maintain some decorum, especially the brigade commander. They did not know that he'd waited until dark, just before they moved out onto the dusty roads again, and slid quietly into the water, under the watchful eye of a provost marshal—not for protection, but as a discreet lookout for Griffin, Warren, or worse, General Meade. It had been cool and delicious, and the uniform dried quickly. Now the uniforms were covered with the signs of the march again. And he knew they remembered the river.

He saw men gathering sticks, small dead trees, and fires began to dot the field, the cooks moving to the fires, the coffeepots hanging above low flames. He dismounted, moved toward the flag bearer, a huge man named Coogan. Chamberlain felt the stiffness in his feet, his legs, tried to flex the muscles. Coogan watched him, still held the flag high, the gathering place for the officers. Chamberlain approached, looked up at the bright sky. Sweat rolled into his eyes and he blinked hard, put a finger to his eye, the hard leather of the glove probing painfully, doing no good. He blinked again as Coogan held out a handkerchief.

"Here you go, Colonel."

Chamberlain took it, nodded, said, "Thank you, Sergeant." He wiped carefully at the teary eye, shook his head. "Summer in Virginia."

Coogan nodded, waited for Chamberlain to return the handkerchief, said, "Not much different from back home. Summer's always like this. We're not that far south." There was a quiet pause and Coogan said, "Sorry, Colonel. I suppose Maine is a bit farther north."

Chamberlain handed Coogan the handkerchief, was suddenly defensive. "Well, we have our summers in Maine too, Sergeant. A hard sweat does a man good . . . sometimes."

The big man was looking at him, nodded, smiled slightly. Chamberlain felt awkward, ridiculous, pawing at the stinging in his eyes. He blinked again, fought it, thought, You have nothing to prove to these men.

"Um . . . you have mountains where you come from, Sergeant?"

"No, sir, just a few hills. My family's in York, southern part of the state, near Harrisburg."

Chamberlain blinked again, the eye better now, said, "Near Gettysburg. Yes, Sergeant, I am familiar with that area."

Coogan nodded, said nothing, and Chamberlain saw the man's look, saw the respect they had all given him. No, you do not have anything to prove to these men.

He could smell coffee now, heard the sound of tin cups, men moving toward the fires. The regimental commanders were coming together, small staffs trailing behind, but they were moving slowly, without urgency. He waited for them, had nothing really to say to them, no new orders. He searched the faces, knew they were all good men, all veterans of the hard fight.

The brigade had been organized by Griffin from units that had fought far apart. Some were from Reynolds's First Corps, which no longer existed, Reynolds himself killed at Gettysburg. The 149th and 150th Pennsylvania regiments were from the old Bucktail Brigade, and the men still wore the furry tails pinned to their hats. But the pride of these men came not just from symbols, but from their good work, from the bloody fields where they'd done their job. It was the one reason that no one objected when this man from Maine was named their commander. No one doubted that Chamberlain was a man to do his job as well.

The officers saluted him. Some were drinking coffee. There were low, quiet greetings. He knew one man was missing, Major Merrick, the newest arrival, commanding the fresh 187th Regiment. He looked around, out over the fields of resting men, then saw him running toward them. Merrick was yelling, waving one arm behind him, pointing. Heads turned, there were small laughs, quiet jokes at the expense of the new officer. Merrick stumbled through the tall grass, and now the soldiers were laughing as well. He stopped, out of breath, still pointed behind him. Chamberlain waited, did not smile.

"Sir! Over there, over that rise . . . rebels! The enemy is right over there, sir, earthworks, spread on a hill . . . guns . . . cannon! We're in the open, sir!"

Heads turned that way and the laughing stopped. Chamberlain stepped forward, moved past Merrick, could see the low rise, motion, the reflection of guns. Merrick was right, they were very close to the rebel lines. He took a deep breath, thought, No one told me. Why were we sent this close? Why were we stopped right here?

There was sound behind them, wagons, horses. Chamberlain turned, saw a row of big guns moving up, men unlimbering them, quick motion from the flashes of red on the uniforms of the artillerymen. Then the guns were moving into place, pointing out over their heads, toward the rise Merrick had seen. Chamberlain moved toward the guns, looked for an officer, someone in charge, saw a man approaching.

The officer stopped, snapped a crisp salute, said, "Captain John Bigelow, Ninth Massachusetts Battery, at your service, sir."

Bigelow was a young man who carried the confidence of hard experience. Chamberlain returned the salute, said, "It seems, Captain, that we are very close to the rebel lines. We were halted here, apparently in clear sight of the enemy."

"Oh, yes, sir, I know. I was told you are serving as a screen for my guns. This is good ground, a good position, clear line of fire. But we are a bit vulnerable, if their infantry should suddenly advance. I was told you are here to protect us."

Chamberlain stared at the young man. Protect you? He turned, looked back toward the rise where the rebels were still moving into position. They can see us, he thought. They can see us right here, can see these guns. He scanned the wide field, the men now beginning to stand, all looking out toward the enemy. He saw his group of officers, standing together, and now it finally came, across the field, the puff of smoke, and he yelled, "Move! Spread out!"

They did not look at him, were watching the smoke, and now the sound came right at him, the sharp scream, and behind the guns the first blast threw up a shower of dirt. His officers began to move now, did not need Chamberlain to tell them not to stand together as one very nice brass target. More screams split the air over his head and there were more blasts behind him, the rebel gunners shooting long, harmlessly, behind Bigelow's guns. The field was filling with shouts from the officers, and the men were coming together, moving into formation. Muskets were being loaded, more shouts from the officers. The rebels always overshoot, Chamberlain thought, but they will adjust. We're too easy a target.

There were more horses now, men coming down the road from the north, and he saw the flags, saw it was General Warren, and then Griffin as well.

The shells were still flying past, and Warren yelled to Chamberlain, "Good, yes, very good. Colonel, good show displaying your men like this. You must protect these guns. We must discourage the enemy from advancing to this position, they must not believe these guns are easy pickings. Keep your men out in front, make the good show. We have two more batteries moving up along this ridge. Good position . . ."

Chamberlain moved closer, thought, *Good show?* The rebel shells now began to fall in front of them, scattering the formations, heavy showers of dirt throwing men to the ground. Chamberlain looked at Griffin, tried to keep his anger from showing as he asked the silent question.

Griffin gazed across the field, said, "General Warren, this is not a good place to defend against the enemy's artillery."

There was a sudden blast, close to the horsemen, and Chamberlain saw a man fly into the air, men now crying out. He looked at Warren, thought, We are just here to be a target? You didn't think they would shell us? We would lie here and drink coffee in plain sight . . . and the rebels would just *watch*? He felt the redness boiling up his neck, felt himself shake, holding it in. Warren looked around, and Chamberlain saw his calm expression change, something, perhaps clarity, come over him, like a window opening into a dark room.

Warren said, "Colonel, those guns are somewhat of a menace. Won't you take your men over there and do something about that?"

Chamberlain stared up at Warren, heard the calm, the matter-of-factness of the request. "Yes, sir. I believe that is a fine idea." He looked at Griffin, who closed his eyes for a moment, his own silent show of impatience. Chamberlain thought, Careful, no sarcasm, not now. He saluted, said, "General, if you will excuse me. General Griffin, with your permission, sir."

Griffin nodded, said, "Take care of it, Colonel."

There were more blasts now, the sharp screams streaking all around them, and Chamberlain moved quickly, shouted to the officers, the faces watching him, waiting for orders. Now the men began to stand, coming together into tight lines, muskets on shoulders.

Chamberlain grabbed for his horse, waved the sword, saw the lines straightening.

In a few minutes they were moving forward, pushing through the thick grass. He could hear a new sound now, the enemy answering the assault with muskets. He rode forward, saw the rebel works, bathed in white smoke now, and he yelled, waved the sword again, pushed the horse, and the smoke began to clear. The blasts and shrieks of cannon fire had stopped. Now the only sound was the voices of his men, the low growling yell of men who know they're close to the enemy. They began to move up the rise, the smoke gone, carried away by a light breath of wind. Behind the works, the rebels were pulling out, the guns rolling away with a last volley from the infantry. His men reached the works, short rows of fresh dirt thrown up around an old fence line, and climbed over, jumping down, stumbling into the empty trenches. Some fired their muskets, a last chance, and then there was a new sound, a cheer. They had driven the enemy away.

Chamberlain dismounted, saw blood, a dark stain flowing from the horse's side, a big spotted gray, the gift from the citizens of Brunswick, the horse he called Charlemagne. He stared at the blood, felt sudden shock, the horse looking at him. He reached out and touched the wetness. The ball had hit the horse's shoulder, and Chamberlain tried to convince himself, thought, It's all right . . . we can fix that. He stepped away as an aide took the reins and pulled the horse back. Chamberlain climbed the mound of dirt then, looking for the flag, for Coogan. He moved out past the fence, could see the last of the enemy flowing up a far rise, disappearing behind more works, another long row of thick dirt. His men were still cheering, and then he saw the flag, the big man holding it high, and he moved that way. Coogan was not cheering, was staring out ahead, holding the flag stiffly. Chamberlain reached him, watched the officers moving through their men.

The fight had been quick and the casualties light. The officers were organizing their troops, the smaller company flags now in place along the fence line. Chamberlain stared across the open ground toward the new rebel works. This is no victory, he thought. They were too far forward, and we just drove them back to the main lines. They were lucky to keep their guns. If we had been a bit quicker . . .

The men were quiet now, the cheering having exhausted them more than the assault. He could see them lining up in the enemy's trenches, but it was not a strong position. The best protection was behind them, since the ground in front was open, cut by small clumps of brush. Still, they were in the enemy's works, had taken the position, and if there was no great strategic gain, it was good for the men. He saw Merrick now, thought, Yes, this is good for the 187th, a shot of confidence. Merrick was following the example of the other commanders, quieting his men, taking charge, spreading them into line in the works. Chamberlain moved toward him, and Merrick saluted, beaming a smile.

Chamberlain said, "Well, Major, fine work. Now your men are veterans."

Merrick glanced down his lines, said, "Yes, sir! We are ready to go again, sir!"

Chamberlain smiled, remembered how anxious he'd been to get into the first fight, the frustration of being in the reserves at Antietam, unused, watching the rest of the army do the bloody work.

"There will be time for that, Major. Patience . . ."

Behind them he could hear the big guns moving forward, more this time, the batteries Warren had mentioned. He climbed the dirt, anchored himself with one foot on a piece of fence line, watched as the men unhitched the guns, other men with shovels throwing dirt in the air. All along the ridge shallow pits were quickly dug behind the crest, and now the guns were wheeled forward, their muzzles just above the ground.

He jumped down, moved to the horses, saw one man beside his Charlemagne. The bloodstain was dark and dry, but the wound had a small white dressing, a plug of cloth stuck straight into the bullet hole. Chamberlain moved close, stared at the dressing, then at the horse. The man said, "He's fine, sir. A grand old fellow. Take more than a musket ball to bring him down. Even got the bullet out of him . . . here." The man showed Chamberlain the flattened piece of lead.

Chamberlain said, "Good, thank you. Fine work. Yes, he's a grand old fellow. Not ready to lose him yet."

He reached out, patted the horse, reached into the saddlebag and brought out his field glasses. He moved back to the old fence, climbed up, stared out over the works, looked through the glasses. The ground dropped away in front of them, and in the low area there was a creek, winding through brush. The banks were steep, but the creek was narrow enough for a man to jump . . . if the ground were hard. He could see where the rebels had crossed, tracks in deep mud. It's swampy, he thought. They must have known where to pull the guns through, the drier ground. He lifted his gaze up the rise, saw the enemy works, motion, the sharp glare from bayonets. There were many bayonets.

The works spread all along the ridge in front of him and far out to the right, disappearing beyond more ridge lines. In front of where he stood, the enemy's lines curved away to the left, the apex of the curve pointing right at him. He lifted the glasses and gazed beyond the enemy's lines, could see church steeples, the tops of buildings. His heart jumped, the sun reflecting off rooftops. It was the town of Petersburg.

There were shouts from behind the works, the sound of a horse, and Chamberlain turned, saw a staff officer climbing over the fence, a face he did not know. The man looked around, followed the hands that pointed toward him, then moved close. Saluting, he said to Chamberlain, "Colonel, I have orders for you, from General Meade. You are to attack the enemy position immediately."

Chamberlain was trying to remember the face, wondered who the man was, then said, "General . . . Meade? What of General Warren? Excuse me, but this is not chain of command . . . um, Colonel . . ."

"Abercrombie. I come straight from General Meade. The commanding general is considerably, um, agitated that his attacks have not been carried out. Your position is the most forward of the army. You are closest to the enemy's lines. You are to attack the position."

"Alone?" Chamberlain was moved to anger again, had begun to wonder if this man was some impostor. He thought, I don't get my orders straight from General Meade. He tried to imagine Griffin's response to a breach in protocol like this, wondered if this man was a spy.

"Colonel Abercrombie, does corps headquarters know of these orders? Has General Warren been informed?"

Abercrombie glanced around, lowered his voice. "Colonel, all I know is what I was told. General Meade has expressed considerable frustration at General Warren's lack of aggressiveness. Your name was mentioned . . . your actions this morning were noted by the commanding general, and by General Grant as well. I do not speculate on General Meade's orders, but there was considerable anger behind his instructions to me."

Chamberlain thought, But we are one brigade. If we assault those works, we will receive fire from all over the field. This is suicide.

He looked past the officer, to where others were beginning to gather. He pointed to an aide, said, "Corporal, a sheet of paper?"

The man hurried forward, pulling a paper from his coat, and handed it to Chamberlain. Chamberlain stepped to the fence, spread the page on a flat board, began to write.

I have just received a verbal order not through the usual channels, but by a staff officer unknown to me, purporting to come from the general commanding the army, directing me to assault the main works of the enemy in my front. Circumstances lead me to believe the General cannot be perfectly aware of my situation, which has greatly changed within the last hour. I have just carried a crest, an advanced post occupied by the enemy's artillery, supported by infantry. I am advanced a mile beyond our own lines, and in an isolated position . . .

He stopped, looked out across the ground, then continued to write, described the ground, the enemy's entrenchments, the position of his troops. The anger grew as he wrote, and he finished the note, signed it:

Very Respectfully, Joshua L. Chamberlain, Colonel Commanding 1st Brigade, 1st Division, 5th Corps

The officer watched him, waited, and Chamberlain folded the paper, handed it to him.

"If you don't mind, take this to your commanding general, and request a response. *Respectfully* request a response."

There was a look of dread on the man's face, and he nodded. "Whatever you say, Colonel. I would suggest, sir, if I may, that judging by the commanding general's mood this morning, you can anticipate these orders will be repeated. Reports of delay have been received at headquarters with some . . . frustration." Abercrombie saluted, moved back toward his horse.

Chamberlain stared out across the open ground, could see movement in the rebel position even without the field glasses, said, "They're still filling the works."

He looked around, the officers watching him. No, be careful, he thought. Keep it to yourself. He looked up at the sun, nearly straight overhead, thought, Plenty of time. We may yet do it. It would be nice, though, if the rest of the army decided to lend a hand.

THE ORDERS CAME BACK EXACTLY AS BEFORE. BUT THE REST OF the army *would* lend a hand. Meade ordered the assault to begin at three o'clock, and included a general assault across the entire front. Chamberlain's position was closest to the enemy works, and his brigade was chosen as the focal point to begin the attack.

Warren's Fourth Division was commanded by Lysander Cutler, an old soldier who saw events very much in his own way. The Fourth was positioned behind Chamberlain's left flank, too far behind to protect it. There was time before the assault, and Chamberlain decided to speak with Cutler himself.

He rode a borrowed horse slowly into Cutler's camp, a staff of unfamiliar faces watching him with no expression. He dismounted, handed the reins to a silent aide, stood in silence, felt strangely out of place.

"Excuse me, but can someone direct me to General Cutler?"

One man pointed to a tent, the only tent, and Chamberlain thought, Why is there a tent? We've been on the march all day. This isn't the time to camp. He stepped forward, saw a sergeant standing stiffly beside the tent, and the sergeant bent low, said something quietly into the tent. Chamberlain waited, then saw the gray hair, the old man emerging slowly. Cutler stood up straight, and Chamberlain was surprised, he looked much older than the near-sixty he'd been told. Cutler stepped forward, looked at Chamberlain with impatience, as though something terribly important had been halted for this meeting.

He said, "Yes, Colonel . . . Chamberlain, is it? What's the problem?"

Chamberlain glanced around, saw little motion, none of the preparation for the great fight that was about to begin.

"General, my brigade has been ordered to take the lead in the general assault. I am sure, sir, you have been told of the assault?" Cutler stared at him, said nothing. "Um, well, sir, you are on my left flank, and that flank is exposed at present. I wish to make you aware of that, sir, that when my brigade advances, we will be in some . . . difficulty, if your division does not advance as well."

Cutler still looked at him, tired black eyes, a gruff gray beard. Chamberlain was becoming annoyed.

"General, with all respect, I would suggest that you could move your men *en echelon*, to support my flank, so that my men are not mown down like grass—"

Cutler lunged forward, startled Chamberlain, put a finger close to Chamberlain's face, growled his words in low anger, "You do not give me orders, Colonel. I am your senior. You will take orders from me!"

Chamberlain took a deep breath, felt the cold silence around him, the staff standing stiffly. "General Cutler, I have my orders, and I suppose you have yours. We are to work together. The entire army is to work together. You are my flank. I am also your flank. I thought it best we understand that."

Cutler turned away, began to move to the tent, said aloud, "I will know what to do when the time comes."

Cutler disappeared into the tent, and Chamberlain felt the staff begin to move again, a collective release of air. He looked around, and the faces were not looking at him. The meeting was over. He felt exhausted, angry. He had lost his patience completely, thought, Yes, I understand the orders now. General Meade, I am grateful I do not have your job.

He moved to the horse and took the reins from the aide, who said quietly, "Best of luck to you, Colonel Chamberlain."

Chamberlain looked at the man, surprised, saw the gentle seriousness in the man's eye, suddenly felt he knew him, the older face familiar, even the voice. "Thank you, Corporal. Do I know you?"

"Don't reckon so, Colonel. But I know you. Some of us . . . we just pay a bit more attention than they give us credit for. We know who the good ones are. It's not important, Colonel. You just take good care."

The man saluted, backed away, and Chamberlain watched him, still felt something familiar, even something in the man's walk, a slow calm step. The man was gone now, beyond the lines of troops beginning to move, the army slowly coming to life. He climbed the horse, tried to see the man again, then he knew, saw another old face, heard the voice in his mind, the thick Irish brogue. It was Kilrain, and he thought, Yes, Buster, there are more of you, aren't there? There are many who see beyond the orders and the flags and the stars on the shoulders. This army still has men like you, men so unlike the rest, men who know how to *think*, who see all that happens around them with such clarity. He thought, I should have asked the corporal's name. But no, it won't matter, after all. He will not survive. The thought gave him a shiver. I know it, I am absolutely certain of it. My God . . . and he knows it too. It's so clear, the calm . . . you can see it in the eyes, hear it in the voice. He will sleep soundly, while the men around him stare nervously at stars. It's the men who know they are going to die who sleep well. If you have doubts, if you are uncertain, then you are afraid. He thought of the man's words. *Take good care . . .*

HE GLANCED AT THE POCKET WATCH, THEN BACK BEHIND THE lines, to the far ridge where they had begun the day. The ground was empty, nothing moving, not one man, not one piece of blue. He lifted the field glasses, searched down to the left, back into the heavier trees, where Cutler's division should be. He tried to focus, strained his eyes, thought, Where are you? He turned, looked now to the right rear of the brigade, saw the long row of guns, waiting, as he was waiting. He looked again at the watch. It was nearly three o'clock. Well, he thought. We won't have to wait much longer.

All along his lines the men were crouched low, a last moment of rest, and he walked out in front of them, saw a solid line of blue in both directions, and they were waiting as well. Most of the faces were looking straight at him, and he was suddenly stronger, felt the power of these men, the strength of their confidence. Yes, we will do the job, he thought. These men will not stop.

The four veteran regiments were to move out in one battle line, with the 187th coming up behind. It would be an assault nearly four hundred yards wide, and if the orders were carried out, they would be supported strongly on both flanks. He'd seen the troops above them, on the right, another strong line, out in front of more big guns. They were not as close to the enemy as he was, but the flanks were secure, and there would be no mistake—when Chamberlain began to move, the rest of the Fifth Corps would move with him. He stood now in front of them, his back to the enemy, looked again down to the left flank, the empty ground. Damn that old man! He clenched his fists, wanted to shout, yell out toward the empty patch of woods. But Cutler had his orders, and he kept hearing the arrogance in the old man's words: *I shall know what to do when the time comes . . .*

He walked down toward the left flank, the exposed end of his line, looked at the faces watching him, wondered if they knew, that without support they would be hit the worst. He glanced far to the left, to a low hill half a mile away. It was on the maps, a small circle on the crude sketches of the enemy positions. The rebels called it Fort Mahone, and he'd seen it with the glasses, had seen the motion of the flags, the small black dots along the edge of the works. The fort was filled with cannon. He looked back to the men, would not see that place now, thought, If Cutler doesn't come up, those guns will have nothing to shoot at but . . . these men.

He saw their faces again. It doesn't matter to them, not anymore, not the men who have done this so many times. There are always guns. Sometimes you see them right in front of you, the sharp bright blast that sweeps away the man beside you, but more often you never see them, you only hear what they can do to you, the high scream, the sudden shattering blast, moving the ground under your feet. But none of that matters, because after all, the guns are far away, and the goal is always much closer, those men out there, the muskets pointing at your heart. That is your target, the goal. If the artillery blast takes you away, that is the hand of God, the poor stroke of Fate. But that man out there, the one looking right at you, you can never look beyond him. He turned, gazed across the wide-open ground, could see the reflection of the bayonets.

It was suddenly deathly still, no breeze, no sound at all. He stared at the enemy's works for a few seconds, then turned back to his men. The faces were watching him still, and he suddenly felt like saying something, speaking to them. He remembered Cutler's strange old corporal, looked down the rows of his own men, thought, How many of you know for certain you will not come back? He stepped closer to the line, walked slowly toward the center of the line. He felt a cloud of words building up inside of him, had to say something . . . if not for them, for himself.

"Gentlemen . . ." The word stuck in his throat, and he was suddenly angry at himself. No, these are not *gentlemen*.

"Men . . . it is close to the time. You are aware that by your successful action this morning, we have advanced well in front of the rest of the army, and so . . . they are looking to us to begin the assault." There were a few cheers, fists punched the air. He waited, continued the slow walk, saw men farther down the line beginning to stand, trying to hear him.

"We have a duty to perform here. It is not that different from the duty which many of you have performed before. You may have wondered . . . how many times, why must we do this again? We have all known men . . . friends, who have fallen on fields just like this one. And all of you know that some of us will not survive this field. If God is merciful, then it will be only a few. Look at the man beside you. Remember him, know that you are fighting together, that each of you has a part in something much greater than yourself. Think about this ground, where it is we *are*."

There were more cheers, men began to shout, *"Virginia!"*

He waited again, then raised his hand, and the shouts quieted. "Yes . . . we are very close to the end of this war. It may be today, it may be by the very action you take today, by the heroism of this very brigade, of these regiments, of the man beside you . . . of *you*. Do we know the name of this place? Will history record what we do here? Did we know that a name like Gettysburg would have such meaning? Take that with you, across this ground. What each of you does here may decide the end of the war. Think of the importance of that. If it matters to you that your nation be proud of what you do, then carry that with you. If you have a family back home, make them proud as well, take inspiration from that. But if all that is very far away, if you can only see the enemy, and you feel alone, or even afraid, then look again, now, at the man beside you. Know that he is there, and the man beside him, and the men all down the line, that what you do today may be the one great effort, the last full measure that God requires of us, to break this unholy rebellion."

Men began to cheer again, and the regimental flags began to move forward. He saw the officers step out in front, saw Coogan now, with the brigade colors, and Coogan nodded, looked at the ground beside him, a quick downward glance, a silent reminder. Chamberlain stared at him a brief moment, then felt a sudden chill, looked at his watch. It was three o'clock.

He looked down the line, both directions, drew his sword, held it straight in the air, then turned, pointed across the wide field, straight at the enemy.

"Attention . . . trail arms!" he shouted. "Double quick! *March!*"

The men surged forward, and he moved with them, Coogan by his side. He felt the wild thrill again, wanted to yell out, Yes, we are unstoppable, a mighty force! He glanced at Coogan, the big man holding the flag steadily, staring straight ahead. Now the voices spread over the field, the low growling sound, rising into one single chorus. They were moving quickly down the long rise, and he could see far off to the right, more masses of blue, the assault beginning for the rest of the corps.

Behind him, the air was shattered by the blasts from the big guns, Bigelow's battery, then more, down the crest of the hill, the other guns of the corps. The shells began to strike the works out in front of them, across the way, flashes of light, great bursts of dirt and timber. The chorus of sound from the men began to slow now, the raw excitement giving way to the hard breathing, the exertion of the charge.

He looked back down to the left, could still see the patch of woods, and there was still no movement, no sign of the Fourth Division. Cutler was still not up. He felt a rage boiling up, felt like blowing a cannon blast into Cutler's smug face. I will have him court-martialed . . . I will march into that damned tent and grab that gray beard . . .

He looked down the hill again, kept moving, pressing forward by the great flow of men around him. He began to feel something else, the quiet anticipation, the voices now silent. As they moved down the hill they all waited for it, knew it would come in a sudden shocking wave, and each man held his jaw tight, pulled his arms in tight against his sides, stepping forward in rhythm with the man beside him. And then it came, the first wave of shells ripping through the lines, solid shot rolling through the men like a hard wind, some streaking overhead, some plowing down into the ground beneath their feet. Then the hollow shells began to whistle past, a different sound, fuses timed to ignite directly overhead. But the fuses were never very good, and the blasts began to fill the air high out in front of them, bursts of fire, and then far behind them, exploding harmlessly over the ground they'd already crossed. But then would be the one good shell, the perfect timing, and the great blinding fire would shatter the air overhead, men punched down, blown away by the shock and the small pieces of iron. There were gaps in the line now, officers screaming at the men, close it up, keep it together.

Chamberlain pushed down through the smoke, could feel the impact of each shell that hit the ground around him, the rumble, the sudden shock under his feet. He looked behind him, saw Coogan, steady, still looking grimly ahead, the flag straight in the air. Chamberlain moved closer to him, waved the sword, the silent command that the men did not need.

He was close to the creek now, felt his boots slip and sink into softer ground, then sticking deep in thick mud. He pulled his feet into each step, forced his boots up and down, could see the winding ditch of the creek in front of him. It was very wet, the ground a mire, and the men began to slow, to reach the creek, some climbing down, some jumping across, stumbling, then standing again. He saw one man stopping, yelled at him, "No, keep moving . . ." But the man was reaching back, pulling another man out of the creek bed, and now more were doing the same, the men gathering now on the far side of the creek, and out in front the officers began to form the line again. Now there was a new sound, the sharp zip of the musket ball, the first volleys from the works up the hill. He tried to see, looked up the hill, across more open ground, stared into the gray smoke, great choking clouds rolling toward them, from the muskets of the enemy. How close, he thought, how much farther do we have to go? He looked out through the smoke, tried to see the faces of the men behind the works, the muskets and bayonets. If we can see them . . . we will keep moving . . .

He stood beside the creek, watching waves of his men flowing across, climbing down then up the soft banks. He looked at Coogan, to give the order, move the flag across, and there was a blast of hot air, a sudden burst of thunder in his face, knocking him straight back. He was still on his feet, the words still in his mouth, but the big man was gone, completely, swept horribly away. Chamberlain stared at the flag. It was standing upright, still, held by . . . nothing. The flag began to fall, and he jumped forward, grabbed it, looked again for the big man, the grim face, dependable. The ground behind him was a mass of churned up mud and smoke, and small pieces of blue. He stared, felt something in him turn slowly, closed his eyes, held it tight, then looked, saw more troops coming up now, Merrick's men, the 187th bringing up the rear, and he waved the flag, held it high, turned, would jump across the creek, looked up, tried to see the enemy again, a glimpse of the musket fire, sheets of red flame pouring down from the crest of the hill. He looked again for Merrick, thought of yelling, something, anything, but the sounds were deafening, and there was nothing he could say now, this was about blood and instinct and the courage of good men. And we will move up the hill . . .

He was spun around, a sharp hot sting in his side, at his hip. He felt one knee give way, and gripped the flagstaff, held himself up, looked down, tried to see . . . what? There was a rip in his pants, blood streaming out of his hip, and he felt the other knee weaken, then give way. He stabbed the ground with the sword, leaned on it, tried to stand straight, but the one leg would not hold him. He tried to pull himself up, lean his weight on the one leg, saw more blood now, on both sides, his pants legs now soaked. He let go of the sword, left it upright in the soft mud, now slowly felt the wetness, touched the torn cloth, thought, I am shot through, clean through. . . .

He let go of the flag and fell forward, his hands in the mud, and now there were hands under his arms, lifting him up, pulling him back. He looked at the faces of young men staring down at him, said, "Thank you . . . I am shot."

He tried to see across the creek, to sit up, but there was no strength, and he looked again at his side, thought, Too much . . . too much blood . . . *you are dying*.

Around him men were shouting, loud frantic voices. He lay back, the hands under his head, easing him down, and now his head was spinning, and the smoke began to drift across again, the thick gray clouds covering him, the fight still around him, the men still moving forward, fighting for each other, fighting for him.

26. GRANT

June 18, 1864

The staff was not talking. The only sounds were the tin forks, the dull knives, the men hacking slowly on the hard meat of the dinner. Grant was not watching them, sat at the head of the table, listening to the soft sounds of the night, the crickets, the calling of the unseen animals as the fading light woke them to duty. He had finished his own meal, still sat at the table, staring into the dark. Down below, along the wide river, the heavy boats were moving against the landings, and he listened for that, for the sounds of wood against wood, the shouts of the officers, the sailors. He looked down at the plate, one piece of meat left, one good bite of crusty black beef. He stabbed it with a fork, held it up and looked it over, admiring it, then stuffed it in his mouth. There was a small plate of fruit on the table, grapes and berries of every kind, dried figs, and his eyes focused on the sweet dates crusted in sugar. He glanced at the staff, reached slowly out, sneaking, eased his fingers around the flaking sugar, pulled the hand quickly back toward him, the guilty pleasure held tightly, out of sight. Good, he thought, they did not see that. He stood, pushed the chair back, and the faces looked at him, the quiet broken only by the sounds of struggle with the overcooked meat.

"Gentlemen, thank you. Colonel Porter, a fine meal, fine. Thank you."

Porter nodded, had seen Grant's grab of the small treat, did not let on. He began to back away from the table.

Grant said, "No, keep your seat, Colonel. I'll have a cigar and wait for General Meade. He should be along any time now."

Porter relaxed, glanced at the closed hand where Grant guarded the small piece of dessert. Grant saw the look, moved his hand behind his back, hiding the evidence. He moved into the dark, glanced around at the fires, could see movement now, small sounds, a few men leading slow horses, coffee cups and tin plates. He glanced over his shoulder, the staff all content to stay at the table, and he slowly lifted the hand, quickly stuffed his treat into his mouth, glanced around again. Now he saw Porter, smiling, turning away, and he clenched his teeth, thought, Porter saw me, Porter knows.

They always were bringing him special food. The quartermasters seemed to search far and wide for what they assumed to be the special tastes of the commanding general. He didn't understand that, knew that for the last few weeks the staff supply duty had gone to Horace Porter, the officers taking turns working with the quartermasters, and even Porter did it, brought all manner of odd and delicate foods to the table. Grant thought, What is it about . . . rank? Am I supposed to become suddenly strange in my eating habits, just because I am in command? Save it for the men, for the soldiers, the ones who earn it. They eat bacon and hardtack, and my mess table is covered with amazing varieties of . . . stuff. He thought of the sweetbreads Porter had found, and it gave him a shudder. He had first eaten them when he was very young, was not partial to the taste, the *feel* of it. Then he learned what part of the animal it was and it made him sick. A few days earlier, Porter had served the staff a tall plate of this odd "treat," and Grant couldn't touch it. While the others feasted, he had sliced a cucumber. They often found chickens, scrawny birds that had somehow escaped the scavenging of soldiers. Grant would not touch that either, could never stop thinking about feathers.

He was perfectly content to feed from the herds of cattle that came from the big boats. When they had beef, which was often now, he watched the men stabbing the bloody meat with lustful enthusiasm, and finally he'd let them know, the subtle hint passed around. The meat will not bleed. He would only eat it nearly burnt to a crisp, and the staff had learned to go along; the man who liked his meat red would have to find another table. But it was the small sweet treats that still made him feel guilty, and he tried not to think about it, didn't really understand anyway. The food is there, on the table, he thought. If it is not eaten, it will just . . . go to waste. But, *sugar* . . . an amazing luxury. There should be no luxuries, not when a war is being fought, not when those men are out there on their backs, spread out on hard dirt, sleeping so close to the guns of the enemy. We have not earned the right, not yet. We sleep in tents, our boots are dry, we can stand straight and stretch our backs without a sharpshooter taking our heads off. That is luxury enough.

The taste of sugar was still in his mouth, and he began to think of coffee, then heard the horses, the commotion across the dark field. He stopped, waited, saw men rising from the mess table, and they knew as well. It was Meade.

The horses stopped, the men began to dismount, and Grant heard the greetings, the staffs talking. He watched the one man, the wide floppy hat, silent, looking around. Grant moved that way, knew Meade was there only to see him, not to socialize with his staff.

"General Meade, here. This way, if you please."

Meade moved quickly, now walked beside Grant, kept his head down, said nothing. Grant waited, knew something would pour out, always expected a flood of hot words, but Meade was quiet.

Grant said, "General, your men have done all they can do, for now."

Meade stopped, looked at him, appeared surprised. "General Grant, I am not certain I share that view. We had our opportunity, and lost it. Petersburg was in our hands, and we allowed the moment to pass. My command did not—"

"General, your command is fine. The attacks were not coordinated well, there was delay when there should have been none. It is something I have become accustomed to."

Meade was shocked, his face illuminated by the firelight as he stared at Grant with his mouth open.

Grant began to walk again, said, "General, it has been six weeks. We have not stopped moving since we crossed the Rappahannock River. Look where we are, how much ground we have covered. We are facing a beaten enemy, an army that is on the very edge of collapse. The only way Lee can fight us is behind dirt. We still have the numbers, we still have the supplies, the guns, the power. If Richmond had any strategic value, I have no doubt it would be in our hands, it would be ours. His defensive lines cannot stretch that far and be much of a defense. He knows that as well. Now we will pick our moments, select our opportunities. If this is to become a siege, so be it."

Meade removed his hat, said, "Sir, there is no excuse for our performance today. I had to issue the same order three times, to get our people to move forward. This was to be one grand assault, we should have pushed them right into Petersburg. But for every unit that went forward, another just sat there, or moved too late to do any good. Half of Warren's corps watched the other half chew themselves to pieces. The Second, Hancock . . . hell, Hancock can't even fight."

Grant stopped again, said, "How's he doing?"

"Not good. The doctors won't let him ride. The Gettysburg wounds have opened up. General Birney is now in field command of the Second Corps." Meade took a deep breath, made a low chuckle, unusual. "Hancock's still pretty mad at Baldy Smith. Wants a court of inquiry, says we should have walked into Petersburg with bands playing. I told him Smith was relieved, but it didn't help him any. He's hurting more than he lets on. Guess I'd be about as mad as he is if the doctors kept me confined to my tent. He's a fighter, no doubt. But . . . without him to give the orders, the Second is as toothless as the Ninth."

Meade stopped abruptly, had crossed a line. Grant said nothing, knew it was still a sore point with Meade, Burnside's Ninth under Grant's direct control, not a part of Meade's command. It was still a problem, as was Baldy Smith's Eighteenth, the corps that technically was still under Butler's command. But the biggest problem that day had been Meade himself, the vague orders, each corps receiving a separate command. There had been no coordination because Meade had not told them to coordinate. Grant had learned now, with these men, these commanders, the orders must be plain and simple and direct. There could be no room for discretion. The fights today had gained little, but the casualties had not been as bad as this kind of jumbled attack could have produced. Lee was now firmly in command of the works around Petersburg, most of his army having completed the move from north of the James.

Grant said, "Let it pass, General. We may have some time now, some room to breathe. The enemy is hard in his defense, and the men deserve a rest. We cannot fault the corps commanders every time a battle does not go according to plan. War is not fought on paper, you cannot draw a line with a pencil and account for what might happen. When change is needed, change is made. Who would *you* place in command of the Ninth? Of the Fifth? Is anyone ready to step into that position?"

There was a quiet pause. Meade said, "I am not especially comfortable with having my orders ignored."

Grant thought, Maybe if the orders were better . . . but no, he would not say that to Meade, knew Meade was still sensitive, still expected to be the scapegoat if anything went wrong. And he knew that some of the worst orders, the disaster at Cold Harbor, those orders had not come from Meade, but from him. Grant also understood that the army was fresh with many new troops, men who did not yet understand that the battlefield is not like the parade ground. Even the veterans were not performing like they should, and the corps commanders were learning that even the best men, the finest and most experienced units, had to take a breath sometime. This powerful army was simply worn-out.

He had seen the newspapers, the names, even those friendly to Lincoln, calling Grant a "hammer," and those who were not friendly using words like "butcher." He tried not to pay attention to that, but many of the officers did, especially after Cold Harbor. Many were questioning if there would be someone else, if that great failure would be like the failure of so many others, and would sweep Grant out of command. But Lincoln had said nothing, there had been no official blame. Grant appreciated that, that what Lincoln had told him months before was still true: *Use the army, and I will leave you alone.* He stared out through the dark, past Meade, thought, Yes, we have used this army. And we have made Lee use his more. Now it's only a matter of time.

JUNE 21, 1864

HE STEPPED ONTO THE DARK WOODEN PLANKS OF THE DOCK, watched the steamer moving closer. Behind him the staff was in their best dress uniforms, waiting along the shoreline. He held the cigar tightly in his teeth, looked up at the black trail of smoke coming from the small ship, and now he heard a voice out on the dock, close to the water, a sentry, a very young man in a sharp blue uniform. "No smoking allowed on the wharf!"

He heard another voice, behind him, Rawlins, heard the boots coming out on the wood, small coughing sounds coming from Rawlins's throat, knew what was about to happen, held up his hand.

"It's all right, Colonel. This man is quite correct. It was my order, after all. We cannot risk a fire."

Rawlins stopped beside him, and Grant glanced at him, saw him still red-faced, knew that if he'd let Rawlins confront the sentry, Rawlins might have thrown him in the river. Rawlins was choking on his own words, staring at the sentry.

"Dismissed, Colonel. Go back to the others. The man is doing his job." Rawlins stepped away, slowly, made some gesture to the sentry Grant did not see. He held out the cigar, freshly lit, and tossed it off the dock, a small hiss as it touched the water. The sentry was aware now, and Grant realized the man was shaking, staring at him with wide eyes. It was obvious he'd had no idea who this plainly dressed officer was who had intruded into his authority. But he definitely knew now.

Grant nodded, and the man saluted, a slight quiver in his hand, said weakly, "Sir . . ."

The boat was alongside the dock now, sailors moving about with ropes, pulling the boat tightly into place. The gangplank was quickly laid, and now Grant saw one man, tall above the others, stepping forward, the long legs carrying him quickly forward onto the dock. He was all smiles, the tall black hat clamped down firmly on his head, moving in long quick strides toward Grant, now holding out the wide hand.

"General Grant, it is a pleasure, sir, a pleasure!"

Grant reached out, felt his hand swallowed up, held on tightly while the lanky arm shook up and down, raw boyish enthusiasm.

"Mr. President, welcome to City Point. Welcome to the headquarters of the army."

THE REPORTERS WERE KEPT BACK, THE STAFF GUARDING CAREfully, and even the small bribe or promise of favor did not tempt the officers to allow anyone within earshot. The two men walked slowly along the high bluff over the river, out in front of the rows of white tents. City Point was at the junction of the two rivers, where the Appomattox flowed into the James, and at this point the water was nearly a mile across. The two men stopped, Grant pointing, and the reporters, and the staff, could only guess what he was telling the President.

The bluff was higher than even the tops of the tall ships, and Grant motioned toward one, just docked, the ropes now securing her to the wharf. "Cattle, probably two or three hundred head."

Lincoln nodded, said, "Indeed. The supply people are doing their job. I hope you agree. The supplies have been . . . adequate?"

Grant pointed to another ship, the decks piled high with brown bundles, men moving about, the piles slowly shifting to the dock itself. "More than adequate. From this place, we can keep the flow constant. The wagons can load up right at the water. We don't even have to rely on the railroads."

Lincoln nodded, said nothing. Grant turned, could see the sea of faces watching them, men scattered across the open yard of the grand estate. The big white house itself was used by the quartermasters, the headquarters tents spread out in neat lines across the open yard. Behind them was the larger mess tent, and down below, beyond the last of the staff tents, the small corral for the horses.

Lincoln still watched the ships, the activity down below. He said quietly, as though unfriendly ears were listening, "If I may ask, what of General Lee's supplies?"

Grant looked at him, surprised at the question. "We're working on that. General Lee has little to rely on *but* the railroads. That's why he's protecting Petersburg."

"Permit me, General, I know I had told you I would never ask. But I am stunned by what I see here, by the size of this effort, by the strength . . . the pure strength of your army. It is an easy thing to sit up there in Washington and forget what is happening here, the magnitude of your effort. I hope you don't hear what I have to endure, the opinions from my opposition, how easy this should be, how quickly we should overrun those rebels. I wish those men, the reporters, the congressmen . . . I wish they could see *this*, this remarkable scene, all the ships, the wagons, the men. I am impressed, General. I have to say honestly, I am impressed. I wonder, though, how strong is the enemy?"

"You mean, sir, does Lee have anything like . . . this?" He waved his arm, a sweeping gesture across the waterfront. "No, he most definitely does not. And, that is the point. I have not done as well with this army as some of your people in Washington would have assumed. I *have* read the papers. Most of them criticize you for what this army has not been able to accomplish."

Lincoln nodded, said, "I do bear the responsibility. No one lets me forget that. The victories are yours, certainly. The failures are mine."

There was something painful in the words, the signs of strain that Lincoln tried not to show. Grant looked at him, the deep lines in the worn face.

Lincoln said, "Been nominated again. Those foolhardy Republicans want me to keep at it until I get it right."

"Yes, sir, I heard about the convention. Congratulations."

"Hmm, well, don't congratulate me yet, General. There's still an election. I hear it might be George McClellan for the Democrats. He's pretty loud about a peace movement, got a bunch of people thinking we should end the war before too many more get hurt. It's the kind of talk that looks good in the newspaper. People beginning to move that way, I'm afraid. You have to give them a reason to believe this will end soon, General." Lincoln stopped, looked down, said, "Sorry, Mr. Grant. I told you I would not interfere."

There was a quiet moment, the sounds from the waterfront drifting up the rise, a light breeze now blowing across the wide stretch of water.

Grant said, "It will take time. It may only take time. This is settling down to a siege. They can't last much longer."

Lincoln looked at him, said, "How much longer? You expect this will end like Vicksburg? That would be quite wonderful, sir." Lincoln was smiling now, the enthusiasm returning.

Grant said, "I don't think it will end like Vicksburg. There's still the railroads, the rebels are still being fed. And Lee is not Pemberton. Lee is not like anyone I have fought against."

Lincoln smiled, pointed to the reporters watching them. "There's a good many of those fellows over there with the pencils in their hands who would enjoy quoting you on that."

Grant did not look. "A few generals too . . ."

Lincoln laughed, removed the tall hat from his head, ran his hand through his hair.

"Yes, we both have our crosses to bear. How long, General?"

The question was serious, and Grant looked at him again, saw the expression changed, the dark eyes looking hard into him. "We will put as much pressure on Lee as we can. We are already extending our lines around the south of the city, and as far as we extend, the enemy must extend as well. They do not have the manpower, and we do. I had hoped it would be over by now. We should have driven him out of the city by now, broken them. . . ." He glanced at Lincoln, saw a frown, knew that Lincoln did not feel comfortable hearing the details. Grant paused, said, "I don't enjoy making a siege. It requires patience. I have learned that predictions are easier made than realized. I don't know how much time it will take."

Lincoln nodded, still serious, then began to smile. "Then, General, we will exercise patience. It will be my job to convince the voters to do the same."

Lincoln stepped forward to the edge of the bluff, looked downriver, saw another ship, moving closer, and in the distance a column of black smoke, a steamer. He waved his hat in a sweep across the waterfront below.

"My God, I cannot get over this. Look at this, General! The strength, the power behind your army. It's right here, right in front of us. These ships come from every port, all the way up to Maine. The entire Union is pouring out not just its men, but its bounty. I wish they could see this, the people who doubt us, who doubt our resolve."

Grant stepped closer to the bluff, followed Lincoln's gaze, could see more columns of black smoke now, the steady flow of supplies for his army. He pulled a cigar from his pocket, began to light it, said, "There's only one person who needs to see this. If there was some way, any way, to bring him here, I'd go myself, a private invitation." Grant pulled at the cigar, the smoke flowing up and away from the river. "If he would stand right here, right on this spot, and watch those boats unloading, the supplies, the food, the guns, if he could see the reinforcements filling the docks . . . if he saw it for himself, what we are bringing to the fight . . . we would not need patience."

Lincoln was running the names through his head, the reporters who plagued him, his enemies in the press, in Washington. "One man? Who, if I may ask?"

Grant looked at him, held the cigar now tightly in his teeth, said, "Robert E. Lee."

THEY RODE OUT IN FRONT OF A COLUMN OF STAFF AND REporters, moved on the hard roads through the camps of the men. The horse that carried Lincoln was large, but not large enough, the man's legs hanging down awkwardly. Grant had not wanted to look, did not want to embarrass the President, knew Lincoln was not as comfortable on the horse as he tried to show. Some of the soldiers were pointing, Lincoln's neat black suit now covered in dust, the pants legs riding up, showing a bit of his bare leg. The soldiers seemed to cheer more at that, at the humanity, the lack of show. They were used to the spectacle of the silken dignitaries, men in perfect suits, embroidered shirts, as though posing for a portrait. But Lincoln was simply one of *them*, awkward and smiling, happy to feel their enthusiasm, and so they shared it with him even more.

They had toured through the camps all morning, and Grant now turned down a smaller road, a sudden shift in direction, guided the procession along a brief cut through thin woods. He glanced at Lincoln, saw the President ducking under a low tree limb, said, "Excuse me, sir. I thought you might enjoy visiting one of the units of the Eighteenth Corps. They equipped themselves quite well in the last fight, captured a good number of the enemy's guns."

Lincoln nodded happily, was clearly enjoying himself, said, "Whatever you say, Mr. Grant. Whatever you say."

The trees now gave way to open ground, and they rode up a short rise, then beyond, rows of tents, and now Lincoln understood, saw for himself why Grant had brought him this way. Through the rows of tents, from around the small fires, men began to move out into the road, filling it, blocking the way, began now to cheer, loud and boisterous, hands reaching out toward Lincoln, his name echoing across the camp like church bells. He touched the hands, reached out as far as he could, and Grant knew, watching them, that Lincoln had already touched each of them, all of them. It was a camp of men who had volunteered as so many had volunteered, to pick up a gun and fight and die for their country.

But there was a difference. That these men would fight, and fight so well, was a surprise to many, and many still would not believe it. But Grant saw it in Lincoln's face, there was no surprise at all, that Lincoln had believed from the beginning that war was color-blind. Grant let the horse drift to the side, let the troops move past him, a wave of blue uniforms, the sea of black faces pushing forward, the cries and the joy and the tears filling the air, flowing up and around the smiling face of the President.

27. CHAMBERLAIN

June 29, 1864

He had very nearly died. He'd even written that to Fannie, a long and tearful letter, words that came from some very desperate place, the part that fights for just a bit more time, enough time to say the right words. He was good with words, but struggled for something more, the sorrow and apology, that somehow she did not know how much he loved her. He'd told himself the letter should comfort her, but when he read it again, he knew he had written it to comfort himself, to relieve the guilt, to make a peace with her for going off to fight, and to God, for not staying closer to the Word.

The doctors had not thought it possible, the wound so severe, cutting right through him. But the surgeons agreed to try, and they spent long hours working and cutting and patching. When they took him away, loaded him on the wagon that would carry him to the hospital steamer, the men in bloody white coats had stopped their work, just for a moment, watched with shaking heads as this man was driven away, to be put on the small grim boat, set gently down among the long rows of wounded.

He did not know where they were taking him, slept through most of the trip, had to be told by a nurse, a very round woman with very bad breath, that he was at Annapolis, the naval hospital. And he would be there for a long time.

In every direction all he could see was white—white walls, a white ceiling, white sheets, women in white uniforms. Next to him there was another man, covered in more white, a man Chamberlain had yet to speak to. When the nurses came around, they spoke in whispers, and it was not because of him. He would lie wide-awake, hoping they would stop and talk to him, break the monotony. But they would only nod politely, and he'd watch their faces, the horrified stares at the bed beside him, and even the whispers would fade away. Now it was beginning to get to him. What was the matter with this man?

There was no trying to sit up or turning to one side. The wounds were still very dangerous, the surgery very fragile. If he made the effort, tried to see beyond the mounds of white that blocked his view, there would be a blast of pain, and he would apologize to himself, try to relax, let himself drift back into the soft white clouds around his head.

After a few days the pains were not constant, the sleep not interrupted, and they had stopped giving him the drugs. Now, when daylight began to fill the room, he tried to keep track of time, to measure what hour it was. His mind made it an exercise, and he told himself it might be the only way he could survive this and stay sane.

He knew it was mid-morning now, he'd been awake for a while, the room brightly lit. He had learned to watch the shadows, a picture frame on the one wall he could stare at comfortably. There was a portrait in the frame, and in the first few days in the bed, when the drugs still clouded his mind, he thought it was Dr. Adams, Fannie's father, a grim portrait that hung in their living room. The shock of that had given way to acceptance, his price for being here, for allowing himself to be wounded. But when his eyes cleared, the face had grown unfamiliar, and he was still not convinced that the painting had not been quietly switched, that the new face was someone else's punishment.

But the frame now held his attention, ornate and gilded. The morning sun cast a shadow on the wall to one side. He had not seen the window, but by now guessed how tall it must be, enough to let the sunlight hit the frame for just so long. The shadow would disappear while the sun was overhead, but sometime in the afternoon it would return, the other way, until finally it faded away with the light in the room. He even began to believe he could see the shadow move, just slightly, shifting as the sun rose and set. It was his secret, his one guilty pleasure. He was beginning to get pretty good at it; it became his game. When the nurses came around, he would ask them the time, and before they could answer, would tell them himself. By now they reacted with feigned surprise, patronizing him, and he knew that, but he also knew they had no idea how he'd figured it out. And so it was still his game.

The shadow was growing weak as the morning went on, and he heard rain. He stared at the picture frame, began to feel a small panic, the shadow fading in the dull light. Scared, he thought, My God, this game is more important than I realized. His mind began to roll over, images flashing as the daylight faded, his concentration not held by the picture frame. Hold on, he thought, what is going on?

The sounds of the rain were growing, the wind began to rattle the windows, and suddenly there was a bright flash and a sharp crack of thunder. He made a sound, a loud short scream, stared at the white ceiling above him, then heard more screams, all down the rows of beds, the storm bringing out the memories, the fear, the horrors of what brought these men to this place. He could feel his heart beating, each pulse a small stab of pain low in his gut. He heard the rain again, the soft sound above him, took a long deep breath, then another. One man was still screaming, no words, just an awful sound, and Chamberlain wanted to sit up, to say something to the man, "It's just rain, just a storm. There are no guns here."

The nurses were moving past him, and now the screaming stopped and he heard women's voices, soft, comforting, and closed his eyes, relaxing again. He tried to imagine how the rest of this place looked, had no idea there were more men in the same room with him, a row of men that stretched out . . . how far, past the one man next to him?

He opened his eyes, heard the voices of the women again, closer, and suddenly was missing her, feeling as empty and alone as he'd ever felt. Then the voices were beside him, and he blinked through damp eyes, tried to see, abruptly saw her face, her hair dripping wet, small drops of water falling on him, and he thought, No, this is a dream, like the portrait on the wall, and he cleared his mind, blinked again. He felt, then, her soft cool hand on his, wrapping around, holding him tightly. She kneeled down beside the bed, a small voice, tears. "Oh, Lawrence, Lawrence . . ."

He tried to squeeze her hand, and there was no strength, and he tried to see her, but his eyes were filled, and he closed them, felt the tears on the side of his face, heard the soft sounds of her voice.

"You're alive . . ."

July 3, 1864

SHE SAT WITH HIM FOR LONG STRETCHES, AND HE FORGOT ABOUT the game, about the shadow on the wall. He still could not lift himself up, the pain still waiting with every motion, and so he lay on his back. He could not see the man beside him. Fannie sat with her back to the man, sat between the beds, would only glance at him when she arrived, a brief look of horror, would sometimes say something, "Oh my," and then turn away, quickly turn her back.

He wanted to know, and some part of him already did, that even if he never saw the man, he had seen the wounds, men shot into pieces, men surviving, amazingly, pieces of them gone, taken away in a horrible moment. The arms and legs were commonplace now, but the doctors were learning, had gotten better, would now try to save men they had always thought could not be saved. It was these men who had the worst time, trying to go home, missing an entire shoulder, or hip, men who had to be carried, or would never leave a wheelchair. Or the faces, men who lost more than an eye, or some teeth. Chamberlain tried not to think on that, fought against it, the faces of scared children, what that would be like, feeling the stares, the horror of your own appearance. But the doctors were saving lives, and men were going home who two years ago would have been left for dead on the field.

And maybe that's a good thing, he thought, not just for those men, but for everyone. Take the war back home, show the citizens. He had often seen the coffins, waiting for the trains to take them home, thought, Dead men in boxes bring grief and crying, gravestones remind us of those we once knew, give us the memories, hold them for us in stone. But these men, still alive, would bring the horror of this war right into their towns, their homes; not some fading memory or sad empty space at the table.

He didn't have to see the man beside him now; the expressions from the nurses, from Fannie, told him all he needed to know. He began to feel he knew the man, and felt affection for him, the man with no voice, who never spoke, and it did not matter why. Go home, he thought, good luck. You gave as much as those who gave their lives. You have to endure, you are the living face of this war, a symbol we must look at and not turn away from. God bless you.

HE AWOKE TO HER SOFT HANDS, TURNING HIM GENTLY, AND had to force himself to relax, to let the movement come from her. The soft cloth rubbed his back, the cool dampness soothed him. Above him, a nurse waited, would help her if she had trouble. But Fannie had learned, was helping whenever they would let her. Now he was turned back, closed his eyes again, relaxed into the pillows.

"Well, what have we here, some kind of hero?"

He opened his eyes, knew the voice, and Fannie stood up, there were hugs. He tried to see, then the face leaned out over him, smiling, the rough beard, the clear blue eyes. It was his brother.

Chamberlain smiled, said, "Tom . . . how . . . you desert?"

Tom stood straight, wounded at the comment, said, "Most certainly not. I'll have you know that not only am I not a deserter, I am now a captain!"

Chamberlain wanted to reach up, to grab his younger brother around the shoulders, to feel that young energy. He lifted one hand, and Tom took it, held it for a moment, said, "We were worried about you, Lawrence, the whole regiment. Just 'cause you command those Pennsylvania boys don't mean the Twentieth Maine forgot about you. Colonel Spear sent me a message for you, said even if you ain't fit to command, there's always a place for you in the Twentieth. You can be our mascot, maybe."

Mascot? Chamberlain didn't know if he was serious or not. He glanced at Fannie, said, "I assure you, young captain, I am no one's mascot. All I need is a bit of rest, and I'll be back on the field." He looked at Fannie again, and she was smiling at him, shaking her head. He knew she didn't take him seriously, that she believed he would never go anywhere but home.

She said, "Lawrence, you have another visitor."

He heard a throat clear, and another man stepped up close to the bed.

Chamberlain saw a familiar face, said, "Well, Major Gilmore, how are you . . . my word, it's been a while."

Gilmore was smiling, said, "Actually, it's Lieutenant Colonel Gilmore, sir. The army seems to enjoy promoting men from Maine."

Chamberlain was feeling very good now, would always remember the stern face of Gilmore, the first combat veteran he'd met, the first day the regiment was organized. Gilmore had been sent to Portland to help organize and drill the new recruits, an efficient and disciplined officer who showed a subtle tolerance for Chamberlain's lack of experience.

"Colonel Gilmore, I congratulate you on your promotion." He looked at Tom again, said, "I congratulate both of you. I have no doubt the promotions were well deserved."

Tom looked at Gilmore now, made a small impatient gesture. Gilmore said, "Colonel, whether Captain Chamberlain is here with permission or not is something I cannot be certain of. However, I am here on official business."

Tom started to protest, and Chamberlain said, "For what? Who—"

"For you, sir. The Department has sent me here to read you . . . this. If you will permit . . ."

Chamberlain felt a sudden dread, thought, A discharge, they're sending me home. "Go on, Colonel, read it."

Gilmore unrolled a piece of paper, read, "To Major General George Meade, Commanding the Army of the Potomac, Major General G. K. Warren, Commanding Fifth Corps, Brigadier General Charles Griffin, Commanding First Division. Colonel Joshua L. Chamberlain, Commanding First Brigade, First Division, Fifth Corps, for meritorious and efficient services on the field of battle, and especially for gallant conduct in leading his brigade against the enemy at Petersburg, Virginia, is hereby appointed Brigadier General of Volunteers, to rank as such from the eighteenth of June, 1864. As provided by Special Orders Thirty-nine, Signed, Lieutenant General Ulysses S. Grant, Commanding."

Gilmore lowered the paper, and out across the white room there was a sudden burst of applause, a few small cheers, from men Chamberlain had yet to see. Gilmore handed him the paper, and he read it over, ran his finger over the seal of Grant's official signature.

He raised one hand, said aloud, "Thank you, gentlemen. I cannot see you yet, and I hope some of you are not here because of me."

He looked up at Gilmore, then at Tom, saw the smiles, and he read the words again, his eye now settling at the top of the page. He said, "This is addressed to General Griffin. His name is at the top. Why?"

Tom looked at Gilmore and began to laugh. Gilmore cleared his throat, leaned down, close to Chamberlain's face, said quietly, "I had hoped not to tell you, actually. You would find it out eventually. Um . . ." He stopped, and Chamberlain could see he was searching for words.

Now Tom leaned over, said with a broad smile, "Lawrence, they think you're dead!"

Chamberlain looked at the paper again, saw the order, all in the third person, not addressed to him at all.

Gilmore said, "It seems so, sir. I was told that General Grant has never promoted anyone on the field before. Ever. The first reports from the Fifth Corps seemed to indicate that you did not survive. When General Grant heard about that, he issued the promotion on the spot."

Chamberlain began to feel sick. He looked at the paper again, said, "This looks official. Can he change his mind?"

Now Gilmore was smiling, said, "Not hardly, sir. It's been

approved by Congress, by the War Department. I believe that by now General Grant is aware that you are among the living. The promotion is official. May I be the first, sir."

Gilmore stepped back, snapped a salute, and now Tom did the same. There were more voices from the room, the applause again.

Chamberlain looked up at the two men, lifted his hand, returned the salute. He stared up at the ceiling then, felt weak. It was the most exertion he had experienced in a while, and he was drained. He closed his eyes, could hear the voices of the women again, whispers, heard the boots on the hardwood floor, moving away. He felt a hand wrap around his, knew it was Fannie. She said in a soft voice, "I am very proud of you, Lawrence. My soldier . . ."

The voice drifted away above him, and now he saw one more face, the old man looking him in the eye, something he rarely did. Chamberlain still felt the piece of paper in his hand, wanted to show it to him, felt suddenly very young, very excited, remembered the question, his father asking him, "You got a chance at bein' a general?" He looked at the old face, the hard eyes, and Chamberlain smiled, said only, "Yes," and now the old face was smiling back at him, something he had never seen, and he felt the old man's hands now holding him, a tight grip on both arms, and Chamberlain said it again.

"Yes."

28. GRANT

July 27, 1864

He sat alone with the cigar, a small camp chair leaning against a thin oak tree. He was in Meade's camp, waiting for Burnside to arrive, but he was thinking about Sherman.

He remembered the conversation with Lincoln, he thought of it often now, what he'd said, the phrase coming to him whenever there were quiet moments like this one. *It is only a matter of time.*

Sherman had said the same thing, had pushed and pursued Joe Johnston from Chattanooga all the way to Atlanta. The pursuit had come when the good fights did not, because Johnston was skilled at retreat, at the careful maneuver, had kept his smaller army away from a general engagement with Sherman's power. Johnston had learned the value of the trench, the heavy mounds of dirt, and his men made good use of the shovel. Grant smiled at that, thought of Sherman's angry impatience. He'd received a steady flow of reports from Georgia, all rippling with the frustration of a commander who wanted the fight, wanted it *now*, and Johnston wouldn't give it to him. Each time Sherman brought his great strength into line, Johnston would simply back away, sometimes with obvious and distinct movements, sometimes quietly in the night. But if Sherman was frustrated, he also understood that he was in fact winning, that with the constant movement forward, the closer he pushed his army toward Atlanta, it was only a matter of time.

Grant had wondered about Johnston, just how long Richmond would listen to the explanations of retreat. He'd read the hostile joking in the southern newspapers, that Davis had already organized a fleet of transport ships at Savannah, ready to receive Johnston's troops, prepared to carry Johnston's retreat all the way to Bermuda. If there was bitterness in the humor, Grant knew that in Richmond no one was smiling, and especially not Jefferson Davis. And then the word had come. To no one's surprise, Johnston had been relieved. What did surprise Grant, and bring a smile to the impatient Sherman, was the name of Johnston's replacement. The defense of Atlanta was now in the hands of John Bell Hood.

No one questioned that as a commander of troops in the field, there were few on either side who could put the fight into his men as well as Hood. But the appreciation, the enthusiasm, for Hood's appointment, came from both sides. The most recent letter from Sherman had made Grant smile, the childlike excitement barely concealed. Sherman knew that Johnston had been relieved because Davis had heard too much of retreats. Sherman also knew that if there was one rebel commander who needed no pressure from Richmond to make a fight, it was Hood. And the one man who had pressed for a fight more than anyone was Sherman. With Hood in command of the enemy, Sherman knew he'd get his fight.

He heard footsteps, turned, saw Porter stepping slowly, quietly forward. Porter would never say anything until Grant saw him first. The staff had come to understand that when he sat alone like this, quiet, the small motion of the cigar, you did not interrupt. Unless there was urgency, they would wait for the moment to pass and for Grant to bring himself back to the business at hand.

Grant held out the cigar, said, "Yes, Colonel?"

"Excuse me, sir, General Burnside is on his way. He should be here any moment now, sir."

Grant leaned back against the tree, nodded, said, "Fine, Colonel. I'll be along shortly."

Porter saluted, backed slowly away. Grant watched him, thought, Yes, you too, Mr. Porter. You want to ride out in front, and lead men into the guns. I am sorry, young man, but it will not happen.

He thought of the others, the good staff, knew most of them were doing a fine job, would always be with him. Rawlins, of course, was the headmaster, had never dreamed of leading combat troops, probably had nightmares about finding himself actually having to look at the rabble of the enemy. Grant smiled, gave a small chuckle, thought, No, Mr. Rawlins, don't ever let yourself be captured. They'd have to build you a special prison all your own. He knew Rawlins was his guardian, the great protector, had appointed himself the keeper of his public image. Rawlins was forever watching him, a small peek through the tent flaps, a bold intrusion into Grant's private moments, something Porter would never have done. He's afraid, Grant thought, afraid of the newspapers, of Lincoln's enemies, afraid of me, of something I might do to embarrass us all. Or to embarrass *him*. He has found his purpose in life, to be a chief of staff, to be the caretaker of our good behavior. But Porter is very different, he has his eye . . . *out there*, beyond the front lines, where the adventure lies. He shook his head, stood up, stretched his back, suddenly thought of his oldest son, Fred. Yes, he would do that too, stare out past the front lines, see only the adventure, the daring, the heroics. But no matter how long this war goes on, and no matter how much he ever begs me, he will not get the chance. He will never see it for himself. The thought gave Grant a cold chill. He had never imagined the war would go on long enough for his fourteen-year-old son to fight. He stared into the dark, saw the boy's face, then remembered another face, at Cold Harbor, the nameless young man who had died right in front of him. No, he thought, my son will not have the chance. What we do here, what I must order this army to do . . . this will never happen again. Once this is over, this country will carry this forever, the faces, the blood, the horror. It will be the last time. It *must* be.

THEY WERE THE 48TH PENNSYLVANIA, STRONG, HARD MEN FROM the deep coal mines back home, and some of them had been in this army since the beginning. For over a month now they dug and carried the dirt, slowly pushing farther into the side of the hill, hammering timbers into place, bracing the soft, wet dirt over their heads. The tunnel was narrow, only four feet across at the base, narrowing around their heads to two feet wide. None could stand up, the tunnel barely four feet tall. They did not mind the tight space, had no paralyzing claustrophobia, did not listen to the observers, men from other units who watched these dirt-encrusted men crawl into the black abyss and called them names like *moles* and *gophers*. It was the work they'd been trained to do before becoming soldiers, work none of them had forgotten. Now their colonel had convinced General Burnside that this was not only the work they were meant to do, but a good plan for the army as well.

His name was Henry Pleasants, and he was a Philadelphia engineer who'd grown up in coal country. He had stood beside the steep hillside, peeked up and over to where the rebels peeked up and over toward him, measured the distance between the sharpshooters as less than four hundred feet. It had been his idea to build the tunnel, a long narrow mine, to reach out underground to the strong rebel position across the deadly space and, with enough explosive force, blow it to pieces.

BURNSIDE HALTED THE HORSE, WAITED FOR AN AIDE TO TAKE THE reins, then dismounted, moved toward Grant.

"General Grant, a pleasant evening. I trust you are in good health."

Grant returned a salute, said, "Quite well, thank you."

Burnside turned to Meade, a slight bow, said, "General Meade, a pleasure as well. Are you in good health, sir?"

Meade nodded, and Grant thought, He's still not comfortable around Meade, probably never will be. Burnside was a large man, every part of him round, and the wide face was accented by the huge tufts of beard that covered his jaw, framing his face like two handles. He was always jovial, tried to bring his own good cheer to every situation, but it was overdone, exaggerated, and he never seemed to be completely at ease. Everyone knew he carried the memories of Fredericksburg in some dark hidden place, but he never spoke of it, and Grant had rarely heard Meade speak of those days either. Now there was strain between the two men.

If there was an awkwardness to the command structure in the army, this was something far deeper, far more personal, between the two men. Burnside in fact outranked Meade, had been a major general well before Meade received his promotion. When McClellan failed at Antietam and allowed Lee's battered army to escape, Lincoln's patience ran out and McClellan had been removed. When Burnside was picked to succeed the popular McClellan, there had been little enthusiasm, but Burnside had always been cordial and polite to all. No one could think of any reason to dislike him, and he carried none of the political harshness of so many of the senior commanders. By rank, he was entitled to have his opportunity to win the war. The resulting disaster at Fredericksburg was laid directly at his feet, and no one knew the depth of his failure more than the man himself. But worse, Burnside had been in command of the Army of the Potomac when Meade's division suffered its worst loss of men. It was Meade who had broken through the strong lines of Stonewall Jackson, and if the breakthrough had been supported, the Battle of Fredericksburg might have gone very differently than the extraordinary defeat it turned out to be.

Now the Army of the Potomac was commanded by Meade, and if

Burnside tried to hide the awkwardness of their relationship by boisterous formality, Meade just let it lie. But he would never forget that while his division was fighting for their lives on that December day, this was the man who could have sent help, who had thirty thousand men standing idly by while Meade's division absorbed a fearful slaughter. The man whose inability to make the decision, to seize the moment, cost not only the lives of Meade's men, but certainly lengthened the war, and the loud joviality of the man's personality would never hide the cloud that would always follow Ambrose Burnside.

Burnside now waited, looked back and forth at the two men, and Grant finally made a small gesture with the cigar, pointed to Meade's tent, and they moved away from the fire. They ducked under the flap, moved into the darkness. Grant sat himself facing the back of the tent, the glow of the fires painting the faces of the other two men. He had long understood that their words alone did not tell the story, and he would always position himself where he could see the expressions on their faces.

Burnside and Meade both removed their hats, and Grant lit a fresh cigar. Grant said, "General Burnside, how is your plan progressing?"

Burnside seemed to inflate, his chest bursting with something Grant thought must be pride. "Splendidly, sir. Splendidly! We are ready on your command, sir! They have reached what Colonel Pleasants tells me is the proper depth. The charges are being placed as we speak, sir. All that is needed is the final coordination with General Meade's command."

Meade made a low sound, and Grant said, "General Meade, your comments?"

Meade shifted in his chair, said, "I have never placed much confidence in this plan, sir. If we are to make a breakthrough in the enemy's position, it should be done with power and with a strike of considerable force, in a narrow front. I do not see how this . . . hole in the ground will accomplish anything toward that goal. I have not changed my position on this since the plan was originally introduced. Sir."

Burnside looked at Grant, said, "Sir, what General Meade is describing is exactly the purpose of the plan, sir. A narrow front, yes, exactly. We have the troops ready, General Ferrero's division has been drilling now for weeks. When the mine is exploded, they will make a quick thrust through the opening, taking full advantage of the confusion. Once the breakthrough is made, the rest of the corps will follow them through, and with General Meade's support on either side, the breakthrough should cut Lee's lines in two. By the end of the day, Petersburg will be ours, and possibly Lee as well."

Grant leaned forward, said, "Ferrero? The Negro division?"

Burnside glanced at Meade, said, "Yes, sir. We have taken great care, they have been training for this mission in great detail, sir. I have absolute confidence that any man in that unit is as capable—"

Grant put up his hand. "General Burnside, I have no doubt about the fighting spirit of General Ferrero's division. I am concerned that this division is new to the army. They have no field experience." He stopped, looked at the small red glow of the cigar. "I am also concerned what might occur when the Negro troops appear behind the enemy's lines."

Meade said, "Yes, if they get that far. It's not a good plan, not at all."

Burnside put his hand on his face, felt the thick brush of whiskers. "Well, they are a fresh unit. But the training has been exceptional."

"Training . . ." There was an edge to Meade's voice. Grant now stood, moved to the opening of the tent.

Burnside leaned closer to Meade, said, "General, I assure you, we have the ability, the means to train these men. There is no reason they cannot perform the duty given them. Just because they are not white—"

Meade stood, his voice booming, "White has nothing to do with it, General. It is *green* I am concerned with. They are untested troops. You are trusting this entire operation to the performance of men who have never been under fire! You have four divisions under your command, three of them with experience! You have chosen the one part of the Ninth Corps that is the least likely to perform in this situation!"

Burnside looked at Grant, the confidence slipping out of his voice. "We trained them well, sir. It would be a message, show the enemy . . . it would be greatly pleasing to the President."

Grant turned now, looked at Burnside, said, "General, it is not your concern what might be pleasing to the President. And it is precisely the message to the enemy that bothers me. Their response to that message . . . might not be what you anticipate."

"Sir, what I anticipate is that the enemy will be defeated, that this plan will create a breakthrough that could end the war."

Grant absorbed the words from Burnside, thought, There is no fire, he sounds like he's reading it in a newspaper. He's not even committed to his own plan. There was a long quiet pause, the sounds of the camp drifting into the tent. The two men were looking at Grant now, and he stared past them, to the back of the tent, watched the shadows moving on the glow of the canvas. He thought, Burnside has never performed, my orders have never moved him into the kind of action we have needed. Now . . . this is *his* plan, and he wants us to believe it will work without a flaw, that the coordination will happen as it must happen.

Meade made another grunting sound, said, "I am still doubtful the mine will even work. How do the miners breathe? My engineers tell me there has never been a tunnel that long, not that narrow. The powder won't burn, there's no air."

Burnside inflated again, said, "Colonel Pleasants is extraordinary. He has devised a duct system, using a fire at the mouth of the mine. I have seen it myself. The fire draws the air through the duct, from the farthest point in the mine. It's ingenious! The explosion will work, I assure you. They have split the end of the mine into a T, and I have, um . . . I have authorized the placement of powder into the mine. It is . . . all ready to go!"

Meade said, "It's complete? They're finished? How do they know it's far enough, that it reaches the enemy's lines? You call a cease-fire so your Colonel Pleasants could measure it?"

Burnside ignored the tone of Meade's question, said to Grant, "Colonel Pleasants has measured the distance using sophisticated engineering methods. I observed him myself. We have absolute confidence that the mine is of the correct length."

Grant had not been as hostile to the idea as Meade, had thought from the beginning that any plan was a good one if it worked. He'd heard the numbers, the amount of powder sent to the mine. Yes, it will make one *big* hole, he thought. But even if the mine worked as the miners said it would, he had the problem of Burnside. He looked at him now, said, "General, you will select another division to lead the assault. I don't see why any veteran unit cannot take advantage of a sudden break in the enemy's line and advance through it. You don't need special training for that. When the enemy recovers enough to try to contain the break, untested men could lose their initiative, and might give back whatever advantage they have gained. General Meade . . ."

Meade was watching him, nodded.

Grant said, "General, you will order the Fifth and Eighteenth Corps to stand ready to advance against the enemy's positions in the event the breakthrough occurs between them. General Burnside's men may very well pull the enemy away from in front of both those corps. I don't want spectators. Your forces must take advantage of whatever occurs, of whatever weakness might suddenly open up to their front."

Meade said, "Certainly. I will see to it, sir." Meade stood up, held his hat in his hand, motioned toward Burnside. "General Burnside, if your boys do as you say, then my boys will be right there with you. You may depend on that."

Burnside stood now, clamped his hat on tightly, said, "This is splendid, gentlemen. I assure you, this will be a magnificent success. Colonel Pleasants has demonstrated the kind of initiative that the Ninth Corps has always been capable of."

Burnside looked at Grant, and Grant knew there was more.

"Sir, when do we blow the mine?" Burnside asked. "When will the army be ready to assist our breakthrough?"

Grant glanced at Meade. "If you say the mine is ready, then preparations shouldn't take long. I would say the assault should commence the morning of the thirtieth. That's three days, plenty of time to organize the assault, instruct the division that will lead the way. Make it early morning, very early. Four A.M. That give you enough time, General Meade?"

Meade said, "The thirtieth. The orders will be prepared immediately, sir."

Grant moved out of the tent, and Burnside waited for Meade, then followed him into the warm night air. Grant looked up at the stars, tasted the smoke of the cigar.

Behind him, Burnside whispered to Meade, "Um, if I may ask . . . do you . . . can you spare, say, a good-sized length of fuse?"

JULY 30, 1864

THEY WAITED IN THE DARKEST NIGHT MANY OF THEM COULD remember, stood side by side, packed together, men already sweating into their uniforms. Most of them had not made a predawn assault, at least not a successful one, and the low hum of nervous voices echoed through the web of trenches. They were Ledlie's division, the First in Burnside's Ninth Corps, and they had not known they were to lead the attack until the afternoon before. Burnside had not ordered them to the job, hadn't measured their will or their ability against his other divisions. The division commanders had debated, argued, and finally, with Burnside unwilling to make the decision, they put pieces of paper into a hat, and so it was by chance that Ledlie's men were standing in the heat of the darkness.

Their inexperience was typical of the many reinforcements to this army who had come south in recent weeks. Many of the men were from the Heavy Artillery units. For many this would be their first real fight, the first taste of crossing open ground with an enemy pointing his musket at your head. They knew of the plan of course, had been told about the mine, and how it would destroy the enemy, a wide-open gap they could burst through with ease. Their commanders had passed the word down—once the mighty blast cleared the way, it would be a simple matter to push through the enemy's position, form a line out in each direction, their backup units flooding through the gap. To those who had been here awhile, the veterans who had seen other great plans unfold, there was little talk, even when the new men wanted to know, had to know, what it was like, what would happen.

The men of Ferrero's division had heard only late the night before that they would not lead the assault they had so eagerly trained for. The Fourth Division would instead come up last, after the other divisions had completed the breakthrough. There was anger, confusion, and immediately the few reporters who kept themselves within earshot of any piece of news began to write down the comments. The mood was angry, bitter feelings about having been so well prepared, the expectations so high, the opportunity for some piece of glory, gone now by the simple decision from somewhere else, a commander most had never seen. The rumors flew easily, and most accepted what seemed obvious. These men would not lead the assault because they were black, because somewhere, someone up the chain of command did not want to give them the chance.

HENRY PLEASANTS HELD UP A SMALL LANTERN, LOOKED AT HIS watch. It was three A.M. He glanced up at the dirty face of Sergeant Reese, the young man moving about nervously in the dark. Pleasants tried to force a smile, looked now at the somber, drawn face of Lieutenant Douty. He tried to say something, his voice choked off in the dust of his throat. He coughed, looked at the watch again, said, "It's three o'clock. It's time."

There were three fuses, each leading to a different part of the mine. They had not been able to secure long lengths of the tight hemp, were forced instead to piece together smaller lengths. The elaborate patchwork was less than a hundred feet long, so Pleasants himself would have to move far into the mine to light the end. Once lit, the fuse would burn for nearly thirty minutes before reaching the kegs of powder.

Pleasants handed the lantern to Douty, and Douty held out a hand. Pleasants took the hand, looked now at Reese, who saluted him. They had been a part of this project from the beginning, had their own experience deep in the black mines of Pennsylvania. Reese had spent more time in this hole than anyone, had directed the placing of the powder kegs, and even through the hot night had been deep inside, checking and rechecking the fuse. Pleasants knew Reese wanted the job, was eager to light the fuse himself, but this was the responsibility of command, and so Pleasants smiled now, returned the salute, leaned down into the opening of the mine, and was gone.

GRANT HELD HIS FIELD GLASSES IN HIS HANDS, NERVOUSLY FINgered them, waiting for the chance to see . . . *something*. He stared into the dark, out toward the place where the great plan was to begin. He turned, looked behind him, thought, The sun will be up soon, very soon. He looked at the watch again, saw it was nearly four o'clock. Well, that's it, let's go. He wanted to look into the glasses, had waited for it now with some excitement. He hadn't allowed himself to feel that, not yet, but here, alone in the dark, away from the staff and Meade and the dismal confidence of Burnside, Grant was feeling the churn in his stomach, the childlike sense that something truly marvelous was about to happen, something spectacular, something no one had ever seen.

He looked at the watch again, tapped it against his leg. Yes, it was working, six minutes after four. He began to move now, small steps, back and forth, impatience growing into anger. No, not this time, we cannot be delayed this time. If it doesn't go . . . nothing good can happen, there can be no assault. He stared hard into the dark, took a deep breath, thought, Why is it . . . can we not do something right even *once*?

PLEASANTS HAD RECEIVED THE URGENT MESSAGE FROM BURNSIDE, but he didn't need a commander to tell him something had gone wrong. The fuses were always slow, but they were consistent. No, there was something else, maybe the dampness of the ground. He cursed to himself, thought, No, we accounted for that, it has to be . . . they've gone out.

Douty looked at his watch, then turned to the east, said in a whisper, "Sir, the sun . . . it'll be light soon."

Reese stepped close to Pleasants now, said, "Colonel, we have no choice. Permit me, sir. I will go in."

Pleasants glanced at the opening to the mine, then looked at the young man's face. There was no fear. Pleasants handed him the lantern, said, "Quickly, Sergeant. Godspeed."

IT HAD BEEN FIFTEEN MINUTES, WAS NEARLY FOUR-THIRTY, AND Pleasants was leaning down, staring at a faint glow from far up in the mine, the light of the lantern growing brighter now. He could see the shadows, blocking the light, the movement of the men. Douty had gone in shortly after Reese. If Reese had a problem, Douty would be there to help. Pleasants stayed behind, counting seconds to himself, nervous, closing his eyes with every bit of sound, flinching at every noise that came from the mass of troops waiting in the trenches behind him.

Now he saw faces, the two men covered in the mud and dirt of the long crawl. Douty emerged first, stood upright, stretched his back, saluted, smiled. Then Reese came out, held the lantern, saluted as well. They stood side by side, and Pleasants wanted to yell, *Tell me!* He had no patience now for riddles. He leaned close to both men, did not return their salute, said in a frantic whisper, *"What happened?"*

Douty was still smiling, said, "It went out, sir. At one of the joints. We repaired it. And then we lit it again. Shouldn't be long now."

Pleasants backed away, eased up the embankment, peeked his head over the top, heard Reese climbing up beside him.

Reese said, "Excuse me, Colonel, but I'd be a-duckin' if I was you."

29. LEE

July 30, 1864

THEY HAD BEEN ON DUTY SINCE MIDNIGHT, REPLACING THE MEN who were there the twelve hours before. It was becoming the normal day now, half the troops manning the front lines, the best marksmen in the units sighting down their muskets, waiting for something, anything, some piece of motion. Sometimes they would fire at nothing, send the deadly message, "Come on boys, take a peek, just one look, and I'll knock your head clean off." For the men who did not fire the muskets, the duty was mostly quiet and tedious. The heat had made the covered trenches pits of hell. Some men fainted, and others just sat, stared at nothing, spent the twelve-hour duty waiting for the relief of sleep and whatever rations they would be given. The shelling would come at regular intervals, the guns firing blindly all along the line, on both sides, not at any target, but just . . . out there, across the way, a calculated guess where the exploding shell might find the enemy.

There was a new weapon now, the mortar, brought to the field by the Yankees first, but now the boys in gray had them too, and so the sport had changed. The mortars would throw a solid shot in a high arc, easily seen, and the gunners would watch it strike down hard, and if it did not bounce on solid ground, the clean miss, it had found the trench, a sudden crushing death to anyone who might be crouching low, believing himself safe.

They knew they were close to the enemy, the lines curving out slightly, the enemy's doing the same. The sharpshooters had the advantage here, could easily see the motion, and the game changed again, the tease, men sometimes testing their opponent, the hat rising slowly on a stick just to the top of the earthworks, and the answer would come, a dozen shots, more, the hat ripped to pieces. There would be laughter. Yes, fooled you, Billy Yank.

The darkness, the wet stinking mud of the covered trenches was home now, and no one had any idea when this might change. They would look for any distraction, the long hours giving way to fantasy, daydreaming, nightmares. In the long quiet times, the dark silence of the ground had given up a new sound, something very faint. The men began to gather, to lean close to the wet ground, some even dropping down and putting an ear to the soft clay. The word had gone to the officers, and most paid it little mind, the madness of boredom, but a few did come themselves, heard the sounds with their men. The word spread all along the line. The Yankees were digging!

The sounds were unmistakable now, made more so by the imagination of the men aboveground. The jokes began, Grant digging his way to the other side of Petersburg, the attack would come from the rear! Maybe a railroad, an underground train, carrying the blue army far behind them. The officers began to give the order, probe, dig down, drive the long steel pike into the soft ground. If there was a tunnel, it would be found. The men probed and stabbed, and when a pit was dug and a man lowered the few feet down, the faint dull sounds would be clearer still. The jokes began to grow quiet, the search became more purposeful, careful, deliberate.

The engineers laughed along with the best of the rumors, knew the sounds were something else, magnified somehow by the lay of the land, a rock formation perhaps, echoing the sound toward them from far away, men in blue digging their own trenchworks. It was not possible, after all, to dig a mine that far, not if you had to begin behind those lines, over there, over four hundred feet away.

Even Porter Alexander, hearing word of the strange sounds, had come easing through the trenches himself, the men standing aside, quiet, respectful. They knew this young man's name, that when it came to positioning the big guns, General Alexander was the best they had, the best on either side. Now he was there, with these poor foot soldiers from South Carolina, and he knelt down, listened to the dull sounds as the muddy faces watched quietly. Alexander heard the skepticism of the engineers, but did not laugh. He moved away with a grim silence. It did not matter if educated men said it was not possible. The enemy was digging a mine.

The gunners of Pegram's battery had heard the talk, but their duty was off to the right of the commotion, and they could not see the men with the shovels and picks searching the ground beneath them with hot frustration. The gunners still focused across the way, the four guns of the battery working with each other, the men enjoying another game, the perfect rhythm, trying to fire the guns in a quick sequence. They did not know if the work was effective, if they were killing the enemy, but the orders were plain, keep it up, adjust the range, a bit shorter, then fire again.

When the sharpshooters were quiet, the gunners were more relaxed, but this morning the Yankees were active, very active, a steady shower of lead, much more than usual. The gunners cursed, kept low. This morning there was no game with their friends, each gun fired on its own, the men waiting for the slight pause in the musket fire, then scrambling to position, loading, firing off a round. On the far right, the fourth gun, the men were flat on the ground, began to rise now, brushing dirt away, laughing. The enemy had nearly gotten lucky, and there were admiring nods, small comments, a close one, a good shot. The shell had come within a few yards of the gun pit, knocked them all to the ground. They moved slowly at first, then the captain barked the familiar command and they were up around their gun, loaded quickly, and all thought, Well, time to return the favor.

One man leaned on the wheel, waited for another man to ram the shell hard into the barrel. He jumped, startled, felt something move under his feet, then felt the gun rising slowly, the wheel in his hand now jumping, lifting off the ground. The men backed away, looked at each other, wide eyes in the gray darkness, and now the sound came up toward them from below, the earth itself rising in one massive mound. Then the mound broke, pushed skyward, the dull sound erupting into a deafening roll of thunder, a great hollow roar. To their left, where the rest of the battery had been, there was only fire and a great column of black smoke. Dirt now blew across them, the air thick with a fiery wind, knocking them flat on the ground. Above them the flames tore at the darkness, the blast carrying the earthworks, the timbers, the big guns and the bodies of men, high overhead. Slowly, the huge black cloud began to rain down on them, the roar still thundering over them, now pierced by the screams of men, the sound of debris hitting the ground around them, pieces of the guns, horses, torn pieces of men.

It was the men from South Carolina, men who had heard the small laughs and the new joke from the men who moved past them in the dark, the shift they had replaced. As they'd filed into the works, some repeated the joke, laughed that the Yankees must have given up. They had huddled low in the trenches, held their ears to the ground, some climbing down into the small pits, listening hard, possessed of a nervous curiosity. These men who had strained to hear the familiar sounds from below, who wondered why just last night the sounds of digging had stopped, felt it first, the ground lifting under them.

LEE HAD THOUGHT IT WAS A MAGAZINE, ONE OF THE CAISSONS maybe, but the sound rolled over him now in a hard wave, and he knew it was no single shell. He moved quickly. The staff was out in the open now, and he could see it, the bright horrible glow, the tall spiral of flame and smoke. The small trees to one side began to lean, struck by a sharp gust of wind, and then the smell blew past him, the choking sulfur, carried by the sudden wave of wind and thick dust. He looked around, and now Traveller was there, and he climbed up, spurred the horse hard, rode straight for the blast.

Men were moving quickly around him, officers yelling orders. Soldiers were emerging from earthworks, the lines farthest from the front, the men grabbing their muskets, surprised faces all staring toward the great sound. Lee heard a new sound then, a steady roar of cannon fire, throwing their shells right into the area of the blast, then out in both directions. The front lines began to erupt in a steady burst of explosions, flashes, and thunderous impacts. He knew it was not his guns, it was the enemy, the line had been shattered, and now the assault was on. He tried to move the horse faster, thought, They are coming, they have broken the line.

He saw a house, a group of horses, more men, and pulled up in the yard, tried to hold the big horse still, stared out, could see the chaos of motion against the dull glow of the sunrise. He heard something new, musket fire, a wave of sound reaching him now, the cheering of men pushing forward, rolling over the narrow stretch of open ground. He raised the field glasses, stared into thick black smoke, a dense cloud of dirt and debris boiling up from a vast hole in the ground, saw a long mound of dirt, ragged, uneven, the edge of the crater itself. Beyond, he saw motion, flags, then the long lines of men, moving straight at him, straight into the horrible place, the hole blown right through his defenses, right through the lines of his men.

Lee looked around, saw Taylor, Venable, the staff now with him, and he said, "We must stop them, keep them from coming through!"

He looked through the glasses again, all down the lines in both directions, tried to see his men, who was there, the response. From both sides of the crater he saw his own troops, gathering now, men stumbling in shock, some just standing and staring. But there were officers, and slowly the lines began to form, and now musket fire was echoing all around, the small flashes from far down the line. If there was no one in the center, nothing to stop the enemy from coming forward, the men on either side understood what was happening, and across the open stretch of ground they had a clear target. Now the sounds of the big guns were close, his guns, throwing their fire toward the mass of the enemy. He still tried to see, but the smoke filled the open space, different, white smoke now, the smoke of the battle, of the fire from the guns.

Men were moving on horseback, he heard voices, frantic, and one man said, "General Lee, the enemy is coming . . . this area is undefended, sir. You must withdraw!"

Lee looked at the man, shook his head, said, "No . . . we must not let them through!"

He turned now, saw Venable, the older man watching him, waiting for instructions. Lee said, "Colonel, go directly to General Mahone. There is no time for chain of command, we cannot wait for General Hill to pass the word. Tell General Mahone he must withdraw from the enemy in his front with great care, but he must use speed. We are in a dangerous situation here. It is my desire that he bring whatever force he can to close this gap." Venable spun his horse, was quickly gone.

The musket fire was increasing now. Stray shots whistled past him, and he pushed the horse forward. Behind him, he could hear the shouts, his staff receiving the messages, the word being passed, the army waking from a stunned sleep, recovering from the shock. He spurred the horse up a small rise, raised the glasses again, could see past the mass of destruction, the torn earth yawning open, ripped from below, piles of dirt and clay spread out in all directions. He could still see the enemy flags, saw them drawing closer together, pressed from both sides by the gathering storm of fire.

Now he could see the men on the other side of the crater, gathering together, a tide of blue, drifting down, following their flags right into the crater. The guns were still firing from far down both sides, and the blue lines that were still out in the open were falling into panic, the lines breaking up, more men moving forward, disappearing into the protection of the great hole. He could see one single gun, very close, just to the right of the big hole, and the men were firing down, an odd angle, the rear of the gun carriage raised, the barrel pointing . . . *down*.

Lee stared, felt something turn in his gut, watched as the gun fired again, saw one man fall beside it, struck down, the others still moving in quick steps, then the gun firing again. He thought of the words, the horrible phrase that only a soldier understands . . . *point-blank.* He moved the glasses slightly, to the crater itself, could only see the far side, not what he knew to be down deep in the hole, a vast sea of blue soldiers, swarming right into a trap of their own making.

Closer, on the near side of the crater, a thin line of blue troops had emerged, coming up out of the hole. They were flowing down into more lines of trenches, firing out at the gray troops on both sides of them. But there were not many, not enough to push forward and sweep out on both sides, and Lee understood, thought, Yes, that was the plan, burst through, push through with great strength, then spread out, both ways, roll up the line. But it didn't work. The crater . . . they can't get out of the crater.

Now the men in blue were drifting back, pushed by growing numbers of Lee's troops, the musket fire slicing through the blue troops from all directions. Lee watched them, the ones who did not fall, saw them backing up, moving back toward the edge of the crater, then over, gone, dropping away, joining the mass of men who did not go forward with them, who did not try to climb out. Lee could see it now, most of the assaulting force had sought the cover of the great wide hole or been stopped by the hole itself, men dropping down, only to find themselves staring up at the crest of the wall of earth in front of them. Peering through the glasses, Lee could feel it, the great thrust, the momentum of the enemy's assault gone. Men were still moving past him, moving forward, forming new lines. Stronger lines. He knew it was the Third Corps, Hill's troops, the division of Billy Mahone. A few cheered him, but most had their eyes on the front, toward the job at hand, the deadly gap in the line. Lee looked again at the edge of the crater, saw the last signs of blue disappear over the edge, saw his men moving forward, closer, the enemy's thrust now contained, held together by Lee's men and by their own plan, by the great hole in the earth.

DOWN IN THE WIDE CRATER, THE MEN COULD SEE WHAT WAS happening, that they could no longer push forward, that the great plan to cut Lee's lines in two had stopped in a mass of confusion and fear. The men were crushed together in a suffocating mass, a solid sea of blue with nowhere to go. The crush was getting worse, more and more men coming forward from their own lines, guided by the deadly fire of the enemy into the only place that was safe. Some continued to fight, aimed their muskets up at the crest, waited for the face of the enemy to appear, the careless man who stood up to see the astonishing sight spread before him. But the blue soldiers who tried to fight were held back, could not even reload their guns, the growing crush of men now pressing them together into a helpless tide.

As more lines of blue came forward, those who saw the hopelessness, the chaos, tried to return to their own lines, the safety of their own works. But troops were advancing in a tight line, through the only places where the men could move, blocking the escape of anyone who tried to run. The officers could see it now, the great mistake, that Burnside had not ordered the front of the earthworks cleared of brush and cut trees, and so there was no way to get back into their own works, as long as men were still being sent forward. Down both sides of the assault the rebel muskets and big guns were all pointing now toward the center, and if the gunners could not see the crater itself, they had a clear view of the open ground behind it, the flat space between the lines. The officers who tried to stop their units from making the deadly mistake, who tried to halt their men before they reached the crater, now found themselves in the open, under the massed guns of both flanks. If a man tried to leave the crater, escape back to his own lines, the rebel muskets were ready, and if the aim was not good, it did not matter, because the blue masses were too great a target, too many to hide from the storm of lead.

As the gray troops reached the edge of the crater, some remembered Spotsylvania, the bloody angle, the horror of knowing your enemy was so close, a few feet away, and some hesitated, crouched low against the ragged mounds of dirt. There was something different this time, something more horrible, even the officers could see it slowly spread through the men. There would be prisoners, thousands . . . yes, the fight was over, the Yankees were trapped, there was nowhere they could go. Those who could see, who eased toward the crater from the sides, understood that this was something truly extraordinary, that right in front of them thousands of men waited, helpless.

But the fight was not over, and along the edge of the crater there were men who still felt the rage, who still saw the Yankee as the hated enemy, who knew only that over the crest of this hole men waited to die, and so they *would* die. Slowly, the noise of the voices rose, the cries of the fight returning. Down the line, rebel gunners were still sending their shells into the mass of blue, most still not understanding how simple a target they had. The gray soldiers could hear the sounds, watched overhead as the high arc of the mortar shell landed beyond the crest, straight down into the packed horde of blue. Now bayonets began to go over the edge, men throwing them like spears, and the ones who could see into the hole watched in horror as the faces stared up, the eyes watching the hand of death reaching right for them, slowly, too slowly, and the men were packed so tightly together that there was no getting away.

There were cries of "Surrender," and many of the gray soldiers moved to the crest, offered to pull the men in blue out and over, offering survival, escape, and many accepted the hand, scrambled out of the crater to become prisoners. But now the rebels began to see the faces of the black soldiers, the shocking reality that many had never seen up close, that those men in blue had put the Negroes into the fight. Many of the blue soldiers were surprised as well, saw the screaming mass around them swell with the men of Ferrero's division, the last troops across the field.

A few voices began to ring out, a sharp cry of anger from some of the rebels, and many of the gray soldiers stopped accepting surrender, stopped taking prisoners, would not accept that the man who was like you, the man you respected as your enemy, would fight beside the Negro, would take up arms against the men they saw as their own kind. Now it was becoming something new, it was not a fight at all, not a battle like any of them had ever seen. In the crater, the black soldiers could see it in the eyes of the men beside them, that if the white men were taken prisoner with the Negroes, the result would be barbaric, ruthless. Some of the Federal soldiers still reached out, waved a handkerchief, anything they could find, still tried to surrender, but when the black soldiers tried as well, they were struck down, if not by the musket of the enemy, then by the man beside them, by the incredible horror of blind madness.

The men trapped in the crater were sentenced to death, a decision that came not from the minds of the rebel commanders, or even the irrational fear and anger that makes wars. Those men in gray, who understood that the fight was over, could only watch in shock, friends watching friends, officers watching the men under their command, helpless to stop the rising flow of blood. The men in blue felt it as well, heard the screaming roar of madness all around them, saw their own men taken down by the bayonet, the sword, stared in utter horror as the muskets began to swing, the bayonets finding the soldier who was your comrade. The faces spread the terror, the savagery, the mindless insanity of the beast, and the men who held on to their humanity stared in utter horror as the rules of war, the last fragile string of human decency, was pushed aside by those whose blind hatred would only be fed by slaughter.

30. GRANT

July 30, 1864

The losses were staggering, nearly four thousand men, most of them struck down in and around the crater. He had not seen Burnside, not yet, but that would come. The reports were being written, but already what was said privately was the most damaging, the personal details that could never be put into official reports.

The First Division, Ledlie's division, had simply panicked, had marched straight into the confusion of the big hole and then stopped. Jim Ledlie himself was the focus of the comments, the speculation. He was the only man in his division who knew what they were supposed to have done, but he never gave the orders, never led his men around the crater, to the side, the clear open advance into the shattered lines of the enemy. Instead his men marched straight ahead, straight into the crater itself, and Ledlie could not stop them, because he wasn't there. Grant began to hear it himself, that Ledlie had been drunk, far behind the awful place where his men went to die. This was not new, not a surprise to the other commanders of the Ninth Corps. Grant was already being told that Burnside knew Ledlie's reputation yet had still allowed the man to command the first wave of the assault.

They were riding back to City Point, another sunset, another horrible day. He rocked with the rhythm of the horse, stared ahead quietly. Behind him the staff was strung out in line, and no one was talking.

They had never heard him explode in anger. He never erupted the way Meade did, the hot words flowing hard into the pale face of the subordinate. But he was feeling it now, building inside of him, boiling up in a raw red fury. He felt his heart beating, held the reins in a tight grip in his hand, stared straight ahead. He was as angry as he had ever been. The names rolled around in his mind, the puzzle had already come neatly into place. The plan had been a good one, and he'd placed confidence in his commanders that it would be carried out, that the instructions would be passed down to the officers, that the men would know what to do, that they would in fact be *led*.

He was angry at himself because he'd allowed Meade to interfere, to criticize Burnside's use of Ferrero's division. Burnside was right, they had trained for weeks, they would have known what to do, they would not have marched straight into that hole. But if the Negroes were angry at not leading the assault, they could not complain about being left out entirely. Burnside had sent them in anyway, when it was already clear that the plan had failed, the rest of the corps massing into a hopeless tangle. If they had missed their opportunity to lead the way, they had not missed their opportunity to die.

He had heard of the decision to send Ledlie in first, the drawing of names out of a hat, and it made his eyes clamp shut. His face held the expression tight, the loud yell held down deep. *Draw names out of a hat?* It was almost comical, an army run by lottery, responsibility by the luck of the draw. But there was nothing comical about the loss of four thousand men.

Burnside will go, he thought. That was definite, the order already etched hard in his mind. He knew Lincoln would allow him to handle that any way he wanted, and if it was to be today, he would have the man flogged, drag him by the collar right into the crater, make him look at the horror of what he had done. He closed his eyes, took a deep breath, thought, No, you cannot give in to that, you cannot just explode.

He forced himself to see beyond the anger. There is the right way to handle these things, he thought, there always has been, especially for the men who have served for so long. There was nothing to be gained by public humiliation, by shaming the man. The letters would be written, sent to Halleck in Washington. Burnside would be given leave, maybe a month, with instructions that his staff could accompany him. There would be no confusion about what was really happening, and Burnside was experienced enough in command to understand that. After the leave expired, he would be told to simply wait for a new assignment. It was the most discreet way to handle the dignity of the veteran commanders. The newspapers would not jump on the story, put the name in shameful headlines, because in fact there would be no story.

He could see the river now, rode across the open ground toward the tents. The camp came to life, the aides began to move out, to take the horses. Grant ignored them, pushed the horse out toward the water, stopped at the edge of the high bluff. He looked across, saw distant trees, the hills turning dark with the setting of the sun. He heard another horse, saw Porter now, slowly moving up beside him. Grant looked at him, knew that Porter would sit quietly, as long as he did, to listen, and that if he wanted to be alone, it would just take a small shake of the head and Porter would be gone.

Grant turned to the water again, felt himself let go, a long slow breath, the anger now giving way. "Colonel," he said, "I never have seen an opportunity such as that, and I never expect to see it again."

Porter said nothing, nodded.

Grant rolled the names through his mind again, thought, No, it does no good. There is nothing to be gained by singling anyone out. The men will know, the officers will know.

He looked at Porter again, said, "It was not the men. Whatever is said about this, from the papers, from Washington, it was not the men. I believe that the men would have performed every duty required of them had they been properly led." He paused, said, "Or had been led at all."

Porter still said nothing, and they sat quietly for a long moment. Grant thought, Another horrible day, another day that could have changed everything. I cannot be there, I cannot oversee every operation, every command.

He stared at the darkening river, saw the lights now on the big ships. Down below, men were beginning to look up at him, could see the perfect silhouette in the last glow of the sunset. Some wanted to cheer, to salute him with a rowdy call. But most were quiet, gathering on the wharf, on the decks of the ships, staring at the distinctive figure, the shapeless hat, the slouch in the saddle. They watched as the dark form slowly turned the horse and moved away. They did not see him take the cigar from his pocket, and they could not hear his thoughts, already moving beyond this awful day, the new plan, the motion of the army already in his mind, the chess game in progress again.

31. LEE

SEPTEMBER 1864

IT WAS ONE PIECE OF PAPER, A FEW SIMPLE WORDS, AND IT CUT INTO him like the violent stab of the enemy's sword. John Bell Hood had evacuated Atlanta. Sherman had won the long fight, the continuous moving battle from Chattanooga.

He had been unusually candid about Hood's appointment, told Davis that he felt disappointment in Johnston's resistance to Sherman, that he'd thought Johnston would bring the fight to Sherman instead of the constant retreat. But he knew Hood was not the man to lead that army. There were none who could put the fire into his troops better than the big Texan. But he understood that Hood was impatient, would try to please Richmond, justify the appointment by doing the opposite of Johnston, taking the fight straight to Sherman's vastly superior army. And it was not once, but three times, three bloody fights, Hood slamming his men into the strength of the Federal forces, until finally there was nothing left to hold Sherman back. Now Atlanta, the great rail center, the gateway for the crops and hard goods of the deep South, was in Federal hands.

Lee read the telegram again, put it down. There was little in the way of detail, no troop numbers, no count of casualties. It did not matter. He stood, moved to the opening in the tent. He saw the men moving about, Taylor at the field table, the paperwork moving through, the business of headquarters. He watched for a long moment, thought, It's as though nothing has changed. The war is the same as it has always been, these boys, these good boys, holding the line against those fellows over there. But it was not the same, and it was growing inside of him like some great sickness.

North of the James, close to Richmond, the enemy had made a

push, a brief strike, with the result that they were now that much closer to the capital. Lee had done what he could, had sent men who could be pulled from the defenses to the south, had summoned Ewell to call out the Home Guard, the cripples and boys and government clerks, to line the trenches east of the city. The Federals had not pressed it, seemed content to make the point, and the point was made clear by what happened down south, below Petersburg.

The Federals had moved west, struck out at the supply artery that stretched straight down from the city, the Weldon Railroad. There had been a good fight, a poorly coordinated assault by the enemy, but in the end it was the numbers, and Lee could not stop it, and so the Weldon was now behind Federal lines. It was one more lifeline, one more way to feed his army, cut off. But it was not from some great strategy or brilliant tactical move by the enemy, it was simply the movement of troops, the extension of the blue lines. With the threat of Richmond, Lee had to pull men away from Petersburg, send them north, and so when Grant moved his men out below Petersburg, Lee had no reserve, no way to meet strength with strength. The earthworks, the solid line of defenses, was over twenty-six miles long, and Lee's army did not have enough men to make any kind of strong defense without pulling men completely off some part of that line.

There was still a chance in the valley. Early's forces, most of the Second Corps, were still intact, the fertile farmlands of the valley still under control. Lee knew that Early was no longer a serious threat to Washington, but the valley was defended, the Virginia Central Railroad still open. It was a force of fifteen thousand men that Lee needed desperately at Petersburg, but just as desperate was the need for the crops from the Shenandoah. Lee had heard that Sheridan was now on his way there, that the vicious David Hunter was no longer in command. Lee did not know Sheridan's strength, thought, They may just stay to the north, around Harper's Ferry, keep Early contained. There is victory even in that. We must not lose the valley.

He had thought of going out, riding the horse, but the day was grim, dreary, still very hot. The lines were an unpleasant place, there was nowhere he could go and feel the pride, hear the cheers, the wide grins coming from hungry men. The front lines were like some horrible wasteland, stripped of green, of any of the beauty that had been this part of Virginia. The trenches themselves were mostly covered, protection from the constant shelling, the impact of the mortars. For miles the land behind and between the lines was barren of life, as though the men had made a new world in the misery of the underground, moved only in tunnels, through the mud and darkness that bred sickness. He would not go there now, would not see the men being carried out, disease taking many more than the guns of the enemy. He turned back into the tent, suddenly felt the weariness, the sadness. He sat on the cot, looked down, thought, Virginia. It was always . . . this is where I chose to fight. It is the only choice I could have made. Look what we have done, what man has done to God's land. There has to be a price for that. God cannot ignore . . . no, He has not ignored. Lee stared into the side of the tent, thought, There has not been one day, not since this campaign began, when there was not some fight, somewhere, when we did not have casualties. There is death every day. The hand of God.

He had been thinking about Richmond, looked at the maps, at the long lines, the miles of defense. He'd seen it clearly for a while now, thought about it again. There is no way we can keep Grant out of Richmond. It will be impossible to stop him if that is where he wants to go. He can send twenty thousand men at the city and simply push his way in. The only defense would be to abandon Petersburg, move the army north. And then . . .

He stood, began to pace, felt the anger, the frustration. I did not expect, ever, to be doing this. To just . . . wait, while the enemy decides what to do next, where the next fight will be. From his first days in command, when the army was so very strong, led by the good men, the men who would bring victory, Lee had made the fight on his terms, found the advantage. He always knew his enemy, understood where the mistakes would come, knew how to strike at opportunity. Now, he thought, we are weak, and we can only . . . respond.

He had sent a letter to Davis, a long and serious plea. There was a great untapped resource of manpower in the South still, men who had not fought at all, some by choice, some by the rule of law. But Lee knew Davis could try to change the law. The age of the soldiers was fixed, from eighteen to forty-five. That could easily be changed, lowered to seventeen and raised to fifty, possibly even higher. There were still men who escaped from the fight by employing themselves in exempt positions, noncombat jobs every army must have. There had been great resistance to arming the Negroes, but there were thousands of freedmen who could be employed as teamsters, railroad workers, thousands of jobs along the lines of supply now held by able-bodied white men the army so desperately needed. It was only a question of organizing, convincing the state governments. Lee had stressed it to Davis, how the army was losing strength every day, but if Davis ever had the power, the persuasion to energize the states to answer the call, he did not have it anymore. Many of the states saw the war now as a simple issue of survival, and if there were men in Georgia who could be brought to the fight, they would stay in Georgia, defend Georgia. Lee was beginning to understand that what had created the Confederacy in the first place, the cooperation of the states, was falling apart as well. As the losses grew, the states pulled away from the larger fight, looked to their own. Lee did not need Davis to tell him that whatever strength the army had now, in the filthy desolate trenches at Petersburg, was all the army he would ever have.

To evacuate Richmond . . . he had not yet suggested that to Davis, not with the force needed to convince him. Davis would not even discuss it, still saw Richmond as the heartbeat of the Cause, and Lee was beginning to understand that Davis was slipping, not just his physical health, but slipping further from the reality of the war. Davis was now talking about liberating Atlanta, had even written that Sherman could still be swept completely out of Georgia, his huge Federal army "utterly destroyed." Lee did not ask him how.

Lee thought of his father, Light-Horse Harry Lee, the great hero of the Revolutionary War, remembered hearing the old man talk about defending Virginia. *If you do not control the water, the ports, the rivers, the only way to defeat the enemy is to move inland, take him away from his base of supply. If you can bring him into the open, then the advantage is to the more mobile force.* The old man spoke of a time when there were no railroads. And the British were a very different enemy, did not know the land, did not know their opponent. But still, the strategy was very sound, very modern. We need open ground, we need to maneuver, to find opportunity, Lee thought. It is the only way there can still be a victory. Grant *can* be defeated, if we can fight him on our terms. He said it again, said it out loud in a low voice, "*On our terms.*"

Holding on to Richmond . . . using our army to sit in one place while the enemy stretches himself slowly around us, like some great fat snake . . .

He felt suddenly like he was suffocating, moved outside, tried to breathe, but the air was no cooler. He stood beside the tent, and the faces were looking at him now.

There was one voice, one man said, "General Lee! God bless you, General Lee!"

He looked for the voice, the man's face, had to see him, abruptly felt the need for that, for the energy of the man. But now there were only blank stares, and in front of Taylor the paperwork began to move again. He still watched them, thought, Maybe I should ride out, move through the men. They always respond, there is always the spirit. He looked toward the horses, suddenly felt very weak, the hollow coldness in his chest, thought, Maybe later. It might be cooler. . . .

He looked toward the town, the church spires, could see damage, small signs that the war was there as well, that they too would not escape. He had heard about Atlanta, the fires, the destruction, thought, It was never like this, this is not the way wars are fought. You do not hurt the innocent, the people who simply get in the way. He remembered Fredericksburg, the Federals allowing the townspeople to leave, time to evacuate. It doesn't seem to matter anymore, he realized. There is no thought to the fighting, the destruction has become so commonplace, we don't even see it now.

When the Federal soldiers had looted Fredericksburg, ransacked the personal lives of the innocent, he'd been furious, outraged at the indecency, the barbarism of that. Now the indecency was simply a way of life, everything they did was barbaric. He had ridden to the crater, had to see it for himself. He was, after all, an engineer, and it was an amazing accomplishment, and he felt oddly inspired by that, thought, I would like to meet them, the men who did that. And then he had seen the hole itself, the wide rip in the earth, and packed into the bottom, the horror of what they had done to each other. He'd looked down on the scene and his mind saw a painting, small shreds of color mingled with the clay, the twists of metal. When he walked away, he felt a strange calm, thought, Yes, it was horrible, horrible indeed. But he had to tell himself that, remind himself to see it that way. There was no sickening revulsion, no outrage, no indignation at the barbarism. It was just one more scene from this war, one more horror, one more mass of death, blending together with all the rest.

32. GRANT

November 1864

He began to feel it, slowly, growing inside of him, not confidence, not the self-assurance he had never lacked anyway, but more. It was enthusiasm, the complete calm, rising up inside, from some very important place. He felt it every day now, every morning when he rode out along the lines, a ride that for weeks now had become that much longer. The army was wrapping farther around Lee, extending to the southwest of Petersburg. Lee's lines were now over thirty miles long. Grant would ride along the new trenches, out along the far flank, sit and watch the workers throwing up the logs and fresh earth. If they could not tell by looking at him, if the soldiers did not know what was coming, he knew it with absolute certainty. The flank would be moved again, farther, stretching Lee's ability to defend, would continue to stretch until Lee could defend no more. It was simply a matter of time.

If there had been confidence around Petersburg, it was still a siege. There could be little excitement in that, in knowing you were slowly starving your enemy. The newspapers, the politicians in Washington, had shown slight praise for a war that clearly was going to take a while longer to end. Grant had begun to despise reporters, had grown weary of reading the fine exploits of the rebel armies, while his own victories were never "complete." There was not to be any satisfaction in the North until the war simply ended. They wanted a time, a date, some careless boast to fill the headlines. Grant knew that even Lincoln did not expect that, had heard too much of it anyway. The progress was slow, but it was progress.

Then came Sherman's message from Atlanta. Grant had been so excited by that he even considered going there himself, to look into the sharp eyes of his friend, to grab him hard by the shoulders, tell him face-to-face, "You have done something truly extraordinary." He did not go, wrote to Sherman instead, a glowing letter filled with the praises of the proud commander and the affection of the good friend. But the letter had not been enough, and the man who did not show jubilation had his army do it for him. Grant ordered a salute, fired from every big gun in every battery that faced the enemy. When the word was passed, it became a celebration that gave a thrill to every blue soldier, and across the way the rebels kept low, absorbed yet another pounding. If the sound of the guns did not carry to Washington, the spirit of the celebration did, and it did not take a message from Grant to tell Lincoln that, "Yes, now it is more than a good fight, it is more than progress. Now, we are *winning*."

There had been another salute, another cannonade. This one was for Phil Sheridan. The cavalry commander had been given charge of the fight in the Shenandoah, to deal with Jubal Early once and for all. Lincoln did not send instructions to Grant, there had been none of the needling telegrams that this army had become so accustomed to, but as long as Early was in force in the Shenandoah Valley, Washington was nervous. The more nervous, the worse it was for Lincoln, and his chance for reelection.

Grant had overestimated Early's strength, had believed the rebels to be much stronger, and ultimately, when Sheridan took command, he was given a considerable force, was able to bring nearly forty thousand men into the valley. The newspapers made great sport of the confrontation, and many made comparisons to the great Stonewall, that Jubal Early would do what Jackson had done, rid the valley of yet another Federal invasion. But Sheridan proved that he was not to be chased away, would not run from a bold attack. At a place called Cedar Creek, Early threw his fifteen thousand men against Sheridan's great force. It was a plan Jackson would have approved, an assault that depended on surprise and audacity. But Sheridan created his own legend, rallied his retreating troops and turned his men southward. Unlike Jackson, this time it came down to numbers, Sheridan finally crushing Early's smaller force. No matter how much praise and legend the newspapers tried to give Jubal Early, he was not Stonewall Jackson.

What was left of Early's forces now hugged close to the big mountains, but they were no longer a threat to Sheridan. The Federals not only controlled the valley, they began to destroy it; not the mindless barbarism of David Hunter, but the methodical and strategic destruction of the farms, the breadbasket of the Confederacy. If Lee's army was to be fed, it would not be from the Shenandoah.

THE ROW OF HEADQUARTERS TENTS WOULD BE REPLACED BY permanent structures, small log cabins. The days were shorter, had become much cooler, and the winds blowing across the wide river had made the tents an uncomfortable home. The cabins were not yet completed, but every day, the logs were dragged close, the carpenters working with clean efficiency, especially when their audience included the commanding general.

Grant was still not comfortable with patience, made the rides along the lines when the weather would allow. The men were becoming used to seeing him, and he was recognized now, as he had rarely been before. If the soldiers were not yet sure, if this plainly dressed officer with the cigar did not catch their attention, it was the young boy riding beside him who did. The lull in the fight meant that finally his family could come down, he could see Julia and the children. Fred was the oldest, and so had the honor of riding out with his father, beside him, and the troops cheered him, laughed and pointed at the boy's wide smile, his eyes wide, too, as the men emerged from the dugouts, from the camps, standing straight with the pride of good soldiers, holding the muskets and swords to their chests, a show the boy would never forget.

GRANT WAS ON HIS BACK, BUCK HOLDING HIM DOWN BY THE shoulders, while down at his feet, Jesse, the smaller boy, sat on his legs. They had been at it for a while now, and Grant was feeling the exhaustion. He looked up at the older boy, felt the strength in the boy's hands, thought, Soon, I won't be able to do . . . *this*.

He grunted, rolled over, carefully moved Jesse off his legs, then wrapped his feet around the boy, pinning him between his legs. Jesse was howling with laughter, trying to free himself, now lying sideways, pushing in vain at the trap that held him tightly. Grant looked at the older boy, and there was something strange in Buck's eyes; it was not play. Buck was still trying to pin him down, grabbing his father's shoulders hard, the face now red and angry, and Grant felt the boy's fingers clawing into him, hurting now. He reached up, held the boy's arms, pulled him away, said, "All right, easy, a moment . . . take a moment. . . ." He was breathing very hard, and the boy let loose now, sat back on the ground.

Grant released Jesse, still giggling, sat up between them, saw the opening in the tent and the face of Horace Porter. Grant laughed, said, "Colonel, you care to give it a go? I feel quite sure the fight isn't over here." Grant looked now at Buck, thought, He is not like his older brother. Fred is so much like Julia, but Buck . . . he is stubborn, a fighter. He is . . . like me.

Buck was actually Ulysses Jr., was just twelve, the second oldest, not yet old enough to ride through the camps with his father. It was a major disappointment, not helped by Fred making sure no one forgot the privilege of age. Jesse was only six, and he knew nothing of the rivalry of his older brothers, was concerned more with the daily torture he received from his sister Nellie, three years older than he, and very capable of making his life pure misery. The wrestling match with his father was a joyous relief, no matter that defeat was only a matter of time.

Grant saw Porter's hands full of papers, looked again at the older boy, said, "No, I don't believe Colonel Porter has time for a game right now. You two run outside for a moment. Buck, take your brother to see the ships. There was a new one coming in just a while ago."

The boy stood and held out a reluctant hand for his little brother, but did not hide his disappointment. He said, "All right. Come on, Jesse, I'll race you. . . ."

Buck waited for the smaller boy to run out of the tent, a respectable head start, looked at Porter, then at his father, said, "You leaving? You going away again?"

Grant said, "No . . . why?" The boy was quickly gone, the race on, and Grant pulled himself up, reached for the chair, sat down, took a deep breath. "He is . . . very serious, for a boy."

Porter moved toward the desk, set the papers down, said, "It's envy. Fred gets the attention. The oldest always do."

Grant glanced at the papers. "No, more than that. He's angry. These wrestling matches aren't a game to him. He's always trying to beat me. I see how big he is now, and I realize it won't be long and he'll be strong enough to do it. I wish he'd . . . laugh more."

Porter said nothing, began to move through the papers.

Grant looked out through the opening in the tent, said, "He's like me . . . I never really saw that until now. At his age, even younger, I wouldn't budge, stubborn, had to do things my own way. Only saw one way of ever doing anything, and if it didn't work, I'd do it harder." He laughed, pulled out a cigar, the end smashed flat.

Porter glanced up, smiled, looked back at the papers.

Grant leaned over, tried to see what held Porter's attention. "How's things at the quartermasters'? Any problem feeding the family? Four kids eat a lot."

Porter seemed surprised, said, "Oh, none, sir. Plenty . . ."

"Well, good. You be honest with me, Colonel. They make themselves too much of a bother, you tell me. No favoritism here, not in this camp."

Porter put the papers down, looked at Grant, smiled again. "Sir, forgive me, but I believe you are entitled . . . it is acceptable for a man in your position to . . . do whatever you please."

Grant pulled out another cigar, saw less damage, said, "No, Mr. Porter, it most definitely is not. You need proof of that, just ask Mr. Rawlins. If I am not certain that something is acceptable behavior, he is my authority on the subject. I doubt he approves of my family having the run of the camp."

Porter looked down, tried to hide a smile, said, "Sir, Colonel Rawlins, um . . . Colonel Rawlins is somewhat nervous by nature, sir. He has taken it upon himself to be our protector. No disrespect intended, sir, but I do sometimes wish that Colonel Rawlins would . . . not look so closely over my shoulder."

Grant nodded. "I share your feelings, Mr. Porter. But he is doing a good job. Keeps the reporters away, knows how to deal with the foreigners. Knows the rules . . . that's it, you need someone who knows the rules, the things you can say, things you can't, what makes headlines, what causes scandal. Never made much difference out West, but here . . . too close to Washington."

Porter looked to the papers again, said under his breath, "He reminds me of my grandmother. . . ."

Grant pulled at the cigar, said, "Well then, Mr. Porter, if anything happens to Colonel Rawlins, have your grandmother report to me immediately."

HE WAITED, LISTENED FOR THE SOUND OF HORSES. HE STOOD now, feeling the impatience, then sat again. He heard motion outside, knew Rawlins was close, a quiet day, nothing to aggravate the chief of staff. Grant shouted, "Colonel, any sign?"

Rawlins was at the tent now, said, "Of . . . what, sir?" Grant looked at him, and Rawlins saw the impatience, said, "Oh, if you mean General Hancock, no, not yet."

Grant nodded, pulled at the cigar, the peak of the tent above him thick with smoke. "What time did he say . . . ?"

Rawlins looked at his watch. "Two o'clock. About . . . now, sir." Rawlins turned away, looked out beyond the tents, said, "It's a wagon, sir. And the flag of the Second. He's here."

Rawlins was gone quickly, and Grant stood again, felt anxious. He did not know Hancock well, knew him at first from pure reputation, had always heard that Winfield Hancock was the best commander in the army. It was something that Meade kept with him like a small burning wound. Meade fully expected that Hancock would succeed him when Grant's patience, or the pressure from Washington finally took Meade away from the army. But it had not yet happened, and now Hancock had sent the word, through Meade first, but then directly to Grant himself. He could no longer lead his troops.

He had requested a personal meeting with Grant, and Grant knew that it was final, that if the wounds did not heal, it could be the last meeting. What had plagued Hancock since Gettysburg, the daily grief of a painful wound, the inability of the doctors to repair once and for all the damaged groin, now became the enemy Hancock could not defeat. The wound had opened up again, so badly that he could not ride, could not be there to direct his troops. Command of the Second was given to Andrew Humphreys, Meade's chief of staff. Humphreys was an older man, an engineering genius, had led troops throughout the war with quiet ability. But Grant already felt the loss, the energy that would slip away from the army when Hancock was no longer on the field.

He moved now to the opening of the tent. A wagon? he thought. Then he saw it. Of course, an ambulance. Hancock would not do that for show, to be dramatic. The wound was serious, and he could not ride. Grant waited, saw the aides move to the rear of the ambulance, hands reaching out, and now he saw Hancock, easing down to the ground, his face pale, drawn, weak. Hancock looked at him, straightened, saluted, and Grant saw the clean white shirt, the sharp blue of the dress uniform, smiled, nodded, returned the salute.

To one side, Hancock's aide tried to assist him, and Hancock barked, "I'm fine. I can walk, dammit!" The aide backed away, and Hancock limped forward, moved toward Grant.

Grant met him with a hand. "General Hancock, it is always a pleasure."

Hancock took the hand, tried to smile, but the pain filled his face, even the short walk a strain. Grant backed into the tent, and Hancock followed. Grant pointed toward the rear of the tent, to the bed, said, "If it is more comfortable, General, please, do not hesitate."

Hancock glanced at the bed, then moved toward the small chair, sat slowly, heavily, made a small groan. "This will do, sir."

Grant sat in his own chair, saw the tight lines in Hancock's face, the big handsome man fighting the pain, holding it away. Grant said, "May I get you anything, General?"

Hancock let out a deep breath, slumped now on the small chair, said, "No, thank you, sir. I won't take up your time. I just wanted to speak to you, before I left, just a moment."

Grant nodded, waited. He had actually looked forward to this, to speaking to this man when there was no one around, when Meade was not there, when the others were not a part of it. There had always been something different about Hancock, an angry impatience, something Grant understood, something Grant held tightly inside himself. Hancock was known for his angry outbursts, but his were not like Meade's; the anger was always focused, and utterly brutal, and he would find the weakness, the mistake, wrap it with intense profanity and launch it back at the guilty man like a missile. Hancock had no tolerance for incompetence, no patience for wastefulness. And if the subject was never officially discussed, Grant knew it was the one thing that would keep Hancock from command of the army: Hancock would never put up with Washington.

Hancock leaned forward now, said, "As you know, sir, I will be leaving for the capital in a few days. I have been informed that a new command has been created. If you had something to do with that, I am grateful."

Grant nodded, said nothing. If Hancock could not lead troops into battle, Grant understood that his name alone could still be very useful for recruitment, to bring the experience of the veterans back into the service, the experience that was so lacking in the new recruits, the new draftees. There would be an official organization to these veterans, a new corps that Hancock would command. It was hoped that if the war was to last much longer, Hancock might again lead good men into a good fight.

Grant said, "I expect we'll see you back here soon."

Hancock nodded. "I would prefer it that way. I wouldn't want to miss it, not again."

Grant said, "Miss . . . the end?"

Hancock nodded painfully, his face twisted slightly. "I missed it once before, in Mexico. The final blow, Chapultepec. I was sick, damned flu, my gut tied up in one big knot. Watched my own men hit that wall, climb those ladders, watched them through field glasses. I pulled myself out of bed, climbed out on a rooftop, sat there like some groaning old woman while my boys went over the wall. I marched them all the way from the coast, all the way to Mexico City, and when the time came . . ." He stopped, and Grant could see the anger in Hancock's face, the memories. Hancock forced a small laugh, said, "Looks like . . . I may miss it again."

Grant thought of Mexico, of the bloody fights against an enemy no one thought would be so strong. "That was a good day . . . Chapultepec. My men captured a couple of guns, put them to good use. . . ." He smiled now, thought of all the faces, so much younger, and the smile faded, the names rolled through his mind, so many of them gone now.

Hancock was looking at him, said, "We've killed more of our boys ourselves . . . than the Mexicans did. Who would have thought . . ." He stared away.

Grant pulled at the cigar, said, "Did you know . . . Pete Longstreet was in my wedding?"

Hancock shook his head. "No, guess I didn't. He's back, I hear. Not like . . . some of the others. I served under General Johnston in California, ran the quartermaster department in Los Angeles." He smiled, said, "Department. Me. One man. Not much happening in southern California in those days. I watched Johnston leave, and Lew Armistead, and Dick Garnett. Going home, fighting for their damned rebellion. Now . . . they're all gone." Hancock stared at the floor for a moment, said, "I always thought John Reynolds would take command, lead us to the end." He looked at Grant now. "No disrespect, sir."

Grant smiled. "I thought so too. Always thought he was the best we had. We killed Albert Sidney Johnston at Shiloh, they killed Reynolds at Gettysburg."

Hancock nodded, said, "Too many others, Phil Kearny, McPherson. Even Sedgwick could have handled the job." Hancock was suddenly uneasy. "I didn't mean to suggest that General Meade is not—"

Grant held up his hand. "If it's all the same to you, General, I'd prefer it if this meeting was unofficial. Speak your mind. I'm going to miss you here. I'm going to miss knowing that out there, somewhere, the Second Corps is where I need it to be, that those men are doing what they're supposed to be doing."

Hancock looked down, seemed embarrassed, said, "Humphreys is a good man."

Grant said, "Humphreys is a brilliant man, maybe the smartest commander in this whole army . . . both armies. But he's—excuse me, General—he's not Winfield Hancock."

Hancock straightened, nodded slowly, said, "Thank you, sir."

There was a quiet moment, and Hancock began to move, stood up slowly, tried to stand straight, leaned slightly to one side. "Sir, I won't take up more of your time. I just wanted to say good-bye. I am in the belief, sir, that the army is in the most capable hands it could be."

Grant stood now, set the cigar aside, felt a sudden wave of affection, something unexpected, thought, There are so few . . . so many of the good ones are gone. He looked at the big man's dark eyes, wanted to say something of comfort, ease the man's pain.

Hancock forced himself upright, saluted, said, "With your permission, sir."

Grant returned the salute, held out a hand, said, "General Hancock, this command is more than grateful for your service. If you miss the end *this* time, that's not a bad thing. It means the end is pretty close."

DINNER HAD BEEN QUIET, THE CHILDREN WERE AWAY, GUESTS of the navy. It had been Fred who insisted on seeing one of the big gunboats that patrolled the James River. Grant had hesitated, but Admiral Porter was anxious to have the young man as his guest. Fred's enthusiasm seemed to wane when Porter requested that all the children join the tour.

Grant had finished dinner, thought of his oldest son, trying to maintain his fragile dignity, boarding the ship, passing by the respectful line of sailors, forced to endure the embarrassment of six-year-old Jesse holding his hand. Grant smiled, held out his cigar, thought, Not every responsibility is a glorious one.

The staff was slowly rising, formal, polite, and there were small polite greetings to Julia. Grant still felt uncomfortable with their efforts, their attention, thought, It should not be, she is here for my own selfish reasons. They should not be so concerned.

The chairs were empty now, and Grant leaned back, pulled at the cigar, looked at his wife. She was smiling, watching him, said, "Well now, that was pleasant."

He nodded, said, "You make it so. They are not usually this . . . kindly."

He stood, held out his hand, helped her from the chair. She stood, wrapped her arm in his, and they walked out into the dark, toward the river, toward the distant lights of the big boats. He moved slowly, let her steps guide him, felt her arm against him, focused only on that, on the small part of her, said, "It won't be much longer."

There was a quiet moment. They reached the edge of the high bluff and she stopped, turned to him in the darkness, said, "I believe you. But you need not worry about us. There are many kind people, we are treated so well everywhere we go. You are a very respected man."

It was an odd word to come from her, and he had not thought of that, had always felt she was removed somehow, from all of this, from the war. He thought of her family, in Missouri, so different from him. Her father still would not discuss the war, and Grant had no reason to ever try. The old man had been a slave owner, and even now it made Grant sick inside, the anger. He tried not to bring it up with her, would keep the anger hidden away—there was no point in attacking the old man, or his politics. He was fighting this war to end that way of life, and the old man was just one more reason why this war was fought at all. He looked at her still, her face illuminated by the small lights from below, thought, Yes, we need this to end, to become a family again, all of us, all the families. She is so patient.

He smiled, looked down, and she said, "What is it? Tell me."

He looked out over the river, said, "It is a fortunate thing that I am not waiting somewhere for *you* to come home. I do not have the patience. No telling what I might do. I'd probably come here and never leave, until you came with me. No. I would not make a good wife."

He laughed, but she did not, still looked at him, said, "No one is happy waiting for you to come home, for this to be over. We do what we must, all of us, all the wives, all the mothers. Everywhere I go, New York, Washington, it's all I see, in every face, every woman I meet. They even ask *me*, as though I know something, some secrets, that because my husband is in command I must know these things. They all ask the same thing: 'How long?' "

Grant reached for her hand, wrapped his fingers around hers. "What do you say?"

"To pray, to have faith, to believe in what their men are doing. It's not always the right thing to say. I have had some . . . anger. The widows, that is the hardest thing, what do you say to someone whose husband is not coming home?"

He looked down, shook his head. "I try not to think about that. It's part of my job, my duty. I make widows. I could not do that very well, talk to them, see the hurt, the tears. I must *not* do that. The war cannot have a face, or a name. I hear about people I have known, back in Mexico, or at the Point, men I have served with. I hear that they are dead, and it shocks me how hard that hits me. I can't tell anyone about that. How do I order men to their deaths if every death causes so much pain?"

She put her hand on his shoulder, whispered, "Because it is who you are. It is why God has put you here. If you did not believe that, then you would not end the war. If the deaths of so many did not bother you, you would not care if it ended. That's why you will survive this war. That is God's lesson. That's why I am patient."

He stared at her, surprised, had never heard her speak like this. She was always devout, had always insisted the children be raised with the strictest religious instruction, but he'd never heard her talk of the war before. He thought of her words, thought, If that is true, if this war, if what I am doing, is some kind of lesson from God, then God must be very pleased indeed.

They stood for a long quiet moment, felt the chill of the darkness, could hear the sounds from along the waterfront. There was a noise behind him, and he turned, saw several men silhouetted by the glow of the campfires, could hear a low murmur of energy, small quiet voices, intense whispers. He felt something cold stab his gut, said, "What is it? What has happened?"

One man stepped closer, and Grant tried to see the face, knew now from the walk, the proper step, that it was Rawlins.

"Sir, forgive the intrusion. We just received word from Washington, sir. President Lincoln has been reelected."

IT WAS LIKE A PARTY, AND IF IT MEANT THE WAR WOULD GO ON, IT meant finally that they would win. The soldiers had cast their own votes, something that had rarely been allowed before in wartime, anywhere. Grant himself had strongly advocated the vote for the soldiers, that these men were not just paid mercenaries whose vote could be swayed by a commander. They read all variety of newspapers, they understood the issues, and each man was very capable of making his own decision. The war itself was to preserve something unique in the world, the rights of men to choose their own leaders. Grant realized that to deny that right to the very men who were fighting for it made no sense at all. There had been no serious objection to that from either side of the political race, the McClellan people believing that their man had been such a popular commander with the soldiers, it could only help his chances. What McClellan did not understand, and Grant clearly did, was that the soldiers were not interested in going home until the war was won. Despite his popularity in the field, McClellan ultimately had not shown his army that he was prepared to win the war. By choosing Grant, and supporting him, Lincoln had.

The victory for Lincoln was no great landslide, and likely the vote of the vast majority of the army won him the election. Throughout the North sentiment was still very high for the war to end. In the end it was confidence that Lincoln would be more likely to preserve the Union. McClellan himself had begun to back away from an outright declaration of peace, that he would simply stop the war. It infuriated some of his own supporters, but as a military man, McClellan understood that simply ending the war meant recognizing the rights of the Confederacy to form their own country. That was a break with many of the Democrats he was supposed to represent. His commitment to the Democratic platform was consistent with the way McClellan had led his troops into battle: he went halfway.

With Lincoln's victory, the morale in the army soared, and at Petersburg the blue troops peered out at the enemy with a new sense of what was coming. There were still some, the veterans from the first disasters of the war, who might still believe that those fat men in Washington would only disappoint, that the commanders of this army did not know how to finish the job. Now the talk was more enthusiastic. Even the most cynical veterans began to see it, to believe what many were saying, that Grant and Lincoln would do the job, would see it through to the end.

33. LEE

November 1864

HE HEARD IT FIRST FROM THE SOLDIERS, FROM THE SHARP-shooters out front. He knew it was still going on every night, the small quiet truce, enemies meeting face-to-face to trade, to pass along newspapers, bits of information. There was still tobacco—the boys in gray had little else to offer, and the Yankees would still trade for it—and each night it might be the only way his men would get anything to eat. But now the word came back, men moving quickly, and at first it sounded like the familiar rattle of rumors, but then there was a newspaper. If an officer took the time to read it himself, he still moved, kept the horse in motion toward the headquarters. The news came to Lee like a cold black wind. Lincoln had won the election.

There had been hope that if the people in the North were listening to their own newspapers, the fiery talk from those who opposed Lincoln, they might respond, the price for the years of blood, the death of so many sons. Davis had believed it absolutely, told Lee that what they'd given up in land, even now, all the cities, the rivers, the ports, in the end would still mean victory, because the price for the North had been the blood of so many of its young men. Davis had already been planning how to deal with McClellan, the terms of the treaty, the independence that was so very close. Lee had not shared his enthusiasm.

Now Lee sat alone in the tent, heard the wind howling outside, the first hard chill, another winter rolling hard toward Virginia, toward the army that sat low in the trenches.

With the change of seasons had come one change in command. Longstreet had returned, the wounds not fully healed, but he would not accept the comfort of a safe position. His right arm was still paralyzed, and he'd learned to write with the left hand. Lee smiled at that, thought, You are still stubborn, and that is what we need right now. Longstreet would command the forces above the James, protecting Richmond. Lee did not believe Grant would strike there. He believed that the small fights, the occasional strong attacks, were meant to distract him from the greater goal, the true plan. Lee understood the maps, saw it plainly, and so would stay close to Grant's real objective—that no matter how much activity the blue troops threw north of the James, they were still extending west of Petersburg. If they kept reaching out, they would soon reach the Southside Railroad, the final artery for supplies south of the Appomattox River. If the Southside fell into Grant's hands, there would be only one course left—to pull away from the capital, and from Petersburg, and move inland. The siege of Petersburg would become something else.

He stared down between his feet, thought, They must not know . . . the men must not feel this as I do. He shook his head, tried to clear his mind, glanced at the newspaper. This is a defeat unlike anything I have been through. Not one shot, not one gun, and yet it is as though we have been . . . what? If it is not a defeat in battle, utter and simple, then . . . it means that nothing will change. Grant will just continue to do what he has been doing since the spring. And we do not have the strength to stop him.

Abruptly, he stood, closed his eyes, clenched his fists. No, this is not what they expect of me. This is not what my duty is about, to sit here and brood, the luxury of self-pity.

He lifted his head, said in a low voice, "*God, protect us. We do not doubt . . . we do not question Your will. . . .*" He paused, searched for words. "*We ask only . . . understanding. Show us the way. If it pleases You, we will do our duty, we will carry on as You have shown us the way. . . .*"

His mind would not focus, the prayer was weak, wandering. No, he thought, we do not look for answers. We do what we must do. That is all He asks of us. There can be no more than that.

DECEMBER 1864

IT WAS ONE MORE INVITATION, ONE HE'D HEARD EVERYWHERE THEY had set up the headquarters. He declined of course, as he always declined, had heard it so many times, the generosity of a people who could afford little, opening their homes, their soft beds, to the commander of their army. He would always be gracious, insist that he keep to the tents, even if they were set up right by the house, right in the yard. But the cold winds were blowing hard across Petersburg, and for the first time there had been argument. It came not from the insistence of the civilians, but from Taylor, who knew what the winter could mean to Lee's health. The young man had stood up to Lee, insisted in a tone that was direct and firm. Lee had been surprised by that, but he was surprised more by the tactics Taylor used. It was a letter from Mary, scolding him into protecting himself from the harsh invasion of the cold. If Taylor did not admit it, Lee knew there was a plot, a conspiracy, and against the united front Lee was powerless. That Taylor was reinforced by the iron will of Mary Lee meant only one outcome. For the first time, Lee accepted the invitation to sleep under the dry and solid roof of a civilian home.

The family was named Turnbull, and their home had been spared from damage, at least so far, from the nightly bombardment of the city by Federal guns. The house was on a gentle hill, west of the town, the land around still scattered with the big oaks, an orchard of apple trees, the fields not yet stripped and scarred by the feet of the armies. It was not a grand estate, but a solid frame home, two stories, with a porch that faced the road, another to the side.

The first night was misery, his back settling onto the soft mattress with great protest, and he'd stayed awake, turned, looked down at the hard floor, thought, Maybe . . . down there, just move the quilt. But he endured. The second night, he slept with the soft sounds of angels, dreaming of those days, forgotten now, when Mary was so young, the playfulness, the glorious calm of the old estates, the lush green of the fields. He could hear the music, the voices perfect, the songs of God, the pure joy of the church service, then afterward, the great feasts of Sunday dinner. . . .

"Sir?"

His face was buried deep in the soft pillow, and he opened his eyes, stared dreamily into the lush white.

"Sir?"

He lifted his head slightly, saw daylight, the room lit by the early dawn flowing through lace curtains. He raised himself up, felt the stiffness, felt the age. He turned, saw Taylor standing in the half-open door, looking down, embarrassed; he would not look at Lee in his bedclothes. Lee blinked groggily, rolled over, sat up, said, "Yes, Colonel, I am awake. What is it?"

Taylor still did not look at him, said, "Forgive me, sir. We have received word . . . from the War Department . . . about General Hood, sir."

Lee took a deep breath, knew from the sound of Taylor's voice this was not good news. "Go on, Colonel."

"Sir, General Hood has been repulsed at Nashville. The reports are unclear how badly his losses were, but the army is in retreat. There is no doubt that he has been forced to withdraw."

Lee was fully awake now, said, "Thank you, Colonel. I'll be out in a minute."

Taylor closed the door, and Lee sat for a moment, looked over to the window, saw motion, and sharp wind in the trees, thought, They should have gone after Sherman. . . .

After Sherman swept him away from Atlanta, Hood insisted on gathering his army and moving north, Davis approving a plan that should have pulled Sherman up after him. Hood had been effective at harassing Sherman's supply lines, the railroads in Sherman's rear, all along the route toward Chattanooga. But Sherman let him go, focused instead on moving his great strength farther east. No one knew for sure what Sherman's intentions were, but Richmond had seen value in taking the offensive, not merely nipping at Sherman's heels. Hood continued to push northward, moved into Tennessee, finally found a hard fight at Franklin, just below Nashville, a fight that by all accounts had been a bloodbath. The Federal troops then pulled away, withdrew to the safety of the strong works at Nashville, and so Hood could claim victory. But it was costly, a disastrous loss of commanders, so many good men, struck down in front of troops that desperately needed good men.

There was value to Nashville, it was a major rail hub. If Hood had taken the city, it would have been a concern to Washington, a dangerous threat to the Ohio River. But as well as Lee knew the reckless aggressiveness of Hood, he knew the Federal commander. It was George Thomas, who had served under Lee in Texas, in the cavalry. Thomas was a Virginian who surprised Lee by staying in the old army, resisting the enormous pressure to join the forces of his home state. It was Thomas who had saved the Federal army a year ago from complete destruction by Bragg's army, allowing Rosecrans to escape into Chattanooga. By his brilliant defense Thomas had earned the nickname the newspapers loved, the "Rock of Chickamauga." If Thomas had now made a reputation for being somewhat slow to move, it did not matter.

He was already in place, in the strong fortifications around Nashville. All he had to do was wait for Hood to move up close. Thomas had been reinforced, greatly outnumbered Hood's exhausted and bloodied army, and so the results were predictable.

Lee moved from the bed, went to the window and held the lace aside. He looked out at tall trees, could see gray clouds beyond. He touched the pane of glass, felt the icy cold, a faint flow of air seeping into the room. Hood will be of no help now, he thought. If Thomas comes after him, he could pursue him all the way to the Gulf. But even if Thomas sits tight, Hood's army will have used itself up. If he has been beaten badly at Nashville, forced into a rapid retreat, it means he has lost guns, left them behind. And how many good men?

He looked up at the clouds blowing over the trees, low and heavy, the light in the room now fading, a dim gray shadow. Winter, he thought. The weather has not been too bad yet, but that will change. A good hard storm, a hard freeze, the armies will sit tight for a while. Grant may be content to just hold his lines. But Sherman . . . there is nothing in his way, he can move in any direction. If he moves *north* . . .

Lee reached for the uniform hanging on a hook by the door and began to dress. There was a high moan, the wind swirling through the trees, and he looked out the window again, heard the panes rattle. He felt a chill, buttoned his coat, stared for a moment, saw a swirl of motion, the first wave of snowfall. Then the wind grew quiet, the snow falling softly. He knew Taylor was waiting, that outside, in the road, the wagons and the horses were moving, the clatter and hustle of headquarters. He did not move, waited a moment longer, watched the snow gathering on the window ledge and beyond, blowing softly through the tall limbs of the big trees.

CHRISTMAS 1864

MEN HAD BEEN LEAVING THE LINES EVERY NIGHT, SOME ON their own, one by one, slipping away from their posts on the skirmish line, sometimes a whole section of picket line. At first the blue sharpshooters had been wary, steady fingers on tight triggers, suspicious of the ragged enemy who approached, the same men they had sought out for so long down the barrel of the musket. But there was no treachery, no fight in these rebels who came across the line, who called out in harsh whispers, who waved small pieces of white in the moonlight. They had simply had enough. Soon, the men in blue became used to it, waited for the small sounds every night, and every night more of Lee's army slipped away, crossed over to the warm fires, the promise of a good meal.

Lee rode slowly, pulled his coat tight around him, the cold wind raising a dust cloud that swirled down through the men crouching in the shelters. He could see the faces, looking up at him from below, from the shelter of their dark holes. He saw one man stand, and Lee stopped the horse at the familiar look, the man staring up at him as the men had always looked at him. This man raised one hand in a crooked salute, and Lee could see he was shivering, his thin coat ripped at the shoulder, exposing bare skin to the wind. Lee returned the salute, the old instinct, and he wanted to say something to the man, thought, Stay low, stay warm. But there were no words, he could not speak, he felt his throat pull tightly into a knot. He raised his hand, motioned to the man, a silent gesture, sit, go back into the shelter, and the man's voice rose faintly through the wind, his arms now wrapped around his frail body.

"General Lee, I'm hungry."

Lee could not control it now, felt the icy wetness on his face, looked down into his gloved hands, wanted to say to the man, "Have faith, God will be here for us . . . God will provide." But still there were no words. He looked at the man again, the gaunt face now turning away, and Lee saw him drop down out of sight, into the shelter. Lee turned the horse, blinked hard at the wetness in his eyes, thought, They deserve so much . . . and I have nothing to give them.

He knew of the desertions, the reports came to him every morning. The numbers were growing, and he knew that through the winter the numbers would grow worse. The army was extended in a line that no army had ever held, and there were fewer men to hold that line every day.

He rode back behind the lines, close to the buildings of Petersburg. He was beginning to know many of the people who were still in the town, familiar faces, the strong-willed citizens who would never accept defeat, civilians who still cheered him. He had appealed to them to give to his men what they could, but the supplies were low for them as well, the cellars and pantries as bare as the farmland around Petersburg.

He rode into the streets now, past the destruction from the Federal bombardments, broken windows, shattered walls. But the people still came forward, faces watching him from the places that could still keep them safe, voices rising from the cellars, calling out to him.

He turned a corner, saw a wagon moving toward him, drawn by

one lame horse. The wagon slowed, and Lee saw an old woman, holding tight to the reins, and she said to him, "General Lee . . . it is a fine day, sir! It is the Lord's day!"

Lee raised his hat slightly, made a short bow, thought, Yes, we must not forget that. "Thank you, madam. Bless you. But please, it is not safe . . . the Federals may start shelling the town at any time."

The woman turned a hard eye to the east, said, "No, General, I don't believe so. Not today."

There was sound now, from a side street, and Lee saw another wagon, followed by an old man, walking, carrying a bundle on his shoulder. Now the sounds came from all sides, the people slowly moving toward the main road, wagons and carts, women, old men, children. Some moved by him, and he stared in amazement, looked now at the old woman.

She said, "Excuse me, General Lee. I got to be goin'." She slapped at the old horse, who lurched, hobbled past him, and then he saw into the back of the wagon, round bundles wrapped in cloth, and the smells rose up to him, the wonderful fragrance, warm bread. He watched the wagon move away, and the others were moving by him now, and there were more smells. He felt his stomach growl, reminded of the great Sunday feasts, the bounty of Virginia.

People still called out to him, the streets busy now. He glanced to the east, felt a stab of fear, knew the big guns were watching them, hoped the old woman had been right.

The people understood that if they had little, they at least had something, and so they gathered the small bits and scraps, the last hidden treasures, and loaded their wagons with whatever their kitchens could create. Lee moved the horse aside, watched the wagons and carts creaking and groaning past him, the people on foot smiling as they shifted their loads, nodding and greeting him, saw the faces filled with the spirit of their faith, of their cause.

He saw one man, younger, walking on a stiff leg, missing an arm, and Lee recognized the remnants of an old uniform, knew the man was a veteran, had been one of his own. The man's one hand held a package, cradled it gently, and he bowed, said, "General Lee, 'tis a fine day indeed."

Lee nodded to the man, looked at the strange bundle, saw now it was sitting on a plate. He said, "Sir, what is that?"

The man stopped, held the plate out toward Lee, said, "It's a turkey, sir. Well, it ain't a for-real turkey. My wife, she built it, so to speak. It's sweet potatoes. Don't it look like a turkey, though?"

Lee stared at the oddly shaped mass, then out to the passing carts. He felt a wave of confusion, said, "What are these people doing? Where are they going?"

The man seemed surprised at the question, said, "Why, General, sir, we're a headin' out to see the army. It's Christmas. It's time for dinner."

34. GRANT

CHRISTMAS 1864

THE LOG HUTS WERE FINISHED, AND NOW, WITH THE WIND AND the harsh wet cold settling over the army, the energy of headquarters became deliberate, patient, the business of running the army. There had been snow, then a melt, and the roads in all directions were a boggy mess. There were still those who tried to keep their routine—the sutlers, whose business would suffer from inactivity, and others, merchants or reporters, who would not always pay heed to the advisories from headquarters, ignored the requests for restricted movement on the roadways. The soldiers knew there would be no activity, that under these conditions there was no way to move men and machine. It had been this way from the beginning, and it was accepted by both sides that winter meant a grudging peace, at least for a while. There had been exceptions, of course. The Battle of Fredericksburg was the most notable, two years ago.

Now, Hood had made the same effort in Tennessee, fought against an ice storm that was as effective at stopping his army in its tracks as anything the Federals could have done. But the result hadn't had as much to do with the weather as with Hood himself. With the smashing of Hood's army, and the threat now gone from Tennessee, most of the focus would be in Virginia, and here there would be no movement until spring.

The cabin was tight and efficient, one small room in the rear, the bedroom, some privacy at least. The main room was the office and the sitting room, the tiny space for whatever important guest might require attention. At least the cabin was warm.

Grant sat quietly at the tall desk, a high cabinet divided into small compartments, cubbyholes for all manner of paperwork, orders and requests, official and informal. There were candles in each of the windows, and Julia had found pieces of colored glass so that each candle gave off a different light. He hadn't noticed, of course, and so had to absorb her gentle scolding. Now he saw the small flickers of color, dancing slowly on the dark log walls, her touch, the one bit of her feminine hand in the stark decor of the headquarters. It was, after all, Christmas.

The children stayed below, on the river, a small steamer. Most of the time Julia was with them, but came up to visit her husband when there was time, when the workdays were shorter, the nights free of the tedious detail of command. Tonight she was there, but it was very late, and she'd given up waiting for him, had been asleep for a while.

The door closed carefully, the aide backing out slowly, very aware that Mrs. Grant was sleeping. Grant sat at the desk, took the telegram apart, unfolded the paper, read it slowly, ran his finger over each word. Now he was smiling, beaming, felt suddenly like a small child. He wanted to cheer, to yell out something, to burst out into the cold night and wake up the whole army. The wire was not even addressed to him, had been forwarded from Washington, directly from the President. It was a message from Sherman, received by Lincoln on Christmas eve.

> I beg to present you as a Christmas gift, the city of Savannah . . .

Sherman had done it, had cut himself off from his supplies, moved across Georgia all the way to the Atlantic. Grant was still smiling, thought of those people in Washington—Halleck, Stanton—the great outcries, predictions of disaster, how Sherman's plan would end in catastrophe, the suicide of his army, starvation, capture, desertion. Grant had refused to listen to that talk, knew Sherman too well, understood what could be gained, what a success could mean, and now what the success *did* mean.

He thought of Lincoln then, the smile on the rugged face, thought, Yes, this is your doing. If not for you, if you did not give me the authority, if it was up to those people in Washington, it would never have happened. Sherman would be bogged down somewhere around Atlanta, taking small pieces of punishment from Hood's army, and he might as well be in a prison. But now Hood was destroyed, no longer a part of the war, and Sherman's sixty-five thousand men were on the coast, healthy and jubilant, waiting for their next move. Grant stared at the last bit of flame on one of the candles, a small dot of red reflected on the window. You already know, my friend, the next move will be *north*.

The plan had been kept secret, and no one knew just where Sherman would end up, where his army, cut off from communication, would suddenly appear. There had been speculation that he would move south, toward Mobile, or even Jacksonville. Some had believed the march was just a ruse, that he still would turn and go back to Tennessee, to pursue Hood from behind. The papers in Richmond did not believe that Sherman would simply pack up and go, with little concern over Hood's great invasion northward. It was considered pure foolishness that Hood could be allowed a free hand in Tennessee, an extraordinary mistake that would surely result in a major breakthrough for the man from Texas, who everyone knew was determined to make a fight. But it was exactly that determination that gave confidence to Sherman's plan.

Hood was looking for anyone, anywhere, to throw his army against, whatever enemy he could find. Nashville was a ripe target, but Sherman guarded it with the most stubborn defender in the Federal army. Hood's invasion north was exactly what Sherman, and Grant, had hoped for. With Hood out of Georgia, moving straight toward the massed guns of George Thomas's defenses, Sherman had no one to slow him down, no force of rebels large enough to even attract his attention. The small numbers of Georgia militia, men who stayed close to their homes, could only pick and stab at this great blue wave that rolled through their state.

If neither Washington nor Richmond knew exactly where Sherman was going, it was clear that he was forsaking his own lines of supply for what he could take from the land. That was the greatest fear in Washington, that once Sherman was cut off, any delay, any obstacle, could cause him to use up whatever food was in reach. There were short memories in the capital, but not at City Point. Grant had done this before, made the march years ago, Winfield Scott's great trek across Mexico, cut off from everything but the goal in front of him. There was no difference now.

There were newspapers on the small table by the window, and he stood now, would read the one column again, the amazing hostility, the vicious attack on the army. It was not a southern paper, but one from New York. It had always been the voice of opposition to Lincoln, but this time the writing was not endless rhetoric about politics and economics, topics of interest to almost no one; this time the attacks were leveled directly at the army, and directly at William T. Sherman. Grant held the paper up to the light, read the words, focused on the amazing descriptions. The article quoted the governor of Georgia and the representatives in Richmond. They were howling mad, claimed the worst kind of barbarism was sweeping across the state, that what Sherman was doing was little more than raping the land, burning and looting the farms and towns of the innocent. Grant turned slightly, let the lamplight wash over one paragraph, one sentence in particular.

> Wars are the exclusive property of the men who fight, and should never injure the innocent civilian.

He had read that the first time with astonishment, read it now with disgust. He put the paper down. Innocent? he thought. Where is the line? Does the man who works in the munitions factory differ from the man who grows the food? Do they not both support the ability to fight a war? He knew how Sherman saw this, how Sherman had responded to the indignant civilians, the small-town politicians who protested his method of war. His response had opened something in Grant's mind, something Grant had not considered. Sherman had told them: If *you* are not affected, if *you* are not hurt by what we do, then *you* will not do anything to stop it. The war will simply continue. As long as it is just the soldiers, these barbaric men with guns who kill each other, as long as the damage is far away, the destruction and death out of your sight, then no amount of hand-wringing and moral outrage will make it end. If *you* are affected, if your farms, your crops are destroyed, your neat buildings in your perfect towns burned to the ground, then there will be a reason to stop this. War is not tidy, it is not convenient, it is *everywhere*, it has to be felt by *everyone*.

Grant had not thought of that, had always assumed you won the war by winning the battle, your guns against their guns. But now he realized that so much had changed, not just the ground, *where* the war was fought, but *how*. The horror of what was written about, the accounts of the bloody fields, the horrible numbers of casualties, were commonplace now, drifting through headquarters as another piece of the daily routine. The angry reports of Sherman's march were in the southern papers first, as though Sherman himself had somehow changed the war, brought some surprising and outrageous barbarism to this gentlemen's disagreement. Grant thought of his friend, the manic energy, thought, Yes, I have no doubt he has been efficient, completely efficient. But if he is a barbarian, then what about the rest of us?

Above the James River, Longstreet was using land mines now, on the roads east of Richmond, explosive charges that did not distinguish between who was innocent and who deserved to die. Hardee had done the same in defense of Savannah, and when Sherman's army approached, men and horses were maimed in horrific ways by hidden charges they never saw. When the weapons are that anonymous, when we can kill our enemy without ever seeing him, then how do we know who the victim might be? he thought. The guns are so good now, we can drop our shells with such precision, the killing happens with such casual regularity. Was it different when we had to look him in the eye, stare face-to-face, comparing our honor and our courage to his?

Grant had been relieved to hear the wounds had allowed Longstreet to come back. But Pete, he thought, you are my enemy. It was not supposed to ever be like that; this was to be nothing more than a conflict over whether or not you fellows could break away, be left alone, govern yourselves any way you saw fit. It was a fight over an idea, an argument over politics, a duel between gentlemen. How naive . . . Did you believe, truly believe, that there would be no blood, that the innocent would be spared? The politicians thought it would take a month, maybe two. The first troops who volunteered signed up for ninety-day terms.

He thought of Beauregard, another veteran of Mexico, another good soldier in the old army. He commanded the gunners at Fort Sumter. So they shell the fort, show us how serious they are, and expect us to . . . what? Just back away? Just allow it to happen, the country to be divided up, the Union destroyed? It seemed so long ago, a lifetime, another world.

He didn't know how much to believe of the reports, whether or not Sherman had been as vicious as many claimed. But of course, he knew what Phil Sheridan had done to the Shenandoah. If the enemy cannot eat, the enemy cannot fight. Is that any more barbaric than blasting twenty pounds of canister through a line of men? Or dropping a thirty-pound iron ball through the roof of a shelter where men sit, believing they are safe?

He went to the candles, pinched each one, then picked up the lantern, raised the glass, blew the light out. He stared out the window, saw snow now reflected in the faint light of the other cabins. He was surprised, thought, They're still awake, still at work, or, no, maybe just talk, card-playing. He watched the snow, felt the dark silence, thought of her now, sleeping in the small room. He looked toward the door, could see very little, a small reflection. What will this be like . . . when it is over? The boys especially, Fred and Buck, all the attention they get as the sons of the commanding general. It would be nice to be just . . . Father.

He thought of the last time he felt at home, like he belonged in some place, some house that was truly his. He shook his head, thought, Maybe it has never been like that. I have never been very good at anything but . . . *this.* This I know how to do. And it makes very little difference what newspapers say, or how indignant politicians become. We will do whatever we have to do to win this war. This can end, any time. There does not have to be any more barbarism, any more death, any more savagery. And if Lee and Davis don't understand that, then it will go on, and there is nothing they can do to stop us. It has never been clearer than it is right now. They cannot win. It is only a matter of time.

He moved to the door, pushed it open, slowly, a small squeak of hinges. It was very dark, no light at all from the covered window. He could hear her breathing now, soft and slow, and he stared into the dark, thought, She rather likes this, being here, so close to all this. She is very aware of my place, my status. He smiled. Yes, she is spoiled. Her father did that, and now . . . I am no better. I would give her anything . . . and I cannot say no to her. Certainly she knows that. So, how will she adjust? What will we do when there is no war, when I am not in command? Will I be able to make her happy?

He felt his way, sat down on the bed, pulled off his boots, set them quietly on the wood floor. She turned, soft motion, and he tried to see her face, his eyes searching the dark. He felt guilty, thought, No, I'm sorry, I should have been quiet. Now her hand touched his arm, her voice drifting toward him, a quiet whisper, *"Merry Christmas."*

35. GRANT

February 3, 1865

THE CARRIAGE WAS ELEGANT, ACCENTED WITH POLISHED BRASS and deep rich leather, led by the best horses that could be found. They moved through the rebel lines first, out into the bleak open ground, then, slowly winding, made their way through the Federal lines. The passengers were not familiar to the soldiers they passed, the men straining to see, officers with field glasses, men climbing on each other's shoulders for a clear look. They were well dressed, they were civilians, and they did not look to the side, did not wave or answer the shouts of the soldiers. It was a show of dignity, of grave seriousness, a clear indication of the importance of their mission. The word flew, propelled by the sudden burst of hope, and the men began to cheer, to shout and yell and laugh, slapping each other, each regiment, each line of entrenchments passing it along, the contagious joy, the raw sense of relief, of what this one carriage, carrying three nameless men, could mean.

The cheers echoed all down the lines, spread through the dark holes and frozen earthworks, the trenches of both armies. The word spread farther, well beyond sight of the carriage, rippled through the trenches like a flood of cool water. From the James River to well below the deep works around Petersburg men began to stand, to listen to the sounds, to show themselves in the deadly space where no man had dared. But the sharpshooters had laid down the muskets, joined the men behind them, waving hats, blowing bugles, beating drums. On both sides of the line the two armies began to yell at each other, a competition, who could yell the loudest, shout it out with the most passion, their voices swollen with the hope they shared with the very few who knew what the mission was about. Even the officers caught the fever, began to speak of it, spreading the great unstoppable word, and the men believed it even more, made more real by the enthusiasm of their own commanders, the men who *knew* what was happening. More men emerged from the ground, stared at each other, at the enemy across the way, some wondering still if the word was real, if the hope would become truth, if the carriage and the civilians meant *peace*.

Grant didn't know the men, didn't know many politicians at all. But the names were now familiar, and they were important. The group was headed by Alexander Stephens, a former United States congressman from Georgia, and now vice president of the Confederacy. The other men were John Campbell, a former Supreme Court justice, now the Confederate assistant secretary of war, and Robert Hunter, who had been the U.S. Speaker of the House of Representatives and was now president of the Confederate senate.

Grant *did* know why they were coming, waited impatiently as the carriage made its way slowly to City Point. He could hear the cheering following the carriage along the road, while in the camp there was no motion, everyone watching the carriage. For a brief moment the business of the army, of the war, had stopped.

The carriage was led now by a Federal escort, and the horsemen pulled to the side, formed a neat row, most eyes focused on Grant. The carriage stopped, and Grant looked at the driver, a small nervous man with huge eyes that darted about in all directions, absorbing all he saw, a man feeling very much alone in the camp of the enemy.

Grant moved forward, watched the three men climb out of the carriage, one much shorter than the others, the small man moving with difficulty under a thick layer of overcoats and scarves. The face meant nothing, but Grant thought, He's Stephens.

He moved closer as the men adjusted themselves from the ride, and the faces now turned toward him. There were smiles, and Grant was surprised, had expected . . . he was not sure, maybe . . . anger?

Stephens stepped forward, held out a hand, and Grant took it, realized just how small Stephens was, the hand feeling fragile, tiny, in his own. Grant bowed slightly, and the others now came forward, more hands, more smiles.

Grant said, "Welcome, gentlemen . . ." He paused, began to feel it now, could still hear the cheering out on the road, the men still infected by the rumor, by the hope, by the power these men carried, and all that it could mean. Grant looked at Stephens again, the pleasant smile, thought, My God . . . maybe it's true. He stepped back, more formal, made another short bow, said, "Gentlemen, welcome to the headquarters of the United States Army."

THE MEN CARRIED THE OFFICIAL DESIGNATION OF PEACE COMmissioners, and had expected to go all the way to Washington. But Lincoln would not wait for them, came by a fast steamer, and hosted the commissioners on a small ship anchored at the mouth of the James River at Fort Monroe. The meeting lasted four hours, small talk and grave discussion, bits of humor and bursts of anger. The men knew each other well, from years of political wrangling, the business of Washington, the common ground of political experience. When it was over, the peace commissioners returned by the same route they had come, and Lincoln came to City Point to see Grant.

"IT WAS NOT A WASTE OF TIME. NOT AT ALL." LINCOLN LEANED back in the chair, stared at the ceiling of the dark cabin.

Grant held the cigar in his hand, watched Lincoln, would not ask. He will tell me if I am supposed to know, he thought. Lincoln rocked forward, leaned close to Grant, said, "But I know them . . . I know Stephens. They brought me a piece of paper that came straight from Davis. Stephens wasn't happy about it, but his hands were tied." Lincoln shook his head, leaned back again, slapped his knee with his hand. "They don't seem to understand . . . it amazes me, like speaking to a blind hound dog. He knows what he's supposed to do. But turn him loose and he runs in circles. That's it . . . they're running in circles."

Lincoln stood now, ducked under a low beam, moved toward the warmth from the fireplace. Grant still watched him, held the cigar in his mouth, turned it slowly with his fingers.

Lincoln stared at the fire, said, "We talked about it until we beat it to death, and it still came back to one point. They don't see coming back . . . coming together as one country. That's Davis talking, holding out till the end. He still believes they can end this thing and become independent. I could see it in Stephens's eyes. *He* knows better, knows it can't be like that." Lincoln straightened, looked at Grant. "One country. That's the first point, the only place to start. We end the war by reuniting. Everything else comes later. All the discussion, all the terms, come later. But Davis . . ." Lincoln looked at the floor, shook his head. "Davis has his dream, and he can't be moved. As long as Davis is in charge, all the peace commissioners in the world won't make a difference."

He leaned over, put his hands on Grant's desk, looked hard into Grant's eyes, said slowly, a grim, quiet voice: "Mr. Grant, I would have given them a blank sheet of paper, anything they wanted, any terms. All they had to do was come back to one country. Even the slave issue . . . they know there's no hope there, not even Davis believes they can maintain slavery. But . . . it was right there, on the table. It was in their hands . . ." Lincoln straightened again, held his hands together, then slowly spread them apart. ". . . and they let it go. It was . . . sickening."

Grant could see the sadness on Lincoln's face, and Lincoln moved to the chair, sat heavily, slumped down, the thin shoulders sagging. Grant could feel his mood, and Lincoln put his hands on Grant's desk, leaned forward, said, "There is only one solution, Mr. Grant."

Grant nodded, said, "Yes. Always has been."

Lincoln looked at him, shook his head. "No, not always. Reasonable men do not do this. History will not consider what we have done to ourselves as reasonable, or necessary . . . or civilized. I am very afraid that God will judge us harshly. If not all of us, perhaps then only some of us. We have paid a terrible price. This country will never recover from this war, there will always be wounds. And it saddens me, Mr. Grant, it saddens me deeply that this must still be *your* affair."

Grant nodded, stared at Lincoln in silence, at the man's great sadness. Lincoln took a deep breath, shook his head again, and there was a change in the man's face, dark, serious, and he looked hard at Grant now, the soft kindness gone from his voice.

"Mr. Grant, I must ask you . . . forgive me, I must *instruct* you. There will be no more conferences, no more meetings with commissioners. You are not to decide, discuss, or confer upon any political question. That authority rests . . . with me." Lincoln paused, rubbed his tired eyes, let out a long breath. "Your job is regrettably simple. The rebels will agree to our terms when their army is defeated. Defeat their army."

Grant nodded, said nothing, was already far beyond the events of the day. He had felt the enthusiasm, the optimism that the peace commissioners might bring something tangible, justify all the cheers, all the energetic hope of the soldiers. But that was past, and now his mind was already working, the new plan, that when the warm weather came again, the reality was grim and simple. The killing would go on.

On the front lines the joy of the soldiers was swept away now by shock. There would be no peace, the deadly spaces between the lines would remain. The men stared across the open ground, one long look at those men, over there, the men so much like them. Now they began to crawl back into their dark holes and huddle below the frozen earthworks in stunned silence. Gradually, some began to move around, reaching for the muskets, loading with slow precision, then peering up, slowly, carefully, looking for any piece of the man across the way. As it grew darker, the deep rumble shook the ground, and the men did not even notice, the sound too familiar, the low thunder, the big guns launching their terrible fire through the darkness.

36. LEE

FEBRUARY 1865

He had been shocked by the letters, by the angry opinions spread out across the pages of the newspapers. The calls had been loud and thoughtless, but they came from desperation and frustration with a war that was slowly destroying their country. Davis had exhausted the patience, and for a long time had been losing the support of the state governments and the governors themselves, particularly in the deep South. But the surprise for Lee was that his own name was so prominent, the solution, the simple answer to what was ailing the country. As the new year had opened, the calls became louder, and Lee began to receive inquiries directly, some quiet, secretive, as though there should be a subtle plot. Some were open, public, voices of influence, and Lee absorbed it all in stunned silence. Sentiment had grown, and the calls became clear and open. What the South needed was a military commander, someone with absolute authority to take charge of the fumbling incompetence of the government.

The horrible tales told by the soldiers, men who simply quit and went home, began to grow and exaggerate, the stories about the scarcity of food now became horrible tales, ridiculous rumors, men eating rats, even shocking reports of cannibalism. In the camps, the soldiers laughed through their hunger, shook their heads at the absurdity, and no one thought the people back home would listen to the foolishness, surely no one would believe these fantasies. But the politicians had used the horror for their own benefit, and the men who never had great loyalty to Davis now blamed him for all of it, and the outcry was tearing the Confederacy into pieces. There was only one man who still commanded respect, even among the most radical, the most vocal enemies of Davis. Robert E. Lee.

It sickened him. Publicly he had responded with a humble declaration that he was not qualified to lead a nation, that for the sake of the Cause, for the country, Davis had to maintain control. But inside himself, the thoughts would not go away, he could not escape the frustration and the pain of knowing that if Davis was removed, it meant the system had not worked. But worse, he knew what the outcry meant, what the loud voices wanted from him. No one used the word, at least not to him directly, but Lee knew the definition, what the power would mean, and it was a word he hoped to never hear: *dictator*.

He did not look out the window, rocked uncomfortably in the seat, the train moving behind the lines of his men, a thin wall of protection that held Grant's army away, allowing the rail line to stay open between Richmond and Petersburg. The train was crowded, filled with soldiers, men in fine suits, men in rags. He tried not to look at them, knew they were all looking at him, and he had closed his eyes, thought he'd nap, but then he would glance up, see the faces, the curious and the concerned, the shy and the devoted. There was a small group of soldiers, bearded men who carried the dust of the field, and Lee thought, Where are you supposed to be? But he let it go, there was no guilt in their faces, and they kept turning toward him, brief smiles, nods.

He looked now at the suits, at the fat men in rich wool, thought of the politicians, the Virginia legislature. They had invited him to visit, made a great show of passing a proclamation, a call for fifteen thousand new recruits. The vote was unanimous, and there had been back slapping and the self-congratulation of men proud of the Good Thing they had done. They made a great show of presenting the paper to Lee, but his weariness had betrayed him, and he'd responded not with the gratitude of the good soldier, but a small scolding, saying, "Passing resolutions is kindly meant, but getting the men is another matter." They had looked at him with a patronizing kindness, a clear message that he simply didn't understand the ways of government. It was just as clear that they had no understanding at all of what this war had done to Virginia. Even if you brought me the men, he thought, they have to be fed. Virginia has given this war all she can give.

He glanced out the window, could see very little, the landscape barren and desolate. The train gave a sudden jolt, and voices responded, the shock of the bad track. Lee could see the signs of a fight now, broken wagons, mounds of dirt, thought, Horses, at least they buried the horses. He thought of the place, could not remember the name, knew the tracks had been wrecked, briefly, but the repair had come quickly.

The faces had turned away from him, were focused more outside.

Yes, he thought, look at it, look at this land. See what we have done, what the war has done.

He could see down the aisle now. Most of the people were up on the seats, staring silently at the scenes of war. Now he saw one man, crippled, a crutch resting between his knees. Lee watched him, but a fog began to fill his mind, he was drifting off toward another nap. Now the man began to move, reaching behind him, trying to pull a coat around his shoulders. Lee's mind suddenly cleared and he focused on the man, watched as the man struggled with the coat, and Lee could see the insignia on the coat now, Virginia, the First Brigade. The man could not turn himself around, and now Lee saw that he was missing a hand, the arm missing below the elbow. The man sagged for a moment, seemed to give up, then reached behind him again, felt for the collar of the coat. Lee looked past the man, people crowding the seat across from him, on all sides, the faces all turned away. Suddenly, Lee stood, wanted to shout at them, fought to keep the words inside, "Look, look at this man! Look what he has given up . . . someone help him!" He clenched his fists, moved toward the man, and faces turned, saw him now, saw the soldier.

The soldier's eyes widened, his mouth opened, and he said, "Marse Robert . . ."

Lee reached behind the man's head, pulled the coat over the man's shoulders, then put his hand on the insignia. There was silence now, the only sound the rough noise from the wheels beneath them. Lee said, "Your unit, soldier. Tell them your unit."

The man glanced nervously at the faces suddenly watching him, then at Lee, said, "The Stonewall Brigade . . . sir."

Lee looked around, saw the eyes now staring hard at this soldier, and Lee said, "Yes, I know. God bless you, soldier."

Lee moved toward his seat, still felt the anger, thought, Yes, look at him, see him, see *all* of them.

THE TRAIN BROUGHT HIM CLOSER TO HIS ARMY, THE MEN WHO were starving, and the anger stayed hard inside him, a black burning disgust with the arrogance of all the mindless words. He'd kept it inside, hidden deep in that dark place that men in Richmond would never understand. He could not wait to leave the capital, to be away from all the talk. They are very good at talk, he thought.

When the failure of the peace conference became known, Lee was amazed at the sudden changes, men shifting their loud opinions in mid-sentence. Now they supported Davis again. That had amazed him, the sudden shift not only in the mood of the politicians, but in the papers as well. Davis had been very careful to blame the failure of the conference on Lincoln, making the most of the demand from Washington that the South accept absolute and utter surrender, total defeat, that no principles of the Confederacy would ever be allowed to continue, no sense of identity, no independence at all. Davis had brought his opposition together, maneuvered them into seeing what the peace process meant for all of them. He used skillful tactics, showing how he alone had held tight to the principles that caused the war in the first place.

Lee had seen the changes, watched the papers with amazement as they all gradually came into line, gave up their reckless calls for Davis's removal and suddenly seemed to unite against the true enemy. It was the same spirit that brought Virginia into the war from the beginning, the outrage that a President in Washington would make the rules, that the wishes, the way of life so strongly fought for, was of no consequence in Washington, and would be dismissed completely before the war could end.

Now, when the eyes came back to Lee, it was not with desperation, not to throw Davis out. It was hope, the last true hope, and Lee knew that it was Davis who had engineered it. He'd seen it in Davis's eyes, saw through the grand speeches in the capital. Davis was more sickly and suspicious of everyone than he had ever been, but he was still a political craftsman. The weight, the responsibility, had been shifted from the president's weakening shoulders. It was now up to Lee, up to the army. The politicians were united now, spouting new oratory, eloquent speeches. The newspapers filled with a different fire, now vented their wrath northward, as at the beginning of the war, calling for the utter defeat of the invader. To them it was a simple matter for Lee to carry it forward.

He could not see the crippled soldier now, the people again filling the aisle. There would be no nap, the train was coming into Petersburg. He felt his pocket, touched the folded paper, the official document. He had not even read it completely, all the flowery words, the grand pronouncements. He ran his hand along the edge of the paper, thought, I am supposed to feel a great honor. These people . . . they will read about this in the papers, and they will know why I was here, on this train, and . . . maybe they will find some excitement in that. I suppose that is a good thing.

Lee had been named General-in-Chief, now commanded all the armies throughout the South, had full authority over Beauregard, Joe

Johnston, all the rest. He accepted it with mild protest, but knew his feelings made little difference. It was ultimately for Davis's benefit. It was Davis's compromise, a concession to the loud voices. Though the opposition had united behind the government, behind Davis, the president's power was still at issue. Lee knew it had been difficult for Davis, but it was a fight he could not win, a price for quieting the voices, for securing his office. The compromise called for a piece of the president's treasured authority over the military to be taken away and placed carefully in Lee's hands.

Lee had been polite and gracious, but the title meant very little to him. His war was still right in front of him, the dismal ground around Petersburg, and he knew that as the weather improved, Grant would come after him again.

THERE WAS NO DIFFERENCE IN THE CAMP, THE STAFF. HE WOULD allow no ceremony, moved quickly and without fanfare away from the train. It was almost desperate, the anxiety growing in his gut, to get back here, to the headquarters, to the familiar.

He had not yet changed his clothes, stood alone in the bedroom of the house, the door closed, felt the blessed quiet washing over him, the jerking motion of the train slowly fading away from his mind. He had spoken to no one, other than a brief word to Taylor. He knew the young man would understand, would keep them all away, at least for now, for a while. The business of the headquarters would wait.

He pulled the scroll of paper from his pocket, held it up in the dull light of the window. He still wouldn't read all the words, the grand formality, the gold seal splashed across the bottom. He shook his head, moved to the foot of the thick bed, rolled the paper into a neat tube, stabbed it down into his trunk.

He stood straight, stretching his back, looked toward the window, saw the wind ripping at the trees, blowing snow now, another gathering storm.

He thought of the newspaper someone had given him, the first mention of his new title. Someone had called for some elaborate—he thought of the horrible word—*coronation*, as though his new position had given him some sort of royalty. They still look for symbols, he thought. I suppose it was always that way. Wars were fought for flags. We still hold tight to that, the men still go after them, the colors of the enemy, as though that is the most important thing. If you take his flag, you take his pride, his honor.

He moved to the side of the bed, sat, looked down, realized that he was still very dusty from the trip, had put a dirty shadow on the white linens. He sagged, let out a long breath, stood up and looked at the dusty impression he'd made. I should not be here, he thought, not in a house. These people . . . so kind. But I should not be in a bed. This is the army, and I am not entitled to any more than what those boys have. He felt the anger coming back, closed his eyes, thought of those men in Richmond. Eat your peanuts and chew your tobacco, pass out titles and pronouncements. But leave the war to the men who understand it.

He glanced down at the trunk, at the rolled-up paper with his name on it, thought of the words "General-in-Chief." Is it too late for that? What does that do for these men? He would not go to the West, or the Carolinas, or anywhere else, no grand tour of his new authority. He would not gather the commanders and issue profound new orders, would not do anything differently than he had before. Beauregard was in Mississippi, commanding a department that was little more than a name on a map. What remained of Hood's battered forces had been assigned to Richard Taylor, who still held control of much of Mississippi and Alabama. Joe Johnston was without a command, and Davis would not even speak his name, the feud now complete and incurable. That is a mistake, Lee thought, it was always a mistake. Johnston might even have held Atlanta, understood what Hood did not, that you must maneuver and outwit a powerful opponent, not throw yourself at him with complete abandon. Now Sherman will have nothing to stop him, will have nowhere else to go but north, and if he reaches Virginia, we are surrounded. Johnston must be used, can still be of great value.

Lee looked at the paper again, felt suddenly awake, thought, I believe . . . I can do that. I have the authority. He smiled, thought of Davis. This will not make you happy, but it is the one thing they have given me. If I am to command this army . . . *all* of this army, then I need Joe Johnston.

He moved quickly now, opened the door, moved out of the bedroom, saw Taylor sitting at the desk in the main room of the house, said, "Colonel, I need to know where General Johnston may be reached. We must send a wire."

Taylor looked at the papers on the desk, thought a moment, said, "Um . . . sir, I don't know where he is. It might be best to ask Richmond."

Lee nodded, said, "Yes, yes, Richmond."

Taylor said, "I can wire the president right away, sir."

Lee looked at Taylor, slowly shook his head. "No . . . not the president. The Secretary of War. Send a wire to Mr. Seddon." His mind began to work, and he thought of Johnston now, was beginning to feel the old energy, that it was possible, that if Sherman could be stopped, hit him while he's strung out on the march, Grant might have to help him, pull troops away from Petersburg. Lee began to move with slow rhythm, his fists slowly clenching, thought of the message, how the wording should go, ran it through his mind, thought, Maybe it's time to play the politician. Johnston . . . no one has the confidence of the people . . . or the army, and I request he be ordered to me . . . for assignment. Yes, good. He moved closer to Taylor's desk, said, "Colonel, if you please, send a message to the Secretary of War. . . ."

MARCH 1865

WHAT WAS LEFT OF THE SCATTERED FORCES IN THE DEEP South were slowly brought together, and even the few troops that followed Beauregard came with their commander to join the odd mix that Johnston would command.

The roads were still thick with the soft mud of an early spring, but Sherman was already in motion, pushing his powerful force northward toward the Carolinas. Johnston understood what Lee needed him to do, would wait for the moment, probe and seek the opportunity, and Lee believed it would happen, that Sherman could be trapped, held in the mire of the swamplands and slowly cut to pieces. Grant would have to respond, could not just allow Sherman to be crushed piecemeal, and that was the opportunity Lee would need. There would be a weakness, somewhere, an opening in the long line around Petersburg. The response would have to be sudden and complete, but the breakthrough could be made. It might not take much, it might not require a total defeat, just a hard shocking blow. Those fellows are on foreign soil, far from home, he thought, and surely, *surely*, they have had enough of this, of missing their wives and children, of the blood and the cold and the loneliness.

He rode the lines again, felt the wind drifting across the muddy fields. The snow was melting, the roads now worse than before, but soon, very soon . . . He saw the faces again, watching him, men peering out from the soggy slop of their muddy shelters, the sickness in their faces, the rags barely hiding the signs of starvation. But still they looked at him, saluted and called out. They know it too, he thought, they feel the change, the spring. We are still here, we are still an army.

It is not up to politicians and conferences. It is right here, it is in these men. He could hear cheers now, echoing down the lines, more men rising up, pointing, and he straightened in the saddle, knew that they felt it, drew it from him; that feeling, he thought, that they are not beaten, that this is not over until *we* end it. He thought of those other fellows, across the bare soggy fields: No, you do not have *this*, you do not feel what these men feel. This is our home, this is our land. And God willing, we will make you *leave*.

37. LEE

March 23, 1865

GRANT HAD NOT YET MOVED, THERE HAD BEEN NO REAL PRESSURE against the defenses Lee could mount around Petersburg. There had been some activity down below, the slow and painful lengthening of the line, the Federal troops gradually pushing out to the west. Lee's lines now spread out nearly forty miles, and in many places the soldiers stood better than six feet apart, and no one had any illusion that if Grant knew *that*, if the blue troops across the way understood how thin the lines were, all it would take was one great thrust.

When he rode the lines now, it was more to the south, and he could see the effects of the lack of food, the weakness of the men. They stared at him with dark hollow eyes, and the officers would tell him, quietly, that the work details, the men who must dig the trenches, were simply collapsing.

He moved off the road, saw familiar flags, moved the horse toward the one tent, the small command post, saw faces he recognized now, men he had not seen since Gettysburg. He reined the horse, slowly climbed down, and he saw a man, a sergeant, hurry toward the tent, ducking inside. Lee waited, said nothing, could hear his aide behind him dismount. Around them it was quiet, no one spoke, no salutes, no cheers. Now there was motion from the tent, the sergeant first, and then the commander. It was George Pickett.

"General Lee. Welcome to my headquarters, sir."

There was cold formality in his voice, and Lee returned a salute, said, "General Pickett, I hope you are well."

Pickett nodded, unsmiling, said, "Yes, sir. I am quite well. My division is ready for a fight, sir." There was no change in Pickett's voice, no life in the words.

Lee felt a sudden wave of gloom, felt it pouring down all through him. No matter the rank, no matter the solemnity of the occasion, Pickett had always been the spark, the man who would make the inappropriate comment, draw the laugh from stern faces. He had always been Longstreet's favorite, exuded a bright and carefree gaudiness, in contrast to the serious warrior that was John Bell Hood. Pickett's behavior had always infected his troops; he was the most popular division commander in Lee's army, and spread a childlike charm over his men. But all that was before, and all that had been changed by Gettysburg. There was no humor in the man now, and Lee saw the eyes looking at him, looking *through* him, an empty gaze. Lee felt suddenly very out of place, uncomfortable, unwelcome. He turned to the horse, climbed up, said, "Carry on, General. We may need you before very long."

Pickett seemed to rock back, a small reaction to Lee's words, and he saluted again, said with cold seriousness, "General Lee, my men have always been where you needed them."

Lee said nothing, turned the horse, began to move, thought, He will never be the same. I cannot remove him . . . he has earned the rank, the command. But he will never be a leader. I must remember that, not to use these men in a critical place.

He rode slowly back toward his headquarters, climbed a long hill, the road straight and dusty. He was very depressed now, thought, No, do not let that man affect you this way. He is not the army, he is one man whose heart is gone, who has had the fight taken from him. We still have the spirit. We can still make the good fight.

He knew he was trying to convince himself, but what had happened to Pickett had happened to many others, Dick Ewell, even Anderson. They would not speak of it, would never say anything to Lee, yet it was there, in their faces, in the way they carried out their orders. If the men on the line gave up, drifted away, they were nameless to Lee, a small dark piece of a much larger picture. But when the spirit left the commanders, it was something he could not ignore. If any general lost the will to fight, he had to be removed. You had to treat him as though he carried a deadly disease, a disease that would infect the entire army. Ewell had been sent to Richmond, Anderson was back under Longstreet's control, north of the James.

Now Pickett has lost the will too, he thought. He felt the sadness of that again. No, give him the chance, he has always been good in the field, can still lead troops. We must not be too quick to judge. And we need all of them, every man. He thought now of Hill. He will still be there; even in his sickness, he has the fight. Hill was gone again, the illness flaring up, but his own home was close now, and so Hill would have the soft care of his family. And he will be back, he has always come back.

Lee could not avoid it now, had tried to keep it from his mind, focusing instead on his problems right here, along these lines. But it was *all* his concern now, and he could not keep it away. He could see the mound of paper, the strange and unexpected flood of dispatches and wires from Joe Johnston. The line of communication was wide open, and with Johnston that was a surprise. But there was a great difference now, and Lee knew it immediately. Johnston accepted his new command and Lee's authority over that command without complaint. Johnston's title was Commander of the Army of Tennessee, but Tennessee had little to do with what was happening now.

Lee had underestimated Sherman, his strength, and his ability to move troops. Johnston had done the best he could, had gathered the scattered remnants of whatever units could be brought to the field, Hardee and Harvey Hill's men, even some of Hood's people. But they counted barely twenty thousand troops, with a wide variety of experience and skill, and now the difference in numbers became clear. The port of Wilmington had finally fallen into Federal control, and the Federal forces there had united with the men who had marched across Georgia. Sherman's army was nearly one hundred thousand strong.

Johnston had to seek out, probe cautiously, wait for the opportunity for Sherman's army to be divided along the scattered roadways. The chance had come, and Johnston struck out at one flank of the blue force, a sharp surprising fight at a place called Bentonville. But Sherman was simply too many, and the surprise did not last. Johnston could not bring enough power to the field to sweep Sherman away. Now Johnston had to rely again on the small bites, the quick stabs at this great and unstoppable force as it gradually pushed north, deeper into North Carolina, closer to a rendezvous with Grant.

Lee could see the house now, the yard of the headquarters filled with horses, the distinct gathering of staff officers, men in clean uniforms in an army that barely had uniforms at all. He tried to see the flag, wiped at his eyes, saw the one man who stood out, stiff in the saddle, back straight, and for one brief flash it was Jackson. Lee's heart jumped in his chest, a cold hard thump. Lee had always been able to spot him, the man never slouching, never bent. It made Jackson awkward on the horse, and no one ever considered him to be a good rider. Lee would never laugh, never smile at Jackson's explanation, so serious to him, so comical to everyone else. Jackson would explain with complete precision why he sat so straight, why he never allowed himself to touch the back of even the straightest chair. He always thought it would crush his insides, that his organs would be pressed dangerously together. Jackson had a lifelong ailment, always the pains in his side, but he would not complain, certainly not to Lee. When his duty kept him away from the hot springs and the water spas, his only treatment was to stay straight upright, keep everything safely, comfortably in order, no matter how uncomfortable it made him on a horse.

Lee could see the man more clearly now, the short narrow beard, and he looked down, felt the sadness even more, scolded himself, No, do not do this. This is no time for daydreaming, for behaving like a foolish old man. If Jackson is here, he will show himself at the right time, he will give something to the fight, to these soldiers. But you will not see him at headquarters sitting on a horse.

He looked up again, saw the men watching him, and the one man moving forward, ramrod straight, the crisp salute. It was John Gordon.

THE MAP WAS DRAWN IN INK, A SYMBOL OF THE TIMES, OF JUST how long they had been in place, on this same ground. Little had changed in a very long time, and now Lee stared at the familiar lines, had listened to Gordon's plan, a concise and eloquent presentation. He looked up at Gordon, saw a tight confidence, the man completely self-assured. Lee thought, It used to be there, in all of them. He thought of the day's ride, the gloomy visit with Pickett. Gordon is not a career soldier, has not learned what so many of them have learned, how to make mistakes, how to be defeated. How strange, he thought, this man was never taught to be a commander, and now he may be the only real commander I have left. He doesn't understand that . . . not yet. And that may be for the best. This is what we must give the men, this is what we must have, all through this army, if we are to succeed.

"General Gordon, your plan is very detailed. I commend you. If you are correct, and your men succeed, we may drive those people into a panic. It has been the best way, always. You may proceed, General."

Gordon saluted, and Lee nodded, his mind already moving away. Now Gordon's men filed noisily from the house, and Taylor closed the door, moved to the desk, sat, waited quietly. Lee did not look at him, moved to the front window of the house, watched Gordon and his staff mount their horses, move away into the road. Lee stared for a long moment, thought, This may be the best we can do now, it may be the only blow we can make. General Gordon believes he has found a weakness, and we cannot wait, we cannot allow General Grant to make the first move.

The cloud of dust spread out from the road, blew slowly into the few trees across the way, Gordon's men gone now. Lee turned, saw Taylor watching him, always watching him.

Taylor said, "It is a good plan, sir."

Lee nodded, moved slowly from the window, toward the soft silence of his room, said quietly, "Colonel, it is the only plan."

38. GORDON

MARCH 25, 1865

HE HAD NEVER FELT THIS WAY BEFORE. WITH JUBAL EARLY, you came to expect the harsh rudeness, the hostile response at every encounter. He had little chance to deal directly with Dick Ewell; Early had always been there, always in the way. Gordon knew that as long as Early was his division commander, he would rarely know the corps commander at all. But now . . . He thought of Lee: *He looked right into my eyes, and it was as though . . . I could feel the weight, the responsibility, and the respect.*

He felt a chill, the excitement had been in him all night long. It was still very dark, and he stood high up on a barricade, looked out into blackness, could barely see the outline of the earthworks across the way. It was very close, less than two hundred yards, a fat mound of dirt. He could see nothing else, did not have to, knew the place well, had studied the ground, had scouted as closely as he could, talked to the pickets, the cavalry, put together every piece of information he could about the place. He knew what they all knew, that it was just one more focal point on the long Federal line, was filled with big guns, infantry support spread out in both directions in a line that led to other forts like this one, like fat knots in a long rope. The other ones carried numbers mostly, Battery Ten, Battery Eleven, but this place had a name, a custom for the Yankees, honoring one of the fallen generals, a man killed during the slaughter at the Crater. It was called Fort Stedman.

Behind him the hill fell away, a long slope, and he turned, listened, heard nothing, not even the small sounds of men. *Good,* he thought. *Quiet, there must be quiet. It is the only way this can work.*

The field in front of him had been a cornfield, still had a few rows of standing corn, left in haste by a nameless farmer, a man long forced out by the spread of Grant's lengthening lines. The field was cut now by small trenches, quickly dug to conceal the single line of riflemen, the skirmishers of both sides, facing each other only a few yards away. There had been the occasional shooting spree here, but not lately, the men now close enough to speak out, the voices becoming familiar. There were no names, all along the line the men were simply known as Billy or Johnny, the common name for the Yank or the Reb. There was little actual contact, no truces, none of the trading of goods that had gone on before. The rebels had nothing left to trade. The talk now was brief, but there was a kindness to it, small questions, brief answers, home, family. But then someone would make a mistake, violate the unspoken etiquette, and a musket would flash, and if the ball did not find its mark, there might be an angry protest, there might even be humor, the playful warning, and none of them could forget that this was still a war, and when the time came, those boys over there would still put the bayonet into your heart.

Gordon knew that right now the Federal pickets were spread out in the field in front of him, knew that if the alarm went up, even one shot, it could alert their entire picket line, and *that* would alert the fort. If the big guns came alive, the attack would be over before it began.

He had ordered the barricades in front of his own lines to be taken apart, slowly, discreetly removed, allowing his men a clear pathway into the open field. The work was mostly complete, but there were still obstacles, and a few workers were slowly slipping by him, quiet steps, whispered voices, pulling and lifting the timbers and wire aside, clearing the open trails for his men to follow.

Close behind him, the first fifty men waited, armed with nothing more than axes, but they understood their part in this. They were hard strong men, and the axes were sharp, and their only job was to cross the field and cut a quick opening in the piled logs and felled trees that pointed out at them in front of the dirt walls of the fort.

Tight behind the fifty axemen were three hundred infantry, each group of one hundred led by a senior officer. They were veterans, handpicked men who had been hardened by battle, and so would move forward without hesitation when the fire flashed in their faces. Their assignment was basic as well. They would immediately take out the skirmishers, quietly, no shooting, and then, when the axemen had done their job, the three hundred would launch themselves straight into Fort Stedman, and there the shooting could begin. Their first goal was the big guns, not just to quiet them, but to *take* them, hold them so that the next men in line, the great mass of Gordon's infantry, could use them, turn the big guns to the side, aim their charges straight down the lines of the Yankees, in both directions. Once the main body of infantry reached the breakthrough, they could push outward, sweeping the enemy out of their trenches, pushing farther down the lines, capturing more of the batteries, more of the big guns. Those guns could be turned as well, widening the breakthrough, driving a deep wedge through the Federal line, cutting off Grant's left flank entirely, panicking the men in blue into a rout.

The three hundred-man companies had another duty. Once the breakthrough was secure, each hundred men would continue to drive straight back, beyond the rear of the Federal line, each company assaulting a fort, a nest of big guns that Gordon believed supported the main blue line. This could not be done by brute force, but only by deception. The officers understood that they would approach each of the forts, identify themselves as retreating Federal officers ordered back out of Stedman. In the dark it could be all they would need to slip into the forts, to surprise the enemy before any defense could be made.

Gordon had explained it all to Lee, every detail, every piece of this amazing plan. Lee had listened intently, had asked a few questions, and Gordon had a good answer to every one, had left nothing to chance. But now, standing alone in the dark, staring out toward the low mound of Fort Stedman, Gordon did not think on details, on conversation, did not remember anything more than Lee's face, the eyes still in his mind. Gordon had believed that he could design an opportunity to push the Federals back, away from Petersburg, shorten their lines, make Grant pull troops back toward City Point.

But there was more in Lee's eyes, and Gordon still felt that, the weight, that Lee had given him something he did not yet understand, some responsibility he did not expect. He had left the meeting with an uneasy stirring, a nervous twist in his gut, that Lee was putting too much into this plan, the hope, the need for absolute success. Gordon had confidence in the plan, would never had taken it to Lee unless he felt it would work. But he did not realize until he left the headquarters how important the plan was to the army, to Lee himself. The Old Man's image was with him now, the white hair, the grim tired eyes. Lee had not offered any suggestions, had made no changes, had given just the simple instructions to proceed. Gordon carried that away from headquarters with a great deal of pride, that he had the faith of the commanding general. Now he thought of that pride, thought, No, it comes down to more than . . . *me.* Lee believes in these men, in what this army can still do. Now it is up to me to see that this plan is a good one.

He opened a small pocket watch, tried to see the face, knew it was still early. He heard a small sound behind him, saw a brief glimpse of white, the small strip of cloth each man wrapped around his arm, the one piece of identification they would carry into the dark confusion of the enemy.

There was a low whisper, "General Gordon, the men are ready. At your command, sir . . ."

Gordon tried to see past the man, but there was nothing but the hollow darkness, and now he looked back beside the barricade, could see the dim shape of one man, the one soldier he had picked to fire his musket, the only signal to the men behind him to begin the attack. The man was waiting, climbed up on the barricade now, slowly, quietly, knew better than Gordon himself that they were both now in the open, that if there were any light at all, they would be completely visible to the muskets of the enemy only a few yards away.

Down in front, a man was carrying a long piece of timber, one of the last obstructions now removed. The man suddenly stumbled, the timber fell against the barricade, a sharp crack. The man froze, waited, and then there was a cold silence. Gordon stared down at the man, clenched his fists but could say nothing, did not have to say anything. No one had to be told of the value of silence. Gordon looked now into the dark field, felt his heart exploding in his chest, the excitement of the moment now crushed by a sudden fear, *discovery.* For a long moment there was no motion, no sound at all, even the breathing of the men had stopped.

Suddenly there was a man's voice, out in front. "What're you doing over there, Johnny? What's that noise? Answer quick, or I'll shoot."

Gordon felt a stab of ice in his gut, looked at the soldier beside him, and the man took a deep breath, said aloud, "Never mind, Yank. Lie down and go to sleep. We're just gatherin' a little corn. You know rations are mighty short over here."

Gordon stared into the darkness, felt himself pulling together, his shoulders hunching low, bracing himself for the shot, the one horrible sound that would alert everyone on the field and end the attack.

The voice came back, relaxed, a small chuckle, "All right, Johnny, go ahead and get your corn. I'll not shoot at you while you're drawing your rations."

Gordon stared at the direction of the voice, felt a smile now, the hard knot inside of him loosening, and he wanted to laugh, looked at the man beside him, thought, A card-player, you must be a very good card-player. He leaned close to the man now, whispered, "All right, soldier. It is time. Fire your musket."

He could see the man looking at him, a small hesitation, and the man now raised the musket, pointed it first toward the voice of the enemy, at the spot where that one man had nearly ended the day. Gordon waited, felt his heart surging again, but the man did not fire the musket, raised it up now, pointed at the air, still hesitated. Now the man lowered the gun.

Gordon said, an urgent whisper, "Fire your gun, soldier!"

The man raised the musket again, and again hesitated, lowered the gun, said in a low hushed voice, "Sir, I can't lie to him. I talk to that Yank every night. It's not right, sir."

Gordon stared in amazement, the excitement changing now to fury. He could not see the man's face, thought, This is not the time. He leaned close to the man again, said, "Soldier, fire your gun! *Now!*"

The man hesitated again, then raised the musket, pointed up at the sky, said, aloud, "Hello Yank, wake up! Look out, we're coming!"

The musket exploded through the silence, the flash ripping the darkness. Now the man jumped down, moving out into the field, where the rest of the pickets lay low. Gordon could not see them, but he knew that they were already moving, fast and silent, heard only small grunts and quick shouts, the bayonet and the butt of the musket doing the deadly work. In the openings on either side of him, Gordon could feel the men surge past, a silent wave, moving as one mass, the axes held against the chests, men with one purpose, one job to do. Now he jumped down as well, began to move with them, felt himself carried along by the great surge, closer, felt himself pushed through the corn stalks. It was a short distance, and he could hear the breathing, the excitement in the men around him, close to their target, then suddenly there was the sound of axes, like a wild beating of drums. The wave had slowed, waiting for the obstructions to come down, and now the men could hold their silence no longer, and the sounds began to swell, the darkness filling with the high terrible scream, the men pushing forward, up and over the dirt walls, driven hard now by their own voices, by the sound of the rebel yell.

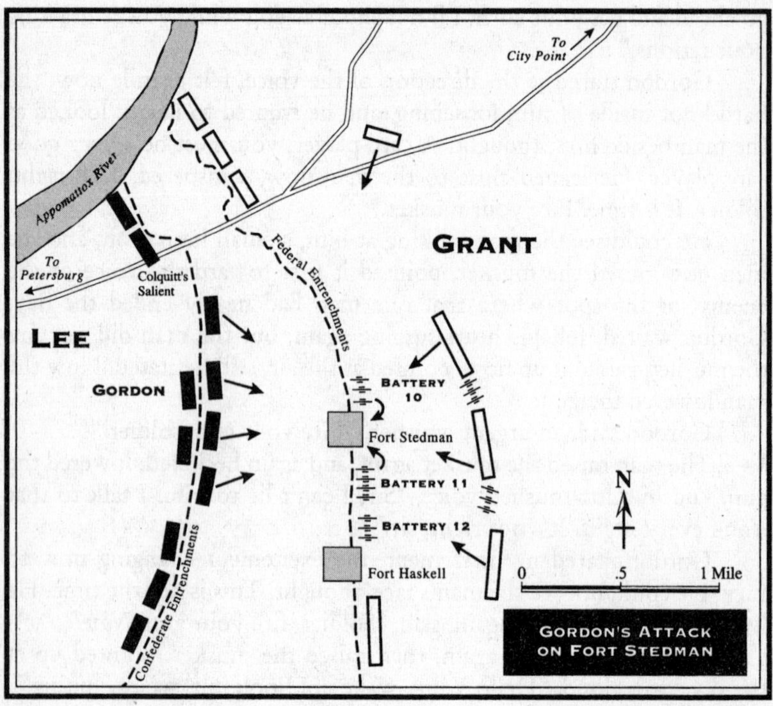

THE GUNS WERE SHAKING THE GROUND, GORDON'S MEN NOW handling them like their own. He could not see far, but the gray dawn was slowly spreading on the barren ground, and as far as his eyes could focus, the men in blue were gone, a quick retreat away from their trenches, or swept away by the sudden blasts from their own guns. The three handpicked companies had already moved to the rear, were gone from view, and Gordon looked in all directions, felt the pure hot excitement, the hard shouts of his men still close, still filling the fort, spreading out in a widening hole in the strength of the enemy, the new ground that was now their own.

Muskets were firing all along the walls, men seeing their targets now. Some of the infantry support had moved into the fort, held there by their officers, waiting for the order to move out.

Gordon was moving forward, could see the faces of his men, the raw excitement, eyes wide, faces red. Now he saw a mass of blue, some men in white shirts. It was the prisoners, the men dazed, stunned by the sudden assault. They were slowly moving belowground, herded into a "bombproof" by the men who had been so effective at interrupting their sleep. He saw one officer, saw the star on the man's shoulder, moved that way, and the man looked at him, wide-eyed, his dirty face now full of the shock of what had happened to his stronghold, his Fort Stedman.

Gordon said, "My compliments, sir. May I know who you are?"

The man nodded formally, said, "Brigadier General Napoleon Bonaparte McLaughlen. My compliments to your operation, sir. You have humiliated a fine command."

Gordon said nothing, thought, Napoleon Bonaparte . . . ? Well, then, your namesake would not be pleased *this* day.

McLaughlen said, "If you permit, sir, I am your prisoner, and wish to remain with my men."

Gordon motioned to the shelter, said, "By all means, sir. We have work to complete."

McLaughlen disappeared into the mound of dirt and timbers, and now Gordon moved quickly toward the rear of the fort, stared out at the growing daylight, lifted his field glasses, searched for the three forts, for the men who would occupy them. He expected to hear more big guns, the men adding to the firepower that was around him, throwing the deadly charges farther down the lines, farther into the rear. He gripped the glasses, turned, swept the horizon, could see some earthworks, flashes of musket fire, but nothing like he had expected, no distinct earthworks, no clear targets for the thrust of the foot soldiers, no sign of the three forts.

There was a sudden blast behind him, the ground ripping under his feet, and he turned,.saw men scattered, bodies torn, timbers and dirt smoking from the impact of the shell. Now more shells came overhead, the high screams from guns far down the line. The ground began to bounce him, more blasts against the dirt walls, then the sharp blow of shot exploding overhead. Now there were screams, men wounded, men with nowhere to go, crouching low, leaning against the dirt walls. He climbed up on the embankment, looked for the three companies through the glasses, for some sign that they had found their own big guns. Where? he thought. Where are you? What is happening?

Suddenly he could see them, men running toward him, dull shadows in the smoke, but he knew they were his men, could see the small scraps of white, the strips of cloth, and he watched them fall, cut down by fire from behind, from both sides. They began to reach the fort, the men saw him now, climbed into the fort, staggered toward him. He jumped down, could hear the whistle and zip of musket balls flying overhead, the slap of lead into the dirt.

One man saluted him, crazily, was breathing heavily, was unarmed. "Sir! We got lost, sir! We couldn't find the fort! There were Yankees all around us! The men are coming back! There's nowhere to go, sir! What do we do?"

Gordon moved past the man, climbed the dirt again, felt the sweat now in his clothes, the fever filling him, a hot sickness. Now he saw more of the men, it was almost fully light. Men were trying to hold a line, firing to the rear, but the Federal fire was coming at them from all directions, and the line dissolved. He looked down the enemy trenches, toward the next massed works, the name flashed in his mind, Fort Haskins, another strong battery, saw the bright flashes, the smoke pouring out in sharp bursts. He knew Haskins should be cleared out, the guns now in the hands of his men, but now he could see his men in line, spread all along this side of Haskins, out in the open. He watched, stared hard, thought, We did not take the big guns . . . they did not get inside. Now those men were falling away, the great clouds of smoke blowing across them, the hot shreds and scraps of metal, the deadly canister, ripping through his troops. He stared, saw glimpses through the smoke, thought, We should be *in* there, those should be *our* guns now.

All along the heavy dirt walls his men were firing outward, in all directions. The big guns still fired, but he looked around, counted, thought, Too few, without the other forts . . . if we did not take the batteries . . . we don't have enough guns.

More men poured up and over the walls, and the musket fire filled the air, his men with more of a target now, the enemy moving closer, the great numbers of Federal troops slowly closing in, tightening down on the breakthrough, the hole in their line. Gordon looked back across the cornfield, saw men moving in one direction, away, the first wave of his troops who would not stand up to the brutal fire. He did not look for more troops. There were no great strong lines of gray ready to cross the field behind him. Everyone had gone in, he'd sent everybody across. Reinforcements . . . he thought of Lee now, of the soft sadness in the old man's eyes. No, there are no reinforcements. From the low ground beyond the cornfield there was silence, no smoke, no great flashes of fire. The rebel artillery was quiet, no batteries had been moved up in support. Gordon stared back toward his own lines, thought, I did not think . . . we would need *our* guns.

More men began to run, escaping back across the open ground, jumping down and across the small trenchworks, across the bodies of the blue pickets. But few made it to the far side. The field was swept completely by the guns of the enemy. Still more men began to pull away from the trenches they had occupied, from out on both sides of the fort. They all knew there was safety beyond the cornfield, and men began to flow out in great numbers now, some dropping their muskets, some moving slowly, stopping to help the wounded. Gordon saw men rushing through the thin rows of corn, saw them suddenly swept away in a bright flash. Now the field began to burn, small fires in the trampled ground, the smoke a spreading blanket, the field alive with the movement of men, the great blasts of dirt and flame.

He felt a man pulling at him, turned, saw a familiar face, the man shouting through the noise. "Sir . . . General Lee orders you to withdraw! Your men cannot hold this position, sir!"

Gordon stared at the man, nodded, looked around again, said, "Yes. Yes, we must withdraw."

The man was gone, swept away in the flow across the field, and Gordon saw an officer, the man watching him, knowing what was coming, and Gordon said, "Find a bugler . . . someone to give the call. We must withdraw. Pull them out! Now!"

The man saluted, was gone into the smoke. Gordon turned, was suddenly on the ground, blown down by a hot rush of wind. He pulled himself up, was on one knee, shook his head, wiped the dirt from his eyes, thought, What could we have done . . . what happened? He tried to stand, felt the ground still shaking, the big guns from all sides closing farther in, driving his men away. He began to move toward the front wall, saw his men climbing out in a mass, and now he saw a man in blue, rising up from the shelter, saw it was McLaughlen, and McLaughlen stared at him, said nothing, just a polite nod, the quiet confidence of a man who understands that his army is just too many, just too strong.

39. GRANT

March 26, 1865

"How close did they come? I heard mention that they turned the guns toward here." Lincoln was grim, serious, concerned.

Grant shook his head, said, "No, not close. It was probably part of the plan, throw us into confusion. A few shells landed down that way . . . nothing to worry about."

Lincoln walked now, a few long steps, stared out beyond the cabins of the headquarters, then turned, looked at Grant. "Lee cannot hold on much longer. Surely, he cannot."

Grant moved out to where Lincoln stood, glanced to the side, to the small group of reporters, the civilians who always seemed to gather around the camp when the President was there.

Lincoln caught the look, nodded, lowered his head, waited for Grant to come closer, said quietly, "Forgive me. I am still accustomed to everyone knowing my business. It is not my place to inform the rest of the world what the situation is here."

Grant smiled, said nothing, moved close to Lincoln now, pulled at the cigar, felt the smoke roll up around his face, glanced again at the people watching them, said, "No, he cannot hold out much longer. It worries me. I wake up each morning and expect to hear that he's gone."

Lincoln tilted his head, looked at Grant with curiosity. "Gone?"

"In retreat, evacuated the city. Moved his army out to the railroads, the Danville line. If he makes it there, he can move south, join his forces with Johnston. Could cause some problems for Sherman. And worse, could make this war last for a while yet."

Lincoln seemed to droop, said gloomily, "How much longer?"

"Don't know. Long enough. He can move faster than we can,

fewer men, fewer wagons, he's on friendly ground. No, I do not want him to leave. We need him right there. The attack on Stedman may have been a sign that he's about to move, put us back on our heels, throw some confusion into our position so that he can slip away, get a good head start. Can't allow that. And he can't do too much more of that. They lost nearly four thousand men yesterday, half of them captured. No, he has to do something else. General Sheridan will be here very soon. We need the cavalry, I'll send them out west, cut Lee off, cut the escape route." Grant stared out toward the river.

Lincoln looked at him, the energy coming back, the smile. "It is your game, Mr. Grant."

Lincoln turned toward the onlookers, saw familiar faces, waved, called out, began to move away. Grant looked back, watched Lincoln move toward the crowd, did not know the faces, the men and women Lincoln began to greet, the handshakes. Grant thought, They're not here to see *me*. He turned again, looked at the river, now heard quiet steps, saw Rawlins moving toward him.

Rawlins was watching Lincoln, moved up close to Grant, said in a whisper, "He's here a great deal now. Puts this place on a bit of an edge, I must say."

Grant did not look at him, said, "No *edge* here, Colonel. I invited him. I imagine this is something of a relief from what he has to endure in Washington."

Rawlins whispered again, seemed suddenly embarrassed at some indiscretion. "Oh, sir, no, I meant . . . I mean, it's as though he is looking over our shoulder, watching everything we do. I have heard it's like he was with General McClellan, same thing."

Grant looked at him now, held the cigar away, stared at Rawlins for a short moment, suddenly felt annoyed, and Rawlins seemed to wilt. Grant said, "I don't know who you have been speaking to, who has given you such good intelligence. I have very little interest in what the state of affairs was in the headquarters of General McClellan. You may rest at ease, however, about the President's spying on us. He has yet to ask me anything about my plans, my orders, or what we intend to do. And, in fact, Colonel, he is the one man on God's earth who has a right to know."

THEY CAME IN A PROCESSION, SLOWLY, EACH HORSE MOVING IN slow jerking steps, pulling their feet out of the mud one step at a time. The man in front kept his back straight, wiped now at his face, at the mud that had splashed up and over him all day. The rains had turned the roads into small rivers of ooze, and on both sides the men and the wagons went nowhere at all. But the horses could still move, and Phil Sheridan had finally come back to Grant's army.

There had been one more fight with Jubal Early, but it was quick and simple, and except for Early himself, what had once been a fine command was now almost entirely gone, buried in the hills of the Blue Ridge Mountains, or marching slowly northward to the Federal prison camps. With little to slow Sheridan down, the horse soldiers had cut a destructive swath across the railroads, canals, and communication lines that still linked Lee's army to anything west of the mountains. Now the cavalry was moving down across the James River, and Sheridan was full of the confidence of a man who knows the power he commands, who understands his own importance.

The staff watched him cross the open ground, the horse still struggling in the mud. Behind Sheridan, his escort, a dozen troopers, pulled off to the side, were already looking toward the wagons, toward the smells of coffee and bacon.

Sheridan still rode forward, finally drew up close to the cabins, dismounted, raised the hat to the staff, made a low bow. "Gentlemen, the cavalry has arrived. We are at your service!"

Rawlins moved forward, beaming, grabbed Sheridan by both hands, shook them, then slapped the small man on the shoulder, said, "Yes! Yes! A pleasure, General, indeed! The commanding general has been expecting you! Now there will be some action, yes?"

Sheridan looked at Rawlins, a hesitant smile, then let down his guard. "Yes, by God, we will see some action now! I expect to run the enemy into nothing short of complete destruction! We will press him until he can stand no more!"

Rawlins backed away, satisfied that the greeting had been appropriately respectful, and he pointed toward the larger cabin, said, "General Grant will be delighted to hear your intentions, sir! Why don't you join him? He is in his quarters now. I know he wishes to discuss your impending rendezvous with General Sherman. Yes, that will put quite a bite on old Joe Johnston!"

Sheridan looked toward the cabin, frowning, looked at Rawlins, said, "Sherman? He wants me to go to North Carolina?"

Rawlins was still absorbing the light of his small piece of privileged information, the official word, did not notice Sheridan's change of mood. "Why, yes indeed, General. First, you and General Sherman put away Johnston, and then, by God, it's back up here to finish off

Lee! A fine plan, I heard General Grant speaking of it myself! I would suggest, sir, you make yourself known to the general. He's in his quarters now. By all means, you go right in!"

Sheridan seemed stunned, glanced at Rawlins's wide smile, said, "Move south . . . to join Sherman? I do not think . . . I must say, I'm not pleased by that plan."

Rawlins's smile vanished. He saw Sheridan's expression now, and his mouth opened, hung there for a brief moment, then he said, "Oh, um . . . no, why of course, General, North Carolina . . . no, not a good idea, not at all. You must convince General Grant to reconsider. Perhaps . . . perhaps I misunderstood the general. . . . No, you should talk to him, now, right now, by all means!"

Sheridan stared at the ground, then looked at Rawlins, said, "Colonel Rawlins, I believe it is better if the general invites me in. It is not proper for me to simply intrude."

Rawlins seemed perplexed, suddenly seemed to have a stomachache, said, "Yes, I see. We should . . . inform the general you are here, perhaps he will ask for you, if he is not busy . . . or perhaps not. Oh dear . . ." Rawlins was red-faced now, felt crushed under the weight of some disastrous blunder of protocol.

Porter quietly moved up behind him, said, "Colonel Rawlins, if I may . . . General Sheridan, General Grant invites you to his quarters, if it is a convenient time, sir."

Sheridan stepped forward, angry, staring ahead, moved past Rawlins, said, "Yes, it is a convenient time. North Carolina . . ."

Rawlins turned, looked at Porter, puzzled.

Porter smiled, said quietly, "I took care of it, sir."

GRANT HANDED HIM THE WRITTEN ORDER, AND SHERIDAN READ quietly, nodded, read again, absorbed the details of the movement of the army, the great final push to the west. Grant would not wait for Lee to make another assault, would not give him the precious time to escape the widening arc of blue.

Sheridan was now under Grant's direct command, eliminating any conflict with Meade. In the field, Sheridan would command not only the cavalry, but the infantry that would move with him in support, the powerful numbers of the Second and the Fifth Corps. The cavalry would lead the way, moving quickly to the west, then north, surrounding Lee's lines, cutting through the Southside Railroad, then farther up, through the Danville as well. If the plan was carried out with speed, and with good movement of troops, Lee's army would be completely cut off from any supply. If Lee did not quit, he would have to come out from the trenches, come out and make the best fight he could. It was exactly what Grant wanted.

The order did mention North Carolina, that if Sheridan's horsemen completed their work with the railroads, he could move south and link up with Sherman. With Lee in a tightening noose, with the defeat of Lee's army so close, it was not Sheridan's choice to move away from the great spotlight, the final bow to the great theater in Washington.

"SIR! I CAN'T JUST . . . I SUGGEST ANOTHER COURSE!" SHERIDAN was red-faced, and Grant did not interrupt him. "Sir, I believe I can best serve this army in Virginia . . . right here!"

Grant looked out toward the staff, said, "General, walk with me, if you please."

Sheridan was still angry. The discussion had been brief, his protests as restrained as he could keep them. Grant had been patient, had let Sheridan blow off some steam, watched him now with amusement as he tried to hold himself together, to keep himself from crossing that line with his commanding officer. Sheridan's face was tight and dark, and Grant moved away, left him standing alone. Grant stepped across the soft ground, turned, looked back at Sheridan, a silent request to follow. Sheridan took short steps, came up beside Grant, and now they walked together, away from the cabins, away from the ears of the staff.

Grant could hear him breathing, the odd hat crushed low on Sheridan's head. Grant began to put the words together, thought of Lincoln, of the man's perfect ability to explain any situation, the humor and the homey stories that would cut through anyone's angry wall, bring down anyone's self-importance. He glanced at the shorter man, said finally, "Please, General, be at ease. I do not wish you to go to North Carolina. My orders . . . there is very little that goes on paper in this army that does not soon reach the newspapers, the eyes of Washington."

Sheridan looked at Grant with confusion. "Washington?"

"General, do you know what will happen, what will happen to *you*, if we do not succeed? We are so close, but this army has been close before, more than once. It is possible that no matter how good the plan, something will happen. Someone will move too slowly, there will be poor coordination."

Sheridan shook his head, smiled knowingly, said, "No, not this time. We have him! My cavalry alone can turn his lines—"

Grant held up his hand, and Sheridan stopped, the smirking smile slowly fading. "Lee has a way . . . a talent for survival. General, you are the best man I have for this operation. But if something goes wrong, something we cannot anticipate, it is you who will pay the price. Washington has very little patience for failure, not now, not after so long. I cannot afford to lose you to the reckless demands of politicians. The order as written says that I intend you to link up with Sherman. That is for the newspapers. It may also be for General Lee. He seems to find out about my orders as fast as they're written. I do not expect you to fail, and I do not expect that this operation will conclude with anything other than the defeat of Lee's army." He paused, thought of Lincoln again. "But I have learned something . . . I have spent a great deal of time with the President. There is something to be said for giving yourself some . . . room to maneuver. If somehow Lee slips away, if your people don't succeed, then we can say, 'Well, it wasn't the plan in the first place.' "

Sheridan looked at Grant with a baffled expression, said, "I don't understand, sir. You are ordering me to go to North Carolina, but . . . not really?"

Grant smiled, lit a fresh cigar. "That's about it, General. Welcome to the world of politics."

MARCH 27, 1865

IT WAS SHERMAN'S IDEA TO TAKE A SMALL STEAMER NORTHWARD, the journey now much shorter than it had ever been. Grant had waited for word of the arrival, finally received a wire from Fort Monroe. The boat had entered the James River and would be at City Point very soon.

He stayed away from the staff, made it very clear that he wished to be alone. They had thought it was because of the seriousness of the meeting, the hard talk of strategy, but Grant had another reason. From the first moment he received Sherman's request, from the time he'd known the tall red-haired commander was on his way, he felt the thrill, felt like an excited child, and it was embarrassing. It had been a year since he had actually spoken to Sherman, the last strategy session in

Cincinnati before Grant came east to take command. It was a year that had changed both men, had made both of them heroes, and, to some, the most horrific villains of all time.

He had been pacing along the waterfront, watched the boat move slowly up the river, and he'd stared at it, a black stare, willing it on, ordering it to push against the current faster. Finally the ropes were thrown out, the crews on the wharf securing the boat tight to the moorings. Grant waited, still paced, small nervous steps, glanced behind him, saw officers, one of them Porter, was suddenly annoyed, thought, I was specific, no greeting party. But Porter was looking toward the boat, smiling, then began to wave, and Grant turned, saw the tall lean figure jump down from the boat, a loud thump of boots on the dock. Before Grant could say anything, Sherman was in front of him, suddenly straightened, saluted with a toothy grin, a small hesitation, the protocol of rank, and Grant laughed now, held out a hand, said, "How do you do, Sherman?"

Sherman was a tall nervous string of energy, every part of him moving in some way. He smiled, said, "How are you, Grant?"

Then both men laughed, and Grant was suddenly overcome, stepped forward and grabbed Sherman by the shoulders, forgot now about the staff, watching from a discreet distance, said, "My God, Sherman, you have done a job! I never had a doubt. . . ."

Sherman put a long finger on Grant's shoulder straps, touched the center of the three stars, said, "Well, my my. Never saw those before. Hard to crowd all those stars on one shoulder. From what I see, those shoulders are holding that weight up pretty well."

Grant was still smiling, said, "It is very different here, these are good men. We've made a good fight . . . mistakes, some things we could have done better. But . . . well, come on, let's don't discuss this war now. That comes later. There's a darling woman up at headquarters who is waiting with some considerable patience to see you!" Grant turned, pulled Sherman by the arm.

Now Porter stepped forward, saluted, said, "General Sherman, welcome to City Point. It is a pleasure to see you again, sir!"

Sherman reached out a hand, grabbed Porter hard by the shoulder, shook him playfully. Porter tried to keep his composure, but the smiles were contagious, and Porter loosened.

Sherman said, "Colonel Porter, if I were you, I'd ask for some leave time. Hell, just hauling cigars for this man is duty enough!"

Sherman laughed now, and Grant felt his face turn red, could not help it, saw Porter share Sherman's good spirits, laughing now as well, throwing a quick self-conscious glance at him. Sherman began to climb the hill, looked out in all directions, turned, stared for a brief moment across the wide river, said, "My God, Grant, you have picked a spot! Hell, I could take a vacation in a place like this!" He cocked an eyebrow at Grant, then pulled Porter up the hill by the shoulder, said, "Colonel, you have to tell me the truth. Now that he's the big man, has he gotten soft? I mean, look at this place . . ."

Grant waited, watched them move up toward the camp, saw Porter turn, still self-conscious, glance back at him, but Sherman was in joyous control, pulled Porter along, the others now moving with him, and Grant began to follow, laughed himself, shook his head, thought, There is no one like him, no one at all.

THEY HAD COME FROM THE RIVER, DINNER WITH LINCOLN aboard his small boat, and the meeting was cordial and serious. Sherman had told his tales already, captured the attention of the staff and the lucky onlookers, a great show around the campfire, glorious stories about his campaign. But with the President, Sherman was more serious, responding to a strange gloom from Lincoln. There was none of Sherman's boundless energy, the endless chatter from the mind that never slowed down. Lincoln seemed removed, spoke only of the end of the war, the slow and difficult healing process, what it would mean for the country, was already thinking far ahead.

They passed by the quarters of the staff, most in bed by now. Reaching the larger cabin, Sherman jumped out in front, pulled the door open for Julia, made another long low bow, had been doing it all evening. Julia glanced at Grant, shook her head, smiled, moved into the cabin. Now Sherman stood straight at attention, said simply, "Sir!" and Grant nodded, a quick smile at Sherman's mock show of formality, and followed Julia into a warm glow. Grant glanced at the well-stocked fireplace, a fire that had not been burning for long. Grant smiled, thought, Porter never forgets a detail.

They sat, a small table covered with maps, and Sherman was suddenly serious, leaned over, pushed one map to the side, studied it for a moment. Julia sat across from him, Grant to one side, and Sherman pointed at something on the map, then suddenly covered the map with his broad hand, looked at Julia with grave suspicion, leaned close to Grant, said, "What do you think, Grant? Can we trust this one? Might not do for the papers to find out a *woman* helped plan our strategy."

Grant smiled, knew that Julia understood the game, said, "Well, you know, Sherman, all the official documents I've ever seen always begin 'Know ye by all men present . . .' Now, in this case, I would suspect it might be better said, 'Know ye by this *one* woman,' because then all men would be certain to hear of it."

Julia huffed, said playfully, "Well, then, gentlemen, would you prefer I not be a party to all your secret planning?"

Sherman rubbed his chin, squinted his eyes, said, "Tell you what, Grant. Let's test her. See what she knows." He leaned forward, the tough interrogator, said, "Tell me, Mrs. Grant, do you know the enemy's present whereabouts?"

Julia fluttered her eyes, put her hand over her mouth, feigning the voice of the belle. "Oh my, certainly, the enemy is in . . . the *South*."

Sherman nodded, said to Grant, "All right, she can stay."

Grant laughed now, pulled out a cigar, winked at Julia, said, "You know, Sherman, I've always said that women should be entitled to vote, in fact, they should have *two* votes, and the men should stay home. That way, there would never be an argument, and no one would ever vote the wrong way."

Julia laughed, said, "And a fine plan it is." Then she stood, said, "Gentlemen, I will leave you to your manly conversation."

The men stood, and she smiled at both, gathered in her dress carefully, moved past the table, disappeared into the back room, eased the door closed.

Sherman said quietly, "My God, Grant. You are a lucky man."

Grant looked at the table, began to move the maps, said, "She is . . . the brightest star in the heavens." He held the cigar out, stared past it. "She knows what's happening. She knows it's time for me to leave. I will be moving with the army, with Sheridan's advance. It's time to go."

Sherman knew the tone was serious now, said, "Lincoln? He's going back to Washington?"

Grant looked up, said, "No, actually, he wants to stay here. He understands that we are very close, that it could happen any time. He wants to be near it all. Can't blame him."

"No. He should be here. He's earned it."

Grant was surprised, said, "Never knew you to be a fan of Lincoln's."

"No, I wasn't. Thought him a bit of a bumpkin, actually. I didn't think he understood what was about to happen, just what a war would mean to this country. He was always spinning yarns, making everything into some kind of joke. But he's changed. I saw it tonight, at dinner. He's a thinker, sees way ahead . . . understands things most of those people in Washington never will. That's a great relief."

Grant nodded, felt the cigar smoke drift up between them, said, "He's no bumpkin. He has endured. We have it easy in some ways, you and me. We control our own situation, we have the power. That's what the military is all about, absolute discipline. Washington . . . no such thing as discipline, as command. The government . . . *our* government can't work that way. And you're right, he's already thinking ahead, already knows what we have to do after the fighting stops. There's a lot of revenge-minded people around Lincoln, a lot of pressure on him to make them *pay*, punish anyone who called himself a rebel. He knows that won't work. We're still one country. Our job is pretty clear, take the fight out of them. His job . . . a lot tougher, the whole business of *forgiveness*. He has to take us forward, heal the wounds."

Sherman stood, moved in nervous motion, stalked slowly around the small room like a cat.

Grant smiled, held the cigar tightly in his mouth, said, "Sit down, General. Let me show you how we're going to end this war."

40. CHAMBERLAIN

MARCH 29, 1865

THE WOUND HAD NOT HEALED, HAD TAKEN HIM FROM THE ARMY again, through most of the winter. There had been operations, difficult days and sleepless nights, but he would not stay there, would not accept the comfort of the hospital. He'd come back finally in February, the hip still tender. But Griffin welcomed him with a wide smile, grateful to have him, and did not hesitate to put him back on his horse, again in command of the First Brigade, First Division, Warren's Fifth Corps.

With the coming of warmer weather had come the healing, and Chamberlain would not aggravate the injury by riding into battle. He could feel it every day, the strength, testing himself on the big horse, the beautiful Charlemagne, grand and majestic.

THEY MARCHED AT FIRST LIGHT, THE ROADS HARDENED NOW BY a blessed break in the rain. He kept in front, stared hard into the woods and low hills, the small stretches of dark swamp. In places, the road had been corduroyed, paved with small trees, forming a miserable carpet, an uneven platform that slowed the horses and men, stepping carefully to avoid breaking an ankle.

They had marched most of the morning now, and the sun was pushing at them from behind. He shifted his weight, tried to find a comfortable place, a part of him that had not yet taken a pounding from the hard saddle.

He could see the ground rising slightly ahead, and the ragged roadbed was smooth again. The horse stepped onto the smooth surface, moving now in the slow, gentle rhythm, and Chamberlain relaxed in the saddle, let out a breath. He could feel the pressure from behind, the men moving well. There had been no straggling, the strong pace of the march picking up even more on the good road, the packed dirt still damp enough so the dust did not yet rise behind him.

The Fifth Corps had broken camp early that morning, the orders to Chamberlain coming directly from Griffin. The word spread quickly to the men—this was not another of those exercises, some mindless drill, some poorly planned scouting expedition. Chamberlain did not have to prod them into motion. There was no grumbling about leaving the misery of the trenches. The deep earthworks had been home through the cold of the winter, but with warmer weather, long days of rain, the holes became pits of mud and misery, and when the order came to strike the camp, to load the supplies, the work had been done with a hum of enthusiasm. There was no sentiment for the camps, for the dismal place they would leave behind.

The orders were to follow the lead of Sheridan's cavalry, move out to the west, well beyond the distant spires of Petersburg. The Second Corps would follow the Fifth, and the word had spread, as it always did, the instinct of the veteran, that this move was something new, a powerful advance by a powerful army, commanded by a fiery little man who would lead them straight into a fight.

The flag bearer rode beside him quietly, a small thin man, clean-shaven, boyish. Chamberlain could not remember his name. He was a sergeant, and Chamberlain wondered about that, if the enlisted men really thought of the rank as a privilege, the promotion as something to be valued. He'd known too many sergeants, had watched too many of them die, and so something in his mind kept him away from this new man, hid the man's name in some safe place. He tried not to think on that, told himself, No, there is no plan here, the man with the flag is not necessarily doomed. He glanced to the side now, and the man looked at him with an excited smile. Chamberlain looked away, thought, He is new, has not ridden up here, at the front of the column. He still thinks it's some kind of honor. I hope he's right.

The low rise began to flatten out, and he could see thick trees on both sides of the road, the sound of a small creek. The blessed smoothness now ended, giving way to more logs, and he sat up straight, lifted himself slightly off the saddle. Out to the side he saw skirmishers falling back toward the front of the column, men pressing and forcing their way through vines and deep mud. Now men came into the road in front of him, emerging in dirty blue from the thick woods.

There was another sergeant, a dark man caked with wet mud up to his waist, and he saluted Chamberlain, said, "Sir, we're moving out into the road. The men can't push through this stuff. If you wish, sir, give us a minute, and we'll move out in front a bit further."

Chamberlain said, "Fine, Sergeant. We'll hold the column for a minute. Have your men advance. Any sign of a . . . problem?"

"Oh, no, sir. Nothing. The rebs are up thataway, for sure, to the north. Nobody down in this infernal place. This is Arthur's Swamp. We scouted it out once before. Mosquitoes as big as birds. Even the rebs stay clear. We'll move up a ways, dry ground up ahead, then spread into line again, with your permission, sir."

Chamberlain was impressed, said, "By all means, Sergeant. Proceed."

The man saluted, and now more of the skirmishers flooded into the road, moved quickly ahead, some stumbling on the roadbed. Chamberlain turned, motioned to the bugler, and the man gave a short blast on the horn, the call to halt. Chamberlain watched the skirmishers move farther away, well in front of the main column, the men who would be the first to see the enemy. He thought of their sergeant, thought, It's easy to forget that, sometimes. We are a very good army, men who have done this before, who know how to do their job, and maybe the most important of all, who know what's up there, in front of them.

Behind him there were small voices, men used to waiting. He watched the skirmishers disappear, moving off the road again, saw the sergeant look back, raise his arm, a quiet signal. Chamberlain looked at the bugler again, nodded, waved his arm forward, and there was another blast from the horn, the men beginning to move.

The horse stepped carefully, but the saddle bounced in one hard jolt, punched him from below, a shock of pain piercing up through him. He was not often bothered by the wound, But no, he thought, it won't let me forget. He tried to hold himself aloft again, a small cushion of space between him and the saddle.

Beside him the flag-bearing sergeant said, "I wonder who Arthur is?"

Chamberlain saw the man gazing into the dense woods, and he flinched from another stab of pain, said, "What?"

The man looked at him, almost apologetic, said, "I meant, sir, he said it was called Arthur's Swamp. I wonder why."

Chamberlain stared at the man, said nothing, the man turning away, not expecting an answer. Chamberlain looked into the woods, thought, A good question. Why would someone want a swamp named after him? Maybe Arthur owned the place. He pondered the possibilities. Maybe someone named Arthur came to some interesting end in this place, a piece of local folklore. He glanced at the man, began to feel a small irritation. Now I will have to find out. Can't let a question like that just pass unanswered. He could see the road ahead smoothing out again, prodded the horse slightly, a silent command, Move forward, please. He glanced at the young man, the flag slapped by a small breeze. Chamberlain said, "What's your name again, Sergeant?"

The man looked at him, said, "Arthur, sir."

IT WAS THE FIRST CLOUD OF DUST HE'D SEEN, THE ROADS UP AHEAD drying out under a high warm sun. The horses moved quickly, came straight toward him, and now he saw the flags, pulled his horse to the side, out of the road, waited, then saluted. It was Griffin.

The horses reined up, and Griffin was sweating, said, "All right, General. We have a job for you. There's a road around this curve, goes up to the right, called the Quaker Road. Take your brigade up that way, keep a sharp lookout. The enemy's flank is north of this position, and we need to know what he's up to. Keep moving north until you find him. You'll come to a creek . . . wait." Griffin pulled out a map.

A man behind him said, "It's Gravelly Run, sir."

Griffin looked at the map, said, "Yes, Gravelly Run. Take good care, General. Keep your pickets close in."

Chamberlain felt his heart thump, looked at the map as though there were some answer there, something Griffin had not told him. He nodded, said, "What do we do if we . . . find them, sir?"

Griffin smiled, pointed at the column moving past them now, said, "How many men reported for duty in your command this morning?"

Chamberlain knew what was coming, felt suddenly ridiculous for asking the question. "Seventeen hundred, sir. Just under."

"Well then, General, you can have yourself one very large dance party. Or you can drive the rebels back as far as they'll agree to go. But advise me first. Lee is likely shifting his weight, knows we're down here. You may run into half the rebel army, and even *your* seventeen hundred men might not be enough. The rest of the division will move up behind and cover your flanks. Keep me informed."

Griffin was not smiling now, and Chamberlain saluted, said, "Yes, sir. We will make contact, and keep you advised, sir."

There was a roll of low sound now, dull thunder off to the west. Chamberlain looked past Griffin, and all heads turned that way.

Griffin said, "Sheridan. The cavalry." He glanced at the map again. "Sounds like he's . . . maybe up here, above Dinwiddie Courthouse." He looked at Chamberlain. "Let's find the enemy, General! We need to know what's up that road."

Griffin spurred the horse, the staff moving away in a thunder of hoofbeats. The troops still marching in the road were watching him. Some had heard Griffin's words.

One man said, "Where they at, General? We close to the rebs?"

He spurred the horse alongside the column, glanced at the voice, all the faces now focused hard on him. He said aloud, "Eyes to the front, gentlemen. It seems . . . we're going to make a fight."

THEY HAD APPROACHED GRAVELLY RUN IN A WIDE LINE, AND there was already a scattering of musket fire from the other side, a rebel skirmish line along the creek itself, men hidden by thick brush, some firing from the thickets of small trees that lined the creek bed. He was still in the road, raised his field glasses, looked up beyond the water, thought, If their pickets are on the creek, the rest of them have to be close behind. He could hear the musket balls zipping past him, felt himself ducking, still stared hard through the glasses, laughed, thought now of Kilrain, something the Irishman always said: *You won't hear the one that gets you.* He lowered the glasses, could see the small flashes of fire, thought, No, not the best place for me to be. Pulling the horse around, he moved back to Arthur, the man with the colors, and the rest of his staff.

Down the line he saw his own skirmishers easing forward, low to the ground, protected by anything they could find. Now the firing went both ways, and he thought, Good, yes, push them back, give us some room. He rode to a small rise, wondered if they should cross the creek. Raising the glasses again, he watched for the thin line of the enemy to pull away, giving up the ground in the face of his great strength. He looked up beyond the creek again, saw a reflection, the flickering motion of bayonets, then a man on a horse. Now he could see fresh fallen trees, logs, dirt, a wide solid line. He scanned along the far side of the creek, down to the right, and saw more men, flags and the reflection of many bayonets. He felt his heart shoot into his throat, thought, This is more than a skirmish line. Yes, we have found the enemy . . . we have found a *lot* of the enemy.

He lowered the glasses, and there was a hush of silence all down the line, the troops dressing the formation, men lining up close to the men beside them.

He could hear horses, turned and saw Griffin, moving quickly. Chamberlain saluted, waited for Griffin to rein up the horse, then pointed out across the creek, said, "General Griffin, as you requested, sir . . . the enemy."

Now there were small shouts along his lines, his men reacting to the small pops of musket fire, the single shots coming from the rebel pickets along the creek. His staff began to gather close to him, the couriers waiting, the horses moving in small jerking motions.

Griffin stared through his field glasses, then smiled at Chamberlain, said, "Well, General, it seems they don't want us to cross this creek. You know what that means?"

Chamberlain absorbed the question, could still hear the sounds of Sheridan's fight off to the west. He looked toward the enemy line, then toward the scattered musket fire of the pickets. "Yes, sir. It means we should cross that creek."

THE BRIGADE WAS SPREAD INTO LINE ON BOTH SIDES OF THE road. Reaching the creek, wide and muddy, the men began to splash across. The left flank moved first, and Chamberlain rode close behind, could hear the great roar of muskets from the right flank, the volleys aimed across the road, a covering fire for the left flank to cross the creek. Behind the low works, the rebels were returning fire, thick smoke pouring down toward the creek in great waves. He pushed the horse through the water, then up out of the creek, moved through small patches of thick brush, could smell the choking sulfur of the smoke, tried to see in front of him, steadied the horse. His men were moving forward, beyond the creek, now reaching the rebel works. He pushed the horse forward, saw the blue wave streaming over the low wall, and beyond, saw the rebels pulling quickly away.

He broke into a clearing, a straight path toward the open field beyond, could see down the line now, his men still pressing forward, the lines wavering but strong. The rebels were stopping to fire, and he could see men falling, could hear the screams now, saw one man drop close to him, clutching his throat, rolling slowly in the grass. Chamberlain stared at the man for a brief moment, saw another man break out of line, move toward him and kneel down. Then the man's sergeant grabbed him by the shoulder, yelled something profane, pulled

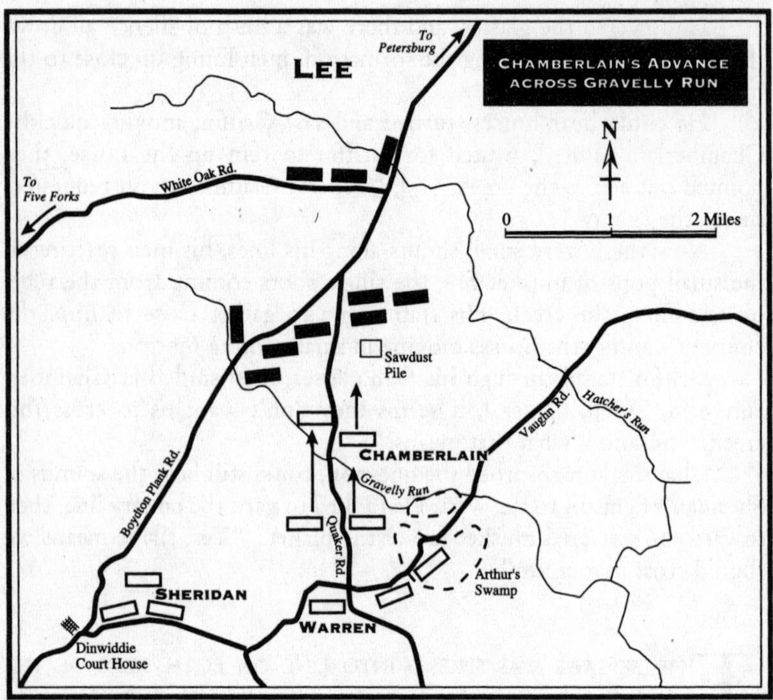

the man back into line. Another job for the sergeants, Chamberlain thought.

He moved the horse, rode to the left, a gap in the log wall, jumped over the shallow trench, could see more horsemen now, the regimental commanders, swords up, pointing forward. His men were still in motion, the rebels in chaotic retreat, no formation, pulling away on their own. The smoke was clearing, a breeze behind him pushing the white fog out before the blue wave, and he reined the horse and just watched, could hear the sounds of his men, the low cheer of soldiers who know they are winning.

Smoke now filled the patches of woods in front of them, each volley sending a blinding cloud toward the enemy. A break, a piece of luck, he thought, the wind is behind us.

He scanned the open ground, could see the wounded, the dead of both sides, some moving slowly, some not moving at all. Suddenly the name came to him, Griffin's orders . . . the *Quaker Road*. He shook his head, thought, No Quakers here on this day. They would definitely not approve.

Out of the thick fog he saw a cluster of men emerging, a slow march across the field, enemy troops moving straight toward him. Chamberlain's heart pounded and he pulled at his pistol, but then saw his own men, the muskets raised, saw that the ragged soldiers were not armed, were being herded to the rear, back toward the creek. They were prisoners. He laughed nervously, thought, Lawrence, have a little faith. As they moved by him, his own men saluted wildly, great toothy smiles. Chamberlain looked at the prisoners, saw bare feet, gaunt faces. They did not look up at him as they moved slowly by, and he thought, They do not look like soldiers, like an army. His own men were shouting out, the pride of the capture, but Chamberlain did not hear them, continued to stare at the prisoners, recalled the great long march toward Antietam, when he'd seen prisoners for the first time. They were ragged then too, torn clothes, the uniforms barely evident. But you could still see the spirit. They had marched past him then with a defiance that said, "We are your enemy, and we will *still* fight you." Now the faces stared at the ground, silent, and he thought, These men look like . . . ghosts.

The fight was moving away from him, his men still pushing forward. He spurred the horse, moved past a line of small trees, saw a wide field, farmland, could see a house now, small white buildings. He moved forward, saw a huge sawdust pile, an old sawmill. His men were in line, kneeling, firing into the thick smoke, rebels holding a line around the sawdust.

He thought, Move forward, get closer, and recalled something Griffin had said long ago, quoting the instructions, laughing, something from some military manual. *The brigade commander shall remain one hundred fifty yards behind the line.*

He could hear the musket balls of the enemy whizzing past him, high, wild shots, men blinded by the smoke, by the pressure, the strong advance of the blue line. He saw officers riding toward him, watching him, and he knew the look, men waiting for the command, making sure. He looked toward the sawdust pile, saw the enemy pulling away, yelled, "Forward! Keep pushing them!" The horsemen moved away, and Chamberlain looked behind him again, then far off to the right, thought, Yes, maybe . . . more strength, coming up on our flank. But he could only see his own men, far down the open field, the line thinning, the men slowing, holding their position.

He looked past the sawdust pile, and then the wind began to shift, the smoke flowing away, across the field. The rebels were still moving away, but he could see woods now, and along the edge, men climbing up and over a wide wall, a thick mass of logs and dirt. Suddenly, the wall erupted in a solid blast of flame, dense smoke pouring forward, and the air around him was alive with the horrible sounds, the piercing whine of the hail of lead. His men were falling all down the line now, there was no cover, no safe place, and the line began to fall apart, men slowly moving back.

The officers were screaming orders, "Hold the line," "Stay together," but the men saw what was in front of them now, what lay beyond the open field. Chamberlain saw the faces of his men, some beginning to run, close to him now, not looking at him, and he pulled out his sword, waved it over his head, felt the hot anger, yelled at one man, a sergeant, "Stop! Pull them together!"

The man looked up at him, and Chamberlain wanted to yell at him again, red rage, but he knew the face, said only, "You . . ."

It was the man in the swamp, the man in charge of the pickets. He looked up at Chamberlain, and Chamberlain saw his face change, the wild panic erased now by an angry black light. The man said nothing, but turned, grabbed a man who was running by him, pulled the man around hard and shouted into his face. Now others began to stop, to fall together, forming a new line, close to Chamberlain, some looking at him. He yelled to them, not words, some sound, thought, *Hold them,* keep them *here*, but his voice faded into hoarseness.

The men were bringing themselves into order, the line strengthening. The officers began to gather, and Chamberlain waved the sword, the silent signal. The officers moved out, still pulling the line together. Some men began to fire back toward the heavy rebel line, and Chamberlain thought, No, wait . . . too far. He could hear the officers shouting the orders to hold fire, and the firing stopped, the sounds now only the voices of the men, the brigade finding itself again, the flags spreading out, men moving to their place in line.

He watched, felt the sudden burst, the energy of pride, *Yes,* you will not brush us away! Now, from the rebel works, there was a new sound, and he stared, had heard it before, that awful scream, and men began to pour over the top of the works, the furious scream rolling forward, the line of rebels coming at them. Chamberlain felt his heart thump in hard cold beats, yelled weakly, "Hold on!"

But the blue line began to roll backward, some men breaking out, running toward the rear, wild eyes, driven hard by the panic, chased by the sounds. Some still held their position, and the orders were shouted, and Chamberlain saw his line explode into one long fire, a massive volley, a sharp blast into the rush of rebels. The rebel yell began to fade, and Chamberlain's men fired again, all along the wavering line. Now the smoke drifted away again and he could see the rebels backing away, withdrawing to their heavy defenses. He yelled, a hoarse sound, a cheer, and his men looked at him, began to understand that they had held, had beaten back the assault.

Chamberlain looked in the direction of the creek, the wide, empty ground, began to feel the heat, the raw fury, thought, We cannot hold here all day. *Where are you?*

He rode a short way toward the creek, the field scattered with his men, many wounded, some men bending low over still bodies. He glanced at the rebel line, saw men moving out in a low crouch, moving toward their own wounded, dragging men back to the works. He took a deep breath, and for one moment there was silence, a complete calm, the smoke gone, and he looked out over the open ground, could see fresh dirt, furrows in the ground. Of course, he thought, it is planting time, but that will have to wait for now. He glanced at the scattered bodies, the dead. If we bury them here, he thought, what then? Is this still a farm? Will you go on as if nothing had happened? He looked at the farmhouse, was suddenly curious, wondered about the people, thought, Probably a woman, maybe children. There would be no man, no able-bodied farmer. He would be gone, maybe dead himself, or maybe . . . right over there, behind those works. Maybe he's fighting on his own property. How odd, you could never have expected this, what must it feel like? Does it make you a better soldier?

No, stop this, he thought, trying to clear his mind. Your brain again, you still think too much. He looked down the line of blue, saw men still falling in, the quiet, the lull, now drawing them up from behind. He looked back toward Gravelly Run, thought, There are still men there, there always are some, hiding, men paralyzed by the panic. He saw troops moving near the water, the provosts, the awful duty, finding the ones who ran, and if they did not return to the line, to arrest them, haul them to the stockade. He shook his head, thought, It is always like that, in every fight. Some men will suddenly come apart, something inside of them suddenly opens up, breaks out in a blinding madness. He recalled the firing squad, the execution of the deserters, the image always there, somewhere deep in his mind. No, we will not do that, not in this brigade, not if I can help it. But if they leave this field, if they run far enough and are caught . . . then I *cannot* help it.

He saw horsemen now, flags, Griffin, let out a breath, *Finally.*

Behind the horsemen came a column of troops, men moving double-time. Chamberlain tried to see the numbers, the strength as Griffin reined up, said, "That's a strong line over there, General. We have prisoners from Anderson's division. They say more are coming, a lot more. No surprise, Lee has to move out this way, can't allow us to keep pushing north."

Chamberlain was watching Griffin's face, thought, We did not do . . . what we were supposed to do. We were repulsed.

Griffin was scanning the rebel lines, said, "Behind those woods . . . the White Oak Road. Very important, it's their main artery from this area back to Petersburg. The Southside Railroad is just above. If we can take the road . . . they have no choice but to pull back, protect the railroad."

Chamberlain absorbed the words as Griffin pulled out a map. Chamberlain thought, He doesn't seem to be too upset that we were pushed back. He felt a sudden wave of relief.

Griffin was already moving beyond what had just happened, looked again at the rebel line, said, "General Chamberlain, we need those works. If you can move the enemy out of there by nightfall, we will be in strength here. The rest of the corps is behind us, and the Second is moving up on our right. We must hold here, keep Lee from pushing us back below the creek." Griffin's voice was calm, matter-of-fact.

Chamberlain watched Griffin still scanning the map, thought, We tried once, but . . . Anderson's whole division? That means we're up against . . . maybe four, five thousand men.

Now Griffin looked at him, said, "Are you not clear about something, General?"

Chamberlain cleared his throat, said, "Sir, how close is the rest of the corps? May we expect . . . support?"

Griffin looked out toward Chamberlain's men, said, "If you can move the enemy out of those works, and hold that line for a while, you'll get all the support you need. There is no time to lose, General. General Sheridan has his hands full. We need to hold on here, keep Lee from moving any farther west."

Griffin was looking at the map again, said something to a staff officer. Chamberlain looked across the open ground, past the farmhouse, the sawdust pile. He raised his field glasses, took in the rebel line, saw flags spread all along the wall, knew each one meant numbers, strength. He thought of Gettysburg then, of that rocky hill, those men from Alabama who had come at him, trying time after time to take that hill. Now that's . . . *us.* At least here . . . it's not uphill.

He put the glasses down, and Griffin patted him on the shoulder, said, "*Now,* General!"

THEY ADVANCED WITHOUT FIRING, THE LINE FIRM AGAIN, MOVing forward quickly. Behind the works, the rebels met them with one solid volley, cutting holes in the blue line, but then Chamberlain's men were up, climbing over the cut trees, men firing their muskets right into the faces of the enemy.

Chamberlain was just beyond the sawdust pile, saw his men still pouring fire straight into the enemy's position, could hear the horrible sounds, the musket fire now replaced by the bayonet and the sword, the clash of steel, the grunts and shouts of men grabbing each other, clubbing with empty muskets, the hollow screams of men driven by the power of the beast, men ripped down by fists and feet, knives and boots.

He moved the horse up closer, pulled his pistol, tried to find a target in the swarming mass of men around him, aimed, then held up, the chaos now complete, the targets swirling together into one mass of confusion. He raised the pistol again, saw a man swinging down hard on a blue soldier with the butt of a musket, a huge man with a bearded face, eyes now looking up at him, staring at Chamberlain with the bloody fire of some terrible demon. The man smiled, staring right at him, and Chamberlain aimed the pistol, pulled the trigger, his hand jumping with the blast. There was smoke, then he saw the man still staring at him, but the eyes were different now, the demon gone, and the man slowly dropped to his knees and fell forward.

Chamberlain heard his name, saw an officer, yelling, waving him away, heard the man say something, then again, now heard the words, "Sir! Get back! Move back!"

He looked into the mass of the fight again, thought, *One hundred fifty yards behind the line . . .*

Men were swarming out on both sides of him, all along the log wall, the fight now all around him. He turned the horse, thought, You damned fool, get out of here. He spurred the horse, crouched low, saw a rebel officer suddenly right in front of him, the face of a boy, a long sword in the man's hand, and the sword went up, the man aiming for the legs of the horse. Chamberlain raised the pistol again, fired into the man's chest, moved quickly past him, did not look back, thought, Keep moving, go!

He saw staff officers now, Sergeant Arthur with the flag, and he turned, could still see the fight across the enemy's works. Men were shouting all around him, officers giving orders, some with wounds. Others now moved back, away from the fight, with bloody faces, torn clothes.

He moved the horse again, could see the woods beyond the wall, men up in the trees, sharpshooters taking slow, careful aim. Then he saw more men moving forward, coming out of the woods, more flags, rebel troops moving right into the fight, fresh muskets, and he could hear more of that horrible sound, a rising chorus of rebel yells.

His men began to climb back out of the rebel works, some crouching low, reloading muskets, some without weapons at all, some snatching up muskets from the arms of the dead. He could still see beyond the wall, a cluster of blue moving across the road, straight into the oncoming rush of the enemy. He felt a thrill, thought, Yes, move ahead. Then he saw the rebels around them and stared in horror, recalling the men who had come by him before, near the creek, and he thought, My God . . . prisoners . . . my men.

Chamberlain turned the horse, saw officers pulling their men back, trying to keep some order, pulling away from the rebel works, but there was no order, men firing blindly, more now climbing away from the enemy. He yelled, pointed, and an officer saw him, moved a few men into one small line. They loaded their muskets, the order was given, a small piece of command, and the muskets swept away a group of rebels climbing over the wall.

His men were beginning to pull away, some organization forming now, small lines of musket fire holding the enemy back, keeping them away just long enough for the blue soldiers to make an orderly retreat. Chamberlain moved away from the road, toward the farmhouse, saw his men in a neat row, kneeling, firing. He rode toward the sawdust pile, saw rebels on both sides of it now, moving forward, pressing the retreat. His men were holding their position, firing in waves, the volleys growing, blowing in both directions, the waves of smoke drifting across. He held tight to the horse, stared for a long moment, and now his men began to move back again, slowly giving ground. The horse abruptly moved forward, pulled him into a cloud of smoke, and he could see nothing, the sounds of the fight suddenly all around him again. He pulled hard at the leather straps, jerked the horse to the side, and now a deafening blast of musket fire blew past him. The horse lurched forward in full panic, dashing through the smoke. He tried to hold it back, pulled hard on the reins. He could see the works again, the logs draped with the bodies of men, and the horse now rose up, threw him back. He lunged forward, grabbed the horse's mane, gripped the thick hair, thought, Damn you, stop! Behind him, he heard shouts, his own men, more horses, heard his name, a staff officer, but the horse still bucked him.

He yelled, "Turn around!" In front of him there was a great flash of musket fire, and the horse rose again, its front legs pawing the air. He felt a hard punch in his chest, then was slammed down hard on the horse's neck. He wrapped his arms around the horse, felt a flood of wetness. The horse was running now, and he gripped the mane, his hat blown off. He could see nothing, the smoke choking him as he held tight to the mane, the blood now soaking his shirt. He could see red spreading down the horse's neck, his face pressed into it. Chamberlain thought, Oh God . . . both of us . . .

He leaned back, out of control, his hand not holding the reins, and he caught a blurry glimpse of the sleeve, the coat ripped into bloody shreds. He tried to grab the reins, could not feel his hand or flex his fingers, his face soaked by the blood of the horse. He thought, No, not an arm . . . please, God, don't take my arm. The horse jerked again, and he dropped the pistol, grabbed at the mane with his right hand, but now the horse reared back and then down, Chamberlain thrown forward, his head slamming hard into the bloody wound on the horse's neck. . . .

HE WAS STILL ON THE HORSE, FELT A HAND INSIDE HIS SHIRT, could hear voices, distant echoes of sound. He tried to shake his head, clear his eyes, felt a rag rubbed across his face, heard a soft voice.

"My dear general, you are gone."

Chamberlain opened his eyes, focused, saw Griffin's face close to his, realized that Griffin was holding him up. He tried to move, felt a sharp pain through his ribs, then looked at his left arm, saw the fingers, thick with dried blood, flexed them, flexed them again, felt a great flood of relief, said, "Well, no, not just yet . . ."

He turned, his ribs screaming, saw a staff officer, and the surgeon who had a handful of bandages and was frowning, waiting to do his good work. Chamberlain gritted his teeth, sat up in the saddle, and Griffin released him, surprised. Chamberlain looked at the horse's neck, saw the hole, the thick blood still flowing. "Is it mortal?" he asked.

The surgeon said, "No, sir, not to worry. The bullet tore your sleeve, punched through your orders book, apparently, and moved . . . around you. Came out . . ." He pointed to Chamberlain's back, touched a tear in Chamberlain's coat. ". . . right here." The surgeon was pleased with himself.

Chamberlain was suddenly annoyed, said, "No, doctor . . . the *horse*!"

"Oh, well, no, sir. The horse took the bullet before you did, probably saved your life. It passed through his neck, but just the muscle. We can patch that up as well."

Griffin was staring at Chamberlain's face, said, "Doctor . . . the blood."

Chamberlain felt his face, the crusty goo, his hair a thick mat, saw now that his shirt was dark red.

The doctor said, "From the horse, sir . . ."

Chamberlain could hear musket fire now, said, "What . . . how are we doing?"

Griffin backed away, still looking at him with horror, and Chamberlain tried to clear his brain again, gazed out toward the sounds.

Griffin leaned closer, took another look at him, said, "We are holding the line, General. A few more minutes and I'll have you a battery. Are you . . . sure you're all right?"

Chamberlain felt the tender ribs again, winced, said, "I am fit for duty, sir."

He could see the smoke now, a new volley of musket fire, thought, We're . . . still in place, they're still behind the works. He looked down at the horse, spurred it lightly, and the horse moved forward, ready for the next command. He touched the neck, and the surgeon handed him a small bandage, rolled into the shape of a plug. Chamberlain stuck the bandage into the hole, and the horse quivered, then snorted.

Chamberlain looked at Griffin, said, "General, when will those guns be here?"

Griffin turned, looking to the rear. "Anytime now. Just . . . hold on."

Then Griffin moved away, and another man rode up, sweating, his face covered with dust. He reined up, looked at Chamberlain with wide eyes, said, "General Chamberlain, we have a problem . . . on the right, sir. The enemy is reinforcing, sir." The man looked closely at Chamberlain's face, said, "Are you . . . all right, sir?"

He thought, I have to see a mirror, reached into his coat, felt the metal frame of the small shaving mirror, pulled it from his pocket, a small shower of glass falling into his hands. He said, "The bullet seems to have made another stop in its travels."

HE PUSHED THE HORSE HARD, FOLLOWED THE WAVE OF HIS MEN, the momentum now driving the enemy away on the flank. For the moment, the crisis was over. They were pressing the enemy back into the woods, and there were small works here too, fresh-cut trees. He wanted to jump the horse across, move closer to his men, thought, *One hundred fifty yards behind the line.* He stopped, looked at the horse, saw the head go down, the strength fading, thought, No, dear God . . . hang on, old man. He jumped down, turned the horse toward the rear, gave him a swat on the rump, and the horse began to move away from the fighting.

Climbing up on the works, Chamberlain saw his men firing, saw bodies everywhere. Right below him, beside him, a man was sprawled faceup against the trees, the eyes wide, ghastly. He made himself look away, jumped down and felt for the pistol, moved toward his men, and suddenly they were not men in blue. The smoke washed past him, exposing different men, wearing ragged brown and tan, men with rough beards, barefoot, screaming. He thought of firing the pistol, turned, suddenly looked at the small black hole of a musket, the point of the bayonet right under his chin. There were voices, more bayonets.

One man said, "You are mine, Yankee. Surrender or die."

Chamberlain stared at the musket, then slowly looked up at the man's face, blackened with dirt, red eyes, no smile, no emotion, just the business of the fight. The man looked at Chamberlain's coat, the dirt and blood blended into dull filth, and Chamberlain saw a moment of doubt, a small question, and said, "Surrender?" He thought of the man's words, the perfect drawl, and said to him in a voice as close as he could to the one he'd just heard, "What's the matter with you? What do you take me for? The fight's . . . thataways!"

The muskets were lowered, the men behind looking toward the works, toward their own line, where the Yankees had pushed them back. Now more rebels were moving past, the flow going forward, and Chamberlain looked at the man, saw the bayonet moving away, the man still looking at him, still not sure. Chamberlain moved then, said, "Come on, boys! Follow me!"

He reached the works, saw his own men on the far side, muskets aimed at him, then the faces, confusion, the muskets again rising toward the men behind him, the rebels following him across the works. He rushed straight at his men, thought, Dear God, let them see . . . Now they moved forward, a sudden lunge, muskets firing, bayonets clashing together, but there were too many men in blue, and suddenly the small group of rebels was surrounded, hands went up, muskets hit the ground. He looked back, saw the stunned surprise, saw the one man, his captor, looking at him. The man slowly nodded, looked to the ground, a quiet salute.

His men began to pull away from the works now. There was another lull, a breath of silence, and he moved with them, saw officers on horseback and walked that way, felt the stiffness in his ribs, the arm throbbing. The officers saw him and there were salutes, men with wide eyes.

One man said, "Sir . . . are you all right?"

He looked at the man, familiar, then recalled his name and smiled; Major McEuen. "I believe so," he said. "Tend to your line, pull them together. We're not through here yet."

McEuen turned, shouted something behind him, and now there was a horse, a heavy white mare. Chamberlain looked at McEuen, said, "Thank you, Major. I'll try to take good care of her."

He climbed up, his side ripping with the pain, and felt the ribs, the wetness. Yes, the bullet was not *that* kind, had ripped into him more than he realized, a neat tear under his shirt, his skin split around his side. He looked at McEuen again, saw the concern, and McEuen said, "You sure, sir? We can have you escorted to the rear. . . ."

Chamberlain heard the sound, the ball coming right past him, heard the impact, the sharp punch. McEuen looked at him with sudden surprise, shocked, his mouth open, now reached out a hand. Chamberlain reached for the hand, McEuen's fingertips just touching his, watched as the young man fell forward, off the horse, hard to the ground. Men were off their horses in sudden jumps, turned the young man over. There was blood now on McEuen's chest, his eyes staring away. Chamberlain closed his eyes, could not look at the face, thought, You cannot . . . you must not stop.

The right had been secured, the 198th Pennsylvania now holding the flank. He looked at the officer kneeling beside McEuen's body, saw the man was crying, thought of words, felt suddenly weak, powerless.

A horseman was coming fast, shouting, "General Chamberlain . . ." He reined, stared at Chamberlain in horror, said, "Sir . . . are you all right?"

Chamberlain nodded wearily, thought, Maybe I should carry a sign reading "Yes dammit, I'm fine!"

The man studied him carefully, said, "Major Glenn is looking for you, sir! We are holding around the road, but the major requests your presence, sir!"

Chamberlain said nothing, turned the horse, wanted to look down, one last glimpse, but he kicked with the spurs and the horse moved under him, taking him away.

He rode back along the line, saw the faces turn, watching him. As they saw him, muskets went down, the fighting stopped, a brief pause, his own men pointing, staring, then a cheer. He moved toward the center again, saw his men in line, ready, a brief lull here as well. The rebels were in their works again, the two sides pausing, licking their wounds, two weary animals making ready for the next assault.

He had not found his hat, rubbed his hand over his head, felt the hair stiff and matted thick with the blood, suddenly thought of Fannie: It is a good thing . . . no women spectators. The men began to cheer him, and he moved toward the sawdust pile. He heard his name, tried not to look at them, focused on the job at hand, on the lines of the enemy waiting beyond the works. There was scattered musket fire, a sudden sharp volley down to the left, and Chamberlain looked that way, began to ride. Another group of his men saw him for the first time, his face a solid mask of deep red, the shirt and coat ripped and still wet. He saw the faces, the horror, changing now to relief, then something else, the cheering rolling along the line as though he was some sort of horrible symbol, their own messenger of death, one horseman of the Apocalypse. Then, across the field, the open ground scattered with men from both sides, rebel troops began to stand up on the works, and he looked that way, saw an officer, sword in the air, and muskets, men raising them high overhead. The sound echoed across the bloody ground, but it was not the rebel yell, the enemy was not coming out again with a new charge. They were cheering *him*.

THE GUNS CAME UP JUST AS GRIFFIN HAD PROMISED, AND THEN the fight turned, the battery adding new weight to Chamberlain's balance. On the flank, more troops from the corps moved forward as well, men who had been delayed by the swollen waters of the distant creeks, who could not be where Chamberlain needed them. Now the rebels began to move away, withdrew from the logs and the woods behind the farm, moved to another strong line, stronger still, reinforced by more of Lee's army, a new defensive line anchored hard along the White Oak Road.

Night had finally swept the field, and Chamberlain rode slowly, felt the unfamiliar rhythm of a new horse. He'd been to the hospital, seen the men who carried the wounds, the men who might yet survive, the ones who would not. He had made a brief visit to the magnificent Charlemagne, now resting, recovering from yet another wound. He looked down in the dark, the white mane, did not know this horse's name, thought it was probably for the best: I'm a curse on horses.

The Fifth Corps had spread into position, and his brigade would now rest in the rear, men gathering in exhausted silence around the small fires, the blessed food. They were fewer now, had lost nearly a quarter of their strength. But Chamberlain had heard from the staff, then from General Warren himself. The rebel prisoners came from four brigades, a force numbering nearly seven thousand of the enemy's troops. Warren had promised him a promotion, a personal note to Washington, then rode away in the splendor of a command that today did not lose.

He is probably a very good commander, Chamberlain thought. But we could have used some help today. It could have been very different. He remembered the prisoners, watching his men marched away, thought, Where are they now? What will happen to them? He'd heard the stories, rumors and poorly written newspaper articles, sensational and dramatic, the rebel prison camps down south, Georgia, one place called Andersonville. No, don't think on that, he told himself. It is a part of it, part of it all. They will survive. They are not like the men in the hospital, the men who will go home broken, leaving something behind.

He had seen the same horrifying sight, always around the hospitals, the great piles of arms and legs, thought again of his own great fear, the shock, believing he'd lost an arm. He reached down, probed the old wound slightly, low in his gut, thought, I always believed it would be . . . in the body. If I went down, it would be there. Usually, that meant you would die. But to go home . . . missing something. He could never admit that fear, not to the men, not to anyone. He marveled at the ones who actually came back to fight, men like Oliver Howard, one sleeve hanging empty. He had heard about Ewell, and John Bell Hood, the horrific wounds, the rebel commanders still riding into the fight, thought, It *must* change them. It would change me.

He had tried not to think of the young McEuen, the body resting under a blanket, laid to one side, one awful corner of the hospital. He would have to write McEuen's father, a doctor in Philadelphia, knew that the memory would stay with him now in that terrible place, where all the memories would stay. The doctor had visited the camp the autumn before, had come to see his son's small command for himself, the pride of the father. He had put his hand on Chamberlain's shoulder, a stern request, to take good care of his boy, as though the boy's safety were Chamberlain's responsibility. Chamberlain had been gracious, smiling, assuring the old man that the boy would return a hero. Now he would have to send a letter, as he'd sent many letters. He was a master at language, at the use of words, but when that time came, when he could see the faces of the men he wrote about, the words dissolved. Nothing he could ever say, no prayers, no tales of heroics, would replace the loss of the son, or the husband. He could not help it now, saw the boy's face, and the face of his father, could see it all, the letter being read aloud, the women weeping, the father trying to comfort. Would there be blame, anger? Would he be cursed by this man, the man to whom he had given the promise? Am I responsible, after all? He stared into the dark, thought, No, the army does not think so, it is all a part of the job. But what do people in Philadelphia know of . . . the *job*?

He was still near the hospitals, could see a long row of lanterns now, wagons moving up the road. The wounded were being taken away, moved to the railroads, back to City Point. After that they would ride the boats north, as he had, to the soft white beds, would stare at blank walls and try to keep their minds alive, wait patiently for the time when they might be allowed to go home or return to the war.

He pulled the horse around, looked up at the stars, but there were no stars. The sky was dull and black, and now he could hear a slight gust of wind, felt the first drop on his face, then more, the sound of the wind now becoming the sound of the rain. He prodded the horse toward the camp, then saw a flicker of light across a wide field. He tried to see, as the rain fell hard around him, and could make out the horsemen, more lanterns, the light reflecting on the flags, the wide column of troops. He nodded to himself, understood now, had received the word from Griffin's headquarters. It would be the Second Corps, Humphreys's command, the men who had fought under Hancock. They would move into line beside the Fifth, and so tomorrow . . . he looked up, closed his eyes, felt the rain on his face, thought of the streams, the muddy roads. Well, maybe not *tomorrow*.

He rode toward the camp, thought of Sheridan, Grant, the great power of this army, knew that very soon they would move again. If they were no longer beyond Lee's flank, could not quite move as Sheridan had wanted, to cut the railroads, to wrap Lee's army up into a tight ball, they would simply drive up hard into whatever Lee put in their path, whatever defense Lee tried to make.

41. LEE

MARCH 31, 1865

THERE HAD BEEN A STRANGE AND CONFUSED FIGHT ALL ALONG the White Oak Road, the Federal troops pushing forward again. Confused and uncoordinated, their attack was made more difficult by the rain, the difficult crossings of the creeks, the small swamps and bogs that were now an impossible barrier to troop movement. Lee's men had broken the first wave of Federal assaults, sent the blue troops racing southward, back across the torrent of Gravelly Run. But he knew this was the Fifth Corps, and to the east there was help from part of the Second, and so Lee had been forced back again, the blue troops finally establishing control along the valuable road.

Lee's men still faced southward, and the White Oak Road would give no one an easy passageway. The men who had fought so well there were now in motion, moving slowly westward, lengthening their trenches. There was a wide gap between the end of the line and the critical crossroads of Five Forks, and Lee knew that the great strength below him would not just sit and wait while he made his defenses strong.

There had been a good fight to the west as well, and he'd waited for it, knew that what had happened at Five Forks was more important than the loss of White Oak Road. The sounds meant that Pickett had arrived, his division nearly five thousand strong, and linked up with Fitz Lee's cavalry, to hold Sheridan away.

Lee had spent most of the last two days along the White Oak Road, and now rode in the rain toward the dull sound of musket fire. The firing had mostly stopped, except for scattered pops, skirmishers getting in the last word. The blue troops were tight against the White Oak Road, and he knew there was nothing he could do about it for now.

He thought it strange that it would be Pickett's division, circumstance moving out of Lee's control, directed by a much stronger force—the hand of God—deciding that Pickett would be in the best position, the fastest way to reinforce the far flank. Pickett's division had been close to the trains, was able to move to the flank quickest. Lee thought hard on that, did not ask why; there was no answer. But if there is some Divine plan, he thought, I can only carry it through. He considered the man himself; he had not seen Pickett again before the move west. What will he do? What kind of fight will his men make? It will matter, after all. Pickett held the flank, the most important position on the long line.

Fitz Lee had been reinforced as well, as much cavalry as could be moved. There were now nearly four thousand horsemen, as strong a force of cavalry as Lee could still assemble. He thought of his nephew, the man who had tried to step into the shoes of Stuart, and had learned to walk with the swagger, the heroic dash, of the horseman. Fitz Lee had proven he could match Sheridan, had fought him all over central Virginia now. But this was not a fight between horse soldiers. Sheridan was supported now by two corps of infantry, forty thousand Federal troops, and Fitz Lee had only the five thousand men of George Pickett.

Traveller moved through the mud, and Lee focused down, the rain flowing off the brim of his hat. It had always been about mathematics, something he'd had to absorb from the beginning, to make the best use of the poor numbers. In front of Petersburg, facing east, John Gordon had barely five thousand men. If Grant knew that . . . but it may not matter now, he thought. Grant is moving west. The forts and trenches that Gordon held was the toughest ground, the strongest defensive position on the field. Grant would know that. No, he realized, I would do the same thing, move out this way, get around the flank, cut the railroad. We must not let him cut the railroad.

The numbers were a blur, and he thought of Davis: You have never understood. If you had used the energy, made the speeches, worked on bringing the states together, uniting their strength . . . But Davis had only alienated those who could have helped, the men in the Carolinas, Georgia. Soldiers continued to drift away, draining the numbers from the army.

He closed his eyes, listened to the rain, the sound of the horse's steps. Did it matter, after all? He had been shocked to hear the numbers from Joe Johnston, had assumed that down south there was good strength, enough force to hold Sherman away. But Johnston could not organize the mix of forces, lost many to the temptations of home, many who simply walked away. Now Johnston could report barely thirteen thousand men in the field, and Lee knew that Sherman had better than sixty thousand.

The staff had put together the best intelligence they could, estimated Grant's numbers at better than eighty thousand, more than double what Lee had left. In Richmond there were still the loud calls from the papers, from the politicians, that together Lee and Johnston could whip either one of the Federal armies, then turn in one great wave and defeat the other. He still considered that, but when the reports came from Johnston, Lee knew that if Sherman simply drove hard to the north, there would be nothing he could do to prevent him from linking up with Grant.

The letters still came into camp, mindless and boastful, advice on military strategy from men who had never seen a fight. Lee had stopped reading them, left it to Taylor to sift through the correspondence, to screen out what was important. He'd hoped to hear more from Davis, but there had been nothing of substance, no help to the army. Davis was holding on to the one piece of the Cause that meant more to him than any other. He was surrounded by it, clung to it with a failing mind, saving it to the end. Lee thought, He believes it, truly believes that if we hold Richmond, we are still winning. If I tell him, he will not hear me. Richmond is a liability, a drain on our strength. Longstreet is there, holding on with what little he can, strengthened only by old men and boys, displaced sailors and crippled veterans. And I need Longstreet here.

It was late in the day, and what fighting there had been was growing silent, held down by the weather and the exhaustion of the men. Lee knew Sheridan had been pushed back to Dinwiddie Court House, good work from Fitz Lee's horses. If we can move out that way, he thought, spread out the line . . .

He could hear the workers, the axes and shovels. He did not ride along the trenches, did not want to see the faces. Not today. The work was more difficult, the men weaker still, the rations even worse than they'd been before. They would still cheer him, but he did not want that now, thought, They cannot do this for me. They must do it for themselves, draw strength from that. *I* cannot be the cause.

Lee moved east, toward Anderson's headquarters, knew that beyond, between Anderson and Gordon, Hill was in place, probably the largest group of fighting men left, the Third Corps numbering about six thousand men. Hill had come back, had left the comforts of his home, the care of his wife, was now somewhere along the lines. Lee thought, Yes, we still have them, we still have good men, Longstreet, Hill. We will need the best they can give, the best fight their men have left.

He reined the horse, turned in the road, the staff gathering around him. Looking out to the west, he thought, With Pickett and Fitz Lee anchored above Dinwiddie, the lines have been stretched another six miles. All we have left to the east is Gordon.

The rain had stopped, the dull gray sky was breaking up, and now there was a glimpse of color, a sunset. Lee straightened in the saddle, pointed, the staff turning to look. Lee said, "There. It is a sign. God is still with us."

Marshall was beside him, the young man behind the round spectacles, and he said, "Yes, sir, God is with *you*, sir. Always has been."

Lee shook his head, wanted to say something, thought, No, we must not do that . . . not anymore.

There was a rider, moving up fast, coming from the west. Lee watched him, forgot about the sunset. The man splashed up, breathing heavily, his face and clothes soaked in the dense mud of the soggy fields.

"Sir, compliments from General Pickett, sir."

Lee returned the man's salute, his chest tightening, said, "Go on."

"The general reports that he was unable to move the Yankees out of Dinwiddie, sir. The general has withdrawn our forces north, to Five Forks. He reports, sir, that the enemy has not followed him, that he is in a strong position there, sir."

Lee stared at the man, waited for more, but the man sagged in the saddle, the report complete. Marshall had pulled out a map, handed it to Lee, who scanned it, thought, I had hoped . . . they could have defeated General Sheridan's cavalry. Even the cavalry would have been a major victory. Now they will have *time*. Sheridan will receive infantry support. He folded the map, handed it calmly to Marshall, felt his gut turn, his jaw tighten.

He said to the courier, "You may return to General Pickett. Remind him that the Southside Railroad is close to his rear. He must not move any further north. Advise General Pickett that he must hold Five Forks at all hazards." He took a breath, felt a hard thump in his chest, looked down, saw a dull reflection in the mud, the last splash of color from the fading sunset, repeated in a low voice, "At all hazards . . ."

42. CHAMBERLAIN

April 1, 1865

THEY HAD MOVED IN THE DARK, CHURNING THE ROADS INTO deep glue, then, off the roads, following the straightest line, moving through the misery of quicksand and blind trails. The orders from Sheridan and Grant and Meade had come in a confusing stream, the lines of communication tangled in the web of Federal command, the structure clouded by divided authority. Grant had given Sheridan command of the field, but where that field began was something Meade did not clearly understand. Finally, word had come, the Fifth would march to support Sheridan, would now be under his command. But orders still came into camp from Meade, and Chamberlain had seen Warren, watched as the small dapper man was slowly beaten down by confusion and contradiction.

They were close to Sheridan's horsemen now, and the sunlight was drying the roads, again. The men were eating their rations, had been given three days of food to carry on the march from White Oak Road. The food was not very good, not what they were normally issued. The long line of wagons mostly carried ammunition, and it was a plain, simple message. Cartridge boxes were clearly the priority, certainly to the commanders, if not to the men themselves.

He sat on a log, finished a cold cup of coffee, stared down into the muddy flow of a creek. Hearing a horse, he turned, saw Griffin, who dismounted and walked slowly toward him. Griffin lifted his hat, rubbed his face with his hand. Chamberlain noticed Griffin's belt, and that he wasn't wearing his sword.

He began to stand, and Griffin said, "No, General, stay put. Drink your coffee."

Chamberlain motioned with the cup, said, "Your sword, sir."

Griffin put a hand on his belt. "Lost it, all the ruckus last night. Some reb probably wearing it this morning."

Chamberlain put the cup down, quickly unbuckled his own sword, held it out to Griffin. "Please, sir, I insist."

Griffin took the sword, looked at it appraisingly, nodded, said, "Thank you. Most generous of you, General. It will be returned."

Chamberlain nodded, thought, More men will follow your sword than mine. "I will find another, sir."

Griffin sat now, and Chamberlain waited, knew there was something happening, could tell from the grim clench in Griffin's jaw that he had something to say.

Chamberlain tossed the coffee cup behind him, toward the fire, saw an aide pick it up, and he nodded apologetically, thought, I suppose I will sit here until he says it's time to move. . . .

"It's going to be a tough day." Chamberlain looked at Griffin, who said again, "A tough day."

Chamberlain nodded, thought, Well, we're sort of used to that by now.

"You know," Griffin said, "we're under Sheridan's command. And this morning General Grant gave General Sheridan the authority to do what he feels is best to maintain this command."

Chamberlain said, "Maintain . . . what do you mean?"

Griffin looked at him, said, "It means General Grant has given General Sheridan authority to relieve anyone he chooses, if he sees fit. The message was specific, actually. General Grant mentioned General Warren by name."

Relieve Warren? Chamberlain thought of the march that morning, leading his column into the open ground around Dinwiddie, seeing Sheridan for the first time. He said, "That explains General Sheridan's reaction . . . what he said this morning."

"You spoke to General Sheridan?" Griffin said.

"Yes, we marched into the fields, over there, along the road, and I saw the headquarters flag, rode over myself, and he came out to meet me. I was . . . maybe I was too relieved at getting the march over with, so I was, maybe, a bit too casual."

Griffin, smiling now, asked, "What the hell did you say?"

"Well, I offered my respects, and reported to him with the lead of the division. He asked where General Warren was. I told him, at the rear of the corps."

"The rear . . . ? I'm sure he found that amusing."

Chamberlain heard the sarcasm in Griffin's voice, said, "He was not terribly amused. He said, 'That's where I expected him to be.' He asked me what General Warren was doing back there, and I tried to explain that we were withdrawing from White Oak Road in the face of the enemy, but—"

"But he didn't want to hear all of that."

Chamberlain shook his head. "No. I don't understand his reaction. General Warren was doing the best he could last night. I had thought . . ." Chamberlain paused, thought, Careful . . . But there were too many hard memories. "I thought . . . we should still be back there. We gave up a lot of good men to take that road."

Griffin looked down toward the creek, said, "We are here because General Sheridan ordered us to be here. General Warren is not popular at headquarters, hasn't been for a long time. Maybe since the Wilderness. I have seen it myself, he often concerns himself with too many details, stirs too many pots, makes too many suggestions where they might not be welcome. And he has been slow, occasionally."

Chamberlain felt words boiling up, held it, thought, Who hasn't been slow in this army? Who can operate with commanders scattered all over the countryside, orders coming in from all directions, no one knowing what is going on?

Chamberlain said nothing, knew that Griffin was probably right, that even the troops had been through the whole range of disgust and frustration, the job in front of them plain and simple, the commands often delayed and confusing. It made things simpler to be out here, far from the main lines, from Petersburg, simpler to be under the command of one man. But Sheridan was quick to anger, reacted often by charging into the fire rather than thinking things through, had a strong eye focused on his relationship with Grant, and thus his relationship with Washington and the newspapers.

Chamberlain said, "General Warren has done all right, if you ask me."

Griffin looked at him again, with a sad smile. "I don't believe General Sheridan will ask *you*."

THE ORDERS CAME LATE IN THE DAY. WARREN'S CORPS WAS TO move close to the cavalry, to strengthen Sheridan's position. But the roads were confusing, and there were delays, communications and troop movements made worse by the dense woods and swampy ground the soldiers had to travel. Sheridan had been furious at the delays, his temper echoing along the slow progress of the men, but by mid-afternoon, the corps had finally come together. If the men did not know of the anger and frustration of their commander, they quickly understood how serious their position had become. To the north, Pickett and Fitz Lee held the intersection at Five Forks, were spread in a strong line east and west along the White Oak Road. On the east end of the line, the gap still remained, a wide space that separated Pickett from the rest of Lee's army. At the eastern end of his position, Pickett had refused the line, turned his men northward at a right angle to the road.

Sheridan's plan was straightforward, and as Chamberlain looked at the drawing, the sketches on paper, he could hear his men moving into line, horses moving past, the sound of an army pulling itself into motion. He ran his finger along the road they would march, thought, Yes, this is a very good plan.

The dismounted cavalry would assault on the left, with the three divisions of the Fifth Corps moving up on the right. The focal point of the assault for the infantry would be the right angle in Pickett's line, with Ayres's division striking right on the point of the angle. Craw-

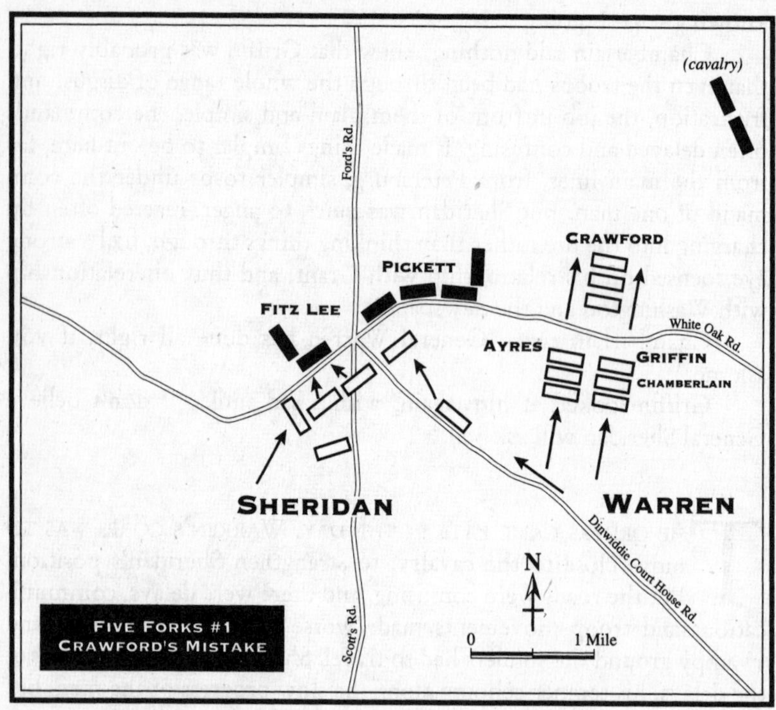

ford's division would lead, and Griffin would follow farther out to the right, moving beyond Pickett's flank, then wheeling to the left, to strike that part of the rebel works that spread to the north. With the cavalry doing the same on the west end, the sheer strength of the Federal assault should envelop Pickett and Fitz Lee's entire position, completely cutting them off from the rest of Lee's army.

They moved forward at four P.M., a quick march on hardening roads. Chamberlain rode again beside the young color bearer, Sergeant Arthur, whose name he would not forget now, had fixed itself in his mind with a strange logic. He could only see it one way, saw it every time he looked at the maps. The sergeant was named after a swamp.

He knew their right flank was vulnerable, that somewhere beyond the low hills, the rest of Lee's army was probably in motion. Griffin had warned him to keep a sharp lookout, and Chamberlain had positioned a small force out to the right, not enough strength to fend off an attack, but at least a warning. They knew now, Lee was out there himself, the prisoners had brought the news, and Chamberlain felt a pride in that, that he'd taken his brigade across Gravelly Run right at Robert E. Lee. But somewhere, locked away inside, was a small breath of relief that he hadn't known it at the time.

There were scattered shots to the left, far in the distance. Our cavalry, Chamberlain thought, out there, moving with us. He felt a thrill now, something different from before, from the assaults of the past few days. There was something about Sheridan, about going into a fight with the power, the good plan. Behind him the men felt it as well, and he turned in the saddle, looked back, saw the faces looking up at him. Men began to smile, the weariness of the march now past, the short rest and the light rations all they would need.

The maps had shown that the road they were on would take them straight at the place where Pickett's line made the turn northward. He could see out to the front now, a wide space of open ground, could see Crawford's division spread into line, moving straight ahead. There was a small bend in the road, and he was staring ahead, and suddenly there was an intersection. He pushed the horse forward, looked in both directions, a long stretch of open road, no troops, no works.

He turned, motioned to an aide, said, "Keep them moving . . . follow Crawford. I have to find General Griffin."

Spurring the horse, he moved to the rear, knew Griffin was close behind. He saw the flags, reined the horse, pulled the map out of his pocket. "Sir," he said, "it appears . . . we are crossing the White Oak Road. There's no sign of the enemy."

Griffin did not look at the map, said, "Don't worry about maps, General. Our orders are to follow General Crawford. We'll find somebody up here. They didn't just go away."

There was musket fire up ahead now, off to the right. Chamberlain turned, said, "Yes . . . there they are!" He listened to the small scattered shots, no sustained volley. Suddenly confused, he said, "But . . . that means we're on the left. The cavalry's on the left, we're supposed to be on the right."

Griffin listened, a silent pause, the shooting still scattered, far up to the right. "That's no fight, just skirmishers. Crawford's just running into some resistance from the east. Could be Lee, pushing this way. Back to your brigade, General. Keep an eye to the right."

Chamberlain saluted, saw anger darkening Griffin's face, thought, Yes, it could be Lee . . . but where is Pickett? He spurred the horse, moved up into the wide road, watched his troops still following Crawford's lines. He reined the horse, thought, If Lee is to the right, then we must be way too far east.

Suddenly, there was a roar, a massive volley of muskets, the sound rolling up toward him from the west, straight down the road. There were big guns now, the hard sounds punching the air, and he raised his hand, motioned to the bugler, the command to halt the line.

He raised his glasses, stared straight down the road, could see nothing, then made out a rising cloud of smoke, the sounds still flowing out in one great wave. He looked behind him, saw the second brigade coming up, Gregory's men, and Chamberlain yelled, "This way . . . wheel them around! We're not where we're supposed to be!"

Gregory began to move, his men flowing over the road, his lines pivoting, swinging toward the west and the vast sounds of the fight. Chamberlain moved in front of his own columns now, waved his arm, his men wheeling about as well. He glanced up above the road, could still see Crawford's division, moving farther away, and now he could see it, understood what had happened. Yes, the maps were wrong, they had reached the White Oak Road well to the right of the enemy's position. But Crawford . . . was still moving away, was moving off in the wrong direction. Chamberlain saw horsemen now, flags, could see Warren, the perfect uniform, the bright gold sash, riding hard, moving out toward Crawford. Yes, Chamberlain thought, he knows as well. Turn them around . . .

His men were in line now, facing west, and Chamberlain looked around, thought, It isn't supposed to be like this. There should be orders. I hope . . . this is the right move.

Then he saw more horsemen, Griffin, with Bartlett, the Third Brigade. Griffin was waving to him, waving the sword Chamberlain had given him, furiously waving his hand, and Chamberlain saw him pointing, the clear sign: yes, go, take them into the fight.

THE CAVALRY HAD BEGUN THE FIGHT, SLAMMING HARD INTO THE rebel front, pushing forward across the road. On the right, Ayres's division, having moved up across the White Oak Road, was suddenly blasted from the left, and moved out just beyond Pickett's flank, where it was hit hard from Pickett's line. Leading two-thirds of Griffin's division, Chamberlain could not see Ayres's fight, rode down through a shallow ravine, then up, in sight of the heavy earthworks Pickett's men had spread up to the north. The volleys were blowing down across the road, Ayres's men pushed back by the surprise, trying to hold their position. On this end of the rebel position, Ayres was the only target, and the rebel muskets ripped his lines, their big guns throwing great bursts of canister into the startled blue troops.

Chamberlain tried to see Ayres, looked for the division flags, but the smoke boiled up from the low ground, the small patches of woods down below the road. In front of him he could see big guns swinging around, the muskets now pointing into his own troops, and Chamberlain turned, yelled, *"Forward!"*

The wave of blue surged down through the shallow depression, then climbed up, and was quickly on the rebel works. Now the smoke was in front of him, the muskets firing all along the works, the sounds whistling past him. His men were climbing the walls en masse. The firing slowed, and there were the awful sounds of men against men, bayonets and clubbing muskets. He still looked for Ayres, thought, I should tell him we are here, tell him what is happening. He glanced up toward the north, could see nothing, no sign of Crawford, of the rest of the corps.

He spurred the horse, moved down a short hill, fought the smoke, climbed up on the road, moved below it. He could see small trees, thick brush, musket fire from below, the fire from Ayres's men. There were big Federal guns there now, and the sharp blasts hit the rebel works hard, shattering the dirt and logs. He pushed the horse on, searching, looking for horses, suddenly saw a different flag, a small man on a huge black horse, stopped, recognized Phil Sheridan.

Sheridan glared at him with black fury, said, "Well, by God, that's what I want to see! General officers at the front! Where's your command, where's the rest of your commanders?"

Chamberlain pointed toward the north, ducked under a sudden blast of wind, the impact of the shell tearing into the brush behind Sheridan. "Sir, General Warren is with Crawford's division. General Griffin instructed me to bring two brigades to support General Ayres."

Sheridan looked toward the north, his anger growing, said, "Ayres . . . I don't know where he is . . . but yes, take your men into the flank, good, yes! Do it! Take command of anyone you see here, any infantry! Break them, dammit!"

Chamberlain started to answer, his arm rising in salute, and there was a sudden blast close behind him, the horse bolting forward. Chamberlain regained control, then spurred the animal, was quickly gone from Sheridan. He moved now below the road, thought, No, I don't want him that angry at *me*. He saw a line of blue coming up from the thick brush, looked for officers, saw a flag. They were from Ayres's division, the Third Brigade. He moved quickly, saw a familiar face, Jim Gwyn, reined the horse. Gwyn's face was red and sweating, with a small flicker of panic.

Chamberlain said, "General Gwyn . . . what are your orders? Where is General Ayres?"

Gwyn looked at Chamberlain with relief, someone who might know something, said, "I have no orders. I've lost General Ayres . . . this brush is too thick. We're cut off."

Chamberlain could hear musket fire again, the sounds cutting the air around him, Gwyn's men now in plain sight of the rebel works. He turned, saw blue on the right, above the road, his men still fighting the rebels up close. He looked at Gwyn, saw a man waiting for instructions, thought now of Sheridan: He told me . . . take command.

"General, come with me. Bring your men forward. I will take responsibility. You shall have the credit. Let me have your brigade for a moment!"

Gwyn saluted him, still waiting for orders.

Chamberlain saw the men watching him and he yelled, "Forward, right oblique!"

Gwyn turned, repeated the order, and the blue line began to move forward, climbing up toward the road, straight into the fight where Chamberlain's men were holding a wide stronghold in the rebel works. Chamberlain moved his horse to one side, waited for the line to move by, then rode up alongside, thought of the salute, thought, He probably outranks me.

He looked farther down, saw more flags, thought, It must be Ayres. He jerked the horse, spurred it hard. He rode behind Gwyn's line, was suddenly surrounded by horsemen, Sheridan again. Sheridan was more angry than before, red-faced, waving a fist close to Chamberlain's face. "What the hell are you doing?"

Chamberlain pointed at the flags, at Ayres now riding toward them, didn't know what Sheridan was asking. Sheridan ignored Ayres, said, "You're firing into my cavalry!"

Chamberlain looked up toward the rebel lines, the fight now swelling into a new roar of sound, Gwyn's men disappearing over the wall. Chamberlain felt the heat rising in his face, looked at Sheridan, held it for a moment, then said, "Then the cavalry is in the wrong place. One of us will have to get out of the way! What will you have me do, General?"

Sheridan stared at him with wide-eyed shock, his mouth moving slowly, and Chamberlain was still angry, thought, Well, that may be the last thing I say to *him*.

Sheridan turned, his mouth still open, looked up across the field, looked back at Chamberlain again, said, "Well . . . don't fire into my cavalry!"

Now Ayres was there, and Chamberlain let out a long breath. Sheridan recognized Ayres, yelled, louder, "General Ayres, you are firing into my cavalry!"

Ayres leaned forward, looked at Chamberlain, and Chamberlain thought, I should tell him, said quickly, a short burst, "Sir, Gwyn is in on the right."

Ayres glanced up, searching, nodded to Chamberlain, looked at Sheridan, said, "General, we are firing at the people who are firing at us! I don't hear any carbine shots . . . those are muskets, the enemy's muskets. I ought to know, General!"

Sheridan's face exploded into red again. Abruptly, he jerked at his horse, rode away through the blue lines moving up from behind. Chamberlain watched him, thought, *My* cavalry? I thought it was *our* cavalry.

Ayres was watching Sheridan as well, then looked briefly at Chamberlain, said, "Fine work, General. We are back in the fight."

Chamberlain saluted. "We're in the works, sir." He turned, the musket fire slowing, said, "I would suggest, sir . . . that way."

Ayres shouted, and a bugler blew out a short command. The wave of blue began to move forward, adding to the strength, pushing into the rebel works, the fight now moving farther above the road. Ayres looked again at Chamberlain, said, "Don't fire into *my* men, General."

HE HAD MOVED PAST THE REBEL WORKS, HIS OWN MEN, strengthened by Ayres's division, now moving the rebels back. There was still a fight, small pockets of rebels, led by officers who would not retreat. The fight had become disorganized, chaotic, and as the men in blue moved forward, there were sudden bursts of fire all around, hand-to-hand fighting rolling across the line as small groups of rebels tried to hold their ground.

He moved again with his own brigade, the staff watching him with relief, men who were becoming used to the man who did not obey what they had all been trained to recite: *one hundred fifty yards behind the lines.*

The fight was in all directions now, rebels suddenly appearing out of small depressions, over low hills. Chamberlain was looking behind them, saw a mass of troops emerge from brush. His heart jumped, and he yelled, "Turn . . . prepare to fire . . . by the rear rank!" The men close to him spun quickly around, saw the rebels moving close and raised their muskets. Suddenly, the rebels began to drop their muskets, hands went up, and the hand-to-hand combat was no longer combat at all.

The rebels gathered around the raised bayonets of the blue troops, men shouting, "Surrender . . . we surrender!"

Chamberlain stared in amazement, saw many rebels now, many more than the men they were surrendering to, and the blue troops were backing up slowly, nervous, unsure. Chamberlain thought, If they see how few we are, any one of them . . . they can just pick up their muskets.

"To the rear!" he shouted, pointing. Glancing down at his men, he motioned with his hand, the urgent silent command, *spread out, move around them.* Quickly, the prisoners were eased away from their muskets, and slowly began to drift back, away from the fight. He watched them for a moment, thought, Now that was interesting . . .

The fight was still in front of him, and he could see more groups of rebels moving to the rear, escorted by the bayonets of their enemy.

He moved forward again, saw a hard line of rebels, stronger. His men were kneeling, firing into brush, small stands of trees. The volleys flew out in both directions now, and Chamberlain moved the horse forward, was surrounded by bodies, down in the tall grass, realized the horse was stepping right across many dead, many more wounded. The sounds began to rise up from the grass around him, the horrible cries that he had heard on so many fields, so many bloody fights. He still moved forward, dropped down into a shallow depression, saw his men huddled close to the ground, a long line now stopped, men holding tight to the muskets, waiting for . . . something, as though if they just held here, in this one safe place, it would end. They began to see him, and men slowly stood, watching him. He pointed up, over the rise in front of them, the strong line of rebels still in place, still full of the fight, said, "Up, move forward! It's almost done! We have broken their flank!"

More men stood, and he looked around, saw officers, a young lieutenant, and Chamberlain said, "Get them up, they want to follow you! Lead them!"

The young man looked at him, dazed, his eyes blank. Chamberlain saw the man's shirt now, saw blood, a dark stain, and the man said nothing, stared past him. Chamberlain looked beyond the man, erased him quickly from his mind, gazed out across the wide depression. There was another officer, familiar. Chamberlain fought for the name . . . yes, Major Glenn, and Chamberlain knew now, these men . . . the 198th Pennsylvania, thought, These are fighting men, there is no line anywhere they cannot cross. He felt a rush of energy. Yes, we will push, or capture them all!

He yelled to Glenn, "Major, get these men up! If you break that line you shall have a colonel's commission!" Glenn saluted, grinning, began to move, and Chamberlain thought, Yes, he always had the fire, then thought of himself, the green commander who didn't know how to do any of this, just that it had to be done. Chamberlain watched Glenn move up the hill. This is *your* time, he thought. Make your mark on these men, take them into the fight!

Glenn shouted, "Boys, will you follow me?"

There was a cheer, the men moving up the rise, a hard surge forward, and now the rebels could see their targets, and a sudden blast poured from the line of logs, but the men did not stop, rushed forward as one wave, were now up and over the low works. Chamberlain spurred the horse, moved up behind them, heard the voices, loud and strong, the sounds of the fight now swept away by the sounds of the fire in his men.

It was over in a few minutes, and he rode forward again, felt a strange pride. I can tell them . . . to do anything. We cannot be stopped! He wanted to laugh, felt alive, the excitement taking over. The job was done, the work, leading the men, commanding the brigade, now something else. He said the word to himself . . . *victory,* wanted to yell it, waved his hat, something he had never done, something from a storybook, the glorious thrill, the pure joy.

Men were falling back now, many with prisoners, small groups, then larger ones. He wanted to count them, thought, No, we will learn that soon enough. But I want to know . . .

Then he saw the wounded, men carrying an officer, and he felt something turn inside him, gripped the hat hard in his hand, saw it was Glenn. The men saw Chamberlain, moved close, lay the young man down, and Chamberlain climbed down from the horse, felt a wave of sickness, leaned over.

Glenn's face was gray as he looked up at Chamberlain. "General," said in a quiet voice, "I have carried out your wishes."

Chamberlain nodded dumbly, could say nothing, thought, I did this. I *chose* him.

One of the men kneeled down close to Chamberlain, said, "He was carrying the colors, sir. The color bearer was down, and Major Glenn . . . he took the flag. It was . . . glorious, sir."

Chamberlain looked at the man, looked past him, thought, *Glorious,* is that what this is?

He looked at Glenn closely now, the man fighting for the one breath, but the fight was past, and Chamberlain saw the soft peace cover the man's face. Chamberlain leaned low, close to the man's face, said, "*Colonel,* I will remember my promise."

He stood then, a last glance at the young man's face, turned to the horse, leaned on the saddle, thought, You *have* to remember . . . you can never forget this. This is what a soldier does, this is what you volunteered for. *You* make the decisions, *you* make the choices, you stand up to God and claim in all your arrogance that *you* are in command.

He closed his eyes, felt a great need to pray, but not here, not on ground like this, not while the fight still echoed around him. He opened his eyes again, thought, No, this is not the time, I cannot do anything but . . . what I have to do.

Crawford's division had finally come into the fight, far up the road that led north, away from Five Forks. It could have been disastrous, Crawford coming in alone, separated from the rest of the corps. But in fact it was the best place he could have been. As the rebels retreated, they ran right into the arms of Crawford's men, and so by dark there was no fight, no enemy left in front of the Federal troops. The rebels that did not find capture simply dissolved into the countryside, the scattered remnants of ten thousand of Lee's most veteran troops. The critical junction of Five Forks was now firmly in Federal

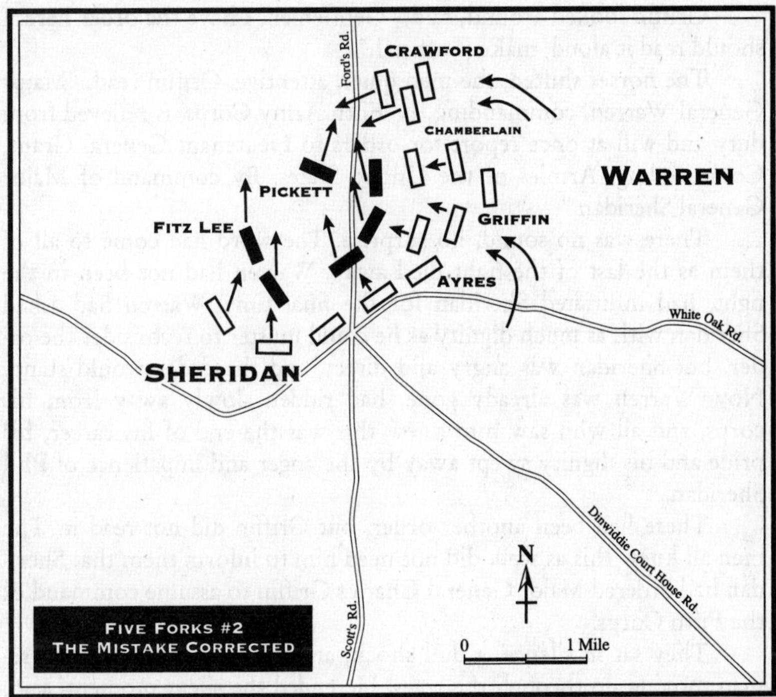

hands, and Sheridan had no difficulty pushing up past the Southside Railroad, cutting Petersburg's last artery of supply.

By the next morning Lee's army was enclosed by a ring of blue that stretched from east of Petersburg, from the Appomattox River, southward, then out to the west, until the tightening cord wound north again and secured its flank on the same river.

In the camps the men gathered in quiet celebration, the complete victory, the crushing blow to Lee's right flank.

THEY WERE IN THE FORKS ITSELF, THE INTERSECTION THAT spread the roadways out in all directions. It was nearly dark, a last glow framing the treetops in the west. Chamberlain sat on the horse, saw the animal licking at its leg, a small hole, another wounded horse that would remember him. Griffin was in the center, surrounded by the rest, Bartlett, Ayres, Crawford. Off to the side of the road the staff officers mingled together in small conversation, low voices.

Griffin looked around, said, "Gentlemen, I have the order here. I should read it aloud, make it official."

The horses shifted, the men quiet, attentive. Griffin read, "Major General Warren, commanding the Fifth Army Corps, is relieved from duty and will at once report for orders to Lieutenant General Grant, Commanding, Armies of the United States. By command of Major General Sheridan."

There was no sound, no surprise. The word had come to all of them as the last of the fight died away. Warren had not been in the fight, had infuriated Sheridan for the final time. Warren had asked Sheridan with as much dignity as he could muster to reconsider the order, but Sheridan was angry and direct, and the order would stand. Now Warren was already gone, had ridden slowly away from his corps, and all who saw him knew this was the end of his career, his pride and his dignity swept away by the anger and impatience of Phil Sheridan.

There had been another order, but Griffin did not read it. The men all knew this as well, did not need him to inform them that Sheridan had ordered Major General Charles Griffin to assume command of the Fifth Corps.

They sat in silence, a dull shock, and Chamberlain saw a horseman moving up through the trees. He ended the silent moment, said, "Sir . . . it's General Sheridan."

The faces turned, and Sheridan rode up quickly, was smiling, filled with the glow of a man who has had his way.

"We have smashed them! This has been a magnificent day!" He paused, saw the subdued looks, said, "Gentlemen, I may have spoken harshly to some of you today. But I would not have it hurt you. You know how it is, we had to carry this place, and I fretted all day until it was done. You must forgive me. I know it is hard on the men too, but we must push on. There is more for us to do together." He looked down briefly, then around at each one of them, said, "I appreciate and thank you all."

He turned abruptly, rode away into darkening woods.

Chamberlain looked at Griffin, saw him staring in surprise, his eyes blinking, disbelieving. Griffin said, "So . . . we have learned something about Phil Sheridan."

There were quiet murmurs, then a pause, and Chamberlain ran that through his mind, thought, We have learned . . . what? That Sheridan is not a man to dig trenches, and not a man to be kept waiting? He felt angry now, thought of Warren, No, he was never the perfect commander, he would never win great battles. But he is a good man, a careful man. Sheridan is not careful. But he is different from Warren, from Meade. Yes, there is the lesson. He is *not* different from Grant.

Griffin said something, a quiet good night, and the men began to ride in separate directions. Chamberlain waited, was alone now, heard the slow sounds of hoofbeats moving away. He thought of Warren again, thought, You were a thinker. You thought too much, you took too much care. He suddenly felt he had learned something new, another lesson. Wars are not won by thinkers. He thought then of Major Glenn, of McEuen, others, Strong Vincent, Buster Kilrain. There were more, many more, and he stopped trying to recall them, thought of this afternoon, of trying to pray. No, there is no time for that, not as long as we do this. That is the lesson. This war will be won by the men who move forward, who do not stop to question what they do or what the consequences will be. It is not cause or country or the fellow beside you. It is simple and direct. The rebels were winning this war when they had men like Jackson. Now we are winning this war because we have men like Sheridan. Whether Warren's removal was justified or Glenn's death was my fault doesn't matter now. Those questions will be answered later. Now, we will simply move forward.

43. LEE

April 2, 1865

LONGSTREET HAD ARRIVED, AND THE LAST OF THE STRONG DEfenses above the James was coming with him, still moving into Petersburg on the rough and battered rail line. Richmond was now defended by little more than scattered remnants of smaller units, cavalry and infantry, plus the home guard, the men commanded by Dick Ewell.

Lee had heard the sounds of the fight from the west, but nothing from Pickett. He had only the scouting reports of the cavalry, the small skirmish line that picked at the great Federal surge on the east side of Five Forks. He'd sent Anderson's troops farther west, at first, to link up with Pickett, to fill the gap in the line on the White Oak Road. But Anderson was too late, could only dig in and face the great force that routed Pickett at Five Forks. Anderson was now the right flank. With Pickett's men swept away, Anderson was the new end of the line.

All night Lee had heard the sounds, the skirmishers firing at his defenses all along the line, all the way from the James River, all down below the city. The big guns had kept up the demonstration as well, and Lee had stayed awake, eyes wide, staring into darkness, uncomfortable now in the soft bed. By late night he knew the worst, that the strong right flank, the force that had kept Sheridan at bay for two days, was now gone, completely erased from the picture. With the first light would come the new reports, what he already knew inside, estimates, thousands of prisoners, a defeat as complete and quick as any he had suffered.

The demonstrations meant something, and Lee had listened to a different sound, not the usual blind bombardment. They were picking a spot, many vulnerable places, the line so weakened that on many of the parapets of the long earthworks, Lee's men stood nearly twenty feet apart. By now Grant knows what happened to us at Five Forks, knows we have stretched this line yet again, stretched it so far that at almost any place he wants to, he can drive a spear, a hard wedge of power, and split us completely apart.

IT WAS FOGGY, THE DULL LIGHT MAKING ITS WAY INTO THE ROOM. Lee sat at a long table, stared down at the smoothness, the polished wood, looked slowly up at the grim face of Longstreet.

Longstreet said, "Is anything known of Pickett?"

Lee shook his head, said, "You mean, the man? No, nothing. He could be captured. He may not have survived. His troops are scattered."

Longstreet held a small pipe, looked at it, said, "He gave it his best. Always did."

Lee leaned back in the chair, was feeling very tired, the long sleepless night dragging on him, his patience frayed, washed away by the frustration of not *knowing*. He'd had doubts about the plan from the beginning, of trusting the important position to a man who wore the shroud of defeat, who had not recovered and learned and grown, who could not be relied upon, not anymore. He was angry now at Longstreet, the blind loyalty, thought, You were not here, you don't know what happened. Your confidence in General Pickett is not justified.

He clenched his jaw, closed his eyes, held it in. No, it serves no purpose. He looked at Longstreet, thought, You have always been where I needed you to be. We must think of *now*. We must move on.

Lee said, "I have not heard from him. I can tell you nothing more."

There was noise from outside, boots on the porch, and the door opened. It was Hill, the small man pale behind the red beard, moving slowly, uncertain. Hill looked at Longstreet and straightened, surprised. He said to Lee, "General, I hope you are well this morning. General Longstreet, welcome." There was a weary softness in Hill's voice.

Longstreet nodded, said simply, "General Hill."

There was a silent pause, an awkward moment, Hill still not certain he should be there.

Lee said, "General Hill, please sit down. We are grateful for your return. You look in fine form, if I may say. I wish I could respond that we are all quite fit, but I am afraid that may not be the case."

Hill sat slowly, looked at Lee, confused, said, "I am fit, sir. Thank you. It is good to be here. The men . . . my troops are full of the fight, sir. It is healing . . . to see that, to hear them salute me like that."

Lee looked down, said, "Yes, General, the men . . . there is loyalty there that still . . . impresses me. I am gratified to hear of the morale of your corps. However, our situation may not be so . . . pleasant." There was an edge to Lee's voice.

Hill glanced again at Longstreet, and Longstreet said, "General Hill, I am glad to see you here. We have serious work in front of us."

Hill nodded, seemed relieved; the conversation was not personal, there was nothing of the old conflict in Longstreet's words.

Lee looked briefly at Longstreet, nodded quietly, thought, Yes, thank you, there is no time for all of the old problems. He took a breath now, said to Hill, "Have you been along your lines this morning? Do you see any sign that the enemy is moving—"

There was a loud commotion outside, and the door burst open, Colonel Venable yelling into the room, "Sir, quick . . . something is happening, sir! We're in retreat . . . quick, sir!"

Lee jumped up, rushed outside, could see men streaming across the open ground, coming up from the defenses below. There were wagons, horses, men in the road, moving up from the far trees and the thickets to the south. He felt for his field glasses, realized he was not wearing them, turned, saw Longstreet reach for his own and hold them out to him. Lee raised the glasses, looked to the southwest, could see more troops, an organized line moving up the broad hill, well past the defensive lines that were still strong, lines that should not have given way. He focused the glasses, strained to see, could not yet tell the uniforms, the fog still holding the sunlight away.

Lee handed the glasses to Longstreet, said, "Can you see . . . ? Is that our people, a retreat? Are we pulling back?"

Longstreet focused, shook his head. "Can't tell . . ."

Lee turned to Venable. "Colonel, you must find out who those people are. Get word . . . find General Heth. I must know if his lines have been broken."

Now Hill jumped down from the porch, climbed quickly to his horse, said, "Sir, General Heth is my responsibility. If his position has been threatened, I will see to it." He spun the horse and moved quickly away, his aide scrambling to follow.

Lee looked at Venable, mounting his own horse. "Colonel," he said, "accompany General Hill! Report any news!"

Venable saluted, galloped quickly after Hill.

Lee felt the energy now fading quickly, felt a dark weariness, a black shroud of gloom, called out weakly, "General Hill . . . take good care. . . ."

THE LINES, MUDDY EARTHWORKS, WIDE TRENCHES, WERE EMPTY. The signs of the fight were all around, but there was no more fight. The men who had held these lines were far to the rear, pursued by most of the Federal Sixth Corps, Wright's men storming into the lines at first light. The men in blue, having little to slow them down, burst through the defenses, as they might have done at any time, the lines stretched thin enough that no concentrated assault could have been resisted for long.

Venable was close to Hill and the two aides, and they moved farther to the west, reached a small rise and could see the road again, a line of cannon, big guns moving slowly away.

Hill focused his glasses, said to Venable, "Colonel, those are our guns. We need them brought back . . . this way."

Venable saluted, rode quickly away. Hill scanned the ground, spurred the horse and moved down into a small patch of trees, the ground wet, a narrow creek twisting through. They moved quickly, pushed past the brush, began to climb up out of the tangle, and Hill abruptly pulled his horse up short. The two aides stopped, seeing two men in blue, muskets dragging the ground, eyes wide, exhausted.

Hill shouted, "Put down your guns. You are prisoners!"

The two aides rushed forward, but the blue soldiers had no fight, the guns slipping from their hands. Hill rode forward, looked at the two men, glanced at his aide, Tucker, who said, "General, what do we do with them?"

Hill looked at the other aide, said, "Private, escort these men back to General Lee. Sergeant Tucker, we must keep on."

THEY WERE A COMPANY FROM SOUTHERN PENNSYLVANIA, MEN who loved Uncle John Sedgwick, who now fought under a man they still didn't know and had rarely seen, Horatio Wright. They had come into the army as an alternative to life in the small towns, as common laborers, possessing the skills of handymen and carpenters. Many laughed when the shovels were passed down the Federal line, had done this work before, and by now many had used the shovels often, burying old friends and new.

This morning their good work had been with the musket, with the quick assault, but when the order came down, they looked at each other, wondered, Why now? What had changed that would make those rebs easier today than yesterday? But the order would never be questioned; the feelings about the officers would come out later, around the campfire, when they would talk more about the friends who did not come back.

They had moved forward at the first light, expected to rush into the blazing hell of the same fights they had rushed into before, but the enemy gave way quickly, without much resistance. Now the men of the Sixth Corps pushed on, chasing the rebels farther than they had before, a fast flight over the rolling fields that would eventually carry them to the railroad and beyond, to the Appomattox River.

His name was Mauk, and he was a corporal, a promotion earned for reasons he still didn't understand. He didn't know much about maps and rivers, had followed the men in front of him, as always, climbed up and over the high walls that he'd watched for months, surprised that when they reached the top there was no one there to stop them.

He had come into the army leaving a family at home, sent his pay to his wife whenever he could. He did not gamble, and if the temptation ever crossed him, he would think of the children, of the small home in the small town, and turn away from the men with the cards, the men with the bottles, and the few dollars would go home instead.

They were separated from the main body now, regiments and companies scattered all along the road, far out into the wide fields. They had moved through the old abandoned winter quarters of the rebels, and some had slipped out of line, an opportunity to perhaps find something, a memento, some piece of treasure.

Mauk stayed away from that, kept moving, a small group of men staying with him. If we keep moving, he thought, we should find the captain, find out what to do now.

What was left of his company was moving, slowly, carefully, through a small patch of damp woods, a muddy swamp. The men spread out behind him were as nervous as he was; they were behind the lines, had broken through into the enemy's ground. The main force was up ahead, somewhere, and Mauk began to scan the ground beyond the swamp, glanced into the sun, now moving higher, thought, No, not that way. He knew enough about direction to know that way was Petersburg.

One man was close to him now, and Mauk saw it was the boy, Wolford, with the freckled face of a child, who everyone thought had lied about his age. Wolford stayed close to Mauk, always, and Mauk had patience, would look out for him, pull him in the right direction, hold him down when the volleys flew thick. Mauk looked past the boy, could see toward the others now, thought they were too far apart and wanted to yell at them to close it up. But then he glanced back across the open ground beyond the trees, thought, Maybe a bit farther, stay quiet, see what might be over that rise . . .

There was a small sound, and Mauk looked at the boy, and the boy pointed, wide-eyed. Mauk heard louder sounds now, turned and saw two horsemen moving along the open hillside. He crouched low, then moved up quickly, slipped behind the cover of a fat oak tree, raised his musket. The boy came up close to him, moved against the trees as well, lower, closer to the ground, pointed his musket as well. They see us, Mauk thought. Looks like officers!

The riders slowed, then stopped, and one, the smaller man, said something to the other, and the larger man rode toward them, closer, shouted out, "Fire and you'll be swept to hell! Surrender, or I will shoot you! Our troops are here, you'll have to surrender anyway!"

The smaller man moved forward now, a thick red beard, and he yelled, "Surrender your arms!"

Mauk glanced down at the boy, said quietly, "I don't see it."

He looked down the barrel of the gun now, thought the smaller man seemed to be in command. He sighted the small metal bead on the man's chest, said to the boy, "Let's shoot them."

Both muskets fired, and Mauk saw his target fall, saw through the smoke that the other man was not hit, had grabbed the fallen man's horse, turned and rode quickly away. Mauk looked down at the boy, said, "I believe you missed."

Wolford nodded, said nothing, and they eased out from the tree, moved up the rise.

Mauk said, "Let's see what we got here. . ."

They moved up to the still body, the gray uniform stained now with a spreading flow of red.

Mauk leaned over, said, "Look here, Wolford. Got him through the heart."

The boy was looking around, nervous still, and Mauk saw the men waving him back into the trees, small shouts, "C'mon." He backed away from the body, said to the boy, "Best be moving on. He's an officer, that's for sure." He moved away, the boy close behind, nodding now, a small piece of pride.

"Yep, got me an officer."

LEE HAD SEEN THE TROOPS CLEARLY BY NOW, DID NOT NEED THE field glasses. They were moving in a slow steady wave, and there was no mistaking that the uniforms were blue.

Longstreet was gone, off to manage the troops arriving on the trains. In the yard around the house, Lee's staff had gathered what they could, but much would be left behind. The Turnbull house was now directly in the path of the Federal advance. Lee still did not know what had happened, how the line had collapsed. He moved to the porch, stepped down toward the big horse, saw Taylor, and Marshall, carrying bundles of paper, tossing them into the waiting wagon. Lee mounted Traveller, heard horses moving quickly up the road from the west. He turned, heard Marshall say, "Sir, it's General Hill . . ."

Lee saw the familiar horse, but the rider was not Hill, and Lee was surprised, then recognized the man, thought, Yes, Tucker, Hill's aide. There were others, Palmer, Hill's chief of staff, but Lee focused on Tucker, and the man's face carried all the message Lee needed. He felt the cold stab in his chest, saw Tucker slide off the horse, waited patiently as Tucker gathered himself, looking at Lee through eyes filled with tearful grief.

Palmer moved forward now, and Lee held up his hand—no, wait—still watched Tucker, and Tucker said, "Sir . . . I am sorry, sir. General Hill is dead. We ran into some Yankees—"

Lee raised his hand again, and Tucker stopped. Lee thought, It does not matter, the details . . . not now. He closed his eyes, pushed it hard, held it away, his throat tight, the stiffness in his chest squeezing away the air. He opened his mouth, tried to breathe, fought for it, and now he looked at Tucker, at Palmer, saw tears on the face of both men, said, "He is at rest now, and we who are left are the ones to suffer."

There was a quiet moment, but down below big guns began to fire, the air overhead ripped with the screaming of shells. Lee looked at Palmer, thought, Hill's home . . . so close to this awful place. He said, "Go, now, to Mrs. Hill. Tell her what has happened. Break it to her as gently as possible."

Palmer saluted, moved quickly away.

Lee looked at Taylor, saw him toss a pile of books into the wagon, said, "Colonel, get word to General Longstreet. Since we cannot locate General Heth, I wish General Longstreet to assume command of the Third Corps."

He looked to the west, could see more lines of blue moving toward the road, the route west, said, "I hope . . . General Heth has been able to join forces with General Anderson. We may not know that for some time."

The orderlies were carrying Lee's small trunk, and Lee saw the telegraph operator now, a small thin man with tiny glasses. The man was moving across the yard, and Lee said, "Sir! Are the lines still up? Do you know if we can still send out?"

The man stopped, glanced nervously at the sounds of the enemy guns, said, "Yes . . . yes, sir. I believe so, sir."

Lee dismounted, grabbed the man by the sleeve, led him up across the porch, back into the house. The man sat at his small desk, pushed away paper, his hand now holding the brass telegraph, and he looked at Lee, waited, a silent urgency for Lee to hurry.

Lee did not look at him, thought of the words, of how the president would respond. He had thought this moment was coming for a long time, something Davis would never discuss. He believes it is the whole cause, he thought. We fight to keep him in Richmond. Lee was angry now, had often thought Davis should come out here, see for himself. There were always reasons; too busy, his bad health. So, this would be a surprise to him. Lee shook his head, looked at his watch, thought, He will be at church, at St. Paul's, and I will interrupt his morning service. A marvelous luxury, sitting in a beautiful church, the peace of a Sunday service. Lee closed his eyes, thought, There is no time for that now. There is no time for luxury.

He looked down at the small man, saw sweat on his face, the hand trembling slightly on the telegraph key. Lee put a hand on the man's shoulder, said, "It's all right . . . there's time yet. You may begin . . . 'To His Excellency, President Jefferson Davis . . .' "

THE HOUSE WAS EMPTY, THE HEADQUARTERS NOW ON WHEELS, the wagon already moving away on the road. Lee saw Taylor and Marshall mounting their own horses, gave Traveller a light nudge with his spurs, the horse now moving across the yard. There was a sudden shattering blast, a shower of brick and wood, a shell hitting the house, and Lee glanced back, thought of the family, the generous people. This is how you are repaid. . . .

He moved the horse into the road, Taylor moving up beside him.

Musket fire could be heard now, close below the house, a new line of blue emerging from the woods, a new line of defense giving way. He stared that way for a moment, could see officers, men waving their troops on toward the house.

He looked at Taylor, said, "Colonel, this is a sad business."

THE ASSAULT HAD COME ALL ALONG THE FRONT. EAST OF TOWN, Gordon had held away the Federal advance as long as he could. The last strongholds were now falling there as well, the men in the small forts holding on until the last desperate moment.

South of the city, Heth and Wilcox had been overrun by the Sixth, and Heth's division was now split in two. What remained of Lee's forces close to Petersburg began to move back in a tight arc around the city. But no one believed there was any reason to stay where they were. Grant's army was pushing still, and there was only one alternative. Lee gave the order. When darkness finally came, the army would move north, cross the bridges over the Appomattox and evacuate the city of Petersburg.

IT WAS A GRAND PLACE, THE MAGNIFICENCE OF STAINED GLASS, THE breathtaking soar of the grand ceiling. St. Paul's Church was usually filled by now, but there were gaps, empty spaces in the pews, many having left the city, gone to the safety of the countryside.

It was the first Sunday of the month, and President Davis sat in his accustomed pew, midway down the aisle, listened to the solemn voice flowing out over the worshippers. He did not hear the words, his mind wandering, thought now of the early days, of cheering crowds, of Varina and the children. . . .

The thought froze him, and he could not help it, glanced beside him, the pew empty. They were gone, had been sent away in a wave of tearful good-byes, had left the city only a few days before. Varina did not want to leave, did not understand why she could not be with him, and he still did not believe it would happen, but the word kept coming, spreading all through the city; the meager defense forces were called out again, manning the works that faced the enemy. They said it was real, and close, and now Longstreet was gone, had taken much of the strength with him. But Davis still believed they would be back. Go, do your job, he thought. Take care of business, then return.

Lee had continued to warn him, insisted he be ready to leave, and

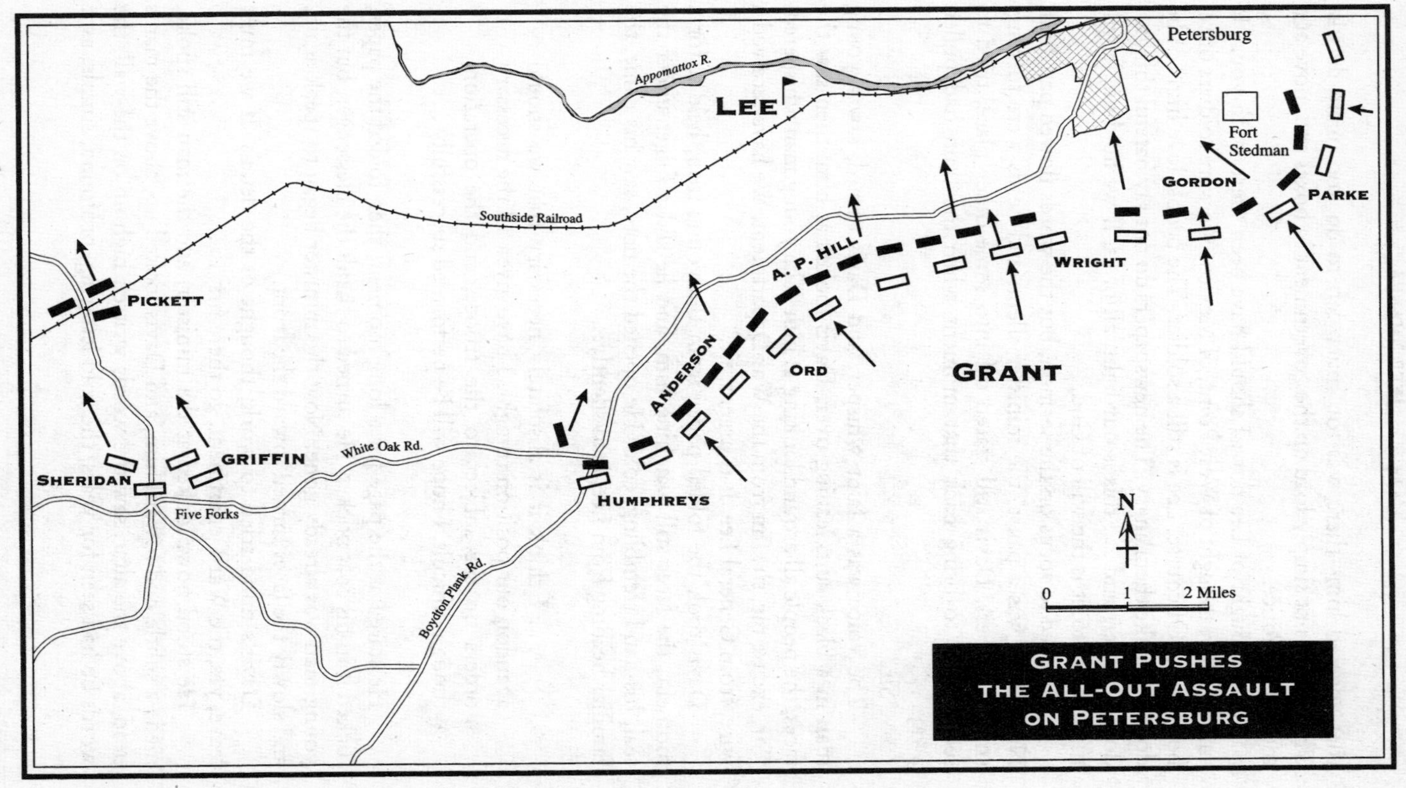
Petersburg
Appomattox R.
Lee
Southside Railroad
Fort Stedman
Gordon
Parke
Wright
A. P. Hill
Ord
Grant
Anderson
Pickett
Griffin
Sheridan
Five Forks
White Oak Rd.
Humphreys
Boydton Plank Rd.
N
0
1
2 Miles
Grant Pushes
the All-Out Assault
on Petersburg

that angered him—there was too much left to do, too many details. They could not simply load up the government in boxes and move at a moment's notice.

He thought of Lee now: I should have been there, with you. He smiled sadly, thought of West Point, of Mexico. We were soldiers once, both of us. Of course, Lee is still a soldier. The people love him . . . he does not make them angry. The newspapers do not say hateful things. I do not understand . . . this is our fight, all of us. If we hold on, it will turn, it has to, it is the will of God.

He tried to focus on the sermon, but the words flowed past him. Now there was a pause, the minister silent, and heads were turning, small whispers. Davis still stared off into some other place, tried to see Varina, to bring back that moment when the train had pulled away. . . .

"Sir."

The voice was a faint whisper, and Davis turned, saw a young man in a black suit, leaning over. Davis looked at him, then saw the faces, the people all around looking at him. The young man whispered, "Sir, excuse me, sir. I'm from the War Department. We have received a wire, from General Lee. It is urgent, sir."

Davis took the folded paper from the young man, held it for a moment, the faces still watching him, and he slid a finger under the seal, his hand trembling, cold. He opened the note, saw his name, the familiar heading from Lee, read silently:

> . . . I think it is absolutely necessary that we should abandon our position tonight. I have given all the necessary orders on the subject to the troops, and the operation, though difficult, I hope will be performed successfully . . .

He stared at the page for a long moment, then folded the paper, tucked it in his coat pocket. He turned to thank the messenger, but the young man was already gone. Now the minister began to speak again, and slowly the faces turned toward the front.

Davis's mind tried to work, thought of the details. If we must leave, yes, the War Department, go there first . . .

He stood now, looked at the minister, and the man still spoke, made a subtle nod toward him, and Davis looked up, above the man's head, above the altar, saw the words written high up on the wall, the words he had seen for years, the gold lettering, profound, simple, as if for the first time. He understood now it was for *him*, had been sent by God as a message to him.

Peace I leave with you, My Peace I give unto you . . .

He turned slowly, his hand on the end of the pew, felt his head spinning for a moment, steadied himself, then slowly walked up the aisle. Beyond the doors of the church, in the streets, the people were already in motion, the wagons and horses weighed down with the precious memories, the symbols of home, of the cause and the country that was collapsing around them.

MIDNIGHT, APRIL 2, 1865

THEY WOULD COME FOR HOURS, LONG COLUMNS OF MEN AND horses, the guns and wagons, crossing the river on bridges that would not survive, that would be burned quickly once the army was across.

He had done this before, sat on the big horse, high above the banks of a river, watching his army move away from a disaster. He kept it hidden away somewhere, would never dwell on that, the defeats, pulling his army off the field where so many good men had been left behind. He had always remembered going north, the Potomac, the glorious marches by men who knew they were winning. Now the hidden places began to open up, and he remembered moving south, the same big river, after the horrifying day at Sharpsburg, and then, after Gettysburg, watching his battered army from a high bluff, sitting on the big horse in the misery of the rain.

Now they were moving north again, but there was no spirit in the army, the men moving in slow motion, creaking wagons pulled by weak horses. He thought of Davis, all the oratory, *the spirit of the fallen*, the bizarre notion that somehow they could energize the army by calling on the memories of all who had gone. It was a fine emotional theme for the politicians, made for a rousing speech in those places where the war had not yet come. But here, Lee thought, here the *fallen* are greatly missed, and the spirit is hard to find in the men who have lost the leadership, who have lost so much.

They did not see him, moved past under dull lamplight, faces locked forward, moving out of the city they had given up so much to protect. Many of these were Hill's men, the Third Corps, and most did not even know that Longstreet would lead them. Many had no thoughts of being led anywhere at all, that what they did now was only for their own survival.

He had heard from Anderson, finally, knew that Pickett was still with the surviving fragments of his division, that Fitz Lee could still bring horses to the fight. Lee had ordered them to move north as well, to link up with Longstreet and Gordon's men, that a good hard march would take them all to the railroad depot at Amelia Court House.

A line of wagons moved by him, and another column of troops, but there was something different about the sounds, men moving with more speed, even some voices, laughter. There was still a spark in these men, and Lee sat up straight, was surprised, looked for flags, saw now, reflected in the dull yellow of the lanterns, these were Gordon's men. He understood now, these men had not been defeated, had held their ground, held the enemy away for a full day so that the rest of the army could make it to the bridges. There is a difference, he thought. This is . . . another march. He had not thought of that—there would be some who would be happy to leave this place. Of course, there is nothing encouraging, he realized, nothing to build the spirit enduring a siege. Now we are moving out, and the enemy will have to pursue us. He smiled, thought of Gordon. The irony . . . that it would take a man who is not a professional soldier to remind us that there is still the duty, the strategy. We can still succeed. They must pursue us, and they will be vulnerable.

Amelia Court House was a forty-mile march, but once there, the Richmond and Danville Railroad could move them quickly away, southward, to link with Joe Johnston. He did not think of it as the last hope, the desperate move. It was sound strategy, might always have been, if they could have pulled out of Petersburg before. Lee thought of Davis, the pressure to preserve Richmond, thought, No, it was always a mistake. We knew there was no value, the city gave nothing to the army. This could all have happened sooner, we should have *made* it happen sooner. Now we will come together again, and there are fewer of us, but those who march, who still follow their commanders, there is still power in that. He knew that Ewell was coming from Richmond, had been instructed to go to Amelia as well. Ewell brought what remained of Longstreet's men, with as much of the home guard as were able, and even some naval units, sailors who had burned their own ships and were taking their fight across the land. Once they united at Amelia, the trains would be waiting for them, great long cars of food, and then they would be strong again, would move on the railroad toward Danville, toward North Carolina. And if Grant continues to pursue us, he thought, we will look for the opportunity, and we will hit him hard in the soft place, drive him back to these cities he holds as meaningless trophies of war.

There was a great rumble, and a bright flash of light, and he squinted, tried to see, the fiery blast shaking the ground. The men on the bridge turned, and there was a cheer. Lee thought, the ammunition, the depots. There were explosions echoing all across the town now, and far to the east the big Federal guns began to open up, a response to activity the Federal commanders could see. The sky was now streaked with bright light, bursts of red and orange, small pops and thunderous booms. There were flames now, patches of fire scattered through the town. Lee did not look at that, gazed up instead, at the billowing smoke reflecting the great flashes of light.

He thought of George Washington, his great hero, the friend of his father, thought of the statue in Richmond, the tall dark bronze, where he used to go and just sit. He had often thought of Washington, the struggle for independence, what the man had endured to see it happen. The statue will survive, he thought, they will not destroy it, even those who would burn and loot the city would not do that. I would like to see that again, take that walk along the wide street and sit in the small park across the road, and just . . . talk to him. He would understand what we are doing here, what this army must still do. We are still fighting for the same things, there is no difference now. The fight is not over until we say it is over, and these troops still have the spirit for the fight, even in the worst of times, something George Washington would have understood.

The sharp blasts from the enemy shells and the slow rumbling fires from the exploding munitions still lit the sky, and he stared up, marveled at the glory of that, thought, It looks like a celebration, Independence Day.

The echoing thunder now fell slowly into a rhythm, a steady roll of drums. He turned the horse, his mind holding the bright and terrible images, and moved away from the bridge, out on the dark road, the road filled with his army, marching again to the sound of drums.

44. LEE

April 4, 1865

THERE COULD BE NO SLOWING DOWN, NO DELAY IN THE MARCH. Lee expected some pursuit, but the great Federal mass converging behind him in Petersburg was not yet on the move. On the left flank, down toward the river, Sheridan's cavalry picked and punched at him all day, but the assaults were more of an annoyance than anything significant.

They moved on roads that had not felt the marching of an army before, good roads, a network that fanned out to the west. Lee ordered the wagons and most of the artillery to move on a separate route, a parallel route above the army, so the foot soldiers would not be held back by the slow-moving horses. The goal was still Amelia, and that meant they would have to cross the river again. Once out beyond Petersburg, the Appomattox made a sharp turn northward. Amelia was below the river, and Lee sent specific word to each column of troops, to Longstreet and Gordon and Ewell, where they would cross the river, where the precious bridges should still be in place.

He rode with Longstreet's command, led a long column of troops in eerie silence. Longstreet had moved ahead, securing the crossing at a place called Goode's Bridge. Lee rode beside his own staff, a few of Longstreet's aides and a man who carried the flag of Hill's Third Corps.

He knew Gordon was behind them, bringing up the rear of the march. It was not planned that way for any good reason, except that Gordon had been farther from the bridges in Petersburg. But Gordon's men were still marching with a strong step, still carried the high morale, and so, from behind, they would prod the rest of the army forward. There were many stragglers now. The spirit of Gordon's men

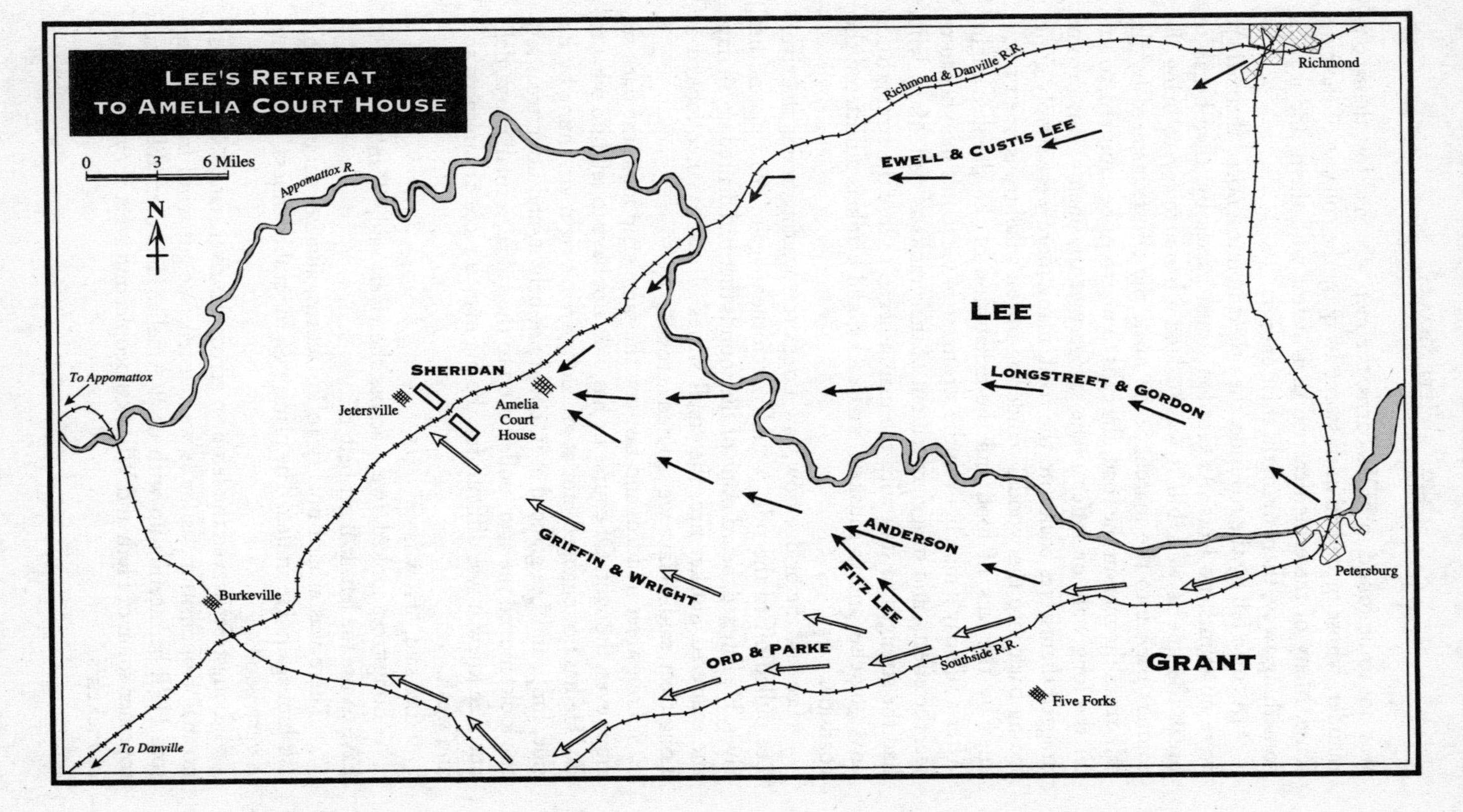
LEE'S RETREAT
TO AMELIA COURT HOUSE
0
3
6 Miles
N
Richmond
Richmond & Danville R.R.
EWELL & CUSTIS LEE
Appomattox R.
LEE
LONGSTREET & GORDON
To Appomattox
SHERIDAN
Jetersville
Amelia
Court
House
ANDERSON
Petersburg
GRIFFIN & WRIGHT
FITZ LEE
Burkeville
ORD & PARKE
Southside R.R.
GRANT
Five Forks
To Danville

was not to be found in Hill's corps, the men who had lost their commander, whose pride had been swept away by the collapse of their defense. Many of these men carried their defeat with them, and it took something away, their strength, their energy.

As men fell by the roadside, the others in line ignored them; there were no taunts, no jeers. As Gordon's men passed by, they began to break the line as well, but it was to lend a hand, to try to bring the soldiers back into the march. Some made the effort, inspired by the talk from the men in the road, the calls to march or be captured, to suffer the long walk or suffer at the savagery of the enemy. But if some dragged themselves back into the road, many more were simply gone, fading back into the woods, wandering off on small trails, men weakened by the lack of food and the exhaustion of the sleepless night. After a full day's march, even the strongest of Gordon's men began to feel the effects, and stragglers fell out of their ranks as well. Many who had the strength to stay with the march began to lose the strength for anything else, and so muskets, knapsacks, and blankets all littered the roadside.

Lee saw the bridge now, saw Longstreet waiting beside the river. Lee pulled off to the side, would watch them again, crossing another river. He listened, heard none of the sounds that had drifted up all day, the scattered musket fire, the small waves of cavalry. Lee looked at Longstreet, said, "Have we scouted across?"

Longstreet nodded, and Lee saw the same grim look, the dark serious eyes, thought, Of course he has, I do not have to tell him what to do. He has not changed, not at all. Longstreet's right arm hung by his side, limp, and Lee glanced at it, could not help it, and Longstreet saw the look, moved the arm, pulled it up to the saddle, a small show, defiant. Lee knew it was difficult for the big man, a piece of him now soft and weak.

Lee said, "How is it?"

Longstreet looked away, across the river, said, "Can't write . . . have to use the left. It'll get better."

There was a hard finality to his words, and Lee thought, Don't ask him again. He smiled. The pride, yes, the stubbornness. Good, that is very good.

Longstreet waved the left arm across the river, said, "We're clear, no major opposition, as far as we can tell. We got word from Anderson. He'll be meeting up with us at Amelia. He's been able to gather together some of Heth and Wilcox's people, and what they could find of Pickett's."

Lee was surprised at that, had heard nothing from below the river. He said, "Do we know how many? What strength?"

There was urgency in the question, and Longstreet looked at him, said, "Not too sure. But there's a fair number. Maybe as many as we have here."

Lee felt a charge, a spark running through him, thought, If that is true . . . we are stronger still. "Are you certain of that?"

Longstreet nodded, said, "According to Anderson . . ."

"That's very good, very good indeed. That means we have nearly thirty thousand muskets . . . and Ewell, he must have . . . several thousand." He looked at Longstreet, said, "That is very good news. I did not expect to find that much strength, once we left the city."

Longstreet pulled the small pipe out of his pocket, and both men turned, watched the column of troops moving across the small bridge. Longstreet said, "I am not sure we can call it . . . strength. I am not sure how many men can be considered effective."

Lee watched the men marching by, and there were few cheers, the men staring straight ahead, slow and mechanical. He said, "They need to be fed. When we reach Amelia, there will be time." He looked around, out toward the south, then back to the east. "General Grant should be pressing us, not just cavalry. And he is not. Surely, he can't be satisfied with just capturing the city."

Longstreet held the pipe in his teeth, said, "No, I expect Sam Grant is moving. Sheridan's not going to sit still either." He waved the pipe, pointed to the south. "They know where we're going. They have to know if we reach the railroad, if we can get to Danville, they have a big problem."

Lee nodded. "Then we cannot allow them to stop us. We must keep moving. We have a full day's march on them. Once we reach Amelia, get these men fed . . . all those people can do is chase us."

HE COULD SEE THE COLUMNS OF BLACK SMOKE, HEARD THE LOW whistle echoing through the woods, rode now up a short rise. He could see the small buildings, the one small steeple, and out to one side, a long row of great black boxes, the freight cars of the blessed supply trains.

He had sent word specifically to Richmond, sent the wire straight to the commissary commissioners—*send the rations*—and there was nothing polite or formal; it was not a pleasant request. It would be the last of the supply trains to leave Richmond, the last way out before the city fell into Federal hands. The food was warehoused there, had been slowly accumulated in anticipation of feeding troops that would still be stationed there. But those troops, Ewell's ragged mismatched command, had made the long march, six thousand men who would soon reach Amelia, joining the rest of the army. Lee had received no reply from the commissary people, but now he could see it for himself, saw another small engine, a belch of black smoke, coming from the northeast, slowly grinding to a halt at the small depot.

The word had passed back along the column, and as they came closer to Amelia, the men picked up the pace, knew that once this day's march was over, there would finally be something to eat.

Now he could hear the men moving up behind him, a low hum of voices, and he glanced back, saw them looking out at the trains, heard one man raise his hands, shout, "Praise God!" The man saw Lee, smiled, said, "Praise General Lee!"

Lee nodded, realized the man had no musket, was carrying nothing at all, and he wanted to say something, but the column moved past quickly, and there were more sounds, some directed toward him. But he did not hear, focused instead on the men themselves, felt his chest tighten, a small cold stab in his gut. He saw that many of them had shed the weight, had made the march on empty stomachs by lightening the load. Many of his soldiers did not have muskets.

The orders were given, and the men began to fill the open fields, some finding a soft place in the thick grass, simply dropping down, ignoring the directions of the officers, the call to stack arms, to stay in line. Lee moved the horse down the rise, toward the town, saw Longstreet approaching, moving slowly up the hill, away from the small buildings. Lee rode up beside him, and Longstreet was staring at him with a deep gloom, then looked at the ground, said nothing. Lee did not stop, moved on toward the depot, saw cavalry, men on thin horses, gathering along the railcars. Lee rode up toward the tracks, saw an officer sitting on a horse, looking up at one man standing in the open doorway of the car.

The soldier did not yet see Lee, said, "Yee howdy, Captain! We got all the ammunition we're ever gonna need. And not one damned thing to eat!"

Lee moved toward the officer, and the man removed his hat, said, "General Lee! Uh, sir . . . this ain't exactly what we was expectin' to find."

Lee climbed down from his horse, moved to the railcar, looked at the soldier, who stared at him with wide eyes. Lee said nothing, reached up, and the man extended a hand, helped Lee into the car. Now Lee could see the piles of boxes, the neat stacks of cloth bags, wooden crates. He took a step forward, leaned down, saw the car was packed with powder, munitions, shot and shell for the big guns. He looked at the man, said, "This is just one. . . . The others, there must be . . ."

The man was nervous now, shook his head. "No, sir. All like this one."

Lee felt a hot fire swell up the back of his neck, turned, jumped down from the car, staggered, and the captain was down now, stepped forward quickly to help him, but Lee straightened, held the man away. He felt sick, his stomach clenching into a hard knot, his throat clamping down hard. He walked to the next car, looked inside, saw the same cargo, one cloth sack split open, black gunpowder spread out on the wooden planks of the floor. He turned, leaned against the side of the railcar.

The cavalry officer said quietly, "You all right, sir? Can I get you something?"

Lee stared ahead, said, "How are we . . . we cannot feed the men. They knew that . . . and they sent me gunpowder."

The captain said nothing, saw a horseman moving through the depot, made a quick motion to the man to come forward.

Lee did not hear the man coming, and suddenly there was a hand on his shoulder and Lee turned. It was Taylor, who said, "There are no rations, sir."

Lee nodded, said nothing.

Taylor was angry, said, "It is treachery, sir! Just like before . . ."

Lee stepped away from the train, moved to the horse, climbed up, sat heavily in the saddle. He looked at the cavalry captain, said in a slow, quiet voice, "Thank you for your assistance."

The man saluted, looked at Taylor, said something Lee could not hear. Taylor moved close to the horse. "Sir," he said, "we will send out the wagons to all the farms around here. There has to be something . . . the people will not deprive their army."

Lee took a deep breath, felt the hot pain in his throat give way, and he nodded again, said, "Yes, Colonel. See to it. Spare no effort. Prepare an order . . . no, a request. We need anything that can be provided."

He turned the horse, moved through the depot, rode close to the tracks, looked into each car, all of them, could not ride away from the trains without seeing it all for himself. He did not pause, moved slowly by each one, saw that every one was filled with the tools and the fuel of war. He passed the last car, turned the horse toward the camps of the men. I do not understand this, he thought, there could have been no confusion. He thought of Taylor's word, *treachery,* but it had not been like that, not since Northrop had been removed, but what explanation could there be? No, it was just . . . a message. God has denied us. I do not understand.

He rode back up the hill, toward the field where more of the army was spreading out, the men still anticipating the relief from the weakness, from the awful emptiness. He could not look at them, at the faces, thought still of Richmond, could see it now in his mind, men in blue adding to their celebration, digging through the great warehouses stacked high with the food that could save his army.

45. GRANT

April 5, 1865

He had spent the night in Petersburg, the staff choosing a pleasant, modest house in the nearly deserted town. Lincoln had come to him there, a short happy visit, but was gone now, had gone back toward City Point. Grant then began the ride with his army, in pursuit of Lee's retreat.

He was west of the city, moving out on the well-worn roads, when the courier reached him, the dispatch simple and direct. Richmond was captured, had been nearly as deserted as Petersburg. The first blue troops into the city had found the last remnants of a violent and destructive departure. Some had made the decision that nothing of value would be left behind, others had simply grabbed whatever was there for the taking, and often that included liquor. Most of the citizens had fled, but they were the people who truly hoped to return. To many it was an escape from the emotion, not from the Yankees. Many simply could not bear to watch the city occupied by the men in blue. As the town emptied, the mobs had taken over, and stores, offices, and warehouses were looted. Many were burning, most from simple arson. Along the waterfront the destruction was different, the fires deliberate and necessary, the gunboats and waterfront storage sheds destroyed by the last of the rebel troops, the horrible duty of burning your own so the enemy can make no use of it.

When the Federal troops moved in, there was no fight, no opposition. The few townspeople who remained stayed mostly indoors, and in the streets there was a strange celebration, mostly Negroes, slaves and free, the people who understood as much as anyone what the fall of this city would mean.

Grant read the dispatch with regret, thought, I wish Lincoln was still here. I wish I could see his face.

Of course, Lincoln would know by now, probably knew before he did. And he knew Lincoln would go there, would have to see it for himself. Grant understood that, did not share the apprehension of some of the others, that Lincoln's life would be in danger. Yes, there could still be stragglers and deserters, men crouching low on rooftops, still determined to strike out at the enemy. If Lincoln were there, out in the open, walking the streets, he could be an irresistible target, and anything could happen. But it will not happen, he thought, because of the man himself, the message he would give to anyone who still remained, the newspaper perhaps, anyone who might represent the government of the state of Virginia.

There had been a movement already, reasonable men who looked to the future, to the mechanism for bringing Virginia back to the Union. Lincoln had encouraged that, had no intention of continuing the war when the shooting stopped, had no patience for those in Congress or the newspapers in the North who insisted on revenge, on a policy of punishment, the recklessness of a hostile relationship with those who had created the rebellion. Lincoln did not fear the streets of Richmond, especially if the cavalry and naval guard kept a sharp lookout. Grant knew Lincoln would find a way, get the message to those who held the authority, communicate that they were still part of the United States. As long as Lincoln was President, it would be as simple as that.

Grant rode farther west now, below the Appomattox River, stayed close to Edward Ord's command, the troops who had once been under Butler. The columns marched along the Southside Railroad, and all along the tracks he saw the workers ripping up one side. But it was not destruction, it was repair, adjusting the rails to fit the gauge of the Federal cars. The quartermasters had insisted, and Grant authorized the work, as long as it did not slow the march of the rest of the army. He did not believe it was really necessary, knew it was a precaution against failure. Only if Lee escaped, only if the war was to last for many months yet, would this army need the railroads.

There was no reason for him to stay close to Petersburg. The war had left that place behind, was moving away again, to a new place, new ground, where the fight would still have to be made. He had given the new orders, but the commanders already knew, the target was the rebel army, that wherever Lee went, they would go.

Much of the cavalry had moved up above the river, kept a close watch on the direction Lee was moving, but there were no surprises.

Grant knew now about Lee's disaster at Amelia, and Federal scouts and small cavalry units were following the wagons that Lee scattered into the countryside. Many were simply plucked up, the drivers captured along with their small weak escorts, and all told the same story, how they had been sent on a desperate search for food, for anything the farm country could still provide.

Whether or not Lee could feed his army, he could not stay long at Amelia. The key was the railroad, and that left only one route for Lee to follow—southwest, toward Danville.

THEY WERE RIDING THROUGH DARK WOODS, A DANGEROUS route close to the camps of the enemy. There had not been time for a formal escort, and it was not the place for it. The commotion of a large security force would have certainly brought on more attention than Grant wanted. Sheridan had sounded urgent, sent a scout in a rebel uniform across miles of open country, bringing the message straight to Grant's headquarters. The message was of troop movements, positions, but it was the last few words that brought Grant and his small escort now into the dark woods: *I wish you were here yourself.*

Sheridan was much closer to Amelia, his cavalry still on the far west of the Federal position, leading the way in the race to cut off Lee's retreat. The Fifth Corps, Griffin's command now, was spread out across the one road that ran out of Amelia to the southwest, the road that ran parallel to the Danville Railroad. Grant had left Ord behind with simple instructions: keep moving. By morning Ord's men would be at Burkeville, also on the Danville line, and so even if Lee somehow ripped through the strength of the Fifth Corps and Sheridan's horsemen, the way would still be blocked.

Grant could see small fires now, flickers of light spread out across a wide field. He felt relief, thought, Finally, we're here. But they did not stop, moved farther, beyond the vast sea of sleeping men, and Grant realized with a quick flash of excitement: Those are not our men, they are the campfires of the enemy.

There were only a dozen troopers with him, led by Sheridan's scout, a grisly looking man named Campbell. They had ridden for nearly four hours, could not stay on main roads, had to rely on Campbell's skills and his memory for faint trails in dim moonlight. Grant rode just behind Porter, the young man silent and nervous, and suddenly the small column halted, held up by the quiet hand of the scout.

Campbell rode back toward Grant, then slowly eased into the woods, his head low, probed for a long moment, then came back into the trail, moved farther back, still searching for something. Grant thought, I hope you are as good at this as Sheridan says you are. Grant could see a small movement now, saw Porter pull his revolver, discreet, ready. Grant could not see the gun in the darkness, but knew Porter held it tightly against his chest. Porter did not trust this strange man, and Grant smiled at that, had known Campbell for a long time, knew he was Sheridan's most trusted scout. He could say nothing to Porter, silence was still essential, but he thought, It's all right, Colonel. He's not going anywhere. There is no treachery here. Now Campbell emerged from the woods again, moved toward the front of the horsemen, motioned to the right, and then ducked again into the woods. The column followed, and Grant saw Porter's revolver go back into its holster. He waited for Porter to move into the woods, then gently spurred the horse and followed the rest of his escort.

The trees parted and there was a visible trail. Campbell turned in the saddle, looked back down the line, motioned to Grant and pointed ahead to a panorama of flickering light. Suddenly there were men, moving quickly out of the shadows, appearing all around them, the sharp sound of metal, weapons cocked, then the column abruptly halted. Grant could see one man looking straight at him, pointing the gun at his face, a carbine. These were Sheridan's men.

The man who blocked the trail said in a low voice, "Well, what we got here?"

There was a lantern now, and another man carried the light forward. Grant began to move the horse slowly to the front of the column, could see the first man was a sergeant, and the man said, "Well, lookee here! We got a reb escorting a dozen prisoners, or we got a dozen men escorting one rebel prisoner. Either way, reb, you must be some seriously important man."

Campbell looked around at Grant, who moved beside him, and now Porter began to move as well, and on both sides the carbines were raised a bit higher.

The sergeant said, "Whoa, easy there. No hurry boys, no one's going anywhere."

Porter said, "Gentlemen, we are here to see General Sheridan. This is General Grant's party. We are here at the request of General Sheridan."

The sergeant looked now at Campbell, laughed. "Well, now,

would *you* be the commanding general? Or are you just his chief of staff?"

There were small laughs, and now Grant leaned forward, took off his hat, said, "Good evening, Sergeant. I am entirely dependent on your professionalism as a soldier. I can offer little except that you recognize me. This is understandably . . . an unusual situation."

The sergeant moved closer, glanced at the man with the lantern, who raised the light higher. Grant leaned over farther, thought, The light, catch the shoulder straps, the stars. The sergeant looked him over, then stepped back, looked again at the rebel uniform, said, "And you would be Mr. Campbell."

Campbell nodded, a slight bow.

The man saluted Grant now, said to the men around them, "Boys, this here is General Grant. I seen you before, sir, crossing the Rapidan River. Mr. Campbell, he's another matter. Don't never look the same way twice."

The carbines were lowered, and Grant said, "Thank you, Sergeant. May we have an escort to General Sheridan?"

The man motioned with his hand, and suddenly two horses appeared, their riders climbing up. The sergeant said, "Just follow these boys, sir. Take you right to him."

The column began to move again, and Grant let out a breath, realized how tense he had been, how easily fate could have made a much different, much more deadly situation.

Porter rode beside him now, said quietly, "Forgive me, sir, I should have been better prepared."

Grant tried to see him in the dark, said, "Prepared for what, Colonel?"

"To protect you, sir. They could have been rebels."

Grant smiled, said, "Mr. Porter, if they had been rebels, we might have been able to spur ourselves around and skedaddle away, and maybe most of us would have made it. If you had done anything to *protect* me with those fellows back there, we'd be dead. Those carbines are seven-shot repeaters."

Porter said nothing, and now they were moving past long rows of sleeping men, the fading embers of small fires. Men began to stir, and Grant looked out over the ground, could see faces coming out from under blankets, a slow ripple of activity, men coming awake in greater numbers.

One man close by said, "Why, there's the Old Man! Boys, this means business!"

SHERIDAN HAD BEEN WAITING FOR THEM, CERTAIN THAT GRANT would answer the request. He'd even waited on his own evening meal.

Grant had chewed on a small piece of burnt roast beef, watched with a hidden smile as Porter and some of the others gulped down a vast pile of boiled chicken, a slab of fat beef ribs.

Now he was riding through the dark again, held a fresh cigar in his teeth, something he could not do on the long ride. But this time he was with Sheridan, and it was a short ride across a field of tobacco. Beyond the field he could see the lanterns in a cluster, a well-lit hub of activity, horses and men moving around a small cabin. Sheridan dismounted first, and the aides stepped back, almost by instinct, had observed Sheridan's hot temper too many times. Grant dismounted, and they began to recognize him. Salutes went up, small greetings. Sheridan did not answer, moved by them, and Grant followed, moved past a man who held the door open, the dull orange light barely filling the small room. Grant looked down, saw Meade lying flat on a small bed, a white shirt, hatless.

Grant moved quickly, leaned down, said, "General Meade . . . I heard you were ill."

Meade looked at him with a flash of anger, but held it, clamped it down, said, "Of course . . . yes. I am ill. I'm flat on my back, while out there Lee's army is waiting for us."

Sheridan grunted, said, "Sir, that's why . . . sir, no, I do not believe General Lee is waiting for us at all." He looked around the room. "A map . . . where's a map?"

Meade raised an arm, pointed toward a small desk, and an aide moved that way, but Sheridan was faster, pushed past the man, grabbed the paper, held it up in the lamplight, said, "Turn up the lamp, I can't see."

The aide looked at Meade, and Meade closed his eyes, said weakly, "Fine. Turn up the damned light."

Grant was still looking at Meade, sweat on his brow, the face drawn, ghostly. He said, "No. We can use this light. Lay the map out, let's have a look."

Sheridan grunted again, spread the map on the desk, said, "Lee has dug in all around Amelia. He has moved some people out this way, drawn up in a line against us. But he is not going to wait for us. He has to keep moving. General Meade has a different opinion. I will not speak for you, General."

Meade sat up now, a groaning struggle, said, "We should wait for all the troops to get up. The Fifth Corps is facing Lee now. The Sixth and Second should be here, ready to move, by tomorrow."

Sheridan said, "And we may advance toward Amelia just in time to see Lee riding away over the next hill."

Grant scanned the map, said, "General Ord will be at Burkeville by tomorrow. There is no way that Lee can use the railroad now. He is cut off from Danville. His only option is to fight . . . or keep moving. If I was in his place, I would be moving . . . right now."

He straightened, looked at Meade, who was on his back again, the small piece of strength now gone. Grant said, "General Meade, the cavalry will continue to move to the west. The infantry will divide, moving west and north. I want to cut him off, get in front of him, not just follow him. There is nothing to be gained by preparing an attack at Amelia. The fight will come when he has no choice but to face us."

Meade nodded, said nothing, and Grant knew he was resigned to it, the illness draining the argument out of him.

Sheridan was already moving toward the door, impatient, and Grant said, "General Sheridan, may I assume you intend to move your people . . . early?"

Sheridan saluted, said, "Sir . . . with your permission, we are *already* moving!"

46. LEE

April 6, 1865

They had found Sheridan's cavalry blocking the road to Burkeville, but Lee had believed Longstreet's men were strong enough to break through, to push them aside. Danville was becoming more important now than merely as the escape route. There was food there, a huge stockpile, and Lee had sent word for the trains to roll north, to bring the rations to the army.

As Longstreet had pushed down toward Jetersville, to drive off the Federal horsemen, he found not just cavalry, but infantry, the strong lines of the Fifth Corps. Scouts reported the Second Corps was moving to join them, and the Sixth was a short march away. It was clear to Longstreet, and so, to Lee, that the road to Danville was closed. The only line of march was west, the town of Farmville. There the Southside Railroad ran out toward Lynchburg, and Lee had two choices. If they could stay ahead of the Federals, the army could again turn south and try for Danville. Otherwise, they could make use of the last leg of the Southside not in Federal hands, and move the army farther west to Lynchburg.

He had camped near the home of Dick Anderson, another fine old estate that would absorb the effects of the long war. Anderson's wife and children were still there, had prepared as much of a dinner as they could for Lee and his staff the night before.

He had started the army in motion well before dawn, and once it was known that the route would have to be west, there would be no delay, no time to lose. There was still no food for the army; the wagons had come back from their foraging mostly empty. The farmers simply had nothing to give. It was the season for planting, for plowing the new fields, and whatever harvest had been stored from the previous autumn had long been exhausted. A small wagon train had escaped Petersburg, and there was a much larger train that Ewell had put into motion at Richmond, but Lee learned that the Federal cavalry had caught up to both of them, and what was not taken by the enemy had simply been burned.

The tent had been packed away, and he was pacing nervously in the yard, impatient. He saw Taylor, then Venable, coming out of the house, and Lee mounted the horse, the clear signal that it was time to move.

Taylor moved toward his own horse, said, "Sir, we have asked General Anderson's family to remain in the cellar. I told them it could be dangerous for them today."

Lee nodded, had not thought of that, could not think of civilians now. His mind was already out on the road, far out with Longstreet, with the advance of his army.

On the road, the men were already moving. He watched them, and there was no cheering, the only sounds the muffled steps of weary soldiers, their short time for sleep broken by the dull pain of hunger. We had the chance, he thought, the opportunity, a good day's start. But here, we had to stop, to wait, to see what the wagons could bring us. And it cost us a day's march. There can be no delays now, none. Sheridan has good horses, while ours drop away from their own hunger. The animals have it no better than the men.

There was a horseman, moving against the slow tide of troops, and Lee did not recognize the man, an odd sight, a neat uniform, clean, something no one saw anymore. The man had an escort, another unfamiliar face, civilian clothes. Lee sat on the horse, waited, and the officer saluted him, and now Lee could see the man's face. It was Isaac St. John.

St. John was now the commissary general, having replaced the incompetent Northrop two months before. St. John had made his reputation for efficiency by good management of the Mining and Nitre Department. Where Lucius Northrop's mismanagement had often left the army hungry, St. John's department always kept the ammunition boxes full. In the weeks before the final collapse of Richmond, St. John had done what he could to salvage something of the commissary. Lee had no reason to doubt the man's good intentions, or his capability. It was just too little too late.

St. John saluted Lee, shifted his weight in the saddle, a painful reminder that he had rarely been in the field.

Lee said, "General St. John, I did not expect to see anyone from your department." There was sarcasm in his voice, and Lee regretted it immediately. He looked down, said, "I assumed you might have accompanied the president."

St. John said, "No, sir. I am not certain where the president is, though I believe he made it to Danville. I came here . . . to find out where you wanted the rations."

Lee looked up, stared at the man in the dim lamplight. "What rations?"

"We have eighty thousand rations waiting at Farmville. I had ordered them to Danville, but when we realized the way was blocked, I sent them on the Southside out to Farmville. Farmville is about . . . eighteen miles from here, sir."

"I know where Farmville is, General. We are moving out that way now. Are you certain?"

St. John seemed surprised at the question, said, "Oh yes, sir. I was wondering if you wanted me to load some wagons and send the rations in this direction."

There was a simple matter-of-factness to the man's words that made Lee smile. St. John showed no signs of nervousness, of the strain of what was happening all around them. Lee shook his head, said, "No. Not yet. The Federals have a large cavalry force, certainly moving toward Farmville. We may be in little more than a race. If you send wagons this way, they may be captured. We will do what we can to get to Farmville."

St. John nodded, shifted his weight again, said, "I did not realize the urgency . . . I had best return to Farmville myself." He looked out toward the road, at the march of the troops. "Godspeed, sir."

Lee nodded, looked at the slow steps of the men, thought, Godspeed, indeed.

THE CAVALRY FANNED OUT TO BOTH FLANKS, WOULD MAKE whatever stand they could against the pressure from Sheridan's horses. Longstreet's men led the march, and Lee knew he did not have to prod him, there would be no need for him to stay up front to keep the column moving. In the center, Ewell's mixed command would move behind Anderson, and behind them was much of the artillery and what remained of the wagon train. The wagons would again be sent on a parallel route, a long circling route to the north, to take them out of harm's way and to clear the road for the more rapid movement of the men. In the rear, John Gordon's troops would hold off any threat from behind, and once the wagon train was out of the way, Gordon would move up and connect with Ewell and Anderson.

Lee had ridden all along the line, tried to see into the faces of the men, to give them something, a piece of himself, some of the cheer that they always seemed to find when they saw him. But the faces were down, staring at nothing, the steps slow and plodding, and all along the road men were falling out, simply collapsing. He moved the horse carefully, the roadside littered again with muskets. There was little else, few blankets, few knapsacks remained. The men had lost all need for comforts, for any personal items that would only require more energy to carry. Without blankets the men would sleep on the ground. Without muskets they could not fight.

He had seen Heth, then Wilcox, Longstreet's commanders, holding their men together as best they could, the numbers dropping by the hour. Now Mahone passed by him, and Lee nodded, smiled, thought of the nickname, Little Billy, another of the men from VMI. Lee had promoted him on the spot for Mahone's brilliant defense after the Crater explosion, and now Mahone commanded Anderson's old division, troops that had been in every major fight since Malvern Hill.

There were some cheers now, a small number of old veterans, hard men who simply treated this as another march. Lee felt some of the energy coming back, saw hats going up, the affection as it had always been. Mahone had stopped briefly, but now was moving on, keeping his men in motion, keeping them tight against the columns in front.

Lee could see a few guns now, small field pieces, horsemen. He rode back that way, crested a small rise, saw men scattered down along the road, some crawling away, moving into the shade of tall trees. He sat straight, could hear it now, a hard roll of thunder, the sounds of a fight echoing in the east. He had expected to see the column of troops, Pickett's men, and Anderson's and Ewell's, but felt a sickness growing in his gut, looked at a road scattered with stragglers. The sounds were louder, rolling over the low hills, and he spurred the horse, began to move across the countryside, dropped down into a small gully, then up another short hill. He stopped the horse, could hear musket fire, great rolling chatter, and he spurred the horse again, rode up that way, thought, The wagon train.

He knew he was moving to the north, far above the main road, saw small creeks, swampy patches of woods. He climbed another rise, the ground falling away in front of him, a wide hill dropping down into tall pine trees, a small creek. The fight was all along the creek. Beyond, along the far rise, he could see great columns of smoke, small patches of flame. He raised his field glasses, tried to focus, saw it was Gordon's men, a rolling assault coming all along Gordon's lines. Lee stared, lowered the glasses, thought, The rear guard . . .

He turned the horse, rode along the crest of the ridge, saw officers coming toward him from the main road, saw Mahone, staff officers. Lee pointed toward the road, yelled, "Where is Anderson? Where is Ewell?"

Mahone reined up the horse, could see the smoke from Gordon's fight, said, "I don't know, sir. They were supposed to be close up behind us."

Lee felt the anger breaking through, could hold it back no longer, said, "Well, yes, General, I know where they are *supposed* to be!"

There was a small group of cavalry now, and they rode along the crest of the hill, the men staring down into the fight along the creek. Lee looked for an officer, saw a young man, a major, said, "Who is that? Who is engaging General Gordon?"

The man saluted, surprised, did not expect to see Lee, said, "Infantry, sir! Looks like the Second Corps, sir!"

Lee stared down the long slope, thought, Infantry? I had thought cavalry perhaps. How did infantry get so close to our rear . . . and where *is* their cavalry?

To the south, near the main road, there was a faint sound of muskets, and Lee turned the horse, said to Mahone, "General, ride with me. We have to find General Ewell."

They moved along the crest of the hill, and Lee saw Venable now, riding hard, waving at him. Venable pulled up, steadied himself on the horse, was breathing heavily, said, "General Lee . . . the wagons have been captured. The enemy's cavalry has broken through the column."

Lee said, "Where is General Ewell? Where is General Anderson?"

Venable shook his head, said, "I don't know, sir. I don't know if they made it across the creek. We have heard nothing." He pointed down the wide hill. "That's Saylor's Creek, sir. There has been a considerable fight there, sir."

Lee turned to Mahone, said, "I may need you, General. This way!"

They rode farther along the crest, then dropped into a shallow depression, climbed up again, and Lee reined the horse, looked down the hill, saw the creek bed snaking through a wide stand of tall pines. Out of the trees, men were flowing in a vast carpet up the hill, wagons without drivers, panicked horses dragging bridles. The men began to fall, collapsing in the open grass, mostly from exhaustion, some with bloody wounds. In the trees below, along the creek, there were scattered pops of musket fire, but the fight was past, whatever had happened to the long column was already done. Lee stared at the great flow of his men, some moving close to him now, men with wild eyes and no muskets, and he felt the horror filling him, the cold stab in his chest, said, in a low voice, "My God . . . has the army been dissolved?"

Mahone said nothing for a moment, the men now moving past them, the ones with enough strength to climb the long hill. Then Mahone shouted at the men, "Turn and fight! Stop . . . fight for General Lee!"

A few faces turned up. Lee saw recognition in their eyes, and some began to gather, to slow the panicked stampede.

Lee looked at Mahone, said, "General, I need you now. We must hold those people back."

Mahone saluted, turned the horse, said, "My men will still fight, sir!" He rode away quickly, and Lee moved down the hill, waving his hat, began to call out to the men, "Soldiers! Fight with me!" Men were moving closer, more now standing, finding their breath.

Lee saw one man holding a battle flag, the man bloody, staggering, and he moved toward him, said, "Here, son, let me. . . ." The man looked at him, dropped to one knee, said nothing, and Lee saw now the face of a child, the sharp eyes, the bright light looking up at him, and the boy released the flag. Lee held it up high, began to wave it, catching the breeze. Now more men fell into line beside him, behind him, and they began to cheer, to yell out his name. He stared below, into the trees, was ready to ride, to move in one hard wave down into the face of the enemy, drive them out, drive them away. The flag was slapping hard around him, catching a sharp gust of wind, the horse staggering to keep straight, and he thought, Yes, we will not be beaten, you cannot take this away from us!

Behind him there was a new sound, men moving over the crest of the hill, a heavy battle line. It was Mahone's men, and all along the hill came the sound of the rebel yell, high and terrible. Suddenly, someone grabbed the flag, and Lee would not let go, looked at the man with hot anger, How dare you . . . saw the face of Mahone.

Mahone still gripped the flag, gave a firm pull, and Lee felt it slip out of his hands. Mahone said, "General, this is *my* job."

THE DAY ENDED WITH THE FEDERAL CAVALRY AND INFANTRY held in check, while Gordon and Mahone slowly backed away. By dark Lee had learned the extent of the disaster at Saylor's Creek. The army had lost nearly eight thousand troops, most of them captured. Many of the commanders had made their escape. But word came to Lee that Dick Ewell had fallen into Federal hands, and then, later in the evening, he learned that most of the Richmond Home Guard had been captured. They now ceased to exist as a fighting unit, would be escorted back toward City Point, along with their commander, Custis Lee. Lee's oldest son was now a prisoner of war.

It was Ewell's mistake that gave the Federals the opportunity to cut through the column of march. The wagon train in front of Gordon had been sent on their northerly detour, but Ewell left no one behind at the intersection to tell Gordon that the wagons were changing direction, no one to tell Gordon not to follow the wagons. Without the crucial instructions, Gordon turned his column, followed the wagon train onto the wrong road.

When Ewell and Anderson slowed their march, to respond to Sheridan's assaults, they did not tell anyone in front of them, did not send word to Mahone, and so the army simply spread out, the column stretching longer, with gaps opening up, large enough for the Federal troops to cut through. The numbers were bad, the losses staggering, but Lee did not focus on that. He had to look instead at what was left, at the army he could still take into a fight.

AS LONGSTREET'S FIRST TROOPS REACHED FARMVILLE, THE blessed rations were put into the grateful hands of starving men. Lee stayed closer to the rear, moved through the scattered troops who still made their way forward. He did not want to hear numbers, had received the reports from staff officers of what was left of the commands, but would not look at them, folded the small pieces of paper and stuffed them into his coat. Most of the commanders were still close by, somewhere, but for many, for Anderson and Pickett, there were no troops left to command.

He rode slowly, thought about his son: I will write Mary. I will have to. They will not harm him, he is too valuable. There is some comfort in that. He knew Rooney was nearby, probably on the flank, riding with his cousin's command. Fitz Lee's cavalry was spread out all over the countryside, rushing to whatever crisis the Federals threw at them, were now gathering together in the same way the infantry was, finding itself, taking the head count, seeing just how much strength they had left.

Lee had seen Rooney earlier that day, and it had been all orders and tactics, the business of command. He knew Robert Jr. was probably up front, near Longstreet, pulling his guns along under Porter Alexander now, guns that could still serve the army. How odd, he thought, the one farthest from the fight, from the war, would be the one captured. Custis was a brilliant engineer, and Lee thought of that, how much alike they were. Lee himself had spent most of his early military service in the Corps of Engineers, knew that his oldest son had the talent for it, but even though Custis had gone to the Point, he was not a soldier, did not have the temperament for it. He was quiet, even shy, nothing like the boisterous Rooney.

The letter was already taking shape in his mind, but Mary would not take it well, no matter how he explained it. Lee knew Custis was clearly her favorite, and Lee was not sure why, thought, He is . . . something like me. But he has also been there, when I have not. She has learned to depend on him. He stared into the darkening trees, past the scattered movement of his men, thought, No, she has never depended on me. There has always been the army, even the early days, the duty always somewhere else, the Carolina coast, St. Louis, the Mississippi River. Then Mexico, the cavalry in Texas, and now . . . something we never could have known. No one had ever believed it would go on like this . . . four years.

It suddenly came to him that he did not know where she was, not exactly. With Richmond now in Federal hands . . . he felt the anxious turn in his gut, forced it away, told himself, No, she is safe. They have been so kind, so many good friends, looking out for her. She has always had that, from the time she was a girl. Then it was her father, now . . . it should be me.

He moved past an open field, the last of the sunlight reflecting on small pieces of motion, men coming out of the woods, still finding the road. He saw one man stop, looking at him, the man shirtless, with no hat, no musket.

The man stared, then said, "Praise God. If I ain't seen Jesus . . . I seen Robert E. Lee."

The man moved slowly away, and Lee felt himself sag, thought,

No, so profane . . . how can they do that? And yet they believe it. They have always believed it. Now look at us, look how few of us there are.

Abruptly, he reached in his pocket, had kept it away long enough, glanced through the brief reports, while there was enough light to see. He thought, The numbers are never good, never, not in any fight, on any ground. We were always up against greater strength. He already knew how many cavalry Fitz Lee had, had heard a brief report, something near three thousand. The infantry was harder to figure, and they were still finding stragglers, men still trying to keep up, dazed, starved. The best estimate was around twelve thousand, mostly under Longstreet and Gordon. There were more men than that, but the reports would emphasize *effectives*, men you could put into a fight. He did not know how many men Grant had, had heard that Ord's people were at Burkeville, and Ord had been above the James, the farthest Federal troops from Petersburg. So if Ord is here, that means . . . *all* of them are here. And that means they are slow. The thought raced across his tired mind, surprised him. They have always been slow. A very big dog, trying to catch a very small cat. He suddenly turned the horse, thought, Yes, that is one thing that has not changed. All we need is time. Even Sheridan's cavalry could only hit us in the middle, not the front.

Gordon had finally been able to pull away from his own fight at Saylor's Creek, would move now up across the Appomattox again, and Mahone would take his men that way as well. Once across the river again . . . he tried to remember the map, did not have it with him. The river is still a great barrier to Grant's people. Once we are across and can burn the bridges, we will have a very good jump on them. We can make the trains at Farmville, move on to Lynchburg.

He rode now toward Longstreet's camp, heard his name, a man calling out, a one man salute, and Lee could not see him, the darkness now deep into the trees. He waved his hat, said aloud, "Rations are at Farmville. You can draw rations at Farmville. Keep moving!"

There were small voices all around him, surprising him, men he could not see, and now he could hear them moving, footsteps in the road, and the word echoed out through the woods, far behind him on the road: *rations!*

APRIL 7, 1865

THE FEDERAL PRESSURE ON GORDON AND MAHONE MADE THEIR crossing of the Appomattox difficult, and Mahone's most important job, to burn the High Bridge before the enemy could seize it, succeeded only halfway. Mahone did set fire to the main bridge, the rail crossing for the Southside, a huge span stretching over a part of the river that was impossible to ford. But the Federal troops came on too quickly, in too much strength, and after a sharp fight, they were able to put out the fire. But worse, what Mahone had failed to do was burn a second bridge, smaller, down below, close to the water. That bridge, designed for wagon traffic, was left undamaged. Humphrey's Second Corps was able to cross immediately, keeping up the pressure behind Gordon and Mahone.

At Farmville, Longstreet camped his men on the north side of the bridges there, prepared to burn them when the last of the army could move across. But with the Federal Second Corps now on the same side of the river, Lee had to keep moving. Below the river, Federal troops under Ord were approaching fast, and so the railcars carrying the food could not stay at Farmville, could not risk being captured. St. John had to move them farther west, out of harm's way. Many of Longstreet's men were still lining up for their first rations in five days when the trains suddenly pulled away.

LEE WAS WITH LONGSTREET, PACING NERVOUSLY. HE HADN'T seen Mahone, knew that he and Gordon were doing their best to hold the Federals away in the rear.

Longstreet was sitting, leaning against a tree, smoking his small pipe. Lee stopped pacing, listened for big guns, the sounds of a fight. Longstreet's camp wagon was nearby. An aide was unloading a trunk, and it fell open with a loud clatter of metal pans.

Lee turned, said, "Quiet! I'm trying to hear!"

There was complete silence in the camp, all faces turning toward the outburst from Lee. Longstreet leaned forward, motioned the aide away.

Lee stared as the man slipped past the wagon, then looked at the faces, turning from him now, averting their glances. Lee took off his hat, rubbed his hand slowly over the top of his head, said to Longstreet, "We have done nothing right. They should have burned that

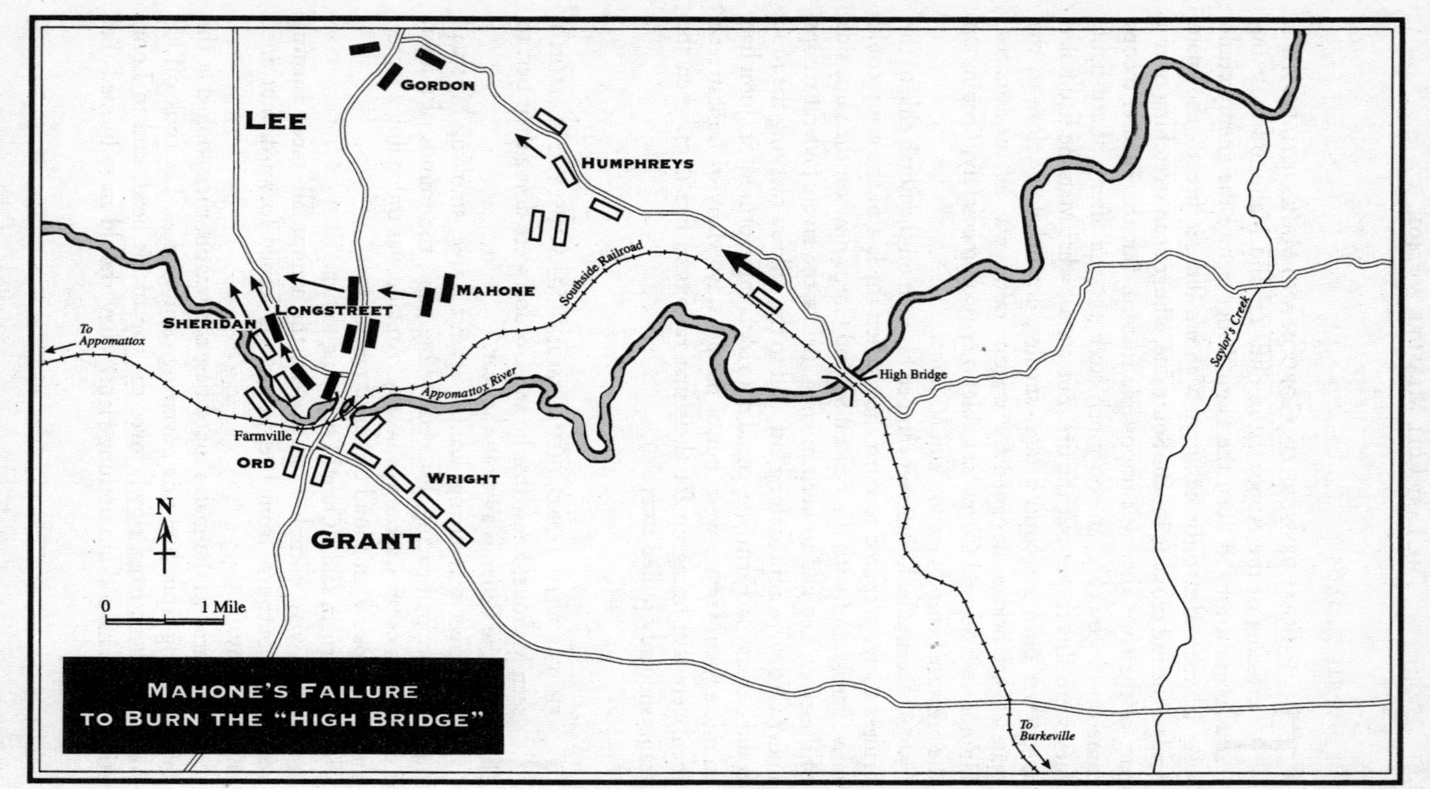

MAHONE'S FAILURE TO BURN THE "HIGH BRIDGE"

bridge. We would . . . they should have . . ." He stopped, the words choked away.

Longstreet said, "Sir, please, sit down. Here . . ." He reached for a small camp chair, set it upright.

Lee moved to the chair and slowly sat down. Resting his arms on his knees, he looked at the ground, then gazed beyond the matted grass, staring deep into some dark place. There was a quiet moment, then he said, "If they were not on this side of the river, we would have escaped."

Longstreet nodded, said, "We have still escaped. There's nothing west of us. There's a big bunch of those boys south of the river, but they can't come across, not for a long while yet. We move quick, we can make it up to the next station, the rations will be there, and all we have to do is keep those boys behind us from making trouble."

Lee looked at him, saw a smile, thought, Something is . . . wrong with him. I have not seen a smile on him since . . . longer than I can recall. He said, "General Longstreet, your mood puzzles me. We are in a serious predicament here."

Longstreet tapped the pipe on the tree behind him, lit it slowly, said, "When have we *not* been in a predicament?"

Lee was still confused, thought, This is the man whose gloom is legendary, and now . . . with the enemy hard on us from two sides, he smiles.

Longstreet saw the look, said, "Sir, we can only do what is in our power. It is still in our power to reach Lynchburg. We might still find an opportunity to reach Danville. If we can keep moving, keep the enemy behind us . . . Gordon's men are still putting up a fight. These boys here . . . Yankee cavalry isn't going to stop them. We make it to the next station, feed them, we have a clear shot to Lynchburg. And *that* will give Sam Grant a problem."

There were horses, a small group of couriers riding into the camp, eyes searching for Lee. Lee looked up, saw Marshall step forward. One horseman saluted Marshall, said something, then reached down, handed Marshall a piece of paper.

Marshall turned toward Lee and, hesitating, moved close and held out the paper. "Sir," he said, "a message has come through General Mahone's lines, sir. It is from General Grant."

Lee took the paper, saw the wax seal, slid his finger slowly under the flap, broke the wax and opened the page. He read slowly, absorbed the words:

General:

The results of the last week must convince you of the hopelessness of further resistance on the part of the Army of Northern Virginia in this struggle. I feel that it is so, and regard it as my duty to shift from myself the responsibility of any further effusion of blood, by asking you the surrender of that portion of the Confederate States Army known as the Army of Northern Virginia.

Very Respectfully, Your Obedient Servant,

U. S. Grant, Lieutenant-General, Commanding Armies of the United States

Lee looked at Longstreet, handed him the paper.

Longstreet read it, handed it back, shook his head and said, "Not yet."

Lee looked up at Marshall. "Colonel, bring me the map. I want to see how far we still have to move to reach . . ." He looked at Longstreet. ". . . the next station, you said, General?"

Longstreet held the pipe in his mouth, said, "Appomattox."

47. GRANT

APRIL 7, 1865

IT WAS NEARLY MIDNIGHT, AND HE'D SPENT THE EVENING ON THE porch of a hotel, the only one in the small town of Farmville. The army was gathering still, and by now word that Grant was here, with them, had fueled a party, a bonfire, men cheering, singing; men exhausted by a long day's march, but not yet ready to let go of the emotion. It was clear to all of them, whether they had seen the enemy or not, whether they'd had any part in the fight, that this army was moving fast and furiously toward something momentous, something grand and joyous.

Grant sat on the porch, alongside Rawlins and Edward Ord. Men were still marching by, some coming into the town for the first time. A few were breaking ranks, moving toward the bonfire, some carrying knots of fat pine, lit now into great torches. The men were cheering Grant as they passed the hotel, and the songs were a strange mix of bad voices and disconnected melody, each unit singing something different, the sounds overlapping into a roar of noise. One group now stepped into the light, the odd uniforms of the Zouaves, the red trousers lit by the light of the great fire. They were singing especially loud, "John Brown's body lies a molderin' in the grave . . ."

Rawlins said, "Inspiring! Indeed, inspiring! 'John Brown's Body' is nearly a hymn to our boys."

Grant listened for a moment, then said, "Is that a song?"

Rawlins seemed surprised, said, "Why, yes, sir. That very song, there. 'John Brown's Body' . . . surely you know that one, sir."

Grant frowned, thought of Julia. The same thing would come from her, the scolding at his ignorance. Grant listened again, shook his head. "No, afraid not. I know two songs. One's 'Yankee Doodle.' " He paused, thought a moment, could recall some very poor harmony in a disreputable bar in San Francisco, the indiscreet words still lodged in his memory. He was suddenly embarrassed, glanced at Rawlins, said, "The other one isn't."

The Zouaves were past now, and the sounds of the great salute were winding down. Grant stood, moved to the porch rail, thought, We should have heard by now. He cannot just . . . ignore it.

There were boots behind him, and he heard Porter's voice, "Sir! Look! It's a rebel!"

Grant looked out into the dark, the dim light of the street beside the hotel. A man came out of the shadows, careful, discreet, saw Grant now, removed his hat. The man moved slowly around the porch, reached the steps and waited, still cautious. Grant could see what was left of a gray uniform, an officer.

Rawlins moved to the top of the steps, blocking the man's way, said, "Who are you, sir? Do you come from General Lee?"

The man flinched, looked at Rawlins as though expecting to be hit, shook his head. "General Lee? Oh, Lord, no. Please forgive me." He looked at the others on the porch, his eyes now focusing on Grant, and he said, "This is . . . my hotel. I am the proprietor."

Rawlins made a noise, said, "Is that a fact? You look more like a deserter to me. How did you get through? We have provost guards on all these streets."

The man smiled now, said, "I grew up here, know my way around. There's a few shortcuts . . ."

Grant stepped forward, put a hand on Rawlins's shoulder, said to the man, "What is your command? Where is your unit?"

The man looked at Grant, glanced again at Rawlins, saw Grant's shoulder straps, the rank, said, "Oh, my. Sir, my unit is . . . gone. There is no command. I didn't see much point in keeping up the fight. I heard there was a mighty lot of you fellows moving through here. I was kinda afraid . . . what might happen to my place."

Grant stepped aside, motioned for the man to move up the steps. "Welcome home, sir," he said. "We appreciate your courtesy. These are fine accommodations. No harm will come to this place."

The man seemed more comfortable now, confident, said, "Finest hotel in these parts, sir. Built it myself."

He looked past Grant, toward the front door, saw more blue officers in the lobby, men now moving past, saluting Grant. He stepped toward the door, then turned, said to Grant, "Can't rightly recall when it's been this busy . . ."

The streets were quiet now, the troops in camp, the bonfire collapsed into a mound of glowing embers. Grant was still on the porch, where he sat alone. He'd tried to sleep, but it was not to be, not yet, not until he heard something from Lee.

There was still activity in the hotel, a card game, but the sounds had quieted now, and he heard footsteps, a low voice, "Sir?"

Grant turned, saw Porter standing in the doorway, lit from behind by the glow of an oil lamp. "Come on out, Colonel," he said. "Have a seat."

Porter moved to a chair, sat down, said, "It might not be till tomorrow, sir. You should get some sleep."

Grant held a cigar out, looked at the faint glow. "By anyone's definition, Robert E. Lee is a gentleman, and an old soldier. He will respond. I'm guessing he has already responded. It just hasn't reached here yet."

Porter sat back in the chair, stared at the dying bonfire. "Do you think it's over, sir? Do you think he'll surrender?"

Two men were riding hard up the street from the east. Grant stood, moved forward, clamped the cigar hard in his teeth, said, "We're about to find out."

The horsemen moved closer, slowed, and one of them pointed toward the hotel, then both saw Grant. The men approached and dismounted. Grant saw one was an officer, a familiar face.

The man climbed the steps, saluted, said, "Sir, General Humphreys sends his compliments and wishes me to pass along to you this letter, which was received into our lines earlier tonight."

Grant said nothing, focused on the paper, reached for it, turned toward the light, scanned the words. He lowered the page, stared into the dark and let out a deep breath.

Porter moved close, said, "What is it, sir?"

Grant did not look at him, held the paper out, and Porter read it quietly.

> General—
>
> I have received your note of this day. Though not entertaining the opinion you express on the hopelessness of further resistance on the part of the Army of Northern Virginia, I reciprocate your desire to avoid the useless effusion of blood, and therefore before considering your proposition, ask the terms you will offer on condition of its surrender.
>
> R. E. Lee, General

Porter looked at Grant now, said, "He's asking for terms. Sir, he's asking for terms!"

Grant looked at the courier now, said, "You men are dismissed. You may remain here, if you like, or return to General Humphreys."

The man saluted again, said, "Sir, thank you. We will return to our camp."

The man moved away down the steps, and both men mounted the horses and were quickly gone. Grant moved to the porch railing, said, "Terms . . . there are no terms." He looked at Porter. "They cannot hold out much longer. This . . . says nothing. It is no admission of anything." He held his anger, flicked the ash from the cigar. "Surely, he doesn't believe he can fight it out. He must think they can get away." He turned now, pointed out toward the west, said quietly, "I want to be sure . . . get word to General Sheridan. I want our people out there, in front of him. I want Lee's army penned up tight. This matter will be concluded." He looked again at Porter, said, "Those are my terms."

He felt the first tightening bloom of a headache, took a deep breath, moved toward the door of the hotel, said, "Colonel, tomorrow morning I will respond to . . . this. Now, I believe I will go to bed."

April 8, 1865

> To General Robert E. Lee, Commanding, CSA:
>
> Your note of last evening, in reply to mine of the same date, asking the conditions on which I will accept the surrender of the Army of Northern Virginia, is just received. In reply I would say that peace being my great desire, there is but one condition I would insist upon—namely, that the men and officers surrendered shall be disqualified for taking up arms against the Government of the United States until properly exchanged. I will meet you, or will designate officers to meet any officers you may name for the same purpose, at any point agreeable to you, for the purpose of arranging definitely the terms upon which the surrender of the Army of Northern Virginia will be received.
>
> U. S. Grant, Lieutenant-General

He rode now north of the river, stayed close to the Second Corps, the tight pursuit of Lee's army. If the response came, it would likely come through those lines, the closest point where the armies met.

He'd had little sleep, and the headache had grown, erupting like some great black fire behind his eyes, fueled by a tight stranglehold on the back of his neck. He had tried to ride, to keep up with the movement of Humphreys's troops, but the movement of the horse only increased the throbbing in his head. Now he was camped at a farmhouse, could only sit and wait while his army kept up the chase.

The army was nearly equally divided, the Sixth Corps moving in behind the Second above the river, while down below, Ord's Army of the James was supported by Griffin's Fifth. Sheridan's horsemen were pushing hard, skirmishing all day with Fitz Lee as they moved closer to the most likely place for Lee to entrench. Sheridan focused on Appomattox Court House, where the river narrowed to an easy crossing, where it could no longer protect Lee from the troops below. By nightfall Sheridan's cavalry had reached the edge of the small town, and the scouts could see the great railcars that waited for Lee's army to arrive.

GRANT WAS STILL AT THE FARMHOUSE, HAD WELCOMED THE kindness of the family there, and his headache had been assaulted by every home remedy anyone in the house, or on his staff, could suggest. He lay on a sofa, stared up at the dark, could still smell the mustard from the compress that had been put on his legs. Outside, it was quiet, the family occupying a small guest house while Grant and his staff used the larger house for the headquarters.

The headache had been relentless, and he tried closing his eyes, but the pressure inside of him forced them open. He knew there would be no sleep, not while he felt like this. He stared up again, and there was a soft knock at the door. He wanted to yell, to shout, the anger at the intrusion sprouting from the flaming agony in his head. The door opened, a small crack, and he heard a quiet voice. It was Rawlins.

"Sir?"

Grant let out a burst of air, said, "Come in. I'm awake. I'm suffering too much to get any sleep."

Rawlins moved in slowly, Porter behind him, with a small candle. Rawlins said, "Sir, we have received a letter from General Lee."

Grant sat up quickly. Porter set the candle down, and Grant took the paper, held it toward the light.

> General:
>
> I received at a late hour your note of today. In mine of yesterday I did not intend to propose the surrender of the Army of Northern Virginia, but to ask the terms of your

proposition. To be frank, I do not think the emergency has arisen to call for the surrender of this army; but as the restoration of peace should be the sole object of all, I desired to know whether your proposals would lead to that end. I cannot, therefore, meet you with a view to surrender the Army of Northern Virginia; but as far as your proposal may effect the Confederate States forces under my command, and tend to the restoration of peace, I shall be pleased to meet you at 10 a.m. tomorrow on the old stage road to Richmond, between the picket lines of the two armies.

R. E. Lee, General

Grant lowered the paper, shook his head, let out a long breath. "What does he think I had in mind . . . that *we're* going to walk away? It appears he intends to fight it out. I will send him a reply in the morning." He lay back on the sofa, closed his eyes, said quietly, "It is quite likely . . . we may *all* reply in the morning . . . with a great deal more than words."

48. CHAMBERLAIN

April 8, 1865

It was pure pursuit, a march quick and straightforward. They had not seen the enemy, but the fight was all around them, the skirmishes with the cavalry, the great roar that had come from Saylor's Creek.

He rode Charlemagne again, the wound now a hard black knot on the horse's neck. They had moved most of the night, and now all of the day. There had been rain, enough to cool the men, enough to soften the roads so the wagon wheels could cut it into long furrows, the hardened ridges just high enough to break the ankles of the men who were too tired to watch their own footsteps.

He had to slow the column down. The road was clogged with another column, more wagons and guns. Ord's troops were up ahead, would share the same route for a while, and Chamberlain reined in the horse, watched as men struggled to push the wagons through a small stream. Behind him the men were in no mood for delay. Suddenly, a dozen men moved past him, toward the trouble in front, splashed down into the water, pushing the wagon up the other side. He moved the horse forward, thought, Yes, good. I suppose I should have told them to do that.

He had ridden for so long now he could not recall his last hour of sleep. The men had no patience, and when the march was slowed by the clumsy struggles in front of them, they would break ranks again and swarm past him to do whatever was necessary. Often there would be a little extra, either the removal of the horses and their drivers by force, followed by an unceremonious toss into the creek or mud, or an astounding flow of profane language. He heard it this time as well, several men yelling in delirious anger at a teamster, the man lashing at the troops with his whip. There were bayonets up now, and Chamberlain was suddenly awake, alert, thought, No, God, don't kill him. But the bayonets merely held off the driver's whip, finally knocking it away completely. The men then drifted back toward him, rejoining the column. No officer said anything, there was no reprimand, and Chamberlain thought, No, we are as tired of this as you are. We just can't do anything about it.

As they moved past him a few glanced up, and there were no smiles, and he could hear mumbled profanities, low voices. He tried to pick out the unique phrases, could not help but smile, the men scowling as they returned to their places in the line of march. A master of language, he thought, and I've never heard *that* before. I should write some of this down . . . but when on earth would I ever use it? An image flashed into his mind, and he saw the dark, frowning face of his father-in-law. Well, that would be interesting, testing Fannie's father's capacity for shock. And Fannie would respond to my eloquent use of these new phrases by . . . what? Some choice phrases of her own? No, that is not a competition I could ever hope to win.

The columns were moving again, the men behind him giving their last word to the crippled wagons on the side of the road. They climbed out of the woods, moved onto open ground, the road much better, and Chamberlain turned the horse, moved to the side, stopped and stared at the wide field.

He'd seen fields like this before, where the great fights had taken place, the violence sweeping over the ground like some horrible storm. But the violence was different now, there had been no fight here, at least no combat.

As far as he could see, there were the broken machines of the rebel army, wagons, heaps of wood and wheels, and guns as well, broken carriages, brass barrels jutting out in all directions. Now the smells began to reach him, and he could see the brown shapes, had thought they were brush and bushes, but no, it was horses, mules, mostly dead, swollen carcasses. There was some motion, animals that had simply collapsed but were still alive, many still strapped into harness, trapped by the weight and the wagons they could no longer serve.

He moved the horse, fought breathing the awful smells, thought, No, keep going. If this is what is happening to Lee, we will soon see much more.

There was another creek in front of them, and the column moved down a short hill, the road muddy again, but the creek was open, wide, with few trees. He could see small pieces of what had once been a bridge, the rest swept away, either burned or chopped to pieces by the men they were chasing.

Ord's column had already moved through, but again wagons were being pushed aside, the foolhardy who assumed the water was shallow. There was a staff officer now, one of Ord's men, directing the column of men upstream, away from the congestion and toward a shallow place where the men could wade across.

His men followed the new path, and he waited until they began to cross at the new ford. They were veterans of this now, boots coming off quickly, suspended by a high bayonet, ammunition held high as well. He turned the horse, moved back down toward the remains of the bridge, had to see why they had moved upstream. There, below, all along the muddy banks, he saw a great mass of debris, more wagons, more guns, but now he could see color too, pieces of . . . *things* in the water, scattered in the mud. There was thick brush downstream, and the creek was clogged by vast piles of something different, not pieces of the army, but of life, home. The broken carts and wagons were not all military. There were small black carriages, trimmed in gold; pieces of fine leather bridles; a broken picture frame, the painting ripped away; pots; and mostly clothes, all colors, lace and silk, hats and black leather shoes. Civilians, he thought. This is a clear picture of the chase, the panic of a people escaping from . . . *us*. He felt a sudden sadness. They must think we are something truly awful, demons. Of course, the bridges were burned by whoever got here first, protecting themselves, with no thought of who might follow. And this was what followed. On the far side of the creek the mud was a vast spread of tracks, shallow and deep, and more color, the dirty refuse of clothing, cast-off shoes and boots.

He turned the horse, moved up along the column again, splashed the horse through the water. His mind was swirling in a daze, from lack of sleep, and he realized now he was very hungry. He instinctively felt his pockets, but there was nothing there, and now he began to feel angry, thought, All the criticism for being slow, Warren's removal, the angry talk about Meade's sluggishness . . . well, somebody better write about *this*, about how we are moving now. He tried to think of distance, had heard someone say thirty-five miles, thought it was probably more.

He climbed another rise, saw a long patch of trees, a farmhouse, and movement caught his eye. He could see men now, gathered around the house, most sitting, leaning against the side of the house. He looked around, thought they might be prisoners, but there were no guards. Someone should—

In the trees close by he heard voices, then saw more of them, scattered all out in the woods, men sitting, some lying flat on the ground. They were calling out to the troops, small greetings, some weak requests, begging for food. He saw muskets then, scattered along the edge of the road, thought, It's an entire unit . . . maybe a company, different companies. He looked for a uniform, something identifiable, saw only an occasional hat, one man wearing a bent sword, a black stripe on a ripped pant leg. The faces were mostly staring out at the road, but there were others, men staring ahead with blank eyes, men close to death, or dead already. No, he thought, they don't need guards. They aren't going anywhere.

The farm was behind them now, and then there was a fork in the road, and a staff officer, another man directing traffic. Ord's people were moving away, and Chamberlain saw Griffin, talking to officers Chamberlain did not know. Griffin saw him, and Chamberlain raised a salute, felt the stiffness in his shoulder, the wound now an ugly bruise along his ribs.

Griffin said, "Take the right fork . . . keep moving, General. Sheridan's up ahead. It's getting pretty tight."

Chamberlain nodded dumbly, asked, "Where's Lee?"

Griffin leaned closer, saw the blinking fatigue, said, "Don't worry about Lee, General. You just keep your men moving on the road . . . this way. If you don't fall off your horse, General Sheridan will find you when he needs you."

THEY FINALLY STOPPED WELL AFTER DARK, THE MEN COLLAPSING on any spot that would make a bed. Some rations made their way along the line, but waiting for food to cook meant more time awake, and so most of the men slept rather than ate. Chamberlain had slid down from his horse, given the order to the bugler, the command to bivouac. The sounds echoed down the line over the heads of men who did not need any command to sleep. Chamberlain had dropped down, spread out right where his feet touched the ground, and slept through the sound of the horse breathing right above him, finding its own rest.

He was very, very small, standing on uncertain legs, reaching up, his hands not quite reaching the tip of the icicle. Now his father was there, the large hand grabbing the ice, snapping it clean from the eave of the house. The icicle was in his own hands now, and he sat in the snow, touched his small hands to the sharp point. His father was laughing, and Chamberlain put his tongue out, licked the icicle, felt his tongue suddenly stick to the ice, the sudden panic, and now he began to cry, and his father's hand was on his shoulder, shaking him . . .

"Sir?"

The hand shook him again, and he stared up at something horrible, ugly, hovering over him, tried to clear his eyes, realized it was the horse's nose. The voice said again, "Sir?" He tried to focus, thought, No, don't talk to me . . . and then saw the face of the man, leaning in close. "Sir? Orders, sir."

Chamberlain blinked hard, thought of sleep again, the snow, the wonderful dream. "Orders? For what?"

The man stood, said, "From General Sheridan, sir."

His eyes were open now, and he sat up, bumped his head on the horse's snout. Charlemagne was coming awake as well, snorting, a hot wet breath on Chamberlain's face. He rubbed a hand over the wetness, rolled over, slowly stood up, said to the horse, "Well, the orders are for you too."

The aide held the paper out, and Chamberlain took it, could read nothing in the dark. The man struck a match, held it in front of the paper. Chamberlain tried to focus, saw the words:

> I have cut across the enemy at Appomattox Station . . . if you can possibly push your infantry up here tonight, we will have great results in the morning.

Chamberlain looked around at the vast field of sleeping men, said to the aide, "Find the bugler. Sound the call to rise. Let's *move*."

49. LEE

Night, April 8, 1865

They were close to the station, and everyone knew the railcars were waiting for them. The march had gone well, Lee staying close to Longstreet, riding with him at the head of the column as he had so many times before. He kept the memories away, tried not to think of those days, now so far behind them, when he would ride beside the big quiet man, pushing the hard power of this glorious army into a weak and badly organized enemy. It was so very different now, and it was not just that his army was so weak, so badly used up, but that the enemy was very different as well. Grant's army had never run, could never have been persuaded to leave by the sheer audacity of Lee's tactics. He thought of that now, of the fight that had been, the long siege, the chase. He wanted to believe that it was the commanders, that if Jackson had lived, or Stuart, or Rodes, or . . . so many others . . .

But it might not have been. Grant had brought something so different to those people, and whatever they had lacked before, whatever had been so terribly wrong with Hooker or Polk or Burnside, had finally been erased. Lee had always feared that, and even after Grant had been given command, he was not sure what it would mean. Always, from the beginning of his command, when Lee knew the fight was coming, when the great blue wave would slowly move forward once more, he never doubted that his army would prevail, never feared defeat. He always understood the mind of each one of those men Lincoln sent after him. He did not ever wonder about that, never asked himself if it was simple instinct, or superior military skills, or the hand of God. But now, riding in front of a slow column of starving men, he had to think of it, could not keep it away. He still did not believe that Grant had brought some strategic brilliance to the field that he could not grasp, or that his men had been outfought. But Grant had given his army something else, had propelled them forward at a horrible cost. Lee wondered about the numbers, what those boys in blue had given up. He had always believed *that* would decide the war, that the wives and the mothers in the North would not have that. But still they came, had come into his guns until his guns could not hold them away. It did not make sense, all the loss; the death of so many did not take away their spirit, but instead strengthened it, made them a better army. He had to admit that if he had underestimated Grant, it was because he had underestimated what the people in the North would allow him to do.

Lee had relieved some of his commanders, made it official, though no one else had thought it necessary. But he knew it was still the army, and there would be protocol. The commanders continued to move with the column, rode beside ragged pieces of their army, but the organization was nearly gone. Many regiments were now so small that they were grouped together with men they did not know, following unfamiliar flags. Richard Anderson, George Pickett, several others, were dismissed from command, and even if the names still drew respect from the men they had led, those men were too few. The army did not need any more generals.

Longstreet was now moved back, and Gordon's command was moved out in advance, closest to Appomattox. The greatest threat was still from the rear, from the Federals who were close behind, and Longstreet's troops were the most prepared for a good fight, now the freshest troops left in the dwindling army. If the race for Appomattox was won, it would be up to Longstreet to hold the blue infantry away. In front of them would be only cavalry. Even Sheridan could not hold his horse soldiers in line against Gordon's infantry.

There had been no delays, another hard march, and no one in the ranks thought they should stop. There was no food, except what waited for them up ahead, and the column was consumed by the forward motion, men sleeping on their feet, driven only by the slow rhythm of their own fading strength. If the rhythm failed, the men simply dropped away, fell to the side of the road. Those who remained did not notice, still moved forward because there was nothing else for them to do.

Lee had felt more energy since the morning, moved the horse along the column now, toward the front, knew that somewhere up ahead they would make some sort of camp, a place for the business of the army. Behind him some of the staff stayed close, Marshall, Venable, and Lee knew that Taylor would have the camp ready when they arrived. Traveller moved slowly, stepping carefully, moving around the men on foot, blinded by the darkness and their own exhaustion. Lee could see the ones who had fallen away, some just sitting on the side of the road, heads low, faces down. He thought, I must still rally them, say something, give encouragement. He called out, "Up, men . . . to the march!" They did not seem to hear, and he realized his voice was only a whisper, barely a sound at all. There was nothing he could say to replace what they had already given up.

Lee rounded a curve, a short rise, could see the moon, bright, bathing the open ground around him in white light. The road was still full of troops, the last of Gordon's men, pushing closer to the town, to the rail station. He spurred the horse, just a bit, a gentle prodding, and Traveller climbed the rise, another curve, reached the crest. The moon was off to the side now, and he could see his shadow, felt the coolness of the air, a slight breeze, and suddenly, far out in front, he could hear the sound of big guns.

He stopped the horse, listened, thought, It is down below, along the river, the cavalry. . . .

He looked that way, toward the south, stared into the dark, but the sounds would not let him turn away, and now he could hear it plainly. The sounds were in the west, from the one place they could not come, where there could not be anyone to block his way. He looked again to the south, thought, No, it's the wind, the lay of the land, the echo tricking me. He moved the horse a short way along the road, pulled off, moved into the wide field, crested another small rise, halted the horse . . . and now he could see the flashes of light, the sounds rolling toward him in louder bursts, sharp waves of thunder. He thought, Gordon has found them . . . cavalry, there is cavalry at Appomattox. He moved the horse quickly now, the staff following closely, his gut closed up tight in a cold ball, and he thought, They cannot be there . . . they cannot take the railcars.

MIDNIGHT, APRIL 8, 1865

THEY WERE BARELY TWO MILES FROM APPOMATTOX COURT House, a small town whose existence was defined by the railroad. The fight had quieted, a hard encounter between blue horsemen and an advanced line of Lee's artillery, big guns put into place by Porter Alexander, men who were suddenly the front line in a fight they were not expecting. Fitz Lee's horsemen, helping to guard the rear of the column, had quickly been sent up, and the fight was softened now by the late hour, the big guns holding the blue cavalry back. But they did not leave; there was nothing about the rebel line in front of them to drive them away. It was George Custer's division, men who had ridden hard for this opportunity. They had won the race, had come hard into the rail center, seen the great prize strung out on the tracks before them, and now the railcars were in Federal hands.

Lee's camp was quiet, many officers spread out on the ground, most just lying flat, staring up at the thick clouds that drifted past the moon. They were mostly staff officers, serving what remained of the command of the army. The men they served—Fitz Lee, Longstreet, Gordon—were all close around the fire, sitting on the ground themselves, faces lit by the glow, staring up at the one man who stood. Lee could not move from the fire, not yet, and they waited, patient, no one speaking. He stared down into the flames, listened to the crackling sounds, and felt the weariness, the energy of the day and of the cool night drained out of him. He turned, saw Longstreet sitting on a log, the small pipe in his mouth, watching him.

Lee looked down at his nephew, made a small motion with his hand, said, "Who is that up there?"

Fitz Lee was looking into the fire, said, "Custer. Maybe Devin."

Lee waited for more, but the young man still stared at the fire, and there were no more words. Lee was now annoyed, felt his patience suddenly fall away, said, "Cavalry? Is that all . . . just cavalry? Are you sure?"

The young man looked up at him, heard the anger in Lee's voice, glanced at Gordon, who said, "There has to be infantry."

Lee looked at him. "Do you have information? Is there something I do not know?"

Gordon said, "No, sir. But they're out there. If they're not up ahead right now, they will be by morning."

Fitz Lee nodded, said, "Probably right. Custer didn't pull away. It wasn't a probe. He meant to dig in, hold his line. He's expecting support."

Lee looked at the fire again, closed his eyes. He had not done this, not in a very long time. He did not believe in councils of war, in calling everyone together at one time. If they were alone, one on one, he could depend on honesty, could feel out each man himself, read the face, read the heart, had always felt they would open up to him. But there was no time now, and after all, it was only these three who really mattered, who really controlled what would happen in the morning. They had spent little time together, had very little in common except that they were the best commanders he had left. He thought, No, that is no accident, there is something of God in this. The weak, those with no heart for the fight, are gone, taken away by Your will. You have left me with the men who can still do this, who can save us yet. Your hand still guides us. If we are to go on, if You will provide for these men, show me . . . something, show me a Sign.

He turned, saw Longstreet, who still watched him quietly. Lee looked out to the officers spread all around them. He moved away from the fire, looked at Longstreet, then the other two, said in a low voice, "Can we break through?"

Longstreet leaned forward, took the pipe from his mouth, said quietly, "We can always break through. If it's cavalry, we can break through easily. If it's infantry, it will be a bit tougher. But we can do it."

Lee nodded, thought of the strange mood, reading the letter from Grant. Longstreet was still criticized by the papers, too slow, too much defense. Even I thought him too stubborn, he thought, and now he understands what I want, what we need to do. Maybe he always knew. Maybe stubbornness is what we need now, more than anything else.

He looked at Gordon then said, "It will have to be up to your men, General. If they are in force . . . if General Grant has infantry blocking the road . . . we may not have an alternative."

There was a silent moment, and Lee waited, could not use the word, had not thought of the word all day, but he had to see it in their eyes, if they understood what he meant—that if they could not break through, the only alternative would be surrender.

Gordon sat up, looked at Fitz Lee, said, "If the cavalry can hold the road, move them back, we can push through."

There was another quiet moment, and Lee looked at Gordon, thought, He believes that. But it is not enough. If those people have moved infantry in front of us, if they have won the race . . . we are not strong enough.

He looked at Longstreet, said, "General, we must march the men now. We cannot wait until morning to see what is in our path. Your corps must close up the ranks, hold away those people in your rear, and stay close behind General Gordon."

Longstreet was looking at him strangely, and Lee suddenly understood, thought, *Corps.* No, do not think of numbers. It does not matter that we do not have the strength. It is God's fight now . . . we will take our strength from Him.

THREE A.M., APRIL 9, 1865

THE MEN WERE MOVING AGAIN, THE ROAD A SOLID MASS OF DULL sounds, shuffling feet. The lines were compact, Gordon's men near the town, moving out into open ground. Close behind, Longstreet's troops faced to the rear, prepared to hold off anyone who came in from behind.

Lee walked away from the small camp, the moon now far to the west, settling toward the horizon. He moved out that way, stepping through soft dirt, fields that had been planted, the seeds trampled by the bare feet of his army. He could see a few stars, but only a few, small flickers of light washed away by the brightness of the large moon. He kept moving toward it, tried not to think of all this, of what was happening, of what had already happened to his army. The commanders had been enthusiastic, were ready for whatever the day would bring them. He felt a great sadness about that, moved in a soft gloom, thought, They will do their duty, as long as I do mine. Their men will follow them as long as they lead. The war can still go on, and they will still fight as they have always fought. I do not understand that.

I had thought it would never come this far, that it would pass on and be done, and we could go home, and be with our families. But Fitz believes . . . probably many others as well, we should take to the hills, keep fighting in every town, every railroad, a guerrilla war. Anyone can shoot a musket, kill someone, a soldier, a politician. You can terrorize civilians, burn crops, destroy tracks . . . but that is not what this is about. We do not fight to simply . . . destroy. There is nothing different now, nothing different from four years ago. The cause is the same, the reasons for this fight are the same. If it is meant for us to stop this, to go home, if God gives us that message, then we must listen, we must obey.

He stepped down into a shallow depression, began to climb up. It was very cool, and he pulled his coat around him, thought, We can still win this . . . we can still pressure them to give up this fight. Grant cannot just make a war against us until we are all dead. There must come a time when they will have had enough, when they will not want any more trains filled with their young men, men in wooden boxes, or worse, masses of men pushed into great scars in the earth. There has always been a simple solution . . . *stop* this, just take your soldiers and leave our land. That's all we have wanted. It should never have been up to the guns, to these men who march on that road, who must still kill their enemy, or die themselves.

He felt a great wave of grief, felt himself letting go, pulled at it, thought, No, not even here, alone in the dark, you cannot lose control. He looked up at a faint star. God is here, right here, and He will grant us what we must have. He glanced out toward the road, could hear faint sounds still, one horse, moving slowly, but he could see nothing. He walked that way, climbed slowly up a rise, thought of the men, of the great fights, the power of the army, the quiet excitement that had filled him, the victory, the cheering of the men, the loyalty, the love. He had to see them, thought, Yes, we are still an army, and we can still do this, and there is nothing but the hand of God that can stop us.

He stepped through the soft dirt, reached the crest of the low hill, looked up at faint stars, then down, all along the horizon, could see more stars, many more, and they were large and bright. He stared, confused, and his eyes began to focus, and now he could see that they were not stars, the horizon was not lit by the glow from the heavens, but by the glow of campfires, a vast sea of light spread along the horizon, a glow from a vast blue force that spread all along the west, then down toward the south, a wide arc extending far beyond where his ragged army was pulling itself together.

He stood for a long moment, stared at the horizon, felt the glow rolling toward him like some hot wind, a sickness boiling up inside of him, pulling his breath away. He knew what the fires meant, thought, They are in *front* of us now.

He looked out toward the road, toward the small town where barely ten thousand men would wait for the dawn, would wait for *him* to lead them to the desperate fight.

50. CHAMBERLAIN

Dawn, April 9, 1865

It was barely light, the chill of the morning broken by the sweat of men who had moved forward in a steady rush. They were in column again behind Ord, and this time the wagons did not slow them, there was no bogging down in soft mud. They were pulled forward by the guns, by the great hard sounds that grew louder as they moved closer, louder still with every cresting of every small hill.

Chamberlain was wide-awake, felt his eyes burning now from the drifting smoke of the field, a light haze flowing through the treetops. He watched it, thought, It is not mist or fog. It is smoke, cannon, musket fire. He was excited now, as excited as he had ever been, held the horse to the side, waving his hand, spurring his men past him. He moved the horse alongside the column, rode up in front again, saw Ord's men keeping good time ahead, thought, Yes, excellent, don't slow us down, don't get in our way.

He felt a strange energy this morning, and for the first time he did not hear the small voice, that small angry place in his mind, the voice of reason, of pure survival, that says, "No, do not do this." The voice was there in all of them, had to be, yet it was the strength in his heart, his own will, that held it away, kept it silent. He had heard the voice many times, always in the face of the guns, and he'd seen the panic, the wild faces of the men who had listened to it, whose will had been swept away by the sound of that voice. He had always feared that one day it would happen to him, feared it even as he rode right into the fight, into the vast clouds of smoke, the horrible sounds. It had angered him, his own lack of faith in himself, that no matter how often he had done this, how many of the great battles and small sharp fights, he could still give in to the panic. But once the fight was hard in front of him, once he was a part of it, the voice was always silent.

It was the same every time, after every fight. There would come the quiet moment, the blessed satisfaction, the reassurance that after all the horrors he had seen, after the painful agony of his wounds, the voice could not turn him away after all. He thought of the word *soldier*. If that is what he had become, if he'd finally learned to ignore the voice, had silenced it, then he would never run away, never hesitate to march straight into the fight.

He was still moving, could hear the sounds rolling past him, louder, Sheridan's field guns, and he scolded himself, Do your job, stop thinking. It was the first time he had no fear of the voice, and he smiled, thought, This is, after all, an adventure.

He could see a man moving back along the column, cavalry, covered in black grime, and the man saw his rank, shouted, though there was no need to shout. "Are you in command? Are these your troops?"

Chamberlain heard the urgency in the man's voice, serious, dangerous, felt his heart suddenly pounding, said, "Yes . . . two brigades of the First Division, Fifth Corps."

The man pointed away from the road, still shouted, "Sir, General Sheridan wishes you to break off from this column and come to his support. The rebels are pressing him hard. Don't wait for orders through the regular channels. General Sheridan says to act on this at once!"

Chamberlain took in the man's excitement, thought, Is he authorized? And he thought of Warren, of the fatal delay, decided, No, I don't believe I will wait. Out through the woods he could hear Sheridan's guns, a new round of firing, and he turned, saw his staff moving close, yelled now himself, "Turn the column . . . follow this man. Leave a courier behind us, tell General Crawford to keep on the road, not to follow us! Move!"

Chamberlain glanced at the man with the bugle, saw the polished brass horn come up, the sounds echoing back to his men. He looked now at the cavalry officer, and the man was already moving into the woods. Chamberlain pointed, yelled again, "There, that way. Let's move!"

THE TREES OPENED INTO A WIDE CLEARING, THE SMOKE DRIFTING toward him in great thick clouds. His men filed into line, began to move ahead in battle formation. Chamberlain tried to see, had no idea where the cavalry officer had gone, guided his men by the sound of the fight in front of him. He rode forward, felt the smoke burning his throat, the heat in his lungs, thought, Keep moving, find out what is going on.

He saw a flag, horses, moved that way, saw the great black horse and the small man. Riding up quickly, he saluted, said, "General Sheridan. I have two brigades of infantry, at your service, sir."

Sheridan stared at him with a black fire, pointed toward the sounds, said simply, "There! Smash 'em up! Smash 'em to hell!"

Chamberlain looked to the front, the smoke drifting slowly away, could see it now, a heavy line of rebels and the blue cavalry, dismounted, a thinning line, falling back, the field scattered with the fallen blue troopers. The rebels were moving forward, slowly, against the men in blue. Chamberlain thought, They cannot hold . . . they need support. He looked around at his men, moving forward in a neat line, felt suddenly ridiculous, thought, Yes, of course, that's *us*.

There was a volley from the rebels, the smoke blowing out toward him, and he spurred the horse, rode back to his men, moved close behind the line. He looked for the bugler, saw officers watching him, waiting for the word. The men could see what lay in front of them now, already knew what was coming. Chamberlain saw the man with the bugle, yelled at him, "Now! Advance!"

The men surged forward, and Chamberlain moved down the line, yelling, "Forward, advance!" But the men were in a good hard line, and there was no wavering, no hesitation. He could see more infantry now, Ord's men, coming out of the trees far off to the side, and they were moving as well, the officers turning them, linking up with Chamberlain's flank, lengthening the line, a solid, growing wave. Chamberlain wanted to say, "Yes, thank you," but there was no need. The movement was automatic now, the fight pulling them forward, the enemy so close, right in front of them. He looked at his own lines, reaching the base of the wide hill, saw the muskets go up in one long motion, the order going out from officers he could not hear, his officers, the volley blowing the smoke back toward the rebels.

He could see the rebel line backing away, climbing up the hill, men still firing, the line breaking up. He looked across to Ord's lines, felt a sudden odd stab in his gut, could see a solid front of blue, pushing forward. He watched them, stared at the great long line of black faces, a Negro division . . . Birney's men. They moved in flank with his own line, pushing the rebels back farther up the rise, a steady advance, the rebels giving up the ground. He was lost for a moment, the sounds now somewhere else as he watched the Negroes begin to absorb the fire of the rebels, men punched back by musket fire, some simply collapsing, opening small gaps in the line. The line tightened up then, the officers and the sergeants pulling their men together, keeping the formation tight. What is this like for them? Chamberlain wondered. What are they feeling? My God . . . this is what we are fighting for . . . at least, it is what *I* am fighting for. And I can never know . . . I will never feel what this means to them.

A hot rush shook him, nearly knocked him from the horse, the sudden blast of dirt behind him, and the horse jumped. He focused, thought, Lawrence, your brain again. Back to work.

He could see his men climbing up the rise now, the rebels pulling away still, back along the crest of the hill, some moving beyond, out of sight. His men were in pursuit, yells echoing where the sounds of musket fire had stopped. He rode up close, thought, No wait, we don't know what is over the hill.

He waved the sword, a silent signal to hold them up, to wait. Now there were horses coming up from the flank, flags, and he looked at the man in front, arms waving, a man he didn't know. He turned that way, saw two stars, thought . . . Ord. Chamberlain saluted, waited.

Ord shouted at him, "General, keep your men off that crest. They will be exposed to fire!"

Abruptly, Ord was gone, the horses thundering away. Chamberlain stared at the cloud of dust, turned, looked up toward the crest of the hill. Exposed to fire? he thought. Isn't that what we're supposed to do? He thought of Sheridan: I do not believe those would be General Sheridan's orders. The words came to him again: *smash 'em up.* No, I believe General Sheridan would rather we advance. He sagged slightly, thought, *Generals.*

He saw the bugler watching him, the line now snaking along the side of the hill, the officers in front, pulling the men together, straightening the line. He nodded to the bugler, said, "Now . . . advance!"

The men began to move again, the line flowing forward, and then they were on the crest. He rode up quickly, thought, Careful, be ready to order the retreat.

The ground fell away in front of them, revealing a wide valley. He saw the small town, a scattering of buildings, a small line of trees snaking through the valley, the river now only a small stream. He reined the horse, heard the sound of one shell, the explosion ripping the ground in front of his line, another streaking overhead. Then there

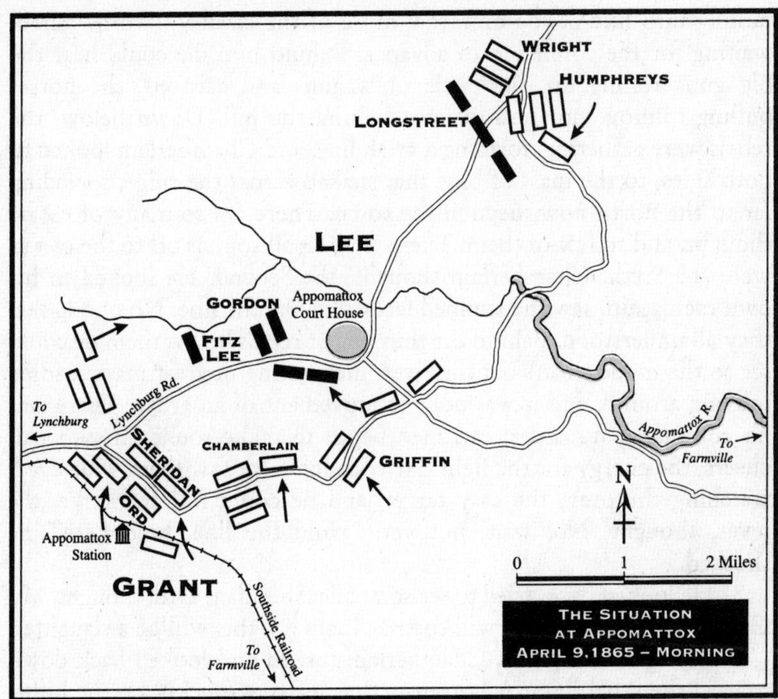

was a sudden breath of silence, and he stared in amazement, felt himself drawn forward, out across a vast field, short rolling hills, small trees. Below the wide hill, spread across the valley, was a mass of guns, wagons, and men; ragged lines, pulling back, drawing up into a defense. He thought, It is a division, and we're exposed. But there was no firing, no organized formation. Many of the guns were parked, neat squares, many of the wagons had no horses, and the troops were not gathering for a fight, were not gathering at all. He could see men sitting now, some standing without muskets, a few staring up the hill at the men in blue with a look he'd never seen before. Then he understood what lay across this small valley in front of him. It was not a division, it was not even a fighting force at all.

It was what remained of Lee's army.

HIS MEN BEGAN TO MOVE FORWARD, SLOWLY, ON THEIR OWN, and there was musket fire, scattered, men crouching low. He could see more of the Fifth Corps now, Crawford's men, pulling into line beside him, saw more of the cavalry, swords raised, waiting for the command to advance. Behind him, he could hear the big guns rolling up, the rattle of wagons and caissons, the horses pulling cannon into position just behind the hill. Down below, the rebels were gathering, forming a weak line, and Chamberlain looked to both sides, to the mass of blue that snaked across the ridge, spreading far to the north now, beyond the town. There are so many of us, he thought, and so few of them. There were small sounds off to the east as well; the Sixth, Chamberlain thought, the Second. He looked to his own men again, saw the stunned faces all along the line. No one spoke, they all understood. Behind the thin line of rebels below them he could see to the muddy banks of the river, men sitting in great masses, some moving around, and it was not the movement of an army. There was no command, no order. His men began to make sounds now, small cheers, the energy for the fight. He rode forward, saw them wide-eyed, watching the prey, the easy target, and he could feel the surge, the fever, thought, No, wait, not yet. "Hold the line, hold here!" he shouted.

He looked back, tried to see someone, Sheridan, Ord, thought, My God, if we attack . . . we will destroy them . . . this will be a slaughter.

Seeing a man point, Chamberlain turned and looked back down toward the rebel lines. A horseman was moving quickly up the hill, a tattered rag of dirty white over the man's head. The man was moving right, then left, and Chamberlain thought, He is looking for . . . someone in command. He is looking for *me.*

He rode forward, and the man saw him. Chamberlain could see the Confederate uniform, an officer, the uniform ragged but intact, and he thought, He is not combat . . . he is a staff officer. The man moved up the hill close to him, stopped, dismounted, held the ragged white cloth in front of him, looked nervously at the blue line. Chamberlain glanced at the muskets of his men, and no one was pointing their gun, there was no threat.

The man said, "Sir, I am from General Gordon. General Lee desires a cessation of hostilities until he can hear from General Grant . . . as to the proposed . . . surrender."

Chamberlain absorbed the man's drawl, could see the pain in his face, and now the word began to fill him: *surrender*. Close to him, the men who heard the man's words began to yell, to cheer, and the word proceeded to flow down the line, the voices growing louder. Chamberlain felt his stomach twist, thought, Can I do this? He thought of his own words now: There has to be the right thing to say. The officer watched him patiently.

Chamberlain said, "Sir, that matter exceeds my authority. I will send for my superior." He felt instantly foolish, the cold words of command, the formality. The man nodded slowly, understood, and Chamberlain turned, saw one of his aides, the man staring wide-eyed. Chamberlain waved him forward, said quietly, "Go to General Griffin. Find him. *Now!*"

He looked at the Confederate officer again, could see the dignity, the sadness, the man doing his painful duty. He thought, I should say something appropriate. . . . What is appropriate? How many times are we in this position? He removed his hat, at least a bit of courtesy, said, "General Lee is right. There is nothing more he can do."

The man nodded slightly, said nothing. Chamberlain's men had quieted, were all watching the officer, waiting. For what, he thought, something else? He looked out past the man, down the hill, out over the small valley. Out of the odd silence, there was a sudden sharp blast from down below, one gun hidden in small trees, and he heard the shell, the hard shriek. Down the line there was a quick rush of sound, a small blast, and he saw a man go down, falling from a horse. Men were gathering, and Chamberlain spurred the horse, moved that way, quickly dismounted. The men cleared away, and he saw a young officer, thought of the name . . . Lieutenant Clark, from New York. There was a hole in the man's chest, blood everywhere, and someone yelled for a doctor, but Chamberlain saw there was no need. He backed away, felt suddenly sick, turned from the horror.

The man in gray walked toward him, toward the body of the young lieutenant. The man said nothing, and Chamberlain looked at him, wanted to feel anger, to scream at him, the words hot in his mind, *This is your truce?* But the man kneeled down, lowered his head, and Chamberlain could see he was saying something, a quiet prayer. He stepped forward then, close to the man, thought of the word again, *surrender,* said quietly, "Pray that he is the last."

51. LEE

Morning, April 9, 1865

The fight had gone exactly as they had planned, Gordon striking hard at the blue cavalry, supported by Fitz Lee's horsemen. They had pushed Sheridan away at first, and for a brief time the road was open, escape possible. But Lee had seen it himself, the sudden ring of blue coming over the low hills, emerging from the woods, and very soon Gordon's men were fighting an enemy on three sides, and Fitz Lee's men became separated from the infantry, cut off out to the west. Gordon sent for help, requested in urgent terms that Longstreet come forward, turn his men to the front, but Longstreet was still holding a weakening line against the hard advance of two Federal corps.

The couriers had moved in and out of camp, the situation growing more clear. All along the front lines men were waiting for the command, to strike out again, to do whatever it would take to drive the enemy away. Lee had spoken to many, sorted through details of what they knew, of what they felt. Some still wanted to fight it out; if the mass of blue was too strong, the army could be divided, scattered into the hills, continue the war by any means. He was surprised at that, knew the passions were still high, but the talk of scattered resistance would only serve the needs of the soldier, of the men who would not end the fight. It would be devastating to the civilians, with the likelihood of brutal reprisals from Federal troops, and to the towns that would have to be occupied by force and governed by martial law. He listened to the passion, but had been firm and clear in his own mind. There could be no end to the blood and the death, and there could be no hope for a just peace, unless the war was stopped.

He had sent for Longstreet, who rode up now, trailed by a flag bearer and one other man, Billy Mahone. They dismounted and walked up the rise to where Lee waited. Lee stood straight, felt the tightness around his waist, the stiffness in the fresh uniform.

He had dressed early, searching through the trunk for the last clean one, and the one he rarely wore, reserved usually for the formality of Richmond. The uniform had not been worn in a long while. He had run his hand through the trunk, searching, finally felt the softness of the silk, an afterthought, had thought, No, too much, but then he put it around his waist, the red silk sash he'd always left in the trunk. The sword was a gift from the state of Virginia, would never see combat, was meant for some glorious ceremony, gold-trimmed, with a carved hilt and an elaborate scabbard. He'd never thought it would be worn, had even been embarrassed to receive it, but now it was there, hooked to his belt, a part of him.

He watched Longstreet move up the hill, taking long slow steps, and then he could not look at him, turned away, felt a sudden wave of sadness. Longstreet's right arm still hung low, the effects of the wound. He stopped, waited for Lee to speak.

Lee still would not look at him, said quietly, "There are heavy troop concentrations blocking our way west. General Gordon has not been able to break through."

There was a quiet pause, and Longstreet moved closer, looked past Lee, toward the sounds of scattered musket fire, a fading battle, said, "Sir, may I ask why you are dressed . . . this way?'

Lee still looked away, the voice still soft, said, "If I am probably to be General Grant's prisoner, I thought I should make my best appearance."

Longstreet let out a deep breath. "Is there nothing left? Surely, there is an alternative."

Lee looked at him now, saw the grim anger in the man's face, the look so familiar. "Do you have a plan, General?" he asked.

Longstreet looked down, and after a moment, said, "Is there anything to be gained by throwing this army forward . . . by making the sacrifice of these men? Can we gain some advantage . . . elsewhere?"

Lee thought of Johnston, and the numbers flooded his mind again, the vast strength that Grant could now send anywhere there was still a fight. He shook his head. "No."

Longstreet stared at him hard in the eye, and Lee felt it, the old power, the cold stubbornness. Longstreet said, "Then, your situation speaks for itself."

Lee nodded, looked back toward Mahone. "General, do you have a view . . . something to add?"

Mahone appeared nervous, moved forward slowly, glanced at Longstreet, said, "Can we not . . . continue the fight, sir? My division is still fit."

Lee looked at the young man, nodded, said, "How many men, General? Four thousand . . . perhaps more?"

Mahone seemed to energize, a show of enthusiasm, "Yes, sir. Absolutely, sir! Four thousand good men!"

Lee could not hide the sadness, looked at Mahone with tired, heavy eyes, thought of the numbers, carried them in his mind like some great wound. Mahone's faith in his division did not change the fact that Longstreet had barely eight thousand men holding the line in the rear, and after the fight this morning, Gordon had far fewer than that. The cavalry could not even be counted, but Lee knew that if his nephew had as many as two thousand troopers, he would be fortunate. He did not know the Federal numbers, but he knew who they were, and at least four corps plus Sheridan's cavalry meant he was outnumbered easily five to one. Lee raised his hand, pointed, motioned to the south, the west. "Do you know how many of those people are out there?"

Mahone thought for a moment, stared at Lee, absorbed his mood, and the young man's energy began to slip away. He glanced at Longstreet, said, "I do not suppose . . . we have enough."

Lee turned away, looked again to the west, out beyond the road that was now held tight inside the hard blue line, thought, It could have been . . . it could have taken us away. He wondered about that, if there were still a chance to escape, to take the army farther west, to take himself away from all of this, from the fight, from the death of his men. God had always been here, he thought, always . . . I felt Him. If He is here now, then I must do what He wants me to do. He thought now of the night before, some sign, some message that would lead them, but the message had come bathed in the hard blue of the enemy that was closing in all around them.

He looked at Longstreet now, felt a cold darkness in his chest, said, "There is nothing for us to do. It is time for me to go to General Grant, and accept the consequences for my acts."

He looked back down the hill, saw staff officers waiting, watching him, and he motioned them forward, his hand resting on the sword. He rubbed his fingers slowly on the scabbard, gripped the hilt, felt the cold weight growing inside of him. This is the message, he thought, this is the only path. He looked at Longstreet, felt the tears, had no strength to hold it away, his hand shaking now, the fingers letting go of the sword, said, "But I would rather die . . . a thousand deaths."

EARLY AFTERNOON, APRIL 9, 1865

THE MESSAGE HAD GONE OUT TO GRANT, WRITTEN FOR HIM BY the young man in the round spectacles, the nervous hand of Charles Marshall. He had no idea where Grant was, had tried to reach him through the lines in the rear, as he had before, but there was no reply, and without a cease-fire, without the entire Federal line accepting a truce, there could be a new assault at any time.

It was the sheer bulk of the Federal forces that had slowed communication, the message passing from one front to the other. The dispatches were now flying back and forth, confused, uncertain, no one taking responsibility for ordering a truce. The word finally came that Grant had been on the move, the long ride down across the small river toward the town, from the rear of the army forward, to Sheridan's front.

Lee sat on the ground, leaned back against an old apple tree. The shooting had stopped, a fragile truce in effect, but still he had not heard from Grant. Around him, the staff had spread out, guards posted, holding the soldiers at a distance. Word of the truce had spread through his men as well as the Federals, and order was breaking down, men looking for him, to protest, to beg for the chance to fight on.

He did not hear it, the sounds of men from across the open ground, calling him, the anger, sadness, tears. He was thinking of Mary, of a letter, months before, while they were still in Petersburg, before the winter had ended. There had been such optimism, the energy for the new spring, for what would come, and the letter had been forgotten, pushed aside by the great flood of words and papers that came with the operation of the army. But now the letter came back to him.

I . . . shall endeavor to do my duty and fight to the last.

He imagined her reading the words, shaking her head, the mild scolding, her sad acceptance that yes, he truly believed it, truly believed the war would still go on, *must* still go on. Now, it would not, and already he was trying to understand that, what it meant.

He thought of Lincoln, had never imagined he would ever see him as . . . President, the commander-in-chief. Of course, Lee would not be in the army, would probably become a prisoner. And Davis . . . he realized now he had no idea where Davis was, or what might become of him. He ran names through his mind, his own staff. Taylor had taken a brief moment to be married, just as the defenses of Petersburg collapsed. Lee shook his head, could not help a smile. Taylor was the most vocal on his staff about continuing the fight, was ready to pick up a musket himself. He thought, No, young man, your life is beginning, something new, something worth going home to. They have that, the young ones. That is where the passion belongs, to yourselves, to creating a new life.

He heard horses now, looked up, saw past the men around him, to Longstreet, riding in a slow rhythm, both hands holding the reins, the good show for his men. Longstreet would still do that, he thought, still not let the weakness show. Lee pulled himself up, waited, and Longstreet dismounted, moved through the staff, saluted awkwardly with the left arm.

Lee said, "We are still waiting, General."

Longstreet nodded, held the pipe in his teeth, looked around, focused across the open ground, and men began to point. Longstreet said, "There . . . a flag of truce."

Lee followed his gaze, saw three men, two of them in blue, and they rode up fast, reined up beyond the cordon of troops. Lee felt a thump in his chest, moved forward, and the guards parted. Lee saw the Federal officer, a brigadier general, one star, and glanced at the man in gray, who saluted him. The third man took the three horses, stayed back. The Federal officer moved up, faced him, nervous, made a bow, removed his hat, said, "General Lee, I am General Babcock . . . of General Grant's staff. I have a letter for you, sir."

Lee took a deep breath, said nothing, nodded, reached for the paper that Babcock now held out. He stared at it for a moment, and opened the envelope.

> General R. E. Lee, Commanding C.S. Army: Your note of this date is but of this moment (11:50 am) received. In consequence of my having passed from the Richmond and Lynchburg Road to the Farmville and Lynchburg Road I am at this writing about four miles west of Walker's church, and will push forward to the front for the purpose of meeting you. Notice sent on this road where you wish the interview to take place will reach me.
>
> Very respectfully, your obedient servant,
>
> U. S. Grant, Lieutenant-General.

Lee folded the letter, glanced at his pocket watch, pulled out a small stub of pencil, wrote the time on the envelope. It was one o'clock. He looked at Babcock, said, "General, I am concerned that the truce . . . will not hold. Can you see that General Grant's people be instructed to observe the truce until . . . our business is concluded?"

Babcock nodded, said, "Certainly . . . absolutely." He felt his pockets, and now Marshall was up beside Lee, handed a pad of paper to Babcock, who said, "Thank you . . . um . . ."

"*Colonel*, sir."

Marshall backed away, and Lee did not look at him, heard the hard emphasis on the word, the pride of the young man still intact.

Babcock felt his pockets again, and Lee now held out the pencil. Babcock smiled weakly, said, "Thank you, sir." He wrote something Lee could not see, and Lee waited, patient, now sensed Longstreet beside him. Babcock said, "There . . . sir, if you will have someone deliver this to General Meade's command, there should be no further hostilities from that part of the field. General Grant is up ahead, and I assure you, sir, that the truce will be observed there."

Taylor now moved up, and Babcock's note was carried away quickly. Lee reached into his pocket, pulled out a folded map, the sketches of roads, troops movements, thought, I suppose this should stay here. He reached out, handed it to an aide, now turned to Babcock, said, "I suppose, General, we should be on our way. Do you have some preference? General Grant is not specific."

Babcock made a short bow, said nervously, "I thought, sir, in the town, we can find a location that is suitable."

Lee said nothing, moved toward the horses, took Traveller's reins from an aide, reached up to the saddle.

Now Longstreet was beside him, said, "Honorable terms . . . unless he offers us honorable terms, we can still fight it out."

Lee stared out to the west, thought, No one here knows General Grant as well as you. He climbed up to the saddle, said, "Do you believe that will be a problem?"

Longstreet thought a moment, shook his head. "No, I don't. Sam Grant will be fair."

Lee spurred the horse, moved toward Babcock, who was climbing on his own horse. Lee glanced around, all the men now looking at him. Seeing Taylor, he said, "Colonel, I wish you and Colonel Marshall to accompany me."

Lee saw another man, recalled his face, Hill's man, the message brought to him on that awful day just a short week ago. Lee said, "Sergeant Tucker, will you accompany us as well?"

Tucker seemed shocked, said, "Yes . . . certainly, sir."

Marshall was on his horse, and Lee saw Taylor, standing close to the apple tree. Taylor was not moving, stared down at the ground, and Lee said, "Colonel Taylor . . . are you ready?"

Taylor looked up at him, and Lee saw the tears. Taylor said, "Sir . . . please, I ask you not order me."

Lee saw the pain, the sadness, in the young man who had been so close, such a part of the army, of Lee himself. Taylor sat now, his head in his hands, quiet sobs, soft sounds.

Lee watched him for a moment, fought it himself, said, "Very well. Colonel, you may remain here."

He turned the horse, nodded slowly to Babcock, and they began to move out across the field.

He could see the town in front of him, the small buildings, the courthouse. They rode out through the lines of his men, men who called out to him, as they always had, the men who never held anything from him, from the fight, from their affection for their commander. He moved through the lines, would not look at them, could not bear to see it in their faces. The sounds were enough, the cries, the sadness, the long years now suddenly closing in, the great long fight now passing, drifting out of them, the last piece of strength, the last emotion from the hearts of his men, pouring out across the field. Then the soft sounds were behind him, following him, inside, staying with him. He could not keep it away, held the sounds hard, tried not to show what it meant, the pain that was gripping him, pulling him back toward them.

He looked up, above the rooftops, looked into a vast sky, imagined the face of God, sad, forgiving . . . and now he saw them, the images on the clouds, the cold steel in the face of Jackson, the laughing playfulness of Stuart. They were his boys; more, they were his sons, and now the tears came, the sadness overwhelming him, the grief for a part of him that was gone forever.

52. GRANT

AFTERNOON, APRIL 9, 1865

HE REACHED SHERIDAN'S LINES, RODE PAST MEN WHO HAD already heard the news. They cheered, wildly at first, but he did not respond, moved quickly, held a cigar tight in his teeth. He was still not sure, could not really know if this was not some ruse, some deception. He had run that through his mind, that for Lee's army, it was the only way, the only escape. If they catch us resting, a lapse . . . but he thought of the letter, the last note from Lee, had read it through the hot cloud of the awful headache that had still tormented him. The letter echoed now in his mind, the cool blessed words.

> I ask for a suspension of hostilities pending the adjustment of the terms of surrender of this army . . .

After he read it the first time, the headache suddenly vanished, the violent fist gripping the back of his neck releasing him, as if chased away by some marvelous miracle. No, he thought, it is genuine, it is not deception. I have to believe that Lee is, after all, an honorable man.

They had ridden hard, along dusty trails and hard roads, the staff trailing out in a long column. He could see flags now, turned the horse, rode toward a group of officers, men who were waiting for him. He reined the horse, saw the faces, the expectations, then he saw Sheridan.

He dismounted, and Sheridan was quickly in front of the others, saluted, said, "General Grant! We should resume the assault, sir! I respectfully request that my men be allowed to finish this job, sir!"

Grant was surprised, said, "General, did you not receive a request for cease-fire?"

Sheridan made a grunt, said, "Oh, yes, I received it. Time enough for the rebels to strengthen their position! Five minutes, sir, five minutes, and this will be over. We have them right in front of us. The boys are itching to go. It will be short work. I guarantee it, sir!"

Grant glanced at the other officers, saw some men with Sheridan's fire, nervous motion, but there were others, sad frowns, small glances at the ground, men who did not share Phil Sheridan's eagerness for an easy fight. Grant said, "Are they moving troops? Have they shown any signs of advance?"

Sheridan shrugged, said, "Not that we can tell. But you know how they are, sir. Give them an opening—"

Grant shook his head, put up his hand, stopped Sheridan's words, said, "General, your precautions are noted. Have you not received something from General Babcock, some word of a meeting with Lee?"

Sheridan's face now fell into a gloom. "He is supposed to be . . . in the town. I didn't believe it, not sure I believe it now. But the message came for you to proceed at General Babcock's request."

Grant chewed hard on the cigar, thought, You would wait until you killed them all before you told me? "General Sheridan, you may accompany me. That should relieve your fears about the enemy's intentions."

Grant climbed the horse, glanced at Rawlins, Porter, the others, and said, "Gentlemen, let's find General Lee."

THEY SLOWED AS THEY MOVED PAST THE HOUSES, THE SMALL buildings, storefronts. Along the hill in front of him, he could see the solid blue line, the sun reflecting off the bayonets, the men spread far out around the town. In the shallow valley below, he could see a line of rebels, and behind, the mass of dull gray, wagons, guns, all that was left of Lee's army. He heard Sheridan behind him, small comments, thought, Yes, five minutes, and the blood would be on our hands for all time.

He saw a man, ahead, waving, the clean blue uniform of an orderly, the man saluting now. Grant reined the horse, the men behind him slowing, the horses bunching up. The man was nervous, saluted again, seemed suddenly overcome, stared open-mouthed at the collective power of the men on the horses.

Grant said, "What is it, son?"

The man pointed, a house to the side of the road, a pleasant brick home, two-story, a small open yard, said, "There, sir! I am instructed to direct you . . . there!"

Grant saw three horses now, riderless, beside the house, and a man holding the reins, wearing a ragged gray uniform, a sergeant. He rode into the yard, dismounted, suddenly felt his hands sweating, looked at the front entrance of the house. It was quiet, with no one guarding the door. He stepped forward, reached the steps, stopped for a moment, turned, looked at the men behind him, thought, maybe . . . I should go alone, but no, it does not matter. They have earned it. This is something we will tell our children about. Say something to them, he thought, keep it dignified, quiet. But he saw the faces, and no one was smiling. He scanned the solemn faces, the weight of the moment keeping them all quiet, and even Sheridan removed his hat now. Grant turned, walked slowly up the steps, the sound of his boots echoing through the quiet of the house.

He passed through the door and into a hallway, did not wait. He saw Babcock off to the left, a warm room, dark, and Grant moved to the doorway, stopped, looked at three men, all standing, waiting for him.

Babcock saluted, and Grant nodded, returned it with reflex. Then he straightened, removed his hat, stepped slowly into the room. He could not help but stare at the calm dignity, the grace, of the man in the gray uniform facing him, straight and tall, the white beard not quite hiding the firm jaw, the dark weariness in the man's eyes.

Babcock said quietly, "Sir . . . General Grant, may I present . . . General Robert E. Lee."

Grant made a short bow, and Lee's expression did not change. Grant realized now how well Lee was dressed, saw the red silk, the extraordinary sword. There was a quiet moment, and Grant felt something odd, something he did not expect, thought, How difficult this must be. What would this be like if it were *me*?

He moved closer, held out a hand, said, "General Lee, thank you for meeting with me."

Lee did not smile, took the hand, a brief, firm grip, said, "General Grant, it is my duty . . . to be here."

Grant heard footsteps behind him, saw officers slowly filling the room, lining up along the wall. Lee glanced at them, and Grant thought, Familiar faces, surely he knows some of them. He looked now at Lee's aide, a young thin man in small round spectacles.

Lee caught the look, said, "General, may I present Colonel Charles Marshall."

Grant nodded, and Marshall made a short bow, said quietly, barely audible, "Sir."

The room was quiet again, the officers now still, and Grant began to realize what he was wearing. He glanced down, saw the mud on the boots, the dust on his clothes, was suddenly embarrassed, wanted to say something, realized he still held the cigar in his teeth. He slowly raised his hand, removed the cigar, said, "I hope you will forgive my appearance. I have ridden all morning to get here. There has not been time to change. . . . I'm not even certain where my trunk is, at the moment." He tried to be casual, relieve the tension, the quiet strain in the room, but no one spoke.

Lee simply nodded, said, "Quite all right, sir."

Grant could not take his eyes from Lee now, began to feel a growing sadness, did not know what to expect, thought, How would we ever know? We will never be in this position again. Lee's face still was hard, firm, and Grant looked for something, some sign, but could see now, thought, No, he will give nothing, he is holding it all in. Is this his way? Or perhaps he believes this is what men must do, something about gentlemen. Grant's mind was beginning to move now, a swirl of frustration.

"General Lee, I recall seeing you in Mexico. Perhaps you remember me? I was with the Fourth Infantry, a captain."

Lee shook his head slowly, said, "No, I don't recall. The Fourth . . . good unit. They were all good."

Grant thought, Of course, how would he know me? How many officers did he meet? He was General Scott's chief of staff. "Yes, all good men. It was a good fight. General Scott was, um . . ." He ran out of words now, frustrated again. What can I say to him about General Scott that he does not know? He glanced around, saw his men watching him, was impatient now, thought, I have never done well at this sort of thing, not even with Lincoln.

Lee now looked to the side, focused on a small oval table, said, "Perhaps, General, we should discuss the matter at hand. I have come to meet you in accordance of my letter this morning, to treat about the surrender of my army. I think the best way would be for you to put your terms in writing."

Grant nodded, scanned the faces, saw Ely Parker, his secretary, a pad of paper, an order book emerging from the young man's blue coat. He felt relieved now, the small talk was past, and he said, "Yes, I believe I will."

Grant moved to a small table, sat, put the cigar in his mouth, stared at the blank paper in front of him. There was quiet motion behind him, and a pencil was placed on the table. Grant picked it up, gripped it hard, stared again at blank paper, thought . . . words. I am not good with words. What is it we want? Then, tell him. He suddenly began to write, did not think, felt his mind pouring out on the pages. He kept writing, the only sound in the room the scratching of pencil on paper. He paused again, saw Lee quietly moving across the room, sitting now at the oval table. Lee's sword bumped the floor, and Grant stared at it, thought, Yes, there will be none of that, the stuff of newspaper stories, the ridiculous dramatics of handing over the swords. He wrote again, another page, then stopped, glanced back at Parker, who stood close behind him.

Parker leaned forward, and Grant held up the book. Parker read quietly, pointed to a word, and Grant frowned, of course, spelling too. He scratched at the word, corrected himself. Parker made a silent nod, and Grant put the book down flat again, took a deep breath. Then he stood, with the book, moved across the room and handed it to Lee.

Lee put the book on the small table, pulled a pair of spectacles from his pocket, wiped them slowly with a handkerchief.

Grant stepped away, nervous again, felt like a student, his words put before the grim judgment of the professor. He scolded himself, It's fine, it's simple, and it's what I want. He is taking his time, of course, give him a moment.

Lee now raised the book slightly off the table, and read.

> Headquarters, Armies of the United States
> Appomattox Court House, Va., April 9, 1865
> General R. E. Lee, Commanding C. S. Army
> General:
> In accordance with the substance of my letter to you on the 8th instant, I propose to receive the surrender of the Army of Northern Virginia on the following terms, to wit: Rolls of all the officers and men to be made in duplicate—one copy to be given to an officer to be designated by me, the other to be retained by such officer or officers as you may designate; the officer to give their individual paroles not to take up arms against the Government of the United States until properly exchanged, and each company or regimental commander to sign a like parole for the men of his command. The arms, artillery and public property are to be parked and stacked, and turned over to the officers appointed by me to receive them. This will not embrace the side-arms of the officers, nor their private horses or baggage.

This done, officers and men will be allowed to return to their homes, not to be disturbed by United States authority so long as they observe their paroles and the laws in force where they may reside.

Very Respectfully,
U. S. Grant, Lieutenant-General

Lee nodded slowly, said, "Your concern for the dignity of the officers, their private property . . . this will have a positive effect on the army." Lee paused, hesitant, then said, "I must mention . . . in our army, the cavalry and artillery men own their own horses. May I request . . . that they be allowed to retain their animals?"

Our army, Grant thought. He must still believe that—that we are not one country. He said, "Under the terms as I have written them, no, they may not."

Lee looked down, and Grant saw the first emotion, Lee closing his eyes, a small glimpse of sadness. Grant watched him straighten, could see Lee fighting himself, holding the calm.

Grant thought, How important is that after all? Those men will go home now, back to the small farms, the land they will need to work to survive. He said, "I suppose it will be acceptable. I will instruct my officers to allow any man who claims a horse or mule to be allowed to keep it."

Lee looked at him with tired relief, said, "That is very kind of you, sir. It is planting season, and these men will need their horses." Lee paused, looked down at the book, said, "It will no doubt . . . be a long winter for many of them."

Lee handed the book to Grant, who turned, gave it to Parker and said, "Colonel, you may copy this in ink."

Officers now were moving outside, some leaving the room. Faces appeared in the doorway, briefly, and were gone. Now new faces appeared, to catch a quick glimpse of Lee, of the event in this modest house.

Grant reached for a chair, pulled it closer to Lee, sat now, said quietly, "General . . . I am aware of the lack of supply . . . of the difficult situation your men may be in. May I offer to assist?"

Lee straightened in the chair, nodded slowly, said, "Your cavalry has been most efficient. We have not had rations for . . . some time."

"If I may ask, General, how many rations would you require?"

Lee shook his head, and Grant saw the eyes close again. Lee said, "I am not entirely certain. Twenty-five thousand perhaps."

Grant turned, looked at Sheridan, said, "General, can you provide twenty-five thousand rations to General Lee's men?"

Sheridan seemed surprised, said, "Twenty-five thousand? That many? Why do they need—"

Grant glared at him. *This is not the time.*

Sheridan absorbed the silent message, said, "Uh . . . yes, sir. It is not a problem. We will make the arrangements."

Grant said nothing, turned to Lee, and Lee now looked up at Marshall, who still stood close behind him. Lee said, "Colonel, you may prepare a response to General Grant's letter."

Marshall sat now, pulled a pad of paper from his pocket, wrote a few lines. Grant waited as Lee read the words and said, "Colonel, it is not necessary to say 'I have the honor to acknowledge the receipt of your letter of such a date.' He is right here. Just say, I accept these terms."

Grant wanted to smile, but there was tension in Lee's voice, the guard coming down just a bit. Marshall wrote again, and Lee scanned the letter, then slowly handed it to Grant.

> Headquarters, Army of Northern Virginia
> April 9, 1865
> Lieut.-Gen. U. S. Grant,
> Commanding Armies of the United States
> General:
> I have received your letter of this date containing the terms of surrender of the Army of Northern Virginia as proposed by you. As they are substantially the same as those expressed in the letter of the 8th instant, they are accepted. I will proceed to designate the proper officers to carry the stipulations into effect.
> Very Respectfully, your obedient servant,
> R. E. Lee, General

Grant looked at the heading, thought, So, this house is now the headquarters of *both* armies. Grant looked back at Parker, who handed him the permanent letter, and Grant read it carefully, leaned down, took the pen from his secretary and signed his name. He moved across the room, handed the letter to Lee. Lee now took Marshall's letter, read it again. Grant watched him, saw Lee staring at the letter but not reading, was staring beyond, past the page, perhaps past this room in this simple house, out past all the men and guns and the horror of the past four years. Grant waited, would say nothing, felt the sadness coming again, the room very quiet now, the men understanding what was happening, what this moment meant. Lee blinked hard, took a pen from Marshall, read the letter one more time, the acceptance of the terms, the surrender of the army. Grant saw the pen shake slightly, saw Lee clench his fist, then slowly Lee signed his name.

GRANT STOOD ON THE PORCH, AT THE TOP OF THE STEPS, AS LEE and his aides moved away, the horses out on the road. The yard was full of men in blue, officers, men who had known Lee from years before, West Pointers, who had hoped to speak to their former superintendent; old soldiers, veterans of Mexico, or from Lee's cavalry command in Texas. Grant watched him move out of sight, looked across the yard, up the long rise, saw the flags, Ord's command, and the cavalry.

Suddenly, a big gun fired, a hollow blast, no shell, just a show of fireworks, and now the word was out all across the field, the men hearing from the officers that it was official, that it was *over*. Muskets began to fire, the voices drowned out by more big guns, and the men in the yard began to cheer as well, right in front of him. The depression, the sadness, still hung over him, and he began to feel the anger, the slow rage filling him. Rawlins was there now, grabbed his shoulder, said something loud, some boisterous cheer. Grant glared at him, looked out at all of them, and above him, on the hill, another big gun opened up, a spray of fire blooming from the barrel. In the yard he saw a man with a bugle, caught the man's eye, motioned for the man to come close, said quietly, "There will be none of this. . . ."

The man did not hear him, stepped up close, smiling, a toothy grin, said, "Yes, sir? Orders, sir?"

Grant stared at the man with grim anger. The man's smile vanished, and Grant said, "Stop this! Blow the call to formation! To inspection . . . anything! There will be *none* of this!"

Now Sheridan was beside him, heard the order, and he was suddenly down the steps, the orders flying. Then men were on horses, moving away in all directions.

Grant moved into the yard, mounted the horse, sat for a long moment, waited, and the sounds began to quiet, the guns did not fire. He was still angry, thought, This is not a celebration . . . there is no dignity, no honor, in humiliation. They do not need to be told they are beaten, they do not need us to tell them *we* have won. He began to move, and the men were quiet now. There were still a few cheers, a few hats waving, but around him men were watching Grant move past, and they began to absorb what was in his face, began to understand. Some were looking down across the fields, toward the camp where the men of Lee's army were lining the road, sad low cries, men gathering now around their leader as he rode slowly back into their lines.

Grant moved the horse in a slow rhythm, thought, I have learned something today, something about dignity, about the power of that, what it means to have respect from your men. He is . . . the *symbol*, he carries it with him . . . everything those men fought for. Even in defeat, even now, he still has the dignity. It is no wonder they fought for him. He had thought of that often, not just the strategy, the frustration with Lee's military mind, but the other, the intangible, They have followed him until they simply could do no more. If we had not . . . subdued them, they would still fight, no matter how few their numbers, whether they had food or guns or nothing at all. You cannot ask for that, you cannot order it. You just go about your work and your duty with absolute honesty, you fight for something you believe in without any other motive. Lee simply did not believe he was ever wrong, or would ever lose.

He thought now of the others, a long list of familiar names, thought, This army, any army, is filled with men who stake their claim, who plan their own place in history. But there is no honor in that—because their name reaches the newspaper does not mean they hold any special power, anything to be respected. You don't create honor, it creates you. I saw that today, I saw it in the man's face, in the eyes, in the man's heart. We prevailed on the field, we defeated his army . . . but we did not defeat *him*.

He looked up along the rise, saw the flags of the Fifth Corps, thought of Griffin and Warren, controversy and conflict, men who deserve the honor and men who don't. Now he stopped the horse, thought for a long moment, remembered one name, the commander who had been wounded . . . thought to be dead, the man who came back, who always came back, the man Griffin always spoke of. Grant tried to picture the man's face, but it was not there, just the name, and something came to him, stuck in his mind. The man was not a soldier, not a West Pointer, had come to the army from a college somewhere in Maine. But he was always there, in front, the hot places, had become a soldier by earning it, not by pronouncement or politics or simple good luck. Grant thought, Yes, that's what we need, not a professional, not someone who is just performing another duty. We need someone who will go back home to his family and tell them how important this is, what we have done here, what it feels like to be here.

He still tried to see the face, remembered something Griffin had said, something about words, language. Grant thought of the surrender document, the struggle for the right words. No, I don't want another military man, I want someone who can tell the people . . . who can use the right words. He turned now, saw Porter, pointed up the hill, said, "The Fifth Corps, go up there, find General Griffin, get word to him that I have chosen the man I want to receive the arms of Lee's men."

Porter moved up beside him, pulled out a crumpled piece of paper, a pencil, said, "Yes, sir, uh . . . the name, sir?"

Grant looked up the hill, said, "Brigadier General Joshua Chamberlain."

53. CHAMBERLAIN

April 12, 1865

It was gray, dreary, and the roads were still soft from the rains of the past two days. He had received the order from Griffin, still did not truly believe it, that *he* would be singled out, or even remembered at all by the commanding general. But Griffin had been clear and direct, and there was no ceremony, no dramatics. Chamberlain had thought, All right, but not just the brigade, it should be all of us, the division, the corps, maybe the whole army. It was not possible, of course, much of the army was already breaking camp, moving away. But the First Division, Griffin's old command, would remain around the town, and Chamberlain had insisted, had been as firm as anyone could be to Charles Griffin, and Griffin had no objection at all. The entire division would line the road, both sides, would be a part of it, of the ceremony none of them would ever forget.

He was on the horse, still wore the same coat, had been embarrassed about that, poked his fingers through the holes, neat and round, punched by the musket balls of the men he would see today. No, it is all right, he thought. No one will notice. And if they do, I suppose that is all right too.

There had been some low voices, nervous talk down the line, and in the distance they could see the rebel camps, the tents coming down, the flags lowered. He could hear their bugle calls, felt the sound in some uneasy place, a sound he had heard before, but the notes were different now, slow calls to order, to formation. The men far down the line could see movement on the road now, the gray column in motion, and a low murmur spread up the road toward him. He felt his gut churn, felt the hard thumping in his chest, and finally he could see them coming up the long hill, marching toward him.

They were led by an officer on horseback, and Chamberlain watched him, the back straight, the uniform clean, as clean as could be in the mud of the camps. The man's face was trimmed by a short beard, a neat point below his chin. Chamberlain saw nothing else now. If this man was in front of the column it was for a reason, a choice made not by chance but by something in the man himself. The horse was moving slowly, with steady steps, and the man was now close to him, looking straight ahead, the eyes cold, dark, accepting the challenge of the moment, and Chamberlain could see it all, the sadness, the courage. He did not know all the flags, how to identify all the gray units, or even how many units were still a part of Lee's army. He saw the red banner, held by another officer, behind this one commander, and now the name came, the recognition of one of Lee's best. Chamberlain felt a sudden rush of excitement: John Gordon.

Gordon moved past him, then reined the horse, and now Chamberlain saw the first of the foot soldiers, felt a small shock, the lines neat, the men marching straight, upright. But their uniforms were rags, pants torn, feet bare. The officers had some faint symbols of rank, but the coats were faded, sleeves frayed. Even the horses were gaunt, bones held together by raw patches of hide. The column was halted, and there was a quick shout. The men stood at quiet attention, and for the first time he could see the faces. They stared hard at the men who faced them a few feet away, who might have faced them on different ground in some very different place. The faces were thin, drawn, rough, and Chamberlain thought, These are the ones who still would fight, the ones who did not fall away, did not lose the strength, who are here now because it is their duty to be here.

There was another quick shout, and the men drew their bayonets, fixed them in one motion down the line, and for one brief moment he had a stab of fear, thought, How many times . . . and they know it too, they know that when the bayonets went forward, we would be close, we would look straight into the eyes, and the better man would win. The word stuck in his mind. No, not *better* . . . there is nothing in that here, this has not been some contest, some test of resolve. Look at these men, look at the faces, the strength in the eyes. They are, after all . . . *us*.

There was another order, and the men stepped forward, began to stack arms, making small pyramids, the bayonets pointing up, locking together. Then cartridge boxes were unhooked from belts, some from pieces of rope, some pulled from pockets. Slowly the boxes were piled beside the muskets, and the men backed into line, waited for the next command. He saw the smaller flag, had not really thought about that, had focused still on the bayonets, on the dull steel he'd seen too many times, but now one man stepped out of line, held the flag above him for a moment, and Chamberlain saw the man was crying, the flag slowly coming down, the man draping it carefully on the points of the bayonets. The man's head dropped and he let go of the staff, moved back into line. Suddenly, several of the men broke ranks, hands went out, small sounds, and now, loud sobs, the hands were touching their flag, men dropping down, kneeling. No one spoke, there were no orders, then slowly the men began to stand again, helping each other, moving back into line.

The line was straightened again, with a quiet look from an officer, the men standing at attention. The faces were fixed again, men fighting for control, for the dignity of the moment. There were still tears, small sounds, faces staring across to the men in blue. Then Chamberlain heard the low sounds beside him, behind him, could hear the quiet respect, the sadness coming from his own men. He looked at Gordon again, who stared ahead, waiting for the appropriate moment, waiting to move on, to bring on the rest of the column, the regiments, the brigades, passing the entire army along this road, every unit repeating the ceremony, with more stacks of arms, more bayonets, more flags.

Chamberlain glanced to the men beside him, saw his young sergeant, the man with the flag of the Fifth Corps now, the red Maltese cross. There was another man beside him, another flag bearer with a larger flag, the stars and stripes, the flag of the army, of the Union, and the flag was fluttering in the slight breeze. Chamberlain saw the faces again, the men in the road looking up at the flag, thought, Yes, it is still yours . . . it has always been yours. Despite all you have done, all of the death and the horror, the anger and the hatred. You have proven you will fight and die for something that you believe in. That is exactly what this flag means, has always meant.

He saw more faces looking up, drawn by the slow wave of the flag. There were still some angry glances, the fight not yet out of all of them, and Chamberlain thought, Well, that might be a good thing. It will take another kind of fight, a different strength now to pull us together, to mend what this war has done. They still have the strength, the will, and there is great value in that, for all of us, for the country, for the future. We are blessed by that, we are blessed that we can welcome them back, that we are all again under one flag. I salute you . . . no, we will *all* salute you.

The words came into his mind, and he did not hesitate, said in a loud voice, *"Carry . . . arms!"*

Men were looking at him, surprised, small voices, and he looked to the side, stared hard at the officers closest to him, would not repeat the order, knew they had heard it, knew they understood. Now the order echoed all along the line, all down the road.

They all knew what the order meant, that the killing anger, the hatred, the blind violence of the beast was gone, and the men who stood face-to-face were brothers after all. Now the order was obeyed, and the men in blue held their muskets up to their chests, the quiet salute, the show of respect.

Gordon was looking at him again, his face changed now, the eyes soft. Slowly, Gordon raised his sword, held it high, then dropped it down, low by his side, the point of the sword to the toe of his boot, the response, the soldier's salute.

54. LEE

April 12, 1865

Headquarters, Army of Northern Virginia

General Orders: No. 9

After four years of arduous service marked by unsurpassed courage and fortitude, the Army of Northern Virginia has been compelled to yield to overwhelming numbers and resources. I need not tell the brave survivors of so many hard fought battles, who have remained steadfast to the last, that I have consented to this result from no distrust of them; but feeling that valor and devotion could accomplish nothing that could compensate for the loss that must have attended the continuance of the contest, I determined to avoid the useless sacrifice of those whose past services have endeared them to their countrymen.

By the terms of this agreement, officers and men can return to their homes and remain until exchanged. You will take with you the satisfaction that proceeds from the consciousness of duty faithfully performed; and I earnestly pray that a Merciful God will extend to you His blessing and protection.

With an unceasing admiration of your constancy and devotion to your country, and a grateful remembrance of your kind and generous consideration for myself, I bid you all an affectionate farewell.

R. E. Lee, General

He had stayed in camp until the surrender was complete, could not yet leave until the business of the disposition of his men was concluded.

He had ridden well beyond what remained of the camp, saw many of his soldiers still scattered about, and many of the men in blue, small groups, larger gatherings, some from simple curiosity, some old friends, veterans of another time, when they had served for the same cause.

He did not ride with the column, would not be a part of the ceremony, had made the excuse to himself, No, it is not necessary, my own surrender is already past.

But he knew it was far more than that, that after all, he would have been more of a disruption than support, that the men would have still rallied around him. The emotion of that, of seeing the flags go down, the faces of the men, would have been more than he could have endured. Already now his mind was moving on, as it always had before, to the great bloody fields. It never could be any other way, not for the commander, not for the man who ordered the men to go forward, to march into the guns. The death of the soldiers could not stay with you, haunt you, you could not hold the faces in your mind. The memories of all the horror, of what had happened to each man, each part of his army, all of that had to be put away somewhere, locked into some deep place. It had always been that way, and it would be that way now, leaving this behind, moving on, to the next place, the next duty, the new responsibility. When he moved the horse out onto the road, heading east, toward Richmond, he tried to convince himself this was no different, that he had already moved past all of this, was guided by the hand of God toward another destiny.

Taylor and Marshall rode with him, and they led a small headquarters wagon, the last of the personal effects. There had been no fanfare, no parting speeches, just the simple text of the General Order that Marshall had penned for him. He hoped to just slip away unnoticed, had absorbed all the overwhelming sadness that he thought possible, the pain of the men, the suffering in their bodies, now, in their hearts. He could not look again at the faces, could not hear the sounds, but he began to see it would not be that simple. All along the road, they began to gather, waiting for him, lining both sides, all out in front of him.

General Gibbon had sent a squad of blue cavalry, an escort, some measure of security for Lee's return to the capital, but Lee declined, knew that in this country, riding through this land, there was no threat, no danger, that there was no place on earth where he felt more at ease. But his own men were changing that, and the sounds were all around him now. He tried not to see, to just take himself away from it, but it was not to be. Finally, he began to acknowledge them, a glance, a small nod, a lifting of his hat.

They were letting it all go, holding nothing back. There was no need for the dignity of the ceremony now, for the decorum of the military. They were all veterans, some showing the effects of the hard march, many marches, but now there were no officers to hold them in line, and as he passed by them, they seemed to just come apart, men collapsing along the road as he passed, whose tears now soaked the ground they had given everything to hold. There were still the wounded, men in bandages who could only reach up with one arm, others who simply stood and stared, whose bodies were used up, their minds a fog of fatigue and hunger.

Some were calling out in anger, and he had expected that, and it burned into him worst of all, the men who still wanted to fight, who would blame him for giving in, for taking that away. They will understand, he thought, they will have to. He wanted to speak to them. If there had been one speech, something to leave them with, it would not have been some inflammatory call to the Cause, that they should keep the fire blazing for what they had fought for, as though, maybe, one day, they could do it all again. No, he thought, I can never say that, it is not in me to do that, not anymore. He had tried to move beyond the sadness of that, fought it with every sound he heard, every voice calling out to him. They need more than I can give them, they need more than words. There must be a healing, to move them forward, as I must try to move forward. You must put all of this . . . emotion, all this energy, toward home, to rebuild your lives, go back to the families that so desperately need you, the towns and states that need your strength. You must understand . . . there can be no other way, the Message is so very clear. It is the will of God that we bring ourselves back peacefully into one country.

As he moved farther from the camps, there were fewer men, and the cheers and crying began to fade. He kept his mind busy with memories, not the grim painful ones, but strategy, things that might have been done differently. But he had little energy for that. It was the sadness that came back, that would not leave him be. He tried to remember the beginning, the enthusiasm, his own doubts about what a war would do, how long it could last. But his mind was drifting, and he could not think of four years, of how long that was, what had been taken from him, from them, from the ones who had survived. The dead were in that wonderful place, and he thought of that, how many times God had nearly taken him, the sounds of the guns, the musket balls so close. But He did not take me, He left me for . . . this. He left me to take all of this home . . . and perhaps that is my destiny . . . my punishment. Perhaps I am to atone for this, that the memories must continue, the horrific numbers, the faces of all the souls who are now at rest. So many of us are with Him now, so many died for something they believed in, an honorable death, and after all, is that not what God rewards?

The thoughts began to run together, the weariness of the last few days now complete. There will be time for this, he thought, time for reflection. But . . . not now, I cannot do this now.

He moved through a stand of trees, could see a farmhouse beyond, an orchard, thought, This year, there will be a bounty, there will not be an army to feed. The land will heal, will become fertile again, God will give us that. The plague is past.

He knew Mary was in Richmond now, a modest house provided by the generosity of friends. He did not know if they would stay there long, if there would be some life for them in the city. He knew that many of the troops would gather there, men who had nowhere else to go, whose homes had been destroyed, whose businesses were gone. I can help them, I suppose. I can do little else. They have given so much to me.

He still had not heard from Davis, knew he was somewhere south, Danville, or maybe farther down. Sherman's army was still looking for a fight with Johnston, and Lee knew there would not be much of a fight now. Johnston understands what all good soldiers understand, he thought. There must come the time when you simply stop the killing. They do not teach that at West Point, it is something a commander feels inside of him. Death is necessary, it is a part of war, of anything worth fighting for. But to butcher your army just so they can fight again tomorrow . . .

He had seen Grant briefly again, a small conversation, polite, cordial. Grant understands as well, he thought, what must happen now, what this country must begin to do. He had been surprised at first, Grant's sincerity, nothing of the madness, the cold anger that many in Lee's army had believed. No, he is no demon, he has been simply and utterly efficient. Once the war became the great horror, what so few had ever understood would happen, once these two great armies brought all the power and passion to the field, there could be no other way to resolve it. The foolishness of the politicians, the fat men with their fiery oratory, their hot words, igniting the people into believing this was the only way . . . once that happened, the die was cast. How few understood that, especially in the beginning. But Grant did understand.

He did not know where Grant was now, thought, Probably on his way to Washington. He deserves all they can give him, all the recognition, the cheers, the celebration. *To the victor go the spoils. . . .*

He thought of Lincoln too, as he had before. There is only one President now, only one country. To some, that will never be, the wounds will not heal quickly. But Lincoln will do much . . . he will try. It is in the man, in everything he has said. He wants this to be behind us . . . *with malice toward none* . . . We can hope for nothing else. As long as he keeps control, keeps the angry voices at bay, those who would seek any excuse to punish, to bring down revenge on us, then the wounds can heal.

The sun was setting behind him now, the gray sky opening a bit, the clouds now bright with color. He did not look back, let Traveller carry him at his own pace. He stared ahead, his mind drifting away, moving far beyond the desolate land around him. He closed his eyes, rocked gently with the motion of the big horse. Yes, there is still time. His mind began to fill with the soft smells and joyous sounds, of lush fields and cool green hills, the voices of children, the memories of all he had missed, all that he had left behind. He was going home.

55. GRANT

APRIL 14, 1865

HE HAD BEEN IN WASHINGTON FOR TWO DAYS, MOSTLY THE official business of the army, but much of the detail could be handled by the various commands, the men in the white buildings. He'd been offered a chance to pass through Richmond, to see the last remnants of the great prize the army had been told so much about. It meant little to him when he took command, and it meant little to him now, and so he felt no need to parade through the destruction, felt no sense of pride or accomplishment that a city lay in ruins.

Wherever he went in the capital, crowds had gathered. There was nothing secret about his return to the city. Since the word of Lee's surrender reached Washington, Lincoln himself had spent much of his time waving to the great flocks that spread into the streets beyond the White House, and now, knowing that Grant had arrived, the crowds were even more enthusiastic. Grant had to move with an escort, could not hope to travel anywhere in the city without a large mass of blue clearing the way. They all wanted to give him something, if only their absolute attention to anything he might want to say, any small speech. When he could ignore them no longer, when the voices swelled loudly enough that he had to wave, even a brief nod, a tip of the hat, there would be a loud cheer.

Now, in the sudden quiet of the White House, the first quiet moment all day, he felt the relief, safety behind thick walls. He waited in a small sitting room to see the man who'd given him so much, the patience and faith that had allowed him to press the fight to its conclusion. He remembered his first visit, the hesitation, the embarrassment, the grand portraits, the artifacts, the history of his country symbolized so deeply in that one place.

He could hear voices behind the great door, laughter, then the door opened and two men in fine wool suits came out of Lincoln's office, filling the quiet space in the small room. Grant stood out of polite instinct, and now they saw him, one man staring as if paralyzed by his good fortune.

"You're . . . General Grant! My word, sir, it is a pleasure! Have you seen the crowd? Have you, sir? You must go to the window, say a few words! The President has been speaking to them all day, I'm sure they would be thoroughly excited! Indeed!"

Grant waited for the rush of words to pass, had no idea who the man was, tried to smile, thought, Yes, this is Washington. "Thank you," he said. "Perhaps I will address the crowd later."

"Ah, well then, I am certain they will wait for you! No one in this town can draw the audience you can, sir! You, sir, are the topic of every conversation!"

Grant nodded politely, said, "Thank you, you're very kind." He looked beyond the man's beaming, bobbing face, saw Lincoln standing in the doorway with a weary smile.

Lincoln said, "Mr. Grant, if you please?"

Grant moved forward, gently pried himself past the two men, said, "Excuse me . . . the President . . ."

The men watched him go, the other man now reaching out, grabbing Grant by the shoulder, a hard grip, said, "Good show! The stuff of Presidents!"

The other man slapped his friend's back, said, "Yes! Absolutely fine idea! Washington has a way of finding the best men!"

Lincoln waited for Grant to move by him, closed the door, the voices of the two men still echoing their enthusiasm. Lincoln moved around behind his desk, sat down heavily, shook his head, said, "Please, have a seat, Mr. Grant. Forgive the show of . . . hero worship, if I dare call it that. They're quite right, you know."

Grant sat, saw past Lincoln, an open window, could now hear the sounds of a crowd. He absorbed Lincoln's words, said, "Right . . . about what?"

"Presidential, Mr. Grant. We love our heroes. Generals have a way of getting out the vote: right from the beginning, Washington, Andrew Jackson, Zachary Taylor. I have no doubt, if you were to make it known, you could walk right in here and take up shop!"

Grant was suddenly uncomfortable, said, "Why? I mean, sir, excuse me, but my place is in the army. This place, this city, has never appealed."

Lincoln sat back, smiled, "Ah, but that's why it would work. You're not a Washington man, you're a hero! Here, look outside . . ."

Lincoln turned in the chair, motioned Grant toward the window. Grant stood, thought, I don't really want to make a speech, moved reluctantly behind Lincoln, took a small peek over his shoulder, and now the sounds outside exploded, loud cheers, calls of *"Grant! Grant!"* Lincoln stood, backed away, and Grant was fully in view now, saw a sea of faces spread all across the White House grounds, all down the street. He stared, amazed, thought, This cannot be, not for . . . me? He raised his hand, a small self-conscious wave, and the noise exploded again, louder still. He backed away, stared toward the window, said, "This is . . . strange."

Lincoln, in his chair again, laughed. "Nothing strange about it. They even cheer *me*. Haven't heard that in a while. I admit I can't help but say a few words, the instincts of a politician, I suppose. These are happy days, Mr. Grant. We have been through the most dreadful time in our history. And we have survived. The rule of law, the Constitution, has prevailed. And that's not just from a politician. Look at those people, look at the newspapers. This is one big celebration!"

Grant sat again, said, "I'm not sure about that. There's some rebels still holding out, Richard Taylor's people, Kirby Smith. May take some time yet."

"Those are details, Mr. Grant. If I may, allow me to pass along a secret. Several of the states are already in contact with us, trying to work out the transition back into the Union. That will spread. Once the southern politicians understand that it can be a simple matter, that there is no restitution, that this is not about punishment, that we in fact welcome all the states with open arms, there will be no long-term problems . . . the Union will become one again."

Grant thought a moment, said, "I have a hard time believing it will be a simple matter. There has to be some bad blood, some open wounds. What about Jefferson Davis?"

Lincoln frowned. "Ah, Davis. If only I could do something about that. He doesn't have to be captured, you know."

Grant was surprised, said, "Of course . . . I mean, sir, I would think his capture is a necessity."

"From your point of view, I understand that. Consider this, Mr. Grant. If he is caught, he will be tried, and convicted, and possibly hanged. Then he becomes a martyr. That's how wounds stay open. The best thing that can happen is if he simply . . . disappears. I would not mind if he, say, crossed into Mexico, maybe found his way to Europe. He no doubt has friends who would expedite all of that. I can't suggest this publicly, of course . . . you understand that, don't you, Mr. Grant?"

Grant nodded. "Yes, I suppose so. But I can't tell my people to just . . . stop looking for him."

Lincoln stroked his chin, rubbed his beard. "No, of course not. But unofficially, Mr. Grant, it would be better all around if he simply . . . left. Solves another problem too. Anyone who still thinks the Confederacy should continue can follow him. Take a lot of starch out of the fire breathers in the South. A government in exile is better than a government coming to its end on a gallows."

Grant shook his head, said, "Never thought of it that way. That's why I'm not suited for this office. Intrigue . . . the intrigue behind closed doors. Forgive me, sir, but this job is in the right hands. My job is much simpler now."

Lincoln nodded, smiled again. "So, I understand Mrs. Grant is here as well?" Lincoln had changed the subject, and Grant felt a small sense of relief.

"Yes, sir, she's at the hotel. I'll be taking her up to New Jersey tonight. We have a house now in Burlington, on the river."

Lincoln frowned. "Burlington . . . the river, yes, lovely place. Well, that's too bad, Mr. Grant. Must you leave so soon? I assumed we would see more of you. This city is positively hungry for your presence."

Grant thought of Julia, of the new home, her impatience to leave the city.

"I will discuss it with her, sir. I know she is anxious to be under way. The children are already up there." He stopped, could see the disappointment in Lincoln's face, was surprised, suddenly felt guilty, thought, Well, maybe we can stay. One more day, surely . . .

Lincoln held up a hand, said, "It's all right, Mr. Grant. Talk to her, and if you can't persuade her to change her mind, I will understand. I am well acquainted with female willpower. Please convey our invitation, however, Mrs. Lincoln and I would be delighted to have your company. And I am quite certain the people would receive you with some enthusiasm." Lincoln laughed. "You might even stop the show."

Grant did not understand, said, "I'm sorry, sir . . . show?"

"Oh, yes, Mr. Grant. We're going to the theater tonight."

THE ABSENCE OF THE CHILDREN WAS MORE THAN SHE COULD stand, and Grant sent word to the White House that his wife's impatience had prevailed after all. The train took them to Philadelphia, then they moved through the city to the wharf along the wide river, where the ferry was taking them to the New Jersey side.

It was late now, and the ferry was just slowly making its way to the far shore. He had thought of spending the night on the Pennsylvania side, waiting until tomorrow to cross the river. But the word was out, General Grant was there, and crowds had begun to gather at the wharf, the atmosphere of a party.

Now, they would find someplace to eat a late dinner, and then board a train, the last leg of the trip up to the town of Burlington, a few miles upriver.

HE AND JULIA WERE IN A SMALL RESTAURANT NOW, A SMALL piece of privacy in a hotel near the river. He'd finally allowed himself to feel hungry, sat now in front of a plate of brown roast beef. His back was to the hotel lobby, and Julia could see the faces, a growing crowd of people, straining to see him. He was cutting the hard beef, tried not to hear his name in the general murmur of the crowd, which was kept away by the efficient energy of a gracious host. Julia still looked past him, was smiling, said, "You know, Ulyss, you could go out and say something to them."

He looked up at her, his mouth working the dry meat, said, "They'd be just as happy to hear from *you*."

She frowned at him, and scoldingly said, "Now, that's not very kind of you! You are quite the celebrity. They are being quite generous. No need to be rude, you know!"

He saw her looking out toward the crowd again, thought, Yes, she truly loves this, the attention. I suppose, maybe for her, I can say something, a few words, maybe get them to go on home. He stabbed at the last piece of meat, stuffed it in his mouth, tried to think of something, words, thought now of Lincoln, the wonderful stories, at ease in any crowd. It was a talent he knew he didn't have. He swallowed the last of his dinner, took a deep breath.

Suddenly there was a man beside him, a neat uniform, but not army, something else, a courier. Grant looked at the man's face, and the man was looking down, said in a quiet voice, "Sir . . . we have a telegram for you."

Grant took the paper, saw the strange look on the man's face, something very wrong, and he thought, What could have happened? He opened it, read the telegram, stared at the paper, the words unreal, thought, No . . . this cannot be true.

Julia was waiting, impatient, said, "What is it, Ulyss? What does it say?"

He looked at her, felt a deep cold hole open in his gut, and he looked at the message again, thought, No, this is wrong, I read it wrong. But the words were clear and brief, and the message was the same. He tried to breathe, looked at her again, said, "President Lincoln has been shot."

THE HOPE, THE JOYOUS RELIEF THAT THE HORROR AND SAVagery was past, that the rebuilding was under way, was now replaced by something else, by the last shocking blow.

The last casualty of the war was not the tragic soldier, the man who fought for honor and a cause, who faced his enemy across the deadly space. It was instead Lincoln's optimism, a belief in a future made glorious by the rights of the individual, that everything planned for this nation by the men who founded it could now go forward, leading the way for the rest of the world.

The death of Lincoln ripped apart the nascent healing of a battered nation struggling to put the deep and bloody wounds behind. In the North the outrage grew, and to many it did not matter that the plot had been little more than the mindless actions of a conspiracy driven by one fanatic, a man named John Wilkes Booth. The voices of reason were swept away, drowned out by emotional cries of revenge, an emotion that would give fuel to the self-serving needs of powerful men in powerful positions. They would now take control of the weaknesses of Lincoln's successor, Andrew Johnson, could easily point their fingers into the heart of what had been the Confederacy, using the emotion and the sorrow of a nation to punish those who could too easily be blamed.

In the South the voices of reason understood that they had lost the one man who was after all not the enemy, that with the muskets stacked and the cannon silent, Lincoln was the only man with the power and the influence to put the war behind them all, who wanted nothing more than to bind up the wounds, to reunite the people into one strong voice, the voice of hope and freedom. Even in the darkest hearts, where resistance to the peace, to the Union, was still hard, it was clear that the assassin's bullet had taken away much more than one man. Now would come the angry times, a new brutality; not the guns and the blood of war, but something subtle, quiet and powerful. What had not been taken away from the southern people by the great crushing weight of the war would now be taken by a new kind of violence, a policy of reconstruction that would do everything Lincoln would not. The wounds would not be allowed to heal, the vision of the bright future would be pushed aside, replaced by a dark vision of revenge. Instead of healing, the wounds would be probed and ripped, would become scars that would never quite close, would be kept alive with anger and hostility for generations.

PART FOUR

. . . that we here highly resolve that these dead shall not have died in vain; that this nation shall have a new birth of freedom; and that this government of the people, by the people, for the people, shall not perish from the earth.

Abraham Lincoln
November 19, 1863
Gettysburg, Pennsylvania

56. LEE

Blue Ridge Mountains, September 1870

They climbed higher, the horses moving with slow grace, up past the small trees and rocks. He led the way, knew the trail well by now, and Traveller did not need to be prodded, the big horse knowing the ground, the long trail, as well as Lee did himself.

Mildred rode Lucy Long, the mare given to Lee years before by Jeb Stuart. The smaller horse did not have Traveller's strength, but Lee knew Traveller's pace, that he would carry them slowly, the steady climb. Lee also knew that Mildred was not afraid to use the whip, that his youngest child had become an excellent rider herself.

Of all the children, he was enjoying Mildred the most now. She was finally grown, as they all were, but as she passed out of the teenage years, she became less of the spoiled aristocrat, had grown to accept life in the valley, the life her father had chosen.

It had not been easy for any of them. Lee had accepted a position that seemed to be more tedious than the quiet retirement everyone felt he'd earned. Washington College had barely survived the war, barely survived the torches of David Hunter. The college was the neighbor of VMI, and when Hunter burned the "halls of treason," the pleasant red brick buildings next door had been looted, nearly destroyed as well. What remained of the college was little more than the will of those who worked to see it survive. The man chosen to lead that campaign had been Lee.

It would have been impossible for him to stay long in Richmond. From the earliest days after the war, he'd been under siege, great long lines of visitors, former soldiers, refugees, men who just had to see him, to look upon him with teary eyes, while others brought gifts, the devotion of a people who still saw him as their symbol. He tried to be kind, but generosity had a price, wearing him down physically, and he could not endure the pressure of the public eye.

The invitation to take on the challenge of rebuilding Washington College had come late in 1865, and at first there was nothing about the position that appealed to him. But the pressure simply overwhelmed him, the political turmoil in Virginia and all through the South, the efforts to bring him out into a public forum, all the pleas for some active role in the political chaos of reconstruction.

The offer to move to Lexington began to feel more attractive for a variety of reasons. There were many young men from his old command, soldiers who needed an education to survive, men who had the youthful energy and the intellect to move themselves forward, to create a new life for their families. Lee knew there was prestige in his name, and to use that to build something of value, to lend his name to the rebirth of an institution for learning, could not be ignored. There had been criticism, surprise that he would accept the position at this shell of a school in the small town of Lexington when larger, more prestigious schools would certainly have welcomed him, had they known he was inclined. But in fact the invitations did not come from these *better* schools, but from this one struggling place at the head of the Shenandoah Valley.

There was another reality, and he thought more of Mary than himself, though it was clear to the children and to anyone who knew him well—he was aging. Mary had become accustomed to the wheelchair, and the deterioration, the crippling effects of her arthritis, had slowed. There was even relief from the pain, and if she still could not walk or use her left arm, with the lessening of the pain came the return of the spirit, the hot anger, the impatience, the spoiled little girl who took command of the household once again. Lee had never shied away from her anger before, had simply endured her jabs, her sharp comments. It was always a fair price to pay for the guilt he carried. He had not been there for her, for the raising of the children; with him, it had always been duty first, the long career in the army.

But now he *was* there, and there was time to be with her, to sit for long hours, have conversations with the children, or endure Mary's long and angry monologues about the politics of the day. That had surprised him, her sudden interest in politics, her knowledge of detail, her passion and opinions about so many of the complicated issues that swirled through the country like some blinding dust storm. There were still times when she would rant to her friends, to their new social circle in Lexington, and her views were usually the popular ones—anger at the abuses endured by southerners at the hands of the northern politicians, the carpetbaggers, those who made opportunity for themselves from the chaos and ruin of war. She would sometimes shock him with hot words, indiscreet assaults on politicians she would fearlessly name.

The move to Lexington was a difficult change for the girls as well. Mary, Agnes, and Mildred had grown up in the shadows of great plantations, great social circles. Now they were replanted in a town that did not have the bright whirl of Virginia society. Here, the men kept a respectful distance; if they actually had the courage to keep company with the girls, it would take audacity to actually court a daughter of Robert E. Lee.

The best times for Lee were the quiet times, evenings when the girls would be at some local gathering, some function, and he would sit alone with Mary. Often they would not speak at all, just look out the windows across the campus at the tall oak trees, the green lawns.

The school had built him a new residence, near the traditional home of the president, the home that had been built for the founder, George Junkin. That had been the home where Stonewall Jackson had lived, long before anyone used that nickname. It was there that Junkin's daughter Ellie, Jackson's first wife, had died, a dark memory that followed Jackson into the war, through the last years of his life. Lee had lived there for a while, but the decision to build the new residence had been a blessing for him, more than he would tell the board, the men who provided the funds. He could never escape what had happened there, could not stand in the small rooms that had been Jackson's and not feel the weight of that, the terrible emotion that still echoed in those walls.

The new home was larger, more spacious, with large windows, and Lee even added a sun porch, a patio enclosed with glass, so Mary could sit in the warmth, surrounded by the greenery outside. He'd been amazed to discover that she had a talent for painting, something he had rarely been around to see. Now he would watch her for hours, her one strong hand still nimbly creating beauty, paint on small canvases, idyllic scenes, forests and water, and scenes of young lovers, mythic celebrations, all enclosed by the beauty of God's world. She was especially skilled at faces, the small details, and he marveled at that, looked at his own rugged hands, and thought, She has paid such a price, and surely He has given her the gift, that through her one good hand will come His blessing, His beauty.

His work at the college had always been difficult, the hours long and the duties expanded as the college became healthy again. Each year the enrollment had grown. The endowment was now receiving funds from surprising sources, many in the North. He took great pride in that, but would not take the credit. The staff, the faculty, had grown as well, and all the energy was forward. Lee knew it was the effort from all of them, the dedication and labor from beyond his own small office, that had built the school's growing reputation.

He would not focus on it, but had felt the quiet illness spreading through him. The same pains and hollow weakness that had come to him during the war were never truly gone. The workload had made it worse. He'd thought often about retiring completely, but his presence was a great force at the college, and he was not yet ready to make the selfish move, give up all the good work, and the good work yet to come, just for his own well-being. Even the rides into the hills were fewer now, the discomfort of long periods on horseback something he found difficult to admit.

They reached the crest of the long hill, and he patted Traveller's neck, thought, You do understand. You were gentle today.

Many times he had come up here, on a pleasant ride past thick green woods, climbing, a long straight trail that would take him to this special place, the extraordinary view of the town and far beyond, the Shenandoah, the Blue Ridge Mountains. He often made the trip alone, but there had been something in him, a voice, caution, and now he would wait, find the right time, days when Mildred was not occupied with something more pressing than a long ride with her father.

He turned, saw the mare bringing Mildred up the last climb, and he dismounted, slowly, felt the stiffness in his back, his arms. He rubbed his hand on Traveller's nose, the horse nodding to the touch.

Now Mildred was down, said, "Oh, Papa, this is . . . wonderful. I forget about this place."

He stared out toward the long line of mountains, said, "Don't . . . forget. Never forget. This is God's place. He has led us here. This is where He wants us to come, to see His work."

She looked at him, saw a small frown and said, "Papa, are you feeling all right?"

He did not look at her, stared at a motion against the distant sky, a large bird, far away, a long slow turn, drifting. He said, "I am fine, child. I wish I could come up here . . . more often. There is no time."

The horses began to nuzzle the ground, pulling at small pieces of green, tufts of grass in the rocks.

Mildred was still watching him, said, "I wish Mother could see this."

There was a quiet moment, and Lee nodded. "I have brought her up here sometimes, in my mind. I have imagined she could ride, that she could see this. I have talked to her, right here, as though she was with me." He was suddenly uncomfortable, had revealed some very private place, looked at her, said, "I'm sorry. That was very personal. I hope I did not embarrass you."

Mildred was smiling, shook her head. "Papa, you have never seen any of us as grown. I'm not a child. Mother is very happy where she is. After all, she has you."

He nodded, knew she was right, that often when he was with his army, he would send letters home to all of them, advice, small bits of knowledge, as though they were all still children. It was something he'd always done, even in the early days, stern letters then, the absent father teaching them from far away.

He moved forward, stood out on the edge of a large rock, peered down into thick brush, saw more birds now, small flecks of color.

Mildred was rubbing the neck of the mare, said, "Are you still writing?"

He sagged, took a deep breath, turned and looked at her. "Not for a while now. It is very hard." He stared out to the mountains again, thought of Taylor, Gordon, Johnston, so many others. There was great interest in his own account of the war, and the letters were still coming, many from men he'd forgotten, commanders who looked to him to complete the task, as though it had to be from him and him alone. There were even letters from up North, from newspapermen and publishers, prompting him to tell his side of the story, a version that otherwise might never be told. He had tried, had asked many of the veterans, the commanders, to send him their own reports, to fill in gaps in the official records, or gaps in his own memory. The papers were stacked high in his study, and on those days when he had the energy, he would begin to read, to make some notes, but the energy would not last. Even when he would force the effort, taking the pen in hand and putting words on paper, something would hold him back. He would stare into some distant place, and the memories would come back, and many of the memories were very, very bad.

He thought now of the men themselves: I cannot judge them, it is not my place. If I tell the truth, there will be controversy, anger. We do not need that now. If a man was not a good commander, or if by some mistake a fight went badly, it is for God to decide the importance of that, not me. They expect me to give them some kind of Final Word, as though only I can tell the absolute truth. No, I do not want that responsibility.

He was suddenly very tired, thought, This is why . . . I come up here. It is far away from all that, from the eyes of the people. He'd received many invitations, social and political functions, places where he would certainly be an honored guest. No, he thought, they do not understand. They still want to talk about the war, to relive the great fights, the grand memories. I do not enjoy that.

Mildred was now close to him, said, "Beautiful . . . the valley."

"Yes . . . this is home. I always knew that."

Mildred looked at him, then down, hesitated, then said, "Mother still believes . . . she still wishes you would reconsider all the offers."

Lee did not look at her, knew very well how Mary felt. "Do you feel the way she does?"

Mildred raised her arms, a long stretch. "I like having you home. If you were governor, you wouldn't be home very much."

He smiled, thought, I should have had her on my staff. There was never any doubt what Mildred's opinions were. He said, "She doesn't understand. She believes that I can do some good, help Virginia get through these times. She only sees one side, my influence, my . . ." He paused, hated the word. ". . . my popularity. She does not consider that I have many enemies. There are so many people in the North who would use me as an excuse to punish Virginia. I have to stay away from that. I am no good at being a figurehead, a symbol. If I thought my presence there would be for the good of Virginia . . . but it can only do harm."

"Papa, you have always been a symbol. You can't change that."

He stared out again, tried to find the great lone bird, saw it now, soaring in soft circles, quiet, without effort, carried on the wind.

"They must go on . . . move forward on their own. I cannot help them do that. The soldiers, the people . . ." He still followed the flight of the bird, saw it move beyond the crest of a far hill, drop out of sight. He felt a chill now, a shiver that Mildred saw, and she moved close to him, put her hands on his arm.

"Papa, you don't have to convince anyone. Everyone knows how much you have given."

The chill flowed all through him now, and he pulled at his coat, his hands shaking, said, "We had better go back."

He turned, looked back, saw Traveller raise his head, the horse rested now, ready for the ride back down the long trail.

SEPTEMBER 28, 1870

THE CHURCH WAS DOWN THE HILL FROM THE RESIDENCE, ACROSS an open lawn. It was dark early now, and he walked slowly up the hill in a steady rain, thought of the meeting, the voices of the men. He had presided over the vestry meetings for a while now, the business of managing the church, and today's meeting had been as routine as any of the others. He rarely took a strong hand at running things, let the members work out the issues for themselves, would exercise whatever authority they had granted him only when there was some impasse. The meeting today was a long one, and it was nearly seven o'clock, past the supper hour. It had been difficult for him, the damp misery of the unheated church cutting into him, his mind drifting, pulling him off into some cold angry place. When he brought his attention back to the voices, his patience had been short, and the meeting concluded as they often concluded, with the announcement of a shortage of funds. He'd seen an opportunity there, to bring the meeting to a blessed close, offered to provide funds himself, to meet the shortfall. It had given the meeting an optimistic tone, and the men filed out with good cheer, while he moved out still feeling the misery of the cold, and clenched his jaw for the uphill walk in the rain.

They were waiting for him. The supper had been delayed until he came home, and he could smell the food when he opened the door. He slid out of his dripping coat, ran his hand through wet hair, moved into the large living room, saw the dining room beyond, the girls moving into their chairs, Mary in the wheelchair. There was laughter, some joking at his appearance, and he still felt the chill. He pulled at himself, wrapped his arms tighter. Mary was watching him, said something, and he looked at her, could not hear her words. He moved toward his chair, and there was silence, they were all watching him, watched him slowly sink into the chair. Mary said something else, and he felt his mind asking . . . what? Why do you not speak up? Now Mary moved her chair closer to him, held out a cup, the steam from the tea drifting up in front of his eyes. He stared ahead, still could not hear them, felt the fog closing across his eyes, his mind now drifting slowly away. He saw them standing now, moving forward, hands touching him, the voices like small bells, echoing through the cold darkness in his brain, the darkness spreading now, covering them all.

OCTOBER 12, 1870

HE HAD BEEN AWAKE MOST OF THE TIME, HAD TRIED TO RISE from the bed, but there were always hands, and he had no strength to fight them. He was in the dining room, had thought that was strange, some odd dream, that the bed was in the wrong place, embarrassing, the privacy violated. But when his mind cleared he could hear them, understood that they'd made the large room his hospital, had seen the faces of the doctors now, familiar, men with warm hands, comforting words.

The medicine was always there, the bitter liquid, and they told him it would help, and so he took it without protest. For two weeks they told him he was getting better, would recover, something about a congestion in his brain, something the medicine would help. For the first few days he believed them, felt the strength coming back, but then would come the bad days, when he could not hear them, when the kind faces would change, showing dark concern, and he knew what they would not say to him, that it was more than a simple illness, more than any treatment could help.

When the sunlight had come into the room through the wide bay windows that looked out to the campus, he'd seen strange faces, thought he was dreaming again, but then his mind would clear, and the faces were real. Outside the house, they had lined up for days, students at first, then people from the town. As word of his illness spread, more people came, many just standing outside the window, watching the activity inside. At night the curtains would close, but the people would stay, many of them sleeping right there, on the lawn. On the good days, he had even waved to them, and they cheered him, joyous tears, kind words. He had seen uniforms, even a flag, a strange surprise, some of his army violating the law, presenting themselves to the man who was, after all, their commander. He had thought, speak to them, tell them they do not have to do this, it is all right. But he never left the bed, and so the faces never left their vigil outside the window.

Through the night, when the brief moments came, when he was awake, he could feel Mary's soft hand holding his. He felt the pains come back, the familiar tightness, the left arm, his throat filled with a dull ache. He wanted to tell them, but there were no words, no sound except the voice in his mind. He tried to see her face, could still hear the sounds flowing around him, but the darkness settled around him, began to push it all away. His mind was still working, and he tried to see through the darkness, thought, It must be . . . the face of God, but the darkness began to open, move away.

He could see new faces, panic, tears, the faces of soldiers, the great hollow sounds of a bloody fight. There was a stone bridge, a creek, red with the blood of the armies, and flowing across the bridge was a great mass of blue, pushing away everything in front of them. He saw Jackson now, the smiling face of Stuart, and they were standing still, beside him, looking at him silently, waiting for him to move, to tell them what to do. He looked around, saw the great blue wave moving close, and he looked at the commanders, and still they did not move, and now he heard a noise, a great cheer, the high scream of the rebel yell, and he turned that way, felt the horse under him, could smell the smoke, the hard sounds of the fight along the creek.

All around him now were row after row of his men, long lines of death, but back behind him the high yell was still coming forward. He looked back, over the hill, saw troops, soldiers, his soldiers, a great wall spreading out to turn away the blue wave. He waved his hat, pulled the horse up high, Yes, come forward, push them, drive them. He could see the men on horses now, the flags, saw the one man in the red shirt, and he thought, Now, do it now! The staff was there now, the face of Taylor, and he yelled, "Tell Hill he must come up!"

In one great surge his men poured down the hill, the blue wave now backing away, a furious fight, the bridge now choked with the blue mass, death spreading all along the creek, the piercing yell of Hill's men still flowing forward. He watched, still waved the hat, felt that glorious thrill of the victory, the blessing from God he never took for granted.

The battle was past now, and the field was changed, the horrible sights, the awful scenes of death were gone. He saw Hill now, and the others, and behind, there were many more faces, all still, quiet, watching him. He wanted to tell them, Fine work, victory is yours . . . but there were no words now, and the faces were all smiling at him, and now he saw strange faces, men who should not be there, who were not at that great awful fight, the struggle for Antietam Creek. There were the faces of many friends, Winfield Scott, Albert Sidney Johnston, many others, all the familiar faces, spread out in a soft white glow. He was not on the horse now, moved forward, the white mist flowing around him, and the faces began to move away. He began to follow them, saw them looking back at him, leading him farther into the mist.

Now the mist began to clear and he saw a vast field, a great tide of men, moving away. He thought, Who . . . which army . . . But there were no uniforms, they were all the same. He watched them, felt more men now moving past him, the flow endless, the faces looking at him with a gentle calm. Some were calling to him, silent words, but he could feel it, thought, I must still lead them. He stared out above them, the bright white of the sky, thought, The face of God . . . it must be. . . . Then he looked again at the men, the endless numbers, still flowing past him, and he thought, Yes, this is the face of God . . . you are all the face of God. He looked behind him now, thought, It is time . . . I must go with them. He looked for his staff, but there was no one there, and he thought, There must be someone . . . I must tell them . . . we must go now. He turned, yelled out the command, the last breath before he moved away, marched again with his men.

"Strike the tent!"

57. GRANT

MOUNT MCGREGOR, NEW YORK, JULY 1885

HE HAD BEEN WRITING ALL MORNING, THE WORDS POURING from his mind in a steady stream that seemed to outpace his ability to put them down. He would pause, resting, feel his own harsh breathing, but the words pushed hard against the dam, and so his hand would move again, releasing them, an unstoppable flow.

His hand began to ache, and he stopped, sat back in the chair, laid his head back, stared at nothing. Outside, he could hear the sounds, the birds, and he looked that way, felt the tightness in his throat, and now his weariness was complete. He looked at the paper in front of him, thought, No more, not now.

He stood, a slow labor, walked to the doors that opened onto the terrace, stared for a moment, could see the birds now, flutters of motion, and below, the road, blessedly empty, no traffic, none of the people who had gathered earlier that morning.

It had annoyed him at first, people coming just to watch him, to stare at him, his private moments. There was kindness in that, he knew, but it was still an intrusion, and the sickness took away his patience. When he needed the break from the work, from the writing, he would go outside, settle into the soft chair, listen to the birds. If there were onlookers, they were respectful, usually quiet, would not disturb him, but he always knew when they were there, and that was disturbing enough.

He'd wondered at first why they came, thought they might be reporters, or old soldiers, someone who knew him once, maybe a long time ago. But he never saw a familiar face. They had the odd habit of just standing, watching, giving a wave, a small greeting. Then it had occurred to him: they are waiting for me to die.

The first pains had come the autumn before, a sudden shock, an assault on his throat from nothing more than eating a piece of fruit. He felt a sting, thought it was an insect, a bee, and swallowed, fighting back, had bathed his throat in cold water, but the pain had not gone away. Julia insisted on doctors, but he would have none of that, had little faith in anything they would do. But Julia had her way, always had her way, and the doctors had come to him with that look that carries its own message. He had cancer of the throat.

Julia would not believe that, sought more doctors, some assurance that it was curable, but Grant did not cooperate, would not be the subject of experiments. He could feel it inside, the disease kept a hold on him every day, always announced its presence. He eventually began to weaken, and then he knew what was happening, that there would be very little time, and that he had one very important job to complete.

The memoirs had not been his idea, but when the offer was made, it seemed to be a miracle. After eight tumultuous years in the White House, after a two-year journey around the world, his gift to the patience of his wife, he had in fact been nearly destitute. He'd been approached to write some articles, a piece for a magazine, and was surprised to learn there was an audience for the stories, for his memories of the war. He was never a writer, had never even thought of putting words on paper, nothing but what came with the job. They paid him anyway, a pleasant surprise, and he'd begun to enjoy it, going back, searching through some of his old papers, the familiar names and places, and even the bad times, the grim fights where many good men were lost.

It had never occurred to him that anyone would pay to read the story of his life, that there was anything about his life that was inspiring, or even interesting. But the numbers had been presented to him, a guarantee of half a million dollars; that if he could produce the memoirs, it would ensure the financial well-being of his family. The articles, brief and to the point, had been fun. Now there was something added—a responsibility. The writing had taken on an urgency because, he knew, more than anyone else, he was running out of time.

The money, the financial security, was inspiring certainly, but there was something more, a growing friendship with the publisher, Samuel Clemens, an unexpected benefit of the simple business deal. That was a new experience for Grant, because his business deals almost always went bad. Through his entire life, the most painful lessons, his faith in man would be shaken not by success or failure on the battlefield, but by how men behaved in business dealings. It was a lesson he still could not accept, not completely, and he still wondered about the criticism he'd received, how naive he was. He had always been too eager to trust, believed that everyone would accept responsibility the way he did. It was simple and logical. If you trusted someone with doing their duty, to do a job, it did not matter if money was involved, the job would be done.

During the last half of his presidency, he had clearly shown too much blind faith in those who worked in his administration. His failure to understand and then to stop the corruption around him had not only been a severe embarrassment, but would haunt him for years after his term expired. It was as it had always been, on the fields of Virginia, or in the white halls of Washington. If he was told the job would be done, he simply believed it.

The memoirs could only be handled by him, and even if he had use of a secretary, someone to correct his spelling, his poor grammar, the words still came from him. His fading energy only gave him a few hours each day, but it had been enough so far. Clemens was confident that he was very close, that in a few weeks, or maybe days, the final pages would be written.

Clemens came more often now, and the visits were more social than professional. He would wait for Grant to complete the day's work, then they would sit and talk, as much as Grant's voice would allow. As weak as he was, as much discomfort as his voice gave him, he enjoyed the visits. It could be wonderfully entertaining, because Clemens himself had no problem filling the quiet spaces with his own words, was a man who did not even require an audience, seemed perfectly happy just speaking out loud, entertaining himself as well as anyone who might be around. Clemens had done a good bit of writing himself, great literary treasures, and Grant always enjoyed hearing about that from a professional, the magical process, where the words came from. He'd always been astounded that this man would actually pay him to write the memoirs, was honored now by the man's friendship, the man most people knew by the name of Mark Twain.

HE MOVED OUT ONTO THE TERRACE, PEERED OVER THE BALCONY, still saw no one on the road. He was grateful for the privacy, moved to his chair, eased himself down. The birds chattered at him, annoyed by his presence, and he sat still for a moment, had come to know that if he sat quietly, did not move, they would soon forget he was there.

He could hear a carriage now, the birds suddenly fluttering away. The carriage slowed, stopped in front of the house. He didn't hear voices yet, listened for the sound of the bell outside the front door. He knew Clemens was supposed to come today, and he'd drawn energy from that. Even the writing had gone well, faster, stronger. He heard footsteps, thought, Please . . . no one else, no reporters, no well-wishers. The bell rang, one sharp clang, and he could hear sounds in the house, Julia moving toward the door. It opened, and he heard her voice, the flirtatious delight, and thought, Thank God, it has to be him. He relaxed then, knew what would be next. Staring out at the trees, he saw the birds gathering again, and then the terrace door was opening. Immediately, he could smell the cigar.

"Still drawing inspiration from those damned birds, eh?"

Grant smiled, and Clemens was now in front of him, the playful teasing a mask for the man's eyes, examining Grant with dark concern.

Grant said nothing, held out a hand, which Clemens took, and then Julia was there, holding a bright cluster of flowers. She said, "Look, Ulyss, he brought more flowers. I must say, Mr. Clemens, you do know how to charm a household."

Clemens winked at Grant, said, "My dear, it is not the household I aim to charm. It is the occupants. And, given that one of them is this fellow here, it is safe to say that my aim is toward his better half."

Julia made a short bow, said, "Mr. Clemens, your aim is accurate."

There was a pause, and Clemens blew a cloud of cigar smoke toward Grant, then made a great show of extinguishing the ash, tapped the cigar on the railing, slid the cigar into his coat pocket.

Julia made a short nod, said sternly, "Thank you, Mr. Clemens. Now, I will go put these in water, and leave you two alone."

When she was gone, the door closing, Clemens sat down next to Grant, peeking around toward the house, the same game played with every visit. He retrieved the cigar, lit it again, and leaned back in the chair.

It was a simple pleasure for Grant now, the wonderful smoke. He could not enjoy his own cigars anymore; the gentle warmth that he'd enjoyed for so long was now a scorching fire in his throat. Julia was considerate of that, had thought it was insensitive of men to smoke around him, a cruel tease. Usually, she was right, but she did not understand that Clemens knew it as well, would smoke only what he knew were Grant's favorites. If Grant could not enjoy the pleasure of smoking himself, Clemens would do it for him. If the men thought themselves clever, like two boys in some guilty misbehavior, they did not know that Julia understood the game as well. As the cloud rolled up between them, and Grant would absorb what he could of the glorious smoke, she would wait, then move up near the door, watching the two men enjoy their small victory over her stern discipline.

They sat for a moment, and Clemens said, "The voice . . . all right today?"

Grant nodded, said, a low scratchy growl, "Not too bad. They want me to take the morphine to help the pain. But it fogs up my brain. Can't do that."

Clemens nodded, blew another cloud of smoke, said, "You're very close. How far you gonna take it?"

Grant shook his head. "The war. I don't see how I can go—"

Clemens held up his hand, said, "The war is fine. Good stuff. That's what people want anyhow. Hard to get anybody excited about eight years in the White House. Anticlimactic." He laughed. "Even *your* White House."

Grant nodded, thought for a long moment, said, "I never would have done that . . . if Lincoln had lived."

Clemens nodded, blew smoke. "You wouldn't have *had* to. You may have saved the country, your enemies notwithstanding. We were out of control. Could have been anarchy. Too bad . . . you could write a lot about that. Teach some people a few lessons."

Grant shook his head no.

Clemens realized what he'd said, knew well that there would be little time. He said, "No, it's not important. Stick with the war."

Grant stared at the birds again. "I had thought, maybe the trip . . . write about that, what it was like . . . especially for her. She was in her glory."

Clemens glanced back toward the house, said, "Never known a woman to be so suited for a man. Pardon me, General, but if not for her, I doubt this visit would be near as interesting."

Grant smiled, closed his eyes, was feeling very tired now. He said slowly, "If I did nothing else, I made her happy. All the attention, the ceremony . . . the gowns, the parties. Everywhere we went, she had to tell the world who I was. Didn't matter much what I wanted." He paused, took a deep breath, tried to relax his throat.

Clemens was looking at him now, said, "Take it easy, General. Save your voice."

Grant shook his head. "No, it's all right. I was just thinking about her . . . anger, if something came up, some crisis, and we had to cancel a social event. She took it as a personal inconvenience. I would like to have written that . . . spent more time writing about her, about our lives. There is so much . . . I have been so blessed."

He closed his eyes again, and Clemens sat back, said, "Maybe, General, she'll do that herself."

JULY 19, 1885

HE HADN'T SLEPT, HAD BEEN UP MOST OF THE NIGHT WRITING. He was beginning to feel a small panic, the first real fear; there was so much left unsaid. It was not death. He had accepted that long ago, even when the doctors were telling Julia that he was recovering. What he feared was the weakness, losing the concentration, the flow of words, the memories. The fear gave him energy, and when the nights were sleepless, he would move himself to the small lamp in their room, where the pad of paper always waited, and would take up the pen again.

He'd been thinking too much of her, remembered Clemens's words, *the war is enough,* but she was there, always, and the memories began to fall together, confused, a jumble of thoughts. He kept an image of her, someplace in Europe, someone allowing her the privilege of trying on crowns, great jeweled headpieces, and her pure joy, the giggling pleasure, and he thought, Yes, she could have been a queen . . . as if there was any more scandal about me the newspapers needed for their editorials.

He focused on the paper again, blinked hard at the dull lamplight. There had been so many details, so many names, the numbers, and now there was little of that. He'd tried to think about how much he'd already written, some way to bring it all together. He drifted off again, thought now of the people, the crowds outside the house, the kindness. There had been hopeful, supportive letters, even telegrams, from all over the country, every state. Some had come from Confederate officers, men who faced him across the bloody fields, and that surprised him at first. But now he understood, it was more than concern for him, for one man, one old soldier, and it was more than the formal show of respect to a former President. The wounds were healing and the uniform did not matter now. All the old soldiers had a common bond, having been through the great horror. There had been great difficulties, great controversies, anger, abuse, injustice, but that was past, and the country was moving on again, strong, united, prosperous. The letters were thanking him for that, and even if he knew better—that his role was one small part—the sad reality of his illness inspired them to reach out, to thank him.

He understood now, in the dull lamplight, stared at the paper, thought, We have learned, we are moving into a new time, and all of us know what we must not ever do again. He wrote now, thought, There is nothing else I can give them, no wisdom, no comfort. It is only a simple request, the hope I can leave to all of them, to their children, to their future.

"Let us have peace."

58. CHAMBERLAIN

GETTYSBURG, PENNSYLVANIA, SPRING 1913

HE HAD COME BACK HERE MORE TIMES THAN HE COULD REMEMBER, would walk the same ground, the same hills. He would find all the special places, stand where Lee stood, watching Pickett destroy his division, wander through Devil's Den, marvel at the huge rocks, wondering how anyone could have fought a battle there. He would find the place where Reynolds went down, a very good man taken away from a war he might have changed, even before Grant. He'd walk through the cemetery, stand in the place where Lincoln had made the speech, read the words, or say them quietly from memory. He wished he had met Lincoln. How curious a man, nothing to ever indicate he was a master of language, had the brilliant use of words. It was a subject Chamberlain knew as well as anyone, and he still marveled at the simplicity of this one small speech, the finest piece of oratory he had ever seen.

He would cover as much of the battlefield as his time allowed, and always save that one place, that special place, for last. He had to prepare for it, would make the long walk up the long rise, climbing along the crest of the rocky hill, as he had fifty years ago, on that one horrible day. Here, he did not wander, knew exactly where he was going, would ease along the trail made first by his men, now made by generations of visitors. Finally he would come to the big rock, the smooth flat surface, his own private place, would stay for long hours, staring out at the distant trees, the thick woods, his mind hard at work on the memories, the magic of the ground.

There would be a celebration of the fiftieth anniversary of the battle, and in Maine there was no one who could better represent the old veterans, the last survivors of this extraordinary place, than Chamberlain. As with every event, there had to be planning, arrangements, conveniences prepared for the fragile soldiers. They were, after all, fifty years removed from the battle.

It had been a long while since his last visit, several years, and it was the pressure from the organizers, from nameless committees, all the attention surrounding the anniversary, that brought him back even now. It would be difficult this time, something he would not explain to anyone else, and it had nothing to do with his age, with any physical problem. This time there were different memories, more than the fight, the horrible thrilling memories of that one day. This time he would bring the memories of Fannie, would remember walking the hills with her, telling her all the stories.

That he outlived her was the most painful experience of his life. She had been through terrible times, her health slowly failing over the years, her eyesight gone completely, and finally, in 1905, the end had come. But for years, even when her health was poor, the blindness nearly complete, she would still come here, hold his arm, move slowly with him through the trees, the small paths through the rocks. If it was a painful ordeal, she would never tell him that, knew how important this was to him, to be here, to share all of that with her. He knew it was a test of patience, the tolerance of a woman who had lost most of her tolerance. Their life together had been long and, more often than not, difficult.

After the war, he'd come home to a hero's welcome, and his immediate popularity had handed him the governor's chair, to which he was elected four times. But Fannie did not go with him to the capital, would not be a part of that, and the job was, after all, a job. He had never really understood her anger, what she was missing in her life, why she seemed to be so unhappy. He struggled with the balance, his responsibility to her, and the responsibility he could never seem to escape, to the people, to his state, and later, to the college.

When he came back to Brunswick, it was not to the quiet privacy of home, but more public attention, the presidency of Bowdoin, a notoriety he accepted and she did not, and it was a burden that would follow them to the end. If his private life was overshadowed by the bright spotlight of his fame, that was an observation made by others, never by him. To her last days, he loved her as he had in the first days of their courtship, the young scholar in agonizing pursuit of the girl whose aloofness kept him just far enough from her heart, just far enough so the pursuit would stay glorious. Throughout fifty years of marriage, the pursuit had still been glorious.

The walk was not simple now, not to a man of eighty-four, but he would not let anyone come with him. The reunion organizers were gathered near the copse of trees, conducting their meeting around the high-water mark, the flat ground near the center of the field. It was the most obvious place, flat open ground, where the cameras could get the best shot, where the old men would have the least difficulty. But he had been through these meetings before, already understood what would take place, what the ceremony would involve, the little speech he would be expected to make. It would be an emotional experience for everyone who saw it.

As at every reunion, the Confederates would make the trek, come across the open ground where Pickett and Pettigrew had led the disastrous charge, and they would slowly climb the long open rise, moving closer to the copse of trees, the low stone wall where Armistead had fallen, where the tide of the war slowly turned them back. Along the wall, the old Federals would wait for them, along the same line where Hancock held, where the firepower and strength had been too great. The two sides would come together with hands held out, arms reaching to arms, old men now lost in those days, some crying out loud, some holding their dignity in some quiet place. They would remember their friends, the men whose blood was still in that ground, and they would speak of it all, the memories, the tearful sadness, cleansing themselves again. There would be many fewer than the last time, and they would look at each other with the soft sadness of age, knowing that if there were another reunion, there would be fewer still.

He had made the simple request, a lone walk, had to be firm with the volunteer, a giggling woman who insisted on escorting him. He would have no one with him, and moved away with purpose, a show of strength, of good legs, leaving the disappointed woman behind. Now his legs were stiff, his breathing hard, and he sensed the soft green around him, the air damp with the spring. He walked with slow purpose, saw a sign, something new, a small wooden plaque: LITTLE ROUND TOP.

He was alone, there were no onlookers, the attention focused back at the center of the great long line. He stopped, took a long breath, felt the pains, small reminders, and he blew out a hard, disgusted breath, said aloud, "Go on, old man!"

He climbed again, found the small trail he'd used before, and now he was among the big rocks, stepping carefully, his focus on that one familiar place, where he could sit, finally, and stare out across the peaceful ground.

He felt his legs, the soreness, thought, How many of the old veterans will come up here? He could see out over the peach orchard, the wheat field. He thought of the old men, the reunion, how many stories, where they would go. He could see the great rocks in Devil's Den, thought, There, they will certainly go there. After the ceremony, old men will lead their grown children and impatient grandchildren, will point at the special place, tell the stories. The children will shake their heads, had heard it many times before. But up here there will not be many, too hard a climb for so many old legs. He felt a pride in that, how he could still come up here, the difficult climb. But then he thought, If they do not come . . . the children might never know. Someone has to tell them what happened here, what we did, how important this was. They cannot forget. He looked to the left, toward the bigger hill, Round Top, looked down into the thick green woods between the hills. Right there, he thought, it was right there. We held the rebels away, and it was important. We must not lose that, can't forget about that. How different it might have been, if not for those men from Maine.

He had grown accustomed to the attention, the individual fame. They had finally awarded him the Congressional Medal of Honor in 1893. He'd humbly accepted it, knew they had to put one man's name on that piece of paper, to identify the great deed with a man, to have someone to make a speech, to go to these reunions. But he knew better than any that it was not the generals, not some singular work of genius or valor. If the men, the privates, the men with the muskets, did not want to go forward, there would be no great fights, no chapter in the history books, no generals to wear the medals.

He still recalled the names, the men who died there, and he'd been adamant about the monument, that the piece of marble would not be some generic statement about location, but would name them, all of them. In all the fights that came after, it had never affected him quite the same way, and he wondered about that, thought, Maybe when I was wounded, I started worrying more about *me*. But, no, maybe there were simply too many to remember. He thought of his promotions, the larger commands, had always wondered if learning how to lead a large group of men meant learning how to be a better fighter. If my regiment made the good fight here, and my brigade made a good fight at Petersburg . . . yes, then that's probably true. If the war had gone on, they might have offered me a division, and sooner or later I could have had Griffin's job. . . .

He did not like thinking of Griffin. If he missed the men in his command, Griffin was the only one above him who left a painful hole. Griffin had not lived long after the war, had gone to Texas, where he was killed by yellow fever. Texas was a long way from Maine, but Griffin's attachment to Chamberlain was stronger than Chamberlain himself understood. The package came one day in 1867, the dying man's request, and Chamberlain was astonished to receive Griffin's hat, and the sword, the same sword Chamberlain had given him at Five Forks. Of all the artifacts of war, it was the most cherished possession Chamberlain had.

He thought of their last meeting, Griffin's disappointment that Chamberlain would not stay in the army, would not accept a peacetime command. He had tried to tell Griffin, "I'm not a soldier," and Griffin actually shouted at him with raw frustration, told him, "You are the finest soldier I have ever known." It was a compliment that meant more to him than he would have expected, because somewhere, deep inside himself, he knew it was the goal, the reason he'd gone into the army in the first place. There was nothing he'd ever done that mattered as much as that, as leading men into the guns. Picturing his father, he thought, Yes, you were right after all. You knew it from the beginning. I should have gone to West Point.

He had thought often about that, the need for the fight, all of that business about the nature of man. He'd tried to discover something about religion, all the different theories, had traveled through Europe, had even been to Africa, the Mideast, to try to learn about other wars, to see for himself if there were differences. He'd wondered, Was it something unique about Americans that makes us fight? Was it inevitable, something in our nature, something about the pioneer spirit, that if there is no enemy in front of us, we will find an excuse to kill each other? But, no, he thought, we are not that exclusive, it is not just us, it is *all* of us, it is the history of man.

He had always believed in the Divine Light, the lesson from his devout mother, that all men held a piece of God somewhere inside, that always, given the chance, that small piece of goodness would prevail. Even after the war, when the country was exhausted, the great wounds still open and bleeding, he had expected the kinder instincts to prevail. But the cruelty, the inhumanity, did not stop with the great fight. He could still see the Irishman's face even after fifty years, the cynical disgust, Buster Kilrain's bitter words, *Where have you seen the divine spark in action?* Perhaps, Buster, it just takes . . . time.

For a long time he had believed, hoped, that surely mankind would learn from that war, would carry the lesson into the future. Our war was different, after all, he thought. Something new, something besides the amazing bloodshed, the horrible efficiency of the weapons. This time, there were *pictures*. If the lesson had never been learned by hearing the stories, or by studying numbers, or even walking among the small white gravestones, this time we could gaze at great thick books, awful collections of photographs. If we start to forget, then *look*, *see* it, the blood, broken pieces of men, the horrible things we can do to each other. That should be enough.

He shook his head. But it is not enough. The rest of the world seems to pay no mind to our lesson, and the guns are still getting better. If God is in us all, then Buster was right. We are killer angels.

It bothered him feeling this way, the cynicism, losing faith. He knew he had not truly felt this until Fannie had gone. He thought of her now, had known he could not keep that away, could not sit up here on this big rock and not have her beside him. It was nothing like the wounds, or the aches of old age; it was a soft pain, spreading all through him, filling his mind. He stared away into blue sky, thought, I don't know how long I will live . . . but I will never lose this. I will miss you always, always in the quiet moments.

He pulled himself back, his brain working again, distracting him, easing away the sadness. He looked down into the thick green, where the men from Alabama had tried to push past the men from Maine. He had thought of it every time he sat here, on this one flat rock. What might have been, what if he'd given way, what if the Twentieth Maine had turned and run away? There were great debates, academic exercises that Chamberlain had attended too often, and the scenarios were always dramatic and profound. Often it began with a discussion of the great Stonewall, if he had been here, on this ground. Chamberlain enjoyed the speculation, kept his thoughts quiet, thought now, Stonewall would have been . . . over there, the far end, Cemetery Hill. Right here, the fight might have been no different. It would still have been up to us. But if we had let them through here, things would have been very different indeed.

He had heard all the theories, if the South had won, how the nation would be split into thirds, the North, the South, and California; how there might have been another war to decide just where the boundary would be out West. There were always Texans talking about their state as a separate country. And the South . . . he thought of Europe, of all the small countries, hot boundaries, small angry kingdoms, quick to fight. It could have become . . . the kingdom of Alabama, the Grand Duchy of Virginia.

He felt a headache growing, tried to pull his mind from all of that, shut down the machine in his brain. You do that every time, he thought, you can never just . . . sit. He remembered Fannie's grim patience, holding his arm while he explained it all to her, the explanations she had certainly heard before. He was feeling the sadness again, thought, How many times will I come back here? How many times will I still have to sit here? What, after all, am I waiting for?

He didn't know if his children would come to the reunion, even to support him, to endure the great speeches, watching the sad old men. He hoped Daisy would come at least, and bring her children. There is value in that, that if my stories and all the newspaper clippings mean very little, they should at least come to this place, walk this ground. It was different with Wyllys, his son never quite finding his place in the world. Chamberlain had tried to help him, had even gone to Florida for a business venture that Wyllys involved him in. It had come apart, as much of Wyllys's life had come apart, and Chamberlain thought of that now: It is my fault, my doing. He has a lot to live up to, the name, the famous father. He doesn't have to prove anything, not to me, but he will never stop trying.

Down below, there was a noise, loud, and he looked out over the rocks, saw black smoke, an automobile, full of straw hats and colored dresses. The car growled and sputtered along the road, moving toward the town, and he thought, *There* is something new, something for the old soldiers to think about. What of armies without horses?

He stood now, slowly, eased the stiffness in his legs. The noise of the auto was still in his mind, the jarring distraction, and he thought, Enough of this. It's time to go.

He moved back along the trail, stopped, paused briefly, saw a tall thin tree where no tree had been. Beside it was a rock, small, flat, oddly round. He moved over, stepped up on the rock, looked out toward the larger hill, Big Round Top, and knew it was one of those places he had stood, watching them, watching the enemy roll up the hill in one screaming tide. He looked across the ground, saw more of the rocks now, knew they had always been there, and he remembered now, this rock, he had done this every time he came up here.

All right, Lawrence, he thought, enough. But something held him, something different this time, and he told himself, No, wait, don't leave, not just yet. It came out of the ground, the rocks, through the deep green of the trees, all around him, the sight of his men, the sounds, the smells. He closed his eyes, and he was swallowed up in all of it, his men, holding them back, holding the line, the smoke and the cries, the horrible sight of his men dropping away, struck down. He could hear the screams and the sounds of the muskets, could smell the hot burn of the smoke, saw the terror in their eyes, and now he felt it, his mind opening to the marvelous memories, the pure raw excitement. If this was the last time, if he could never come back, he knew, seeing it all again, it was the most alive he had ever been.

JOSHUA LAWRENCE CHAMBERLAIN DOES NOT ATTEND THE FIFTIETH Reunion at Gettysburg, is stricken with illness. On February 24, 1914, he dies in Portland, Maine. He does not live to see the events that will follow six months later, when, across a wide ocean, another conspiracy, another assassination, will shatter the peace. Once again a glorious army will march with banners unfurled, the colorful flags slapping in the brisk wind. This time it will be the French, and they will still remember the ways of Napoleon, still march in neat lines, a grand parade, officers leading their men, energized by the lust for the glory of war. They will not march into the rifled musket, but something new, the ever-changing technology providing a weapon even more deadly, more efficient. This time, the glorious charge will take them straight into the machine guns of the Germans. The Great War will last another four years, and again the blood and the numbers will horrify the world. And again they will not have learned.

AFTERWORD

"War is for the participants a test of character; it makes bad men worse and good men better."

— JOSHUA LAWRENCE CHAMBERLAIN

"It is history that teaches us to hope."

— ROBERT E. LEE

JULIA DENT GRANT

Regarded with great affection, she seems born to the attention that surrounds her husband's amazing career. Pious yet charming, her White House years leave Washington with a clear image of the perfect social hostess. She writes her memoirs, an odd mix of touchingly affectionate descriptions of her romance with her husband and a strident attack on the myths that surrounded him, including his presumed difficulties with sobriety. Her focus, and thus her personality, is revealed with charming clarity, as much of her reminiscences concern their two-year journey through the capitals and palaces of the world. Her book is not published in her lifetime, and only reaches a public audience in 1975. She dies the dignified widow of an American hero in 1902.

THOSE WHO WORE BLUE

MAJOR GENERAL WILLIAM TECUMSEH SHERMAN

A man with few friends in the press, his reputation for eccentric behavior continues. He is often accused of insanity, or at the very least, a brutal insensitivity to human life. But the few who know him well understand that this is a man with a deep respect for excellence, and a man of high intellect—in 1859 he founds what later becomes Louisiana State University. Promoted to Lieutenant General in 1866, and then Full General in 1869, he succeeds Grant as general-in-chief of the army. He thus is blamed or praised for the army's behavior during the great Indian conflicts throughout the expansion of the American West during the 1870s. Despite a notorious disregard for criticism, he wearies of controversy, and retires in 1884. He dies in 1891, a week after his seventy-first birthday.

MAJOR GENERAL PHILIP H. SHERIDAN

A man who likely would have faded into obscurity without the opportunities provided him by Grant, he continues to invite controversy for his brusque manner and hot temper. The month after the Appomattox surrender, he is assigned to Texas, to confront the supposed threat from Mexican Emperor Maximilian, brought to power as a puppet of the French, who support Maximilian with French troops. Sheridan's force of nearly fifty thousand men is a successful deterrent, and the French pull out of Mexico, leaving Maximilian to the angry Mexican citizenry. Sheridan is made military governor of Texas and Louisiana during Reconstruction, but displays such brutality to the civilian population, he is recalled to Washington after a short term of office. Promoted to Lieutenant General in 1869, he later travels to Europe and represents the U.S. as an observer in the Franco-Prussian War. In 1884 he succeeds Sherman as general-in-chief of the army, and dies four years later at age fifty-seven.

BRIGADIER GENERAL JOHN A. RAWLINS

Grant's conscience, if not his tormentor, he is still Grant's close friend, and remains close after the war. Seen by many as a hypochondriac, his suffering becomes real, and he contracts the tuberculosis that had previously killed his wife. Still with Grant, he accepts the cabinet post as Grant's first Secretary of War, but his failing health causes his term of office to be brief, and he dies in mid-1869. It is a letter to Grant, written by Rawlins early in the war, that lends the most credence to Grant's supposed drunkenness. The letter, which Grant never saw, is made public in 1891, and in part reads, "I find you where the wine bottle had been emptied, in company with those who drink, and urge you not to do likewise." The message reflects the hovering attention to detail and proper protocol for which Rawlins was well known, and includes the additional note, which is often ignored by Grant's enemies, that this advice was "heeded, and all went well." There is no evidence whatsoever that during any campaign where the safety of the army was an issue, or during any time when Grant's decision-making was critical, was Rawlins's commander ever indulging in the destructive practice that affected the abilities of so many men of both armies.

MAJOR GENERAL WINFIELD SCOTT HANCOCK

Grant describes him as "the most conspicuous figure of all the general officers who did not exercise a separate command," and the man whose name was "never mentioned as having committed in battle a blunder for which he was responsible." Hancock still receives the deepest respect and affection from his subordinates, but the nagging wound keeps him from returning to active command of troops in the field. At the end of the war he is officially Commander of the Department of West Virginia, and has command of the Middle Military Division, the position originally created for Sheridan in the Shenandoah Valley. He remains in the army, and his command places him in the uncomfortable position of military executioner for the assassins of President Lincoln. Despite grave misgivings, Hancock reluctantly oversees the execution of Mary Surratt, who he believes to be an innocent victim of the conspiracy.

In 1866, at Sherman's request, Hancock is named commander of the Military Department of Missouri, and moves again to Kansas, where he had spent so much of the 1850s. His duty in Sherman's controversial Indian conflicts is short-lived, concluding with a feud with General George Custer, whom Hancock arrests. In 1867 Hancock is reassigned and succeeds Sheridan as Military Governor of Texas and Louisiana, where his sympathy for the rights of the former Confederate citizens creates enemies for him in Washington. He is eventually given the thankless post commanding the Department of Dakota. Feeling the pressure of Democrats to represent their political interests, he makes an attempt at a presidential nomination in 1868, but Grant's popularity prevents any hope of success. He assumes command of the Department of the Atlantic under the new president, still keeps his political interests alive, and in 1880 receives the nomination. But Grant's corrupt administration has shifted the mood of the country away from military heroes, and Hancock loses the election to James Garfield.

Hancock then suffers the extraordinary loss of both his children, then loses the final fight for his own health and dies in 1886.

Major General Gouverneur K. Warren

The unfortunate victim of Sheridan's wrath spends the rest of his life trying to correct the record, and is supported by Joshua Chamberlain for his actions along the White Oak Road and Five Forks. Pleading his case for a Court of Inquiry, he is finally granted a hearing in 1879, which clears him of wrongdoing and faults Sheridan's judgment for relieving him from command of the Fifth Corps. But the damage is done, and Warren dies in 1882 still believing his potential for a brilliant army career was stripped away by a grave injustice.

Major General Horatio G. Wright

Sedgwick's successor to command of the Sixth Corps performs with competence, though he never rises to the esteem or the affection that the men had given "Uncle John." He remains in the army after the war, is assigned Chief of the Corps of Engineers in 1879, retires in 1884. He survives until 1899.

Lieutenant Colonel Horace Porter

Grant's most trustworthy and efficient staff officer remains in the army after the war, is promoted to Brigadier General. He resigns in 1873, returns to Pennsylvania to become an executive for the railroad. He is a frequent contributor to magazines whose audiences hunger for the "real" stories of the war, and in 1897 he writes his own memoirs, considered one of the most accurate and readable accounts of life with General Grant. He survives until 1921.

Major General George Gordon Meade

He is described by Grant as "an officer of great merit, with drawbacks to his usefulness that were beyond his control . . . no one saw this better than himself, and no one regretted it more." Meade remains in the army after the war and is named to command the Division of the Atlantic. Congress's Reconstruction policies place the military in command of the southern states, and he becomes Military Governor of Florida, Georgia, and Alabama. When Sheridan alone is promoted to

Lieutenant General, Meade vents his anger in public at both Sheridan and Washington for being passed over. He resigns his Reconstruction position, returns to Philadelphia to again command the Division of the Atlantic, and dies in 1872 of pneumonia.

Major Tom Chamberlain

Joshua Lawrence Chamberlain's youngest brother remains in command of Company G, Twentieth Maine, throughout the last half of the war. After Appomattox he is promoted to Lieutenant Colonel, and for a short while serves on Chamberlain's staff at division command. When the Army of the Potomac is officially disbanded in late June 1865, Tom returns to Maine, finds little to substitute for life as a soldier. He marries his ex-sister-in-law (widow of brother John) in 1870, and tries to follow his older brother's example by joining Joshua and Wyllys Chamberlain in their unfortunate business venture in Florida. He returns to Maine, saddens his family by establishing a dismal reputation for drinking and womanizing. Those who served with him during the war remember only a man who was an excellent soldier, but his civilian life can never measure up to the extraordinary esteem enjoyed by his famous brother, and he dies in New York City in 1896, at age fifty-five.

Those Who Wore Gray

Colonel Walter H. Taylor

Lee's most loyal officer was arguably the most hardworking and efficient staff officer in either army. After the war, he settles with his new wife in Norfolk, Virginia, and raises eight children. He prospers first in the hardware business, eventually enters banking, becomes president of the Marine Bank of Norfolk. He serves briefly as a state senator to the Virginia legislature, which labors to carry the state forward through the difficulties of Reconstruction. He maintains contact with his former commander, and is one of those called upon to assist Lee with material for the memoirs Lee never writes. Taylor understands Lee's fondness for those small bits of luxury Lee himself would rarely reveal, and so the young man frequently surprises Lee with gifts from the seacoast, most notably great boxes of fresh oysters, for which Lee has a weakness.

Taylor serves on the board of his alma mater, the Virginia Military Institute, and three of his sons attend the school.

His book, *General Lee, 1861–1865,* is possibly the most insightful and least egocentric memoir of any staff officer of the war. Throughout his life he is well known in Norfolk not only as the staff officer of the South's greatest hero, but for his own quiet accomplishments as well. He dies in 1913, at age seventy-four. His obituary in the *Richmond Times-Dispatch* concludes: "Few men have been more honored in life than Col. Walter H. Taylor . . . and few are more honored in memory than he. To have lived so that all men gave him reverence to the day of his death is memory fine enough, but to have lived so that in his youth he was the trusted adjutant of Robert E. Lee sets his name apart and emblazons it. His books, his work in later years, his service to his community will live after him."

Lieutenant General James Longstreet

Possibly the least understood and most maligned commander in the South, "Old Pete" was decades ahead of his time with his defensive tactics, the development of trench warfare.

After the war, he and his wife Louise settle in New Orleans, where he goes into the cotton brokerage business and later founds an insurance agency. Often blamed for the loss at Gettysburg, his close relationship with Lee diminishes after the war, and he pursues a lifelong effort to vindicate his actions, which often results in controversy, since much of his writing and explanations come after the death of Lee. There is still controversy and disagreement as to what role his ego and desire for independent command played in his relationship with Lee. It is indisputable, however, that Lee relied upon Longstreet more than anyone under his command, and no one performed in difficult situations with the consistency of Old Pete.

Proving, however, to be his own worst enemy, Longstreet writes that "we are a conquered people" and should "accept the terms that are now offered by the conquerors." Though conciliatory in sentiment, it is an unwise statement to make publicly. He becomes a Republican during Reconstruction, believing sincerely that he can better aid the South by cooperation with the powers in Congress, and thus alienates many southerners who otherwise would have supported him. He accepts a job from his friend, (now President) Grant, and in 1869 becomes Customs Surveyor for the Port of New Orleans. This further outrages many who feel that he is a direct pawn of the hostile administration. His old friend, and former subordinate, Daniel Harvey Hill writes, "[Longstreet] is the local leper of the community."

He finally leaves New Orleans in 1875 and settles in Gainesville, Georgia. Later he serves as United States Minister to Turkey, but has never had skill as a diplomat, finds the position disagreeable at best, and returns to become a U. S. marshal in Georgia. He retires from government service in 1884 and settles into a pleasant life as a farmer. In 1889 he endures disaster as his home, and many of the precious artifacts of his wartime service, are destroyed by fire, and then later in the same year, his wife Louise dies. She had borne him ten children, only five of whom survived to adulthood. He eases his grief by writing his memoirs, creating yet more controversy. His view of events is described by many as flawed, either by the passage of years or his continuing need to defend his service on the field.

He shocks friends and family in 1897 by marrying thirty-four-year-old Helen Dortch, a woman younger than he by forty-two years. Gradually, though, he rekindles the affection of many of the old soldiers, attends reunions and celebrations, and is cheered with great enthusiasm by the men who remember him, after all, as Lee's war-horse. He dies in 1904 of pneumonia, having never regained the use of his right arm; he is just shy of his eighty-third birthday. Helen Dortch Longstreet survives until 1962.

The controversy that has surrounded his name is made poignant by the fact that it is not until July 1998, 135 years after the battle, that the first monument to him is scheduled to be placed on the field at Gettysburg.

MAJOR GENERAL JOHN B. GORDON

The lawyer-turned-soldier returns to his home state of Georgia after the war, and serves two terms as a United States senator, then one term as governor of the state. Always active in Confederate causes and reunions, he serves as commander-in-chief of the United Confederate Veterans. Long after the war, after most of its participants are gone, he writes his memoirs. As with Longstreet, the accuracy of the work is criticized, and again, much is made of the span of years between the events and the writing. Some suggest there are some indiscreet motives behind some of Gordon's accounts, and so, much of his reminiscences are regarded with great skepticism. Lee biographer Douglas Southall

Freeman writes that it is often difficult "to know where General Gordon's memory ended and where his imagination began."

LIEUTENANT COLONEL CHARLES MARSHALL

The grandson of the illustrious John Marshall, the fourth U.S. Chief Justice, the young man who serves Lee so well was in reality the author of many of Lee's most famous documents, including the General Order Number 9 (Lee's farewell to his troops). After the war he settles in Baltimore and establishes a successful law practice. He is often called upon to speak at dedications to Lee monuments around the South, and continues to eloquently defend the southern cause. As the years pass, he becomes equally as outspoken in the cause of healing the wounds of the country. He speaks at the dedication of Grant's Tomb in New York, where he says, "Men who were arrayed against each other in deadly strife are now met together to do honor to the memory of one who led one part of this audience to a complete and absolute victory over the other, yet in the hearts of the victors there is no feeling of triumph, and in the hearts of the vanquished there is no bitterness, no humiliation."

He survives until 1904.

MAJOR GENERAL WILLIAM MAHONE

At the time of the surrender, "Little Billy" was regarded by many as Lee's finest commander. His troops identify themselves as "Mahone's Division" at reunions and gatherings for decades, despite the brief duration of his command. He becomes president of the Southside Railroad and prospers in the business of operating the very line that his troops had fought to defend. He becomes a United States senator from Virginia in 1880, survives until 1895.

MAJOR GENERAL FITZHUGH LEE

After Lee's army exhausted any hope of escape at Appomattox, Lee's nephew, "Fitz," insisted that surrender was not an option, and without telling his commander, led what remained of his cavalry command away from the town, intending to continue the fight as a guerrilla. He changed his mind, returned, and surrendered his cavalry at Farmville two days after Lee and Grant have met.

He establishes himself prominently in Virginia politics, becomes governor in 1885, but his greatest peacetime notoriety comes as U.S. Minister to Cuba, handling the difficult duties of diplomacy prior to the Spanish-American War. On the basis of his excellent service, he applies for and is granted commission as Major General of Volunteers in 1898, commands the Seventh Army Corps during that war. He retires in 1901, and dies in 1905.

MAJOR GENERAL GEORGE WASHINGTON CUSTIS LEE

The oldest and the only one of Lee's sons who seems destined not to be a professional soldier, the shy and self-effacing man is released from capture on orders from Grant at Appomattox. He moves to Lexington, Virginia, around the same time as his father, and becomes a professor of engineering at VMI. When his father is near death, the board of Washington College votes to allow Mary Lee lifelong occupancy of the President's Residence, which she refuses. Though qualified and certainly suitable for the post himself, the board's earnest desire to assist Lee's widow plays some role in Custis's election to the presidency, succeeding his father. Since he will live in the residence, it solves the dilemma for Mary as well, who remains with her oldest son until her death in 1873. If nepotism is a motive, it proves to bring exceptionally good fortune to the school, which is soon named Washington and Lee University. Custis serves as a much-respected administrator until he retires in 1897. He survives until 1913.

LIEUTENANT GENERAL RICHARD S. EWELL

As the successor to Stonewall, no commander in Lee's army had the opportunity for lasting fame as much as "Old Baldy." It remains a mystery why he could not rise to the challenge, though blame is often given to the dominance of his wife. His harsh temper, constant illness—real or imagined—drained all the fire of the Cause from him. After the war, he fades into obscurity, and dies in Virginia in 1872.

LIEUTENANT GENERAL JUBAL A. EARLY

"Old Jubilee" was finally relieved of service by Lee just prior to Appomattox, and he became a commander without a command. He disguises himself and goes to Texas, to bring what forces he can to assist Kirby Smith. After Smith's surrender, Early hops the border into

Mexico and continues to fight the war in his own mind. He goes to Canada, where he writes his memoirs. Finally returning to Virginia after Lee's death, he becomes embroiled with Longstreet in the controversy over blame for the loss at Gettysburg. Considered vain, ill-tempered, and vindictive, it is likely that his unfortunate behavior did much to diminish the reputation he earned with his troops as an excellent field commander. He never marries, and dies in 1894.

GENERAL P. G. T. BEAUREGARD

His unfortunate vanity and hunger for the limelight is a combination that makes enemies, and so throughout the war he was never allowed to remain long in any command where serious fighting took place. Considered an able commander of troops in the field, and noted particularly for his brilliant defense of Petersburg against extraordinary odds, he has an unfortunate talent for making ill-advised demands and exaggerating his own military situation. His single-minded need to put himself in the center of the war made his superiors uncomfortable, notably Jefferson Davis. He still offered a steady flow of grand plans and military strategies, none of which showed any rational hope of success. He was assigned to Joe Johnston's command in the Carolinas, must endure being the subordinate again, but the war ended before he could alienate yet another commander.

Afterward, he serves briefly as a railroad executive, but astonishingly, his reputation for greatness is expanded abroad, and he is offered command of armies in both Egypt and Romania, which he turns down, though with some regret. He writes extensively on his role in the war, creates considerable controversy by giving a slanted and wholly inaccurate account of his communications with Lee prior to the Petersburg campaign, putting himself in the best possible light, and harshly criticizing Lee's generalship. The articles are not published until after Lee's death. He survives until 1893.

PRESIDENT JEFFERSON DAVIS

Despite great effort, he does not fulfill Lincoln's wish that he escape, and thus fade into obscurity. He maintains some semblance of a Confederate government, traveling first to Danville, Virginia, then Charlotte, North Carolina. Johnston's surrender to Sherman turns all energy to Davis's capture, and finally, desperate and on the move, he is captured near Irwinville, Georgia, on May 10, 1865. He is imprisoned at

Fort Monroe on the Virginia peninsula for nearly two years, subjected to humiliating and inhumane treatment. But what Lincoln had feared is realized, and the publicity that begins to spread creates an uncomfortable situation for the government. Ultimately, he is simply released, and the scars that would be opened by a public trial are avoided. He travels to Europe, but feels some bitterness at what he sees as the betrayal of the powers that could have given so much aid to the Confederacy. He settles in Memphis in 1869, and accepts a position as head of an insurance company, which fails in 1873. Then he moves to Mobile, where he begins a long and bitter dispute with Joe Johnston, their wartime feud now expanding. In 1881 Davis completes his memoirs, much of which is devoted to disputing Johnston's own book. It is suggested by friends that Davis apply for a congressional pardon, to participate in the healing that has helped many of his former subordinates in their new lives. He responds, ". . . repentance must precede the right of a pardon, and I have not repented." He continues to insist that though the war showed secession "to be impracticable, this did not prove it to be wrong." He dies of malaria in 1889 at the age of eighty-one.

Lieutenant General Richard H. Anderson

Even before his crushing defeat at Saylor's Creek, Anderson's zeal for the Cause of the Confederacy had faded, and by the war's end he shared none of the political fire that still inspired men like Jubal Early. He returns to his family's old homestead in South Carolina, and, unlike Billy Mahone, he never makes the effort to fit himself into the new opportunities that open up in the rebuilding of the South. He settles into a difficult life as a farmer and suffers financial failure. He eventually endures humiliating work as a day laborer, earning a meager living from the sympathy of his neighbors. He dies in poverty in 1879, at age fifty-seven.

Traveller

Purchased by Lee in 1862 for two hundred dollars, he is possibly the best known horse in American history. He outlives his master, but in death, as in life, the two remain close companions. Traveller is buried close beside the Lee Chapel at Washington and Lee University, which houses the final resting place of Robert E. Lee and his family.

About the Author

Jeff Shaara was born in 1952 in New Brunswick, New Jersey. He grew up in Tallahassee, Florida, and graduated from Florida State University in 1974. For many years he was a dealer in rare coins, but sold his Tampa, Florida, business in 1988 upon the death of his father, Michael Shaara.

As manager of his father's estate, Jeff developed a friendship with film director Ron Maxwell, whose film *Gettysburg* was based on *The Killer Angels.* It was Maxwell who suggested that Jeff continue the story Michael Shaara had begun, the inspiration that produced Jeff's novels *Gods and Generals* and *The Last Full Measure*. He is also the author of *Rise to Rebellion, Gone for Soldiers,* and *The Glorious Cause*.

Visit the author online at www.JeffShaara.com.

And don't miss Michael Shaara's Pulitzer Prize–winning novel at the heart of the trilogy

"My favorite historical novel . . . A superb re-creation of the Battle of Gettysburg, but its real importance is its insight into what the war was about, and what it meant."

—James M. McPherson
Author of BATTLE CRY OF FREEDOM

"Shaara carries [the reader] swiftly and dramatically to a climax as exciting as if it were being heard for the first time."

—THE SEATTLE TIMES

The complete trilogy—GODS AND GENERALS, THE KILLER ANGELS, and THE LAST FULL MEASURE—is also available as a handsome boxed set in a special slipcase!

Available in bookstores everywhere.
Published by Ballantine Books.
The Ballantine Publishing Group
www.ballantinebooks.com

"JEFF SHAARA HAS SUCCEEDED BRILLIANTLY. *GODS AND GENERALS* IS EVERY OUNCE AS FINE A WORK AS HIS FATHER'S WAS."

—Detroit Free Press

"The Battle of Gettysburg featured a cast of characters dramatically and poignantly portrayed in Michael Shaara's *The Killer Angels.* This new novel by his son, Jeff Shaara, describes the interconnected paths that brought these men together at this crossroads of our history. Readers of *The Killer Angels* won't want to miss *Gods and Generals.*"

—JAMES M. MCPHERSON
Author of *Battle Cry of Freedom*

"*Gods and Generals* is an honorable, readable sprawl of a book. . . . Shaara's best service in *Gods and Generals* is to take men who now stand as unnoticed monuments outside courthouses and humanize them."

—The Philadelphia Inquirer

"The strength of this work is its personalization of the struggle. The action both draws in the reader and illustrates the gravity of each situation. . . . There is also a certain poetry to Mr. Shaara's introspection and narrative."

—The Dallas Morning News

"Pick up and read *Gods and Generals.* . . . The pen of Shaara has put life into Lee, Jackson, Hancock, and Chamberlain. We almost get to know them personally through their thoughts and feelings as they lived through our great American tragedy."

—The Civil War News

"Shaara has created human beings of the myths and cold facts."

—St. Petersburg Times

WINNER OF THE ALA AWARD FOR BEST MILITARY NOVEL

Please turn the page for more reviews. . . .

"VERGES ON THE MIRACULOUS . . .
Against all odds, Jeff Shaara's *GODS AND GENERALS* succeeds in leading you back to *The Killer Angels*."

—GABOR S. BORITT
Director of the Civil War Institute, Gettysburg, PA

"In *Gods and Generals* [Shaara] writes in the same spare but elegant prose style his father did, and measures up to Michael's genius for crafting exciting fiction against a historically accurate backdrop. He conveys to the reader the same vivid sense of battle as his father and builds characterization with wonderfully believable dialogue."

—*Houston Chronicle*

"Civil War buffs and fans of the hefty historical novel will find plenty to enjoy in *Gods and Generals*. . . . Historical detail and depth of character carry the book, which examines the viewpoints and vulnerabilities of one of the most fascinating collections of military minds ever assembled on a single battlefront."

—*Minneapolis Star-Tribune*

"This heartbreaking story offers an understanding of man's fascination with battle and made me marvel at how wave after wave of soldiers marched into sure death. The portraits of the battlefield are vividly horrid, of the men profoundly emotional, and of the war, intense. I wept as I turned the pages."

—*Anniston Star*

"Shaara hits his stride as the political debate turns to armed conflict. The early days of war and the epic battles at Fredericksburg and Chancellorsville come to life on the pages of *Gods and Generals*. Not only the main characters in the novel, but the secondary and subsidiary ones contribute to a fine portrait of a people and a nation in conflict."

—*Chattanooga Times Free Press*

"[*Gods and Generals*] did something *The Killer Angels* did not; it made me cry."

—*The Nashville Banner*

"AN HONORABLE EFFORT AND A CLEAR INSIGHT INTO U.S. HISTORY."
—Fort Worth Star-Telegram

"A highly engaging book . . . Shaara weaves together a coherent battle narrative, conveying the difficulties of moving troops and the near-chaos of fighting in the days before modern communications."

—*The Commercial Appeal*

"Writers, like athletes, from time to time find themselves in that elusive 'zone' where everything seems to go right, and they surpass their greatest expectations. . . . In writing his bestselling Civil War novel *Gods and Generals*, author Jeff Shaara often found himself in that zone."

—*Sun-Sentinel*

"In every sense, even when compared with the father's celebrated work, the son's uncommon skill has produced a Civil War novel that stands out among all others. . . . *Gods and Generals* is truly more epic in scope than *The Killer Angels*."

—*BookPage*

"A robust portrait of the early years of the war . . . Like *The Killer Angels*, this novel displays an impressive grasp of the particulars of the conflict. . . . Shaara's wonderful command of detail and his generally shrewd depiction of character make for an impressive debut."

—*Kirkus Reviews*

"Shaara treats his material with the kind of respect it deserves and does not try to remake his characters to appeal to modern sensibilities. . . . He is, in every sense, faithful to his material and to the legacy of his father."

—*American Way*

Please turn the page for more reviews. . . .

"SHAARA IS AN EXCELLENT WRITER
who pays tribute to his father with a fine first novel."
—*The Orlando Sentinel*

"Jeff Shaara does shine when he writes about Jackson, and the general's death is the most moving part of the novel."

—*The Indianapolis Star*

"The battle scenes are remarkably easy to visualize and haunting in their ability to stay with you long after you have put down the book."

—*The Highlands Ranch Herald*

"Shaara tells a tale impressive in its sweep, depth of character, and historic verisimilitude. . . . Like his father, Shaara gets deeply into the minds of his protagonists. . . . The Shaara genes, it seems, are in fine shape."

—*Publishers Weekly*

"I truly enjoyed this fictitious but historically accurate work by the son of one of my favorite authors. Jeff's style is much like that of his father, and for that I was pleased; it was like visiting with an old friend again. I only hope the young Shaara finishes this trilogy of America's great conflict."

—JAMES N. VOGLER, JR.
Confederate Veteran

"The Civil War has been a popular subject for novelists virtually ever since the guns fell silent. Only a partial list of titles would include such highly acclaimed works as Stephen Crane's classic *The Red Badge of Courage*, Shelby Foote's *Shiloh*, Tom Wicker's *Unto This Hour*, Gore Vidal's *Lincoln*, and William Safire's *Freedom*. Jeff Shaara's *Gods and Generals* belongs in the company of these other masterful novels. It's fascinating reading that brings the heart of the war closer to you."

—*The Shelby Star* (NC)

"A DELIGHT TO READ . . .
If you are interested in the Civil War and have a hankering for trying to understand the psyches of the major players, I highly recommend you to go out and buy the book and keep it next to *The Killer Angels* on your shelf."

—COL. JOHN P. GLASGOW, USMC (Ret.)
Marine Corps Gazette

"*Gods and Generals* is a very fine book that will lead many readers to Michael Shaara's *The Killer Angels*. The two books belong together, and father and son, though years apart, reveal the consistency of their vision, expression, and relation."

—*Stars and Stripes*

"Whereas historians can only recite their actions, skilled novelists like Michael and Jeff Shaara can re-create—with surprising empathy and acceptable accuracy—their moods and emotions, their feelings, and their faith."

—*Newport News*

"His writing style is a lot like his old man's—soft but direct, cotton-wrapped iron. . . . *Gods and Generals* can stand on its own . . . as a very good historical novel packed with vivid word pictures."

—*The Palm Beach Post*

"*Gods and Generals* is as good as *The Killer Angels*, maybe better. Jeff Shaara has written a masterpiece."

—MORT KÜNTSLER
Historical Artist

"*Gods and Generals* will delight and entertain."

—*Savannah Morning News*

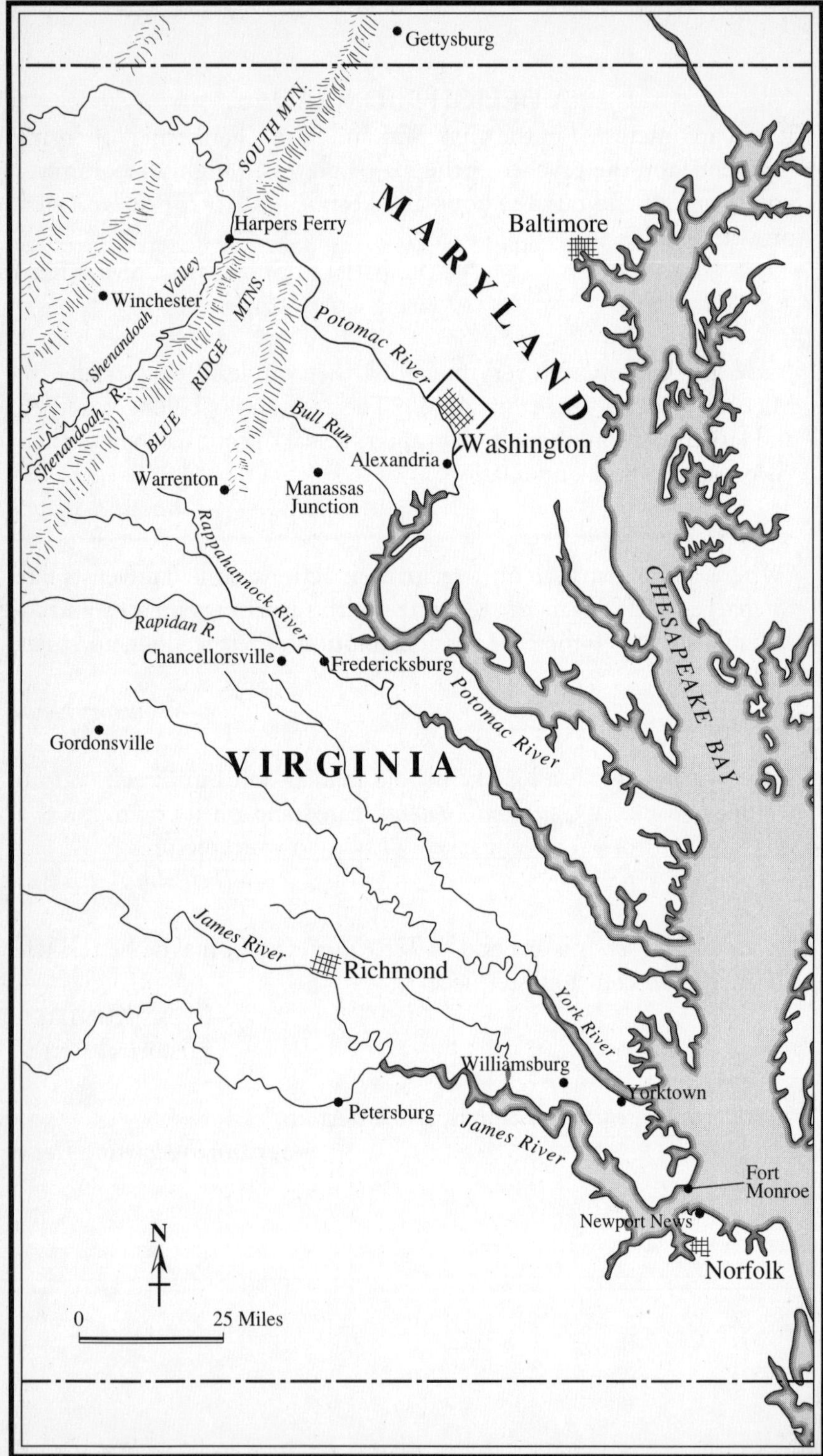

Gettysburg
SOUTH MTN.
MARYLAND
Baltimore
Harpers Ferry
Winchester
Shenandoah Valley
BLUE RIDGE MTNS.
Potomac River
Shenandoah R.
Bull Run
Washington
Alexandria
Warrenton
Manassas Junction
Rappahannock River
CHESAPEAKE BAY
Rapidan R.
Chancellorsville
Fredericksburg
Potomac River
Gordonsville
VIRGINIA
James River
Richmond
York River
Williamsburg
Yorktown
Petersburg
James River
Fort Monroe
Newport News
Norfolk
N
0
25 Miles

GODS AND GENERALS

JEFF SHAARA

BALLANTINE BOOKS
NEW YORK

To Lynne

A Ballantine Book
Published by The Random House Publishing Group

www.ballantinebooks.com

Library of Congress Control Number: 97-92954

ISBN 0-345-40957-4

Text design by Michelle T. Gengaro

Manufactured in the United States of America

First Ballantine Hardcover Edition: July 1996
First Trade Paperback Edition: May 1997
First Mass Market Edition: June 1998

20 19 18 17 16 15

TO THE READER

IN 1974, MICHAEL SHAARA PUBLISHED *THE KILLER ANGELS*, A novel about the men who led the fight at the Battle of Gettysburg. It was not an attempt to document the history of the event, nor was it a biography of the characters who fought there. Both have been done, many times, before. What Michael Shaara did was to tell the story of the battle by telling the story of the men, from their points of view, their thoughts, their feelings. It was a very different approach, and it was possibly the first novel of its kind. It also won the Pulitzer Prize. Michael Shaara died in 1988. He was my father.

The impact of his approach, the feeling that the reader truly *knows* these characters, has drawn an emotional response from a great many people. Over the years, many have expressed their appreciation for my father's work, whether in letters or in person. They continue to do so. Some have ancestors who shared the battlefields with Lee or Chamberlain, some are people who have simply come to know these characters well, to understand the impact that these men had on the history of this country and on our lives today. And there have been others who have said "I never liked history, but I loved these characters." It is to all these people, but especially those who learned their American history in often impersonal textbooks, that this story is written.

This is primarily the story of four men: Robert E. Lee, Thomas Jonathan "Stonewall" Jackson, Winfield Scott Hancock, and Joshua Lawrence Chamberlain. Woven throughout the story of these men are the stories of many others, their wives and families, the men who served with them on the field, names many of us know well: James Longstreet, Winfield Scott, "Jeb" Stuart, George McClellan, and characters important not just to the telling of this story, but to history as well: Jefferson Davis, Sam Houston. As *The Killer Angels* gave readers a connection to the characters *at* Gettysburg, this story takes them further back, to the first rumblings of the Civil War, the tragedies and successes of their personal lives, and their experiences as soldiers, to paint a picture of each character as he might have understood his own world. In 1861 every American was faced with the horror of watching their young nation divide, and every soldier—and a great number of civilians—had to make an extraordinary decision, a question of loyalty, of principles, of duty. Those individual decisions in many ways changed our history as a nation. Each character in this book is faced with the same choice, and each makes his decision for different reasons.

This story begins in late 1858 and concludes in June 1863, just prior to the Battle of Gettysburg. I have tried to follow a time line that accurately describes the history as it follows each character. That history and the events that propel this story are true. Most of the dialogue, the thoughts, the characterizations of the men and women, are my offering, my gift to the memory of these extraordinary individuals.

JEFF SHAARA

ACKNOWLEDGMENTS

INSPIRATION FOR A WORK SUCH AS THIS IS A DEEPLY INDIVIDUAL EXperience, yet my own adventure in bringing this story from some unknown and unexplainable place to the printed page suggests that there is much more to be said.

I am deeply indebted to Ronald Maxwell, who was the first to suggest that I could, and should, continue the story that my father began. Ron held the torch high for *The Killer Angels* for fifteen years, until his own dream of bringing that story to film was realized. His screenplay and his directing talents gave the world the film *Gettysburg*, and so he too is continuing my father's legacy.

For assistance with the considerable research for this project, I must thank the following:

Patrick Falci, of the Civil War Round Table of New York, who is a tireless source of information and materials, and whose willingness to open doors for this project is most appreciated.

Lieutenant Colonel Keith Gibson, of the Virginia Military Institute, and his wife, Pat Gibson, who opened up their home and allowed me to explore their considerable insight into these characters.

Ms. Michael Anne Lynn, of the Stonewall Jackson House, in Lexington, Virginia, for her gracious hospitality, and her willingness to impart her own suggestions for research materials.

Dr. Jeffrey Pasley, Department of History, Florida State University, for his enthusiastic assistance in providing valued sources of reference.

Ms. Clare Ferraro, publisher, Ballantine Books, for her extraordinary support, and her belief that this book could stand beside *The Killer Angels.*

Mr. Doug Grad, editor, Ballantine Books, who has listened with much patience and has lent a skilled hand to guiding a first-time author through this process.

I give most special thanks to my wife, Lynne, who proofread my hasty typing, and always, *always* gave me unqualified support throughout this often unnerving process.

Finally, there can be no greater acknowledgment than to my father, Michael Shaara. His long career as an accomplished writer, the highs and lows, are strong memories from my earliest years. Ultimately, his greatest achievement, *The Killer Angels*, opened an enormous door for me, allowed my apprehensions to be set aside, and brought forth the first words of this book. His greatest wish, what drove him through a difficult career all his life, was the desire to leave something behind, a legacy to be remembered. Dad, you succeeded.

GODS AND GENERALS

INTRODUCTION

TWO EXTRAORDINARY EVENTS OCCUR IN THE MID-1840S. FIRST, the United States Military Academy, at West Point, in a stroke of marvelous coincidence, graduates several classes of outstanding cadets, a group of young men who at the time are clearly superior to many of the classes that have preceded them. The second event is the Mexican War, the first time the armed forces of the United States takes a fight outside its own boundaries. The two events are connected, and thus, together, they are more significant than if they had occurred separately, because the events in Mexico served almost immediately as a brutal training ground for these cadets, who are now young officers.

They are a new breed of fighting man, the college-educated professional soldier, and the Mexican War is the first war to which West Point has given commanders. It is not a popular war, is seen by many opponents as nothing more than a land grab, the opportunity for the United States government to flex its muscles over a weaker enemy, and thus gain the spoils: South Texas, New Mexico, Arizona, California. What no one can know at the time is that the experience these young soldiers receive will have a profound effect on the battlefields of their own country in 1861. Not only do these men bring home the terrible visions of death and destruction, the experience that wars are not in fact great and glorious exhibitions, but they bring home something more—the discovery that the old way of fighting a war, the Napoleonic School, is becoming dangerously outdated.

The discovery comes from the use of the latest improvements in technology, for the rifleman and the cannoneer, for the observer and the bridge builder. Mexico is very much a testing ground for the new killing machines: greater range, accuracy, and firepower. And so, these young officers are schooled not only in the skills of traditional command and tactics, but in the vastly improving knowledge of the art itself, of engineering and mathematics.

The effect that all of this will have thirteen years later, on the battlefields of our own country, cannot be underestimated. One of the many great tragedies of the Civil War is that it is a bridge through time. The old clumsy ways of fighting, nearly unchanged for centuries, marching troops in long straight lines, advancing slowly into the massed fire of the enemy, will now collide with the new efficient ways of killing, better rifles, much better cannon; and so never before—and in American history, never since—does a war produce so much horrifying destruction.

But this is not a story about the army, or about war, but about four men. Three of them serve their country in Mexico, two of them spend the decade of the 1850s in a peacetime army with very little constructive work to do. They are not friends, they do not share the same backgrounds. But their stories tell the stories of many others, weaving together to shape the most tragic event in our nation's history, and so their story is our story.

ROBERT EDWARD LEE

Born 1807, Lee graduates from West Point in 1829, second in his class, with the unequaled record of never having received a single demerit for conduct in his four years as a cadet. He returns home to Virginia to a dying mother and a scandal-laden family, and so resolves that his life shall bring atonement. Lee possesses an unwavering sense of dignity, and is thus often considered aloof, but his dedication to duty and his care for those around him reveal him to be a man of extraordinary compassion and conscience. His faith is unquestioning, and he believes that all of his accomplishments, all events around him, are the result of God's will.

Lee marries Mary Anne Randolph Custis and has seven children, but he is rarely home—the sacrifice of being a career soldier. He distinguishes himself as a Captain of Engineers, goes to Mexico, and his reputation lands him on the staff of General in Chief Winfield Scott, the grand old man of the army. Lee performs with a dedication and a skill that makes heroes, and Scott promotes him twice, to Lieutenant Colonel. After the war he is named Commandant of West Point, finds it stifling, finds himself growing older with little prospect of advancement beyond his present rank, and he is not a man who will pull strings, or play politics for favors.

In 1855 the army forms the Second Regiment of Cavalry in Texas, and Lee astounds friends and family by volunteering for command. He sees this as his last opportunity to command real troops in the "real" army, and thus spends five years in the cavalry, which ultimately becomes another thankless and unsatisfying job. Serving under the harsh and disagreeable thumb of General David Twiggs, Lee asks for and is granted leave, after receiving word that his father-in-law, George Washington Parke Custis, the grandson of Martha Washington and the patriarch of his family's home, has suddenly died.

WINFIELD SCOTT HANCOCK

Born 1824 in Pennsylvania, one of twin boys, he graduates West Point in 1844. Hancock serves in Mexico with the Sixth Infantry, but only after waging war with his commanders to let him fight. He leads troops with some gallantry, but misses the army's great final victory at Chapultepec because he has the flu. He watches from a rooftop while his friends and fellow soldiers, Lewis Armistead, George Pickett, James Longstreet, and Ulysses "Sam" Grant, storm the walls of the old fort.

After the war, Hancock marries Almira Russell of St. Louis, considered in social circles, and by most bachelors there, to be the finest catch in St. Louis. She is beautiful and brilliant, and accepts her role as the wife of an army officer always with good grace and a superb ability to charm all who know her. They have two children, a son and a daughter.

Hancock, a large, handsome man, has the unfortunate talent of making himself indispensable in any assignment he is given, possessing an amazing talent for the drudgery of army rules and paperwork. This launches him into a dead-end career as a quartermaster, first in Kansas, then in Fort Myers, Florida, where the Everglades assaults the soldiers there with crushing heat and disease, snakes and insects, and the constant threat of attack from the Seminole Indians. He soon is transferred back to "Bloody Kansas," as the army tries to maintain control of rioting civilians confronting each other over the issue of slavery. Moving farther west with the army, he is named Quartermaster for Southern California and assumes a one-man post in the small but growing town of Los Angeles. But Hancock is never content to be a quartermaster, cannot forget his days in Mexico leading infantry, and aches for duty as a real soldier.

THOMAS JONATHAN JACKSON

Born 1824, Jackson arrives at West Point as a country bumpkin with homespun clothes and no prep school training, unlike the brilliant George McClellan or the aristocratic Ambrose Powell Hill, and has great difficulty at the Point. Jackson struggles with the studies, but has no vices, and so spends his time improving, and acquires a reputation as rigid and disciplined, and graduates in 1846 in the upper third of his class. All who know him there are certain that if the courses had gone a fifth year, Jackson would have reached the top.

In Mexico, as an artillery officer, he quickly shows his commanders he is not only suited for the heat of battle, but thrives on it. Jackson leads his two small guns into the fight with an intensity that puts fear into the enemy, and into many who serve with him. He is promoted three times, more than anyone in the army, and returns home a major.

After the war, Jackson grows weary of peacetime army life and applies for a position as an instructor at the Virginia Military Institute, in Lexington, Virginia. He is far from the most qualified candidate, but his war record and the fact that he is a native of western Virginia, and might assist in drawing recruits from that area, gain him the job. Thus he resigns from the army in 1851; he becomes a major in the Virginia Militia and embarks on a career in academics, for which, justifiably, he will never receive praise.

Jackson becomes a Presbyterian, and earns a reputation in local circles as a man of fiery religious conviction, if not a bit odd in his personal habits. He is seen walking through town with one hand held high in the air, thought by many to be constantly in prayer, and he is often sucking on lemons. He violates the law by establishing a Sunday school for slave children in Lexington, and justifies it by claiming it is the right of all of God's creatures to hear the Word.

In 1854 Jackson marries Eleanor Junkin, daughter of the president of Washington University, but a year later she dies in childbirth, as does the baby. Jackson's grief overwhelms him. He takes a long tour of Europe to recover emotionally, but his physical health, and his eyesight, give him constant trouble.

In 1857 he marries again, this time to Mary Anna Morrison, the daughter of a minister who is the founder of Davidson College in North Carolina. Their first child survives only a month. The tragedies of this time in his life place him more firmly than ever into the hands of his God, and he sees every aspect of his life, every act, as only a part of his duty to please God.

Joshua Lawrence Chamberlain

Born in 1828, Chamberlain graduates from Bowdoin College, Brunswick, Maine, in 1852. He is considered brilliant, with an amazing talent for mastering any subject. He enrolls in the Bangor Theological Seminary, considers the ministry as a career, but cannot make the final commitment, for though he often preaches Sunday services, he does not hear the calling. Chamberlain returns to Bowdoin as a teacher and is named to the prestigious Chair formerly held by Dr. Calvin Stowe. Chamberlain is now Professor of Natural and Revealed Religion, and speaks seven languages.

While part of Stowe's circle, Chamberlain becomes well acquainted with Stowe's wife, Harriet Beecher Stowe, who at that time is working on *Uncle Tom's Cabin*. The book has considerable influence on Chamberlain and causes him to see far beyond the borders of Maine, to the difficult social problems beginning to affect the country.

He falls desperately in love, and marries Frances "Fannie" Adams, daughter of a strict and inflexible minister. Fannie is a complex and difficult woman, burdened by her own family's awkward collapse—her father marries a woman barely older than she is. Fannie is moody and seemingly hard to please, but Chamberlain loves her blindly. While his distinguished position and title satisfy her, he begins to slide into a long period of discontentment and to focus more on the gathering tide of conflict, the loud and bloody threats to his country.

PART ONE

1. LEE

November 1858

THE COACH ROLLED THROUGH THE SMALL IRON GATES, UP THE slight rise, toward massive white columns. Lee had not seen Arlington for nearly three years, saw again the pure size, the exaggerated grandeur. It was the home of George Washington Parke Custis, the grandson of Martha Washington and Lee's father-in-law, and the old man had built the mansion more as a showplace for the artifacts of President Washington than as a home for a living family. The design was cold, impractical, but to Custis, the impression was the important thing, the shrine to his revered ancestors. But now Custis was dead.

Lee had received the wire from his wife, the first news from her in many weeks. They had written often, always, and he sent letters to all of them; not just Mary, but his children as well. He had missed a father's great joy of watching his children grow and learn, and so all he could do was offer the steady stream of advice and counsel, and try not to miss them too much, try not to think about what his career had done to his family. For several weeks the letters had been few from Mary, which was unlike her, but Lee had not thought much on it. He focused instead on his work, the absurd job of the cavalry, chasing Comanches over the vast Texas wilderness, *their* wilderness.

But there had finally come a letter, a wire, special courier, unusual, and the shock of the news hit him hard—that Mary now had no one, could not possibly manage the old estate—and so the army had granted him emergency leave, and he was returning home to Virginia.

He rode closer to the grand house, felt a chill, realized how much the house looked like a tomb, pulled his coat tighter around him. He was not yet accustomed to being away from the Texas heat, and November had settled in around Arlington like a gray shroud. As he climbed the slight rise, he could see out over the lands and untended fields. There had been little planting that year, and ragged brown grass filled the fields in matted lumps. Lee tried to think back, to recall the beauty, but he could not recall the lush green, the neat rows of corn, knew it had never really been like that; the old man had never been much of a farmer.

He wheeled the coach now to the short steps, reined up the horse, and stepped down onto dirty white brick. He looked, all directions, saw no one, thought, Very strange, there was always some activity, even the field hands, Custis's slaves, and though they did not spend much time in the fields, they could usually be seen out and around. He walked up the short steps, stood between the absurdly huge columns. The porch was empty, no chairs, and none of the white clay pots had been planted. There was no sign of any life anywhere. Lee began to feel the coldness; not the Virginia weather, but more, deeper.

He went to the doors, tried to see first through the small glass panes, could not—curtains lined the inside, and so he thought of knocking, felt a hesitation, then felt foolish. This was his home too, and he turned the large brass knob and walked into the house.

He slowly closed the door behind him, the silence broken by the sharp squeaking of the hinges, the sound startling him. He moved farther into the vast hall, looked toward both side rooms for anyone, then finally heard a voice, a girl. Lee turned, saw a whirl of black lace, and down the wide round stairway came his daughter Agnes.

She stopped, stood for a brief second with mouth open, a look of shock, said only, "Oh!"

Then she ran down, bounded past the last few steps and threw herself hard against her father's chest. Lee wrapped her in his arms, held her, felt her crying, her soft sobs buried into his coat, and he rocked her slightly, was suddenly uncomfortable, had not expected this. He lifted her away, put his hand out and touched her soft hair.

Agnes said, "Oh, Papa, Papa," and he felt her let go. She pressed to him again, pouring the pain out against him.

"It's all right, child, I am home now," he said. "Home." She began to loosen her hold, lifted her head and looked at him through swollen red eyes. She laughed then, a short sweet sound, and he put his hand on her cheek, realized now how much she had grown, thought, She is sixteen, and soon she too will leave and be gone.

"Papa, it was so . . . sudden. Why did God take him? He is buried next to Grandma. You must see the grave. Oh, Papa, it makes me so sad to go there." Her words began to pour out in quick bursts, overwhelming him.

He held her by the shoulders, said, "Wait, slow, slow, my child. We will talk . . . we have time to talk now. But where is your mother? I have not seen her."

Agnes felt words boiling inside of her, wanted to tell him so much, but saw his face, the lines, the gray hair, began to see him as older, different.

"She is upstairs. In her room. Your room. Oh, Papa, I am so glad you are home."

She hugged him again, and he turned, did not want her to start crying again. Moving toward the stairs, he looked up, expected to see Mary at the top, tall thin Mary, smiling and scolding him. She must have heard Agnes crying, he thought, and felt a chill—it was odd she hadn't come to greet him.

He climbed in quick steps, stared up toward the railing that led away from the top of the stairs, expecting still to see her. He reached the broad, open hallway, moved quickly to their room, saw a closed door and knocked, a gentle tap. She must be asleep, he thought, and pushed the door open, another squeaking hinge, and frowned because he did not want to wake her.

"Robert. Is that you?"

He stepped in, looked at the bed, thick and white, but she wasn't there. Then he saw her, sitting by the window, and he made a sound, a small gasp. He couldn't help himself, felt his knees give way, then stiffened, gained control, said, "Mary . . . are you not well?"

"No, Robert, I am not well."

She sat in a small leather chair, leaned slightly to one side, and Lee saw her right arm, hanging down, the hand twisted in a grotesque curl.

"I am sorry I did not greet you at the door. I saw you ride up. It is difficult for me to walk."

Lee stared at her, did not understand, did not know what to say.

"Please don't look at me like that."

"I'm sorry, but what is wrong? Are you getting better?"

"I have arthritis. The doctor says I will likely get worse. It's been a year or so. I could not tell you. I am ashamed that you should see me like this."

"No, no, it's all right. I am home now, I will take care of you."

"For how long?" Lee felt the edge in her voice, had heard it before, the bitterness she tried to hide, that the letters *did* hide. But now it could not be concealed, and he felt a sudden wave of guilt, as though if he'd been here, she would not be this way, it would all be different.

"I am . . . I have a two-month leave. General Twiggs . . . the army was very understanding."

"Understanding? I doubt the army has ever understood what it is like around this house."

Lee turned away from the argument, felt only the need to help, to mend the wounds.

"I was shocked at the news. I did not realize your father was ill."

"He wasn't. It was pneumonia. He had only a few days. We were with him . . . the girls were with him when he died."

She tried to stand, raised herself up with her left arm, pushing against the chair. He rushed forward, held her, lifted her under the arms, pulled her against him and felt the frail stillness, the dead right arm. She groaned suddenly, pulled back.

"I'm sorry. It hurts. It . . . always hurts. I just wanted to see outside."

Gently, he reached for her again, could feel her bones, had a sudden fear he might break her, and she turned, left his hands and faced the window.

"Would you please ask Agnes to bring me some tea?"

He backed away, still held his arms out toward her, and she moved closer to the window, a slow painful step, placed her left hand on the sill and looked out toward the gray sky. He watched her, felt sick inside, shut out. Behind him, in the hallway, he heard soft steps. He turned, said, "Agnes? Are you there?"

There was a silence, and then the girl answered, "Yes, Papa." Lee opened the door, stepped into the hallway and, in one motion, went to his daughter and held her, felt her strength and gave her back some of her tears.

HE SAT AT THE OLD MAN'S DESK, SURROUNDED BY HIGH WALLS and thick oak shelves. The dark office was suffocating, every space occupied by some memento, some piece of history, and Lee had begun to feel it all as a great weight.

He read through a stack of papers, the massive confusion of the old man's will. Custis had drawn it up himself, had felt no need for lawyers, and now Lee agonized at the contradictions, the grand pronouncements and the wholly impractical way Custis had divided his holdings. But it was the first page, the first paragraph that had given Lee the greatest dread, because the old man had named Lieutenant Colonel Robert Edward Lee as the principal executor of the estate.

There was land, thousands of acres on three plantations, and Lee's sons, Custis, Rooney, and Robert, Jr., inherited that. Then there was cash to be paid to the girls, but there was no cash in the estate: the money was to come from the farming operations of the lands. So, if the older sons were to come home and give up their careers to manage the farms, they would do so only to raise funds to give to their sisters. And, as Lee continued to plow his way through the documents, he noticed that Custis had not made any mention of existing debts, of which there were plenty. Thus, funds first had to be raised to settle those, or the Virginia courts would not approve the final settlement of the estate.

All of this was challenging, but Lee had the experience to handle it—he'd managed complicated budgets and administered financial dealings both in the Corps of Engineers and at West Point. The only thing he needed was time.

He studied the mound of papers for most of the afternoon. His eyes and his concentration began to wander, and so he left the study, walked through the large house, became acquainted again with the odd design, the vast clutter of artifacts. He stopped at the main parlor, admired the portraits, Custis and his wife. The old man was fiercely proud of his legacy, considered the home to be of great value to his country, a place where the name of George Washington would forever be preserved in the souvenirs of the first presidency. Lee began to see the artifacts differently now, the pieces of silver, large porcelain plates and tall vases, the small and large portraits cluttering the walls. He turned slowly, looked in detail around the room, the fireplace mantel, the shelves and glass cabinets. How strange to live in a museum, he thought. It took something away, some part of home. He hadn't noticed that before, and so had never missed it. He looked at the portraits again, saw a smaller painting and looked closer at the small gold frame. It was Mary as a girl, probably done when she was Agnes's age.

He knew she was never beautiful, not by the standards of the other boys. But he'd loved those things that were there, clearly, in the portrait: the frailty, a girl who needed caring for—*his* care.

Her father had not been happy with this young Lieutenant Lee, had thought his daughter fit for a husband of considerably higher breeding. Lee's own father, the great hero of the Revolution, Light-Horse Harry Lee, had died in shame and exile, with huge debts and failed dreams, a great soldier with no talent for business, and it was a disgrace and a reputation that haunted the young soldier. His mother had suffered as well, and when Lee graduated from West Point, he returned home to a dying woman, a woman worn away by the scandals, who had only one pride now, the success of her son. She died soon after, in his arms, and left him with soft words and the deep hurt of a mother's love, and he had told her, the last words she would hear, that he would make her proud.

Lee had pursued the young Mary despite the old man's hostility, and it was finally Mary's mother who had intervened, knew her daughter would do well to be cared for by this serious and soft-spoken young gentleman, and so finally they were allowed to be married.

He smiled at the memories: Mary the spoiled girl, his own easy patience, her mother scolding her for her carelessness, her inability to do anything for herself, and years later, her daughters scolding her again for the same reason. Lee remembered waiting, late for church, and she was never ready, would not come, had more "fixing" to do. So he and the children would go off anyway, and Mary would finally arrive in a flutter of mismatched colors, and the girls would ask her what it was she had "fixed."

He left the portrait, walked into the huge front hall, the cavernous entranceway that added no comfort to the house. He turned toward the back, went past small sitting rooms, a hallway, and then outside, where he stood on the small rear porch and looked out over the fields. It would be spring soon, the planting season, and there was no one here to handle it. He thought of the will, the debts, the old man's generous gifts to his grandchildren, gifts that would never be given, unless someone took charge. Lee stepped down to the brown grass, the thick patches of old, dirty snow melting now. He thought of the army. He would have to request further time, an extension of the leave, and realized that he had friends in Washington. That came from years of being the good soldier, never asking for the favors others sought with regularity. Walking out through the yard, toward a small stone wall, he thought of names, men he had known well, served well in Mexico. He did not have the political stomach for reminding his superiors what he had done, had done for *them*, and so he was a lieutenant colonel still, and probably would be for the rest of his career.

Sitting on the rough stone, Lee looked away, down a long clear hill to a row of far trees and beyond, to the wide river, the Potomac, and the buildings of Washington. He thought of General Scott, so much like his own father had once been. Scott was the finest soldier of his day, a man you could trust absolutely, who would fight for his cause and his men, and a man who had little use for the double-talk of politics. But in the peacetime army there was no other place for Scott to be than across the wide river, in those white buildings, surrounded by men who saw him as an outdated annoyance. He was still in command of the army, however, and Lee knew Scott was his friend. And he would only need a few months. . . .

He looked again, closer, at the near fields, and thought, What would it be like to be a farmer?

2. JACKSON

September 1859

Major Jackson stood with a solemn stiffness, facing the seated rows of cadets. The classroom was small, with white walls, a solid oak floor, and one tall window, toward which the cadets would occasionally gaze, though not for long. He had completed today's lesson, a thorough explanation of the practical applications of geometry on the trajectory of artillery. He had recited the lesson exactly as he'd memorized it the night before.

"So, gentlemen, you will see that with a proper grasp of the principles I have laid before you today, you may eventually apply these principles with great effectiveness in your own field experiences, and indeed, these principles may be applied to a great many other practices as well."

Eyes were fixed on him in a daze, and there was no sound. The room was a small tomb, and he led the class with a somber intensity that invited no comment from his students.

"Sir?" A hesitating voice rose from one side of the room, from the sharp glare of the window.

Jackson stopped, tried to see the boy's face, obstructed by the sunlight. "Did someone speak?"

"Yes, sir. I am a bit confused, sir, about your principle of application. Do you mean that we may apply mathematical principles to the pursuit of, say, romance, sir? Or perhaps the appreciation of a beautiful girl can be explained by one of these formulas, sir?"

Jackson stared in the direction of the question. There were a few stifled giggles, and Jackson knew this boy, knew the reputation as a clown, and had no use for it.

"Cadet, have you found yourself in a position to pursue romance?"

There was more stifled laughter, all heads turned toward the boy. Jackson could see him now, his eyes had pierced the glare. The young man looked at his professor with a slight sneer, the cockiness of the aristocrat.

"Well, sir, of course, some of us are fortunate in the pursuit of the fairer sex." He smiled, glanced around at his audience.

Jackson stared at the boy, felt his neck turn red, looked back toward the class. Faces turned back to him, and he said, "Gentlemen, if you are going to succeed at this institution, you have one common goal—to learn your lessons. If you are placing your energies elsewhere, you will not succeed, either with me or with your careers as military officers."

The laughter had stopped, the joke was over, and the young cadet by the window made a low comment, which Jackson could not clearly hear.

"Does Mr. Walker have another valuable thought to share with us today about the usefulness of the principles of geometry?" The question held no sarcasm. Jackson did not play the game, had only one purpose in this room, to impart the lesson.

"No sir, I have nothing further. Um, except, sir, I am confused about the principles regarding the application of triangulation in the placing of the observation sights for artillery." It was a serious question. Jackson knew that this cadet, for all his bluster and arrogance, was not doing well in his lessons. He sagged, thought, This is inexcusable, a clear lack of effort from the boy. He knew others in the class were having some difficulty as well, and he often received questions that had the unnerving effect of disrupting his presentation.

"Mr. Walker, I am forced to conclude that I must repeat this lesson tomorrow, word for word, and if you, if all of you, will pay a bit closer attention, perhaps it will be understood. We are out of time today."

There was a low groan, and the cadets understood that Jackson was serious, that tomorrow's lesson would be the same as today, *exactly* the same, and they would absorb the words again, or try to, and there would be little room for questions.

He turned, reached toward the small desk behind him, picked up his copy of the large gray textbook which all the cadets carried. They rose, a great collective sigh, and filed from the room.

Jackson was annoyed. He had spent the greater part of the previous evening memorizing today's lesson, had spoken it aloud to himself in the dim lamplight of his room. It was perfectly clear to him, and he had recited it with the same clarity today. He turned back, watched the cadets, frowned. Many of these young men would not survive the academic load at VMI. He saw the fault lying with the outside influences, recalled West Point, the local taverns that had attracted so many of his classmates. Lexington, Virginia, was not as sophisticated, there was not a bustling social scene, and so it mystified him why these young men were so distracted, why they could not seem to grasp the lessons that were so clear to him.

He held the heavy book under one arm, waited for the last cadet to exit, then walked out into the hallway. He saw many faces watching him, heard some laughter, comments, the brashness of boys who are briefly anonymous, out from your control. He did not look at them, had heard it before, walked past the building's wide oak doorway and to the cool air outside. He stopped, took a deep breath, then another, tried to rid himself of the stale air of the classroom. It has been going fairly well, he thought, most of them do want to learn. He could not understand the others, could not understand why they made the effort to be here if they had no sense of duty.

Major Jackson walked again, with long loping strides, kept the book tightly under his arm, allowed the other arm to swing freely. Conversations stopped when he passed, cadets pointing, more comments. He didn't see them, kept his eyes straight ahead in an intent stare—he had an appointment to keep.

Moving out across the wide parade ground, he glanced once toward the row of brass cannon, *his* cannon, which he used to teach the skills of artillery. It was the one part of their lessons the cadets enjoyed. Jackson's reputation in the classroom was clear and appalling. He was nicknamed "Tom Fool," a teacher with no talent for teaching, whose daily routine tortured his cadets, but out here, with the guns, there was something else, something the cadets could feel. The professor was, after all, a soldier, and with his beloved guns his lessons became animated, energetic. Though he forced them through the torture of the classroom, they knew that out here, in the open air, Jackson and his guns would show them a small glimpse of the *fire.* Out here they did not ridicule him, and though many of these young men would never become soldiers, they would know at least what a soldier *was.*

He moved beyond the gates now, passed through the campus of Washington University, which spread out alongside VMI. The atmosphere here was very different. There was laughter, young people moving in pairs under great sweeping trees. He did not look at them, stared straight ahead, moved in long strides toward a distant church steeple.

He was uncomfortable now, would not look around, would avoid the modest brick home that sat in the center of the campus, the home of Dr. Junkin, the university president. Jackson had lived in that home, had married Junkin's daughter, Ellie, and it was a part of his life that he put aside, kept far away. Ellie had died in childbirth, and the pain of that moment filled him when he was weak, when he could not wall it away. The Junkins were still his family, but he had married again, to Anna Morrison, the daughter of a minister, and his life had begun again. But he was not safe from the unspeakable, from the sad face of God, and he stared hard ahead, but knew the house was there, *right* there, and he tried, braced hard against the pain, pushed it away into some untouchable place.

He glanced up, saw the sharp point, the small cross at the top of the distant steeple, lowered his eyes again. Looking down the dirt street, he moved quickly now, with purpose, thinking, I will not be late.

The little girl had been only a month old, a small piece of pure light, and Jackson had thought, This is our reward, God is pleased and has allowed us to feel this joy. But this baby too did not live, was suddenly gone, and he felt the loss as if a piece of him had been torn away. Blessedly, Anna had survived, and no, there would be no pain, God had shown him something important, a lesson he must not forget. And so, while Anna had grieved, and her health had suffered, Jackson had gone back to his classroom.

He had often struggled with the notion of God, was not raised with any strict adherence to one church, but the gradual ending of the war in Mexico had taken something from him. When the duty that had driven him with such pure energy was drifting away, his real search began. He even considered becoming a Catholic then, defying the prejudice that many of the soldiers held. He learned Spanish and spoke often with local priests. But there was something about the papacy he found uncomfortable. He had difficulty accepting that authority, preferring to pursue instead a more personal service to God. In the peacetime army his duty was stripped down to mundane and pointless tasks, and so his religion had given him a new purpose, another place where his duty was clear. If he could not serve the army, he would serve God, and his enemies would be any temptations, any distractions, from that course.

He was in the street now, away from the campus. Cresting a short hill, he glanced at the high steeple. He felt excited, thinking of Dr. William White, the Presbyterian minister who had given him a comfortable home for his young religion, a man who did not insert himself into Jackson's worship, who understood that God was to be found well beyond the walls of White's own church.

Jackson did not look at the people along the street, did not feel the eyes watching him, staring at the sharp uniform, the crisp white pants, the blue jacket, brass buttons tight to the neck. He did not feel them staring as he reached into his pocket, felt for the hard round ball, pulled it free and shifted the book to his other arm. He reached into another pocket for a small knife, and then, with a quick slice, cut the ball in half and abruptly stuffed one piece, dripping and sticky, into his mouth. It was a lemon.

It was another experience from Mexico—the variety of strange and exotic foods. He had discovered lemons, tasted the sour tartness with the enthusiasm of a child, allowed himself one small piece of pleasure. He felt some guilt even for that, but knew, unlike many of the others, he had kept his path straight, that God had perhaps given him this small gift, this one small treat. Now, as the sharp ribbon of juice filled him, he thought of the baby. The pain tore through him, and he stopped, closed his eyes, said quietly, "No . . ."

Now he saw the people, their eyes, and he nodded, touched the brim of his cap, and continued his walk toward the church.

HE STARED DOWN, BETWEEN HIS KNEES, THOUGHT OF WORDS, how to begin. Dr. White sat behind the old desk, a thin man, slightly bent, waiting, patient.

"I am in something of a turmoil, Doctor. I was hoping I could have a few moments of your time to dig through it, or, perhaps, help me understand what is happening."

White sat silently, waited for Jackson to continue. The silence lasted over a minute, and White finally said, "Major Jackson, I have always considered you not only a guiding force in this church, but I have also considered you my friend. There are few in this congregation who share my devotion to doing God's good work as much as you. Please do not hesitate to freely discuss with me anything, anything at all. I had hoped you would visit me sooner. You have suffered a loss that no one can realize unless they have lived through it."

Jackson sat without moving, stared at White's desk, then looked up, into his eyes. "I have heard . . . that God punishes us for loving each other too much. There are those . . . who have come to visit . . . friends . . . I suppose. They offer kind words, advice. I have been told . . ." He stopped, tried again to form the words.

"I have been told that if we do not suppress our love for human things, and give more to God, He . . . makes us pay with great pain. I . . . am not sure I believe that. And yet . . . I am finding it harder to keep the pain away."

"It's an interesting doctrine, but I must say, not a very comforting one. Do you feel you and Anna have been punished?"

Jackson thought, glanced at the ceiling, then around the room.

"I . . . well, no. God has His reasons . . . Anna has suffered a great deal. I have told her we must try harder to please Him, that He has given us a lesson. It does not seem to help her. The path I chose, marrying Anna, was the correct one. I truly believe that. But I may love her too much. Is it possible . . . God has given us . . . a warning?"

White put his hands together, under his chin, and looked down.

Jackson continued. "If it is wrong for me to love anyone but God . . . if I have to, I can do that."

White looked up, said, "You have made a giant leap of interpretation there, I must say. You are accepting what has happened in your life as a direct result of an act of God. Step away, Major, back away from your own pain, and look around you. Your loss is not yours alone. What of your family? What of the people in your life, who share the pain of your loss? And, excuse me, Major, but what of the baby?"

"The baby?" Jackson stiffened, did not want to think about the baby.

"Was the baby punished because you gave it love? Major, I do not know why God does the things He does, but I believe you have the same duty to God as you have always had: to follow the right path, to live your life with a clear conscience. If God decides to inform you why He is doing whatever it is He chooses to do, then please come and tell me. But I suspect, Major, that you may only learn the Great Answers when He calls you away from this life."

Jackson pondered again, absorbed the words, began to feel a release, a load removed. He had assumed an awful guilt for the baby's death, had assumed it was his fault. He sat silently, scolded himself for his ego, his presumptions.

After a long, quiet pause, White said, "Major, do you miss your mother?"

The question caught Jackson by surprise. He looked at White, puzzled, thought about his mother. "I suppose . . . well, I try not to. It serves no purpose. She died when I was very young. God would not want me to dwell on that . . . the pain."

"Well, maybe. But do you miss her? Do you ever talk to her, pray to her? If we believe that all our departed loved ones sit with God, then maybe it is *she* who watches over you, who might provide you some guidance."

Jackson stared at White, fought, pushed away the image of his mother. "I . . . don't think I can do that. It seems odd to pray . . . not to God."

"Don't look for answers, Major, look for guidance, for comfort. And do not fear love. I believe that God would be happy if you sought out the guiding hand of someone who loves you as much as your mother loves you."

Jackson thought again, did not like thinking of her. When she entered his mind, the brief glimpses, the memories, always brought pain, so he did not pursue it. But if it would please God . . .

"Doctor, thank you." Jackson stood abruptly, and White leaned back in his chair, saw the look he had come to know as Jackson's own, the face that says, It is time to move on, to take the next step.

SHE STOOD HIGH ON THE SMALL PORCH, ABOVE THE HARD DIRT street, watched him slap at the horse. The carriage lurched, then began to roll slowly away.

He saw the look, the dull pain, and tried to make her smile, waved foolishly, exaggeratedly, then stood up precariously. Now she laughed, softly, and shook her head. He sat back down on the small wooden seat, pulled at the horse, and the carriage stopped.

"It will be soon. Really."

She nodded. "I know, Thomas. It is a good thing. . . ."

"You can come along . . . still. . . ."

"No. This is for you. I will be fine. The garden needs tending."

He turned to the horse, nodded quietly, thought, Yes, the garden . . . that will also please God. He looked at Anna again, thought, There will be comfort for you as well. She waved now, the smile faded, and she began to back away, into the house, and he knew it was time to go.

He drove the horse with a long whip, bounced along, holding straps of worn soft leather in his hand. There were high hills and thick woods, then a farmhouse, orchards, vast fields of ripening corn. He rode down the Shenandoah Valley, northward, through the most beautiful land he had ever seen, the treasured land of home. He would gaze, marveling at a farmer's good work, the neat rows that covered the countryside, and then in the distance the high mountains, the Blue

Ridge, the Alleghenies. He rode with purpose, the passion of the good mission. He did not feel the painful bouncing, did not fight the dust. It was bright, and warm, and perfect, and he stopped only to rest the horse. After many hours and many miles, he reined up, saw a small wooden sign with crude letters, HAWK'S NEST.

He stepped down from the carriage, looked for . . . something, not sure what. He saw no people, a few small wooden buildings, one of old brick, a general store, a broken sign hanging loosely over the door. He walked stiffly over, working the kinks out of his legs, patting his chest and pants, freeing the dust.

The store was dark, with one small, dirty window. It did not appear to be open for business, but behind a dust-covered counter sat an old man, deep wrinkles in dark, weathered skin. He slept on the floor, propped up against a sack of flour. Jackson leaned over the counter, studied the strange old face, the etchings of long hard experience. The old man let out a muffled noise, a small snore, twitched a wiry shoulder, and Jackson thought, Let him be, and began to turn away. But the weight of his boots sent a loud squeak from the worn wooden planks of the floor, and the old man suddenly woke, snapped to, looked at Jackson with the fear of a wounded animal.

"Who are you . . . what . . . ohhh." The old man grabbed his head, looked away in obvious pain, then back at Jackson, the fear now annoyance.

"What can I do for you, there, stranger? Pardon me for not getting up . . . bad leg. Bad most everything else too. Damned apple cider . . . A word to you, friend. Don't mix good corn whiskey with bad apple cider."

He closed his eyes, groaned again, one hand on top of his head, holding it in place. Jackson stood quietly, wanted to leave, but this was the only person he had seen.

"Pardon my interruption, sir. I am Major Thomas Jackson, of Lexington. My mother is buried here, around this place. I am trying to find her grave."

"Your mother?" The old man squinted up at Jackson's face, tried to recognize him, didn't. "What's her name? When was the funeral? Indians get her?"

Jackson thought, Indians?

"Her name was Julia Neale Jackson Woodson. She died in 1831."

"Twenty . . . uh . . . twenty . . . some-odd years ago?" The old man laughed, wiped his nose. "You just now find out about it?"

Jackson did not smile, did not want to explain, had not expected difficulty finding the gravesite.

"Is there a cemetery here, a churchyard?"

"I don't reckon there is, son, um . . . Major, you say? Woodson? You in the army? Indian fighter?"

"It's Jackson, my mother married again just before she died. I'm Virginia Militia. I'm a professor at VMI."

"VMI—what's that? A professor?" The old man was obviously disappointed. "I'm an old Indian fighter myself, Texas, the cavalry. Back then, well, we had it really rough, not like these boys today. You see them fancy repeating revolvers? Well, Major . . . Jackson, I don't know no one with any of them names around here. Check with the lieutenant outside, we have our troops stationed here, all good men, good Indian fighters. Just come back from Texas, you know, cavalry. Watch that cornfield over there, they sneak up every now and again. Arrow flew in here just . . . well, there, over there. Dang near got me too. Stay down here, the floor, safe." The old man made a cracked wheeze, coughed.

Jackson followed the man's gesture, saw no arrow, began to understand.

"Thank you, sir. The . . . the lieutenant seems to be off duty. Can you tell me where I might find someone who can tell me more?"

"Yep, check with old McLean . . . yep, McLean, he's around the town most of the time. Old guy, older than me even, hee. Gray head. Jake it is, Jacob McLean."

The old man coughed again, kept talking. "You bring a regiment with you? I heard drums last night, they're planning something, I tell you that. I stay here, on the floor."

Jackson nodded, turned, and stepped gratefully back into the sunlight. Across the road, away from the few buildings, was a huge cornfield, stretching to the hills beyond. He walked to the edge of the field, thought, Maybe a farmhouse, saw no one, and a voice behind him said, "You, hey, you there! You aim to steal some corn?"

Jackson turned, saw an old man, bent, gray, with a crooked cane. The man was well dressed, dark wool suit, looked out of place.

"Sir, I'm trying to find some information . . . a man named McLean. I'm looking for—"

"Well, you found him, son. I seen you come outta the store, there. You been talking to Jasper?"

"I didn't get his name," Jackson said. "He told me to watch for Indians."

The old man laughed, shook his head. "Yep, old Jasper brought all those Indians home with him from Texas. Brought a good love of the strong spirits too. There's a lot of that around here. If these people ain't shootin' at their neighbors, they're drinking themselves crazy. We had to take his gun away, his old musket. He was prone to takin' a potshot over that countertop every now and again. Doubt he'd ever hit anything, but it weren't good for the mood of the town."

The man began to laugh, stopped, eyed Jackson again. "We don't see many newcomers around here. Not a place many people happen on . . . visitors usually stay to the east of here, on the big road."

Jackson began to feel the frustration, wondered if everyone here did nothing but talk, felt a warmth creeping up the back of his neck.

"Sir, if you please, I am looking for the grave of my mother. Julia Neale Jackson Woodson, died near here many years ago."

The smile slowly left the old face, and Jackson saw clear eyes looking him over, studying him.

"Julia was your mother?"

"Yes, sir. My name—"

"You're Tom. Her youngest boy. I remember you, see it in your eyes."

Jackson felt a rush of relief. "Yes, yes, did you know her? Do you know where she is buried? I'm here to see her . . . to see her grave. I haven't been back here since . . . since then."

"I reckon I oughta know. I helped dig the grave." The old man turned, pointed his cane down a rough trail. "Down this way, a mile or so, by the river."

"The river?" Jackson didn't recall water.

The old man turned, looked at him. "I reckon it has been a while since you been here, eh, son? The New River, at the end of this road here. Not much of a river actually. Dries up now and again. But a nice spot for a grave. As I recall, she picked it out herself."

Jackson looked down the dim road, branches hung low across, barely room for a carriage to pass.

"Would you mind showing me . . . taking me there?"

"Well, no, I wouldn't mind. Wouldn't mind a'tall."

Jackson led him toward the carriage, and the old man walked around to the far side, warily eyed the climb up.

Jackson mounted, reached out a hand to the old man, who struggled, grunted, then, with Jackson's help, reached the seat. He looked at Jackson and studied him, but Jackson was looking toward the small road, the high grass. He slapped the horse with the leather straps.

The old man steadied himself against Jackson's arm as the carriage rolled onto the old road, then said, "You don't live around here . . . I'd know it. What you doing here, son? Why you come back here after so long? This is not a place people just happen by."

Jackson drove the carriage, didn't speak. They bumped along past thick clumps of bushes and tall trees, and Jackson felt the delicious coolness of the thick woods, realized he was sweating, anxious. He felt the old man's hand, holding on to his arm, could not think of the right thing to say, the answer to the old man's question.

"I came back here to see her. I miss her."

The old man nodded, said, "I reckon we all miss somebody."

The road became muddy, and Jackson knew the river was close. The old man put up a hand. Jackson stopped the horse.

"I believe . . . wait, no . . . there, over this way." The old man pointed the way, and Jackson steered the carriage through the woods.

The carriage splashed through a thick muddy bog, the horse kicking black mud in the air, and then the road appeared again, a slight rise. They entered a clearing and Jackson could see flat ground, the edge of a small river, a small meadow of green grass, a huge oak tree, and across the meadow, on the far side, before the old man could point to it, the depression in the earth, the unmarked resting place of his mother.

Jackson reined the horse and stepped off the carriage, jumping down onto soft ground. His hands were sweating and he felt his heart pound.

The old man said, "If you don't mind, I'll just sit here. I 'spect you want to be alone anyhow."

Jackson didn't answer, walked softly, silently, toward the sunken grave. At the lower end, away from the river, he stopped, knelt, reached out a hand and touched the grassy ground. He ran his hand along the edge of the depression, felt the lush grass between his fingers, the cool moisture wetting his hands, and put a hand to his face, touched the wetness to his cheek. He sat now, closed his eyes. He thought of Dr. White, tried to pray, not to God, to her, but it would not come, he could not talk to her. He sat quietly, thought back, stared at the small sounds of flowing water, began to remember her, the strong arms, the soft voice.

His mind began to carry him, drifting through the sweet smells of her kitchen, the clear summer days and the snows of the winter. He could see his sister, just a baby, and began to feel what it was like, being the great protector of her tender helplessness. He saw the small bedroom, saw himself, just a young boy, seven, and his sister, older now, holding on to him, reaching up to grip his hand, and they were very quiet, staring at her in the bed . . . *and now he was* there, *and it was real, and he saw the pain, the awful hurt in his mother's dying face, and he leaned over, touched her face, held her now, felt her breath fading away, and she reached for him, wrapped him in her arms, and spoke, soft words, but he could not hear and he tried to answer, and she spoke again, the words coming in clear, quiet sounds, and now he heard, understood, he felt her warmth, her love, and he knew that God was there, and it was all right. . . .* He began to pull away, remembered it all now, gently closed the dark and silent place, felt the dampness of the grass again, knew now that she sat with God and loved her children still.

3. CHAMBERLAIN

November 1859

It was cold, very cold, and he felt the sting in his cheeks, a slight burning pain in the edges of his ears, the delicious feeling of being totally alive, every nerve, every part of you totally awake, every breath of the cold air filling you with the sharp and wonderful bite of the Maine winter. In front of him the hillside stretched far below, spread out in a deep white carpet broken by clusters of dark green, the tall fir and spruce trees, branches holding on to clumps of snow. He looked farther out, over to the next hill, saw more trees, a solid, thick mass, the snow hidden underneath.

He had climbed the wide hill, moved slowly across the crest, resting between slow, deliberate steps, sinking into the deep powdery snow. He began to move downhill now, and stopped, stared at the tall ridges in the distance. How high are we, how far up? he wondered. He took a long, cold breath, thought, Easier going down, and . . . I am tired—Tom is so much younger.

Chamberlain turned, looked sideways across the wide slope for the figure of his brother, knew the boy would be moving through the smaller trees to the left, the short, thick ones where a man could hide his movements, sneak through, then suddenly glimpse the far side without detection. He waited, heard nothing, and realized, Yes, you can hear *nothing*. He listened hard, focused on any sounds, and there were none, no birds, no breeze. Remarkable, he thought. How many places can you go where you hear nothing?

He kept watching the cluster of small trees, suddenly saw movement, the trees first, a small shower of loose snow from the low branches, and then a quick brown flash, and a deer burst out, ran along the hillside toward him. He did not move, and the deer stopped, looked back to the trees, then raised its long, thick, white tail and began to make long prancing strides right toward him, still not seeing him. Chamberlain stood completely still, and the deer stopped again, now saw him, stared at him from a few yards away, and Chamberlain stared back, looked into the large round eyes, saw, not panic, but intense curiosity. They stood motionless for several seconds, and the deer suddenly raised its tail again, the thick flag, had seen enough of this unknown thing, and jumped quickly into motion, ran off, down the hill, away from him, and then darted below through the larger trees.

He watched the animal, could still glimpse the high bounding tail, thought, How odd, they hide so well, masters of camouflage, and then display their tail so everything in the woods can see them.

"Lawrence . . . did you see him?"

The boy emerged from the small trees, running now, fought his way through the deep snow, and he looked down, saw the tracks of the deer, then looked at Chamberlain, called out, "Lawrence, he ran right by you. Did you see him?"

He watched the boy, plowing his way closer, and Tom looked again at the tracks punched through the snow, a solid line leading away down the hill.

"Yes, Tom, I saw him. He went off, down there." He pointed a gloved hand down the hill.

"Well, yes, Lawrence, I can see where he went. Did you get a shot? I didn't hear you shoot."

Chamberlain looked down at the musket, the long barrel of the old flintlock, had not even thought of using it. "No, I didn't get a shot."

"Lawrence! You let him go. God in heaven, you did it again! I been trailing that fellow from clear across that last valley, and he flushed out right by you . . . and you let him go. I swear, Lawrence, you do cause me some aggravation."

The boy was out of breath, and Chamberlain swung the gun up, laid it backward on his shoulder, said, "We best be getting back. Over there, some clouds moving up. Could be more snow."

The boy looked toward the thickening sky, then stared back at Chamberlain, and suddenly kicked at the soft snow.

"Phooo! I am never going hunting with you! Not ever again! If you wasn't going to shoot the deer, why'd you come along anyway?"

Chamberlain turned, began to walk, stepping slowly through the snow, up the broad hill. He looked back, saw his brother following, holding his musket firmly in both hands, ready, always ready. Chamberlain stopped, smiled at the boy, who puffed up the hill and moved up beside him, short bursts of steam from tired breathing.

"Why do you come out here if you don't want to shoot anything?"

Chamberlain raised his free hand, waved it about, a grand sweeping turn, said, "I love it. I love hunting. The woods, all of this. I don't need to shoot, it's more than that . . . it's just being here."

The boy let his gun drop into one hand, rested the butt in the snow. "I reckon I understand that, Lawrence. There's something out here, something in these hills that makes everything else seem . . . all right, somehow."

Chamberlain looked at the boy, surprised. "It's good you see that. You may need this someday. You may need to get away from . . . something. I hope you always have . . . all of this."

"Get away? What you getting away from, Lawrence? My God, you've got everything a man could want. You're a teacher, a big-time college professor. You make good money, I bet. You got a wife . . . a real beauty too, and that baby, Lawrence, I swear . . . I only hope I can have what you have."

Chamberlain looked at the boy, saw red cheeks and wide eyes, saw a young piece of himself. "You're only eighteen," he said. "You've got plenty of time to make your own life. Just don't forget about this place. No matter where you end up, and you may move very far away someday . . . come back here when you can. Climb up here, and listen to the silence."

Tom frowned, did not understand, saw something, a dark mood in his older brother he had not often seen. "Lawrence, you telling me you're unhappy? I can't hardly believe that."

"No, no, certainly not. Let's go, those clouds are getting a bit darker."

They walked together, did not speak, followed their own tracks back through the soft snow, over the crest, began to move down, into the chilling shade of the taller trees, and Chamberlain suddenly felt a brief flash of depression—he was going back down, back to the real world.

He knew that Tom was right, that there was much to be thankful for. He had been named to the prestigious Chair, vacated by the famous Calvin Stowe, with the title of Professor of Rhetoric and Oratory. It was a stunning accomplishment for a man in his mid-twenties, and the prestige focused even more attention on this brilliant young man with the certain future. He thought, Yes, I have so much . . . Fannie is so happy. And he thought of the baby, the precious little girl, and the tiny face gave way to images of classrooms and the pages of black writing, the lectures he had already prepared for next week.

He kicked his boots through the snow and saw the dark hallways of Bowdoin, endless tunnels in gray buildings, and he felt something, a small twist in his stomach, and he did not understand: What is wrong with me?

As he moved down the long hill, the trees became thicker, darker, and the walking was easier, the snow harder and thinner under the great pines. His brother moved ahead of him, darting between the trees along the familiar trail. Chamberlain watched him slide over the small slick patches, the glazed areas of ice, hardened by many footsteps. He began to pay more attention to his own feet, the treacherous footing, and he marveled at his brother's recklessness, slipping, nearly falling, then upright again. Chamberlain moved carefully, feeling his way over the glassy ground, and soon Tom was gone, farther down the hill, and Chamberlain could hear him, faint whoops as he ran and slid, closer to the house of their parents. He'll make it without a bruise, Chamberlain thought, and I'll move slow and easy, and break my leg.

He leaned against a thick fir tree, held on to low, stiff branches, steadied himself, listened, knew Tom was at the house by now, and he caught a faint smell, smoke, from the chimney. He looked back up the hill, through the dark trees, saw heavy clouds, there *would* be snow tonight, and he released the branches, slid a few inches, took a step down, tested the firmness, then thought, No, I'm not ready to leave, not yet. He turned, looked out through the trees, carefully took a long step up, out of the trail, climbed up to softer snow, began to move away from the trail, from tree to tree, felt better footing now, the snow not hardened by the constant travel.

He walked along the dark slope, felt his way over fallen branches, old stumps. The weight of the gun was tiring him, and he thought of laying it down, leaning it against a tree. But no, not a good idea, he might not find it until spring, and his father would go through the roof, so he raised it up, rested it on his shoulder, and moved farther along, into the trees. He came to an old flat stump, capped with thick snow that he pushed away with a sweep of his arm, and sat down.

He knew the house was just below, maybe a hundred yards, and he could see them, could imagine the scene: Fannie was there, with the baby, and his other brothers, Hod and John. His mother would be in sublime control, preparing the great dinner, and Fannie would offer to help, a polite and insincere gesture, and his mother would say, "No, it's all done," and the young men would sit impatiently in front of the fire, waiting for the feast, and make conversation about very little, and yet the whole house would be filled with a common feeling, a sense that they were all loved, all of them, by each other, and as one family. And by now Tom was there, shaking snow from his boots and excitedly telling them all about the deer and his older brother, the hunter who would not shoot, and Chamberlain knew that his father would say nothing, make some small gesture of unspoken hopelessness, another disappointment.

He should have gone to West Point. That was the first disappointment. He had heard that now for years, especially after his graduation from Bowdoin, when he enrolled instead at the Theological Seminary. It had been the happiest day of his mother's life, her dream that her oldest son would become a man of God, and his father had just turned away, did not share his wife's closeness with the Almighty. But Chamberlain did not find the great spark, the powerful commitment to his faith, and so after his courses at the seminary, he had gone back to Bowdoin, and not to West Point, to teach the subjects he had so mastered; and so, to his father, there was another disappointment.

He was named Lawrence Joshua Chamberlain, but had switched the two, thinking "Joshua Lawrence" had a more formal sound, a better rhythm, and yet in a stroke of illogic preferred to be called Lawrence. His father preferred it as well—he had named him to honor the famous military hero of 1812, Commodore Lawrence, the man forever known for the quote, "Don't give up the ship." His mother would not relent, preferred the more biblical Joshua, and though both his father and grandfather had been named Joshua, his father had settled on calling him Lawrence, and Chamberlain had always wondered if it was because his mother did not.

He stared down the hill, closed his eyes, felt a great weight of gloom.

By now they would begin to wonder. Fannie would say something, ask Tom to go out and see what was keeping him, and he felt guilty, did not want them to worry, but knew they had no idea, could not understand why he sat alone on a cold stump in the thick, darkening woods.

Everyone, he thought . . . all of them, even my father, they're all happy for me, they see me now as a success. But he did not feel like a success. This should be the happiest time of my life, he thought, and he searched for it, tried to feel the self-satisfaction, the sense of standing at the entrance to a long and prestigious career, a doorway to great academic achievement, and he felt nothing, no sense of thrill, no anticipation. He thought of Tom's comment, back on the hill, "You make good money," and he smiled. Any salary would seem like good money to someone who had never had a job. But Chamberlain was not pleased with the meager living he was offered for his teaching, had even added to his own workload, was now teaching languages as well, anything he could do to supplement his income. He scolded himself: There is something foolish about all this, I am, after all, in the very position I had sought. This was what he was meant to do, clearly. He was a natural scholar, could master any discipline put before him, but when he thought of that, he felt it again, the twist in his stomach.

I need to come up here more often, he thought, the hills, the great wide silence. Give it time.

Fannie had been reluctant to marry him, had worried about his career, their ability to raise a family. But Fannie was already happier, and there would be more children. He smiled at that, thought, A son, I would truly love to have a son, to bring him up here, show him this world, maybe even teach him to hunt, if he wants to. He might be better at it than I am.

He felt a cold wetness coming up through his pants, the melting dampness from the icy stump, but he did not move, sat still for a while longer, felt a great weariness, the need to go back. He looked down at the musket, cradled in his arms, looked along the dull metal of the barrel, saw rust spots, small brown circles, thought, Better work on that, I will certainly get the blame. He straightened his back, began to reach his arms up, a long stretch, and in the thick silence he heard a noise, a slight crunch of snow. He turned quietly, saw movement a few yards away, behind a tree, and then a deer emerged, a few short steps, and was clear of the tree.

Its head was down, searching along the ground, prodding small openings in the snow, for some small piece of brown grass, and Chamberlain saw he was huge, antlers wide and tall and heavy, and a thick neck, a chest like a brown barrel, larger than any deer he had ever seen, and the deer eased along, did not yet see him, and he brought the gun slowly up to his shoulder, pulled the hammer back with his thumb, slowly, slowly, and the hammer clicked lightly into position. The deer raised its head, froze, looking at him, and he sighted down the barrel, placed the small metal bead on the animal's shoulder and pulled the trigger. There was a loud snap, and the gun did not fire. Chamberlain had leaned forward, anticipating the heavy recoil from the old gun, nearly fell off the stump, and there was a quick flash of the white tail and the deer was instantly gone.

He stood up, his heart pounding heavily, thought of running after the deer, another chance, but knew it was pointless. He looked at the gun, said aloud, "Well, I'll be damned," and he started walking, began to move back through the woods, toward the trail.

They will never believe me, he thought, and laughed nervously, stopped, felt his hands shaking. An icy chill ran down his legs, and he knew it wasn't just the cold; he had never felt like this before. He had never enjoyed shooting anything, but this had been pure instinct, without thought—he had never wanted to kill something so badly in his life, and now it shook him, frightened him. He started walking again, quickly followed his own tracks back toward the trail, smelled the smoke again. He reached the trail, began a quick stumbling descent to the house. Far above, drifting down through the tops of the tall trees, it began to snow.

4. LEE

November 1859

At last the house was quiet. He had tried to do some work, sat at the desk in the old man's study, but the girls seemed especially playful that morning. Young Robert, Jr. had been their victim, and the joyous cries had echoed through the vast rooms like the sound of bells. Lee hadn't stopped them, would not interfere, had just sat back in the old chair and listened with a quiet smile. It was Monday morning, and the schools were calling, and Lee wondered if the chance of getting out, of spending time away from the grim house was having an effect.

Mary was still upstairs, and Lee knew she was still in bed. The nights were difficult, the pains kept her awake for long hours, and Lee could do nothing to soothe her, to stop the pain.

Now the children and the happy sounds were gone, outside and away, and once again the house was still. Lee picked up a sheet of paper, ran his finger down a long list of materials, the lumber and hardware still needed for repairing the house.

Of all the tasks he was facing, the repairs came slowest. The fall harvest was completed, and there was more time, and so he looked to the house, the work that had been put aside for the more important job of getting the farm into production.

He rechecked the list of lumber, refigured the roofing for the outbuildings, and heard a carriage, the sound of a horse on the bricks of the front entranceway. He stood, put on the dark gray coat that hung across a chair and went out into the barnlike foyer. He could see a figure through the glass, a soldier. The man did not ring the brass bell, had seen Lee coming, waited.

"Yes, what is it?" Lee pulled the door open, then straightened in surprise. "Well, my word. Mr. Stuart, Lieutenant Stuart! Quite a surprise!"

"Sir! I am honored to see you again, Colonel."

Lee opened the door wide, stepped back and motioned the young soldier into the house.

"Lieutenant, I regret to say you have just missed the girls. They have grown up . . . and I'm sorry, my wife . . ."

"Yes, Colonel, I heard about Mrs. Lee. I am dreadfully sorry for her condition. Please pay my respects, sir, when you are able."

Lee led the young cavalryman into the study, felt a flood of energy, had not seen him since he graduated from the Point. It was no secret that J.E.B. Stuart had been Lee's favorite cadet.

"I heard you had been assigned out West, but after I went to Texas, I didn't hear much more. My word, it is good to see you!"

Stuart was embarrassed, was not used to a show of emotion from Lee. He held a plumed hat firmly at his waist and clutched the brim with both hands.

"Yes, sir, I was in Kansas. Sent to fight Indians, spent more time chasing the guerrillas, the insurrectionists. Quite a mess out there, sir. The army seems caught in the middle . . . seems like no way to make people get along. Sad, bloody place. But, sir, I have news!"

Lee smiled. Stuart always had a way of turning the conversation, any topic, back to himself.

"Sir, I am married! And, a child! Perhaps you know Colonel Cooke, Philip St. George Cooke, a Virginian, of course. I married his little girl! And, well, we have come back here . . . a visit . . . the colonel was helpful in arranging a leave for me so that he could see his new grandbaby."

"Well, Lieutenant, it seems you have been busy. I never doubted that . . . not for a moment. I am honored you found the time to call on me."

Stuart suddenly brought a hand up to his mouth. "Oh, sir . . . no . . . thank you, but I am here officially, from the War Department, actually. I was there this morning, hoping to arrange a meeting with the Secretary. I have this invention, you see, a means of attaching the sword—"

Lee knew he would have to steer the young man back to the main subject, gently interrupted, "Lieutenant, the War Department? You have a message for me?"

"Oh . . . yes, sir. I was sitting in the clerk's office, waiting for the chance to see the Secretary, when Colonel Drinkard suddenly appeared, handed me this." He reached into his coat pocket and brought out a small envelope. "He asked me if I knew the way to Arlington. I have been instructed to give this to you."

Stuart looked at the note, studied it for a brief moment, then suddenly remembered his duty, came to noisy attention, and handed it with a snap of his arm to Lee.

Lee could not help a smile. "Thank you, Lieutenant, you may stand at ease."

Stuart complied, then leaned slightly forward, looked at the envelope, waited impatiently for Lee to open it.

Lee unfolded a small piece of linen stationery, read aloud, for Stuart's benefit. " 'From the chief clerk, Colonel Drinkard, at the request of the Secretary of War, Mr. Floyd, Colonel Lee will report to the Secretary's office with all haste.' "

Lee looked at Stuart, and Stuart said, "That's it? Just . . . report?"

"Appears so. Well, Lieutenant, would you be obliged to give me a ride over the bridge? We can leave . . . right now, actually."

"But your uniform, sir. You are not dressed."

Lee looked at his civilian clothes, the dark wool suit. "Nothing in the note about a uniform, Lieutenant. They seem to prefer haste to dress. I suspect the Secretary will forgive the oversight."

Lee pointed the way, and Stuart went quickly to the front door and held it stiffly open. Lee stopped and looked up, glanced at the top of the vast stairway, knew Mary was sleeping, would stay in bed all day. A note, he thought. I should let her know.

He moved back into the office, pulled out a sheet of clean paper, wrote a few words, paused. Stuart had moved to the office doorway, watching him, and Lee looked at the bright young face, eager, full of life, then finished the note: "I might be gone awhile." He wondered how she would react to that. He was always to be gone for just a while. Without speaking, he folded the note, passed Stuart and moved quickly up the stairs toward the silence.

THEY CLIMBED THE CLEAN WHITE STEPS THAT LED TO THE OFfices of the Secretary of War, and above them, from the wide doorway, came Secretary Floyd himself, leading a cluster of young clerks.

"Ah, Colonel Lee, greetings, yes, left a message upstairs for you. We are off to the White House, please accompany us."

Lee said, "Certainly, at your service, sir," thought of asking more, knew it would wait for now. Behind him, he heard Stuart, a rough whisper, and Lee understood, asked Floyd, "Do you mind if we are accompanied by Lieutenant Stuart? He is serving as my . . . aide."

Floyd nodded, did not look at Stuart. "Fine, fine, let's move a bit, shall we?"

The crowded carriage rolled quickly to the President's home, and the group of men walked swiftly into the building, Stuart jumping in front to open doors.

Lee had met President Buchanan at social functions, really did not know much about him, about the man. But he realized that all this commotion was serious; there was none of the social banter of politicians.

Lee and Floyd were escorted past guards into the President's office. Stuart, knowing he had to remain outside, sat deeply into a thick chair, pouting silently.

Lee followed Floyd into a wide office, sunlight pouring through great windows. Aides were moving away, and Lee could see Buchanan sitting across a vast desk.

The President said, "Colonel Lee, welcome. Allow me to dispense with pleasantries, if you will. Colonel, we have what seems to be an emergency, a situation. We need you to command a military force, to lead troops against . . . well, we don't know what. A revolution, an insurrection, call it what you will."

Lee's eyes widened. He had heard nothing of any trouble.

Buchanan continued, "Harper's Ferry . . . from what we have heard, the Government Arsenal has been captured, trains have stopped running. We've heard as many as five hundred, maybe more, a slave uprising."

Floyd nodded vigorously. "Five hundred at least, slaves rising up, yes, a great deal of bloodshed."

Buchanan glanced at Floyd, impatient, went on. "Colonel, you are to take command of a company of marines that is currently en route, and three companies of infantry from Fort Monroe that are preparing to move. The militia has been called out as well, mostly Maryland men, I believe, some Virginians."

Floyd nodded sharply. "Yes, Maryland and Virginia."

Lee sat quietly, absorbed, waited for more.

"Is there a problem, Colonel?"

"No, not at all, Mr. President, I am honored to be your choice . . . but I am confused why—"

"Because you are *here*, Colonel. Washington is full of ranking officers who haven't led troops in decades. There's no time to bring in anybody from the field. According to General Scott, you're the best man we've got, under the circumstances. There should be no further need for explanation, Colonel."

"No, sir, certainly not. I will leave immediately for Harper's Ferry. Do we know anything about . . . any idea who or what this is about, who we are dealing with?"

Floyd spoke up: "Kansas ruffians, insurrectionists, slaves. That's all we know. It's chaos, Colonel."

Lee thought, There are few slaves at Harper's Ferry. But . . . the Arsenal—if there was an uprising, it was a prime target, a huge store of guns that could supply a massive revolution. But something nagged at Lee, some feeling that he had heard this before: the rumors that flew through Texas, huge hordes of Indians terrorizing the plains, frightened civilians, the constant alert for a crisis that was never there. Still, there was the Arsenal.

"Good luck, Colonel. Keep the Secretary posted on events, if you don't mind. It seems that real information is in short supply."

"Yes, Mr. President, I will do my best."

The meeting was over, and as the men left the President's office, passing through the heavy oak door, Stuart jumped to his feet, his eyes imploring Lee for details, and Floyd stopped, turned to Lee and said, "I don't have to tell you what this means, Colonel. This could look very bad for us here, very bad for . . . the President. The public is very nervous. All this talk of slave revolts, and now . . . my God." His voice quieted and he leaned closer to Lee. "You must protect us!"

Lee slid away from Floyd, said, "Will the Secretary provide us a ride to the train station? We will secure a car immediately. And perhaps a courier. I should . . . could you please send word to my family."

Floyd nodded, excited. "Certainly, Colonel. Right away."

Lee turned away, moved past the huddle of clerks, past grand portraits on stark white walls, down the wide steps to the lush green lawn, Stuart following close behind. He heard Stuart comment, a low curse, something about politicians. Lee did not answer, let it go by, thought now of Mary, tried to see the soft face, but the image would not come, and so he began to think of his new command.

THE MARINES WERE UP AHEAD, WAITING FOR THEIR NEW COMMANDER. Lee had wired to the station in Baltimore, told them he was close behind, instructed them to stop at Sandy Hook, just outside Harper's Ferry. It was long past dark when Lee and Stuart caught up, and as the two men stepped from the train car, a young officer approached, saw only Stuart's cavalry uniform, saluted him with a puzzled look.

"Sir, are you. . . ? I was told to expect a Colonel Lee."

"I am Colonel Lee, this is Lieutenant Stuart, my aide. Forgive my appearance, Lieutenant, there was not time for proper dress."

"Yes, sir. I understand, sir. Lieutenant Green at your service. I am to turn command of the marines over to you."

"Very well, Lieutenant, I assume command." Lee looked past the young man, saw neat rows of crisp blue, men waiting for orders. "Lieutenant, is there anything you can tell us?"

"Well, yes, sir. The bridge over to Harper's Ferry is wide open, no resistance that we can see. We've heard a few shots, but nothing major."

Lee was not surprised. A more accurate picture was beginning to form in his mind.

"And over there, Colonel, state militia has been arriving since we've been here, several companies. I don't know who is in command there, sir."

Out beyond the station platform Lee saw troops gathering in the darkness, a ragged formation of volunteers, numbers swelling by the minute, and he had an uneasy feeling, did not look forward to commanding men who were not used to command. He stepped down off the platform, walked out toward the uneven groups of men, saw someone who appeared to be in charge.

"Excuse me, sir, are you in command of these men?"

The man turned, gave a quick glance to the older man in the dark suit, sniffed with the air of a man of importance.

"Pardon me, sir, but I have no time for interviews. I must organize these men here—"

"That's good to hear, sir. I am Lieutenant Colonel Robert E. Lee, and by order of the President I am assuming command of your militia."

The man turned again, looked Lee over doubtfully, said, "I do not know you . . . Colonel. Forgive me if I'm somewhat cautious. We don't know who the enemy is here. Have you some orders, some documentation?"

From the platform behind him, Lee heard the voice of Stuart, calling out, "Colonel, a wire for you. The infantry is in Baltimore, awaiting your orders. And the marines are ready to move out on your command, sir."

The militia commander began to respond, puzzled, then realized Stuart had been talking to Lee.

"Well, forgive my suspicions, Colonel. I am Colonel Shriver of the Maryland militia. I suppose . . . my men are at your disposal."

"Thank you, Colonel. Perhaps you can tell me exactly what we are confronting here."

"From what we have learned from the townspeople, sir, there is a group of men barricaded in the Arsenal, with some hostages, local citizens."

"How many, Colonel? How many men, how many hostages?"

"Perhaps twenty, or more."

"Hostages?"

"Oh, no, sir, the insurrectionists, the rioters. There may be ten or twelve hostages. The insurrectionists fought with some local militia for most of the day, and then holed up in the engine house, inside the Arsenal."

"Any notion who is in charge?"

"I have heard, a man named Smith . . . something like that."

"Very well, Colonel. Have your men fall into line behind the marines. Keep them together, good order. Let's move out."

Stuart had walked down toward the road, the wide bridge over the Potomac. He turned, ran back up the short hill, met Lee at the platform, motioned to the bridge.

"There are people, Colonel, wagons, moving across the bridge, both ways. Looks awfully . . . normal."

"I know, Lieutenant. I believe this situation will soon be under control. Would you please go to the telegraph window and wire the Baltimore station my orders to return the infantry to Fort Monroe. I don't believe we will be needing an army here."

"Yes, sir, right away."

"And, Lieutenant, send a wire to Secretary Floyd. Tell him his revolution has an army of twenty men."

"Sir?"

"No, you had better just tell him the situation is in hand and not as serious as rumor would suggest."

"Yes, sir, I understand."

Lee walked over to the lines of marines, saw curious faces watching him, said, "I am Lieutenant Colonel Lee, Second Regiment of Cavalry. Forgive my lack of uniform. I don't know what you have heard about what is happening over that bridge, but I assure you, it will not be as bad as you've been told. Now, gentlemen, if you will move out behind me, we may proceed."

Lee glanced at Lieutenant Green, who saluted, and put the men into motion, then Lee walked down and away from the platform, toward the dim lamplights of the bridge.

THERE WERE SEVERAL DOZEN CITIZENS ARMED WITH OLD MUSkets, some with pickaxes and shovels. As Lee approached, the crowds moved aside, cheering the troops. They had made a makeshift barricade around the engine house, overturned wagons and broken barrels. He saw a man point a rifle, fire blindly into the dark, then an answering shot came from the engine house, and the civilians ducked behind their crude wall.

Lee halted the men behind the barricade, and Green and Stuart began to move the people back. There were shouts, mostly toward the engine house—curses, taunts of what they were going to get now.

Colonel Shriver walked up beside Lee, said, "It's been like this all day, Colonel. Potshots back and forth. There was a good scrap earlier, before they holed up. A couple of their men didn't make it inside, killed by civilians. The hostages are mostly workers, Arsenal workers who walked right into the fight."

A woman suddenly appeared out of the dark, older, bent, head wrapped in an old scarf. She looked at Lee, then Shriver.

"Who's in charge, one of you?"

"I am Lieutenant Colonel Lee, madam, in command."

"Well, *Lieutenant Colonel* Lee, one of the men inside that building is my good friend, and a distinguished gentleman. He tried to stop this, wanted to talk to them, and they kept him! Took him prisoner! He's kin to President Washington, he is. Lewis Washington. You take care with him in there, Lieutenant Colonel Lee."

Lee knew Lewis Washington well, his wife's cousin, the President's grandnephew. He sagged, looked at the engine house. Putting a familiar face on the hostages should not have made a difference, but he could not help it. His first plan had been to storm the building immediately, but in the dark and in the confusion it was likely that there would be more blood than necessary. He turned to the young marine.

"Lieutenant Green, have your men take up position here, spread behind these barricades. Colonel Shriver, would you please deploy your men in a wide circle around the building. I want it perfectly clear to these people they are surrounded. Make some noise, be obvious about it, but keep your heads down. And Colonel Shriver, before you go—we will be moving in at daylight. Would your men like the honor of capturing these troublemakers?"

"Thank you for the offer. I am honored, sir. But, well, these men are volunteers, they have wives . . . families. Your soldiers here . . . the marines . . . are paid for this sort of thing, are they not?"

Lee looked at the fat face, lit by dim firelight. "Of course, Colonel. The marines will handle this."

Lee saw Green placing his men, waited until he had completed the job, then motioned to Stuart to join him with the young marine.

"Lieutenant Green, I want you to pick out a dozen men, good men. They will be the assault team. Lieutenant Stuart, I will prepare a message to the insurrectionists, which you will deliver. It will say that they are surrounded, and I will guarantee their safety, and so forth. When they accept the terms, the marines will move in quickly and subdue the men, removing their weapons. Once they understand the hopelessness of their situation, this should end quickly. Now, post guards, Mr. Green. Let the others get some sleep. We will talk again at daylight."

There was a commotion down the line, a marine guard held a man roughly by the arm, brought him toward the officers.

"Excuse me, Colonel, Lieutenant. This man claims to have information."

Green excused his man, and Lee watched the civilian in lamplight, adjusting himself from the gruff treatment by the marine.

"Colonel, my name is Fulton, I'm a newspaperman, from Philadelphia. I know who your man is, there." He pointed toward the engine house.

"How do you know, Mr. Fulton?" Lee asked. He looked the man over, saw a good suit, dark gray wool, like his own.

"I've been in Kansas, covering the trouble there. I have interviewed many of the insurrectionists, Colonel, they seem to favor reporters. I suppose we provide them a soapbox, if you will. Colonel, I have no doubt that the man you are facing is Mr. John Brown."

It was a name faintly familiar to Lee, did not carry great weight. But Stuart said, "John Brown? Here?"

Lee looked at Stuart, heard the pitch in his voice. "What do you know of the man, Lieutenant?"

"He is trouble, Colonel. He led some of the radical antislavery people out West. Slipped through our fingers more than once."

Fulton said, "He is a violent man, Colonel, a man who will not hesitate to kill himself and everyone around him for his cause."

"He's right, Colonel. Brown is . . . well, I think he's crazy. Wants the slaves to rise up, thinks he can start a revolution. I saw a paper, something he spread all over Kansas, telling the white people, his *own* people . . . they were all going to die."

Lee stared at Stuart, let it sink in. "Mr. Fulton," he said, "how can you be so certain?"

"Colonel, I've been following Brown for some time, written a few stories about him. He didn't seem to mind me snooping around. I knew he was headed this way, might try for the Arsenal."

Stuart's voice rose. "You knew he was coming here, and you didn't warn anybody?"

Lee put a hand on Stuart's arm, said, "We're here now, gentlemen, let's work on solving our situation here. Mr. Fulton, thank you, you are excused."

"Thank you, Colonel. Best of luck." Then the man slid away, was gone in the dark.

Lee thought of the hostages. His mind began to work, he absorbed the new information, the uncertainty of a man like Brown. His simple plan might result in a bloodbath. He felt his stomach tighten, a chill in the cool night.

"Gentlemen, this is a new situation. Our priority is the safety of the hostages. Lieutenant Stuart, if Mr. Brown rejects the terms, and I suspect he will, you are not to negotiate. The marines must storm the entrance immediately."

Both men nodded approval, and Green said, "Sir. Begging your pardon, sir, but we need a signal, something to tell us when to move."

Lee looked at Stuart, who touched his hat.

"If they . . . if Brown rejects the surrender," Stuart said, "I will remove my hat, drop it downward. That will be the signal to move in."

"Very well," Lee said. "Mr. Stuart, I will have the message ready for you shortly. Mr. Green, we must use the bayonet. We do not know the situation in there—we cannot have your men firing at will."

"I understand, sir. It will be bayonets. I will have the men prepare a battering ram. We will make good work of it, sir."

"Very well. Get some rest, Lieutenant, I will speak with you at dawn."

"Sir!"

Lee found a wooden box, sat down. Stuart grabbed a lantern, a careless target left sitting on top of the barricade. He brought it closer, out of sight of the engine house, and Lee pulled a pen from his pocket, the same pen he had used that morning to figure his list of lumber, and wrote out the terms of surrender.

IT WAS JUST DAYLIGHT, A COLD, THICK MORNING, FOG ROLLING OFF the river into the small town. Lee climbed up a small hill, a short distance behind the barricade, to find a clear view, and was suddenly aware that the hills around him were covered with people. In the night, the town had poured from its homes, and now everyone, Lee guessed a thousand, maybe more, was watching the proceedings. He looked back to the engine house, saw the militia stirring, forming into line all around, a toothless presence that might at least intimidate Brown into surrender. Through the mist he saw the blue form of Lieutenant Green, moving up the hill toward him.

"Colonel. Good morning. We are ready when you are, sir. We await the order."

Below, Stuart was tying a white handkerchief to a short pole with quick, nervous motions, and then he turned, saw Lee and ran up the hill. "All set, Colonel!" Stuart was breathless, shivering.

Lee looked at Green, gave him a nod, and the young marine went toward a small group of men, his handpicked troops. Lee waited for him to leave, out of earshot. Then he put a hand on Stuart's arm, a brief clench from his cold fingers. "Lieutenant," he said, "it would please me if you would use some caution this morning. We have no way of knowing how this man Brown will respond."

"Colonel . . ." But there were no words, both men knew it was just duty. "I await your order, sir. Let's take these people out."

Lee nodded. "You may proceed, Lieutenant."

Stuart ran back down, picked up his flag of truce, pulled Lee's message from his pocket, and, with a glance toward the waiting marines, walked past the barricade, across the open ground, to the engine house door.

Lee heard Stuart's voice, firm and unshaking, and he held his breath, said to God, *Please, let there be reason, protect him from harm.* Suddenly, the door opened, a slight movement, and Lee could only see a dark, faceless crack.

Stuart looked into the slight gap, saw a short barrel of a rusty carbine pushing out through the opening, pointing at his head. He focused on the small black hole, the end of the barrel, stood without motion, said quietly, "I have a message . . . a request from Colonel Robert E. Lee. Please allow me to read it."

There was noise from inside, hushed sounds. Stuart could hear people moving, and from behind the rifle came a face, smeared black dirt in a wild mass of tangled beard, and Stuart recognized the glare of the deep black eyes, the face of John Brown.

Stuart showed the paper, held it up, could not look away from the eyes, and Brown said with a quick burst, "Read it!"

Stuart began, emphasized the part about their safe passage, the impossible nature of their position. Lee's words were brief, to the point, and as Stuart read, he glanced at Brown, at the small black hole pointing at his head, wished the message had been shorter.

Brown began to make a sound, a hissing grunt. The barrel of the rifle stuck farther out, closer to Stuart's face, and Brown began to speak, a quick stream of words, his own terms, his version of the day's fighting, a flurry of talking that Stuart tried to follow. Behind Brown there were other voices, joining in, and Stuart knew the situation was falling apart, felt the tightening in his body like a coiled spring, and said, "Colonel Lee will hear no discussion. . . ." and Brown began again, made demands for safe conduct, mentioned the hostages. The voices became louder behind Brown, hostages were calling out, pleading for help, the voices blending together in a dull roar, and Stuart began to feel overwhelmed, stared into the barrel of the rifle. Then one voice, clearer, older, yelled out, and even Lee heard the words, the voice of Lewis Washington.

"Never mind us, fire!"

Stuart backed away one step from the rifle, said, "Colonel Lee will not discuss your demands," and suddenly the rifle was gone, back into the dark, and the door closed with a loud thump. Stuart stared at the door, then turned, looked at the marines, took a deep breath, reached his hand up, a slight quiver, and removed his hat.

From the barricade the marines rushed forward, and men in sharp blue uniforms began to pound on the thick wooden door. After several heavy blows the door splintered and a hole was punched through. Green threw himself into the hole. Behind him, his men lined up, pushing their way in one at a time.

Lee saw the marines disappear inside, a painfully slow assault. Then there were shots, and Lee knew it would not be the marines.

Inside, Green was frantic, he had only a sword, and he saw the face of the man who had spoken to Stuart, focused on him, saw the rifle, and hurled himself in a screaming rush. He brought the sword down and knocked the rifle away. Brown lunged at the young man, tried to grab him around the neck, and Green raised the sword again, brought it down heavily on Brown's head. The sword hit sideways, the blade bent at a useless angle, and Brown tried again, grabbed for Green's neck, but the young man turned the sword, swung the heavy handle against Brown's head, and with a cry of pain Brown went down.

Behind their lieutenant the marines made use of their bayonets. The shooting stopped and men lay wounded all around the inside of the building. Green turned, saw the hostages huddled in a group against one wall, then looked back to the door, daylight through the ragged opening, and he saw blue coats, two of his men on the ground. They had just made it through, were shot down just inside the door, and Green went to the men, saw the blood and yelled out. They were dragged aside, the door was pulled open, and the rising sun flooded the dark space. It was over.

Brown was held in a secure room in the Arsenal, and now the politicians came, to see for themselves how the great rebellion had been crushed. Lee stood aside, performed his official duties, while Brown was questioned by anyone who had the influence to see him.

Lee and Stuart went about the business of identifying Brown's cohorts, dead and alive, captured a small store of arms Brown had accumulated, but to Lee, his work was done. He notified Secretary Floyd that the matter was concluded, that in his opinion there was little for Washington to be concerned about.

The marines and Lieutenant Green remained in Harper's Ferry as security, and served as escort when Brown was moved to Charlestown for trial. Despite wild rumors of new riots elsewhere and threats of attempts to free him, Brown was tried and convicted without incident, and was sentenced to be hanged.

5. JACKSON

NOVEMBER 1859

THE DIRT SIFTED THROUGH HIS FINGERS LIKE FINE BROWN SUGAR. Jackson sat, dug his hands into the soft soil again, held it up, watched it pour down. It was his, his dirt, his land. From where he sat, he could look across the twenty-acre patch, down the long straight rows, the newly planted winter crops. The green sprouts of the collards and turnips had broken the soil a few weeks before, and now the new life in the garden was stronger, ready for the coming cold. He slid along on the seat of his pants, between the thickening green lines, plucked out the intruders, the errant weeds. Winter was sliding across the mountains, and he looked up, toward the west, saw the cold gray line of thick clouds. There will be snow tonight, he thought, and frowned, looked out over the patch, concerned.

He stood up, stretched, raised both arms above his head, reached upward, felt the pressure in his back, scolded himself for sitting so long on the cold ground.

"Not healthy, not at all," he said aloud.

These days his health seemed to come and go, the pains in his side, his poor vision. He had taken trips to the hot springs and water spas over the summer, but it was Anna who worried him. She had still not recovered from the baby's death, and he missed her quick energy, her playfulness. She had taken the water treatments with him, had seen the same doctors, but seemed to be no better.

He stood stiffly, put his hands on his hips, made dirty handprints on his cotton trousers, looked out over the garden. Surely, this will please God, he thought, an offering, the labor of new life. He bent down, rubbed his fingers along a short green stem, prickly and rough. These are Your children too, he thought.

Townspeople had passed by throughout the day, small carriages and lone riders, and at midday he had seen the stage to Staunton. There were friendly greetings, and he had acknowledged them, returned waves. There was space behind his home, a fine spot for a small garden, but it was not enough, and so he had bought this piece of plain land, barely outside the expanding boundary of the town, a flat field hugged by the rolling hills, and people would stop just to admire, to point and wave at the major, this odd professor who so thoroughly groomed his small farm.

He looked again at the clouds, the dark movement, thought of home, the good smells of supper, wiped his hands on an old rag and began to step past the neat rows, toward the main road, when he heard a shout.

"Major! Major Jackson!"

It was a cadet. Jackson could see the uniform bouncing on the back of a horse, riding wildly toward him from the town. The boy was waving one arm, then had to use it to steady himself, then waved again. Jackson thought, Not a very good rider, something we should work on . . .

"Major Jackson, sir!" The boy reined up, jumped from the saddle, stumbled sideways and landed in a heap of gray and white. The horse did not stop, ran on a short way, contemptuous.

The boy gathered himself, grimaced, felt a knee, then stood at attention and saluted. Jackson returned it, though, as the boy quickly noted, his ragged farming clothes did not present him as any kind of officer.

Jackson waited for the boy to catch his breath, then said, "You all right, cadet? Nasty fall."

"Yes, sir. Not my horse, sir, had to grab the closest one, and well . . . Sir, I have been instructed by the commandant, by Colonel Smith himself, sir, to request in the strongest terms that you report to the colonel as soon as is possible, sir."

Jackson straightened, wiped his hands again. "Now? Is there some problem?"

"Sir, I have only heard reports that we have been called to duty, sir. By the governor."

"The governor? Well, all right, then. You return to Colonel Smith, report that I am right behind you. You are dismissed."

"Yes, sir. Thank you, sir."

The boy walked gingerly toward the horse and took the reins. The horse allowed him to mount, and with a quick yelp from the boy, it turned and carried its rider toward the town.

Jackson started down the road at a quick pace. His house was on the way to the institute, and it would not take him long to dress. Behind him, in the west, the thick clouds rolled forward, the unstoppable flow of the coming storm.

IT WAS DARK WHEN JACKSON ARRIVED AT THE COMMANDANT'S OFfice. There were other officers there, small quiet talk, anxious whispers. Jackson closed the heavy door behind him, stood in the entranceway, nodded to the others, saw both dress and casual uniforms, a hasty assembly.

From down the hallway there was a voice. Cadets moved quickly by, saluting the officers. Jackson watched the young faces, tried to recall the names, as Colonel Smith stepped noisily into the room.

"Gentlemen, as you were. Sorry to call you out like this, evening meal and all, I know . . . but we have received some orders, a rather important assignment. Allow me to read it."

He reached into his vest pocket, drew out a folded paper, opened it, and Jackson could see a ribbon, the seal of some importance.

> "From: The Honorable Henry A. Wise, Governor, the Commonwealth of Virginia.
>
> To: Colonel Francis H. Smith, Commandant, Virginia Military Institute.
>
> By Special Order, the Officers and Corps of Cadets, Virginia Military Institute, shall report to Charlestown, Virginia, on the twenty-eighth day of November, 1859, for the purpose of maintaining the general security, for the protection of the town and its inhabitants, and for the prevention of any violent uprising from interfering with the execution by hanging of Mr. John Brown."

Jackson felt a sudden lump in his stomach. The insurrection that John Brown had attempted was a hot topic, and reckless rumors had flooded over the countryside after his capture. But he had believed the Federal Army would handle the matter. Someone spoke, Jackson turned and saw Major Gilham.

"Colonel, are we to be the only security?"

"Let's just say, Major, we're the only *organized* security. The governor has already issued a call for militia, and units from all over the state have been assembled, but I would not place much stock in their ability to do anything more than cause trouble. Oh, and there's one more thing." Smith looked back to the paper, found his place, stopped.

"Well, no need to read it all, point is, not only are we to provide security, but it appears the good governor has decided that I am to be the executioner in charge. I don't have to tell you that, in fact, our Corps of Cadets, with you gentlemen in command, may find itself up against . . . well, God knows what."

Jackson felt a low fire deep in his gut, thought of his guns, the artillery crews. They were very young, and some of them were not very good, but he began to run the faces through his mind, assess the skills.

"Gentlemen," Smith continued, "your commands will cover your areas of expertise, of course. In the morning, we will issue the order to the corps to move out. Major Jackson . . ."

Jackson's thoughts scrambled, he snapped to attention and stared straight, past the colonel.

"Major, you will bring a two-piece battery of your cannon. Pick some good boys, Major. This could be a difficult assignment."

"Yes, sir. Already working on it, sir."

Smith spoke to the other officers individually, and Jackson did not hear, had his orders. Then they were dismissed, and he moved back outside, felt the cold chill of the night, looked across the parade grounds, the wide space guarded by his guns. He looked at them, each one, and nodded, a brief greeting to the heavy brass, then he graded, appraised, silently chose the two he would take, and smiled, a quick, cold clench of his mouth. Then he turned and marched home through a starless night.

ON THEIR FIFTH DAY CAMPED AROUND CHARLESTOWN, THE cadets woke to an early breakfast and new orders. Then there were drums, a slow cadence, giving a rhythm to the troops, who marched in line, filed into a large field, and formed their units. The artillery were first, had set up on the high ground, and Jackson stood by one of his cannon and faced the tall wooden scaffold, looking across to his other gun, pointing out, away from the forming troops. The units of cadet infantry filed in behind the scaffold, a vast rolling field, neat blocks of bright red, new field uniforms the cadets were wearing for the first time. Jackson's handpicked gun crew stood at rigid attention, and there was no talking, no looking about. From the vantage point of the rise, Jackson could see all the others, the ragged formation of volunteer troops, and beyond, the buildings of the town. A crowd of people filled the road with the temper and bluster of a careless mob, following a wagon, and Jackson knew the cadets could not control a riot, that they had to depend on these people to control themselves.

The wagon climbed the rise, rolled closer. Jackson could see a soldier on horseback leading the way, and then the wagon itself, carrying several officials and the local sheriff. High up above the rest, the figure of John Brown sat on the head of his coal-black coffin.

The wagon rolled on slowly, approaching the scaffold, and Jackson watched with a tense gripping in his gut. The first chilling days of December had arrived without incident, but to the experienced officers, the wild rumors had become troublesome; the cadets could be easily spooked. There was talk of a vast number of Negroes, arming, heading in a crazed mass toward the town to free their leader. It was said that the Federal Army had abandoned the area, had assumed the worst and fled, leaving these boys to fight off a revolution.

Jackson knew of rumors, had heard a continuous stream of them in Mexico, knew they followed an army like flies. He did not believe there was a revolution, that there would be a fight here. But if there was . . . he glanced at the polished brass of his big gun. The townspeople spread out, people scrambling for the good view. Then they began to quiet, a great weight pressing down upon them all, any sense of celebration pushed away by the presence of the troops, these quiet boys with guns.

The wagon passed close to Jackson, turned, and stopped at the scaffold. He tried to see Brown's face, to get a close look at the eyes. How different this was from war, he thought, to wait for death slowly, to know with total certainty it was coming, would not catch you in the heat of action, snatching you suddenly from your duty, but was there in front of you, and you approached it with slow, steady steps. He felt an odd respect for that, watched Brown move deliberately from the wagon up the wooden stairs. As he reached the platform, Brown smiled, made a comment to the sheriff, and said something to Colonel Smith, who stood somberly to one side. Jackson looked up at the few men now on the platform, saw no minister, no man of God, and he was surprised, could not understand that, the rejection of God. Jackson thought, He seems . . . cheerful, does not show any sign of fear, is not appealing for mercy. . . .

Now Colonel Smith gave a quiet order to the sheriff, who said something to Brown, then placed a white cap over Brown's head, covering the smiling face. The crowd now began to move, the slow pulse of expectation, and Jackson heard the anxious muffled voices. It would be very soon.

Colonel Smith then read from a document, and Jackson could not hear the words, knew it was the death warrant, the governor's order. Then Smith motioned to the sheriff, a brief nod, and the sheriff leaned toward the colonel, made certain, and Jackson saw the sheriff's hand, the simple instrument of death, saw the blade flash, cutting the rope. The trapdoor, the floor beneath Brown's feet, opened with a clatter that startled the crowd, made them all jump in one sharp beat. Brown's body dropped down quickly, then caught, and Jackson heard the small sound, the rope tightening, and Brown's arms jerked up, bending at the elbows, small twitches in the stillness, and then down again, and then no motion. The body hung with a stillness that froze all who saw it. There was a light breeze, and the body began slowly to turn, to spin, and Jackson looked down and said a prayer. *Dear God, let this man pass over and be with You, even if he did not ask . . . did not understand . . . he is Your own.*

Then he heard a voice, a mad scream from the crowd, "Burn in Hell!" and others followed, hard shouts and small cries for damnation.

He looked back to Brown's lifeless body, thought, Perhaps it is meant for him to pass below, into the fires of Hell. Jackson clenched his fists. He could not bear that, could not believe that men could be judged to be so wicked, and that others would be so eager to condemn their brothers to a flaming eternal death.

6. HANCOCK

September 1860

THEY RODE IN SINGLE FILE, TWELVE OF THEM, DRESSED IN THE bright colors of the Spanish army, or what they knew of that army, so far away. Wide red sashes were wrapped around their waists, and their hats sprouted long thick plumes, plucked long ago from birds no one here had ever seen. They rode slowly, deliberately, on horses that had been decorated with as much care as their riders. As the men passed the front of Hancock's house, they turned their heads, faced the house, a fixed stare, fierce and defiant.

"This is very odd."

Hancock reached out an arm, and Mira moved closer. He pulled her to him, wrapped his arm around her shoulders. They watched from inside, through the wide front window of the house, as the procession moved past. Hancock watched each man carefully, looked for weapons, any sign the display would turn into something else, something more aggressive.

"I've been expecting this, actually. General Banning told me about this—this custom."

"What does it mean? Is it a threat?" She turned, looked instinctively toward the small cradle where the baby lay sleeping.

"Probably not, but it could be the first step. They're showing their displeasure against the authority of the government, and . . . I guess that's me."

He had been here only a few months, ordered to the new post from up north, Benicia, near San Francisco, the headquarters of the California command. It was a promotion, if not in rank, at least some prestige, a reward to a man who had demonstrated great skill in managing property, a flair for the paperwork of equipping an army.

They had come to California nearly by accident. The Sixth Infantry had moved west from Fort Leavenworth, Kansas, a long march to the Utah Territory, to confront the rebellious Mormons, who were threatening to reject the authority of the federally appointed governor. But with the show of force closing in, the Mormons had avoided the fight, had finally agreed to accept the government's authority, and so the Sixth Infantry, under the new command of General Albert Sidney Johnston, had been ordered to keep going, farther west, and provide manpower for the new Department of California.

The march had taken many months, and in all had covered over two thousand miles, the longest overland march by infantry in military history, and it was the job of this young quartermaster, Captain Winfield Scott Hancock, to supply the troops. And, as he had done from his first days of service, he had exceeded the army's expectations, had arrived at Benicia better equipped than when they left Kansas. It was an extraordinary accomplishment, and so Hancock had been appointed to command the new Department of Southern California, which consisted of . . . him.

His first concern had been the Indians, the Mojaves, but there had been no trouble, and Hancock had even become acquainted with some of the tribal chieftains. But the Spanish residents had deep loyalties to the old territorial government, a government that had been forced to surrender control to these new Americans, one great price for the defeat of Santa Anna in Mexico, and it was a control that most in Southern California never recognized, because little around them had changed.

The protesters had completed their ride past his house, sped up their horses and disappeared down the street, toward the older buildings of Los Angeles. Hancock turned from the window, went into his small office, opened a desk drawer and pulled out a small pistol.

Mira came in behind him, saw the dull metal of the old gun. "Win, are we in danger?"

He didn't answer, was thinking about the warehouse, the piles of government stores, weapons and powder, as well as the various hardware, tents, and blankets. He always thought it foolish of the army to store these supplies in Los Angeles, with only one man, one quartermaster, as the military presence in the area. The Quartermaster's Depot was a simple storage building, a barnlike warehouse with a wide door, secured by crude strap hinges and one old lock, and the nearest military unit was over a hundred miles away, the cavalry detachment at Fort Tejon.

He held the pistol, felt the solid power, ran his fingers over the oily surface, then turned and handed it to Mira.

"How long has it been since you fired this?"

She pointed it down to the floor, turned her hand sideways, then back.

"Kansas. Mr. Benden took me out to the cornfields, set up a box. He was concerned that with you gone I might need it."

He watched her handle the gun, thought of the huge Irishman, the man he had hired to look after her. Kansas was a dangerous place, had become a war zone, the issue of slavery for the new state a source of growing conflict. Hot-tempered radicals on both sides of the issue were crowding in, hoping to vote the issue their way, whether the state would be free or slave. The conflicts had become vicious and bloody, and the army had been squarely in the middle. Hancock knew that an officer's wife could be a vulnerable target, and he had hired Benden, a fierce giant whose fists had long ago earned him a reputation as a man you did not confront. Benden had taught Mira how to shoot, and she had a knack for it, a steadiness, could outshoot many of the officers. But she did not enjoy guns, saw them as the tools of the soldiers, did not understand the compliments the men gave her.

"Maybe we can go out, the big field down the road, set up a target."

She looked at him. "You didn't answer my question. Are we in danger?"

"I'm not sure. We are certainly vulnerable. I need to learn more about these Spaniards, this . . . protest. In the meantime, it can't hurt to be prepared." He reached for his coat.

"Where are you going?"

"To see Banning. He deals with these people, maybe he's heard something."

She put the gun down on his desk, reached up, and he caught her hands, pulled them into his chest, held them.

"If there is any trouble, it will certainly be at the warehouse, not here. I won't be long . . . don't worry."

He lifted her hands up, kissed them, and then turned and went out through the front door. She followed him, leaned against the open doorway, watched him cross the hard dirt street, then closed and locked the door.

General Phineas Banning was not a general at all, had not been a military man, but had come to Los Angeles some years earlier, recognized the great potential for shipping and commerce, and organized the first modern port facilities. His command of engineering projects, his natural ability to organize the local workers, had given him the military nickname. Banning had a strong appreciation for the army's usefulness, as did most of the Americans in the area, and so the Hancocks had been warmly received. Hancock knew Banning better than most in the area, knew that his close involvement with the larger community, the Spanish-speaking community, could provide him with a clearer picture of what was going on with the protests.

Hancock was well known now in the town, the only blue uniform that anyone saw walking the street. People smiled, polite, as he passed, though most did not speak English and there were few words of greeting. Banning's office was a large adobe house, had been converted from an old Spanish villa, and sat on the main road that led out to the coast. He reached the open yard, saw several young men sitting on the steps. Hancock guessed them to be laborers, men waiting for their foreman, for instruction. They were short and brown, tough, hard-looking men, heavy arms and broad chests, and they watched Hancock with quiet black eyes. He climbed the stone stairway to the veranda, reached the door and turned to see a dark face watching him closely; there was no politeness, no smile.

Inside, he heard voices, the first words of English since he had left his house. He called out, "Hello? Mr. Banning?"

From a dark hallway he heard a sound, then a door opened and light filled the long space. He saw two men walking toward him, carrying papers, rolled-up drawings. One of them was Banning.

"Well, Captain Hancock, a surprise! Come on back, please." Banning waved the other man away, said something briefly in Spanish, and the man was out the door. Hancock heard commotion outside, the stirring of the men.

"Forgive my visit, I'm sorry if I have interrupted your work. I do need to talk to you."

"Nonsense, always time for a few words."

Hancock followed Banning down the hall, turned into a large office containing a huge, heavy desk and windows filled with pots of flowering plants. Banning went around the desk, sat in a heavy leather chair, wheeled it closer, folded his hands in front of him in a gesture of attention.

"Now, Captain, what's on your mind?"

Hancock sat in a wooden chair, saw reflected sunlight in a rich mahogany glare, did not put his hands on the desk.

"We had a demonstration today, in front of my home. It was as you had described: men dressed as Spanish soldiers, formal uniforms, riding by and staring."

"Hmmm, so. It's been coming. A lot of talk. Anything happen, any problem?"

"No, they didn't approach the house, just rode by, then took off."

"That's the way it works. The key is, what happens next."

"That's what I was hoping you could tell me."

"Captain, have you seen Hamilton's newspaper this week? The *Star*?"

"No, missed it."

"That damned idiot. He's filling his paper with all kinds of stories about what's happening back East, the election and all. I know him, he thinks he's fair, I suppose. But he's the only news these people have about Washington. I get letters, some correspondence from Delaware, friends in New York, a great deal of commotion about the election, none of it too positive, but then I read about the same events in Hamilton's 'news' and I see his slant, his opinions coming through. And that, Captain, is where your trouble might come from."

"About the election? What kind of trouble?"

"This fellow Lincoln, this Republican . . . he's got a strong following in the North. Too strong, probably. The Democrats are splitting up, fighting it out with each other. From what I can gather, the Southern cause is hurting itself. But when you read Hamilton, you see Lincoln as the devil himself, and the election as a vote to preserve the American way of life. That kind of rhetoric talks to people's passions, not their good sense. You a Democrat, Captain?"

"Yes, I suppose I am. My father had pretty strong views on politics, can't say I ever disagreed with him much, but most soldiers I know are Democrats. What is so dangerous? It's just an election."

"There's more and more talk that if Lincoln wins, the country could divide up, fall apart altogether. The slavery business, the government sticking itself into the affairs of the states, there's a good many people who see Lincoln as the man who will destroy the country. And you've got loose cannons like Hamilton throwing this stuff out at people like it's the word of God. Around here we're pretty far removed from what the government says, Captain. Things like 'law' and 'Union' don't mean much to people who don't even speak your language. Sounds pretty scary to me, Captain."

"And, the Spanish . . ." Hancock paused, began to understand.

"The Spanish, the Mexicans, are sitting back, taking it all in. I tell you, Captain, if the country splits apart, there's talk, right outside this damned window, these boys don't think I know what they're saying. . . . They're waiting for the day, because the bet is they can walk right in and grab California away from the army. Hell, they already know there's American soldiers who are talking about quitting, going home to their states. You scared yet, Captain?"

He looked past Banning, out the wide window. He had heard some talk, most of it coming from San Francisco, from Benicia, the angry talk of politics. He had never been too political, had supported the Democrats because it was what his father had done. He felt there was some logic in their issues, the right of the states to determine their own course. But . . . the collapse of the Union? It seemed too far beyond reason, too irrational to be taken seriously.

"You expecting any help here, Captain, any troops?"

"I haven't asked for any. There has never been any trouble." He realized now he sounded naive, that the demonstration in front of his house could be far more serious than he wanted to admit.

"The local boys might need some discouraging, Captain, so keep the lid on. If they start feeling their strength, thinking they can push the army a little harder, they will."

Hancock began to think, his mind seemed to come awake, clear. The warehouse . . . the property of the army . . . the munitions . . . could not fall into the hands of anyone.

"Phineas, you could do your country, and me, a great service."

Banning smiled, nodded. "At your service, Captain."

"Spread the word. There's cavalry coming, several squadrons, no, a regiment. Captain Hancock is . . . outraged . . . that local citizens would defy the military authority, by the . . . the . . . disgraceful lack of respect paid to me and my wife, the threats against my home. How's that?"

Banning laughed. "I must say, Captain, I have never seen such fury from a military man. It could be . . . my God, the army could be coming here to . . . oh, my Lord, it could be a massacre!"

Hancock felt the rush of energy, but did not laugh with Banning. It had to work, a show of bravado, throw uncertainty into a growing mob. It would slow them down, at least until he could send to Tejon for real troops to back up his rumors.

Hancock stood, made a slight bow. "You are a friend, Mr. Banning. Thank you for your time."

Banning sat back in his chair, and Hancock saw he was already planning how he could spread the word. He said quietly, "Hamilton," and Hancock knew, of course, the newspaperman would jump on this story, a military invasion, full-scale occupation, martial law . . .

Hancock left Banning's office, walked out into hot sunlight, thought, Go to the warehouse, just to be sure. He turned a corner, passed several new shops, with Spanish and English signs, then made his way out beyond the street where his house sat, where Mira waited for him. He reached the long wooden building surrounded by a short picket fence with flaking white paint, saw the sign over the wide doors, U.S. ARMY SUPPLY DEPOT. He suddenly felt naked, very weak, unarmed. He pulled keys from his coat pocket, found the one for the old brass lock, swung open the thin wooden door. Inside were stacks of goods, high piles in neat rows, cloth and canvas. This is insane, he thought. All this, enough to equip, what? A small army? At least, to supply a good-sized bit of trouble. In a far corner he saw a wooden box, large and square, and he leaned over, pulled at the wood planking. It came loose, and he put his hand inside, felt through thick straw, worked his fingers in until his hand touched hard steel. He pulled the large pistol out through the top of the box, held it up toward the open door of the warehouse, aimed at nothing, then tucked it in his belt. He reached back into the box, pulled out another, then paused, thought, Maybe one more.

The wide flat door began to move, pushed by an afternoon breeze, and he jerked to attention, startled, and grabbed at a pistol. He laughed at himself, felt his heart beating with icy quickness, and thought of Banning. Are you scared yet, Captain?

THE SPANISH "SOLDIERS" HAD COME AGAIN, MORE OF THEM THIS time, another absurd parade, and there had been others with them, people on foot, following along, yelling at the house, at *him* as he watched from the window. He could still see the faces, the infection spreading in the crowd.

They sat together in the fading light. Mira had brought him supper, and he was finishing the last piece of bread, drinking a cup of coffee. Outside the cavernous warehouse the last bit of orange glow was fading on the flat western horizon.

"You had better leave soon. It's already dark."

She took the plate from his hand, set it on the ground, slid closer and leaned against him. They sat on the wooden box that held the pistols, and he wrapped his arms around her, leaned back against the side of the building.

"In a moment, there's no hurry. Consuela stayed late today, probably has the children in bed by now. She's been a godsend, really."

Hancock thought of the sweet old woman Mira had found to help with the house. She knew almost no English, but he could see in her hands, her touch, an understanding. She seemed to know just how to deal with the children, what they needed. Hancock had never actually spoken with her. She would not look at him, always looked at the floor when he was there. Very strange, he thought, and he wondered if it was fear, respect, or just old Spanish custom. She had been in Los Angeles since she was a child, and Hancock guessed she was maybe sixty-five, seventy years old. He began to think out loud.

"I wonder what these people think of us."

Mira stared ahead, still pressed against him. "What people, you mean the Spanish, the Mexicans?"

"Yes. We won the war, took over their government here, and they just go on like they always did. Maybe they never considered themselves Mexicans, any more than they consider themselves Americans."

"It's the Church. They worship at the same place they have since they were children, the same priests. I don't think Consuela even understands what the government is. She talks about the priests as the authority."

"She told you this?"

"In not so many words. The priests always were in control here, even before the war. If the people have problems, that's who they see."

"And now the Americans are having problems, and the priests see an opportunity to regain control."

She sat up, turned, tried to see his face in the darkness.

"Do you really think it's the Church?"

"I don't know. Someone is organizing this resistance, the protests. Those people today, the protesters, they have leaders, behind the scenes. They're smart enough not to show us who they are. All it takes is one, one man who knows how to use words, charismatic, who commands their respect, a man like Santa Anna."

"Surely not the Church . . ."

"I don't know. We may never know."

She stood, stretched her arms upright, and he could barely see her. We should have a lantern, he thought, but no, if they come, they must not know I am in here. It's the only advantage I have.

The word was out, Banning had seen to it, and the Spanish citizens were buzzing, hostile and afraid, and Hancock knew it had been a risk, but no one had come near the warehouse, not yet. But now the rumors came back at him. At a meeting, even a rally, tonight, the militant leaders of the Spanish community were going to take their own actions. Many of the locals had been speaking out, calling for a rebellion, taking back control from the Americans.

And though his rumors had seemed to work, and slowed down the hot talk, there were still no American soldiers, they had not come, no great military presence to keep down the talk of rebellion. He had sent a message to Tejon and a civilian courier to Benicia, but it was slow, no telegraph, no railroad. There had been a squad of infantry passing through, going to Arizona. They stopped briefly for provisions, the normal function of the Quartermaster's Depot, but they had not stayed, could not. Their captain had orders, an Indian raid near Yuma, did not see Hancock's problems as a priority, and so they loaded a few wagons with supplies from the warehouse and were gone.

"This is all because of the election."

She bent down beside him, put a hand on his, and she knew he wanted to talk, did not want her to leave, not yet. "What do you mean?"

"This trouble—it's all because of the election, all the talk in the paper, Hamilton's damned newspaper, his great oratory about the collapse of the country if Lincoln is elected. It's madness, pure idiocy."

She sat quietly beside him. "It's his right, he can print anything he wants," she said. "I don't think people pay much attention to that kind of talk."

"But they do. They are—it's not just Hamilton, it's the South . . . the states. The infantry unit that just came through, their captain told me that soldiers at Benicia are talking about going home, quitting the army if Lincoln wins the election. The newspapers come from back East and fights break out over pieces of news. They are talking about the slave states pulling out of the Union, making a new country . . ." He paused, lifted his hat from his head, ran his hand through thick hair, and she sat closer again, next to him, felt his tension.

He took a deep breath, said, "We have a system, a democratic system, and if one man is elected, it's because the people choose him. But not this time. This time if the wrong man wins, the system gets torn down. And not just back East, but right here. Most of the local Americans are Southern sympathizers. Hamilton speaks to them, they listen. Banning . . . at least Banning is reasonable, some of the others I guess, too. But if the Union collapses, what will these men do? We are so isolated, so far from the Federal government. It's not just the Spanish who want California to be independent, it's men like Hamilton. How easy it is to be so reckless, to make grand pronouncements about rebellion and independence, when the authority, the system, the responsibility is so far away." He paused, held her gently away from him, stood up and began to pace, feeling the nervous energy.

"I wear the uniform of that authority, I'm the only piece of the government here, and this post is *my* responsibility. No one will start any rebellion with *these* guns."

She watched in the dark, felt his movement, and then he stopped, leaned down and took her hand, helped her stand.

"You had better leave, go on home, before it gets much later."

"Please, Win, please, be careful. These are just . . . *things*. The army can replace them."

He hugged her, held her hard against him. "It's all right. Besides, it's only rumors. You know what rumors are like. Help should be here soon anyway. It's probably just for tonight."

He didn't sound convincing, knew it, didn't believe it himself. He was glad she could not see his face; he could never lie to her.

"All right, my dear husband. I'll be back in the morning, I'll make a big breakfast for you."

"Wait, do you have—"

"Yes, Captain, I have the pistol right here. I will be fine."

He walked her over to the doors, pushed them open slowly, quietly. The moon was coming up over the far trees, and he was relieved to see the street was not as dark as the inside of the warehouse and it would be a short walk to their house. She kissed him, quickly, did not want to draw it out, make it worse than it was, and then she moved away. He followed her with his eyes until she was gone in the dark.

He went back inside, pulled the doors together, could see the moonlight coming in between them, through an opening a half-inch wide. He felt his belt, the pistols, felt a little foolish, thought, You must look like some kind of buccaneer. He sat down on the box, adjusting the pistols, a one-man army. He leaned back against the hard wall, maybe would try a nap, but he was wide-awake, began to listen to the silence. He looked away from the doors, from the small sliver of moonlight, tried to see in the dark, the high stacks of supplies, up to the tall ceiling. He thought of wild animals, the night creatures. What was so different about their eyes? Damned dangerous beasts if they could see in this.

He did not know how much time had passed, could not see his watch. It was late, near midnight, certainly. He stood up slowly, flexed stiff knees, walked toward the crack of the doors. He peered out, saw nothing, no movement, and felt relief, confident Mira had made it home all right. He thought of the children, told himself, purposefully, they would be fine, there would be no danger to them, it was the supplies they would want, the munitions. He went back again to his corner, to the open box of pistols, sat and leaned against the wall, listening to the quiet night.

His hand rested on something, a tin cup, his coffee. He brought it up, smelled it, took a small sip of cold mud, made a face Mira would have scolded him for, set the cup back down on the hard ground beside the box. He heard a horse whinny in the far distance, and a dog barking. He froze, listened hard, heard nothing else, leaned his head back now, his hat a thin pillow against the wood siding.

He heard a horse again, closer this time, and he sat up, felt a burst of cold in his stomach, and quickly he was standing. He moved over against the far wall, listening, and now there were more. He heard the dull rhythm of slow hoofbeats. The cold spread through his body, his heart pounding his brain into a clear alertness. He pulled a loaded pistol from his belt, touched the cartridge box in his coat pocket, moved in a silent glide to the doors, peeked out and waited.

The horses came closer, outside the picket fence, and he saw them now, saw the riders, could not tell much, just gray shadows, no voices. He watched the men dismount, tried to count . . . five, six. One man walked to the gate, pushed it open, and they began to move toward the building, to the wide doors, quiet slow steps, and Hancock stood straight, took one step back from the crack, raised the pistol, could see one man's form moving up closer, blocking out the moonlight, and he held the pistol with both hands, felt a rising heat, his heart sending a roar of sound through his head.

He set the barrel of the pistol in the crack of the door, aimed at the man's chest, and the man stopped and said in a loud whisper, "Captain Hancock? Captain, you in there?"

It was Phineas Banning.

Hancock pulled the pistol back, stood for a moment in the dark, fought the urge to laugh, then slid a steel bar through heavy metal rings on the door and pushed it open.

"Captain? We heard you were in here. I called on your house earlier, saw your wife. She damn near shot me. Guess it was late . . . sorry . . . but she said you were here, standing guard."

"What are you doing here? Who is with you?"

Hancock tried to see faces, now others began to speak, familiar voices, men he knew well from the town. Banning quieted them, said, "Captain, we have been hearing things, talk of trouble, and we're here to help."

Another man spoke, Joseph Brent, a lawyer, a man who dealt with the Spanish people.

"Captain, you are in some danger here. There is organizing going on, men gathering west of town, talking about a raid on this warehouse. We got together to see what we can do to help."

"Gentlemen, this is dangerous business. I can't . . . I'm not authorized to issue guns to civilians. This is the army's problem, I can't ask you—"

"Captain, we can't have the army treated like this. It's bad for business." Banning laughed and pulled back his coat. Hancock could see the reflection from a pistol in his belt. Now he saw other guns, men held up rifles, old muskets.

Another man spoke, Ben Wilson, a rancher. "Captain, we are your friends. Just tell us what to do. We're here to help."

Hancock looked at the faces, tried to see them in the dark, began to feel a sense of confidence, of strength. He pointed to the fence, said with a quiet firmness, "There, one of you in each of the four corners of the fence. One at the gate, one with me, here, by the doors. Use your ears, you'll hear them before you see them. Don't hesitate. If you hear anything, call out, be loud. Let them know we're here. And, gentlemen, don't shoot at anything without my order. No innocent casualties. Are we clear?"

There were short murmurs, nods, and the men began to spread out. Banning moved up and stood beside him.

Hancock said, "Phineas, thank you. I am fortunate to have such friends."

Banning put a hand on his shoulder. "So are we, Captain, so are we."

THE RAID DID NOT COME. HANCOCK SAT QUIETLY, A FEW FEET from Banning, leaned against the wooden doors of the warehouse, began to see the bright glow in the east, heard the men begin to stir, standing, stretching, and now it was light enough to see faces clearly. He called them together, watched as the small army assembled. He wanted to say something, something more than a thank-you, but from down the road, away from town, there were hoofbeats, many horses, and a cloud of rising dust. His men turned, started to move, and Hancock listened, felt a rising alarm at the growing sound of many horses; too many. Then he saw them—a small flag, dull blue coats in the dim morning light: it was the cavalry.

The front of the column stopped at the picket fence, the line stretching down the road and around a curve, a full squadron, maybe a hundred men. Hancock's civilian army came back together, stood in their own kind of formation, and he felt their pride, his friends standing at attention—they were being relieved.

An officer dismounted, came through the gate and saluted Hancock, a gesture of greeting, not rank.

"Captain William Lorman, at your service, sir. Second squadron of cavalry, Fort Tejon. Understand you have a bit of a problem here, Captain?" Lorman glanced at the civilians, saw the weapons, and looked back at Hancock, puzzled.

"Captain Lorman, these men are good citizens of Los Angeles, and have provided volunteer service to their country in time of crisis. They are to be commended."

Lorman looked over the men again, shrugged. "Whatever you say, Captain. They may be excused now. We have been ordered to encamp here, to act as security for your command until the infantry arrives." He looked again at the line of men, saw the ancient Tennessee rifle held by the rancher, Ben Wilson, said to Hancock in a low voice, "They didn't have to shoot anybody, did they?"

"No, Captain, all is peaceful here for now. Their presence was a deterrent, I am certain of that. Please have your men set up their camp around the depot, as you see fit. Did you say *infantry*?"

"Yes, Captain, I am to tell you that a regiment of infantry under the command of a Major Armistead is being sent down from San Francisco."

"*Major* Armistead?"

"That's the message I was given. You know him?"

"I know him as *Captain* Armistead." Hancock smiled, shook his head. Chasing bandits around Benicia must have its rewards, he thought. He turned back to his friends, who had eased their stance, were watching the horse soldiers dismount.

"Well, Captain," Banning said. "Looks like you don't require our services anymore. My word, it is a good feeling, isn't it?"

"What's that?"

"The army . . . the troops. Calms things down a bit, I'd say. Gives me a bit of credibility too. Now, our friend Hamilton will really pay attention when I bring him some news. Could be very useful indeed." Banning laughed, gave Hancock a crude salute, and the others, smiling now, yawns and more stretches, began to move away in a weary stagger back to their homes.

He watched them leave, then turned to find Lorman again, to offer assistance, when he heard her voice, then saw a bright wave. Mira came to the gate, the soldiers parting with an admiring stare, letting her pass. She didn't rush to him, knew about decorum, the dignity of officers. Hancock glanced at Lorman, who had moved up to ask for something, and Lorman caught the look and backed discreetly away, then barked something to his men Hancock did not hear. Mira held out her arm, which Hancock hooked into his, and she led him out, through the gate, back toward their home and their waking children.

7. LEE

September 1860

His oldest son, Custis, had arrived home the night before. Lee had secured a post for the young man in Washington so he could live at Arlington, and continue the good work Lee had started managing his grandfather's estate.

Lee sat at the breakfast table, a hand on his round stomach, groaned, thought, I should not have eaten that last biscuit. Custis sat at the other end of the table, still eating, reached again toward the plate of biscuits.

Lee looked at the young man, tried to see his own face, but saw so much of Mary. Mary sat at the table as well; the arrival of her son had been an effective tonic, and she had come to breakfast for the first time in weeks.

Custis finally sat back, stretched. "Oh my, how I've missed Aunt Becky's biscuits!"

Rebecca was the old black servant and cook who had been at Arlington since Mary had been a child. Now frail and half blind, she was devoted to Mary, a valuable help to her, as much as Mary would allow.

Custis yawned, stood, raised long arms over his tall frame. "So, Father, when do you report to Texas?"

"I will leave this week, probably on Friday. They want me there as soon as possible, though I can't . . . well, they need a commander, somebody to fill the office. General Twiggs will be back down there before much longer. The command is his and he won't stay around Washington for long. I will make the best of it, temporary as it may be."

Custis smiled. "Well, you have no worries here. Your reinforcements have arrived."

Lee rose from the table, made way for Rebecca as she cleared the table. He went to Mary's chair, but Custis intervened.

"Excuse me, Father, but Mother and I have made plans for this morning."

The young man slid Mary's chair back, and he helped her stand. Lee saw a faint smile cross her worn face. "Yes, my son and I are going for a ride."

Lee thought it was not a good idea, she was so frail, but he saw his son's firm grip, the two of them standing close, and he felt Mary's enthusiasm, so rare now.

"Well, you be careful. Custis, you drive—"

"Robert, enough!" Mary said. "I have managed around here without your help for too long. I believe I can take care of myself, and my son too!"

She was teasing him, but the words stung. Lee nodded, backed away, and walked down a wide hallway to the study. He stood at the large desk and looked at the ledgers and the paperwork. He thought, I will sit with Custis later, go over the records. He sat down heavily in the soft leather chair, rocked back, felt great relief that his son was home, then thought again of his post, of San Antonio and Fort Mason.

He knew it would be more of the same, uneventful and frustrating, and his career still had little chance of advancement. While in Washington, he had learned that more than twenty colonels were ahead of him in seniority, and the news struck him like a hammer, made him think of retirement. But he could not sit still at Arlington and grow corn. And so, his long leave was finally expiring, and he was assigned to fill the temporary vacancy left by General Twiggs's prolonged visit to the capital, appointed mainly because he was the only colonel currently assigned to a post in Texas.

He had gone there for one reason, volunteered for the cavalry because it was the only chance he might ever have to be a soldier again; the satisfaction that came from the praise, the respect from General Scott, the good work in Mexico. He had spent three years as Commandant of West Point, appointed over many others, a job politicked for by men who sought the prestige, the opportunity to grow old in the quiet surroundings of their own authority, absolute control over a corps of cadets. But Lee had tired quickly of the mundane responsibilities, the annoying administrative duties, conflicts over ridiculous infractions of outdated rules. It had been no better than his long career as an engineer, and to the surprise of all who knew him, he jumped at the opportunity to command the newly formed Second Regiment of Cavalry, an honest command of real troops, and so he'd gone to Texas.

But Texas was not like Mexico, and he was under the authority of General David Twiggs, a thoroughly disagreeable and bitter old man, who had a complete dislike for Winfield Scott. The Department of Texas was Twiggs's private domain, and Lee learned quickly that Twiggs had little regard for his abilities and a great suspicion of his warm relationship with General Scott.

The Second Regiment was stationed far from the comforts of San Antonio, far into the miserable heat and incredible hostility of the wilderness. And if Lee was to receive no support from Twiggs, he would receive less help from the elusive Comanches he was sent to control. But contemplating the coming winter, the changing seasons, the fresh chill of the Virginia winter, he thought, I do miss Texas . . . and I am not a farmer.

"Colonel Lee?"

It was Rebecca.

"Yes, what is it?" It came out gruffly, and he was instantly sorry. "Is there something I can do for you, Rebecca?"

The old woman padded slowly into the study, pointed out toward the front door. "Colonel, there's a visitor, sir. It's Nate, ol' Nate."

Lee did not know who she meant. He stood and walked past her and to the front door, opened it and faced a huge black man, with broad shoulders and thick neck, one of Custis's former slaves. As Lee looked up at the massive frame, the name came back to him.

"Nate! Yes, yes, Nate, why, come in. It's been a while since you left."

The man leaned slightly, stepped through the front door, seemed shy, hesitant, and Lee realized he had probably never come through the front door before.

"Thank you, Colonel. I comes to ask you somethin' if you have the time." He spoke slowly, with a deep cavernous voice, did not look Lee in the face. Lee motioned for him to follow, went into the study, saw Rebecca looking at the familiar black face, squinting, trying to see him clearly. Nate leaned over, gave the old woman a gentle hug, said only, "You ol' woman."

Lee could see that Rebecca was moved, teary-eyed, and she quickly turned away, moved down the hall, scolded, "Now you don' take up the colonel's time, you heah?" and she was gone, back toward the kitchen.

Lee had often wondered how old the woman was. She didn't know herself. He turned to the big man, said, "It appears she misses you."

"Sweet ol' woman, that she is, Colonel. Hope she lives forever. Reckon she will as long as she has Miss Mary to tend to."

"You may be right. What can I do for you . . . Nate?" Lee realized that was the only name he could recall, did not know his last name, felt foolish.

"Colonel, you did me a great thing, sir, when you gives me my papers. I wanted you to know, I done real good. The man you sent me to, Mr. Van Dyke, they is good Pennsylvania folk, they right happy to have ol' Nate on their farm. I been blacksmithin'."

It all came back to Lee now. He had heard there were opportunities in the Pennsylvania Dutch country for freedmen to find work, vast new farms in a rugged land, and he had inquired, learned of several farmers who would hire good help. Nate had been one of the first, one of the most able men the old man had, and Lee had watched him leave with mixed feelings. But Arlington could not afford to hire the freedmen.

"Colonel, the reason I come back here . . . I raised some money. They payin' me good. Never been . . . not good at spendin' much money . . . it just gatherin' up. So's I come back here to ask you about my brother, Bo. I wonder, sir, if you would allow me to buy him."

Lee had been listening to the man's deep voice, and noticing his clothes, a nice homespun suit, well made. Now, he looked up at the dark, rugged face, let the words sink in, began to feel awkward.

"You want to . . . buy your brother?"

"Yes, sir, he's not fit for much. He been crippled up most of his life, not much good to you here."

Lee realized now who Bo was, the man with a missing foot, bad farm accident long ago. He hobbled about with a cane, did odd work for the other field hands, work that didn't require much mobility.

"Nate, the people who are still here are not for sale. I am pleased, greatly pleased, to allow any of them to leave, who want to. The problem has always been that most of them have nowhere to go. It was . . . easier finding work for you, you are . . . well, quite fit. Men like Bo, and the women like Rebecca, they don't have much hope of finding any work."

"But sir, Bo don' have to work. I can take care of him now. I done talked it over with Mr. Van Dyke, he say it all right."

Lee sat down at the desk, reached for a blank piece of paper, pulled out his pen and began to write, then stopped, stared down for a moment, said, "Nate, forgive me. I don't recall your last name."

The man smiled, a wide toothy grin. "They give me a name. Mr. Van Dyke says when he first seen me, he thought I was black as coal, so they calls me Nate Cole. I even hear some people call me *Mistuh* Cole."

"Well, Mr. Cole, I suppose your brother should have the same last name, so . . . here." Lee wrote out the document, signed it with a broad stroke. "Here are his papers. He's a freedman."

Nate kept smiling, shook his head, wanted to say something, still felt reserved in front of Lee, took the paper and held it up to his face.

"I reckon I cain't read this, Colonel, but I knows your name, your signin'. I looked at the papers you give me . . . still looks at 'em, carries 'em here." He tapped at his wide pants pocket. He folded the new paper carefully, the tender freedom of his brother, put it into the same pocket, started to go, then stopped. "Colonel, how many you gots left here?"

"You mean, how many still work the land? How many . . . hands?" Lee felt a sudden cold shock. He could not say the word slave to this man, had almost never used the word at all. "Thirty . . . or so, I believe."

"When they gonna be freed, if you don' mind me askin', Colonel?"

The question sank deep into Lee. It was the same question he had asked himself when he first read the old man's will. The will called for release of all Custis's slaves within five years of his death, and Lee had seen the mandate as a relief, the added incentive to take care of an unpleasant burden. But there had always been a problem. Many of the slaves simply did not want to leave, had no thoughts of any other home, but once freed, they would have to be kept on as paid labor, and Arlington had enough financial struggles as it was.

"I'm working . . . hard at it, Nate. You know those people. Most of them have no idea what lies beyond these hills. I cannot just . . . send them away. Where would they go?"

"I didn' know about much of nothin' either, Colonel. Now I'm doin' good. I knows some of 'em . . . they been hearin' about Africa . . . this Liberia. I knows some of 'em wants to go there."

"I'm happy to hear that—Liberia is a good solution. But it's expensive. I cannot . . . Mr. Custis's estate does not have the money to pay for that. Not now."

Nate looked down, rubbed his chin with a hard hand. "Colonel, you think there ever come a time when everybody . . . do like you?"

"You mean, give all the . . . slaves their papers?"

"Yes, sir. Everywhere."

Lee thought, ran a hand through his hair, said, "I believe . . . the Negroes are where God wants them to be, and when God wants the Negroes to be free, then He will free them. God has set you free, through my hand. He has set your brother free through your hand. There will come a time—"

"Colonel, you is a good man, a decent man, and I thanks you for what you done for me, and for Bo. But forgive me, Colonel, not meanin' no disrespec', this here is *your* name on this paper, not God's. If'n we waits for God to set all of us free, we be waitin' for a long time."

Lee stared now into the man's eyes, the deep lines in the black face. "You may be right about that. It may be a long time. But I must do what I believe God wants me to do. I can't do anything else."

"It ain't you, Colonel, that I'm talkin' about. You done good, you *is* doin' good." Lee began to see a small light, a flash of anger in the dark eyes. "But they is plenty of white folks who don't depend on God for much of nothin'. They ain't about to change the way things is."

"Nate, all I can say . . . well, I promise you that God will decide one day it is time, and it will happen."

Nate nodded, but Lee saw he did not agree, did not have the faith that Lee so cherished.

"Colonel, I be goin' now. I gots to find my brother, then I be on my way. Thank you, Colonel, I hope God blesses you."

The man turned and was quickly gone, soft respectful steps. He went out the front door, closed it quietly behind him.

Lee sat back against the soft leather, stared toward the hallway, felt something strange, a new sensation. He had never had such a conversation with one of . . . them. He thought, God has had a hand here, in this. He thought of John Brown, the reckless calls for abolition made by people who did not live with slaves, who took no responsibility for what happened to them. But the speeches went on, and there was great anger in the South, especially down in the cotton states, where there were many more slaves than here, around Arlington. Nate is right, he thought. These people are not letting God decide. There had been blood in Kansas, blood at Harper's Ferry.

Lee stood, walked toward the small window that looked toward Washington. *God, please let them see reason. . . .*

San Antonio had not changed, and Lee spent his brief time of command once again swallowed up by the same monotony and aggravations that he had left. As he'd expected, Twiggs came quickly back from Washington and assumed command of the Department of Texas once more, his ego too tender to spend much time that close to his commanders in Washington. So Lee found himself back in command of the Second Regiment, and Twiggs had sent him north, to Fort Mason, back to the routine Lee thought he'd missed.

As Lee's coach rolled into the dusty walls of Fort Mason, he did not wait for the escort to open the door or even the coach to stop before he was out, moving across the hard dirt of the compound. He needed no greetings, no introductions. It was all too familiar. He reached the door to the headquarters offices, paused, looked around. He was surprised there were not more troops around. Only a few groups of men were scattered about, and no formations of drilling squadrons. The fort was a good deal quieter than he had left it more than a year ago.

He pushed open the door and walked into a thick cloud of cigar smoke. Behind the small desk sat a corporal reading a newspaper, feet up on the desk. The man had a huge cigar stuffed in one side of his mouth, did not look at Lee.

Lee waited, felt an unusual lack of patience, drained away by the heat and dust of his trip.

"On your feet, soldier."

"What . . . ?" The man looked up, annoyed at the interruption, did not recognize Lee's face, finally absorbed his rank, and placed the paper gently across the desk. He stood noisily then, pushing back the chair.

Lee stared at the cigar, still poking through the man's mouth, and the man caught Lee's look, removed the cigar, raised his hand in a sloppy salute, and dropped it down prematurely, not waiting for Lee's response.

"Excuse me, Colonel. We don't get many visitors around here."

Lee felt a hot rush, a sudden impatient anger, wanted to tell the man who he was, how long he had served this army, all the good things he had done, only to be treated with such lazy lack of respect. Seconds passed, and the man looked down at the cigar, then reached for it, and Lee suddenly felt great despair. He continued to watch as the man grew impatient, painfully wanting to return to the chair and his newspaper.

Looking around, Lee felt embarrassed now at his anger, saw the door to the smaller office open, *his* office, asked, "Is Major Thomas here?"

"No sir, he's out right now. But if you would like to leave your name, I'll see he gets your message. You do have a message for him, sir?"

"Yes, Corporal, you may tell Major Thomas that Colonel Lee has returned. And if you don't mind, Corporal, you may retrieve my bags from the coach outside, put them in my quarters, and then—"

"Right . . . Colonel . . . Lee . . ." The man was writing on a corner of the newspaper; Lee's name meant nothing to him.

Lee wanted to say more, to put this arrogant little man in his place, remind him he was in the army, but he sensed the futility, felt swallowed up in the heat, abruptly had no energy.

"Uh, Colonel, you want me to get those bags now?"

"Now would be helpful, Corporal. If you don't mind telling me, just when may we expect Major Thomas to return?"

"Any time now. He's gone over to find a bite to eat, at the mess. Do you know where the mess is, Colonel?"

"Yes, I do, Corporal. Thank you for your help."

Lee turned and walked back into the sun. He saw a few men moving about now, followed a young lieutenant into a low white building. The man did not see him until they were inside, then said, "Oh, sir," and saluted.

Lee saw recognition, a familiar face, tried to think of the man's name.

"Welcome back to Fort Mason, Colonel. Please, would you join . . ." The man looked around, tried to find reinforcements, saw one table in the rear with a group of officers and motioned nervously for Lee to follow. "This way, sir. Please, join us."

Around the table were four men, faces Lee did not know, except for his old friend and second in command, George Thomas. They were quietly arguing, had not noticed him.

The lieutenant spoke up. "Gentlemen, please. It's Colonel Lee."

Thomas turned around, surprised, rose suddenly, knocking his chair back, a noisy clatter. "Colonel, forgive me. I didn't know you had arrived. Good to see you again, sir."

"Thank you, Major. Please, sit down. I just came in to let you know I was here."

"Have a bite to eat, Colonel. Some bread left, not too hard."

He seemed rattled to Lee, but still, it was a friendly face, and Lee suddenly was very glad to see him. "Well, I'm sorry to interrupt your conversation, but a bit of bread might do, yes."

The men spread their chairs, made room for Lee and the young lieutenant, and Thomas made introductions, names Lee did not recall. The men greeted him with formal respect and few smiles.

Lee said to Thomas, "I was wondering, it seems there are not many troops here. Are they out on patrol, something up?"

Thomas glanced at the others, looked down at the table. "Colonel, there aren't many troops here at all. The men have been assigned, scattered out all over Texas, spread pretty thin. Begging your pardon, sir, but since you've been gone, the situation here, all over, has gotten a good deal worse."

"Worse than before?"

Thomas nodded. "The army won't send any more men, they say it's money, but I'm guessing they just don't see we're doing much good out here. We've got new outposts clear up . . . well, just about everywhere there's Indians. We're spread out so much, even the forts themselves aren't safe anymore. We lose horses and mules every day. Forgive me, Colonel, but, well, I'm glad to have you back in command, but I'm not sure just what your command is."

Across the table a man with a dark, full-bearded face and deep-set, angry eyes, introduced to Lee as Captain Barlow, said, "The reason is pretty clear, Colonel. What George isn't saying is that Washington has bigger problems than a bunch of wild Indians. We all know what you did to John Brown. What George doesn't seem to understand, Colonel, is a lot of us folks from up North see that Brown fella as a symbol of what's wrong, what's got to change in the South. If it comes down to it, a lot of us . . . the army is willing to do what it takes to straighten things out."

Lee was shocked, had no idea anyone outside of Washington knew anything about the Brown raid. He looked at Barlow, saw anger, saw the deep feeling directed at *him*.

"Captain, John Brown was just . . . it was a group of rioters. There was no uprising, no slaves."

"Colonel, John Brown was hanged because he tried to educate the slaves, tried to unite them in a cause of justice. Read the papers! I'm from New Jersey. I get the Trenton papers every week, and there's a lot of people, Colonel, who want the South to own up to its responsibilities."

Lee felt shaken. Surely, he thought, this man does not speak for many. He looked at the big man, tried to sort through the hostility.

"The South? You are referring to the slave states as one . . . community? Captain, I am from Virginia, as is Major Thomas. I do not consider Virginia . . . to be united in some way with any other states, whether Alabama or New Jersey, except by the Constitution."

Thomas saw the look on Lee's face, knew Lee did not understand the man's anger. "Colonel, have you not heard the news, about the elections?"

Lee realized he hadn't been reading much. He had received some Virginia papers from his son, but could not recall any mention of John Brown.

"I'm sorry, I have not paid much attention. I have been rather . . . my duties in San Antonio kept me rather involved . . . the Mexicans, mainly, the bandits. I have spent a great deal of time in the field."

Another man spoke, older, gray-haired, a lieutenant, and Lee heard the distinct drawl of the southern accent. "Colonel, the Republicans are going with Abraham Lincoln as their candidate. Many in the South see Lincoln as nothing short of a threat to this nation."

Lee said, "I have always assumed Mr. Breckenridge . . . I always felt he was the popular choice and would be elected without . . . controversy."

"Controversy?" Barlow laughed. "Colonel, since Harper's Ferry there is nothing *but* controversy. The abolitionists and the moderates have united, the way is clear. Mr. Lincoln will be elected, and the talk of secession will grow."

Lee had heard the word before, secession.

"I am not very political, Captain. God would not allow . . . I always had the faith that this country would elect those who knew best, who could follow the best course through any situation. I certainly never thought what happened at Harper's Ferry would be seen as such a political—"

Thomas interrupted, "The problem, Colonel, is that the army is becoming divided as well. What Mr. Barlow is saying is that we may be asked to take action where we may find it difficult. I have talked to men from South Carolina. . . . There is much talk that if the Republicans are elected, South Carolina will withdraw from the Union, will secede. If that happens, what would you expect the officers from South Carolina to do? What would we do if it were Virginia?"

Lee was becoming overwhelmed. "Surely you gentlemen are overstating the situation. I cannot believe that one state would withdraw from the Union just because a Republican is elected President. And, Virginia . . . Gentlemen, I have heard nothing of this kind of talk. Virginia is certainly not a part of this destructive talk, talk that does nothing but stir emotions. No, gentlemen, I believe you are wrong, I believe reasonable men will find a reasonable path and that all this talk of secession is just talk. What of Texas, what of right here?"

The older man spoke again, in a quiet tone. "Colonel, there is no support for Mr. Lincoln in Texas. We consider him to be quite the enemy. And that, sir, is the point."

"The President of the United States is your commander, Lieutenant!" Barlow had stood, and his voice boomed.

Lee looked at the man, then rose, moved his chair away from the table, said, "Gentlemen, please. I am a soldier in the United States Army, as are all of you. I cannot believe that any of us will be called on to fire upon any state. I would never allow myself to bring violence upon my home of Virginia, and I believe there are enough men of reason in this country who feel the same way."

Barlow glared at Lee and leaned forward, his palms down on the table. "With all due respect, Colonel, I am not sure I understand your blind loyalty to your home, but my home is the United States of America, and I believe that what is going on in the South is a threat to our country, and I will do everything I can to preserve the integrity of the Union. If there is a rebellion against a legally elected President, whether he be Lincoln or Breckenridge or my aunt Mary, then I will serve my country by putting down that rebellion!"

Now the gray-haired lieutenant stood, said to Barlow, "Captain, there *will* be a rebellion against a government that illegally inserts itself into the private, constitutionally protected affairs of the states. . . . The Federal government has *no* right—"

The two men faced each other, and Lee raised his hand, looked into Barlow's black eyes, felt helpless, saw a deep chasm between him and these men who carried such passion. "Gentlemen, we are all officers here."

They looked at him, stared, waited. He wanted to say more, to end this, but there was nothing else he could say. He had calmed them, however, their tempers softened. As he turned and moved toward the door, the men sat down again, watched him leave, then resumed their discussion.

ON NOVEMBER 6, 1860, ABRAHAM LINCOLN WAS ELECTED President. Within a few weeks the state of South Carolina had called a convention, to vote on withdrawing from the Union.

The governor of Texas, Sam Houston, was in San Antonio to

confer with the army. Lee had been summoned to the meeting, and made the dusty trip back from Fort Mason once more.

General Twiggs sat behind his huge desk, reached out and with a flourish of motion straightened an imposing stack of official papers. When Houston wired him of the need for a meeting, Twiggs insisted it be here, in his office. So, the three men sat, with Twiggs clearly in control.

Lee had great admiration for Houston, the great hero of Texas's fight for independence from Mexico, and the *first* to defeat Santa Anna's army, ten years before Scott. In person, Lee could see that Houston fit all the legends, all the great tales. He was a large, handsome man whose presence dominated a room. Of course, Twiggs would not allow himself to be dominated.

"Colonel Lee," Houston said. "I'm glad you could be here. I have wanted to meet you for some time."

"Thank you, Governor."

Twiggs sniffed, brought the meeting back to the subject at hand. "Governor, the army has learned that it is likely the state of Texas will secede very soon. This office is concerned that the transition proceed smoothly and that violence is minimized. I would like to hear your thoughts on how this might best be accomplished."

Houston shifted in his chair, glanced at Lee and said, "General, there will be a vote on this issue within a few days, and I am reasonably certain that despite my strong desire for Texas to remain a part of the Union, there is a great deal of strength on the part of those who would pull us apart."

It was a politician's words, Lee thought, but he also saw a painful look on Houston's rugged face.

Twiggs said, "Well then, let's make this a simple matter. The army is prepared to vacate the forts and turn over all equipment at your request."

Lee was stunned. Twiggs was offering the surrender of the army's property and territory, when secession had not even been called to a vote. He felt words boiling up, could not stay quiet.

"General, forgive me, sir, but has General Scott approved this transfer?"

Twiggs glared at him. "Colonel Lee, General Scott is busy in Washington sitting on the right hand of God. He does not know the situation here, he is not in a position to make the best decisions."

"General, have you notified anyone in Washington of your offer to the governor?"

Twiggs stood and leaned out over his desk, toward Lee. "Colonel, I do not need any instructions from you on how to perform my duties. You are in attendance here today because you command a regiment that will be involved in the transfer. There is nothing else for you to say."

Lee clearly remembered Mexico. There was always the deep rift between Scott and Twiggs, the jealousy that Twiggs had for command, for the popularity of the troops. Twiggs was making a last grand show now, Lee thought, displaying an independence in his command that would never be tolerated in Washington. He was an old man, had voiced his opinions for weeks that the Union would be dissolved, and Lee realized that if the pressure came down on him, he would simply leave, retire, and return to his home state of Georgia. By complying peacefully with the Texas secessionists, he would be able to return to Georgia in a positive light, a friend of the South. It was all very neat, very convenient, and Lee felt a fire crawl up the back of his neck. He gripped the arms of his chair. Twiggs was right, there was nothing else he could say.

Houston sat without speaking, watched Lee. He was a good soldier as well as a politician, and he also understood what Twiggs was doing.

"General," he said, "I believe we should meet again, once the convention vote is taken. It is perhaps premature to plan any specifics."

Houston rose, made a slight bow to Twiggs, then turned to Lee, who caught a glance, a meaning in the look. Houston walked to the heavy oak door, paused, turned back to Lee and said, "Colonel, please, if the general will permit, will you accompany me?"

Twiggs had not expected the meeting to be this brief, had not finished basking in his own importance, and he tried to speak, to rescue the situation. "Governor, we have much to . . . there are many details—"

"Yes, General, I will call on you when the matter is more clear. Thank you for meeting with me. Do you mind if Colonel Lee is excused?"

Twiggs glanced at Lee, then looked back at Houston, said nothing, but nodded dumbly. Lee stood then, and in an awkward moment saluted Twiggs before moving toward the door.

In the outer office, he waited for Houston, curious. Twiggs's aides stood as Houston came out, and the two men walked through the outer door, where Houston's aides were waiting, three men in identical gray suits. They rose in unison from their chairs.

"Gentlemen, please remain here for a few moments," Houston said. "I would like to speak to Colonel Lee."

The men sat back down, expressionless, and Houston led the way outside, down the stone steps, into the cool December air.

From a distance, Lee saw people stop, staring. There were waves and greetings. Houston was the most beloved Texan of his day, and Lee could see it in the faces.

"We may draw a crowd, Governor."

"They'll keep their distance, they usually do. I never get tired of hearing the calls, though, the warmth. I just wish these people would understand . . . they are on a reckless course."

Lee did not speak, knew there was a reason for this, felt very comfortable speaking with the big man.

"I take it you and General Twiggs do not often confide."

Lee nodded. "No, I believe he sees me as General Scott's spy."

"Are you?"

Lee smiled. "Certainly not. I rarely see the commanding general these days. General Scott is a good man, Governor. It is a shame to see him grow old."

"We are all growing old, Colonel. The important thing is to grow old doing the right thing. Forgive me for saying so, Colonel, but I do not believe your commander here is doing the right thing."

"General Twiggs? I do not pass judgment on my superiors, Governor."

Houston laughed. "Well put, Mr. Lee."

They walked around a corner, and Lee glanced up, knew Twiggs's office window was just above them.

"Tell me, Colonel. As a Virginian, are you sympathetic to the Southern cause?"

"Governor, forgive me, but I have learned that with events, emotions, as they are now, it is best for a military commander to keep his opinions to himself. It seems there is a lot of hostility in the air. An army that is swayed by politics and rumors stops being much of an army."

"Colonel, I regret to say that these days we are all swayed by politics, whether we choose to be or not. And it is not a rumor . . . your army is falling apart around you. Your commander is about to jump ship and throw his command to the wolves. And I believe the new President is about to send troops to stop a rebellion . . . maybe right here."

Lee stopped walking and said, "Do you really see that . . . do you think this lack of reason will prevail?"

"Colonel, you heard what I said up there. The state of Texas is about to vote to withdraw from the Union. I have spoken with the governors of four other states, all of whom support secession, and all of whom expect their states to follow South Carolina."

This was all new to Lee. He suddenly felt very small. "Governor, will God allow this to happen?" Lee knew it was a question Houston could not answer.

"Colonel, I know of your duty in Mexico, your duty here. I know you to be a good soldier, and I believe you are a decent man. I must admit to feeling a good bit isolated these days. I am wondering if I am the only one around here who believes that there is a bountiful surplus of stupidity in all this."

Lee glanced up, toward Twiggs's office, thought of the harsh talk from his officers, the rising anger, the feeling that the world was falling out of control.

"Governor, allow me to say you have a gift for words."

8. HANCOCK

December 1860

"Come in, Captain, thank you for coming. Pleasure to finally meet you."

Hancock felt wary, moved into the small office slowly, and the man said again, pleasantly, with a warmth Hancock did not expect and did not trust, "Come in, please."

"I received your invitation, Mr. Hamilton. The note said you had a message for me."

"Yes, yes, we'll get to that in a moment. Please, sit down. We have some coffee, if you would like. Cigar?"

"No, that's all right, thank you."

Hancock looked around the newspaperman's cluttered office, saw clippings tacked to the wall, some framed, some loose, large headlines, small columns. There were pages from cities back East, from papers Hancock had read in St. Louis and Philadelphia.

"Surprised we haven't actually met before now."

Hancock looked at the man, saw a small bald head on a short round body, and he studied the face, looked for something, some sign. Hamilton was not what he had expected.

"Fine uniform you have there, Captain. I've heard you've been a captain for quite a while. Any chance of a promotion soon? Certainly you deserve one. You're in charge of a wide area, a good deal of responsibility, and a good reputation too. A man who knows his duty."

"Staff officers aren't promoted as quickly as the line, the men in the field. If there's a vacancy above me, there's always a chance I will be considered."

A brief look on Hamilton's face betrayed him, and Hancock now saw he wanted more, wanted him to say something about the army, make some complaint. He stiffened in his chair, felt foolish for having given the man even a small piece of information. He was cautious now, felt that behind the charm, the polite banter, this man could not be trusted.

"Well, Captain, I hope your fortunes change. That is, in fact, why I asked you to stop by. Have you heard the news from back East? The election?"

Hancock said nothing, knew the word would be received soon, it had only been three weeks.

"No? I thought not. I seem to get the news before most here. My job, you know. A newspaperman learns to talk to a great many people, make a great many friends, people who love to pass along information. Fact is, Captain, there's a steamer anchored this morning on the coast, just arrived from the Isthmus. The captain brings me the newspapers, and in return he goes home with a little gold. A fine arrangement, works with most of those fellows, certainly works for me. Let's see. . . ." Hamilton bent down, reached under his desk, lifted up a newspaper and pretended to read. Hancock knew there was some game being played, some little piece of strategy that Hamilton was enjoying.

"Mr. Hamilton, I should return to my post. You said you had a message for me?"

"Oh, certainly, Captain, forgive me. It's just, well, when events happen around us that are certain to change our lives, well, it's momentous. Today is such a day!"

"How? What has happened?" Hancock began to lose patience, leaned forward with his hands on the desk. Hamilton did not flinch, and Hancock thought to himself, Careful, this man does not intimidate, too much arrogance. Find out what he knows.

"Captain, the election, as you know, was held just a few weeks ago. What we greatly feared has happened. All of us who value the sanctity of our freedoms, those of us who treasure the sacred right of the American people to determine our own futures, are sickened, sir, mortified at the outcome. Mr. Abraham Lincoln has been elected President of the United States. The Democrats beat themselves, split their vote between Breckenridge and Bell, a foolish, fatal mistake."

Hancock absorbed the news, had not believed it would happen, had thought Breckenridge would carry the vote.

"I take it by your silence, Captain, you do not approve of Mr. Lincoln?"

Hancock stood up. "Is there anything else, Mr. Hamilton? I really must be leaving."

"Please, Captain, a moment more. Please, sit."

"If you have a point, sir, please make it."

"Really, Captain, there is no need for that tone. I have no ill feeling toward the army, and certainly not toward you. I have an instinct for these things, Captain. I sense you have your own strong feelings about Mr. Lincoln, and I know that you are in fact a Democrat."

Hancock felt a curiosity, wanted to leave, but more, wanted to know what Hamilton was up to. "Go on."

"Captain, I'm sure you have heard, from your own sources, that the army is going to face a severe crisis because of this election. I know that in San Francisco this news is going to be received, *is* being received, with a great deal of anger, and I also know that many good men, officers of high rank, will resign from the army and return to their homes in the southern states. Many men, men you know well, I'm sure, anticipate hostilities to break out. Mr. Lincoln is a misguided fool, a puppet for the radical elements in the North who want nothing less than total domination and control over the South." Hancock said nothing.

"Forgive me, Captain. I didn't mean . . . I didn't ask you here to preach to you. The point is, where do you stand, Captain?"

"I'm an officer in the United States Army. I took an oath to defend my country—"

"Please, Captain, set aside the standard doctrine for a moment. We are a long way from West Point. Your army is about to dissolve, fall to pieces. The commanders, generals, colonels, men to whom you place your admirable loyalty, are about to resign. The reality is that the southern states will secede, forming their own independent nation. What do you think will happen to California, Captain? Let me tell you. The good people of California have no more loyalty to Mr. Lincoln's government than do the people of South Carolina, or Alabama, or Texas. California will become an independent nation, Captain. A rich nation, welcoming all those who recognize the great bounty we have here. A man like yourself, a man of strength, duty, a man who understands order . . . we will need order, Captain. There is a place for you here, a command, a position of great prestige. California will need her own good soldiers."

"Mr. Hamilton, California is governed by the laws of the United States government, as are you, sir. If I believed you had the authority to offer me any such position, I would arrest you for treason."

"Captain Hancock, when you leave here, look around you. Count the flags you see, the illegal flags of the Bear Republic. The only

American flag you will see is on your own building, and when the army leaves, that flag will come down. That is the reality, Captain."

"Please excuse me, Mr. Hamilton. I have duties to attend to." He began to back away, reached behind him for the door, still watched the round little man.

"The offer stands, Captain. Don't place your loyalties foolishly. You have a family to think of—their future . . . their safety. . . ."

Hancock felt something break inside him, lunged forward, put one knee up on the desk, reached across and grabbed Hamilton's shirt, pulled him forward heavily onto his desk. He stared a long second into the man's eyes, expected fear but did not see it.

"If you . . . if anyone comes near my children . . . my family, I will kill them. I will shoot them dead, Mr. Hamilton. Do you understand?"

He released the man's shirt, and Hamilton slid back down into his chair, smiled slightly.

"No one is threatening your family, Captain. I'm just a newspaperman. This was a friendly conversation, that's all. I thought a man in your position should hear the latest news, the election. I'm always here, Captain, my door is always open."

Hancock backed away, stared at the man's face, the cold smile, the maddening smugness, and he wanted to grab him again, suddenly felt very weak, powerless, and left the office. He rushed outside through a narrow doorway, felt the coolness, the December breeze, and a motion caught his eye. He looked up, across the street, saw up on a building the short pole and, snapping crisply in the wind, the flag of the Bear Republic.

CAPTAIN LORMAN'S CAVALRY HAD BEEN CAMPED AROUND THE supply depot now for several weeks, longer than expected. Hancock knew that the longer the infantry was delayed, the greater chance the cavalry would be needed somewhere else and called away. He had sent inquiries to Benicia, asking when the infantry would arrive. Messages were moving back and forth to Fort Tejon, and from there communications were being received from Benicia. It was the only communication line the army had, but there was no definite word about the infantry. It was a five-hundred-mile march down a coastline used by many bandit groups, and no one expected the army to pass through without some problems. All Hancock knew was that they were on the march.

It had been only three days since his meeting with Hamilton, but by now everyone knew of Lincoln's election, and the men had begun to react here, just as everywhere else.

Hancock knelt on the hard dirt floor, his head close to the ground, reading faded labels on wooden boxes, making notes on a thick inventory pad.

"Captain? Oh, there . . . do we have the tents?" Lorman stepped up beside him, leaned over.

"No problem, Captain," Hancock replied. "Some of them are here, underneath. It would be helpful if your men could lend a hand, moving this stack, maybe . . . over there, that empty corner."

"Sure thing, Captain." Lorman turned, moved back outside, called to his men, and instantly soldiers were around Hancock, waiting for instructions. He stood up, pointed to the tents, and the men began to work, lifting boxes, shifting piles. He could feel the energy, a new eagerness. The men knew they would not be here much longer, had begun to itch for a change, the return home to Tejon, or a new assignment.

Hancock watched the labor, saw it was handled, began to leaf through the inventory sheets, and Lorman said, "Captain, a minute, if you don't mind?"

"Certainly." They walked outside, Hancock following Lorman's lead. Lorman was a younger man, clean-shaven, smaller than Hancock, with a sturdy build and the compact stance of a good horseman. They walked out to the picket fence, and Hancock saw the men moving about, tending their horses, cleaning rifles, the daily chores of camp.

"We received new orders, Captain," Lorman said. "This morning. Colonel Blakely is sending us to the coast, south of here a ways. The navy has been losing some property to bandits around the San Diego Mission. They don't have the manpower, or the inclination, to chase them around the countryside. The colonel has told me specifically to defer to your judgment. If you feel it is too dangerous for us to leave just yet, we can delay a few days."

"That's very good of the colonel. But . . . it seems a little unusual to send your men out without returning to Tejon first. Other units could—"

"Captain," Lorman said, "I don't question the colonel's orders."

"No, certainly, I didn't mean that. I just—" He stopped, could see the look on Lorman's face, knew there was more, something the young man was not saying. Hancock glanced around the depot, waited.

Lorman said, quietly, barely above a whisper, "Captain, we don't need to go back to Tejon, not now. The colonel feels we need to keep the men moving, keep them out in the field. Until . . . the tempers calm down."

"Do you think they will calm down?"

"As long as my men stay busy, they don't talk. As long as they have a mission, they all point in the same direction."

Hancock listened to the man's words, tried to hear an accent. "If you don't mind, Mr. Lorman, where are you from?"

"Illinois. My family's up near Lake Michigan."

"Pennsylvania, myself. Please, forgive my personal question. I was just . . . well . . ."

"You were wondering if I was one of the Southerners. It's all right, Captain. We're all asking the same questions. I have men I've served with for five years, men I thought I could always depend on, who were always where you put them, doing their job. I have a lieutenant, there, that tall fellow with the red beard, Calloway, been with me from the beginning. He says he's going home, quitting, says he has to defend Alabama. I ask him, defend them from what? He says, Lincoln. Do you understand this, Captain? What are they defending?"

Hancock looked at the ground, thought of Hamilton, the fierce oratory, pulling people along by their fears.

Lorman put a hand out, rested it on the fence rail. "You know, I thought it would be best if I supported Mr. Lincoln, nice to see someone from Illinois that made good like that. I never gave much thought to being a Republican or a Democrat or anything else, I figured it was the right thing to do, and now I hear men talking like he's the devil. I don't see what it is he's done that people hate him so."

Hancock saw the innocence, saw himself, a soldier who learns late the dangerous power of politics, said, "There's been too much talk, I think. Too many loud voices. If someone disagrees with you, you shout back a little louder, and so he does the same. The words get nastier, the threats grow . . . and that's how wars start."

Lorman looked at him, and Hancock said the word again, to himself: *war.*

"But . . . we're all on the same side," Lorman said. "One country—"

"Mr. Lorman, you and I are from one country. Maybe your lieutenant from Alabama doesn't see it that way. These people here, these Californians, don't seem to see it that way. I don't know how you change that."

Lorman turned, and Hancock saw a man running over, calling out. "Captain, a rider . . . a courier."

They turned toward the sound of hoofbeats, saw a blue uniform riding up, but from a different direction, not the road to Tejon.

The two officers moved toward the gate, and Lorman said, "He's not cavalry—the uniform, infantry."

The man dismounted, looked around, saw the officers approaching, saluted and said, "Lieutenant Phillips, sirs, Sixth Regiment of Infantry. Begging your pardon, I have a message for Captain Hancock."

Lorman gestured in Hancock's direction. "Right here, Lieutenant."

"Sir, Major Armistead sends his compliments, wishes me to inform you that units of the Sixth Regiment will be camping just north of town this evening. He also requests . . ." The man felt in his pocket, pulled out a rumpled piece of yellow paper. "Major Armistead respectfully requests an invitation to dinner with the captain and his commanding officer, Mrs. Hancock."

Hancock laughed, startling the dusty lieutenant, who said, "Excuse me, sir, but may I assume that the captain understands the major's message?"

"Quite well, Lieutenant. Please pay my respects to your major. Tell him . . . the commander will expect his presence at seven o'clock. It's all right, I'm authorized to speak for my . . . commanding officer."

The man saluted, climbed back on his horse, and with a quick graceful spin, a self-conscious move in the face of a crowd of cavalrymen, spurred the horse down the road, into a dusty cloud.

Lorman waved his hat at the dust. "I assume, Captain, we may begin to break camp. Sounds like you are in capable hands. And, forgive the personal observation," he said, smiling, "it sounds like this Major Armistead is a good friend of yours."

Hancock watched the dust rising on the road, turned, looked at the young man from Illinois.

"That he is, Captain."

9. LEE

February 1861

At Fort Mason the officers had given up on maintaining good order and discipline in the troops. The tensions were high, fights were common, and it seemed that no one gave much thought to Indians, or any other aspect of their duty.

Lee sat alone in the commander's office. He still allowed Major Thomas to share the small space, felt it relieved the boredom by having a companion, especially someone from Virginia. But Thomas was away now, and Lee passed the days in painful ignorance. Occasional newspapers would make it to the fort, passed through San Antonio, and always now the news was bad.

He turned his chair toward the small window, looked out beyond the wall and saw the Lone Star, the flag of an independent Texas flying from a high pole, placed purposely, defiantly, where the soldiers would see it.

What will happen? he wondered. Will we become prisoners, or will they simply tell us to leave? He reached out, ran his finger along the windowsill, pushed up a small line of gray dirt, the dust of the frontier. He felt a part of some great disaster, some great piece of history, and yet, he was not part of it, was not connected. He turned back to his desk, wiped his hand on his pants, said aloud, "I have always been too far away."

He suddenly felt very lonely, thought of Mary, his family, wondered what they knew, what news they heard, what wild rumors were cascading through Virginia. Of course, there would be rumors. There were always rumors. But no rumor could be any worse than what already *was*, nothing could make less sense. The country was falling apart, and he was helpless, could do nothing, was stuck in Indian country.

"Sir?"

It was the voice of Sergeant Morgan, a small, cheerful man who did not seem affected by all this, which Lee found curious and a bit entertaining. He simply loved being a soldier.

"Yes, Sergeant, come in." Lee leaned back in the chair, stretched, did not feel like a commander.

"Forgive the interruption, sir, but a message has come for you."

"Read it to me, Sergeant, if you don't mind."

"It's sealed, sir. From General Twiggs's office, sir."

"Read it, Sergeant. Not much in the way of military secrets passing through there these days."

Morgan broke the seal with a flourish, sent a piece of wax flying past Lee, hitting the window.

"Oh, sorry, sir. I'm not used to opening these things."

Lee tried to smile, felt very tired, didn't have it in him. "Go on, read it, Sergeant."

"Yes, sir, 'To Lieutenant Colonel Robert E. Lee, dated February fourth, 1861, by direct order of the War Department, you are hereby relieved of duty with the Second Regiment of Cavalry and are hereby ordered to report in person to General in Chief Winfield Scott in Washington, prior to April first.' Good God."

Abruptly, Lee was awake. He reached out, and Morgan stared at the order, reluctantly handed it to him.

"I assume, Sergeant, that last comment is from you, not from the War Department?"

"Oh my God! Oh . . . yes, sir. Sorry, sir. I never read one of these before. You have been . . . relieved of command, sir? I'm terribly sorry. What did you do?"

"Sergeant, I have no idea. But it appears my services here are . . . concluded."

He looked at the order, and saw there were no added remarks from Twiggs, he had simply passed it along, and Lee thought, probably with pleasure. He stood, pulled his blue coat from a hook on the wall, put it on.

"Sergeant, thank you. That will be all."

Morgan saluted, said, "Colonel, I'm . . . I have enjoyed serving in your command. You will be missed, sir."

"Thank you, Sergeant. You are dismissed."

The man left the office, closed the door gently behind him. Lee smiled, thought, I should have told him to keep this quiet.

He went to the window, bent over, put his hands on the dirty sill, looked out, saw nothing moving, no troops. He straightened, pulled down on his coat.

"I don't suppose it makes much difference anymore."

As his coach entered San Antonio, Lee knew immediately there were changes. The streets were filled, people carrying all manner of weapons, a ragged army caught up in the passions he had feared.

The coach approached the hotel, his stopover for the night. He planned to leave the city the next day, making the roundabout trip back home, to Washington, and to Arlington. There was a late winter chill, a cold wind that washed down the streets, and as Lee stepped from the carriage, he drew attention. Several armed men approached, and Lee saw they were all wearing red armbands.

"Whoa, there, we got an officer here!" Lee looked at the man, saw a rough face, ragged clothes, and a rusty rifle. The man stepped closer, looked Lee over, did not point the rifle, but held it high, ready.

Lee saw others, more rough faces, and he thought, Get inside the hotel, now. Then another man moved up and onto the steps, blocking his way, and Lee turned to the first man, said, "Who is in charge here? Do you have a . . . commander?"

"Yep, reckon we do. Ben McCulloch. Now, soldier, if I was you, I'd be a-moving on out of here real soon."

Lee knew the name. McCulloch was commander of the Texas Rangers, a man who certainly would side with his home state.

"Gentlemen, I have no intention of staying here any longer than it may take me to arrange transportation."

He looked across the wide street, toward the buildings that belonged to the army and the one building that had briefly been his office. On top he saw a new flag, moving slowly in the cold breeze, the Lone Star.

Up on the wagon his driver, a corporal, waited for his instructions, and Lee saw the young man's growing fear, knew that could be bad. He nodded silently to him in an attempt to reassure, then turned back to the man closest to him.

"Excuse me, gentlemen," he said, polite, respectful. "May my aide and I be allowed into the hotel?"

The man moved closer. His face hardened as he stared at Lee. He took another step closer, put his hands on his hips and leaned forward, his face close to Lee's. It was a taunt, bait for a hotheaded soldier, a clear clean shot at the man's chin.

Lee knew the man wanted him to swing, to take a shot, and he stood still, said quietly, "Sir, may we pass?"

The man straightened up, looked at Lee with disappointment, then backed away. The others stood aside, and Lee sensed the mood clearly, the itch for a confrontation, and knew he must not give them one. The young corporal jumped down from the wagon, did not bring his rifle, and Lee nodded again to him, thinking, Good, good, leave it there, let them have it, the spoils of the fight. The corporal picked up his bags, and they moved with deliberate steps up into the hotel.

LEE WALKED BACK DOWN INTO THE BUSY STREET. HE HAD CHANGED, now wore civilian clothes. He moved quickly across, did not look into faces. He climbed the steps into his old headquarters, saw three men, civilians with red armbands, and no other men, no blue uniforms anywhere.

"Well, howdy, here's another dandy! Something we can do for you, mister?"

"I was wondering if you men could tell me where I might find General Twiggs?"

The men laughed, short and without humor, and Lee suddenly felt very alone.

"Twiggs is gone, friend. He packed up and flew out of here this morning, he and his flock of blue birds." The man made a raw laugh, and the others, enjoying the moment, joined in, one man slapping the other's shoulder.

Lee had to know more, to find out, but knew these men would not show much patience.

"Is the army . . . gone? I have been away, just come from Fort Mason. May I be told what is happening?"

From behind, Lee saw another man, coming out of the office in the back, Twiggs's old office. The man walked up beside the others, looked Lee over carefully, and Lee saw familiarity, recognition.

"You are Colonel Lee, are you not?"

Lee was relieved. The man seemed reasonable, he sensed some authority. "Yes, I am Lieutenant Colonel Robert E. Lee, formerly commanding the Second Regiment of Cavalry, Fort Mason. I would like to speak to General Twiggs, if that—"

"Colonel Lee, I am pleased to tell you that your kind General Twiggs has surrendered to the authority of the state of Texas. The state of Texas now controls all property formerly held by the United States Army. Including, I might add . . . you."

So it was done. Lee felt a rising anger, felt his hands shake, and he clenched his fists. "Sir, I am not a participant in this . . . madness. The War Department has ordered me back . . . to leave here, to leave Texas. With your . . . permission, I will arrange for transport and be on my way. I am trusting in your good judgment, and your courtesy, not to prevent my leaving."

"Colonel, the services of the United States Army are no longer required in Texas. You *will* leave immediately. However, your equipment, your weapons, your possessions, will remain the property of the state of Texas."

Lee's fists clenched harder, his nails dug into his palms. He spoke in a slow hiss, fought the urge to explode at this man. "I have no equipment. I have only my personal belongings, my clothes, books. *Surely*, you will—"

"Colonel, I have made myself clear. You will leave Texas immediately. You may keep the clothes you are wearing. There is nothing else to discuss."

Lee looked at the others, who stood leaning against the desk, watching his moves. He thought, I have been given a chance to leave, to get out. They are in control, can do anything they want. Thank God for this one reasonable man.

He looked back to the man in charge, nodded, and backed slowly toward the door. As he turned toward the street, he felt the tightness in his fists and slowly spread them, loosening the clench. It was beyond his control, beyond sanity. There was nothing he could do but go home.

MARCH 1861

HE STOPPED BRIEFLY IN THE HALLWAY, WAITED, TOOK A breath, then opened the heavy door and stepped into the dark outer office, meeting the gaze of Colonel Keyes.

"Well, Colonel Lee, we have been expecting you. Tell me, how was your experience in Texas? I understand you and General Twiggs performed an admirable job, a flawless surrender."

Lee took another breath, did not speak, looked at the sharp eyes of Keyes, a man named to a position Lee had turned down years ago, secretary to Commanding General Scott.

Lee understood, he was back in Washington. All the reasons he had for not settling into a position here were more plain than ever. Opinions rattled through these offices like dried bones, and facts were often disregarded if they caused a conflict with rumor.

"I have an appointment with the commanding general. Will you kindly inform him I am here?"

Keyes stood, could not hide a sneer, retreated behind a door and then returned, saying, "Colonel, the general has decided to see you now."

Lee did not answer, walked past Keyes's desk and into the bright, sunlit office of General Winfield Scott.

Scott sat in a huge leather chair, watched Lee with a slight tilt of his head, then stood with a painful effort. Lee saw the stiff movement, the slow struggle. Scott held out a huge, worn hand, smiled with a warmth Lee remembered well, and the two men sat, facing each other across the shiny plane of Scott's oak desk.

"I see that look, Colonel. It's the same look I get from the President. I'm what is referred to around Washington as an old soldier. There is no kindness in the description. Most of these fools have no idea what old means to a real soldier. They assume it means it's time to retire. I rather take it as an accomplishment, a mark of survival. There are a *lot* of *young* soldiers."

Lee studied the old red face, the deep lines, the gray hair now thinner, and realized that he had never seen Scott so fragile . . . so unkempt.

"Sir, it is good to see you again. I must say, things are . . . difficult . . . in the field. I hope the general is maintaining his command—"

"Enough, Colonel. I'd prefer it if you didn't speak to me like you're speaking to Davy Twiggs. Yes, we have some problems. Big problems. But we have good men in this army, men who are used to *solving* big problems. Men like you, Mr. Lee. That's why you're here."

Until this moment, Lee did not know why he had been recalled from Texas, had considered many alternatives: his own weak performance, Twiggs's dislike of him, the shifting politics in Washington. It had not occurred to him that Scott had called him there for a specific duty.

"General, I am happy to be at your service."

"Well, maybe so, maybe not. Tell me, Colonel, what are your feelings about this rebellion? Your home is in the South. How do you feel about what is going on?"

"Sir, forgive me, but I am curious why so many people assume that because Virginia sits below the Potomac, we are in a tight alliance with the cotton states. I do not see Virginians making speeches such as anything prevailing in South Carolina or Mississippi, or Texas. Since my return, I am relieved to see that Virginia does not have the secessionist passion that has infected the deep South."

"There is slavery in Virginia, Colonel. How do you feel about that?"

"I believe in emancipation, but I believe it is ultimately in God's hands. I do not agree with the radicals of the deep South. And, I must say, General, I also do not agree with the talk in the North, the calls for radical abolition, made by people who have no involvement with the situation, who propose no solution to the problem."

"Colonel, how did you feel about General Twiggs giving in so easily to the rebellion in Texas?"

Lee looked down at his hands, turned his palms up, then over, said in a low voice, "I was outraged, sir."

"I'm glad to hear that, Colonel. You might be interested to know that General Twiggs has been relieved. Damned fool."

"I had not heard that, sir."

"Colonel, if you had been in command there, in Texas, what would you have done? Would you have held out, possibly confronted by an armed force? Would you have fired on civilians?"

Lee absorbed the question. He had hoped he would never make that decision, had considered the utter lunacy of being placed in that position, had tried to maintain his faith that it would never happen.

"I take it, Colonel, that by your hesitation in answering, it would have been a difficult decision."

"Yes, sir. Most difficult, sir."

"It should be. Damned difficult. These people are American citizens. Imagine, Colonel, what kind of courage it takes to make that decision. I happen to believe that you have that courage."

"Thank you, sir. But I have never—"

"Colonel, they don't believe I can run this department anymore, that my days are numbered. But—they don't know how to run it either."

"They . . . ?"

"The President. The new administration. Let me tell you, Colonel, they have their hands full of troubles. Full. This man Lincoln . . . good man, I think. If he gets the chance to . . . well, if the radicals don't drown him out . . . There's quite a few people around here that think old Davy Twiggs is a traitor, would have him shot.

Would probably have had *all* of them shot. Probably wouldn't have hesitated, like you just did."

"But . . . why?"

"Who knows, Colonel—moral outrage, the love of country, the damned flag? People like to be inflamed, get their dander up, and the problem is, it's too easy. It's too easy to make a speech up in New York and scream about killing the rebels when you don't have to look 'em in the eye. Hell, Colonel, you've seen men die. It's not something you get all fired up to enjoy."

"No, sir. But I believe there is some of that same . . . passion in the South. I saw it in Texas, men who just want to fight, to strike out at something, you can see it in the eyes."

"That's what I like about Lincoln. He's done his damnedest to keep all sides of this apart, find a solution, make everybody happy. Hell, he's a politician, that's what they're supposed to do. The problem is, Colonel, it isn't working. Not this time. And that too is why you're here."

Lee sat up, straightened his back, looked at the hard old face.

"I need some help, Colonel. I need a second in command. The President hasn't told me directly, but he will. He will come to me and with that politician's smoothness, that comforting look, he will say that I am too damned old to run this army, that things are likely to get out of hand faster than a feeble old soldier can handle. And, Colonel, he may be right."

"Sir, I know of no one in this army more qualified—"

"Colonel, I'm seventy-five years old. I wake up each day with new pains, new weaknesses. I've got this great big office, with these damned great big windows, and you know what happens when the sun shines in here in the afternoons? I take a damned nap. Fall asleep, right here in this chair. Can't help it. You should see your friend Keyes out there when somebody important calls. He peeks in first to make sure I'm awake."

Lee could feel Scott's mind moving away, drifting from the subject, and he saw the anger, Scott's disgust for politics, for Washington. He remembered President Polk, the long arm of the administration reaching down to Mexico, trying to control Scott, to fight a politician's war. It was no way to handle a good soldier, not then . . . not now.

"General, you are offering me . . . a position as your second in command?"

"What? Oh, yes, Colonel. There's going to be a great deal more trouble with this rebellion before much longer. A great deal. You familiar with Fort Sumter? Charleston?"

"Yes, sir. I spent some time in that area, before Mexico."

"Well, Mr. Lee, the President is going to use Fort Sumter as the justification, the spark that lights the powder."

"I'm not sure I understand, sir."

"The army still controls the fort—Major Anderson there hasn't been as gracious to the rebels as your General Twiggs. So far, it's been a standoff. But they're running out of supplies. I have advised the President to withdraw the men, pull out of the fort. It's a regrettable move, another surrender, if you will, but for the time being it will preserve the peace. But the President is going to send down a ship, into the harbor, not to evacuate, but to resupply the troops. I can't argue with the fact that it is Federal property, but, Colonel, there are a number of rebels in Charleston sitting on some very big guns who aren't going to let that ship in, who aren't going to allow the fort to be supplied. And there, Colonel, is your spark."

"The President knows this?"

"Of course. This is his game: politics. The army can't fire the first shot, and so far, nothing violent has happened."

"But General, if the fort is fired on, the army will respond. They will have to."

"You have the picture, Colonel. Now, think back to all that moral outrage that's spreading like a plague in the North, and . . ." Scott raised his hands, a slow, rising motion, then spread them apart. "Boom."

"A war."

"Yes, Colonel, a war. But at least the President can say it's a *good* war, a war for what is right. And so . . . we will need commanders who will accept that as the truth, commanders who will understand their duty, their loyalties, who will not hesitate if ordered to fire on American citizens. What do you say, Mr. Lee?"

"A war . . . will involve everyone. There will be no neutral ground. If Virginia sides with the southern states . . . General, I cannot fire upon my home."

Lee stood, walked to the window and looked out, across the Potomac.

"General, my home is right there. My family is spread all over this part of Virginia." He turned back, felt a shock, the clear vision. "If you . . . invade the South, this is where it will happen. Your enemy territory will be there . . . right across that river, and so, that is where it will begin. I would not . . . I could not accept that assignment, General."

"Colonel, you said yourself there is no great cry for secession in Virginia. I do not believe it is a foregone conclusion that Virginia, or Tennessee, or Arkansas, or Kentucky will join in the rebellion."

"I hope you're right, General. I pray you are right. But if there is fighting, many things could change. I must request time to consider your offer. Please, allow me some time."

"All right, Colonel. Think about it. You know where to find me."

Lee sensed an abruptness, knew it was time to leave. He moved toward the door, then stopped. "General, please understand, I am honored you would consider me—"

"Colonel Lee, there is a great deal more at stake here than honor."

April 1861

On April 12, P.G.T. Beauregard, a man who had served with Lee as a fellow engineer in Mexico, commanded the Confederate troops who opened fire on Fort Sumter.

Major Robert Anderson had held solidly to the fort for two days, with no loss of life, but ultimately had to concede to the hopelessness of his position.

In Richmond, the state convention to debate the calls for secession met secretly. Lee heard that the voices of reason dominated the sessions, and he was confident Virginia would remain neutral. On April 17 he received an urgent request to come to the house of Francis P. Blair, father of an old friend from Lee's days as an engineer in St. Louis, before the Mexican War. He was also a close acquaintance of President Lincoln.

Early the next day, Lee rode his small carriage over the bridge into Washington. The river flowed peacefully beneath him, and along the banks, rows of young trees were speckled with the fresh buds of a new spring. He could see couples, lovers walking along the water, wrapped with the sublime peace of romance. For a moment he felt lost, away from all the turmoil. He left the bridge and rode through the wide streets, feeling as good as he had in weeks. It must be the air, he thought, and had a sense that everything would be all right, the troubles would pass.

Then he reached the Blair house, climbed out of the carriage, and saw an old man standing on the porch. The look on the man's face, a stony, sobering stare, brought Lee back down, back to the place and the time. It was Francis Blair.

As Lee reached the porch, Blair turned, without speaking, walked into the house and held the door open for Lee, who followed. Lee was ready with a warm greeting, inquiries about Blair's son, still in Missouri, but the old man did not speak. He led Lee into a study, a large and impressive room with shelves filled with hundreds of books.

Lee looked around the room admiringly, and finally Blair said, "Colonel, have a seat. Welcome to my home. I thank you for your promptness."

"Thank you, Mr. Blair. I am happy to see you. I would like to hear about your son—"

"Colonel, allow me to get to the point. I have been authorized by President Lincoln himself, with the full blessings of the War Department, to offer you the position of Major General, in command of an army, an army that is being formed to put down the rebellion and preserve the Union."

Lee had not expected anything of the sort, did not know Blair was that close to the President. His mind danced, jumped in all directions, and he sat for a long moment before replying. "I am . . . grateful, but an army? Where . . . when is this army being formed . . . ?"

"The President is issuing a call for volunteers, from every state. *Every* state. The President expects to build an army of seventy-five thousand men, maybe more. You are the choice, his choice, for commander of that army."

"But, General Scott . . . ? Has he . . . ?"

"The general still retains the title of Commanding General, but it is only a title. The President will not remove the general from his post. He feels that General Scott is entitled to leave his command in his own fashion. The general is also strongly in favor of your appointment to this post.

"If you don't mind, Colonel, the President is in somewhat of a difficult position. This army must be raised, equipped, and organized as quickly as possible. I'm sure you are familiar with the difficulties of that. We require your acceptance of this position . . . well, immediately."

Lee stared at the old man, tried to think, to clear his mind. "I am assuming, Mr. Blair, that this army is to be used to . . . invade those areas . . . to eliminate the rebellion by force."

"Of course, Colonel. The Federal government has been violently attacked by elements of an unlawful band of criminals, who have been most effective in turning the sentiments of several state legislatures against their central government, against the Constitution. The President has no choice. The situation is quite clear."

Lee stared at the wall beyond Blair's desk, the rows of books, then looked down, looked at his own hands, realized he was shaking. He said a small prayer. *God, how can You have let this happen?* But it *was* happening, and he was being asked to sit in the center of it all. He thought of the long, dull years spent wondering if there would ever be the satisfaction, the reward for a good career, the advancement he so wanted but could not politic for. And now it was there, from the President himself, and with it came the horror of what he would have to do. He prayed again, silently asked God, *Why must there be such irony?*

He looked at Blair, saw patience. The question had been asked. Lee broke the silence with a small cough. "Sir, would you please convey my deepest sense of honor and gratitude to the President, but I must decline your offer. Please understand, I am sorely opposed to secession, as I am opposed to the violent path that the southern states seem bent on following. I decided months ago that my greatest loyalty is to Virginia, to my home. I would rather resign from the army and return to my fields at Arlington than to lead an invasion such as this. I hope, with all prayers to God, that Virginia stays within the Union, but I fear that with this call for an army, this building of an invasion force . . . I fear that the President will now unite his enemies. And that may include Virginia. Please tell him, please be clear, I have never taken my duties lightly, not to my country nor to my home. But I have no greater duty than to my home, to Virginia."

Blair did not speak, sat with his head down, rubbed an old hand on the back of his neck, then looked up and nodded. "Well, Colonel, we have your answer. I hope . . . in the end . . . your home is a safe place."

He ran up the steps to General Scott's office, did not stop outside the door, pushed through and halted at Keyes's desk.

Keyes jumped, startled. "Oh! Colonel . . . I am not aware you have an appointment—"

"Please, Colonel, may I see the general? It is very important."

Keyes knew instinctively that Lee was serious, would not be there to waste anyone's time. He opened Scott's office door, said something Lee could not hear, then opened the door farther and stood aside.

"Thank you, Colonel Keyes. I am grateful."

Scott sat back in his chair, watched Lee pull the door shut, and Lee saw there was no humor in the man's face.

"General, forgive the intrusion. I have just spoken with Francis Blair. Permit me to be blunt, General, but I must assume you knew of this meeting."

"Yes, Colonel, I knew. I also had a fairly clear notion of how you would respond."

"Sir, I did not accept the offer. I could not . . . take up arms. . . ."

"An explanation is not necessary, Mr. Lee. I know your position. You are aware how much I admire you as a soldier. I believe the country has lost an opportunity here, the best use of perhaps its best commander."

He stopped, and Lee saw his face grow darker, a sadness he had not seen before. Scott looked at him through red, tired eyes, the eyes of a man whose time is past.

"I also believe, Mr. Lee . . . Robert, if I may . . . that you have made the greatest mistake of your life, but I feared . . . it would be so."

Lee sat down, did not want this, did not want the old man feeling this. "I regret if I have disappointed you. I understand that my duty . . ." He paused, carefully picked the words. "I understand that by stating my reasons for turning down this post, I have compromised my effectiveness as a commander. I have expressed my conclusion that I will not raise my sword against my own people. If I remain in the army, I may be asked, again, to do just that. It would force me to resign under orders."

"Yes, Colonel, it would, and your career would conclude with disgrace. The army does not have room for those men who cannot answer the call. You have stated your position. Now you have only one course. I have always known you to be a man who would do what is right."

Lee knew the next step, what he must do. He thought of his career, the years, the slow advances and thankless jobs. And Scott could not understand, could not see a soldier's loyalty replaced by a different loyalty, to his home, his family. Lee thought, I have not been there, for Mary, for the children, but I must be there now.

"Sir, I will prepare a letter, which I will forward to you as quickly as possible."

Lee did not want to look at the old man's face. The bond that had always been between them would now be gone. He stood, stared down at the desk, bowed slightly, and Scott did not move, stayed back, sunk deeply in the big chair. There were no words, nothing was said, and Lee looked up, saw the old face once more, turned, softly wiped his eyes and went to the door.

ON APRIL 20, THE SAME DAY LEE SENT HIS LETTER OF RESIGNATION to General Scott, the Virginia convention, in response to the President's call for troops, voted overwhelmingly to secede from the Union.

10. JACKSON

April 1861

THEY WERE STUDENTS, A HUNDRED OR MORE, BUT JACKSON knew it was more like a mob. The flagpole of Washington University now carried the new flag of the rebellion, the Confederate flag, and the students cheered wildly as it waved with a sharp snap in the brisk spring breeze.

Jackson kept his distance from the crowd, moved past unnoticed, heard young speakers, voices of careless protest, the bravery of the untested, and he continued on, toward the home of the university president, Dr. Junkin.

There were a few students gathered outside the Junkin home, some calling out rude, hostile remarks. Jackson pushed his way through. They saw his uniform and there were a few cheers. The door was locked, but it immediately opened partway, and he was invited in with a brief greeting. It was Julia, Junkin's youngest daughter, and Jackson saw the dark eyes, the fear. She took his hand, a brief squeeze.

"Major, thank you, thank you for coming. Father is—"

And from behind her, an unsteady voice, the bitterness of a man who has seen too much.

"Major, glad you could make it. A wonderful day, truly. The enlightened students, the leaders of our intellectual future, are screaming for the destruction of our nation."

Jackson watched the old man turn away, walk into the parlor. He noticed a slight bend in his back, a weakness in the bones. The old man had lost three of his children, and Jackson still shared the horror that was in this house, of the terrible black night when his own dear Ellie had died giving birth. He tried to push it away again, but here, inside the house, the memories were everywhere. He watched the old man, thought, You are with this every day . . . *always.* He shook, a brief, cold jolt. God must be of comfort, he thought. Junkin was a deeply devout man, and they had spent great, long hours discussing their faith. The old man had always been there with the right words, and now, Jackson thought, it is *my* turn to provide the comfort, the words.

"Come in here, Major, if you please. Take a seat."

Jackson followed, and Julia went away, toward the rear of the house. Jackson wanted to say something to her, something consoling, but she was gone. He moved into the parlor, sat across from the old man, could still hear the calls, the loud voices from outside.

"Sir, are you all right? Have you been assaulted?"

"Oh yes, Major, very much so. My university, my students, have assaulted me in ways they don't even understand. Those children out there," he waved a thin arm to the front of the house, "they think they know what is best for this country. They read about some fancy politician in South Carolina making some flaming ridiculous speech about revolution, and off they go. They have no sense of what . . . no sense of the reality . . . My God, what is happening to us, Major?" He stopped, put his head down, rested his face in soft, open hands.

Jackson thought of words, but nothing came. There were not many in Lexington who were still holding on, who had heard of the secession votes and were still fighting it, who did not share the loyalty to the new cause, the defense of Virginia.

"Sir, President Lincoln is raising troops, says there will be a war, there will be an army sent here, we are to be attacked. . . ."

The old man raised his head, looked at Jackson with red eyes. "You miss the point, Major. All of that is . . . out *there*, somewhere. What is right here is our lives, our homes. *My* home. Right now the students of this school are openly preaching the overthrow of our country. The townspeople here are gathering themselves into militia units. People are talking about Virginia as though she is some sort of Holy Land!"

"But the President . . . Lincoln is—"

"What Lincoln is doing is responding. There are vast numbers of . . . idiots—yes, that's the word—in these state governments, who believe that they can make a good speech, rouse the people into a rebellion and defy . . . defy the word of God!"

Jackson sat still, absorbed the old man's words, felt confused. "The word of God?"

"Major, this country was founded by good Christian men, on the principles of equality, justice, and all of it *under God.* That has never been done before, *never*, in the history of the world! This country is God's model, God's message to the rest of the world. '*Look here!* We are God's chosen land, this is how God intends man to be governed.' "

The old man's voice cracked, he was losing control, trembling. Jackson waited, leaned forward, caring.

"Point is, Major—the *real* point, that is—the reason I wanted to see you: I'm leaving."

"Leaving . . . the university?"

"Leaving Virginia, Major. Going up to Pennsylvania. I have already resigned my position. These young fools outside don't even know it yet. I cannot live in a place that does not want me. Any control I have in this university is gone. It has been made quite clear to me by a good number of the local citizens that my views are *treasonous.*"

"Doctor, you cannot . . . just *leave.* This is your home, your family. . . ."

"My family is in shambles, Major. My children . . . those that are . . . not gone . . . my sons are scattered . . . my wife sits now with God . . . and you may be assured, Major, be assured, *they* understand why I am leaving." He stopped, wiped at his nose, and Jackson saw the old man was crying.

From the hallway, Julia quietly walked in, sat softly by her father, looked at Jackson. "Major, my father has been through . . . well, you know. It is not right for him to spend the rest of his life fighting a war. He has given all he should have to give, all God ever expected him to give."

Jackson nodded, did not see things the way the old man did, did not see the blessings of God on Mr. Lincoln's war, but he was not prepared to argue with the old man. If he could not be of comfort, could not say the right words, he would have to just say nothing and let them go.

"When will you be leaving?"

Julia looked at her father, and the old man took her hand, smiled weakly at her, turned to Jackson.

"She's going with me, you know. So much like her mother . . . I suppose this old man needs to be looked after."

Julia said, "We'll be leaving this week, Major. We have some family waiting for us. The sooner, the better, wouldn't you agree?"

Jackson heard more voices outside, louder now, saw Julia look toward the front windows, saw the fear, and he stood.

"Doctor, we all must do what we believe God wants us to do. I have prayed for this country, I have prayed that God would stop this, would end all this talk of war, of this rebellion. . . ."

He paused, suddenly realized this would be the last time, that the old man would never come back. But he could not let it go, could not let the old man leave without understanding why he himself would stay. He knelt down on one knee, close to the old man.

"I have spoken to the church, to Dr. White. Many others . . . We have tried, we have prayed and asked all good Christians to pray, that this might not go any further. How can a nation founded on the principles of the Almighty allow this . . . destruction? I have no answer to that . . . except that we do not make the war. The God-loving people of this country are not making this war. The people up there . . . Mr. Lincoln . . . this is their . . . they are . . ."

He stopped. The old man's eyes were not looking at him, he did not hear him, and Julia looked at him pleading no, not this, not now, and Jackson understood, he could not make this fight with the old man. He stood up, held out a hand to Julia, and she rose.

The old man said, "What, you leaving, Major? Well, my my . . . there it is, I suppose. . . ." He tried to stand, struggled, and Jackson leaned to help him, lifted him under the arm.

The old man straightened himself, looked at Jackson, stared straight into his eyes and spoke very slowly, deliberately, "Major, I will only say . . . you are wrong. God will damn all those who fight to destroy this country."

"Father, please!" Julia said, and looked at Jackson. "He doesn't mean that . . . really, Major. You must understand. They have taken his school from him. It's all he has left. You must understand."

Jackson nodded, put out a hand, let it hang in the air toward the old man, a last gesture. The old man looked at the hand, then looked at Jackson's face, a part of his family still, and he took the hand, gave it a weak shake, let go, turned and walked slowly out of the room.

Jackson watched him go, did not speak, and gave a short prayer: *God please watch over him, he has always been Your good servant.* Then he turned to Julia, who was crying silent tears. He wanted to say the right thing, to heal the hurt, but it was not there, there were no more words, and so he turned away and went to the front door.

The students began to cheer him when he stepped out, and a young voice called out, "Did you straighten him out, Major?" and others joined in.

Jackson stopped at the edge of the porch, looked at a small sea of youth, said, "There is nothing for you to do here. Go back, join your friends at your celebration."

He stepped down through the small crowd, and they followed

him. He made his way toward the open green, where the larger crowd still cheered the new flag, and now more people noticed him, the uniform, began to call out to him. He looked up at the flag, and they cheered again, assumed he was with them, and he felt sick, a twisting in his gut. He stepped up on a marble platform, the base of the flagpole, thought for a moment, looked over the crowd, was surprised to see some uniforms, cadets, but then he saw the faces, the fire, the pure untarnished lust for the glorious fight.

"You are all quite eager for a war," he said, and there were whoops, a jumble of hot words and the loud cries for blood. He waited, wanting to tell them, to give them some of the wisdom that had been taught to him only where the blood flows and men scream, the horrible sounds of raw death.

"In Mexico . . . I have seen a war. You do not know what . . ."

But they had stopped listening, heard only each other, the growing pulse, the throbbing rhythm of passion, the voices now together in one long, high, frightening sound. Jackson stepped down, moved through outstretched hands, the deafening cries of a world gone mad, and walked away, left the noise, a swelling horror, behind him. He walked toward the town, felt his mind drift off, floating away, out past the hills, thought of his path, his duty to God. He weighed again, as he had so many times, why he would fight, why it was the right thing to do, but all the politics and causes ran together, scrambled his mind into a mass of confusion, and the one clarity was that God was here, was with him, had shown him the Path, and the reasons men gave no longer mattered.

ANNA ROSE EARLIER THAN USUAL, THE SUN JUST OVER THE TREES on the eastern rim of the mountains. Jackson was already gone, out for his morning walk, and she dressed quietly, with special care, with respect for the Sabbath. She thought, The services will be good today, a break from the turmoil of the past week.

Jackson had been occupied with preparations for the deployment of the cadet corps, the readiness required to send these boys off to train an army, a new army. The week had ended with nothing definite, though constant rumors had kept the entire town on edge.

Anna walked down the stairs that wound through the center of their home. She stopped midway, stood on the small landing, paused to listen, could hear her husband's footsteps, the unmistakable rhythm. She listened, waited for him to climb the back stairs, and heard his every motion, could see him in her mind, removing his boots, the long, high stretch, organizing his body, seeking out the pains and probing them. Then he quietly opened the back door and padded inside.

He came into the hallway, tiptoeing, would not wake his little *esposita*, rounded the base of the stairs. Anna stood above, looked down on his tall frame, and he saw her suddenly, smiled up at her. She did not smile in response, did not share his good mood.

"My darling, you startle me. Did I wake you? I'm sorry."

"No, Thomas, I . . . just fell awake, had to be up. This is a special Sunday."

"Why? Oh, forgive me, I know it is special. I have missed the good prayer sessions, the good company. . . ."

"No, Thomas, this is special because you will be leaving soon. We both know that. All the prayers, all our hopes, have not been answered. There will be a war."

He was surprised at her gloom, tried to put it aside. "There is no war yet. I am still here, with you. There is still hope. The Almighty may yet make them see, may turn us away from this course. It can still happen."

"No, Thomas, it will not happen. God does not change our course, that is for us to do. All we have done is plan one course, and only one course, and there is only one end."

He was stunned, had not heard her speak this way before. He realized he had been so busy this week, had spent so much time at the institute, he had not been with her, had not been of much comfort. She heard the rumors, all the buzz in the town, and he understood how rumors affected people.

"We are preparing, we must be ready. But that is not for today. This is the Lord's day, and we shall spend it with Him, you and I together."

He started up the stairs, to be close to her, but she passed by him, to the bottom of the stairs, said, "I expect we should start with breakfast," and she disappeared around the corner. He watched her, wanted to tell her . . . something, make her understand that his duty was his greatest responsibility to God, that God would protect them as long as he did his duty. He felt a pain in his side, reached up high with his left arm and stretched. The pain lessened, but did not go away. He began to climb up to the bedroom, to change his clothes and make ready for the Sunday services, at least there would be that, the comfort of church, and he thought of Dr. White. Maybe Dr. White could talk to Anna, help her understand. But we will have this day, at least, he told himself, this blessed day.

They both heard the sharp noise from the small brass bell at the front door. Anna stood in the kitchen, heard the bell ring again, heard the urgency, the strain on the thin metal. She could not go, could not answer the door. There could be nothing good about a caller this early on Sunday morning.

Jackson hurried down the stairs, opened the door and saw: a cadet.

The boy snapped to attention, said with crispness, unsmiling, "Good morning, Major. This just arrived for you."

Jackson took the envelope, saw the wax seal, thought he should wait and send the boy away, but he could not stop himself from opening it. He felt his hands shake, looked up at the boy, embarrassed, but the cadet was staring straight ahead, was not seeing, the good discipline of the soldier.

The paper slid out into Jackson's hands, clean and white, and there were only a few lines, the beauty of the skilled pen. Jackson read the message silently, looked back behind him, looked for Anna, and she was not there, had not come out, and he knew she had expected this, had seen it coming sooner than he had, already knew what it said.

Jackson turned back to the boy, said, "Cadet, return to the institute. Give Colonel Smith my compliments, and inform him that I will be at his office within the half hour."

The boy saluted, said simply, "Sir," and in one quick motion was down the steps and gone.

Jackson looked again at the message, the neatly scribed words:

> You are ordered to report immediately with the Corps of Cadets to Camp Instruction, Richmond, to begin the formal training and organization of the Provisional Army, for the defense of the Commonwealth of Virginia.

He turned, did not look for Anna, ran up the stairs to find his uniform.

Anna stayed in the back of the house, the kitchen, prepared a small meal for herself, knew he would not eat now. Then she heard him, the heavy boots on the old stairs. He called out, said something, she couldn't hear it all, and then he was gone.

She walked out to the back, down the porch steps, looked across the yard, the new furrows in the clean brown soil, the bed of the new spring garden, waiting for the seeding, the new crop, and she knew he would not be planting it, that he would not be working his beloved field outside of town. She looked up to the porch, saw the cloth bags, the seeds. She had just bought them this week, had hoped to sit with him, to poke small fingers into waiting dirt, the beginnings of the new life, and she thought of him, the look of pure joy, sitting in the dirt, part of it, brown smudges all over his clothes and face; thick, caked dirt on his hands. He loved it, would ask her to sit with him, share the feeling, the good work with God's earth.

She stood in the yard for a long while, lost track of time. She could hear noises drifting over the town from the big hill to the north, where the cadets were preparing. She could hear drumming, the hollow sounds echoing through the streets, and the townspeople, excited voices. She went back to the porch, sat on the steps. Looking up, she saw the spring birds flying past, circling, landing on the freshly turned soil, then away in a flutter, spooked by the noises from the street, and then she heard him, calling out in his playful Spanish from the front of the house, and she stood, hurried up the steps and inside.

"My *esposita*, I have only a few minutes. I must get back . . . we have a church service. . . . Dr. White is going to lead . . . then we are moving out, to Richmond." He was out of breath, and she knew he had run all the way from the institute.

"Come, before I leave, we must sit, read together. There is a verse . . ." and he led her into his study, found his Bible, hurriedly thumbed through. "Yes, yes, here. Corinthians, Second Corinthians, chapter five, please, sit by me. I have been thinking about this verse."

Anna sat, put her hand on his, and they read it together.

"For we know that if our earthly house of this tabernacle were dissolved, we have a building of God, a house not made with hands, eternal in the heavens . . ."

When they had finished, he turned, knelt before her, looked at her with a softness she had never seen, then closed his eyes and said, "I pray, O Almighty God, I pray that You feel our love, You feel that we do only what You ask, that our path is the right one, and that we may sit by Your side . . ." He went on, a long and earnest plea, and Anna pulled her mind away, watched him, saw the passion, the determination to do *right*, and she lay a hand gently on the side of his face, waited.

He finished, the final Amen, then she pulled him closer, and he opened his eyes, and she knew it was to be, his way was clear. They rose, stood with hands together, and she smiled. He saw the first smile from her today, and suddenly he hugged her, clamped his arms around her, pulled her into him and held her . . . and then it was done.

She stood at the open door, watched him move in a quick motion down the steps, watched the long strides marching up the street, away. He turned, one more wave, and she tried, could not raise her hand, watched him crest the hill and drop out of sight. She looked up then, tilted her head toward a bright sky, the sharp unblemished blue, and asked aloud, "How could You make this day so beautiful?"

11. LEE

April 1861

HE STARED OUT THE WINDOW OF THE MOVING TRAIN, SAW THE buildings of Richmond grow in size and number. He had not been through this part of Virginia in years, and he marveled at the changes, the vast number of new houses, the sleepy farmlands absorbed by a spreading city.

Barely two days after his resignation, Lee had received a messenger from Governor Letcher, a request that he accept the command of the Provisional Army, the defense forces for the state of Virginia.

The train ride was his own idea. He did not receive an invitation to meet personally with the governor, but assumed it would be best if he was closer to the rush of events that would certainly follow the secession vote.

As the train began to slow, Lee continued to gaze intently at the buildings, stately homes of red and white brick with tall, peaked roofs. They reached the station, and the train lurched to a stop. He climbed down onto the platform into a fever of activity, the hot energy of people moving with a purpose. Through the moving crowd he spotted a line of horse-drawn taxis, carried his one leather bag and climbed aboard, alone and unrecognized. The taxi began the climb up the streets of the city in turmoil, toward his temporary home, the Spottswood Hotel.

The Spottswood was a grand place, and as such, the focal point for important meetings and gatherings. Lee walked slowly through the hurried clatter of the lobby, saw groups of men, some huddled in intense conversation, others waving big cigars, broad-chested men with loud voices, proclaiming their opinions with the mindless flourish of those who share no responsibility for the consequences of their grand ideas. Lee stopped briefly, listened to one such speech, felt uncomfortable and began to wonder what reckless policies and self-indulgent planning was going on elsewhere.

His room was large, with white walls and dark oak furniture. He placed his bag on the bed, deciding to unpack later, for he wanted to waste no time before seeing the governor. From the large window he gazed down at the streets, saw tightly packed carriages, men on horseback, noticed that everyone was hurrying, the wagons and carts bouncing about on the rough cobblestones. He began to feel anxious, excited, could not help but be caught up in this, whatever it was.

There was a mirror hanging on the wall across from the window, and Lee checked his appearance, the fine dark suit, looked down at the fresh polish on his black leather shoes, and with quick, precise steps, went out to meet the governor.

The walk to the capitol was longer than he had anticipated. He climbed hills and walked down streets that intrigued him. There was much of his own history here, and he felt a strong sense of kinship, the revolutionary spirit that had filled this place nearly a century before. He kept a brisk pace, felt the cool spring air, and up ahead could see a statue, a man on a horse, standing high in the middle of a circle, a wide plaza. He approached with curiosity, then saw: George Washington.

He stopped. People were walking past, few looking at the tall figure, the sharp bronze features. Lee felt himself breathing heavily, the exhilaration of the walk, and he looked into the face of Washington, thought, We too are in the midst of a revolution. He wondered what Washington would do in his situation, and felt, of course, he *had* been in this same situation, accepting the cost of fighting for independence.

Lee spoke, in a low voice unheard by people dashing past. "What has changed? Why has it not worked?" He began to think of history, the great men: Hamilton, Franklin, Adams. They did not design a government to control the people.

He shook his head, looked around at the crowded street. He watched a family, a young mother pulling along two reluctant children, then saw more children, a small park across the plaza, parents sitting on benches while children crawled about in thick green grass.

I have so missed that . . . all of that, he thought. But I did that myself . . . the army, my whole life.

Now he thought of Mary, watching him write his letter to Scott, giving up his career. He'd cried, put his head down on his arm there at the big desk and wept, and she was there, put a frail hand on his shoulder, tried to help, and he realized for the first time what she had given up. She had married a young soldier, had shared the life that his career demanded. She was confined to a wheelchair now, could barely walk at all, and now he was gone again, leaving behind advice, as he always had, to move the family, take the girls and leave Arlington. He knew, as she could not comprehend, what a war would do to his home.

And so, Lee knew he would accept this command, would defend his home, because in the end he had nothing else, he had given up all of it.

He looked back up at the face of Washington. We are all revolutionaries, he thought. If we understand that, we will have great strength, we will defend our homes, we *will* prevail.

He turned, began to move through the crowds, toward the capitol.

LEE WAS SURPRISED HOW QUICKLY HE WAS ESCORTED INTO Governor Letcher's office.

"Colonel Lee, a surprise, to be sure. Good of you to come, however. Please, please, be seated. Cigar?"

"No, thank you, Governor. I received your gracious request, and thought it best that I come here. . . ."

"Excellent, yes, Colonel. Oh . . . excuse me, I don't believe I should refer to you . . . excuse me, *Mister* Lee."

"It's quite all right, Governor. I still refer to myself as Colonel."

"Well, Mr. Lee, I would prefer to call you Major General Lee. Are you, um, pleased with that title?"

Lee began to feel swallowed by the energy, the enthusiasm, of this man who, he suddenly thought, did not look much like a governor. He thought of the imposing figure of Sam Houston, the image pressed into his brain, a contrast to the bald man with the puffy red face who sat across the wide desk. Around the wide office sat several others whom Lee did not recognize, men in dark suits. There was a sense of celebration, and Lee wondered, Has something else happened, what have I missed?

"Sir, I am honored that you would offer me the position."

"Well, you come highly recommended, most highly. This won't be official of course, there's the convention . . . the formalities. Your name must be brought before the body, then voted. Well, it's all very ceremonial."

"Whatever is required, sir."

"Good, good. This is a ghastly business, Mr. Lee. We did everything,

everything to convince the convention to stay neutral, but as I'm sure you were made aware, when Mr. Lincoln called on us, on *Virginians*, to supply troops to *his* army, well, sir, the response was . . . well, I must say, even I began to feel the call to secede, to defend against this kind of tyranny. Well, I seem to be making a speech."

There was laughter from around the office, good-natured jabs at Letcher's political side. Lee tried to relax, to flow into the good feelings, but could not, felt himself pull together, deflecting their good humor.

"Sir, may I inquire as to my first duties? Do you . . . is there a plan, a strategy? Pardon my directness, sir, but I need to be informed on just what is happening."

"Yes, certainly you do, Mr. Lee. The government of the new confederation of southern states is currently quartered in Montgomery, and is seeking to reach an agreement with Virginia to relocate here, in Richmond. They are also requesting that the Provisional Army forces, which you will command, be incorporated into a central army, a joining of all the state forces. This matter is still under some discussion."

Lee heard murmurs from around the room, sensed this was a difficult topic.

"I believe you are well acquainted with the President of the Confederated States, Mr. Davis, Jefferson Davis?"

"Yes, sir, we attended West Point together. I haven't been in touch with him in a number of years."

"No matter. He has great respect for you, Mr. Lee, and I expect you will be working closely with him and his people on establishing our defense. It is likely, Mr. Lee, as you may already know, that with Virginia's siding with the Southern cause, we are clearly the front door to any invasion force. Your first duties will be quite explicit. Form a line of defense."

There were some nods of approval, and one man, a large, round man with a deep raspy voice, said, "Hit them. Hit them hard."

Another round man, shorter, with a higher-pitched voice, said, "Yes, we must attack them, quickly. Show them they can't push us!"

Lee listened, respectfully, said nothing. Of course, it would be popular to go on the offensive, the people would cheer the marching troops, the call to battle.

Letcher cut off the discussion, saying, "Good, good, well, Mr. Lee will begin his duties as quickly as we can formalize the post. If there is nothing else, Mr. Lee?"

"Gentlemen, I look forward to serving the Commonwealth of Virginia, and I will defend her from harm as best I can."

There were more murmurs, approving, confident. He stood, ready to leave, waited for others to rise. As he reached the wide door, the big man placed a heavy arm on his shoulders and breathed a thick voice into his ear.

"Remember, hit them hard!"

12. HANCOCK

May 1861

The route started west in Kansas, Fort Leavenworth, where the last of the telegraph wires stopped. The man rode hard and fast and as long as the horse would carry him, then, trading one horse for another, climbed toward the great mountains, following the trails through the high passes. The horse carried him quickly over the shrinking ice fields, slippery patches of melting snow that were just now warming under the springtime sun. There were stations along the way with fresh horses, small and crude outposts, and the man would hand over his heavy cloth sacks, the precious mail, newspapers, to a new man, who would take a fresh horse farther, higher, then down through the hard red rocks of the western flatlands, across the plains of Utah and Nevada, along the edges of small rivers that cut through the dry sands. He would climb again, into California, the breathtaking views across the Sierras, more snow now, and the horse slowed, could not move as quickly as the rider pushed him. Often it did not survive, brought the rider to the next station, only to collapse, dead from brutal exhaustion. Once across the mountains, the ride became easier, the green hills and valleys of northern California, a blessed relief to the man who had begun the trip hundreds of miles back, had survived the dangers of the mountains.

At last, there was the Sacramento River, the wide, calm waters that fed San Francisco Bay. Here, the rider knew, there would be time to rest, to play a bit, the wild and restless city, where the prospectors drank beside the rough men of the sea. But there was no play until the sacks were delivered, and the rider pushed his horse just a little harder as the town of Benicia, the walls of the old fort, appeared over the low hills. He dropped the sacks into the hands of a waiting officer, and both men saw relief in the eyes of the other, the rider because his duties were over, and the officer because they had some news.

Now, letters and papers went south, to Los Angeles, held by the leather pouches of the army, carried by soldiers this time, not the free and rugged civilians who brought the news across the great expanse of prairie and mountain and desert. Now they rode in numbers, protection from bandits who did not know what the pouches carried but knew there could be value, there could always be value. The soldiers were well armed, rode only during the day, and arrived at Los Angeles more rested, with horses that could take them back home.

Lewis Armistead saw them first, a cloud in the distance rising above the narrow road from the north. He was on his horse, had just left the Hancock home, stuffed with a truly marvelous dinner, and was now riding back toward the depot, the camp of his men.

The soldiers rode up fast, saw his uniform and slowed. He saw the faces, men who had ridden all day, hard dust on their burnt faces, the horses sagging, soaked in the lather of the hard ride.

The soldiers pulled up beside him, saluted, and he saw one officer, a captain, an unusually high rank for this duty.

"Major . . . Captain Billings, sir. Company D, Sixth Infantry. Oh . . . Major Armistead, sir."

"That's right, Captain. You're a long way from home."

"Major, these are handpicked men, a security detail. My orders came from General Johnston himself. We are to deliver these pouches to Captain Hancock, and in your presence, sir, if that is possible. The general was quite insistent in his instructions, sir."

Armistead felt a twinge, deep in his gut, a small icy hole. "Gentlemen, I have just come . . . well, follow me. Captain Hancock's house is just . . . there, up this road."

He led the men up the narrow strip of hard dirt, halted his horse in front of the small house with stucco walls and low, flat windows. The men dismounted together, stood ready, looking out in all directions, away from the house, standing guard. Against what? Armistead wondered.

He led the captain to Hancock's door, pulled back a rickety screen and knocked.

It was Mira who greeted them, smiled at Armistead and started to say something funny, a joke, to tease him about his appetite. Then she saw the captain, the brown leather bags, saw past them to the horses, soldiers with guns, and stepped back, pulling the door open wide. She nodded for the two officers to enter, then went to find her husband.

Armistead led the captain inside and waited with him. From the rear of the house, the room where his children had been put in bed, Hancock came out in civilian clothes, smiling at the words of his son. Armistead looked at his friend, but did not smile, said, "Captain, this man has ridden from up north, has some information."

"Captain Billings, sir. Company D, Sixth Infantry. I have orders from General Johnston to give this to you personally, and in the presence of Major Armistead."

Hancock took the bags, looked at Armistead, the smile gone. "Thank you, Captain. Is this . . . all?"

"Yes, sir. This concludes my mission. If you will excuse me, I will escort my men to a convenient campsite, and we will return to Benicia in the morning."

"Captain," Armistead said, "two companies of the Sixth Regiment are camped about a quarter mile from here, at the supply depot, just down the main road you were on. Please take your men there, they can have a decent meal and a tent. See Lieutenant Moore, tall, thin fellow, tell them I said to fix you up."

Billings saluted, nodded. "That is most kind, Major. Thank you." He backed toward the door, took a last glance at the bags hanging over Hancock's arm, and left.

Hancock felt the weight of the bags, smelled the old leather, the gray dust rubbing off on the sleeve of his white shirt. "Well, Lewis, shall we have a look?"

Armistead had often come to dinner, had made it a habit years before, in Fort Myers, Florida, on the edge of the Everglades, when the Sixth Infantry had been sent to the worst place any of them had ever seen—suffocating heat, bugs and snakes, quiet diseases—to pursue and contain the Seminoles. Mira had been the only woman on the post, and the officers took turns for the wonderful opportunity to share the Hancocks' dining table, but it was Armistead who always seemed to have his place set, and the friendship between the two men was understood. They had served together even before Florida, in Mexico, and Hancock had known Lewis Armistead as the jokester, the Virginia gentleman who could feign the embarrassed look of the proper aristocrat and then, with a sly grin, embarrass the unsuspecting victim with his own crude wit.

Armistead was older, had carried with him the shameful reputation of having been booted out of West Point, the jokes then having done more harm. The shame did not come from him, however, but from the others, the gentlemen. Those like Hancock, who knew him well, knew that West Point had wasted its heavy-handed discipline on a fine soldier.

After Mexico, the post around Leavenworth had been a happy time for all of them, but that was before the conflicts over slavery, and before the *influenza.* It was a word most of them had never heard, and it took away the joy, and many of the laughing faces, and one of them was Armistead's wife. Hancock and his own family had been spared, and the bond between them had grown solid then, strengthened by the terrible loss of one and the knowledge that it could have been any of them.

Mira stood quietly behind Hancock as he opened one of the bags and pulled out a heavy brown envelope stuffed with papers, letters, the usual contents of the mail run. He set the contents down on a chair, opened the second bag, and saw a round bundle, newspapers wrapped with string and enclosed by a letter, with the seal of General Albert Sidney Johnston.

"What's this?" he said, sliding the string off. A newspaper slipped out and fell on the floor, the front page with a headline bigger than any he had ever seen, one word, wide letters of black ink: **WAR!**

They stared at the paper, then Armistead bent down, picked it up and read.

"Oh, dear God . . . dear God . . ."

Mira came forward, put her hands around Hancock's arm, and he unrolled the other paper, held the official letter aside, and saw another headline, not as large. FORT SUMTER FIRED UPON!

Mira said, "Fort Sumter?"

"South Carolina . . . Charleston harbor." Hancock read further, scanning the words. The room began to fill with a thick silence, and after a long minute he put the paper down and said to Mira, "They've done it. The southern states have started a war. Major Anderson . . . held his ground, wouldn't surrender the fort . . . so they shelled it."

Armistead stopped reading. "It says no one was killed, no casualties."

"Does it matter?"

"It might. There could still be a way to settle it—much harder once there is blood."

Hancock looked now at the official letter, straightened it out, read it aloud.

> "To, Captain Winfield S. Hancock, Chief Quartermaster, District of Southern California. From, General Albert S. Johnston, Commanding, Department of California.

You are hereby advised that a condition of war now exists between the United States of America and a confederation of states that have elected to withdraw their allegiance to that union. Those states are: South Carolina, Georgia, Texas, Alabama, Florida, Mississippi, and Louisiana. There is great sentiment in this army for men to adhere first to the loyalty they feel is appropriate to their homelands, as taking a greater priority, and being a greater cause than their oaths taken in service to this army. This office shares those sentiments, and I have advised the War Department of my resignation, to be effective only when the department may appoint a replacement for this office, and only when such a replacement is able to take official command of this office. By my example, I hope to inspire the officers and men under my command to delay hasty action, perform your duties as good soldiers, and pursue with care and dignity whatever action is dearest to your conscience. May God have mercy on us all."

Hancock put the letter down, and Armistead said, "He's resigned. Dear God. But, of course, he's a Texan. But . . . he's the commanding general."

Mira picked up a newspaper, said, "It could be all over by now. This paper is dated April fifteenth, that's over two weeks ago."

"Damn the mails . . . damn the distance." Hancock tossed Johnston's letter into a chair and angrily began to pace, taking long steps in the small room. Mira backed away, gave him room.

Armistead read the paper again, said, "It doesn't say anything about Virginia."

Hancock stopped, looked at Armistead with a fierce glare. "Is that important? If Virginia was on that list, would you quit too?"

Armistead felt Hancock's anger, moved away to an empty chair, sat. "I would have to, Win. I could not go to war against my home. How can anyone do that?"

"Your home? Your home is the United States of America! You took an oath to defend her from her enemies."

"Virginia is not anyone's enemy."

"No, not yet. But Mira's right. Two weeks . . . a lot can happen in two weeks. Seven states! Now what happens? Read the letter: 'A condition of war' exists. This is not an argument, this is not a matter of disagreement between points of view. They fired cannon at a government installation. All right, no one was killed, but this is just the beginning. Have you ever seen a war where no one is killed? There will be a response, there has to be: Lincoln . . . General Scott . . . they won't just turn away and say, fine, you shot first, so you win this little war. Now go and form your own country. Damn the distance! We are so far away!"

Armistead leaned forward, rested his arms on his knees, stared down at the newspaper still in his hands. "I don't think . . . I can't believe Virginia would side with the rebels. No one wants this. The last letter I received, my friend Hastings, in Richmond? He said the legislature is solidly pro-Union. No one wants a war."

Hancock began to move again, pacing back and forth like an angry cat.

"No one wants a war? I'm sorry, my friend, but you're wrong. There's two sides to this, two sides that have been pushing us toward a war for months. One side says, 'It's Lincoln! He's the cause!' And the other side says, 'It's slavery! That's the cause!' And the people out here want me to believe it's simply a need for independence, keep the government from telling us what to do. And so, pointing fingers become pointing guns, because nobody listens to fingers."

He looked at Mira, staring down at the other paper, and moved closer to her. "We can't stay here," he said. "Our country is falling apart, and I'm the custodian of a pile of blankets. I have to know . . . we are too damned far away!"

She looked up from the paper, and he saw tears. She nodded, but did not say anything. He looked at Armistead, who put down his paper, stood, slowly moved to the window and looked out to growing darkness.

"General Johnston is right," Armistead said. "May God have mercy on us all."

Within a week another group of riders came down with more official letters, and with them the news that Armistead had not wanted to hear. Virginia, along with Arkansas, Tennessee, and North Carolina, had joined the confederation of rebellious states. There was other news as well, Lincoln's call for troops, the organization of a Confederate Army, and the inauguration of Jefferson Davis.

The rumors of threats to American control of California came more frequently now, and so the infantry stayed at Los Angeles, at

Hancock's discretion. Other supply posts in far-reaching districts, not easily protected, were dismantled, brought to Los Angeles, and added to Hancock's command.

Armistead was with his men, slept in his tent, when he heard the commotion, the sounds of another fight.

"Yaah . . . that's it! Get him! Yeeahhh!"

He rolled off his cot, grabbed his jacket, heard more yelling now, men gathering. Poking his head outside, he saw the crowd, men in uniform and out, surrounding a dusty struggle. He pulled on his pants, grabbed his pistol, and moved unsteadily into the early morning sunlight.

There were other officers approaching, from other directions, and they pulled the spectators back, away from the fight, tried to get closer to the action. Armistead could see the men now, rolling on the ground, torn clothes, one very bloody face, and he pushed past more men, raised his pistol and fired.

The onlookers backed away, and Armistead stood alone over the combatants, kicked lightly at one, rolled him over, looked at the faces. He didn't know them, thought one face familiar, and then other officers were there, lifting the men up. They looked at Armistead through beaten eyes, swollen red faces, one man bleeding furiously from his nose.

"Good morning, gentlemen. Do we have a problem here?"

One of the men, wiping at a cut on his lip, replied, "Major, sir. We was . . . having a disagreement, sir."

The other man, smaller, felt the blood on his face, held his sleeve up against his nose, then said, "He called me a shit-kicker. Said my whole family was shit-kickers. Ain't gonna take that from any man. Sir."

Armistead heard the man's distinctive accent, the deep drawl. "Where you from, soldier?"

"Miss'ippi, sir."

"And you, soldier, you consider that a good reason to insult the man's family?"

"Sir, begging your pardon, but we all knows what's happening. The Southerners are deserting the army, quitting. Heard talk that even you, Major . . ."

Armistead looked at the man's face, saw the cold anger, looked back at the man from Mississippi, who said, "Major . . . I ain't decided if I'm going back home or not. We got a farm . . . my folks . . . my wife is raisin' the kids, the livestock. I don't want to fight nobody. But the army's breakin' up. That's all we been hearin'. I hear tell you headed back to Virginia too, Major."

The other man grunted, and Armistead could tell he had the better of the fight. He was a bigger man, older, with heavy, broad shoulders.

"He's just like the others," the bigger man said, "begging the major's pardon. This here unit's going to pieces because of this war. I been in this outfit since Mexico, sir. I seen you join this outfit, seen you move up from a wet-eared cadet to command of the regiment—"

A lieutenant, holding the man, snapped him up under the arms, said "Watch your mouth, soldier."

Armistead raised a hand. "No, Lieutenant, let him talk. Talking is one thing maybe we all need to do. You may speak freely, soldier. What's your name?"

"Corporal Garrett, sir. Thank you, Major. I just want to say . . . it makes me sick, sir, to see what's happenin' to this army. These farm boys got no understanding, no respect, it seems mighty easy for some to up and quit. I never been much in the South. I ain't never spent no time around the darkies, I got no call to tell nobody what they oughta do. But this here's the army. We got a duty . . . we all got the same duty, all of us, Major."

Armistead looked up, spoke louder, to the broad circle of men. "I know many of you have been with this regiment for a long time . . . some of you, like Mr. Garrett, from the beginning. You are known in this army, you have a reputation, you have always conducted yourselves with honor. To those of you who do not understand why some are leaving, I can only say, it is honor as well. Since both of these men seem to have heard about my decision, I will tell you all. No more rumors. Yes, I have resigned my commission. I will be returning to Virginia as soon as my duties here can be concluded. You men may also be aware that General Johnston has also resigned, as have many of the officers of the Sixth Infantry. I will not defend this decision. It is a personal one, and is the most difficult decision I have made in my life. If you have served under my command as long as Mr. Garrett, then you will know this to be true."

"You plannin' to fight against this army, Major?"

"Mr. Garrett, I plan to go home, to Virginia, and if necessary, I will defend Virginia. Some of you might be going home looking for a fight. The point is, we must all do what we believe is right."

"That ain't a good answer, Major. No disrespect, sir, but it just ain't. This here farm boy I had a go with, he's just a dumb soldier like me. But you're an officer. This army follows you, does what you tell it to do. No sir, I can't accept your answer, Major. You can put me in the stockade, but I reckon I can't salute you no more."

Armistead saw pain in the man's eyes, a deep hurt, and he realized that he had taken something away from the man, from all of them. He had not felt before how much they had respected him, he just took it for granted they followed him because of the uniform he wore, the rank he carried. Now he saw it was much more, and he had pulled it away. He could not look at the man's face anymore, said slowly, in a quiet voice, "Lieutenant, release Mr. Garrett. There will be no punishment for these men. Clean them up, let's get the day started, shall we?"

He turned, looked toward his tent, and the men parted, let him pass. He heard small comments, did not listen, knew what they were feeling now. Reaching the front of his tent, he lifted a flap, and heard a rider, men calling out, and saw a man dismount and men pointing toward him, directing the man his way. The soldier moved with the official step of a staff officer, clean uniform, and Armistead saw a young face covered in freckles.

The man said, "Major Armistead, sir, you are requested to report to the home of Captain Hancock. General Johnston has arrived."

HANCOCK STOOD AT HIS FRONT WINDOW, LOOKED OUT AT THE wagon in his yard, the covered carriage that had brought Johnston and his staff to Los Angeles. He turned to a room full of blue coats, Johnston's staff, who milled around, not used to having nothing to do.

"Captain, your hospitality is most gracious, indeed. My compliments to Mrs. Hancock as well."

"Thank you, General. I would have made better preparations. We were not informed you were coming."

"Please, Captain. We will not intrude on your privacy for very long. I have instructed the men to begin the search for a house."

"A house, you mean, a residence? Are you moving here, General?"

"Gentlemen, please sit down! Good Lord, you're like a hive of bees!" Johnston's voice boomed through the small house, and from the back he heard Mira, trying to quiet the baby's cries. The aides sat around the room, some in chairs, some on the floor. For a brief moment the room was completely quiet, and Hancock heard a horse, looked out and saw Armistead, who rode up beside the carriage, peeked curiously inside, then came to the front door and made a formal knock.

Hancock said, "That would be Major Armistead, sir. Excuse me." He went to the door, pulled it open and saw a look on Armistead's face, a question: Why? Hancock gave a slight shrug, knew only that Johnston had simply arrived.

"Ah, Major, good to see you again!" Johnston stood, held out a hand, and Armistead took it, smiled weakly, looked around the room at the assembled staff.

"General. Welcome."

Johnston went back to his chair, sat heavily on the creaking frame, said, "I was just telling Mr. Hancock about my search for a house. I am moving here. Heard a great many things about the area, better climate than the bay, warmer."

Hancock moved back to his window, stepped over the legs of the seated men.

"Excuse me, General, but are you moving your headquarters . . . down here?"

Johnston stood up again, tried to move around the room, stepped on a young lieutenant's foot, stumbled, said angrily, "All right, enough. Out of here, all of you! Outside! This is the man's home, not a damned staff room."

The officers jumped up, filed quickly out the front door, and Hancock smiled. He looked at Armistead, who watched Johnston, followed him with his eyes back to the chair.

Armistead said, "You have been replaced."

Johnston looked up, did not acknowledge Armistead's words. "They're like damned children," he said. "No, not true. Children will go off and do what they damned well please. They're more like pets. Won't move a bit until you tell 'em to."

There was a quiet pause. Johnston leaned back, rested his hands on his thighs, looked at the floor.

"They're good men. A good staff. Finest in the army. Wish I knew what to do with 'em. They're too damned loyal. Gave up their careers to stay with me. Not very smart, but to a man, not one of them would listen. They all resigned."

Armistead sat in one of the vacant chairs, said again, "You've been replaced."

"Yes, Major, I have been replaced. No, no, make that I have been *removed*. A quick, clean operation. They were afraid, I guess." He stared down again, sagged into the chair, and Hancock saw now a growing sadness.

"Excuse me, General, but they were afraid of . . . what?"

"Captain, let's get one thing straight right here and now. I am no longer 'General.' I am *Mister* Albert Sidney Johnston, private citizen. Your new commander is old Bull Sumner himself. They sent that old man out here to boot me out of my office. No formal notice, no notice at all, he just . . . arrives. Comes busting into my office . . ."

Hancock said nothing, thought, Of course, they were thinking of Twiggs, the surrender of Texas, and had to act quickly so that Johnston would not do the same. But Johnston was not Davy Twiggs.

"Damn them. Damn them all. I kept my honor, gentlemen. I did my duty, just like I said I would. I had no mind to leave until I was replaced, even offered to stay around awhile, help the new people get settled in. They snuck up on me. I thought . . . hell, I thought for a while they were going to arrest me! Hell of a way to end a career."

They sat without speaking, a long pause until Armistead said, "You're going to stay here? What about Texas . . . your home?"

"My home is gone, Major. Burnt down. Got a letter from my cousin. Local militia most likely, thought I was staying loyal to the army. Might go back there yet, but thought this might work out, might be a nice place to live."

"What about the rebel . . . the Confederate Army? I saw a newspaper, your name on a list, possible commanders."

Johnston looked at Hancock, and Hancock suddenly realized this conversation could be dangerous, that Johnston's plans could be information he might have to report. And Johnston knew it.

"Tell me, Captain, are you planning on joining Mr. Lincoln's war?"

"If you mean, am I planning to leave California? I hope so. I have requested a new assignment. Forgive me, General, but I sent the request directly to the War Department, and to General Scott. I thought there might be a greater delay if I sent it through your office."

"Don't explain, Mr. Hancock. We're all looking out for our own best interests these days. And what about you, Major? I *did* receive *your* resignation."

Armistead shifted in his chair, and Hancock knew he felt uncomfortable. It had been unspoken, until now. Hancock knew the papers had gone north, but they had not discussed it, would not argue.

"I will be leaving in two weeks. There's a ship stopping here, on the way to the Isthmus." He looked at Hancock. "I'm sorry, Win. I just learned of the ship yesterday. It seems like the best opportunity."

Hancock stared at him, had known Armistead's decision was made the instant the news of Virginia reached them, had gone through all the feelings, the anger, the sadness, the gut-wrenching frustration that this was all complete and utter madness.

Armistead looked at him, then away. "What else am I to do? Tell me, Win."

Hancock glanced out the window, to the cluster of blue coats sitting around Johnston's wagon, the show of perfect loyalty to their commander. He looked back, across the small room, saw both men looking at him, felt the weight of the gaze, as though it was *him*, he was the one not doing the right thing.

"Gentlemen, I offer you no advice. I will fight for my country, my whole country. I do not believe we are a collection of independent states, but one nation, and my duty is to preserve that nation. I do not sympathize with your pain, or the torment of your decision. Your conscience must guide you, and in the end only you will know if your decision was the right one."

Johnston stood, went slowly to the door, pulled it open, turned to Hancock and said, "Captain, we are all men of honor. Remember that. God will judge our choices."

Hancock moved to an empty chair and stood behind it, resting a hand on the back. He rubbed the smooth dark wood, looked up and into the face of his former commander. "Sir," he said, "it is not God who will assemble us on the battlefield, nor position our troops, nor place the cannon, and it is not God who will aim the musket."

13. LEE

May 1861

In the days that followed Lee's official appointment, he presided over an extraordinary effort at organizing a defensive line across northern Virginia. Governor Letcher had provided him with a long list of volunteer officers, with many names from the old army. He began the delicate balancing act of placing good men in key positions, while tolerating the political appointments given to "distinguished citizens," whose grasp of military service was usually limited to their ability to look good on a horse, wearing a dashing new uniform.

He was alone in his new office, across the street from the governor's offices, pondering the most recent list, the names from which he would organize an army. His finger slid down the pages, stopping at names he recognized, and he thought, Good, good, yes, this is very good indeed.

It was not surprising to Lee that most of the Virginians who had served in the old army would rally to their state's defense, and his confidence began to build as he saw the names, the experienced officers: A. P. Hill, Dick Ewell, George Pickett; men who had been in Mexico. He searched for some names in particular, and was surprised at their absence—his friend George Thomas from Fort Mason—and Lee thought, Well, there is still time.

The offices around Lee's were buzzing with a mild chaos, and Lee knew his next priority would be the formation of some sort of staff. The paperwork on his desk began to pile ominously, the requests for appointments, local dignitaries from smaller towns, who had organized their own units with themselves at the top, letters of recommendation for friends and relatives from those with political pull. The experienced officers did not make the requests—they would wait for their assignments.

Lee made notes on a separate page, checked a map that hung on the wall to his side, and saw a man standing in his doorway, stiff, silent. The face was familiar. Lee said, "Yes, hello, may I be of assistance?"

The man stepped into the office. He was tall, lean, and sturdy, wearing a dark blue coat, knee-high cavalry boots, and a small billed cap, which Lee could now see carried the insignia of the Virginia Military Institute.

"I believe I know you. . . ." Then Lee remembered Scott's grand review in Mexico City, the great victory celebration in the center of the capital.

Scott had wanted them all together, would shake the hands of the officers, and so the army had lined up in formation, the troops spread out down the streets to the square, and this one man, this young artillery officer, had stopped the procession, had received a loud and personal congratulations from Scott. It was recognition of more than just duty, but of an officer who had taken his small guns up close, to the face of the enemy, had led his men out in front of the slow advance of the infantry and moved the enemy back on his own, pushed away the Mexican guns that stood in their way. Lee remembered clearly now, had sat on the podium behind Scott, watching the embarrassed face of this rigid soldier. The young man had been promoted three times, began as a second lieutenant fresh from the Point, and left Mexico as a major.

Lee smiled at the sharp face, the deep blue eyes watching him carefully, and he nodded quietly at the face of a hero. "Yes, you are Thomas Jackson."

"Sir." Jackson gave a crisp salute, which Lee returned, and Lee pointed to a chair, heaped in papers. "Major, please, sit down. Excuse the mess. Things are a bit hectic."

Jackson went to the chair, set the papers on the floor, sat down, straight, did not touch the back of the chair.

"General, I am reporting with the Corps of Cadets from VMI. The young men are prepared to assist in the training of the new volunteers, sir. I, however . . . I have received orders of a different nature. Please allow me, General . . ."

Lee saw a look on Jackson's face, discomfort, urgency.

"What is it, Major? Is there a problem?"

"General, the concerns of one officer do not have priority where duty is concerned, however, I feel I may have been . . . I seem to have been made a Major of Engineers. General, I am not an engineer."

"Who made you an engineer?" Lee was puzzled.

"The Executive War Council, sir. However, I have received a letter from Governor Letcher." He reached into his pocket, drew out an envelope, handed it to Lee.

Lee felt a small anger at these people who were throwing commissions around the state like prizes at a county fair, with little understanding of the value of experience. He read the letter. ". . . recommend that General Lee appeal the appointment, and place Major Jackson in field command, at the rank of colonel . . ." At the bottom, he saw the now-familiar signature of John Letcher, Governor.

"This should not be a problem, Major. The council has been somewhat hasty with many of their appointments. In fact . . ." Lee turned and looked at the map on the wall, lines of red X's marking those places requiring the most troop concentration. "You are familiar with the area around Harper's Ferry, Major?"

"Yes, sir, quite familiar. My home . . . my family is from the valley area."

Lee thought, Of course, this is ideal. "Major, you will soon be commissioned colonel in the Virginia Provisional Army, and as such I am placing you here." He reached out to the map, placed a finger on Harper's Ferry.

"You will assume command of the volunteer units forming there. Organize them into brigade strength and defend the Arsenal there, until we can remove the equipment to a safer location."

Jackson stood, went closer to the map, squinted. "Sir, I am honored. I will hold the position as long as necessary."

"Major, I don't believe you should concern yourself with digging in there. The area is not defensible. The town sits in a low bowl, if you will, surrounded by high hills. But we need the machinery in the Arsenal. If we can maintain some strength there, just long enough to keep the Federal forces hesitating, we will have accomplished a great deal."

"I understand, General. I will leave immediately." Jackson turned, took long noisy steps toward the door, then stopped abruptly, made a neat turn back toward Lee and said, "Excuse me, General. A very good friend of mine, he's my brother-in-law, actually . . . no, he's my wife's brother-in-law. . . ." Jackson stared at the ceiling, spoke to himself, "No . . . well, yes, he's married to Anna's sister, so . . ."

Lee winced, No, not this one too, a good soldier who should know better.

"He is nearly my brother-in-law. He is a professor of applied mathematics at Davidson College . . . a very intelligent man, not lacking in a sense of duty. I believe if he were to be asked, he would return to the army."

"Return . . . ?"

"Yes, sir. He was in Mexico, left the army as a major."

Lee let out a light breath. At least this brother-in-law had some experience. "What is his name, Major?"

"Daniel Harvey Hill, sir."

Lee nodded, the name was familiar to him. He looked down the list on his desk, turned a page, then another. Jackson stood stiffly, watched, curious about what Lee was doing.

"Ah, yes, right here. Major, this army thanks you for your efforts on Mr. Hill's behalf, but it is not necessary. He has already volunteered."

Jackson nodded, said quietly, "Good . . . he knows his duty," then he turned again.

Lee said, "Major, wait."

Jackson froze, realized suddenly he had not saluted, spun around with his hand to the bill of his cap.

"No, Major, I mean . . . I just wanted to say, the state of Virginia is pleased to have your services. You are a valuable asset to her defense."

"General, duty has called me, and I can think of nothing that will please the Almighty more than my performing my duty. I will do whatever I must do to defeat my enemies."

Lee watched the serious face, saw something new, a grimness he had not seen before, had not seen in the others.

"Major, the men you will command are signing up for one-year terms. Most here say that is far too long, that this will be a brief affair, that we may be done with this business after one good scrap. It is the consensus among the political leaders here that the Federal forces will not fight, that with our first good show of strength, they will turn and run. I do not share their view, I would not count on that, Major. Nothing would please me more, but I fear this fight will not be brief."

"General, I will do everything in my power to make it as brief as possible. If they do not run, then they will die."

Lee saw the stern face, staring beyond him, looking at the wall above his head. "Very well, Major. May God be with you."

Jackson turned once more, marched from the office, and Lee heard him speaking, heard soft words hidden by the sharp sound of his boots on the oak floor, and Lee could tell only that it was a prayer.

THE NEW CONFEDERATE ADMINISTRATION UNDERSTOOD THE strategic need to defend Virginia. Lee's decision to occupy the key geographic points, from the western mountains to the vulnerable coastline and river systems, was supported by Davis's government. Lee had quickly established strong posts at Harper's Ferry and at the naval yards at Norfolk. The Federal Army had abandoned both positions, had attempted to burn what equipment was left behind, but alert militia units had rescued the materials, which were vital to Lee's plans for equipping his troops.

It was only logical that since Virginia was of such general importance to the defense of the rest of the Confederacy, their relationship should be formalized. Lee and Letcher had been able to convince President Davis that Virginia would bear the brunt of the Federal Army's moves, and thus they had few objections when, after Lee had established effective lines of defense, the rapidly organizing army of the Confederacy began to assume control.

As this balance shifted, Virginians whom Lee had appointed, men who filled necessary commands in the Virginia forces, began to make the transfer, accepting equivalent rank and positions in the Confederate Army. While politically minded men jockeyed for positions of command, Lee spent his days with the vast mundane details of building an army, and while the growing corps of officers began to make grandiose plans for the quick defeat of their enemy, Lee was struggling with finding enough flour, blankets, and cartridges for the men.

By early May, Lee had reached a point of near exhaustion and a sense of growing frustration with his own duties. There was simply too much to do.

On the floor beside his desk was an old brown cardboard box, and Lee tossed another pile of letters down, watched them bounce and flood over the sides. He thought, I will need another box. He began to sort another stack, separating the official messages from the governor and President Davis from troops reports and other military matters. Into the box had gone the private letters, the flowery recommendations, the long insistent lessons on warfare from people who had read about Napoleon, or who had their own theories for whipping these soft soldiers to the north. Occasionally there was the simple prayer, the sincere hope for peace, for a bloodless struggle, but those were rare. Across the office, Lee saw another bag on the one chair, a pile of mail he had not yet sorted, but all addressed to him.

He stood, stretched, loosened stiff bones, said aloud, "Enough."

He went to the door, pulled his coat from a hook, and walked out through the hallway, past offices of noisy officers. He avoided the faces, thought, Please, allow me to get away, just for a while. And then he was safe, outside, walking down the hill away from the building, from the government. He took deep breaths, walked under the full green canopies of the trees, opened up the dark creases of his mind to the warming spring breeze.

He walked to the Spottswood, still his home, thought of something cool to drink, just for a moment, a guilty pleasure. He reached the grand dining room and was relieved to find it nearly empty. He saw the perfect spot, a delightful corner table, and hurried, as though racing against unseen competitors vying for the same chair, then sat down, the victor. A waiter approached; no, not a waiter, a soldier, a tall, thin boy in an officer's uniform, the uniform of Virginia.

"Sir . . . you are General Lee, are you not, sir?"

Lee knew the escape was over, felt his duty creep back out, pushing away the sunlight. "Yes, Lieutenant, I am."

"Oh, sir, it is a great pleasure to meet you, sir. I am at your service."

"Service?" Lee thought of the waiter again, looked past the boy, trying to find someone to bring him . . . something.

"Yes, sir. Lieutenant Walter Taylor, sir. I have been assigned to your staff. My orders, sir."

Taylor pulled an envelope from his pocket, held it out, and Lee saw the governor's seal, looked at the boy's face, handsome, the eagerness of the young.

"My . . . staff. Yes, it appears the governor is providing for my assistance . . . hmmm." Lee finished reading the orders, returned them to the waiting hand.

"Tell me, Lieutenant Taylor, do you know how to write?"

"Write? You mean, can I read? Well, yes sir, certainly, sir."

"No, I mean, write letters. Capture a good phrase, the gracious message."

Taylor was puzzled, thought, then said, "Well, yes sir, I believe I can. I write home . . . as often as I can."

"Good. Then by all means let's get started." Lee stood, put aside the thoughts of a cool drink, and Taylor backed up a step, not sure what was happening. Lee put a hand on the boy's shoulder, turned him around gently, said, "Follow me."

Taylor glanced over to his own table, his food untouched on a plate, just delivered the moment he saw the general enter the room. He made a quick sidestep, grabbed a piece of bread, stuffed it into his pocket, then galloped after his new commander, who was already outside, returning to his work.

By June, Lee had assisted in the transfer of all the Virginia forces into the Confederate Army. While he assumed there would be a place for him in that army, once again he did not have the political outspokenness to grab a choice position for himself. As he entered the new offices of the Confederate government for a meeting with President Davis, Lee knew he was now in command of a nonexistent army.

He passed through large double doors, and there was no one in the outer office, no voices, none of the manic activity that seemed to fill his own building. He slowed, eased toward Davis's office, then knocked. There was a muffled sound from inside, a voice, and Lee turned the old brass handle, opened the door.

"Yes? What is it? Oh, General, do come in."

"Thank you, Mr. President. I didn't see . . . there's no one out here."

"Yes, I know. Sent them home."

Davis was a tall, angular man. His face carried a fierce expression that rarely softened. He sat behind an enormous desk, signing documents in steady succession.

"Sir, do you have a moment? If this is not a good time—"

"No, do come in, General. Just finishing up some orders here, you know how it is. There, that will hold those people for a while. Damned nuisance, these supply people."

"Sir, if I can assist—"

"This is the Confederate Army supply, General. I would imagine your hands are full worrying about your own state."

"Well, sir, that is precisely why I came to see you. It seems that my duties in command of Virginia's army are coming to a close. The army has been incorporated into the Confederate Army, and the strategic positions along the northern border have been secured by your generals. It has not been entirely smooth, but the job—"

"The job has been handled, General, handled most efficiently. I thank you. So, you have a run-in with Joe Johnston, eh? I heard he took over your men in Harper's Ferry, bit of a problem. He is not . . . well, he has his own way. Good man, though, good man."

Joseph Johnston had been the only high-ranking Virginia officer in the old army to sign up immediately with the new Confederate Army without first joining the Virginia forces. Lee knew Johnston always had a keen eye for politics, and so had secured himself a senior position immediately. Now, he commanded the newly promoted General Jackson and the other forces around Harper's Ferry, and did not recognize Lee's authority, would not even correspond with him.

"Sir, permit me to . . . be direct." Lee was growing more uncomfortable. There should not be this formality, he thought. We have a long history . . . I knew this man when we were at the Point. We were . . . well, not close, but . . . there should not be this wall, this political boundary. This was all too familiar to Lee, the coldness of politics, the lack of recognition, being ignored in favor of the men with louder voices. He felt very alone, very unsure. But as the responsibilities had gradually passed to the other commanders, he had stiffened, vowed to himself he would not allow this to simply slide by.

Davis looked up at Lee, looked into his eyes for the first time. Davis had assumed the role of commander in chief with a fanatical attention to detail. He tried, often at great expense of energy, to control all aspects of his government, and often had no trust for subordinates, and so his aides were usually left with nothing to do, while Davis assumed command of even minute details. It was Lee who seemed to win his confidence, because Lee was the only commander who did not challenge Davis's authority, who did not confront Davis with a great ego.

"General, you have performed an admirable . . . well, you have proven to me anyway that you were just the man we needed."

"Thank you, sir." Patience, Lee thought, be careful.

Davis continued, "Yes, of course. We're old soldiers, you and me. I understand what you've done, what steps had to be taken. There has been some talk, talk that you have been too gentle on our enemy, talk that we should have launched a full-scale attack into Washington, stopped this thing in its tracks. There has been some criticism of your defensive strategy."

"Sir, do you believe we should have attacked?"

"No, no, of course not. That's the point. You can't attack an enemy until you can take the fight *to* him. We weren't ready for that, didn't have the means. Now, however, I believe we do. That's why I'm glad to have men like Joe Johnston and Beauregard up on those lines. They may not be exactly . . . thinkers. But they will fight."

"Sir, I do not have a position in the Confederate Army."

"What? Of course you do, here, wait." Davis slid papers around on his desk, lifted one tall stack, shoved it aside, sent pieces fluttering away to the floor.

"Yes, right here. Mr. Lee, you have been named one of five brigadier generals commanding Confederate forces. Your Governor Letcher was most insistent, helped me convince the convention. There, that what you wanted?"

Lee thought, No one told me . . . I should feel honored. But he felt hollow, an emptiness.

"Thank you, sir. May I ask, what are my orders? What troops do I command—where do I go?" He scolded himself for being too anxious.

Davis looked through papers again, began to read, absently, and Lee saw distraction.

"Sir, do you have duty for me?"

"What? Duty? Of course, General, right here, with me."

"Here . . . ?"

"You're too valuable to the operation of this army—the supplies, the detailed work. Can't have you up there, in the middle of the fighting."

Lee sank into his chair, felt a great weight press him down.

Davis shoved papers aside again, looked at Lee. "Invaluable, General. You are what we need here. Behind the scenes, running the show. No one better at it, no one at all."

Lee stood, pulled himself slowly from the chair. "Thank you for your confidence, Mr. President. I have to get back to my office . . . a great deal to do."

"Yes, I'm sure, General. Busy times, busy indeed. Keep me informed."

Davis turned back to his work, and Lee moved slowly out through the quiet offices, back to his own vast piles of paper.

14. HANCOCK

June 1861

"Nothing. Not a word, not a damned word!" He sat on the floor, shuffled again through the mail pouch, scattered the letters around him.

Mira stood over him, put a hand on his shoulder. "It takes time. They haven't forgotten you."

"Are you sure? We're a long way from Washington, a long way from the war. I'm just another officer who happens to be far enough away that he can be overlooked. What do I have to offer? Right now they're looking for fighters, company commanders, brigade commanders. I'm a supply officer. They've probably got men lined up in the street for the field positions. Damn!"

He gathered the mail, straightened the bundles, put them back into the pouch, and she knelt down, picked up a handful of letters, mail for the soldiers of the Sixth, Armistead's men, helped him put them in order.

"Is there anyone else you can contact?"

"I've written General Scott, the War Department, the Quartermaster General's Office. I suppose I could try Governor Curtin. He knows my father well, might be able to find me something in the Pennsylvania volunteers."

"When will the next mail run be?"

"Hard to say. They're a bit quicker now, maybe three, four days. All we can do is wait."

He got up off the floor, lifted the pouch over his shoulder, reached for his hat.

"I'll be back soon. Once I deliver this, I'll come help you get the house ready. Anything you need?"

"No, I have it all. It should be a nice dinner, we'll try to make it a fun evening. The piano should be here soon; the church is sending it over in a wagon."

"The piano?"

"I thought it might be nice, some music . . . this doesn't have to be a sad evening."

"But it will be. This whole thing is sad. But yes, music will be nice. You've been practicing?"

"Win, if you came to church more regularly, you would hear quite an improvement in my playing. If I know soldiers, and my playing is not satisfactory, there will be at least one of you who will show me how it's done."

He laughed, pulled open the door. "Soon."

She pushed the door closed behind him and locked it, her habit now. Her mind began to work, to plan. She mentally counted heads, went back to the kitchen, the pantry, lifted a small sack of flour, put it down heavily on the thick wood table. She reached up to a high shelf, brought down a large clay bowl, set it by the flour, then paused and thought of Armistead, waiting with a bright smile, the eagerness of a child, as she kept him waiting, waiting for the cookies to cool. He would eat an entire sheet full if she let him, and so she would make him wait, torture him playfully with the smell, until he begged, please. Then finally she would produce the flat pan, and he would gobble the first one in one bite, then savor the rest, slowly. Win would have to wait until Lewis picked out the ones he wanted, the big ones, before he could get to them. She smiled, thought, yes, I'll make those too. It would be good to see him smile again.

THEY BEGAN TO ARRIVE ABOUT SIX. HANCOCK ANSWERED THE door, opened to see officers in civilian clothes.

"Mr. Garnett, Mr. Wiggins, welcome, come in."

"Thank you, Captain. Mighty fine of you to do this. Most kind." The men entered the house.

Hancock pointed to a small table, bottles and glasses, said, "Wine, gentlemen? Help yourself. Mrs. Hancock will be bringing out some trays of food . . . ahh, here."

Mira entered from the kitchen, brought a large platter of bread and cheese, set it down on another table, and the men bowed to her, a short, formal greeting, and then reached for the wine.

Hancock heard a carriage, looked out through the screen, saw

Johnston climbing down with a large bundle of flowers wrapped in brightly colored paper. Hancock did not see the staff officers, and felt relief, for there would be plenty of food now, the house would not be so crowded. With generals, you never knew what they assumed. Johnston came to the door, Hancock stood back, and Johnston held out a large hand. Hancock took it, and both men knew they were not yet enemies.

"Please, allow me to present these to our hostess."

"Certainly. She is back in the kitchen . . . come. . . ."

"No, I'll wait here. Don't want to interfere."

Mira appeared again, brought another bottle of wine, and Johnston made a great show, a low sweeping bow. "On behalf of all the new civilians who have gathered here this evening, we offer you this gift, our warmest thanks for your fine hospitality."

"Well, goodness, Mr. Johnston, thank you, these are quite impressive."

She took the flowers, saw the variety, knew this had taken some time, and carried them back into the kitchen to find a vase.

"Tell me, Captain, in all honesty. This party was her idea, was it not?"

Hancock was still by the door, looking outside for one more guest.

"Well, now that you mention it, yes, I must confess. I'm not a big party man myself."

"Quite all right, Mr. Hancock. I don't believe any of us have felt much like celebrating, certainly not now. I appreciate your wife's sense of sentiment. It's important we don't forget . . . that we can do this . . . that we are all still friends."

Outside, horses rode up, two more officers in civilian clothes. Hancock tried to recall the names, men from Benicia. Johnston moved up closer, followed Hancock's gaze, said, "Ah . . . Captain Douglas . . . that is, Mr. Douglas. Mr. Harrison. Good, good. Hope you don't mind, Captain. They came down this morning, on the steamer. I asked them to join me here."

"Not at all, *General*." Hancock laughed, and Johnston got the joke, nodded.

"Yes, well, we do cut a wide swath, Captain."

Hancock welcomed the men, and after greetings were exchanged all around, Hancock said to Johnston, "Will there be more, *sir*?"

"No, not tonight. There's a few more arriving tomorrow, another boat." Johnston seemed more serious now.

Hancock said, "So, when do you leave?"

Johnston looked at him, and the sound of voices behind him grew, the talk of soldiers, glasses of wine moving about. He said quietly, "How did you know I was leaving?"

"I have many good friends here, Mr. Johnston."

"It's not what I had hoped for. This place doesn't offer what I had . . . well . . . it's not important."

He turned, left Hancock at the door, went to the table where the half-empty wine bottle waited. He poured a glass, the others gathered around him, and Johnston joined the party. Hancock turned, looked outside again, the sun was on the far trees, and the light was slipping away.

Mira appeared again, brought out more wine, to the great happiness of the men, and Hancock watched them toast her, a rowdy salute. She glanced at him, knew he did not share the mood, and he turned again and looked out, waiting.

The horse came at a slow trot, and Hancock did not recognize him at first, had not seen him in civilian clothes for a long time. He pulled the horse into Hancock's yard, dismounted by the others, unhooked a hanger, a thin bag, from the side of the saddle, carried it carefully above the ground, then saw Hancock standing, waiting at the door.

"Good evening, Captain. Sorry to be late. I had to stand over my aide to get him to clean this just right. Couldn't give it to you dirty."

Armistead passed through the door, did not look at Hancock's face, and Hancock closed the door, followed him into the party.

The men gathered around the new arrival. A glass was presented, and Mira came out of the back, the men parting. She hugged him, and the others began to make the sound, the rowdy hoots, then saw that she was crying and quickly stopped. The room was silent for a long pause.

Mira stood back, smiled through red eyes, said, "Gentlemen, we have a great deal more wine."

The men began to loosen again, and Armistead raised his free hand, said, "No, wait. I have a special presentation to make." The men quieted again, and Armistead turned to Hancock and held out the hanger. Hancock took the cloth bag, slid it from around the contents, saw: Armistead's uniform.

"Captain Hancock, it is the sincerest wish and boldest prediction of those present that you will not remain a captain forever. In anticipation of the army's wisdom, and in the interest of eliminating the normal administrative delays, I present you with the uniform of a major. Congratulations in advance."

There was applause, and Hancock ran his hand over the blue cloth, saw the gold oak leaf on the shoulder, looked at Armistead, who held up a glass of wine and nodded slightly. Hancock smiled and looked at Mira, who applauded as well, and he moved forward, closer to the men, and joined the party.

IT WAS CLOSE TO MIDNIGHT.

"Gentlemen, another toast, to our hostess."

"Yes! Hear! Hear!"

Mira had finished her work, had let the empty platters and used glasses gather in the kitchen. Her only distraction now was the children, and she slipped away, back to their room, checking, astonished at the soundness of their sleep, what with the noise from the front of the house. She watched the angelic faces, thought, We will pay for this in the morning, probably very early in the morning.

She went back to the front room, saw the door opened, men saluting with a drunken stagger, laughing and good humor, and the party grew smaller, then smaller again.

There had been piano playing earlier, lively songs and bad singing, and Mira had been right, the men had taken over, some reminiscing about old drinking halls and indiscreet women, brought to life again with poor examples of musical skill.

There were only a few remaining. Johnston sat in the corner, propped up by a firm grip on an empty wineglass, nodding peacefully to the conversation of the others, betrayed only when he could not rise to salute departing guests.

Hancock was closing the door, moved toward the wine bottle, and now Mira saw Armistead across the room, watching him. They had not spoken, had not been together all night, and she knew it would come, that it was too close, too deep to share with the others. Then she remembered, turned quickly and went back to the kitchen. She reached behind the cloth curtain of a high cupboard, brought out a straw basket, white linen, a soft cradle for the batch of cookies. She carried them gently, moved back toward the party, and Armistead was waiting for her.

"I wondered how long it would take."

"You knew I made these?"

"I smelled them the minute I entered the house. You live around soldiers as long as I have, the smell of anything else is a piece of heaven." She pulled back the flap of linen, and he reached in, grabbed one, stuffed it in his mouth, then grabbed a handful, counted the remainder.

"Hmm, there's . . . six more. Two for Win, two for you . . ." He glanced over his shoulder, saw no one else worthy. "I guess the last two are for me." He reached for a cloth napkin, wrapped his treasure gently, pulled a small parcel from his coat pocket, making room for the feast. He held the parcel up, stared at it, said slowly, serious now, "My dear Mrs. Hancock, I have something for you. I would be honored if you would be the caretaker of this. . . ." He handed her the parcel, wrapped in layers of white tissue, tied with a small string. "There are some things I wish you to keep. Please . . . would you see to it that this be given to my family . . . in the event I do not survive this war?"

"Certainly, Lewis." She took the parcel, looked at him, thought, He is not drunk. She had watched him sip from a single glass of wine for over an hour.

"Lewis . . . when are you two going to talk?"

"My dear Mrs. Hancock, would you do us the honor of playing some more? This party seems to have dwindled a tad." He exaggerated the soft drawl, and she nodded, knew not to push. She looked across the room at her husband, who stood over Johnston, a meaningless conversation so that he did not have to face Armistead.

She moved to the piano, gathered in her dress, sat on the small bench and looked up at Armistead. "What would you like to hear?"

"Something quiet . . ." He looked over at Hancock. "Something . . . appropriate."

She thought, flipped through the music books that had come with the piano, came to one book, thin and coverless, and the book fell open at her touch. She saw the title, "Kathleen Malvourneen," and softly touched the keys, began to sing quietly. She did not want to interrupt the others, the conversations. Suddenly, the room was quiet, her voice calling them together:

"Kathleen Malvourneen, the gray dawn is breaking,
The horn of the hunter is heard on the hill,
The lark from her light wing the bright dew is shaking,
Kathleen Malvourneen, what? Slumb'ring still?
Kathleen Malvourneen, what? Slumb'ring still.
Oh, hast thou forgotten how soon we must sever?
Oh, hast thou forgotten this day we must part?

It may be for years, and it may be forever;
Then why art thou silent, thou voice of my heart?
It may be for years and it may be forever;
Then why art thou silent, Kathleen Malvourneen. . . ."

Hancock moved close to her, stood by her side, and he looked at Armistead, the tanned, rugged face, and saw that Armistead was crying, staring down at the piano, at Mira's soft hands on the keys. Hancock moved around behind her, put a hand on Armistead's shoulder, and Armistead looked up. Hancock saw the pain, saw him shake slightly. Armistead fell forward, put his head on Hancock's chest, and Hancock wrapped his arms around his friend, felt his own tears, could not ignore it any longer, knew this would be the last time.

Mira played the song again, did not sing, felt them standing behind her, heard the soft sounds, and after a minute Armistead took a deep breath, composed himself and stood back, keeping his hand on Hancock's shoulder.

"I must do what I am meant to do. I hope you will never know . . . you will never feel what this has cost me. If I ever . . . raise my hand . . . against you . . . may God strike me dead." He looked down, saw Mira's upturned face, the soft eyes, said again, *"May God strike me dead."*

HE RODE HARD, SPURRED THE BLACK MULE DEEP IN ITS haunches, leaned forward as the animal strained its way up the steep hills, the rocky ground. Behind him was the town, the tile roofs of Los Angeles, smaller now and far below. He rode up higher, along any trail that led up, any trail the mule could climb. He reached a long crest, could see the other side now, to the east, the wide, flat desert, and he stopped, felt the mule breathing under him, gasping for thin air.

He climbed down from the tired animal, felt better now, relaxed, his anger drained by the long climb. He looked around, was not sure exactly where he was, looked back to the west, over the town, could see the coastline, the distant islands off the coast, and he thought, My God, this is a beautiful spot.

He climbed a big rock, pulled himself up with his hands, found a flat place on top and sat down. It was cooler now, he was far above the choking heat of the summer sun. He looked at the mule, grateful, and the mule seemed refreshed as well, began to poke its nose around the rocks, looking for anything green.

He turned back to the east again, to the dull flatness, thought of the Indians, the only people out there, wondered how far you would have to go to see a white man. But you would not go, because before the Indians would bother you, the desert itself would take you, bake you in suffocating heat. He turned slightly, could see more to the south, long rows of mountains fading, smooth and round, not like the stark roughness he had seen in Wyoming, in Utah. He gazed over the smaller peaks, toward the far trails that had carried some of them back East, the long routes through Arizona and Texas where the new soldiers of the South would be welcomed to the new war.

He reached into his coat, pulled the envelope from his pocket, opened it again, held the letter up to the sunlight behind him, read it again, calmer this time, no surprises.

> Captain Winfield S. Hancock, Chief Quartermaster, Department of Southern California.
>
> You are hereby ordered to report to the Quartermaster General, Washington, pursuant to your assignment as Supply Officer, the Department of Kentucky, General Robert Anderson, Commanding.

He read it again, stared at the words "Supply Officer." He looked up, stared out at the wide, clear space, said aloud, *"Damn!"*

He folded the letter, put it in his pocket, thought of Mira. She had always been right, always said, "You are too good at your job." He wondered how many old soldiers, former soldiers, friends of politicians—anyone looking for a place in the new pages of glory—how many had volunteered to be *supply officers*? And worse, Hancock knew that without good supply officers, the army would not function, and so, of course, that was where they would send him. But it was not where he wanted to go.

He thought of Mexico, of his long fight to be sent there. He had been assigned as a recruitment officer, to sign up new volunteers for the war, and he was too good at that as well, made himself indispensable. Finally, after long months of tormenting his superiors, he had been assigned to the Sixth, and had accompanied some of his recruits south to join Scott's army. He'd been in the good fight too, the key battles around Mexico City, had led infantry into stupid assaults, ordered by bad generals who did not understand that you did not push your outnumbered troops straight into fortified positions, and so many had died. Hancock had brought that home with him, would always know what it was like, *out there*, in front of the lines. And so it was difficult to live with the peace, more difficult than he could ever admit to Mira. He tried not to see Armistead's face—he was gone, probably in Virginia by now—but Hancock knew: Armistead would *fight*, it was all he was, and unless Washington noticed him in the great crowd of the growing army, Hancock would have to settle for being a supply officer.

He stood up, high on the perch, felt a sudden breeze, balanced himself, could see down, through a small canyon, sharp, steep rocks. Steady, he thought. No need to end up down *there*. He eased himself down from the big rock. The mule was ignoring him, had found a small patch of coarse grass, tugged at it noisily, and Hancock put his hand on the animal's back, looked back to the town, thought, I suppose we will miss it here, the weather, good friends. But I have never been in one place for long, that's just not the way the army works.

He climbed up on the mule, which raised its head and turned to look at him. Hancock saw something that looked like annoyance, and he laughed, patted the animal's neck, said aloud, "Yes, my friend, you have your duty as well. Now, I would appreciate it if you would remove us from this big damned hill without any major injury. Then you may carry me home. I have to tell my wife we're leaving."

15. LEE

July 21, 1861

Lieutenant Taylor moved with noisy haste, bounded up the stairs to the old office building, his boots echoing in heavy steps down the wide hallway to Lee's office. Lee heard him coming, looked up from his writing to see the young man stumble around the corner, supporting himself against the doorway, gasping for breath.

"Lieutenant, are you all right?"

"Sir . . . the War Department . . . it's an attack . . ."

"Slowly, Lieutenant. There's been an attack on the War Department?"

"No, sir . . ." Taylor panted, then adjusted himself, took a long, deep breath. "Sir, I was just at the War Department, delivering the dispatches as you requested. There is a great deal of . . . activity there. I stayed as close as I could, and heard the staff relaying messages from General Beauregard. It seems, sir, that he is being attacked. I heard them talking about General McDowell moving against our forces at Manassas Gap, sir. Beauregard . . . that is, General Beauregard, is calling urgently for reinforcements from General Johnston."

Lee stared at the young man, who was still trying to catch his breath.

Lee knew the attack made sense, the Manassas Gap Railroad was a key strategic position below the Potomac. McDowell's Federal forces had stayed to the north far longer than Lee had expected, and he assumed that the same political pressure that the Confederate Army had endured, the wild calls for mindless attack, had been just as loud in Washington, and so McDowell's forces finally were moving southward.

Joe Johnston had withdrawn out of Harper's Ferry, south to Winchester, protecting the Shenandoah Valley, but now it was apparent that McDowell had focused closer to Richmond, on Manassas, and so Johnston would be called to move in next to Beauregard.

Lee thought it through, glanced up at the map on his wall, the markings of troop placements. If McDowell's troops pushed through the Confederate line, there would be little to stop the Federals from marching straight into Richmond. Lee stood, closer to the map, went over the defensive lines again, thought, We are in place, we have the ground. Now we will find out if we have an army.

Taylor watched Lee, knew when to be quiet. Finally, Lee turned to him, said, "I suggest we make our way over to the President's office."

"Yes, sir, right behind you, sir."

Lee led the young man through the hall, down the steps, and immediately there was a sense of action. The street was alive, everyone was in a hurry. He moved quickly, felt the energy, began to run now, a bouncing step up into the administration building. Taylor stayed close behind, marveled at Lee's enthusiasm, smiled a wide grin, felt, finally, this was what it was about, the real duty of a soldier.

Lee approached the wide doors of Davis's office, saw couriers, a steady flow of men moving from the office, new orders and fresh legs, and finally made his way through the noise and activity. Davis was standing tall above the others, and Lee waited, thought, Wait for the right moment.

Then Davis saw him, his eyes fierce, flashing, and he shouted above the others, "General Lee, we are in a fight!" Lee moved closer, and the office began to clear out, quieter, and Davis said, "I'm heading up to the front, to Manassas. I can't just . . . sit here. I have a train leaving immediately."

Lee waited, felt the intensity, knew Davis shared his anxieties, which most of the others did not feel—that they were an unorganized, untested force, and that one great battle could decide the issue; the entire rebellion could end here.

Lee felt a strange urge, suddenly held out his hand, a warm gesture, affection for a man who did not show affection. Davis took the hand, political reflex, did not look at Lee, passed by him, hurried out. Lee turned to Taylor, saw a puzzled look, and then they both knew what was happening, that Davis was gone.

Lee moved out, past Taylor, into the outer office, and saw the last of Davis's staff close the broad door.

"Sir, we must . . . we can't stay here."

"Lieutenant, it is clear that this is our post. Our duty is in Richmond."

"But, sir, there is an attack. . . ."

"We have good men in command, Lieutenant. It is their battle now."

Lee felt the energy drain from his body, the familiar hollowness. Do not focus on this, he thought. This was, after all, not the issue. He walked outside, saw wagons and horses moving, streams of people, all moving toward the trains, all rushing to the great battle.

"Sir, with your permission."

Lee turned to Taylor, saw the youth, the wounded look, knew he had to go, to be a part. He nodded. "Yes, Lieutenant, you are authorized to join in the fight. Find an infantry unit, give the commander my compliments. They will find a place for you."

"Sir!" Taylor saluted, made a high yelp, turned and ran toward the depot. Lee watched him, all long legs and wild leaps, and he turned toward his office and walked across the wide street, against the flow of people rushing out from his building.

THERE WAS A DEATHLY SILENCE. LEE STOOD AT HIS WINDOW, above the empty street, felt amazingly alone. The city seemed abandoned. He had spent the day in feeble attempts at work, could not sit, went to the window every few minutes, and when there was nothing to see, would return to his desk and try again to attack the papers.

He stood back from the window, went, again, to the map, considered the lines, *his* lines, the defensive design he had put into place, now being commanded by others, others who would receive the credit if the positions were good, if he had chosen the right ground. No, he would not think of that. It does not matter who does the duty, he thought, if the duty is done. I am here because God wants me here, I will serve in other ways. He repeated that, had repeated it all day, trying to ease his feelings, the sense that he was out of place.

The long day began to dim, and he watched the sunset all the way to the darkness, and still there had been no news. He realized for the first time that there were people still, downstairs, in some of the other offices, but no one brought him any information. They probably did not know he was there. Hungry, he decided to go back to the

Spottswood, pondered the long walk, heard a long low whistle, and from the north saw a distant flicker of light. The train moved closer, into the station beyond the buildings. Lee stared, listened, heard more whistles now, and then he saw a rider in a furious gallop. The man rode up close to Lee's building, dismounted and yelled something Lee could not understand, then was gone, into the offices below. Lee started for his door, waited, heard more noise, another rider, several horses now. People began to come out, to fill the street. He went back to the window, was surprised to see so many, had assumed most of them were gone. There were cheers, wild cries, and he could not stand it anymore, left his office and went down to the dark, lamplit street.

Spotting a uniform, a young bearded man covered in dirt, he asked, "Soldier, do you bring news of the battle?"

The man looked exhausted, regarded Lee with wild joy. "We whipped 'em, we whipped 'em good. They's a-runnin' back to Washington, hee hee."

Lee put his hands on the man's shoulders. "Please, can you be more detailed?"

Lee felt the man squirm, itching to get away, to join the growing celebration in the street around them, but he stilled under Lee's grasp.

"Yes, sir. It was General Jackson. Saved the day, he did. Drove them bluebellies all the way back to Washington! They's sayin' he stood his men up like a stone wall!" The man slipped away, a quick turn and Lee could not hold him. He let the man go, but he could not celebrate, had to know more than rumors.

He left the street, went back up to his office. Through the window he could see wagons now, crowds of people returning from the battle. He heard another train whistle, knew this would go on all night, and he would have to wait till tomorrow to find out the details. He sat back in his chair, stared at a dark ceiling, thought of the lone soldier, his only piece of news, and kept hearing the words: General Jackson saved the day.

The Federal forces had fled from the first major battle of the war in a complete panic. The troops under Beauregard and Johnston did not pursue, ordered into inactivity by generals who did not understand how completely they had won the day. The lack of action now spread over the armies like a thick blanket. Thousands of spectators had lined the edges of the battlefield at Manassas, only to view incredible horrors that none had anticipated. After the battle both sides seemed infected with a gloom, a sense that this was now very real, the abstract political rhetoric replaced with the clear, sickening knowledge that many men were going to die.

16. HANCOCK

SEPTEMBER 1861

THE CARRIAGE BROUGHT THEM TO THE FRONT STEPS OF THE Willard Hotel, a white brick building that stood over a wide square. Mira was helped from the carriage by the firm hand and pleasant smile of the doorman, a tall black man in a foolish top hat, who bowed deeply as he released her. Hancock climbed out the other side, watched as the man picked their bags from the rear of the carriage, thought of offering to help, but the man was gone, up the short stairs, into the hotel.

"Well, my husband, this is not at all what you expected, is it?"

He looked around, saw people in all forms of dress, some hurrying, some in a leisurely stroll through the square, down the broad streets of Washington.

"No. This is . . . strange."

From the moment of their arrival in New York, and all during the train trip to the capital, they had heard the rumors: a city under siege, the savage rebel army on the outskirts, a general panic. Hancock knew not to trust rumors, but in some ways they made sense. He had read of the early skirmishes, unprepared armies colliding in sloppy battles like two small children in a fistfight, swinging wildly, arms flapping in a flurry of misdirected motion. But then there were the reports from Manassas, what the northern papers called Bull Run, where there were too many troops and too many bad generals, and one general in particular, Irvin McDowell, who believed the cocky assurances from the men in expensive suits, the congressmen and dignitaries who happily followed the army in grand carriages, who brought along their women, sitting under brightly colored parasols, watching the splendid event from a hillside; an eager audience, picnicking and partying as their gallant heroes under fluttering flags would crush the dirty riffraff of the rebellion.

It was McDowell who learned that the dirty little rebel army had come to fight, would not run from the loud brass bands or the neat lines of blue troops, and were not there to perform for his audience. The bloody rout sent the Union troops back through their admirers in a panic, and the stunned audience was swarmed by the real sounds of war, loud piercing screams, the cries of wounded and terrified men. They saw blood, great bursts of red covering the troops and the ground, and the men in the fancy suits did not cheer, but pulled their women back, moving with the great flow of panic back into the city, pursued by the brutal honesty of death.

And so, the rumors had flown. This army of savages was on the brink, ready to overwhelm the decent people of Washington. But the attack hadn't come, and while Hancock had not expected the rumors to be accurate, he was amazed at the calmness, the jovial mood of the people, still so close to the bloody fields.

"Very strange." He moved around the carriage. Mira took his arm and they went up into the hotel.

The man behind the desk glanced at his uniform, noticed it was not new, seemed surprised, and Hancock now saw that the lobby was filled with officers, men with loud voices, crisp blue coats, the men of the new army. No one noticed him, and he did not think of saluting anyone, though he passed by men of high rank, men who were strutting about like swollen birds.

"Excuse me, we have sent word . . . we have a room, I believe?"

The clerk looked at him again, then saw Mira. His eyes brightened and he nodded in her direction. "Name?"

"Captain Winfield Hancock. And Mrs. Hancock."

"Hmmm, let's see . . . oh, here. Yes, you have Room 6D."

The man motioned to a waiting bellman, another black man in a formal gray suit and red hat, who had been waiting for the cue. The man picked up their bags and led them to the stairway. Hancock paused, glanced out through the noisy throng of uniforms, thought there might be someone he knew, some familiar face. But he recognized no one, saw officers speaking to civilians, men with pads of paper, reporters, of course. He turned back to Mira, who was waiting for him, smiling.

"Let's go up to the room, please. I'm covered with dust."

He felt her arm in his again, and she pulled him along, following the bellman. The man led them up to their room, pushed open the heavy oak door and led them inside. Mira directed the placement of the bags, and Hancock went to the window, looked out to the street, the rooftops, saw the larger buildings, the grand spectacle of the Capitol building, the great white monuments to the government he served. He began to feel a hopelessness, a dark futility, surrounded not by the symbols of his country, the great cause of the Union, but by men sealed away in their offices, men who made decisions based on the preservation of their jobs, men who would distrust Albert Sidney Johnston and could never understand the passion of Lewis Armistead, and so they did not understand that they were in great danger, that this army was in for a real fight and could not be run by puppets and peacocks.

He did not notice the bellman leave, suddenly felt her hand, sliding up his back to his shoulder. He wrapped an arm around her waist, pulled her in tightly, and she said, "It seems so quiet . . . like there is no war at all."

"I know. A few weeks ago, the bloodiest battle ever fought on this land took place a few miles from here, and they have already forgotten."

"Maybe it's better forgotten."

"No, it is better remembered. Because if they don't, it will happen again, and keep on happening until they realize . . . this is a war. The Southerners are not an unruly mob that comes at us with sticks and torches. They have leaders, men who know how to take men into combat. Those men downstairs . . . in the lobby . . . those men have never led anything . . . and they will learn what that can cost."

She looked up at him, saw his hard stare, and she felt him tighten, his jaw clench. She said, "You won't be content to be a supply officer. . . ."

There was a long pause, and he took a deep breath. "I have never been content to be a supply officer."

"Then *tell* them. Volunteer for something else."

He dropped his arm, turned away from her, from the window. "I'm not a politician. I don't have the friends, the pull, that those people . . . downstairs have. I have been given a job, and ultimately it comes down to that, to do what the army orders me to do."

She moved toward him, and the sun came in behind her, silhouetting her. He reached out, touched her face with gentle hands, and there was a knock at the door.

He stared at her a moment longer, then turned, pulled open the heavy door, and was surprised to see an older man, an officer.

"Forgive me . . . are you Captain Hancock?"

"Yes, please come in."

The man moved quickly, then saw Mira and looked uncomfortable. "Forgive the intrusion, Captain, they told me downstairs you just arrived. We've been waiting for you."

"We, being . . . ?"

"I am Colonel Randolph Marcy, General McClellan's chief of staff."

"General McClellan?"

"Yes, Captain. The general has sent me to request that you not report anywhere until the general can see you."

"Forgive me, Colonel Marcy, but I am not familiar with a *General* McClellan. I knew of a McClellan in Mexico, knew him at the Point. . . ."

"You have had a long journey, Captain. General George McClellan has been appointed Commander of the Army, to assume those duties General Scott is . . . no longer . . ." He paused, did not want to say the words. "You *are* familiar with General Scott?"

Hancock nodded. "Of course, sir. Forgive me. I have been out of touch."

"Quite all right, Captain. Events occur at a rapid pace these days. The President feels that General McClellan is more suited to the operation of an effective fighting force than is General Scott. General Scott is . . . beyond his time, wouldn't you agree?"

"If that is the President's judgment."

"General McClellan will send word to you here. Again, forgive the intrusion." He turned to Mira, bowed, said a curt "Madam," and backed out the door.

Hancock went back to the window, began to feel hot, blood rising in the back of his neck. "So, we have a real war, and they shove aside the only real warrior we have."

"What do you suppose General McClellan wants with you, dear? He said they were waiting for you. It sounds terribly important."

"McClellan. I remember him now, feisty little fellow, a couple years behind me. Brilliant . . . graduated at the top of his class, should have stayed in the army. I think he went up north somewhere, ran a railroad or something. Now he's the commanding general?"

"And he wants to see *you*."

THERE WAS CONSTANT MOTION, MEN MOVING IN ALL DIRECTIONS, office doors opening and closing in a jerky rhythm, the manic activity of headquarters. Hancock felt suddenly embarrassed, saw the clean blue coats, the sharp gold braids, knew his uniform was a bit ragged. There had not been time to have it cleaned, the call from McClellan coming the morning after Marcy's visit. The best he could do was a clean white shirt, and he saw they all had clean white shirts.

"This way, Captain. The general can see you now."

He was led by a young major, another new uniform, past aides and piles of paperwork, desks covered with lists and figures, paperwork he knew well.

McClellan sat behind a massive desk, shiny mahogany trimmed with gold-painted strips of wood shaped like the braids of a rope. The office was full of men, and McClellan was signing orders and requisitions, handed to him by each man in succession. Hancock was instantly impressed, knew the efficiency of motion, felt he was indeed in the presence of a commander.

"General, sir, this is Captain Hancock."

McClellan looked up, did not rise, pointed to a chair without speaking, and the major followed the instructions, pulled the chair out, motioned for Hancock to sit.

McClellan did not stop working, did not send the men away, and Hancock knew that whatever the reason for this visit, it would not be private.

"Captain, we are building an army here. A good army. A goddamned big army. You understand that?"

Hancock cleared his throat, tried to make himself heard above the noise of the staff.

"Yes, sir. I can see that, sir."

"Do you know what goes into this, Mr. Hancock? Well, of course you do, you're a damned quartermaster. Best in the army, I've heard."

Hancock did not feel complimented, instead felt a small, cold hole in his stomach. He thought, He wants me to be a quartermaster general. A tremendous need, and you can do it, you're the right man for it, for quite possibly the worst job in the army. He waited for more, saw the papers flow across McClellan's desk in a smooth stream, stopping only for a brief glance, a short explanation, and a quick stroke of black ink.

"They don't understand, you know. They have no idea."

Hancock looked at the face, the eyes that were not looking at him but darted at the papers, piercing and aware. Hancock said only, "Sir?"

"The politicians. The President. They have no idea what this army needs. *None.* No idea what this war is about . . . what we are up against. You cannot command from an office, from a comfortable backside, Mr. Hancock. I believe you know that."

"Yes, sir. I suppose I do."

"The President has called for seventy-five thousand troops. We need three times that, and more. The rebel army that sits right out there, right across that river, numbers over two hundred thousand, gets stronger every day. If we don't move on them, and move with a well-trained, well-equipped, and well-commanded force, we will be massacred. You hear about Bull Run?"

"Yes, sir. I read the reports on the trip east."

"Bloody disaster. Could have been worse . . . they could have marched right into Washington. Hell, they could have marched all the way to New York! Point is, we weren't ready, and they were. No more of that. This is my command now."

Hancock was beginning to relax, began to feel part of the office, the flow of activity, knew McClellan understood. "How may I help, sir?"

McClellan looked at him, shifted his attention away from the papers for the first time. "You know why I called you here?"

"No, sir. I assume, sir, because you want me to assist the quartermaster—"

"Quartermaster? That's for clerks. I have plenty of clerks, Mr. Hancock. I need soldiers. I need men who fought in Mexico, who know what gunfire sounds like, men who don't run when the enemy shoots at them. So far, this army hasn't shown much stomach for a real fight. This whole damned city is filling up with officers, men who can't wait to be heroes, who have no idea *how*. We need leaders, Mr. Hancock. I believe that includes you."

Hancock sat up straighter, felt a new stirring in his gut, said, "I have received orders . . . to report to General Anderson . . . as his supply officer. Does the general have a new assignment for me?"

"Anderson? Good man. Held on at Fort Sumter without losing a man. So, now the War Department sticks him out there in Kentucky, when we need him right here. Mr. Hancock, do you know General 'Baldy' Smith . . . William Smith?"

"Not well. He was at the Point, a year behind me. I can't say I've heard anything about his career in the army."

"Of course not. He barely has one. But he has friends in important places, and so the War Department has given him a division. Never mind that he's barely led anybody anywhere. The department specializes in rewarding politicians. Point is, Smith needs some brigade commanders, men who *do* know how to lead, men who can keep him out of trouble. That's you, Mr. Hancock. I am recommending to the President that you be promoted to Brigadier General and assigned to General Smith's division."

"Brigadier General? Sir, I'm only a captain."

"There is a war, Mr. Hancock. Look around you. You can't fire a cannon down any street in Washington without hitting a newly appointed general. Your promotion will have no difficulty. You are, after all, one of the few around here who is a real soldier. I am grateful for your service, Mr. Hancock."

McClellan turned back to his papers. Impatient aides moved closer to the desk, and the procession began again. Hancock felt overwhelmed, wanted to say something appropriate, saw that the moment was passing, the army was moving on in front of him.

"Sir . . . General, I am honored."

"It is we who are honored. We have a difficult job to do, Mr. Hancock. We have enemies in front of us and behind us. It is the army, alone, that must win this war. Are you with me, Mr. Hancock?"

Hancock did not understand McClellan's concerns, but let the words go, understood that he had been given an extraordinary opportunity, the chance, again, to be a soldier. He stood, saluted, said, "Certainly, sir. I am with you."

McClellan glanced up, returned the salute, then the young major was by his side. He placed a hand on Hancock's arm, a subtle pull, and Hancock knew it was time to leave. He turned, nodded to the young man's expressionless face, then made his way through the blue coats, passed through the maze of offices, past a line of well-dressed civilians, waiting to see Someone Important. He found the crowded stairway which led him back outside, into the clear September morning.

Hancock moved with long strides, passing statues and small patches of green grass, crossing the wide streets, dodging horses and wagons carrying soldiers. He knew Mira would be waiting for him, anxious, staring out the window of their room, looking at the soldiers, trying to spot him in the crowds below. He hurried now, hopped up the curb, glanced up at the windows of the hotel, could not see her, too much glare. He pushed into the lobby, saw more blue coats, women in bright dresses gathered around the men who posed and preened, and he made his way toward the stairs, rounded a corner and bumped into a man, a uniform.

The man turned, saw Hancock's insignia, sniffed, said, "Watch where you're going, there, *Captain*. I'm the new *colonel* of the Forty-ninth Ohio Volunteers. I suggest that if you are going to survive in this army, you learn to respect your superiors."

Hancock stepped back. "Sorry," he said, then looked at the soft, pale dough of the man's face, the short round body, recalled McClellan's words, thought, Which way will *you* run when the cannons fire?

AS THE MONTHS PASSED, THE CONFEDERATE ARMY ALLOWED ITS first great advantage, the hot surge of momentum, to slip away, and Lee had been right after all, the war would last well beyond the twelve-month terms of the volunteers.

As Lee had experienced in the new Confederate Army, the clash of egos, the struggle of ambitious men with private agendas, had rendered quick actions and smooth organization impossible. It was no different in the North. General McClellan had finally been persuaded to make another major move, a new offensive strategy designed to capture Richmond. Moving his entire army by boat to the Virginia peninsula, he would invade from the east coast, up the rivers, driving the small Confederate forces inland. It was a long winter of inactivity, while both sides waited for McClellan to finally do something with his huge army.

17. LEE

April 1862

THROUGHOUT THE WINTER MONTHS, LITTLE HAD CHANGED FOR Lee. He had officially been named Davis's military adviser, which still meant that he continued to perform those duties that Davis didn't want.

Joe Johnston was named commander of all forces in the northern Virginia area, and Beauregard, whose ego would predictably clash with Johnston's, was transferred to command of the army of northern Mississippi. With the new movement by McClellan, the threat to Richmond had changed directions. There was a growing lack of confidence that McClellan's huge Federal force could be stopped.

Lee was the last to enter Davis's office, saw the men seated in a half-circle. He had grown accustomed to meetings such as this being affairs that were anything but friendly and sociable. Davis sat behind the big desk, rested his lean face sideways against one hand, appearing tired to Lee, and impatient. As Lee reached his own chair, he nodded to Joe Johnston, who sat upright, combative, glancing at Lee but not smiling. To Lee's right sat Secretary of War Randolph, a man Lee respected for his reasonableness and his seeming lack of political ambitions. Lee felt he could freely discuss his problems and strategies with Randolph, who, like him, could not escape the stranglehold that Davis maintained on military decision-making.

There were two other men, seated behind Johnston, and both of them stood when Lee entered. Lee knew one to be General Gustavus Smith. The other was introduced by Davis.

"General Lee, General Johnston has been accompanied by two of his ranking commanders. I believe you are acquainted with General Smith."

Lee nodded, Smith sat down, and Lee regarded the other man, much larger, a grim serious man who had been close to the fight.

"This is General James Longstreet."

Longstreet made a brief nod, Lee returned it pleasantly. Longstreet seemed surprised, curious at Lee's cordial greeting.

Both men sat, and Davis said, "Gentlemen, General Johnston has brought to Richmond grave concerns. He does not feel . . . well, General, I will not speak for you. Please inform us as to your need for this meeting." There was nothing pleasant in Davis's voice.

Johnston, who had small features and a short, pointed beard, stood and turned slightly, facing Lee and Randolph. Lee noticed the slight to Davis, saw Davis quietly move his chair to see Johnston's face.

"We are in the midst of the greatest crisis of our rebellion, the greatest crisis of my command. General McClellan is massing his entire army on the peninsula and will very soon be able to make a broad sweep, brushing our meager forces out of the way, until he sits gloating in this very office!"

There was no reply; Lee knew Johnston would have more.

"Our army is scattered so far and wide that we cannot possibly concentrate enough manpower to stop this assault. As we speak, the forces of General McDowell are moving toward Richmond from the northwest, clearly aiming to join flanks with McClellan's. When this happens, Richmond will be surrounded, cut off. It is clear to this command that we have but one alternative, and that is to pull forces from the southern coasts, from the Shenandoah Valley, the Carolinas, Tennessee . . . from any areas where troop positions are strong, and concentrate them for a great defense, the defense of Richmond!"

Lee looked at Davis, who did not speak. It was Secretary Randolph who broke the silence.

"General, do you propose to abandon Yorktown and Norfolk?"

"Of course. We cannot possibly hope to hold back McClellan's forces along the coast. His superior artillery will destroy our defenses there in short order."

Randolph spoke again. "Sir, I must disagree with your plan. If you pull out of Norfolk, we will lose the naval yard, the ships that are currently under construction. We will concede the absolute domination of the seas to the Federal navy. Their gunboats would then move up the James River unimpeded and be in position to shell the city."

"General Lee?" Davis said. "Do you have an opinion regarding General Johnston's plan?"

Lee knew that Johnston was too stubborn to hear alternatives, could not be persuaded away from his own plans. The friction between him and Davis was largely a result of Davis's insistence on keeping a hand in Johnston's operations. Johnston, rather than argue, would simply cut off communications, leaving Davis and Lee totally ignorant of planning and troop movements.

"Mr. President, I do not believe it is a wise course to remove our forces from the Southern coastline. We would be offering the Federal Army uncontested control of Savannah and Charleston. We are in a serious situation in Tennessee and Mississippi, and troops cannot be spared."

Davis nodded, said nothing. Johnston still stood, glared at Lee, said, "We have no choice but to concentrate our forces here, to defend Richmond, and if possible to strike out at the Federal Army from a strong position."

Lee glanced at Longstreet, knew of his good work at Manassas. He looked back to Davis, waited for some sign, some hint that Davis was going to take a stand. But the president sat still, leaned his head against his hand and stared straight ahead. Now, Lee realized that Davis would act when Johnston was not there. He had been pressed into silence by Johnston's grand pronouncement, would not enter into simple squabbles, on which Johnston seemed to thrive. Lee realized that this was Davis's way of maintaining control. The orders would be issued after the meeting was over, and Davis would not have to explain, could be direct, authoritative on paper, and not be challenged.

Lee felt a growing frustration, a sense that no one here was really in charge, that Johnston would go back to his troops and do precisely what he wanted, and if Davis pushed him, he would simply ignore it. Finally he spoke, carefully picking his words.

"General Johnston, it is my feeling that if we begin mass withdrawals, we will announce to the enemy our plans to settle into a defensive posture around Richmond. We will open up all avenues for him to move his troops, concentrating at his own pace and with his own methods. Is it not possible that, since we have already seen that General McClellan is prone to great caution, we might delay him even further by vigorously defending the peninsula? Is it not possible that we could then find opportunities to attack him, far from Richmond?"

Johnston smiled slightly, said, "Well, General Lee, I suppose from your vantage point here, that may seem like a workable strategy, but you can be sure that for us in the field, who confront the guns of the enemy, these decisions must take into account the overwhelming forces that face us. . . ."

Lee clenched his teeth, did not look at Johnston, heard the words flow out with oily smoothness, the patronizing tone that Johnston would use to disarm any disagreement to his plans. The men had been friends for thirty-five years, had gone through the Point together, through Mexico, and now Lee knew it would never be again. Johnston was alone, had cut off everyone, had placed himself in an isolated position from which he could not be moved.

Randolph spoke again, repeated his position, and General Smith made a comment, lamenting the thinness of his lines. Lee withdrew further, began to see the others from a long distance, the voices hollow and droning. Davis still would not speak, and Lee again watched Longstreet, who focused on each speaker with a determined stare.

The meeting lasted all afternoon, and finally Davis suggested a break for the evening meal. The men rose, limbered stiff legs, and began to file from the President's office.

As Johnston reached the door, Davis said, "General, Yorktown must not be abandoned."

Johnston spun around, faced Davis and said, "If I fight there, I will be pushed back, and then they will have Yorktown anyway." Davis did not speak, and Johnston turned and left the office.

Lee sensed Davis's anger, knew the two men would expend great energy on their differences, that Johnston had made it clear he would have his way, something Davis would not swallow. Lee suddenly realized that there might be an opportunity, and his mind began to move, the wheels of the engineer, as he formulated his own plan.

LEE AGREED WITH JOHNSTON THAT MCDOWELL'S FORCES WOULD try to link up with McClellan, that McClellan had shown he would not move forward until he had every piece of strength available. There was an opportunity to delay McClellan from moving by keeping McDowell away. The man in a position to do this was General Jackson.

McDowell's army was spread over an area that began in front of Jackson, in the Shenandoah Valley, and arched eastward, up toward Washington, then down near Fredericksburg, where they were a short march down the Rappahannock River from McClellan's right flank.

Lee was not in a position to give direct orders to Jackson, could not assume that authority without stepping on the toes of both Johnston and Davis. But he had seen Jackson's reports, his urgent requests to be allowed to attack the Federal forces in front of him. While Johnston

FEDERAL POSITION—
McCLELLAN'S INVASION OF
THE VIRGINIA PENINSULA
SOUTH MTN.
MARYLAND
Harpers Ferry
Baltimore
Winchester
Shenandoah Valley
BLUE RIDGE MTNS.
McDOWELL
Washington
Manassas
Junction
CHESAPEAKE BAY
Fredericksburg
Potomac River
Gordonsville
VIRGINIA
Rappahannock River
McCLELLAN
James River
Richmond
York River
Williamsburg
Yorktown
Petersburg
James River
Fort
Monroe
Newport News
Norfolk
N
0
25 Miles

maintained actual command over Jackson, and over General Ewell's division, which was positioned across the Blue Ridge near Jackson, Lee assumed that Johnston would be completely absorbed in his plans on the peninsula.

Because of his distance from Johnston, Jackson had been operating more or less as an independent force, and Johnston's lack of concern for correspondence included Jackson and Ewell. Thus, for long stretches the two commanders had no direct orders from Johnston. Lee saw the opportunity to fill that void.

Lincoln, and his Secretary of War, Stanton, had made it clear that the protection of Washington was a top priority. This was frequently discussed in Northern newspapers, which Lee occasionally saw. He began to reason that if Lincoln felt Washington was threatened, McDowell's troops would be withdrawn from Virginia and brought back closer to the capital. The best way Lee saw to convince Washington there was a threat was to allow Jackson to move aggressively north, attacking McDowell's forces at the mouth of the Shenandoah Valley.

Jackson had sent his own letters to Johnston, which had passed through Lee's offices, in which he stated his desire to attack the forces to his front. His reasons were clear: to stall any movement by McClellan. It was not difficult for Lee to "suggest" to Jackson what his course of action should be.

Jackson's small force had been used primarily to observe the movements of Federal troops in that area, but by adding Ewell's division, he would have nearly sixteen thousand troops, a sizable force when commanded by a man like Jackson, whose single-minded sense of aggression Lee was coming to appreciate.

The greatest threat to Lee's quiet plan was a sudden southward move by McDowell into the center of Virginia, down through Fredericksburg, which would cut off Jackson from Richmond and effectively cut Virginia in half. This was a risk Lee accepted, confident that the Federal commanders would remain as sluggish as they had always been.

JACKSON ACCEPTED LEE'S SUGGESTIONS AS THE AUTHORITY HE needed, and began a campaign that resulted in the defeat of four Federal armies, including Generals Milroy and Fremont, who threatened the valley to the west, plus the complete destruction of the forces under Generals Banks and Shields. With his force of sixteen thousand men, Jackson defeated and drove from the valley Federal forces numbering nearly seventy thousand. The defeat of Banks was so complete, and the retreating troops so panicked, that Banks's force was pushed all the way back across the Potomac. The response from Washington was as Lee had predicted. McDowell's movements were reversed and his forces were recalled to the defense of what Lincoln believed was Jackson's imminent assault on Washington. McClellan did not get his reinforcements, and so, true to form, McClellan did not attack.

In the newspapers and among the troops, both North and South, the name of Thomas "Stonewall" Jackson was becoming legendary.

LEE STOOD AS SECRETARY RANDOLPH ENTERED, THEN THE TWO men sat across the vast desk from President Davis.

Both men had been given a frantic summons, and Lee could see that Davis was not well. His thin face appeared hollow, his eyes dark and heavy. Davis sat with his hands under his chin, supporting his head only a few inches above the desk.

Randolph had just returned from Norfolk, to see for himself what dangers were threatening the naval yard, and his report to Davis had only added to the President's anxieties. While at Norfolk, Randolph received a courier from Johnston, ordering the troops there to withdraw from Norfolk. The message contained no other information, did not even advise where they should go. It was plain to Randolph that there was no Federal force threatening the city and there was no need to abandon the equipment at the yard. Randolph furiously issued an order countermanding Johnston's, so the valuable machinery could be moved before the city was evacuated.

Davis lifted his head, spoke slowly. "Gentlemen, my authority . . . is it plain to the two of you that I am the commander in chief?"

Lee glanced at Randolph, who nodded, said, "Yes, sir, of course."

"General Lee? Is it plain to you as well?"

"Certainly, Mr. President."

"Then can either of you explain to me why I am unable to persuade our General Johnston, our commanding general in the field, to inform us what he is doing? Have either of you been able to communicate with the general?"

Randolph said, "No, sir. It is most . . . difficult, sir. We have sent wires, couriers to his headquarters requesting his position . . . his intentions. He does not respond."

"Gentlemen, as you may know, we have received word that

Yorktown has been abandoned. General Lee, do you have some idea where our army might be headed?"

Lee had received only one communication from Johnston, a suggestion for a full-scale invasion of the North by an assembly of all the troops in the East, with a similar invasion of Ohio by the troops of the West. The suggestion had been so irrational, and without serious regard for the actual problems of moving troops, that Lee had not shown the letter to Davis. Lee now saw that regardless of the kind of collapse that was affecting Johnston, Davis was falling apart as well.

"Mr. President, I have not been informed of General Johnston's plans. We have . . . My staff has spoken with soldiers . . . men who have come from the front. . . . We have tried to put together some information from these stragglers—"

"Stragglers?" Davis's voice rose, cracked. He looked away, past the two men, spoke to no one. "We rely on the word of stragglers."

"Sir . . ." Randolph spoke with a gentle tone. "Sir, we must consider that if the general is in a full-scale retreat, the Federal Army could appear at the outskirts of Richmond at any time. This might well throw the city into a panic. It may be prudent for us to consider evacuating the city."

Lee stiffened. Randolph continued, "The general abandoned Yorktown because he had great fear of the Federal artillery, the guns from their ships. Those same guns will most certainly follow him up the James River. We cannot hope to defend Richmond against that kind of assault. The city could be destroyed."

Davis stared ahead, then turned to Lee. "General Lee, is it time for us to . . . evacuate?"

"I don't believe it is necessary quite yet, Mr. President. I agree that we must not make Richmond a battlefield, and it may be that General Johnston feels he is retreating from indefensible positions, but I do not share that view. If he has withdrawn completely from Yorktown, he may have established a defensive line at Williamsburg, using the fortifications constructed by General Magruder. If so, that should slow McClellan's advance even further. If he withdraws from Williamsburg, there are a number of other strong positions, still far enough from here to keep the city safe. Frankly, sir, I am pleased to see McClellan sitting where he is. His forces are spread across a part of Virginia that is very difficult for the movement of troops. The swamps, the wide creeks . . . he is vulnerable. If we can persuade General Johnston to stand his ground, McClellan will never get as far as Richmond."

Randolph looked at Lee, said, "We don't know where our troops are. How can you be sure we are capable of making a stand?"

"There are lines of defense . . . . every river, every stream—not only can we make a stand in that country, Mr. Secretary, but I believe that General McClellan can be pushed back, driven off the peninsula altogether. We have some good commanders leading good troops. We must persuade General Johnston of that fact."

Randolph turned back to Davis, shook his head. "I don't see how we can persuade General Johnston to do much of anything. We can't even get him to respond to our inquiries."

Lee looked at the faces of the two men, saw Davis staring blankly away. A sense of defeat hung in the air like a dark mist, and Lee could not sit still.

"If you will permit, sirs, I must return to my office."

Davis did not speak, continued his stare, and Randolph raised one hand slightly, a weak gesture, said only, "Good, General."

Lee walked across a darkening street, knew this day was over, nothing more would happen. He climbed up to his office and saw that his staff had already gone. He went to his window and looked out, past the government buildings. In the street below came a small group of soldiers, men who carried the dirt of the Virginia swamps, men who had left their army but had not walked far.

18. HANCOCK

April 1862

He sat on his new horse, a grouchy mare he called Annie. His men filed from the steamer, marched gladly down the long ramp, happy to leave the cramped ship. They formed in companies on the wharf, in front of the walls of Fort Monroe. They had come down the Potomac, had reached the mouth of the James, and now the pieces of McClellan's army would wait for the rest, until it was all assembled and the commander would begin his invasion up the peninsula.

Hancock watched them, the tight formation, the smooth movements. He had spent the long Washington winter training these men, and he knew that regardless of McClellan's fear of the enemy's superior preparations, his brigade was ready to fight.

Gradually, all four of his regiments were formed and began to march away from the wharf, creating space for more troops. He pulled his horse toward the colors of the Fifth Wisconsin, the first regiment to move out, rode up beside Colonel Amasa Cobb, a distinguished political leader before the war who had learned the art of drill only under Hancock's direction.

"Colonel, it's a fine morning, is it not?"

"General Hancock, sir, this unit is prepared. You shall be proud of us, sir."

Hancock looked back over the neat lines, the steady marching, officers on horseback riding beside the lines of fresh troops, men who now felt like soldiers. He pulled his horse out of the line, sat alongside the moving men, thought, Let them see me, let them feel the pride. He sat tall in his saddle, gave them each a look, and the men responded with waves and some cheering. The company commanders, young captains and smooth-faced lieutenants, saluted him crisply as they rode by, made a show of tightening the lines of their small commands. Hancock thought, These men will not run. It's in their eyes, their step. General "Baldy" Smith had come through the camps throughout the winter, had given the customary speech, the rousing call to the flag, the great honor in duty, and the men were always enthusiastic, always responded. Smith, and the others, men who tried to inject some great spark of patriotism into the troops, would ride away satisfied that they had done their bit to train the men, to prepare them for the bloody war. Hancock stood at the front, always listened with respect, and watched his men, knew that this was not what made them soldiers, that if the fight were not in them already, no great speech about loving the flag would change that. He did not understand why the generals did not see, would not accept, that those other fellows, those boys in the ragged uniforms who wanted to burn your lovely flag, had already shown they could hurt you, would stand up to your patriotism and put the bayonet through your beloved uniform. But still the words came, and Hancock began to understand. It was all they knew how to do: make speeches. Very few of them had ever led troops under fire, had ever led troops at all. And when the time came, many of them would fail, and many men would die because they did not have leaders.

His head began to feel heavy—he'd had little sleep since they boarded the steamer—and he slumped in the saddle, looked down at the ground, the short grass his horse was now exploring . . . *the ground a smooth, shining carpet of red, soaked in the blood of the army, a man was screaming, then more, many more, thick gray smoke and burning powder, and the sounds of artillery shells exploding and the stench of death—*

Hancock jerked awake, sat up straight, felt his heart pounding. He looked around, saw his troops in line, forming again in a wide field, and felt foolish for the small, terrifying daydream. Then he thought, No, it is foolish if you lead these men into the face of the enemy and are not prepared for them to die.

Across the field he saw Cobb again, directing his men, and the order was given to make camp. The men began to spread out, unloading the wagons. Hancock saw a flag moving quickly up the road that came from the walls of the fort, saw General Smith and a group of aides, and they spotted him and rode in his direction. Hancock met the general with a salute.

Smith said, "General Hancock, greetings to you, sir. Your men are positioned well, yes. This field will be filling up over the next few days, we hope to have the entire corps here by Wednesday."

"Corps, sir?"

"Yes, Mr. Hancock, have you not heard? We have been placed under the command of General Sumner. General McClellan has organized the army into corps. Better use of the chain of command and all that. I suppose I should have told you."

Hancock thought, Yes, that's your job: chain of command. He thought of Sumner. Edwin "Bull" Sumner, the man who had gone to California to remove Albert Sidney Johnston—interesting coincidence.

"Sir, my men are ready for orders, at your discretion."

"Very good, General. Our next move is up to General McClellan. Once the army is all here, I expect we will begin some real action, probably sweep on into Richmond."

Hancock wondered if they all believed that, that the rebel army would simply be brushed aside like so many bugs. He nodded, polite, said only, "We're ready for a fight, General."

"Good, good. Well, I'll keep you informed. Got to check on my other commanders, General. Good day to you."

Smith rode away, the aides trailing behind, and Hancock prodded the horse, which protested mildly, then moved toward the spreading troops and the fresh campfires. The afternoon was wearing on, and he looked out to the west, beyond the field, to great thickets of trees, miles of nothing, except . . . out there, somewhere, men waited with bayonets.

HANCOCK'S BRIGADE WAS ENCAMPED IN THE WIDE FIELD FOR nearly a month. McClellan made it plain, both to his commanders and to Washington, that he believed his army to be greatly outnumbered, and that a rapid, forceful move up the peninsula would result in certain disaster. As the army formed in front of Yorktown, McClellan's force of over ninety thousand men faced the Confederate general Magruder's command of fifteen thousand. Rather than assault this force, McClellan decided to lay siege to the city, and sent a continuous stream of requests to Washington for more men and more guns. When on May 4 he finally reported to the President that Yorktown was in his possession, he did not mention that it was a Confederate withdrawal that had handed it to him.

The army was finally put into motion, moving several miles inland, through the abandoned positions of Joe Johnston's retreating army. As they advanced to Williamsburg, they met the troops of the

Confederate rear guard, a strong solid line that had been placed before them by General Longstreet.

Hancock's men were well back in line, and he knew little of what was in front of him, except for the scattered sounds of skirmishes. He rode beside the lines of his men, spoke with each commander as they passed, answering the same questions with a simple, "I have not been informed."

The roads were sandy and soft, and he watched a small squad of men helping push a wagon through a bog. He looked at the sky, thought, No rain today, thank God. They had sat in the mush of a campground, softened by days of rain, a hard, soaking spring storm that had drowned the fires and dampened the enthusiasm of the whole army.

Up the line in front of him, his men were stalled again by some obstruction he could not see, and he spurred the horse, rode forward feeling a boiling wrath. He moved the horse along the edge of the road. The men moved aside, the waves and shouts muted now; the men had an instinct for the mood of their commander. Along with Hancock, they all were wondering if this army had any idea where it was going.

He heard a shout behind him, turned the horse and saw a courier, a man covered in mud. The troops watched the man pass, began to laugh, called out, mocking the man's obvious distress.

"General Hancock, sir. I have a message, from General Smith." The man paused, took some air, and Hancock saw a stream of brown water flowing from the man's boots, the blue pants smeared with shiny brown sludge, saw eyes looking at him through a wet paste of brown goo. He began to smile, felt himself let go, a tightness in his chest loosen, and now he laughed, and around him his men took the cue, laughed as well.

The courier glanced at the men, then back at Hancock, who saw the man's embarrassment growing and said, "Are you all right, Captain?"

"Sir, I had an accident. My horse doesn't seem to care for this sand, and he threw me. Forgive my appearance, sir."

"At least wipe off your face," Hancock said, laughing.

The man felt his face with his hand, saw the mud on his fingers, said, "Oh," and pulled a handkerchief from his pocket, wiped painfully at the drying crust.

"Sir, if I may . . . General Smith is at the rear of this column, and he requests your presence as soon as possible. He has orders deploying your men, sir."

Hancock stopped laughing, turned away from the stalled troops, who were continuing to gather, and motioned to the man to follow. They rode off the road, through a small gap in the brush, and Hancock turned back, spotted a lieutenant leaning back in his saddle, allowing the men to break their lines. He shouted at the man, "You there! Lieutenant! Get these men back into line. Prepare to move them forward. We are on the march, not in camp."

The man jumped up straight in his saddle, began to shout at the men, who were already moving back in place, straightening their lines on the road.

Hancock looked at the courier, could now see his face, said, "Captain, in the future you will impart your messages to me out of earshot of the troops, do you understand?"

"Sir? Yes, sir. I didn't see any need—"

"Captain, we are in the enemy's country. Have you ever heard of spies?"

The man stiffened, glanced around, said in a whisper, "Spies? Do you really think there are spies?"

Hancock stared at the man, felt the rage beginning to build again. "Captain, we are at war. . . ." Then he thought, No, let it go. He took a long breath. The man leaned closer to him, whispered again, "Sorry, sir. I will pay more attention next time. General Smith requests your presence. He is in the rear of this column, with General Sumner, sir."

Hancock turned his horse, climbed back to the road, began to move toward the rear. He did not see where the courier went, and did not care. He thought, Maybe, *finally*, something will happen.

MAY 4, 1862

HE HAD MET GENERAL SUMNER SEVERAL TIMES, HAD SERVED under him briefly in St. Louis, had even seen him in California, but he did not expect the man to have aged so badly.

"General Hancock, do come in, thank you." Sumner was an old man, and Hancock saw now that he might be too old. His headquarters was a large tent, and he sat alone at a small table. Behind him was a map, hung between two thin sticks, small trees that had been cut and pushed into the soft ground. General Smith stood beside Hancock, nervous, clasping and unclasping his hands. He greeted Hancock only with a small nod.

Sumner turned in his chair, motioned to an aide, who handed him a pointer, and he held it up to the map, waved it unsteadily.

"Gentlemen, this map is all wrong. It's the only map we have, but it's all wrong. Turns out, the roads we've been using don't go where they're supposed to go. Damned nuisance." He stopped, coughed, turned back to the men in front of him.

"We've got the enemy in front of us, dug in, ready for a fight. General McClellan is not here. He is . . . God knows . . . back there, somewhere, trading complaints with Washington. So, I am in command of the field. This is not my choice, but it is the circumstance. General Smith?"

"Yes, sir."

"General, you must deploy your division across the roads in front of you. Then push out through the woods to the right. General Hancock, I would like that to be your job. Take five regiments, yours and some from . . . from whoever General Smith designates. Move north, out on our right flank. There's supposed to be some fortifications out there, part of what they call Fort Magruder. You know John Magruder? Artillery man, hell of a fighter. Did some fine work in Mexico."

Hancock nodded, said, "Yes, sir. I am familiar with him."

"Well, that place could be a threat to our position. The enemy is dug in heavily around their so-called fort. General Hooker is in contact with the direct center of the fortifications. He probably has his hands full. General Hancock, I want you to take this man here."

He raised a thin arm, and Hancock looked toward a cavalry officer, standing to one side, who stepped forward.

"I'd like him to go with you, be my observer. He has scouted the woods already, may be of some help."

Hancock looked at the young man, saw blond hair falling in loose curls, a red scarf tied loosely around the man's neck, a long feather sprouting from the band in the man's hat. The man saluted, said, "It will be an honor to serve with you, General."

Sumner coughed again, and Hancock stared at the strange cavalry officer a moment longer. Then Sumner said, "General Smith, are you yet engaged?"

"Sir, we have forces in our front, and . . . well, yes, we have been moving against them. Not fully, though. Shall I give the order to advance, sir?"

Sumner stared up at Smith, leaned back in his small chair, paused for a long moment and said, "General, have you heard fighting on your left?"

"Yes, sir. About an hour ago. Seems to be somewhat heavy."

"Well, General, that fighting involves two divisions, Hooker and Couch. I imagine they are expecting you to move up in support. Does that seem like a reasonable plan to you?"

Smith felt the sarcasm, glanced at Hancock self-consciously, said, "Yes, sir. Right away. If you will excuse me, sir. I will move my units up in support and engage the enemy."

Smith hurried out of the tent, and Hancock saluted Sumner, followed Smith outside. Smith climbed up on his horse, turned around unsteadily, said, "General . . . best of luck. This day may make heroes of us all."

Hancock wondered if he was serious, said nothing. He looked over to the young cavalryman, who pulled his horse up beside Hancock's. "Do you have a name, soldier?" he asked.

"Lieutenant George Armstrong Custer, at your service, sir."

"Well, Lieutenant Custer, shall we get started?"

FOR OVER A MILE THEY SLID BETWEEN HUGE LIVE OAKS, PUSHED through the thickets of scrub pine. Behind them, off to their left, they could hear the sounds of a growing battle, the deep rumble of artillery and the high chatter of musket fire.

Hancock stayed on foot, led the column through the woods, Custer his guide. The battle sounds were solid now, no wavering, no gaps. If it goes badly, Hancock thought, if they push the rest of Smith's division back, if Hooker doesn't hold his ground, we are out here by ourselves, cut off.

The woods began to thin, and he saw an opening, the trees spreading far apart now. The woods ended suddenly, giving way to a wide-open plain more than a mile long. He put his glasses to his eyes, heard Custer say, "There it is," then saw their objective across the long, undulating field: the small dam. Behind him the regimental commanders had been assembled, and Hancock turned, saw the troops stretched out in ragged lines, disappearing back through the thick trees.

"Gentlemen, we have to cross this field and reach that dam. I don't see any sign of the enemy, but the field has some elevation, some depressions, they could be waiting for us anywhere. Once we reach the dam, it's a tight line over the top, only a few feet wide, and from what Lieutenant Custer tells me, the enemy's entrenchments are on the other side. We will form battle lines here at the edge of the woods, then move across the field as quickly as we can. Keep the noise to a minimum, and no firing."

He scanned the faces, saw an aide, Hughes, with small round glasses on a long point of a nose. "Lieutenant, send word to Colonel Wheeler: I want his batteries brought forward to the edge of these trees, focused on that dam. If we can't get across it, we'll blow it to hell, maybe drive 'em out with a flood of water. Any questions?"

There were no questions. He looked at the faces, the commanders he had trained, knew they were ready. He focused the field glasses out across the open field, and the men went back to their units, began moving them up.

Custer stepped out of the trees, walked out into the open, then turned and said, "Give me a squad, General, a picket line maybe. Let me ease across and draw their fire. I can't see anybody, but those far trees could be full of artillery."

Hancock thought, Yes, good, it could work. Tempt some nervous gunner, a sweating hand holding a tight lanyard, and they could start a reckless fire that would reveal the entire position of the enemy. He nodded, waved back to another aide, said "Give Lieutenant Custer fifty men, tell them to keep low, move fast, cross that field."

The man ran back, and men quickly came forward, men who had not yet seen the enemy, who would be the first.

They moved out into the open. Custer spread them into a thin line, spaced a few feet apart. Then, with a quiet wave of his arm, they were moving away through the field. Behind them the regiments poured neatly out of the trees, began to form in lines three deep, then moved forward, made room for the units behind. Hancock climbed on his horse, rode out to Custer, watching, looking ahead for the small puff of smoke coming well before the sound, the first telltale sign of an impatient gunner, the high screech of the shell that would rip the air as it tumbled toward them. But there was nothing.

"Proceed, Lieutenant. With speed."

Custer saluted, waved to the line of men, and they began to move in a quicker step, jogging through the thick green grass, moving up a slight incline. Hancock braced, waited for the volley, but it did not come. The men were now out of sight and he was watching an empty field, then they came up again on a far rise, still in line, still with the quick step. Now the regiments began to move, the slow, steady march, and Hancock rode along the front, watched the officers spread the

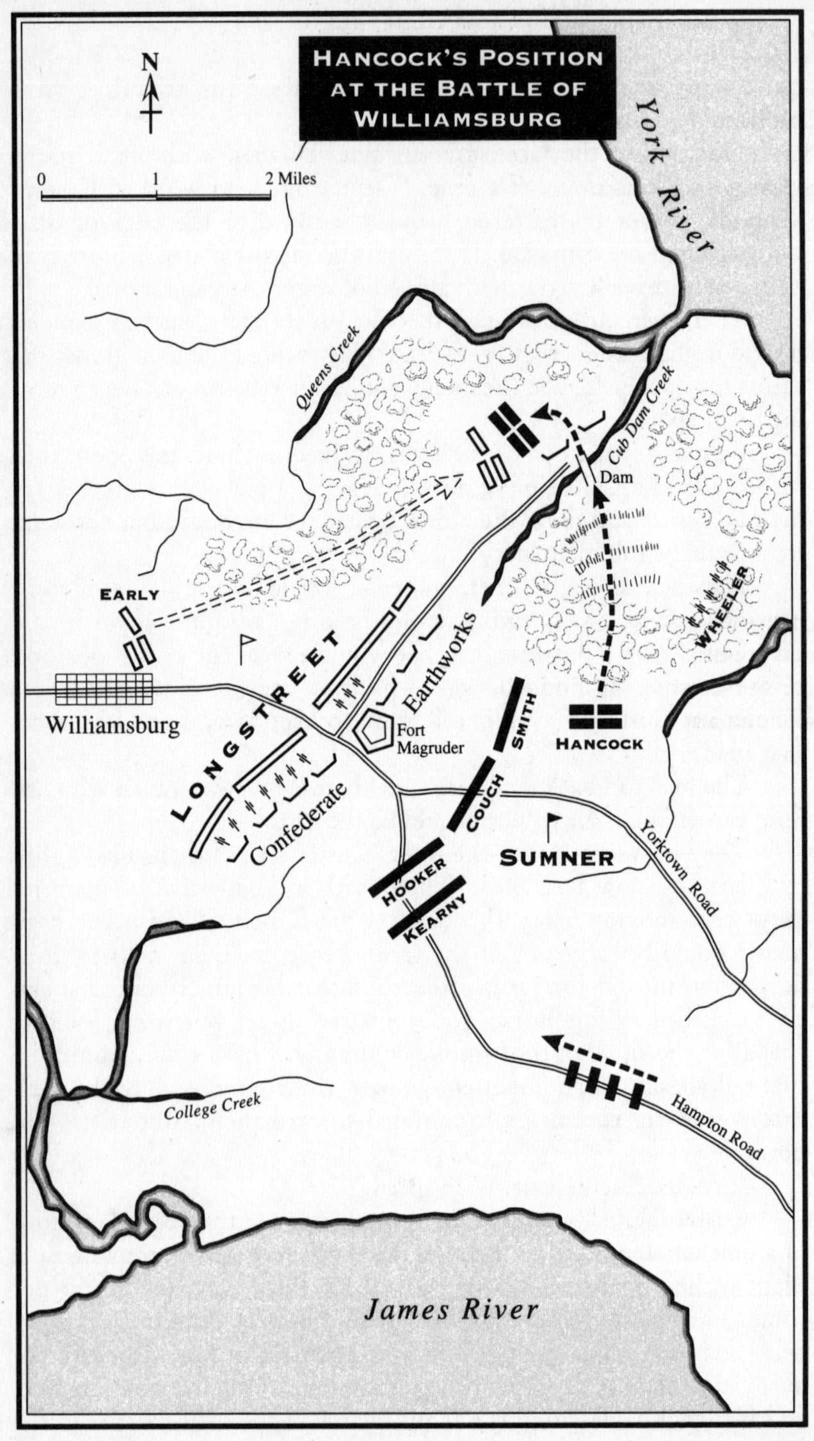

HANCOCK'S POSITION AT THE BATTLE OF WILLIAMSBURG
N
0
1
2 Miles
York River
Queens Creek
Cub Dam Creek
Dam
EARLY
WHEELER
LONGSTREET
Earthworks
Williamsburg
Fort Magruder
SMITH
HANCOCK
COUCH
Confederate
SUMNER
HOOKER
KEARNY
Yorktown Road
College Creek
Hampton Road
James River

formations. He prodded the horse, moved quickly down the lines, and the men waved hats. There were some careless cheers, quickly silenced by the officers.

He rode out now to the top of the first rise, could not see Custer's men, and so rode farther, dropped down, then climbed the gentle slope to the next rise, and then they were there, very close to the dam now, a small dirt ridge blocking an unseen creek. He looked behind him, saw the troops coming up over the first rise, then studied Custer through the glasses again, saw them reach the dam. He held his breath, felt the pounding in his chest, careful, careful, but there was still no sound, and now he saw Custer, saw the ridiculous hat held high in the air, waving, and now the small line of men were on the dam and moving across.

He rode forward again, down the slight hill to the long flat plain, could see the dam plainly now, and behind him the men were up the second rise, spread out in a beautiful wave of blue. He saw movement on the dam, held up his glasses and saw Custer standing in the middle of the dam, waving crazily, both arms, and he understood, knew what they had done.

The fighting behind them continued to be steady, and he listened carefully, could not detect any movement, any change in the flow. Good, he thought, hold your ground. He rode now to the dam.

The troops were coming up behind him, across the flat ground, and Custer ran toward him, waving the men forward. "Sir! It's empty!" he said, excited, panting. "There's no one there! We can cross the dam and occupy the fortifications!"

Hancock dismounted, handed the reins to an aide and walked quickly across the soft dirt of the dam. He saw his men, the first ones across, in line behind a great round wall, a wide trench. Then he saw more trenches, spreading out in several directions, and he climbed up on a high mound of brown dirt. The men waved, threw hats quietly in the air, and he thought, This is incredible, we have flanked the enemy and no one knows we're here.

Beyond the earthworks there was shooting, distant musket fire, and the men began to move in that direction. Rifles came up on the far side of the works, pointing out at the scattered shots. Hancock walked along the top of the earthworks, and now other officers were eyeing their front, toward the shooting, and he saw an officer motion to him, a quiet, urgent wave. He jumped down into the trench, moved to the man's position and followed the man's point with his glasses.

Across the wet grassland, dotted with small marshy ponds, he saw lines of brown, Confederate troops in line, moving to the left, toward the battle they had been hearing. Beyond those troops were more earthworks, larger, heavier, the walls they called Fort Magruder. Light musket fire was increasing in their direction, and Hancock lowered his glasses, saw, closer, another fortification, trenches and earthworks, smaller, like this one. He saw a rebel officer, a man in a tall black hat, pointing the rifles of the troops in a new direction, *their* direction, aware now of this new threat.

Hancock called for a courier, and a red-faced lieutenant scurried over the dirt embankments and saluted clumsily. Hancock said, "Go, now, to General Smith. Tell him we have flanked the enemy. We are only lightly opposed, but that will change. If he can shift his units in this direction, we can assist both him and General Hooker. We might be able to push the enemy out of the fortifications to Hooker's front. Stress the point: we are on the enemy's flank. Move *fast*, Lieutenant."

His troops were nearly all across the dam, and the trenches were filled, became lines of solid blue. Hancock spied the closer troops again, saw thin lines, maybe one regiment, and he shouted at the other officers, "Up . . . over the wall, advance on those troops! Tell your men to hold their fire until you order it. Move out!"

The officers shouted the orders, and men began to climb the earthen walls. They slid down into the tall grass, lines formed, and they moved forward. There was more noise now, shots coming in quicker succession, the balls whizzing by, some high over his head. He sat on the wall, heard the balls thumping the sides of the thick dirt. His men continued to move out, a spreading swarm of blue down through the grass, and within minutes they had reached the lines of the enemy. Suddenly, they stopped, poured a volley of thick fire into the rebel troops, and instantly he could not see, the lines hidden by a thick white cloud. He slid down, jumped into the thick grass, pulled his pistol and began to move forward with his men.

He stumbled, followed the shouts of the men in front of him, was not sure of distance, how far he had come. Then the smoke gave way, the shooting slowed, then stopped, and he was climbing another wall, a low, thick hill of dirt. In front of him his men were pushing on, through the new fortifications, and now he saw the first bodies, men in gray and brown uniforms, those who did not escape the assault. He did not wait, ran over the tops of the earthworks, reached the far side, saw his men ready to climb out, to press on, and he waved them back, no, not yet.

He saw the rebels moving away, no more than a hundred men, and he realized they had pushed back only a small outpost, an isolated unit. He looked toward Fort Magruder again and the heavy sounds of battle, and saw nothing to their front, nothing to stop them from pushing on, into the side of the Confederate position.

He turned, looked back toward the distant dam, said out loud, to the reinforcements that were not yet there, "Come on, dammit!"

Then he saw a horseman, a man riding on the dam, a tricky move, and the man came forward, a different face, not his courier, and he began to walk back through his gathered troops.

The courier saw him, dismounted, and climbed the wide dirt wall. "General, sir. General Sumner orders you to withdraw from your position. You are in a tenuous spot, General. You are ordered to withdraw back to General Smith's lines . . . back there. You are too far in advance, sir."

Hancock stared at the man, disbelieving. He saw the snotty confidence of the untested staff officer, the smug arrogance of a man with a big message and no responsibility for it, and he moved closer to the man, leaned hard into the man's face.

"Listen, son. You go back and you tell General Sumner . . ." He paused, felt the anger screaming in his ears, and the man's face changed, the arrogance turned to fear. Hancock was surprised, and a voice in his head said, No, careful, be careful. He turned away, looked for another courier, saw his aides now, gathering around, and no one was talking, they were all watching him. He pointed at one, the young Lieutenant Crane, motioned him closer.

Crane moved up, saluted, and Hancock took a slow, deep breath, loosened the tightness in his jaw, said, "Lieutenant, you will take a message to General Sumner. You will inform the general that we are on the open flank of the enemy, and that reinforcements have already been requested from General Smith. You tell General Sumner that I do not understand his . . . order for withdrawing these troops. I would like it made clear. Do you understand, Lieutenant?"

"Yes, sir. Perfectly," and the man was off, ran to a waiting horse and rode quickly away.

Sumner's man watched Hancock warily, like a trainer watching an angry lion, and Hancock ignored him, moved forward, toward the eyes of his men, stepped through the earthworks and climbed up, studied the heavy Confederate lines, still in place, through his glasses. The battle had begun to slow, the volleys were irregular, but the sounds still came from in front of the fort, no big push either way: it had been a stalemate. He thought, It won't be a stalemate if we hit them from here. But he knew Longstreet would react, his presence was known by now. He looked at his watch, nearly three o'clock. Plenty of time . . . if Smith would just come.

"Sir, a rider!"

He looked around, saw a horseman coming through the thick swampy grass, a different man, not one of his, and the man dismounted, ran in a crouch over the earthworks, hearing a battle that wasn't there.

"General Hancock, sir, General Smith regrets to inform you that he has been ordered by General Sumner not to send any troops to your position. General Smith understands that you have been ordered to withdraw. General Smith is of the opinion . . . sir . . . that you may withdraw at your convenience, sir. At a time you see as best, within the limits of General Sumner's order." The man paused, and Hancock saw his discomfort.

"Sir, the general is not in agreement with General Sumner's order, and wishes you to know that. But General Sumner is in command of the field."

Hancock nodded, knew Smith was playing it as carefully as a good politician can.

"Please return to General Smith and thank him for his intentions. You may tell the general that I will remain here until such time as General Sumner's orders are clarified. I did not completely understand them the first time. His courier was . . . vague."

"Yes, sir. Thank you, sir." The man ducked low again, moved back across the earthworks.

Sumner's man stood with Hancock's remaining aides, and stepped forward, prepared with a mild protest.

"Sir, General Sumner's orders—"

"You may return to General Sumner. Relay to the general that our position here continues to be strong. We are in a position to carry the field. Request General Sumner to repeat his order. You were *vague*."

The man swallowed his protest, mounted his horse and was quickly gone.

Hancock went back to the front wall, continued to glass the far positions. The shooting began again, a fresh volley, then slowed, and now there was silence. From behind him, he heard another horse, turned and saw Crane. The look on the young man's face told him what he did not want to hear.

"Sir, General Sumner has ordered you again to withdraw from your position. He is insistent, sir."

Hancock turned away from the man, felt a heavy fist inside his chest, pressing down hard on his own disgust, forcing it down deep inside him. You do not criticize generals, you obey them, he thought. But this is pure stupidity. We are losing our opportunity. A glorious piece of good luck has been erased by the hesitation of a cautious old man.

He looked at his watch, five o'clock. Now there was not much time, and it was clear that no more troops were coming from General Smith.

Men began to call out, pointing, and Custer suddenly appeared, climbing over the far end of the earthworks, plucking at briars on his hat.

"I hope you, for one, have enjoyed this day, Lieutenant. Gone for a walk in the woods?"

"General, sir, I have been doing a bit of reconnaissance. The enemy is beginning to move this way. At least two regiments, maybe more, are forming behind those woods to the right. They appear to be units of Early's brigade, sir."

Hancock thought, We can hold out here for a while, but this fortification is too small, we are too tightly bunched. If they should bring up artillery . . .

"Good work, Lieutenant." He motioned to Crane, sent him to the commanders, gave the word to begin pulling back, out of the fortifications, back toward the dam.

The orders were called out, and men began to climb out, going back the way they had come, and he saw the looks, the disappointment. They didn't understand either, he thought. Even the troops knew they should have kept going.

He followed the last of the companies through the winding trench works, then climbed up and over the dirt embankment, and now the earthworks were empty, except for the neat row of Confederate dead, which his men had arranged respectfully. They moved quickly back through the thick grass, reached the first fortification, filled it, and Hancock climbed up on the wall, watching his men. He looked out past the works, back across the dam to the great open field, the plain of green grass that they had first crossed, saw a rider suddenly appear on one of the low crests that ran across the field. It was Smith's man again, and he knew there would be nothing he wanted to hear. But he watched the man disappear again, between the crests, completely out of sight. Then the man topped the second crest, came down across the flat plain toward the dam.

Hancock turned, suddenly, shouted, "Regimental commanders . . . I need the commanders here . . . *now*!"

The word went out, and through the trenches below him he saw the officers approach, snaking their way through the troops. Behind him Custer was glassing the fortification they had abandoned.

"General, the rebels have returned."

Hancock turned, put his glasses on the flags that were moving into the works, saw three, four, then men on horses, more troops, and now shots began, from out of the woods, closer to them, from the right, where Custer had seen the units forming.

He turned, saw the faces of his colonels, said, "Gentlemen, we have been ordered to withdraw. So, we will withdraw. Right now, lose no time, move across the dam as quickly as you can. Lots of noise, let them know we are leaving. We are running away, their numbers are overwhelming us." He laughed, and the officers did not understand, looked at each other, and Custer stood up beside him, followed his gaze out to the wide-open field.

Hancock said to his commanders, "Gentlemen, when you top that first rise, form your men into battle line . . . facing *this* way. Then you will wait for my orders."

The officers spread out through the troops, and the column formed quickly, began to cross the dam.

Hancock saw Lieutenant Hughes, called him over and said, "Lieutenant, are Wheeler's batteries where I wanted them, in those far trees there?"

"Yes, sir. Colonel Wheeler understood your orders plainly, sir."

Good, he thought. Very damned good. Wheeler would not move his guns without word from him first, no matter who sent the order.

"Lieutenant, I want you to ride like hell across that field, find Colonel Wheeler and tell him to prepare for an assault. Tell him we are withdrawing across his line of fire, and to keep a sharp watch on our movements. I will give him a signal. I will wave my sword in the air—tell him, once we pass across his line of fire to keep watching me. He will know what to do."

"Yes, sir." Crane moved toward the dam, pushing through the line of men, and Hancock watched him ride out across the open grass.

Behind him rebel troops, Early's troops, were cutting their way through the dense woods, and now the pickets had made it through, began to fire at the blue coats filing out of the works. Hancock pointed Custer in their direction, and the young lieutenant ran toward the sound of the muskets, collecting men, placing them on the dirt wall, and quickly they fired a volley, then another, and the annoying fire was slowed, the pickets driven back into the cover of the dark woods.

Hancock pointed the glasses back toward the other earthworks, saw lines of men moving out, toward him, blending into the tall swamp grass. The rebels were now in pursuit of his retreating troops.

Custer ran toward him, and Hancock saw they were nearly alone in the earthworks. The last men were crossing the dam, and his troops were marching in ragged formation across the field, beginning the slight climb up toward the first crest.

"Excuse me, General, but there are rebel troops on two sides of us, advancing rapidly. I suggest, sir, it is time to leave."

Hancock hopped up on the wall that faced the woods, saw lines of men pouring out through the trees, easy musket range away, and he jumped down, said, "Yes, Lieutenant, we must join the retreat. Try to look as panicked as you can."

"Sir?"

"Let's *move*, Lieutenant."

Hancock ran across the dam, Custer close behind. The balls began to fly by now, poorly aimed at a rare target. They reached the horses and received the reins from a very nervous aide, who quickly ran toward the withdrawing lines of his own unit. Hancock spurred his horse, thought, This is not the time to be stubborn, old girl, and the mare moved in a quick jump, began to glide up the long incline, past the swiftly marching troops.

He stopped at the crest of the hill, could see it all now. The Confederate troops had swarmed over the works, were crossing the dam, hard in pursuit. He saw the whole picture now in his head, the plan came to him like a clear blue light, like a window opening in his brain, a sudden flow of clean, cool air, and he smiled. Yes, *yes*. He turned, looked back to the line of trees that had brought them there, felt the presence of the big guns, Wheeler's guns, and he knew Wheeler was watching him, somewhere, up in a tree. Keep watching, my good man, you are about to see it unfold.

His troops reached the crest of the hill, began the descent into the trough between the two crests, and quickly the officers directed them into line. Hancock watched as they filled the depression, a solid blue wall growing stronger as each man came over the hill.

He glassed back down toward the dam, saw cannon being rolled up on the other side, then scanned down to the lines of gray troops coming up the hill. Their cannon will not fire, he thought, it is too close to their own men, right over their heads, and now they can't see

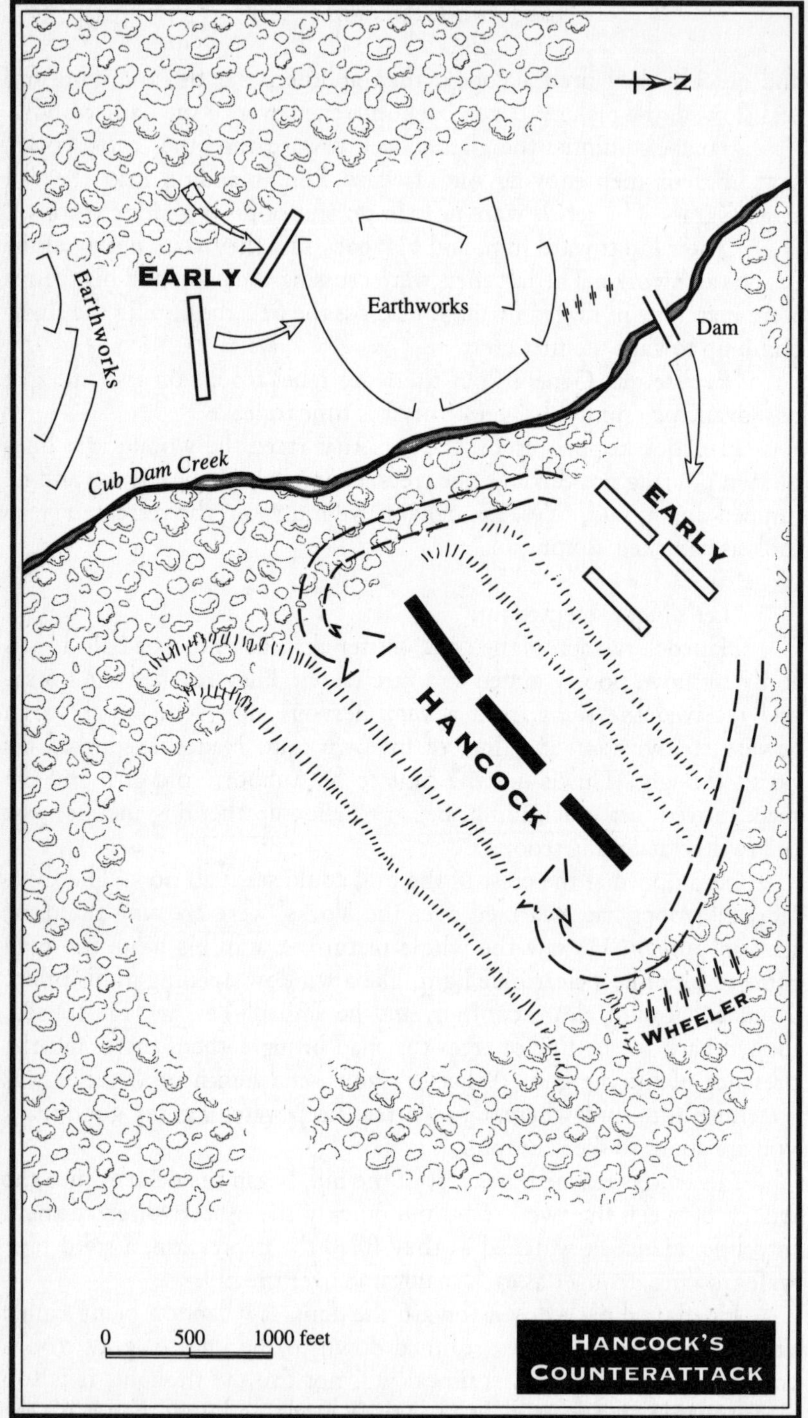

Z
EARLY
Earthworks
Earthworks
Dam
Cub Dam Creek
EARLY
HANCOCK
WHEELER
0
500
1000 feet
HANCOCK'S COUNTERATTACK

us at all. He looked back to the trees, saw motion through the low branches, and took one last glance at the lines of men chasing him. Then he grabbed at his belt, felt the solid brass handle, pulled his sword from the scabbard and waved it in a wide circle over his head.

In an instant puffs of smoke blew out from the line of trees, and shells began to scream across, in front of the crest, and into the lines of rebel troops. He sat high on his horse, just enough to peer over the top of the hill, saw the cannon far below turning, taking aim on his guns, of course, they would try to duel the artillery. They could not shell the troops. He waited until the rebel guns began firing, smoke grew in a thick cloud over the dam, shells began to burst back in the trees to his right.

The lines of rebel troops were moving faster now, began a wild yell, feeling the full effect of the cannon fire. Wheeler's shells continued to burst among the rebels, flashes of fire and smoke began to blur the lines, and now the first gray troops made it to the top of the hill and faced the solid blue line. The first volley went out, a thousand muskets opened together, a long, thin line of white smoke pouring their shot into the first lines of gray troops. The rebels stopped cold, only a few yards from the lines of blue, began to turn back into themselves, and more men reached the top, saw what lay on the other side, and another volley was fired, and the rebel lines fell to pieces. Hancock watched the collapse of the attack, saw the rebels backing down, off the crest, and he turned, yelled to Custer, gave the order, yelled for him to carry the order through the lines, then yelled to Colonel Gray and Colonel Cobb, whose men waited in line close beside him, *"Charge!"*

His men moved up the gentle slope in one motion and met the jumbled and broken lines of gray troops at the crest of the hill. The strong advance by his deep rows of men, visible now across the open field as one long blue wave, sent the rebel lines back down the slope in complete confusion. Hancock's men crossed over the rise, began to pursue the rebels back toward the dam. He rode to the top of the crest, could see nothing for the thick smoke, gradually pushed his horse forward, rode slowly for several minutes down the gradual slope, over the bodies of the Confederate troops, a bloody carpet across the entire ridge. The sounds of the battle faded. The only musket fire came from far away now, across the dam, and now his men began to come back up the hill. The chase was over, the rebel soldiers were pushed back to their defenses.

The smoke began to clear, and he noticed for the first time that it was nearly dark. A light breeze blew toward the trees where Wheeler had his guns, and now the field showed the signs of battle, a stark change to the way he had first seen it, the smooth green grass pockmarked by the craters of exploded shells, the heaped dead and crawling wounded, nearly all from the Confederate side. He saw an officer running toward him, holding a flag, saw: Custer. The young lieutenant came up the hill, had lost his hat, and his hair flew about in a great blond tangle.

"General, sir, I have captured this here flag. Took it right out of the man's hand. He just . . . gave it to me. I reckon we won this one, General. That was some fine work, if I am allowed to say, sir."

"Thank you, Lieutenant. We have a fine brigade here. They should be proud. But I may have some explaining to do at headquarters."

As Hancock's men pulled back from their field of battle, they sent nearly six hundred Confederate prisoners to the rear, with a total loss to their own forces of barely thirty men. McClellan arrived at Sumner's headquarters in time to learn of Hancock's battle, and rode immediately to the scene. His first order was to General Smith, to reinforce Hancock's position. McClellan understood what Hancock had tried to do, and planned an assault to complete the job. But Longstreet understood as well, as did Joe Johnston, and the following morning, when the Union lines moved forward, they found Fort Magruder abandoned and the Confederates again in retreat.

19. LEE

JUNE 1862

HE ENTERED HIS OFFICE, SAW TAYLOR BEHIND HIS DESK, THUMBing through a stack of letters. The new title that had been given to Lee, Military Adviser to the President, a title with nothing of significance attached, no real duty other than remaining near Davis, also provided for promotions for his staff. Taylor had received a commission of Major.

Lee paused, watched the young man, smiled at the quick movements, the efficiency. He is just a boy, Lee thought, and he's a major. It took me nearly twenty years. . . .

"Oh, good morning, sir. You're early, I didn't expect you this soon."

"Good morning, Major. Any news? Anything from General Johnston's headquarters?"

"Sorry, sir, nothing. I spoke this morning with some men from General Hood's brigade . . . Texans."

Lee smiled, could not hide the reaction to the name, saw the huge man, John Bell Hood, the bright blond hair and beard, the only man Lee knew from his days in the cavalry who actually *liked* it there, chasing impossibly elusive Indians through the suffocating dust.

"You certain it was General Hood's men?"

"Yes, sir. They came from Seven Pines, sir."

"Seven Pines? So, our army is closer still."

"Yes, sir. They told of being whipped at Williamsburg, said General McClellan had pushed them out of the trenches at Fort Magruder."

"They said that? We have abandoned Williamsburg?"

"Yes, sir. They didn't know much else, so I talked to some others, and they said pretty much the same thing. McClellan is apparently hot on their heels."

Lee turned, went to his window, expected to hear something, cannon, some sign. There was no sound. He thought, This is madness. McClellan has never been hot on anybody's heels. And did Davis know this, know of losing Williamsburg?

"Major, I am going to take a ride. It is not necessary to inform anyone in what direction I am riding."

Taylor was puzzled. "Direction . . . ?"

"Major, I can no longer stay here and endure General Johnston's silence."

Lee heard the heavy sound of boots in the hall, then a young man, Major Marshall, another boy with the new responsibility of a senior officer, entered. Marshall stopped, startled to see Lee, and saluted, jarring his wire-rimmed glasses to one side.

"General, sir. Please forgive me for being late, sir."

He glanced at Taylor, asked quickly under his breath, "*Am* I late?"

Lee's mind was moving ahead, beyond the office, and he stepped toward the door, put a hand on Marshall's shoulder. "Let's go, Major, we're taking a ride."

Marshall trailed after Lee, then turned back to Taylor, still confused. Taylor laughed, seeing the young man's awkward expression, waved him away with a loud whisper, "Good luck on your mission, Major!"

THEY WERE NOT FAR FROM THE CITY WHEN THEY CAME UPON the first troops, men of Gustavus Smith's brigades. The men were down, lying about in large clusters, trying to avoid the vast patches of thick mud from the hard rains that had soaked these swamps the last few days.

Lee and Marshall rode on, passed more resting troops, then reached an intersection where a large building was identified with a makeshift sign, THE OLD TAVERN. Across from the tavern was a farmhouse, and Lee stopped, saw horses, officers moving in and out. To the east, in the distance, he heard the sound, the soft rumble of artillery, then a steady rattle, a flow of musket fire.

"This way, Major."

Lee dismounted by the horses, and the men coming from the house stopped and gave a surprised salute. Lee led the young man in, looked through a doorway into one of the rooms and saw staff officers, Johnston's men. He motioned to Marshall to wait there, and the young man went in. Lee moved away from the pleasantries shared by officers who did not dirty their uniforms. He went toward the other doorway, peered in, and saw Joe Johnston.

Johnston looked up, did not stand, and Lee felt the tension, the dense air of trouble. He saw Gustavus Smith, nodded, and Smith made a quick unsmiling acknowledgment. There was a third man, General Whiting, another Johnston favorite, another quick nod. There had been no talking, and Lee sensed he had not caused an interruption. The men sat apart, did not face each other.

Lee broke the silence. "General, have you heard the firing?"

Johnston looked up, and Lee saw nothing in the eyes, a cold stillness. He made a quick wave with his hand. "Some artillery. Nothing to be concerned about."

Surely he has heard the muskets, Lee thought. He saw an empty chair, sat down, and still no one spoke, no attempt at conversation. Lee waited, had not expected this kind of reception. He studied Johnston, who did not look at him, did not look at anything, sat staring at the floor.

From outside there was the sound of a horse, a shout, and through the house came a burst of noise, a courier, who stopped in the doorway and began a frantic recital of his message: "General, sir, General Longstreet offers his compliments and wishes to report that he is engaged with the enemy and is moving them back. He requests with some urgency that the general provide support on his left flank."

Johnston rose, passed quickly by Lee and was gone, then the others were up, and Lee heard Johnston call to his staff. There was a flurry of activity, men running for horses, and in a few seconds Lee was alone. He still had no idea what was going on.

He walked outside, found Marshall watching the men leave, and then from up the road, from the west, the road to Richmond, he saw a group of men and a familiar rider. It was President Davis, who rode closer, spotted Lee and smiled; in a good mood, Lee saw, which was strange.

"Well, General, I see you have also decided to use the direct approach with Joe Johnston. Have you learned what is happening? I hear musket fire."

Lee could still see Johnston in the distance, and Johnston looked back, then spurred his horse and rounded a bend, out of sight.

"Mr. President, it appears that General Johnston has a full schedule today. He did not take the time to reveal his plans."

"Yes, well, I know he saw me, I watched him leave. I suppose we have no choice but to follow along. Would you please accompany me, General?"

The men rode down a muddy road through thick woods. Troops were moving up on all sides, and Lee saw the flags, the units from Hood's brigade. He looked about, hoped to see their commander, but the woods were too thick, and Lee knew it would not be a good time for conversation. From straight down the road came a sudden burst of musket fire, and in the distance smoke began to rise.

Davis pointed, said, "That's Fair Oaks."

Now cannon fire began to slice the air, heavy thunder poured toward them, and Lee knew the sound: Federal guns.

They rode forward, staying on the road, then came to a wide-open field filled with lines of moving men. To their front the woods turned thick again, and they watched the lines move forward, disappearing into the thick mass. Smoke began to fill the open spaces, and Lee heard units coming together, men screaming in confusion, officers trying to direct the lines, and he knew this was not good, there was no order.

After a few minutes men began to pile out of the woods, filling the road. Lee saw a flag: Texas, more of Hood's men. The firing had moved away now, farther down the road. Lee saw an officer, a colonel, and yelled to him, "What are your orders?"

The man rode closer, saw Davis, saluted and shouted back, "We cannot locate General Longstreet's flank, it is too thick. I'm trying . . . the men cannot fight through these woods!" The man saluted again, rode quickly away, tried to push his horse back into the trees.

The cannon fire continued in uneven bursts, and the daylight began to fade until the trees became a solid gray wall. Lee knew it would not go on much longer. Davis was speaking to the troops, a crowd had begun to gather around them, and then the wounded began to appear, carried out of the woods, and the sounds of battle were replaced with the cries of the men.

There was nothing left for them to do. Soon they would see the commanders and there would be answers to the confusion. Through the soldiers that crowded the road came a horseman, yelling, waving his hat, an officer Lee had just seen, one of Johnston's men. The foot soldiers cleared a path, and he rode closer.

"Sirs, General Johnston is wounded," he shouted. "They are bringing him . . . there." The man pointed across the open field, where the smoke was beginning to clear.

Johnston was carried by two of his staff, who laid him down under a tree as Davis and Lee rode up. Davis jumped down, kneeled, put his hands on Johnston's shoulders, and Lee stayed back, watched from behind. There were shells still falling, mostly in the distance, and Lee could not hear the men speaking, but he saw Johnston's face, saw he was awake.

Davis turned and glanced at Lee, said something to Johnston, then mounted his horse. "We must find General Smith. He is in command now."

They began to move back toward the farmhouse, would wait for the officers to come together, out of the dark.

Gustavus Smith was already at the house when they arrived and went inside. Smith was pacing, a manic display. "There was no . . . communication. I had no idea what we were . . . Longstreet was not on the road. . . ."

Davis did not speak, and Lee stepped forward, said to Smith, "What was General Johnston's plan?"

Smith stopped moving, looked at Lee, glanced past to Davis, said, "General, I don't know. He didn't tell me."

Smith began to pace again, looked at Davis, then Lee. "Where are my men? What do we do now?" He turned to Lee, and Lee saw a wildness in his eyes, a man not in control. "What do we do now? The men are all over. The Federals are right . . . out there!"

Lee backed away and followed Davis outside. Davis mounted his horse, motioned to him.

"General, would you please ride with me?"

"Of course, Mr. President."

They rode slowly through the dark. The sounds of the wounded filled the woods, and small flickers of light were moving about. Lee could smell the mud, the rain, knew the weather was again turning wet. Good, he thought. It would slow down the troops, swell the rivers. There would be time to regroup, to make new plans.

They moved farther from the troops, toward the west, closer now to the city, and the signs of battle were gone. The only sounds were those of horses stepping through the thick mud.

Davis had his head down. Lee thought he was sleeping. Abruptly, Davis sat up straight, leaned toward Lee and said, "General Johnston is not mortally wounded. He will survive."

"I'm relieved to hear that, sir. He is a valuable man."

"Maybe. He is a good soldier. I am not sure he is a good commander."

Lee didn't answer. They rode in silence again, and Lee began to think back, to drift away, Johnston in Mexico, at West Point, the fiery temper, which would give way to a quick joke, a big laugh.

"General, I am placing you in command of the army."

Lee was jolted from his thoughts. "Sir?"

"This army needs the right man to lead it. These men . . . they want to fight. I have no doubt you are the man to give the commands . . . make the decisions."

Lee felt his heart pound, looked at Davis through the dark, tried to see, to be sure. Davis said nothing else, and Lee took a long, deep breath, said, "Sir, I will do my best."

They rode on, toward the dark shapes of Richmond, the horses moving in a slow rhythm. Lee stared at the flickering lights, distant lamps and streetlights. His mind was turning, moving beyond the night to the days ahead. It began to rain then, a steady, cool mist, but he did not notice, was deep into thought, and feeling very, very good.

PART TWO

20. LEE

July 1862

It had been just seven days, the last of June and the first few days of July. Each day had brought a new fight, at places they would remember as Frayser's Farm and Gaines Mill, Mechanicsville and Malvern Hill. The armies fought and struggled and moved about and made blind and stupid mistakes and brilliant and heroic attacks, and for both sides the losses had been staggering. But now McClellan had pulled his army back down the peninsula, away from Richmond, and in Washington his political enemies had their day. He had not taken Richmond, despite fighting battle after battle, though he had not once been truly defeated or even driven from the field. McClellan had pulled away by his own choice, backing toward the safety of the big gunboats, escaping from demons that Lee did not command.

Lee knew he had missed an opportunity, that McClellan in his retreat had repeatedly left himself open to assaults at a variety of places, but Lee had discovered his own army's weakness, his reliance on his commanders, and those commanders had not always been up to the task. Troop movement was inconsistent, communications were poor, attacks had been uncoordinated. The great weakness of choosing generals through politics had shown itself, and now, with McClellan tightly bound away from Richmond, Lee finally had both the authority and the breathing space to reorganize the army.

His headquarters was at the home of an old woman, the widow Dabbs, whose large house sat in the midst of an old, underused farm. His office was one of the smaller rooms, at the back of the house, and he had his own entrance so he could go outside when he chose, to slip away when he needed the rest or to just take a short walk.

The room reminded him of his office at Fort Mason, small and plain, the low ceiling and close walls, with one small window, but outside, he faced a stand of thick trees, saw the rolling green hills he loved. Beyond, the narrow, soft roads led out toward the bloody fields.

It had been a long day, couriers moving rapidly in and out, officers moving through the little office in a steady stream. Major Taylor had learned, had grown into the job, and Lee was grateful for the endless flood of minute details Taylor handled, diverting them from his attention.

For the first time, the army began to acquire an identity. Johnston had commanded units that he felt were his alone. Other generals not directly associated with Johnston's command, such as Magruder, incorporated their own aura of political importance to the running of their commands. Thus, the army had been a group of smaller armies, where coordination and communication was a matter of both ego and convenience. Lee understood the necessity of eliminating the independence of division commanders, and thus formed a system over which he had more control, and more confidence. Longstreet had been the backbone of the Seven Days' battles, had shown an ability to both move his troops and carry the fight, and Lee felt an instinctive trust for his abilities. Jackson had not performed as well during the series of fights, but Lee knew him well enough to know that given a specific task, there was no one who would move forward with more energy or ruthlessness. These qualities persuaded him to place Longstreet and Jackson in command of two large wings, bringing the various division and brigade commanders closer together and under his central authority. Others, men who simply had no place leading large numbers of troops, were removed, delegated to commands in distant fronts, out of harm's way.

The most immediate difference between Lee and Johnston, however, came in Lee's communications with Davis. Lee sent a continuing stream of messages to the President, kept him informed all through the Seven Days, and now passed along messages of all kinds, from important command decisions to the more mundane. Lee knew this would put Davis in a better frame of mind, and though Davis insisted on providing him with constant advice, Lee knew that simply by the existence of the open lines, Davis would convince himself he was still in tight control, while Lee did his job in his own way.

In Washington, the administration had heard enough of McClellan's strange logic, and the general's paranoia about those who conspired against him became reality. He was relieved of command, and the Army of the Potomac was given to General John Pope.

21. CHAMBERLAIN

JULY 1862

THE UNIFORMS WERE FRESH AND BLUE AND SHARPLY CREASED, and most seemed to fit their wearers well, but occasionally the taller boys or the shorter would self-consciously glance at their too-short pants legs or the sleeves that rode down over their hands. They marched down the main street, and people came out from the shops to watch and admire. There had been no great patriotic fever in Brunswick, no loud breathers of fire, abolitionist orators, radical Unionists screaming out from soapboxes, but these boys, this new company of clean-faced boys, the sons of the shopkeepers and bankers and longshoremen, the boys who had responded to the calls for volunteers, stirred something in them, brought them together in a new way, and so they watched quietly as the slightly uneven lines paraded by.

Chamberlain had come into town to see the tailor. He now carried his package, a bundle of new shirts, all crisp and white and neatly folded, encased in a tight wrapping of brown paper. He tossed the parcel up onto the seat of the small carriage, began to pull himself up, and heard a drumbeat, a rhythmic pounding that surprised him. Then he saw the line of blue rounding the corner a block away. There was a flag, held up high by a boy in front of the line, and beside him was the drummer, who bounced the drum awkwardly in front of him, suspended by a thin strap around his neck, somehow maintaining the steady beat. Chamberlain climbed up into the carriage, sat sideways on the small seat and waited, saw the townspeople now, the small crowd gathering along the edge of the street. Then he saw the flag, a bright red A on a blank field of blue. They marched four abreast, and the line stretched back, still emerging from around the corner. He began to count, and made a quick guess, maybe two hundred. They reached him and passed at a deliberate march, the drummer setting the pace. He saw the faces, felt a cold thump in his chest; they were the faces of children.

Chamberlain had built a reputation at Bowdoin for respecting his students as much as they respected him. He advocated less strict discipline, and more equal exchange of ideas, and this put him in conflict with the old professors, the men who treated the students with a mindless rigidity, an inflexible doctrine of study and examination. The attitude appalled him, and he did much to show the students that they not only had the right to question their instructors, but were obligated to do so. He taught them to accept the responsibility for their own education, because, sadly, many of the professors would not. Now he saw the same faces, the young men he had taught, several marching in line alongside the local boys, the farmers' sons who did not go to school, who had been taught only that they would do as their fathers had done. But now there was a war.

As the troops marched by him, some of the students saw him, turning discreetly, nodded in his direction. And he saw the looks, the pride, and he thought, No, they are too young. They are not old enough to become an army. But the uniforms were new, shining buttons and black leather belts, and he turned away, felt a sudden sickness, knew the image would be with him for a long time, boys and their uniforms, marching happily to war. He waited for the last of the troops to pass, slapped the horse with the leather straps, turned the carriage toward his home.

THERE WERE EMPTY CHAIRS, GAPS AMONG THE CROWD OF SEATED students. He walked to the front of the classroom, placed his notes down slowly, on the podium, and looked out at the young faces. They watched him as they always did, the talking stopped, and there was a moment when there was no noise at all.

"Some of you are missing. I did not realize, until today, why attendance was falling off. Forgive me, I feel somewhat foolish."

There were a few giggles. He saw heads turning to look at empty chairs, and he lowered his eyes, stared down at the podium.

"Some of you have decided to fight in this war. Some of your friends are on their way to join the army, have already joined. President Lincoln's call for volunteers is being answered. To many of us, this is a surprise. Not because we did not believe people would join the fight, but because so many of them—so many of *you*—would do so with such . . . enthusiasm.

"I am embarrassed to tell you that I am among those who never believed this country would fall into this situation. I always have felt that we are a nation that is very different . . . unique, perhaps. We were founded by thinking men, brilliant men, men who designed a system where conflicts were resolved in debate, where the decision of the majority would prevail. These men had confidence in that majority, they had faith that the design of the system would, by definition, ensure that reasonable men would reach reasonable conclusions, and so we would govern ourselves, all of us, by this new type of system, a system where our conflicts and differences would be resolved by civilized means. There is no other system like this, anywhere. And if this war is lost . . . if the rebellion is successful, it is possible there may never be another."

He paused, cleared his throat.

"Forgive me, I did not intend to talk about this . . . I do have a lesson prepared here. But . . . and you may know of this, the new regiments are being formed, and they are marching off to war, and of course . . . I knew that, I have been reading the papers, just like you. But I watched them today. They marched right by me, and I saw . . . *you*. And I felt a sense of history, of familiarity . . . as though I have seen this before, great columns of troops, men with strong, proud hearts and polished weapons, marching . . . just the same as they have done for centuries, since the dawn of man. Some of us have been naive enough to believe it would not happen again, that we have gone beyond that. We were wrong.

"I don't mean to sound . . . political. I've never been one who gives much weight to the opinions of politicians, but we are living in a time when those opinions threaten the existence of this nation. That's . . . extraordinary, but it is true. Those who lead the rebellion are trying to prove a point . . . a point that we are not one nation, that we are a group of separate countries, we are Maine, and Vermont, and Virginia and Georgia and Texas and New York . . . and that if any one of us disagrees with the policies of the Federal government, we have the right to erase whatever binds us together, disregard the existence—or the importance—of the Union. They have simply said, 'We quit—and if you don't approve of our right to quit, then you will have to send a great army down here and point your bayonets at us and maybe shoot us, and you may expect that we will do the same thing to you.' If that seems a bit simplistic, forgive me. I know some of you are students of Dr. Coleman, who is imminently better qualified to explain political science."

There were giggles, a few heads were shaking no, and he paused, scanned their faces, wondered why he was doing this, but they still watched him, waited silently.

He moved away from the podium, walked toward the tall window, looked out across the grounds of the college.

"We are so far removed, and yet, it is right here, right out there. We are all a part of it."

He turned back to the faces. "Does this mean we are simply patriots? If we say you cannot destroy the Union, you cannot simply cut the ties that hold us together, is that a reason to pick up a rifle? Do any of you believe that President Lincoln has the right to ask you to . . . kill someone? I believe Dr. Coleman would agree that this nation was founded on the notion of self-determination, that we are all individuals with the right to choose, and so, how much responsibility do we have to politicians? But . . . look around you. It is more than that . . . more than politics, more than Mr. Lincoln, more than some vague principle that you might be required to recite for Dr. Coleman. A great army has come together, has *volunteered* to fight for this union. I have heard numbers . . . hundreds of thousands of men. It's astonishing. And so, if you live up here in Maine, and you never go outside New England, and you have never seen a slave, or even read the Constitution . . . you must take notice. When you see the faces of these soldiers, in their new uniforms and their shining bayonets, try to understand why this is important. If you don't feel it here, in your heart, then feel it here." He tapped the side of his head with a finger.

"If you believe something is truly important, you have an obligation to fight for it. How many times have we heard words like that, especially from great figures of authority, like . . . our parents?"

There were nods, laughter.

"And how many times have the words really meant anything? Well, my young friends, if it has never mattered before, it matters now. And if I did not believe that I would ever see young men—the men from the empty seats in this room—if I did not believe I would ever see any of you put on a uniform and pick up a musket, well, I saw it today. And . . . if there are more of you who plan on doing the same . . . God bless you."

He stopped in the doorway of the small office, saw an older woman, a tight bun of silver hair, thick glasses, sitting behind a small desk. "Excuse me," he said. "Is the meeting . . . in here?"

"What? The meeting? Yes, there, in Dr. Woods's office. Are you a member of the faculty?"

"Yes, madam, I am Professor Chamberlain. I am the—"

"Can't say I'm familiar with you, young man. No matter, I forget faces all the time. If you say so . . . go on in."

He moved warily through the small room, approached the old dark door to the president's office, stood for a moment, reached slowly for the knob, turned it quietly, and behind him the woman startled him.

"Go on in, son. They won't bite you."

He had rarely been in the president's office, had never had reason to call on Dr. Woods personally. There was a distance between them, mainly in age, but Chamberlain had respect for Woods, knew the president was at odds with most of the older faculty, men who rejected the modern notions of education. Woods had been gradually pushing through a policy of enlightenment with respect to the students' off hours, their free time. Many had felt their behavior should be regulated around the clock, that students should be monitored closely, lest they succumb to the horrors of unspeakable temptations, most of which were not identified.

"Ah, Mr. Chamberlain. Good, you made it."

Woods stood behind his desk, and there were a half-dozen men in the large office, men whom Chamberlain knew, some by reputation, others socially. There were always faculty meetings, mostly informal affairs, and Chamberlain had learned early on that attendance was rarely an issue, but this time there had been a memo directed to him, by name, a specific invitation.

He saw the always grouchy Dr. Caldwell, who nodded without smiling, and Grodin, the philosophy professor, a tiny man with a high, nervous voice, a man not much older than himself. Grodin came forward, held out a small friendly hand, which Chamberlain shook.

"I think we should begin," the president said. "Gentlemen, if you can find a chair." Woods sat down in his tall, cushioned chair, pulled himself forward, closer to the desk, leaned out toward the others, waiting for them to find seats. Chamberlain slid a straight-backed wooden chair out from the corner of the room, sat to the side of Woods's desk.

"Good, now gentlemen, let us begin." He turned and looked at Chamberlain, and Chamberlain felt the sudden stares of the others, wilted slightly.

"Professor Chamberlain, we have received some . . . somewhat disturbing reports. Please understand, this administration is not attempting to guide you in any direction. In fact, it is widely known here that your teaching is top of the line . . . first-rate. You are highly thought of . . . most highly."

Chamberlain waited, began to get impatient. "Sir, if you don't mind, can you tell me the nature of these complaints?"

Woods looked uncomfortable, glanced over to Caldwell, who said, "Professor Chamberlain, I have the highest regard for your abilities. But several of the faculty members have been hearing reports of some unusual discussions . . . unorthodox goings-on in your classroom. It is said that your views on this war—"

"Your views on this war are causing some disruption in this school." Chamberlain looked for the voice, saw a man lean forward from the far corner, Dr. Givins, the old mathematics professor, thin wisps of white hair scattered over a pale spotted scalp.

"Professor Chamberlain?" Woods saw the need to speak up, and took charge. "Have you been advising your students to volunteer for the army?"

Chamberlain looked around the room, saw the stern old faces, and the small smiling face of Grodin. He looked at Woods, saw the weary expression of a man who has better things to do.

"President Woods, I have expressed to my students that there is a significance to the events down South . . . that it is quite likely our nation is in jeopardy. I have not had to recommend to anyone on what course they should follow, they are quite capable of deciding for themselves."

"Ridiculous!" It was Givens, and he stood up, a bent old man, pointed at Chamberlain and said, "Wars are not fought by children! Young man, if you care about the well-being of this institution, then your time could be better spent teaching these students to consider the greater good!"

Chamberlain stared at the man, tried to understand what he was talking about. "The greater good?"

"This college! The enrollment. What is going to happen to this fine institution if the students rush off and join the army? It's madness! What of their futures? You're teaching them foolishness!"

Woods raised his hands, leaned toward Givens, said, "Please, Doctor, we are all gentlemen here. Your point is understood—"

"No, Dr. Woods, I'm afraid his point is not understood at all." Chamberlain stood up, could see Givens now, small in his distant chair.

"Wars are indeed fought by children, by young people who have little say in where they are sent to die. The greater good? These students may not have a greater good if this nation is dissolved. If this war goes on, we will all feel the consequences, whether we understand them or not. It is our job, our responsibility, to prepare these young people for life out there . . . outside these buildings. And right now that life is very uncertain. I'm sorry if you feel your responsibility ends in your classroom."

Caldwell stood, did not look at Chamberlain, spoke to Woods. "I'm sure that Professor Chamberlain will concede that there is not much that any of us can do that will affect the outcome of this war. The government's problems go well beyond the needs and influences of one small college. Dr. Woods, we have made a great deal of progress in building the reputation of Bowdoin as a place where students may come to receive a modern and practical education. Professor Chamberlain has contributed greatly to that reputation, and will continue to do so. Certainly he can understand the benefits of not allowing himself to be sidetracked by issues that are so far removed from that goal."

"With all respect to you, Dr. Caldwell . . ." Chamberlain paused, spoke slowly. "If we attempt to teach these students that the most important lessons they will learn are the lessons to be found within these buildings, then we have done them a most serious injustice. And they will discover that quickly, once they leave here. You . . . some of you may be satisfied with the job you do, you may pat yourselves on the back after your daily lectures and sit back in your offices, confident that you have done some great service for our young people, but I am having an increasing difficulty with that. Right now . . . there are professors, men just like us, just as educated, and just as experienced, who are facing their students at the University of Georgia, or the University of Virginia, and telling them that the course their rebellious states are following is the right one, and that they are growing up into a world where the concepts of the United States and a Federal government, and the Constitution, and . . . even the concept of individual freedom for all men, will have no meaning, are obsolete. They will study the history of the United States of America just as we now study the history of England. I'm sorry, gentlemen, I cannot stay focused on my lectures on oratory, or my lessons in German semantics, and pretend that the outcome of this war has no significance."

Woods stood, said, "Gentlemen, let us adjourn. Mr. Chamberlain has made some valid points, and I believe little else can be served by debating these issues here. I, for one, do not believe that anything of Mr. Chamberlain's ideas hold any threat to either this college or his students, and that accordingly, the matter is settled. This meeting is adjourned."

The others sat for a moment, surprised by the quick end to the meeting. Chamberlain continued to stand, thoughts pouring through his mind, a great tide of energy, and he felt he could have gone on, had a great deal more to say, and then realized Woods knew that as well. Gradually, the men rose, went to the door, and there were glances, small voices, and Givens moved by him with fragile old steps, did not look at him, and then Grodin, who held out the hand again, smiling again, and Chamberlain could not tell if he had even heard anything he'd said, wondered if any of them had.

"Mr. Chamberlain, would you remain? If it is not inconvenient . . ." Woods was motioning to the chair, and Chamberlain looked at him, saw kindness in the old face, something fatherly, and he sat down, waited. The last of the others filed out, and the door was closed behind them. Woods put his hands on his head, rubbed his temples, as though wiping away a headache.

"They probably haven't been lectured to in a long time, Mr. Chamberlain. They're not used to it."

"I'm sorry, I didn't realize I was lecturing."

"No matter. They'll recover. No doubt I'll hear from one or two of them privately, the friendly advice of my colleagues, that maybe I should talk to you myself, set you straight." He laughed, prodded the headache again.

Chamberlain watched him, pulled his chair over toward the front of the desk, felt himself heating up again, said, "So, is that what this is? Are you going to tell me that I should watch what I say, that I should pay no attention to my instincts, my fears about the war? I should not disrupt the blind serenity of Bowdoin College?"

"Certainly not. Mr. Chamberlain, I share many of your concerns. Unlike many of those distinguished men, I have traveled somewhat throughout the South, and I know that what you are saying is probably true. But I also know that these men are right, that there is very little that any of us can do to affect these matters, and that if we open up our worst fears, if we convince these students that our nation is in a deep crisis, it is possible, don't you see . . . they may take that seriously. They may stop applying themselves, what's the use, and so forth. Some of them will go off and be soldiers—young people are good at that sort of nonsense—but it's the rest that concern me, the ones who stay, who look to us for a foundation, something they can build on. It is possible, Mr. Chamberlain, that what you are telling them is taking that foundation away."

Chamberlain felt suddenly betrayed.

"But you said you agreed—"

"Yes, Mr. Chamberlain, I do agree. I understand, and I share your concerns. That much is true. But I question the wisdom of sharing those concerns with young minds."

"There is no one else better suited to solve these problems. Certainly, you don't believe this office full of gray-haired academicians is going to solve anything." He looked at Woods's gray hair. "My apologies, sir."

"No, you are quite right. But my concern is you. I believe you need something . . . to take you away from these distractions. This war is not likely to last very long, you know. And when it is over, we will need to get back to the job at hand, which is teaching these young people. Right now, you are distracted. I would like to propose a possible solution."

Chamberlain waited, watching the kind old face, then realized he was about to be fired, felt a sudden lump in his stomach.

"Mr. Chamberlain, I would like you to consider a leave of absence. Have you ever been to Europe?"

"Europe? No, sir, I haven't."

"Well, this might be the perfect time. Take a leave of absence. We'll grant you two years. Travel, study, visit the great universities, the museums, the cathedrals, immerse yourself in the culture. You have a great talent for languages, so use it. It should be easy for you . . . and your family. It will be the opportunity of a lifetime for them. When it's over, come back here, to your Chair, and I am confident your attitude will have tempered. The war will certainly be over, and all this . . . disruption will be gone."

"Two years?"

"That should be plenty of time. It's an opportunity, Mr. Chamberlain. A rare opportunity."

"I would like to think about it, if you don't mind, discuss it with my wife."

"Of course, I'm not looking for an answer right now."

"Thank you, sir." He stood, felt a fog in his brain, a sudden numbness, his mind flooded with the idea of leaving, and . . . Europe . . . and he nodded, went slowly to the door.

Woods said to him, "It's the opportunity of a lifetime!"

HE HAD GIVEN HER AN ABSURD EXCUSE, FELT GUILTY IMMEDIately, but she would not understand, and there would be time for explanations later.

Augusta was a short coach ride from Brunswick, and he had wired a request, had received a positive response, and so today he would see the governor.

The coach reached the city, and he saw immediately the government buildings, the state capitol. There was little about the town to impress, but he felt impressed anyway, had never dealt with a seat of power, did not consider that these were just politicians, but the men who were close to it all, who had the facts, had up-to-date knowledge of the war and made their decisions accordingly. He felt childlike, excited.

He had excused himself from his classes for a couple of days, and Woods, and the rest, did not know where he was. It was assumed he had taken some time to be with his family, to weigh the great decision of accepting the leave. He told Fannie that he had to attend a meeting in Augusta, but did not mention the governor, said something that he could not even remember, some fictitious name of an academic conference. It had been a lie, and he knew it, and she had said nothing. He thought, She knows. But then, No, she knows you the same way they all know you, you're the bright young scholar, the man with the future firmly planted in academics, and they have no idea what it is doing to you.

The coach hit a pothole, lurched through the rough stone streets of the capital. He watched the unfamiliar scenes roll past, shops and bakeries and offices. She would never understand this, he thought, and none of them will listen, they will tell me I'm a fool, a college professor who knows nothing of life beyond academics, who has no business anywhere close to the war.

The coach slowed, pulled into the depot, and he stepped down, could still see the top of the capitol building, high above the rows of shops and houses, and he moved quickly in that direction. He looked at his watch: one-thirty. He was early, had time, but did not slow down, would sit and wait for hours if he had to. He paid little attention to the people, the storefronts, kept his eyes on the capitol, then finally he turned a corner and saw the entire building, perched in the center of a square, waiting for him to arrive.

"SIR, GOVERNOR WASHBURN CAN SEE YOU NOW."

He was startled, had let his head fall, sleepily, and he snapped awake, stood, saw the young man holding the door for him, and he tried to say something, his mouth dry and thick. "Thnn uuu," he said, and cleared his throat, stepped through the door.

Washburn sat behind his fat desk, framed by heavy flags, the state of Maine and the Stars and Stripes. It was a picture that Chamberlain had expected, what a governor's office should look like. Washburn was a man of medium height, showed signs of a prosperous life; a large roundness pushed his coat forward. He wore glasses, peered over them at the young professor, then glanced over to another man, a thin, older man in a blue uniform, who sat beside the great desk, examining Chamberlain carefully.

"Professor Chamberlain. We received your request.... A bit unusual, but these are unusual times. I understand that you wish to volunteer for service. Exactly what did you have in mind?"

Chamberlain stood stiffly, said, "Governor, I would like to volunteer for military service in whatever capacity you consider appropriate. I am an educated man, I have considerable experience instructing young people, and I am willing to serve where the army considers me the most useful. Sir."

"Professor, that's a fine offer. Are you familiar with General Hodsdon, our adjutant general for the state of Maine?"

Chamberlain looked at the man in the uniform, who nodded pleasantly, and Chamberlain stiffened again, said, "No, sir."

"Well, Professor, General Hodsdon has the unenviable responsibility of organizing and equipping our volunteer regiments, and seeing that they are staffed with commanders who may lead them out safely beyond the border of our state, so they may lend a hand to President Lincoln's army. General, would you like to ask the professor here some questions?"

"Certainly, Governor. Professor, I took the liberty of wiring your President Woods, asking about you. Nothing too personal, of course, but we do need to know what we are dealing with here."

Chamberlain looked at Hodsdon, felt a lump forming in his stomach.

"Professor, in all honesty, I was surprised to find that President Woods did not seem to be aware that you were making this visit."

"No, sir, I did not inform him."

"May I ask why?"

"Because, sir . . ." He paused, sorted the words. "I am considered to be a good teacher. I have a prestigious position at Bowdoin. It is unlikely that Dr. Woods would appreciate my desire . . . to leave."

"You're quite right about that, he did not seem to appreciate it at all. However, he did respond to my inquiry with some highly positive comments. I don't mean to embarrass you, Professor, but he considers you a brilliant man. He made mention of your value to the college, and he considers you to be the . . . how did he put it . . . the 'new light of the future' or something like that."

"Dr. Woods is very kind. I do not consider myself destined, however, to remain behind the walls of a university. I have a strong belief in the need, our need, to win this war."

"That's good, Professor. Tell me, do you have any military experience?"

He paused again, thought of just saying no, but considered that anything might help. "Sir, when I was younger, I attended Major Whiting's Military Academy." He felt instantly foolish. He had been barely a teenager.

"Yes, I'm familiar with Major Whiting. Is there anything else?"

"No, sir. But before you pass judgment, please allow me to express that . . . I will accept the challenge of studying military tactics, and I will apply myself to training as I have applied myself to . . . many things."

Chamberlain stared straight ahead, looking past Washburn's head, heard a slight chuckle.

Hodsdon said to Washburn, "Governor, President Woods gave me a lengthy description of this young professor. He speaks seven languages, teaches four different disciplines, and Woods says he will likely master any subject that is placed before him."

"It's no wonder President Woods is unhappy with your running off to join the army." Both men laughed now, and Chamberlain nodded slightly, felt himself relaxing.

Washburn waved his hand, said, "Professor, it is not necessary for you to stand at attention. You're making me nervous. Sit down, please, over there."

Chamberlain turned, saw a wide dark chair, sat slowly down, thought, At least, keep your back straight.

Washburn moved some papers on his desk, studied one, said, "Professor, I have an order here from President Lincoln, requesting five new regiments of infantry. *Five.* We're talking about five thousand men. General Hodsdon has already sent them fifteen regiments, but it's not enough."

Hodsdon said, "Professor, what do you know of the war?"

Chamberlain considered the question, said, "I know that we are fighting against a rebellion that . . . if we are not successful—"

"No, Professor, the *war*. The fighting."

"I have seen newspapers, some reports."

"Professor, what the newspapers will not tell you is that the Federal Army has shown that when it confronts the forces of the rebels, when we bring superior numbers and superior armament against an enemy that is poorly equipped, underfed, and outnumbered, *we lose*. The war could well have been over last July, after that mess at Bull Run, had the rebels marched on into Washington. They sent our troops scurrying back across the Potomac like a bunch of schoolchildren. We are in sad shape, Professor. I for one am pleased to accept your offer. We are in desperate need of good officers."

Washburn said, "General, how about this? I see here . . . we have no one yet in command of the Twentieth Regiment. Professor, how would you like to be commissioned the rank of colonel and placed in command of the Twentieth Regiment? How does that sound?"

Chamberlain stood again, looked over at Hodsdon. "Well . . . Governor . . . thank you, but . . . commander? I must admit, I would have no idea how to begin. I had thought, maybe a lower position . . ."

Hodsdon leaned across the desk, pointed at something in Washburn's papers that Chamberlain could not see, then said, "Governor, I believe the professor is correct, perhaps immediate command of a regiment may be a bit premature. As you can see, here, we have Colonel Ames arriving back here next month. I had expected to appoint him to command that regiment."

"Hmmm, all right, yes I see." Washburn nodded, then looked up over his glasses at Chamberlain. "Well, then, Professor. How about Lieutenant Colonel? You would serve as second in command, the Twentieth Maine Regiment, under the command of Colonel Adelbert Ames."

Chamberlain absorbed the words "Lieutenant Colonel," felt a bursting need to yell at the top of his lungs, run around the wide office, and he pulled himself together, knew he was smiling, could not help it.

"I am honored to serve, sir. May I ask . . . when would I—"

Hodsdon said, "You will receive orders within a few weeks. Most likely, you will report to the adjutant's office in Portland, it's the closest to you. This should give you enough time to arrange your personal affairs."

Washburn stood, held out a thick hand. "Good luck, Professor. Oh . . . one piece of advice."

"Yes, sir, please."

"When you take command of your troops, it might be better for discipline if you're not smiling like that."

THE COACH RIDE FROM THE CAPITAL SEEMED TO TAKE FOREVER. Now he walked, and sometimes ran, from the depot, and reached his house in a panting, sweating excitement.

He stopped outside the front door, said to himself, Slow, calm down, and let his body breathe heavily. He waited a moment and then opened the front door. Inside he heard the cries of his small son, Wyllys, now barely three, and he stopped, was struck by a wave of guilt, felt that he had somehow betrayed his family. He listened to the boy, the sound echoing through the house, and then heard Fannie, saying something, trying to calm him. Chamberlain walked slowly through the house, went down the hallway, toward the sounds, reached the doorway into the children's room and paused.

Fannie sat on the floor beside the boy, holding something, a toy, waving it toward him in a playful tease, and the boy quieted. Up on the small bed, Daisy, who was now five, watched them both, began to laugh as the crisis passed. They did not see him, and he stayed quiet, framing the scene before him like a treasured picture, one he knew he would carry with him.

Fannie had given birth to four children, and two had not survived. There had been doubts about Wyllys's health as well, and his first year had been difficult. Chamberlain had grown weary of doctors, of somber pronouncements and vague predictions, and through it all he had feared more for Fannie. Their home had become the warm nest she needed, and the deaths of the children had shaken her, but Chamberlain was amazed that she had come back, had learned to smile and laugh and play again. Even after the second death, it was as though she had expected it, a price for the happiness, and so it too had passed, and now the boy was growing, the problems were behind them, and the family was complete.

"Daddy!" Daisy saw him now, jumped off the bed, ran to him and clutched his leg.

Fannie turned around and smiled, saw his expression, and the smile faded. She turned back to the boy, made sure he was all right, then stood up and said, "You're back so soon. I wasn't sure . . . you said it might be a couple of days."

"Yes, it did not take long. The ride is fairly short. Come, we need to talk."

"Let me get them ready for bed. It's been a rather long day. They seem to have some new energy these days, or maybe . . . I have less." She forced a small laugh, and he knew she was preparing herself for something, some news, his face had betrayed him. He went outside, to the small front porch, sat in a rickety chair, saw lights now, the day was done. He pushed back carefully, felt the chair twisting, groaning, and he looked up, saw the first stars, looked back on his day, his meeting, what he had done, and realized now that he actually felt alive, and happy, and it shook him, he had not felt this way in years. Now he would have to explain that to her.

It was not long, a few minutes, and she came out, had wrapped a sweater around her shoulders, moved in front of him, to the other chair. He could barely see her now, her silhouette in the dim lamplights of the town.

"I don't think I could have gotten them to bed if you had not come home. That's all I heard this afternoon, 'Where's Daddy?' "

They sat quietly, and Chamberlain felt himself tensing up, felt his heart beating. His hands began to sweat, and he took a deep breath, then another. Fannie heard him, knew he was finding the words, waited a few minutes, then said, "Are we moving?"

"What? Moving?"

"I thought . . . maybe you have been offered a new position."

"Well, no, but . . ." He stopped, could put it off no longer. "I saw the governor today, Governor Washburn."

"The governor? Really?" She laughed, "My father calls him Old Breadball."

Chamberlain smiled, knew many reasons why he did not discuss politics with Reverend Adams.

"The governor has offered me . . . a commission. He has offered me a command position, a lieutenant colonel's rank . . . in the Maine volunteers."

She sat up straight, and he felt her eyes. "Why would he do that?"

"Because I requested it. I volunteered for service."

She stared at him in the dark, and he leaned forward, brought the chair slowly back down onto four legs.

"You volunteered . . . to join the army? Why on earth . . . you mean, you want to leave here? Leave us?"

"No, I didn't do it for that. Please. I love you, I love you all. But . . . this has been coming for a long time . . . maybe since the war started."

"You can't mean this, Lawrence. You're not a soldier."

He heard the edge in her voice, knew she was not going to take this well. He turned in the chair, faced her.

"The closer I came to doing this, the more I thought about it, the more I knew it was something I had to do . . . I wanted to do. I cannot let this war happen without doing something. If I don't do . . . something . . . I will regret it for the rest of my life."

Her voice was quiet, softer. "But what about your career? You can't just . . . quit. Have you told them?"

"No. I will do that tomorrow. They already know, probably. Woods knows. I'm sure I will hear a lot of . . . criticism. Those old men, they have no idea what this is about. I doubt I could ever convince them, so I won't try. They can't stop it. They've granted me the leave already."

"I thought we were going to Europe, I thought that was the news. You haven't told me if you were accepting the leave or not. It's been weeks, and I thought, finally, you had made up your mind. I did not expect you to join the army. How could you do this . . . without discussing this with me first? Do I not have any say in this?" She was angry now, and he looked away from her, out into the dark, did not have an answer for her, had never been able to tell her that he was simply . . . unhappy.

"I'm sorry. Please try to understand. . . ."

"I thought we were finally . . . doing so well. I thought you enjoyed . . . doing what you did. You never gave me any notion that you would ever do anything like this."

He looked at her again, tried to see her face in the dark, said, "I had come to believe that I would grow old standing in front of students, reciting my lessons, and that it didn't matter if I was happy or not. If this is where I am supposed to be, then I would accept that. But . . . something changed. I look into their faces, and they expect answers, and I began to realize that the answers they want are the same ones *I* want. My colleagues . . . they stopped asking about anything a long time ago . . . they know all they need to know, and their lives are as complete as they will ever be, and that works for them. I am not ready to grow old, to accept that what I am today is what I will always be."

She stood, moved away, to the edge of the porch, leaned against the thin railing, stared out to the night sky. "So, that's it."

He stood, moved toward her. She lowered her head, said slowly, her voice calmer now, "So . . . when do you leave? How long will you be gone? What will you be doing?"

"I'm not sure . . . of any of that. They'll send me orders . . . soon . . . a few weeks. It's a new regiment, the Twentieth. I'll be serving under a fellow named Ames, Colonel Ames. I expect we have a good deal of training to go through. I have a lot to learn."

"You'll learn it. If you want to do this, you will learn it."

He smiled, thought of Woods, Hodsdon. "They seem to believe that too."

He moved close behind her, wrapped his arms around hers, held her against him. They stood quietly together for a long moment, then she said, "What of us, the children? Are we to stay here?"

"Well, yes . . . I suppose so. I will be able to send money home, my salary. We'll have to see . . . it's up to you, really."

"Up to me?" He heard the anger again, her voice cutting through him. "How much of anything is up to me? You have made a decision that will change all our lives. A soldier . . . my God, you may be injured . . . you . . . might never . . ." And now she began to cry, shook against him softly. He reached into his pocket, pulled out his handkerchief, held it out to her, and she wiped her eyes.

"No, no . . . don't think on that. I will probably be sent to some office somewhere, writing speeches for some general."

He tried to sound convincing, but she turned in his arms, faced him now, said, "No, Lawrence, that is not what you will do. That is not why you volunteered." She had stopped crying, stared at him hard in the dark. "Go, do this thing . . . but be honest about it. Do not tell yourself that everyone here is happy for you, that you are doing something wonderful for us all. I will not spend my nights happily thinking about what could be happening to you. I will not send you away from here with a lie. If you are not happy, then change that, but remember that what you are doing may have a price for the rest of us . . . for me. . . ." She began to cry again, sobbed hard against him.

He held her, put his head down gently against hers and said, "I will try to be careful . . . I *will* be careful. I *will* come home to you. I will miss you . . . I will miss the children."

She grew quiet, still leaned tightly to him, then he felt her stiffen, pull away slightly, and she said calmly, "I know you will. And I know you will write us, and I know we will be all right. There is my father, and your family too." She moved away from his arms, along the porch, turned back and said, "Lawrence, when you come home, you will be a different person. I am afraid for . . . what that will be like. I don't want you to change. But if you must do this, then go do it, and we will pray for you, and when it is over, your family will be here."

He nodded quietly, knew it was all she could give him, that he had done something for himself, and that not all of them could understand, not even she.

To the east, out toward the vast open water, the moon began to climb above the treetops and the peaks of the houses, and he could see her face reflected in the faint light, said in a whisper, "I *will* come home . . . and I *will* make you proud."

He went to her then, pulled her up to him, and she softened against him, and he kissed her, a soft and long caress. Far off, beyond the town, the hollow wail of a great long train cut through the night, the cars heavy with men in rich blue uniforms, sharp creases and polished buttons, rocking in a steady rhythm down the southbound tracks.

22. LEE

August 1862

"SIR, IT APPEARS THAT THINGS ARE A BIT MORE QUIET. DO YOU have any orders?"

Taylor stood in the small doorway, and Lee turned away from the window, studied the young man for a moment, said, "No, Major . . . actually, I don't. We seem to have . . . a pause. It's been a long time. I'm waiting to hear more of Pope. Have we heard from General Stuart today?"

"No, sir. I will inform you when he arrives. Sir . . . might I suggest . . . begging your pardon, sir."

Lee waited, knew Taylor was still slow to speak frankly, often treated him as he would an overly stern father who would lash out angrily if the words did not come out just right. Lee did not understand that, had never been angry or harsh with him.

"Please, Major, you have something to say?"

"Sir, we feel it might be a good opportunity for you . . . to visit your wife, sir. It's a short ride . . . and you could be back by dark. We can handle anything that comes up today. You said yourself . . . it's pretty quiet, sir."

Lee looked at him, saw a slight smile, knew the young man was trying to be helpful, and he thought of Mary, living now at the Spottswood. Taylor was right, it was a short ride into Richmond.

"Thank you for your suggestion, Major. However, we are in the midst of organizing a new army . . . new commanders, a new way of doing things. It is not appropriate for me to suddenly leave . . . make a journey to Richmond for my personal benefit."

"Sir, only for the day—"

"Major, thank you for your concern. You are dismissed."

Taylor looked hurt, like a scolded pet, and Lee watched him turn, disappear from the doorway. He does not understand, Lee thought.

Mary had come to Richmond, carried through Union lines by the generosity of McClellan. The plantations were under Federal control now, and months before, Arlington had been ransacked and vandalized, despite assurances from General McDowell that the historic home would be protected. Though McClellan had guaranteed she would be safe at her son's home, it was risky, and McClellan was receiving criticism for providing a guard for the wife of the enemy commander. So, she had been granted safe passage. More fragile and crippled than ever, she made the journey to Richmond without incident. Lee met her there, saw her for the first time in months, and her condition was worse. The visit had not gone well, and seeing her had depressed him. His appearance had changed as well—he now was fully gray, and had grown a full, short beard. The change made him seem older, and she absorbed that reality poorly. Now, he was deep into his command, had buried himself totally in the running of this army, and could not bear to think of her . . . could not face what they had become, the permanent distance between them.

Lee turned back to the window, stared out at the trees, watched the heavy branches sway slightly, the leaves flickering in a summer breeze. He thought of going out, walking down to the small grove of apple trees that stood at the end of a far field, a field that had once grown corn and wheat, but now, after the marching feet of his troops, was only patches of thick short grass, dotted with bare spots of dried mud. He tried to stand, felt suddenly weak, saw her face again, the younger face, the way it had been before. But it was not a clear memory, and the early years, when the children were small, the brief times together, did not seem real, did not even seem to be his. The only life that was real to him was this one, the army.

He heard horses, several, riding hard up to the house, and he knew from the sound it was too fast and too much show: *Stuart*. He smiled, heard loud voices and took a last look out the window. How strange, he thought, I feel more like a father here than anywhere else. They are all my children: Taylor, Stuart, sometimes . . . even Jackson. Maybe this whole army . . .

Is that not what a commander must do, earn respect, give them discipline and . . . love them? The thought jarred him. He felt suddenly guilty, thought, No, it's all right, I do not love my own family any less. But I have not been a good father . . . and now God has placed me here, to redeem myself. And if my own children don't know . . . then these men will. He turned back toward the doorway, waited for the inevitable burst of Stuart.

But it was Taylor first. "Sir, General Stuart has returned, and has asked to see you."

Lee was still smiling, tried to hide it, said, "Of course, Major, send him in."

Stuart was instantly through the door, and Taylor backed out. Stuart had kept his hat on, rich gray felt and a long black plume, waited for the right moment, removed it with a flourish and made a deep bow to his commander. Lee let him go through the routine, could not hide the smile. Abruptly, Stuart came to attention, slapped his heels together sharply.

"Sir, with your permission, may I present the latest newspapers from the North." He reached into his coat, withdrew a handful of clippings, laid them carefully on Lee's desk. Lee leaned forward, picked through them, all items about McClellan and Pope and the recent battles.

"Good, General, thank you. I see there's quite a bit about their new commander."

Stuart made a sound, a grunt, and Lee looked at him, questioning. "With the general's permission," Stuart said, "I have heard of General Pope's dispatches, sir. He has ordered his men to pursue a policy of barbarism, sir, pure barbarism. His army has been instructed to take whatever they can from our farms, from our stores. He has ordered anyone conversing with any of our people to be arrested as a spy." Stuart began to move, pacing in the small space, obviously angry. Lee sat back in his chair, watching, surprised. "General Lee, this man is no gentleman. McClellan . . . at least you could depend on him to conduct himself like a civilized man . . . but this fellow Pope is . . . a barbarian!"

Lee picked up one of the clippings, read briefly, *My headquarters shall be in my saddle.* Lee paused, knew there would be jokes about that. He read on, a message Pope had given to his troops, trumpeting his victories in the West, which Lee stopped to consider, some minor battles that had little influence on the war. He read on, *I come from where . . . we have always seen our enemies from the rear . . . let us not talk of taking strong positions and holding them, lines of retreat, bases of supplies.* The story quoted him further, bombastic statements about crushing the enemy with quick and direct blows, and Lee looked up at Stuart, who was still moving about.

"Well, it seems we have a new problem."

"Sir, I have learned that General Pope has taken command of the forces under Banks and Fremont, and has at his command, sir, something over fifty-five thousand men. General McClellan has not yet left his base on the James River, but according to . . . those reports, there, sir, in the Washington paper . . . the wounded from his forces have already been seen coming up the Potomac. If General Pope is planning a large-scale operation, he will need General McClellan's forces. It's only logical, sir. . . ."

"Yes, General, I see that." He pushed through more of the clippings. "It seems that McClellan is no longer a priority with Mr. Lincoln. Certainly, his troops will begin to move, to unite with Pope's."

"Sir, they cannot be allowed to treat our civilians with such lack of respect."

"There's more to it than that, General." Lee felt something, an uneasiness in his stomach, thought, Pope is a dangerous man, a man who will say anything to create a name for himself, who will say and do anything to rally support from Washington.

"General Stuart, please excuse me . . . you are dismissed."

"But sir, I have . . . I have other details . . . troop positions—"

"It's all right, General, we will talk in a little while. I just need a few moments."

Stuart snapped to attention again, saluted, and left the room. Lee turned back to the window, thoughts rolling through his mind in waves. He took a deep breath, began to sort out a plan, thought, This is a great opportunity. We can use Pope's own ego to trap him.

He pondered, watched the slow motion of the big trees, then turned, said in a loud voice, "Major Taylor," and instantly Taylor was in the doorway. Lee looked at the bright face, said, "Major, send for General Jackson."

BY LATE AUGUST, POPE'S ARMY WAS CENTERED IN THE AREA BEtween the Rappahannock and Rapidan Rivers, north of Fredericksburg. Lee ordered Jackson's troops north, to move between Pope and Washington, which would have the easily predictable effect on Lincoln, who would see Jackson's move as a direct threat to the capital. Pope would certainly be called upon to move back to the northeast, removing his pressure on central Virginia. Lee also suspected that Pope would convince himself he had been given a glorious opportunity, that Jackson's army by itself was no match for his superior numbers. By assuming correctly that Pope would focus completely on Jackson, Lee knew he could maneuver the rest of his army, under Longstreet, and bring the attack to Pope while he was exposed.

The move by Jackson's troops also achieved a direct benefit for his own forces. Their sudden advance put them quickly at the Manassas Gap railroad junction, where Pope's supplies were stored. The small number of troops guarding the depot were easily routed by Jackson's surprise arrival, and so they not only disrupted the flow of material to Pope's army, but found themselves awash in vast stores of food and equipment. Pope reacted as Lee had predicted, and began to move back up to crush the greatly outnumbered Jackson, with little regard for the rest of Lee's army, which, unknown to Pope, had moved by a slightly different route, to unite with Jackson's forces.

McClellan's troops were indeed being withdrawn from the Virginia peninsula, and were moving up the Potomac to join with Pope. Thus, Lee knew his opportunity for meeting Pope on more even terms was a brief one. But Pope was in a hurry as well, would not sit and wait for the rest of his army to arrive while the ripe target of Jackson sat alone.

LEE AND LONGSTREET RODE TOGETHER, IN FRONT OF THE LONG columns, quietly, feeling the August heat. Out in front, nervous skirmishers, a handpicked squad of Texas sharpshooters, cleared the way of any Federal snipers and scouted the advance of the army for detachments of Federal troops who might have been sent to scout the Confederate positions. They were the only advance guard the two men had. Behind them, Hood's division led the long column.

Lee rested his head, his hat pulled low, and appeared to be sleeping, but he was very awake, his mind focused on what might be ahead of them and where Jackson might be. They had received no word since last night, knew only that Pope's army was scattered, the result of a hasty march, and that somewhere, up ahead, Jackson was preparing for the assault.

They had climbed a long hill, had crested the top, surrounded by the familiar signs of a bloody fight. It was Thoroughfare Gap, where General John Buford's Federal cavalry had slowed the march, holding the pass against a brigade of Georgians, commanded by George Anderson. Buford's cavalry had been stubborn, had held up the march for nearly half a day, but finally General Hood had been sent over the mountain through another route, a nearby pass, and the flanking movement had worked. Buford's men and a small detachment of supporting infantry finally gave way.

Now, the Federal troops were gone, pulling back, to unite with Pope's larger army, and so Longstreet's men kept moving forward, up and over the mountain, toward their rendezvous with Jackson.

They rode slowly, a steady rhythm, and behind them the officers were shouting now, for the hills were steep and the heat was draining the men. Lee could hear the commands, "Keep up," "Stay together," and he sat up straighter, crested the hill, saw shattered trees and broken wagons, noticed the fresh smell of yesterday's fight. Along the wide ridge, in the rocks and beyond, the bodies of men still lay, exposed. Lee saw the uniforms, both sides, a vicious fight in a tight area, and the army was now pushing through, quickly, too soon for even the burial parties. They had marched nearly thirty miles in thirty hours, and so it was not just the heat that deadened their steps.

Lee saw the Texans moving below, keeping a tight line, spread far to each side, and he smiled, thankful. Behind him, he heard voices, then one voice, the deep, booming sound of John Bell Hood.

"Well, dammit, move them along! It's just a hill!"

Lee turned, saw Hood approach, a small staff following.

"General Lee, forgive me, I had meant to ride with you earlier. We're having a bit of trouble getting these men up this damned hill . . . begging your pardon, sir."

Lee nodded, and Longstreet turned in his saddle. Hood abruptly saluted, and it was an awkward moment. Longstreet was Hood's commander, and Hood knew he should have spoken to Longstreet first. It was a small error, one of those annoying pieces of military etiquette that Hood had not yet mastered.

"General Longstreet, I have ordered the company commanders to push the men hard, get them up this hill with all speed."

"That's good, General." Longstreet spoke from under a wide-brimmed hat, pulled low so his face was half hidden. Hood looked at Lee, and Lee saw the eyes, the wide, excited face, the thick blond beard, and he thought of Texas, knew Hood had not changed. He had performed brilliantly as a commander, had led his Texans with a fire that infected them all, and Lee knew that if it was critical, if one man could be sent into the furnace, could face the deadly hell and turn the tide, it would be Hood.

Hood said, "I'd best get back down the line . . . see how we're doing." He saluted, Longstreet returned it, and Hood glanced at Lee with sharp, smiling eyes. Lee nodded, knew that Hood remembered Texas too, the shared experiences, unspoken feelings men have when they both know they are good soldiers.

Lee turned to Longstreet, who was staring ahead, peeking out under the brim of his hat.

"We shall need him, I believe, before this is through. Make good use of him, General."

Longstreet did not turn, kept staring to the front, said, "I've seen him work, General. He will have his chance again."

Lee followed Longstreet's stare, tried to see what held his attention. He had seen the look before, as though Longstreet were seeing something far away, well beyond the horizon.

Longstreet was partially deaf, and others who did not know him well often mistook it for aloofness or simple rudeness. He was not a man for fluent conversation, did not join in around the campfire, the jovial, drunken revelry that too often surrounded the headquarters. Lee had learned to respect him as a commander, knew Joe Johnston had relied on him often. He had not known Longstreet long, had not known him at all before the war.

Longstreet came home from Mexico with a wound that hadn't healed for a long time. He settled into a career as a paymaster in the old army, had spent most of the peacetime years out West, in El Paso and Albuquerque, and never had shown the ambition to press further. At the start of the war he was a major, and had come back to the South expecting nothing more, volunteering for a job as paymaster again. But President Davis knew him from Mexico, knew that Longstreet had led infantry, the great assault on the big fortress of Chapultepec, knew of his training at West Point and his abilities to command, and so Longstreet was surprised to be commissioned a brigadier general. Only a few weeks after his arrival in Virginia, he was leading troops at Manassas.

But Lee knew something had changed, there was a new darkness in Longstreet's eyes, in his moods, and Lee tried to understand it. The cause seemed obvious at first. During the previous winter, while his family was staying in Richmond, all four of Longstreet's children had contracted a fever. Within a few days three of them died. All of Richmond was shaken by this news, and no one expected that he would return to duty so quickly, resume command of that part of the army that would play such a large part in turning McClellan away.

Lee had heard the earlier stories, the poker playing, the long nights of drinking and bawdy storytelling, and he could not believe any of that, did not see those things in this big, dark man. There was a hollowness, a deep opening in the man's soul, and Lee had wanted to talk about that, to be of some . . . comfort. He didn't know if

Longstreet was particularly devout, had never heard him mention God, thought, If he knew that God is with him, that all of this . . . his tragedies, are part of a Plan . . . But there was never the right moment; the two men did not share that kind of close conversation. To Lee, that sort of closeness had never been easy, but he'd grown very fond of Longstreet, was not even sure why, and so wanted to do . . . something. They often were together now. Longstreet seemed to gravitate toward Lee's headquarters, but the conversations were brief and military, strategy and planning, and Lee sensed an edge, as though Longstreet held himself in some tightly bound, angry place. Longstreet seemed to know it himself, and Lee began to hear more caution in his planning, more need to avoid the big risks.

Jackson was very different. Lee had come to understand that if left alone, Jackson held nothing back, would operate with a fury and an anger that was simple and straightforward. He was given credit for military genius. The newspapers referred to him as the greatest general in either army, though Jackson never seemed to pay attention to that kind of praise. Around Lee he was like a young child, eyes wide, eager to please the fatherly Lee, and so Lee had learned to treat him that way. But he did not see just a child. He saw a very strong and dangerous animal that would do whatever you asked him to do, with complete dedication and frightening efficiency.

Lee did not know how Longstreet and Jackson felt about each other. There had never been a dispute, or any other reason to examine their relationship. Longstreet clearly considered himself the ranking officer, which technically was true: his commission had come first. Jackson had often deferred to that seniority when the two were together, but Longstreet understood Jackson's value, and if he thought Jackson reckless and headstrong, he did not express it to Lee.

The strength of the forces under the two generals was now nearly equal, due mainly to the transfer of Ambrose Powell Hill's division from Longstreet's command to Jackson's. A. P. Hill was a difficult, moody, and egotistical man, and a dispute had arisen between him and Longstreet after the Seven Days' battles. A correspondent for the Richmond *Examiner* had written glowing and exaggerated accounts of Hill's role in the army's confrontations against McClellan, indicating that Hill's division was responsible for most, if not all, of their successes. Longstreet responded angrily by authorizing his chief of staff, Major Moxley Sorrel, to write a letter to a rival newspaper, the *Whig*, setting the record straight. After heated and nasty correspondence between Hill and his commander, Longstreet finally had Hill arrested, which so inflamed Hill that he challenged Longstreet to a duel. By this time Lee had no choice but to intervene. The solution was simple, and served a useful purpose. Hill's division was moved, increasing Jackson's strength, and Longstreet was relieved of a headache.

The columns were closing up behind them, and still Longstreet stared ahead, not moving. He spurred his horse then and moved slowly forward, starting down through the gap. Lee followed, and Longstreet stopped again, and now Lee heard it. There was a rumble, straight ahead, the rolling thunder of cannon, and Lee knew it was Jackson.

They began to move again, and behind them the column of soldiers reacted to the distant sounds, the men quickening their steps with a new flow of energy. Lee strained toward the horizon, looked for smoke, and then from below he saw riders, the gray hat and the tall plume: *Stuart.*

The horses reined up, and a cloud of hot dust followed, enveloping the group of men. Lee closed his eyes, waited, and Stuart said, "General Lee, General Jackson is engaged, in a line facing to the southeast. He is deployed along an unfinished railroad cut and is in a position of some strength. I suggest, sir, that you direct this column to his right flank. There is a small town, Gainesville, where you may turn to the left, taking the Warrenton Turnpike toward Groveton. You will find General Jackson's right flank anchored there."

Stuart was breathing heavily, and Lee waited for the flood of words to pass, then said, "General Stuart, my compliments. We will proceed as you have suggested. Can you advise us as to the concentration of General Pope's army?"

"Sir, General Jackson is facing a heavy concentration of troops. We have located three corps, with at least three more corps approaching the field."

Longstreet rubbed his nose, said quietly, "That's near seventy thousand men. Jackson has twenty-two thousand. I hope that railroad cut is a deep one."

Lee turned to Longstreet, said, "General, I have confidence that General Jackson will not engage the enemy unless he is confident of holding his lines. It is up to us now. We still have an opportunity. Let us move forward."

Longstreet saluted, turned his horse around, saw the approach of Hood, who was hurrying toward the group of commanders.

Longstreet said, "General Hood, your men will lead the column, and speed is a priority. We will proceed to Gainesville, turning left and filing out in a line away from General Jackson's right flank."

Instantly Hood was away, riding back to his officers with the instructions, and now Lee said to Stuart, "General, take your men out to the right, to the northeast, see if you can determine if more troops are close to joining Pope's forces. McClellan's army is out there somewhere, and if they are moving this way, we need to know. Be mindful that your position will also serve to protect General Longstreet's right flank."

Stuart smiled, nodded. "Sir, I have a squadron out that way now."

"Good, General. You will keep me informed?"

Stuart removed the hat, made a sweeping motion. "I serve only you, *mon Général*."

Salutes were exchanged and Stuart rode back down, away from the column. Lee turned, saw the men pressing forward, motioned to his staff, the waiting couriers. He could feel the movement from behind, the pressure of the column, unstoppable, and he spurred his horse, leading them forward. Down the hill he saw the lines of sharpshooters, watching, waiting for him to begin moving again, and now they continued forward, down through the thinning trees.

Longstreet rode alongside, still stared out ahead, toward the low sound of the guns, which was now constant. He pointed, but Lee had already seen a flat cloud of smoke beginning to rise over far trees.

Lee said, "General Stuart has proven himself valuable again."

Longstreet said nothing, and Lee knew he did not approve of Stuart's style, the flair for the dramatic.

Lee waited, then said, "He is of great value to us, General."

Longstreet nodded, said, "I do wish . . . begging your pardon, General, but he needs to be kept on a shorter leash. He has a great love of headlines. It may cause some problems."

"General Stuart has his ways . . . certainly different from our ways, you and me. But he is young, and he inspires the men. And if the newspapers love him, then he can inspire the people as well. There is no harm in that."

Longstreet said nothing, and Lee focused again to the front, could see small buildings now, a few houses, and he motioned behind him. A staff officer rode up, the young Major Marshall, and Lee said, "Major, ride forward into that town, make certain there is an intersection, and determine that a left turn will lead us toward that fighting."

"Sir!" and Marshall was quickly gone.

Longstreet looked over at Lee, smiled slightly. Lee stared straight ahead, said, "I have great confidence in General Stuart. But, General, there is no harm in being certain."

As Longstreet's men reached the field, Jackson absorbed a daylong pounding from Pope's forces. Waves of Federal troops poured against Jackson's lines, were beaten back, and then replaced by fresh troops. As Jackson held to his precarious position, Longstreet's troops spread out to the right, at a slight angle forward, so that by the next morning, Lee's army lay in the shape of a V, with Jackson on the left and Longstreet on the right. The bulk of Pope's army lay just outside the mouth of the V.

That night, Lee called the commanders together. He had set his headquarters up just behind the junction of the V, and his staff had secured an old cabin for him to sleep in. Jackson, Longstreet, and Stuart all arrived at eight o'clock, as requested. Lee rarely issued orders for his meetings, made the more cordial suggestion of when they should attend, but there was no confusion in the minds of his generals. Now, they had all gathered, their staffs at a respectful distance, and Lee emerged from the cabin, paused, stared up into the dark sky. It was a warm and humid night, and he welcomed the relative cool of the old log house. Stuart was the last to arrive, had just dismounted, and Jackson and Longstreet had made themselves crude seats from a pile of cut firewood.

Lee stood at the door of the cabin, adjusted his uniform, saw the three men outside watching him, lit by the bright glow from the nearby fire. Taylor stood to the side, waiting. Lee asked, "Coffee, gentlemen?"

Stuart said, "Thank you, yes, if it's all right, sir." Taylor moved quickly away. Lee looked at the other two.

Longstreet shook his head silently, and Jackson rose, said, "Thank you, General, I do not partake."

"Of course, General, no matter, please, be seated." He walked out among them, found his own seat, a thick-cut log propped upright on the bare ground. Taylor appeared, handed Stuart a tin cup and then moved back, behind Lee, and sat on the ground, his back against the side of the cabin.

Lee spoke first, always spoke first. "General Jackson, your troops performed an admirable service today. How are they faring?"

Jackson rose, stood stiffly, said, "General, I have pulled most of the units back, into the cover of the thick trees. They are somewhat battered, but they will hold their lines."

"Back . . . into the trees? You pulled them away from the railroad cut?"

Jackson glanced at the others, then looked back at Lee. "Yes, sir. It should be better for their . . . relief. They will be ready tomorrow."

"General, what do you suppose will happen if General Pope discovers the railroad cut has been abandoned?"

"I did consider that, sir. It can only be to our advantage. My troops can move out of the trees quickly if he attempts an advance."

"Yes, I know. This is not a criticism, General. It might be a good plan. Our best advantage lies in the ground we now hold. It is up to General Pope to advance against that ground."

Jackson sat, and Longstreet stared down, scratched at the ground with a stick, said slowly, "General Lee, I do not believe General Pope knows our disposition. Our deployment on the right was barely contested. He does not seem to have made any serious move to confront our lines."

Lee stared at him, could not see his face for the wide floppy hat. All that afternoon, Longstreet had been in position to advance into the battle, could have possibly relieved the great mass of pressure on Jackson, but had not done so, had told Lee that it was not a good time, that there were too many uncertainties about the ground, about the location of Pope's other units, those not pressing Jackson. Lee had been frustrated by the lack of action, but now it was done, and he could do nothing but look ahead. Lee knew, if Longstreet was right, if Pope did not realize the strength that lay behind the trees to his left, he might be inclined to make a very serious mistake.

"General Longstreet, are you prepared to advance your troops in the morning?"

Longstreet knew there was something implied in the words, let it go. He did not share Jackson's raw lust for plunging ahead, had not been comfortable in an area where rolling hills and thick lines of trees made visibility difficult.

"General, we are prepared to meet the assault."

"General Stuart, have you observed any additional forces coming our way?"

Stuart stood stiffly, held the big hat in his hands, had quickly tossed the cup aside. The presence of Jackson and Longstreet had a subduing effect on him; the brutal seriousness was intimidating. He began slowly. "General, yes, we did observe a column of troops moving down from the northeast . . . at least a corps. By dark, they were still several miles away."

"Good. I do not expect that General Pope will receive much more assistance on this field, not by tomorrow. These are, after all, General

McClellan's troops marching toward him. They are likely to be somewhat . . . slow to advance."

Longstreet looked up, and Lee saw his face in the firelight. Longstreet said, "General Pope is not a well-liked man. Even at the Point he had a way of talking too much, saying the wrong thing. If he has even met with his own commanders, it is likely he has very little . . . coordination."

Lee stared at him. "What do you mean, General?"

Longstreet tossed the stick aside, stood up, stretching his back. "I mean, General, that even if General Pope is seeking the advice of his commanders, he is not likely to listen to it. He does not have confidence in anyone's ability to lead his forces . . . but his own."

"If you are correct, General, then he may yet pursue General Jackson's 'retreat.' That will be our opportunity."

Jackson stood again, following Longstreet's lead, said, "General Lee, I did observe on my way here . . . there are a large number of

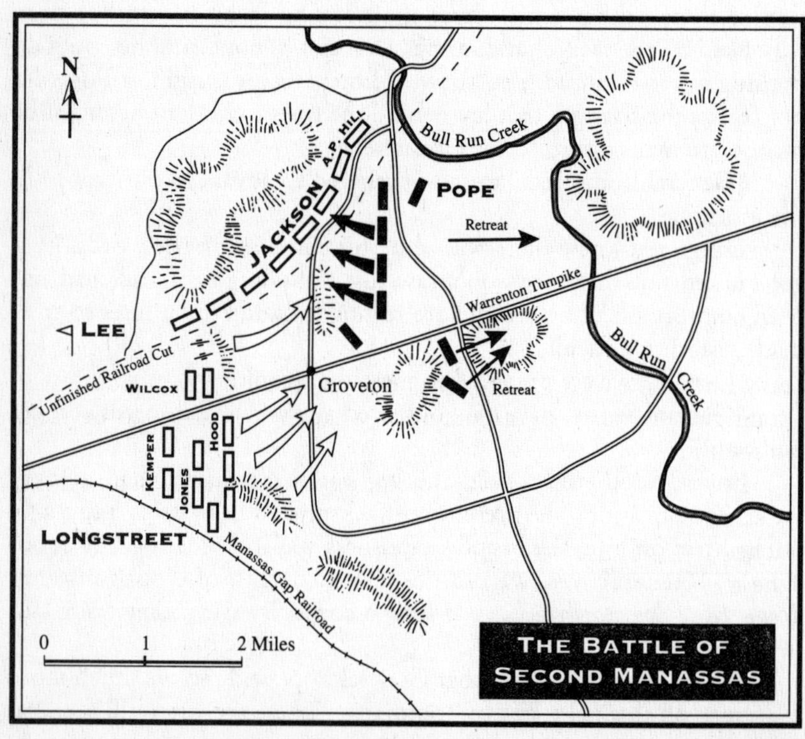

General Longstreet's batteries digging in on my right flank. These could be very useful if I am attacked."

Lee smiled. "Yes, General, General Longstreet and I have placed a heavy concentration of guns at the junction of your two lines. There is a slight rise at that point. They may have a clear view of the field, and so far it appears that General Pope is not aware they are there."

"Then, General Lee, let us hope he provides them with a fine target."

August 30, 1862

Pope had indeed convinced himself that Jackson was in retreat, and despite the observations from Generals Porter and Reynolds, who cautioned against Longstreet's position, Pope believed that the bulk of Longstreet's strength had moved back behind Jackson, not alongside him. The next morning, after long hours of conflicting advice and his growing impatience at what he believed was Jackson's potential escape, he ordered his men forward.

Lee sat on a flat stump, still behind the center of the V. He had simply waited, nervous, praying, hoping that Pope would bring the attack forward. It was now past noon, and he stood, began to pace again, as he had done all morning. He knew his location was important, he should stay between the commands, but he could not see anything. In front of him the batteries were spread along a wide ridge, hidden by a thick line of trees, but it was these trees that kept him blind to the field. Suddenly, he heard a loud and distant noise. He had expected guns, an artillery barrage first, but this was not cannon, it was . . . men. Out to the left, in front of Jackson's waiting troops, heavy lines of Federal infantry had emerged from the far woods, over distant ridges, and were in pursuit of what they believed to be Jackson's withdrawal.

Lee started forward, began to run up into the trees. Behind him, his staff was moving quickly, grabbing horses, following him. He reached the tree line, and the men on the guns turned, cheered him as he moved past. He did not look at them, focused in front, trying to see. Finally, he stood at the edge of the trees, the ground dropping away in front of him, a long, shallow bowl, and he saw three lines of blue, moving from right to left, toward the railroad cut. Then he heard another sound, one he'd heard before, the sound of Jackson's men, a high, steady, terrifying chorus. Farther to the left, behind the cut, the gray lines flooded forward, out of the trees. The field filled quickly with smoke, the sound of voices replaced by that of muskets.

"Sir!" Lee turned, saw Taylor and other staff officers. He looked back at the guns, saw the men moving, ready, and he motioned to his staff, started back to the rear. The orders came, and the guns began their deafening fire. Flashes of light and thick smoke filled the tree line. Lee watched from behind, could no longer see the great lines of troops, but knew what was now happening to them.

The Federal forces pushed hard against Jackson's left, the troops of A. P. Hill. Once the shock of Jackson's surprise advance had worn off, the reality was that Hill's forces were outnumbered, and the Federals kept pushing, kept coming. Pope sent more strength into the assault, and Jackson knew that Hill was in trouble, was beginning to waver.

Lee sat again on his stump, waited anxiously. There had been little word from the fighting, and he thought, Jackson must not hesitate, he *must* ask for help. This time we have the troops. Behind him, Taylor stood, holding two horses, his and Lee's, the beloved gray the general called Traveller. Lee thought, I should ride up, try to see something, and he turned, motioned to Taylor. Down to the left he saw a rider, coming hard. It was Henry Kyd Douglas, of Jackson's staff.

Douglas dismounted, saluted hastily, said, "General Lee, General Jackson sends his compliments, and requests reinforcements, sir. He requests at least a division on his left flank, to support General Hill, sir!"

Lee looked at Taylor, said, "Major, tell General Longstreet to move. . . ."

He paused, saw another rider to his right, one of Longstreet's staff. The man pulled up but did not dismount. "General Lee, General Longstreet is advising that he believes the time has come to advance his army into the attack, sir. He believes that the Federal Army is exposed to a counterattack from his position."

Lee felt his heart thump, the cold chill of the moment. "Yes, tell General Longstreet to advance with all speed. Major Douglas, return to General Jackson, tell him General Longstreet is advancing in force on his right."

Both staff officers were quickly gone, and Lee looked at Taylor, saw the young man moving around with jumpy, nervous energy, and Lee said, "Major, this could be a glorious day!"

THE EFFECT OF LONGSTREET'S SUDDEN PUSH INTO POPE'S FLANK caused an immediate collapse of the Federal lines. While small pockets of blue troops fought stubbornly, the tide of the battle had turned for good, and now Jackson's weakened lines pushed forward as well. Within a couple of hours Pope's army was in a panicked retreat toward the Potomac.

Lee rode Traveller out through the line of trees, followed close behind Longstreet's advancing infantry. Smoke filled the air, and he could not see the Federal troops, only the backs of his own lines. They continued the rapid advance, and the solid roar of musketry deafened him. Behind him, Taylor raced to keep up, yelling out, trying to convince Lee this was not the place to be.

He climbed up a long ridge, reached the top, and his men were moving ahead down the other side, pursuing the Federals down a long hill. Now he could see across to another ridge. A steady stream of blue flowed over the hill, men in a dead run, moving away without firing. He stopped, sat high on Traveller and watched the scene. The sunlight was starting to fade, heavy clouds darkening the fields. His mind was racing, filled with thoughts and pictures.

He thought of Pope, where he might be. Was he watching this as well, or was he caught in the flow, pulled away by the tide of a beaten army? He thought of Longstreet, who had delayed yesterday, would not attack until the time was right, and now it did not matter because the time was right today. He knew Jackson would be out with his troops, pushing them forward. He turned back, looked to the row of trees where the artillery was, saw the gunners standing along the ridge, waving, cheering, and then he thought of the lone soldier, the man who had come back into Richmond after the first battle, the man he had tried to talk to, who spoke only of Jackson's great success, and he wondered if he was here, today, a year later, and had seen it all again.

Taylor was beside him now, and Lee looked at the young man, said, "Remember this, Major. There are not too many days like this . . . when you have swept your enemy from the field and you can watch him run. You don't need official reports or newspapers or the gossip of stragglers . . . you don't need anyone to tell you what has happened."

Taylor nodded, staring wide-eyed at the frantic withdrawal of Pope's army.

Lee pulled on the reins, turned the horse around, said, "We had best get back . . . they will be looking for us." Then he paused, looked out one last time, saw his own troops now, moving over the far ridge, still in pursuit, a deadly chase that would last until it was too dark to see.

IT RAINED ALL NIGHT AND ALL THE NEXT DAY. LONGSTREET'S fresher troops were assigned the dismal task of burying the dead, and the men dug their way through the soft ground of the farmlands, now turned to vast seas of thick mud. The pursuit of Pope's army had been bogged down by the rain and by the arrival of more of McClellan's troops, which Pope now used as a rear guard as he limped his way slowly back toward Washington.

Lee's staff gathered at the edge of a stand of trees. They had just come across Bull Run Creek, following the slow advance of the army, pressing closer to the Federal troops. Out in front, the advance lines had confronted the Federal skirmishers, who did not run, and so both armies moved sluggishly in the rain, staring at each other like two tired animals, one slowly backing away.

Lee stood beside Traveller, holding the reins, and around him the rest of his staff waited for further news of Pope's movement. Taylor stood near Lee; the others mostly sat on their horses. There was no dry place, and the thick black rubber of their raincoats wrapped each man like a glistening shroud. Lee focused, tried to hear, caught the occasional dull pop of musket fire from the distant skirmish lines, but it was infrequent and had no meaning. There will be no fight today, he thought, and even with McClellan's reinforcements, Pope would not make a stand. He would go back to Washington and tell of a great battle where he was lucky to rescue his troops, could only back away because his troops were sadly underprepared or overmatched, and he would inflate the enemy's strength and claim he fought the good fight against tall odds, because that was the kind of man he was. He will not tell his President that he stumbled blindly into a disaster, Lee thought. That observation would be made by others.

Lee put his hand on Traveller's neck, felt his uniform pull at him, soaked by the wetness, the hot and stifling humidity, held hard against him by the dripping raincoat. He patted the horse's thick, wet hair, and the horse turned slightly, cocked his head. From behind, a man came through the trees, said in a quick yell, "Yankees!" and a shot rang out, the ball whistling over Lee's head.

Traveller jumped, lunged forward, and Lee's hands were still holding the reins, were tangled in the tight leather straps. He was suddenly pulled, snatched ahead by the motion of the horse. His knees dragged the ground, and he tried to release the reins but could not, and then quickly the horse was stopped, grabbed by Taylor.

"There, boy, whoa . . . calm down." And now Taylor looked toward the soldier, saw others moving up with him, muskets raised, yelled out in an angry burst, "You damned fool, this is General Lee!"

The men put their guns down, saw now that the horsemen in the black raincoats were not Yankees. A sergeant emerged from the men, came closer, saw Lee and said, "Oh, my God . . . oh, my God."

They helped the general up, and he found his feet, his hands loosening from the straps. The officers were quickly around him and he was held under the arms, carried to the trunk of a fallen tree, sat down on soggy wood. Now he looked at his hands, felt the pain twisting through his hands and arms like fire. He heard someone call out, and from the woods men began to gather. He heard someone yell for a surgeon, and he stared at his hands, thought, this is bad . . . and it is very very painful.

A man was pushed through the crowd of soldiers, and Taylor brought the man forward, said, "General, this is a doctor."

Lee looked at the man, saw an older face, gray beard, felt some comfort in that, and the man said, "Dear me, General, what have you done to yourself?"

Lee rested his elbows on his legs, and the doctor put his hand under the elbow, lifted it gently.

"You have a broken bone in your hand, General," the doctor said. "I can set that . . . and the other one. . . ." He lifted the other arm, bent down, looking it over. "Nothing broken, it seems, but quite a sprain." He looked at Lee's face, and Lee was staring down, was trying not to look at his hands. The doctor said, "General, you are in a great deal of pain. Let me get you something—"

"No," Lee said, shaking his head. "You cannot drug me, Doctor. Not now. I will be all right."

"Whatever you say, General. But I do have to set that bone. You will feel better if you at least drink something. I have some whiskey, here, always carry it. Just a small swig—"

"Thank you, Doctor, no. Just do what you can."

The doctor handled the arms carefully, and Lee stared ahead, past the men, who were now being scattered, sent away by his staff. The pain in the right hand, the hand with the broken bone, was not nearly as bad as the other, and he wondered at that: bending is worse than breaking, he mused, I would not have thought that . . . but . . . either way . . .

He tried to focus on other things, Pope, the battle, but the pain was enormous, and he felt as if the one arm was on fire. Now there were bandages and splints, the doctor working quickly. Taylor stood behind, looking over the doctor's shoulder, and said, "It's all right . . . it's all right," and Lee knew Taylor was convincing himself.

He turned, tried to see the young face, said, "Yes, Major, I will be fine." But his voice shook, betraying the effect of the pain, and he thought, Of course, this is punishment . . . God's way of saying every victory has a price. Yesterday was . . . too easy. It must never be too easy.

The doctor finished his work, and the staff lifted him up, helped him to a wagon, an ambulance that had been brought up. He was helped aboard, sat on a thin mattress, and the driver saw his face, recognized him, snatched his hat from his head and held it against his chest as he began to cry, "Oh Lord, what has happened to General Lee?"

There was an embarrassed pause, and Lee looked at the man, surprised at the outburst. "Soldier," he said calmly, "I have been inconvenienced, that's all. It is a small price for the inconvenience we have given General Pope."

POPE CONTINUED TO PULL BACK, AND HIS TROOPS FILED NOW into the massive fortifications near Washington. Lee did not pursue, there was too much strength. McClellan's army was united with Pope's, and for now they were safe. Lee knew there would be no fighting for a while, that it would take a fresh start of some kind, a new Federal commander, new bluster and new pressure from Lincoln. For now, he began to look toward his own troops and the serious problems confronting his own army. A majority of the men had no shoes at all, or wore pieces of cloth wrapped around their feet. Clothing was becoming an embarrassment—many of the men were covered only partially by rags that were barely strung together. The only uniforms visible were on the officers, and those had become so worn that most showed rips at the knee and frayed cuffs and sleeves. But it was not their clothing that affected the men's ability to fight—it was food. The farms of Virginia had been assaulted not only by the needs of the army, but by the pillaging of Pope's army as well, and what crops and livestock were available were barely able to support the needs of the civilians.

Lee rode everywhere now in the ambulance. He could do nothing with his bound hands without great pain, and so relied completely on his staff. Taylor became ferocious at protecting him from unnecessary visitors. They tried to make him comfortable, made the ambulance a rolling office, and he was thankful there was a lull in the fighting—he knew that if things were hot, he would have to turn the command over to someone else, probably Longstreet.

The ambulance hit a deep pothole, bouncing him high off the fat cushion that served as his seat. The driver stopped, peered back through the flaps, worried, said, "Begging your pardon, sir. It's a bit rough since the rain."

Lee nodded, said nothing. It had been several days, and the discomfort did not bother him anymore. His hands had stopped hurting with every movement, every small gesture, and now it was just the wait, the healing, and the frustration of not having the freedom to move, to take Traveller out through the tall trees, to ride with dignity among the men. He loved that the men were inspired, cheered when he rode past, and he saw it as a blessing, the good fortune of high morale in these men who knew the joy of victory. Now, they watched him go by with a painful silence, an occasional yell of condolence, good luck. He understood the importance of that intangible spirit the commander carries with him, riding with his staff and the flags, the response that comes from the hearts of men who have no shoes and little to eat. And if there was to be no enemy in front of them, there must be something else, to make the best use of the opportunity. They could not sit on this same trampled ground and wait for another big fight.

Jackson arrived first, rode up on his little sorrel carrying the dust of many days. Lee watched him from the back of the wagon, his legs dangling. Jackson rode alone, upright in the saddle, stiff, never seemed comfortable on his horse. He still wore the old small-billed cap from VMI, which now sat flat on his head like a crushed tin can. The bill was pulled forward, came down barely over his eyes, and as he rode he cocked his head slightly back, in order to see. Lee smiled, thought, He could ride right past Federal sentries, and they would never know who he was.

Jackson dismounted, and an orderly took the reins. The general tossed something aside, and Lee smiled, saw it was a lemon, spent, crushed into a flat mass. Jackson walked quickly with long strides, and now Lee saw something in the sharp face, a painful sadness. Jackson reached out a hand, then froze, awkward, wanted to touch Lee's bandaged hands, could not.

"General Lee, I pray you are not in pain."

"Thank you, General, it is better now. I must keep them wrapped for a while, though. We heal slower with age, an unfortunate fact."

There was a voice behind the wagon: Major Marshall. "Sir, General Longstreet is arriving."

The horses thundered closer, Longstreet and his staff. Jackson backed away from Lee, saluted toward the sound, and Lee waited, could not see where Longstreet was, then heard the heavy steps, the slow, deep voice.

"Afternoon, General Jackson." Then Longstreet was around the back of the wagon, saw Lee. "Well, my word . . . you look a fright, General, begging your pardon. I heard you went at Pope's rear guard with both fists." He laughed, a quiet chuckle, and Lee smiled, was surprised, had not seen Longstreet in such a jovial mood for a long time.

"I will leave the hand-to-hand to the men from now on, General. It is not a pleasant thing for an old man."

They both were smiling, and Jackson stood stiffly, puzzled, did not share the joke.

"Come, gentlemen, if I may be assisted . . ." Marshall was there quickly, lifted Lee off the wagon, and he settled on the ground, arched his back, stretched slightly. "This wagon is not for comfort. Let us walk, gentlemen."

The three men moved away from the horses and the staffs, walked out into a field, stubs of cornstalks, now pressed into drying mud. It was hot again, and they moved away from the shade trees.

Longstreet said, "The weather should break soon, cool things off."

Lee adjusted his hat, turned now to face away from the sun. "General, do you believe General Pope will attempt another advance before spring?"

Longstreet kicked at a spot of hard ground, knocked thick mud off his boots. "General, I don't believe we will see General Pope again, not in the spring, or ever."

"You may be correct, General, but his army is still there, and now they are safe and so they will refit and resupply, and Mr. Lincoln will send them out again. The question is not so much who will lead them, but when they will come, and where."

Jackson said, "We should have pressed them back to Washington. They were running. God sent the rain, to slow us. He wishes us to fight again, in a better place."

"I don't know if there is a much better place than this one," Longstreet said. "That army left this field as quickly and as completely as any army ever has."

Jackson tilted his head back slightly, looking at Longstreet. "But we did not destroy him. We must still destroy him."

Lee nodded, looked at both men. "General Jackson, as much attention as I would like to devote to the Federal Army, we have a closer problem at hand, the condition of *this* army. I have been thinking . . . it's about all I have been able to do. Our greatest need is to feed this army, and we can do that in either of two ways. We can withdraw, to the Shenandoah Valley, where the crops are still in good supply. That would expose this part of Virginia to occupation by the Federal Army yet again. While this army could restore its health in friendly country, the damage to the morale of the people could be great. It is also likely that President Davis would not approve of that move."

Jackson shifted his feet. "Nor would I, sir. We would lose what we have gained by chasing the Federals back into Washington. You have a second plan, sir?"

"Yes, General. I propose we advance our army north, into Maryland. The farms there are plentiful and nearly untouched. With the fall harvest, we can feed our troops well. And there is one other consideration. The people of Maryland have expressed neutrality. It is my belief that the constant use of their land by Federal troops is felt as a hostile occupation. It is quite possible that our intervention there will be viewed as a liberation. We might receive a great deal of hospitality, and we might even receive a number of volunteers for service in the army."

"General, if they have proclaimed neutrality," Longstreet said, and paused, "would we not be seen as an army of occupation as well?"

"I don't believe so, General. The invasion of Virginia, of the entire Confederacy, by Federal forces, made clear to any neutral party that the Confederacy is not the aggressor here. We did not bring this war, and we fight now only to free the South of Federal occupation. If Washington will end their side of the fighting, and recall their armies . . . General, this war will be over. And, gentlemen, that is another reason why I believe this plan can succeed. By moving into Maryland and strengthening our forces, we will then be in a position to push into Pennsylvania. If Mr. Lincoln sees that we are threatening to cause destruction against the Northern cities, Philadelphia, even New York, there will be a great outcry in the North to stop this. So far, gentlemen, the bloody fields are Southern fields. If we threaten to bring that blood into the North, there will be great pressure on Mr. Lincoln to end this war. We might not even have to fight, just our presence, just the threat, could be sufficient."

Longstreet stared down, spoke from under the brim of his hat. "General, we would be cutting ourselves off from our base of supply, from communications. We would be vulnerable from the rear."

"General Longstreet, you did march with General Scott, into Mexico, did you not?"

"Yes, sir."

"And did not General Scott cut himself off from his supplies, from all communication, and by doing so, did he not bring a rapid end to that war? And did he not accomplish all of that in a foreign land? Well, this is not a foreign land, and the citizens will see that we do not come to terrorize, as did General Pope. We come to end the war, quickly and without any need to conquer or subdue anyone. We have proven our superiority on the battlefield. The threat of that superiority may be all we need."

Jackson began to fidget, rocked back and forth on stiff legs. "My men are ready to move on your command, General."

"General Jackson," Lee said, "we do have one problem, which I will need you to address."

Longstreet said, "Harper's Ferry."

"Yes, General, you are correct. There are nearly twelve thousand Federal troops quartered there, and they could add to those numbers easily by moving men up the river. That would be the danger to our rear. Harper's Ferry must be secured. General Jackson, I want you to move your forces down that way, surround the town from the heights and secure it by any method that will ensure success. I will accompany General Longstreet's forces across the Potomac, masking our movements behind the mountains. We should be well into Maryland before anyone in Washington can do anything to impede us."

Longstreet said, "General, we are already greatly outnumbered, and by dividing the army . . . there is considerable risk, sir."

"This plan could end the war, General. Is that not worth risk?"

Jackson looked at Longstreet, said, "General, my troops will move on Harper's Ferry and reunite with your army in short order."

Longstreet kicked at the dirt, said, "We need cavalry in the mountain passes, masking our movement, and in our rear, to keep anyone from following us."

"General Stuart will be so ordered. I will inform President Davis of this plan, and provide both of you with detailed written orders by tonight. It is a slow process. . . ." He held up his hands. "I must dictate everything to my staff."

Lee turned, began to walk back toward the wagons, and the

others followed close behind. They reached the edge of the shade, felt the cooler air, and Lee paused, said, "Gentlemen, you were both on this field a year ago. We won a great victory then, quite possibly could have ended this war, and we did nothing, we did not follow it up. That is why we had to fight here again, on this same ground. It is a lesson learned, gentlemen. It is time to take this war out of Virginia."

23. CHAMBERLAIN

August 1862

They stood in groups, sat in small circles. Some were lying on the ground, some slept. He had walked from the train station, through the streets of Portland, had seen other men moving in the same direction. No one noticed him as he made his way into Camp Mason, the first assembly point for the volunteers of the Twentieth Maine.

He saw the faces of the young, the same kind of faces he had seen in the streets of Brunswick, but there were others too, older men, men with rugged, worn faces, big men, log cutters, farmers, and he was surprised, but it made him feel better. This was not, after all, an army of boys.

There were tents lined up in neat rows at the far end of the grounds, and he began to move that way, lugging a heavy cloth bag over his shoulder. He had thought of bringing his usual small trunk, then decided it would be too conspicuous. He did not want to appear to be too green. At least make a good first impression, he thought. He walked past the groups of men, heard conversations, most about where they had just come from, what was left behind, a few comments about the war, where they might go next. He heard a few accents, Irish, Scottish, but clearly, they were all Maine men, and they did not yet know that he would lead them.

He reached the tents, saw a man, an officer, the only uniform he had seen so far, sitting at a small table. The man was writing on a long sheet of paper, and Chamberlain said, "Excuse me, I'm looking for my tent. I'm Lieutenant Colonel Chamberlain."

The man looked up, glanced him up and down quickly, then stood, saluted.

"Sir, I am Major Gilmore, formerly of the Seventh Maine. I have been sent here to assist you . . . and . . . this regiment."

"Fine, Major, it's a pleasure to meet you. You are a veteran, then?"

"Yes, sir. Fought in General Hancock's brigade, on the peninsula, General Smith's division."

"We can use some experience here, Major, myself included. Are you the only officer here?"

"There are others, sir, the company commanders, but the uniforms have not yet arrived."

"And Colonel Ames?"

"The colonel is expected at any time. I have taken the liberty, sir, of preparing a schedule . . . a routine for the drills. I had thought Colonel Ames would want to begin as soon as possible. They're a pretty rough bunch, sir. If you'd like, we can begin right away, get a bit of a jump on it before the colonel arrives."

Gilmore handed him the paper. Chamberlain saw a list of march steps, formations, and column movements, and he examined the list with an attempt at a critical eye, hoped Gilmore did not realize that he would have no idea how to begin drills.

"Yes . . . well done, Major . . . but, this is Colonel Ames's command. I think we should let him decide the training schedule."

"Whatever you say, sir."

Chamberlain began to look around, studying the faces, the clothes, the mix of city and country, then turned toward the tents, said, "Major, can you point me—"

"Begging your pardon, sir, yes, you are over there . . . that large one, with the open flaps."

"Thank you, Major." He began to move that way, felt a childlike excitement, his own tent, sleeping right out here, on the ground, then he felt silly, forced himself not to smile. He leaned over, into the empty tent, saw only one small cot. He threw his bag toward the back, then gazed at the camp again, thought, Maybe I should walk among the men, introduce myself, get to know them. Then he thought, Well, no, maybe a commander shouldn't do that. But the officers . . . I should find the officers. . . .

"Beggin' yer pardon, sir, but I heared you was a perfessor?"

It was a comical voice, with a crude, exaggerated accent. Chamberlain turned, saw a man coming from between the tents, a small, thin man in baggy clothes. The man had spoken out from under a wide, floppy farmer's hat, then the hat lifted and he saw: Tom!

"What . . . you come to see me off? What are you doing here?"

"Lawrence, I joined up. I'm in this regiment. I'm going with you." Then he snapped to attention, threw up a crooked salute, said, "Colonel, sir!"

"How did . . . did Father approve this? How will he run the farm?"

"Lawrence, once he heard you was gonna be a colonel, he couldn't say no. You know him, he'll be all right, they both will. I just gave him one less thing to cuss at. And Mama said so many prayers for both of us . . . we got nothin' to worry about."

"Well . . ." He looked at the clean smile of the boy, felt the pride, then a hard tug in his gut. His brother, his little brother, was a soldier. "Well, I guess I have one more responsibility—I have to look after you."

"Me? Lawrence, Mama told me to look after *you*."

Chamberlain smiled, could picture that scene, his mother wrapping the tight arms around her youngest son, the last gift of pious advice, and his father standing to one side, grim and silent, maybe one nod, one grudging show of affection.

"This is really something, eh, Lawrence? Look at all these men. And you're gonna tell 'em all what to do. Think they'll listen to you? You're just a professor."

Chamberlain felt a sting, said, "They'll do what they have to do . . . it will take some time. But one thing has to change right away."

"What's that, Lawrence?"

"Stop calling me Lawrence."

HE LAY ALONE AND QUIET, HEARD NOTHING, THE CAMP DARK and silent. He thought, I had better sleep . . . I have to be sharp tomorrow. But there was no sleep, and he tried to move, lay on his side, hoping it would be more comfortable. But the stiff cot would not give in, and he rolled onto his back again, staring at white canvas. He sat up, stuck his head out through the flaps, saw the stars, a clear, lovely night, and stepped outside, stretched, looked out over the sea of tents. Nearly a thousand men, he thought, waiting for someone to tell them what to do. Waiting for *me*. No wonder you can't sleep. He looked farther out, saw a lone figure moving, walking, then toward the other side, another one: sentries. Major Gilmore had posted guards, something Chamberlain would not have thought of. Guarding against what? We're still in Maine. But, of course, the guards were there to keep these men *here*.

He thought of taking a walk, strolling through the cool air, but no, it would be a bad example. Try to get some sleep, Colonel, he told himself, and he moved back into the tent, sat on the cot. His brother was there. He had not counted on that. It shouldn't change things, he thought, but it does.

Stretching out on the cot, he stared up again, at the blank canvas. He tried to relax his mind, heard himself breathing, and then saw Fannie—God, I miss her already. He thought of the many nights he would reach over to her, run his hand gently over her arm, touch her hair. . . .

It was a terrible screeching, a dying animal, some horrible demon tearing through his brain, a hellish whine in his ears. It was dawn . . . and it was a bugle.

Chamberlain turned over, tried to find the floor, rolled off the edge of the cot and hit the hard ground with his whole body. Then he pulled himself up, tried to stand, and his head bumped the canvas above him. He tried to see, stumbled toward the opening in the tent, saw it was still dark, a faint white glare beyond the far trees. The bugle continued to blow, a broken and tuneless flow of sounds, and men were moving now. He heard voices and curses, and he backed into the tent, looked through the darkness for his clothes, realized he was already dressed, had never taken them off. He turned again, fought his way out through the tent, stood outside in the chilly morning and saw a man on a horse, a sharp silhouette in the faint light. It was Gilmore, and beside him, standing, was the man blowing the bugle. Chamberlain began to move that way, thought, I really do need a uniform, and as he approached, Gilmore saw him and saluted stiffly. Behind him, Chamberlain saw a horseman sitting stiffly, a smaller man in a wide-brimmed hat. The man moved his horse up beside Gilmore, the major said something, and, blessedly, the bugle stopped.

Then Gilmore said, "Colonel Ames, I am pleased to present Lieutenant Colonel Chamberlain."

He felt confused, then realized it was him, and he saluted in the man's direction. He could not see the face, but he heard, "Colonel Chamberlain, please accompany me to breakfast."

Food? he thought. "Yes, sir. When, sir?"

Ames stared down at him, said nothing, and now the men were gathering in numbers, most of them up and out of the tents.

Gilmore shouted, "Line up . . . here, across here."

The men began to fall in, and Chamberlain heard the voices, "Where's the coffee?" "Kill that bugler," and he thought, Yes, a brave man carries the bugle.

Gradually the men came together, a sea of bodies in the faint light, and Gilmore shouted, "Quiet! Men of the Twentieth Maine Regiment of Volunteers, this is your commanding officer, Colonel Adelbert Ames."

There were some cheers, applause, and Gilmore waved his arms frantically. "Quiet! You do not applaud your commander. You will learn to salute him. Now, here . . . this is Lieutenant Colonel Chamberlain, your second in command."

There were more cheers, and Chamberlain bowed, then heard Gilmore again. "Quiet!"

The noise lessened, and the men began to mumble, talking among themselves, waking up in a rising steady hum, and Gilmore yelled again, "Quiet!" and it had only minor effect.

Ames said, "Major, it's their first official morning. We'll give them a bit of slack today. You won't have much of a voice left if we don't. Let them eat . . . then we begin the drills. Colonel Chamberlain, come along, if you please."

Ames moved his horse away, and Chamberlain walked behind, was not sure where they were going, remembered breakfast, and thought, I really do need a horse.

"COLONEL, YOU WILL SHARE MY TENT."

"Sir?"

"It will work out better. We can spend our time more efficiently, teaching you the fundamentals."

"Certainly, sir."

They sat at a small table, under a flat open tent, and Chamberlain was holding his first cup of army coffee, was attacking it bravely, determined. It was his greatest challenge so far. The tent began to fill with other men, the officers of the regiment, who had learned that the officers ate separately from the men. They came slowly up, with some shyness, approached the mess table where assorted piles and pots of food were waiting. Chamberlain watched them come, stuffed a hard biscuit into his mouth, knew immediately it was a mistake, too large and too dry, but could not remove it. He saw Ames watching him, and so took a hard gulp from the coffee cup, washed it down.

Ames smiled. "Welcome to the army, Colonel."

Ames was a small, thin man. He had a wide, round face with a thick mustache, and Chamberlain was surprised to see he was young, much younger than he. He had graduated from West Point only a year before, and had seen action immediately at the first big fight, Bull Run. His assignment to command this new regiment was a questionable reward, but he was an ambitious man, and took his own advancement as seriously as he took his need for discipline.

"I've been told quite a bit about you, Colonel. General Hodsdon has a great deal of faith in your abilities. It's my job to teach you how to be a commander."

"Thank you, sir. I will do whatever it takes."

"We'll start immediately. This regiment is about as raw as any I have seen. That will not last, Colonel. They will learn how to be good disciplined soldiers, or they will be slaughtered."

Abruptly, he stood, said loudly to the other men under the tent, "Gentlemen, in fifteen minutes I want the regiment formed in lines of four, company A on the left, and so on down the line. We cannot waste time getting these men in shape."

Chamberlain looked at the other officers, saw nods, uncertain faces, and there was a noise off in the distance, the shouts of men, a line of wagons. A man ran to the tent, saw Ames's blue coat, said, "Sir, the uniforms are here!"

The officers rose from their breakfasts and the tent emptied as they moved quickly toward the small line of wagons. Men had crowded around, there were happy shouts, and now the officers took control, began to yell instructions, herding the men into formation.

Chamberlain stayed with Ames, following his lead, and Ames climbed on his horse, moved the animal slowly toward the forming men. Chamberlain walked behind, watched the officers waving and pointing, with minimal success. Men still gathered at the wagons, and suddenly Ames rode forward, pushing his horse through the men. Reaching the first wagon, he pulled his sword and yelled something Chamberlain couldn't hear. The men scattered, moved toward the familiar, less-threatening faces of their company commanders. Now the columns began to show some shape, rough formations, and Ames turned the horse around, rode to the front.

Gilmore rode up, began speaking, then Ames followed, giving instructions of what was expected of them, how the training would go. The company commanders were instructed to appoint a quartermaster officer, who would issue the uniforms. Chamberlain listened to the words, the commands, watched the strange mix of men standing before him, some looking up at Ames, some at him, some staring away into some distant place, and he began to get a feeling of dread, a feeling that this wasn't going to work. These men were not an army. Surely it was different in other units, men with a sense of order, an inherent knowledge of how to do all this. These were Maine men, a different breed, men used to a hard, tough life, a life as individuals, men who never had to listen to anybody tell them anything, and so many of them were not listening now.

He tried to spot Tom, looked for the floppy hat, did not even know what company he was in, and his eyes ran up and down the rows, past all variety of dress and stance and expression. Are they better than we? He thought of General Hodsdon's words, and he wondered if the rebel army was so much better, what it was that won battles. He still felt the dread, a sense of doom, and then he saw Tom, the bright face. He was not wearing the ridiculous hat, was smiling at him, directly at him, and Chamberlain could not stare back at him, because he would begin to smile as well. But he felt the look, the energy of youth, the enthusiasm, and now he began to see others, the faces that were staring to the front, listening to Ames's words, absorbing them, and he saw there were a lot of them, men who did not yet know how, but would learn, men who understood after all, what this meant, what they had to do.

He began to feel better, the dread slipping away, and imagined himself wearing the uniform, the deep blue, seated high on a horse, before neat rows of men with their own uniforms, straight lines of rifles, shining bayonets. He glanced up at Ames, heard the voice of the commander, and thought, No, they are not better than we, and we *will* have our chance.

SEPTEMBER 1862

THEY WERE AT CAMP MASON LESS THAN A MONTH WHEN ORDERS arrived to board the trains, trains that would pass through other towns and other states, adding carloads of men and equipment, bringing them all out of the cool hills of New England, toward the flat, hot plains around Washington.

Chamberlain had his horse finally, a gift from the town of Brunswick, a wonderful surprise. It was light gray, dappled with white spots, and he rode slowly, grandly, through the formations, watching the men of the regiment turning themselves into soldiers. And they had watched him as well, as he was taught and drilled night after night by Ames. Now, as they rode the long rails south, there was a feeling, shared by all of them, that they were ready for the only real test. Ames still pushed them, rode them hard, drilled them so often that they began to curse him, hate him, but they continued to learn, and if Ames was despised, they also knew he was a good soldier.

In Washington they continued to drill, lines and formations, columns of march and lines of battle, the bugle commands and the hand signals of the officers. Then they were issued muskets and ammunition, backpacks and blankets and canteens. Around them, in camps spread throughout the city and well beyond, great fields of blue troops and white tents, horses and wagons, began to move together, toward and across the river, lining up and flowing out along the narrow, hard roads. The men knew it was their turn, fresh troops for a battered army, and they began the march, not to the south, as they had thought, but northwest, toward a far corner of Maryland.

CHAMBERLAIN HEARD THE REPORTS, THE RUMORS AND GOSSIP, and sorted through it all, began to feel an instinct for what was accurate and what was absurd. Then there was the official announcement, passed along formally to each regiment: General Pope was gone, relieved. The reckless and pompous fool had been replaced, after he had led his army to a bloody disaster, another costly and painful embarrassment on the same ground that they knew as Bull Run, and it was the beloved McClellan who was getting his second chance.

What his troops, and General Lee, did not know was that an extraordinary piece of good fortune had fallen upon McClellan. Lee's Special Order 191, which detailed to his generals their movements and objectives, had been issued to all his commanders, and when they began to move away, units of the Federal Army had felt their way cautiously out, moving slowly over the ground the Confederates had left. It was here that a pair of soldiers, walking the abandoned camps, found a prize, three precious cigars, rolled up inside a piece of paper. They may have considered the cigars more valuable than the paper, but had the good sense to turn it over to an officer, who quickly took it to McClellan's headquarters. It was a copy of Special Order 191. So now there were no more ghosts, no great, unseen obstacles to McClellan's mission. He knew Lee's plan, his troop strengths, and their positions: that his army had been divided, Jackson to Harper's Ferry, and Longstreet moving north into Maryland.

Now they were marching in a great blue line, and Chamberlain rode the grand horse, crested the small rolling mounds, could see the vast army in a long curving line in front of him, the dark blue snake spotted by patches of white and brown, clusters of wagons and cannon. Behind him he saw more, much more of the same, his own troops, and behind them, a long cloud of thick dust, the rest of the great army.

They marched through farmlands, fields of corn, some just picked. The farmers, anticipating the destruction from a hundred thousand marching troops, had made a frantic effort to save what they could, because they did not believe the army's assurances.

Maryland was a neutral state, and though most were against the cause of the rebels, they did not welcome the blue-coated troops as their own. They did not want this war fought on their lands. But if they protested and anguished over the presence of the great blue masses, they regarded the move northward by Lee's rebel army as even worse, a hostile invasion, a violation. The warm welcome from the liberated people of the state that Lee had so expected was nowhere in evidence. And so both armies were now on neutral ground.

McClellan was moving with unusual speed, to avoid panic in the North, a speed that Lee did not anticipate, and when the armies began to find each other, Lee spread his greatly outnumbered troops along a small tributary of the Potomac, Antietam Creek, and waited for the assault McClellan was pushing toward him.

In Maryland, September is still summer, and there had been no break from the heat. Chamberlain rode in a thick daze, his body moving with a slow rhythm with the steps of his horse. There was no breeze, and he felt as if there was no air at all, just a thin mist of dry dust. He could see down to the surface of the road, saw the moving feet of the men in front of him, saw little puffs kick up from each foot, the tiny clouds rising slowly, coming together into one continuous line of hot, dry, choking dirt. Most of the cloud did not quite reach him, as it did the men on the ground, he was just high enough to escape most of it, but he knew the men behind him were breathing nothing but, and he felt guilty, avoided looking down at the hoofprints of his own horse, knew he was helping to choke his own men.

He looked out across a cornfield, wondered, Why don't we just . . . move over there, no dust? But he knew there was a reason, some reason, and thought, Of course, fences, and ditches, and we do not march for the convenience of the men.

Ames rode beside him, had said nothing for a long hour or more. Chamberlain wanted to look at him, wondered if Ames was sweating as much as he was, but thought, No, keep it to the front. So he drifted off again, now began to think of Maine, knew it was a bad idea, could not help it. September . . . the cool streams, the cool shade, his mother's cool apple cider . . . He sat up straight. Stop that!

Behind him the heat was pressing his men down hard, and men were falling out on the side of the road, lagging behind. This was their first real march, and if they were sturdy and fit and strong, they were not ready for this heat. The officers behind had tried to keep them in line, and there were shouts and cursing, but it had stopped now. The veterans knew this was the way it went, and tonight most would catch up and find their camps. By tomorrow they would begin it all again. They would be lighter as well—all day Chamberlain had stared at a continuous stream of discarded equipment lining the edge of the road, backpacks and blankets, small cloth sacks, boxes and pouches. Some of it was personal, the treasured memories of home, but most was army issue. New soldiers did not yet understand . . . they would issue you as much as you could carry, and the more you marched, the less you would carry, for even the precious gifts and memories lost meaning in the heat.

Chamberlain could see wider, fatter hills now, deep green mounds, and they began to climb, a slight incline. Down the road, coming toward him, was a line of men, walking slowly, with heads down, kicking through the dust, and he saw: prisoners.

The men were mostly barefoot, torn and ragged clothes hung loosely from thin bodies. There were pieces of an identifiable uniform. He saw one man who seemed to be an officer, and the man looked up at him as they passed by, glanced at the fine fat horse, and Chamberlain wanted to stop, talk to the man, but they were gone. Then there were more, thirty, forty, and they did not look up, moved steadily, their guards walking alongside with long bayonets they did not need. Chamberlain wondered, Are they still at war? Am I the enemy, even now? Their war is over . . . maybe. Or maybe it will never be over.

In front of him the line of troops began to climb the larger hill. He could see the blue moving up, toward a small pass, a slight break between two taller mounds. Please, he thought, let us reach those hills, let us stop up there, it would be cooler, it has to be. The sun hung just above a long line of low mountains that stretched far away, to the left. His mind drifted again. He began to focus on the sun now, talking to it: go on, move . . . down . . . He closed his eyes, willing it lower.

The climb became steeper. He had to lean forward now, and Ames suddenly pointed, stuck an arm out in front of him. Chamberlain focused, saw a tree split and shredded into a great pile of white splinters, and now there were more, and the smell of fresh earth, scattered sprays of dirt, small holes, then larger ones, and now beside the road there were broken and crushed wagons, pushed aside by the lead troops, pieces of lumber and metal, and some twisted forms that Chamberlain eyed with fascination.

Ames said, "A good fight here yesterday . . . Turner's Gap, they held us up for a while. Gibbon's 'Black Hats' pushed them back."

Chamberlain saw more evidence of the fight now, a small farm, the house burned, a thin line of black smoke still rising, drifting away finally, high above. Beyond, there was a shattered barn, torn into pieces, great rips in the thin walls. He saw men out in a field, working . . . a burial detail, a long line of fresh, open dirt, and he looked for the bodies, the dead, saw some blue and white and brown . . . things—they were too far away to see clearly. Now they were inside the gap, cresting the wide mountain, high hills rising on both sides of them.

He had seen a tornado once, just for a few brief moments, a hard storm of wind and rain, and a thick black funnel dropping down like some great evil claw. It had touched down only for a minute, had torn through the fields near his family's farm. He had stayed out in the fields, watched it through stinging bites of cold rain, until it lifted again, pulled back up into the blackness. He never forgot that, had followed with pure amazement the clean path it had cut, the total destruction weaving through the fields and woods and then suddenly stopping. Now, here, he saw it again, the total obliteration of trees and bushes and wagons and cannon, torn and ragged pieces of raw death alongside the untouched, the perfect.

It was cooler now. The sun had dropped behind the big hill, and he turned around in the saddle, looked back down the line of men, saw fewer than he had expected. The line seemed stretched out, pulled from the rear, and the faces of the men were down, the steps heavy and automatic. Soon, he thought, just a bit more.

They were moving downhill now, and he saw the sun again, the last piece of orange over far hills, and then there was a bugle, from far up ahead, and the lines in front of him began to slow. He pulled his horse up, saw a flood of blue spreading in both directions away from the road, filling small open spaces under great wide trees. The bugles became louder now, came down the line, closer, and the sound filled him with a vast joy, soothing notes. His own men had stopped, began to bunch up again. Ames said something to the color bearers, and a bugle rose up, blew loud and clear, the call to fall out, stack arms. They were done for the day.

September 17, 1862

The bugles began early, before dawn. He rolled off the cot, stared ahead into black nothing, tried to focus his brain. Ames was already gone, up before the bugle, and Chamberlain could make out the empty cot, thought, Is that what it takes to be a commander? He reached for his uniform, laid carefully at the end of his own cot, struggled with the brass buttons, his clumsy fingers not yet awake. He tried to stretch, reached his arms out wide, could not raise them up, so he moved out of the tent, and heard the sounds of men moving, the slow hum of the army coming alive.

"A good mornin' to ye, Colonel."

"Huh?" He tried to see the face, a short man, thick, built like a bull, and the man held out a tin cup, steaming hot.

"Colonel Ames sent me to get you, Colonel. Says you might be needin' a touch of the elixir."

Chamberlain stared at the man, heard the accent, the hint of the Irish.

"Thank you . . . uh . . ."

"Kilrain, sir. Sergeant Kilrain. Glad to be of service, sir. The boys—we been a-watchin' you with some interest, that we have. You come a long way. Becomin' a pleasure to serve under you."

Chamberlain took the hot cup, drank a painful gulp, could see the face now, faintly in the first light, broad, round, familiar, maybe. There were so many.

"Thank you, Sergeant. Do I know you? You say you've been watching me?"

"Aye, Colonel. We ain't properly met, but bein' you're the second in command and all, and not long of this army, we have been takin' an interest, don't you see? Fact is, Colonel, when we go into line against those rebels up there, we need to know who's up front. We was a bit leery of you, some of us older gents. I been tellin' em you'll be turnin' out all right."

"You a veteran, Sergeant?" He realized from the gravelly voice, the heavy face, Kilrain was older, maybe near the limit, forty-five.

"Aye, Colonel, I suppose you could say that. Did me duty in the regular army for a while—made the great long walk with General Scott, down South. Not very many of us back then, and we did a mighty fine job, if I do say. A great many more of us now, and we're not doin' such good work."

Chamberlain could see now, across the sea of tents and men and wagons, and he felt clearer, not sure if it was the dawn or the coffee. He wanted to ask this sturdy little man some questions, felt something . . . some curiosity, as though this man had something he could use, some knowledge.

"It's a pleasure to meet you, Sergeant. Perhaps we can talk later." Chamberlain held out a hand, an old instinct.

Kilrain saluted, said, "Best be gettin' back, Colonel. We be movin' shortly. There's a mess of rebs up there, just a ways. Enjoy your coffee, Colonel."

Chamberlain watched him leave, then turned and began to look for Ames, thought, Maybe I should tell him what Kilrain said, about the rebs . . . the Confederate Army. But Ames would know, of course, and Chamberlain was still feeling slightly left out of things, too high above the flow of rumors and gossip of the men, too far below the official reports. But if Kilrain were right . . . it could be their first fight.

He tossed the last bit of coffee out of the cup, began to walk. Off to the west, down the hard, dry road they would march again, came a rumble, a brief burst of distant thunder, and he thought of rain, an early morning storm, but the men around him stopped moving and the faces turned, and he knew that it was not thunder, it was guns, the big long-range cannon. The sounds came again, more this time, some closer, the answering rounds, and the men began to move again, quicker now. He saw Ames talking to the company commanders, and he cursed quietly, trotted over, embarrassed for not being there sooner.

". . . and we will remain near this road . . . staying in reserve of the rest of the corps until needed. Tell your men . . . be ready, stay in formation." Ames turned, saw Chamberlain, said, "Good morning, Colonel."

"Sir, I'm sorry, I woke with the bugle—"

"If I had needed you, Colonel, I would have awakened you. I have just informed the officers that we have been instructed to remain in place, in our position in line of march. The army is spreading out in front of us, a couple miles up. The enemy is dug in behind a small creek, Antietam Creek, just this side of Sharpsburg. We may be put into the attack at any time. For now, get the men to step it up, finish their breakfasts, then wait for the orders to move. Got that?"

"Certainly, Colonel." He paused, listened again. The rumbling had stopped. "Colonel, whose guns are those? Is the attack begun?"

"Likely it's the first feeling out, probing, testing the strength. It's like a game to the artillery boys, letting you know they can hit you when the time comes. Let's grab some breakfast, Colonel."

Ames moved away, and Chamberlain followed, toward the wagons and the plates of food. The fare was much simpler now, hardtack, the thin bread with the consistency and flavor of old bricks, and bacon, nearly raw. He caught the smell: a steaming pot of thick coffee. He felt his stomach turn slightly, did not feel hungry, but he saw Ames putting hardtack in his pocket, thought, If today is the day . . . there might not be a mess wagon later. He grabbed a handful of thick, greasy bacon, stuffed it in his mouth, then the hardtack, and he followed Ames's lead, put a few pieces in his pocket, kept one out to eat now. He held out the tin cup Kilrain had given him, the mess orderly filled it, and suddenly there was a bugle, their own, and the men began to flow away from the tents and the wagons, and his stomach turned again. He looked at the coffee, tossed it out, and ran toward the front of the gathering troops.

THEY REACHED A SMALL VILLAGE, PORTERSTOWN, AND MARCHED through wide streets, the townspeople standing in doorways, leaning out windows, some waving, others just staring. Farther ahead, on the creek itself, was the Middle Bridge, held by the Confederate division of Daniel Harvey Hill. The rebel forces were dug in, back, away from the creek, and to their front the Federal Army was spreading out, into lines of attack, were crossing the creek and preparing for the assault. The battle had begun on the far right, just after dawn, and now, as the sun began to rise up behind them, Chamberlain could hear the steady rumble, and as they moved closer, the sharp sounds of single cannon. He sat high on his horse, moving along with the same slow rhythm of the march, but now the men did not fall out, did not feel the weight of the hot September morning, but stared to the front, marching steadily, closer to the sound of the guns.

He heard the steady clatter of muskets now, still off to the right of the road, to the northwest. The battle is not in front of us, he thought. Strange that we should move this way . . . not up there.

In front of them Chamberlain saw a rise, a long, wide hill, and as they began to move up, he saw guns, rows of black cannon set into shallow, round depressions before the crest of the hill. Just then they began to fire, quick bursts of gray smoke, and a sudden shocking boom that startled him and his horse. He bounced around on the road, had to grab the horse hard to calm him. From over the hill he saw Ames, riding hard, past lines of troops that were moving away now, to the right, toward the sounds of the battle.

Ames reined up his horse, and Chamberlain saw he was sweating. "Colonel, we're here, right here. Keep the men in column lines. Let's move them out into this field. Wait for further orders. We are part of the reserve."

Chamberlain turned, and Ames rode past him, into the columns of men, and gave the command to the bugler. With the signal, the men moved quickly off the road. Then Ames rode up again, toward the front of the column, slowed his horse as he reached Chamberlain, said, "Colonel, keep them tight, keep them ready. I am to survey the field to our front."

Chamberlain watched him ride away, up the long hill, turning his horse to the side behind the rows of black cannon. The guns began to fire again, a loud and thunderous volley, and the hill became a great, thick fog bank.

He stayed on his horse, saw now across the road, on the left, vast numbers of troops, lines disappearing into a distant grove of trees, and the men not moving, keeping their formations. He rode out the other way, to the right, into the grass, saw more troops farther out that way, a great field of blue, waiting. He looked to his own men, saw the companies staying in their formations, coming off the road, and he rode up to the head of one column, saw Captain Spear of Company G, a small, sharp man who had also been a teacher. He had a narrow, thick beard, sat on a horse, watched Chamberlain approach, puffed on a large round pipe.

"Well, Colonel, do you think we will get our chance?"

Chamberlain looked back to the crest of the hill, could still not see through the smoke, and another volley thundered out, shaking the ground, startling his horse again.

"Whoa, easy . . . We'll see, Captain. Right now we must be ready . . . be ready to move forward on command!" He felt a little foolish, a vague order, felt again as if he were left out, didn't know what was happening. The battle sounds had continued to the northwest, and he wondered, Are they moving away, around us? He glanced at Spears, said, "I'll be right back . . . just going up the crest a ways, take a look maybe."

"We're right here, Colonel."

He turned the horse, then decided to dismount instead. This wasn't a parade. He jumped down, felt his belt, his pistol, began to walk toward the thick cloud of smoke.

The guns continued to fire, every minute or so, and he wondered, How far away is the enemy? There had been no explosions, no incoming shells, none of the sounds he'd been told about, coached about, by Ames, just the deadening thunder of their own big guns.

The smoke began to envelop him, and he kept moving. Suddenly he could not breathe, felt suffocated by the thick smell of burnt powder. He stopped, coughing hard, tried to see, caught a glimpse of one gun, saw men moving around it like ghosts, and then, abruptly, they all moved away and the gun fired, jerking backward with the recoil. He felt his ears deaden, shattered by the sound of the blast. He went farther, was moving up between the guns now, and suddenly the smoke cleared in front of him, a light breeze sweeping up the far side of the rise, blowing the smoke away to the rear. Down below he saw the wide, flat plain, farms and roads and trees, cornfields and small distant buildings. And to the right, far across the curving lines of the creek, there was more smoke, great, flat clouds of white and gray. The sounds of the battle were steady and loud now, and on either side of him the big guns boomed again, the shock knocking him off his feet.

He lay on soft grass, thought, I'm hit . . . then, No, but I'm damned near deaf. He raised his head, could still see down, the fields and woods. Now, from the sounds of the battle, he saw his first troops, thick lines of blue, uneven and ragged formations, moving toward a cornfield, and then smoke, solid lines of gray, and in a few seconds the sound reached him, the chattering musket fire, and the blue lines were in pieces, men moving back, some still advancing, some not moving at all. He saw more lines now, solid blocks of blue spreading wide, advancing, and more smoke, and more sounds, and then, farther away, a glimpse through the smoke, other lines of men, some moving, some firing, quick flashes of white and yellow, and the big guns beside him firing again.

He saw down to the left the arch of a stone bridge, crossing the creek to the south. Down in front of him, where the creek swung closer to the base of the hill, he could see the Middle Bridge, saw troops moving across, a steady advance, and then he saw the rebels on the far side, moving into position, and he understood: the attack is moving, shifting this way, we will begin now, *here*. He turned to watch the men working the cannon, and was startled to see more men, his men, watching the battle, lying on the ground, creating a neat blue patch on the hill. He had not thought anyone else would be up here, should not have been up here; *he* should not be up here, but he knew they could not just wait, could not sit behind some big hill and hear it all and not see.

Chamberlain stood up, began to wave his arms, fast and high, motioning to the men, and another blast came from the guns. He braced himself, did not fall, kept waving, back, move back, wondered if they saw him or were ignoring him. He moved along the hillside, tried to yell, but the sound of the guns took his voice away, and suddenly he heard a high, distant scream, louder now, whistling toward him, dropping down on him from behind. He turned, saw nothing, but the sound pierced his ears, and the ground suddenly flew high around him, dirt spraying him, knocking him down, and he lay still, shook his head . . . checked, all right, but . . . a bad day for the ears. Then another scream, overhead, and behind the hill, down where the rest of his men sat waiting, there was another explosion, and he tried to see, but it was beyond the crest.

Suddenly, someone had him under the arms, lifting him, and he said, "No, I'm all right," and he saw the face of an officer, a man with black crust under his eyes, around his mouth and nose, glaring at him with eyes of cold steel.

"You are bloody well not all right, you damned fool! Get these men back off this hill. You're drawing fire to my guns!"

Chamberlain saw the uniform, a captain, realized suddenly he had done a supremely stupid thing, and the man turned away, was gone through a new cloud of smoke.

Chamberlain crouched down, ran along the hill, yelling at the men, "*Back, get back*, we're giving the enemy a target!"

They were watching him, understood, and moved fast and low, back over the hill and away from the guns.

He slowed as he came down out of the smoke, saw his men moving back in their lines, where most of the others, the ones who did not have to see, were down on the ground, resting. He saw the still smoking earth, the round fresh hole from the enemy shell, and he thanked God it had not gone farther, had not gone into the rows of men.

Captain Spear was standing, talking to another officer, and they looked at him, questioned silently, saw the dirt, the black grime that covered him, and he said, "The battle may be moving our way. Keep them ready!"

They nodded, looked at him without expression, and he wondered if they knew what he had done, that he had stood up high on a hill, out in front of his own carefully placed cannon, and waved his arms like some idiotic fire-breathing evangelist.

He moved away, felt thirsty, looked for his horse, his canteen, and saw a sergeant, the short and sturdy Irishman, Kilrain, standing, leaning on the barrel of his musket.

"Well, now, Colonel, did you get a fine look at what we're facin'?"

Chamberlain wiped at the dirt on his face, said, "Quite a sight . . . right over that hill, it's a few hundred yards, all of it."

"Impressive, ain't it, Colonel? Watchin' them line up and walk right into the fire."

"Yes . . . impressive." He stared back up the hill, the big guns quiet now, the smoke clearing, and he could see them again, lining the crest of the hill. The cannon are hidden, of course, he realized, hard to get the range on them that way. I will damned well remember *that.*

"The word is, Colonel . . ." Kilrain said, and Chamberlain turned, looked into the heavy face. "The word is, we'll be sittin' here all day. The boys reckon we been left behind. I been tellin' em, don't be in such a damned hurry . . . the time will come."

"I'm not sure. It looks like the battle might swing back this way. We had better be ready." He had said it again, felt foolish again. Telling them to be ready won't make them ready.

Kilrain looked up toward the hill, said, "It's already in front of us, Colonel, there."

Chamberlain listened, realized the noises to the right had faded, replaced now by a wave of new sounds, over the hill and out in front of where he had been. And now the cannon fired again and did not pause, and the smoke began to flow down the hill toward them and above them, darkening the sky. He heard the scream again, the whine of the incoming shell, and up on the hill the shell burst, a new thunder, and he felt the ground shake under his feet. More shells came high overhead, and behind him the men began to move nervously, some standing, some crouching, and the officers were shouting, keeping them in line—there was no other place to go.

The sounds were much closer now. He stared at the hill, wondered if this would be the place, if suddenly the rebels would pour over the hill, rush past the cannon and down. Easy, he thought . . . there's a whole army out there . . . we're in back, behind them all.

The cannon kept up the waves of firing, and the enemy's shells continued falling around them, but only a few, and not aimed at them . . . just chance . . . the shells that were missing their targets. He sat down now, and the men who had stood, expecting . . . something, sat as well, and there was nothing to do but wait.

It was now past noon, and out on the road men and wagons were moving back, away from the fight. The troops stared at the long procession, the solid line of wounded, heard the sounds, the wails and screams, and some would not look, turned their faces away, and others stared hard. Chamberlain had stood at first, a show of respect, but this too was not a parade, and he sat again and listened to the battle work its way along the creek far out in front of them. Now there was fire down to the left, toward the stone bridge, and it seemed to grow more quiet in front of him, and he had the strange feeling that the battle had been like some great, horrible wheel, rolling slowly from right to left, right in front of them, right past them.

It is not coming after all, he thought. This is what the reserves do, they sit back behind it all and hear the sounds, and wait for an attack that does not come. He realized then that he felt disappointment. He looked down along the lines, saw the faces that had been watching the hill, that like him had been expecting something and who now began to look elsewhere. There were a few fires, coffee being made, more laughing.

Well, then, it must be going well, he thought. They don't need us. He began to move toward the new smells, was suddenly very hungry. He brushed dirt from his pants, stepped around a small crater, then another. The men were letting go now, the tension releasing, and there was more laughter, a big sergeant teasing a small man with glasses.

Chamberlain did not feel like laughing, felt something dead, hollow in his gut. The hunger had become something else, more painful now. He stopped at a fence post, cupped his hand over the top, suddenly pulled hard on the post, pulled it down, the base uprooting from the soft dirt. He stood back, looked around, felt embarrassed, but more, he felt angry, denied. He turned toward the hill, looked up to the guns, silent now, the fight drifting, too far away.

24. HANCOCK

September 17, 1862. Early afternoon.

THE BATTLE HAD MOVED AWAY, OFF TO THE LEFT. HE HAD BEEN up front, in the center of the entire Federal line, for only an hour or so, and he expected a fight, a good fight. He could still see the gray lines spread out on the far side of the field, but they did not come.

He did not know Israel Richardson, knew only that the man was down, presumed dead by now, a terrible wound. It had happened just after noon, when the fighting was heaviest in front of where Hancock now stood. Richardson was the commander of the First Division, Second Corps, and McClellan had come immediately to Hancock, had brought the promotion as if asking a question, in that respectful way he spoke to those whom he trusted. Hancock had accepted with a thin veil over his eagerness. He did not forget that the position was vacant because a man had just been killed. His own brigade had not been engaged, had been placed by Baldy Smith around the division's batteries, who had tried to lend support to the first attack on the far right. Hancock had time for brief good-byes, had taken his staff with him, and now was in command of his own division, right in the middle of it all.

He had ridden his horse quickly to the front lines, had met the brigadiers in a hasty greeting, had passed along a message from McClellan, an embarrassing note that Hancock read flatly and without comment: "We will push them into the river, before the sun sets." But in front of him, across the narrow field, no one was running, and he had already sent a courier back, asking for instructions, had expected the word to come down the line, push ahead, advance. The Confederate lines were badly bruised, had withstood an assault by overwhelming numbers all morning, but the attacks were never coordinated, were fought piecemeal, and it was clear that Lee had been able to shuffle his units back and forth, meeting the greatest point of attack.

Now, the only serious fight was down to the left. He looked that way, heard big guns and muskets, thought, It has to be Burnside, trying to cross that damned bridge. He could not see it from where he stood, but he knew the location, knew Burnside's orders, and could only listen as one more small piece of McClellan's massive army was sent against Lee's thin lines.

He climbed back up on his horse, could see more clearly the lines across from him, and a musket ball whizzed by, above his head, then another, and he thought, Best not sit in one spot. Spurring the horse, he rode back over a small rise and dropped out of sight of the Confederate lines.

He dismounted, his small staff following him, and saw an officer, trailing aides, one holding aloft a bright green brigade flag. It was General Meagher, Thomas Meagher, of the Irish Brigade.

"General Hancock, sir, are we to be movin' forward now? The men . . . they're waitin for a fight."

Hancock stared behind, back toward headquarters, saw no one coming, no courier. "General Meagher, I have no orders to advance. The last word I received from General McClellan himself was that we were to hold this position against an assault by the enemy. General, have you seen any signs that the enemy is preparing to assault?"

"Not hardly, General. There's a pretty thin line out there in front of my men. Unless Bobby Lee's got a herd of ghosts backin' them up . . . I believe we have a good chance of bustin' right through."

Hancock looked again at the empty ground behind him, removed his hat, rubbed a hand across his head, felt a throb, the birth of a headache, the back of his neck tightening, squeezing up and over the top of his skull. He said aloud toward the empty field, "Dammit!"

Meagher watched him, understood, said, "General, I'll be gettin' back to my men. I will wait for word, General. We'll be sittin' tight."

Meagher spurred his horse and rode off, leading his aides, and Hancock watched him leave, saw the green flag in a quick flutter as it dropped away over the rise. He began to feel truly angry, once more the frustration of the commander who has the men, the strong position, and must wait while someone else sits in a fog. He turned, looked at the faces of his staff, saw Lieutenant Hughes, knew he was the best horseman, would move quickly.

"Lieutenant, go to General Sumner's headquarters. Maybe they decided to attack and forgot to tell us."

Hughes moved his horse closer. "Sir, might I word that differently? General Sumner is—"

"Lieutenant, please pay our *respects* to General Sumner, or General McClellan, or whoever else might be in charge of this damned army, and request some instructions. Tell them that we can hear General Burnside's activity on our left and are wondering if we should go to his aid. Please inform them that the lines in front of us can be pressed without much difficulty, if we are so ordered. You more comfortable with that, Lieutenant?"

"Yes, sir." Hughes jerked the horse, moved away over the open field, and Hancock pulled his horse the other way, eased up the rise until he could see the Confederate lines again. There was no movement.

McClellan's orders were repeated: "Hold position, and prepare to receive an assault." Burnside's forces finally broke through and crossed Antietam Creek late in the afternoon, only to have their strong advance routed by the sudden arrival of the troops of A. P. Hill, the last of Jackson's forces to rejoin the army after the capture of Harper's Ferry.

Sumner, who commanded the Second Corps, had seen his divisions punished at the center of the Confederate position, at a place known as the Bloody Lane, but he had managed to push through, until Lee's more mobile units strengthened the position. Now, neither side had moved the other from the field, and the aging commander convinced himself that this amounted to a success. McClellan seemed to accept that logic, absorbed it himself, and so once Burnside was halted and the daylight began to fade, McClellan's preference was to wait and see if perhaps Lee would give them a better opportunity tomorrow.

25. CHAMBERLAIN

September 17, 1862. Late afternoon.

The sun was dropping toward the crest of the hill when Ames rode up and dismounted.

Chamberlain stood, and Ames said, "We won't be needed today, Colonel."

Chamberlain looked at him, waited for more, and Ames turned, stared up the hill to the guns. Other officers began to gather, and Ames turned back to them, said, "The Fifth Corps was not needed today, gentlemen, not in the judgment of the commanding general. The battle has been extremely costly. The enemy has been pushed back, at great loss to both sides, and from what we can observe so far, we have gained little. It is possible that tomorrow the fight will resume." Ames stopped, looked slowly at the officers.

"I have been ordered to announce to you that the commanding general feels that this battle has been a great victory. Certainly I would not presume to dispute or contradict the words of General McClellan. I would only caution you to prepare your men for tomorrow, for what may yet follow." He moved away, began to walk out into the field, looking over the sight.

The company commanders spread out to their men, and the order was given to stack arms and make camp. Chamberlain watched the men unload the wagons, watched the camp form, the tents and new fires. Beyond the hill there were still faint sounds of the battle, scattered firing, and he had to see, to walk back up. He stepped through the thick grass, up toward the positions of the guns, and saw now they were being moved, their crews hitching them to the caissons and the horses pulling them away from their shallow pits. He looked for the captain, the man who had ordered him off the hill, to apologize, to tell him it was his mistake, but he could not see the faces. The teams were beginning to move away, toward the road and down closer to the battle.

Chamberlain reached the top of the hill, looked down again across the quiet fields and saw great masses of men, long battle lines, and small groups in formation, appearing just as they had that morning. Now the light was fading, and he watched, waiting for something to happen, expecting movement, some noise. The men did not move, however, and he felt a sudden wave of horror, realizing he was looking at long lines and vast fields of dead soldiers, the unspeakable conclusion, the bloody aftermath. He forced himself to look, felt a hot sickness rising in his gut, scanned the wide fields from the far right, where the sounds had first come, down toward the stone bridge, where it had ended. Every field, every open space, was dotted with clusters of the dead, every fence draped with dark shapes, every road a solid black line. He saw the cornfields, flattened and spotted with the dark shapes, and then he saw movement, the few men who wandered among them, and he felt sick again, thankful he was not down there, one of them. He wondered what they were doing, what they were thinking, what they were looking for. He stood for a long while, felt the breeze against his face, could still smell the smoke and powder, but not the dead. Not yet, he thought. The sun had dropped below the horizon, a distant line of trees, far behind the army in ragged gray uniforms that was still out there, was still facing them. Now the fields began to darken, the ghastly sight began to fade from his view, and he thought, They did not need us today . . . but the enemy is still out there, and there is still a war. . . . Could we not have helped?

THE FOLLOWING DAY THE TWO ARMIES FACED EACH OTHER without moving, like two fighters who have beaten each other senseless and don't know what else to do. McClellan outnumbered Lee's forces by better than two to one, had been given the best opportunity he would have to end the war, but he waited, again pleading with Washington for more reinforcements.

Lee realized his invasion to the north was no longer feasible, that even though his army had fought to a bloody draw, his smaller forces could not win that kind of war. And so, after bracing for a new attack from McClellan's army, an attack that never came, he waited until dark, and during the night of September 18 withdrew his badly bruised army back across the Potomac, into Virginia.

26. HANCOCK

September 19, 1862

"Sir, they're gone."

It was just light enough to see, a cool morning. Hancock had reached the front lines, had ridden through a fine foggy mist until he saw the green flag.

"They're gone, General," Meagher said again. "The lines are empty."

Hancock did not stop, rode his horse past the shallow trenches, up over the low mound of earth that had protected his men, rode into the open field between the lines. Meagher rode out with him, and they guided their horses carefully, avoiding the scattered black masses, the bodies of the dead. Behind them the officers began to shout and men climbed up from the trenches, began to move out with the commanders, some running farther, to the advance, screening the generals. But there was nothing to screen against. They reached the Confederate lines, saw down long rows of shallow ditches, saw bodies piled out in front of and behind the lines; and in the trenches themselves, broken muskets, pieces of clothing and equipment, and nothing else.

Hancock stared at the empty ground, said aloud, "We let them get away."

"Aye, General, that we did."

Meagher moved his horse closer, and the two men sat quietly for a long minute. Finally, Meagher said, "We lost many a good man. Did ya know General Richardson, sir?"

"No, I'm sorry, I didn't. I heard he was a fine commander."

"Maybe . . . A general that gets himself killed isn't much good to anybody. We had a good fight of it, though, maybe better than some, maybe worse. I will say, beggin' your pardon, General, we was all pleased when we heard you was takin' over."

Hancock nodded, said nothing. He knew the reputation of the Irishmen, knew they had indeed given the good fight. And they will again, he thought, if someone will give them the chance.

Meagher looked at Hancock for a long moment, said, "You know General McClellan, do ya, sir?"

"Yes, I know him. He's a good friend, opened a mighty big door for me. More than once."

"Aye. Do ya think we can win this war, General?"

Hancock looked at the heavy, round face and the sharp, honest eyes that hid nothing. "You mean, do I think General McClellan can win this war?"

"Is it not the same question, General? This army wants Mac to lead it, they've shown that. And who else can we follow?"

Hancock looked away, did not want to think about it, had felt this way before, the sense that no one was really in command.

"Forgive me for speakin' freely, General. If you'd rather I'd button it—"

"No, General Meagher, your concerns . . . are good ones. We have all been taught how to follow orders. I just wish someone was back there who understood *opportunity*. I have been in this position before, General. I watch this army fight and maneuver itself into great advantage, and then we just stop, as though someone, somewhere, does not truly believe we can finish this. I am loyal to General McClellan because he is our commander. I have always believed he knows what is best for this army, what is best for his troops. That's why the men love him . . . he is *their* general. And that may be his problem. He may love them too much."

"I don't know about much of what goes on back there, sir, under those big tents. But my men, General, these tough old micks . . . they been watchin' each other get shot up for over a year now, and it seems that nothin' ever comes from it. General, forgive me for sayin' it, but these soldiers . . . they would have won this war by now if it weren't for the generals, maybe me included."

Hancock laughed quietly, but the humor passed quickly. "I expect Mr. Lincoln might agree with you."

LEE RETURNED TO CENTRAL VIRGINIA, MOVED HIS FORCES INTO the fertile comfort of the Shenandoah Valley. McClellan remained around Sharpsburg and Antietam Creek for over a month before the prodding from Washington had an effect. Lincoln himself had come to McClellan's camp, pushing him to make some pursuit of Lee's bloodied army, and so by the end of October, McClellan finally started the chase. While Lee's escaping army had crossed the Potomac in one night, McClellan took eight days. And now, while he marched slowly and carefully down the Blue Ridge, Lee had time to move east, placing Longstreet between the Federal Army and Richmond, so that McClellan would again stall, and begin the persistent calls to Washington for more troops.

November 1862

"Well, gentlemen, I feel we have little to fear of old Robert Lee now! Look, outside!"

Hancock turned, with the others, saw what McClellan was pointing to: snow. It had turned colder all day, and the army camp had begun the first preparations for winter quarters. The troops had started digging the small square pits over which they would build whatever form of shelter they could find. There were mixed feelings about the winter break. Some of the men welcomed the rest, the opportunity to write letters, play cards, nurse sore feet or small wounds. Others despised the waiting, the weeks of inactivity, and, if the weather was bad, the necessity of staying cramped together inside these small, makeshift shelters.

Hancock watched the new snow, thought, We have waited for over a month, and now here is the first honest excuse. Behind him the large, single room was glowing from the warmth of a large fire. One end of the simple house was a huge stone hearth, framing an enormous firebox. As the fire grew, the men had begun moving away, toward the other end of the long room. They were all familiar to Hancock, mostly generals, brigade and division commanders of the Second Corps, who were camped near McClellan's headquarters. Most had come through the recent campaigns weighed down with a sense of self-defeat, and privately, each man believed he had done the best that could be done, as though it was no one's fault. Excuses filled every conversation: the weather, the ground, the government, some mysterious power that seemed to be with Lee. No one talked now of the end of the war, there were no longer any grand predictions, no more fat boasting to the newspaper reporters. The sense of gloom was affecting the troops as well, spreading out through the entire army. But tonight, here, the mood was oddly buoyant. Men were laughing and talking, and McClellan himself sat on an old wooden chair, behind a crude table, smoking a cigar, the center of attention. A bottle of brandy had made its way around the room, was emptied, and another had appeared, began the same route.

Hancock knew the faces, men mostly around his age, many with long careers, and now some tough experience, and he did not feel attached, did not share the pleasant air of camaraderie, still stared out the window watching fat snowflakes and wondered, Why are they laughing?

He looked back into the room, through a haze of cigar smoke and blue coats, saw one man watching him. General Couch had been placed in command of the Second Corps after the apparent failure of Bull Sumner to again appreciate the value of initiative. While everyone bore some share of the failures at Antietam, Sumner had controlled the entire center of the line, and by keeping up the pressure, could have split Lee's army in half. When the time had come, he simply quit, and the talk began quietly that he had run out of nerve. Even McClellan had understood that Sumner had only one advantage that gave him seniority in the army, and that was his age. He was simply the good old soldier, the career man who had spent his long life rising gradually through the ranks. At the start of the war neither Winfield Scott nor the War Department had any reason to assume that Sumner was not qualified to lead large numbers of troops into battle. It finally fell on McClellan to pull him off the line.

Darius Couch was slightly younger than Hancock, a small man of light build. He had come out of West Point in 1846 with the same class that produced McClellan and Jackson. He left the army after Mexico, but returned to serve with his friend McClellan, and had shown a fiery competence for leading troops.

Hancock returned his look, saw Couch glance toward the door, a silent signal, and Hancock moved that way, followed Couch outside into the blowing snow. They walked out a way from the house, toward the camps of the troops, and Couch stopped, reached a hand out, his palm catching the snow.

"Winter."

Hancock nodded in the dark.

Couch said, "Nothing will happen now. We have wasted the last good month of the year. Have you spent much time in Virginia, General?"

Hancock looked out through the snow, toward a large field, a wide sea of small fires and huddled men.

"No, sir."

"A miserable place to move an army. The roads . . . after a snow like this, it will probably warm up, melt it all, and the roads will turn to deep mud. Doesn't get cold enough to freeze solid, so the cycle repeats. We'll probably sit right here for months, until someone persuades our commanding general to get started again . . . if he is still our commanding general."

"Yes, sir." Hancock held himself back, did not know Couch well, but there was something in the man, something quiet and dark and dangerous, something he had begun to see in a few of the others, had seen it now in himself, that nameless *thing*: Men who advanced with their troops and did not hear the muskets and stepped over their dead without looking down. He also sensed that Couch did not fit into that great warm celebration behind them, powerful men who drank too much brandy and toasted each other's empty successes. Couch pulled at his coat, wrapped his arms around his thin frame.

"I know how much Mac appreciates your work, General. I know he appreciates mine. He's a good friend, and once he's in your corner, he'll go all the way to Hell to back you up. There're a lot of people in this army who have never even met him, and they feel the same way, that he's their friend too." He paused. "I wish he was a better fighter."

Hancock could not see his face, knew the words were difficult, that since their days at the Point, Couch and McClellan had always been close.

Hancock felt the cold now as well. Snow was blowing into his collar. He said, "Well, excuse me, General, I believe I'll head back to my quarters."

Couch turned, held out a hand, said, "Good night, General," and Hancock took the hand, then started away.

There was a sound of horses on the road, between the house and the vast field, and Hancock saw four men. They rode up along the rail fence, reached the gate, where a guard halted them, then from a small shelter more guards appeared, and one horseman said, "Special courier, I have a message for General McClellan."

The guards gathered closer. One man lit a match, tried to see the man's papers, and Couch walked over, said, "Excuse me, gentlemen, I am General Couch, Second Corps commander, and this is General Hancock. You may give the message to us, we will take it to General McClellan."

The man who had spoken said, "Begging your pardon, General. I am General Buckingham, from Secretary Stanton's office. These men are my escort. I am to deliver this personally to the commanding general. If you will examine the seal . . ."

Couch stepped forward, took the papers, saw the heavy wax seal of the War Department, said, "General, please follow me. General McClellan is there, inside the house."

The men dismounted, and Buckingham stepped up beside Couch and waited.

Couch looked at Hancock, said, "Well, General, still off to bed?"

"No, I suppose not. Maybe one more look at the fire . . ."

The three men walked toward the cabin, and Hancock held open the door, moved into the big room behind the other two. The noise did not stop, no one paid attention. Couch and Hancock waited by the door, and Buckingham made his way to McClellan and announced himself quietly. McClellan looked up at the man, nodded without smiling, and Hancock saw Buckingham hand him the paper. McClellan pushed his thumb through the wax, unfolded the letter, read for a few seconds, then stood up.

"Gentlemen . . . please. May I have your attention? Quiet, please."

The talking wound down, faces turned, and McClellan said, "Is there any brandy left? This man is from the War Department. He has ridden hard through this weather and appears to need a drink."

A bottle moved from the far side of the room, was placed on the table in front of McClellan. He poured the last of the contents into his glass, handed it to Buckingham, and Hancock saw that the man's hands were shaking. He raised the glass slowly, said, "Thank you, General."

"Gentlemen, this man has braved this miserable night at the request of the Secretary of War. I could read the letter out loud, but it is simpler to just say that I have been relieved of command. Effective immediately, this army is under the command of . . ." He paused, and Hancock sensed it was dramatics, McClellan making the best of his last moment in the spotlight. ". . . Major General Ambrose Burnside."

There was a moment of stunned silence. The men began to look at each other, and Hancock dropped his head, stared at the floor, felt briefly sick, took a deep breath. Couch's hand was on his shoulders and he said, "We can only do our jobs, General."

TO THE TROOPS, BURNSIDE'S APPOINTMENT WAS NOT AS IMPORtant as McClellan's dismissal. Rumors began to fly immediately, angry men making big talk. The most radical story was that McClellan was to lead an armed force into Washington, unseating Lincoln. There was more widespread talk of a milder protest, men refusing to serve, resigning. The officers were more discreet. Most understood that angry talk was dangerous talk, and if rumors led to action, the effectiveness of the army could dissolve.

Hancock felt McClellan's dismissal as a blow, but understood that the affection he held for the commander did not mean that McClellan was the best man to lead the army, and so when the angry talk reached him, he was quick to put it down. He was, after all, a career soldier, and he had no doubts that his loyalty lay to the nation, not to any one man.

The troops considered Burnside just another in a line, a man who held a title, who inspired nothing else. To the commanders, Burnside's appointment was a serious mistake. Even Burnside himself had doubts, had been as surprised as the rest that his name had come down from Washington. He was thought of in the high ranks as a reasonably capable commander, a friendly, generous man with no particular talents. He had been as culpable as anyone else for the failures at Antietam.

Burnside immediately made two decisive moves. He reorganized the army, creating three large "Grand Divisions," putting them under the commands of the ambitious and temperamental Joe Hooker; William Franklin, Hancock's original commander from the Sixth Corps; and, surprisingly, Bull Sumner. Burnside did not explain his logic, and Hancock assumed that by creating a buffer of experience between him and the corps commanders, Burnside would be able to shield himself from direct criticism, and perhaps direct blame. Hancock's division, under Couch's Second Corps, was placed in Sumner's Grand Division.

Burnside's second decision was to abandon the pursuit of Lee's army through central Virginia, and instead make a sudden surprise move to the left, to the southeast, along the Rappahannock River, crossing below Lee's army, placing the Federal Army between Lee and Richmond. Burnside assured the President that this would bring a speedy end to the war, as Richmond would fall before Lee could react. The place he chose to make the crossing was the town of Fredericksburg.

THEY HAD MARCHED FOR TWO DAYS, WOUND THEIR WAY ALONG the high banks of the Rappahannock River. Hancock rode at the head of his division, and today Couch rode with him. They were in the lead, and would reach their destination before dark, the town of Falmouth, across the river from Fredericksburg.

The weather had warmed slightly, and Hancock rode without his heavy coat. The men moved at a good pace, knew the march was a short one, stepped through a layer of mud on the road that gradually deepened as more of the army passed. Couch had said little, stared away, toward the other side of the river.

"There's a few more."

Hancock looked across, saw gray-clad troops at what had been a bridge crossing, burned timbers now poking at angles out of the water. There was a shot, then two more, and Hancock turned around and watched the column. The men did not break ranks, kept up the smooth march, and now a small squad of skirmishers formed along the bank, fired back across at the rebel troops, and they quickly vanished.

"I wonder if Lee knows by now."

Hancock looked at Couch, said, "I expect he does. I heard earlier, a report of some cavalry watching us. Probably Stuart's men. They're keeping an eye on us."

"I have to admit," Couch said, "I think this might work. If we can get across the river quickly, move down toward Richmond . . . Lee will have a problem."

Hancock thought of Lee, tried to form a picture, had only seen him once since Mexico, at a party in Washington. He was a quiet Southern gentleman, graceful and proper, and he had given Mira some advice, had told her to go with her husband to California, to keep the family together. It was a brief conversation, but there was a quiet sincerity to the man that had caught Hancock's attention, and the advice had an impact on Mira as well. She had not told him of her doubts about going to California, but revealed something in conversation to Lee, and Lee's words carried a sadness, an awareness of what his own career as a soldier had cost him. Now, Hancock tried to see the face, wondered how Lee might have changed, what it was that made him such a good leader. So much has happened, he thought, we never could have known it would become this bloody insanity.

He thought of Albert Sidney Johnston and their last night, the party at his home. Johnston had already pulled away before he left California, his loyalties had already made him cautious. He was the first to understand that he was to be the enemy, and now Johnston was dead. Mira had written him, relaying the story from the papers, a battle at a place called Shiloh. There will be more, he thought, more familiar names, and he tried to stop it, said to himself, Do not do this. But he could not avoid it, saw now the rugged face of Lew Armistead. He'd heard little about him, knew he had been with Longstreet in the Seven Days' battles, but there was no real news. And he thought of Couch's words: "We all have our jobs to do. And our job now is to move this big damned army as fast as we can, and outsmart Robert E. Lee."

From down the road a rider came up, saw the colors behind them, pulled his horse alongside and saluted. "General Couch, sir. I am Major Spaulding, of the Engineering Corps. I am to guide your column into position for the crossing."

Couch nodded, said, "Very good, Major. You anticipate any problems?"

"Not at all, sir. The river is calm, and there appears to be little if any opposition on the other side. All we need are your pontoons, sir."

Couch looked at Hancock, puzzled, and said, "What pontoons, Major?"

Spaulding laughed, tried to be part of the joke, said, "Why, General, we can't send this army across the river without your pontoons."

Couch did not laugh, and Hancock saw the face of the engineer slowly change, the smile fading. "General, we have been waiting . . . we have orders from General Burnside to lay the pontoon bridges as soon as your corps arrives. I assumed, sir . . . you have them."

"Major, you had better look elsewhere. There are no pontoons with this column."

Spaulding's red face, bitten by the cold air of the fast ride, now drained of color. "General, we have already checked. . . . General Burnside requested the pontoons be delivered over from Harper's Ferry. The request went straight to Washington, to General Halleck. I heard him discussing it myself, sir. The pontoons were to be . . . were to arrive at the same time as your column. General Burnside was very plain on this, sir. I have my orders. I have to build a bridge."

Couch looked at Hancock, said, "General, you see any pontoons? Anybody in your division hiding any pontoons?" His voice began to rise, angry and without humor, and Hancock now understood. They would sit still again, the great power of this army would be held up one more time because something went wrong.

Spaulding abruptly saluted, said, "General, if you please, I have to return to Falmouth."

"Of course, Major, go about your business. We will arrive shortly."

The man turned, sent mud spraying over them as his horse kicked away, and Hancock said, "So, we have no way to cross the river."

"No, General, of course not. The plan was a good one too."

"They may find them yet, sir. Hard to lose something as big as a pontoon train."

"Oh, we'll find them, General. They'll make their way to Falmouth eventually. They might even get us across the river in time to do some good. But I have a feeling, General . . . surely, you share it. You've been with this army long enough." Couch stared ahead with dark eyes, and Hancock said nothing, now could see the small town, buildings, a church steeple, small neat houses, and to the right, down a long, steep embankment, the wide river, and across it, Fredericksburg.

IT SNOWED THROUGHOUT THE NIGHT, SLOW AND STEADY, AND early in the morning when he left his tent, the ground was covered with a thin white blanket. He walked through the camp, felt the cold, knew winter had yet to really show itself, that this army was preparing to move in what might be the worst conditions imaginable.

It had been two weeks, and the pontoons had still not come. The word came from Burnside to just sit and wait. Couch had gone to headquarters every day, meetings and informal gatherings of the higher ranks, but Burnside was adamant: They would cross the river at this place. The missing pontoons were simply an inconvenience.

Hancock walked downhill now, toward the river. He saw a thin glaze on the water, the first signs of ice, thought, If we wait long enough, we can walk across. He felt the ground soften, slippery mud under the thin layer of snow, and he backed away, thinking, Don't fall into that mess *this* morning. Mighty damned uncomfortable. He eased along the bank, looked across to the larger town of Fredericksburg, saw a long hill behind, stretching down to the left. The hill had the same layer of snow, and he stopped, admired it as he would a painting, a beautiful scene. Church spires rose sharply above the town, and the riverfront buildings were packed together in a neat row. He guessed at the distance, three hundred yards, maybe less.

Above him, upriver, there was some rough water, a few rocks breaking the smooth flow. He stopped, saw something moving among the rocks, waited, and now he could see. It was a cow.

Several more cows moved into the water on the far side, breaking through the thin ice as they moved out into the middle of the river. The first one had reached the near bank, climbed up through the black mud, disappeared into thick grass and short trees. He watched the others, watched the depth of the water, saw they did not go down more than three feet, and he turned, ran back up through the snow, toward the headquarters of General Couch.

Couch was eating breakfast, a pile of steaming hotcakes, and Hancock caught the smell, the butter, felt a hungry turn in his stomach. Couch watched him approach, saw the look, said, "Ah, General, news travels fast I see. A gift, from a local farmer . . . white flour and butter, and even a few eggs. No need to hurry, there's plenty. Join me, please."

Hancock stopped at the table, was out of breath, said, "No, oh no, sir . . . that's not why . . . sir, we can cross the river. Upstream, a quarter mile. It's shallow enough to ford."

Couch stuffed a forkful of hotcakes into his mouth, syrup dripping down his chin. He stared at Hancock, swallowed hard, said, "Ford the river? It's a long way across, General, and it's damned cold. You sure it's shallow?"

"Sir, I just watched a herd of cattle cross the entire way, no more than three feet deep. We can have the whole corps across by tonight."

Couch stood, glanced down at the hotcakes, looked over to a waiting aide and said, "Enjoy these, Captain," and the man leapt forward, picked up the fork and attacked the plate without sitting down.

Hancock followed Couch away from the table and the smells, and they walked quickly toward the grand house, the stately home overlooking the river that had once belonged to the family of George Washington. It was Sumner's headquarters.

Guards saluted as they passed, and Hancock glanced around the yard, saw vast gardens, vine-covered walkways, brown stems peeking out through the snow. They entered the house, and Hancock caught the strong smell of cigar smoke. Standing in the middle of the main living room, among a cluster of clean blue coats, was General Burnside.

Burnside was the only one wearing a hat, tall black felt with a wide brim, and from underneath, his thick whiskers washed down the sides of his round face. He turned toward the opening door, smiling, and Couch said, "Excuse us, General, we did not know you were here. We came to see General Sumner. General Hancock has some information you may find useful."

Burnside looked at Hancock, held out his hand, said, "Yes, General Hancock, a pleasure. Please, gentlemen, let's go this way. . . . I just left General Sumner in his office."

They moved away from the larger crowd, and Hancock saw civilians now, men with pads of paper: reporters. They passed into a smaller sitting room, were alone now, and Burnside peered around the corner of what had been a bedroom, said, "General Sumner? We have visitors."

Sumner stood, seemed annoyed at the interruption, and they crowded into the small room. It was dark, because Sumner had closed the curtains, and there was only one other chair, which Burnside offered to Couch.

"No, General, please, you are in command here."

Burnside nodded, smiling, said, "Quite right, quite right," and sat in the chair.

Sumner looked up at the other two, said, "What is it, Couch?"

"Sir, General Hancock reports that it is possible to ford the river, upstream a short distance. The crossing appears to be a fairly simple one. With your permission, we could begin moving the men right away."

Sumner stared at Couch with no expression, and Burnside chuckled quietly, said, "General Hancock, I certainly appreciate your efforts at reconnaissance, but that possibility has been considered and rejected. The pontoons will be here at any time, and then we will be able to not only send the men across, but the wagons and supplies as well. It would be foolhardy to send the men without the wagons."

There was a silent pause, and Hancock said, "Excuse me, General, but am I correct in my observation that there is little force opposing us across the river?"

"Yes, General, you are correct. As I have planned, we have caught old Bobby Lee by surprise."

"Well, then, sir, if I may suggest . . . it is possible that General Lee is moving this way. Certainly he is aware of our intentions. If we were able to occupy the town, it would make our job much easier when the bridges do arrive, sir."

Sumner grunted, and Hancock looked at the old face, and there was still no expression. Burnside said, "General, that's a bit risky, I'm afraid. Those men could be cut off. This weather . . . the river is already rising a bit. It will be best, I assure you, if we wait until the entire army can proceed across. I am not worried about General Lee. He will not move against such a large and formidable force as we have here." He paused, laughed, pleased with himself. "I do not share General McClellan's tendency to inflate the enemy's strengths. We have General Lee just where we want him."

Hancock said nothing, looked again at Sumner, who was staring at Burnside with a look that said they had already had this conversation. Beside him, Couch began to shuffle, and Hancock heard a deep breath come from the small man.

Couch said, "General Burnside, if we cannot cross the river very soon, I am confident that General Lee will make every effort to impede our movement to do so. I feel fairly certain that he will also make great efforts to prevent us from moving toward Richmond. We do not know the disposition of General Jackson's forces, and we could find them on our flanks if we move on toward Richmond prematurely. It is important, sir, that we make some attempt to gain even a small advantage by occupying the town, and possibly the heights beyond. Allow me, sir, to send at least General Hancock's division across the river. Surely, they can carry enough supplies with them, and the artillery from this side can protect them from any aggression by Lee—"

Burnside raised his hand, cutting him off, still smiled. "Gentlemen, please, we have beaten this to death. We will cross the river when the bridges arrive, and not before. You must understand, I do not have the luxury of deviating from the larger plan. The President has approved my strategy, and I will stick to it. Once this army is across the river, I assure you, General Lee will have little chance to do any more than nip at our heels as we move down to Richmond. Now, if you please, gentlemen, my presence is required outside."

Burnside stood, did not wait for salutes, was quickly gone. Sumner leaned back in his chair, rubbed at tired eyes, said, "Someone should tell him he can deviate from any plan he chooses. I've already done all the talking I can. This is his operation, and he means to make it work."

Couch pulled at Hancock's arm, moved toward the door, said, "Let's hope, General, that we get those bridges soon."

Outside, the growing bite of the November wind rolled down the long valley of the river. Behind the hills around the headquarters, great fields of troops built fires from whatever wood they could find, passed the time huddled together in tents, and most now expected they would sit here through the winter, that another opportunity had been missed, and so the work began again on the construction of winter quarters. Far upstream, long miles away, teams of horses pulled lines of heavy wagons, bringing the pontoons down the soft roads toward the army.

The two men walked out from the grand old mansion, down the short steps, and Hancock stopped, stared out across the river, to the hills that lay beyond the peaceful town, the pleasant scene he had admired that morning. We should be over there, on those hills, he thought. Couch was watching him, turned to see where Hancock was focused, and started to say something but let it go and left Hancock alone. Turning away, he moved back to his headquarters.

To the west, far behind the hills, the clouds began to grow darker. Another winter storm was moving toward them, more snow, and Hancock pulled at his coat, saw Couch moving away, down the slope. He thought again of the hotcakes, and began the walk back to his camp.

NOW, BEHIND THOSE HILLS, BEHIND THE PEACEFUL TOWN, OUT of sight of the men in blue, there was movement, a steady stream of men in ragged clothes and worn coats, horses and wagons and flags, moving up the sides of the hills, spreading along the ridges covered by the clean snow. They began to dig, long trenches and shallow artillery pits, and now one man rode to the top of the hill, sitting on a tall gray horse, and looked out across the river, toward the high bank, to the place where the generals had just met, the grand old house that had belonged to George Washington, and so had belonged to the family of his wife. Lee had arrived.

PART THREE

27. LEE

November 1862

He straightened his stiff legs, stood high in the stirrups, the big gray horse not moving under him. The hill around him was mostly bare. A few trees broke the clean snow, and in front of him the slope was steep, dropping away toward the town. He could see clearly, see it all, the wide gap of open land the attackers would have to cross, broken only by a few fences, and one deep canal, which would disrupt any quick advance of troops. Fredericksburg itself was spread out against the edge of the river, and he knew he would not hold it, it had no value to the army, but even if he had wanted to, the Federal cannon were massed across the river, on top of the long rise known as Stafford Heights, perched high above the river, and so would control any movement in the town and make any defense there impossible. No, it was back here, these hills. He looked around, saw the troops working, dirt and snow flying, a few trees felled and moved into place. The cannon had arrived now, and the shallow pits prepared, and his own guns were moving into position. They too would control the ground, the open fields the Federal troops would have to cross to reach them. He looked back to that ground, the flat grassy plain, saw a few small houses, knew they would offer little protection.

Across the Rappahannock, on the far hills, he saw the camps, the masses of blue, and could see some movement, though not much detail. The heights were nearly a mile away, and the only really clear image was the house, the mansion, the ancestral home of George Washington. He glanced that way, did not want to look at it, avoided it, knew that again this war had taken something from him. He looked down, patted Traveller's neck, said a small prayer: *Please, don't destroy this one too.* He knew it was not just the war, that Mary's health was failing for reasons beyond what he was doing now, but he could not help the feeling that if this were over . . . if they were at home and he could be with her, she would be better. He realized he did not even know where she was these days, somewhere in Richmond, safe, for now. But across the river from him sat another piece of her, another symbol of loss, and he could not look at it, knew that there were other matters at hand.

He focused again, looked back to the open ground at the base of his hill, saw straight down to a deep road bed, a long stone wall that ran along the base of the hill. Surely, he thought, they will not do it here, not *here*. He looked to his right, to the south, along the ridge of the hills, saw his men working far into the distance, digging in. This is too . . . perfect. He felt a nagging sense of alarm: No, it will not happen here. Burnside is not a fool. But . . . there they sit, across the river, a great assembled force, and they are not moving.

The Federal Army had marched with uncharacteristic speed, had surprised him, slipping down the river this far. He hadn't expected the fight to be here, had waited for them to come at him from farther upriver, crossing at the shallow fords to the north. But Stuart followed their movement, the advance down to Falmouth, watched them all along the way, and they continued to move south, reaching the hills across from Fredericksburg a full day before Lee could move any troops in their direction. Lee then quickly brought Longstreet's army to these hills, and now Jackson had been recalled from Winchester, from the valley, and was on the march. Everything pointed to one conclusion: Burnside's plan was to cross here, he would fight here. And we have the good ground, Lee thought. Longstreet's army had grown to nearly forty thousand men, its greatest strength of the war. But Burnside had nearly three times that, and Lee knew that if they moved quickly, came across the river soon, even the good ground would not be enough. Jackson was on his way, with another thirty-five thousand, and if he arrived in time, it would be the largest force Lee had yet commanded, but Jackson had been nearly 150 miles away.

He turned Traveller around, began to ease him along the top of the ridge, moving slowly down to the south. The hills fell away slightly, down into thick trees, and he could see downriver now. The space between his troops and the river was even wider there, another large flat plain, completely open. This cannot be, he thought. No, this must be a feint, a ruse. They will start moving, downstream, a few miles, maybe Skinker's Neck, possibly down to Port Royal. But that would be the last chance. Below Port Royal the river widened to over a half mile, and was deep enough for larger boats. And, as the river snaked far down below the plains of Fredericksburg, there were thick woods lining both sides and any crossing would be difficult, easily defended with smaller numbers of troops. He stopped the horse, looked back across to the heights. And so there they sit, he thought. And it will be . . . *here*.

Above Stafford Heights he saw something, the sun reflecting off an object high in the air. He had heard of the balloons, the new observation platforms held aloft by the big bags of hydrogen. And now he saw more of them, downriver, and he knew they were watching him, knew by now he was digging in. He shook his head. They were waiting for . . . what? Does Burnside think I will attack *him*? he wondered. No, he is coming. And we will be patient.

Behind his hill more men were moving up, wagons were unloaded, more guns were pulling in. He saw horses climbing up toward him, saw Taylor, and another man, a red hat: artillery. It was Colonel Porter Alexander. They reached him, saluted, and Alexander said, "General Lee, a fine day, sir."

"Appears so, Colonel. What do you think of this position?"

Alexander smiled, and Lee saw the youth, a man not much older than Taylor, saw a bright and efficient student of war. Alexander said, "General, we have batteries all along the hill, we have a solid anchor on the north, covering the river, and by tomorrow the batteries will be positioned in those trees down to the south. We will be able to cover the entire open ground, all of it." He paused, looked down toward the town, then closer, the bottom of the steep hill, the stone wall.

"General Lee, do you think they will come at us here?"

Lee looked again to the river, said, "Colonel, the Federal Army is massed together across that river watching us prepare for them. If I were General Burnside . . . no, I would not attack here, I would move back upstream, come across above us. But General Burnside is not a man with the luxury of flexibility. He is being pushed from behind, by loud voices in Washington, by newspapers who demand quick action. We are here, and so he will attack us here."

"General, we have positioned guns to cover every inch of the open ground. If they try to cross that canal, it will slow them down, and we will hit them from every angle. Sir, a chicken could not live on that field."

Lee looked at the young man, saw the intensity, the enthusiasm for the deadly job. He suddenly felt excited, a quick rush, looked back down toward the town, thought, Yes, let them come.

To the south, along the ridge, a lone horseman worked his way along, through the lines of laboring soldiers. Taylor motioned, and Lee turned his horse, watched the man move closer, then saw Captain James Power Smith of Jackson's staff.

Smith saluted, knocking a thin crust of mud off his hat, said, "General Lee, sir. General Jackson sends his respects, and advises that his corps will begin deploying to the south of this position by tomorrow, per your instructions, sir."

Lee nodded, looked back across the river, raised his eyes and looked into the dull gray sky. He gave a prayer then: *Thank You for this place, for this ground.* He lowered his gaze, stared at the blue mass across the river, covering the distant hillside, the patchwork of white tents and black guns, thought, You had your chance, General. Now we are ready.

28. JACKSON

December 1862

IT HAD BEEN A GOOD DAY, THE MEN HAD KEPT THE COLUMNS TIGHT, moving with good speed. There was no dust, the roads crusted each morning with a thin frost, a light cover of snow. He had sat on his horse, watching them pass, had seen the bare feet, the bloody impressions, and he felt a deep pain, a sadness. He did not talk about it, did not show what he was thinking, and his staff had learned to keep their distance; that when he moved away from the column, sat alone like this, watching the men, there would be no orders, no messages; that he would stay in one spot for a long while, just watching. The troops would often cheer him, recognized him now, knew the worn and ragged coat he wore, the same major's jacket he had worn at VMI, the small crumpled cadet hat he pulled tightly down on his head, shading his eyes.

Today he sat off to the side of the road in the shadows of a tall pine tree, and they did not know he had cried, talking quietly to God. He sat upright in the saddle, stiff, feeling the sharp burning in his side, knowing it was sent there by God, a lesson in the pain of his men. He had pleaded, *Please, make it stop, yes I understand, I see them. They are all good men, and I have so little to give them.* But the pain had not stopped, had been with him all day, and now, after the march, the cold night covered them all. Finally, as he sat alone in his tent, the pain had gone away.

As they rested in the comfort of the Shenandoah, his army had grown. If there was one success from the Maryland invasion, it had been to rid northern Virginia of Federal troops, and the farms had prospered, the harvest had been a good one, and so the army had been fed, had grown much healthier, and new recruits and veterans with healing wounds had added to the numbers.

He did not want to go to Fredericksburg. From his position in the valley he was still a threat to Washington, and he had tried to convince Lee that this was the greater value. But Lee had finally been firm, had ordered him to march, and so he moved his men with the same energy they had come to expect. He did not understand the importance of Fredericksburg. There was no way to pursue a beaten enemy back across the Rappahannock. He had favored a line farther south, along the South Anna River, and Lee had agreed, but now Burnside had taken that option away. The fight was to be at Fredericksburg, and so he did not question, began to see it now in his mind, his guns and his troops flowing forward to strike the enemy again with all the fire and deadly energy God would provide.

Outside the tent, his staff gathered around a sack of mail, dropped by a weary courier. There was a light snowfall, and the air was quiet and cold. They would not disturb him when he was in his tent, had learned that he would often pray for long periods, but now there were nods, and it was his chief of staff, Sandie Pendleton, who moved toward the tent.

He stopped, stood at attention by the canvas wall, said, "Sir? Forgive me, General. . . ."

Jackson sat inside on a small wooden stool, had been staring at the back of the tent, staring at the glow from a small oil lamp. He turned toward the voice from outside, did not speak, and Pendleton waited. After a moment Jackson focused and his mind returned to the tent, absorbed the young man's words. He said, "You may enter, Captain."

Pendleton lifted the flaps, leaned into the warmth of the dull light, said, "There is a letter for you, General. It's a bit late, but the courier was slow today. I thought you would want to see it, sir."

Jackson reached out, took the letter from Pendleton's outstretched hand and glanced at the envelope. It was a woman's writing, but not Anna's.

Pendleton said, "Good night, sir," and was gone, the flaps dropping back down to seal out the cold.

He stared now at the letter, felt a cold lump in his stomach. Anna had been pregnant again, and he had not seen her since he heard the news. They had been together briefly the previous spring, in Winchester, prior to the great battles, his great triumphs over the Federal armies in the valley. He had not mentioned the pregnancy to anyone, not even his staff, had feared if word got out, God would not be pleased, would punish him somehow. His fear for Anna was so great that he would not think of her at all, would coach himself to think instead of God. If he revealed too much, if God knew that he was afraid for her, if he did not trust completely in God's care, He would take her from him, as He had taken Ellie, as He had taken his daughter.

Jackson did not recognize the writing on the envelope, saw that it was from North Carolina, where Anna had gone to spend the long months with her family. He took a deep breath, tore open the envelope. His hand shook slightly as he held the paper out, catching the lamplight.

> My Own Dear Father,
>
> As my mother's letter has been cut short by my arrival, I think it but justice that I should continue it. I know that you are rejoiced to hear of my coming, and I hope that God has sent me to radiate your pathway through life. I am a very tiny little thing. I weigh only eight and a half pounds, and Aunt Harriet says I am the express image of my darling papa . . .

Tears filled his eyes, and he wiped with his sleeve, then began to search down the page, came to the line he had sought:

> My mother is very comfortable this morning . . .

He put the letter down, smiled, wiped more tears away, then looked up, through the walls of his tent, said in a low voice, *"You did not take her from me. Thank You, thank You."*

He sat staring for a minute, then read the letter again, saw the final words, signed: "Your dear little wee Daughter." He smiled again, stared into the walls of the tent, closed his eyes, staring far away into the dark, and saw the face of his mother, her face with a smile like he had not seen before, a glow from her that filled him with a sudden energy, a bright light deep inside him. He knew it was a gift, that his new and precious daughter would fill that place, the lonely dark hole that his mother had left, and he thought, Yes, she will be named for you, she will be called Julia. Then the image began to fade, but deep inside he felt her smiling still.

HIS MOOD WAS DIFFERENT. HE DID NOT RIDE OUT TO WATCH the troops. He rode at the head of the long column, stared out to the front. The staff noticed, but no one asked about the letter. They had learned early what he expected of you and what you did not do. His division commanders had served with him long enough to witness his irritability and intolerance for inefficiency. Now, he too was involved in a conflict with A. P. Hill; the fiery temper and fragile ego that had plagued Longstreet were now tormenting him as well.

Hill had shown a tendency to march his division with too much haste, stringing out his men into a sloppy line, leaving behind many stragglers. On the march into Maryland, Jackson had ordered one of Hill's brigadiers to halt, to allow the unit to close up and regroup. Hill had furiously protested, and Jackson responded by having him arrested, had ordered him to march at the rear of his division. In the weeks that followed, Hill had been granted a brief reprieve, the opportunity to lead his division at Antietam, but even his timely heroics there had not changed Jackson's mind about his need for discipline, and a long series of letters and accusations from both men had poured across Lee's desk.

Lee tried to soothe feelings on both sides, with little success. Jackson was unbending, and Hill demanded a full court of inquiry, a disruption even in the best of circumstances, and Lee knew the army could not afford to be tied up with such administrative energy. And, despite Jackson's anger, and Hill's talent for annoying his superiors, Lee knew that Hill was an essential division commander. Faced with the inevitable assault by Burnside's superior numbers, Lee needed all the capable commanders he had at hand. Thus, the conflict had to simmer until Lee chose to pursue it further. He had no plans to do so.

A month earlier Lee made the corps system in his army official. With the approval of President Davis, Longstreet and Jackson were promoted to the rank of Lieutenant General. Longstreet was still the senior, which Davis had heartily approved, since he had never been comfortable with Jackson's independent spirit. Lee understood that Davis had to be convinced that Jackson was not a threat to Davis's sensitive illusion that he held tight control over the army. Lee had insisted that Jackson was as important to the army as Longstreet, and he had finally defused Davis's uneasiness.

Jackson received the news of the promotion without comment, saw no reason to change his routine. His staff had wanted to offer some celebration, but he would not have it.

He still carried the letter in his pocket, had ridden all day without telling anyone, did not want the congratulations, did not want God to see too much happiness. Now, as this day ended, they were approaching the hills of Fredericksburg. He ordered them into camp, resting the army within a short day's march from Longstreet's defensive lines.

After the evening supper, he returned to his tent, read the letter again, had waited all day for the quiet moment. He thought, I must answer, there will be time tonight. Tomorrow they would begin the deployment of the troops, spreading the divisions to the south of Longstreet's strong solid line.

He rose from his small hard seat, stepped out into the camp, saw the campfire, and his staff noticed him, began to gather. He walked stiffly to the fire, raised his hand high over his head, stretching his back, feeling for the pain in his side. He looked at the faces, saw Pendleton, tilted his head, asking a silent question, and Pendleton nodded, bowed slightly, was quickly gone. The others watched, did not understand. Jackson held his hands up to the fire, absorbing the heat.

Captain Smith moved closer, said, "General, I have seen the deployment of General Longstreet's troops. We are in a very strong position, sir."

Jackson looked at him, said nothing, then looked past, saw Pendleton hurrying back toward the fire, carrying a small wooden box. Jackson waited, and Pendleton lifted the lid, revealing small yellow balls nesting in a soft bed of straw: lemons. Jackson reached for one, held it up in the firelight, pulled out his pocketknife and sliced it in half. Smith glanced at Pendleton, who replaced the lid on the box, slid away toward Jackson's tent, placed the box inside the flaps, then returned to the fire. Smith watched Jackson stuff the half lemon into his mouth, looked again at Pendleton.

Pendleton said under his breath, "A gift . . . from Florida. They come all the time . . . from the same place. . . ."

Smith whispered, "Who . . . ?"

"Don't know. I don't ask."

Jackson paid no attention, stared deep into the fire, bathing his throat with the tart juice.

Pendleton turned toward a noise, and now there were voices, and they saw the rider, the huge German, Von Borcke, from Stuart's camp. He rode clumsily, his wide girth spilling over both sides of his straining horse, seemed ready to tumble to the ground with every step of his much pitied animal.

"Greetings, vat ho!"

Hands were extended, and Von Borcke looked past the men toward Jackson, who still stared into the fire.

"General, goot evening. I come . . . bringing you a present!"

Jackson's head jerked up, suddenly aware, and he stared at the huge man with wonder. Heros Von Borcke was unlike any man in the army. He was still an officer in the Prussian Dragoons, had slipped through the Federal blockade at Charleston, had crossed the Atlantic with a strange obsession to fight with the rebel army, finally arriving in Richmond with much fanfare and a public plea to be allowed to fight.

It was Stuart who had caught Von Borcke's attention. He had read of colorful and daring and often exaggerated exploits in the Richmond papers, and Stuart recognized a fine opportunity, as well. Von Borcke's adventures would be fine entertainment for the European newspapers, and so, despite Von Borcke's limited use of English, Stuart insisted that the Prussian serve with him as a staff officer. Impeccably dressed, with all the trappings of military ceremony, he had become Stuart's favorite messenger, and his arrival always resulted in a gathering crowd. Stuart had been so impressed by his enthusiasm for service that he recommended Von Borcke receive an official commission in the army, and now it was Major Von Borcke.

Jackson began to smile, and his staff caught the mood. Von Borcke laughed along with the others, who were laughing at him, and he waved to the growing number of men who had moved closer to this odd spectacle.

"General Chackson . . . I am *grreatly* pleased to bring you this present from General Shtuart. The general has gone to *grrreat* lengths to secure for you . . . this!"

Von Borcke held out a package wrapped in brown paper, and Jackson stared at it, did not move. Pendleton reached out, took the package, said, "Would you like me to open it, sir?"

Jackson looked up at Von Borcke, then at Pendleton, nodded silently, and Pendleton tore at the paper and held up the neatly folded gray of a new uniform.

"Wowee, General, this is some fine material. Look here, there's gold braid. . . ."

Jackson stared at the gift, began to reach out a hand, to touch the new cloth, then stopped, withdrew. "Major, you may tell General Stuart that I deeply appreciate his present. Please assure him that I will regard it with the greatest of care, and will see that no harm comes to it. Captain Pendleton, will you kindly place the uniform in my tent, and keep it neatly folded."

Von Borcke's expression changed, the smile faded. "No, General, no, you do not understand. General Shtuart vas most insistent that you try it on. He will certainly ask how vas the fit. Please, General. Try it on."

Jackson looked at Pendleton, who smiled broadly, holding the uniform out to him. Jackson reached out slowly, felt the material, then took it, cradling it with both hands, and without speaking turned and walked to his tent.

In the dark, men began to move closer, and Pendleton turned, motioned for quiet. Officers began to appear and there were questions. They saw Von Borcke, and so the men were kept at a distance, but were allowed to stay.

A few minutes passed, and the impatient Von Borcke walked thunderously over to Jackson's tent, did not have the staff's wariness of Jackson's moods, called out loudly, "General, can I be of assistance?"

There was no sound from the tent. Then the flaps were pushed back and Jackson stepped out into the firelight, stood up straight, placed a large black hat on his head.

"*Mein Gott*, you are a splendid sight!" Von Borcke made a deep bow, and around the fire his staff began to applaud, weakly at first, uncertain. Then, as Jackson noticed the gathered troops, he raised the hat, held it high above his head, and the men exploded into cheers. He stood still for a long moment, could not hide a smile, then placed the hat back on his head.

He said to Von Borcke, "You may tell General Stuart that I thank him deeply for this gift. The hat . . . my wife sent it to me, and I never thought . . . it was quite right. . . ."

"General, it is perfect . . . perfect! Please, General, allow me to leave. I will report to General Shtuart that his gift is a success."

"Yes, certainly, you are dismissed, Major."

Von Borcke hurried heavily to his horse, climbed up with a great grunt, began to move away through the crowd of men. Some of the troops followed after him, calling out, and he waved wildly, nearly falling from the horse.

"*Vat ho!*" And the men yelled it back to him, none having any idea what he meant.

Pendleton moved closer to Jackson, admired the gold buttons, the gold stars on the collar, the elaborate braiding on the sleeves.

"General Stuart must have gone to a great deal of trouble, sir. This is fine work, probably came from Richmond."

Jackson had stopped smiling, stared at the young man, said, "We will move at dawn, Captain. General Lee will be expecting us."

Pendleton knew the festivities were over. He took a step back, raised a salute, said, "Yes, sir. Good night, sir."

Jackson removed the hat, leaned over into the tent, and the flaps closed behind him. He tossed the hat down on his blanket, thought of Anna, the silly gift that he thought he would never wear. I am a lieutenant general, he thought. She is proud. I must tell her, No, do not be proud of me—thank God for what He has given us. He ran his hands down the smooth material of the uniform, so different from the old ragged jacket that lay now on the ground by his feet. He began to undo the buttons, thought of sleep, the day ahead, then he saw the laughing face of Stuart, thought, I suppose I cannot insult the kindness of General Stuart. But it is clear he has too much time on his hands. We will have to see what we can do about that.

He sat on his blanket, leaned over to the small lamp, snuffed out the light. He lay down, pulled the blanket over the fine gray cloth, and now it was dark and quiet and the cold began to seep into the tent. He stared up, began to think of Fredericksburg and the wide river, of bayonets and flashing cannons and driving the enemy back, over the edge, into the icy water.

29. HANCOCK

December 1862

THE PONTOONS HAD FINALLY COME INTO FALMOUTH THE LAST few days of November, came piecemeal, a convoy that had stretched itself thin on the softening mush of the roads. Now they lay in long rows on the bank of the river, patrolled by nervous engineers, the men who would push them out into the icy water and lash them together side by side, until they reached the far shore. Once in place, planks would be laid on top, and the huge army would begin to cross on a narrow strip of bouncing wood. Hancock had walked among them, had heard the comments. They had waited for nearly two weeks for the pontoons to arrive, and now that they were there, the order had not come. There was only silence from Burnside's headquarters.

Hancock had stayed away from headquarters, from the frequent meetings, meetings that Burnside also avoided, choosing instead to hear a summary of the comments from his staff, feeling out the mood of his commanders. When Burnside did attend, it was to persuade his subordinates that loyalty was their primary concern, not the soundness of his plan. Now, there had been another meeting, and Hancock had been summoned specifically, had gone with no expectations, and the crowded room had been loud and hostile, the commanders speaking their minds more openly now, criticizing their commander's strategy. The meeting was chaired by Sumner, and the old man had finally given up, had dismissed them with a weary wave of his hand. As the men flowed out of the grand old house, no one spoke, the mood of the generals reflecting the mood of the army. Hancock had paused, waiting for Couch, but Couch passed by him with red-faced anger, did not want to talk, and the others had gone quickly as well.

Now Hancock stood alone in the winter ruins of the wide garden, stared far across the river toward the heavy lines of Bobby Lee, admired the scene again, the snow on the wide-open fields, the pleasant waterfront town, and felt like this was all unreal somehow, that there was no war, that nothing would happen to disturb this peaceful countryside.

He put one foot up on a low brick wall, thought, No, this is very real, and we do not have a leader. Behind him he heard a voice, turned, saw Sumner coming toward him. The old man was pulling on a heavy coat, his breath in short bursts of white, and he walked closer to Hancock, who pulled his foot from the wall, turned, stood at attention.

"Easy, General. Saw you out here, wondered what you were doing. You didn't say much this morning, but there's a lot in your face. A lot of them . . . they're getting pretty casual with what they're saying about General Burnside. Not good . . . not good for an army to let down like that. The disrespect . . . He is *still* the commander."

Sumner stared out across the river, and Hancock looked at the old face, the heavy eyes.

"General, we can go inside if you like. No need to stand out here in the cold . . ."

Sumner looked at him, shook his head. "Makes no difference, General. Sometimes, I feel the cold worse inside than I do out here. Old bones . . . this old coat . . ." He raised an arm, and Hancock saw the dull brass buttons on the sleeve, an old army design he had not seen before. "Had this old coat since . . . hell, I don't know, since the beginning. No West Point back then, no place for a soldier to get any training except out here, the field. It was better . . . smaller . . . simpler. A general gave commands and the army carried them out, and the job was done. You in Mexico, General?"

Hancock nodded. "Sixth Infantry."

"Oh, so you were with Scott. Winfield Scott . . . now, there was a commander." Sumner paused, looked again at Hancock. "Your name . . . you were named after him."

Hancock smiled. "Yes, sir. My father had a great admiration for him. I even met him once. He came to West Point. He asked for me, for *me* in particular, saw my name on the list of cadets. He told me we had a responsibility to each other . . . said he'd promise not to disgrace my name if I didn't disgrace his. He scared me to death."

Sumner laughed, a rough cough, and Hancock realized he'd never seen him smile before. But the smile did not last, and Sumner shook his head, said, "It is a different army. General Scott didn't have to hold meetings to find out what he should do, to tell him what people thought . . . he didn't give a *damn* what people thought. He was the *commander*, and everyone understood that, even the President. Hell . . . several Presidents. But he made a great mistake—he got too old, and now they replace him with this damned Halleck, a politician. Runs the army like a puppetmaster, pulling strings. If he thinks you're in his corner, he supports you. If he doesn't, you don't get your damned pontoons when you're supposed to. Scott would never have done that . . . that foolishness." He turned sharply to Hancock, leaned closer. "This bother you, General? You think maybe I'm talking out of turn?"

Hancock shook his head. "You're saying what a lot of the men have been saying, General. Even the foot soldiers seem to feel the same way, seem to understand what a mess we're in."

"You think we're in a mess . . . here?"

Hancock paused, told himself to be careful. He knew he had better choose his words. "We might have a difficult time taking those hills, General."

"General Hancock, last week I showed General Burnside a map, given to me by one of the engineers. It showed a deep canal, cutting across that open field behind the town, the field we will have to cross. I pointed out the location of the canal, that it will present a difficult obstacle in the face of artillery fire. General Burnside looked at the map, then looked at me, and said there is no canal in that location, that the map was wrong. I thought, well, he could be right, I suppose he has access to better information than I do. So I came out here, stood on this spot with field glasses, and looked across the tops of those church steeples, and pretty plain I could see it, right where the engineer said it was. Now, General, what am I supposed to do? I have spent over forty years in this army accepting the word of my commander as gospel, carrying out my duty." He paused, wiped at his nose with a handkerchief. "The commanding general says we are to cross this river and take those heights. So, that is what we will do."

Hancock nodded, said, "It's possible. Down to the left, we could push through, maybe turn Jackson's lines, push him back, trap Longstreet on top of the hill, surround him. It's possible."

Sumner cocked an eyebrow, chuckled again, said, "You trying to be a politician too? Turn Jackson's lines? No, General, we will meet him head-on and it will be a bloody mess. And we will march up to that hill over there, and we will eat their artillery fire all the way across that field. But the important thing is, regardless of the outcome, we will be able to look at ourselves in the mirror and say we are good soldiers, we did what we were told. And if we are not successful, we can say, well, it was a good plan, but there were . . . circumstances, and Mr. Lincoln and General Halleck and Secretary Stanton will pace in their offices and fret over what we should do next. And *you*, General, can one day go back to your hometown and tell the families of your men that they died doing their duty. And they might even believe you."

Hancock felt the cold numbing his hands and feet, began to move slightly, nervously. "Is there no way to change his mind? We should have crossed upriver, at the shallow fords."

"Oh, certainly that has been suggested, General. Try to imagine President Lincoln's response if General Burnside said to him, 'Sir, if you don't mind, we're turning the army around, going back up where we just came from and starting over.' " He chuckled, rubbed his chin with the handkerchief. "I'd like to be there for that . . . ought to be a good one."

Hancock nodded, tried to smile. Sumner turned, began to move back toward the wide doors of the house. He paused, kicked softly at the snow, turned up something with his foot, and Hancock saw color, bright yellow, red, a child's toy. Sumner bent over, picked it up, shook off the snow and held it for a long moment. He said nothing, and Hancock waited, then moved closer to the old man, saw his face, saw red anger, hard red eyes, and Sumner tossed the toy out of the garden, over the low brick wall.

"General, we will be moving across the river very soon. There has been too much talk . . . too much loose talk. I want it shut off, stopped. Any further criticism of General Burnside's plan of attack will be considered insubordination and will be dealt with severely. Am I clear?"

Hancock stiffened, felt the old man's anger, said crisply, "Yes, sir. Very clear, sir."

"Good. Now, return to your division, General. The engineers will be receiving their orders very soon. Be ready." He climbed up the short steps, reached for the door, did not look back, and Hancock watched him disappear inside. He stood still for a minute, absorbing what Sumner had said, thought, Of course, he has no choice, it is all he has ever been. The rest of us . . . we have the luxury of youth, of better education, of better choices after all this is over. He's just an old soldier, and his time is up. And he will go out doing his duty.

He turned toward the river again, to the far hills, felt a shiver flow across his body, pulled his coat tighter. He walked over to the low wall again, looked down the hill, saw the deep scars in the snow where the toy had rolled, saw broken pieces, the remnants, and he thought of Pennsylvania, and going home to the families of his men.

30. BARKSDALE

December 11, 1862

It had been a steady stream, a solid sad line moving slowly, by foot, by cart, out and away from the town. They were old and young, women and children and their grandparents, the sick and infirm. Some were veterans of earlier fights, men who carried their wounds. Some were fit to be soldiers but had escaped, by politics or by money, but now they were all part of the same tragedy, moving together, and they all understood, they were giving up their homes, leaving behind them all that they could not carry, because the great destruction of the great war had finally come to crush their town, and the two armies, who squatted on the hills around them, could not offer them safety, but only ensure them that if they stayed, they would suffer the most.

He had kept his men by the side of the road, allowing the long line to pass, making room for squeaking carts and richly upholstered carriages, and the people looked at him as they went by, some saluting the uniform, but few said anything, there was no cheering, no mindless patriotism.

The civilians had grown used to seeing the war through the newspapers, sipping tea on sunlit porches, boasting of the great Lee and the mighty Jackson, cursing the demon Lincoln. They had read of the horrors of other cities, Charleston, Norfolk, pitied the people in the smaller towns, Sharpsburg, Manassas, Harper's Ferry. Some of them worked on the river, loaded goods from boats and barges to trains and wagons, watched the food and supplies move away, sustaining their soldiers off in some far distant field, some other valley. Some had expected this, were prepared, neatly packed boxes, wagons piled high, and others did not believe it still, wanted to stay, fight the Yankees just by being there, showing their spirit. But the order had come from the hills beyond, from Lee himself, and so they would not disobey. Across the river they could see the big guns and the mass of blue, and they understood at last that all they could do was leave, get out of the way.

He moved his men into Fredericksburg before dark, quietly, with no fanfare, and they did not have to work, no trenches or earthworks, but had filled the basements and the lower levels of the houses and stores perched along the riverbank. Every window, every small gap in old brickwork, any place a man could fire a rifle, was filled with the men of his brigade. Sixteen hundred rifles pointed at the river, and during the long dark night, they made coffee and played cards, and talked of the Yankees across the way.

Barksdale stood at the edge of the water, at a small boat launch, the hard street flowing right down into the water. It was still early, there was no light, and he could feel the thick, cold air, the heavy fog that filled the valley. He strained his eyes, stared across the quiet water, listened hard for any sound. There were small voices, conversation, then the sound of tin, coffee cups and plates, and soon the voices became louder, more intense. The conversation had become official, commands and replies, and now there were new sounds, tools and heavy wood, and still he could see nothing.

The fog began to glow, a light gray, the dim light of dawn finding its way down to the streets and the water, and now he watched his boots, had perched his toes right on the edge of the smooth glaze of ice, gauging the motion of the slowly moving river. He looked out again, and still there was only the fog, and after a minute he looked down again, and saw: his boots were wet—the water had come out from under the ice, a small disturbance on the still water, pushed toward him by something . . . something wide and heavy moving into the river from the other side.

He turned quickly, ran up the short hill to the quiet streets, and now he saw his staff, the men waiting for the order, and he sent them fanning out through the houses and stores, passing the word to the men: the Yankees were coming across.

He walked back to the edge of the river, stared hard into the fog, heard now the splashing of oars, heavy boots on hard wood, the orders of the engineers. He tried to measure the distance, had memorized the far bank, the positions of the idle pontoons, now began to draw a bead. There was no breeze, and so he knew the sounds were true and straight. He raised his pistol, pointed blindly at the sound of a man's voice, held the pistol steady for a long second and fired a single shot.

On both sides of him, his men responded to his signal, and a volley of rifles opened with bright flashes, sending a shower of lead toward the unseen voices.

There were splashes, the sound of cracking ice. Men screamed and orders were yelled, and suddenly the voices moved away, back in the distance: they had gone back to the far shore. He waited, listened; there was no sound from the river, no movement on the water. He took off his hat, waved it high above his head and gave out a whoop, a single piece of rebel yell, and from the basements and windows came the muffled reply, the cheering of his men.

Barksdale's brigade of Mississippians had been ordered into the town as the first line of defense, and the division commander, Lafayette McLaws, had told him there would be no support. Barksdale's orders had been simple and brief: delay the building of the pontoon bridges, then retire back to the safety of the high hill, the hill above the stone wall known as Marye's Heights.

William Barksdale had come to the Confederacy with the background as a newspaperman and a hard-line secessionist. He was gray-haired and clean-shaven, a neat and educated man, and had shown an unusual ability to lead troops, unusual because Lee had learned through bitter experience that the more political a commander, the less likely he was to be a good soldier.

The fog showed no signs of lifting, and now he heard the noises again, more heavy boots on hard wood, sharp voices and cracking ice, and he waited, let them begin work again. He tried to picture the scene in his mind, the engineers scrambling over the fat pontoon boats, pulling them together into a line, hauling the long planks, laying them across. He knew they would be looking his way, wondering where the shots had come from and when the next volley would come. He smiled, raised the pistol again, and fired into the fog. And from all along the riverfront his men responded with their rifles, and the cries were louder this time, more men fell into the ice, collapsed into the boats. He did not yell, heard his men take up the refrain on their own, and he knew this would work for a while, but he was only one brigade, and surely someone over there would do something to push him out of the town and away from the river.

Barksdale stared hard at the fog, could see out into the river now, maybe forty or fifty yards. It was fully daylight, and the fog was beginning to lift. Now the noises returned, and he could hear men farther down the river, another bridge, knew he had men stretching far enough to cover the entire waterfront, that any landing along the town would be a hot one. He raised the pistol again, picked out a single sound and took aim, and suddenly there was a loud rush of sound, a low scream, and behind him a shell exploded, digging a hole into the hard street. Then another one fell into the building on his left, splinters and bricks scattered across the street, and he heard voices, his staff behind him, and he turned and ran up the short street. Men were waving at him, and he went that way, and another shell hit the street, then another went through the porch where his men had stood, and he was hit with a spray of broken glass and shattered timbers. He saw more men and moved that way, ran with his head down and reached a stairway, dropping down below the level of the street. He jumped toward the bottom, fell hard and then felt himself pulled by the arms into the dark coolness of a basement.

The shelling kept up for several minutes, and when his eyes grew accustomed to the dark space, he counted seven men, all huddled against the heavy walls. Above them the terrible screams of the shells were muted, the sharp explosions dulled by the thick mud of the walls.

He could see faces now, smiles, nods, the heavy sounds from above blotting out their voices. He ran his hands over his legs and arms, no wounds, felt a painful ankle from the long jump down. He thought, It is just like this, all along the river, men in small groups, sitting in low crouches, waiting. But the cannon will have to stop, or soon they will hit their own men, the men on the lengthening bridges, and so we will just sit and wait.

The shelling began to slow, then abruptly stopped. He stood up, reached for the low ceiling with his hand, could not quite stand upright. He went to the small window, looked to the river, and saw the first glimpse of the men on the water, one ghostly figure standing in a shallow boat. Suddenly, there were shots, a scattered volley from his men, who did not wait for the signal. They could begin to see on their own now, and he saw the man fall, a splash of water and thin ice. Now he could see more, straight out in front of him, could see the buttons of their coats, officers yelling and pointing and their men moving in quick, short motions, scampering over the boats like big blue mice, trying to find cover in the wide-open middle of the river. His men kept firing, and now the figures disappeared back into the thinning fog, pulling away again, and his men stopped firing and he waited, knew what was coming, listened for the first high sounds. Then they came, shrieking overhead, shattering the walls of a house on the street behind them. He sat back down on the cold floor, saw the faces watching him in the small dark space, and he nodded, smiled, and they waited again.

31. HANCOCK

December 11, 1862

THEY WERE TIGHT TOGETHER, A SEA OF MEN STANDING TOgether by regiment, muskets pointing high, and they could not move.

They had begun to form along the edge of the river at midmorning, moving through the thinning fog. The engineers had started earlier, and the bridges now reached well out into the river. All morning the musket fire from the far side had whistled past them, blindly piercing the clustered masses of men who waited on the bank. The officers kept them together, and they all knew there was nowhere to hide, no cover, that if the small lead ball was meant for you it would find you, and they flinched and ducked and held their position.

Hancock had watched it all, had been out early with the engineers. The order to begin laying the pontoons came the night before, passed through his hands, and it seemed something positive was happening at last, and he saw they would finally have their chance, and thought it might work. Then, as he stared into the fog, watching the workmen falling into the ice, the angry shelling of the town that drove no one from their holes, his excitement faded and he began to feel angry, a boiling fire of fury.

He looked back, over the heads of his own men, up the hill to the mansion, said aloud, "You won't move them out with guns!" and his men heard and cheered him, an outburst that betrayed their mood.

He saw Sumner now, riding down the hill, below the firing of the guns, thought, Fine, come see for yourself. The general's staff followed close behind, made an elegant procession. Hancock pulled his horse through the crowd of men, slowly, carefully, moved to meet him. Couch came down the hill as well, from another direction, and now Hancock saw Oliver Howard, another of Couch's division commanders, making his way to the spot where they would meet.

Now there was a pause in the shelling, and behind him the engineers tried again, more visible now to the riflemen on the other side. Hancock did not watch, stared ahead to the gathering commanders.

Sumner was in a new uniform, sat tall in his saddle, his back straight, the thin face set square and firm, and Hancock suddenly knew that this would be all for him, the last fight. He knows that this will not work, Hancock thought, but he has no choice. He suddenly felt pity, watched the old man's face with a great sadness.

Sumner looked at him, showed nothing, no emotion, said, "General, are your men ready to move across?"

"Quite ready, General."

Sumner turned to Howard, who was trying to steady his horse, said, "And you, General? I want you to be the first. Move your division through the town, spread them out on the streets, protected from those far heights. Keep them inside the line of buildings."

Howard said, "Yes, sir, we await the order to move, sir."

Hancock looked at Couch, who was staring down toward the river. "They're coming back again."

They all turned, and Hancock saw the men running along the wobbling pontoons, toward the safety of the near shore. Now, from above, the shelling began again. The ground rumbled, and across the river they could see the flashes of light, black smoke rising through thinning fog.

Hancock looked at Sumner, wanted to say . . . something, thought again of suggesting the crossing upriver, coming into the town from above, clearing out the sharpshooters from behind. Sumner stared at the river, and Hancock said nothing, let it go.

A rider yelled out, the man pushing his horse through the crowded troops. There were shouts, indignation, and the man kept moving, forced his way closer.

"General Sumner, Colonel Coppersmith of General Franklin's staff. General Franklin has asked me to report, sir, that we have completed the laying of the pontoon bridges downriver. If you are ready to cross, sir, we will move on your signal."

Sumner looked at the man, did not change his expression. "We are not ready to cross, Colonel. Tell General Franklin that he can begin his own crossing at his convenience. We will move across when we can. We have a bit of a problem up here."

"Well, sir, General Franklin has not been successful in convincing

General Burnside that he should not wait. General Burnside has expressed to General Franklin that the army move together. I was there, sir, when General Burnside said that we should . . . 'sweep across as one mighty wave' . . . sir."

A smile escaped from the man's face, and Sumner said nothing.

The man cleared his throat, said, "General, if I may return to General Franklin, I will advise him of your situation."

Sumner nodded, and the man saluted, turned his horse and began to push again through the lines of men.

Hancock looked at Couch, questioning, and Couch shook his head, looked at Sumner. Sumner turned again toward the river, to the clearing scene on the far side. The houses could be seen now, and the impact of the shelling.

Sumner said, "They are still there." He turned to Couch, said, "Pick some men who know how to row a boat. Send them across directly, with good speed. It might help to clear out those damned riflemen."

Couch said, "Immediately, sir," and Hancock saw his expression, a sudden flood of energy. Hancock turned his horse, his men clearing a path, and Couch moved quickly down toward the river.

The regimental commanders were assembled, and Hancock gave the instructions. Within minutes men were filling the pontoons and the wide boats were moving out into the river. Hancock watched them from the bank, saw the small flashes coming from the far side, from small holes under piles of debris, the sharpshooters still in place. More boats moved out from the shore, farther up, the oars breaking through the thin ice, and the rifle fire came across the river again, aimed this time at the boats. But the pontoons were heavy and the men kept low, and soon boats had reached the other side, men pouring up the banks into the town. Now the firing did not come across the river. Rebel soldiers began to appear, emerging out of their holes, moving back through the streets. There were more orders, loud voices beside him, and the engineers started forward again, the workers moving with new courage, without their officers prodding them.

Hancock rode back up the hill, glassed farther down the river, could see Franklin's bridges stretching across the still water, saw no troops, no lines of blue. There was no crossing. He thought, Another day, we have lost another day.

It was after dark before Sumner's men could begin moving into town. Howard's division crossed as ordered, and set up camps in the streets. But the army had run out of time, and Hancock's men would have to wait until the next morning, and so he lay on his blanket, staring past the walls of his tent, thinking about the sharpshooters across the river, the small brigade that had kept eighty thousand men from moving all day. Outside, the fog began to fill the valley again, and across the way more gray troops arrived to fill the high ground.

32. JACKSON

December 11, 1862

He did not like digging trenches, but put his men to work all down the line. They did not have Longstreet's great advantage of the steep hill, the stone wall. They were in the trees, mostly thick woods, and so they cut and dug and piled tree limbs and dirt, and soon they would be ready. The flat plain in front of him was nearly two miles across, and there was no cover, and so when Sumner's engineers were being killed by Barksdale, Jackson could only watch as Franklin's engineers did their work, laying their pontoons across the icy water. He had wanted to advance, place a line of rifles along the bank, but the Federal guns on Stafford Heights made that impossible. He watched through his field glasses as the long bridges gradually found their way to his side of the river.

They had not known what Burnside was going to do here, below the town. Lee thought he might cross lower, downstream, at Skinker's Neck, and so he sent General Early there, commanding the division of the wounded Dick Ewell. Daniel Hill had been sent farther down, protecting the crossing at Port Royal, and Jackson's own division, commanded now by William Taliaferro, set up close by at Guiney's Station. Only A. P. Hill's division was below Longstreet's lines, around the place where Jackson sat, across from the new bridges.

As the fog lifted and the bridges grew, Burnside finally showed his hand. Now the instructions came from Lee: Jackson would bring the corps together. He had sent his staff out quickly, the call for his units to come together here, below Longstreet, forming a heavy line down through the trees. Below Fredericksburg the river curved away slightly, and the plain between the woods and the river was wider than in front of Longstreet. But it was open and flat and there would be nowhere to hide.

On his left, toward the base of Marye's Heights, he linked up with Longstreet's right, the division of John Bell Hood. It was slow going in the thick trees, but if the Federal crossing was not rapid, if they did not mass an attack today, there would be time.

The new uniform stayed behind, in his tent. Jackson had thought about it, felt the fine material again, rubbed his fingers gently over the new gold braid, but it was not time. He did not want to appear too . . . taken with it, with the grand appearance. He would wear it for the men, had seen how it inspired them, but not today; today they were working, their duty was clear, and so there was no need.

He sat stiffly on the small horse, stared through the glasses, focused past overhanging branches, bare and brittle, but behind him the trees were thick enough to hide his men. The ground rose up toward him, and he was high enough to see the white of the water and the thin lines of pontoons, the new bridges. He focused closer, scanned across the wide, flat ground, and it made him ache. It would have been so simple, such a good place to form strong lines, cover the river with thousands of muskets and cut them to pieces as they came across. But then he raised the glasses, looked to the far heights above the river, saw the vast cluster of black, more than a hundred long-range cannon, better guns, more accurate than the Confederate batteries, and he knew they would have to wait, sit back in the trees while the Federal Army crossed at will, unmolested.

It was getting late now, the light fading fast. He scanned the horizon far down to the right, downstream, saw balloons, wondered how much Burnside knew, how much he could see. The trees were thick along the river there, and any troop movement might be exaggerated, the numbers inflated by nervous observers. Small units had been left to guard the crossings downstream. They were ordered to keep moving, marching back and forth, showing themselves in the small openings in the trees. It had always worked with the Federal lookouts, who seemed anxious to embellish their reports of vast gray armies prowling the ground in front of them.

Jackson knew that today he had been vulnerable, too spread out, but it had to be—at worst, the divisions had been within a day's march of each other, could delay the crossing at any point long enough for support to arrive. But then, gratefully, Burnside did not cross at all, sat still while Lee played the chess game, watched Burnside's plan unfold, and now Jackson was moving everyone into place, and through the trees down to his right more men were filling the lines.

He saw movement, glassed toward the river, saw troops, blue dots appearing suddenly on his side of the river, climbing up, reaching the top of the steep embankment that lined the river there. He looked beyond, to the bridges, expected to see great masses of troops, but there was only a thin line now, men moving across in single file. So few, he thought, why are they not coming? It's nearly dark, but . . . there is no opposition, they have a free passage.

He put the glasses down, rested his eyes, thought, Are they waiting for dark? But he knew the Yankees did not like to march in the dark. He shook his head, it made no sense. Upriver, to his left, the heavy shelling in the town had long stopped, and now the street fighting slowed. There was no mass crossing there either, he thought. Barksdale's muskets held them up. So, it would be tomorrow.

He looked to the right, down his own lines, saw movement on the long narrow road through the darkening trees, wagons and guns and new flags. It was Early's men, and they were spreading out, deploying into the woods. Jackson smiled, nodded silently, thought, We are stronger still.

Behind him Sandie Pendleton was directing the couriers, the men returning from the distant units, placing them at a discreet distance from Jackson, telling them to wait for further orders. There was a commotion in the trees, riders moving through the troops, and Pendleton saw the flag of D. H. Hill's division, and Hill himself, leading a small staff.

Pendleton called out, "General Jackson, sir, General Hill . . . *Daniel* Hill . . . is approaching."

Jackson turned, smiled, saw the small frame of his brother-in-law moving up the rise toward him. Hill threw up a formal salute, which Jackson acknowledged.

"General Hill, it is a pleasure to see you. Ride with me, if you please."

The two men moved away from the staffs, rode forward, out of the woods, down into patches of snow and tall brown grass and a fading glimpse of sunshine in the cold blue sky.

Jackson turned to look at Hill, saw the hair more gray, the forehead taller, the bright professor's eyes a bit more weary, and he said, "How are you, Daniel? How is Isabella?"

Hill was surprised at Jackson's personal question, concern for his wife, nodded. "Very well, thank you. Allow me to congratulate you on the birth of your daughter."

Jackson turned abruptly, glanced over his shoulder, still had told no one. He wondered how Hill knew, and Hill saw his surprise.

"Isabella wrote me, the letter came this morning." He was puzzled by Jackson's glare, and then Jackson returned to the smile, nodded. "Of course. Anna's sister . . . Isabella. Women must reveal all, I suppose."

"Is it a secret, General? Be assured, I will tell no one." Hill turned away, hiding a smile, looked across the clean white of the field, knew Jackson well enough to understand that there need be no explanation for Jackson's secrecy.

"Daniel, it is best if we keep good news . . . happy news . . . to ourselves. If we spend our energy spreading these . . . things . . . God is liable to take them away. I would rather use my good feelings thanking Him for the gift." He turned toward the river, spoke, thinking out loud. "I must tell Anna. Do not put our precious daughter at risk. We must not be too happy. Thank God, thank Him."

Hill lifted his field glasses, was watching the river. "They're on this side," he said. "They're coming across."

"No, not yet. Too few of them, maybe a skirmish line. They will cross tomorrow."

Hill put down the glasses, looked at Jackson, said, "Do you think it's a feint? Maybe they're still going to move downriver. We have pulled out of Port Royal. I could turn the men around. . . ."

"No. Once they began building the bridges it was settled. How could they go anywhere else? It is too easy here, they control the open ground with their guns. We cannot even slow them down from back here. How soon will your men be up, be ready to deploy?"

"By morning, first light."

"Good. It will happen tomorrow. They will do nothing more tonight."

Jackson pulled at his horse, and Hill followed. They rode back up toward the trees, quietly, and Jackson thought of Lexington, of Hill the professor, and he turned, smiled at Hill. Hill did not understand, and did not ask, and saw Jackson pull something yellow from his pocket.

33. LEE

December 13, 1862. Dawn.

It did not happen as Jackson had hoped. A full day passed, and the attack did not come. The Federal troops had finally crossed the bridges, slow, thick lines marching on fragile ribbons of wood, finally gathering on Lee's side of the river, but they did not advance, stayed close to the water, spreading out on the plain in a huge sea of blue. The fog had shielded them at first, then lifted late in the morning, and by then the spectacle of it was immense, and Lee had sat on the top of his hill and watched with barely concealed excitement. It was a grand show, and Burnside was doing exactly what Lee wanted him to do. The chess game was over, now it was straightforward and honest and brutal, and Lee would do no more now than watch and wait.

In Fredericksburg the streets had filled with Federal troops, and Lee could see them crowding between the buildings and the houses, setting up their camps in the shattered ruins. He did not give the order to the artillery, would not do as Sumner had done—would not shell the town.

The day had passed, and the armies watched each other, one growing, feeling its strength, while the other sat back firmly against its hills. Lee made no attempt to move forward, knew the guns on Stafford Heights were still there, would still control the open fields, and so he spent the day moving men about, small adjustments in a line that needed very little adjusting. When the darkness came, there had been nothing, only slight noises from the town, no campfires, Burnside making sure his men were not seen from Lee's hills. Lee had thought, How foolish, depriving your men of the warmth of their fires, while bitter winds hurled down the valley. It was an order straight from some textbook, and Lee knew that in the morning, the Federal troops would be weary and stiff and grumbling.

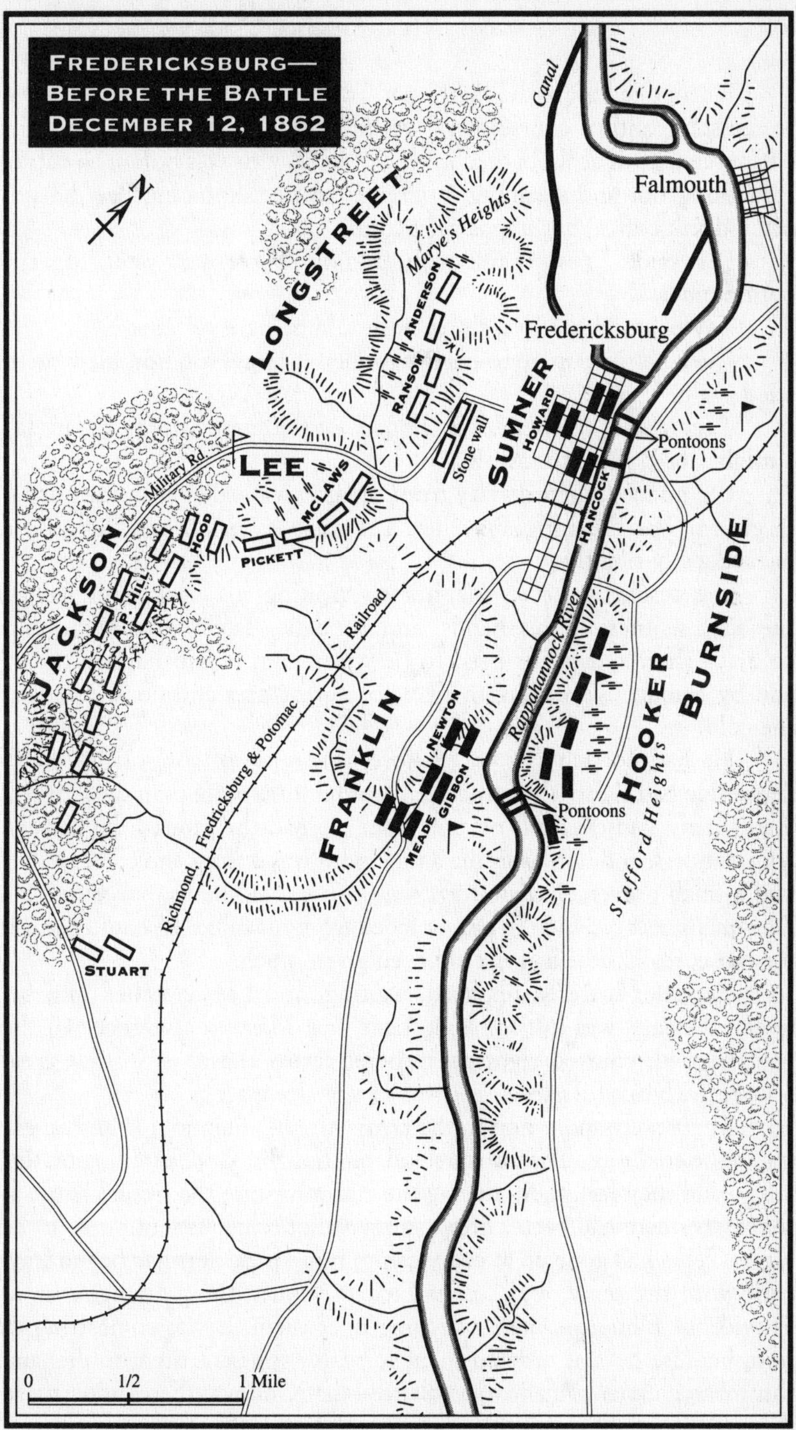

Fredericksburg—
Before the Battle
December 12, 1862
N
Canal
Falmouth
Marye's Heights
Longstreet
Anderson
Ransom
Fredericksburg
Sumner
Howard
Stone wall
Pontoons
Lee
McLaws
Military Rd.
Hood
Pickett
Jackson
A.P. Hill
Hancock
Railroad
Rappahannock River
Burnside
Hooker
Franklin
Newton
Gibbon
Meade
Richmond, Fredericksburg & Potomac
Pontoons
Stafford Heights
Stuart
0
1/2
1 Mile

He awoke before the light, met Taylor beside the small fire, tried to see stars, and of course there would be none. The wide valley, the entire scene, was again bathed in thick fog. Taylor was holding a cup of something hot and steaming, offered it to Lee, knowing Lee did not often drink coffee, but it was very cold.

Lee said, "Yes, thank you, Major. Have you sent for the commanders?"

Taylor nodded. "Yes, sir, they should be here very soon."

Lee held the cup up to his lips, pulled it away, too hot, blew on it, tried again.

Taylor said, "General, I do hope we have some activity today. It's a mighty cold place to just sit."

Lee nodded, turned away from the fire, walked over to the horses. A groom was brushing Traveller. Lee raised a hand, and the groom backed away silently.

Lee reached out to the horse, stroking his neck, still feeling the sore stiffness in his hands, and thought, Taylor was right, this cold . . . these old hands need to be warm. But it will happen today, and by tonight we will again sit before great fires and not care about the cold.

He had not felt this way before, this sense of comfort, of confidence. He had eighty thousand men around him, more than the Confederate Army had ever put on one field. He had the ground, he had the commanders, and he was facing a man who was unsure and cautious. He said a small prayer, *By Your mercy, we will not lose many, our friends . . . Please deliver us . . .* and the prayer faded from his mind, he could not ask for more, realized he had already been given much.

Traveller lowered his head, waiting, and Lee scratched him between the ears, was lost for a moment, saw Mary, the younger girl he had married, courted right over there, across the river in that great house, the beautiful gardens. It was so very long ago. . . .

There were more noises, the army stirring, men joking and laughing in the cold mist. They understand, he thought, God is smiling on this army, and they feel it. All during the autumn, since the second battle at Manassas, there had been a growing revival of religious sentiment in the army. Tents had gone up at every camp, more preachers had begun traveling with the army, and Lee had felt the spirit, the growing sense of Providence filling the men, watching over them. It was comforting to him, because he still ordered them forward, still sent them to die, and this made it easier somehow, a balance—that God was there, understood their cause, would watch them, keeping them a little more safe.

There were few trees on his hill, and the light began to find the ground. He could see movement, men walking about in the dull gray of the morning. He turned, looked for Taylor, saw the fire and walked over. Taylor was quickly there, chewing on something. He tried to swallow too quickly, and Lee raised his hand as if to say no, it's all right, please continue eating. But he knew Taylor, was thankful for his pure devotion, and Taylor cleared his throat, was red-faced, embarrassed, caught his breath.

"Sorry, General . . . I was just—"

"Major, please, go and finish your breakfast. We have little to attend to until the others arrive."

Taylor saluted, still rubbed his throat, moved away to the wagon where the other staff had gathered. Lee thought, A biscuit would be good, maybe one more for his pocket, and he followed behind Taylor. Down the hill, from the south, came a horse, the first loud sound of the morning, the true beginning of the day. Lee watched, saw the figure approach in the fog, the wide black-plumed hat, the grand entrance of Stuart.

Lee raised a hand, a quiet acknowledgment, moved quickly to the breakfast wagon and grabbed a pair of biscuits. Stuart waited close to the fire, warming gloved hands. Lee climbed back up the rise, said, "General Stuart, are you well this morning?"

"Quite well, General, quite." The voice was high, excited. "Sir, we are extending the far right flank of General Jackson's line. I have scouted forward, determined that the Federal position rests along the river, then out toward General Jackson to a point near the Richmond Road. The way is open for the enemy to attempt to flank—"

Lee held up his hand, said, "Wait for your report, please, General. I would like the others to be here, to hear what you have learned. It will be just a few minutes, I am certain."

Stuart stopped, began to look past Lee toward the food, the smell of coffee. "General, if you will permit? It was a rather chilly ride up this way."

"General, help yourself to some breakfast."

Stuart moved quickly toward the table, passed Taylor, who came up beside Lee, to the fire.

"General Stuart is full of energy this morning. His cavalry will serve us well today."

Taylor tried to speak, his mouth distressingly full again, and he made a small grunt. Lee hid his smile as behind them another horse approached, at a slow deliberate trot, from the opposite direction. Lee knew without turning it was Longstreet.

Longstreet dismounted, moved to the warmth, and now Lee could see the face clearly, the fog had a bright glow, and Longstreet saluted, removed the floppy-brimmed hat, was smoking a short cigar.

"Any movement to your front, General?" Lee asked.

"Nothing. Can't see anything . . . just like up here . . . but there's some sounds. The picket line sends back regular reports . . . they're eating breakfast, most likely. Won't do much until the fog clears. Nothing to shoot at yet."

Lee stared down at the fire, said, "They are all so . . . cautious. I often wonder if God has done that . . . made them slow. It evens up the fight a bit. They have the numbers . . . the guns."

Longstreet stared at Lee, put the hat back on, moved the cigar in his mouth. "Could be," he said. "Could be they just don't have the heart for this fight. The generals, I mean. The troops . . . they're the same boys we served with before. I've talked to some of the prisoners. Not much different from these boys up here. They go where they're told, shoot when they're told to shoot. But they don't have much respect for the officers. And the officers don't have much respect for the generals. It's not very . . . healthy."

Lee watched the fire, thought of the troops, said, "No, General, they are not the same. These men . . . our men are fighting for something that means more to them than obeying their orders. I feel sometimes like God is with us . . . God is protecting these men. He knows they are looking to Him."

Longstreet chewed on the cigar, said, "Maybe. I'm not sure if God is in all the places we want Him to be."

It was an odd statement, and Lee still looked down, thought, No, He is with you too, General. He thought of Longstreet's children, how Longstreet could not even plan the funeral. It was George Pickett, his old friend, who had made the arrangements, and Longstreet had not even attended, could not watch his children laid in the ground, and so did not hear the words of the minister, the comforting blessings, the lesson of God's will. Lee thought, It was a mistake, he should have been there, God would have given him peace.

Lee also thought that Longstreet had come back too soon, returned to duty too quickly. But Longstreet would not speak of it, would not talk of his wife, of the experience. Instead he pulled himself into a quiet darkness. Lee felt pain for him, wanted to give him something . . . some comfort from God, show him that God would help him but there was no opening, and so Lee knew there would always be that difference between them, a different way of seeing . . . everything, the enemy, the war.

Jackson appeared now, at a quick gallop from the same direction as Stuart. Lee thought, No, it can't be. Then he saw the face, the sharp nose and glaring blue eyes from under a wide black hat, and yes, it was he, but . . . he was dressed in a new uniform, gold buttons shining down the front of his coat, crisp gold braiding on his sleeves, a gold braid around the wide black hat. Lee did not know what to say, thought, This is very strange.

Stuart was back, held a heaping plate of food, said loudly, "Well, General Jackson, you are a beautiful and most gallant sight this morning. Von Borcke told me it was a fine fit, but I had no idea . . . the uniform suits you most elegantly."

Jackson did not speak, seemed embarrassed, moved toward the fire and removed his hat, saluted Lee. "Thank you, General Stuart. Your gift was appreciated. Very kind."

Longstreet had said nothing, began to laugh, said, "General Jackson, this was a gift? Well now, was there some special occasion? I apologize for not being better informed."

Stuart began to move about, excitedly, spilling food from the plate. "No, General, it was just . . . something I felt this army could use. We have a quite famous man in our midst. It seemed appropriate for him to dress the part."

Jackson frowned, and Longstreet said, "Well, yes, I understand that. The papers up North are giving our good Stonewall here credit for bad weather in New England and a poor harvest in Illinois. Certainly, he should dress the part."

Jackson put the hat back on, stared down, hiding his face, which was bright red. Lee was still speechless, had never known Jackson to look like anything other than a rugged mess.

"I must say, General," Lee began, "the change is . . . a positive one. Yes, General Stuart, you are to be commended for your good taste. It puts the rest of us . . ." He looked down to his own simple gray coat. "Well, let us say that we had best be careful walking among the troops . . . there will be confusion as to who is in command." It was a rare joke from Lee.

Jackson looked up, concerned, said, "Oh, certainly not, sir. Forgive me, General Stuart, but perhaps this was a mistake. I did not mean to suggest anything of my own . . . I did not wish to appear grandiose. . . ."

Longstreet was still laughing, said, "Nonsense, General. I feel today that you are the new symbol of this army—gold braid and all. You have truly inspired us. Perhaps I will go and polish my boots."

This was very good, Lee thought, they are all in good spirits. But he knew this would go on until he stopped it, and he said, "Gentlemen, we must address the matter at hand. Please join me." He motioned, and they moved toward a small table.

Taylor jumped ahead of them, unrolled a map, and Lee said, "General Longstreet, please show us where your troops are positioned."

Taylor held a small piece of pencil, laid it on the map. Longstreet tossed the cigar aside and began to make short straight lines with the pencil.

"We are anchored on the north by Anderson's division, up on the bend in the river, then General Ransom's division is in several lines along and below the ridge of Marye's Heights, with Cobb's brigade dug in down on the road, behind that stone wall. To their right is General McLaws, and farther down, in the woods to the right, are Pickett and Hood. General Hood is my right flank, and is connected in those heavy trees with General Jackson's left. Up here, on the heights, are the Washington Artillery, with Colonel Alexander's batteries in support. It is a very strong line, General."

"Very well, General. General Jackson, would you please extend the line for us?"

Jackson took off the hat again, leaned forward slightly, said, "General Hill . . . A. P. Hill is on the left, adjoining General Hood. His position is supported . . . here . . . by General Taliaferro and General Early. To the right flank and behind is Daniel Hill. General Lee . . ." He paused, ran his finger along the map. "We have completed construction of a road, running behind the lines for our entire length. We can move troops as is necessary. If the enemy penetrates our line at any point, the reserves—Taliaferro and Early—can change their position rapidly. If the enemy makes an attempt to cut our center, or if General Pickett is pressed, we can move to his aid. Our right flank is anchored here." He pointed to a straight line, a road that led away from the river, out to the west. "General Stuart has advised that the enemy has placed his flank on this road, and does not threaten farther southward. Daniel Hill is positioned to move farther down if the enemy changes his direction."

Lee stared at Jackson, and there was a brief silence. Jackson had not built his reputation by defensive tactics, and even Longstreet nodded, impressed, said quietly, "Good, very good."

Stuart was moving impatiently, and Lee said, "General Stuart, are you protecting General Jackson's flank?"

"Yes, sir. We are covering the enemy's position from the river, as far out as General Daniel Hill's position. If the enemy begins to threaten downriver, to turn General Jackson's line, we can block his advance until the line is moved."

"Very well." Lee leaned over the map, studied the positions, the ground. "General Jackson, there is a large area of trees extending out toward the enemy from the center of your line. That area could be vulnerable. There could be good cover there for the enemy's advance."

Jackson leaned forward, squinted, said, "A. P. Hill is dug in along that position, sir. I will confirm that he is aware of that possibility."

Lee nodded. "Very well. I have confidence in General Hill. He will not leave himself at a disadvantage."

Behind the men, out toward the open field that stretched toward the town, the batteries of the Washington Artillery were set into shallow pits. The men were manning the guns, watching the fog slowly drifting in the growing breeze, a fine, cold mist. The sun was higher now, and across the river the far heights could be seen, the flags of the Federal headquarters, the closely spaced guns of the enemy. Now, the fog had settled downward, into the town, and rising above the dense gray were church spires, the only sign that there was a town there at all. The meeting was concluded and the four men walked out toward the guns, walked behind the crews, who stood stiffly, quietly, reverent respect for the four generals.

Lee moved closer to one of the guns, placed his sore hand on a spoked wheel, said aloud, "How odd. The fog is lower. . . ."

Now other pieces of the town began to appear, the rooftops of the taller buildings, and he began to see some of the destruction, the black skeletons of burnt-out houses. A breeze blew sharply up the hill, and below, the fog was moving, breaking into smaller layers. Thick puffs of white began to move past the town, clearing the plain, and suddenly they could see far below, down the river.

Stuart said, "My God. They're coming."

On the wide plain in front of Jackson's woods, a vast checkerboard was taking shape. Neat formations were moving out slowly on the clean snow-covered field, the sharp squares of blue spreading out on the stark white, and Lee stared, amazed, had never seen anything like this. The troops had nothing to protect them, nothing to hide them except the fog, and now it was clearing rapidly.

Longstreet moved up next to Lee. "Beautiful."

Lee said nothing, stared down from the hill, resting on the wheel of the big gun. The soldiers around them were still quiet, absorbed by the stunning sight, and he began to count, the regiments, the strength. From the river's edge out into the plain he tried to estimate, could see . . . fifty . . . sixty thousand troops. They were not advancing yet, were not spread into battle line, and so it was like a grand review, some great blue parade.

There were always trees, hills, obstructing the view. You saw them coming in pieces, sometimes wide lines, maybe a whole brigade. But the smoke would come, the battle would be on before the rest came forward, and so you knew the strength, knew the numbers in your head, would make a good guess where they would hit the hardest, where the farthest units would be thrown in at your own lines, but you would never see all of them, the whole army. Not like this. He even saw the reserves, more blue masses across the river, crowding the bank. And he thought, Longstreet is right, God help us, but it is a beautiful sight.

Guns began to fire now, far down the line, Jackson's guns, but not many. Lee knew it was reckless, would be stopped quickly, and from the far heights the Federal guns answered, and he could see it all, the bright specks of light streaking across the river, landing in the woods. The great blue masses began to move forward, thinning out, shaping into long lines, and the Federal guns opened again, more of them, a massed artillery barrage on the woods where Jackson's men crouched. Lee turned, saw Jackson looking through field glasses, said, "General, it seems that your men will open the day."

Jackson turned, put down the glasses, and Lee saw the look, the blue fire, the raw, silent screaming in the eyes. Jackson did not speak, gave a short salute, and Taylor was there, had his horse. Jackson climbed up and pulled his hat down low on his head, hiding his face.

Longstreet said, smiling, "General, there's an awful lot of them out there. Don't they scare you just a bit?"

Jackson tilted back his head, glared at him, said, "We will see if now I will scare *them*." He turned the horse, and with a quick flash from his eyes, a last glance at Lee, he was gone down the hill, toward the growing thunder filling the trees.

Lee turned back to the blue troops, to the steady sound of the Federal cannon. Far out, beyond the lines, down where Stuart's troops were holding the flank, he saw something, movement, a small team of horses, then another, wheeling two guns out into the open field. He put his glasses up to his eyes, heard Stuart say, "My God, those are *our* guns . . . it's Pelham. Those are Pelham's guns."

Lee strained to see. The guns were firing now, small dots of men scrambling around them, then firing again. The first wave of blue was advancing toward Jackson's woods, moving out through the open fields, and now puffs of smoke came from their lines, the impact of Pelham's shelling, the firing right into their flanks, right down the long blue lines.

Stuart began to cheer. "Hoooeeeee, that's Pelham all right. Hoooeeeeee!"

Lee focused on the two small guns, saw a great ball of smoke and fire near them, a Federal gun directing its fire in their direction. Quickly, the horses were hitched and the guns moved a short distance. Then their crews were back on them and both guns began to fire again. Lee looked closer, toward the Federal lines, saw gaps opening, the line wavering, and still Pelham's guns kept firing. Now more Federal guns were pointing that way, trying to find the range. Once again the horses were hitched and the guns shifted. Lee saw one explosion, a bright flash of light, and one of the guns was in pieces, and he thought, Well, it's over, but it was a good effort. Now the smoke cleared and he was amazed. He saw the other gun, still moving, and now firing again, and the Federal line was breaking up, pulling back. Lee focused on the blue mass, saw the lines behind through the smoke, trying to advance, bogging down, stopped by the shattering of the line in front.

Stuart was still yelling, and the men around them, the gun crews, began to cheer as well. The Federal lines were still well away from Jackson's position, but were being delayed and disrupted by the one man, John Pelham, one gunner from Stuart's command. Now Stuart grew quieter, said, "All right, pull out . . . that's enough . . . save the gun. You've done enough."

Lee could still see the lone gun firing, shells impacting around it, close, and Pelham moving again, still firing. He turned to Stuart, said, "General, you had best return to your troops. I don't want that gallant young man to fight this battle by himself."

Stuart was smiling, saluted. "At your service, *mon Général*." Then he reached for his horse, climbed up, and with a wave of his tall hat rode away toward the battle.

Longstreet was glassing down toward the town, saw little movement, said, "It's all down that way . . . nothing is happening in front of us. It's Antietam again. One piece at a time."

Lee looked toward the town, glassed the buildings, saw masses of blue in the streets, knew Longstreet was right. The fight was not here, but down there, on the right, and Burnside would wait and see what happened there first. Lee shook his head, turned toward the sounds, searched again through his glasses for the lone cannon, the heroic gunner. "It is well this is so terrible," he said. "We should grow too fond of it."

34. JACKSON

December 13, 1862. Early morning.

He saw the red shirt from a distance, rode that way. Shells were still falling in the woods to his left, out toward the front of the line and the edge of the wide plain. Military Road, which the soldiers had built through the thick trees, was clear, open; the shells had not reached that far back. He rode quickly, kept looking toward the sounds of the explosions, felt the earth bouncing under the horse, the horse not flinching at all.

Jackson reached the group of men, the man in the red shirt, A. P. Hill, directing the rest, and he pulled the horse up. He tried to hear what was being said, and they turned to him, Hill saluting. But the sound of the artillery barrage drowned out the voices. Hill was pointing toward the front, said something to Jackson he could not hear, and Jackson motioned to him: move back, behind the road, away from the shelling.

Hill mounted his horse and followed Jackson back into the trees. They passed over lines of crouching men, Taliaferro's lines, and the men saw him, began to cheer, waving hats. Jackson tried not to notice them, and Hill looked self-conscious, usually heard the same thing from his own men, but not from the rest, and it was clear they were cheering Jackson, not him.

When they reached a small clearing, two of Jackson's staff, Pendleton and Smith, rode up quickly from behind. Both men were sweating in the cold air, and Jackson reined his horse and waited.

Pendleton said, "General, we were told you had returned. Sir, we have a gap in the line, you need to see this. . . ."

Jackson looked at Hill, who said, "Yes, yes, it's that swamp, the thick trees. Do not worry, General, no sizable force can move through that ground. It's a wide creek bed, the ground is a muddy swamp. I spoke with a local farmer. He told me he never uses that land. With respect to your staff, General, my lines are sound."

Jackson said nothing, reached for the piece of paper offered by Pendleton, a small, crude map showing the units, the woods. He studied it, and there was a long, quiet moment, a lull in the shelling. "I must ride out," Jackson said. "I must see what is happening. Mr. Pendleton, you will stay with General Hill. You may find me on this road, or forward, at the edge of the trees. Captain Smith, please accompany me."

Jackson spurred his horse and Smith followed. They were quickly beyond the clearing, moving toward the front. Hill still offered a salute, which Jackson did not see, then dropped his hand with a sarcastic flourish.

Now, the shelling began again, still in the trees in front of them. They reached the road and Jackson pulled the horse, moved farther down to the right. He turned again, eased the horse to the left, up off the road, forward through the brush, and came to a shallow trench filled with Hill's men. Carefully, he jumped the trench, and the men cheered him again. Smith waved at them furiously, quieting them, because now they could be heard by the enemy.

As they reached the edge of the trees, the shelling came in to their right, down the line. Jackson raised his glasses, tried to find the blue line, the advance of the Federal troops.

"I can't see. Too low. Let's move forward." And he spurred the horse out into the clearing, into the tall grass. Smith rode out beside him, then to the front, and Jackson did not notice that Smith was placing himself between him and the enemy lines.

They reached a small rise. Jackson stopped, brought up the glasses again, said aloud, "Over there, they're coming toward the point of trees."

The blue lines were barely visible, stretched out for several hundred yards, but they were moving forward again, still a long way off. Behind him there was no sound. The shelling from the Federal guns had stopped and Hill's guns were not firing, not yet. He turned, looked back to the line of trees, could see nothing, no sign of his men, and he turned toward the advancing enemy, said, "They don't know where we are. Let them come . . . much closer. We must get back to General Hill, tell him to hold his fire, keep the guns quiet until they are much closer."

He pulled on his horse, and Smith said, "Look!"

Out to the front, two hundred yards away, a single soldier, a blue

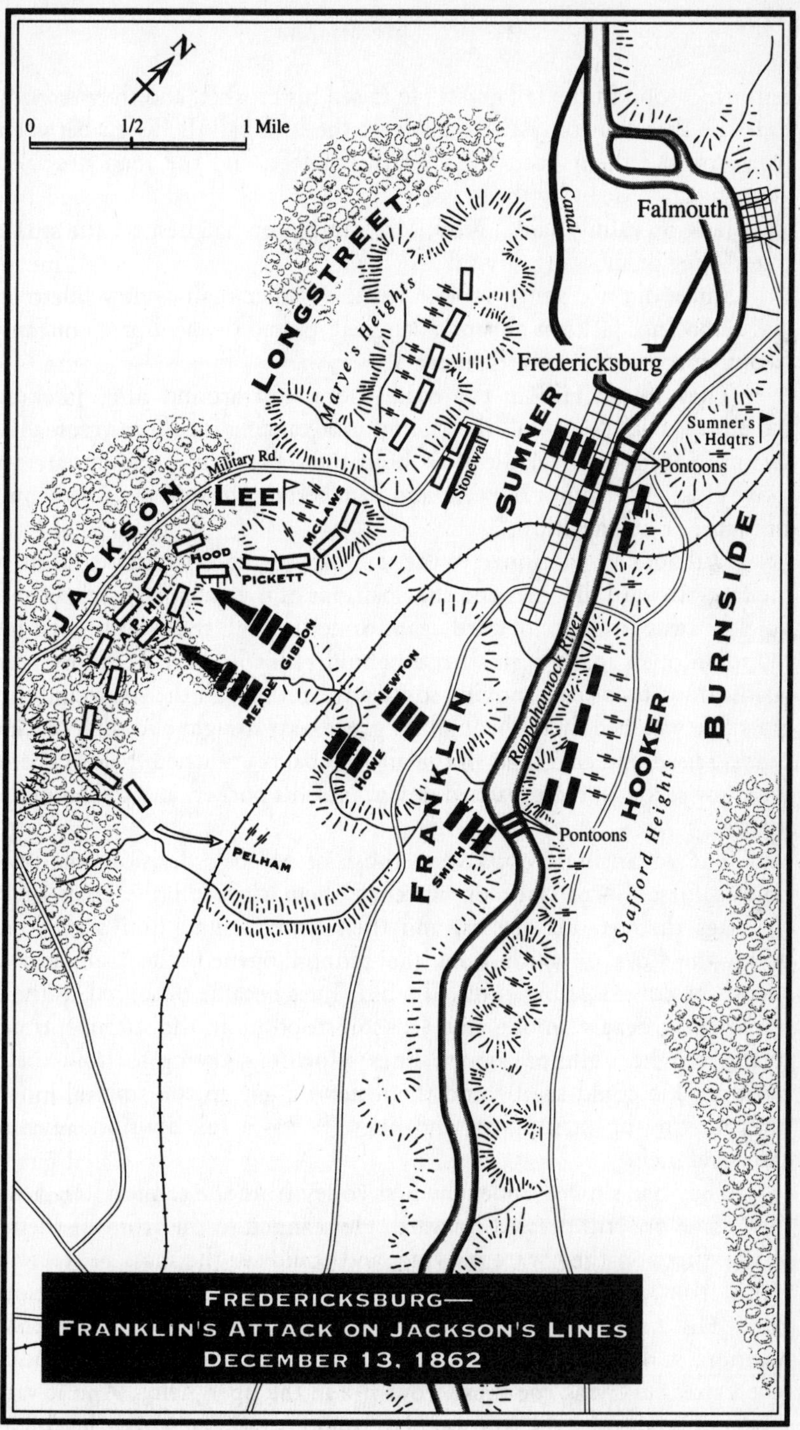

FREDERICKSBURG—
FRANKLIN'S ATTACK ON JACKSON'S LINES
DECEMBER 13, 1862

uniform, stood in the tall grass. He raised his musket, and they did not hear the shot, but only the whistle of the lead ball. It hissed between them, missed them both by a couple of feet, and the man dropped down again, hidden by the grass.

Jackson calmly said, "Why, Mr. Smith, you had best return to the trees. They're shooting at you!"

Smith did not smile, looked for the soldier again, knew the man was reloading. Jackson abruptly laughed, pulled on his horse, and the two men rode back into the trees.

They found Hill in the road, more staff around him. Jackson pulled up, said, "General, the enemy is advancing on those trees, that swamp. Order your artillery to hold their fire, allow the enemy to move close. We cannot be seen, and I am certain they do not know our strength, or our position."

Hill nodded, motioned to the staff officers, and they rode out into the trees, toward the lines and the positions of the guns. Jackson turned quickly away, moved forward again, rode through the woods until he found an open space, a small rise behind Hill's lines. The enemy was visible now, blue coats moving toward them through the snow and the grass. He watched them through his glasses, sat straight and high on the horse, raised one arm high in the air, the palm upturned, held it there for a few seconds, then reached down, into his pocket, and pulled out a lemon.

The advancing troops were those of Meade's division, of Reynolds's First Corps. Jackson watched them close on the trees, saw the flags through his glasses, and then from behind him and from down the lines on both sides the cannon opened, the thunderous sounds of dozens of big guns. The blue lines became obscured, bathed in the thick deadly smoke, and Jackson stood up in the stirrups, tried to see, caught a glimpse of the lines reforming, trying to hold their position. He could see behind them now, a gap in the smoke, more lines moving up in support, and knew it was a full division, several thousand men.

They had slowed under the first volley from the cannon, but now they came on, still pressed forward. He scanned to the front of them, in the direction they were moving, and could see the mass of trees to Hill's front, the swamp Hill had so confidently dismissed. Jackson knew Hill had been wrong, they were going into the woods at that position, it offered the best cover, was the first safe place they could reach after surviving the murderous fire in the open fields. And it was *winter*. The swamp, the soft muddy ground, would be frozen hard. He snatched his hat off his head and yelled out a furious sound. Behind him Pendleton moved forward, looked at him, waiting for instructions, but Jackson continued to stare ahead at the long point of trees that split Hill's lines.

From each side Hill's muskets began to fire, squeezing the blue lines together, pressing them with the deadly fire, and so they would reach the trees even more compactly, moving where the fire was the least, where Hill had no muskets. Jackson saw it happening, saw the gap in Hill's lines suddenly filling with a strong flow of blue. They began to move into the swamp, pushing forward, driving a wedge between Hill's brigades.

Jackson pulled on the horse, began to move back toward the road. Smoke was drifting across now, and he could see very little. The sounds of muskets filled the woods, and he did not see Hill. He moved down the road, toward the point where the blue advance would come, saw General Maxcy Gregg and the troops that lay behind the swamp, that would next feel the thrust of Meade's advance.

"General, prepare for the assault. The enemy is cutting our lines . . . they are pushing through the swamp, between the brigades of Archer and Lane."

Gregg nodded. "Yes, General, we have seen them coming. Can we expect some support?"

Jackson turned, saw his two aides following up close behind him. "Captain Pendleton," he said, "go to General Early. Tell him to advance his men here, toward these woods. He may direct himself by the sounds of the battle. Captain Smith . . . go to General Taliaferro, tell him to advance his men here as well." He turned back to Gregg, who saluted and was quickly gone.

The battle was closer now, the minié balls clipping leaves and small branches around him, high shots from lines of men who knew they were breaking through the enemy, men who would not stop unless you *made* them stop. He looked down the road in both directions, still did not see Hill, and now in the road in front of him, not a hundred yards away, smoke boiled out of the trees, a fresh volley from moving troops. He saw a cluster of blue, the men pouring out into the road like the flow from a great blue wound, lining up against Gregg's troops, who were moving up from the woods in the rear.

Suddenly, he was blinded by a swirling cloud of smoke, the hot sulfur smell. Jackson turned the horse, rode back into the woods, tried to find a clear spot, someplace he could see. In front of him and to the side new smoke poured from the lines of muskets, and he could hear nothing but the steady crack of the rifles, the enemy yells, and the screams of his shattered troops.

He rode farther back, tried to escape the smoke, to find someone, Early. We have the reserves, he thought, we are strong. They never should have pushed this far, cut through our lines. He thought of Hill, felt a violent twinge, saw the man's small figure, the ragged beard, the red shirt that he now saw as obnoxious, foolish bravado, and he wanted to kill him, grab him with his fists and squeeze the life from him.

He jerked the horse through the trees, ducked under low branches. He rode up onto a small ridge, could see out through the woods, thinner trees, the dense clouds of smoke hanging in the branches. The sounds kept moving, a steady flow, pushing his men back, and he knew this was bad. If they send in more strength at the gap, he thought, they can turn our lines completely, cutting behind the bigger hills, surrounding Longstreet's position. He faced the sounds, tried to determine the direction, glanced up at the sun, now high in the sky, and gauged the direction. No, they had not turned yet, were still coming straight through, straight across the road.

The firing began to slow now, the men deep into dense woods, seeking out a target. For a short few minutes the Federal troops had no organized lines in front of them, no enemy they could see. Jackson heard the shouting, officers calling to their men, trying to bring them back together, forming the companies into some organized shape. From his right he heard a new sound, a piercing shrillness, a long, high wail that he had not heard since Manassas. He moved the horse, prodded it along the ridge, toward the sound. Taking off his hat, holding it high, he stared at the sound with the blue fire in his eyes. . . . It was the rebel yell.

From back behind the heavy trees a new force was advancing into the confused positions of Meade's men. It was Early's division, and they flowed into the woods, strong, heavy lines of fresh troops. Now the muskets began again, and Jackson felt it, felt the surge. *Yes*, push them back. Close in front of him he heard new sounds, of the wounded and dying, and of blind panic, and the sounds began to shift back toward the road. Meade's men were falling back.

EARLY'S DIVISION PUSHED THE FEDERAL ADVANCE COMPLETELY back out of the trees, and then the Confederate position was strengthened, units moved out into the frozen swamp. The gap was sealed, the reserves brought forward, and the Federal forces wilted under the steady barrage of cannon and muskets. Alongside Meade, Gibbon's division, which had pushed up against the brunt of Jackson's defense, could only hold its ground in front of the line of trees, and now was pulling back as well. It had not been pressed as hard, but Gibbon had expected help, support from the vast number of troops behind him.

For most of the morning the rest of Franklin's Grand Division, the rest of the sixty thousand men who had crossed the river, stood in formation, ready to follow Meade across the plain, into the woods. The plan had been for Meade to push through and break the lines, but when he tumbled back out of the woods, flowing back out into the plain with broken lines and panicked troops, Franklin watched without responding, and did not order a new advance. The call went instead across the river, to Burnside, a request for new instructions, and from high up on Stafford Heights, from the man who still believed in his own plan, no orders came. If Franklin's troops could not carry the day, could not push through Jackson's woods, then it would be Sumner and the troops in the town.

Outside Burnside's headquarters, while Franklin's courier waited for instructions, the commander stared through his glasses toward the hills beyond the town, where Sumner's troops would make the final push, a glorious assault that Burnside knew would sweep Lee's army from the hills in one broad stroke.

35. HANCOCK

December 13, 1862. Midday.

THEY MOVED THROUGH THE STREETS, BEGAN TO FORM ON THE edge of town, out past the last of the houses. They could still hear the guns down to the left, the destruction of Meade's division, but their attention was focused on the hill a half-mile across the open ground in front of them.

Hancock rode through the forming lines, stared out at the field, could see fences, rows of posts and rails that would slow and therefore devastate his lines when crossed. Farther, he could now clearly make out the canal, crossing the field at a slight angle, the canal that Burnside said did not exist.

Out beyond his lines the division of William French was already in battle formation, would be the first across the field. Behind him, still strung out down the streets of the town, Oliver Howard's division would follow Hancock. This was Couch's Second Corps, and on them would fall the responsibility for salvaging Burnside's great plan.

Hancock rode back into the town, saw the last units of his men gathering, easing slowly through the last rows of buildings. Officers were prodding the slow movers, and when they saw him, their pace quickened. He rode toward the river, glanced up at the heights beyond, to the Federal headquarters, to the silent guns. He lowered his head, thought of the irony. The great force of artillery that had blasted so much of the town to ruins was now totally useless. The range of the guns commanded the flat ground they would cross, but could not reach the hills, and so, since Lee had not moved forward, had not made any attempt to cross that ground, the big guns had nothing to shoot at, could only point silently above the backs of his men as they marched toward the high ground.

He saw a flag, quick riders: Couch. Hancock moved that way, and Couch saw him, halted the group, motioned for him to ride forward, leaving the staff behind.

"General," Couch said. "Your division about set?"

"They are. French is ready as well. Howard should be able to move out once we start forward."

"Good."

Hancock saw the face, tight and grim, said, "Any further word . . . from over there?" He motioned back across the river.

"Sumner has been ordered to remain in his headquarters. He will not accompany his Grand Division in the fight."

Hancock stared up at the far mansion, thought of the old man, said, "Burnside ordered him to stay back?"

"I think General Burnside feels that General Sumner is at risk today, might do something . . . dangerous. General Sumner is not pleased with the order."

"No, I would imagine he is not pleased at all." Hancock waited, expected something further from Couch, but Couch said nothing, looked downriver toward the sounds of the fading battle. Hancock followed the look, said, "It did not go well, I expect. Jackson held his lines."

Couch took off his hat, held it up, blocking out the sun. "They did not expect General Jackson to put up much of a fight. They tried to drive him back, break his defense with two divisions, two of Reynolds's divisions. They left the bulk of Franklin's forces idle. General Smith's corps was ordered to guard the bridgeheads . . . his *entire* corps. Guarding them . . . from what?" Couch lowered the hat, slapped it against his leg, said, "Burnside's order said to keep the lines of retreat open. Have you ever received an order like that? Your commander emphasizing your need for retreat?"

Hancock stared away, thought of Reynolds, a good man, a general who knew how to command a field, all his fight taken away by a weak commander. How could they not expect Jackson to put up a fight? He shook his head, said, "Was it bad?"

"Don't know. Heard Meade made a good advance, but Franklin didn't support him. Had Hooker sitting across the river with thirty thousand reserves and didn't use them. Now, they're *our* reserves. Likely, by tonight, they'll still be over there."

Hancock looked toward the hill and Lee's army, said, "We'll try, though. It's all we can do."

Couch looked at him, turned to his staff and waved them

forward. "General Hancock," he said, "return to your division. I will give General French the order to advance, and you will allow him to move out approximately two hundred yards, then you will move your men in line behind him. The orders you received this morning still apply. You will advance in brigade front, spacing your brigades that same distance. Your objective will be the stone wall at the base of the hill. You will drive the enemy from his position and move up the hill." He stopped, stared away, back across the river. "Do you understand, General?"

Hancock nodded. "Yes, sir, I understand."

Couch turned toward him and his expression changed. Hancock saw something, concern, a soft look in the eyes, and Couch suddenly put out a hand, said, "Take care, Win."

He took the hand, embarrassed; the staff was watching, lines of marching troops were passing by. He released the hand, snapped a salute, said, "General . . . we will see you this evening . . . up on that hill."

Couch nodded, said nothing, and Hancock turned and rode through the streets toward his men.

He moved the horse carefully, and the men in the street gave way, moved respectfully to the side. There was some yelling, a few catcalls, nervous comments from the men who would do the bloody work. He did not look at them, did not know them—they were Howard's men. He could see his own lines now, the formation nearly complete, and he rode out among them, into the open field. Beyond the end of his lines he saw Couch, riding quickly through the last row of houses, moving forward, toward French's lines.

Suddenly, the hills in front of them began to speak, small flashes and puffs of white. There was a silent pause, a frozen moment, the men turning, waiting, and now came the sounds, the high screams, the whistles and shrieks. The shells began to fall, shaking the ground, blowing quick holes in the neat blue lines. French's men moved forward, wavering slightly from the impact of the explosions. Gaps had already opened in the line, men dying before they could even begin the attack. Hancock saw Couch riding back toward the town, the order given, the assault under way.

Hancock moved the horse up through his own lines. Sam Zook, one of his brigade commanders, another Pennsylvanian, was waving at French's men, leading a cheer, watching them move away. Then he saw Hancock. "You're the first line, Sam. Clear the way."

Zook was smiling broadly, ready for the fight, and he yelled out,

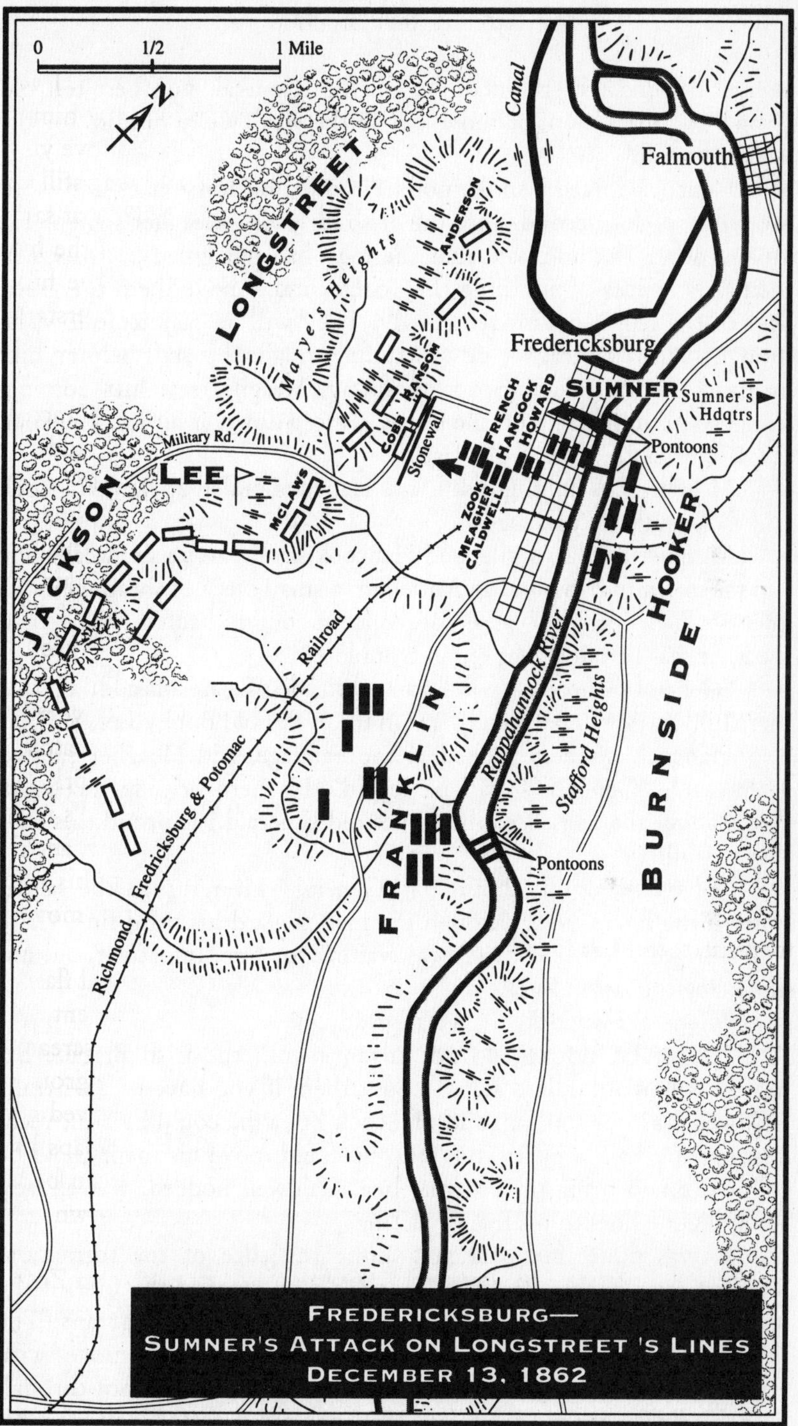

FREDERICKSBURG—
SUMNER'S ATTACK ON LONGSTREET 'S LINES
DECEMBER 13, 1862

over the sounds of the incoming shells, "General, you best tell old French to hurry it up, or move out of the way! We're headin' for the top of the hill!"

Hancock forced a smile, nodded, pulled his horse back and faced the front of his second line, the Irish Brigade—Meagher's men. He looked down the line, saw that the men had put green . . . *things* in their hats, pieces of anything they could find. Above them the green flags of the regiments moved slowly. They will be easy to follow, he thought. He saw Meagher now, standing, fragile, his staff helping him up onto a horse, and he rode that way. Meagher saw him coming, straightened himself up on the horse, glanced down at his leg. Hancock saw a wide cloth, a thick bandage.

Meagher was holding a salute as Hancock pulled up, and Hancock said, "General, are you fit?"

Meagher tried to smile, and Hancock saw he was pale, weary. He had taken a minor wound at Antietam, a small piece of shrapnel in his knee. It had been no cause for concern, but it hadn't healed, and the knee was bad now, the leg in trouble.

"General Hancock, I will lead me brigade. We are a-headin' up that there hill, and I will personally spit in the eye of old Bobby Lee. Sir."

Hancock nodded, looked at the bandage, and Meagher saluted again, said, "General, I *will* be leadin' this here brigade. Have no doubt about that, sir. We will do the old Emerald Isle proud this day, that we will."

"I have no doubt about that, General." He returned the salute, spurred the horse, rode through the men toward his third line, Caldwell's brigade. John Caldwell was waiting for him, impatient, did not like being the last in line.

"General Hancock, sir, we are ready."

"General Caldwell, do not advance until the Irish Brigade has moved out two hundred steps. Count them if you have to, General." Caldwell was not smiling, and Hancock knew he could be a bit reckless, too much in a hurry, but still, he could move his men, could be counted on to bring up a strong line. Caldwell nodded, was already watching the lines to his front, waiting.

It was done. He rode out along the edge of the formation, watched through his glasses as French's men reached the first of the fences, the lines slowing, men pulling down the wooden rails. The shelling was following them out, like a violent storm that moves with you, the gunners adjusting the range, hurling their solid shot through French's lines with vicious effect. Hancock saw a great black mass hit the ground, splattering dirt and men, and the black ball still coming, rolling and bouncing across the patches of snow and grass, then burrowing into the lines of his own men. He moved his horse forward, looked down the rows of his lead brigade and saw Zook riding out in front, waving his sword. Now the whole thick line, the First Brigade, began to move, and Hancock moved forward with them.

Up ahead French's men were still holding their formation, but the fences were slowing them down. Zook's brigade began to close the gap between them, the artillery taking a heavier toll, the blasts and rolling shot cutting through the bunched-up lines. The smoke began to hide the hill, and Hancock could see French himself, riding down through his men, waving and yelling, and now he understood. They had reached the canal.

Men began to drop down, out of sight, then Hancock saw them coming back up, climbing a short embankment. There were small bridges, thin rails, and the rebels had removed the planking, so the men could only cross single file. The gunners on the hill had been prepared for that, had the range and were close enough for the smaller shot, the grape and canister. Men began to fall into the canal, blown apart by the unseen swarms of hot metal.

The smoke was thicker still as Hancock reached the canal. He could not see French's lines at all, wondered if there were any lines left. His men began to jump down into the freezing water, nearly waist deep, splashing through the thin ice. Down the line he saw Zook, raising his sword at a small group of men who were moving back, pulling away from the canal, and Zook turned them around and over they went, pushed along now by the second line, closing the gap again. He thought, No, this is not good, wait, and he saw the green flags, saw men moving toward him with the green in their hats. He looked for Meagher, other officers, saw one man leading a company, rode to him through the clouds of smoke.

"Wait . . . hold them up, slow the line!" Hancock shouted. "You're moving up too fast!"

The man looked at him, stunned, did not understand, and Hancock saw: a lieutenant with the face of a scared child. He looked up, tried to see farther down the line, saw Meagher now, riding toward him, and Meagher was yelling, telling his men to wait, let the front clear out. Hancock watched him, admired him until a shell hit the ground between them, a blinding flash. A mound of dirt blew straight up in the air, and he could not see. He thought, Keep moving, General.

Some of his men had found makeshift planking for the bridges, had laid it across the rails, and now the men were quicker. Many of them did not have to jump down into the frozen icy stream. Hancock dismounted, moved with the men over the bridge, holding his horse. Once across he could see through the smoke, a ragged line out in front. French was still advancing, was moving past a small farmhouse, and Hancock rode quickly to the front of Zook's men, saw the lines straightening, the last of the barriers cleared. It will be faster now, he thought. We are getting close. He turned toward the hill, looked up the long slope, saw the mouths of the big guns pointing down at his men, the gaps still blowing through the lines, and felt a new rush of blind fury. He yelled out . . . something . . . not words, turned and saw Zook leading them on, laughing madly, wild eyes, and now they moved past him, toward the face of the hill.

Behind him, he watched for Meagher, saw the specks of green coming on, saw horsemen, the officers, bright flags in the wall of smoke, and then he saw Meagher, rode quickly toward him.

Meagher waved, had his sword high, yelled above the steady roar, "There she be, General. We're a-gettin' close. It's a hot one, that's for sure!"

Hancock did not speak, looked toward the hill, at another small farmhouse, the last of the structures. Then he could see the base of the hill and French's men out in the open, moving faster now. Some men began to run toward the hill. He saw a short stone wall, a long line running along the base of the hill. There was movement from the wall, and suddenly the entire front of the hill was a sheet of flame, a single crushing blast of massed musket fire. French's lines simply collapsed, melted away in the shower of lead. Smoke flowed across the open ground from the face of the hill. Hancock could not see, but he heard the sound again, another volley, and the balls were reaching his men now. Men were going down, small cries and grunts, the horrible slap and crack of the balls against flesh and bone, and he could begin to hear the wounded, sharp screams, and there was another volley, and around him his men were dropping down, some firing blindly toward the hill, some beginning to run away from the terrible flashes.

From the smoke in front of him, men were moving back toward him, the survivors of French's lines, lines that were completely gone. Across the field, through small clearings in the smoke, Hancock could see bodies everywhere. He looked behind him, saw his own lines still holding together, still advancing, and he yelled out, waved them on. The men saw him, still cheered him, raised their hats and held their muskets high. They moved steadily toward the great mass of guns that waited behind the stone wall. They began to pass French's men, the men who had survived by lying flat on the ground, trying to hide from the rifles. They had found a slight depression in the ground—the last hundred yards to the stone wall was up and over a small rise, and the men had found blessed cover.

Hancock saw that this was a good place to reform the lines, bring them together for the last push. He rode forward, could see over the rise to the wall, thought, Not too close, remembering Meagher's words: "A general's not much good to anyone if he gets himself killed." Zook's men were gathering below the rise now, and some of French's men were regrouping, standing with them. He saw Zook calling to them, and they began to move again, up the hill. They reached the crest and now stood within fifty yards of the wall.

Many of the men were stopping to fire, their first chance to see the clear face of the enemy, and then they were wiped away, whole groups falling at once. Hancock watched from below the rise, yelled, "No, do not stop!" but there was no one to hear him.

Behind him, dropping now into the depression, came the Irish Brigade, and he saw Meagher waving the men on, and then Meagher was falling, awkwardly, from the horse, and Hancock rushed that way and dismounted.

Meagher was surrounded by his men, the men in the green hats, and he waved them away. "No, go on, I'm all right!" He saw Hancock, pointed at the knee, the dirty bandage, and Hancock saw a neat black hole. Meagher said, "I'll be a-takin' this leg off, that's for sure. Damned thing keeps drawin' fire."

Hancock leaned over him, and Meagher looked around, began waving at his men. "Go on, move! You're almost up the hill! Go!"

He's all right, Hancock thought, and joined the line of Irishmen moving forward on foot.

They went to the crest, saw the wall, and the men kept going, broke into a run, did not stop to shoot. He watched them close in, saw the faces of the men behind the wall, many, many faces, and there was another volley, and then another, and again he could not see, and now behind him it was Caldwell's brigade. He did not see Caldwell, but still screamed at the men, and they obeyed, climbed up, moved forward with the rest. Now he had no one else to send, tried to see through the smoke, through eyes watering from the thick smell of burning powder.

He expected to see the blue coats, his men, climbing the stone wall, moving over the top, pushing the rebels out. But the smoke was too thick and the muskets were still firing. He dropped down to his knees, moved up, out into the open, crawled over a body, then another. There was a lull, and the smoke was drifting back, over his head, and now he could see, and the faces were still behind the wall, looking out over the field with the black and hungry stare of men who have not had enough, the ground in front of him spread with a vast carpet of blue.

36. CHAMBERLAIN

December 13, 1862. Late afternoon.

HOOKER'S RESERVES DID FINALLY CROSS THE RIVER, MARCHING shakily across the bouncing pontoons and through the burning and shattered town, forming their lines at the edge of the open field. It was late afternoon, and Sumner's attack had run its course. Steady streams of bloodied and hobbled men now crossed the field toward them, many passing right through the lines without speaking, others cursing their own luck, or warning the fresh troops what awaited them out there, beyond the low rise. Chamberlain did not watch them, kept his eyes to the front, stared out across the smoky plain toward the half-hidden hills, the steady roar of the muskets, the constant pounding of the big guns.

There had been no official word. No report had come down this far, but they knew the day was not a good one. Before, from across the river, they could not see what was happening in front of the stone wall, but now, as the broken units out in front of them hugged the ground and broken men flowed from the field, Chamberlain understood. His men were the reserves, and they were being sent in.

The Twentieth Maine was part of the Third Brigade of Griffin's division, Fifth Corps. Griffin's other brigades were already moving out, and Chamberlain watched them go, growing smaller and fading into the drifting smoke. Now he heard new bugles, and Ames, down the line, the familiar voice, "Advance . . . the Twentieth!" and the line began to move slowly forward.

They marched in lines three deep. Chamberlain looked to the side, down the short rows, thought, We are not very many, and this is a big damned field. To his left he saw the other regiments, men from New York, Pennsylvania, Michigan. Men like these, he thought, just farmers and shopkeepers, and now we are soldiers, and now we are about to die. The thought struck him as a certainty, and it shocked him. He did not feel afraid, felt no emotion at all, only the slow rhythm of his steps kicking through the thick grass, small, hard lumps of snow.

He had been hearing the constant sounds all day, and nothing had changed, and so it did not affect him. The sounds were closer, maybe louder, but they were the same sounds. He became curious, thought, We will see, now, won't we? We will learn something, what this is like, what it has been like for the men in front of us, the men who were in front of us at Antietam, who have done this before.

From the brigade in front of him he saw a man break, turn and run back toward him, closer, and he saw the face, the animal eyes, the pure terror. Down the line his men began to yell, taunting, and he suddenly knew that it was his job to do . . . something.

He felt at his belt, grabbed his pistol, pulled it from the holster and pointed it at the man's head. The man looked at him, the eyes clearing for a few seconds, and he stopped running, stood a few yards in front of him. Chamberlain was still moving forward, his feet in a rhythm by themselves, and the man stared at the pistol, abruptly turned and began to walk forward again, by himself, out in front of the regiment.

Chamberlain lowered the pistol, amazed, heard cheering from his men, and he stared ahead at the back of the lone soldier, thought, All right, it's all right. The instinct is in all of us, to save ourselves. But what happened to that man, what was it that made him suddenly turn?

He began to feel afraid now, a sudden wave of sickness filling him. What if *I* run? No, do not do that. You think too much. This is not about thinking, it is about . . . instinct, a different instinct than survival. He tried to think of the *cause*, yes, focus on that . . . the reason for . . . all of this. He tried to picture it, slavery, the rights of all men. . . . But the men . . . why are they doing this? No, this wasn't working. His mind was numb, he felt no great fire, no passion for any cause. Where had it gone, the excitement and enthusiasm for doing something that was so . . . necessary, his trip to the capital, to the governor? It was all vague, faint memory . . . and out in front of him the puffs of smoke and the small flashes were all that was real.

The shells began to reach them now, and the rhythm of his steps was jarred, the ground rolling and bouncing him up, and dirt spraying him, pushing him aside with a breath of hot wind. But he did not fall, looked back toward the explosion, saw . . . nothing, a gap in the line. He turned to the front, the rhythm returning, thought, There had been a man there . . . several. But his mind would not let him focus on that, and he stared ahead, saw the backs of the men out in front of him, saw the lone soldier still marching by himself. The noises were growing now, loud hisses, high screams. The ground began to bounce again, and now he could hear something else, the sounds of men, and he still focused ahead, saw the lines in front bunching up, the men gathering together, crossing a canal, and for the first time he said something, made a sound, called out to his men.

"Hold up the line, halt!" They were looking at him, would do what he told them to do, and he thought of that, of being in command, felt a strength, a new rush of energy.

He held them back, moved out by himself, closer to the canal, looked at the small fragile planks, the last of the Second Brigade crossing, forming again on the far side. He turned back, raised his sword, looked along the line, then saw, off to his left, toward the right flank of the regiment, beyond, saw . . . *nothing*. There had been other units on the right flank, two more regiments, and they were not there. He suddenly felt a cold panic, moved over that way, looking back, then saw the lines, lagging a hundred yards behind, and he saw Ames with them, in front of them, yelling angrily, bringing them on, and he felt a sudden rage, impatience. This is no time for mistakes, for stupidity.

He yelled aloud, over the heads of his men, "Get up here, on the right flank! Step it up!" and his men were turning, looking back with him, and now he saw: Ames was moving them up. Other officers, their own officers, were yelling and moving quickly along the lines, closing up the brigade.

He turned back toward the canal, felt his hands shaking, the rhythm broken now. He walked forward, stepped onto the small bridge. He waved the sword forward, and they began to form a line, began to move across on the planks. To the other side, the left flank, he saw the other regiments, saw there were no bridges, and the men began to move along the canal toward him, to the one dry crossing. No, he thought, it won't work, and he saw other officers waving swords, and now the men began to jump into the water, moving across where there was no bridge. He looked down into the canal, thick masses of blue, like piles of rock, but the men were walking around them, careful, and he saw the rocks had arms, the bottom of the canal was deep in the bodies of blue-coated men. Suddenly his stomach turned, and he shook, held it in, looked up, away, fought for control.

There was a loud rush of sound, a sudden splash, and he was sprayed with cold water. He looked down again, and there were more bodies, fresh bodies. At the far end of the canal he saw a bright flash, a rebel battery firing straight down the canal. Another great splash of water blew over the small bridge and men below him were suddenly swept away. His men began to cross with more speed, and the men now down in the canal pushed across, climbing out quickly, knowing this was not a place to wait, this was not cover. Now he was caught up in the heavy flow of men, pushed through, moved out in front waving his sword. They began to spread out again, forming the lines, and again they marched forward.

There was no rhythm now, each step was deliberate. He tried to see, to find the men in front, and there was nothing, a field of thick gray smoke. Then a hand was on his arm. It was Ames.

"You have command of the regiment! I must take charge of the right side of the line. The commanders are down. . . . God help us!" and he was gone.

Chamberlain suddenly felt awake. He climbed out of his thoughts, saw the faces looking at him, waiting for him to lead them. He pointed the sword toward the thick unknown, yelled, "Men! Forward! Keep it up!"

The sounds came by him one at a time now, the single terrible whiz of the musket ball, the hot whoosh of streaking shrapnel, the air hitting him in short, hot bursts. He still could not see, moved forward through the thick smoke, did not look at the bodies as he passed, the red and blue poured out into great heaps over the white snow. He looked back to his men again. They were still with him, and he gripped the sword hard, dug his fingers into the steel of the scabbard, but it was not enough. He reached for the pistol, held it tightly in his other hand, still moving forward.

There was a break, a small gap in the flowing smoke, and he could see a wide depression in the ground and a shallow rise, men in blue crouching down, some with muskets, firing, reloading, vast numbers that were just . . . bodies. Beyond, he saw a stone wall, and he raised the pistol, his hand shaking with a boiling rage. He was not thinking, his mind did not tell him what to do. He began to yell, screaming now at the muskets pointing at him from behind the wall, the face of the enemy, and his voice blended with the great roar around him. There was a burst of flame from the wall, and around him men fell, and he aimed the pistol, fired, and fired again.

THERE WERE MEN ALL AROUND HIM, VOICES AND CRIES, AND HE lay without moving, staring up at the darkness, the night sky. What was left of the regiment, and of the brigade, was lying flat around him in the depression, out in front of the stone wall, and for today it was over.

He could feel the cold of the ground under his back, felt it creeping up, into his hands and arms and feet, and he thought, This is not good . . . we will freeze to death. They had heavier coats, of course, had left them in the town, had left everything in the town except what they would need to fight. But they were still out here, still facing the enemy, and would have to wait through a freezing night before anything else would happen, before there could be any relief.

He began to shiver, flexed his fingers, wrapped himself with his arms, and now shivered more. He raised his head just slightly and looked around him, saw a great field of black shapes. He began to move, slid along the hard ground, moved up alongside one of the shapes, said in a low, hoarse voice, "You, there. Are you wounded?" He waited, then reached out a hand, touched the blue cloth, prodded harder, poked the man's stiff body, and he understood.

"Truly sorry, old fellow. But . . . I need to . . . " He slid closer, pressed his body up against the mass, grabbed the man's loose coat, unwrapped the body slightly, pulled a flap out over him and lay still again, but it was not enough. He rose up, saw another mass a few feet up the rise, pulled himself along, prodded again, and again, there was no reply. As he slid back down, he grabbed the man's foot, pulled him down the hill, put the man on the other side of him, pulled another flap of coat out over him. Now he lay between them, thought, All right, so now you will be warm. He pushed up hard against one man, pulled the other closer still, then lay his head down, his hat for a pillow.

It had been dark for about an hour, and he began to hear new sounds, the numbness of the shock, the natural anesthetic of the wounded giving way to the raw pain. The sounds began to grow, spreading out over the entire field, soft cries broken by short screams, words and meaningless noises, curses and prayers. The sounds filled his mind, there was no shutting them out, and he stared up at the stars, tried to see beyond the sounds, but they pulled him back. There were other voices now as well, the men who were not wounded, who were scattered through the others, through the lifeless forms, as he was, and they began to shout, some of them yelling at the wounded to stop, to be quiet. Some were angry, loud hostile screams, others begged, pleaded. He kept staring up, distracting himself, trying not to hear, but the sounds were now filling every space, and his head began to throb . . . *the sounds were coming from inside, louder now, no voices, no words, but a steady, high scream, and he felt his head would burst, his mind shattering, blowing into a thousand pieces, the pieces of the men around him. . . .*

And then he was suddenly awake. The sound was gone, and he felt the cold again, felt the hard masses pressing on him from either side. Above him there was a face, a man crouching low over him, and the man pulled the flaps back, looked at him, and Chamberlain said, "Excuse me, but I was sleeping. . . ."

The man jumped, lurched back, said in a burst, "For the love of God!" and crawled away, sat for a moment in the dark, said in a whisper, "Sorry. I thought you was with the Beyond."

Chamberlain raised himself up, could see across the field now. The moon had come up, and men were moving around, crawling among the dead, pulling off coats and shirts and boots. There were men with stretchers, lifting some of the wounded, carrying them back toward the wagons waiting far behind the lines. The sounds of the wounded were still there, but not as many, softer sounds, and he thought, Many have died, maybe the lucky ones.

He propped himself up on his elbows, told himself, You are in command, maybe you should . . . This had never been discussed; Ames had not told him what to do in this situation. Ames . . . he wondered if he was alive. He crawled out from the shelter of the bodies, slid along painfully, then saw more of the stretcher bearers, standing, and he rose to his knees, tried to look around. He wanted to say something, to call out, how many were still alive . . . Tom. *Tom!* He felt a burst of cold in his gut.

"Tom!" The noise exploded through the cold night, and he listened, waited, and then he heard other voices, other yells.

"Tom!" and laughing, and he looked that way, over the hill, toward the stone wall, and now there were more voices.

"Tom! You home, Tom?" and along the hill, across the field, his own men began to take up the call.

"No Tom here!"

"Hey, Tom! You got a message!"

He felt a rush of anger, wanted to yell again, and now he heard another voice, one single sound from below him, down in the bottom of the wide depression:

"Lawrence!"

He started to rise, to stand up, thought, I can see, the moon is bright, maybe I can see where he is . . . and suddenly there was a flash, several more, and he dropped down, lay flat, and around him other men began to yell, "Keep it down, stay down. You'll draw fire!"

He lay still for a minute, raised himself up slowly, thought, He is alive, thank God. He turned, crawled back up to his bed, slid in tight between the bodies, pulled again at the flaps of cloth.

There were clouds now, moving across the face of the bright moon, and he could see fewer stars. There was a new sound, the wind, a steady growing breeze, and he thought, No, please, no storm, no snow, not tonight. But the clouds were thin, and the moon was still there, shining through. The breeze flowed across the field, and he rose one more time, felt the sharp chill, lay back down, said in a low whisper to the bodies, to his shelter, "God forgive me."

He lay still for a long time, watched the clouds slide past the moon, and the wind began to change, to shift direction, and suddenly there was a noise, a rustle, a knocking. He sat up, looked to the side, up over the rise, saw a dark shape in the distance, a battered house. The noise came from there, but he could see nothing. He lay back down, and the noise kept coming, and he tried to imagine what it was, pictured a house in his mind, the wind, thought, A *window*. And he knew it was a curtain, a blind, slapping against an open window frame. He felt relief, let out a long breath. He lay still again, and the noise still came, the sound growing, pushing everything else away, and his mind was filled again, and the noise became words, a hard, cold whisper.

"Never, forever . . . never, forever . . ."

HE WOKE TO THE DIM LIGHT OF A FOGGY DAWN AND THE sound of muskets. There were scattered shots, small protests from the stone wall, and his men learned quickly that they had no choice but to stay low, keeping their heads barely above the surface of the ground. The depression gave them cover, broke the clean line of fire from the wall, but higher up, on the face of the hill, the big guns still watched over them, and so Chamberlain stayed put.

The word had been passed, the Ninth Corps would advance, come up behind them, renew the attack, a strong force moving up to replace them. It had the logic of something official, and so he believed it, did not distrust that it was only the wishful thinking, the careless fantasies of pinned-down officers. By mid-morning there was no attack, only the scattered firing, and he could see up the rise, across the shallow hill, could easily pick out the men who were still alive, the ones who held a musket as they took their careful shots, reloaded while lying down, then took aim again. There was little action anywhere else, no distant sounds, no long-range guns. He began to think about the army on the hill in front of them, wondered if they were coming, to sweep away this small line of troops who lay flat in the thin snow.

He tried to reach a better vantage point, make some reconnaissance, slid on his stomach, and a rifle ball plowed into the snow beside him. He backed down the hill, said to himself, All right, so much for *that*. He passed beside more bodies, pulled one down with him, lay it on the uphill side, above his head, toward the enemy, thought, He would understand, I would want them to do this with me. Then he pushed that from his mind, was not at all sure if it was the truth.

There was no reaching Tom, and he had not seen Ames. He heard some talk that orders were being issued, and it sounded like Ames was moving about, farther back, on safer ground. He realized that Ames might think he was dead. I need to get word to him somehow, he thought, find out what I should be doing. Suddenly, there was a flurry of musket fire, and he turned, looked out over one of the bodies and saw a line of gray soldiers moving beyond the crest of the hill, coming out, forward, firing into the open flank of the men in the depression. He yelled out, a warning, and others were yelling as well, and now the shots were being answered, his men firing at the new line of skirmishers. He pulled the pistol out, laid it across his chest and raised his head slightly, just to see past the body beside him. He saw a man raise a musket, spotting him, and he dropped his head down, heard the crack and the dull slap of lead against his protector. Now there were other shots, balls whizzing inches above him, and more lead hit the man beside him, thuds and thumps. He could feel the impact, the shock passing through the man's body, and he wanted to sit up, fire the pistol, felt a new anger, wanted to yell out, "For the love of God, let him lie in peace." There was more firing now, from below him, and he heard yelling and new sounds, and a line of his own men began to push by him, toward the rebel line. Now the volleys were slow and scattered, and he could hear his men, talking, yelling, they had pushed the rebels back.

He sat up, saw the blessed blue coats moving slowly back down the hill, spreading out just above him, and he said, "Hey! Good work . . . good work, thank you!"

A man moved down toward him, slid heavily along the ground, and he saw the round face of the Irishman, Kilrain.

"Well, Colonel, me laddie, we was a-wond'rin' if you was still among the living." He looked at the bodies on either side. "Got to hand it to you, Colonel, you have a talent for pickin' your friends. This one's . . . done his bit. . . ." He reached across, rolled the other man toward him, and Chamberlain saw the expression change, the bright smile vanish, replaced by a look of recognition and horror.

Kilrain said, "Oh, Mother of God." He let the man go, turned away, stared down at the ground.

Chamberlain wanted to ask who it was, felt the bulk of the man still pressing against his side, thought, No, don't, let it go.

Kilrain shook his head, looked at Chamberlain, said, "We lost many a fine man . . . a few fine *boys* too. Don't seem like we can do much of anything today. Nobody coming up to help us, it appears. We're scattered out all over this field, the whole division, more. The rebs . . . they seem pretty happy to sit tight. We run off that one bunch. A few of them didn't make it back. . . . Don't expect they'll try *that* again."

"Sergeant . . . I need to get back . . . to find Colonel Ames. Can you . . . is it all right to move back down the hill? You seem to have been able. . . ."

"Come on, Colonel, just keep your head down. The rest of ya too. Stay low."

Chamberlain slid out from his human shelter, fought the urge to look at the face of the man Kilrain knew, and they began to move down the hill. Others were moving up now, strengthening the skirmish line, and across the wide hill he saw the men in a solid snaking line, lying just below the crest, just out of the line of fire from the wall, and most were waiting, ready. He wondered, Will the order come, the new attack? He was beginning to feel the excitement of a new day, thought, Yes, we can do it again . . . we're already here. There just aren't very many of us. He could see back across the field, all the way to the town. There were still vast numbers of men, some in formation, strong lines of blue, and the sight thrilled him. Yes, come on!

They reached the bottom of the depression, and Kilrain led him along, over the mass of bodies, and now Chamberlain could see horses, officers, flags, some organization, back out of range of the muskets. He began to walk upright, heard a musket ball whiz overhead, and he ducked.

Kilrain watched him, said, "Colonel, me darlin', if that one was meant for you . . . there'd be no need to be duckin'."

He stood upright again, looked at the officers, finally saw Ames. He felt another thrill, wanted to run up to him, show him he had survived after all, and Ames looked at him, nodded, a quick, short smile. Chamberlain understood, saw now General Griffin, and Colonel Strong Vincent, of the Eighty-third Pennsylvania. Griffin was speaking.

". . . while Stockton is unable. Colonel Vincent, you are now in command of the Third Brigade. Keep the men in position here until dark. You will be relieved as soon as possible."

Vincent saluted, said, "Yes, sir," then noticed Chamberlain, stared for a second, said, "Colonel . . . are you all right?"

Chamberlain nodded, said, "Yes, sir. I was pinned down . . . up on the rise . . . the wall." He felt suddenly very tired, looked at Ames, who smiled again.

Ames said, "General Griffin, Colonel Vincent, this is Lieutenant Colonel Chamberlain. I spoke of him earlier."

Griffin held out his hand, caught Chamberlain by surprise, and he stared numbly. Griffin waited, kept the hand out, and Chamberlain reached for it weakly.

Griffin said, "Fine work, Colonel, keeping your men up close like that. Not many men made it that far . . . fine work."

Chamberlain felt the hand release, and he nodded, felt himself smiling, a big stupid grin, tried to control it, saw the faces of the others watching him, said, "Thank you, General. Are we going to attack?"

There was a silent moment, and the others looked at Griffin, who stared down at the ground, then looked hard at Chamberlain. "Colonel," he said, "there are no new orders. The commanding general has not given instructions to General Hooker, and General Hooker has not given instructions to me. You have done your job, Colonel. All of these men on this field have done their job. Unless something changes, that job is complete."

Chamberlain stared at Griffin's face, saw deep lines and tired eyes, and he looked at Ames, and Ames raised his hand, cocked a finger, a small quick signal to move away, *follow me.*

Ames moved slowly, stepped over bodies. Chamberlain struggled to keep up. His legs were not working well. "Colonel," he said, "what happened? How can we be through?"

Ames stopped, said, "Because we are. It's over. We sent forty thousand men across this field, Colonel, and it was not enough. They are still up there." He pointed to the hill, and Chamberlain could see it clearly now, the entire hill in front of him, the guns perched high on top, small flags waving. "They're waiting for us to try again. It was suicide, Colonel. It would be still."

Chamberlain stared at the hill, then looked down, across the wide field, the crouching lines and small groups, the living and the dead, and he felt something swelling inside him, something painful and sickening, and he wanted to be angry, to say something important, some loud pronouncement against the raw stupidity, the tragedy of the waste, sorrow for the dead. But he had nothing left, he had given all he had the day before, and Ames turned away, moving toward the long rise. Chamberlain began to understand, to accept the truth, that there was nothing left to do but wait for the sun to drop and the field to grow dark. Then they would lead the men back across the field and pull away from the guns of the enemy.

37. LEE

December 14, 1862

As the sun went down, it began to rain, cold, hard drops, and he found shelter, stayed near his tent. He had been at the top of his hill all day, waiting, watching. His eyes were worn, tired from the long hours of looking through the field glasses, and he felt a great need for sleep. Taylor had brought him a plate of food, and he sat now just inside the flaps of his tent, gave a silent blessing, *Thank You*, ate gratefully, and thought again of the great open field below him: *Thy will be done.*

He had expected a new attack, all of them had, and the sunken road behind that wonderful stone wall was lined with fresh troops, anxious men who could see the field in front of them, the horrible piles of blue bodies, and they were ready for more, ready to resume the slaughter.

He thought of Thomas Cobb, the fiery clean-cut Georgian whose brigade had first filled that road, and Maxcy Gregg, the charming, educated man from South Carolina—both were dead. There had been many . . . good soldiers, good leaders. Where would they come from now?

He cleaned the plate, wiped at thick gravy with a hard biscuit. It was still raining, and he pushed back the flap of the tent, looked out, saw men around a sputtering fire, thick smoke.

Taylor saw him, came over quickly, splashing through mud. "General, can I get you anything?" he asked. "Was the supper acceptable?"

Lee nodded, handed him the plate, said, "Thank you, Major, it was fine, quite good. I would like to speak with General Longstreet. Please send someone to his camp. Be sure to express my apologies for bringing the general out in this weather."

"Sir!" Taylor stood upright, saluted, and moved toward the fire. Lee watched, saw one of the staff move quickly away. He let the flap drop again, moved over to his cot, lay down and closed his eyes for a moment, just a quick rest, his mind drifting out . . . *over a wide flat ocean, thick waves of blue, rolling against a rocky shore, the sweet soft rumble of the surf, and the voice of* . . . Longstreet.

"General, forgive me for waking you."

He blinked, tried to see, sat up and shook his head. "No, please, General," he said. "I will join you." He stood, pushed aside the flaps, stepped out into the chill. The rain had stopped, giving way to a light breeze. Longstreet stood towering before him in a heavy overcoat, his face hidden by the wide floppy hat. Lee moved to the fire, held out his hands, felt a thick cloud of smoke engulf him. He backed away, said, "Too wet. Winter . . . we should not be out here."

"We won't be, much longer."

Lee looked toward the voice. "General, do you have some information?"

Longstreet removed the hat, pulled out a short cigar, lit it behind his dirty white gloves, said, "They spent all afternoon digging trenches, by the town. Those men out there, in the field: they will be gone by morning. The skirmishers down below have been talking to them, taunting them a bit . . . you know how it goes, sir. 'Come and get some more,' all of that. The Yanks are talking pretty freely about . . . about all of it, I suppose. Mainly, they're pretty sure they've been left out there alone. Not many kind words for Burnside. General McLaws brought me a prisoner, an officer, Pennsylvania man, says he's not going back, thinks he's been led by fools, a lost cause. Says there's no attack coming, the generals have no stomach for another day like yesterday."

Lee stared at the struggling fire, said, "Dangerous talk from an officer. You believe him?"

"He says they're expecting us to advance, drive them back. That's the reason for the trenches. They think we'll try to push them across the river."

Lee shook his head, rubbed his fingers through his beard. "No, there will be no advance. We have no cause to move off the good ground. We have beaten them from this ground . . . we will do it again."

"I don't believe they will give us the chance."

"I hope you are wrong, General. This has been a war of missed opportunities. We have let them get away before. I do not wish to make that mistake again. We cannot continue to lose men . . . good officers. . . . We cannot trade casualties with an enemy that has much greater numbers and much greater resources. If we are to win this war, we must strike a decisive blow . . . force him to admit defeat." He turned away from the fire, walked slowly toward the crest of the tall hill, toward the wide, dark field. "He will try again . . . maybe to the south, below General Jackson. It should have been his plan from the start . . . not here, not against these hills. We must tell General Stuart to observe him closely, watch for movement by Franklin's forces. General Reynolds is down there. He is a good commander, knows how to position his troops."

Longstreet stayed close behind him, and Lee still moved forward, reached the crest and began to walk down, between the batteries. The clouds were thinning now, the moon reflecting on the flat plain. There were scattered shots from below, from the base of the long hill to the left, the men in the sunken road firing at motion in the moonlight.

Longstreet chewed on the cigar, put the hat back on his head, said, "Sir, John Reynolds will not move anywhere Burnside does not tell him to move. It is still Burnside's army. We have beaten him. There will be another day, but it will not be here."

Lee said nothing, watched the shadows of the small clouds move across the field, and suddenly there was a bright flash, a searing band of color jumped out of the sky, and he flinched, raised his hand up to his face. But there was no sound, it was completely silent, and now he saw a wide sheet of green, and the light spread out over him, rippled, then was gone. To the north there was another, turning slightly red, and around them the men began cheering, yelling.

Longstreet said, "The aurora . . . the northern lights."

Lee kept staring up, the lights dancing and flickering, then spreading out wide, then moving away. "My God . . . I've never seen anything like this before. Are you . . . certain, General?"

"Oh, yes, sir. Used to see them once in a while in Pennsylvania, when I was at Carlisle. Quite a show sometimes." Longstreet began to chuckle, was enjoying the spectacle.

Lee said, "No . . . it is more than that, General. It is a sign. We have pleased God. He is honoring the dead. A sight like this cannot be . . . just an accident. This is Sunday . . . the Sabbath. No, it is no accident."

Longstreet said nothing, stared upward, and the calls were echoing now, across the field, soldiers on both sides absorbing the wondrous sight. Longstreet looked down at the flat ground, saw the colors reflecting off what was left of the snow, thought, We are all sharing this . . . both sides. If God has smiled on us, then He will also smile on them.

DECEMBER 15, 1862

THE FOG RETURNED, AND HE WOKE TO MORE WET COLD, AND AN army still shivering. Lee pushed out of the tent, could see up toward the top of his hill, rolling mist and dark shapes. He looked for Taylor, for the others, saw no one, thought, They cannot be sleeping, must be . . . breakfast. He thought of going toward the food, tried to pick up the smells, but the heavy mist was in the way, and he walked the other way, back up over the crest. He saw small groups of men gathering around the guns. Someone saw him and hats were raised quietly. They knew by now not to shout, not to alert the enemy. Down the hill he could see nothing, just a sea of thick gray, and he listened hard, heard voices, movement, the sound of tin coffee cups, nothing else.

He turned, climbed back up to the crest, toward his tent, saw a man kneeling, working on the fire, wet wood and quiet curses. The smells began to reach him, coffee, fresh bread. He shivered, felt a growl in his stomach, saw men moving toward him, carrying plates, and Taylor quickly hurried up to him.

"Sir, I have been looking for you. A courier is here, from General Jackson." He turned, looked for the man, and Lee spotted him, the young Pendleton, carrying a plate piled high.

Pendleton saluted with his free hand, cleared away a mouthful of food, said, "Good morning, General. Sorry . . . we have not yet had breakfast in General Jackson's camp. Sir, General Jackson offers his respects and reports that the enemy is no longer in front of our position, sir. The general made a reconnaissance in force early this morning, hoping to catch the enemy in the fog . . . and they were no longer there, sir."

Lee looked for a stool, moved over, sat, said, "Are you referring to the forces under General Franklin? Captain, you're talking about sixty thousand troops. They did not just vanish. Has the general spoken with General Stuart . . . have they scouted downriver?" His voice began to rise and he felt a tightening in his chest.

"General, the enemy has withdrawn back across the river. When our troops found no resistance, they kept going. They reached the edge of the river and they could hear the enemy, on the other side. The sound carries very well in the fog, sir. The pontoon bridges are gone, sir, cut loose from the bank."

Lee stared up at the young face, thought, It cannot be . . . Longstreet was right. He straightened his back, said to Taylor, "Major, summon General Longstreet. I want to know what is down below us here. I do not wish to wait for the fog to lift to find out. Captain Pendleton, you may return to General Jackson. Please express my appreciation for his diligence. And please remind General Jackson that we do not wish to give the enemy an opportunity by exposing our troops to those guns on the heights. When the fog lifts, your advance will surely receive a concentration of artillery fire."

Pendleton saluted, nodded. "Yes, sir. General Jackson has already ordered the men back. There is only a line of pickets at the river, sir."

Lee thought, He has done all this . . . so early? He remembered the joke, passed along by his staff: to Jackson, dawn is one minute after midnight.

"Very well, Captain. You are dismissed."

Pendleton slid the contents of the plate into his pockets, moved quickly to his horse and disappeared in a flurry of muddy hoofprints. Lee leaned forward, rested his arms on the tops of his thighs, felt another shiver. Longstreet will be here soon, he thought, and I must know. He stood, flexed the stiff, sore hands, moved toward the warmth of the growing fire.

THE MEN AT THE BASE OF THE HILL ALREADY KNEW. MANY HAD ventured out, another night of scavenging, taking from the dead what they no longer needed. But this time they found that most were buried, shallow and crude graves, dug with bayonets and shell fragments. It was one thing to strip a dead man, but once he was in the ground, in the earth, it was a line they would not cross, and so they had come back to the safety of the wall with few new prizes.

McLaws had ordered more of them out now, a more organized line, probing, easing slowly along, down the slope of the incline, into the depression. Like Jackson's men, when they did not find the enemy, when there was no rifle fire, no obstacle, they pressed on, gradually picking up speed, stalking less quietly and with more courage. They had gone all the way to the edge of the town, crossed over the trenches dug the day before, and once they knew there was no one there, they began a party, a feast on the spoils left behind, knapsacks and blankets.

Word had gone back to McLaws, then to Longstreet, and Longstreet had come to Lee.

The fog was nearly gone now, and the sky began to clear, cold and blue. Lee and Longstreet reached the edge of the town together. Lee moved Traveller carefully down, across the fresh trench, and Longstreet followed, and in front of them nervous skirmishers began to move out through the streets of Fredericksburg, probing through the remains of the houses, making sure there was no one waiting.

Longstreet pointed, said, "Over the river . . . they're back on the heights. They may begin to shell us . . . the town."

Lee stopped the horse, stared over to the far hill, said nothing. From the right, toward the far edge of the town, they heard horses, and the foot soldiers dropped down and raised their muskets. Lee saw a flag and a man in a tall, plumed hat. In the street an officer yelled out to hold fire. It was Stuart.

"Good morning, General! General Longstreet. I heard you were riding into town. I hope you don't mind if I join you."

Lee nodded, said, "Of course, General, you are always welcome." He saw a broad smile, a man full of victory. "General Stuart, it was risky for you to ride across that plain with your flag. The enemy could certainly see you clearly."

Stuart bowed. "Thank you for your concern, General. We did not unfurl the flag until we reached the safety of the buildings. Besides, General, my staff and I have a way of escaping the guns of the enemy. Their marksmen are no match for a good horseman."

Longstreet made a sound, and Lee did not look at him, said, "All the same, General . . . there are too few of us to present the enemy with careless opportunity."

The smile faded and Stuart nodded solemnly, a scolded child.

Lee moved the horse forward, saw an officer running through the streets toward them, waving, yelling. "General . . . it's barbarism! The devil himself! You have to see . . . !" The man turned, waved them on, ran back down the street.

They rode ahead, followed the man's path, rounded a corner and reached the first row of houses, many still partially intact. Lee stared, looked down the street to heaping piles of debris, saw many more piles beyond, shattered furniture. He dismounted and the others followed. He walked toward the homes, felt the cracking of glass under his feet. The street was covered with the contents of the houses. There were mirrors, smashed from their frames, paintings ripped and torn, clothing—dresses, men's suits, a bridal gown—soaking up muddy water. He turned, walked down a side street, saw more of the same, began to move quicker, to the next main street, saw a huge pile of broken furniture, pieces of porcelain, grand vases and small pitchers, dishes, cups, all shattered into pieces. In front of one house a pile of books lay in the mud of the yard, covers ripped off, bindings split, and finally he stopped, felt the hot anger tighten his chest. He clenched his fists through the soreness, lowered his head.

"God . . . " He fought the anger, felt the sharp edge of the curse rising inside him, held it hard, pushed it back, away. "God, *forgive* them for what they have done."

Longstreet moved up beside him, and Lee still stared down, his eyes closed now, and Longstreet tried to think of something, said, "It's a real war. This is what war can do."

Lee did not look up, said, "No, General. This is not the work of soldiers. That man was right . . . it is the devil himself. It is the rape of the innocent." He raised his head, looked around again, and Longstreet saw tears, red swollen eyes. Lee turned then, walked back through the great piles of destruction. Longstreet heard a voice, Stuart, raw indignation, angry sounds, and he came up beside Longstreet, wanted to say something to Lee. Longstreet held up an arm, held him back.

Stuart said, "The whole town . . . barbarism . . . everything is destroyed! He has to do something about this!"

Longstreet watched Lee mount the horse, said, "He will, General, he will."

38. HANCOCK

December 15, 1862

The snow was nearly gone on the heights, the warmer rain washing much of it away into the river, and the hillside was slick and muddy. All day the troops had moved up the hill, forming camps behind the long rise, spreading out behind the guns. What was left of his division was now far back in the trees, behind the old mansion.

He had spent most of the morning with the paperwork, his great talent, and this time it was not supplies he counted, but men, the casualties. Word came up, passed from the squadrons, to the companies and regiments, and then to the brigades, and while other commanders were still tending to their own staffs, or the replacement of horses, Hancock was working with the papers. He had to know.

He had taken over five thousand men to the stone wall, taken them to within twenty-five yards, the closest anyone had gotten, and all three of his brigades, Zook and Meagher and Caldwell, had been decimated. They had lost nearly forty percent of their strength, over two thousand casualties. Once he saw the figure, he handed the report to his staff, could not complete it, not yet, and left the men behind. He walked back to the river, passed through the undamaged batteries that still watched the town, the guns that could not help them.

Hancock moved with careful steps, his boots sliding in the soft mud and small patches of ice. He walked upriver, away from the army, walked to the place in the river he had seen before, where the cattle had come across, where his men could have crossed days earlier. A decision, he thought. A command decision.

He understood command, understood the value of discipline, it was the most basic lesson a soldier could learn. If you were asked, you offered your input, your suggestions, and in the end you did what the commander told you to do. It was simple and straightforward, and it was the only way to run an army. And this time it had been a horrible disaster.

He found a rock, climbed up, found a dry spot and sat down. Across the river he could see the burnt and crushed buildings in Fredericksburg, the debris piled along the streets, the scattered ruins of people's lives, lives that were changed forever. His men had done that. Not all of it, of course. The whole corps had seemed to go insane, had turned the town into some kind of violent party, a furious storm that blew out of control, and he could not stop it. The commanders had ordered the provost guards at the bridges to let no goods leave the town, nothing could be carried across the bridges, and so what the men could not keep, what they could not steal, they had just destroyed. And now, he thought, the people will return, trying to rescue some fragile piece of home, and they will find this . . . and they will learn something *new* about war, more than the quiet nightmare of leaving your home behind. They will learn that something happens to men, men who have felt no satisfaction, who have absorbed and digested defeat after bloody stupid defeat, men who up to now have done mostly what they were told to do. And when those men begin to understand that it is not anything in *them*, no great weakness or inferiority, but that it is the leaders, the generals and politicians who tell them what to do, that the fault is *there*, after a while they will stop listening. Then the beast, the collective anger, battered and bloodied, will strike out, will respond to the unending sights of horror, the deaths of friends and brothers, and it will not be fair or reasonable or just, since there is no intelligence in the beast. They will strike out at whatever presents itself, and here it was the harmless and innocent lives of the people of Fredericksburg.

He stared at the town for a long moment, the church steeples that still rose high and had somehow survived. At least you will have that, he thought. He wondered how strong their faith could be, after . . . He glanced up, looked toward God, something he rarely did, said to himself, *All right, help them. Give them some strength to start over, rebuild what they have lost. If this is Your will, then explain that to them. I surely cannot.*

He could see rebel soldiers in the town, men on horses, flags, but they were not in force, were not there to set up a line of defense. The big guns were still up here, after all, and by now Lee would know there was no need for a defense. It was over.

In the river below him the pontoon bridges were still fastened to the near shore, but had drifted down with the current, lay flat against the bank, and he could see men moving beside them, starting their work, untying them, salvaging what was worth keeping. He laughed, a humorless chuckle. It will be a long time before this army crosses a river on those things again, he thought. Maybe we should just cut them loose, let them drift in long strings down the widening river. They might make it all the way to the ocean, or hang up, clogging the river, preventing supplies from moving up this way. Might be a better weapon than these damned guns.

He rubbed his face, told himself to keep it under control. He knew he was angry, and an officer cannot be angry, does not have the luxury of the good old-fashioned cleansing temper, of walking up to headquarters with a pint of whiskey and two hard fists, kicking down the door and launching a bolt of lightning through the face of the man who did this. He felt himself shake. Yes, that would be very damned nice. The whiskey would be easy, there was always some around. He could even picture the scene, the whole thing, the staff officers moving to stop him, and he would brush them aside, the pale and weak men who did not dirty themselves with soldiers' work, and there would be Burnside, the fat round face staring up at him with raw terror, and he would pull him up by the collar . . . no, he would grab the sides of his face by those ridiculous whiskers, and Burnside would scream out, "Have pity, mercy!" And he would say, "They are all gone. You sent them across that river and watched them die . . . *you fat, bloody idiot.*"

He laid his face down in his hands, felt it pour up out of him, tried to cry, felt his eyes fill, and then it cut off, would not come. He could still see the looks on the faces, the pieces of broken and blasted men, *his* men, still running at the wall, right into the face of the muskets; and after the blinding flash, if they were still standing, they still ran forward. How can we expect them to keep doing that? It is not just training, you do not train a man to face death, he either will or he won't. And so many of them *will*.

He thought of Burnside again, thought, At least he knows what he did. Hancock still loved McClellan, would always consider him a friend, but McClellan did not understand, did not seem to grasp why a battle was lost, that he might have done something differently, better, faster. He would never blame the men, of course, but always looked behind him, to Washington, always found a conspiracy, some way to blame . . . *them*. But Burnside had accepted his failure, had even tried to lead another assault, ride out in front of his old Ninth Corps by himself, lead them up to that damned stone wall, die as the others had died.

It was a foolish gesture, and no one ever considered letting him go, and even he had understood that the absurd plan would kill a great many more good soldiers in yet another suicidal assault.

Lincoln will certainly replace him, Hancock thought. He went through the names: Franklin, Sumner, Hooker. None of them seemed to inspire much of anything. There was Reynolds, Baldy Smith, even Couch: a better group than the first, probably. But there was always the issue of rank, of seniority. And this was still the army.

He saw clouds forming now, a long low bank far to the west, back behind Lee's hills, more dark winter. We will do nothing for a while, he thought. Good, let them rest. Christmas . . . He thought of his son. My God, he is nearly ten years old. And he wants to be a soldier. He remembered Mira's last letter, the toy gun, fighting imaginary rebs in the backyard. No, he will not get the chance. The war may last . . . but he will not go, not *ever*.

He stood up, stretched, felt a stinging pain, his stomach, a wound he had not even noticed until it was over. Something . . . a ball, shrapnel, had torn his shirt, grazed a raw red line on his skin. Lucky man, he thought. If it had been an inch closer . . .

He stepped down from the rock, slid in the mud, steadied himself. Best get back, he thought. They're probably looking for me. Ought to find Couch, talk to him. And Meagher, his leg. He started back along the hill, was surprised to see a man higher up the hill, sitting against a tree, a civilian. The man was writing, had a pad of paper perched on his knee, and Hancock turned, climbed up closer, and the man looked up, surprised.

"Hello . . . you're . . . a general. One of the *leaders* of our fine young men." There was heavy sarcasm in his voice, and Hancock let it pass, nodded.

"Hancock. Winfield Hancock."

The man looked up again, wide eyes, said, "Oh, General Hancock. It is a pleasure to meet you. Not too many generals on this field to whom I could say that. You are very highly regarded, General . . . which is also a rare comment."

Hancock watched the man, who kept writing; a small man, older, thin gray hair, wire-rimmed glasses.

"I don't know you, sir. Are you an artist?"

The man laughed, put down the pen, said, "Well, yes, certainly I am. In the same way as you, I suppose. Anyone who rises to the top of his profession must have some artistry. In fact, I am a reporter. Have you heard of the *Cincinnati Commercial*?"

"No, sorry, I'm from Pennsylvania."

"No matter. There's a good many in Cincinnati who haven't heard of her either."

"You're writing about what happened here?"

"What happened here has already been dispatched. By this morning my paper, and most others, have already given the people the news. Another chapter of disaster in the ever lengthening tragedy. No, General, I am writing a column, a commentary. From time to time there are people in Cincinnati who actually seem to care about what I think."

"So, may I ask?"

"What I think? What does it matter, General? You have only one duty, only one opinion to guide you, that of your commander. We civilians have little influence over either your actions or your thoughts. My audience is interested in hearing the point of view that does not flow through a headquarters, is not censored by the official rationale that, alas, war is a necessary evil, and thus any tragedy or idiocy is just a small part of the greater curse, which of course you all deplore. The people have heard all that, General. What they do not often hear is some honesty, the uncensored view of someone outside of your bloody little fraternity."

"I assure you, Mister . . ."

"Bolander, Cyrus Bolander."

"I assure you, Mr. Bolander, we do not all share the same official view of events. The commanding general has a responsibility to speak for his army, but he does not tell us what to think."

The man looked at his pad, then back at Hancock, said, "Hmmm, well that may be, General. All right, fine. Here." He handed the pad up to Hancock. "That's my column. Forgive me if you find my words a bit harsh."

Hancock turned the pad around, saw the writing of a skilled hand, neat straight lines, and he began to read. "It has never been possible for men to show more valor, or generals to manifest less judgment . . ."

He stopped, looked at Bolander, said, "No, sir. I do not find your words too harsh. Perhaps they are not harsh enough."

PART FOUR

39. CHAMBERLAIN

JANUARY 1863

CHRISTMAS HAD BEEN WHITE AND COLD, AND THEY DID NOT talk about the men who were no longer there. Griffin's division moved out away from the river, spread out into winter quarters around an obscure place known as Stoneman's Switch.

They had dug shallow pits in the hard ground, piled logs around for short walls, then capped the huts with what had been their tents. It was cramped and dark, but it kept them warm. But the warmth also softened the ground beneath them, and so the huts became soggy dens of mud and sickness.

They did not celebrate the New Year. Burnside would not allow the army to sit quietly while his great failure haunted him, and so he sent troops out, up the river, small reconnaissance patrols and larger probes, as though by the effort he could somehow discover some soft vulnerability in Lee's lines, some undiscovered part of the countryside where the army could redeem itself, and thus redeem him. Chamberlain led the regiment on such a probe, had done nothing to create any miracle, only the men having passed the time over the New Year without having to huddle together in the crude huts.

His feet were cold. They were always cold. He walked among the huts, could hear the squishing sound of his boots now, the ground softening, the weather warming slightly. He looked up to the sun, thought, So, what now? An early spring? The weather over Christmas had been brutal, a heavy, wet cold that even the men from Maine found miserable. Now he felt a slight warmth, looked into the bright glare above him. Damned strange. He thought of Maine, the dependability of the winter. By November it was there, without doubt, and the snow would come, and it was consistent and definite, and you worked around it, understood it was simply part of life. It would stay there often until April, and then you began to think once more of spring. He thought of the simplicity, the four seasons. It was a good system. But in Virginia there was no system. The cold gave way, a day or two of warm air, and the snow would melt, turning the ground to soft glue, and then without warning it would snow again, sometimes a foot or more, or a hard freeze would catch them by surprise, torturing the men, who had begun to lighten their load, letting down their guard. And so they would prepare for the worst again, scramble into the huts, and then it would warm up again. Chamberlain thought, I will not miss this.

They were nearly three weeks into the new year, and did not believe anything serious would happen until an honest spring came upon them, but now there were orders, and most of the huge army was stirring around them, new activity. Ames had come around early, told Chamberlain to bring the men together. They were to begin a new march.

There were no announcements, no send-off, and even the bands were quiet. All they knew was that Burnside had a new plan, and they were to move back up the river, to cross the Rappahannock where many had insisted they cross two months before, the shallow fords above Fredericksburg.

Again Burnside assumed he would outsmart Lee, would make a bold and quick assault from the north, catch Lee by surprise, coming at him from behind. Burnside waited until the roads were firm, the weather fair, and now he would lead his men to the victory they had no chance of finding in December.

Chamberlain did not ride, led his men on foot, and they filed into place on the wide road that would lead them along the river. He heard little talking; there was no sense of adventure now, the energy drained away. He saw Ames, on his horse, sitting beside the road ahead. Ames was talking to another officer, a man missing an arm. Chamberlain walked toward them, stepped down off the surface of the road, and his feet slid suddenly away, slipped sideways into the depression that ran beside the road. He caught himself, one hand landing hard in the wetness, and Ames saw him. The other man said something, laughing, then rode away.

"Are you all right, Colonel?"

Chamberlain straightened, shook his hand, looked for something to wipe the mud away, and behind him, a voice: Tom.

"Lawrence, you hurt? Here . . ." Tom had a handkerchief, held it out, and Chamberlain took it, grateful, and wiped his hand.

Chamberlain looked at Ames, said, "Just a clumsy fall, Colonel. These roads are a bit of a mess."

"No, they are not, Colonel. I have just been told—that officer was Colonel Markey, of General Griffin's staff—these roads are now ideal for a new and glorious advance of this army. That is, in so many words, part of General Burnside's orders. So, Colonel, you see, you did not slip in the mud. There is no mud."

Chamberlain stared at Ames, heard the bitterness, something new, looked at his hand again, the handkerchief. "No, sir. No mud here."

Ames abruptly turned his horse, rode away along the edge of the wet road.

Tom said, "He's in a fine spirit today, eh, Lawrence?"

Chamberlain handed the cloth back to his brother, realized Tom was wearing a new uniform. "So . . . it's official."

"Ain't it grand, Lawrence? Got it this morning. Look . . ." He pointed to the shoulder, the gold bar of the lieutenant. "Lawrence, I tell you . . . it's real different. They *salute*. Even those boys from Bangor—the Capper brothers? I was always afraid they was gonna whip me for no good reason. Now, they call me *sir*!"

It had been Ames, and Captain Spear, who had recommended Tom for promotion. Chamberlain had stayed out of it, knew better, but it was clear that Tom had done his job well enough to attract the praise of the others. And now there were many vacant positions for officers.

Chamberlain smiled, said, "A uniform does strange things to people. Good things, I suppose. It has meaning . . . we're trained to accept that. We see that bar on your shoulder . . . the eagle on Ames's. We don't even have to see the face, the *man*. I guess that means we're soldiers."

"Lawrence, I was gonna write to Papa today, tell him about the promotion . . . the new uniform. Anything you want me to say?"

Chamberlain watched the line of troops moving past, momentum pushing them into the rhythm of the march. "I suppose . . . tell him we did good. You and me both. We did as good a job as soldiers are supposed to do. He'll appreciate that. Probably mean as much to him as anything else we could say."

"All right, I will. They're proud of both of us, Lawrence, you know that."

Chamberlain watched the last of the regiment move past, saw new officers, the next unit in line, knew they had better move along, catch up. "Yep, I know that. But please, stop calling me Lawrence."

Tom smiled, saluted, then turned and ran, falling into line at the rear of his company. Chamberlain climbed carefully up to the road bed, walked with a quick step alongside the lines of troops, thought, We follow symbols, we follow the commands of men who have stars on their uniforms. The man doesn't matter, the face or the name. Unless . . . he makes some bloody awful mistake, then the stars are given to someone else. He looked at the ground, felt his boots sink slightly into softening dirt, thought of Ames's words. Of course, Ames understood, it is happening again.

He passed Tom, kept moving forward, moved by the other familiar faces, made his way toward the front of the line. He glanced over to one man, saw Kilrain, who was looking up, and Chamberlain followed the look, a brief glimpse toward a thick gray sky, and then he felt it, hitting his cheek, one cold drop of rain, and he looked back toward Kilrain. The heavy round face was looking at him, the hard look of a man who also understood, who had seen all the stupidity, who knew, after all, that the gold stars were often mindless decoration, that the army was led not by symbols, but by the fallible egos and blind fantasies of men.

IT RAINED ALL NIGHT AND ALL THE NEXT DAY, AND STILL DID NOT stop. On the far side of the river Stuart's men watched from under the dripping rims of wide hats as Burnside's new plan, the quick and daring assault, was swallowed by the deep ooze of the Virginia mud. The great lines of wagons pulling the salvaged pontoons, the small field guns and heavier cannon, the tons of food and supplies, sank deeper and deeper, until Burnside had no choice but to halt the march and give the order to return the army back to Falmouth and the winter camps across the river from Fredericksburg.

By the end of January the army had settled into a new sense of gloom, defeated not only by Lee and Jackson, Stuart and Longstreet, or by the forces beyond the control of man, the rain and the cold. They had been defeated by the mind of one man, a kind and affable man who had a disastrous lack of talent for command. And thus Lincoln again made a change. Burnside was removed, as was Franklin, and Sumner was forced to retire. Fighting Joe Hooker was given command of the army. Lincoln's appointment to the new commander concluded, "Go forward and give us victories."

40. LEE

FEBRUARY 1863

THE WAR WAS SPREAD NOW OVER MOST OF THE SOUTH, AND there were new threats to the Atlantic coast. Burnside had been given his Ninth Corps again, and had been sent by boat to the southern coast of Virginia, below the James River. This effort could open a new front which would threaten the valuable supply routes that came from farther south, the fragile system of railroads through the Carolinas and Georgia. There was still the fear that by occupying southern Virginia, the Federal troops might again push inland, south of the James River, and once again threaten Richmond, this time from below.

The Federal threats to the Southern coast had never been serious enough to warrant Lee splitting up his army. He had found this part of the Confederacy a convenient place to send those commanders who had proven they were not fit to lead large armies in times of major crisis. Gustavus Smith, Chase Whiting, and even Beauregard, whose ego did not mix well with Lee's style, were in command in various regions along the coast. But with the new threat, Lee knew he had to send someone who could hold the line against a serious advance, and at the same time hold the various Confederate commands together into some sort of cohesive unit, not governed by each general's temperament.

He had first responded to the Federal move by sending Daniel Hill to North Carolina, to organize new volunteers into some sort of effective defense. Additional troops had been sent down under General Robert Ransom, and while Lee knew that neither man had proven himself in independent command, both were diligent and trustworthy soldiers. The detachments from Lee's already outnumbered army, which still looked across the Rappahannock at the massive Federal force, did not satisfy the agitation that the new threat had given Jefferson Davis. Davis believed the threat to Richmond called for a more drastic response, and so, despite Lee's small numbers, Davis insisted the army be divided further, and that a much larger force be sent to southern Virginia.

THERE HAD BEEN SNOW AGAIN, A FEW INCHES, AND THE HILLS and fields were again a solid white, a clean blanket for the fresh graves and torn earth of the great battle. Lee walked along his hill, Taylor behind, and the gun crews came alive, stood suddenly, shaking off the cold, a show for the commander which he did not need. He raised his hand, nodded to the men, and hats were raised, cheers went down the line. The sounds carried below, to the troops in their cold-weather camps, and the men crawled out from snow-covered hideaways, knew what the sound meant. No matter how often they saw him, they would give up the small warm place in the ground to see him again.

He moved back over the hill, dropped down behind the lines, saw a huge fire. There were few big fires now, there was no wood left, the trees and fences long gone. The men had formed details, hauling firewood over the rough country roads from farther and farther away. As the army sat in one place, it pulled at the country like some great dirty sponge, soaking up a widening circle of food and fuel.

The big fire was slowing, and the men saw him coming now, more cheers, and now he saw it had been a wagon; one spoke wheel leaned crookedly from the edge of the black ash. There was one officer, a captain Lee did not know, and the man was hesitant, saluted with a glance toward the fire, and Lee nodded, did not speak, did not ask if the wagon was usable or not.

He stood close to the shrinking heat, looked at the men who spread along the far side of the fire, away from him. They would not get too close, though more than once, when he would ride through the camps, someone would approach, carefully, a dirty hand extended, just to touch him, to touch the horse. He did not understand that, it always embarrassed him, but he rarely stopped them, left that to the officers or his staff, who might keep the men away with a shout, or the empty threat of a raised sword. He stared beyond the fire now and saw the faces of the men, the faces of his grand and wonderful army. Now there were more faces, to the side, behind him, men gathering from all directions, all along the hill, and he looked out, to all the dark eyes that watched him quietly, and he felt his throat tighten, could not swallow, fought it, said a silent prayer, *Thank You, for the love of these men.* Yes, he thought, I love them as well.

He tried not to look at the faces, saw the army instead, saw the filthy rags most were using for clothes, the small pieces of cloth many had wrapped around their feet, but not all—there were many bare feet, red and hard on the snow. He saw now the thin frames of men who did not eat because there was little to go around. The soft sadness gave way now, replaced by anger, toward the Federals, toward this war. And toward Davis, who would not come out here, who did not see these men in their rough and cold camps, and so did not take seriously his urgent requests, and those of others, to provide better for these men, soldiers who spent their time now in basic survival, a glorious fighting force that was slowly starving to death.

HE WAS IN HIS TENT, HOLDING A GIFT FROM A LOCAL MERCHANT in the town, an old man, a candlemaker, who had brought his family back to their home and found their whole lives reduced to the litter of war, scattered into the streets of Fredericksburg. The man had crossed the canal, climbed the hill, looking for Lee, asking, following the sad directions of weak soldiers, and finally had found him. He had come only to give him the one piece of his family's history that he had found intact, their Bible. The old man looked at Lee with eyes that unsettled him, eyes that dug deep inside, a man whose faith was now firmly with this army, and so he accepted the gift without protest. Now, he sat alone and read the inside cover, crude handwriting, the old man's simple message: "To General Robert E. Lee, May God bless you, and the good work you do."

Work. He did not think of what he did as work, not as a job. When he had been back in Richmond, in the drab office with the piles of paper, that had been work. Leading these men . . . he shook his head, thought, Maybe that is what we need now: work. These men do not need generals now, they need someone who can supply them, feed them, the work of the people who stare at piles of paper. And those people have not done a very good job.

He rose, put the Bible down on his cot, pushed out through the flaps of the tent and looked for Taylor, who was standing over two men, trying to keep a small fire lit.

"Major, if you please." Taylor turned toward him, began

to move, and Lee said, "Major, please send my respects to General Longstreet, and request that he meet with me as soon as he is able."

Taylor nodded, began to move again, and Lee said, "And . . . please request that the general bring along two of his best . . . no . . . that is vague. Request that the general be accompanied by General Pickett and General Hood."

Taylor absorbed the message, nodded again, and Lee went back to the warmth of the tent, began again to read the old man's Bible.

IT WAS LATE IN THE AFTERNOON, AND MORE CLOUDS WERE MOVING in, more thick gray, and Lee knew there would be snow yet again. He heard them first, a dull rumble, then saw the horses coming up the rise from the direction of the larger hill, Marye's Heights. Longstreet wore the wide floppy hat, held the reins with a new pair of white leather gloves, and Lee smiled, thought, It has to be a gift, he would not wash the old ones.

Behind Longstreet the other men were a marked contrast. Lee knew the bulky form of Hood, a bigger man than even Longstreet, and beside him Pickett, the small, thin frame topped by rolls of curling hair bouncing below his small cap. They reined up, dismounted heavily, and Lee stood, hands on his hips, stretched his back, then felt a tightness in his chest.

He pushed his arms out wide, said, "Gentlemen, it is a pleasure. Please, let us go inside, it's a bit warmer."

Lee backed into the tent, and Taylor held open the large flaps for the others. Longstreet bent, moved inside, and Lee pointed to a small stool. Longstreet did not speak, sat down with a small groan. Hood moved inside, quickly found a place on the ground, and now Pickett, and suddenly the tent was filled with a smell, and Lee felt his face contract, bombarded by the peculiar odor.

"My goodness . . . what is that . . . ?"

Longstreet laughed, pointed a gloved hand at Pickett, who said, "General Lee, with all respect, I come today wearing the latest gift from my dear Sallie, a sample of the finest and most recent import from Paris. It is called *'Fleur de . . . Fromage,'* or something. . . ."

Lee thought, Flower of cheese? and Longstreet said, "General, please forgive General Pickett, he does not have a gift for French. And as for his taste . . ."

"My taste is quite the envy of Richmond, sir. I assure you, if the other gentlemen in this army would allow themselves to partake of the good life that still abounds, it would make for a much more pleasant if not high-class atmosphere."

Hood moved slightly, increased the distance between him and Pickett, said, "General, it is not often my good fortune to share such close quarters with you . . . for which I am now grateful . . . but I respectfully point out that there are a great many fine officers in this army who are *not* gentlemen, and who would not be caught dead smelling like that."

Pickett looked at Hood with surprise, then frowned. "Pity . . ."

"Gentlemen," Lee said, interrupting. "We must address matters at hand. I, for one, will accept General Pickett's . . . adornment. However, it compels me to make this meeting a brief one."

Hood nodded, said, "Bless you, sir."

Lee looked at Longstreet, who waited, was not smiling now, had removed the gloves and pulled a short cigar from his coat. "General Longstreet, we are faced with a problem . . . two problems, actually. The first, and most immediate, is the supplying of this army. This is my priority. The second problem concerns the Federal advance along the Virginia coast, below the James River. That is President Davis's priority. I believe we have a means to deal with both situations. We must begin by dividing this army. . . ."

AS THE FIRST TRUE SIGNS OF SPRING BEGAN TO SPREAD OVER the hills and farms of Virginia, the march began. The two divisions under Hood and Pickett would move to the trains, travel south, establish a defensive front below the James River, and unite the efforts of the other commanders there to prevent any further Federal advance. Longstreet was placed in a position of independent command, with two important conditions. One was that he begin immediately to secure supplies for the army from an agricultural area that was still relatively abundant, and send a steady flow of these supplies to northern Virginia. The second condition was that Longstreet be prepared, at quick notice, to make use of the railroads, and return his troops to Lee's command if Lee required it. Lee was now left with a force of only fifty-five thousand, less than half the size of the Federal Army that sat in winter quarters above the Rappahannock, a Federal Army with a new commander, who had a sharp eye toward the end of the miserable winter.

HE HAD RIDDEN INTO THE TOWN, AN INVITATION FROM A GROUP of women. It was a brave show of normalcy, a formal and social gathering by citizens crushed by the weight of destruction and rebuilding, and Lee could not refuse them.

The snow was gone now, the wide field beginning to fill with large patches of deep green. There were still signs of the battle, many signs, and he rode past them now without looking down. He looked up to his hill, to the long row of hills, thought, Will they do it again? It was hopeful, but he knew it would not be. The new Federal commander would not follow the same disastrous path of his predecessor.

He began to climb, and the gun crews waved to him, welcoming him back. He stopped the horse, climbed down, had a sudden need to walk, to kick through the new growth. Behind him, his staff was surprised, began to climb down as well, and he turned, waved them on, said, "No, go ahead. I just want to walk."

Taylor stayed behind, sat on his horse, holding Traveller's reins, and the others rode on up the hill, between the big guns.

He began to climb, quick short steps, a fresh energy, his boots digging into the soft dirt, and he looked down, saw bees dancing among the first of the new flowers, small yellow circles climbing out of the layer of thick brown. He was breathing hard now, paused, reached down, thought of Mary, flowers in her hair, and there was a sudden pain in his throat. He tried to straighten up, felt the pain moving into his left arm, a sharp burn, and looked at the arm, the hand, expected to see blood, a wound, but the gray coat was unchanged. He sank to one knee, held the arm, massaging, feeling, but the pain did not go away. He looked up the hill, to the guns, saw the troops watching him, coming toward him, and from deep inside he felt something swell up, long icy fingers wrapping around, gripping his heart, and he looked down, saw the flowers, saw them fading behind a cold black curtain.

HE WAS ON HIS COT, STARING INTO A GLOW OF LIGHT, THE REflection of the sun on the canvas. He saw Taylor, and Walker, and now he saw more, realized the tent was full of people, and there was a doctor . . . the man who had set his injured hands. He tried to turn his head, felt the pain in his throat, froze into stillness.

The doctor said, "Hello, General. Welcome back. We were a bit concerned, I must say."

He said nothing, looked at Taylor, saw teary-eyed relief, then tried to turn, and again the pain stopped him cold.

"Easy, now, General. No need to move about."

"What . . . ?"

Taylor bent over him, said in a hushed tone, "We thought you had left us, General. You collapsed . . . we brought you to your tent. The doctor says you'll be all right. Just rest. If you need anything . . ."

There was a sound outside the tent, a voice, yelling. "He's awake. He's all right!" and now there was more noise, the sounds of cheering, and Lee listened, did not move, looked at the doctor, a question.

The doctor said, "General, if I may have a private word?"

Lee looked at Taylor, who turned, spoke to the others. "Out! Leave the general alone now. We must leave him."

The men began to file out, and the tent seemed suddenly cavernous, hollow. The doctor sat down on the stool, said, "General, I believe you have a problem with your heart. You seem better now . . . actually, you seem in perfect health. But sometimes it can sneak up on you. The best advice I can give you is take it a bit easier."

Lee spoke quietly, testing his voice. "Doctor, there is an army out there. They are not likely to allow me much of a rest."

"General Lee, I can only offer that you will not serve our cause well if you are flat on your back. The best way for you to get back on your feet, or onto your horse, is to rest now. Your young Mr. Taylor seems to be quite capable of managing this headquarters."

Lee stared at the canvas, nodded slightly. "Doctor, can we do anything to keep this matter somewhat . . . private?"

The doctor laughed, said, "Actually, no."

Lee smiled. "No, I suppose not."

The news that he was not seriously ill spread through the army with the same speed and energy that propels word of a great victory. The troops began to find ways to pass by his headquarters more often now, and gifts began to flow into the camp, from the town and from the countryside. He did not stay on his cot long, and within a few days even Taylor could see no difference, none of the tormenting signs of age. Lee began to ride again, to move among the troops, to ride down the broad hill, through the guns and the fields of flowers, staring hard at the hills across the river.

41. JACKSON

April 1863

He stared down at the paper, held the pencil tightly, frowned. There were no words. Abruptly, he stood up and walked around the small table, a quick search for inspiration, then sat back down, stared again at the blank page. He tried to recall the battle, could see it all, the smoke and the men, could hear the violent sounds. But . . . he could not write it down, the simple explanation of what happened.

He had gone too long without tackling this job, the painful and annoying paperwork of command. Lee had insisted. There was a lull in the fighting, the army was still in winter quarters, and there would be no better time. But Jackson was not a writer.

He stood again, thought, Pendleton will help, of course. He wondered why he had not thought of that before—his staff. They had been on all the fields, they saw most of what he saw. They would know whose regiment and whose brigade led which advance. To Jackson, once the sounds of the battles had rolled across the field, it was all automatic. The troop movements and the positioning of the lines were instinctive. He did not ever recall thinking that he would have to write it all down afterward.

Yes, he thought, I will tell them: Pendleton . . . Smith. They can do this. I will read what they recall, and if it seems accurate, I will sign it. He nodded, pleased with himself, his aggravation resolved. He thought of lemonade then, realized he had a great thirst, knew the women in the house would always accommodate him. He looked around the tent, spotted the wide black felt hat that Anna had sent him, reached for it, and heard a small sound outside. He stopped, silent, peered toward the flaps, saw a small movement along the bottom and smiled, then moved quietly closer to the sound with slow, light steps. He could hear the sound again, the small giggle, and through the flaps came a small pink hand, then more, the tiny face, a beaming smile. Jackson knelt down, surprised the little girl with a quick grab, pulled her up and into the tent, and she burst into loud and happy laughter. He held the child up above him, toward the top of the tent, and the surprise passed. She was smiling now, reached for the hat on his head, and he set her down.

"No, child, you cannot have my hat. It might be a bit large. . . ." He removed it, saw the strip of gold braid that wound around the hat, pulled, and it came loose in his hand. He tossed the hat aside, wrapped the gold braid around the girl's head and tied it up around the fine golden hair.

"Well, now," he said, "I believe that suits a young girl better than an old soldier."

She laughed again, touching the braid.

"Now, I was just about to go for some lemonade. I would very much like the company of one beautiful five-year-old girl."

She nodded, smiling brightly, and he led her out of the tent. He picked her up and set her gently down on his shoulders, her oversized dress bunching up, covering his face, and he stumbled about. "Oh no, I cannot see," he said. "How shall we find the house?" She began the high sweet giggles again, and he staggered unevenly across the yard, went up to the porch and into the house.

In the yard, near the other tents, Jackson's aides had watched the scene, and Pendleton said, "No soldier, on either side, who has ever shared the field with Stonewall would ever believe what we have just seen."

The others laughed, heads were shaking, and the group began to disperse, attending to their own duties. Pendleton went toward Jackson's tent, held a handful of new reports, ducked inside, looked for a place to set them down and then saw the blank paper on the table. He understood Jackson's difficulty with battle reports. There were small dots—a dozen pencil marks where Jackson had tried to begin writing. Pendleton sat down in Jackson's chair, thought of what he'd just seen out in the yard. Around the fires, at dinner, Jackson would sit quietly while the staff joked and kidded, and when he would laugh, it was sudden and awkward, and Pendleton thought, He laughs like a man who doesn't know how. Yet, out there, with the little girl, he had been as open and free as a child himself, nothing reserved, no shy withdrawal. Pendleton picked up the pencil, began to write:

The Official Report from the Second Corps, Lieutenant General Thomas J. Jackson Commanding: The Battle of Fredericksburg . . .

THEY WERE CAMPED ON THE VAST GROUNDS OF MOSS NECK, A plantation spread out a few miles below the plains of Fredericksburg. It was the home of Richard Corbin, his wife and child, and his larger family, some of them refugees from other places, places now consumed by the war. Corbin himself was away, assigned to duty with the army, and so the women commanded the household, and the little girl, five-year-old Jane, commanded General Jackson.

Jackson had been invited to stay in the house itself and declined. He'd had the staff tents pitched across the wide yard. On occasion, however, he would allow himself and the staff to enjoy the luxury of a supper on the white linen of the Corbin dining room. Mrs. Corbin was a most courteous hostess, but it was her daughter who brightened the long days of winter quarters.

They stood in the hallway, at the kitchen door, waiting. The request had been made, and Jackson stood at attention, the little girl reaching her hand high to hold his, and together they filled the doorway. The girl's aunt, Kate Corbin, was busy stirring a pitcher.

"My, General, we do appreciate the gift. Where do you get all these lemons?"

Jackson stared ahead, said, "It is a kind Providence that provides kindness. . . ." He paused, tried to rephrase that.

"Why, General, you are quite the poet!"

He was suddenly embarrassed, said, "No, it is God who provides. . . ."

"Yes, General, I know what you meant. Here, for goodness sakes, enjoy your lemonade."

She handed a tall glass to him, and a small cup to the little girl, and he stepped away from the door and bent over, a formal bow to bright blue eyes. Jane bowed toward him, then they both drank from their glasses. Afterward, wiping at wet chins, they repeated what had become their ritual, closed their eyes and together said, "Mmmmmmmmmmmm!"

Kate wiped her hands with a small towel, said, "I swear, General, if you spoil your own child like that . . . you will have your hands full."

He looked at her, and Jane suddenly leapt forward, grabbed his leg and wrapped one arm tight around his knee. "Miss Corbin," he said, "it will give me great pleasure to spoil my daughter. I intend to give her many opportunities to spoil me as well." He looked at the small bundle now clinging to his leg, and he drank from the glass again. "How easy it is to forget . . . all that we must do . . . all the horrors that we have seen . . . simply by staring into the face of a small child. There is Providence here . . . in that. The children are blessed."

He reached down, pulled the little girl up, lifted her onto his shoulder. She still held the small cup, splashed lemonade on his uniform.

Kate said, "Oh goodness, here, General, let me put a damp cloth on that."

Jackson glanced at her, a gleam of blue mischief in his eyes, said, "Oh, that won't be necessary, Miss Corbin, because Jane and I . . ." He paused, grinned devilishly at the little girl, and giggles rolled over him. Suddenly, he was running down the hall, out the front of the house, carrying her at all angles. He gently set her down in the green grass and rolled on the ground beside her, and there were gales of laughter from both of them.

A few feet away, Captain Smith was staring in utter amazement, then turned toward the sound of an approaching rider.

THE FEDERAL ARMY HAD BEGUN TO STIR. WHILE THERE WAS NO clear evidence of a plan, Lee knew that the new commander, Hooker, under the stern eye of Washington, could produce a quick threat, and so he ordered Jackson to move his camp up from Moss Neck, to be closer to the hills behind Fredericksburg. Stuart's vigilance along the river above the town had given Lee some hint that the Federal Army would again plan a move in that direction, and he took a chance, pulling Jackson's corps away from Port Royal. He anticipated that Hooker would do what Burnside should have done from the start, cross the river to the northwest, behind the hills, using the convenience of several shallow fords. Below the crossings, the roads ran together, intersecting with the main roads leading westward out of Fredericksburg. The intersection was named for the family that lived there, was called Chancellorsville.

The tents had been struck, the troops moved well up the road, and Jackson rode his horse back along the line of moving men, went toward the house for the last time. Kate Corbin was on the porch, had watched the troops leave. The last of the staff was cleaning up the yard when she saw Jackson and waved sadly. He rode up close to the porch, dismounted and said, "Miss Corbin, if you please, I would like to say good-bye to your niece. I shall miss her."

"Certainly, General. She is not feeling well today. There seems to be some illness in this house. All the children have come down with a fever. Please, come in."

He followed her into the house, he felt the heavy layer of quiet, and lightened his steps, self-conscious of his boots on the hard floor. She led him into a small parlor, and he saw Mrs. Corbin, Jane's mother, bending over a small blanket. She turned, looked at him, smiled weakly, and he went to the little girl, saw the blond hair spread over a small white pillow.

"Well, now, what is this? How can I play with my friend if she insists on staying in bed?"

He waited for the laugh, the small giggle, but she only smiled up at him, held up a hand and tried to reach his short beard. He saw the look in her eyes, suddenly straightened, said to Mrs. Corbin, "I will have my doctor, Dr. McGuire, attend to her. I will send him immediately." She nodded, grateful, and he backed away, saying, "I must return to my men. I will send Dr. McGuire."

Then he turned and marched from the house.

THEY WERE CAMPED NOW IN A LARGE FIELD, IN SIGHT OF THE broad plain where Jackson had held his lines against Meade. The staff filed from the small mess tent, had enjoyed the unusual and rare gift of a smoked ham sent to the headquarters from a local farmer, who clearly had a talent for hiding his bounty. Jackson was last out of the tent. He rubbed his stomach, listened to the casual talk from the others, how long they would be in this spot, the warmth of the spring weather. He thought of writing a letter, had received a new note from Anna detailing the joys of his tiny daughter, and he began to form his words, maybe a prayer, but heard the sound of horses. There were two riders out on the road. It was Pendleton . . . and Hunter McGuire.

McGuire was not much older than the young staff officer, had come to Jackson's staff from Winchester, a choice made mainly because he was well known among the others. He was a well-educated man, even by medical standards, had received formal training at the University of Pennsylvania. By now he had built a solid reputation for medicine, advised many of the older surgeons, and no one doubted he was the best man Jackson could have chosen for the job. Jackson had an instinctive respect for the neat and efficient young man, and as Pendleton and McGuire walked toward him, there was something in the doctor's face that turned Jackson cold. He did not move, waited. Pendleton saluted, and Jackson did not look at him, kept his eyes on McGuire.

The doctor glanced down at the ground, said in a low voice, "It was scarlet fever. The children are all right. I gave them some . . . they will be fine. Except . . . I am terribly sorry, General. The little girl . . . Jane . . . did not survive. She has died, sir."

Jackson stared at him, did not speak, fixed his eyes on McGuire's face, and McGuire turned away, could not look back at the sharp glare of Jackson's eyes. Abruptly, Jackson stepped away, marched out between the tents, out into the field. Pendleton began to follow him, the others as well, but they slowed, stayed back, watched as he moved away through the thick green grass. Then suddenly he sat, on a short stump, put his head in his hands and began to sob.

Pendleton stayed a short distance away, felt McGuire's hand on his arm. "What is it?" Pendleton said. "He's never cried before . . . not for all the blood and all the death. There was something about that little girl. . . ."

McGuire nodded quietly, said, "A general cannot cry for his men. They cannot even cry for each other now. This army has cried all its tears."

"But he has not."

They stood, and around them troops gathered, curious. They saw Jackson now, and no one spoke. They watched in silence as Jackson poured out his grief, and they did not move, stayed quietly around him as the dark night filled the field.

42. CHAMBERLAIN

April 1863

THERE WAS NO OTHER EXPLANATION: THE SERUM WAS SIMPLY bad. He did not understand medicine, knew that his unit had done well compared to others, that they made it through the winter without losing many. Now, Hooker had made it a priority: the army would improve its health. Hygiene would be practiced, the camps would be cleaner. And . . . there would be vaccinations, protection against the always present danger of smallpox. Except . . . the serum had been bad.

Around the camp, officers were working quickly, men in white masks directing the troops, digging the small signposts into the soft ground. Chamberlain moved closer, saw the troops back away, keeping their distance, and he walked around, saw the sign: DO NOT ENTER—QUARANTINE AREA.

He waved at the men. "Hello, how are you today?" and smiled, thought of the absurd bad luck. The serum could possibly have infected the entire regiment with the disease, and so, of course, they would have to stay put, together, no contact with the rest of the army until the danger was past. He stared at one man, a doctor who was waving the troops away, their work done.

Chamberlain walked over to another signpost, where a man was nailing up fence wire. "Enjoy your work, do you?" he asked.

The man looked at him, covered his mouth, said, "For the love of God, man, stay away! I got a family!"

Chamberlain turned, walked toward the tents, shook his head. If the enemy cannot kill us, he thought, the army can.

The rest of the army had begun to move, along the same roads that had swallowed them up in January. Hooker had done much for morale, for the sense that maybe—this time—it would be different. Chamberlain did not know the mission, knew the army was moving away to the northwest and that the Twentieth Maine was not going anywhere.

He had not seen Ames, who was not in camp, and he wondered if quarantines applied to the commanders. It brightened him for a moment. Maybe he could somehow just order the disease away, the privilege of rank.

He saw men on horseback approaching the edge of the camp, then dismounting, and he moved toward them. They were officers, among them a major, who stepped back. It was a reflex Chamberlain was beginning to find extremely annoying.

"Sir . . . you are Colonel Chamberlain?"

"Certainly am, Major."

"Sir, I have a message for you . . . from Colonel Ames. Under the circumstances, Colonel . . . would you mind if I read it? I am not to cross the quarantine line, sir."

Chamberlain nodded. "Fine, Major, read the message."

"Thank you, sir."

> To Lieutenant Colonel J. L. Chamberlain . . . I am pleased to inform you that I have received appointment to General Meade's command, as a staff officer. I deeply appreciate your fine work as second in command and wish to advise you unless I return, you are in command of the Twentieth Maine Regiment of Volunteers. I regret that the regiment, which has performed with consistent valor, should have been victimized by such an unfortunate turn of events. However, I have been assured that in a few short weeks the quarantine will be lifted and the regiment may return to active duty. Please assure the men that they are in my thoughts. Signed, Colonel Adelbert Ames.

"That is all, sir."

Chamberlain nodded. "Thank you, Major. You may return to the land of the unafflicted."

He walked toward his tent, thought, So Ames *did* escape. And he made certain I did not. Men were watching him, some had heard the order, and they began to gather. He stopped, stood with his hands on his hips.

One man said, "Colonel, sir, how long are we to be kept here? They're treatin' us like prisoners."

Others began to speak, angry questions, and he held up his hands, said, "Please, quiet." More men moved up, they were in a circle around him, and he saw Tom and the other officers. "The army is on the march, and we cannot go with them, not for a while. It's as simple as that. You already know the danger, why we are behind a fence. There is simply nothing we can do about it."

"Colonel . . . " Ellis Spear moved forward, through the men. "I've been talking to . . . well, sir, the Eighty-third Pennsylvania is under the impression that they are moving up to meet the rebs pretty quick, they're expecting a good fight. My men . . . they feel like we're gonna miss out on something big. Surely the army can find something for us to do."

The men responded, the voices rising, and Chamberlain held up his hands again, said, "If we're going to have a fight soon, then we are going to miss it. I have no say in this. General Hooker himself knows of our predicament. I did volunteer us . . . that we be allowed to lead the attack. If we were to infect the enemy, it might be an effective way to end the war." There was laughing and men nodded.

"But the high command did not think it a practical and humane strategy. Wars should be fought by noise and violence, not by subtle diseases. So . . . we will stay behind."

He began to move through them, and their protests faded, the officers breaking them up, moving away. He reached his tent, heard a sound, music, listened. It was a band, far out on the road, leading another column of men away. The sounds faded, and he thought, So, we will miss this one, and maybe . . . there will not be any more, maybe it will end here, one more great fight. And we can go back home and say . . . nothing. We weren't there. He leaned into the tent, realizing what a terrible thing it was to hope for . . . that the war go on just so they could be a part of it. But he could not help it, sat on his cot now, stared at the side of the tent, remembered the stone wall, the smoke, the screams. His heart began to pound, and he thought, Please, someday, let us have one more chance. . . .

43. HANCOCK

THURSDAY, APRIL 30, 1863

HE HAD BEEN WRONG ABOUT THE PONTOONS. THEY WOULD BE used again, were already in place when he led his division to the site, the wide clearing along the river. There had once been a bridge here too, at this place called, strangely, United States Ford. As at every good crossing, the bridges were long gone, small burnt memories lingering in crooked shapes. But here there was no opposition, no hidden muskets on the far bank, and the men crossed quickly and easily, and Hancock knew they were ready for a fight.

Hooker had done for the army what Burnside could not. He had put them into position, quickly, with efficient use of engineers and time; put them into position to crush Lee's army from the rear. The plan was basic military logic: keep Lee occupied by a large force, Sedgwick's corps crossing the Rappahannock again below Fredericksburg, threatening to move across the same fields where Jackson had defended against Meade, while Hooker moved the larger bulk of the army upriver, to the shallow fords. By occupying all three of the main crossings, the army would move with more speed, down separate roads, converging due west of Lee's position, to his rear. With pressure then from Sedgwick, Lee would be caught along his row of hills in a vise grip of nearly 140,000 Federal troops.

By now Sedgwick was in place, a formidable blue mass that was already on Lee's side of the river, and their complete parade-ground visibility would clearly demonstrate that it was a large enough force to hold Lee in place, a threat he could not ignore.

Hooker had given the army something else besides another good plan. In the months of waiting, while the ground hardened and the warm air of spring filled the valley, the army had been trained constantly, their diet improved. He did away with Burnside's system of Grand Divisions, bringing back the more efficient corps system. And, knowing the sad state of troop morale, Hooker devised a symbolic, though effective means of instilling pride. Each corps was given its own identifying insignia, with the color of that insignia reflecting the specific divisions. The new insignias were sewn on the soldiers' hats, and the response was immediate and positive. The men eagerly accepted this small bit of identity, and the officers knew that in the heat of battle, it would be much simpler for the men to stay with their own units, or locate them after the fight.

The new commander also dealt with poor morale by pardoning deserters and stragglers, and guaranteeing the men that they would have a predetermined opportunity for leave, so that desertion would no longer be necessary. For all of Hooker's shortcomings, he had done a great deal to bring the army back up to fighting form. Now, with the new spring and the new march, Hancock understood that something good had happened to the army, to his division. Now they would learn if Hooker could satisfy Lincoln's request to "go forward and give us victories."

The army was spreading below the river quickly, moving down the roads toward the hub of the wheel, the intersection of Chancellorsville. Hancock's division was now the First, still a part of Couch's Second Corps, and in the new organization of the army, Couch was an informal second in command to Hooker. Hancock felt some comfort in that, some sense that at least Couch would be there, would hear it all and have his say, and surely, *surely*, they would not stumble into another bloody disaster.

They marched south, left the river, and the road led them through a thick and dense woods. Couch rode beside him, and they led the column, trailed by the staffs and Sam Zook's brigade.

"This is rather like Florida."

Couch looked toward Hancock's gesture, said, "Really? I would imagine Florida to be more . . . green."

"Green, yes. And thick, impossible to see. Down there, it was palmettos, and some kind of damned thick sticker bush, something called catclaw. This looks about as bad—you can't see anything."

Couch looked toward the other side of the road, saw more of the same, said, "It's called the Wilderness. I heard it wasn't always like this, but the big trees were all cut—there's some ironworks around here, use a lot of wood fuel, and after the trees were cut, the woods just grew up

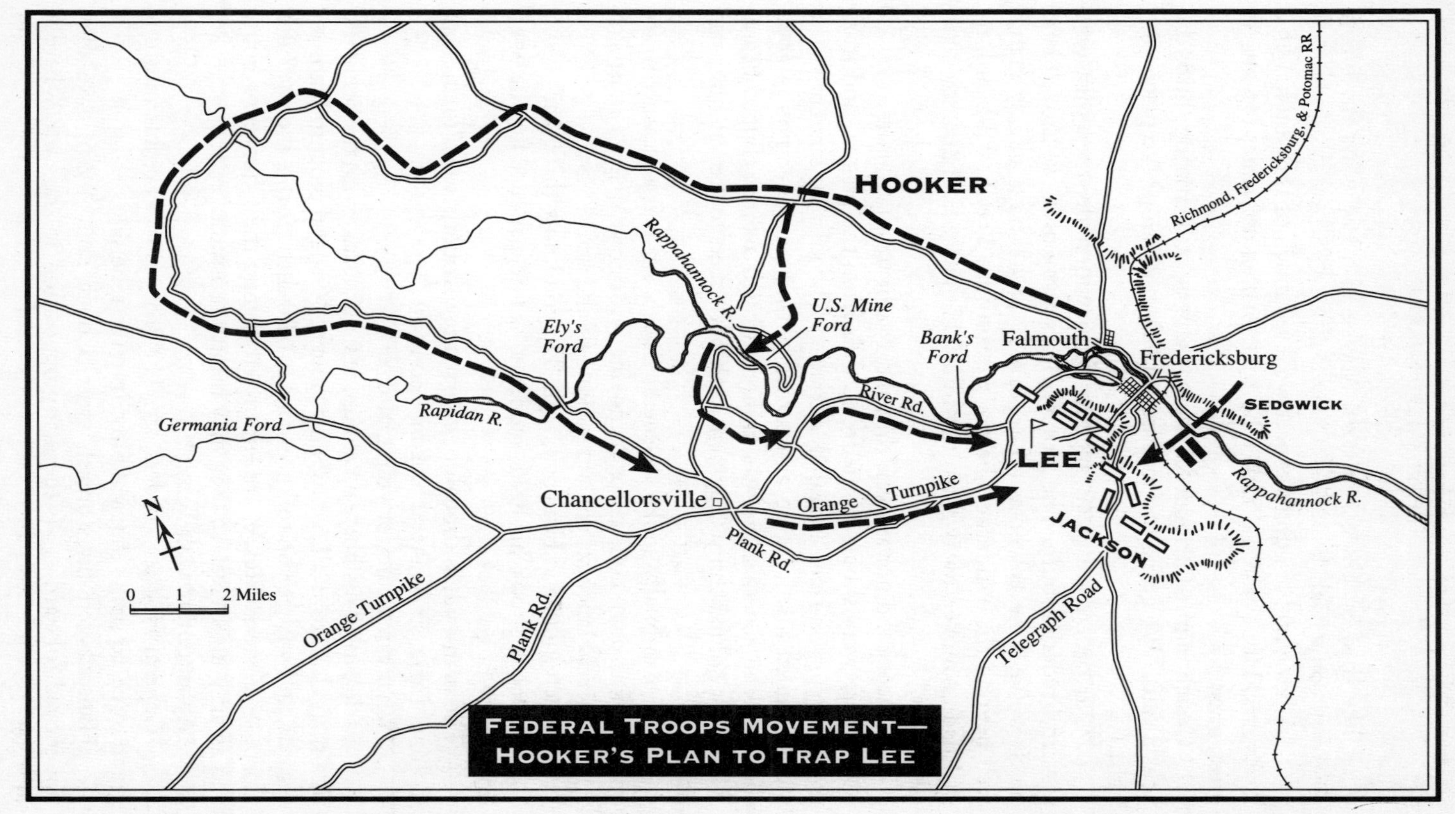

HOOKER
Richmond, Fredericksburg, & Potomac RR
Rappahannock R.
U.S. Mine Ford
Ely's Ford
Bank's Ford
Falmouth
Fredericksburg
SEDGWICK
River Rd.
Rapidan R.
Germania Ford
LEE
Chancellorsville
Orange
Turnpike
Rappahannock R.
Plank Rd.
JACKSON
N
0
1
2 Miles
Telegraph Road
Orange Turnpike
Plank Rd.
FEDERAL TROOPS MOVEMENT—
HOOKER'S PLAN TO TRAP LEE

thick like this, bushes, scrub trees. Maybe in a few years the bigger trees will come back."

"A few years . . . don't expect we'll see much of this country in a few years. Hope not. I'd rather be back in Pennsylvania, looking at green grass."

Couch smiled, nodded. Hancock was still staring into the brush, said, "We going to move out of this stuff soon? No place for a fight."

"Our orders are to advance to Chancellorsville, then turn east, toward Fredericksburg. The ground clears away once we move east a bit. If we've done as well as the reports say, we'll have an easy march well beyond the Wilderness before we run into Lee. Last I heard, he still hadn't moved away from the hills." He paused. "This may actually work."

Hancock did not answer, thought, I've heard that before.

There were shouts to the front, calls from the pickets, and from around a curve a rider appeared, a courier. The man sat straight in the saddle, pulled his horse up and turned with expert precision, a good show for the generals. He was smiling through a short clipped beard, waited for some acknowledgment, and both men looked at him, said nothing.

The man finally spoke. "General Couch, sir! It is a pleasure to see you this fine day. Your corps is moving with great speed, I must say! And General Hancock, you are looking fit and well."

Couch looked at Hancock, said, "Do you know this man?"

Hancock shook his head, suddenly had no patience for the overdone show of good cheer.

The man said, as though of course they would recall, "Lieutenant Colonel Earle, sir, General Slocum's adjutant."

"What can we do for you, Colonel?"

Earle pulled his horse up alongside Couch, said with the smugness of a man close to it all, who knows much, "General Slocum sends his regards, and wishes you to know that his Twelfth Corps, and the Fifth Corps of General Meade, are encamped around the Chancellor house and await your arrival, so they may begin the assault."

"Await our arrival? Why?"

"General Hooker's orders, sir. The army is to assemble into one grand force, to strike the fatal blow into the rebels!"

Hancock felt his stomach twist. Couch said, "Why have they not moved forward . . . is there any opposition to the east? Where is Hooker?"

The colonel's expression began to change. Couch's response to his good news was not what he had expected. "Uh . . . I am not sure, sir. General Hooker has not yet arrived on the field. Perhaps the general would care to accompany me back to General Slocum? It is a short ride now, sir."

Couch glanced at Hancock, said, "Keep your column moving, General," and spurred his horse, moving quickly away, leaving the colonel behind. Earle jerked his horse forward, and then both men were gone in a spray of dust.

Hancock turned, saw the puzzled faces of Couch's staff, said, "Don't worry, he'll be back. It seems the plan has changed."

"GENTLEMEN, THIS IS A GLORIOUS DAY INDEED!"

There were nods, some low sounds, and Hooker held his glass high, waited, and gradually the arms went up, the others joining in the toast.

Hancock and Couch stood under a great chandelier, and the large room was filled with the elegance of the great plantations and thick with the smell of cigars. Hooker had arrived after dark, a grand show, taking personal command of the attack, which now would begin the next morning.

Hancock held his glass high, had said nothing, glanced at Couch, who was not smiling, and he felt the shared anger, the sense that yet again they were led by a man who did not inspire respect. There was something else about Hooker that made Hancock uneasy. Unlike the personable and mildly buffoonish Burnside, Hooker was a man clearly focused on his own goals, behaving more like a politician than a soldier. Hancock heard it in the idle talk, the conversation of the others: Hooker was generally disliked by everyone who served close to him. They had respected his treatment of the army, but the rise in morale had not spread through the headquarters of the commanders. They would wait, instead, for the results of this new plan. Their gloom was lifted by the quick march, the efficient crossing of the river, but now, despite Hooker's attempt to create a party, a celebration of some unnamed success, Hancock felt it clearly, through the toasts and the bouyant salutes. There was nothing yet to celebrate.

The troops were camped close to the small town, spread out in tiny clearings that dotted the thick Wilderness. Hancock understood, they all understood, that had they pushed on, turned to the east, they would be out in the open ground, closer to Lee's position, where they could see what lay in front of them. There had been no official explanation from Hooker why he had slowed them down, just some vague talk of uniting the army. And so the afternoon had passed without contact with any major force from Lee, nothing to slow down the assault except the sudden caution of Joe Hooker.

The toast was concluded, and suddenly there was a wooden box, a case of whiskey, a common commodity around Hooker's headquarters. There were more toasts, and Hancock knew this would go on for a while yet. Other corps commanders had arrived, his friend Oliver Howard, who now commanded the Eleventh, and Dan Sickles of the Third. The great room was filling quickly, and Hancock felt a stifling heat, a need for air. He left Couch's side, began to move toward the wide front door of the grand house. There was a sudden shout, a man calling for quiet, and slowly the talk hushed. Hancock waited, turned to see Hooker's aide standing on a chair, holding a paper.

"Gentlemen, you have all received the commander's General Order Forty-seven, but . . . on this occasion, I feel it should be read aloud."

There were nods, mostly from the junior commanders, who had not yet seen the order.

" 'It is with heartfelt satisfaction the commanding general announces to the army that the operations of the last three days have determined that our enemy must either ingloriously fly or come out from behind his entrenchments and give us battle on our own ground, where certain destruction awaits him—' " He was interrupted by cheers, a show of enthusiasm that Hancock tried to share.

Now Hooker spoke up, raising a glass, and shouted above the voices, "God Almighty will not be able to prevent the destruction of the rebel army!" There were more cheers, but they faded quickly, and Hancock saw stunned and uncomfortable expressions, the men who held dearly to their faith, who were absorbing what their commander had just said.

He had heard enough, quickly opened the door, passed by eavesdropping guards, stepped down away from the light. He climbed up onto the horse, moved the big mare along the road, thought of the ridiculous boasting, daring God to stop them, felt suddenly very sad. He tried to convince himself it did not have to depend on those men

. . . the real success could still come from the good work of these good soldiers. We do have the numbers, he thought, and we may have indeed surprised Bobby Lee. He rode on toward the camps of his men, thought of Hooker's words, wondered if Lee would ever be pursuaded to "ingloriously fly."

44. LEE

April 30, 1863

He was still on the hill, looked down toward the river, to the spreading mass of blue, a force too strong to be a simple diversion. But they were not coming, not advancing toward the woods where Jackson's men waited, again.

Jackson was watching him, sat on a log, then stood, felt the itch of the new fight, paced for a moment, then sat again. Lee walked alone, still stared at Sedgwick's troops, then turned and moved back up to the crest of the hill, toward Jackson's impatience.

"That is not the main attack," Lee said. "They are waiting for something."

"We should punish them, now. Hit them before they can get set."

He turned to Jackson, saw the fire, the violence in the sharp face. "No, General, the guns, remember the guns. They are still on Stafford Heights, it would be a costly advance if we showed ourselves across that plain. It is no different now than it was in December. We must wait for *them*."

Jackson looked toward the far hills, across the river, knew of course that Lee was right. He put his hands behind him and his shoulders sagged slightly.

Lee said, "General, I must know where the rest of them have gone. We must wait for General Stuart. Sedgwick has come across with only one or two corps. Hooker would not repeat Burnside's plan. Do not focus your energies on those troops."

It was not a command, but the softer advice, a father to an over-eager son. Lee understood the impatience: the target was in plain sight, open and vulnerable. That was exactly why he did not believe it, did not believe Hooker would attack with just those troops.

Stuart had observed heavy columns moving above the river, out to the northwest, and Lee knew they would cross somewhere upstream, as they should have done in December. To the north and slightly west of Lee's left flank lay Bank's Ford, where the river made a sharp U downward, and he understood that there must be no crossing there, it was dangerously close to his rear, and so he had strengthened that position, sent Anderson's division back, off the hills.

Richard Anderson commanded one of the two divisions of Longstreet's corps that had stayed with Lee, and Lee knew that though Anderson was not one for ingenuity, he could be counted on to stand his ground. Lee had instructed him to push out farther west, as far as the next major crossing, United States Ford. It was there that Anderson met the first of Hooker's strong columns, advancing southward. As instructed, he pulled back, and now was spreading his division in a north-south line, protecting both Bank's Ford and the two main roads that led from Chancellorsville straight into Lee's position. But Lee still did not know how many troops Hooker was pushing across the river there, or just where they might be heading.

Jackson was still frustrated, paced again. The meeting seemed to be over, and he looked for his horse, was ready to return to his troops, and Lee held up his hand, said, "General, please, sit down. We can do little else until we hear—"

There was a shout, the voice of Taylor, running along the hill. "General . . . it's Von Borcke, Major Von Borcke!"

Lee saw him now, the huge form riding with some difficulty up the side of the hill. He was on a large black mule, and the mule seemed intent on moving in other directions than where the Prussian intended.

"Vat ho! General Lee . . ." Suddenly the mule turned, began to go back down the hill, and Von Borcke jerked the head around, gave a heavy kick to the mule's side, and it began to climb slowly again.

Jackson moved up close to Lee, and Taylor stepped forward and grabbed the reins of the mule. Abruptly, Von Borcke swung a huge leg over and leapt from the mule in a great awkward flight, landing thunderously on both feet.

"Only vay I can get off the damned thing. He shtill vants to run off to play." He looked now at Lee, saw no smile, saw the deep glare from Jackson, straightened himself, said, "Forgive me, Herr General, I am not used to riding such animals as you have here. I beg to report on behalf of General Shtuart, that a column of the enemy has crossed the river at Germanna Ford, and is moving south, toward Chancellorsville.

General Shtuart has determined it is the Twelfth Corps. He has also observed units of the Eleventh."

Lee said nothing, looked at Jackson, and Jackson said, "They would not move two corps that far behind us for a feint."

"No, they would not." Lee nodded toward the big German, said, "Major, you may return to General Stuart, and request in the strongest terms that General Stuart join me here. Please go now, Major. I regret your difficulty with your mule. We do not have the luxury of thoroughbreds." It was not a criticism, but Von Borcke suddenly felt foolish, complaining to a man who clearly knew of all the army did not have. He backed away, saluted, and Taylor held the reins tight as Von Borcke struggled up to the mule. Then he moved quickly away.

Lee did not watch him leave, turned again toward the south and the blue stain that spread along the edge of the river.

"General Hooker expects us to stay here, watching *them*. And that is the trap."

Jackson nodded, said nothing, understood now that Lee had been right.

Lee motioned to Taylor, said, "Major, my horse please," and then turned to Jackson. "General, we do not yet know where General Hooker is intending to lead his army. He is either intent on holding us here, assaulting us from behind, or he may move farther south, toward Gordonsville. He could easily cut the Orange and Alexandria Railroad, and cut us off from the Shenandoah. If he drives in that direction, we will have to withdraw from here, move down to the South Anna River and make our defense there."

He felt an anger rising up from deep inside, thought, How much more must we do? All the grand successes, the great bloody efforts to push them out of Virginia, and now they were coming again, unstoppable, into the heart of his home. He suddenly kicked at the ground, sent a spray of dirt flying, was breathing heavily, closed his eyes. No, keep control.

Jackson stared at him, and Lee turned toward him, looked hard into the sharp blue eyes. Jackson did not look away, and Lee said, "General, once again God is challenging us, offering us another opportunity. We must strike the enemy before he can go any farther." He looked away now, across the open fields, the town, the river. "I had thought . . . we had done enough . . . that He would be pleased. . . ."

Jackson stared at him, at the soft white beard, the face of a man growing old, then he looked up, beyond, said, "General Lee, if it will please God, we will kill them *all*."

IT WAS DARK WHEN STUART REACHED LEE'S CAMP. HE LED HIS troops through lines of marching infantry, Lee's men withdrawing from the great safety of the long row of hills, moving out now toward the west. Stuart's route had taken him along the roads that ran below Chancellorsville. He understood the necessity of staying clear of the Federal positions, but had still met a regiment of Federal cavalry, a short and confused fight on a dark road, and so it was becoming clear that Hooker was not passing them by, was not moving away toward Gordonsville, but was spread out around Chancellorsville, had stopped in the vast, thick Wilderness. Lee had not heard the shooting, but Anderson had, knew it was more than nervous skirmishers. He had sent word to Lee, and so when Stuart finally reached Lee's camp, Lee had not been sleeping, but anxious and alert.

The infantry was still moving down off the hill, would move all through the night, and Lee heard the shouts, tried to see in faint firelight, to see the man on the horse, the hat held high in the air, absorbing the cheers of the troops.

Stuart finally saw Lee, dismounted, made a deep bow. "General Lee, I am at your service."

"I am pleased to see you, General. I understand you had some difficulty tonight."

Stuart was grinning. "That we did, sir. The Virginians did themselves proud, both regiments, the Third and the Fifth. We sent a good-sized flock of Yanks scurrying back home!"

"That is good news, General, but I do not need you engaged with the enemy just now. You must be of greater service to this army."

Stuart bowed again, serious, said, "Yes, sir, I understand. Fact is, General, we did not look for the fight. We just ran into them. There's not many places to hide on these roads, sir. The Wilderness is not a place for horses."

"Very well, General. Do you mean to say that the Federal cavalry is advancing below the main body of infantry?"

Stuart seemed surprised, said, "Oh, no sir. They're *gone*. We ran into a regiment . . . just one regiment . . . some boys from New York. The main body, most of Stoneman's entire strength, is moving away, down south. I sent your son . . . that is, I sent General Rooney Lee to keep after them, stay close, and keep me—the army—informed." He stopped, Lee waited for more, saw the smile again. "General Lee, I believe that General Stoneman is trying to ride clear around this army, sir." He waited for Lee to absorb that.

Lee said, "General, are you suggesting that General Stoneman is attempting to duplicate your . . . accomplishments?"

"All I can tell, sir, is he's taken several thousand men, is moving down along the Orange and Alexandria Railroad, trying to tear up whatever he can, and he has already sent some units toward the east, well below us, sir. By now he is completely cut off from General Hooker's command. They may even be heading toward Richmond, sir! Maybe General Stoneman . . . well, maybe he wants to see his name in the Richmond papers."

Stuart was glowing now, and Lee could not believe it. If Stuart was right, Hooker's cavalry, the critical eyes of the Federal Army, was on their own, possibly to make a sweep through central Virginia that would be an annoyance, but little else. Stuart had made the same type of ride, twice before, had severely embarrassed the Federal command by riding completely around their army without any serious obstacles, and without any substantial gain. It was not something of which Lee approved, but the grand show, the sheer audacity of it, had been of great benefit to morale and was trumpeted loudly by the newspapers, both North and South. Surely, Lee thought, there is more than that . . . this cannot be just a glorified parade.

"General, please keep me informed what the young Mr. Lee reports. I do not want ten thousand Federal cavalry suddenly appearing on our flank."

"There will be no surprises, General."

Lee turned, walked over to a small fire, and Stuart followed. It was very late, and Lee suddenly felt a great need for sleep, a thickening fog in the brain. Taylor was poking the fire, trying to stifle a yawn. Lee said, "Major, you may retire. We will have a long day tomorrow."

Taylor stood, felt another yawn coming, clamped it down, saluted, and quickly moved away. Lee felt his own yawn building, and he stretched his back, twisting slightly.

"General Stuart, in the morning, General Hooker will find that we have moved out to meet him. We are constructing a line of defense from the river to the north, down across the main roads. I do not believe the force that is below Fredericksburg is a threat at this time. I have ordered General Jackson to move his corps away from these hills, to support General Anderson and General McLaws. General Jackson will be in command of the field."

Stuart looked out along the top of the hill, started to say something, and Lee said, "We are not abandoning these hills, General. I have placed General Early's division up here, spread out in a thin line. He will do what he can to convince General Sedgwick that we are still up here in force." The fog in his brain had cleared. He felt a rush of energy, and the words came quickly. "I do not believe General Hooker wants the fight to be below Fredericksburg, and so I do not believe General Sedgwick will advance against us. But I do not want General Hooker to move the rest of his army any farther south. General Stuart, you will do what you can to impede his movement that way, toward Gordonsville. If there is to be a fight, we must make it quickly, before General Sedgwick learns we have pulled away from him. If he sees there is only weak opposition, he will certainly move up and occupy these hills. We cannot fight a battle in two directions. . . ."

Stuart listened hard, stared at Lee. It was plain and clear, and Stuart suddenly felt overwhelmed, felt something rising in him, loud and excited. He smiled again, wanted to put his hands on Lee's shoulders, show him the affection, but it would not happen, and he tried to hold it in, abruptly made another deep bow, swept the ground with his hat.

"Yes, sir. I will keep you informed, sir."

Lee nodded, was finished. The words had drained him, and he felt the fog returning in a heavy wave. He turned away from the small fire, moved wearily toward his tent and with a soft voice said, "You are the eyes of this army, General."

45. HANCOCK

Friday, May 1, 1863

THE FOG HAD BEEN THICK, WAS NOW BURNING AWAY. THE MEN had been up since first light, had formed early and waited in the roads, but there were no orders. Now, finally, the word came from the old mansion and they began to move.

They were to advance eastward on three roads, the two direct routes toward Fredericksburg, the Orange Turnpike and Plank Road, and by a third route, River Road, which left the Wilderness above and moved in a direct northeast line toward Bank's Ford. Two divisions of Meade's Fifth Corps had this assignment, with the intended goal of opening up that crossing for Federal troops and creating a more direct line of communication and supply between Hooker's main force and Sedgwick's corps below Fredericksburg. Slocum's Twelfth Corps would advance on Plank Road, to the south, supported by Howard's Eleventh, and between these two routes, George Sykes's division of Meade's corps would lead the way, followed by Couch's Second Corps, with Hancock in front, close behind Sykes. The Third Corps, led by Dan Sickles, would remain north of Chancellorsville, acting as a general reserve. This advance involved a force of nearly seventy thousand troops.

Hancock rode behind the last of Sykes's column, watched thin clouds of steam rise out of the thick brush on both sides of the road. The fog had given way to a light rain, but it had been brief, thankfully, had not mired the roads, and now it was clear and warm, and nearly noon.

They would not have far to march before the Wilderness would break, give way to the open fields, precious room to maneuver, to place the cannon where they could actually see their targets . . . if there were any targets.

Couch had been with him earlier, before the march, expecting the quick order to move out, and when the orders did not come, Couch had gone back to see Hooker. Hancock did not know if the orders had finally come because of anything Couch had done, but he knew—all the commanders knew—something was wrong at headquarters. The soldiers still had the high spirit of the day before, knew they had done something important, a quick and successful march by this huge army, and the campsites had been lively places. This morning they had not delayed falling into line, were moving now with the quick step of men who have the sense that this time they had the upper hand, that the fight would be theirs.

The line in front of Hancock began to make a long slow climb toward a slight rise that lifted the ground far out on both sides. He could see the advance now, up in front, small flags, and suddenly there was a long thin line of smoke, but not heavy. It was the skirmish line, the first opposition to their grand sweep toward Lee. Sykes's column

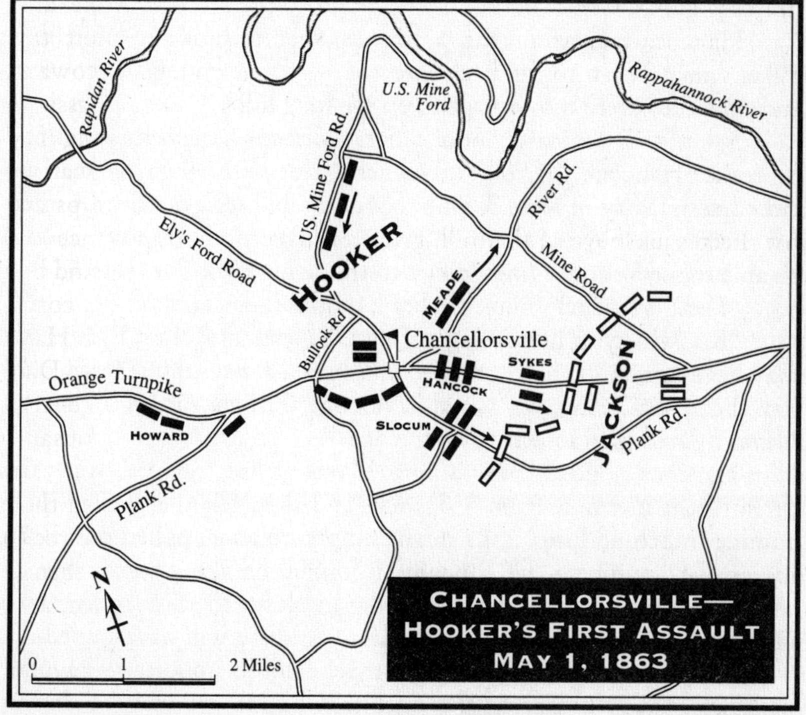

CHANCELLORSVILLE—
HOOKER'S FIRST ASSAULT
MAY 1, 1863

began to disperse, moving with difficulty off the road and into the wiry brush. Hancock rode forward, past shouting officers, intent on finding General Sykes, to see if he knew yet what was in front of him.

There had been no word from either of the other advance columns. The terrain made it impossible for communication, but there were no sounds, not yet, no deep thunder of the battle, and so they would press on.

Sykes's lines did not slow, pushed the rebel skirmishers back up the long hill, and Hancock still rode forward, past more troops. He saw Sykes now, a cluster of blue uniforms, and Sykes was directing his officers, spreading the companies out across the road.

Sykes saw Hancock, raised a hand, said, "Ah, good morning . . . good day, General. All is well so far. We seem to have awakened a few rebels. No matter, they've scattered away."

"A skirmish line, General?"

"Barely. They didn't really try to slow us down, just took a shot and moved out. Probably a scouting party. Any word from the rear?"

"Not yet. I expect General Couch to return soon. Have you heard anything—"

"From Meade? No, and nothing down below us either. Looks like easy going, General."

Hancock focused on the far woods, tried to hear . . . something. Sykes's men began to file back into the road, reforming the column, and now they were moving again, up the long hill.

Sykes was waving to more officers, directing them forward, and he said to Hancock, "If you can, General, ride with me. Your men are close behind, stay in front for a bit. We should break out of this infernal thicket just beyond that hill, give us a little room to move. Should be able to see Slocum's lines, down to the right. How does it feel?"

"Feel?" Hancock shook his head, didn't understand.

"Knowing you're running right up the back of Robert E. Lee? We may have him this time . . . finally have him. I always thought it would have been McClellan, we would have done this, ended this with Mac. Never figured Joe Hooker to be the one."

Hancock nodded, said nothing. Maybe it was true. If Lee felt the threat from in front, from Sedgwick, and then felt the greater force coming in behind him . . . he might simply be gone, pulled out. With his smaller numbers, he thought, it might be the smart move to withdraw south of Fredericksburg, dig in closer to Richmond, make Hooker bring the Federal Army *to* him. And we will have gained . . . what? he wondered. Ground? But maybe more important, Hooker will have driven Lee back, and once that begins, we may be able to keep driving him back. He is outmanned, outgunned, outsupplied. And maybe today he was outmaneuvered.

Hancock began to feel some excitement, thought, Yes, it is working, the quick march, dividing the army. He looked at Sykes, who was focused to the front, to the moving line of troops.

"Yes, General, press on! My men are anxious to see the backs of Lee's army!" He felt foolish saying it, the kind of mindless boasting heard so often around the camps, around the headquarters of bad commanders.

Sykes looked at him, smiled. "Yes, and don't forget that Stonewall. Let's see how fast he can run!"

There was more firing now, a rolling wave of muskets, and toward the front of the line the men were spreading out again. Sykes began to ride, moving forward, and Hancock followed, sped the horse closer. Now they could see the crest of the hill. Spread on both sides of the road, out through a narrow clearing in the deep brush, was a solid gray line, and the muskets began again, fresh and regular volleys, and Sykes was yelling, directing the men. Hancock saw that this was not a skirmish line, Lee had come out to meet them, was waiting for them. He stared ahead for a moment, then turned the horse, rode back down the hill toward the front of his division. His staff was there, waiting, expectant faces, and he thought of the ridiculous conversation with Sykes, the arrogant notion that Stonewall Jackson would ever run.

THEY HAD MET THE LINES OF ANDERSON AND MCLAWS. JACKSON did not want to wait, knew that once the Federal columns came out of the Wilderness, they would have the advantage of mobility. While Jackson's own divisions were quickly moving toward the field, preparing to link up with Anderson, Jackson was already there, had reached the strong defensive lines Anderson had prepared during the night, the trenches and felled trees. It was a strong line, but Jackson would not wait for the slow advance of the Federals, had ordered Anderson and McLaws forward, out of the trenches, toward the edge of the Wilderness.

Hancock pointed from the center of the road, spreading his regiments out into the woods. He could still see Sykes's lines moving forward, still climbing the hill, and now his own men were ready, began to advance up, close behind Sykes. The sounds were steady now, a dull echo in the dense mass of brush. Down to the south he could hear more sounds: Slocum was engaged as well; Jackson's lines were spread down across both roads.

Hancock stood in the stirrups, tried to see beyond the brush, but it was hopeless. How can they put up that much of a front? he wondered. His mind began to turn quickly. If Lee is here, he thought, if he has come out to meet us, then who is on the hills in front of Sedgwick? So, if Lee has turned this way, then it is up to Sedgwick to come up over and around the hills, and we can still squeeze Lee between us.

His men were pushing slowly through the thickets, still moving up the hill, and now he saw a flag, riders. It was Couch.

Couch pulled the horse up, stared forward toward the crest of the hill. "General Hancock, are your men engaged?"

"No, sir. But Sykes is pushing them back. He appears to have control of the high point of the hill. The clear open ground is not far beyond. If we can advance out of this mess, we will have an open field of fire."

Couch turned to the south, listening. Hancock said, "Slocum is engaged as well. If the rebels are giving way, it must be a thin line in front of us. We have the momentum, and it seems we have the strength."

Couch nodded, looked back to the north. "Meade is still advancing on the River Road. I left headquarters when we heard the first sounds from out here. But so far Meade is unopposed. Lee will surely have some force guarding Bank's Ford, but with two divisions, Meade should be able to clear them out." Couch was staring hard, intense, bright flashing eyes, and Hancock did not recall seeing the small man with such energy, such animated movement.

"Sir, what of Sedgwick? Is he advancing?"

Couch did not answer, still stared ahead to the fight.

"Sir, is General Sedgwick advancing on Lee's position? If Lee has moved a strong force this way, the hills above Fredericksburg could be taken without—"

"General Hooker has ordered Sedgwick not to attack, to just make a demonstration. General Hooker has ordered Sedgwick to dig in, to prepare to *receive* an attack."

Hancock leaned forward, stared at Couch, was not sure he understood. "An attack? From where?"

"From Jackson . . . from Lee's forces on the hill."

Hancock was confused, said, "Then who is that in front of *us*?"

Couch waited, looked again to the north, heard nothing, said, "If we had some cavalry, we might have the answer to that."

Ahead of them the fighting began to slow, and they could see blue troops on the crest of the hill. Couch began to ride forward, and Hancock rode with him, leading their staffs. The crest of the hill was covered with bodies, and the dead were being pulled aside, off the road. All around them wounded were being attended, men from both sides. From the top of the hill they could see to the east, out past the edge of the Wilderness. Well below, the gray lines were reforming, had been pushed back, but now the Federal forces had the high ground, and far in the distance they could see the dark shapes of the hills between them and Fredericksburg.

The ridge ran north and south for miles, and down to the right they could begin to see Slocum's lines, also in numbers too great for the thin line of Jackson's defense.

Couch was looking through field glasses, watching the emerging lines of blue. Hancock saw Sykes riding up toward the crest, back from the advance lines of his troops.

Sykes saluted, said, "General Couch, welcome to the field, sir. We have won the day . . . we have prevailed! The rebels have been pushed back to the edge of the open ground, and I am ordering my guns up to this hill. Have you heard from General Meade, sir? I must report to him."

Couch shook his head, pointed toward the north. "He's still up there, as far as I know. If he's had as good a day as you have, he may be sitting at Bank's Ford."

Sykes looked toward the rear of his lines, saw horses bringing up the first of his field guns. There was an officer leading, and Sykes yelled, "Here, over here, there's a small clearing. . . ." The horses moved that way, a clatter of wheels, and Sykes said, "General Couch, do you have any orders, sir? Should we press the attack?"

Couch turned, looked back at Hancock's troops, who had filled the road behind them, down along the hill. Hancock looked with him, thought, Yes, we cannot be stopped. We are too many.

In the distance there was a man on a horse, moving awkwardly along the side of the road, pressing hard up the hill toward them. Couch said, "That's Loveless . . . from Hooker." They waited, and the man made his way up the hill, waving a piece of paper.

"Sir . . . your orders, sir!"

The man had called out with unusual energy, was looking now to the front, cautiously, where a few bursts of musket fire still echoed through the woods.

Couch took the paper, read quietly, and Hancock watched his face, tried to see. Couch's expression did not change. Suddenly, he gripped the paper hard, crushing it, stared ahead at nothing. "We have been ordered to withdraw."

Hancock waited for more, said, "You mean, my division?"

Couch looked at him, grim and hard, said, "No, General. Both divisions. The *army*. General Hooker is recalling all units back to Chancellorsville. We are to form a defensive line, back where we began this morning."

Sykes stared at Couch, his mouth open slightly, and he turned to the east, pointed. "Sir, we have pushed the enemy back! The field is ours, we must advance . . . General Meade . . . I must find out if General Meade knows—"

"No, General. The order clearly names your division as well. There is no mention of General Meade. I would assume he has received an order just like this one."

Hancock looked to the south, toward the far clearing where Slocum's troops could be seen. "They're leaving. Slocum is withdrawing already."

Couch followed Hancock's gaze, said, "Of course, he follows orders. We all follow orders."

Sykes was shaking his head, waved an arm wildly, said, "No! If Slocum pulls back we are exposed! Our flank is open!"

Hancock was still looking toward the south and the small sounds of distant muskets. He looked to the clearing beside the road, to Sykes's cannon, the men unhooking and turning the guns, pointing toward the east. He looked back at Couch, who was listening to Sykes still protesting, his voice getting louder.

Men were beginning to gather, men who knew their commander to be a solid leader, a soldier who led a tough division, mostly regulars, veterans of many bad and costly fights. Now the men were beginning to understand, heard Sykes say, "We cannot withdraw! General, we simply cannot!"

The soldiers began to close in around the men on the horses, and Hooker's courier was glancing sharply around, nervous. A man yelled out, "We ain't turnin' back! We got the rebs on the run!"

There were more calls now, and men began to shout at Couch, at Hancock, knew their own commander would not back away, not from a fight they were winning.

Couch looked out at the faces, said nothing, then looked at Hancock, and Hancock now understood. The order was clear and direct, and they would obey. Couch turned to Sykes, who was silent now, in wide-eyed disbelief.

Couch said, "General Sykes, you will form your division and march in column toward Chancellorsville. General Hancock's division will protect your flanks and rear and then will follow your column."

Sykes looked at Hancock, then back to Couch, and around them men were yelling, angry and defiant. Sykes started to say something, waved his arm again, and Couch raised his voice, said with a dark anger, "There will be no further discussion! You will carry out your orders, General!"

Sykes nodded, looked at Hancock, and Hancock could not stay still, pulled his horse away and moved back down the hill, toward his own troops. Behind him officers were giving the commands to Sykes's men, and suddenly there were horses moving quickly by him—Couch and his staff riding hard, back to the west, toward the headquarters of their commanding general.

HE MOVED BY REFLEX, HIS MIND IN A FOG AS HE DIRECTED HIS men through the small clearings east of the Chancellor mansion. They still faced toward the enemy, had now joined alongside Sykes. He gave the new orders, and the company commanders supervised the labor—trenches and earthworks were dug, trees cut.

His division was now fully deployed, and Hancock rode back along the road, toward the Chancellor mansion. He still did not believe it had happened; there had to be something else, some major piece of the puzzle missing, some great disaster. Of course, it could have been Sedgwick. Perhaps Sedgwick had been beaten back across the river. Longstreet could have returned; his divisions could have surprised Sedgwick from the south. And there was Meade, up along the river. There could have been a major obstacle there, something unexpected. But—and there were many buts—there had been no sounds of battle, no distant rumble of guns from Fredericksburg. Meade had not been engaged, the sounds would have been clearer still. He caught himself, realized this had happened before. McClellan had often done it, magnified Lee's strength into huge numbers, great numbers of the enemy everywhere at once, had talked himself into seeing the ghosts of an army that wasn't there. But today they *were* there, Hancock thought. We were right in front of them, and there weren't that many . . . it was our field. And we gave it back to them. Now Lee will move his guns up to that high ridge, will look down on us while we sit tight in our trenches, wondering what to do next.

Hancock reached the grand house, saw officers standing in small groups, men leaving on horses, others arriving. He climbed down, moved slowly, heavily, up to the porch. A guard opened the door, and Hancock saw blank and pale faces, then heard voices, loud and angry. His mind cleared and he moved in noisy steps on the hard floor, went into the large living room, the room with the chandelier. Couch was waving his arms in the air, red-faced; and sitting behind a large table, Joe Hooker.

Hancock did not hear what Couch had said. He stared at Hooker, surprised, did not see anger. The clean-shaven face was staring up at Couch with a small, weak smile. Suddenly Hooker stood up, looked around the room, looked at Hancock without seeing him, looked past several other men, said, "It is all right, General Couch. Gentlemen, it is all right. I have got old Bobby Lee right where I want him. Now he will have to come to us, on our own ground!"

Couch stood still for a moment, then abruptly turned and moved quickly toward the door. He passed Hancock, saw him, a quick glance of recognition, and Hancock followed him outside.

Couch went to his horse, and his aides began to gather. He looked at Hancock, said, "He ran out of nerve. When he learned that we had run into opposition, he stopped believing in his own plan. He just ran out of nerve. Meade . . . Meade had nearly reached Bank's Ford . . . *unopposed*, when he was called back. Howard's corps never even had time to leave their camp. Sedgwick still doesn't know what happened. Now we're digging in . . . as though Almighty God Himself is leading an army against us!"

Hancock wanted to say something, knew Couch was as angry as he had ever seen him, and Couch put a hand up on his horse, grabbed at the leather straps, turned again to Hancock, calmer now. With a long, slow breath, he said, "He is a whipped man."

Couch climbed up on his horse, and his staff moved in behind. Without speaking, he turned and rode away.

It was nearly dark, and Hancock climbed on his own horse, moved slowly across the yard, nodded at familiar faces. He moved out onto the road, felt completely drained now, like waking up from a long and deep sleep, rising slowly out of a horrible nightmare, but now there was no relief, no feeling that it was over, only the same heavy dread that they had done this before, the utterly foolish mistakes, and if the leaders had not learned, certainly the soldiers had—that these mistakes would always turn into bloody disasters.

46. JACKSON

Friday, May 1, 1863

He reached the intersection, looked down both roads. Troops were everywhere, small fires and stacks of arms. He did not yet see Lee. He pushed the horse along, and the men saw him now, hats went up, and the subdued cheers. They were, after all, a tired army, a stiff march and a good sharp fight, and Jackson tried to see the faces, the men who had done their duty. He glanced upward, raised a hand, said a silent prayer, *We do all we can to please You*, and he felt a calm satisfaction, knew God would be pleased by such a day as this.

He had thought it too easy, the heavy columns of Federal troops pulling away, giving him the field, abandoning the fine, long ridge from where the guns could find the long range. Now his own three divisions were in place, alongside Anderson and McLaws, and he knew that with this army, no one could stand in their way, that Hooker must know that as well and would pull away, completely, back across the river. He nodded silently, pulled a lemon from his pocket. *Yes*, you had best be gone tomorrow or we will give you the bayonet.

He stopped the horse, looked around through a small grove of pines, saw more troops, watching him, and now he saw Lee, riding slowly through the grove, heard the new cheers from his men. Lee dismounted, raised a hand, a warm greeting, and Jackson pulled the horse off the road, into the grove.

Lee's staff was arranging something to sit on, old wooden boxes marked U.S. ARMY, and three boxes were placed together, two chairs and a table. They were near a fire, and a dim glow spread over the flat wood. Lee moved toward one of the boxes and sat down.

Behind him, Jackson's aides had moved up, closer, and someone took the reins from his hand. He walked on soft ground toward the fire, tossed the flattened lemon aside, sat down on the other "chair," watched Lee from under the short bill of the old cadet cap.

Lee removed his hat, ran a stiff hand through gray hair, glanced toward the fire, and Jackson saw the old face in the firelight, heavy, tired eyes. Lee said, "Fine work, today, General. We were in a difficult situation. It could have been very different."

Jackson did not respond, absorbed the words, was not sure what Lee meant. He leaned forward, put his hands out on the box between them, as though holding it down in place, said, "We pushed them hard, and they ran away. There was nothing difficult about it."

Lee looked at him, hid a smile. "General, from what we have observed . . . there are nearly seventy thousand Federal troops beyond those trees, digging in around Chancellorsville. Sedgwick has nearly forty thousand spread out along this side of the river in front of General Early. There are possibly thirty thousand more back along the river, north of here, that we have not yet located. I give you credit for a fine day's work, General. But we are not in a position of strength here. We owe a great deal to the unexplainable, to the mystery of General Hooker. He has allowed us to maneuver freely between two parts of an army that is more than twice our strength. I am concerned, General, that we do not yet understand his plan."

Jackson leaned back, looked at Lee again from under the cap. "He has no plan. He is waiting for us to take the fight to him. He is, right now, digging trenches, building a defensive line. He is already beaten."

Lee nodded. "Perhaps. He may yet be planning a move toward Gordonsville, move around below us, cut us off from Richmond. We must not forget about General Sedgwick, on the river. He shows no signs of moving, but that could change."

Lee turned, motioned to Taylor, who stood beside the fire, and the young man came close, handed Lee a rolled-up paper, which Lee spread on the box. It was a map, faint pencil lines on wrinkled paper, and Jackson leaned closer, tried to focus in the dim light.

Lee pointed to the Rappahannock, to a point above them, said, "They are anchored against the river, up here. Their line is continuous, down below Chancellorsville, then curves along . . . here."

Jackson nodded. "Yes, we observed that . . . their lines curve around these open clearings . . . then toward the west."

"Then what, General? Do you know where their right flank is, where they are anchored to the west?"

Jackson stared at the map, said quietly, a small defeat, "No. Not yet."

"We must know that, General. If he begins to march in that direction, he could threaten our flank, or be gone toward Gordonsville before we can react."

Jackson shook his head. "If he moves, it will be north, across the river. . . ."

Horses came at a fast gallop on the road, and both men turned, saw a small squad of cavalry and the tall dark plume on Stuart's hat.

Stuart jumped from his horse, moved quickly toward where the men sat, removed the hat with the usual flair, said, "General, may I be allowed to join your meeting?"

Lee smiled slightly, nodded, and Stuart looked around for his own box to sit on, saw nothing, then moved around, away from the fire, so as not to block the light, and leaned over the map.

"General, I have some interesting news."

Jackson leaned his head back, tried to see Stuart from under the cap, said, "They are digging in."

Stuart looked at him, nodded, "Oh, yes, sir, they are digging in. But that's not the interesting part." He looked at Lee, put his finger on the map. "Out here, to the west . . . along the turnpike here . . . their right flank is completely exposed. It's the one place where they are *not* digging in. Clearly, they do not expect any pressure there. Their flank is completely in the air."

Lee glanced at Jackson, leaned closer to the map, said, "Who is on their flank?"

"The Eleventh Corps, Oliver Howard."

Lee continued to look at the map, reached a hand out. "Are there any roads, down this way, below the turnpike?"

Stuart began to move now, shifting from one foot to the other. "Yes, sir, indeed there are. Good roads." He pointed. "That's Catherine's Furnace, and there's a road . . . wait . . ." He pulled a stub of a pencil from his pocket, drew a ragged line. "Here, there's a road, over this way."

Jackson said, "Then we will hit them *there*. We can move around their flank." He looked up at Lee. "And they will have nowhere to go but back across the river . . . or we will destroy them."

Lee nodded, said, "Those roads . . . they are too close to their lines, they will observe any movement. We must find another road, farther down. Do we have someone here, someone we can trust, who knows the area?"

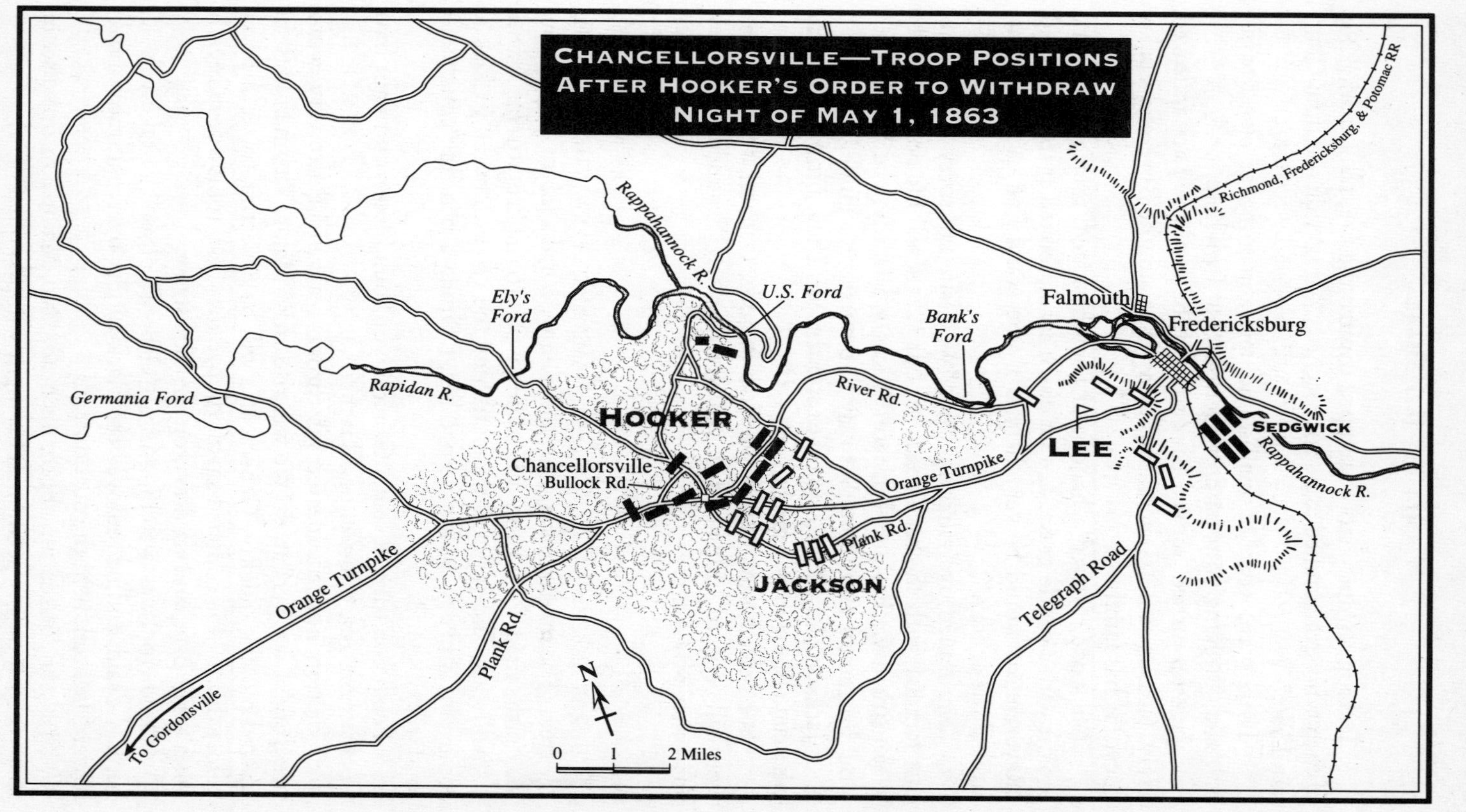

Chancellorsville—Troop Positions
After Hooker's Order to Withdraw
Night of May 1, 1863
Richmond, Fredericksburg, & Potomac RR
Rappahannock R.
U.S. Ford
Ely's Ford
Bank's Ford
Falmouth
Fredericksburg
Rapidan R.
Germania Ford
River Rd.
Hooker
Lee
Sedgwick
Rappahannock R.
Chancellorsville
Bullock Rd.
Orange Turnpike
Plank Rd.
Jackson
Telegraph Road
Orange Turnpike
Plank Rd.
To Gordonsville
N
0
1
2 Miles

Jackson abruptly stood, stepped toward the fire, to a small group of men who straightened as he approached. "Mr. Pendleton, find Chaplain Lacy."

There was a voice, a small sound, and a man moved closer to the fire, said, "Begging your pardon, General, but I am here, sir."

Jackson turned, moved back toward the map and Lacy followed, shyly. Jackson said, "General, this is my chaplain, the Reverend Tucker Lacy. He has family in this area, sir."

Lee stood, offered a hand, and Lacy hesitated, then reached out, took it with a gentle grasp. Lee sat down again, looked at the map, said, "Reverend, it would be very helpful if you could find us a safe route around the enemy."

Lacy leaned over slightly, said, "Well, sir, I'm sorry . . . I'm not that familiar with the back roads . . . but . . . there." He pointed to the spot marked Catherine's Furnace. "I know a family, the Wellfords. I would suggest a visit there. We may find ourselves a guide."

Jackson said, "Please go there at once, Mr. Lacy. Find us someone who can tell me how I might proceed."

Lee smiled, said, "Then we have decided, General, that this mission will be *yours*." He nodded, smiled to himself. "I would not have it any other way."

IT WAS SURPRISINGLY COOL—A DAMP MIST BLEW THROUGH THE trees. The meeting was over, the men who had a job to do were out on the road. Pendleton was adding wood to the fire, stirring it with a small stick, and Jackson was searching the ground, began to kick at some pine straw, pushing it together, forming a bed. He coughed, a loud, raspy sound.

Pendleton turned, said, "General, you sound like you might have an affliction. Are you feeling all right?"

Jackson nodded, cleared his throat, realized he felt very weak, tired, and it was very late. "We will rise early, Major. The men must be up and moving quickly. General Lee will be expecting to see me well before dawn." He coughed again, rubbed his chest, took a deep breath, felt a slight pain, and sat down on the pine straw.

Pendleton was watching him. "General, please . . . take this . . . here," he said, and he removed the black rubber overcoat, moved over toward Jackson, held the coat out.

Jackson looked up, shook his head. "No, Major. Do not discomfort yourself on my account. This night will pass quickly."

Pendleton began to pull at the coat, separating the long lower flap from the topcoat, a series of small metal snaps.

"At least, sir, take the bottom part. I will not need more than this."

Jackson saw the young face, genuine concern, and he nodded. "All right. Thank you . . . bless you, Major. Now, let us get some sleep."

He lay flat on the straw, felt something hard, realized he had not removed his sword. He sat up, unbuckled it, then turned and reached out toward a tall pine, leaned the sword upright against the trunk of the tree. He saw Pendleton, lying still now near the fire, and he said a prayer, a quick thought for the boy. Above, the wind blew the thick mist down through the trees, a sharp, cold breeze. Jackson fought against a cough, stood, walked quietly to where Pendleton lay, heard the faint, steady breathing of the tired young man. He draped Pendleton's coat over the young man's legs and moved back toward his own bed. Jackson stretched out on the damp straw, another small cough, and he rolled over, lay on his side, the side that did not hurt. Now a new breeze came through the tops of the pines, a hard whisper, swirling toward the sleeping soldiers. The sword, held by the glow of the faint firelight, was lifted by the voice of the wind, suddenly slid away, dropped down hard on the straw-covered ground.

Saturday, May 2, 1863

He was a boy, but he had spent his young life in these woods, had seen the brush thicken into a vast tangle, covering the old trails, and so he had made new ones, had explored the creeks and climbed the hills. Now he would guide the army, the army he was too young to join. He would lead them away from the eyes of the Yankees.

Jackson had been up for a while, had barely slept at all, and now he was on his horse, moving slowly among his troops, the troops that would soon be on the march.

Lee was still asleep as Jackson eased toward the pine grove and dismounted. In the faint light he could see one of the staff, working on the fire. He walked through the grove, and the young man watched him, nodded, said nothing. Jackson eased closer to the dark form on the ground, paused, watched the slow breathing, then said, "General Lee?"

There was motion, and Lee's bare head peeked from under a blanket.

"What? Time? Oh . . . thank you, General. Be right with you."

Jackson backed away, moved toward the boxes. The map was there now, spread out by the young aide, and the man went quietly back to the fire.

Lee, in the firelight now, putting on his coat, looked up at thick darkness, said, "General, your Mr. Lacy came to me . . . late . . . earlier this morning. He told me there is another road, a road that will take you well below the Federal lines."

Jackson sat, leaned over to the map, said, "Yes. The boy—the Wellford boy—has explained it to me. He knows the route. He will ride with me."

Lee sat back, glanced toward the warmth coming now from the growing fire.

Jackson was still staring at the map, said, "There. We will march to that point, where this road rejoins the turnpike. Then we will turn east and attack the flank."

"Very well, General. And what do you propose to make this movement with?"

Jackson looked up, seemed surprised at the question. "Well, General, with my whole corps."

Lee was not surprised at the answer, flexed his stiff hands in the cool air.

"And what will you leave me?"

Jackson looked at the old face, thought he saw a smile, said, "Why, the divisions of Anderson and McLaws."

Lee stood, walked to the fire, began to understand. Of course, it was the only way. The risk was extraordinary. He would be left with barely twelve thousand men, spread in a thin line facing Hooker's mass of seventy thousand. But if the plan were to work at all, Jackson would need the strength, a sharp hammer blow to the Federal flank, enough force to do more than surprise. If Hooker had already shown a reluctance to charge into a hot fight, Jackson's assault could unnerve him enough to fulfill Jackson's prediction and withdraw back above the river.

It was Jackson's job to lead thirty thousand troops quietly and discreetly through the countryside, and it was his to keep Hooker from realizing how weak the forces were that he was defending against. If Hooker pushed out of his trenches, even a short and brief advance toward Lee, or if he made an aggressive move toward Jackson's marching column, he could destroy not only the plan, but possibly the army.

Lee held up his hands, warmed them toward the fire, shook his head. And of course, there was still Sedgwick along the river. . . . How long would he sit and stare at a near-empty hill? This is not an accident, he thought. We are led by Divine hands. He turned, saw Jackson standing now, saw the familiar look, knew Jackson was anxious, ready to leave, and Lee nodded, said, "Well, go on!"

It was after daylight, dangerously late. The march would cover twelve miles, an easy distance for Jackson's foot cavalry if there was no obstruction and no opposition.

They filled the road quickly and quietly—instructions had gone down, all the way to the lowest levels—this was a quiet affair. There would be no cheering, no shouts, and no stragglers.

The three divisions would march in a column of fours, led by Daniel Hill's men, commanded now by Robert Rodes. Behind Rodes were Jackson's own division, led now by Raleigh Colston, and in the rear, the division of A. P. Hill.

Lee sat on Traveller at the edge of the trees, watched them forming column lines, and now he saw Jackson, riding with a hard, fixed

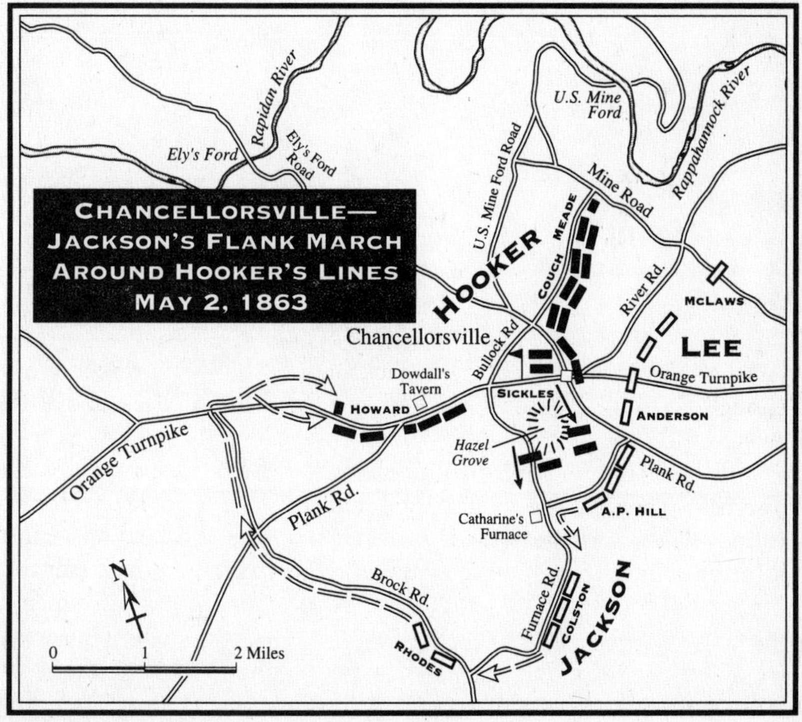

stare, moving alongside the troops. The men did not respond. The mood was clear, something was going on, the march would not end with tents and rations, but a hot and bloody fight. If they did not hear it in the orders, they saw it in Jackson's face.

He rode up to Lee, tilted back his head, was still wearing the old cap, and Lee saw the eyes, nodded sharply, did not smile.

There were few words, small nods, and suddenly Jackson reached out an arm, pointed down across the intersection, to the route they would take. Then he spurred the small horse, Little Sorrell, moved out across the road. Lee watched him move away, lowered his head, a small prayer, *God be with you, General,* and in front of him the great column began to move.

47. HOWARD

May 2, 1863. Midday.

He let the empty sleeve hang loosely, did not roll it up and pin it as most of the others did. The arm was lost at Fair Oaks, on the peninsula, and the loose sleeve reminded him constantly. He did not want to forget. And it made a good show. The Eleventh Corps did not accept his appointment with enthusiasm, and with this bit of dramatics, the loud message that he was a veteran, had made the sacrifice, he thought they might respect him a bit more.

The Eleventh had been identified as Sigel's corps, had consisted mainly of German immigrants, farmers and factory workers, mostly from New York and Pennsylvania. The men of the Eleventh were an untamed and rugged bunch and had pride in their heritage. When Sigel was relieved, the corps was given to Howard, a disciplinarian and a devout Christian. Neither trait opened any doors.

Oliver Howard had earned the promotion, served well under McClellan and since. He was the first division commander, under Couch, to enter Fredericksburg the winter before. He was a man with no outstanding talents, but he understood command, and it was a natural progression for him to eventually lead a corps. But even he understood that command of the Eleventh was a questionable reward. The Germans were not highly regarded as fighters, and were rarely put into the thick of the action. Now they were the far right flank of Hooker's army, well out of harm's way, the last line of defense, facing an empty section of the Wilderness.

They had finished breakfast, and the men were not looking for a fight. There were small groups, circles of blue, card-playing mostly, some stretched along the side of the turnpike, the opportunity for extra sleep. The trenches they had dug faced south, alongside the turnpike, and they were not deep. The fight was well to the east, far off to their left.

To the north, above the turnpike, the river was three miles away. There were no troops positioned above them. It was the far rear of the Federal position, the safest place on the field.

Howard rode slowly down the line of trenches, was met by small nods, the trained show of respect. It had only been a month, and he still did not know many of them, the regimental commanders, long and unpronounceable names. He had been patient with the accents, but often they would speak German around him, and he would say nothing, stare them down, and they would return to English, or say nothing at all.

He rode on the turnpike itself, toward the west, came to the end of the line, saw two brass guns pointing straight down the road, out toward nothing. It was the only place guns could be positioned; the road was the only clear line of sight. He turned toward the right, moved the horse off the road, saw the flags of two regiments, not quite a thousand men who lined up at a right angle from the road, refusing the line to the north. Here, they had not dug trenches at all. He rode alongside the distinct edge of the thickets, tried to see out through the dense tangle, and he saw a man, emerging with curses, carrying an armload of wood. The man tried to free himself from a thorny vine, dropped the wood, said, "Dammit, tore my sleeve."

He saw Howard, did not salute, bent over to retrieve his firewood, said, "No fit place for a man, General. Damned near got lost."

Howard nodded, did not smile, pushed the horse along.

There was a flurry of noise back on the turnpike, and he turned in the saddle, saw riders, flags. He spurred the horse, moved closer, saw now it was Hooker, his staff stretching out behind him like a small parade. Hooker raised his hand, stopping them. Howard rode up onto the road, saluted with his left hand.

Hooker said, "Good morning, General Howard."

Hooker was smiling broadly, in high spirits, and Howard forced a smile, said, "General Hooker. I am honored by your presence."

Hooker accepted the flattery, sat straight up in the saddle, looked out to the trenches, the official eye of the inspection. Men were standing now, lining the edge of the road, and Hooker said, "Yes, good. Good, indeed. Very strong, very strong."

Abruptly, he turned the horse around, moved through his staff, followed closely by his color bearers, and shouted back, "Keep it up, Howard!" and the parade moved quickly away.

The men began to spread out again, the show was over, and Howard stayed up on the road, pushed the horse slowly, followed the direction of Hooker's ride, moved back toward his own headquarters.

Howard did not move with any haste, expected few official tasks to fill the day. He let the horse walk slowly, gradually approached the building, the old tavern known as Dowdall's. In front there were horses, those of his staff, and another, which he did not recognize. He was still up on his horse, and an officer emerged from the tavern.

"General Howard, I am Major Montcrief of General Hooker's staff. The general has sent me to alert you, sir. There is a movement of rebel infantry and wagons on the roads south of this position."

Howard stared at the man, an unfamiliar face. "General Hooker . . . was just here, not an hour ago. He said nothing—"

"No, sir. The news just came from General Sickles. There is a heavy line of rebel activity moving south and west of General Sickles's position. General Hooker is most pleased to advise you, sir, to be alert for this activity."

"Pleased?"

"Why, yes sir. The general has expressed his congratulations to his men for prompting the retreat of the rebel army."

He thought, Of course, it has to be. They are moving away, probably toward Gordonsville. Stoneman's cavalry raid likely did serious damage to their supply and communications lines.

"Thank you, Major. You may return to General Hooker and convey to him that we are prepared to pursue the enemy on his command."

The man jumped down the steps, climbed his horse, and with a quick salute was gone.

Howard sat back in his saddle, thought, Yes, this army is finally moving in the right direction. He thought of going inside, maybe some coffee, but suddenly he felt stronger, awake, and he pulled the horse around, moved back down the turnpike, to once again ride along the strong lines of his men.

HE JOINED THE MEN AROUND THE SMALL FIRE, ASKED SLOWLY, "Might I enjoy a cup of your coffee?"

They had stood quietly, watching him approach, dismounting from the horse. There were nods, looks between them, and a cup was offered.

"Thank you, it has been a while since I had a cup of *real* coffee."

He put the cup to his mouth, felt the rush of steam. "Ah, yes. Thank you."

He looked to the faces that were looking at him, uncertain, curious, and now more men were moving closer, word was spreading, the aloof and hard commander was down with the men.

"Gentlemen, you may not know this yet, but this is a day to remember." He paused, heard voices, men saying "Sir," and he looked around, saw General Devens, the commander of the division, moving through the men.

"Ah, Devens, hope you don't mind my taking the liberty . . . I smelled the coffee, had to stop."

Devens saluted, glanced at the men, said, "No, General Howard, certainly not."

"General Devens, do any of your men climb trees?"

There was a pause, and one man said, "I been a good climber since I was a boy. Never seen a tree I couldn't top."

There were laughs, small jibes, and Howard said, "Well, that's mighty fine. I tell you what, soldier. You go over there, across the road, and pick out one of those tall ones, and when you get to the top, you tell me what you see."

The men were talking and moving now, accepting the challenge, and Devens moved closer to Howard, more curious, but Howard would say nothing, was enjoying the moment. Yes, this was a fine day indeed.

The soldier pulled off his coat, wrapped hard hands around the trunk of a tall, thin tree, began to shin his way up the limbless trunk. Men circled around the tree, cheering him on, and the man reached the first of the small limbs, pulled himself up quicker now, and Howard stood in the middle of the road, looked up through the branches, said, "All right, soldier. Anything to report?"

The man looked around, parted the leaves with his free hand, and then looked down at Howard, shook his head, and Howard raised his hand, pointed to the south, said, "How about that way?"

The man slid around the trunk of the tree, parted more leaves, and suddenly he stood up higher, leaned out away from the tree, said, "Hoooeeee. It's rebs! A whole army!"

Faces turned to Howard, and now other men began to move up the tree, and other trees, some without success.

Howard rocked on his heels, listened to the sounds of the men, and the excitement spread all along the lines.

Devens stood beside him, said, "May I assume, sir, that the rebel army is in retreat?"

Howard smiled at him, said, "Yes, you may, General." He looked around, saw one of Devens's staff, said, "Captain, please take a message to General Hooker."

The man moved up, pulled a pad of paper from his pocket, and Howard said, "Tell the General . . . from General Devens's headquarters, we can observe a column of infantry moving westward. . . ."

THE SOUNDS CAME RUMBLING UP THROUGH THE BRUSH, FROM down to the southeast. Howard was back at his headquarters, at Dowdall's, had returned from the woods to the south, from the direction of the fight. Sickles had been watching the enemy movement all morning, could stand still no longer, and so had sent a division down, toward Catherine's Furnace, to drive hard into the moving column. Howard had received a request from Hooker to lend a hand, to move one of his units down in that direction, protecting Sickles's right flank. The orders were carried out, and now Howard was back at his headquarters, stood outside the tavern, listened to the sounds of the fight, smiled. Yes, Bobby Lee, we will chase you after all.

He had wondered why Hooker did not begin to form the army, move out in pursuit, but Hooker had seemed content to stay put, let Lee move away. The victory, the great success of his plan, was to be savored.

Sickles had pressed down, into a portion of A. P. Hill's division, and Hill had brought his long line together, pinching at Sickles from both sides. Within a short time the battle had faded, and Sickles had the token reward of a regiment full of prisoners and the satisfaction of a man who has pressed the action, who, unlike his commander, was not content to watch the enemy flee. Since the bulk of the rebel column had already passed on the Furnace road, Sickles was content to settle his forces down in their new position, well below the rest of the Federal defenses. The brigade that Howard had sent for support had left a wide gap on the east side of his lines, but with Sickles down below, there would be no need for strength at that point. His men in the treetops could still see the rebel column moving far away to the west.

He thought again of coffee, maybe something stronger. It was mid-afternoon now, and he was not a drinker, but . . . it was such a glorious day, for an army that did not have many glorious days. He climbed up the steps, and now there was a rider coming from the west, and the man seemed anxious, was yelling.

"General . . . General . . . Please!"

Howard watched the man dismount in a tumble from his horse, and the man came forward in a rush, saluted wildly, said, "General, Major Rice reports that the rebel column has turned and is now to our west, sir. The major requests instructions, sir!"

Howard held up his hand, said, "Easy, young man. I am aware of the rebel movements. Tell your major to keep his eye on them. There is no cause for alarm. Have you reported this to General Devens?"

The soldier stared at him, said, "No, sir. The major thought this was . . . a high priority, sir."

"You tell Major Rice that in the future he will report his observations to his division commander. I do not have the time to entertain every courier from every outpost."

The man nodded, said, "Yes, sir. Sorry, sir. I will tell him."

He backed away, climbed up on the horse, and Howard raised the hand again, trying to ease the man's agitation. The man saluted, calmer now, and Howard returned it, nodded, and the man rode back to the west.

DEVENS WAS WATCHING THE MAN IN THE TREETOP, BALANCED precariously, and the man was struggling, trying to stay upright. Below him others were shouting, *"Hang on!"* and suddenly the man fell, down through the branches, dragging the thin limbs with him, and another man, below him, tried to slow the man's fall, and he began to fall as well, and there was laughing, and in a slow jerky motion, limbs cracking one by one, they slid downward, the two men grasping each other, then dropped into the clear, fell the final few feet to the ground. The crowd of men cheered now, and the men were helped to their feet, limping and scraped. Devens smiled, saw no major damage, except of course to their pride. He looked through the crowd of men and the men beyond, thought, This is very good, this has been very good for morale. Now . . . we may finally see some change, some real success.

He walked back up to the turnpike, looked at the pair of brass guns, pointing away down the far road, and he heard the voice of his aide. "General Devens, sir, a messenger."

He looked for the voice, saw his young lieutenant, and another man in a heavy sweat. The man saluted him, said, "General Devens, sir,

Major Rice reports that a large body of the enemy is to his front. He suggests . . . he respectfully advises . . ." The man paused. "General, he ordered me to say . . . 'for God's sake make some disposition to receive them.' "

Devens stopped smiling, said, "Sergeant, have you seen this large body of Major Rice's enemy?"

"Well, no sir. I'm the courier, sir. The major commands the lookout, sir. Don't care much for heights myself."

"Well, then, Sergeant, you go back and tell Major Rice that there is no need in trying to panic either you or this division. I will forward this report to General Howard. But I would suggest you return to Major Rice and tell him to calm down. If he cannot perform his duties with appropriate decorum, we may have to find someone else for the job. Is that clear?"

The man snapped to attention, said, "Perfectly clear, sir. Please allow me to return to the outpost, sir."

Devens returned the man's salute, said, "Dismissed, Sergeant." He stared wearily at the lieutenant, rested his hands on his hips. "I suppose you should ride to General Howard's headquarters. Tell him of the report. Tell him I have seen no evidence that the enemy is doing anything more than leaving."

The man hurried away, mounted his horse, and galloped down the road, then slowed, rode the horse at a trot, knew that when he reached Howard's headquarters he would hear the same reproach, would receive the wrath of the annoyed commander: that these observers, the men who watch the enemy, are always jumpy, always exaggerate, and that the commander certainly understood the situation—it was his *job* to know what was going on.

48. JACKSON

MAY 2, 1863. LATE AFTERNOON.

HE STEPPED QUIETLY THROUGH A CLUSTER OF SMALL BUSHES, thick and green, and the ground suddenly dropped away, down a long flat hill, and there, along a wide road, was the Federal line.

He had never been this close, felt like giggling, a wild adventure. His guide, the man who had brought him to this spot, was beside him: Lee's nephew, Stuart's brigade commander, Fitz Lee.

"There they be, General. The whole lot of 'em."

They were sitting around small fires. Some were reading, playing cards, and back, behind them, a small herd of cattle was being lined up, the preparation for tonight's dinner. Jackson rubbed his hands together, wiped them on his pants leg. This was an incredible sight.

Lee backed away, through the bushes. Jackson didn't want to leave, but knew he had to get back, to move the column farther to the west. This was the point where they had thought the flank could be assaulted, but there were too many blue troops, and the line ran farther west, along the road. So the march would continue, until his men were far around the last of the Federal lines.

He followed the young Lee back to the horses, said nothing. Lee climbed up, smiling, waited for the compliment, the acknowledgment of a fine piece of scouting. He was well taught in the Stuart school of soldiering, appreciated the glamour of the cavalry; they all basked in the bright light of Stuart's reputation. But Jackson had climbed up on the horse, was already far away, and Lee frowned, would have to find the pat on the back elsewhere.

They moved quickly back to the road. A squad of cavalry was waiting, and Jackson looked past them, pulled the horse around, began to move alongside the marching column of troops, toward the front of the line.

He reached an intersection, the last leg that would take the men up to the turnpike, and saw Robert Rodes and the young boy who had guided them. Rodes's division was now crossing the intersection, and Jackson rode close beside the men, said, "Keep it up, move up."

They looked up at him. Most were smiling, and he did not notice the hollow eyes, a toll from the warm day and the lack of food. There had been few rations for the march, and those men who had not eaten early that morning had likely not eaten since the morning before. Despite Jackson's enthusiasm, and the constant pressure from the officers, the march was taking far longer than he had expected.

He pushed through the line of troops and moved up beside Rodes. Raleigh Colston came quickly along the road, followed by a small staff, and Jackson waited. When Colston reined up, Jackson said, "Very soon now. General Rodes, you will begin to deploy your men on either side of the turnpike, brigade front. General Colston, how soon will your men be up?"

"We're right behind, General."

Jackson nodded, was now seeing beyond the men, out past the thick tangle of woods, already watching what was yet to come.

Colston and Rodes had both been instructors at VMI, and both were well acquainted with Jackson's manner and his moods. Neither man spoke, and they glanced at each other as Jackson stared quietly beyond the road. Suddenly, he reached into his pocket, pulled out a small pencil, a rough piece of crumpled paper, held the paper flat against his saddle and wrote a brief message.

". . . I hope as soon as practicable to attack. I trust that an ever kind Providence will bless us with great success . . ." He concluded the note, stared at it, and behind him Pendleton moved closer, anticipated the order. Jackson started writing again, a small postscript. Pendleton had motioned for a courier, and the man was up quickly, held out his hand when Jackson turned with the note. Jackson stared at him, thought he should know the man's name. He had forgotten it, stared for a long minute, tried to recall. The man glanced at Pendleton, uncomfortable, and Jackson abruptly handed him the paper, said, "Take this to General Lee."

Pendleton said something to the man, precautionary instructions that Jackson did not hear, and then the courier was quickly moving, leading the horse back along the edge of the road.

There were more horses now, Fitz Lee's squadron of cavalry

moving past, alongside the road, and Jackson turned and watched them. Lee slowed, waved the men on, and Jackson looked at him from under the cap, said, "Take your men up past the turnpike. You must observe the roads that go to the river, protect our flank."

Lee saluted, smiled. "Already on our way, General."

Jackson watched the cavalry move away, sat back in his saddle and smiled. He looked at the two men, said, "The Virginia Military Institute will be heard from today!"

Rodes smiled, glanced at Colston. Both men had wondered often if Jackson even recalled their former relationship.

The column reached the turnpike, and Rodes quickly led a line of skirmishers out, down the turnpike to the east, toward the farthest point of the Federal position. The men filed out into the brush, began to feel their way through. Jackson sat high in the middle of the road and watched. Now he could hear the guns, from far out in front of him, a roll of low thunder. He gauged the distance, knew it was Anderson, McLaws, and Lee on the far side of the Federal position, and he nodded, thought, Good, they are still engaged, still in place. He felt the thrill again, the excitement of knowing the entire Federal Army was right in front of him, between him and Lee, *right there*. Others were beside him now, his own staff, and now Rodes was back, and his division was filling the road, spreading out in thick battle lines into the woods.

Jackson began to rock in the saddle, a small rhythm, back and forth, pushing the men into position. With each forward movement he said to himself, Go, move forward. The men were having some difficulty, it was slow going, and he wanted to yell, tell them to hurry, but there could be no noise, and so he prodded them from inside his head, leaned out over the horse's head, then back in the saddle. It was getting late, but he would not look at the sun, far behind them now, dropping quickly toward the distant trees. He saw his own shadow on the road, long and dark, and closed his eyes, would not see it, kept pushing them, rocking.

It was Colston now, and the second division moved into lines behind Rodes, the men swarming past Jackson's horse. Most did not look up now, knew it was soon. Then Colston was beside him, wanted to say something. He was nervous, had not led a division into battle before, and still Jackson rocked, his eyes closed. Colston watched him, let it go, turned to his troops again.

Jackson suddenly stopped moving, looked sharply behind him, saw Pendleton and said, "Where is Hill?"

Pendleton was startled, moved closer. "General Hill will be up with his lead brigade very soon," he said. "He is not more than a mile behind. His last two brigades are well back, sir. They have not been able to make up for the lost time, for the fight with the Yankees."

Jackson turned, closed his eyes again, was suddenly furious, felt a stab of pain in his side. His chest tightened and he tried to breathe, opened his mouth, and the tightness gave way. *Hill again.* It was good Hill was last in line. They could move without him if they had to.

Rodes was still close by, heard the brief conversation, felt defensive about Hill, said, "Sir, General Hill was pressed by a large force of Federals. I am certain he is bringing his men up as quickly as he can."

Jackson stared at him, a withering glare, and Rodes looked away, had crossed a dangerous line with his commander. Jackson closed his eyes and slowly began to rock again. Colston's lines were almost in place now, and Jackson spurred his horse, moving down the road toward the back of Rodes's troops, with Rodes moving quickly to catch up with him. Jackson reached the line of men, leaned over and tried to see out into the thick brush. The line disappeared in both directions, the men slowly moving forward with small noises, the officers keeping them in line. Jackson heard curses and nervous laughter, could hear the sounds of the brush, the men stepping through the tangle. He looked down the road, lifted his field glasses, stared ahead and saw two small black eyes, the silent stare of Howard's cannon. Lowering the glasses, he reached into his pocket and pulled out a small gold watch: five-fifteen. They would have two hours of daylight.

Rodes said nothing, waited, and Jackson now looked at him, hard, tried to see into the man's soul, measure the strength of his heart. Rodes still waited, felt the power of Jackson's cold blue stare.

Jackson said, "Are you ready, General Rodes?"

"Yes, sir." Rodes did not pause.

"You can go forward, sir."

Rodes turned, and there was a quick shout and a bugle sounded, and out in front the first line began to crush through the tangle of briars and thickets. From far out in both directions came the sound, the high, screaming wail, of ten thousand men; a solid line a mile wide pushing and clawing through the brush in one great mass of motion. The terrible sound echoed far in front of them, carried forward by the wind, and before them, beyond the brush, in the wide clearings along the road, heads began to turn, and plates of hot food were spilled, and the men in blue coats stood, staring at the impossible, the impenetrable thicket, stared as the deer and the rabbits and the birds ran and darted and flushed out before the great wave. Before the first man was seen, or the first musket aimed, the men in blue were swallowed by the sound, by the raw terror, and they began to run.

HE RODE CLOSE BEHIND THE FIRST HEAVY LINE, PUSHED OUT into the first clearing. His men stopped, raised their rifles in one sweeping motion, and there was a long blast, the echo filling the space. In front of them the flight of many soldiers was cut down. They ran on again, passed untouched stands of muskets, campfires and tents and wagons. They could see the enemy in a desperate scramble to get away, and, like the hound who finally sees the prey, they quickened their pursuit.

Devens's division was in total chaos, stampeded past the trenches of Schurz's division, the next in line. Schurz's men turned, formed a line of fire, and a volley came at the front of the gray wave, but it was the poor aim of panic, and the tide quickly rolled over them, driving those who could run into the escaping mob.

There were more trenches now, earthworks dug by men who had expected a fight, and they were quickly covered by the swarm. Jackson rode up, pushed the horse onto a long mound of dirt, could see his troops far in front, continuing to press on. Men were coming up behind him, Colston's first line.

Jackson turned, yelled, "Press on! Forward!"

They looked at him, and he saw the fire in their faces, *his* fire, and they went over the embankment, fighting their way through felled trees. Shots whistled past him now, return fire from small pockets of men in blue, the few who stood to fight. But even the most determined, those who would never run, soon realized that the line washing over them was too wide and too many, and if they did not finally move out, join the great wave, they would be quickly captured.

He pushed on, rode through the earthworks, saw beyond to the next obstructions, and there was more solid fire now, coming through the thick brush, splintering branches and limbs. His men slowed, the lines ragged now, and there were new shouts from officers. Jackson yelled to them all, "Form the lines! Keep it up!"

Now there were more volleys, from both sides, and he saw men falling, right in front of him, Rodes's men—*his* men. He rode past them, toward a building, glanced at the sign, DOWDALL'S, and reined the horse. Across the road he caught a glimpse of blue, hidden by the brush, and a roar of muskets blew into the line behind him. He turned back, saw a dozen men, a neat straight line, still pointing their muskets forward, and the men were all down, had fallen together. Now there was another sharp blast, farther behind him, toward the brush, screams, and men stumbled out toward the road, blue coats and new stains of red, and his line moved on by, kept going. He looked at the fallen men, men from both sides, a few feet apart, and raised his hand, held it high, the palm up, a silent prayer. Colston's second line was passing by him now, watching him, and suddenly there was a cheer, echoing down through the roar of the guns and the rising smoke. It spread, grew into a high scream, rolled into a new chorus of the rebel yell, and he watched them now, shouted out again, "Keep it up! Move forward! Stay together!"

The smoke was heavier now, shells ripping the air, bursting in the road, tearing through the brush. Federal batteries were turning, meeting the wave, and his lines began to shatter. He turned to the side, rode along a thick patch of the dense woods, saw a small group of men standing, unsure, and an officer. He yelled to the man, "Get them together, press them on!"

The man looked at him, appeared stunned, and Jackson yelled again, "Get them into line!"

There was a hot rush of air, and the brush in front of him was suddenly swept away; then a bright flash, a deafening, horrible sound, and the officer and men were gone. He had started to yell again, his mouth open, the words forming, and he stopped, turned, would not see, would still push them on.

Jackson jerked at the horse, moved back into the clearing, to the road, began to follow the line again. Now the firing was more to the front. They were still pushing the Federal troops back. He looked behind him, to the tavern, saw a farmhouse and knew they had come two, maybe three miles. He spurred the horse, moved up quickly, did not look at what lay around him, the vast spread of debris, shattered guns and wagons, and the broken bodies of men. He moved out toward a grove of trees, saw there were blue soldiers, crouching, aiming, and a volley ripped by him, struck men moving up behind. He saw a line, Colston's men, moving into the grove, and there was another volley, in both directions, a thick mass of smoke spreading out right in front of him. He strained to see, raised his pistol, ready, then saw the blue bodies, swept from their cover. Colston's men moved forward, and now Jackson saw one man, with the face of a boy, still standing, facing the oncoming line. He was trying to reload, and now Colston's men were on him, and the boy was trying to raise the rifle, and there was a flash of steel, the quick rip of the bayonet, and the boy was down. Jackson turned away, the image hard in his mind, thought, We must kill the brave ones, we must kill them *all*.

Far in front of him, beyond the heavy lines of smoke, one man sat high on his horse, held a billowing flag, the Stars and Stripes, taken in a rush from his headquarters. He clamped it tight against his body with the stump of his arm, the empty sleeve waving wildly, held his pistol high with the other hand, yelled, screamed, pleaded with the men who ran by him, "Stop, for God's sake . . . turn and fight!"

They did not stop, would not look into the face of their commander, knew only that behind them was the certain terror of hell on earth, and somewhere, if they kept going, they would find the river, would get back across, to where it was safe; that maybe they would fight again, become an army again, but not today.

49. HANCOCK

May 2, 1863. Late afternoon.

"Colonel Miles, they're coming again!"

The young man followed the extended arm, saw movement deep in the brush, the wave of brown and gray, and raised his pistol. All along the skirmish line the other officers yelled out the order, and now the line exploded into a single blast, a careful volley that stopped the advance cold, and the gray lines melted back into the dense brush.

They were beside a long, narrow creek bed, had spent the night digging shallow trench lines, clearing the woods to their front for a clean line of fire. Behind them, back up the rise, the main body of Hancock's division was dug in as well, waiting for the grand assault by Lee's army.

Hooker had ridden by earlier in the day, full of pomp and compliments. Hancock had been polite and formal, endured the inspection as a soldier had to endure inspection, but Hooker's predictions had not come true, there was not yet a heavy attack, just this constant skirmishing, wave after small wave, against the strong lines that had so pleased Hooker, the lines that would butcher Lee's army.

Hancock heard the new assault, the brief volleys, saw the thin line of smoke rising, again, from the trees below. He saw an officer moving in a run up the rise, and the man stopped, the young face smeared with mud and the gray stain of battle. He spoke through heavy breaths, saying, "General, it's nothing but . . . more of the same. They've been beating us up all day with a single line of skirmishers. It doesn't make sense, sir."

Hancock stared across the wide depression, past the trees that covered the creek bed, toward the position of Lee's unseen troops, and now, to the south, in front of the Twelfth Corps, a new burst of artillery, shells bursting in the air, shattering trees, and far down in the woods there was a rebel yell and a clash of muskets, and both men watched, waited, and then it stopped.

Hancock looked down at the dirty face, found the clear eyes. "Colonel Miles, I will send you a bit more strength, beef up the line again. But I don't believe you will be pushed very hard. Not now . . . it's too late in the day."

Miles looked back down the hill, said, "Doesn't make sense. You can't get anything done with a skirmish line."

Hancock looked across the crest of the ridge, the trenches and heavy lines of troops, his division, still waiting, rifles still pointing toward the trees below, rifles that had been quiet most of the day. They had not moved, had kept the sharp eye to the east, where Lee's army had moved in close the night before. All day, Lee had just . . . played with them.

He waved an arm, and an aide moved closer. Hancock said, "Go tell General Meagher to pick out another squad, have their commander report to Colonel Miles, down below."

The man saluted, began to move along the crest of the ridge.

"Go on back to your line, Colonel," Hancock said. "I'm sending you some Irishmen this time."

Miles raised a dirty hand, saluted, and Hancock turned his horse and rode to the south, toward the sounds of the last assault. He could see the turnpike now, saw a long, deep line of blue, the trenches of the Twelfth Corps, and riding up the ridge toward him, a flag, a small parade. It was Slocum.

"General Hancock, greetings. How are things up this way?"

It was a rhetorical question. Hancock had not known Slocum long, had never received a good impression, but Slocum had impressed someone in Washington enough to secure command of a corps, and seemed to enjoy the show of it, the long trail of staff under the flutter of flags. He was a small, wiry man, with a short clump of beard perched below a long, thin face, and he smiled pleasantly, waiting for Hancock's rhetorical answer.

"We're looking at the same thing you are, General. They're just bumping into us every so often."

Slocum still smiled, waved an arm slowly, toward the east. "Ah, but it would have been glorious. It could have happened right here, right on this spot. We could have ended it all."

Hancock watched him, sat quietly. Did Slocum really believe Lee would throw himself against this position? he wondered.

"So now, tomorrow, we have to start chasing them . . . all the way to Richmond, I imagine."

Hancock said, "What? What do you mean?"

Slocum looked at him, smiled again, said, "Why, they're gone, in full retreat. Have you not heard?"

"No, I haven't. I've been attending to this fight in front of me."

"General, I'm surprised. I received word from General Hooker's headquarters hours ago. The Confederate Army is in full retreat, toward Gordonsville. They've been marching west all day. I thought you knew."

"No, I have not heard that. Is this . . . certain?"

"Definitely, General, I heard from my own lookouts early this morning, and Sickles moved some units down to harass their supply trains, and ended up capturing an entire regiment of Georgians. He was too late to disrupt the retreat further, they were already by him. My latest orders are to prepare to pursue in the morning. As I said, General, it's a shame we couldn't fight them right here, from this wonderful position."

Hancock looked to the east, down toward the woods where Miles was strengthening his lines.

"General, if Lee is in retreat, who is it that keeps charging my lines?"

Slocum rubbed his chin, said, "Well, to tell you the truth, that question had occurred to me. Not like Lee to leave anybody behind."

Hancock thought, Lee has never *had* to leave anybody behind. "Excuse me, General, I must return to my division. And it seems clear that I must find General Couch."

Slocum watched him go, still smiled, and down below, in the trees, there was another high yell, and the trees came alive again with the rattle of the muskets and the sounds of a new charge.

COUCH HAD RIDDEN ALONG THE LINES EARLIER, SHORTLY AFTER the tour by Hooker. Hancock thought, It's not like him to keep me in the dark. Why had he not sent word?

Hancock rode toward the orange glow of the sun, lowered the brim of his hat, let the horse keep herself in the road. Behind him there were more shells bursting, a new artillery barrage, and he thought, If Lee is gone . . . would he leave his guns behind? He began to feel a small rumble in his gut, a small clench, thought of Slocum's words, then suddenly reined up the horse, stopping in the middle of the road.

He looked down, toward the south, recalled the map, the roads that led away, then ran parallel, far out to the west. There were more shells falling now, all along the ridge where his troops waited, a steady roar from a heavier assault, heavier than he had heard all day, and he thought, This could be it, I should go back. He rode hard back to the crest of the hill, pulled up, listened, and the shells slowed, stopped, and now the sounds of the skirmish came again, exactly as before, all along Miles's line. He waited, expected to hear much more, but in a few minutes it was over again.

He stared down the hill, watched the white smoke gradually clearing, and the rumble in his gut began again, and a familiar word suddenly flowed into his brain, a word from the textbooks, from old lessons. Suddenly, he felt utterly stupid, knew they had all listened to Hooker, had accepted instinctively, blindly, what the commander told them, and even if they did not truly believe it would happen, that Lee would hurl his army against a solid wall, they still waited, firmly in their trenches, inflexible and mindless. The word came into his brain again: *demonstration*. Now he understood why the attacks were regular and brief, with just enough muscle to hold his division in their trenches. Now he understood what Lee had done.

He spurred the horse hard, jerked the reins, and began to gallop into the deep glow of the sun, toward the Chancellor mansion where the generals waited. It was a short ride, and he pulled into the yard, jumped down hard, stumbled, and men were watching him, some were laughing. He stood, felt a sharp pain in his knee, looked up toward the porch, saw, sitting at a small table, holding a teacup, Joe Hooker.

"General, try to maintain a bit of dignity. There are enlisted men present."

There was laughter, and Hancock saw the faces of the others. Officers and their aides spilled out onto the porch, drawn by the commotion, and he saw Couch now, coming out of the house. Couch saw the look on his face and did not laugh. On the road behind him there was a sound, the clatter of wheels, and he turned, followed the gaze of the others, saw a horse, a fast gallop, pulling an empty wagon, and there was no driver. He watched the wagon move past, heard more laughter, looked back to Couch, would talk to him, find out what was happening, the truth. On the porch, one man looked past Hancock, looked toward the last of the sunlight, through the trail of dust from the single wagon, said, "Good God . . . here they come!"

Hancock turned, saw on the road, across the clearing on both sides, a ragged mass of troops, no coats, no hats, without guns. There was the rattle of another wagon, then many more, still without drivers, terrified horses, pulled along by a growing tide of running men.

On the porch Hooker yelled out, and men began to move. Above the house, in a wide clearing, there was a line of resting troops, a reserve division of Sickles's corps, and now orders were flying, the men scrambling into formation. Hooker shouted from the porch, "Move into line, move around, move into line! Give them the bayonet!"

Hancock grabbed his horse, jumped up and spurred the big animal out into the road, saw now that this was not the enemy, these were men in blue. *Our* men, he thought, and felt the great weight of the wave. If they keep going, they will run right over the backs of my men.

He could hear guns now, well to the west, scattered cannon, but mostly muskets, the vast flow of sound finally reaching the clearing. There were more wagons, men on horses, and the mad stampede was moving past the mansion. Hancock looked for officers, someone in control, saw the line of Sickles's fresh troops swinging around, moving toward the road, trying to stop the panicked mob. From the thicket below the road more men appeared, torn uniforms, still running, and he raised his sword, swung it down hard, hit a man flat across the shoulder, knocking him down. The man looked at him with raw terror.

Hancock shouted, "Get up! Stop running!" and the man was back on his feet, seemed to understand. But then another rush, and the man was caught up and gone again. Hancock turned the horse, rode quickly down the road, fought his way with the tide, moved past, tried to get out in front, to reach his trenches before the tide swept over.

He crested the hill, turned back, saw fewer men running now. Many had simply collapsed with exhaustion. But others came on, and now they reached his own troops. His men were turning, standing, surprised, and muskets were raised, but they saw it was blue troops, not the enemy, and did not shoot. The first of the wave poured away, down the hill, into the woods, across the stream where Miles's men waited, and many still ran, farther, plunging through the vines and the brush and into the arms of Lee's astonished troops.

50. JACKSON

May 2, 1863. Evening.

THE VOLLEYS WERE SLOWING NOW. THE BIG GUNS STILL THREW shell and canister toward him, but the dark was spilling heavily over the ground, had filled the thick woods, and even the open clearings were growing dim. He saw Colston, and rode that way. Colston was yelling at an officer, directing the man to form his company, saw Jackson and stared with wild eyes.

"We have stopped, sir! Can't see! The lines are tangled . . . we're mixed in with Rodes's men. It's confusion, sir! We need Hill to come up . . . Hill's men can move on by us!"

Jackson turned, looked to the rear, tried to see past the dark thickets. He heard the sound of troops, fresh troops, said, "Yes, General. Try to form your men. I will tell General Hill to push on! We must not stop! They are running. They will keep running if we press them!"

He turned the horse, rode back toward the oncoming lines, now saw A. P. Hill leading his staff. Hill saluted, unsmiling, and Jackson stared hard into the thin face. "Keep them moving, General," he said. "Keep the pressure up. We have broken their flank. We can crush them now, cut them off. We must not give them time to organize. Take your division forward, then press on to the north, toward the river. Move toward United States Ford . . . they must not escape!"

Hill stared at him, said, "General . . . it is dark. I don't know the ground."

Jackson turned around, looked, saw his own staff beginning to come together, saw Captain Boswell, the engineer, and yelled out, "Boswell, report to General Hill. Find a way through the woods . . . to the northeast. Find the rear of the enemy's position. We will cut them off!"

Boswell moved up, saluted Jackson, and Hill looked at him, knew there would be no argument.

Jackson turned away now, his orders clear, and he rode forward down the dark road. In front of him a sudden burst of shelling was answered from both sides, the woods cut down by aimless blasts of metal. He rode farther, listening, looked up into the black, wanted to ask God to please let them keep on . . . but he did not, thought, *You have given us much today.* To the south, away from the turnpike, he could see a red glow, and then another. Now, the staff eased up closer behind him.

A voice said, "Fire . . . the woods are burning," and they waited, watched.

Another man said, "Oh my God . . . the wounded . . ." Jackson held up his hand, waved them back, pushed the horse forward, listened. The shelling had stopped now. Scattered musket fire echoed through the trees, and he watched the fire, could hear it, fueled by the dry and dense brush.

He wanted to ride forward, to the confused tangle of Rodes's and Colston's lines, to tell them not to stop, to keep going, move forward . . . but he felt the sudden deadweight of hopelessness, could not see anything at all in front of him, knew they could not as well, that a night attack rarely made sense, not in a place like this. He looked up, said another prayer, *Thank You for our success,* and through the tops of far trees, saw a white light, the great brightness of the rising full moon. Around him the light was cutting through the shadows, and now he could see the shapes, the wide path of the road. Yes, he thought, God is still showing us the way!

He turned, and the staff came up again. He saw the boy, the young man who knew these woods so well, and Jackson said, "Is there a road . . . that way, toward the United States Ford?"

"No, sir, not here. There's some old trails, but farther up, there's the Bullock Road. Some trails off that . . ."

Jackson nodded impatiently. "Show me! Now . . . we must not waste time!"

The boy moved forward, Jackson followed, and the staff trailed behind.

They turned down a small road, moving slowly in the growing moonlight, and Jackson strained to hear, stopped the horse, heard troops out in front of him, digging in. There was the clear sound of axes, the chopping of trees, and so they would be Federal troops. Still, he thought, sound carries far at night, they might not be as close as the sounds, there must still be a way. The boy was watching him. He motioned, and they began to move along the trail again.

Behind them there was the deafening blast of a big gun, one of Hill's, a pointless blind shot toward the Federal lines. Then came the answer, several bright flashes, and around them limbs shattered, dirt flew up, and both sides turned quiet, nervous fingers wrapped on tight triggers, waiting for some movement, some telltale sound.

Jackson felt the chill of the night, the damp sweat in his uniform, reached behind the saddle for the black rubber overcoat, pulled it quietly over his shoulders, and they kept moving, into solid dark broken by small pieces of moonlight. Behind him the staff drew up, closer. A burst of fire came from the Federal troops, a short volley from a line of muskets exploded in the woods from the right, then he heard a low voice behind him, and a hand touched his shoulder.

It was Lieutenant Morrison, Anna's younger brother. Morrison said, in an anxious whisper, "Sir . . . we are beyond our lines. This is no place for you, sir."

Jackson stopped the horse, raised his hand, halting the group. He understood now, it could not go the way he had hoped. It would have to be in the morning.

"You are correct. We will return to the road."

He turned the horse, began to move quickly now, and the others followed. Now, below them, close in the thick brush, a man's voice. "Halt! Who is that?" and another voice, a sharp command, "It's cavalry! Fire!"

There was a quick sheet of flame, and behind him, Jackson heard the cry of horses and men falling.

One of the aides rode toward the troops, shouted, "No, stop firing . . . you're firing on your own men!"

Then came a strong hard voice, the voice of a veteran who has seen cunning and deceit, and who understands that his men are the front of the line, and that before them is only the enemy. "It is a lie! Pour it to them!"

The second volley was better aimed, the moonlight silhouetting the men on horseback. Jackson spun around, tried to reach the shelter of trees beyond the trail, and he felt a hard tug at his hand, a hard, hot punch in his shoulder. The horse lunged, terrified, began to run away from the noise, jumped and jerked, and now it was Morrison, beside him, grabbing the reins that Jackson had dropped. He felt himself sliding, tried to reach for the saddle, could not grab with his hand, slid down the side of the horse and fell hard to the cold ground.

There was more yelling now. Horsemen were coming toward them on the trail. It was Hill and his staff, and Hill yelled toward his lines, said, "Hold your fire. These are your men here!"

His staff rode quickly toward the line of rifles. Hill came forward, saw the bodies scattered beside dying horses, and he dropped down from the horse, moved through the dark, said, "Oh God . . . what have they done?"

He saw one more man on the ground, and another man kneeling and Hill said, "Who is this?" He saw the face of young Morrison then, and Morrison was crying.

Hill moved around. A small piece of moonlight crossed Jackson's face. "Oh . . . God . . . General . . . are you hurt?"

"I am afraid so, I am hit in the shoulder . . . and . . . here." He raised his right hand, turned it in the faint light, tried to see it, to see where the pain began.

Now there were more shots, from above the trail. The Federal lines were moving forward, and Hill turned to one of the aides, said, "Get an ambulance . . . a litter! We need a litter!"

The aide hesitated, stared at the blood flowing from Jackson's shoulder, soaking into his uniform, said, "Oh my God . . ."

"Move!"

The aide looked at Hill, then turned and was gone.

"We must leave here, General. Can you walk?"

Others had gathered, and a tourniquet was wrapped high around his left arm. He bent his knees, tried to stand, and there were hands around him, pulling him up.

They began to move quickly down the trail. He tried to run, felt the hands holding him up, saw others coming up the trail toward them, carrying a litter.

He stared at the soft, dirty cloth, thought, No, I will walk, heard a familiar voice, Captain Smith, and tried to see the young man's face. But the hands pulled him down, laid him down, and now he was on his back.

Smith leaned close to his face, said, "General, are you in pain? Can I give you something? Here . . . take this, it will help."

He put a small bottle to Jackson's mouth, and Jackson thought, No, I don't need anything. The liquid wet his tongue, burned his throat, and he wanted to say no, but the liquid burned down deep, the warmth spreading through him. Then Smith took the bottle away, and Jackson smiled at him.

"Mr. Smith, I should have a word with you about this. . . ." He felt himself rising, lifted up, could not see Smith's face now, only the tops of the trees, the moonlight, small specks of light, the stars. He tried to feel the pain, could not, knew it was not just the whiskey, thought, Thank You. He tried to lift his head, but the litter was bouncing, and he remembered . . . Hill . . . fresh troops. We should not have stopped.

There was a sudden roar of fire, a new burst of light. Federal cannons were firing blindly into the rebel positions, and now the men dropped down, lay flat. Overhead, limbs and small branches flew into pieces, wood and dirt rained over them. A body was suddenly across his, and now he saw Smith's face, close, shielding him from the debris. He wanted to speak, to say something to the young man, tell him thank you, but there was no voice, and he knew he was now very very weak. I will die here, tonight, he thought. He tried to see God, to ask why . . . this place? But his mind was foggy, swimming, he could no longer see the trees.

The shelling stopped, and they rose in unison, picked up the litter, and four men held the corners as they again moved toward the road. Now, musket fire, more Federal troops, and there was a small, sharp crack, lead against bone, and one of the men suddenly grunted and crumpled, dropping the litter. Jackson rolled off to the side, landed hard, felt a sharp pain in his side, slicing through him. He was suddenly alert again, tried to twist, to roll off the pain, his mind screaming inside, Make it stop, and the hands were on him again, and he was mercifully on his back and they were moving again.

They reached the road, and now more soldiers were around them, the lines of his men. Hill was suddenly moving quickly, saw an officer, a captain, the man questioning, and Hill said, "Tell your men nothing. It is a wounded Confederate officer." The man looked past him, tried to see, and Hill heard horses, the ambulance, and he pushed the man aside.

The man went over to the litter, looked down into the face of Jackson, suddenly dropped to his knees, said, "No, oh dear God, no . . ."

Jackson heard the man, but his mind was now moving far away, and he turned his head, could see beyond the trees, the rising red glow of the fast-moving fires. He looked to the man again, tried to see, but the face was framed by the wall of red, and Jackson stared hard, eyes wide, saw the flames now moving toward him, laughing and dancing, and he looked back to the face, wanted to say . . . to ask . . . would talk . . . must talk to God, but now the face went away, and there was only the fire, the pain burning him from inside, and he was too weak to stop it, to fight it, and his mind finally gave in, and he drifted further away now, beyond the fire, felt the strong hands lifting him again, and he slept, believing that it was God's hands, and He was lifting him toward Heaven.

THE LITTER WAS UP AND IN THE AMBULANCE, AND HILL LOOKED at Smith, said, "Where will you—"

"Dr. McGuire is at Dowdall's. We have sent word. I will keep you informed, General."

Hill nodded, turned, saw his aides and moved toward his horse. He knew it was his responsibility now, that this army was in confusion, that daylight would bring a dangerous fight from a huge number of Federal troops, troops that were digging in hard in front of them. He sat in the saddle, looked past the trees in front of him, then pulled the horse, moved down across the turnpike. Beyond, there was more scattered shooting, and he dismounted again, waved a courier forward, thought, I must find Colston and Rodes, get word to Stuart . . . and Lee. He began to put words together, forming the messages, and the courier followed. Hill looked up to the trees, the moon, tried to pinpoint the sounds of the guns, to get some bearing.

Now the heavy roar of the cannon filled the woods around him. Suddenly, there was a ripping pain in his legs. His knees gave way and he rolled forward, made a sharp cry. His men were quickly down, holding him, and he tried to feel the wound, touched the backs of his legs, felt the blood, nothing deep. He looked up at the faces, said, "No, it's all right . . . just my legs, it's all right." They tried to lift him up, and his legs would not hold him, he could not stand, and he fell back down, fell forward onto his hands, stared into the dark, thought, I am in command . . . I must . . . I am in command. . . .

He tried to stand again, and there was no feeling in his legs. He rolled to the side, sat, thought, So, God is with Stonewall after all. If *he* cannot command, then it is not to be me. He looked at the faces around him, said, "The command of the Second Corps should pass now to General Rodes. But General Lee would not place him in that position, he does not have the experience. Captain Adams . . ."

The man bent over, said, "Yes, sir, what can I do, sir?"

"Take a message to General Stuart, he is up at Ely's Ford, I believe. Tell him of our situation, and request that he ride here as quickly as possible. He must take command of the corps. And send a message to General Lee, for his approval. I do not see what other choice we have, but General Lee might disagree."

"Sir . . . right away!"

There was a flurry of motion, and horses began to move away.

He put his hands around the wounds on his legs, tried to feel. . . . He reached into his pocket, held up a gold watch, tried to catch the moonlight, saw . . . nearly three A.M.

"Well, we will soon learn if Joe Hooker is still running."

DR. MCGUIRE WAS TALKING TO HIM. "WE'LL GET THIS TIGHTened up first." And he felt a tugging in his shoulder. McGuire looked at him, saw the sharp blue eyes. "Well, General, welcome back. Can you hear me? How are you feeling?"

Jackson tried to see the shoulder, and a sharp pain stopped him. He opened his mouth, made a sound, "Ummghh." His tongue felt like cotton.

McGuire reached out, brought a cup up to his mouth. "Here, this may help. . . ."

It was cool and wonderful, and he tried to swallow, felt his throat harden into a knot, and the water spilled down the sides of his face. McGuire lifted the cup, and Jackson shook his head, tried to lift up.

McGuire said, "All right, here, try again."

This time he swallowed, just a bit, then more, and now he laid his head back, moved his tongue, said, "I . . . am I not dead?"

McGuire laughed. "Certainly not! I may take offense at that, General. You are in my hands now."

Jackson tried to smile, then saw other faces, more men, and the faces were dark and serious. He suddenly realized he was on a bed. "Where am I, Doctor?"

"Field hospital. For tonight, anyway. Tomorrow, we'll move you away from the . . . fighting."

McGuire was not smiling now, knew the word would have an effect. Jackson suddenly tried to sit, to pull himself up. He reached for the edge of the bed, saw his right hand was bandaged.

"What . . . I'm shot. . . ."

"General, the hand is minor. The ball lodged under the skin. It is the other wounds. . . ." He paused, looked up at the other men, and Jackson heard the sound of a table being moved, saw the faces closer now. "General, you were wounded twice in your left arm. The artery in your upper arm has been severed, the bone is broken. You were very fortunate you did not bleed to death. In cases such as this, the removal of the arm is . . . required." McGuire paused, waited for a reaction. The other men were around the top of the bed now.

Jackson said, "Doctor, I have absolute faith in your abilities. You must do what is necessary."

McGuire nodded slowly, said, "We have chloroform . . . it will make this much easier for you." Jackson shook his head, and McGuire said, "No argument this time, General. You will not please God if you endure pain needlessly. This is not a test of courage."

Jackson smiled, knew that McGuire understood him well. He closed his eyes, a brief prayer, *Forgive me . . . but I must follow orders.* He looked again at McGuire, and now the smiles were gone. McGuire said something to one of the other men, and there was a hand above him, and a white cloth, and Jackson closed his eyes, felt the soft cotton against his face, took a long, deep breath.

His mind began to spin, a swirl of light, and above him, far away, he heard music, faint, soft. Then it grew, swelled into a loud and glorious march, deep and rhythmic, the smooth and regular cadence of soldiers on the move, men who could do anything. . . .

51. STUART

Sunday, May 3, 1863

He saw Rodes first, rode up quickly toward the larger tent. Then the others came, Colston, Harry Heth, and more, men he did not know.

He had ridden alone, left his men up at Ely's Ford, a crossing that was now dangerous because it offered the Federal Army a clear route behind their new position, the ground they had won by the collapse of the Federal flank. Late in the day, Jackson had sent him up to prevent anyone from coming that way, if there was a Federal commander who recognized the opportunity. They were surprised to find the ford already occupied by a large force of Federal cavalry, Averill's brigade, and Stuart knew he did not have the manpower to drive them away. But this night, there was much edginess, and it would only take a good, solid surprise to hold them back, keep them nervously dug into one spot.

But the attack had begun without him. A. P. Hill's courier had reached him with the message, and he did not wait, gave Von Borcke the job: strike fast, retreat, then strike once more.

He had pushed the horse hard, reached the turnpike at a fast gallop, pulled up now at the new headquarters, near Dowdall's, close to the former center of Howard's position, but now well behind their own lines.

He did not bow, did not sweep the ground with the ridiculous hat, looked hard at the men waiting for him, saw the eyes of confident soldiers who know they need direction.

There were salutes, and they let him pass by, followed him into the tent. It was warm, from the dull heat of an oil lamp. He saw a small table, a wood chair, sat and motioned to small seats spread around the tent. They followed, quiet now, looking at him, waiting.

"Do we know if General Jackson is alive?"

Rodes looked at the others, spoke up. "He is seriously wounded, his arm . . . not sure where he is now, but we have not heard more since he was taken from the field."

"General Hill was with him." Heth stood now, tall, nervous. "General Hill was wounded shortly after . . . not seriously, but he cannot walk. He has appointed me. . . . As senior brigade commander, I have assumed command of his division. If you do not object, sir."

Stuart motioned. "Please, General Heth, please sit. This is a difficult time for us all. We must pause, say a prayer for General Jackson, and keep our heads cool. Yes, I quite agree with General Hill. Unless General Lee requests otherwise, you are now in command of Hill's division."

Heth sat down again, all knees and elbows, stared at the ground, said, "General, have you been informed who it was . . . how General Jackson was wounded?"

"Is it important? Our concern is with his recovery and his return to the field. Revenge cannot be—"

"Sir, it was our own troops. General Lane . . . it was the Eighteenth North Carolina."

Stuart stared at him, absorbed, said, "My God . . . are you certain?"

Heth nodded, still looked down. After a long moment Heth said, "They are aware . . . it was dark and they were close to the enemy. It was a dangerous place for the general to be."

"The Eighteenth North Carolina . . ." Stuart felt sick, took a long, deep breath. "They will carry this with them for the rest of their lives."

Heth looked up with sad, tired eyes. "We all will, sir."

Colston cleared his throat, said, "General, we have all been praying for General Jackson. The whole army . . . word has spread, it could not be helped. I suppose that even the Yankees know by now. We may be in serious trouble."

Stuart did not know Colston well, knew only that he was new to command and had risen through the ranks of Jackson's own men, the division that Jackson himself organized two years earlier: the heartbeat of the entire corps, the Stonewall Brigade.

"General Colston, the sun will rise very soon on a field where the enemy has been beaten badly and is of a mind to withdraw. The advantages are all ours."

Colston seemed unsure, looked at Rodes, and Rodes said,

"General Stuart, we welcome your authority to command this corps. We will do what you order us to do, sir. But these men . . . my division is scattered all over these woods, sir. I don't even know how many men I can put into line. General Colston has the same situation. The only fresh troops we have, men who have even had something to eat . . . are Hill's . . . General Heth's division. The Federals are digging in, building heavy defensive lines. They are expecting us to advance against them at daylight. I'm not sure we have much to send against them."

Stuart looked at Heth, said, "General, is your division in place? Can you press forward an organized attack?"

"Yes, sir. The men were not heavily engaged yesterday. They will be strong."

"Good. Then they will lead the attack. Gentlemen, I do not believe General Jackson would have had us sitting here moaning about our problems. He would have one word, for all of us: *attack*. That is what we must do. Once we can see . . . once we can determine what the enemy has done to prepare for us . . . then we will find his weaknesses, and move against him."

There were nods, and he stood, led them back out of the tent. Riders were coming into the camp. He looked at faces, and saw his own men, reports of the success at Ely's, and then he saw Sandie Pendleton, Jackson's chief of staff. Pendleton climbed from the horse slowly, and Stuart watched him, was suddenly very afraid, waited.

Pendleton said, "General Stuart, I come from General Jackson's bedside. I reached the general just after he awoke from surgery. Dr. McGuire has amputated his left arm. . . ." He paused, choked on the words.

Behind Stuart, Colston said in a soft whisper, "Good God."

Stuart stepped forward, raised a hand, some comfort, and Pendleton straightened, felt the hand on his shoulder, continued.

"Sir, General Jackson has been informed of General Hill's wounds, and of your taking command, sir. The general has every confidence in your abilities."

"Can you tell me, Major . . . does the general have any orders?"

"He said only for you to do what you think is best, General. It is your command."

Stuart turned to the others, and they waited. He thought, No, Stonewall is still in command, they will do it for him, they will do what he would want. I must remember that.

"Gentlemen, this has been a difficult . . . a long day. I suggest we tend to our troops, try to get them fed, and find some breakfast for ourselves."

They looked past him now, to another rider. He turned and saw Jed Hotchkiss, Jackson's mapmaker. Hotchkiss limped from the horse, moved tenderly, held out a paper, said, "General Stuart, I have a message for you, sir, from General Lee. Please forgive me. . . ." He slumped, fell to one knee, and Pendleton was down beside him.

"All right, Hotchkiss, all right. Does Lee know . . . ?"

"Yes, yes, he had been informed by Wilbourn when I got there. I had to ride down a long way." He stood, steadied himself on Pendleton's arm, and Stuart unfolded the paper, read quietly, then turned to the others, read aloud.

" 'It is necessary that the glorious victory thus far achieved be prosecuted with the utmost vigor, and the enemy given no time to rally. As soon as it is possible, they must be pressed, so that we may unite the two wings of the army. Endeavor, therefore, to dispossess them of Chancellorsville.' "

He stopped, there was a silent moment, and he said, "The plan is clear, gentlemen. We will form in lines to press hard to the east, toward Chancellorsville, and by doing so, we can move our right flank around to the southeast and link up with General Lee's lines. The enemy has already demonstrated a great willingness to leave this field. We will do what we can to speed them along."

The meeting was over, and men and horses began to move away. Hotchkiss sat down beside a small fire. Pendleton watched him, lowered his voice, said to Stuart, "It has been difficult for us all. Captain Smith is with the general now . . . I had best get back as well. I will keep you informed."

Stuart nodded, patted the young man's shoulder again, said, "Tell General Jackson that we will finish the work. This day too will be ours."

Pendleton tried to smile, nodded, moved slowly toward the horse. Now both men turned, saw it together, the first white glow of the dawn.

HE HAD RIDDEN OUT FIRST TO THE SOUTH, TO THE RIGHT FLANK of their lines, followed the advance as it pushed forward, smashing with full fury into the first of the Federal positions. The right flank was little more than a mile from Lee's left, but in between, Sickles's corps had dug in, well below the turnpike, and so

Stuart could not reach Lee without first confronting the deep lines of the Third Corps.

Heth's lines were nearly two miles wide, and they swept forward in a continuation of the assault the day before, straight down the turnpike, toward Chancellorsville. Colston's lines were moving up behind, and in the rear, Rodes was organizing what was left of his division. Stuart knew that he could count on barely twenty-five thousand exhausted and underfed troops, and in front of him was an army of nearly ninety thousand men, many of whom—the men under Reynolds and Meade—had yet to see any action at all.

To the north, Reynolds's First Corps and Meade's Fifth had worked all night, dug a long solid line, blocking any advance toward the river, the advance that Jackson would have pressed the day before had he not run out of daylight. Around Chancellorsville, Couch and Slocum were entrenched in a near circle, Slocum facing south and west, and Couch facing east. Between his headquarters and the Confederate lines, Hooker had dug four solid lines of entrenchments.

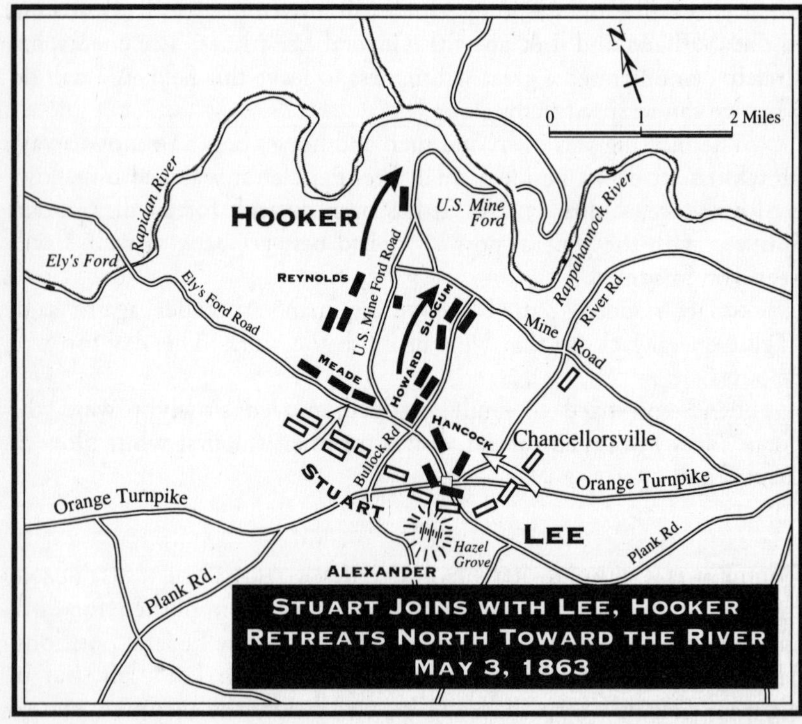

STUART JOINS WITH LEE, HOOKER RETREATS NORTH TOWARD THE RIVER MAY 3, 1863

Stuart rode close behind the first line, as Jackson had the day before. He waved his sword, yelled, "Remember Jackson," and they watched him, shouted back. They all knew it was not yet a victory, that the long day ahead of them would prove whether the great, bold plan, the sheer audacity of Lee and Jackson, would be enough after all.

They could see the abatis now, the great piles of thick brush, cut trees, spread high in front of the first entrenchments. The lines kept moving, pushed ahead through smaller thickets, short clearings. He pulled the horse along, stepping over the unburied dead, tried to pick his way through the roar of musket fire. Behind him, he could not see the next line, hidden in the thick brush, and he turned the horse, called out and waited. Then came the great rumble, from the batteries far in front, and low screams, the high whistling shrieks, and the brush began to fly apart around him. Great blasts of splinters blew by him, and he turned again, ducked low on the horse, saw the backs of his men pushing forward, yelled, "Keep moving, forward!"

He rode back to the south, toward the right flank, looked for officers, horses. The orders were plain, Lee had sent another message: link their two armies together, move around below the Federal lines. He pushed the horse into a thick mass of vines. The horse stopped, and he yelled, *"Move!"*

A shell tore through the brush behind them, a sharp spray of dirt hitting him in the back, and suddenly the horse lurched, tore through the last of the thicket, and he was in the open. I know, he thought, this is not what cavalry horses do. He laughed now, patted the horse's neck, moved farther. Smoke was filling the clearings. He saw a man on a horse and rode that way. The man was directing his men through the thickets, and now the troops in front of him were gone, out of sight in the dense brush.

Stuart reached him, saw he was a major, said, "You'll have to dismount! Move with them . . . stay with them!"

The man looked at him without recognition, and Stuart was quickly past. The man stayed on the horse, and Stuart was looking in all directions, could see no other horses, just lines of moving men. He saw the major again, thought, He might know . . . where his commander is.

The man was watching him now, yelled, "This is no place for a fight . . . we can't stay together!"

"Dismount! Move into the brush with your men, Major. The fight is in front of you!"

The man stared at him, still not moving, and now another man rode up, through the thickening smoke, said, "General Stuart! Please ride down this way . . . General Archer is pushing the flank, sir!"

Stuart jerked the horse, moved with the man, and the major stared, wide-eyed, was quickly down from the horse, began to plunge into the brush after his men.

Stuart followed Archer's aide closely, their horses still stepping over scattered bodies. Then he saw Jim Archer, a vague, ghostly form in the smoke. The heavy shells were whistling higher overhead now, finding the lines behind them, and now in front of them a steady rattle of muskets began, from places they could not see.

Archer saluted Stuart, yelled hoarsely through the sounds, "Good morning, sir! It is an honor to be under your command, sir! We have a strong position in front of us, it appears. The Yankees are still in these woods! We did not expect to find them this far below the roads!"

Stuart tried to see to the front. The musket fire was growing still, and now the men behind them were moving up, the second line, and hats went up, cheers. Stuart waved, but did not yell, knew these men did not need anything else to inspire them.

There was another officer beside them now, a captain, and he was pointing up to the left, from where Stuart had just come. "General, we have lost contact with McGowan's flank! We are in the open, sir! It's too thick to see!"

Archer spurred his horse, said, "Excuse me, General, I must see to my flank," and he rode forward, moved quickly through a grove of short trees.

Stuart watched him. It could be like this all along the line, he thought, hard for them to stay together, to see each other. He dug hard at the horse's side, rode farther down to the right, toward the end of the line. He could see a long clearing now, then up a large hill, in front of them, and on top the steady flashes of the Federal guns, a high and clear position, a perfect place to throw fire into the oncoming lines of his troops. Stuart heard more guns now, down in front, farther east, and he thought, *Lee's* guns. Lee was pressing the attack as well.

He turned the horse and rode back toward the turnpike, passing between lines of gray troops, all moving east. He came to a small road, was amazed to see a long line of guns, *his* guns, strung out far down the road, men on wagons and horses, just sitting, waiting. He thought, No, something is wrong. Why are they not in line, firing? He saw an officer, a red cap, and the man rode toward him, saluted, said, "General Stuart, we are ready, sir. We need that ground!"

Stuart stared at the man, then recognized him, it was Porter Alexander.

"Colonel, why are these guns not in position? They should be answering those batteries up on that hill!"

"General, that is exactly where we're going . . . that hill. All I'm waiting for is your troops to clear those batteries away. We will advance as soon as we can."

Stuart looked toward the hill, could see only smoke, and the musket fire below was a strong and steady roar.

"Colonel Alexander . . . you are assuming—"

"Yes, General, I am. We will push them back, and clear that hill. That is the objective, isn't it, sir?"

Stuart nodded, yes, of course. The infantry must move against the hill, push on up. He thought of the cavalry, the plan . . . go around, ride in quick and surprise them from the rear, but this was not cavalry, and he had no one to send except the foot soldiers. He was beginning to appreciate the infantry commanders. There was nowhere else to go but right *there*, straight ahead.

"Colonel, prepare your men to move! I will give you that hill!"

Stuart turned the horse, rode along the small road, followed the sounds of the muskets. Now there was a new sound, high and loud, and he saw men all around him, yelling, some beginning to run. He stopped, saw a long bare pile of dirt, and men flowing across, down into the trenches beyond. They had reached the first entrenchments, had pushed the Federal soldiers out and away, and many of his men were still going, pushing forward, disappearing into the smoke.

He rode behind them, felt the ground rising, knew they were on the big hill, and he stopped, tried to hear. There were more muskets farther to the left, some back behind, and he had a sudden burst of cold in his gut, thought, We are not together, there are no lines. The fight is . . . *everywhere*. He turned now, rode along the base of the hill, suddenly saw a clearing and a line of blue troops, firing into the brush beyond. He jerked the horse, rode farther to the rear. He saw lines of his own men now, moving toward the Federal troops, and they were not watching him now, did not focus on the men on horses, were driving forward, staring in one direction. Men were stopping, firing, and others falling, dropping down in solid heaps or flying back, arms wild, heads back. He pulled the horse again, fought more vines, more brush, and now he was in the clear and back on the turnpike.

The shelling was coming from the north now, and from the east, from Chancellorsville. The trenches dug by the Federal troops the night before were behind them, and he could see ahead, to the next line of trenches. His men were moving that way, shrouded by the smoke.

Colston's lines were advancing past the first entrenchments now, and they moved by him. Many hats went up and they began to yell. Stuart sat still, beside the road, suddenly stood in the stirrups and waved his hat in a wide circle, began to yell himself. They felt it, began to run, pushed through the woods in a new wave. Now, in front of them, where the muskets met across small spaces, and men stared into the faces of their enemy, the gray wall pressed and pressed. The men in blue pulled out, left the second entrenchments, swallowed by the screaming wave of gray.

It was no longer the stampede of raw panic, and the gray wave began to slow. There were more muskets in front of them now, heavier, solid blue lines. He rode into a small clearing, saw his men moving out beyond the second trenches, and now straight in front the trees exploded with one mighty flame, and canister tore through the brush and through the lines of his men. He stared, could see nothing through the new wall of white smoke, turned, and the horse would not run, was suddenly limping. He looked down, saw a flow of red, thought, No, not here, I must get to the road. The horse began to move, stepping awkwardly. He guided the animal past mangled bodies, heaps of men, reached the road and dismounted. It was a bright gash, a deep and deadly wound. The horse dropped its head, one knee buckled, and he patted the soft neck, stepped back, took off his hat, pulled out his pistol and ended it.

Men were running back along the road now, the wave had turned, and the shells began to fly past, heavy shot and the hot whistle of canister. He ran down into the trees, began to yell, "Stop . . . turn and fight!" He could not see, did not know what was happening, but could not move on the road. It was the one clear line of sight for the Federal gunners, and they were sweeping the road with steady firing.

He moved back, reached the first line of trenches, saw they were filled now with his men, most with heads down, shielded from the vicious firing.

"Up, you men. Up! You must keep moving forward! On your feet!" Men were looking at him. Some began to rise, officers appearing, and he watched one man, grabbing at the men around him, pulling them up, and he yelled, "Yes! Stonewall would be proud! Do it for Jackson!"

Now more were moving, forming a solid line, and they began to move out of the trench. In the trees a blast of muskets rolled over them, an advancing line of blue troops, and the men melted back, down into the trench. The firing went both ways now, blue soldiers behind trees, moving forward in small groups, and the men in the trenches, and Stuart knew this was not where he should be. . . .

He reached the edge of the road again, past the bodies of many men, had stepped across solid layers of men. Bodies were scattered in a thin layer all across the road. He saw a group of officers and ran toward them. They watched him come, stared at him, and there were loud shouts, commands, and suddenly he was handed the reins to a horse.

"Do you have orders, sir?" It was Rodes.

He steadied himself on the horse, sat straight in the saddle, said, "General Rodes, we must advance with all our strength. We are being driven back. We do not have the numbers, the defenses are too strong. Are your men ready?"

Rodes looked behind him, saw officers riding along the edge of the woods, pointing, shouting orders, and he said, "We are ready on your command, sir."

"Then, advance your men. Fast. Press them hard. If we do not push them back they may counterattack."

"Sir, for General Jackson." He saluted, turned to the officers behind him.

Stuart spurred the new horse, pulled him back toward the roar of the muskets, said under his breath, "Yes, for General Jackson."

ARCHER'S BRIGADE CONTINUED TO PRESS UP THE LONG RISE, toward the top of the wide hill known as Hazel Grove. Beside him McGowan's brigade did the same, but it was two separate attacks, a fight by two units who could not stay connected to each other. Gradually, the lines of Federal soldiers withdrew all along the hill. Sickles had asked for help, to strengthen that part of the defense, but his lines were well below the main strength of Hooker's trenches, and Hooker was more inclined to pull Sickles back, tightening the circle around Chancellorsville. As Archer's men reached the top of Hazel Grove, they saw Sickles leaving, the heavy guns pulling away, the shallow gun pits empty and waiting for Porter Alexander to climb the hill.

"HERE! SIR!"

Stuart heard the voice, saw the wave, rode toward the man in the red cap. Around him the guns were unlimbering, men scrambling down from caissons and wagons, and Stuart saw Alexander pointing, holding his arm out straight. Now Stuart saw, pulled up the horse, stared across the green thickets below them, toward the northeast: a short mile away, toward the next rise, another hill, open, a wide clearing, and one large and imposing mansion: Chancellorsville.

"My God . . ."

"Yes, sir. As I said, sir. We will begin firing very soon now. This should take the pressure off the infantry, quite a bit, I'd say, sir."

Below them, down in the trees, the musket fire was steady and spread all around them. Stuart rode forward, did not feel like a commander. There was no control to this battle . . . it was being fought by small groups of men, regiments, led by low-level officers. He had tried to find many of the commanders himself, found small units that did not know who was leading them. So many of the officers were down, so many of the names he knew were either separated from their units, lost themselves, or dead. Companies were being led by sergeants, regiments by captains. Frank Paxton, the only general that Colston had under him, the man picked by Jackson to lead the Stonewall Brigade, was dead. Stuart stared out across the sounds, to the grand old house, thought, This must end soon. We are running out of men.

The order was yelled, there was a shot from a pistol, and the batteries began to fire, thundering across the wide hill. Stuart moved back, stood beside Alexander, raised his field glasses and saw the first puffs, the small flashes of light. He nodded. Yes, Joe Hooker, he thought, we have found your headquarters. Quickly, the house was covered with smoke, and he could see small fires, knew the house would not last long. It was, of course, the first target for men who had been waiting for a target.

Now all the batteries were firing, and the ground was shaking under him. He steadied the horse, tried to see. The wide fields around the house were alive with the impact of the shells, and smoke covered most of the hill. Federal batteries began to answer, from new positions beyond the house, and around them a few shells were beginning to land. He turned to Alexander, said, "Colonel, this is your hill. You know what to do."

Alexander was smiling, said, "If you happen to see General Hooker, please thank him for this wonderful gift."

Stuart nodded, smiled, began to move the horse, would move back up to the north, toward the turnpike. He thought, I must try to form them . . . some kind of line, press them forward. Then he saw riders coming from the east, moving out of the woods, into the clearing. They were officers, men in gray. He stopped, waited, then spurred the horse, rode hard toward them, waved the hat high.

"General Lee!"

He pulled up, jumped from the horse, made the low bow, and Lee said, "Well, I did not expect to find you up here. Very well, General. It seems we have joined the two corps. Anderson's division is below us now, and I believe they have located General Heth's flank. How is the fight here, General?"

Lee was not smiling, and Stuart stood at attention, said, "Sir, we have pressed the enemy hard. We have beaten him back from his defenses, but . . . we are outmanned, sir. They have pushed us back."

"We are always outmanned, General. We need to press on." He stopped, saw now the focus of the guns, saw Alexander riding up.

"This is a fine position, Colonel. Your guns will do good work from here."

Alexander saluted, was still smiling. "We will do our best, General."

Lee looked down at Stuart, who reached for the horse, pulled himself up, said, "General, perhaps I should return to my . . . to General Jackson's troops."

Lee nodded. "That would be a wise decision, General. Press them. Press them *hard.*"

Stuart saluted and moved the horse away, back down the wide hill, where the guns continued to fire in a steady rhythm.

Lee watched him, thought of Jackson now. The mention of his name sent a hard, dull pain through his chest. We have lost many . . . so many, he thought, and God does not judge one man better than the next. But I cannot help it. *Dear God, You must save General Jackson. This army has no better man.*

Lee put it from his mind, would not see the face, the sharp blue eyes, stared out in the direction of the cannon fire. He raised his field glasses, saw the house, burning now, tall flames and black smoke, and he thought, General Hooker has lost his headquarters, and so he must move, and when he moves, he will take the army with him.

52. HANCOCK

May 3, 1863. Late morning.

They had been pressed since first light, heavier waves coming out of the woods to the east, and it was clear that no one had retreated from in front of his division.

The fight was coming now all along their lines, down, across the front of Slocum's position, then in a wide arc to the right, in a wide U-shaped front, and from the crest of the ridge he commanded he could hear the worst of it back behind him, toward the west.

He had put the young Colonel Miles in command of the first lines, had given him enough troops to spread out in a heavy skirmish line all along his front, dug into their muddy trenches. Lee's troops had pushed and charged and sent volley after volley against them, and Miles did not break. This part of the line will hold, Hancock thought.

He rode along the crest, down toward his flank and the junction with Slocum, heard more steady musket fire and a few big guns. He saw Slocum, who moved toward him, waving, his staff riding at full speed to keep up. Slocum slowed the horse, yelled, "General, we are running out of ammunition! Have you any reserves?"

Hancock looked at him, saw no smile now, only the dirty sweat of the battle. "We are holding our lines . . . but . . . no, I have received no supplies. The wagons are up above the mansion. Have you sent back to headquarters?"

Slocum waved his arms, seemed frantic. "Of course I've sent to headquarters! There is no support there! Hooker will not send any aid . . . says we are fighting for our lives!"

Hancock saw the look, a man who believed they were done, a commander who would infect his men.

"General Slocum, we are not giving way! There are not enough rebel soldiers to drive us from this ground! Can you hold your position?"

Slocum stared now down toward his lines, then turned to Hancock with a new look, a dull sadness. "We will hold out as long as we can. If Sedgwick does not come to our aid . . . it cannot last."

Hancock thought, Sedgwick? Why do we need Sedgwick? Is he still on the river, below Fredericksburg? He was feeling the old anger again, the heat rising in his chest.

"General Slocum, I must tend to my division. I am sorry that headquarters is not cooperating with you. I will try to find General Couch. He may have some help to give."

He pulled the horse away, left Slocum sitting, rode back toward the turnpike, toward headquarters, the Chancellor house.

There were guns now, long lines, wagons and caissons, moving up into the wide clearing, coming from the south and the west. They moved up past the house, to the north, began to unlimber, officers screaming orders, gunners pulling their cannon into position. He reined the horse, thought, Why are they back here . . . and suddenly, in front of him, a bright flash, a hard slap of wind, and the air came alive, bright red streaks, blinding explosions. Now he understood: We have pulled back, the lines are closing in.

He pushed the horse, could see the house, saw a shell hit directly into the walls, shattered brick blown high in the air, a stone chimney collapsing. Men were running, scattering, riderless horses were galloping toward him. He tried to keep going, the house now hidden by smoke, and he heard men yelling, approaching, saw flags now, officers. He waited, thought, Keep moving, but no, there will be no one there now, and that whole damned clearing is a target. He heard his name then, a hoarse voice. He turned toward the sound, saw men on horses, *Couch*. Other officers were trailing behind him, and they were moving fast, away from the house, toward the east, moving closer now, toward the turnpike. He pulled the horse around, met them on the road.

Couch said, "Are your lines holding, General?"

"Yes, we have not withdrawn from our original positions. Where are the rebel guns firing—"

"From Hazel Grove. We have pulled back. Our commander has decided we are too weak, and so we are concentrating the lines. *We* are too goddamned weak!"

He saw Couch's face, red rage, knew that it was all falling apart, and Couch said aloud, as more men gathered around them, "General Hooker has been injured. It is not serious . . . he seems to be stunned.

He was at the house when the shelling began and was struck . . . quite possibly by the hand of God." There were nods, small laughs from the men, and Hancock saw that Couch was not smiling.

"The general has transferred command of the field to me. His last orders were . . . that the army be withdrawn . . . that we seek the safety of the river. It is the commanding general's feeling that this army has been beaten on this ground. I do not agree with that assessment . . . but the order has been given. I have sent word to Sickles and to Slocum to begin pulling back from contact with the enemy."

Hancock stared down to the south, toward Slocum's lines. He could see wagons moving, men filling the road. Behind them, around the burning house, shells continued to fall, and the Federal guns there were now answering. From the far side of the clearing, from where the stampede of the Eleventh Corps had come the day before, columns of troops were marching toward them, Sickles's men. Couch watched silently, and the men around him did not move, waited. Hancock looked at Couch, thought, He wants to turn them around, to fight . . . he cannot just *leave*.

Couch turned, said, "Gentlemen, let us move to a safer place. We will soon be the front lines."

He spurred the horse, and Hancock looked east, toward his troops, could hear nothing, sounds drowned out by the fierce chorus of blasts from the clearing.

He yelled toward Couch, rode quickly to catch up, and Couch slowed, looked at him. Hancock saw the face of a man who had had enough, the anger now fading, replaced by deep sadness. Couch said, "You will protect our flanks. . . . We will pull back to the north, toward the river. Reynolds will cover the west flank, you will cover the south and east."

Reynolds? he thought. "Sir, did the First Corps give way? I did not know they had engaged—"

"The First Corps did not have the chance to give way. They have not yet seen action. General Reynolds is dug in above the turnpike, and will withdraw toward the fords above him."

Hancock stared blankly at Couch. Reynolds . . . the First Corps, maybe the best they had . . . *was not even engaged.*

Up the road leading toward the river, riders appeared, came through the smoke, turned, moved toward them. Hancock saw the flag of the Fifth Corps, the Maltese cross. It was Meade, and with him, John Reynolds.

The aides stayed back, and Couch moved forward. The three men began to speak, and Hancock waited, could hear nothing. Then Couch turned, motioned to him, and he pushed the horse closer. Meade was staring away, toward the sound of the guns, and Reynolds was looking at him, hard, cold.

Couch said, "General Hancock, do you understand your orders?"

"Yes, sir. I am to protect the withdrawal of the army."

Reynolds was still staring at him, said quietly, "The withdrawal of the army . . . gentlemen, this is pure madness. General Hooker is not in control. Couch, you can override him, you are in command of the field. I can advance my men in line to the south, flank the enemy to the west. It is not too late to save this!"

Meade was still looking away, watching the lines of troops moving up the road, away from the sound of the guns. "We did not even have a fight." He turned, stared at Couch. "We did not even have a fight! Most of them . . . my men never even *saw* the enemy!"

Couch nodded, spoke with slow, careful words. "Gentlemen, General Hooker's last order was clear. The general made his decision because . . . General Sedgwick did not pursue the enemy with vigor. General Hooker feels that had Sedgwick come in behind Lee's lines, we would not be forced to withdraw. But we have already begun the withdrawal. It is now . . . the only course left to us."

Reynolds leaned forward, glared at Couch. "Sedgwick? So . . . that's to be it, eh? Sedgwick is the cause? We will blame one corps?"

"Gentlemen . . ." Couch raised his hand. "You may all prepare your own reports of this battle. But we have our orders. They will be carried out. General Hancock . . ." He turned, and Hancock looked again into the sad eyes. "You may return to your division."

They held the line until the troops behind them had passed, moving quickly now, the retreat pushed hard by the panic of defeat, the spreading disease of fear—that the enemy was coming, right behind them, that if they did not move quickly, the massive army would be crushed. On the roads the columns had little order, and the guns, from Hazel Grove, from the main roads in both directions, poured a steady stream of solid shot and exploding shells into the ranks. Many of the units lost all order. Men began running into the thick brush, away from the deadly open roads, knew that if they just kept moving north, they would find the river.

Those who did not share the panic, the corps and division commanders, were now coming to understand that this tragic and expensive defeat had not come from the weakness of the troops, but from the collapse of one man.

Hancock stayed on the turnpike, watched the stream of blue move over the wide fields, past their own guns, still firing, punching holes in the advancing lines of Lee's army, slowing the pursuit. To the south one division was holding a solid line, a rear guard, withdrawing more slowly than the others. It was Geary, of Slocum's corps, and now he was being flanked. The lines had broken, and they came out of the brush in a run, guided by the high column of smoke from the big house. Hancock knew it was time to pull his own people in, back along the ridge, wrap their lines across the wide field, hold the advancing rebels away until the army could reform itself behind him, protect the crossings at the river.

Below him, along the creek, Miles was still holding out. There had been no breakthrough there, but he had sent the word down: withdraw, move up to the trenches on the ridge.

He waited, watched the trees below, and they were not coming. He looked for a courier, the staff following him closely now, yelled out, "Go down there, repeat my order to withdraw! No delays . . . they could be cut off!"

The man saluted, a young lieutenant, began to gallop down the rise. Then Hancock saw horses, and a blue line emerging from the trees, and behind the horses, men were carrying a litter. The lieutenant reached them, turned, waved back at Hancock, and he spurred the horse and moved down. Shells began to fall around him, up behind, along the trenches, and he knew Lee's guns were closing in.

Hancock reached the horses, did not think, just followed the man's wave, pointing, and he saw officers, a captain, and the man saluted him, ran up to the horse.

"General, Colonel Miles is wounded, sir. . . ."

He jumped from the horse, moved to the litter. Miles was black with mud, his face barely recognizable, and he saw Hancock now.

"General . . . why are we pulling out, sir? The line is strong. . . ." He turned his head away, and Hancock saw the blood, the front of his uniform, a dark stain flowing down onto the litter. Hancock looked to the captain, saw no answers. They were waiting for him to say something, and he looked below, into the trees, saw Miles's men coming, moving slowly up the hill.

He said to his lieutenant, still on the horse, "Find the surgeon! Now! Tend to the colonel!" The man pulled the horse away, galloped up toward the crest of the hill. Now Hancock looked at the others, saw another officer, a familiar face, and men were stopping around him. They had heard that Miles was down, most had not seen him until now.

"Gentlemen, we must not delay. Keep the units in line, rejoin the division. We are the rear guard. We are covering the retreat." He paused, saw muddy faces and no expressions, and he could not let it go, had to tell them.

"You men performed as well as any army ever has. Officers . . . tell your men, make sure they all know this. You did not lose this fight! The soldiers . . . in this division, in other divisions . . . you did not lose this fight! I am honored to command you." Miles raised an arm, and Hancock stared down, surprised, did not know he was still conscious. And Miles put a dirty hand to his forehead, made a weak salute. Hancock turned, suddenly could not look at him. There was nothing he could say. He climbed onto the horse, spurred it hard, moved quickly up the hill.

Blue troops were still coming up from the south, and there was little order, men running alone and in small groups. Now the musket fire was growing, and men were falling. Hancock could not yet see, but knew from the sounds that Lee's advance was closing in, a tightening circle in the thick brush. He stayed on his horse, moved behind the new lines, could see the last of the flames from the mansion below him, now out in front of the lines. The guns were pulling away behind him, could no longer support his troops, the fight was coming in too close. He watched the muskets, bayonets pointing out, all down the line. They were not firing, no targets yet, and then he saw horses, officers, a fast gallop toward his lines, more men in blue. There was shouting, and his men were standing, gathering. He rode in that direction, heard the frantic, screaming voice.

"Charge, you cowards! Charge! They're right behind us!"

It was John Geary. Hancock moved closer, and Geary kept yelling, was turning back, looking toward the thickets and the last of his own retreating men. They moved by, passed through Hancock's line, many with wounds, moving slowly, and Geary yelled again, at Hancock's troops.

"Charge them, you cowards!"

Soldiers were closing around the horse, and Hancock saw a musket raised, pointed at Geary. A soldier said, "There are no cowards in this line!" and others began to yell at Geary as well, angry taunts. Geary was staring at the musket, the point of a bayonet.

Hancock moved up, said, "General Geary, I am in command here. You will not give orders to my men. These men have had their fill of watching this army retreat. I would suggest you retire to the rear with your troops."

Geary stared at Hancock, mouth open, and Hancock turned the horse away, had nothing else to say, knew he could not pour out his anger on this one man, a man who after all was doing what he was told.

He heard hoots, yelling behind him, knew it was directed at Geary, the men calling after him as he rode back, away from the fight. Now there were new voices, men calling out, and he felt a sudden rush of hot wind, a high zip of a musket ball, then more, rushing past him on all sides and below, down past the last dying flames of the mansion, they came from out of the brush, a row of muskets, bayonets, and the ragged lines of the enemy.

The long lines on either side of him erupted instantly, a quick and heavy volley, and a thick blast of smoke rolled across the wide field. Now the answer came back, and he began to move, looking for the commanders. He had not seen Meagher for a while, and Caldwell was up ahead somewhere. He rode quickly, and the smoke stayed out in front of them, like fog rolling down a hill, so the firing from below was blind, balls whizzing over him, high and wild. He saw Caldwell on his horse, moving down the line, and Hancock motioned, back, away from the lines, and Caldwell turned and moved with him toward a small grove of trees. Hancock turned the horse, tried to see, and felt a quick shiver from the horse. The horse was searching the ground, plucking slowly at the green grass. Hancock jumped down, saw a steady trickle of blood, a clean shot through the head. He stood back, watched the animal, grazing, thought of the talk of the wounded, men who are dying, who fade slowly away, drifting back to some other place, some peaceful memory, and he thought, You too, old girl, and the front legs quivered, then buckled, and the horse fell over on its side and did not move.

Behind him, Caldwell's aide had grabbed another horse, led it to him. Hancock stared at the animal, much smaller than his, and climbed up, his boots nearly brushing the ground.

Caldwell was staring back at his own lines, the smoke drifting toward them, and he said, "General, we cannot hold out against a strong assault. Where are the reserves?"

Hancock pulled the horse around, said, "You will hold your lines until I tell you to withdraw. There are no reserves, the rest of the army is withdrawing to the river."

Caldwell stared, wanted to ask, saw the hot glare in Hancock's eyes and nodded. "I understand, sir."

Hancock spurred the horse, and it moved toward the smoke. He was suddenly engulfed in a thick cloud of sulfur and ash. He tried to turn, to move off to the left, but was swallowed now, felt himself choking. He moved farther, kicked the horse hard, and saw a clearing and his other lines, facing east, and below, a new volley, a fresh wave of the enemy coming from the woods where Miles had held them away. Then it was Meagher's lines, and he rode forward, saw the green flag and Meagher pointing, shouting. There was a long, single explosion of muskets, and quickly, another. He moved up behind the line, could see down, a thick mass of men pouring out of the heavy trees, coming toward them. They were stopping to shoot, then running again, and he heard it now, the high, terrible scream of the rebel yell.

He rode back toward the black skeleton of the mansion, could see the gray troops moving in one long mass up that side of the rise, and now he knew it was done, his men could not stay here, were being pressed from both sides. He moved quickly, waved to the couriers trailing behind and yelled, "Go to the commanders! Pull back, to the north. Retreat in line, keep firing!"

The men were away, and he rode up the road toward the north, where the rest of the army was crowding the banks of the river, digging in, a quick defensive line protecting the withdrawal from the rushing tide of Lee's tightening ring.

He turned, saw his men falling back on both sides of him, the lines backing toward each other, the distance between them closing rapidly, the deadly fire from the rebel muskets now striking his men from behind, some shots flying farther, reaching out and dropping men far across the field, in the lines of their own advancing troops.

The smoke came toward him again, and he pulled the horse away, slowly, stayed on the road. His men were still moving back, a good solid line, no break, no panicking flood. He halted the horse, sat still now, and suddenly the light wind shifted again, cleared the smoke away, and now he could see it all, his men moving backward. He felt himself shake, an icy stab in his chest, that this was some kind of absurd, horrible joke. He kept staring at them, watched them come closer, backing toward him, and now he felt a sudden release, the small hard place inside him that he could not open, could not touch months before, on the muddy banks of the Rappahannock. But now it came, an unstoppable flow of grief, the weight inside him pouring out, and it was not for the dead, for the men who would hurt no more, but for these, the living, the men in front of him now, men no different from him; soldiers who would carry this with them for the rest of their lives, who would always know that they ran in the face of the enemy they should have beaten, not because they were cowards, or because there was weakness in their hearts. They ran because they were told to.

53. LEE

MAY 3, 1863. MIDDAY.

HE HELD THE HORSE BESIDE THE ROAD, ALLOWED THE GUNS TO pass, the sweating mules and creaking wagons. He saw the clearing now, rode farther, his staff behind, climbed the short rise and could see across the wide-open ground. The remains of the grand house were a smoldering mass of twisted black. He moved that way.

His army was already ahead of him, had pushed beyond the clearings, concentrating on the withdrawal of the Federal troops. Now, guns from Hazel Grove, from the batteries to the west, were moving up, repositioning. It was barely past noon, and he watched them, thought, We can still do it today, there is plenty of time.

He dismounted, walked by himself toward the ruins of the house, stopped close to the edge of the smoldering ash. He tried to feel some joy, the familiar thrill, the wild pursuit of a routed enemy, the glory of victory. It would not come. Men were passing around him, keeping a respectful distance. He heard the shouts.

"We whipped 'em good!"

"The bluebellies are still runnin', General. . . ."

He looked toward the voices, men waving at him, hats and muskets high, and he waved back, weakly, stared down again into the ashes.

Taylor kept the rest of the staff back, on their horses, and moved forward slowly, walked the horse up behind Lee and stopped. Lee did not look up. Taylor said, "Doesn't seem right that General Jackson isn't here to see this."

Lee shook his head, said, "No, Major. It doesn't seem right at all. But it is the will of God."

Lee tried to pull himself away, thought about the army, Jackson's troops coming together, reorganizing, the regiments and companies reuniting now after the massive confusion, the headlong rush through the thick woods. He had seen the face often, peering out from under the old cap, and Lee had to keep telling himself, He is all right, he just lost an arm. Lee had even sent a message, tried to be lighthearted: "Rejoin us on the field, won't you, General?" But it was not sincere, there could be no joy, and then he had said, "You have lost your left arm, I have lost my right. . . ." And he knew somewhere deep inside, that was the truth, that no matter what happened now, Jackson would not return, would not be here to carry the fight.

And there was still a fight. Sedgwick had finally pushed hard into Early's forces, moving up into Fredericksburg and then out, across the same ground where Burnside's army had marched into a massacre. But this time Early was too few, and Sedgwick understood that if the men kept running, did not stop in front of the stone wall, did not try to shoot their way across, the wall could be reached and overrun. So now Early was pushed back, withdrawn safely down to the southwest, below the hills, and Sedgwick controlled the heights and was moving out this way.

Lee had turned McLaws around, marched him out the turnpike to meet Sedgwick's advance head-on. They still held Bank's Ford, on the river just northwest of the town held by Cadmus Wilcox's brigade. McLaws would now spread south, in a heavy line, a long, high ridge that ran beside a small brick building, Salem Church. Sedgwick would find that he was not advancing against the vulnerable and unsuspecting rear of Lee's position, but was moving instead into the teeth of a division full of the good fight, men who had learned that no matter what the enemy sent them, they would turn him around.

Wilcox had used his men to delay Sedgwick as long as he could, withdrawing slowly back toward the church, and Sedgwick found himself strung out in long lines of march, could not organize in the face of Wilcox's tormenting skirmishers. When McLaws showed himself and the volleys began, Sedgwick's lead units were run piecemeal into the fight.

Lee could hear the sounds of battle now, from the east. He turned and stared out. Taylor said, "McLaws . . ."

Lee was moving, went quickly toward his horse, climbed up, said, "Major, send a courier to find General Anderson. I do not want General McLaws overrun."

Taylor moved toward the waiting staff, and a man was quickly out, moving back down the rise. There were more riders now, from the south, a small flag, and they rode toward Taylor and stopped. There were salutes and low voices. Taylor turned, moved toward Lee.

"General, it is Captain Hodges, sir, a message from General Early. He has reformed his division, sir, behind the Fredericksburg hills, and he requests—"

Lee raised his hand, stopped him. "Captain Hodges, you may come closer. Please tell me what you have observed, what General Early has on his front."

Hodges removed his hat, seemed hesitant, said, "General Lee, sir, the Yankees . . . the enemy has pulled most of its force to the northwest of the heights . . . up near the river. General Early believes, sir, that they are moving now toward . . . here." He looked around, saw no entrenchments, no defensive lines.

"Captain, you may return to General Early and tell him this: McLaws's division is in contact with the enemy, between here and the heights, at Salem Church. I am sending reinforcements to assist his efforts. Please request that General Early move northward with all speed. I believe, Captain, that General Early will discover that he has a great advantage in front of him. He may find he can close on the enemy from their flank and rear."

Hodges looked toward the new sounds of battle, nodded, said, "Thank you, General, it will be done, sir." He threw up a salute, made a short bow, and led the group of riders away in a gallop.

Taylor was laughing, said, "Pardon me, sir. He rode up here and started whispering, said he didn't want to disturb you, sir."

Lee watched the small flag disappear on the road, said nothing. He looked toward the low thunder in the east, growing, spreading, and now he saw Anderson, more riders, and Anderson was moving slowly, a calm procession moving up the turnpike. Lee stared, thought, Was I not clear? There is a fight growing behind you. . . .

He heard a loud whoop from the other direction, turned and saw Stuart, another staff and more flags. Stuart reached him first, stayed on the horse.

"Greetings, *mon Général*! It is a fine day, sir! We have done Old Stonewall proud!"

Lee felt a rush of anger, his hands clenched on the reins of the horse, and Anderson was close now, lifting his hat to the men around them, basking in his own glow. Lee felt his jaw tighten, said, "Gentlemen, if you please. This day is not over. We have a fight on our right flank. Sedgwick's corps is on the move, has pushed General Early from the hills and is moving to join forces with General Hooker. And, gentlemen, before we engage in celebration, let us be reminded that just north of our position here, we are attempting to contain an army that outnumbers us by three to one."

Stuart lowered his head, again the scolded child, said, "General Lee, the Second Corps is reforming in a tight arc, sir, and will move against Hooker's forces at your command, sir!"

"No, General, rest them for now. They cannot continue to press the attack without some replenishment. This is not the cavalry, General, we must make time. Get the smaller units together, determine who is in command. We have lost a great many fine officers." He paused, took a deep breath.

"It is our objective to drive General Hooker against the river. If we bring a strong line against his forces, we may cause them considerable discomfort. They can no longer withdraw in a slow methodical retreat. They will be very limited in how quickly they can cross the river, and then we will have them. We have an opportunity to destroy them, gentlemen, with their backs to the river. General Anderson, you must take your division back to the east, toward Salem Church, and strengthen General McLaws's lines. Early's division will be advancing from the south. If we can tie up Sedgwick until General Early arrives, we may be able to press him hard against the river as well." He was suddenly very excited, putting it into words. He realized now the magnitude of the opportunity in front of them. Anderson saluted, backed the horse away, and Lee stared out to the north, where the Federal Army was digging in to their last line of defense.

He heard Stuart move up closer, beside him, and Lee said, "God has given us an opportunity. It is very clear now. There is a much greater prize, we can do so much more than merely claim this field. If we can crush the enemy right here, against the river . . . we may force him to surrender. We have paid the price . . . what God has taken . . . is General Jackson. It is a message. He is saying, 'Here is your opportunity, and here . . . is the cost.' " He looked at Stuart, and Stuart was watching him with wide, round eyes, the eyes of a small boy absorbing the words of his father.

"Remember that, General, there is always a price."

EARLY DID NOT REACH SEDGWICK'S POSITION UNTIL VERY LATE IN the day, and Anderson's lines were slow in spreading, and so by dark Sedgwick had concentrated his forces, made a strong defensive line backed up against Bank's Ford. In front of Stuart, Hooker's army was tightly in place, a sharp U, with its back toward the United States Ford.

All the next day, McLaws, Anderson, and Early pounded hard against Sedgwick's position, but it was difficult ground, and the numbers were nearly even. Sedgwick was pushed harder into his defensive line, but could not be moved. Around Hooker, the divisions of Jackson's corps harassed and threw light punches all day. Hooker could have pushed out of his own defenses at any time, but Lee had guessed correctly that Hooker would not attack, that still he was waiting for Sedgwick, had pinned all hopes of any Federal victory on one small separate piece of his army.

The next day, Tuesday, May 5, it began to rain, a hard, soaking storm, and so both armies lay down hard in their muddy positions, waiting. Lee could feel his greatest opportunity to end the war flowing away, like the fresh streams of mud that poured away into the river. That night, with Hooker himself already across, the Federal Army made its way over the rocking pontoons. Lee had his men fed and their guns ready, and in the first light of the new day he sent out the fresh and rested troops, the final crushing blow, and they would push out hard and fast and find only empty trenches.

54. JACKSON

WEDNESDAY, MAY 6, 1863

DAYS BEFORE . . . HE HAD LAIN AWAKE, LISTENING TO THE steady roar, the thunder of the big guns in the woods beyond the field hospital, and then muskets, waves of shooting, and sometimes, he thought, It had been very close. McGuire gave him something . . . he had wanted to ask, but his mind would cloud, thick fog, and the pain would be stopped. He could see McGuire's face, calm, confident, and so he would not object, would accept the medication, the prick of the needle. It had been Sunday . . . the Sabbath. We should not have to do that . . . to fight on His day, he thought, but now he lay quietly, did not know what day it was . . . how long it had been.

The fog had cleared, gradually. He could see the room, saw something new, a white ceiling, remembered, We are no longer in the field. . . . His eyes followed a small crack in the plaster, a long curving line, and he stared at it for a long time. The voices and the men were around him, and then it was quiet. He did not know if he was awake or asleep, but then the thin line would grow, move closer, heavier . . . *and he saw now it was a snake, blue and fat, and he watched it move and twist, injured, wounded, rolling madly, convulsing, and he saw men, soldiers, bayonets, and the snake would not die, kept twisting* . . . and then he knew he was awake, because now the snake was gone, was just a long, thin crack in the plaster.

The hospital had been a dangerous place. The shifting flow of the battle had put it close to the shelling, and McGuire and Smith had made arrangements for him to be moved. Jed Hotchkiss and the engineers had led the way, cleared the small road of the refuse of the fighting, shattered trees and sharp holes, and the steady flow of men and wagons had stood to the side, men with hats in their hands, sad salutes and soft crying as the ambulance had passed.

McGuire had received permission directly from Lee to accompany Jackson away from the field. He had hesitated to ask, knew of the common practice of men of high rank, who often treated their army's doctors as their personal physicians, the foolish exercise of privilege that left wounded soldiers unattended. But Lee had no hesitation, had ordered the move, knew that if Jackson was to recover, there was no one better than McGuire to guide him through it.

The Chandler house lay along the railroad line, below Fredericksburg, at Guiney's Station. The war had made Guiney's a busy place, and the Chandler plantation had suffered, as did all the rich farmlands of central Virginia. But for now it was safe and comfortable, and Jackson had agreed, remembered many kind invitations to make their home his headquarters. Now it would be his hospital.

They had brought him to a small building below the main house, a simple, square two-story structure, two rooms down and two up, and in one of the lower rooms, a bed had been placed, with fresh linens. He was carried there, could see out a tall, narrow window to the trees beyond and the bright warmth of the sun.

He was beginning to feel stronger, was awake more, less drugged sleep. McGuire set up the other downstairs room for his medical office, bandages and dressings, and he was completing his examination of Jackson's wound, the surgery.

"Hmm . . . yes, General, very good. It is healing nicely. Is there any pain . . . here?"

Jackson felt the probe, the pressure in the shoulder. "No. No pain."

McGuire stood, nodded. "All right, then, we'll dress that again, and I'll check it in the morning. How's the hand?"

Jackson raised the clump of bandages, turned it, moved the fingers. "It seems fine, Doctor."

"It was not bad, should heal completely . . . sore for a while, but you'll have full movement in a week or two."

Outside, there were horses, voices, and the outer door opened, boots on the wood floor, and Jackson heard a quiet voice.

"Is it all right, Doctor?"

McGuire moved away from the bed, said, "Certainly, Captain Smith, please come in. The general is doing quite well today."

Smith moved toward the bed, bent down to one knee, said, "General? You feeling better?"

Jackson looked at the young face, the sad eyes, said, "Don't concern yourself about me, Mr. Smith. I am in God's care now. But . . . tell me . . . how are we faring . . . ?"

"The fight? Oh, General, the enemy is gone, across the river. We've secured the high ground around Chancellorsville . . . and along the river. General Stuart did well by you, sir. And the Stonewall Brigade . . . right in the middle of it, sir. They were fighting for Stonewall, I heard that all day."

Jackson nodded, smiled, thought, Why must they do that? "Captain, I would appreciate it if you would not refer to me that way. There is too much of the self-seeking . . . the name Stonewall belongs to the men who earned it, the men who fought at Manassas. God would not be pleased if I carried a label I do not deserve."

Smith looked down, stared at the floor, smiled to himself. This man would never be known as anything but Stonewall.

"Sir, the men . . . they honored you . . . a good fight. They all think of you, sir."

"The men . . . Captain, many years from now those men will be able to recall this war with the unique pride of the soldier, something no one will ever take away. They will be proud to say they served in the Stonewall Brigade. But they did not serve me . . . they served God."

Smith nodded. "Yes, sir." There was a silent pause, and Smith stood up, said, "General, I have the ball. Dr. McGuire allowed me to keep the musket ball he took from your hand, sir. It is a round smoothbore, sir. It has to be one of ours."

Jackson nodded. "Yes. I heard . . . they thought I was asleep. Pendleton . . . I heard them talking. It could not be helped. There is no blame in war. God understands, we must all forgive."

"Yes, sir . . . it was the Eighteenth North Carolina—"

Jackson lifted the bandaged hand. "No . . . it was the war. We will not place blame. Tell them . . . do not be sad . . . they were doing their duty."

He began to feel weak, the alertness fading, and he turned, stared at the blank wall. Smith watched him, said, "Sir . . . ? Are you all right?" He stepped back, went to the door, called across to the other room, "Doctor? The general—"

McGuire moved past him, went to the bed, said, "General? Are you getting tired? We can leave you now. You should be resting . . . let the strength return."

Jackson looked at him, saw the dark heavy eyes, said, "I'm fine,

Doctor. Tired. I should rest now. Tell me, Doctor, when was the last time *you* slept?"

McGuire smiled. "I'm not certain. We should all be concerned with . . . less duty and more care for ourselves. Captain, would you mind leaving us for a while?"

"Not at all, sir." Smith bent down again, one knee on the floor. "I'm right outside, General."

Jackson looked at him, tried to focus, but the fog was flowing through his brain again, and now the strength was gone, and he felt himself rising, drifting out . . .

. . . he heard the shots, the fresh volley, heard the hard slap of lead, splitting the skull of the man beside him, and the man crumpled, dropped in a solid mass, and the litter turned, spilling him, and he hit the ground hard, on his side, and the pain tore through him, burning, the hot hard stab of the bayonet, and now he was staring up into the dark, could not see the treetops . . . and now saw the shadows, the window, thought, I'm still in the bed, the clean white room. But the searing blast of pain did not fade, was still there. He reached over, tried to feel it with his left arm, the hand not bandaged, felt the hand move across his body. He tried to touch the hurt and could not, tried to probe with the fingers, could feel them moving, and he held the hand up to his face, but there was nothing there, no dark shape. Now he was awake, his mind clearing, and he knew there was no hand . . . no arm. But . . . he had felt it . . . the fingers . . . and he tried to feel it again, but . . . the pain would not stop. Now he moved the other hand, the heavy bandages, touched the side, pressing, but the pain was deep inside, a burning hole in his lung. He lay still, tried to breathe, deeply, a slow rhythm, calm, heard now other breathing, tried to see, the foot of the bed . . . McGuire was there . . . sleeping on a small, hard couch. He relaxed again, thought, No, do not wake him. It will pass. He stared up at the dark, prayed, *God, please give comfort to them all. They care for me . . . the men are concerned . . . too much. It must not turn them away from their duty.*

The pain began to ease, and he kept his thoughts focused away, the men . . . General Lee. There is more for me to do. God does not want me yet. The enemy is still there . . . waiting. . . .

. . . the field . . . the thick brush, the dense tangles. His heart was racing, and he thought . . . the high ground, we must place the guns. He saw the lines now, his men, rolling forward, the enemy falling back, the edge of the river, falling, jumping in, panic, and his men were there, at the edge of the water . . . the river churning hot and red, and he could hear the yells, the screams of the enemy, and now they began to move across, his troops,

marching across the river, above the bodies of the enemy, pressing on, into the tall trees on the other side. . . .

THURSDAY, MAY 7, 1863

SHE HELD THE BABY, STEPPED DOWN FROM THE TRAIN, HELPED now by men in dirty uniforms. They stood aside, made a clear path for her. There was a carriage, and a man held the door. She nodded, tried to smile.

Her brother was behind her, held a large cloth bag, motioned up to the top of the carriage, and other bags were lifted, tossed up. He climbed in, sat beside her. They did not talk, and the carriage began to move.

He knew it was his responsibility to bring the news, to bring her here. They both knew that Jackson had allowed him to serve on his staff because of her. She did not want him near the fight. This way he could still be a soldier, and, even if Jackson took his own fight close to the front of the lines, something she tried not to think about, his staff, and her brother, would be safe.

It had taken him two days to reach her, the delay caused by Stoneman's cavalry raid. The train that brought them was heavily armed, would fight their way through if necessary, but finally the tracks from Richmond had been cleared, and now they had reached Guiney's Station.

There were troops in the yard, small groups, dirty, ragged, and officers, some familiar. She saw women now, coming out on the porch of the big house, waiting for her. She was led, a gentle arm, soft words and sad faces. She watched her brother moving away toward the small cottage, and men saluted, and she thought, I should see him now, but they were pulling her away. She looked into the faces now, saw the concern, the deep sadness, and knew something was happening, something her brother had not told her, and she tried to turn, said, "I must see my husband. . . ."

Mrs. Chandler nodded, said, "Yes, my dear, yes. You should talk to Dr. McGuire first."

She stopped, turned, knew they were not going to tell her anything, and she said, "Please, take me to him." The baby began to cry now, and she looked at the small face, thought, It has been a difficult trip. She looked at Mrs. Chandler.

Now, a girl moved closer, said, "Please, Mrs. Jackson, allow me to put the baby in bed. We have a place made up special, for both of you."

Anna saw the eagerness, soft kindness. "I suppose . . . all right," she said. "I will rest a bit."

They led her into the house, up to her room, and she laid the baby down in a small bed. Her bags were there now, and she looked at the faces of the women again, and began to feel overwhelmed, the anticipation, the stress of the trip passing.

She sat wearily on the edge of the bed. "I must have a moment . . . please. Thank you for all your kindness."

The girl was leaning over close to the baby, and Mrs. Chandler said, "Lucy, let us allow Mrs. Jackson to rest. Please, excuse us, Mrs. Jackson. . . ."

The woman nodded, a faint smile, and Anna looked to her bags, and the door closed softly behind her. She stood, felt a deep yawn rising in her, moved to the baby, sleeping again, and she smiled and said in a whisper, "Soon . . . we will be a family again . . . this will be over. . . ."

She moved toward the sunlight, a tall window, looked out over the thick green grass of the wide yard, saw troops, men with shovels, and they were digging hard, throwing dirt into a wide pile, and she felt a sudden cold shock. *They are digging a grave.* She tried to see, could not, her eyes thick with tears. She stayed at the window, thought, Why have they not told me? Behind her there was a soft knock at the door. She turned, angry now.

"Yes?"

The door opened, and she saw the face of the young doctor. He bowed slightly, said, "Hello, Mrs. Jackson, may I be allowed to come in? I would like to speak to you before you visit your husband."

"Visit him?" Her voice was rising, tears running down her cheeks. She pointed toward the window. "So, am I allowed to visit my husband before he is buried?"

McGuire was puzzled, looked toward the window, said, "Buried? He . . . is not . . ." Now he saw the men, the shovels. "Oh my . . . no, no, Mrs. Jackson. That is not a grave. Well, it is . . . but, not, oh no. . . ."

She wiped her eyes, looked out, watched them working again. Now men jumped down into the hole, began to lift something, and she felt her stomach turn slowly, thought, What is happening? A long box appeared, was slowly lifted, and several other men moved closer, lifted it farther, away from the hole.

"Ma'am, that's the body of General Paxton, Frank Paxton. He was killed during the fighting. His body is being moved, taken back to his home in Lexington."

She stared down at the box, said, "Yes, I know Mr. Paxton . . . General Paxton. He is our neighbor. His wife . . . she cried when he left. I suppose she knew something like this would happen." She was calm now, looked at McGuire, waited.

"Lieutenant Morrison . . . your brother has told you about your husband's wounds. We removed his left arm, patched his right hand . . . it is healing well, I am very pleased. But . . . there is a new problem. I believe he now has pneumonia."

She stared, felt the words, said slowly, "May I see him, Doctor?"

"Certainly. He is weak, I have given him medication, to help him sleep. He is in some pain. The medication makes him . . . drift away . . . in and out. He may not recognize you, but I am certain your presence would be most welcome."

McGuire stood aside, and they moved downstairs together. Anna suddenly stopped, a familiar smell, saw the young girl and said, "Oh, Miss Chandler . . . Lucy . . . do I smell lemons . . . lemonade?"

The girl smiled, said, "Yes, ma'am. We received a box of lemons yesterday . . . a gift . . . someone from Florida. Mother is making lemonade for the soldiers. Would you like some?"

Anna smiled, said to McGuire, "Please, go on ahead, Doctor. I wish to prepare a surprise for my husband."

SHE SAW HER BROTHER, AND CAPTAIN SMITH, AND SHE WALKED toward them, carried the tray carefully, and now her brother moved to her quickly, said, "Anna . . . here, let me. Very kind—"

"No, Joseph, it is not for you, it is for Thomas. Before I see him . . . would you please see if he is awake, and offer him this glass? I would like it to be a surprise."

He smiled, said, "Of course. Captain Smith, may I take this inside . . . for the general?"

Smith bowed, nodded to Anna, tried to smile, said, "Please do, Lieutenant. I heard the general talking just a few minutes ago. He is awake."

McGuire was beside the bed, saw the lieutenant come in, and the young man nodded, motioned to the glass. McGuire understood, said, "General, we have a treat for you, something you may have been missing."

Jackson lifted his head, saw the glass, said, "Another of your medications? Very well, Doctor."

"No . . . well, not mine, actually. But should do you some good." He held the glass, lowered it to Jackson's mouth.

Jackson took a short drink, then turned his head, said, "Ahhhgggg, it is so *sweet*. Too much sugar. Always the problem with my *esposita's—*" He stopped, and McGuire was smiling, and Jackson saw Morrison now, and he said, "She is here."

"Yes, General. Lieutenant, would you please escort Mrs. Jackson in?"

Morrison went out, and now McGuire backed away, waited, and the young lieutenant had his sister's arm, led her into the room.

She stared down at the clear blue eyes, saw the weakness, something she had never seen, and suddenly she could not look at him, at the wounds. She dropped down, laid her head on his chest, held his right arm, careful not to touch the bandages. Behind her McGuire made a small noise, motioned, and the two men left the room.

He felt her, soft sobs, and he wanted to wrap his arms around her, pull her into him the way he always had, and he tried to feel the left arm, pull it over her. It would not move, and he began to cry now, softly, small tears falling onto the pillow, and he closed his eyes, said softly, "*Esposita . . . esposita. . . .*"

Sunday, May 10, 1863

. . . H*e was staring out at the river, and across, the enemy was lining the banks, preparing, long battle lines, and he felt the horse rear back, and he waved the sword, and now the guns began, a solid line of fire poured across the river, and his men moved forward, over and across the water, and the sounds rushed around him, the rebel yell, the steady roar of muskets, and the enemy faded back, away, the lines utterly destroyed. Now his men pushed on, into the far woods, and the yells continued, echoing, softer now, drifting back toward him. Around him, more lines, his men still coming up beside him, and he yelled out. . . .*

"Order A. P. Hill . . . prepare for action! Pass the infantry to the front!"

McGuire heard the words, moved closer, listened. Jackson had not slept well, had burst into long streams of speech, nonsensical, gasping, and McGuire understood, the medications, the morphia, were no longer effective. He listened to the breathing, the short quick rhythm, worse now, worse each day.

He moved out, through the doorway, into the other room, where his equipment, the towels and bandages, lay in organized rows. He stopped, stared at the instruments, a black leather pouch laid open on the table, shining steel blades, tongs, small, pointed scissors. He folded the pouch, rolled it up, carefully tied it closed with the small attached ribbon.

He went to the window, looked out toward the big house, saw more troops, a whole company of men. There was no fight now, and the army was regrouping. Many of the men had come here without permission, and the officers did not question them. There were no bands playing now, no typical sounds of the camps, and each morning the men had been given a prayer service, led by Chaplain Lacy. But now Lacy was gone, had returned to the corps to lead services for the army, observing Jackson's emphatic belief in the importance of the Sabbath.

He saw Anna now, coming down from the porch of the house. She carried a bundle, and he shook his head. No, he thought, this is not a good idea. She had insisted, said it could only help, and McGuire understood that he had no place to deny this, that it was for them, both of them, that even if Jackson was far away, did not know them, the mother would always be able to tell the child—he saw you before the end.

He moved to the door, and it was opened. He saw Smith and Anna's cousin, Dr. Stephen Morrison, who had been Jackson's personal physician before the war, and now Sandie Pendleton was there, from the corps headquarters. They all came in, quiet, and McGuire looked at the child, the small soft face, and the child smiled at him, waved its arms in a quick flurry of motion. He felt something deep, pulling at him, and they passed by him and continued into the room where Jackson lay.

The only sounds came from Jackson, high and quick and rasping, and no one spoke. The men stood close behind Anna, glanced at McGuire. They did not know what to expect, waited, would be there, unless . . . she asked them to leave.

Anna bent over, held the baby out, set her down on the bed. The baby made a small noise, and Jackson's eyes opened and he stared up, far away. McGuire moved closer, thought, He could make a sudden move, but then he saw something in Jackson's face, and Jackson's eyes turned to the side, and now they were clear and sharp, and he looked at Anna, then turned, saw the small blanket and the moving hands, and closed his eyes, smiled, said, "My sweet daughter . . . my little Julia . . ."

Anna reached out, sat the baby up, and the small hands began to wave, the high sounds came again. McGuire moved closer, stood at the foot of the bed, felt something now, in the room, looked around, the plain simple walls, and the room was suddenly alive, the dreary darkness fading, the sun suddenly flowing in, clearing out the dark spaces. McGuire looked back to the bed, watched them both, heard the sounds, Jackson's hard, short breaths, and the sweet small sounds from the smiling child.

Jackson began to drift away again, his eyes turning dimly toward the ceiling, and Anna picked up the little girl, glanced at McGuire and nodded, a quiet thank-you. He looked at the child, thought, She was right, it can only do some good . . . a small piece of life to break through the darkness of this terrible place.

The group filed back outside, and soldiers began to move toward them, expectantly, waiting for some word. Smith waved them back, silently, and Anna carried the child back to the big house.

McGuire did not go with them. He moved to the small, hard couch, sat in the growing shadows, watched Jackson breathing. Minutes passed, and he heard the door again, did not stand, saw Anna alone. She looked at him, said, "Dr. Morrison tells me that it will be over soon, that it is certain. Is that so?"

He nodded, resigned.

"Does he know?"

McGuire shook his head, said, "I have not told him."

"Then I will. He must know. He must be prepared. He must know it is the Sabbath, it will comfort him."

He looked toward the bed, said nothing, understood now, for the first time, that his job was truly done, that he was no different now from the rest of them, the soldiers outside, the chaplains, praying for miracles, and the newspapermen, gathering slowly in the distance. There was nothing to do now but wait.

. . . H*e could still smell the baby, the scent was still beside him, and he tried to see her again, tried to focus, but there was nothing, only a soft white, the glow of sunshine through the thick woods. The sounds began to come back, the fight now distant, but the low thunder still reached him, and he thought, No, I am too far away, they have gone ahead . . . too fast. He stared now at the river, his army was far across, and around him there was no one, a quiet calm, and he caught the baby's scent again, and he saw something, out in the river, a figure, a woman, and he wanted to say . . . no, it's dangerous, the fighting . . . but now the sounds had gone, the army was far away, and* *he watched the woman, drifting across the surface of the water, moving slowly toward him. He stood motionless, waited, and now he knew her. It was his mother, young, the face as it had been, before, without the pain, the illness, the woman who laughed and played with him. He stared, tried to speak, but there was no sound, and she smiled, moved closer still, and now he reached out, and she shook her head, no, not yet. Suddenly he was very small, and they were at the swing, and he was pushing his baby sister, and his mother was laughing, a sweet sound like soft music, and he turned to her, and she said something, playful scolding, that's enough, it's time to go. He turned now, and the swing and his sister were gone, and he was not a child, saw now, the uniform, his hand, the bandage, the empty sleeve, and she was leading him out of the woods, out to the water. He saw the trees beyond, filled now with a soft light, large wide oaks, a carpet of soft leaves, and she held her arms up to him, spoke to him, faint, soft words, It is time, He is waiting. In the trees, the light began to glow brighter, and he could feel her now, all around him, her warmth, her happiness, and there was no pain, no sickness, and he put his hand on his chest, no bandage now, suddenly felt the last hard breath, the last hard stab of pain, and the light from the trees began to wash over them and she spoke to him again, and he could hear her now, from deep inside, her voice filling him.*

"Let us cross over the river, and rest under the shade of the trees."

THEY ALL STARED, HEARD THE WORDS, AND NOW THERE WAS SIlence in the room. On a small mantel a clock was ticking, and McGuire looked at it, had not heard the sound before, saw: three-fifteen. Anna was sitting beside the bed, reached out, touched the bandaged hand, then leaned both arms onto the bed, put her head down. Pendleton stood behind her, looked at McGuire. The doctor nodded, and Pendleton eased away with quiet steps, left the room and went outside.

In the yard, men had gathered, most stood, with hats off, waiting, and now Pendleton stopped, looked at the faces of the men, and no one spoke. He said, "The general has died."

The sounds began to flow across the open spaces, low and heavy, and men began to cry. Some collapsed to their knees. Now, Smith came out, said to Pendleton, "We must wire General Lee."

Pendleton nodded, said nothing, and Smith waited, said, "I can take care of it . . . I'll go to the station."

Pendleton looked at him, put a hand on his shoulder, nodded, still did not speak, and Smith moved away, slowly, past the soft sounds of the men.

Anna sat up now, stood, and around her the others still said nothing, would wait for her. She looked around the small room, said, "Thank you . . . for all you did."

Dr. Morrison moved closer, said, "May I escort you back to the house, to your room?"

"Thank you, Stephen." She looked at her brother, standing at the foot of the bed, and the young lieutenant moved around, took her other arm, and she turned, a last look at her husband before they led her slowly from the room. McGuire waited, heard the outer door close, then moved closer to the bed and pulled the blanket up, over Jackson's face.

Outside, Anna saw Tucker Lacy, climbing down from a carriage, and Lacy moved quickly, alongside them, said to Dr. Morrison, "I just heard . . . men, out on the road." He looked at Anna, moved in front of her, said, "Take comfort, he is with God now."

She looked at him, deep black eyes. "There is no comfort in this, Reverend. My husband is dead . . . my child has no father."

Lacy held up his hand. "Seek comfort in God . . . He is there for you."

"Is He, Reverend? All I have ever asked is that He give me back my husband . . . allow him to survive this war and come home to his family. There is nothing else I have ever wanted."

Lacy lowered his head, said, "Please . . . rely on your faith, do not turn away. He will comfort you."

"Will He? Would it not be of greater comfort if He did not allow this war to happen at all? How much comfort must He give . . . how many wives and children need His comfort now?"

Lacy lowered his head, and Dr. Morrison said, "Please, Anna, let us get some rest. This has been hard for all of us."

She felt a sudden wave of weakness, slumped against him, and now both men held her and they moved past Lacy, who wanted to say more, raised the hand again, but she was gone now, up the steps, into the house.

McGuire was alone in the dreary room, sat down on the hard couch, stared at the bed, at the lifeless form. He heard the outer door open, and now Pendleton was there, stood in the doorway, looked at the bed, then moved to a corner of the room, sat on the floor and stared down between his knees.

"What will become of us now?"

McGuire looked at the young officer, said nothing, did not know what soldiers were supposed to do, it was not a question he could answer. He listened to the ticking of the clock, began to think about the arrangements, the casket, the memorials, the funeral, imagined a long procession through weeping crowds. . . .

Suddenly there was a new sound, from outside. He looked toward the window, and Pendleton raised his head, and the sound began to fill the room, loud and piercing. Outside, the soldiers had gathered close to the cottage, and through the tears their voices rose together in one high chorus—the rebel yell.

55. LEE

SUNDAY, MAY 10, 1863

He had sent them away, Taylor, the others, reporters and well-wishers, was alone now in the tent. The desk was covered with paper, a hundred requests, promotions, supply, and he could not look at any of it, sat in the small, stiff chair and stared at the blank walls of the tent.

On the table was also a wire, from Jefferson Davis, requesting he come to Richmond, discuss the new strategy. He would go, of course, do it all again, knowing that soon Hooker would be gone and someone else would fall into the role, and the war would start up, all over again, as though none of it had happened before.

He had tried not to think of Jackson, of the death, had kept his mind on the papers, but there had to be the moment, this moment, when the distractions would fade, when he must talk to God, to ask, *Why?* There would be no reply, of course. The answers were all in his faith, that it was all God's will, and that there was nothing else he could do but go on believing, and accepting that in the end there was a Plan. But he had never thought . . . there were already so many challenges, they had overcome so much, fought the good fight when anything less would have cost them the war, when it all would have been lost. He could not help but wonder . . . have we done something wrong? Has the cause become something else, some misguided effort? And he could think of nothing that had changed, why he was fighting, why the war must go on.

Now, the face came to him, the clear image, and he let it come, could not block it out, saw the lightning in the ice-blue eyes, the old cap, and he felt something inside him give way, and he leaned forward, put his face in his hands, and began to cry.

MAY 20, 1863

TAYLOR WAS STANDING BESIDE HIM, AND TOGETHER THEY WERE reading the lists for promotion. They heard the horses, and Lee stood up, moved outside the tent, the sun high and hot, and he saw the big man dismounting, the short cigar.

Longstreet had returned to the bloody ground around Chancellorsville several days after the fighting had ended, and the ultimate result of the excursion south had not been so positive. He had succeeded in sending sorely needed supplies north, but his own goal of pushing the Federal presence out of southern Virginia was not realized, and he had reluctantly pulled his troops away from the outskirts of Suffolk, which the Federal Army still occupied. It had taken a firm order from Lee to bring him back, but now Pickett and Hood had added to the strength of Lee's recuperating forces.

Lee had spent several days in Richmond, had found Davis to be more fragile than ever, infected with a growing paranoia about the defense of the capital, and so Lee now knew there would be no further support, no reinforcements. Davis would not interfere in Lee's strategies, but any plan Lee had would have to be accomplished with the troops he had on hand. After the difficult fight in the Wilderness, many in the army had gone home, many were no longer fit to serve, and so even with Longstreet's return, he had little more than forty thousand effective troops. In the North a paralyzed Hooker was still in command. The wheels of change were slow, and so Lee knew the next move would be his.

"General Longstreet, welcome."

"General." He touched the hat, and Lee suddenly held out a hand, something he rarely did, and Longstreet took it, and there was a short, quiet moment. Longstreet said, "I am deeply sorry for the loss of General Jackson."

Lee nodded, motioned toward the tent, and the two men went inside.

They sat, Lee behind his small desk, and he stared at the piles of papers, said, "We should not regret the loss of General Jackson. He is sitting with God. There is no unhappiness in that." Longstreet looked down, said nothing, and Lee watched him, said, "Still . . . we may grieve. God does not deny us that."

Longstreet nodded, looked at Lee, felt a sudden wave of affection, said, "How are *you*, sir?"

Lee saw the soft look, the concern, tried not to look away, felt suddenly emotional, weak, thought, No, there has been too much emotion. He stared hard at the papers, said, "The army is well, General. With the return of your divisions, and the confidence of these troops now, we have an opportunity."

Longstreet let it go, knew that Lee would not reveal much, said, "We have had many opportunities."

Lee nodded. "Perhaps. Each one is different. And there will not be many more. We cannot continue to win these fights and allow the enemy to escape. We do not have the reserves, the wealth of supply. We cannot continue to fight this war on our own ground, destroying our own land. We have bloodied him and swept him from the field, but there is no victory to be gained by simply pushing him away time and again. He will return, he will always return, with more men and more equipment, and eventually . . . they will find someone, a commander who understands . . . who is capable. They do have many good men. I have been grateful. God has blessed us with their choice of commanders. I have never understood any of the choices . . . not since George McClellan."

Longstreet said nothing, thought, We have been very very lucky. If it had been Couch . . . or Reynolds . . . or the reckless Sickles . . . He thought of McClellan finding Lee's orders, the one time Lee's luck was bad, said, "We tried moving north. . . ."

"It was not the right time. God showed us that. But now . . . if we are to end this war, we must *win* this war, and I believe it is the only way."

He stood, straightened stiff legs, stepped around the small desk. Longstreet watched him, and Lee said, "President Davis has agreed . . . we must not only take the fight out of Virginia, but we must take it out of Tennessee and Carolina and Louisiana as well. In Virginia we are winning the battles. Elsewhere, it has not gone as well. The more time that passes, the more we are simply used up, and so, General, we are losing the war, and that will not change unless we take the war . . . unless we strike them right in their heart. We must point our guns straight into Lincoln's door, and then it will end."

"Attack Washington? Directly? Sir . . . the fortifications—"

"No, General. We do not have to attack the city. We just have to convince them that we *can*, that if they do not end this war, we *will*! Lincoln is already under pressure . . . great pressure. Their own generals hang their heads in public and ask forgiveness as the dead fill their cemeteries. The *people* have had enough of this. We have paid a terrible price, and so God has opened the door. We must march through it."

Longstreet stared at him, was surprised at the show of anger, sat quietly for a moment, said, "We can move up, as we did before, Maryland, then Pennsylvania. They will not know where we intend to strike."

Lee looked at him, waited, had hoped he would finally agree to the plan.

Longstreet thought again, said, "All we need is some luck . . . didn't have it last time, McClellan learning about the plan . . . but we can push the army fast, good roads, good time of year, move around to the northeast, cut off Washington from Philadelphia . . . New York. Even if they react, move to meet us quickly, we will be on *their* ground."

"Yes, General. And the civilians in the North will not stand for that, nor will the politicians."

Longstreet nodded, and now he glanced toward the opening in the tent, said, "General . . . forgive me, sir, but have you chosen a new commander for the Second Corps?"

Lee moved around the desk, sat again, pushed through the papers, held up one, studied it, said, "It is a difficult situation, General. We have lost so many. I do not believe we have one man who can assume that level of command. This is what I have proposed to President Davis, and it will become official very soon."

He handed the paper to Longstreet, and Longstreet studied it. His eyes widened. "Two corps? Dividing it into two corps? A. P. Hill . . . Dick Ewell. Ewell has returned?"

"Yes. He is healthy again, has a wooden leg now. General Jackson placed great confidence in General Ewell. And General Hill . . . there is no denying that he is a fine commander . . . in the field."

Longstreet nodded, a small laugh. "Now the only superior officer he can aggravate is you."

Lee had no humor, was weary of the conflicts with Hill. "That is the new system, General. There will now be three corps. General Stuart will resume command of the cavalry."

"Have you told him that? He might not be too happy—"

"General Stuart understands that he is better suited for that command. He acquitted himself adequately in General Jackson's absence, but he is eager to return to the cavalry. And if we are to succeed, we will require General Stuart's talents."

Lee stood, the signal that it was over, and Longstreet was up, ducked out through the tent. Taylor moved up, saluted, said, "Sir, the newspaper reporters are waiting . . . they keep asking about the rumors, sir. I don't know what to tell them."

"Rumors?" Longstreet looked at Taylor, and Taylor said, "Yes, sir. There's talk in the North . . . the papers, that General Lee is going to invade Washington, that the capital will be under siege." He looked at Lee. "Please, sir, will you speak to them? Or . . . please tell me what to say to them. They are mighty persistent, sir."

Lee looked at Longstreet, smiled slightly, said, "Major, tell them I am too busy at present to speak with them, and that it is . . . imprudent of us to discuss our plans."

"But, sir, what about the rumors? Do I tell them not to print—"

Lee raised his hand. "Major, I would never tell these men what they should not print. There will always be rumors. Sometimes, that is not all bad."

JUNE 1863

THEY DID NOT SPEND TIME IN MARYLAND. THERE WERE NO longer hopes that the neutral state would provide help to their army. So he rode the tall horse, and they moved quickly and with purpose. The papers in the North began to tell of the new invasion, and the Federal Army drew in closer to Washington, but Lee did not move that way, drove north, crossed the border into Pennsylvania. He led a great column of men who understood it would end soon, they were moving up to strike the deciding blow, and there were none among them who doubted they would do it. This was an army that had never been beaten, and that knowledge made them all stronger still.

It was hot now, and even the green hills did not give them relief, but they carried the memory of Jackson, and they knew how he would have pushed them, and so stragglers were few, and the strength of their morale gave them a shield against the hot march.

It was late in the day, long shadows crossed the road, and in front of them was the town of Chambersburg. He had ridden with Longstreet, had sent Ewell and Hill on a parallel route, farther east, and though they had met no opposition, he was beginning to feel concern, to wonder about the movements of the Federal Army.

Longstreet had ridden back, had sent word down the line, Keep a sharp eye, had sent his own scouts away, into the countryside. Now Lee heard him coming, pushing the horse quickly along the edge of the road. Then Longstreet slowed, moved beside him.

"Still nothing from Stuart. Not a sign, not a word!"

Lee heard the anger in his voice, said, "We will hear from him soon. I am certain of that. He understands the importance."

"He is not where we need him to be."

Lee stared ahead, did not answer, thought, General Stuart understands his orders. . . .

Far to the east, Stuart's cavalry raced northward, separated from Lee's army by the advancing column of Federal troops. He was trying, again, to make the glorious ride, encircle the blue army, reclaim the reputation, now that he was again with his own beloved horse soldiers. But Lincoln had moved again, and the Federal Army now had a new commander, George Gordon Meade, a man who did not suffer from the heavy burden of defeat, whose troops withdrew at Fredericksburg because they had not been supported, who had withdrawn at Chancellorsville because Hooker had collapsed. But now the army was his, and they were on the move, above the capital, moving with a new energy to confront the invasion. And this time Stuart could not ride fast enough. It was no longer a weak, lethargic army around which he was playing.

Lee rode out, toward the edge of the camps, looked across the church steeples and small buildings of the quiet town. He stared out to the east, to the deep and quiet darkness, thought, Any time now, there will be horses, the high yell, and he will ride in, jump down in front of me like a small excited boy, bend over and sweep the ground with that hat. But there was still the quiet, the dark, and somewhere, deep inside, he felt a dark hole, small but growing, the enthusiasm for this army's great mission, the final crushing blow now slowly slipping away. He reached down, patted Traveller on the neck, then pulled on the reins, turned the horse back toward the camp. It will be tomorrow, he thought. He will certainly be here tomorrow, and then . . . we will know: where the enemy is, what is in front of us.

Miles beyond the trees, past low hills and thick green woods, another army was in its camp, and their cavalry was already out in front, feeling out, seeking, and tomorrow they would ride forward again, probing the roads in front of them. They would crest a long rise and pause at a small cemetery, high above the peaceful farms and quiet streets of a town called Gettysburg.

AFTERWORD

"... *And Thou knowest O Lord, that when Thou didst decide that the Confederacy should not succeed, Thou hadst first to remove Thy servant, Stonewall Jackson.*"

— BENEDICTION GIVEN BY FATHER HUBERT, OF HAYS'S LOUISIANA BRIGADE, AT THE UNVEILING OF THE JACKSON MONUMENT IN NEW ORLEANS, 1881

Mary Anna Morrison Jackson

She is the widow now of the South's most beloved hero, and readily accepts the responsibility of that role. From the first memorial services in 1863, throughout the rest of her life, she represents her husband's memory at ceremonies, presentations, statues, and monuments for Jackson and for the Confederacy. Her daughter Julia survives only to age twenty-six, dies of typhoid fever, leaving a husband and two children. Anna retires finally to North Carolina, and never considers remarrying. While covering her invited visit to President Taft in Washington, D.C., in 1910, a Washington newspaper reported:

> Those who had the great honor of meeting Mrs. Jackson found her a fragile little woman with keen bright eyes, and the alert air which characterizes those whose interest in life and its best endeavors is undimmed by sorrow or the passing years. Time seems to have passed over her lightly. Having known her worst grief when life was young, she had been enabled to take up the thread again and to weave some brightness into what was left. She delights in recalling old

days and she speaks now with calmness which comes only from Christian resignation.

She dies in March 1915 of heart disease and is buried beside her husband and her two children beneath the Jackson Memorial in Lexington, Virginia. (Jackson's first wife, Ellie, and her stillborn infant are buried nearby.) One of Anna's funeral party is the Reverend James Power Smith, the final surviving member of Jackson's staff.

Mary Randolph Custis Lee

She outlives her husband, maintains a home in Lexington, Virginia. The great mass of the memorabilia of George Washington had been confiscated by the Union occupiers of Arlington, is stored after the war in Washington. She petitions the government for the return of her family's cherished heirlooms, but Congress still regards Lee as the enemy, and refuses. Widowed by her husband's death in 1870, she yearns for one last visit to the old homestead of Arlington, and even as an invalid, makes the difficult journey with her youngest son, Robert, Jr. In 1872, returning to Lexington, she is with her daughter Agnes when Agnes is stricken ill and dies. Mary Lee thus outlives not only her husband, but two of her daughters (Annie had died in 1862). Her grief at this irony is overwhelming, and Mary dies soon after, in November 1873.

Almira Russell Hancock

Left nearly penniless after Hancock's death in 1886, she receives an outpouring of generosity from his many friends of influence, and is provided several homes, finally settles in New York City, where she writes her own memoirs of her remembrances of Hancock's life and career.

Hamilton Fish, an old friend, and the Secretary of State to President Ulysses Grant, wrote of her that "she was always so bright, so gay, so full of sunshine." Known always as a woman who stood close beside her husband throughout his extraordinary career, she is considered the shining ideal of the Soldier's Wife. Thus, when she dies in 1893, it is a strange and unexplained contradiction that she is buried not beside her husband, but in the Russell family plot in St. Louis.

Frances "Fannie" Adams Chamberlain

Her marriage is never without great stress. At the conclusion of the war, she receives her husband's return from the army with much graciousness, but his subsequent political career, and thus frequent absences from their home, take a serious toll. Withdrawing often into long depressions, she even confides to her closest friends of the unthinkable possibility of divorce. She is eventually stricken with blindness and failing health, but their marriage endures until her death in 1905.

Those Who Wore Gray

Major General Daniel Harvey Hill

Jackson's brother-in-law serves in the defense of Richmond while the battle rages in Gettysburg. Promoted to Lieutenant General of North Carolina after the battle, he is sent to Tennessee to assist Braxton Bragg in the defense of Chickamauga, and is embroiled in a controversy by claiming Bragg is incompetent. But President Davis supports Bragg, and so relieves Hill and refuses to recommend Hill's promotion to the Confederate Congress. He serves the remainder of the war in command of volunteers in North Carolina. Returns then to academics, and in 1877 becomes president of the University of Arkansas. Later, he heads the Georgia Military Academy, until his death in 1889.

Major Alexander Swift "Sandie" Pendleton

After Jackson's death, is appointed by Lee to General Ewell's staff, in the newly organized Second Corps, and Ewell promotes him to Lieutenant Colonel. However, the cordial relationship between Ewell and Jackson's former staff quickly dissolves, as the men who were accustomed to Jackson's aggressiveness observe Ewell's sluggishness at Gettysburg and his monumental failure to capture the high ground of Cemetery Hill. Pendleton writes, "Oh for the presence and inspiration of Old Jack for just one hour!"

When Ewell's health begins to fail, Jubal Early is given command of the Second Corps, and Pendleton is one of the very few who gains the respect of the disagreeable Early, serving with him through the campaigns of the following year in the Shenandoah Valley. In late 1863 he receives a brief leave, and marries Kate Corbin, the young aunt of the tragic five-year-old girl who had so captured Jackson. In September 1864, during a battle for the town of Winchester, he is mortally wounded, and dies the next day. He does not ever see the son that Kate bears him the following November. The infant is named Sandie, but does not survive his first year.

Of Pendleton, his friend James Power Smith writes: "His intellectual powers were of the highest order . . . the readiness with which he approached his duty . . . was equaled by the celerity and skill with which he performed it. As a staff officer he had no equal."

Dr. Hunter H. McGuire

From his early association with Jackson's first command of the First Virginia Brigade (the Stonewall Brigade), his reputation exceeds that of any other medical officer in the Confederate Army. After Jackson's death, he serves in Ewell's corps, and thus will return to his beloved Shenandoah, where he is eventually named Medical Director for the Army of the Valley. After the war, his career continues to earn him great honor and respect. He establishes the College of Medicine at the University of Virginia, serves there as Professor of Surgery until 1878, and later is named President of the American Surgical Association, and then of the American Medical Association. He survives until 1900.

Major General Joseph E. Johnston

Recovers from his wounds at Fair Oaks, returns to command the Department of the West. His feud with Davis, and his lack of cooperation and communication, continue, and he is thus blamed for the defeats at Vicksburg and Chattanooga. He cannot bring enough forces to the field to impede Sherman's assault on Atlanta, and so is relieved in July 1864 by John Bell Hood.

After the war, he goes into private business, serves briefly as a congressman, and eventually settles in Washington, D.C., as a railroad commissioner. He dies of pneumonia in 1891. It is observed that he is in many ways the complete opposite of George McClellan: great skill in the field, with a total lack of administrative abilities.

Brigadier General William Barksdale

At Chancellorsville his brigade fights alongside Early's division on Marye's Heights, which eventually gives way to the vastly superior numbers of Sedgwick's corps. He leads his decimated forces into battle on the right flank during the second day at Gettysburg, engages Sickles's corps at the Peach Orchard, where he is mortally wounded. He dies the following day.

BRIGADIER GENERAL ROBERT RODES

After Chancellorsville, Jackson's former colleague is promoted to Major General, leads his division with distinction at Gettysburg and afterward. Assigned to the Shenandoah Valley with Early's corps, he is killed at Winchester the same day as Sandie Pendleton.

PRESIDENT JEFFERSON DAVIS

Continues to deteriorate mentally as the war goes on, pulls all available troops close around Richmond, and so, around himself. When Richmond falls, he moves the Confederate government to Charlotte, North Carolina, and finally is captured in May 1865 at Irwinsville, Georgia. He is imprisoned for two years, but never stands trial, is released by a government anxious to move beyond the lingering taste of the war. P.G.T. Beauregard later writes that the Confederacy "needed for President either a military man of high order, or a politician of the first-class without military pretensions." Regrettably for the Great Cause, Davis proved to be neither. He survives until 1889.

THOSE WHO WORE BLUE

GENERAL IN CHIEF WINFIELD SCOTT

He is given no significant role in the war after the first appointment of McClellan in 1861, and thus the grand old man of the army spends much of the war years writing his memoirs. He dies in 1866, at the age of eighty, and is buried at West Point. For his extraordinary abilities as both a strategist and a leader of men, he is still regarded as one of the greatest soldiers this nation has ever produced.

COMMANDING GENERAL GEORGE B. MCCLELLAN

Runs unsuccessfully for President against Lincoln in 1864, later becomes Governor of New Jersey. He writes an autobiography, defending his military decision-making and emphasizing his success in organizing the army. But even his staunchest supporters concede that his genius as an administrator was never carried forward to the battlefield. He survives until 1885.

MAJOR GENERAL AMBROSE E. BURNSIDE

Reassigned to the Army of the Ohio, he performs adequately through several engagements, though at Petersburg is again blamed for poor command decisions. After the war, he becomes a successful railroad administrator. In 1866 he is elected Governor of Rhode Island, and after two terms is elected United States Senator, serving until his death in 1881.

Ulysses Grant describes him as "an officer who was generally liked and respected, he was not, however, fitted to command an army. No one knew this better than himself."

MAJOR GENERAL DARIUS N. COUCH

On May 22, 1863, he requests a leave of absence, tells the War Department he can no longer "lead his men to senseless slaughter" under Joe Hooker. When he is turned down, he tenders his resignation. His service to the army is considered too valuable to allow him to retire into civilian life, and so in June 1863 he is appointed commander of the new Department of the Susquehanna, and given the duty of organizing local militia to defend Pennsylvania against the threatened Confederate invasion. After Gettysburg he goes west, commands a division in Tennessee. Following the war, he resigns from the army, runs unsuccessfully for governor in Massachusetts, and later enters private business, though he still serves in the volunteer army until his death in 1897. After Chancellorsville, Couch is replaced as commander of the Second Corps by Winfield Scott Hancock.

COLONEL NELSON A. MILES

Surviving his wounds at Chancellorsville, he is eventually promoted to brigade and then division command under Hancock. He receives the Congressional Medal of Honor for his brilliant stand against Lee's continuous attacks at Chancellorsville. He is promoted to Brigadier General in the spring of 1864, then after the war, to Major General. He is appointed custodian of the prisoner Jefferson Davis, and afterward moves to the West to continue building his solid reputation as a fighter in the Indian wars. Named General in

Chief of the Army in 1895, he commands the victorious U.S. forces during the Spanish-American War. He retires from the army in 1903, one of this country's most decorated soldiers, lives the peaceful life of the dignified hero until 1925. He is one of four pallbearers at the funeral of General Hancock.

MAJOR GENERAL JOSEPH HOOKER

Relieved of command in June 1863, he is reassigned to command under the forces of Ulysses S. Grant in Tennessee, where, surprisingly, he distinguishes himself at Lookout Mountain and Missionary Ridge, receives a commendation for gallant and meritorious service at the Battle of Chattanooga. Grant, however, writes of him: "I regarded him as a dangerous man . . . he was ambitious to the extent of caring nothing for the rights of others." Paralyzed by a stroke in 1868, he survives until 1879. Of the disastrous failure at Chancellorsville, Hooker later confides to a friend that he had simply lost confidence in Joe Hooker.

MAJOR GENERAL EDWIN V. "BULL" SUMNER

The old loyal soldier, who shares none of the political egotism of his colleagues, is not named in Burnside's sweeping indictment of his commanders after the debacle at Fredericksburg. By staying back across the Rappahannock River, he is therefore spared much of the stigma the other commanders will carry. However, his personal failures weigh heavily, and in the spring of 1863, less than two months after his forced retirement, he dies.

COLONEL ADELBERT A. AMES

On May 20, 1863, he is promoted to Brigadier General after a vigorous campaign on his own behalf, and receives command of a brigade in the Eleventh Corps, under Oliver Howard. He is later awarded a Congressional Medal of Honor for his gallantry at First Manassas (Bull Run). After the war, General Grant assigns him to Mississippi as the military provisional governor. In 1876 he is forced to resign by an uprising in reaction to his unpopularly liberal views. Returning to the army, he commands a brigade in the Spanish-American War. He dies in 1933, at age ninety-seven, and is thus the oldest surviving general officer of the Civil War.

Brigadier General Thomas F. Meagher

His Irish Brigade is so decimated after Chancellorsville, he resigns from command, believing his usefulness to the army has passed. By December 1863 he is given command of forces under William T. Sherman. After the war, he receives a gold medal from the state of New York for his brilliant leadership of the Irish Brigade. But he leaves the postwar turmoil of the East, goes to Montana, becomes Territorial Governor. He dies by drowning in the Missouri River in 1867.

And from These Pages

Robert E. Lee, James Longstreet, Lewis Armistead, A. P. Hill, John Bell Hood, George Pickett, J.E.B. Stuart, Porter Alexander, Harry Heth,

and

Winfield Scott Hancock, Joshua Lawrence Chamberlain, John Reynolds, George Gordon Meade, John Buford, Oliver Howard, Dan Sickles

In July 1863 they will share the field again, the low hills and open farmlands around Gettysburg, for the three bloodiest days in American history. But that is another story. . . .

© Lynne Shaara

About the Author

Jeff Shaara was born in 1952 in New Brunswick, New Jersey. He grew up in Tallahassee, Florida, and graduated from Florida State University in 1974. For many years he was a dealer in rare coins, but sold his Tampa, Florida, business in 1988 upon the death of his father, Michael Shaara.

As manager of his father's estate, Jeff developed a friendship with film director Ron Maxwell, whose film *Gettysburg* was based on *The Killer Angels*. It was Maxwell who suggested that Jeff continue the story Michael Shaara had begun, the inspiration that produced Jeff's novels *Gods and Generals* and *The Last Full Measure*. He is also the author of *Rise to Rebellion*, *Gone for Soldiers*, and, his latest novel, *The Glorious Cause.*

Visit the author online at www.JeffShaara.com

"THE BEST CIVIL WAR NOVEL EVER WRITTEN . . . The descriptions of combat are incomparable; they convey not just the sights but the noise and smell of battle. And the characterizations are simply superb. . . . Shaara has managed to capture the essence of war, the divided friendships, the madness, and the heroism of fratricidal conflict."

–Stephen B. Oates
Author of *With Malice Toward None*

"[Shaara] writes with clarity and power. . . . His descriptions of the battle scenes are vivid and unsparing."

–*Newsday*

"Akin to Hemingway . . . [and] Stephen Crane's *Red Badge of Courage.*"

–*The Houston Post*

"A compelling version of what America's Armageddon must have been like . . . Surefire storytelling."

–*Publishers Weekly*

"You will learn more from this utterly absorbing book about Gettysburg than from any nonfictional account. Shaara fabulously, convincingly brings characters such as Robert E. Lee to life and makes the conflict all too real."

–*Forbes*

"Literary wonders will never cease. Would you think it possible that after all the hundreds of books written about the battle of Gettysburg, both fiction and non-fiction, that . . . [this] novel about the battle could come out fresh, utterly absorbing, with the strong possibility that it may even turn out to be a classic? Well, read Michael Shaara's . . . *The Killer Angels* and find out."

–*Frederick News-Post*
(Frederick, Maryland)

"Narrated as expertly as though Michael Shaara had been a participant in the battle of Gettysburg."

–*Fort-Wayne Journal-Gazette*

"It's at one and the same time an excellent, historical novel, a bitter anti-war tract, and a story filled with an amazing case of beautifully realized characters."

–*Daily Sun*
(Hudson, Massachusetts)

"An approach so fresh it is stunning."

–*St. Louis Globe-Democrat*

"*The Killers Angels* could well be the best Civil War novel of this decade."

–*News Leader*
(Richmond, Virginia)

"All in all it is a feast of reading, the best you will find for a long, long time."

–*The Chattanooga Times*

"What makes Shaara's novel an admirable effort, and one worth reading, is its sensitiveness to the time-spirit of the era. What it reveals is primarily men in context, men in action, and thought within the changing scenery of events. It is a genuinely appealing book."

–*The Charlotte Observer*

"This is one of the best novels of the Civil War that I've read."

–*Daily Press*
(Newport-News, Virginia)

THE KILLER ANGELS

Other novels by Michael Shaara

The Broken Place
The Herald
For Love of the Game

THE KILLER ANGELS

A Novel

Michael Shaara

Ballantine Books • New York

A Ballantine Book
Published by The Random House Publishing Group

Published in the United States by Ballantine Books,
an imprint of The Random House Publishing Group,
a division of Random House, Inc., New York, and simultaneously
in Canada by Random House of Canada Limited, Toronto.

This edition published by arrangement with David McKay Co., Inc.

www.ballantinebooks.com

Library of Congress Control Number: 96-96190

ISBN 0-345-40727-X

Cover painting by Paul Philippoteaux
Confederate High Tide at Gettysburg courtesy of Gettysburg National
Military Park.
Cover design by Michelle T. Gengaro
Maps by Don Pitcher

Manufactured in the United States of America

First Ballantine Books Trade Edition: July 1996

19 20

To Lila (old George)
. . . in whom I am well pleased

TO THE READER

This is the story of the Battle of Gettysburg, told from the viewpoints of Robert E. Lee and James Longstreet and some of the other men who fought there.

Stephen Crane once said that he wrote *The Red Badge of Courage* because reading the cold history was not enough; he wanted to know what it was like to *be* there, what the weather was like, what men's faces looked like. In order to live it he had to write it. This book was written for much the same reason.

You may find it a different story from the one you learned in school. There have been many versions of that battle and that war. I have therefore avoided historical opinions and gone back primarily to the words of the men themselves, their letters and other documents. I have not consciously changed any fact. I have condensed some of the action, for the sake of clarity, and eliminated some minor characters, for brevity; but though I have often had to choose between conflicting viewpoints, I have not knowingly violated the action. I have changed some of the language. It was a naïve and sentimental time, and men spoke in windy phrases. I thought it necessary to update some of the words so that the religiosity and naïveté of the time, which were genuine, would not seem too quaint to the modern ear. I hope I will be forgiven that.

The interpretation of character is my own.

MICHAEL SHAARA

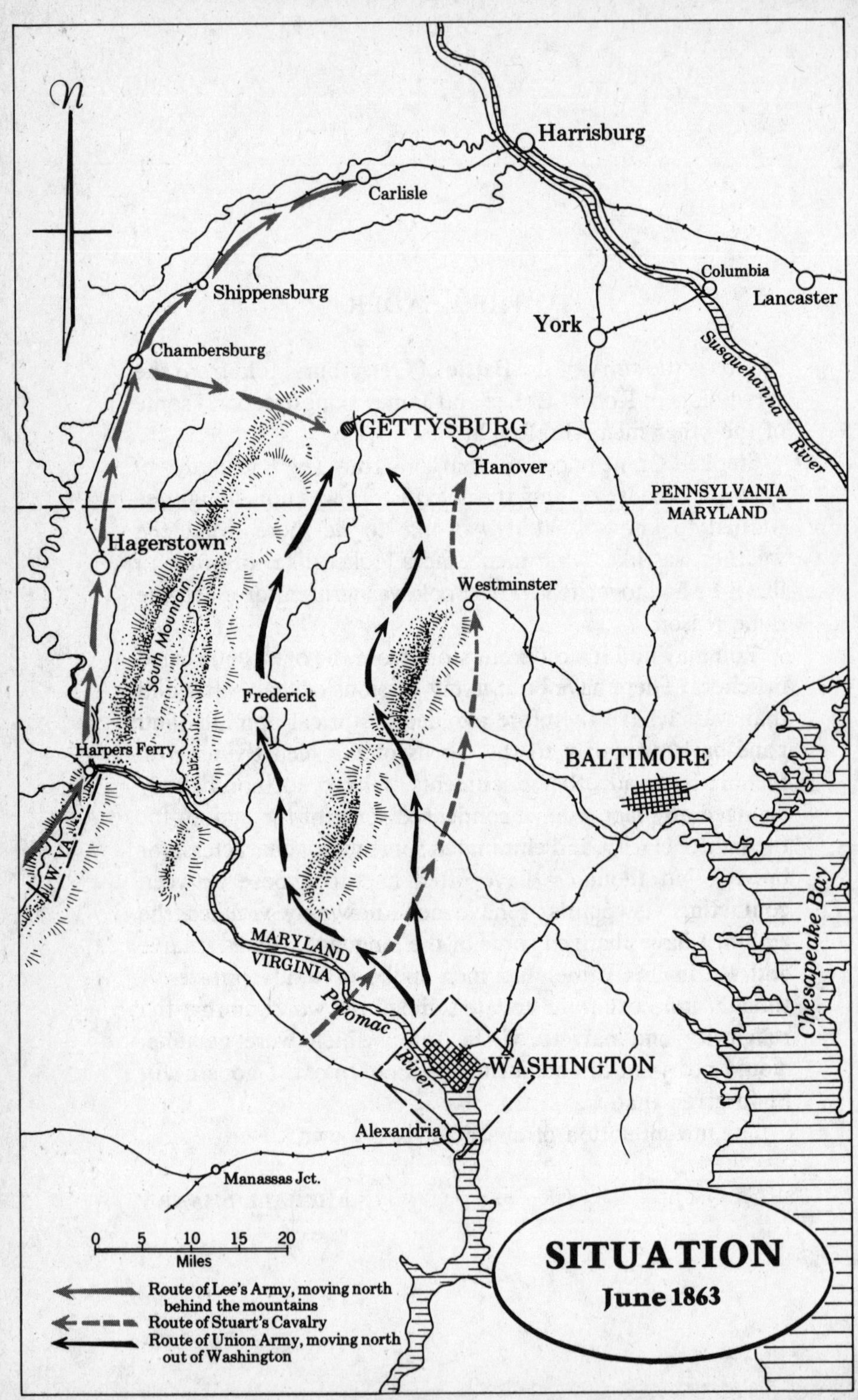

Harrisburg
Carlisle
Columbia
Lancaster
Shippensburg
York
Chambersburg
Susquehanna River
GETTYSBURG
Hanover
PENNSYLVANIA
MARYLAND
Hagerstown
Westminster
South Mountain
Frederick
Harpers Ferry
BALTIMORE
W. VA.
Chesapeake Bay
MARYLAND
VIRGINIA
Potomac River
WASHINGTON
Alexandria
Manassas Jct.
0 5 10 15 20
Miles
Route of Lee's Army, moving north behind the mountains
Route of Stuart's Cavalry
Route of Union Army, moving north out of Washington
SITUATION
June 1863

FOREWORD

June 1863

I. The Armies

On June 15 the first troops of the Army of Northern Virginia, Robert E. Lee commanding, slip across the Potomac at Williamsport and begin the invasion of the North.

It is an army of seventy thousand men. They are rebels and volunteers. They are mostly unpaid and usually self-equipped. It is an army of remarkable unity, fighting for disunion. It is Anglo-Saxon and Protestant. Though there are many men who cannot read or write, they all speak English. They share common customs and a common faith and they have been consistently victorious against superior numbers. They have as solid a faith in their leader as any veteran army that ever marched. They move slowly north behind the Blue Ridge, using the mountains to screen their movements. Their main objective is to draw the Union Army out into the open where it can be destroyed. By the end of the month they are closing on Harrisburg, having spread panic and rage and despair through the North.

Late in June the Army of the Potomac, ever slow to move, turns north at last to begin the great pursuit which will end at Gettysburg. It is a strange new kind of army, a polyglot mass of vastly dissimilar men, fighting for union. There are strange accents and strange religions and many who do not speak English at all. Nothing like this army has been seen upon the planet. It is a collection of men from many different places who have seen much defeat and many commanders. They are volunteers: last of the great volunteer armies, for the draft is beginning that summer in the North. They have lost faith in their leaders but not in themselves. They think this will be the last battle, and they are glad that it is to be fought on their own home ground. They come up from the South, eighty thousand men, up the narrow roads that converge toward the blue mountains. The country through which they march is some of the most beautiful country in the Union.

It is the third summer of the war.

II. The Men

Robert Edward Lee. He is in his fifty-seventh year. Five feet ten inches tall but very short in the legs, so that when he rides a horse he seems much taller. Red-faced, like all the Lees, white-bearded, dressed in an old gray coat and a gray felt hat, without insignia, so that he is mistaken sometimes for an elderly major of dignity. An honest man, a gentleman. He has no "vices." He does not drink or smoke or gamble or chase women. He does not read novels or plays; he thinks they weaken the mind. He does not own slaves nor believe in slavery, but he does not believe that the Negro, "in the present stage of his development," can be considered the equal of the white man. He is a man in control. He does not lose his temper nor his faith; he never complains. He has been down that spring with the first assault of the heart disease which will eventually kill him. He believes absolutely in God.

He loves Virginia above all, the mystic dirt of home. He is the most beloved man in either army.

He marches knowing that a letter has been prepared by Jefferson Davis, a letter which offers peace. It is to be placed on the desk of Abraham Lincoln the day after Lee has destroyed the Army of the Potomac somewhere north of Washington.

James Longstreet, Lieutenant General, forty-two. Lee's second in command. A large man, larger than Lee, full-bearded, blue-eyed, ominous, slow-talking, crude. He is one of the first of the new soldiers, the cold-eyed men who have sensed the birth of the new war of machines. He has invented a trench and a theory of defensive warfare, but in that courtly company few will listen. He is one of the few high officers in that army not from Virginia.

That winter, in Richmond, three of his children have died within a week, of a fever. Since that time he has withdrawn, no longer joins his men for the poker games he once loved, for which he was famous.

They call him "Old Pete" and sometimes "The Dutchman." His headquarters is always near Lee, and men remark upon the intimacy and some are jealous of it. He has opposed the invasion of Pennsylvania, but once the army is committed he no longer opposes. Yet he will speak his mind; he will always speak his mind. Lee calls him, with deep affection, "my old war horse." Since the death of Stonewall Jackson he has been Lee's right hand. He is a stubborn man.

George Pickett, Major General, forty-two. Gaudy and lovable, long-haired, perfumed. Last in his class at West Point, he makes up for a lack of wisdom with a lusty exuberance. In love with a girl half his age, a schoolgirl from Lynchburg named LaSalle Corbelle, to whom he has vowed ne'er to touch liquor. Received his appointment to West Point through the good offices of Abraham Lincoln, a personal friend, and no one now can insult Abe Lincoln in Pickett's presence, although Lincoln is not only the enemy but the absolute utterest enemy of all.

On the march toward Gettysburg Pickett's Virginia Division is by a trick of fate last in line. He worries constantly that he will miss the last great battle of the war.

Richard Ewell, Lieutenant General, forty-six. Egg-bald, one-legged, recently married. (He refers to his new wife absent-mindedly as "Mrs. Brown.") Eccentric, brilliant, chosen out of all Lee's officers to succeed to a portion of Stonewall Jackson's old command. But he has lost something along with the leg that a soldier sometimes loses with the big wounds. He approaches Gettysburg unsure of himself, in command of twenty thousand men.

Ambrose Powell Hill, Major General, thirty-seven. Has risen to command the other part of Jackson's old corps. A moody man, often competent, bad-tempered, wealthy, aspires to a place in Richmond society, frets and broods and fights with superiors. He wears a red shirt into battle. He should be a fine soldier, and sometimes is, but he is often ill for no apparent reason. He does not like to follow orders. At Gettysburg he will command a corps, and he will be sick again.

Lewis Armistead, Brigadier General, forty-six. Commander of one of George Pickett's brigades. They call him "Lo," which is short for Lothario, which is meant to be witty, for he is a shy and silent man, a widower. Descended from a martial family, he has a fighter's spirit, is known throughout the old army as the man who, while a cadet at the Point, was suspended for hitting Jubal Early in the head with a plate. Has developed over long years of service a deep affection for Winfield Scott Hancock, who fights now with the Union. Armistead looks forward to the reunion with Hancock, which will take place at Gettysburg.

Richard Brooke Garnett, Brigadier General, forty-four.

Commands the second of Pickett's brigades. A dark-eyed, silent, tragic man. Followed Jackson in command of the old Stonewall Brigade; at Kernstown he has made the mistake of withdrawing his men from an impossible position. Jackson is outraged, orders a court-martial which never convenes. Jackson dies before Garnett, accused of cowardice, can clear his name and redeem his honor, the honor which no man who knows him has ever doubted. He comes to Gettysburg a tortured man, too ill to walk. He believes that Jackson deliberately lied. In that camp there is nothing more important than honor.

J. E. B. Stuart, Lieutenant General, thirty. The laughing banjo player, the superb leader of cavalry who has ridden rings around the Union Army. A fine soldier, whose reports are always accurate, but a man who loves to read about himself in the Richmond newspapers. His mission that month is to keep Lee informed of the movement of the Union Army. He fails.

Jubal Early, Major General, forty-six. Commander of one of Ewell's divisions. A dark, cold, icy man, bitter, alone. Left the Point to become a prosecuting attorney, to which he is well suited. A competent soldier, but a man who works with an eye to the future, a slippery man, a careful soldier; he will build his reputation whatever the cost. Dick Ewell defers to him. Longstreet despises him. Lee makes do with the material at hand. Lee calls him "my bad old man."

These men wore blue:

Joshua Lawrence Chamberlain, Colonel, thirty-four. He prefers to be called "Lawrence." A professor of rhetoric at Bowdoin University, sometime professor of "Natural and Revealed Religion," successor to the chair of the famed Professor Stowe, husband to Harriet Beecher. Tall and rather handsome, attractive to women, somewhat boyish, a clean and charming person. An excellent student, Phi Beta Kappa, he speaks seven languages and has a beautiful singing voice, but he has wanted all his life to be a soldier. The University will not free him for war, but in the summer of 1862 he requests a sabbatical for study in Europe. When it is granted he proceeds not to France but to the office of the Governor of Maine, where he receives a commission in the 20th Regiment of Infantry, Maine Volunteers, and marches off to war with a vast faith in the brotherhood of man. Spends the long night at Fredericksburg piling corpses in front of himself to shield him from bullets. Comes to Gettysburg with that hard fragment of the Regiment which has survived. One week before the battle he is given command of the Regiment. His younger brother Thomas becomes his aide. Thomas too has yearned to be a soldier. The wishes of both men are to be granted on the dark rear slope of a small rocky hill called Little Round Top.

John Buford, Major General, thirty-seven. A cavalry soldier, restless and caged in the tamed and political East, who loves the great plains and the memory of snow. A man with an eye for the good ground, already badly wounded and not long to live, weary of stupidity and politics and bloody military greed. At Thorofare Gap he held against Longstreet for six hours, waiting for help that never came. Too good an officer for his own advancement, he rides a desk in Washington until luck puts him back in the field, where he is given two brigades of cavalry and told to trail Lee's army. He is first into Gettysburg, where he lifts up his eyes to the hills. He is a man who knows the value of ground.

John Reynolds, Major General, forty-two. Perhaps the finest soldier in the Union Army. Like Lee before him, a former commander of West Point, a courteous man, military, a marvelous horseman, another gentleman. His home is not far from Gettysburg. He has fallen in love late in life, but the girl is Catholic and Reynolds has not yet told his Protestant family, but he wears her ring on a chain around his neck, under his uniform. Early that month he is called to Washington, where he is offered command of the Army. But he has seen the military results of maneuvering by armchair commanders Halleck and Stanton, and he insists that the Army cannot be commanded from Washington, that he cannot accept command without a free hand. He therefore respectfully declines. The honor passes to George Meade, who is not even given the option but ordered to command. And thus it is John Reynolds, not Meade, who rides into Gettysburg on the morning of the First Day.

George Gordon Meade, Major General, forty-seven. Vain and bad-tempered, balding, full of self-pity. He takes command of the Army on a Sunday, June 28, two days before the Battle. He wishes to hold a Grand Review, but there turns out not to be time. He plans a line of defense along Pipe Creek, far from Gettysburg, in the unreal hope that Lee will attack him on ground of his own choosing. No decision he makes at Gettysburg will be decisive, except perhaps the last.

Winfield Scott Hancock, Major General, thirty-nine. Armistead's old friend. A magnetic man with a beautiful wife. A painter of talent, a picture-book General. Has a tendency to gain weight, but at this moment he is still young and slim, still a superb presence, a man who arrives on the battlefield in spotlessly clean linen and never keeps his head down. In the fight to come he will be everywhere, and in the end he will be waiting for Lew Armistead at the top of Cemetery Hill.

All that month there is heat and wild rain. Cherries are ripening over all Pennsylvania, and the men gorge as they march. The civilians have fled and houses are dark. The armies move north through the heat and the dust.

MAPS

"When men take up arms to set other men free, there is something sacred and holy in the warfare."

—Woodrow Wilson

"I hate the idea of causes, and if I had to choose between betraying my country and betraying my friend, I hope I should have the guts to betray my country."

—E.M. Forster

"With all my devotion to the Union and the feeling of loyalty and duty of an American citizen, I have not been able to raise my hand against my relatives, my children, my home. I have therefore resigned my commission in the Army. . . ."

—from a letter of
Robert E. Lee

Mr. Mason: How do you justify your acts?
John Brown: I think, my friend, you are guilty of a great wrong against God and humanity—I say it without wishing to be offensive —and it would be perfectly right for anyone to interfere with you so far as to free those you willfully and wickedly hold in bondage. I do not say this insultingly.
Mr. Mason: I understand that.

—from an interview with
John Brown after his
capture

MONDAY, JUNE 29, 1863

Mine eyes have seen the glory . . .

1. The Spy

He rode into the dark of the woods and dismounted. He crawled upward on his belly over cool rocks out into the sunlight, and suddenly he was in the open and he could see for miles, and there was the whole vast army below him, filling the valley like a smoking river. It came out of a blue rainstorm in the east and overflowed the narrow valley road, coiling along a stream, narrowing and choking at a white bridge, fading out into the yellowish dust of June but still visible on the farther road beyond the blue hills, spiked with flags and guidons like a great chopped bristly snake, the snake ending headless in a blue wall of summer rain.

The spy tucked himself behind a boulder and began counting flags. Must be twenty thousand men, visible all at once. Two whole Union Corps. He could make out the familiar black hats of the Iron Brigade, troops belonging to John Reynold's First Corps. He looked at his watch, noted the time. They were coming very fast. The Army of the Potomac had never moved this fast. The day was murderously hot and there was no wind and the dust hung above the army like a yellow veil. He thought: there'll be some of them die of the heat today. But they are coming faster than they ever came before.

He slipped back down into the cool dark and rode slowly downhill toward the silent empty country to the north. With luck he could make the Southern line before nightfall. After nightfall it would be dangerous. But he must not seem to hurry. The horse was already tired. And yet there was the pressure of that great blue army behind him, building like water behind a cracking dam. He rode out into the open, into the land between the armies.

There were fat Dutch barns, prim German orchards. But there were no cattle in the fields and no horses, and houses everywhere were empty and dark. He was alone in the heat and the silence, and then it began to rain and he rode head down into monstrous lightning. All his life he had been afraid of lightning but he kept riding. He did not know where the Southern headquarters was but he knew it had to be somewhere near Chambersburg. He had smelled out the shape of Lee's army in all the rumors and bar talk and newspapers and hysteria he had drifted through all over eastern Pennsylvania, and on that day he was perhaps the only man alive who knew the positions of both armies. He carried the knowledge with a hot and lovely pride. Lee would be near Chambersburg, and wherever Lee was Longstreet would not be far away. So finding the headquarters was not the problem. The problem was riding through a picket line in the dark.

The rain grew worse. He could not even move in under a tree because of the lightning. He had to take care not to get lost. He rode quoting Shakespeare from memory, thinking of the picket line ahead somewhere in the dark. The sky opened and poured down on him and he rode on: *it will be rain tonight: let it come down.* That was a speech of murderers. He had been an actor once. He had no stature and a small voice and there were no big parts for him until the war came, and now he was the only one who knew how good he was. If only they could see him work, old cold Longstreet and the rest. But everyone hated spies. I come a single spy. Wet single spy. But *they* come in whole battalions. The rain began to ease off and he spurred the horse to a trot. *My kingdom for a horse.* Jolly good line. He went on, reciting *Henry the Fifth* aloud: "Once more into the breech . . ."

Late that afternoon he came to a crossroad and the sign of much cavalry having passed this way a few hours ago. His own way led north to Chambersburg, but he knew that Longstreet would have to know who these people were so close to his line. He debated a moment at the crossroads, knowing there was no time. A delay would cost him daylight. Yet he was a man of pride and the tracks drew him. Perhaps it was only Jeb Stuart. The spy thought hopefully, wistfully: if it's Stuart I can ask for an armed escort all the way home. He turned and followed the tracks. After a while he saw a farmhouse and a man standing out in a field, in a peach orchard, and he spurred that way. The man was small and bald with huge round arms and spoke very bad English. The spy went into his act: a simple-minded farmer seeking a runaway wife, terrified of soldiers. The bald man regarded him sweatily, disgustedly, told him the soldiers just gone by were "plu" soldiers, Yankees. The spy asked: what town lies yonder? and the farmer told him Gettysburg, but the name meant nothing. The spy turned and spurred back to the crossroads. Yankee cavalry meant John Buford's column. Moving lickety-split. Where was Stuart? No escort now. He rode back again toward the blue hills. But the horse could not be pushed. He had to dismount and walk.

That was the last sign of Yankees. He was moving up across South Mountain; he was almost home. Beyond South Mountain was Lee and, of course, Longstreet. A strange friendship: grim and gambling Longstreet, formal and pious old Bobby Lee. The spy wondered at it, and then the rain began again, bringing more lightning but at least some cooler air, and he tucked himself in under his hat and went back to *Hamlet.* Old Jackson was dead. *Good night, sweet Prince, and flights of angels sing thee to thy rest . . .*

He rode into darkness. No longer any need to hurry. He left the roadway at last and moved out in to a field away from the lightning and the trees and sat in the rain to eat a lonely supper, trying to make up his mind whether it was worth the risk of going on. He was very close; he could begin to feel them up ahead. There was no way of knowing when or where, but suddenly they would be there in the road, stepping phantomlike out of the trees wearing those sick eerie smiles, and other men with guns would suddenly appear all around him, prodding him in the back with hard steel barrels, as you prod an animal, and he would have to be lucky, because few men rode out at night on good and honest business, not now, this night, in this invaded country.

He rode slowly up the road, not really thinking, just moving, reluctant to stop. He was weary. Fragments of *Hamlet* flickered in his brain: *If it be not now, yet it will come. Ripeness is all.* Now *there's* a good part. A town ahead. A few lights. And then he struck the picket line.

There was a presence in the road, a liquid Southern voice. He saw them outlined in lightning, black ragged figures rising around him. A sudden lantern poured yellow light. He saw one bleak hawkish grinning face; hurriedly he mentioned Longstreet's name. With some you postured and with some you groveled and with some you were imperious. But you could do that only by daylight, when you could see the faces and gauge the reaction. And now he was too tired and cold. He sat and shuddered: an insignificant man on a pale and muddy horse. He turned out to be lucky. There was a patient sergeant with a long gray beard who put him under guard and sent him along up the dark road to Longstreet's headquarters.

He was not safe even now, but he could begin to relax. He rode up the long road between picket fires, and he could hear them singing in the rain, chasing each other in the dark of the trees. A fat and happy army, roasting meat and fresh bread, telling stories in the dark. He began to fall asleep on the horse; he was home. But they did not like to see him sleep, and one of them woke him up to remind him, cheerily, that if there was no one up there who knew him, why, then, unfortunately, they'd have to hang him, and the soldier said it just to see the look on his face, and the spy shivered, wondering, Why do there have to be men like that, men who enjoy another man's dying?

Longstreet was not asleep. He lay on the cot watching the lightning flare in the door of the tent. It was very quiet in the grove and there was the sound of the raindrops continuing to fall from the trees although the rain had ended. When Sorrel touched him on the arm he was glad of it; he was thinking of his dead children.

"Sir? You asked to be awakened if Harrison came back."

"Yes." Longstreet got up quickly and put on the old blue robe and the carpet slippers. He was a very big man and he was full-bearded and wild-haired. He thought of the last time he'd seen the spy, back in Virginia, tiny man with a face like a weasel: "And where will your headquarters be, General, up there in Pennsylvania? 'Tis a big state indeed." Him standing there with cold gold clutched in a dirty hand. And Longstreet had said icily, cheerily, "It will be where it will be. If you cannot find the headquarters of this whole army you cannot be much of a spy." And the spy had said stiffly, "*Scout,* sir. I am a scout. And I am a patriot, sir." Longstreet had grinned. We are all patriots. He stepped out into the light. He did not know what to expect. He had not really expected the spy to come back at all.

The little man was there: a soggy spectacle on a pale and

spattered horse. He sat grinning wanly from under the floppy brim of a soaked and dripping hat. Lightning flared behind him; he touched his cap.

"Your servant, General. May I come down?"

Longstreet nodded. The guard backed off. Longstreet told Sorrel to get some coffee. The spy slithered down from the horse and stood grinning foolishly, shivering, mouth slack with fatigue.

"Well, sir—" the spy chuckled, teeth chattering—"you see, I was able to find you after all."

Longstreet sat at the camp table on a wet seat, extracted a cigar, lighted it. The spy sat floppily, mouth still open, breathing deeply.

"It has been a long day. I've ridden hard all this day."

"What have you got?"

"I came through the pickets at night, you know. That can be very touchy."

Longstreet nodded. He watched, he waited. Sorrel came with steaming coffee; the cup burned Longstreet's fingers. Sorrel sat, gazing curiously, distastefully at the spy.

The spy guzzled, then sniffed Longstreet's fragrant smoke. Wistfully: "I say, General, I don't suppose you've got another of those? Good Southern tobacco?"

"Directly," Longstreet said. "What have you got?"

"I've got the position of the Union Army."

Longstreet nodded, showing nothing. He had not known the Union Army was on the move, was within two hundred miles, was even this side of the Potomac, but he nodded and said nothing. The spy asked for a map and began pointing out the positions of the corps.

"They're coming in seven corps. I figure at least eighty thousand men, possibly as much as a hundred thousand. When they're all together they'll outnumber you, but they're not as strong as they were; the two-year enlistments are running out. The First Corps is here. The Eleventh is right behind it. John Reynolds is in command of the lead elements. I saw him at Taneytown this morning."

"Reynolds," Longstreet said.

"Yes, sir."

"You saw him yourself?"

The spy grinned, nodded, rubbed his nose, chuckled. "So close I could touch him. It was Reynolds all right."

"This morning. At Taneytown."

"Exactly. You didn't know any of that, now did you, General?" The spy bobbed his head with delight. "You didn't even know they was on the move, did ye? I thought not. You wouldn't be spread out so thin if you knowed they was comin'."

Longstreet looked at Sorrel. The aide shrugged silently. If this was true, there would have been some word. Longstreet's mind moved over it slowly. He said: "How did you know we were spread out?"

"I smelled it out." The spy grinned, foxlike, toothy. "Listen, General, I'm good at this business."

"Tell me what you know of our position."

"Well, now I can't be too exact on this, 'cause I aint scouted you myself, but I gather that you're spread from York up to Harrisburg and then back to Chambersburg, with the main body around Chambersburg and General Lee just 'round the bend."

It was exact. Longstreet thought: if this one knows it, *they* will know it. He said slowly, "We've had no word of Union movement."

The spy bobbed with joy. "I knew it. Thass why I hurried. Came through that picket line in the dark and all. I don't know if you realize, General—"

Sorrel said coldly, "Sir, don't you think, if this man's story was true, that we would have heard *something?*"

Sorrel did not approve of spies. The spy grimaced, blew. "You aint exactly on friendly ground no more, Major. This aint Virginia no more."

True, Longstreet thought. But there would have been something. Stuart? Longstreet said, "General Stuart's cavalry went out a few days back. He hasn't reported any movement."

The spy shrugged, exasperated, glooming at Sorrel. Sorrel turned his back, looked at his fingernails.

Longstreet said, "What have you heard of Stuart?"

"Not much. He's riding in the north somewhere. Stirring up headlines and fuss, but I never heard him do any real damage."

Longstreet said, "If the Union Army were as close as you say, one would think—"

"Well, I'm damned," the spy said, a small rage flaming. "I come through that picket line in the dark and all. Listen, General, I tell you this: I don't know what old Stuart is doing and I don't care, but I done my job and this is a fact. This here same afternoon of this here day I come on the tracks of Union cavalry thick as fleas, one whole brigade and maybe two, and them bluebellies weren't no four hours hard ride from this here now spot, and that, by God, is the Lord's truth." He blew again, meditating. Then he added, by way of amendment, "Buford's column, I think it was. To be exact."

Longstreet thought: *can't* be true. But he was an instinctive man, and suddenly his brain knew and his own temper boiled. Jeb Stuart . . . was joyriding. God *damn* him. Longstreet turned to Sorrel.

"All right, Major. Send to General Lee. I guess we'll have to wake him up. Get my horse."

Sorrel started to say something, but he knew that you did not argue with Longstreet. He moved.

The spy said delightedly, "General Lee? Do I get to see

General Lee? Well now." He stood up and took off the ridiculous hat and smoothed wet plastered hair across a balding skull. He glowed. Longstreet got the rest of the information and went back to his tent and dressed quickly.

If the spy was right the army was in great danger. They could be cut apart and cut off from home and destroyed in detail, piece by piece. If the spy was right, then Lee would have to turn, but the old man did not believe in spies nor in any information you had to pay for, had not approved of the money spent or even the idea behind it. And the old man had faith in Stuart, and why in God's name had Stuart sent nothing, not even a courier, because even Stuart wasn't fool enough to let the whole damned Army of the Potomac get this close without word, not one damned lonesome word. Longstreet went back out into the light. He had never believed in this invasion. Lee and Davis together had overruled him. He did not believe in offensive warfare when the enemy outnumbered you and outgunned you and would come looking for you anyway if you waited somewhere on your own ground. He had not argued since leaving home, but the invasion did not sit right in his craw; the whole scheme lay edgewise and raspy in his brain, and treading here on alien ground, he felt a cold wind blowing, a distant alarm. Only instinct. No facts as yet. The spy reminded him about the cigar. It was a short way through the night to Lee's headquarters, and they rode past low sputtering campfires with the spy puffing exuberant blue smoke like a happy furnace.

"'Tis a happy army you've got here, General," the spy chatted with approval. "I felt it the moment I crossed the picket line. A happy army, eager for the fight. Singing and all. You can feel it in the air. Not like them bluebellies. A desperate tired lot. I tell you, General, this will be a factor. The bluebellies is almost done. Why, do you know what I see everywhere I go? Disgraceful, it is. On every street in every town, able-bodied men. Just *standing* there, by the thousands, reading them poor squeaky pitiful newspapers about this here mighty invasion and the last gasp of the Union and how every man must take up arms, haw." The spy guffawed. "Like a bunch of fat women at church. The war's almost over. You can feel it, General. The end is in the air."

Longstreet said nothing. He was beginning to think of what to do if the spy was right. If he could not get Lee to turn now there could be disaster. And yet if the Union Army was truly out in the open at last there was a great opportunity: a sudden move south, between Hooker and Washington, cut *them* off from Lincoln. Yes. Longstreet said, "What do you hear of Hooker? Where is he?"

The spy stopped, mouth sagging. "Oh by Jesus. Forgive me." He grimaced, shook his head. "I done forgot. There was an item in the newspaper this morning. Saying that Hooker was replaced. They gave the command to Meade, I think it was."

"George Meade?"

"Yes, sir. I think."

"You're sure?"

"Well, it was Meade the newspaper said, but you know them damn newspapers."

Longstreet thought: new factor. He spurred the horse, but he couldn't move fast because of the dark. Lee must listen. God bless the politicians. Reynolds was their best man. Why did they go to Meade? But I'm sorry to see Hooker go. Old Fighting Joe. Longstreet said, "It was Meade, then, and not Reynolds?"

"Rumor was that Reynolds was offered the job but wouldn't have it on a plate. That's what the paper said."

Old John's too smart to take it. Not with that idiot Halleck pulling the strings. But Meade? Fussy. Engineer. Careful. No genius for sure. But a new factor. A Pennsylvania man. He will know this country.

The spy chatted on amiably. He seemed to need to talk.

He was saying, "Strange thing about it all, thing that bothers me is that when you do this job right nobody knows you're doing it, nobody ever watches you work, do you see? And sometimes I can't help but wish I had an audience. I've played some scenes, ah, General, but I've been lovely." The spy sighed, puffed, sighed again. "This current creation, now, is marvelous. I'm a poor half-witted farmer, do you see, terrified of soldiers, and me lovely young wife has run off with a drummer and I'm out a-scourin' the countryside for her, a sorrowful pitiful sight I am. And people lookin' down their noses and grinnin' behind me back and all the time tellin' me exactly what I want to know about who is where and how many and how long ago, and them not even knowin' they're doin' it, too busy feelin' contemptuous. There are many people, General, that don't give a damn for a human soul, do you know that? The strange thing is, after playing this poor fool farmer for a while I can't help but feel sorry for him. Because nobody cares."

They came to Lee's camp, in the grove just south of Chambersburg. By the time they got there Longstreet knew that the spy was telling the truth. Young Walter Taylor was up, annoyed, prissy, defending General Lee's night's rest even against Longstreet, who glowed once with the beginning of rage, and sent Taylor off to get the old man out of bed. They dismounted and waited. The spy sat under an awning, grinning with joy at the prospect of meeting Lee. Longstreet could not sit down. He disliked getting the old man up: Lee had not been well. But you could lose the war up here. Should have gone to Vicksburg. News from there very bad. It will fall, and after that . . . we must win here if we are to win at all, and we must do it soon. The rain touched him; he shivered. Too damn much rain would muck up the roads.

Lee came out into the light. The spy hopped to attention. Lee bowed slightly, stiffly.

"Gentlemen."

He stood bareheaded in the rain: regal, formal, a beautiful white-haired, white-bearded old man in a faded blue robe. He looked haggard. Longstreet thought: he looks older every time you see him. For a moment the spy was silent, enraptured, then he bowed suddenly from the waist, widely, formally, gracefully, plucking the floppy hat from the balding head and actually sweeping the ground with it, dandy, ridiculous, something off a stage somewhere designed for a king.

"General," the spy said grandly, "*à votre service.*" He said something else in a strange and southern French. Longstreet was startled at the transformation.

Lee glanced at Longstreet: a silent question. Longstreet said, "Beg pardon, sir. I thought this urgent. The man has information."

Lee looked at the spy silently. His face showed nothing. Then he said formally, "Sir, you must excuse me, I do not know your name."

"The name is *Harrison,* sir, at present." The spy grinned toothily. "The name of an ex-President, ex-General. A small joke, sir. One must keep one's sense of humor."

Lee glanced again at Longstreet. Longstreet said, "The man has the position of the Union Army. He says they are very close. I have a map."

He moved to the map table, under the awning. The spy followed with reproach. Lee came slowly to the table, watching the man. After a moment he said to Harrison, "I understand that you are General Longstreet's"—a slight pause—" 'scout.' " Lee would not use the word *spy.* "I believe we saw you last back in Virginia."

"That's a fact," the spy worshipped. "I been kind of circulatin' since, amongst the bluebellies, and I tell you, General, sir, that it's an honor and a priv—"

Longstreet said, "He claims their lead elements are here.

He says there is a column of strong Union cavalry not four hours off."

Lee looked at the map. Then he sat down and looked more closely. Longstreet gave the positions, the spy fluttering mothlike behind him with numbers and names and dates. Lee listened without expression.

Longstreet finished. "He estimates perhaps one hundred thousand men."

Lee nodded. But estimates meant nothing. He sat for a moment staring at the map and then bowed his head slightly. Longstreet thought: he doesn't believe. Then Lee raised his eyes and regarded the spy.

"You appear to have ridden hard. Have you come a long way?"

"Sir, I sure have."

"And you came through the picket line after dark?"

"Yes, sir—" the spy's head bobbed—"I did indeed."

"We are in your debt." Lee stared at the map. "Thank you. Now I'm sure General Longstreet will see to your accommodations."

The spy was dismissed, had sense enough to know it. He rose reluctantly. He said, "It has been my pleasure, sir, to have served such a man as yourself. God bless you, sir."

Lee thanked him again. Longstreet instructed Sorrel to see that the man was fed and given a tent for the night and to be kept where Longstreet could find him if he needed him, which meant: keep an eye on him. The spy went out into the dark. Longstreet and Lee sat alone at the table in the rain.

Lee said softly, "Do you believe this man?"

"No choice."

"I suppose not." Lee rubbed his eyes, leaned forward on the table. With his right hand he held the muscle of his left arm. He shook his head slowly. "Am I to move on the word of a paid spy?"

"Can't afford not to."

"There would have been something from Stuart."

"There should have been."

"Stuart would not have left us blind."

"He's joyriding again," Longstreet said. "This time you ought to stomp him. Really stomp him."

Lee shook his head. "Stuart would not leave us blind."

"We've got to turn," Longstreet said. His heart was beating strongly. It was bad to see the indomitable old man weak and hatless in the early morning, something soft in his eyes, pain in his face, the right hand rubbing the pain in the arm. Longstreet said, "We can't risk it. If we don't concentrate they'll chop us up."

Lee said nothing. After a moment Longstreet told him about Meade. Lee said, "They should have gone to Reynolds."

"Thought so too. I think he turned it down."

Lee nodded. He smiled slightly. "I would have preferred to continue against General Hooker."

Longstreet grinned. "Me too."

"Meade will be . . . cautious. It will take him some time to take command, to organize a staff. I think . . . perhaps we should move quickly. There may be an opportunity here."

"Yes. If we swing in behind him and cut him off from Washington . . ."

"If your man is correct."

"We'll find out."

Lee bent toward the map. The mountains rose like a rounded wall between them and the Union Army. There was one gap east of Chambersburg and beyond that all the roads came together, weblike, at a small town. Lee put his finger on the map.

"What town is that?"

Longstreet looked. "Gettysburg," he said.

Lee nodded. "Well—" he was squinting—"I see no reason

to delay. It's their army I'm after, not their towns." He followed the roads with his finger, all converging on that one small town. "I think we should concentrate in this direction. This road junction will be useful."

"Yes," Longstreet said.

Lee looked up with black diamond eyes. "We'll move at first light."

Longstreet felt a lovely thrill. Trust the old man to move. "Yes, sir."

Lee started to rise. A short while ago he had fallen from a horse onto his hands, and when he pushed himself up from the table Longstreet saw him wince. Longstreet thought: go to sleep and let me do it. Give the order and I'll do it all. He said, "I regret the need to wake you, sir."

Lee looked past him into the soft blowing dark. The rain had ended. A light wind was moving in the tops of the pines —cool sweet air, gentle and clean. Lee took a deep breath.

"A good time of night. I have always liked this time of night."

"Yes."

"Well." Lee glanced once almost shyly at Longstreet's face, then looked away. They stood for a moment in awkward silence. They had been together for a long time in war and they had grown very close, but Lee was ever formal and Longstreet was inarticulate, so they stood for a long moment side by side without speaking, not looking at each other, listening to the raindrops fall in the leaves. But the silent moment was enough. After a while Lee said slowly, "When this is over, I shall miss it very much."

"Yes."

"I do not mean the fighting."

"No."

"Well," Lee said. He looked to the sky. "It is all in God's hands."

They said good night. Longstreet watched the old man

back to his tent. Then he mounted and rode alone back to his camp to begin the turning of the army, all the wagons and all the guns, down the narrow mountain road that led to Gettysburg. It was still a long dark hour till dawn. He sat alone on his horse in the night and he could feel the army asleep around him, all those young hearts beating in the dark. They would need their rest now. He sat alone to await the dawn, and let them sleep a little longer.

---

2. Chamberlain

He dreamed of Maine and ice black water; he awoke to a murderous sun. A voice was calling: "Colonel, darlin'." He squinted: the whiskery face of Buster Kilrain.

"Colonel, darlin', I hate to be a-wakin' ye, but there's a message here ye ought to be seein'."

Chamberlain had slept on the ground; he rolled to a sitting position. Light boiled in through the tent flap. Chamberlain closed his eyes.

"And how are ye feelin' this mornin', Colonel, me lad?"

Chamberlain ran his tongue around his mouth. He said briefly, dryly, "Ak."

"We're about to be havin' guests, sir, or I wouldn't be wakin' ye."

Chamberlain looked up through bleary eyes. He had walked eighty miles in four days through the hottest weather he had ever known and he had gone down with sunstroke. He felt an eerie fragility, like a piece of thin glass in a high hot wind. He saw a wooden canteen, held in the big hand of

Kilrain, cold drops of water on varnished sides. He drank. The world focused.

". . . one hundred and twenty men," Kilrain said.

Chamberlain peered at him.

"They should be arriving any moment," Kilrain said. He was squatting easily, comfortably, in the opening of the tent, the light flaming behind him.

"Who?" Chamberlain said.

"They are sending us some mutineers," Kilrain said with fatherly patience. "One hundred and twenty men from the old Second Maine, which has been disbanded."

"Mutineers?"

"Ay. What happened was that the enlistment of the old Second ran out and they were all sent home except one hundred and twenty, which had foolishly signed *three*-year papers, and so they all had one year to go, only *they* all thought they was signing up to fight with the Second, and Second only, and so they mutineed. One hundred and twenty. Are you all right, Colonel?"

Chamberlain nodded vaguely.

"Well, these poor fellers did not want to fight no more, naturally, being Maine men of a certain intelligence, and refused, only nobody will send them home, and nobody knew what to do with them, until they thought of *us,* being as we are the other Maine regiment here in the army. There's a message here signed by Meade himself. That's the new General we got now, sir, if you can keep track as they go by. The message says they'll be sent here this morning and they are to fight, and if they don't fight you can feel free to shoot them."

"Shoot?"

"Ay."

"Let me see." Chamberlain read painfully. His head felt very strange indeed, but he was coming awake into the morning as from a long way away and he could begin to hear the bugles out across the fields. Late to get moving today. Thank God. Somebody gave us an extra hour. Bless him. He read: . . . *you are therefore authorized to shoot any man who refuses to do his duty.* Shoot?

He said, "These are all *Maine* men?"

"Yes, sir. Fine big fellers. I've seen them. Loggin' men. You may remember there was a bit of a brawl some months back, during the mud march? These fellers were famous for their fists."

Chamberlain said, "One hundred and twenty."

"Yes, sir."

"Somebody's crazy."

"Yes, sir."

"How many men do we now have in this Regiment?"

"Ah, somewhat less than two hundred and fifty, sir, as of yesterday. Countin' the officers."

"How do I take care of a hundred and twenty mutinous men?"

"Yes, sir," Kilrain sympathized. "Well, you'll have to talk to them, sir."

Chamberlain sat for a long moment silently trying to function. He was thirty-four years old, and on this day one year ago he had been a professor of rhetoric at Bowdoin University. He had no idea what to do. But it was time to go out into the sun. He crawled forward through the tent flap and stood up, blinking, swaying, one hand against the bole of a tree. He was a tall man, somewhat picturesque. He wore stolen blue cavalry trousers and a three-foot sword, and the clothes he wore he had not taken off for a week. He had a grave, boyish dignity, that clean-eyed, scrubbed-brain, naïve look of the happy professor.

Kilrain, a white-haired man with the build of an ape, looked up at him with fatherly joy. "If ye'll ride the *horse* today, Colonel, which the Lord hath provided, instead of walkin' in the dust with the other fools, ye'll be all right—

if ye wear the hat. It's the *walkin',* do you see, that does the great harm."

"*You* walked," Chamberlain said grumpily, thinking: shoot them? *Maine* men? How can I shoot Maine men? I'll never be able to go home.

"Ah, but, Colonel, darlin', I've been in the infantry since before you was born. It's them first few thousand miles. After that, a man gets a limber to his feet."

"Hey, Lawrence. How you doin'?"

Younger brother, Tom Chamberlain, bright-faced, high-voiced, a new lieutenant, worshipful. The heat had not seemed to touch him. Chamberlain nodded. Tom said critically, "You lookin' kinda peaked. Why don't you ride the horse?"

Chamberlain gloomed. But the day was not as bright as it had seemed through the opening of the tent. He looked upward with relief toward a darkening sky. The troops were moving in the fields, but there had been no order to march. The wagons were not yet loaded. He thought: God bless the delay. His mind was beginning to function. All down the road and all through the trees the troops were moving, cooking, the thousands of troops and thousands of wagons of the Fifth Corps, Army of the Potomac, of which Chamberlain's 20th Maine was a minor fragment. But far down the road there was motion.

Kilrain said, "There they come."

Chamberlain squinted. Then he saw troops on the road, a long way off.

The line of men came slowly up the road. There were guards with fixed bayonets. Chamberlain could see the men shuffling, strange pathetic spectacle, dusty, dirty, ragged men, heads down, faces down: it reminded him of a history-book picture of impressed seamen in the last war with England. But these men would have to march all day, in the heat. Chamberlain thought: not possible.

Tom was meditating. "Gosh, Lawrence. There's almost as many men there as we got in the whole regiment. How we going to guard them?"

Chamberlain said nothing. He was thinking: How do you force a man to fight—for freedom? The idiocy of it jarred him. Think on it later. Must do something now.

There was an officer, a captain, at the head of the column. The Captain turned them in off the road and herded them into an open space in the field near the Regimental flag. The men of the Regiment, busy with coffee, stood up to watch. The Captain had a loud voice and used obscene words. He assembled the men in two long ragged lines and called them to attention, but they ignored him. One slumped to the ground, more exhaustion than mutiny. A guard came forward and yelled and probed with a bayonet, but abruptly several more men sat down and then they all did, and the Captain began yelling, but the guards stood grinning confusedly, foolishly, having gone as far as they would go, unwilling to push further unless the men here showed some threat, and the men seemed beyond threat, merely enormously weary. Chamberlain took it all in as he moved toward the Captain. He put his hands behind his back and came forward slowly, studiously. The Captain pulled off dirty gloves and shook his head with contempt, glowering up at Chamberlain.

"Looking for the commanding officer, Twentieth Maine."

"You've found him," Chamberlain said.

"That's him all right." Tom's voice, behind him, very proud. Chamberlain suppressed a smile.

"You Chamberlain?" The Captain stared at him grimly, insolently, showing what he thought of Maine men.

Chamberlain did not answer for a long moment, looking into the man's eyes until the eyes suddenly blinked and dropped, and then Chamberlain said softly, "*Colonel* Chamberlain to you."

The Captain stood still for a moment, then slowly came to attention, slowly saluted. Chamberlain did not return it. He looked past the Captain at the men, most of whom had their heads down. But there were eyes on him. He looked back and forth down the line, looking for a familiar face. That would help. But there was no one he knew.

"Captain Brewer, sir. Ah. One-eighteen Pennsylvania." The Captain tugged in his coat front, produced a sheaf of papers. "If you're the commanding officer, sir, then I present you with these here prisoners." He handed the papers. Chamberlain took them, glanced down, handed them back to Tom. The Captain said, "You're welcome to 'em, God knows. Had to use the bayonet to get 'em moving. You got to sign for 'em, Colonel."

Chamberlain said over his shoulder, "Sign it, Tom." To the Captain he said, "You're relieved, Captain."

The Captain nodded, pulling on the dirty gloves. "You're authorized to use whatever force necessary, Colonel." He said that loudly, for effect. "If you have to shoot 'em, why, you go right ahead. Won't nobody say nothin'."

"You're relieved, Captain," Chamberlain said. He walked past the Captain, closer to the men, who did not move, who did not seem to notice him. One of the guards stiffened as Chamberlain approached, looked past him to his captain. Chamberlain said, "You men can leave now. We don't need any guards."

He stood in front of the men, ignoring the guards. They began to move off. Chamberlain stood for a moment looking down. Some of the faces turned up. There was hunger and exhaustion and occasional hatred. Chamberlain said, "My name is Chamberlain. I'm Colonel, Twentieth Maine."

Some of them did not even raise their heads. He waited another moment. Then he said, "When did you eat last?"

More heads came up. There was no answer. Then a man

in the front row said huskily, in a whiskey voice, "We're hungry, Colonel."

Another man said, "They been tryin' to break us by not feedin' us." Chamberlain looked: a scarred man, hatless, hair plastered thinly on the scalp like strands of black seaweed. The man said, "We aint broke yet."

Chamberlain nodded. A hard case. But we'll begin with food. He said, "They just told us you were coming a little while ago. I've told the cook to butcher a steer. Hope you like it near to raw; not much time to cook." Eyes opened wide. He could begin to see the hunger on the faces, like the yellow shine of sickness. He said, "We've got a ways to go today and you'll be coming with us, so you better eat hearty. We're all set up for you back in the trees." He saw Glazier Estabrook standing huge-armed and peaceful in the shade of a nearby tree. "Glazier," Chamberlain said, "you show these men where to go. You fellas eat up and then I'll come over and hear what you have to say."

No man moved. Chamberlain turned away. He did not know what he would do if they did not choose to move. He heard a voice: "Colonel?"

He turned. The scarred man was standing.

"Colonel, we got grievances. The men elected me to talk for 'em."

"Right." Chamberlain nodded. "You come on with me and talk. The rest of you fellas go eat." He beckoned to the scarred man and waved to Glazier Estabrook. He turned again, not waiting for the men to move off, not sure they would go, began to walk purposefully toward the blessed dark, wondering again how big a guard detail it would take, thinking he might wind up with more men out of action than in, and also: what are you going to say? Good big boys they are. Seen their share of action.

"Gosh, Lawrence," Tom Chamberlain said.

"Smile," Chamberlain said cheerily, "and don't call me

Lawrence. Are they moving?" He stopped and glanced pleasantly backward, saw with delight that the men were up and moving toward the trees, toward food. He grinned, plucked a book from his jacket, handed it to Tom.

"Here. This is Casey's *Manual of Infantry Tactics.* You study it, maybe someday you'll make a soldier." He smiled at the scarred man, extended a hand. "What's your name?"

The man stopped, looked at him for a long cold second. The hand seemed to come up against gravity, against his will. Automatic courtesy: Chamberlain was relying on it.

"I'm not usually that informal," Chamberlain said with the same light, calm, pleasant manner that he had developed when talking to particularly rebellious students who had come in with a grievance and who hadn't yet learned that the soft answer turneth away wrath. *Some* wrath. "But I suppose somebody ought to welcome you to the Regiment."

The man said, "I don't feel too kindly, Colonel."

Chamberlain nodded. He went on inside the tent, the scarred man following, and sat down on a camp stool, letting the man stand. He invited the man to have coffee, which the man declined, and then listened silently to the man's story.

The scarred man spoke calmly and coldly, looking straight into Chamberlain's eyes. A good stubborn man. There was a bit of the lawyer about him: he used chunky phrases about law and justice. But he had heavy hands with thick muscular fingers and black fingernails and there was a look of power to him, a coiled tight set to the way he stood, balanced, ugly, slightly contemptuous, but watchful, trying to gauge Chamberlain's strength.

Chamberlain said, "I see."

"I been in eleven different engagements, Colonel. How many you been in?"

"Not that many," Chamberlain said.

"I done my share. We all have. Most of us—"he gestured out the tent flap into the morning glare—"there's some of them no damn good but most of them been all the way there and back. Damn good men. Shouldn't ought to use them this way. Looky here." He pulled up a pants leg. Chamberlain saw a purple gash, white scar tissue. The man let the pants leg fall. Chamberlain said nothing. The man looked at his face, seemed suddenly embarrassed, realized he had gone too far. For the first time he was uncertain. But he repeated, "I done my share."

Chamberlain nodded. The man was relaxing slowly. It was warm in the tent; he opened his shirt. Chamberlain said, "What's your name?"

"Bucklin. Joseph Bucklin."

"Where you from?"

"Bangor."

"Don't know any Bucklins. Farmer?"

"Fisherman."

Former Sergeant Kilrain put his head in the tent. "Colonel, there's a courier comin'."

Chamberlain nodded. Bucklin said, "I'm tired, Colonel. You know what I mean? I'm tired. I've had all of this army and all of these officers, this damned Hooker and this goddamned idiot Meade, all of them, the whole bloody lousy rotten mess of sick-brained potbellied scabheads that aint fit to lead a johnny detail, aint fit to pour pee outen a boot with instructions on the heel. I'm tired. We are good men and we had our own good flag and these goddamned idiots use us like we was cows or dogs or even worse. We aint gonna win this war. We can't win no how because of these lame-brained bastards from West Point, these goddamned gentlemen, these *officers.* Only one officer knew what he was doin: McClellan, and look what happened to *him.* I just as soon go home and let them damn Johnnies go home and the hell with it."

He let it go, out of breath. He had obviously been waiting

to say that to some officer for a long time. Chamberlain said, "I get your point."

Kilrain announced, "Courier, sir."

Chamberlain rose, excused himself, stepped out into the sunlight. A bright-cheeked lieutenant, just dismounted, saluted him briskly.

"Colonel Chamberlain, sir, Colonel Vincent wishes to inform you that the corps is moving out at once and that you are instructed to take the advance. The Twentieth Maine has been assigned to the first position in line. You will send out flankers and advance guards."

"My compliments to the Colonel." Chamberlain saluted, turned to Kilrain and Ellis Spear, who had come up. "You heard him, boys. Get the Regiment up. Sound the *General,* strike the tents." Back inside the tent, he said cheerfully to Bucklin, "We're moving out. You better go hurry up your eating. Tell your men I'll be over in a minute. I'll think on what you said."

Bucklin slipped by him, went away. Chamberlain thought: we're first in line.

"Kilrain."

The former sergeant was back.

"Sir."

"Where we headed?"

"West, sir. Pennsylvania somewhere. That's all I know."

"Listen, Buster. You're a private now and I'm not supposed to keep you at headquarters in that rank. If you want to go on back to the ranks, you just say so, because I feel obligated—well, you don't have to be here, but listen, I need you."

"Then I'll be stayin', Colonel, laddie." Kilrain grinned.

"But you know I can't promote you. Not after that episode with the bottle. Did you have to pick an officer?"

Kilrain grinned. "I was not aware of rank, sir, at the time. And he was the target which happened to present itself."

"Buster, you haven't got a bottle about?"

"Is the Colonel in need of a drink, sir?"

"I meant . . . forget it. All right, Buster, move 'em out."

Kilrain saluted, grinning, and withdrew. The only professional in the regiment. The drinking would kill him. Well. He would die happy. Now. What do I say to *them?*

Tom came in, saluted.

"The men from the Second Maine are being fed, sir."

"Don't call me sir."

"Well, Lawrence, Great God A-Mighty—"

"You just be careful of that name business in front of the men. Listen, we don't want anybody to think there's favoritism."

Tom put on the wounded look, face of the ruptured deer.

"General Meade has his *son* as his adjutant."

"That's different. Generals can do anything. Nothing quite so much like God on earth as a general on a battlefield." The tent was coming down about his head; he stepped outside to avoid the collapse. The General and God was a nice parallel. They have your future in their hands and they have all power and know all. He grinned, thinking of Meade surrounded by his angelic staff: Dan Butterfield, wild Dan Sickles. But *what do I say?*

"Lawrence, what you goin' to do?"

Chamberlain shook his head. The Regiment was up and moving.

"God, you can't shoot them. You do that, you'll never go back to Maine when the war's over."

"I know that." Chamberlain meditated. "Wonder if *they* do?"

He heard a flare of bugles, looked down the road toward Union Mills. The next regiment, the 83rd Pennsylvania, was up and forming. He saw wagons and ambulances moving out into the road. He could feel again the yellow heat. Must remember to cover up. More susceptible to sunstroke now. Can't afford a foggy head. He began to walk slowly toward the grove of trees.

Kilrain says tell the truth.

Which is?

Fight. Or we'll shoot you.

Not true. I won't shoot anybody.

He walked slowly out into the sunlight. He thought: but the truth is much more than that. Truth is too personal. Don't know if I can express it. He paused in the heat. Strange thing. You would die for it without further question, but you had a hard time talking about it. He shook his head. I'll wave no more flags for home. No tears for Mother. Nobody ever died for apple pie.

He walked slowly toward the dark grove. He had a complicated brain and there were things going on back there from time to time that he only dimly understood, so he relied on his instincts, but he was learning all the time. The faith itself was simple: he believed in the dignity of man. His ancestors were Huguenots, refugees of a chained and bloody Europe. He had learned their stories in the cradle. He had grown up believing in America and the individual and it was a stronger faith than his faith in God. This was the land where no man had to bow. In this place at last a man could stand up free of the past, free of tradition and blood ties and the curse of royalty and become what he wished to become. This was the first place on earth where the man mattered more than the state. True freedom had begun here and it would spread eventually over all the earth. But it had begun *here.* The fact of slavery upon this incredibly beautiful new clean earth was appalling, but more even than that was the horror of old Europe, the curse of nobility, which the South was transplanting to new soil. They were forming a new aristocracy, a new breed of glittering men, and Chamberlain had come to crush it. But he was fighting for the dignity of man and in that way he was fighting for himself. If men were equal in America, all these former Poles and English and Czechs and blacks, then they were equal everywhere, and there was really no such thing as a foreigner; there were only free men and slaves. And so it was not even patriotism but a new faith. The Frenchman may fight for France, but the American fights for mankind, for freedom; for the people, not the land.

Yet the words had been used too often and the fragments that came to Chamberlain now were weak. A man who has been shot at is a new realist, and what do you say to a realist when the war is a war of ideals? He thought finally, Well, I owe them the truth at least. Might's well begin with that.

The Regiment had begun to form. Chamberlain thought: At least it'll be a short speech. He walked slowly toward the prisoners.

Glazier Estabrook was standing guard, leaning patiently on his rifle. He was a thick little man of about forty. Except for Kilrain he was the oldest man in the Regiment, the strongest man Chamberlain had ever seen. He waved happily as Chamberlain came up but went on leaning on the rifle. He pointed at one of the prisoners.

"Hey, Colonel, you know who this is? This here is Dan Burns from Orono. I know his daddy. Daddy's a preacher. You really ought to hear him. Best damn cusser I ever heard. Knows more fine swear words than any man in Maine, I bet. Hee."

Chamberlain smiled. But the Burns boy was looking at him with no expression. Chamberlain said, "You fellas gather round."

He stood in the shade, waited while they closed in silently, watchfully around him. In the background the tents were coming down, the wagons were hitching, but some of the men of the Regiment had come out to watch and listen. Some of the men here were still chewing. But they were quiet, attentive.

Chamberlain waited a moment longer. Now it was quiet in the grove and the clink of the wagons was sharp in the distance. Chamberlain said, "I've been talking with Bucklin. He's told me your problem."

Some of the men grumbled. Chamberlain heard no words clearly. He went on speaking softly so that they would have to quiet to hear him.

"I don't know what I can do about it. I'll do what I can. I'll look into it as soon as possible. But there's nothing I can do today. We're moving out in a few minutes and we'll be marching all day and we may be in a big fight before nightfall. But as soon as I can, I'll do what I can."

They were silent, watching him. Chamberlain began to relax. He had made many speeches and he had a gift for it. He did not know what it was, but when he spoke most men stopped to listen. Fanny said it was something in his voice. He hoped it was there now.

"I've been ordered to take you men with me. I've been told that if you don't come I can shoot you. Well, you know I won't do that. Not Maine men. I won't shoot any man who doesn't want this fight. Maybe someone else will, but I won't. So that's that."

He paused again. There was nothing on their faces to lead him.

"Here's the situation. I've been ordered to take you along, and that's what I'm going to do. Under guard if necessary. But you can have your rifles if you want them. The whole Reb army is up the road a ways waiting for us and this is no time for an argument like this. I tell you this: we sure can use you. We're down below half strength and we need you, no doubt of that. But whether you fight or not is up to you. Whether you come along, well, you're coming."

Tom had come up with Chamberlain's horse. Over the

heads of the prisoners Chamberlain could see the Regiment falling into line out in the flaming road. He took a deep breath.

"Well, I don't want to preach to you. You know who we are and what we're doing here. But if you're going to fight alongside us there's a few things I want you to know."

He bowed his head, not looking at eyes. He folded his hands together.

"This Regiment was formed last fall, back in Maine. There were a thousand of us then. There's not three hundred of us now." He glanced up briefly. "But what is left is choice."

He was embarrassed. He spoke very slowly, staring at the ground.

"Some of us volunteered to fight for Union. Some came in mainly because we were bored at home and this looked like it might be fun. Some came because we were ashamed not to. Many of us came . . . because it was the right thing to do. All of us have seen men die. Most of us never saw a black man back home. We think on that, too. But freedom . . . is not just a word."

He looked up in to the sky, over silent faces.

"This is a different kind of army. If you look at history you'll see men fight for pay, or women, or some other kind of loot. They fight for land, or because a king makes them, or just because they like killing. But we're here for something new. I don't . . . this hasn't happened much in the history of the world. We're an army going out to set other men free."

He bent down, scratched the black dirt into his fingers. He was beginning to warm to it; the words were beginning to flow. No one in front of him was moving. He said, "This is free ground. All the way from here to the Pacific Ocean. No man has to bow. No man born to royalty. Here we judge you by what *you* do, not by what your father was. Here you can be *something*. Here's a place to build a home. It isn't the land —there's always more land. It's the idea that we all have value, you and me, we're worth something more than the dirt. I never saw dirt I'd die for, but I'm not asking you to come join us and fight for dirt. What we're all fighting for, in the end, is each other."

Once he started talking he broke right through the embarrassment and there was suddenly no longer a barrier there. The words came out of him in a clear river, and he felt himself silent and suspended in the grove listening to himself speak, carried outside himself and looking back down on the silent faces and himself speaking, and he felt the power in him, the power of his cause. For an instant he could see black castles in the air; he could create centuries of screaming, eons of torture. Then he was back in sunlit Pennsylvania. The bugles were blowing and he was done.

He had nothing else to say. No one moved. He felt the embarrassment return. He was suddenly enormously tired. The faces were staring up at him like white stones. Some heads were down. He said, "Didn't mean to preach. Sorry. But I thought . . . you should know who we are." He had forgotten how tiring it was just to speak. "Well, this is still the army, but you're as free as I can make you. Go ahead and talk for a while. If you want your rifles for this fight you'll have them back and nothing else will be said. If you won't join us you'll come along under guard. When this is over I'll do what I can to see that you get fair treatment. Now we have to move out." He stopped, looked at them. The faces showed nothing. He said slowly, "I think if we lose this fight the war will be over. So if you choose to come with us I'll be personally grateful. Well. We have to move out."

He turned, left silence behind him. Tom came up with the horse—a pale-gray lightfooted animal. Tom's face was shiny red.

"My, Lawrence, you sure talk pretty."

Chamberlain grunted. He was really tired. Rest a moment. He paused with his hands on the saddle horn. There was a new vague doubt stirring in his brain. Something troubled him; he did not know why.

"You ride today, Lawrence. You look weary."

Chamberlain nodded. Ellis Spear was up. He was Chamberlain's ranking officer, an ex-teacher from Wiscasset who was impressed with Chamberlain's professorship. A shy man, formal, but very competent. He gestured toward the prisoners.

"Colonel, what do you suggest we do with them?"

"Give them a moment. Some of them may be willing to fight. Tom, you go back and see what they say. We'll have to march them under guard. Don't know what else to do. I'm not going to shoot them. We can't leave them here."

The Regiment had formed out in the road, the color bearers in front. Chamberlain mounted, put on the wide-brimmed hat with the emblem of the infantry, began walking his horse slowly across the field toward the road. The uneasiness still troubled him. He had missed something, he did not know what. Well, he was an instinctive man; the mind would tell him sooner or later. Perhaps it was only that when you try to put it into words you cannot express it truly, it never sounds as you dream it. But then . . . you were asking them to die.

Ellis Spear was saying, "How far are we from Pennsylvania, Colonel, you have any idea?"

"Better than twenty miles." Chamberlain squinted upward. "Going to be another hot day."

He moved to the head of the column. The troops were moving slowly, patiently, setting themselves for the long march. After a moment Tom came riding up. His face was delighted. Chamberlain said, "How many are going to join us?"

Tom grinned hugely. "Would you believe it? All but six."

"*How many?*"

"I counted, by actual count, one hundred and fourteen."

"Well." Chamberlain rubbed his nose, astounded.

Tom said, still grinning, "Brother, you did real good."

"They're all marching together?"

"Right. Glazier's got the six hardheads in tow."

"Well, get all the names and start assigning them to different companies. I don't want them bunched up, spread them out. See about their arms."

"Yes, sir, Colonel, sir."

Chamberlain reached the head of the column. The road ahead was long and straight, rising toward a ridge of trees. He turned in his saddle, looked back, saw the entire Fifth Corps forming behind him. He thought: 120 new men. Hardly noticeable in such a mass. And yet . . . he felt a moment of huge joy. He called for road guards and skirmishers and the Twentieth Maine began to move toward Gettysburg.

---

3. Buford

The land west of Gettysburg is a series of ridges, like waves in the earth. The first Rebel infantry came in that way, down the narrow gray road from the mountain gap. At noon they were in sight of the town. It was a small neat place: white board houses, rail fences, all in order, one white church steeple. The soldiers coming over the last ridge by the Lutheran Seminary could see across the town to the hills beyond and a winding gray road coming up from the south, and as the first gray troops entered the town there was motion on that southern road: a blur, blue movement, blue cavalry. They came on slowly around the last bend, a long blue smoking snake, spiked with guns and flags. The soldiers looked at each other across vacant fields. The day was very hot; the sky was a steamy haze. Someone lifted a gun and fired, but the range was too long. The streets of Gettysburg were deserted.

Just beyond the town there were two hills. One was wooded and green; the other was flat, topped by a cemetery. The Union commander, a tall blond sunburned man named John Buford, rode up the long slope to the top of the hill, into the cemetery. He stopped by a stone wall, looked down across flat open ground, lovely clear field of fire. He could see all the way across the town and the ridges to the blue mountains beyond, a darkening sky. On the far side of the town there was a red brick building, the stately Seminary, topped with a white cupola. The road by the building was jammed with Rebel troops. Buford counted half a dozen flags. He had thought it was only a raiding party. Now he sensed power behind it, a road flowing with troops all the way back to the mountains.

The first blue brigade had stopped on the road below, by a red barn. The commander of that brigade, Bill Gamble, came up the hill on a muddy horse, trailed by a small cloud of aides, gazed westward with watery eyes. He wheezed, wiping his nose.

"By God, that's infantry."

Buford put the glasses to his eyes. He saw one man on a black horse, waving a plumed hat: an officer. The Rebel troops had stopped. Buford looked around, searching for other movement. He saw a squad of blue troopers, his own men, riding down into deserted streets. Still no sound of gunfire.

Gamble said, "That's one whole brigade. At least one brigade."

"Do you see any cavalry?"

Gamble swept the horizon, shook his head.

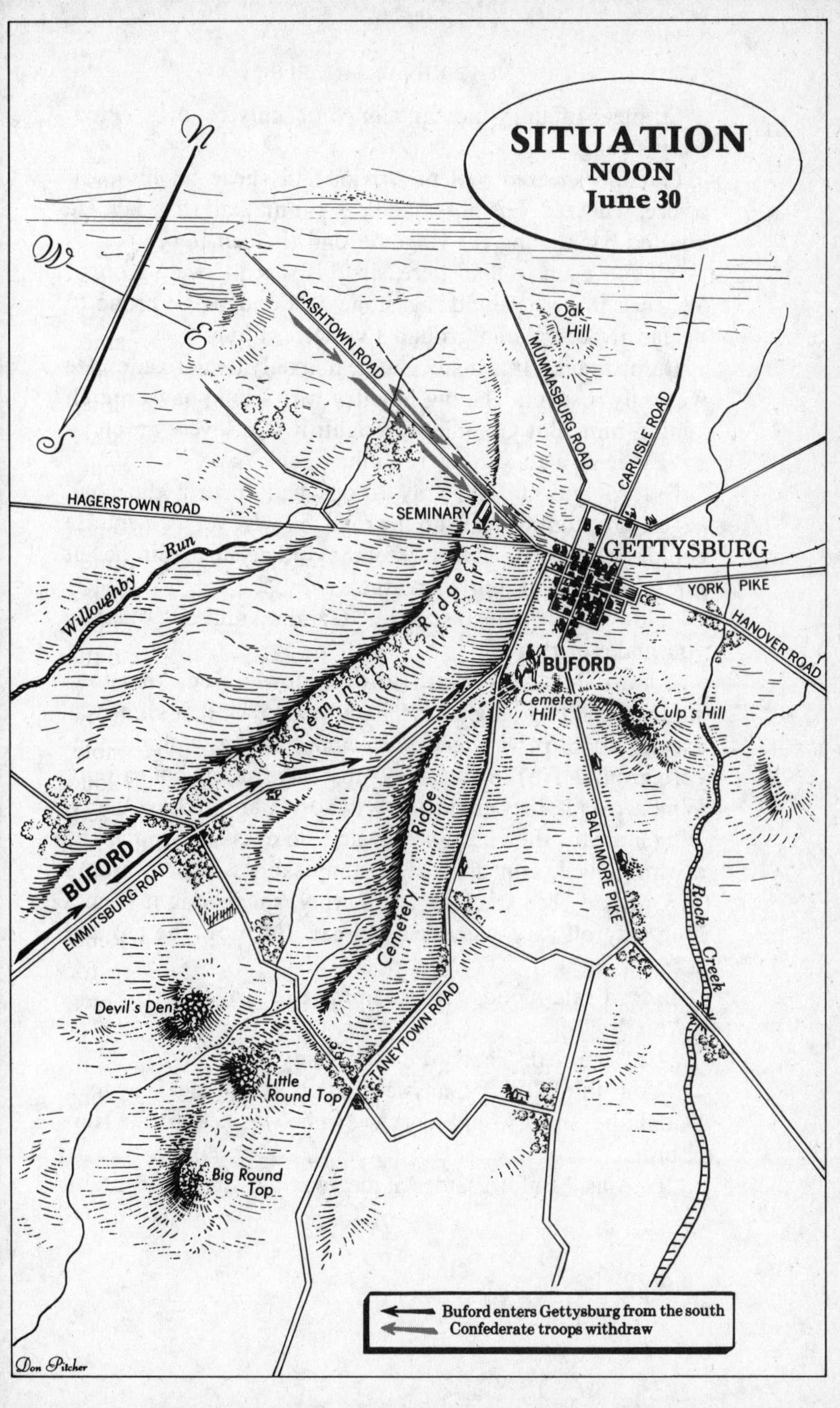

SITUATION
NOON
June 30
N
W
E
S
CASHTOWN ROAD
Oak Hill
MUMMASBURG ROAD
CARLISLE ROAD
HAGERSTOWN ROAD
SEMINARY
GETTYSBURG
YORK PIKE
HANOVER ROAD
Willoughby Run
Seminary Ridge
BUFORD
Cemetery Hill
Culp's Hill
BUFORD
EMMITSBURG ROAD
Cemetery Ridge
BALTIMORE PIKE
Rock Creek
TANEYTOWN ROAD
Devil's Den
Little Round Top
Big Round Top
Buford enters Gettysburg from the south
Confederate troops withdraw
Don Pitcher

Strange. Infantry moving alone in enemy country. Blind. Very strange.

Gamble sneezed violently, wiped his nose on his coat, swore, wheezed. His nose had been running all that day. He pointed back along the ridge beyond the cemetery.

"If you want to fight here, sir, this sure is lovely ground. We tuck in here behind this stone wall and I'd be proud to defend it. Best damn ground I've seen all day."

Buford said, "It is that." But he had only two brigades. He was only a scout. The big infantry was a long day's march behind him. But Gamble was right: it was lovely ground.

"By God, I think they're pulling back."

Buford looked. The gray troops had turned; they had begun to withdraw back up the road. Slowly, very slowly. He could see back-turned faces, feel the cold defiance. But he felt himself loosen, begin to breathe.

"Now that's damned strange." Gamble sniffled. "What do you make of that?"

Buford shook his head. He rode slowly along the stone wall, suspending judgment. There was no wind at all; it was exactly noon. It was very quiet among the gravestones. Superb ground. He thought: they must have orders not to fight. Which means they don't know who we are or how many. Which means they have no cavalry, no eyes. He stopped by a white angel, arm uplifted, a stony sadness. For five days Buford had been tracking Lee's army, shadowing it from a long way off as you track a big cat. But now the cat had turned.

Buford said aloud, "He's coming this way."

"Sir?"

"Lee's turned. That's the main body."

"You think so?" Gamble mused, wriggling his nose. "Could be. But I would have sworn he was headed for Harrisburg."

"He was," Buford said. An idea was blowing in his brain.

But there was time to think, time to breathe, and he was a patient man. He sat watching the Rebs withdraw, then he said, "Move your brigades into town. That will make the good citizens happy. I'm going to go have a look."

He hopped the stone wall, rode down the long slope. He owed a message to Reynolds, back with the infantry, but that could wait until he was sure. He was old army cavalry, Kentucky-born, raised in the Indian wars; he was slow, he was careful, but he sensed something happening, a breathless something in his chest. He rode down through the town and out the road the Rebs had taken. There was no one in the streets, not even dogs, but he saw white faces at windows, a fluttering of curtains. There were no cows anywhere, or chickens, or horses. Reb raiding parties had peeled the land. He rode up toward the brick building with the cupola and topped a crest. Off in the distance there was another rise; he could see the Reb column withdrawing into a blue west. He saw the lone officer, much closer now, sitting regally on horseback, outlined against a darkening sky. The man was looking his way, with glasses. Buford waved. You never knew what old friend was out there. The Reb officer took off his hat, bowed formally. Buford grimaced: a gentleman. A soldier fired at very long range. Buford saw his staff people duck, but he did not hear the bullet. He thought: they'll be back in the morning. Lee's concentrating this way. Only one road down through the mountains; have to come this way. They will all converge here. In the morning.

He turned in his stirrups, looked back at the high ground, the cemetery. The hills rose like watchtowers. All that morning he had seen nothing but flat ground. When the Rebs came in, in the morning, they would move onto those hills. And Reynolds would not be here in time.

Gamble rode up, saluting. Tom Devin, the other brigade commander, arrived with a cheery grin. Gamble was sober sane; Devin was more the barroom type.

Buford walked the horse back and forth along the rise. He said aloud, "I wonder where their cavalry is."

Devin laughed. "The way old Stuart gets around, he could be having dinner in Philadelphia."

Buford was not listening. He said abruptly, "Get your patrols out. Scout this bunch in front of us, but scout up north. They'll be coming in that way, from Carlisle. We've got a bit of light yet. I want to know before sundown. I think Lee's turned. He's coming this way. If I'm right there'll be a lot of troops up the northern road too. Hop to it."

They moved. Buford wrote a message to John Reynolds, back with the lead infantry:

> *Have occupied Gettysburg. Contacted large party of Reb infantry. I think they are coming this way. Expect they will be here in force in the morning.*

The word would go from Reynolds to Meade. With any luck at all Meade would read it before midnight. From there it would go by wire to Washington. But some of Stuart's cavalry had cut the wires and they might not be patched yet, so Washington would be in the dark and screaming its head off. God, that miserable Halleck. Buford took a deep breath. The great joy of the cavalry was to be so far away, out in the clean air, the open spaces, away from those damned councils. There were some moments, like now, when he felt no superior presence at all. Buford shook his head. He had been badly wounded in the winter, and possibly as you got older you had less patience instead of more. But he felt the beautiful absence of a commander, a silence above him, a windy freedom.

The last Reb infantry walked away over the last rise. The Reb officer stood alone for a moment, then waved again and withdrew. The ridge was bare.

Buford sniffed: distant rain. The land around him was hot and dry and the dust of the horses was blowing steadily up

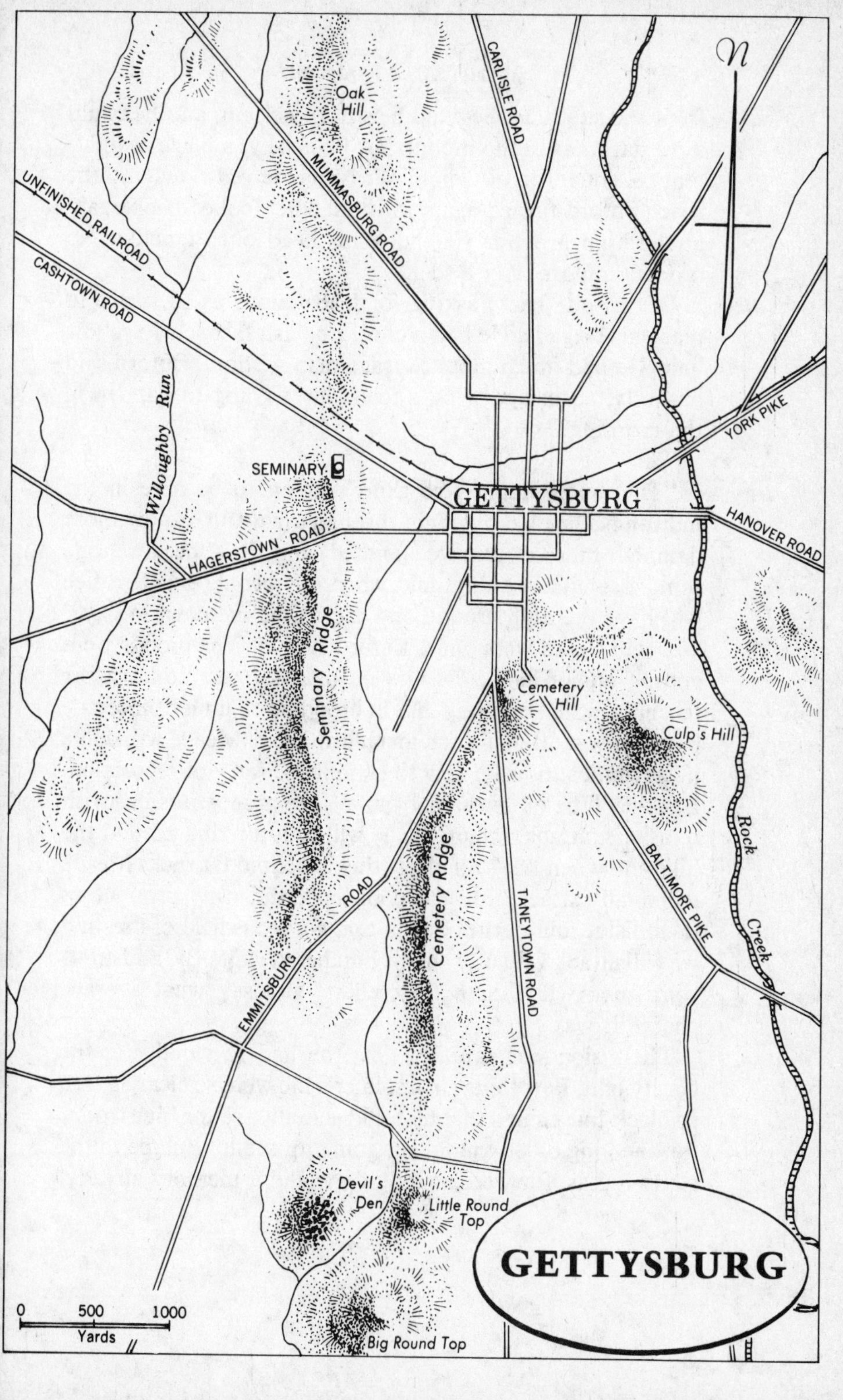

GETTYSBURG
Oak Hill
CARLISLE ROAD
MUMMASBURG ROAD
UNFINISHED RAILROAD
CASHTOWN ROAD
Willoughby Run
SEMINARY
GETTYSBURG
YORK PIKE
HANOVER ROAD
HAGERSTOWN ROAD
Seminary Ridge
Cemetery Hill
Culp's Hill
Cemetery Ridge
TANEYTOWN ROAD
BALTIMORE PIKE
Rock Creek
EMMITSBURG ROAD
Devil's Den
Little Round Top
Big Round Top
0
500
1000
Yards

from the south as the wind began to pick up, and he could see a darkness in the mountains, black sky, a blaze of lightning. A squadron of Gamble's cavalry moved slowly up the road. Buford turned again in the saddle, looked back again at the high ground. He shook his head once quickly. No orders: you are only a scout.

Devin rode back, asking for instructions as to where to place his brigade. He had a cheery boyish face, curly yellow hair. He had much more courage than wisdom. Buford said abruptly, accusing, "You know what's going to happen in the morning?"

"Sir?"

"The whole damn Reb army's going to be here in the morning. They'll move right through town and occupy those damned hills—" Buford pointed angrily—"because one thing Lee aint is a fool, and when our people get here Lee will have the high ground and there'll be the devil to pay."

Devin's eyes were wide. Buford turned. The moods were getting out of hand. He was no man for war councils, or teaching either, and no sense in brooding to junior officers—but he saw it all with such metal brilliance: Meade will come in slowly, cautiously, new to command, wary of reputation. But they'll be on his back from Washington, wires hot with messages: attack, attack. So he will set up a ring around the hills and when Lee's all nicely dug in behind fat rocks Meade will finally attack, if he can coordinate the army, straight up the hillside, out in the open in that gorgeous field of fire, and we will attack valiantly and be butchered valiantly, and afterward men will thump their chests and say what a brave charge it was.

The vision was brutally clear: he had to wonder at the clarity of it. Few things in a soldier's life were so clear as this, so black-line etched that he could actually see the blue troops for one long bloody moment, going up the long slope to the stony top as if it were already done and a memory already, an odd, set, stony quality to it, as if tomorrow had occurred and there was nothing you could do about it, the way you sometimes feel before a foolish attack, knowing it will fail but you cannot stop it or even run away but must even take part and help it fail. But never this clearly. There was always some hope. Never this detail. But if we withdraw—there is no good ground south of here. *This* is the place to fight.

Devin was watching him warily. Buford was an odd man. When he rode off there by himself he liked to talk to himself and you could see his lips moving. He had been too long out in the plains.

He looked at Devin, finally saw him. He said abruptly, "No orders yet. Tell your men to dismount and eat. Rest. Get some rest."

He rode slowly away to inspect the ground in front of him, between him and the Rebels. If we made a stand here, how long do you think we could hold? Long enough for John Reynolds to get here with the infantry? How long would that take? Will Reynolds hurry? Reynolds is a good man. But he might not understand the situation. How do you make him understand? At this distance. But if you hold, you at least give him time to see the ground. But how long can you hold against Lee's whole army? If it is the whole army. These are two very good brigades; you built them yourself. Suppose you sacrifice them and Reynolds is late? For Reynolds will be late. They're always late.

Think on it, John.

There's time, there's time.

The land was long ridges, with streams down in the dark hollows. Dismounted, along a ridge, with all night to dig in, the boys could hold for a while. Good boys. Buford had taught them to fight dismounted, the way they did out west, and the hell with this Stuart business, this glorious Murat charge. Try that against an Indian, that glorious charge, sabers a-shining, and he'd drop behind a rock or a stump and shoot your glorious head off as you went by. No, Buford had reformed his boys. He had thrown away the silly sabers and the damned dragoon pistols and given them the new repeating carbines, and though there were only 2,500 of them they could dig in behind a fence and hold *anybody* for a while.

But could they hold long enough?

Wherever he rode he could look back at the hills, dominant as castles. He was becoming steadily more nervous. Easy enough to pull out: the job is done. But he was a professional. Damned few of them in this army. And he would not live forever.

Rain clouds blotted the western sun. The blue mountains were gone. Gamble's first scouts rode back to report that the Rebs had gone into camp just down the road, about three miles out of Gettysburg. Buford rode out far enough to see the pickets for himself, then he rode back toward the green hills. He stopped by the Seminary and had a cup of coffee. The staff left him alone. After that he deployed the brigades.

He had made no plans, but it didn't hurt to prepare. He told Gamble to dismount and dig in along the crest of the ridge just past the Seminary, facing the Rebs who would come down that road. He posted Devin in the same way, across the road from the north. Three men in line, every fourth man to fall back with the horses. He watched to see that it was done. They were weary men and they dug in silently and there was no music. He heard an officer grumbling. The damned fool wanted to charge the Reb picket line. Buford let loose a black glare. But it was a good line. It would hold for a while, even old Bobby Lee. If John Reynolds got up early in the morning.

It was darker now, still very quiet. No need to make the decision yet. They could always pull out at the last minute. He grinned to himself, and the staff noticed his face and relaxed momentarily. Buford thought: one good thing about cavalry, you can always leave in a hell of a hurry.

Buford turned and rode back through the town, anxious for news from his scouts. People were moving in the streets. He collected a small following of happy boys, one small ragged girl with a beautiful, delicate face. He smiled down, but in the square ahead he saw a crowd, a speaker, a circle of portly men. He turned quickly away. He was no good with civilians. There was something about the mayors of towns that troubled him. They were too fat and they talked too much and they did not think twice of asking a man to die for them. Much of the east troubled Buford. A fat country. Too many people talked too much. The newspapers lied. But the women . . . Yes, the women.

He rode by one porch and there was a woman in a dress of rose, white lace at the throat, a tall blond woman with a face of soft beauty, so lovely that Buford slowed the horse, staring, before taking off his hat. She stood by a vined column, gazing at him; she smiled. There was an old man in the front yard, very old and thin and weak; he hobbled forward, glaring with feeble, toothless rage. "They's Johnny Rebs eva-where, eva-where!" Buford bowed and moved on, turned to look back at the beautiful woman, who stood there watching him.

"Go back and say hello, General."

A coaxing voice, a grinning tone: lean Sergeant Corse, a bowlegged aide. Buford smiled, shook his head.

"Widow woman, I betcha."

Buford turned away, headed toward the cemetery.

"If ye'd like me to ride back, General, I'm sure an interduction could be arranged."

Buford chuckled. "Not tonight, Sergeant."

"The General could use a di-version. Beggin' yer pardon, General. But ye'r too shy a lad, for yer age. Ye work too hard. These here now quiet towns, now, nothin' ever happens here, and the ladies would be so delighted to see you, an important adventurous man such as you, who has seen the world, now, ye'd be doin' 'em a gracious favor, just wi' yer presence."

Buford smiled. "I'm about as shy as a howitzer."

"And similarly graceful. Begging yer pardon."

"Zackly." Buford began the slow ride up the hill to the cemetery.

"Ah," the Sergeant said sadly, "but she was a lovely lass."

"She was that."

The Sergeant brightened. "Well, then if the General does not mind, I may just ride on over there meself, later on, after supper, that is, if the General has no objections." He pushed the glasses back up on his nose, straightened his hat, tucked in his collar.

Buford said, "No objections, Sergeant."

"Ah. Um."

Buford looked.

"And, ah, what time would the General be having supper, now?"

Buford looked at the staff, saw bright hopeful eyes. The hint finally got to him. They could not eat until he had eaten. They trailed him wherever he went, like a pennant; he was so used to their presence he did not notice their hunger. He was rarely hungry himself these days.

The Sergeant said woefully, "The folks in this here town been after us for food. The Rebs didn't leave them much. The General ought to eat what we got while we got it, because the boys is givin' it away." He glared reproachfully at the other officers.

"Sorry," Buford said. He pointed to the cemetery. "I'll eat right here. A little dried beef. You gentlemen have some supper."

They rode on into the cemetery. He dismounted at last, first time in hours, sat down on stone in silent pain. He thought: body not much good but the mind works well. Two young lieutenants sat down near him, chewing on corn dodgers. He squinted; he did not remember their names. He could remember if he had to, duty of a good officer; he could fish in the memory for the names and pull them up out of the darkness, after a while, but though he was kind to young lieutenants he had learned a long time ago it was not wise to get to know them. One of these had wispy yellow hair, red freckles, he had a strange resemblance to an ear of corn. The other was buck-toothed. Buford suddenly remembered: the buck-toothed boy is a college boy, very bright, very well educated. Buford nodded. The Lieutenants nodded. They thought he was a genius. He had thrown away the book of cavalry doctrine and they loved him for it. At Thorofare Gap he had held against Longstreet, 3,000 men against 25,000, for six hours, sending off appeal after appeal for help which never came. The Lieutenants admired him greatly, and he could sometimes overhear them quoting his discoveries: *your great fat horse is transportation, that's all he is, with no more place on a modern battlefield than a great fat elephant.* He turned from eager eyes, remembering the cries for help that never came. That time it was General Pope. Now it was General Meade. Make no plans.

He sat watching the lights come on in Gettysburg. The soldiers bordered the town along the west and the north in two long fire-speckled fences—a lovely sight in the gathering dusk. The last light of June burned in the west. He had one marvelous smoke—a dreamy cigar. Tomorrow he will come, old Bob Lee himself, down that western road, on a gray horse. And with him will come about seventy thousand men.

One of the Lieutenants was reading a newspaper. Buford saw rippled black headlines: CITIZENS OF PENNSYLVANIA: PREPARE TO DEFEND YOUR HOMES! A call for militia. He smiled. Militia would not stop old Bobby Lee. We have good old George Meade.

Now now. Have faith. He might be very good.

The hell he is.

Buford peered quickly around, not knowing if he had said that out loud. Damned bad habit. But the Lieutenants were chatting. Buford looked past them to the silent town. Pretty country. But too neat, too tidy. No feel of space, of size, a great starry roof overhead, a great wind blowing. Well. You are not a natural Easterner, that's for sure. Extraordinary to think of war here. Not the country for it. Too neat. Not enough room. He saw again the white angel. He thought: damn good ground.

He sat on a rail fence, watching the night come over Gettysburg. There was no word from the patrols. He went around reading the gravestones, many Dutch names, ghostly sentinels, tipped his hat in respect, thought of his own death, tested his body, still sound, still trustable through a long night, but weaker, noticeably weaker, the heart uneven, the breath failing. But there was at least one good fight left. Perhaps I'll make it here. His mind wandered. He wondered what it would be like to lose the war. Could you ever travel in the South again? Probably not for a while. But they had great fishing there. Black bass rising in flat black water: *ah.* Shame to go there again, to foreign ground. Strange sense of enormous loss. Buford did not hate. He was a professional. The only ones who even irritated him were the cavaliers, the high-bred, feathery, courtly ones who spoke like Englishmen and treated a man like dirt. But they were mostly damn fools, not men enough to hate. But it would be a great shame if you could never go south any more, for the fishing, for the warmth in winter. Thought once of retiring there. If I get that old.

Out of the dark: Devin.

"Sir, the scouts are in. You were right, sir. Lee's coming this way all right."

Buford focused. "What have you got?"

"Those troops we ran into today were A. P. Hill. His whole Corps is back up the road between here and Cashtown. Longstreet's Corps is right behind him. Ewell's Corps is coming down from the north. They were right in front of Harrisburg but they've turned back. They're concentrating in this direction."

Buford nodded. He said absently, "Lee's trying to get around us, get between us and Washington. And won't that charm the Senate?"

He sat down to write the message to Reynolds, on a gravestone, by lantern light. His hand stopped of itself. His brain sent nothing. He sat motionless, pencil poised, staring at blank paper.

He had held good ground before and sent off appeals, and help never came. He was very low on faith. It was a kind of gray sickness; it weakened the hands. He stood up and walked to the stone fence. It wasn't the dying. He had seen men die all his life, and death was the luck of the chance, the price you eventually paid. What was worse was the stupidity. The appalling sick stupidity that was so bad you thought sometimes you would go suddenly, violently, completely insane just having to watch it. It was a deadly thing to be thinking on. Job to be done here. And all of it turns on faith.

The faces were staring at him, all the bright apple faces. He shuddered with vague anger. If Reynolds says he will come, Reynolds will come. An honorable man. I hope to God. Buford was angry, violently angry. But he sat down and wrote the message.

He was in possession of good ground at Gettysburg. If Reynolds came quick, first thing in the morning, Buford could hold it. If not, the Rebs would take it and there was no ground near that was any good. Buford did not know how long his two brigades could hold. Urgent reply.

It was too formal. He struggled to make it clear. He stared at it for a long while and then sealed it slowly, thinking, well, we aren't truly committed, we can still run, and gave the message to the buck-toothed lieutenant, who took it delightedly off into the night, although he'd been in the saddle all that day.

Buford felt the pain of old wounds, a sudden vast need for sleep. Now it was up to Reynolds. He said to Devin, "How many guns have we got?"

"Sir? Ah, we have, ah, one battery, sir, is all. Six guns. Calef's Battery, that is, sir."

"Post them out along that west road. The Cashtown road."

Buford tried to think of something else to do but it was all suspended again, a breezy vacancy. Rest until Reynolds sends the word. He sat down once more, back against a gravestone, and began to drift slowly away, turning his mind away as you shift a field of vision with your glasses, moving to focus on higher ground. He remembered a snowstorm. Young lieutenant delivering military mail: days alone across an enormous white plain. Lovely to remember: riding, delivering mail. He dreamed. The wound began to hurt. He woke to the Sergeant, bowlegged Corse: the man dragged drearily by on a spattered horse, raised disgusted eyes.

"The husband, by God, is an *undertaker.*"

He rode mournfully off. The sound of music began to drift up the hill from Gettysburg. A preacher from the Seminary began a low, insistent, theological argument with a young lieutenant, back and forth, back and forth, the staff listening with admiration at the lovely words. The staff began to bed down for the night. It was near midnight when the buck-toothed boy came back from Reynolds, panting down from a lathered horse. Buford read: *General Buford: Hold your ground. I will come in the morning as early as possible. John Reynolds.*

Buford nodded. All right. If you say so. The officers were up and gathering. Buford said to the buck-toothed boy, "Did he say anything else?"

"No, sir. He was very busy."

"How far back is he?"

"Not ten miles, sir, I don't think."

"Well," Buford said. He faced the staff: the eager, the wary. "We're going to hold here in the morning." He paused, still fuzzy-brained. "We'll try to hold long enough for General Reynolds to come up with some infantry. I want to save the high ground, if we can."

There was a breathy silence, some toothy grins, as if he had announced a party.

"I think they'll be attacking us at dawn. We ought to be able to stop them for a couple of hours."

At Thorofare Gap we held for six. But that was better ground.

Devin was glowing. "Hell, General, we can hold them all the long damned day, as the feller says."

Buford frowned. He said slowly, "I don't know how long will be necessary. It may be a long time. We can force them to deploy, anyway, and that will take up time. Also, that's a narrow road Lee's coming down, and if we stack them up back there they'll be a while getting untracked. But the point is to hold long enough for the infantry. If we hang onto these hills, we have a good chance to win the fight that's coming. Understood?"

He had excited them. They were young enough to be eager for this. He felt a certain breathless quality himself. He ordered a good feed for the night, no point now in saving food. They moved out to give their orders. Buford rode out once more, in the dark, to the picket line.

He posted the lead pickets himself, not far from the Rebel line. There were four men along the bridge: New York and Illinois, two of them very young. They were popeyed to be so near the Rebs. Closer than anybody in the whole dang army.

Buford said, "They should come in just at about first light. Keep a clear eye. Stay in there long enough to get a good look, then shoot and run. Give us a good warning, but fire only a few rounds. Don't wait too long before you pull out."

A corporal said stiffly, "Yes, sir, General, sir." He broke into a giggle. Buford heard a boy say, "*Now* aint you glad you jined the calvry?"

Buford rode back to the Seminary. He made his headquarters there. In the morning he would have a good view from the cupola. He dismounted and sat down to rest. It was very quiet. He closed his eyes and he could see fields of snow, miles and miles of Wyoming snow, and white mountains in the distance, all clean and incredibly still, and no man anywhere and no motion.

---

4. Longstreet

In Longstreet's camp, they were teaching the Englishman to play poker. They had spread a blanket near a fire and hung a lantern on a tree and they sat around the blanket slapping bugs in the dark, surrounded by campfires, laughter and music. The Englishman was a naturally funny man. He was very thin and perpetually astonished and somewhat gap-toothed, and his manner of talking alone was enough to convulse them, and he enjoyed it. His name was Fremantle—Lieutenant Colonel Arthur Lyon Fremantle—late of Her Majesty's Coldstream Guards, observing for the Queen. There were several other foreigners in the group and they followed Longstreet's headquarters like a small shoal of colorful fish. They were gathered around the blanket now, watching Fremantle perform, and everyone was laughing except the Prussian, Scheiber, a stocky man in a stained white suit, who was annoyed that no one could speak German.

Longstreet sat with his back against a tree, waiting. His fame as a poker player was legendary but he had not played in a long time, not since the deaths of his children, and he did not feel like it now; but he liked to sit in the darkness and watch, passing the time silently, a small distance away, a member of it all warmed by the fire but still not involved in it, not having to talk.

What bothered him most was the blindness. Jeb Stuart had not returned. The army had moved all day in enemy country and they had not even known what was around the next bend. Harrison's news was growing old: the Union Army was on the move. Longstreet had sent the spy back into Gettysburg to see what he could find, but Gettysburg was almost thirty miles away and he had not yet returned. Longstreet dreamed, storing up energy, knowing the fight was coming and resting deliberately, relaxing the muscles, feeling himself loose upon the earth and filling with strength slowly, as the lungs fill with clean air. He was a patient man; he could outwait the dawn. He saw a star fall: a pale cold spark in the eastern sky. Lovely sight. He remembered, counting stars at midnight in a pasture: a girl. The girl thought they were messages from God. Longstreet grinned: she loves me, she loves me not.

"Sir?"

He looked up—a slender, haughty face: G. Moxley Sorrel, Longstreet's chief of staff. Longstreet said, "Major."

"I'm just back from General Lee's headquarters, sir. The General has retired for the night. Everything going nicely, sir. General Lee says we should all be concentrated around Gettysburg tomorrow evening."

"Nothing from Stuart?"

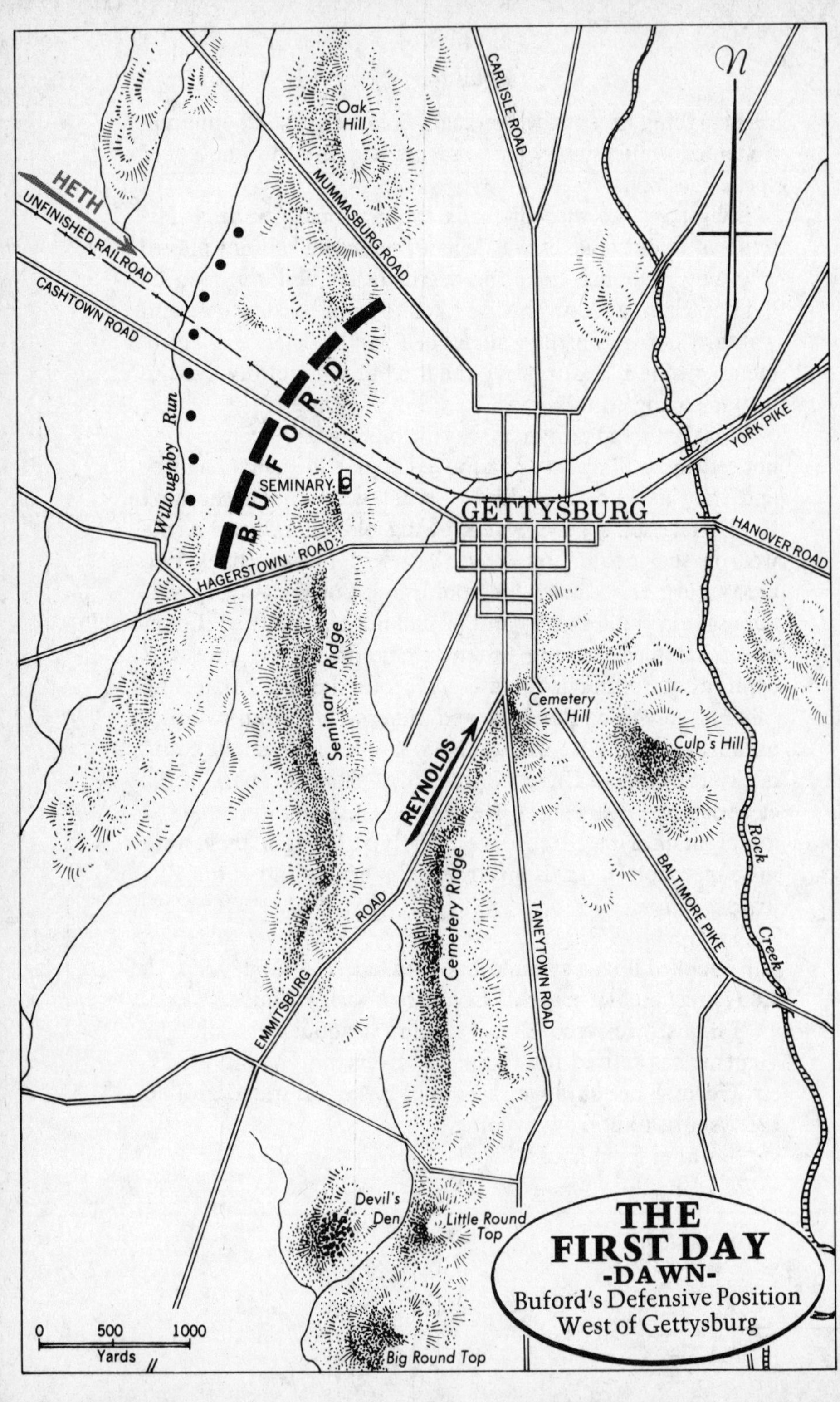
THE FIRST DAY
-DAWN-
Buford's Defensive Position
West of Gettysburg
GETTYSBURG
HETH
UNFINISHED RAILROAD
CASHTOWN ROAD
BUFORD
REYNOLDS
Oak Hill
MUMMASBURG ROAD
CARLISLE ROAD
YORK PIKE
HANOVER ROAD
SEMINARY
Willoughby Run
HAGERSTOWN ROAD
Seminary Ridge
Cemetery Hill
Culp's Hill
Cemetery Ridge
EMMITSBURG ROAD
TANEYTOWN ROAD
BALTIMORE PIKE
Rock Creek
Devil's Den
Little Round Top
Big Round Top
0 500 1000
Yards

"No, sir. But some of General Hill's troops went into Gettysburg this afternoon and claim they saw Union cavalry there."

Longstreet looked up sharply. Sorrel went on: "They had orders not to engage, so they withdrew. General Hill thinks they were mistaken. He says it must be militia. He's going back in force in the morning."

"Who saw cavalry? What officer?"

"Ah, Johnston Pettigrew, I believe, sir."

"The scholar? Fella from North Carolina?"

"Ah, yes, sir. I think so, sir."

"*Blue* cavalry?"

"Yes, sir."

"Why doesn't Hill believe him? Does Hill have other information?"

"No, sir. Ah, I would say, sir, judging from what I heard, that General Hill thinks that, ah, Pettigrew is not a professional and tends to be overexcited and perhaps to exaggerate a bit."

"Um." Longstreet rubbed his face. If there was infantry coming, as Harrison had said, there would be cavalry in front of it.

"What does General Lee say?"

"The General, ah, defers to General Hill's judgment, I believe."

Longstreet grimaced. He thought: we have other cavalry. Why doesn't the old man send for a look? Tell you why: he can't believe Stuart would let him down.

"Have you any orders, sir?" Sorrel was gazing longingly toward the poker game.

"No."

"The men are anxious to have you join the game, sir. As you once did."

"Not tonight, Major."

Sorrel bowed. "Yes, sir. Oh, by the way, sir, General

Pickett sends his compliments and states that he will be dropping by later this evening for a chat."

Longstreet nodded. There'll be a complaint from old George. But good to see him. Sorrel moved off into a burst of laughter, a cloud of lovely tobacco. Longstreet sat brooding.

There was an odor of trouble, an indefinable wrong. It was like playing chess and making a bad move and not knowing why but knowing instinctively that it was a bad move. The instincts were yelling. As they used to do long ago at night in Indian country. He gazed out into the black. The stars were obscured. It was the blindness that bothered him. Cavalry in Gettysburg? Harrison would know.

"Sir?"

He looked up again. In soft light: Fremantle.

"Beg your pardon, sir. Most humbly, sir. I'm not disturbing you?"

"Um," Longstreet said. But there was something about the man, prepared for flight, that made Longstreet grin. He was a scrawny man, toothy, with a pipelike neck and a monstrous Adam's apple. He looked like a popeyed bird who had just swallowed something large and sticky and triangular. He was wearing a tall gray hat and a remarkable coat with very wide shoulders, like wings.

He said cheerily, "If I am disturbing you at all, sir, my most humble apologies. But your fame, sir, as a practitioner of poker, is such that one comes to you for advice. I hope you don't mind."

"Not 't'all," Longstreet said. Sometimes when you were around Englishmen there was this ridiculous tendency to imitate them. Longstreet restrained himself. But he grinned.

"What I wanted to ask you, sir, is this. I gather that you are the authority in these matters, and I learned long ago, sir, that in affairs of this kind it is always wisest to go directly, *straightway,* may I say, to the top."

Longstreet waited. Fremantle relaxed slightly, conspiratorially, stroked a handlebar mustache.

"I am most curious, General, as to your attitude toward a subtle subject: the inside straight. On what occasion, or rather, under what circumstance, does one draw to an inside straight? In your opinion. Your response will be kept confidential, of course."

"Never." Longstreet said.

Fremantle nodded gravely, listening. There was nothing else. After a moment he inquired, "Never?"

"Never."

Fremantle thought upon it. "You mean *never,*" he concluded.

Longstreet nodded.

"Quite," Fremantle said. He drew back, brooding, then drew himself up. "Indeed," he said. "Well, thank you, sir. Your most humble servant. My apologies for the disturbance."

"Not 't'all."

"I leave you to more important things." He bowed, backed off, paused, looked up. "Never?" he said wistfully.

"Never," Longstreet said.

"Oh. Well, right-ho." Fremantle went away.

Longstreet turned to the dark. A strange and lacey race. Talk like ladies, fight like wildcats. There had long been talk of England coming in on the side of the South. But Longstreet did not think they would come. They will come when we don't need them, like the bank offering money when you're no longer in debt.

A cluster of yells: he looked up. A group of horsemen were riding into camp. One plumed rider waved a feathered hat: that would be George Pickett. At a distance he looked like a French king, all curls and feathers. Longstreet grinned unconsciously. Pickett rode into the firelight, bronze-curled and lovely, hair down to his shoulders, regal and gorgeous on a stately mount. He gestured to the staff, someone pointed toward Longstreet. Pickett rode this way, bowing. Men were grinning, lighting up as he passed; Longstreet could see a train of officers behind him. He had brought along all three of his brigade commanders: Armistead, Garnett and Kemper. They rode toward Longstreet like ships through a gleeful surf, Pickett bowing from side to side. Someone offered a bottle. Pickett raised a scornful hand. He had sworn to dear Sallie ne'er to touch liquor. Longstreet shook his head admiringly. The foreigners were clustering.

Pickett stopped before Longstreet and saluted grandly. "General Pickett presents his compliments, sir, and requests permission to parley with the Commanding General, *s'il vous plaît.*"

Longstreet said, "Howdy, George."

Beyond Pickett's shoulder Lew Armistead grinned hello, touching his hat. Longstreet had known them all for twenty years and more. They had served together in the Mexican War and in the old 6th Infantry out in California. They had been under fire together, and as long as he lived Longstreet would never forget the sight of Pickett with the flag going over the wall in the smoke and flame of Chapultepec. Pickett had not aged a moment since. Longstreet thought: my permanent boy. It was more a family than an army. But the formalities had to be observed. He saluted. Pickett hopped out of the saddle, ringlets aflutter as he jumped. Longstreet whiffed a pungent odor.

"Good Lord, George, what's that smell?"

"That's me," Pickett said proudly. "Aint it lovely?"

Armistead dismounted, chuckling. "He got it off a dead Frenchman. Evening, Pete."

"Woo," Longstreet said. "I bet the Frenchman smelled better."

Pickett was offended. "I did not either get it off a Frenchman. I bought it in a store in Richmond." He meditated.

"Did have a French name, now that I think on it. But *Sallie* likes it." This concluded the matter. Pickett glowed and primped, grinning. He was used to kidding and fond of it. Dick Garnett was dismounting slowly. Longstreet caught the look of pain in his eyes. He was favoring a leg. He had that same soft gray look in his face, his eyes. Too tired, much too tired.

Longstreet extended a hand. "How are you, Dick?"

"Fine, General, just fine." But the handclasp had no vitality. Lew Armistead was watching with care.

Longstreet said easily, "Sorry I had to assign you to old smelly George. Hope you have a strong stomach."

"General," Garnett said formally gracefully, "you must know how much I appreciate the opportunity."

There was a second of silence. Garnett had withdrawn the old Stonewall Brigade without orders. Jackson had accused him of cowardice. Now Jackson was dead, and Garnett's honor was compromised, and he had not recovered from the stain, and in this company there were many men who would never let him recover. Yet Longstreet knew the quality of the man, and he said slowly, carefully, "Dick, I consider it a damned fine piece of luck for me when you became available for this command."

Garnett took a deep breath, then nodded once quickly, looking past Longstreet into the dark. Lew Armistead draped a casual arm across his shoulders.

"Dick's been eating too many cherries. He's got the Old Soldier's Disease."

Garnett smiled weakly. "Sure do." He rubbed his stomach. "Got to learn to fight from the squatting position."

Armistead grinned. "I know what's wrong with you. You been standing downwind of ole George. You got to learn to watch them fumes."

A circle had gathered at a respectful distance. One of these was Fremantle, of Her Majesty's Coldstream Guards, widehatted, Adam's-appled. Pickett was regarding him with curiosity.

Longstreet remembered his manners. "Oh, excuse me, Colonel. Allow me to present our George Pickett. Our loveliest general. General Pickett, Colonel Fremantle of the Coldstream Guards."

Pickett bowed low in the classic fashion, sweeping the ground with the plumed hat.

"The fame of your regiment, sir, has preceded you."

"General Pickett is our ranking strategist," Longstreet said. "We refer all the deeper questions to George."

"They do," Pickett admitted, nodding. "They do indeed."

"General Pickett's record at West Point is still the talk of the army."

Armistead hawed.

"It is unbecoming to a soldier, all this book-learning," Pickett said haughtily.

"It aint *gentlemanly,* George," Armistead corrected.

"Nor that either," Pickett agreed.

"He finished last in his class," Longstreet explained. "Dead last. Which is quite a feat, if you consider his classmates."

"The Yankees got all the smart ones," Pickett said placidly, "and look where it got them."

Fremantle stood grinning vaguely, not quite sure how to take all this. Lew Armistead came forward and bowed slightly, delicately, old courtly Lo, giving it a touch of elegance. He did not extend a hand, knowing the British custom. He said, "Good evening, Colonel. Lo Armistead. The 'Lo' is short for Lothario. Let me welcome you to 'Lee's Miserables.' The Coldstream Guards? Weren't you fellas over here in the discussion betwixt us of 1812? I seem to remember my daddy telling me about . . . No, it was the Black Watch. The kilted fellas, that's who it was."

Fremantle said, "Lee's Miserables?"

"A joke," Longstreet said patiently. "Somebody read Victor Hugo—believe it or not I have officers who read—and ever since then we've been Lee's Miserables."

Fremantle was still in the dark. Longstreet said, "Victor Hugo. French writer. Novel. *Les Miserables.*"

Fremantle brightened. Then he smiled. Then he chuckled. "Oh that's very good. Oh, I say that's very good indeed. Haw."

Pickett said formally, "Allow me to introduce my commanders. The elderly one here is Lewis Armistead. The 'Lothario' is a bit of a joke, as you can see. But we are democratic. We do not hold his great age against him. We carry him to the battle, and we aim him and turn him loose. His is what we in this country call an 'Old Family'—" Armistead said briefly, "Oh God"—"although doubtless you English would consider him still an immigrant. There have been Armisteads in all our wars, and maybe we better change the subject, because it is likely that old Lo's grandaddy took a potshot at your grandaddy, but anyway, we had to let him in this war to keep the string going, do you see? Age and all."

"Creak," Armistead said.

"The next one here is Dick Garnett. Ah, Richard Brooke Garnett."

Garnett bowed. Pickett said, "Old Dick is a good lad, but sickly. Ah well—" Pickett made a sad face—"some of us are born puny, and others are blessed with great natural strength. It is all God's will. Sit down, Dick. Now this next one here—" he indicated stoic Jim Kemper—"this one is not even a soldier, so watch him. Note the shifty beady eye? He's a politican. Only reason he's here is to gather votes come next election."

Kemper stepped forward, hand extended warily. He had been speaker of the Virginia House and he was not fond of foreigners. Fremantle took the hand with forced good will. Kemper said brusquely, "Look here now, Colonel. Been wondering when you people were going to get out and break that damned Yankee blockade. How about that?"

Fremantle apologized, grinning foolishly. Now the Prussian was here and the Austrian, Ross. A crowd was forming. Pickett went on to introduce some of his staff: Beau Harrison, his IG, and Jim Crocker. Crocker was moodily sentimental, already a bit drunk. He was returning now after an absence of thirteen years to his old alma mater, Pennsylvania College, in Gettysburg. Someone suggested they drink to that, but Pickett reminded one and all soulfully of his oath to Sallie, schoolgirl Sallie, who was half his age, and that brought up a round of ribald kidding that should have insulted Pickett but didn't. He glowed in the midst of it, hairy, happy. Fremantle looked on, never quite certain what was kidding and what wasn't. He produced some brandy; Armistead came up with a flask; Kemper had a bottle of his own. Longstreet thought: *careful.* He sat off to one side, withdrawing, had one long hot swig from Armistead's flask, disciplined himself not to take another, withdrew against the trunk of a cool tree, letting the night come over him, listening to them talk, reminiscing. He knew enough to stay out of it. The presence of the commander always a damper. But after a few moments Pickett detached himself from the group and came to Longstreet.

"General? A few words?"

"Sure, George. Fire."

"By George you're looking well, sir. Must say, never saw you looking better."

"You look lovely too, George." Longstreet liked this man. He was not overwhelmingly bright, but he was a fighter. Longstreet was always careful to give him exact instructions and to follow him to make sure he knew what to do, but once pointed, George could be relied on. A lovely adventurous boy, forty-two years old and never to grow older, fond of adventure and romance and all the bright sparkles of youth. Longstreet said happily, "What can I do for you, George?"

"Well, sir, now I don't mean this as a reflection upon *you,* sir. But, well, you know, sir, my Division, my Virginia boys, we weren't at Chancellorsville."

"No."

"Well, you know we were assigned away on some piddling affair, and we weren't at Fredericksburg either; we were off again doing some other piddling thing, and now they've taken two of my brigades, Corse and Jenkins, and sent them off to guard Richmond—*Richmond,* for the love of God—and *now,* General, do you know where I'm placed in line of march? *Last,* sir, that's where. Exactly last. I bring up the damned rear. Beg pardon."

Longstreet sighed.

Pickett said, "Well, I tell you, sir, frankly, my boys are beginning to wonder at the attitude of the high command toward my Division. My boys—"

"George," Longstreet said.

"Sir, I must—" Pickett noted Longstreet's face. "Now, I don't mean to imply *this* command. Not you, sir. I was just hoping you would talk to somebody."

"George." Longstreet paused, then he said patiently, "Would you like us to move the whole army out of the way and let you go first?"

Pickett brightened. That seemed a good idea. Another look at Longstreet's face.

"I only meant, sir, that we haven't—"

"I know, George. Listen, there's no plot. It's just the way things fell out. I have three divisions, right? There's you, and there's Hood and McLaws. And where I go you go. Right? And my HQ is near the Old Man, and the Old Man chooses to be here, and that's the way it is. We sent your two brigades to Richmond because we figured they were Virginia boys and that was proper. But look at it this way: if the army has to turn and fight its way out of here, you'll be exactly *first* in line."

Pickett thought on that.

"That's possible?"

"Yup."

"Well," Pickett mused. At that moment Lew Armistead came up. Pickett said wistfully, "Well, I had to speak on it, sir. You understand. No offense?"

"None."

"Well then. But I mean, the whole war could be damn well over soon, beg pardon, and my boys would have missed it. And these are Virginians, sir, and have a certain pride." It occurred to him that Longstreet not being a Virginian, he might have given another insult.

But Longstreet said, "I know I can count on you, George, when the time comes. And it'll come, it'll come."

Armistead broke in, "Sorry to interrupt, but they're calling for George at the poker table." He bowed. "Your fame, sir, has preceded you."

Pickett excused himself, watchful of Longstreet. Pickett was always saying something to irritate somebody, and he rarely knew why, so his method was simply to apologize in general from time to time and to let people know he meant well and then shove off and hope for the best. He apologized and departed, curls a jiggle.

Armistead looked after him. "Hope he brought some money with him." He turned back to Longstreet, smiling. "How goes it, Pete?"

"Passing well, passing well." An old soldier's joke, vaguely obscene. It had once been funny. Touched now with memories, sentimental songs. Longstreet thought: he's really quite gray. Has reached that time when a man ages rapidly, older with each passing moment. Old Lothario. Longstreet was touched. Armistead had his eyes turned away, following Pickett.

"I gather that George was trying to get us up front where we could get shot. Correct? Thought so. Well, must say, if you've got to do all this damn marching at my age there ought to be some action some time. Although—" he held up a hand—"I don't complain, I don't complain." He sat, letting a knee creak. "Getting rickety."

Longstreet looked: firelight soft on a weary face. Armistead was tired. Longstreet watched him, gauging. Armistead noticed.

"I'm all right, Pete."

"Course."

"No, really. I . . ." He stopped in mid-sentence. "I am getting a little old for it. To tell the truth. It, ah . . ." He shrugged. "It isn't as much fun when your feet hurt. Ooo." He rubbed his calf. He looked away from Longstreet's eyes. "These are damn good cherries they grow around here. Wonder if they'd grow back home."

Laughter broke from Pickett's group. A cloud passed over the moon. Armistead had something on his mind. Longstreet waited. Harrison had to be back soon. Armistead said, "I hear you have some word of the Union Army."

"Right." Longstreet thought: Hancock.

"Have you heard anything of old Win?"

"Yep. He's got the Second Corps, headed this way. We should be running into him one of these days." Longstreet felt a small jealousy. Armistead and Hancock. He could see them together—graceful Lo, dashing and confident Hancock. They had been closer than brothers before the war. A rare friendship. And now Hancock was coming this way with an enemy corps.

Armistead said, "Never thought it would last this long." He was staring off into the dark.

"Me neither. I was thinking on that last night. The day of the one-battle war is over, I think. It used to be that you went out to fight in the morning and by sundown the issue was decided and the king was dead and the war was usually over. But now . . ." He grunted, shaking his head. "Now it goes on and on. War has changed, Lewis. They all expect one smashing victory. Waterloo and all that. But I think that kind of war is over. We have trenches now. And it's a different thing, you know, to ask a man to fight from a trench. Any man can charge briefly in the morning. But to ask a man to fight from a trench, day after day . . ."

"Guess you're right," Armistead said. But he was not interested, and Longstreet, who loved to talk tactics and strategy, let it go. After a moment Armistead said, "Wouldn't mind seeing old Win again. One more time."

"Why don't you?"

"You wouldn't mind?"

"Hell no."

"Really? I mean, well, Pete, do you think it would be *proper?*"

"Sure. If the chance comes, just get a messenger and a flag of truce and go on over. Nothing to it."

"I sure would like just to talk to him again," Armistead said. He leaned back, closing his eyes. "Last time was in California. When the war was beginning. Night before we left there was a party."

Long time ago, another world. And then Longstreet thought of his children, that Christmas, that terrible Christmas, and turned his mind away. There was a silence.

Armistead said, "Oh, by the way, Pete, how's your wife? Been meaning to ask."

"Fine." He said it automatically. But she was not fine. He felt a spasm of pain like a blast of sudden cold, saw the patient high-boned Indian face, that beautiful woman, indelible suffering. Children never die: they live on in the brain forever. After a moment he realized that Armistead was watching him.

"If you want me to leave, Pete."

"No." Longstreet shook his head quickly.

"Well, then, I think I'll just set a spell and pass the time of day. Don't get to see much of you any more." He smiled: a touch of shyness. He was five years older than Longstreet, and now he was the junior officer, but he was one of the rare ones who were genuinely glad to see another man advance. In some of them there was a hunger for rank—in Jubal Early it was a disease—but Armistead had grown past the hunger, if he ever had it at all. He was an honest man, open as the sunrise, cut from the same pattern as Lee: old family, Virginia gentleman, man of honor, man of duty. He was one of the men who would hold ground if it could be held; he would die for a word. He was a man to depend on, and there was this truth about war: it taught you the men you could depend on.

He was saying, "I tell you one thing you don't have to worry on, and that's our Division. I never saw troops anywhere so ready for a brawl. And they're not just kids, either. Most of them are veterans and they'll know what to do. But the morale is simply amazing. Really is. Never saw anything like it in the old army. They're off on a Holy War. The Crusades must have been a little like this. Wish I'd a been there. Seen old Richard and the rest."

Longstreet said, "They never took Jerusalem."

Armistead squinted.

"It takes a bit more than morale," Longstreet said.

"Oh sure." But Longstreet was always gloomy. "Well, anyhow, I've never seen anything like this. The Old Man's accomplishment. Incredible. His presence is everywhere. They hush when he passes, like an angel of the Lord. You ever see anything like it?"

"No."

"Remember what they said when he took command? Called him Old Granny. Hee." Armistead chuckled. "Man, what damn fools we are."

"There's talk of making him President, after the war."

"They are?" Armistead considered it. "Do you suppose he'd take it?"

"No, I don't think he would take it. But, I don't know. I like to think of him in charge. One honest man."

"A Holy War," Longstreet said. He shook his head. He did not think much of the Cause. He was a professional: the Cause was Victory. It came to him in the night sometimes with a sudden appalling shock that the boys he was fighting were boys he had grown up with. The war had come as a nightmare in which you chose your nightmare side. Once chosen, you put your head down and went on to win. He thought: shut up. But he said:

"You've heard it often enough: one of our boys can lick any ten of them, that nonsense."

"Well."

"Well, you've fought with those boys over there, you've commanded them." He gestured vaguely east. "You know damn well they can fight. You should have seen them come up that hill at Fredericksburg, listen." He gestured vaguely, tightly, losing command of the words. "Well, Lo, you know we are dying one at a time and there aren't enough of us and we die just as dead as anybody, and a boy from back home aint a better soldier than a boy from Minnesota or anywhere else just because he's from back home."

Armistead nodded carefully. "Well, sure." He paused watchfully. "Of course I know that. But then, on the other hand, we sure do stomp them consistently, now don't we, Pete? We . . . I don't know, but I feel we're something special. I do. We're good, and we know it. It may just be the Old Man and a few other leaders like you. Well, I don't know what it is. But I tell you, I believe in it, and I don't think we're overconfident."

Longstreet nodded. Let it go. But Armistead sat up.

"Another thing, Pete, long as the subject is up. I've been thinking on your theories of defensive war, and look, Pete, if you don't mind the opinion of an aging military genius, just this once? Technically, by God, you're probably right. Hell, you're undoubtedly right. This may be a time for defensive war. But, Pete, this aint the *army* for it. We aren't bred for the defense. And the Old Man, Lord, if ever there was a man not suited for slow dull defense, it's old R.E."

Longstreet said, "But he's a *soldier.*"

"Exactly. And so are you. But the Old Man is just plain, well, too *proud.* Listen, do you remember when he was assigned to the defense of Richmond and he started digging trenches, you remember what they started calling him?"

"The King of Spades." God, the Richmond newspapers.

"Right. And you could see how hurt he was. Most people would be. Stain on the old honor. Now, Pete, you're wise enough not to give a damn about things like that. But Old Robert, now, he's from the old school, and I'll bet you right now he can't wait to get them out in the open somewhere where he can hit them face to face. And you know every soldier in the army feels the same way, and it's one of the reasons why the morale here is so good and the Union morale is so bad, and isn't that a fact?"

Longstreet said nothing. It was all probably true. And yet there was danger in it; there was even something dangerous in Lee. Longstreet said, "He promised me he would stay on the defensive. He said he would look for a good defensive position and let them try to hit us."

"He did?"

"He did."

"Well, maybe. But I tell you, Pete, it aint natural to him."

"And it is to me?"

Armistead cocked his head to one side. Then he smiled, shook his head, and reached out abruptly to slap Longstreet's knee.

"Well, might's well be blunt, old soul, and to hell with the social graces. Truth is, Peter, that you are by nature the stubbornest human being, nor mule either, nor even *army* mule, that I personally have ever known, or ever hope to know, and my hat is off to you for it, because you are also the best damn *defensive* soldier I ever saw, by miles and miles and miles, and that's a fact. Now—" he started to rise—"I'll get a-movin', back to my virtuous bed."

Longstreet grunted, found himself blushing. He rose, went silently with Armistead toward the crowd around Pickett. Moxley Sorrel was on his feet, pounding his palm with a clenched fist. The Englishman, Fremantle, was listening openmouthed. The Prussian, Scheiber, was smiling in a nasty sort of way. Longstreet caught the conclusion of Sorrel's sentence.

". . . know that government derives its power from the consent of the governed. Every government, everywhere. And, Sir, let me make this plain: *We do not consent.* We will *never* consent."

They stood up as Longstreet approached. Sorrel's face was flushed. Jim Kemper was not finished with argument, Longstreet or no. To Fremantle he went on: "You must tell them, and make it plain, that what we are fighting for is our freedom from the rule of what is to us a foreign government. That's *all* we want and that's what this war is all about. We established this country in the first place with strong state governments just for that reason, to avoid a central tyranny—"

"Oh Lord," Armistead said, "the Cause."

Fremantle rose, trying to face Longstreet and continue to listen politely to Kemper at the same moment. Pickett suggested with authority that it was growing quite late and that his officers should get back to their separate commands. There were polite farewells and kind words, and Longstreet walked Pickett and Armistead to their horses. Kemper was still saying firm, hard, noble things to Sorrel and Sorrel was agreeing absolutely—mongrelizing, money-grubbing Yankees—and Longstreet said, "What happened?"

Pickett answered obligingly, unconcerned, "Well, Jim Kemper kept needling our English friend about why they didn't come and join in with us, it being in their interest and all, and the Englishman said that it was a very touchy subject, since most Englishmen figured the war was all about, ah, *slavery,* and then old Kemper got a bit outraged and had to explain to him how wrong he was, and Sorrel and some others joined in, but no harm done."

"Damn fool," Kemper said. "He *still* thinks it's about slavery."

"Actually," Pickett said gravely, "I think my analogy of the club was best. I mean, it's as if we all joined a gentlemen's club, and then the members of the club started sticking their noses into our private lives, and then we up and resigned, and then they tell us we don't have the right to resign. I think that's a fair analogy, hey, Pete?"

Longstreet shrugged. They all stood for a moment agreeing with each other, Longstreet saying nothing. After a while they were mounted, still chatting about what a shame it was that so many people seemed to think it was slavery that brought on the war, when all it was really was a question of the Constitution. Longstreet took the reins of Pickett's horse.

"George, the army is concentrating toward Gettysburg. Hill is going in in the morning and we'll follow, and Ewell is coming down from the north. Tomorrow night we'll all be together."

"Oh, very good." Pickett was delighted. He was looking forward to parties and music.

Longstreet said, "I think that sometime in the next few days there's going to be a big fight. I want you to do everything necessary to get your boys ready."

"Sir, they're ready now."

"Well, do what you can. The little things. See to the water. Once the army is gathered in one place all the wells will run dry. See to it, George."

"I will, I will."

Longstreet thought: don't be so damn motherly.

"Well, then. I'll see you tomorrow night."

They said their good nights. Armistead waved farewell.

"If you happen to run across Jubal Early, Pete, tell him for me to go to hell."

They rode off into the dark. The moon was down; the night sky was filled with stars. Longstreet stood for a moment alone. Some good men there. Lo had said, "Best defensive soldier." From Lewis, a compliment. And yet, is it really my nature? Or is it only the simple reality?

Might as well argue with stars.

The fires were dying one by one. Longstreet went back to his place by the camp table. The tall silent aide from Texas, T. J. Goree, had curled up in a bedroll, always near, to be used at a moment's notice. For "The Cause." So many good men. Longstreet waited alone, saw one falling star, reminding him once more of the girl in a field a long time ago.

Harrison came back long after midnight. He brought the news of Union cavalry in Gettysburg. Longstreet sent the word to Lee's headquarters, but the Old Man had gone to sleep and Major Taylor did not think it important enough to wake him. General Hill had insisted, after all, that the reports of cavalry in Gettysburg were foolish.

Longstreet waited for an answer, but no answer came. He lay for a long while awake, but there was gathering cloud and he saw no more falling stars.

Just before dawn the rain began: fine misty rain blowing cold and clean in soft mountain air. Buford's pickets saw the dawn come high in the sky, a gray blush, a bleak rose. A boy from Illinois climbed a tree. There was mist across Marsh Creek, ever whiter in the growing light. The boy from Illinois stared and felt his heart beating and saw movement. A blur in the mist, an unfurled flag. Then the dark figures, row on row: skirmishers. Long, long rows, like walking trees, coming up toward him out of the mist. He had a long paralyzed moment which he would remember until the end of his life. Then he raised the rifle and laid it across the limb of the tree and aimed generally toward the breast of a tall figure in the front of the line, waited, let the cold rain fall, misting his vision, cleared his eyes, waited, prayed, and pressed the trigger.

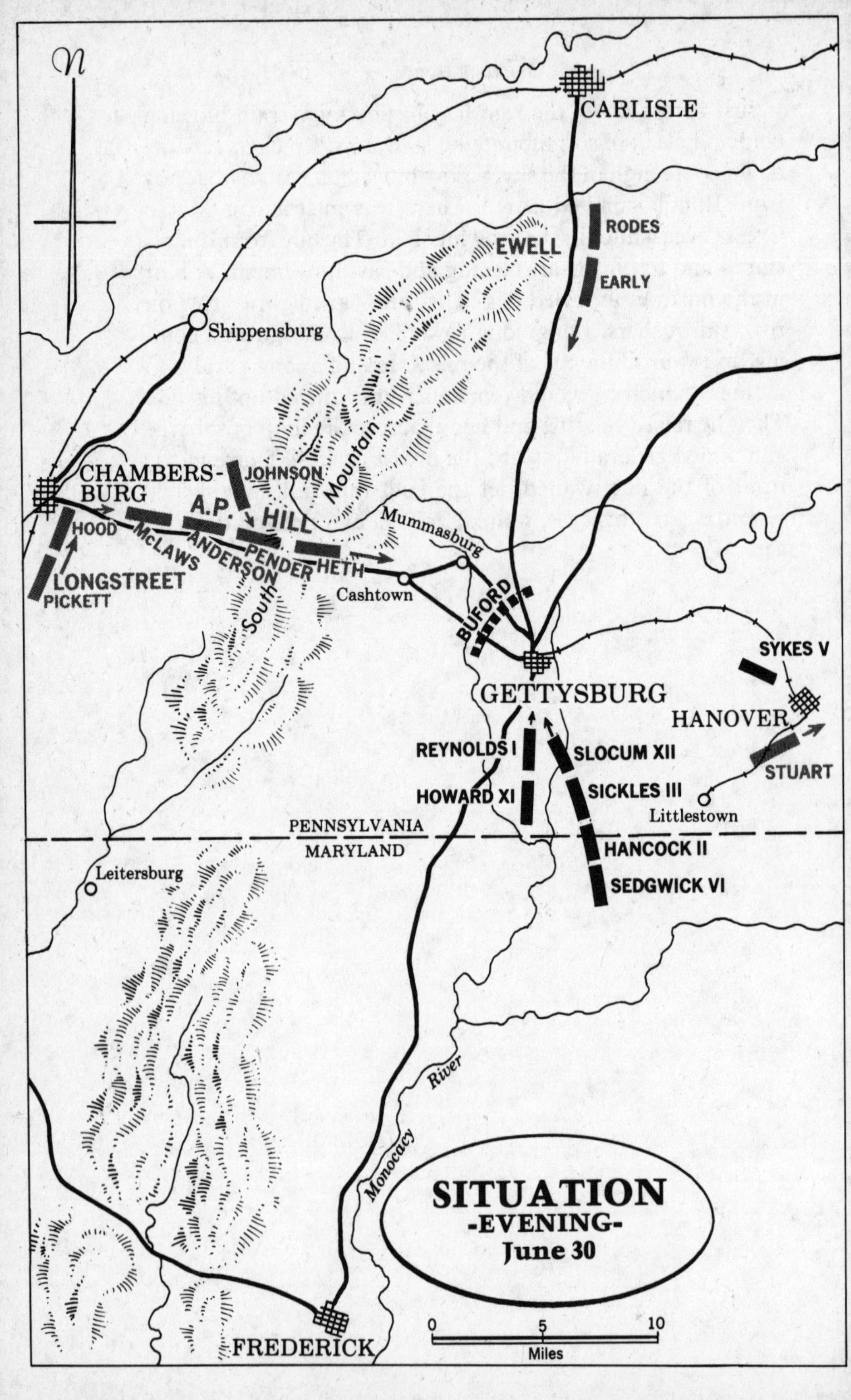

N
CARLISLE
RODES
EWELL
EARLY
Shippensburg
Mountain
CHAMBERS-
BURG
JOHNSON
A.P.
HILL
HOOD
McLAWS
ANDERSON
PENDER
HETH
Mummasburg
LONGSTREET
PICKETT
South
Cashtown
BUFORD
SYKES V
GETTYSBURG
HANOVER
REYNOLDS I
SLOCUM XII
STUART
HOWARD XI
SICKLES III
Littlestown
PENNSYLVANIA
MARYLAND
HANCOCK II
Leitersburg
SEDGWICK VI
River
Monocacy
SITUATION
-EVENING-
June 30
0
5
10
Miles
FREDERICK

WEDNESDAY, JULY 1, 1863

THE FIRST DAY

. . . of the coming of the Lord

1. Lee

He came out of the tent into a fine cold rain. The troops were already up and moving out on the misty road beyond the trees. Some of them saw the white head and came to the fence to stare at him. The ground rocked. Lee floated, clutched the tent. Got up too quickly. Must move slowly, with care. Bryan came out of the mist, bearing steaming coffee in a metal cup. Lee took it in pained hands, drank, felt the heat soak down through him like hot liquid sunshine. The dizziness passed. There was fog flat and low in the treetops, like a soft roof. The rain was clean on his face. He walked slowly to the rail where the horses were tethered: gentle Traveler, skittish Lucy Long. Stuart had not come back in the night. If Stuart had come they would have wakened him. He said good morning to the beautiful gray horse, the great soft eyes, said a silent prayer. He thought: tonight we'll all be together.

Troops were gathering along the rail fence, looking in at him. He heard a man cry a raucous greeting. Another man shushed him in anger. Lee turned, bowed slightly, waved a stiff arm. There was a cluster of sloppy salutes, broad wet grins under dripping hats. A bareheaded boy stood in reverent silence, black hat clutched to his breast. An officer moved down the fence, hustling the men away.

Lee took a deep breath, testing his chest: a windblown vacancy, a breathless pain. He had a sense of enormous unnatural fragility, like hollow glass. He sat silently on a rail, letting the velvet nose nuzzle him. Not much pain this morning. Praise God. He had fallen from his horse on his hands and the hands still hurt him but the pain in the chest was not bad at all. But it was not the pain that troubled him; it was a sick gray emptiness he knew too well, that sense of a hole clear through him like the blasted vacancy in the air behind a shell burst, an enormous emptiness. The thing about the heart was that you could not coax it or force it, as you could any other disease. Will power meant nothing. The great cold message had come in the spring, and Lee carried it inside him every moment of every day and all through the nights—that endless, breathless, inconsolable alarm: *there is not much time, beware, prepare.*

"Sir?"

Lee looked up. Young Walter Taylor. Lee came slowly awake, back to the misty world. Taylor stood in the rain with inky papers—a cool boy of twenty-four, already a major.

"Good morning, sir. Trust you slept well?"

The clear black eyes were concerned. Lee nodded. Taylor was a slim and cocky boy. Behind Lee's back he called him "The Great Tycoon." He did not know that Lee knew it. He had a delicate face, sensitive nostrils. He said cheerily, "Nothing from General Stuart, sir."

Lee nodded.

"Not a thing, sir. We can't even pick up any rumors. But we mustn't fret now, sir." A consoling tone. "They haven't got anybody can catch General Stuart."

Lee turned to the beautiful horse. He had a sudden rushing sensation of human frailty, death like a blowing wind: Jack-

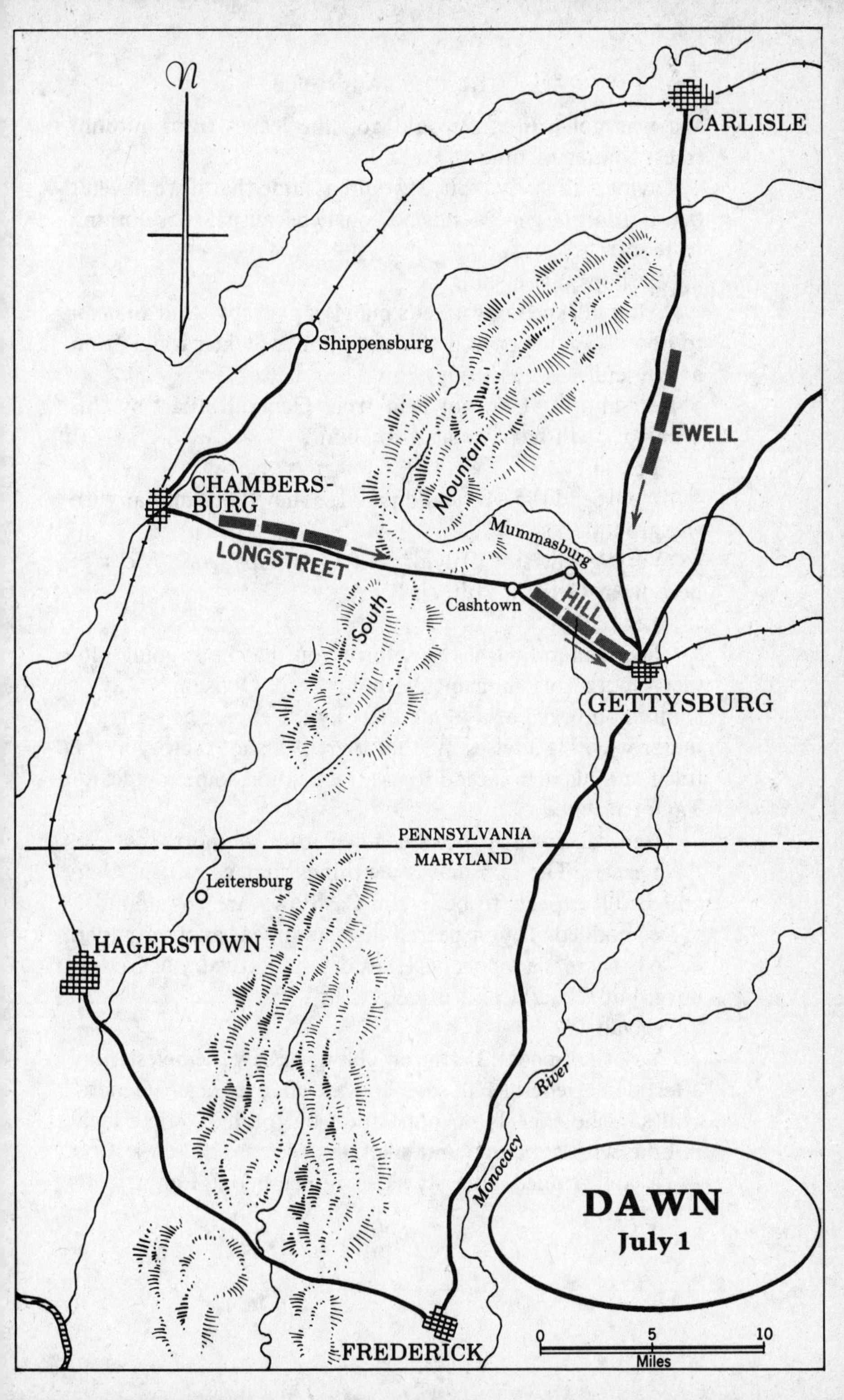
N
CARLISLE
Shippensburg
EWELL
CHAMBERS-
BURG
Mountain
Mummasburg
LONGSTREET
Cashtown
HILL
South
GETTYSBURG
PENNSYLVANIA
MARYLAND
Leitersburg
HAGERSTOWN
River
Monocacy
DAWN
July 1
FREDERICK
0
5
10
Miles

son was gone, Stuart would go, like leaves from autumn trees. Matter of time.

Taylor said airily, "Sir, I would assume that if we haven't heard from the general it is obviously because he has nothing to report."

"Perhaps," Lee said.

"After all, sir, Longstreet's man is a paid spy. And an *actor* to boot." Taylor pursed his lips primly, flicked water from a gray cuff.

Lee said, "If I do not hear from General Stuart by this evening I will have to send for him."

"Yes, sir."

"We'll send the Maryland people. They'll be familiar with the ground."

"Very good, sir." Taylor shifted wet papers. "Message here from General Hill, sir."

"Yes."

"The General wishes to inform you that he is going into Gettysburg this morning with his lead Division." Taylor squinted upward at a lightening sky. "I expect he's already under way. He advises me that there is a shoe factory in the town and his men intend to, ah, requisition some footgear." Taylor grinned.

"General Ewell is moving down from the north?"

"Yes, sir. The rain may slow things somewhat. But General Ewell expects to be in the Cashtown area by noon."

Lee nodded. Taylor peered distastefully at another paper.

"Ah, there is a report here, sir, of Union cavalry in Gettysburg, but General Hill discounts it."

"Cavalry?"

"Yes, sir. General Pettigrew claims he saw them yesterday afternoon. General Hill says he was, ah, overeager. General Hill says he expects no opposition but perhaps some local militia, with shotguns and such."

Taylor grinned cheerily. Lee remembered Longstreet's

spy. If it is Union cavalry, there will be infantry close behind it. Lee said, "Who is Hill's lead commander?"

"Ah, that will be General Heth, sir."

Harry Heth. Studious. Reliable. Lee said, "General Hill knows I want no fight until this army is concentrated."

"Sir, he does."

"That must be clear."

"I believe it is, sir."

Lee felt a thump, a flutter in his chest. It was as if the heart was turning over. He put his hand there, passed one small breathless moment. It happened often: no pain, just a soft deep flutter. Taylor was eyeing him placidly. He had no fear of the Army of the Potomac.

"Will the General have breakfast?"

Lee shook his head.

"We have flapjacks in small mountains, sir. You must try them, sir. Fresh butter and bacon and wagons of hams, apple butter, ripe cherries. Never seen anything like it, sir. You really ought to pitch in. Courtesy of mine host, the great state of Pennsylvania. Nothing like it since the war began. Marvelous what it does for morale. Never saw the men happier. Napoleon knew a thing or two, what? For a Frenchman?"

Lee said, "Later." There was no hunger in the glassy chest. Want to see Longstreet. Up ahead, in the mist, A. P. Hill probes toward Gettysburg like a blind hand. Hill was new to command. One-legged Ewell was new to command. Both had replaced Stonewall Jackson, who was perhaps irreplaceable. Now there was only Longstreet, and a thumping heart. Lee said, "We will move the headquarters forward today, this morning."

"Yes, sir. Sir, ah, there are a number of civilians to see you."

Lee turned sharply. "Trouble with our soldiers?"

"Oh no, sir. No problem there. The men are behaving very well, very well indeed. Oh yes, sir. But, ah, there are some local women who claim we've taken all their food, and although they don't complain of our having paid for it all in the good dear coin of the mighty state of Virginia—"Taylor grinned—"they *do* object to starving. I must say that Ewell's raiding parties seem to have been thorough. At any rate, the ladies seek your assistance. Rather massive ladies, most of them, but one or two have charm."

"See to it, Major."

"Of course, sir. Except, ah, sir, the old gentleman, he's been waiting all night to see you."

"Old gentleman?"

"Well, sir, we conscripted his horse. At your orders, as you know. I explained that to the old man, fortunes of war and all that, but the old gentleman insists that the horse is blind, and can be of no use to us, and is an old friend."

Lee sighed. "A blind horse?"

"Yes, sir. I didn't want to trouble you, sir, but your orders were strict on this point."

"Give him the horse, Major."

"Yes sir." Taylor nodded.

"We must be charitable with these people, Major. We have enough enemies."

"Oh yes, sir." Taylor made a slight bow. "The men have the strictest orders. But I must say, sir, that those orders would be easier to follow had the Yankees shown charity when they were back in Virginia."

"Major," Lee said slowly, "we will behave ourselves."

Taylor recognized the tone. "Yes, sir," he said.

Lee rested against the rail fence. He noticed at last a struggling band: "Bonny Blue Flag." A brave but tinny sound. He bowed in that direction, raised his coffee cup in tribute. A tall thin soldier waved a feathered hat: the music bounced away. Lee said, "I would like to see General Longstreet. My compliments, and ask him to ride with me this morning, if he is not otherwise occupied."

"Breakfast, sir?"

"In a moment, Major."

Taylor saluted formally, moved off. Lee sat for a moment alone, gazing eastward. Cavalry. If Longstreet's spy was right, then there could truly be cavalry in Gettysburg and masses of infantry right behind. We drift blindly toward a great collision. Peace, until night. He rubbed the left arm. Must show no pain, no weakness here. The strength now is in Longstreet. Trust to him.

He saw the old gentleman, who thanked him with tears for the return of the blind horse. A Pennsylvania woman flirted, asked for his autograph. He gave it, amazed, wondering what good it would do her in this country. He met with his aides: angry Marshall, gray-bearded Venable. Marshall was furious with the absent Stuart, was ready to draw up court-martial papers. Lee said nothing. The courteous Venable drew him politely away.

"Sir, I have a request to make."

"Yes."

Venable: a courtly man, a man of patience. He said, "Could you speak to Dorsey Pender, sir? He's had a letter from his wife."

Lee remembered: beautiful woman on a golden horse, riding with Pender on the banks of the Rappahannock. Lovely sight, a sunset sky.

"Mrs. Pender is, ah, a pious woman, and she believes that now that we have invaded Pennsylvania we are in the wrong, and God has forsaken us—you know how these people reason, sir—and she says she cannot pray for him."

Lee shook his head. God protect us from our loving friends. He saw for one small moment the tragic face of his own frail wife, that unhappy woman, the stone strong face of his mother. Venable said, "I think a talk might help Pender, sir. Another man would shake it off, but he's . . . taken it badly. Says he cannot pray himself."

Venable paused. "I know there are others who feel that way."

Lee nodded. Venable said, "It was easier in Virginia, sir. On our home ground."

"I know."

"Will you speak to him, sir?"

"Yes," Lee said.

"Very good, sir. I know it will help him, sir."

Lee said, "I once swore to defend this ground." He looked out across the misty grove. "No matter. No matter. We end the war as best we can." He put his hand to his chest. "Napoleon once said, 'The logical end to defensive warfare is surrender.' You might tell him that."

"Yes, sir. Thank you very much, sir."

Venable went away. Lee felt a deeper spasm, like a black stain. I swore to defend. Now I invade. A soldier, no theologian. God, let it be over soon. While there's time to play with grandchildren. It came too late. Fame came too late. I would have enjoyed it, if I were a younger man.

He moved back to the map table. The guilt stayed with him, ineradicable, like the silent alarm in the fragile chest. Swore to defend. Misty matters. Get on with the fight. He looked down at the map. The roads all converged, weblike, to Gettysburg. And where's the spider? Nine roads in all. Message from Ewell: his troops were on the move, would be coming down into Gettysburg from the north. Lee looked at his watch: eight o'clock. The rain had stopped, the mist was blowing off. He thought: good. Too much rain would muck up the roads. The first sun broke through, yellow and warm through steaming tree leaves, broad bright light blazed across the map table. Lee began to come slowly awake, blinking in the blaze of morning.

Out on the road the troops were moving in a great mottled stream: Longstreet's First Corps, the backbone of the army, moving up behind Powell Hill. The barefoot, sunburned, thin and grinning army, joyful, unbeatable, already immortal. And then through the trees the familiar form: big man on a black horse, great round shoulders, head thick as a stump: James Longstreet.

It was reassuring just to look at him, riding slowly forward into the sunlight on the black Irish stallion: Dutch Longstreet, old Pete. He was riding along in a cloud of visitors, bright-clad foreigners, observers from Europe, plumes and feathers and helmeted horsemen, reporters from Richmond, the solemn members of Longstreet's staff. He separated from the group and rode to Lee's tent and the motley bright cloud remained respectfully distant. Lee rose with unconscious joy.

"General."

"Mornin'."

Longstreet touched his cap, came heavily down from the horse. He was taller than Lee, head like a boulder, full-bearded, long-haired, always a bit sloppy, gloomy, shocked his staff by going into battle once wearing carpet slippers. Never cared much for appearance, gave an impression of ominous bad-tempered strength and a kind of slow, even, stubborn, unquenchable anger: a soft voice, a ragged mouth. He talked very slowly and sometimes had trouble finding the right word, and the first impression of him around that gay and courtly camp was that he was rather dull-witted and not much fun. He was not a Virginian. But he was a magnificent soldier. With Jackson gone he was the rock of the army, and Lee felt a new clutching in his chest, looking at him, thinking that this was one man you could not afford to lose. Longstreet smiled his ragged smile, grumbled, jerked a finger over his shoulder.

"Her Majesty's forces in the New World passed a restful night."

Lee looked, saw the ludicrous man in the lustrous hat and

the wide gray coat. The man made a sweeping, quixotic bow, nearly falling from the horse. Colonel Fremantle was up. Lee gave a formal bow, smiling inwardly.

Longstreet observed with sloe-eyed surprise. "After a while, you know, he actually begins to grow on you."

"You're keeping him entertained?"

"Not exactly. He's got his heart set on a cavalry charge. Drawn sabers, all that glorious French business. He was horrified when I had to tell him we didn't use the British square."

Lee smiled.

"But he's a likable fella." Longstreet took off his hat, scratched his head. "Can't say he's learning much. But he seems to like us, all right. He says you have a great reputation in Europe."

Lee said, "There'll be no help from there."

"No."

"President Davis has hope."

"Well, I guess that won't do him any harm to hope."

"At least we'll be good hosts." Lee felt a sudden strength. It came out of Longstreet like sunlight. Lee said happily, "And how are *you* this morning, General?"

"Me?" Longstreet blinked. "I'm all right." He paused, cocked his head to one side, stared at the old man.

Lee said happily, "You must take care of yourself."

Longstreet was mystified. No one ever asked him how he felt. His health was legendary, he never tired.

Lee said diplomatically, "The Old Soldier's illness is going around."

"It's the damned cherries," Longstreet gloomed. "Too many raw cherries."

Lee nodded. Then he said softly, "General, in the fight that's coming, I want you to stay back from the main line."

Longstreet looked at him, expressionless. Black eyes glistened, bright and hard under hairy eyebrows. Impossible to tell what he was thinking.

Lee said, "You are my only veteran commander."

Longstreet nodded.

"If I should become once again indisposed," Lee said.

"God forbid." Longstreet stared. "And how are *you?*"

Lee smiled, waved a deprecating hand. "I am well, very well. Thank God. But there is always . . . a possibility. And now Jackson is gone, and we must all do more than before. And I do not know if Hill or Ewell are ready for command, but I know that you . . ."

He paused. Hard to speak in this fashion. Longstreet was staring with cold silent eyes. Lee said sternly, "You have a very bad habit, General, of going too far forward."

Longstreet said, "You cannot lead from behind."

"Well. Let me put it plainly. I cannot spare you."

Longstreet stood silent for a moment. He bowed slightly, then he grinned. "True," he said.

"You will oblige me?"

"My pleasure," Longstreet said.

Lee rubbed his nose, looked down at the table. "Now, let us look to the day. Nothing will happen today. But we have an opportunity, I believe."

"Nothing from Stuart?"

Lee shook his head. Longstreet grumbled, "The Federals are closing in."

"I have no new information."

"When Stuart comes back, if he does come back—which he will eventually, if only just to read the Richmond newspapers—you ought to court-martial him."

"And will that make him a better soldier?"

Longstreet paused. He said, "All right. What will?"

"Reproach, I think. I must let him know how badly he has let us down."

Longstreet chuckled. He shook his head, gazing at Lee. "Yes, by George. Maybe. Reproach from *you.* Yes." Longstreet grinned widely. "Might do the job. But me . . . I'm no good at that."

"Different men, different methods. Docile men make very poor soldiers."

Longstreet grinned wryly. "An army of temperamentals. It isn't an army, it's a gentlemen's club. My God. Remember when old Powell Hill wanted to fight me a duel, right in the middle of the war?"

"And you ignored him. You did exactly right."

"Yep. He might have shot me."

Lee smiled. His heart rolled again, a soft sudden thump, leaving him breathless. Longstreet was grinning, staring off toward the road, did not notice. Lee said, "One new item. I have confirmed some of your man Harrison's information. The new commander is definitely George Meade, not Reynolds. The news is carried in the local newspapers."

Longstreet reached inside his coat, extracted a fat cigar.

"You can trust my man, I think. I sent him into Gettysburg last night. He said he saw two brigades of Union cavalry there."

"Last night?"

"I sent you a report."

Lee felt a tightening in his chest. He put his hand to his arm. He said slowly, "General Hill reports only militia."

"It's cavalry, I think." Longstreet chewed, spat.

Where there is cavalry there will be infantry close behind.

"Whose troops?"

"John Buford."

Longstreet meditated.

"Meade's coming fast. Looks like he's trying to get behind us."

"Yes." Lee thought: the direction does not matter. Fight him wherever he is. Lee said, "We have an opportunity."

Longstreet chewed, nodded, grinned. "Yep. Objective was to get him out of Washington and in the open. Now he's out. Now all we have to do is swing round between him and Washington and get astride some nice thick rocks and make him come to us, and we've got him in the open."

Take the defensive. Not again. Lee shook his head. He pointed to Gettysburg.

"He has been forcing the march. The weather has been unusually hot. He will arrive strung out and tired, piece by piece. If we concentrate we can hit him as he comes up. If we ruin one or two corps we can even the odds."

He was again breathless, but he bent over the map. Longstreet said nothing.

"He's new to command," Lee said. "It will take him some days to pick up the reins. His information will be poor, he will have staff problems."

"Yes, and he will have Washington on his back, urging him to throw us out of Pennsylvania. He has to fight. We don't."

Lee put his hand to his eyes. He was fuzzy-brained. Longstreet loved the defense. But all the bright theories so rarely worked. Instinct said: hit hard, hit quick, hit everything. But he listened. Then he said slowly, "That move will be what Meade expects."

"Yes. Because he fears it."

Lee turned away from the table. He wanted no argument now. He had been down this road before, and Longstreet was immovable, and there was no point in argument when you did not even know where the enemy was. Yet it was good counsel. Trust Longstreet to tell the truth. Lee looked up and there was Traveler, led by a black groom. The staff had gathered, the tents were down. Time to move. Lee took a deep, delighted breath.

"Now, General," he said, "let's go see what George Meade intends."

They moved out into the open, into the warm sunlight. It was becoming a marvelous day. Out on the road the army flowed endlessly eastward, pouring toward the great fight. Lee smelled the superb wetness of clean mountain air. He said, "General, will you ride with me?"

Longstreet bowed. "My pleasure."

Lee mounted in pain, but the hot sun would heal the old bones. They rode out into a space in the great gray bristling stream. Another band played; men were shouting. It was lovely country. They rode through soft green rounded hills, a sunny morn, a splendid air, moving toward adventure as rode the plumed knights of old. Far back in the woods there was still fog in the trees, caught in the branches like fragments of white summer, and Lee remembered:

> Bow down Thy Heavens, O Lord, and come down,
> Touch the mountains, and they shall smoke.

He closed his eyes. Blessed be the Lord my strength, which teacheth my fingers to fight and my hands to war. Amen.

They rode several miles before they heard the first thunder.

Lee reined to a stop. Silence. Motion of ragged white clouds. He said, "Did you hear that?"

Longstreet, who was slightly deaf, shook his head.

"It might have been thunder." But Lee waited. Then it came: low, distant thumping. Ominous: angry. Longstreet said grimly, bright-eyed, angered, "I don't hear too well any more."

"That was artillery," Lee said. Longstreet gazed at him with black marble eyes. "You don't think . . ." Lee began, then stopped. "I'd better ride forward," he said. Longstreet nodded. Lee looked at his watch. Not quite ten in the morning. He left Longstreet and rode toward the sound of the guns.

2. Buford

Just before dawn Buford rode down the line himself, waking them up, all the boyish faces. Then he climbed the ladder into the white cupola and sat listening to the rain, watching the light come. The air was cool and wet and delicious to breathe: a slow, fine, soaking rain, a farmer's rain, gentle on the roof. The light came slowly: there were great trees out in the mist. Then the guns began.

A single shot. He sat up. Another. Two more widely spaced. Then a small volley, a spattering. A long silence: several seconds. He stared at white air, the rounded tops of smoky trees. Men were moving out in the open below him. An officer paused on horseback in the road. The firing began again, Rebel guns, farther off, but not many. Buford was cold. He shuddered, waited.

The first attack was very short: a ragged fire. Buford nodded, listening. "Yes. Tried to brush us off. Got a bloody nose. Now he'll get angry, all puffed up like a partridge. Now he'll form up a line and try us for real, and he'll hit the main line." The mist was lifting slowly, the rain was slackening, but Buford could not see the line. He felt the attack come and turned his face toward the sound of the guns, judging the size of the attack by the width of the sound, and he sat grinning alone in the cupola, while the Rebel troops pushed his line and drew back, bloody, and tried again in another place, the firing spreading all down the line like a popping fuse, and then there was another long silence, and Buford could feel

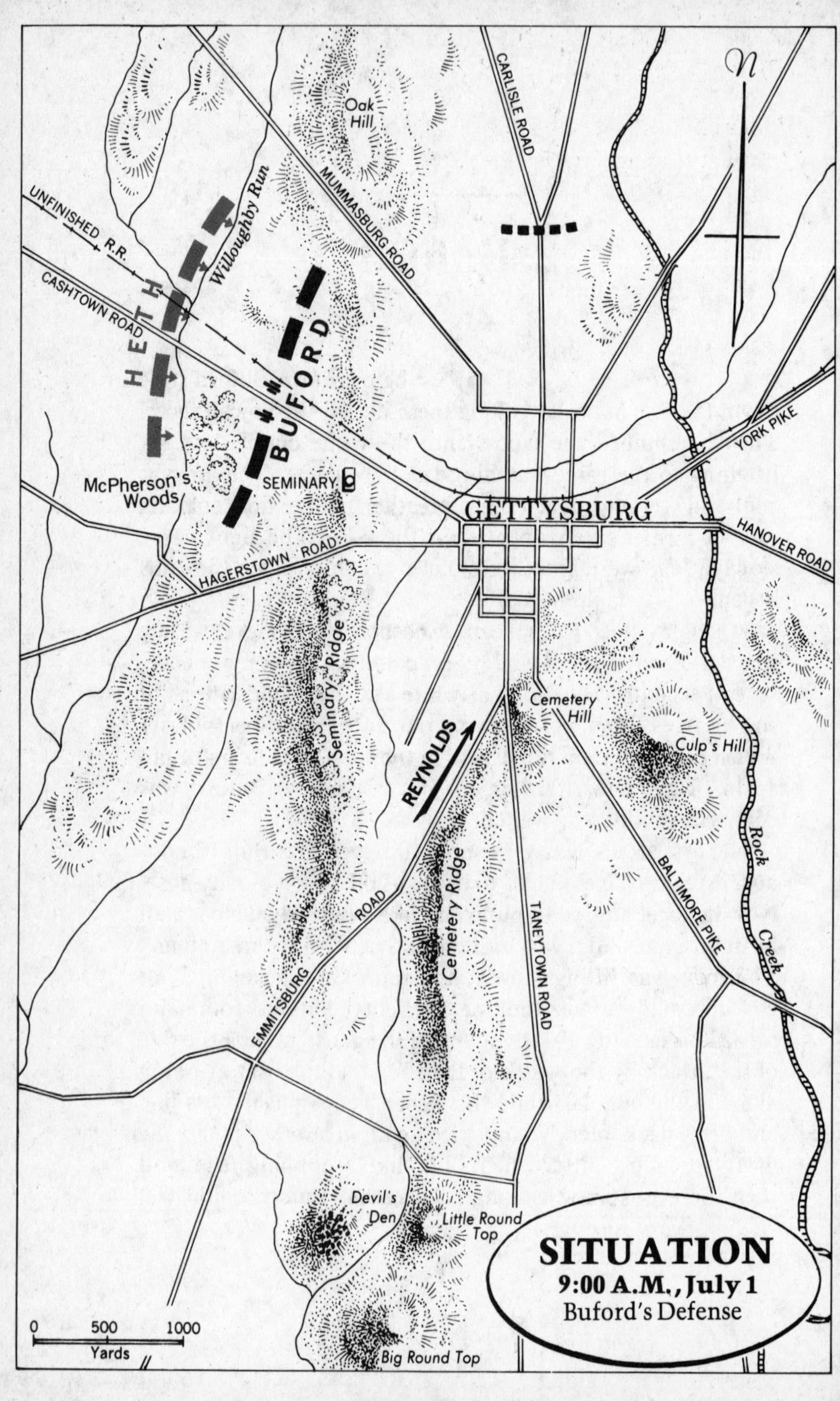
SITUATION
9:00 A.M., July 1
Buford's Defense
GETTYSBURG
Oak Hill
CARLISLE ROAD
MUMMASBURG ROAD
UNFINISHED R.R.
Willoughby Run
CASHTOWN ROAD
HETH
BUFORD
McPherson's Woods
SEMINARY
HAGERSTOWN ROAD
YORK PIKE
HANOVER ROAD
Seminary Ridge
Cemetery Hill
Culp's Hill
REYNOLDS
Cemetery Ridge
EMMITSBURG ROAD
TANEYTOWN ROAD
BALTIMORE PIKE
Rock Creek
Devil's Den
Little Round Top
Big Round Top
0 500 1000
Yards

them reforming again, beginning for the first time to take this seriously. The next assault would be organized. He looked at his watch. Reynolds should be awake by now. They will have eaten their breakfast now, the infantry, and maybe they're on the march.

There was a silence. He climbed down out of the cupola. The staff waited whitefaced under dripping trees. Buford asked for coffee. He went back inside the Seminary and waited for the firing to begin again before sending his first word to Reynolds. It took longer than he expected. If whoever was out there attacking him had any brains he would probe this position first and find out what he was attacking. Buford listened for the scattered fire of patrols coming in, moving along his flanks, outlining him, but there was nothing. A long silence, then a massed assault. Buford grinned, baring fangs. Damn fool. He's got a brigade in position, that's all. He's hitting me with one brigade, and I'm dug in. Lovely, lovely.

He wrote to Reynolds: "Rebel infantry attacked at dawn. Am holding west of Gettysburg, expecting relief. John Buford."

The fire was hotting up. He heard the first cannon: Calef's Battery opening up down the road, grinned again. No Reb cannon to reply: not yet. He sent the messenger off into the mist, climbed again into the cupola.

The light was much clearer. He saw speckles of yellow fire through the mist: winking guns. The road ran black through misty fields. He saw one black cannon spout red fire at the limits of his vision. On the far side of the road there was a deep railroad cut—an unfinished railroad; he had not noticed it before. He saw horsemen moving behind the line. Then he heard that ripply sound that raised the hair, that high thin scream from far away coming out of the mist unbodied and terrible, inhuman. It got inside him for a suspended second. The scream of a flood of charging men: the Rebel yell.

It died in massive fire. There were still no cannon on the other side. Calef's Battery blasted the mist, thunder among the lighter fire. The assault began to die away.

The wounded were beginning to come back off the line. Buford went down from the cupola, restless, found Bill Gamble in the field by Calef's Battery, checking ammunition. There was blood on his left sleeve. His nose was still running. He grinned wetly at Buford.

"Hey, General. That was quite a scrap."

"How are your losses?"

"Not bad. Not bad at all. We were dug in pretty good. We got 'em right out in the open. Really got a twist on 'em. Arrogant people, you know that? Came right at us. Listen, we got some prisoners. I talked to 'em. They're Harry Heth's Division, of Hill's Corps. That's what I've got in front of me."

Buford nodded. Gamble was talking very quickly, head moving in jerky twitches.

"Sir, as I remember, Heth's got near ten thousand men. They're all within sound of the fight, back that road, between here and Cashtown."

Buford squinted. The rain had quit but the sky was still low and gray. He could see a long way off through the trees, and there were ragged bodies in the fields, groups of men digging, cutting trees for cover.

Gamble said, "Sir, he'll be back with all ten thousand."

"It'll take him a while to deploy," Buford said.

"Yes, but he's got Hill's whole Corps behind him. Maybe twenty-five thousand. And Longstreet behind that. And Ewell in the north."

"I know."

"Thing is this. When John Reynolds gets here, he won't have the whole army with him, only a part of it. Point is—" he sniffled, wiped his nose—"as I see it, the Rebs will be here this afternoon with everything they've got."

Buford said nothing. Gamble sniffed cheerily.

"Just thought I'd mention it. Now, what you want me to do here?"

Buford thought: if it was a mistake, God help us.

"Heth will be back in a bit," Buford said. "If he's got any brains at all, and he's not stupid, he'll know by now that he's got a brigade in front of him. Don't think he'll wait to get his whole Division in line. That would take half the morning."

"He doesn't need his whole Division."

"Right. Does Devin report any activity on his front?"

"Not a thing."

"All right. I'll have Devin pull some of his people out and leave a cover in the north and have him dig in alongside, lengthening your line. When Heth comes back he'll run into two brigades. That should hold him until Reynolds gets here."

"Right," Gamble said. He peered up at the sky. "Glad the rain is gone. Don't want anything to slow up Reynolds."

"Take care of yourself."

"You know me: the soul of caution."

Buford moved off toward the north. He sent a second message to Reynolds. He pulled Devin out of line in the north and brought him in alongside Gamble: two thousand men facing west. All that while whenever he came near the line he could see enemy troops moving in the fields across the way, spreading out as they came down the road, like a gray river spreading where it reaches the sea. If Heth was efficient and deliberate he had the power to come straight through like an avalanche. Buford could hear the artillery coming into place on the far side, heard the spattering of rifle fire from probing patrols. He looked at his watch; it was after eight. Reynolds had to be on the road. The infantry had to be coming. He rode back and forth along the line, watched Devin's men digging in, heard bullets clip leaves above him as snipers crawled closer. *We cannot hold ten thousand. Not for very long.* If Heth attacks in force he will roll right over us, and we lose the two brigades and the high ground too, and it will have been my fault. And the road in the north is open; they can come in there and they'll be behind us, on our flank.

There was nothing he could do about that; he had no more troops. But he pulled a squad out of Devin's line and put the young Lieutenant with corn-silk hair in charge and gave him orders.

"Son, you ride on out that road to the north about five miles. You squat across some high ground, where you can see. First sign you get of enemy coming down that road, you ride like hell this way and tell me. Understand?"

The squad galloped off. A cannon shell burst in the air nearby, raining fragments in the wet leaves around him. The first Reb cannon were in position, limbering up easily, casually, getting the range. Now Buford had a little time to think. It all depends on how fast Reynolds comes. It all depends on how many men he's got with him and how fast Lee is moving this way. Nothing to do but fight now and hold this line. But he kept looking at his watch. There ought to be some word. He galloped back to the Seminary and climbed the cupola and gazed back to that southern road, but there was nothing there. A short while after that he saw the enemy come out in the open, line after line, heard the guns open up, dozens of guns, watched his own line disappear in smoke. The big attack had come.

Gamble was down. The first report was very bad, and Buford rode over and took command, but it was only concussion and Gamble was back on his feet in a few moments, ragged and dirty. There was a breakthrough on the right but some junior officers patched it. Lone infantry began bending around the right flank. Buford mounted some men and drove them off. There were moments in smoke when he could not see and thought the line was going; one time when a shell burst very close and left him deaf and still and floating, like a bloody cloud.

On the right there was another breakthrough, hand-to-hand fighting. He rode that way, leaping wounded, but it had been repulsed when he got there. One by one Calef's guns were being silenced. No one had yet broken away, no one was running, but Buford could feel them giving, like a dam. He rode back to the Seminary, looked down the road. Nothing. Not much more time. He felt the beginning of an awful anger, an unbearable sadness, suppressed it. He rode back to the line. The fire was weakening. He stood irresolute in the road. An aide suggested he go to cover. He listened. The Rebs were pulling back, forming to come again. But the Reb cannon were pounding, pounding. He heard the great whirring of fragments in the air, saw air bursts in bright electric sparks. He rode slowly along the smoking line, looking at the faces. The brigades were wrecked. There was not much ammunition. They were down in the dirt firing slowly, carefully from behind splintery trees, piled gray rails, mounds of raw dirt. They had maybe half an hour.

Pull out before then. Save something. He rode back toward the Seminary. He climbed the cupola, looked out across the field of war. Wreckage everywhere, mounded bodies, smoking earth, naked stumps of trees. He could see a long way now, above the rolling smoke which had replaced the mist, and the road coming down from the far-off mountains was packed with soldiers, thousands of soldiers, sunlight glittering on jeweled guns. He looked toward the south—and there was Reynolds.

He was coming at a gallop across the fields to the south, a line of aides strung out behind him, cutting across the field to save time. No mistaking him: matchless rider gliding over rail fences in parade-ground precision, effortless motion, always a superb rider. Buford blinked, wiped his face, thanked God. But the road behind Reynolds was empty.

The General rode into the yard below, dismounted. Buford waited in the cupola, weariness suddenly beginning to get to him in waves. In a moment Reynolds was up the ladder.

"Good morning, John."

An immaculate man, tidy as a photograph, soft-voiced, almost elegant. Buford put out a hand.

"General, I'm damned glad to see you."

Reynolds stepped up for a look. Buford explained the position. In all his life he had never been so happy to see anybody. But where was the infantry? Reynolds swung, pointed a gloved hand.

The blue line had come around the bend. Buford saw with a slight shock the first column of infantry, the lovely flags. Reynolds said softly, "That's the First Corps. The Eleventh is right behind it."

Buford watched them come. He leaned against the side of the cupola. Reynolds had turned, was surveying the hills to the south. There was a set, hard, formal look to him, but a happiness in his eyes. Buford thought: he has brains to see.

Reynolds said, "Good job, John."

"Thank you."

"This is going to be very interesting."

"Yes," Buford said.

"They seem to be forming for another assault. That's Harry Heth, isn't it? Very good. He'll come in here thinking he's up against two very tired cavalry brigades, and instead he'll be hitting two corps of fresh Union infantry." Reynolds smiled slightly. "Poor Harry," he said.

"Yes, sir," Buford said.

"You can start pulling your boys out. As soon as we set up. Well done. Well done indeed. You can put them out on my flanks. Keep an eye on that north road. I expect Dick Ewell to be coming in shortly."

"Yes, sir."

They went down out of the cupola. Reynolds mounted a beautiful black horse. Buford came out into the open, saw his staff tidying itself up, combing hair, buttoning buttons. Shells were falling on the ridge nearby and bullets were slicing leaves, but Reynolds sat astride the horse in a motionless calm, looking out toward the fight, picture of a soldier, painted against the trees. Reynolds called in one of his officers. He said slowly, somewhat delicately, pronouncing each word in turn, evenly, machinelike, "Captain, I want you to ride as fast as you can to General Meade. Tell him the enemy is advancing in strong force and that I am afraid they will get the heights beyond the town before I can. We will fight them here inch by inch, through the town if necessary, barricading the streets. We will delay them as long as possible. I am sending messages to all my commanders to come to this place with all possible speed. Repeat that."

The Captain did, and was gone. Reynolds sent messages to other commanders: Doubleday, Sickles. Then he said, to Buford, "I think I'll move over and hurry the boys along."

"Obliged," Buford said.

"Not at all." He wheeled the horse gracefully, still something of that elegant quality of display in the fluid motion, and rode off. In the direction he took Buford heard music. A blue band was playing. Buford issued his own orders. The great weight was off him. Now it belonged to Reynolds. And there was no regret. Through most of his life he had resented the appearance of higher command. Now it came to save him. A new thing. He did not mind at all. Must be the age. Well, you have gone to the limit, lad. You have reached your own personal end.

Tom Devin was up. He was annoyed to be pulled out. Buford looked at him, shook his head. In a moment Reynolds was back, leading blue troops at double time through the fields, tearing down rail fences as they came. Buford's heart was stirred: the Black Hats, Simon Cutler's Iron Brigade, best troops in the Union Army. An omen. They began to move out onto the road by the Seminary, regiment after regiment, moving with veteran gloom, veteran silence, steady men, not many boys. One man was eating cherries hurriedly from a mess tin; another had a banjo on his back which was bothering him, and he swung it around to cover his front and banged the man in front of him, who complained, to peculiar laughter. One man asked one of Buford's aides loudly which way was the war and offered to go the other way, and an officer turned and began sending them into line along the crest Gamble had held. Then Reynolds was back.

The Rebel shells were beginning to pass overhead. They had seen new troops coming and some of the fire was falling now on Gettysburg. Reynolds summoned another aide.

"Lieutenant, get on into town and tell these people to stay in off the streets. There's liable to be a fair-sized dispute here today, and give anyone you meet my compliments, along with my suggestion that every person stay indoors, in cellars if possible, and out of harm's way. Especially children." He peered at the aide. "Joe, how do you see with those things on?" The aide wore glasses that were very muddy. He took them and tried to clean them and smeared them with jittery fingers. A shell hit a treetop across the road and splinters flickered through the grove and spattered against the brick wall. Reynolds said pleasantly, "Gentlemen, let's place the troops."

He motioned to Buford. They rode out into the road. Buford felt a certain dreamy calm. Reynolds, like Lee before him, had once commanded the Point. There was a professional air to him, the teacher approaching the class, utterly in command of his subject. Reynolds said, "Now, John, he's got a good fifteen thousand men out there, wouldn't you say?"

"Yes. Be a lot more in a little while."

"Yes. Well, between us we can put almost twenty thousand in the field in the next half hour. We're in very good shape, I think."

"For a while," Buford said.

Reynolds nodded.

He turned in his saddle, looked back toward the hills. "Isn't that lovely ground?" he said.

"I thought so."

"Keep at it, John. Someday, if you're spared, you may make a soldier." He bowed his head once slightly. It came over Buford like a sunrise that he had just received Reynolds' greatest compliment. At that moment it mattered very much. "Now," Reynolds said, "let's go surprise Harry Heth."

They rode out together, placing the troops. The First Corps moved into line on the left. The Eleventh Corps moved in behind them, swung out to the right. Through all that the Reb cannon were firing steadily and smoke was filling up the hollow between the armies and no one could see the motion of the troops. The Eleventh was still not in line when the new Reb attack came rolling up out of the smoke. Reynolds moved off to the left, close to the line. Buford heard music, an eerie sound like a joyful wind, began to recognize it: "The Campbells Are Coming." He recognized Rufus Dawes and the Sixth Wisconsin moving up, more Wisconsin men behind them, deploying in line of skirmishers and firing already as they moved up, the line beginning to go fluid as the first Reb troops poured over a partly deserted crest, and met the shock of waves of new troops coming up from the south.

Buford got one last glimpse of Reynolds. He was out in the open, waving his hat, pointing to a grove of trees. A moment later Buford looked that way and the horse was bare-backed. He did not believe it. He broke off and rode to see. Reynolds lay in the dirt road, the aides bending over him. When Buford got there the thick stain had already puddled the dirt beneath his head. His eyes were open, half asleep, his face pleasant and composed, a soft smile. Buford knelt. He was dead. An aide, a young sergeant, was crying. Buford backed away. They put a blanket over him. Off to the left there was massive firing. There was a moment of silence around them. Buford said, "Take him out of here."

He backed off. Across the road a woman was chasing a wild-haired child. A soldier ran past her and caught the child and gave it to her. Buford went to a great shade tree and stood in the dark for a moment. Too good a man, Reynolds. Much too good a man. Buford wandered slowly back out into the light. It was very hot now; he could feel sweat all down his face.

A detail from a New York regiment carried Reynolds away, under a blanket. Buford's aides came to him, back to the shepherd. There were no orders to give.

The battle went on without a commander. The men fought where Reynolds had placed them. Buford slowly withdrew his cavalry, as Reynolds had ordered. All the rest of that morning gray Rebel troops came pouring down that narrow road. No messages came. The line continued to hold. There did not seem to be anyone in command, but the line held. After a while Buford mounted what was left of his cavalry and rode slowly out that road to the north. He could not hold for long, but he could hold for a little while, and the yellow-haired lieutenant was out there alone.

3. Lee

They had stripped the rails from both sides of the road, to widen the passage, and some of the men were marching in the fields.

The road was already going to dust and the dust was rising, and there was nothing to see ahead but troops in the dust toiling upward toward the crest of a divide. The bands played as he went by. He nodded, touching his cap, head cocked, listening, searching beyond the music and the noise of rolling wagons and steely clinking of sabers and guns for the distant roll of artillery which was always there, beyond the hills. They came to a narrow pass: rocky country, dark gorges, heavily wooded. He thought: if there is a repulse, this will be good country to defend. Longstreet could bring up his people and hold this place and we would shelter the army back in the mountains.

He began almost to expect it. He had seen retreat. There would be clots of men out in the fields, out far from the road, moving back the other way, men with gray stubborn faces who would not listen. Then there would be the wounded. But here they would block the road. No room to maneuver. If Longstreet's spy was right and there had been masses of cavalry ahead, what the blue cavalry could do to his packed troops . . .

Lee knew that he was worrying too much, recognized it, put a stop to it. He bowed his head and prayed once quickly, then was able to relax and compose himself. He rode up into the pass and the country began to flatten out, to go down

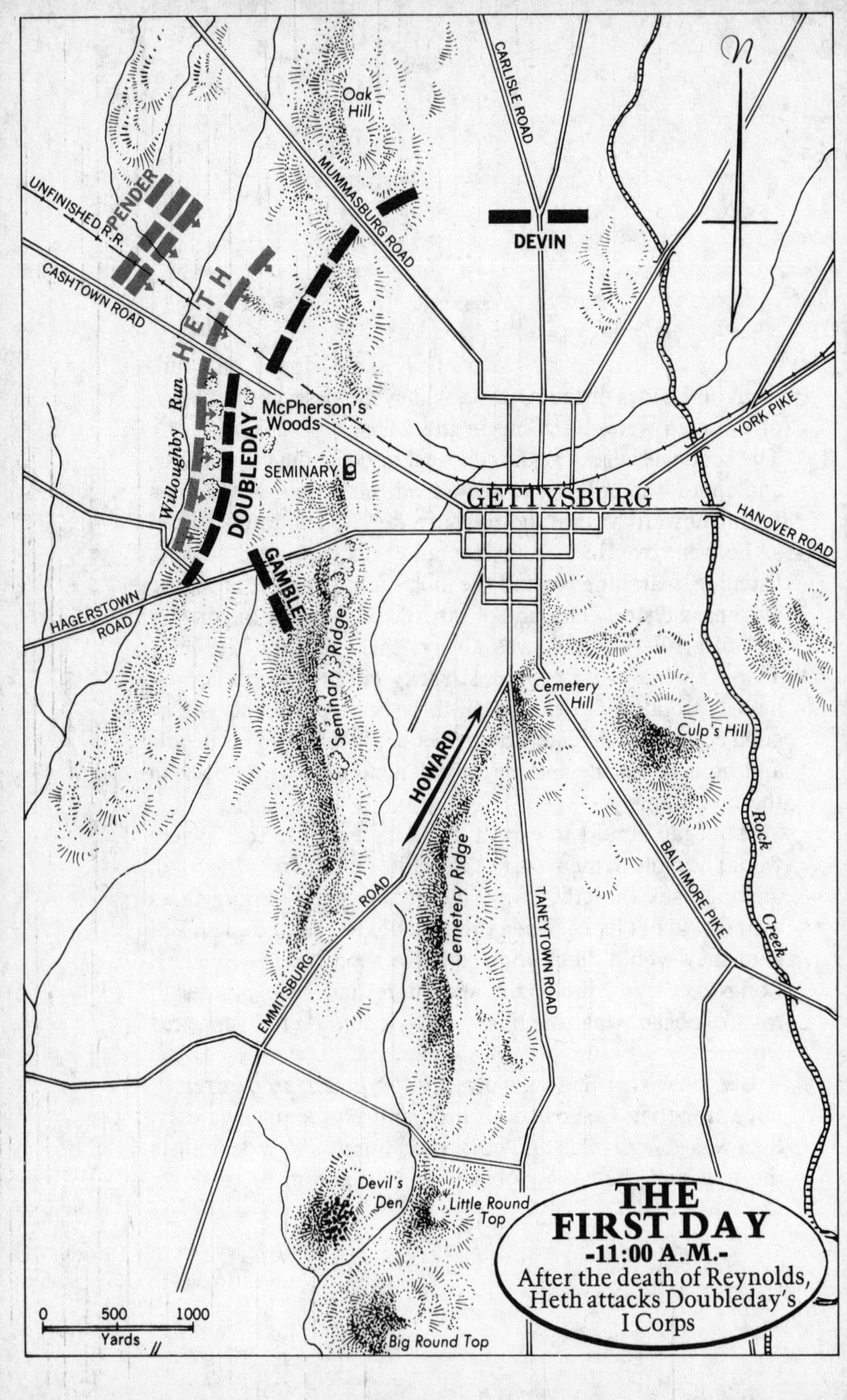

Oak Hill
CARLISLE ROAD
MUMMASBURG ROAD
PENDER
UNFINISHED R.R.
CASHTOWN ROAD
HETH
DEVIN
McPherson's Woods
DOUBLEDAY
Willoughby Run
SEMINARY
GETTYSBURG
YORK PIKE
HANOVER ROAD
GAMBLE
HAGERSTOWN ROAD
Seminary Ridge
Cemetery Hill
Culp's Hill
HOWARD
Cemetery Ridge
EMMITSBURG ROAD
TANEYTOWN ROAD
BALTIMORE PIKE
Rock Creek
Devil's Den
Little Round Top
Big Round Top
0 500 1000
Yards
THE FIRST DAY
-11:00 A.M.-
After the death of Reynolds, Heth attacks Doubleday's I Corps

toward Cashtown. The day was hazy and he could not see far ahead. He began to pass empty houses, dark doors, dark windows. The people had fled. He entered Cashtown and there at the crossroads, mounted, watching the troops pass, was Powell Hill.

Hill was sitting with his hat down over his eyes, slouching in the saddle, a pasty illness in his face. He smiled a ghostly smile, drew himself up, saluted, waved toward a brick house just off the road.

Lee said, "General, you don't look well."

"Momentary indisposition." Hill grinned weakly. "Touch of the Old Soldier's Disease. Would you like to go indoors, sir?"

Lee turned to Taylor. "We will establish temporary headquarters here. All dispatches to this place." To Hill he said, "What artillery is that?"

Hill shook his head, looked away from Lee's eyes. "I don't know, sir. I sent forward for information a while back. Harry Heth is ahead. He has instructions not to force a major action. I told him myself, this morning."

"You have no word from him?"

"No, sir." Hill was not comfortable. Lee said nothing. They went to the brick house. There was a woman at the gate to whom Lee was introduced. Near her stood a small boy in very short pants, sucking his thumb. Lee was offered coffee.

Lee said to Hill, "I must know what's happening ahead."

"Sir, I'll go myself."

Hill was up abruptly, giving instructions to aides. Lee started to object, said nothing. Hill was a nervous, volatile, brilliant man. He had been a superb division commander, but now he commanded a corps, and it was a brutal military truth that there were men who were marvelous with a regiment but could not handle a brigade, and men who were superb with a division but incapable of leading a corps. No way of predicting it. One could only have faith in character.

But to be ill, on this day—very bad luck. Lee watched him. He seemed well enough to ride. Good. Hill was gone.

Lee began work on a plan of withdrawal. Moments later Walter Taylor was in with General Anderson, who had just come into town to look for Hill. Anderson's Division, of Hill's Corps, was stacking up on the road south of town, moving in behind Pender and Heth. Anderson had come to find out about the sound of the guns. He knew nothing. Sitting in the house was galling. Lee was becoming agitated. Anderson sat by hat in hand, watchfully.

Lee said abruptly, impulsively, "I cannot imagine what's become of Stuart. I've heard *nothing.* You understand, I know nothing of what's in front of me. It may be the entire Federal army."

He stopped, controlled himself. But he could wait no longer. He called for Traveler and moved on out of Cashtown, toward Gettysburg.

Now he could begin to hear rifle fire, the small sounds of infantry. He touched his chest, feeling a stuffiness there. So it was more than a duel of artillery. Yet Heth was not a fool. Heth would have reasons. Suspend judgment. But Jackson is not here. Ewell and Hill are new at their commands; all in God's hands. But there was pain in his chest, pain in the left arm. He could see smoke ahead, a long white cloud, low, like fog, on the horizon. The troops around him were eager, bright-faced; the bands were playing. He came out into a field and saw men deploying, moving out on both sides of the road, cutting away the fences: Pender's Division. He put his binoculars to his eyes. Troops were running in a dark grove of trees. Taylor said that Gettysburg was just ahead.

Lee rode left up a flat grassy rise. Below him there was a planted field, rows of low green bush, rolling toward a creek, broken by one low rail fence and a few thick clumps of trees. Beyond the stream there was a rise and atop the rise was a large red building with a white cupola. To the left was an open railroad cut, unfinished, a white wound in the earth. There was smoke around the building. A battery of artillery was firing from there. Lee saw blue hills to the south, in the haze, but now, sweeping the glasses, he could begin to see the lines of fire, could sense by the blots of smoke and the pattern of sound what had happened, was happening, begin piecing it together.

Heth's Division had formed on a front of about a mile, had obviously been repulsed. The Union infantry was firing back from a line at least as long as Heth's. There did not seem to be many cannon, but there were many rifles. Was this the whole Union force or only an advance detachment? Ewell was off to the north; Longstreet was miles away. What had Heth gotten himself into?

The fire from Heth's front was slowing. His troops were not moving. Lee could see many wounded, wagons under trees, clusters of men drifting back through a field to the right. Aides began coming up with messages. Taylor had gone to look for Heth. Lee was thinking: how do we disengage? how do we fall back? where do we hold until Longstreet comes up?

He sent a message to Ewell to advance with all possible speed. He sent a note to Longstreet telling him that the Union infantry had arrived in force. But he knew Longstreet could do nothing; there were two divisions in his way. Lee looked at his watch: well after two o'clock. Darkness a long way away. No way of knowing where the rest of Meade's army was. Possibly moving to the south, to get between Lee and Washington.

And here, at last, was Harry Heth.

He rode up spattering dust, jerking at the horse with unnatural motions, a square-faced man, a gentle face. He blinked, saluting, wiping sweat from his eyes. He had never been impulsive, like Hill; there was even at this moment something grave and perplexed about him, a studious bewilderment. He had been the old army's leading authority on the rifle; he had written a manual. But he had gotten into a fight against orders and there was a blankness in his eyes, vacancy and shame. Lee thought: *he does not know what's happening.*

Heth coughed. "Sir, beg to report."

"Yes."

"Very strange, sir. Situation very confused."

"What happened?"

Lee's eyes were wide and very dark. Heth said painfully, "Sir. I moved in this morning as directed. I thought it was only a few militia. But it was dismounted cavalry. John Buford. Well, there weren't all that many and it was only cavalry, so I just decided to push on it. The boys wouldn't hold back. I thought we shouldn't ought to be stopped by a few dismounted cavalry. But they made a good fight. I didn't expect . . . They really put up a scrap."

"Yes." Lee was watching his eyes.

Heth grimaced, blowing. "Well, sir, they wouldn't leave. My boys got the dander up. We deployed the whole division and went after them. We just about had them running and then all of a sudden I see us moving in on infantry. They got infantry support up from the south. The boys got pushed back. Then we reformed and tried again, couldn't stop there, sir, but there's more infantry now, I don't know how many. But I don't know what else we could have done. Sir, I'm sorry. But it started out as a minor scrap with a few militia and the next thing I know I'm tangling with half the Union army."

"Who are they?"

"Sir?"

Lee was watching the fight, which was now relatively quiet. The smoke was clearing, blowing toward the north. He could see blue troops moving in the trees on the Union right, moving out on the flank. He looked north, but he could see nothing beyond the ridge. The blue troops seemed to be pulling back that way, retreating, reforming. Strange. The battery up by the cupola had stopped firing. Riding up through the haze: Dorsey Pender. Letter from a pious wife.

To Heth Lee said, "What units have you engaged?"

"The cavalry was Buford, sir. Two brigades. They really fought. Then there was the First Corps, the black hats, John Reynolds' old corps. Then there was another corps, but we still haven't got it identified."

At Lee's shoulder, Taylor said quietly, insistently, "General, you are in range of the enemy batteries."

Lee said, "It's quiet now." He looked once more at Heth; his anger died. No time for blame. But there *must* be information.

Taylor insisted, "You gentlemen are standing together. May I suggest that you move at least to the shelter of the trees?"

There was a sudden fire on the left, a burst in the north. Lee felt an acute spasm of real anger. He clutched his chest. *I know nothing.*

Heth said, "I'd better look to my flank." He moved away. A rider came up—a courier from Rodes.

"General Rodes' compliments, sir. I have the honor to inform you that the General has joined the engagement with his entire division and is attacking the Union right. He begs me to inform you that General Early is behind him and will be on the field within the hour. Do you have any instructions, sir?"

Lee felt a thrill of delight, mixed with alarm. Rodes had come in right on the Union flank; the blue troops were turning to meet a new threat. And Early was close behind. A flank assault, already begun. Lee sat staring north. No way to tell. He could order forward the entire army. Heth was here and Pender. Rodes' attack might almost have been planned.

But he did not know how many Federals were ahead. Rodes might be attacking half the Union army. Another Sharpsburg. And yet, and yet, I cannot call him back; he is already committed. Lee said, "Nothing for now. Wait here."

He turned to Taylor. "I want all possible knowledge of the enemy strength. Ride forward yourself and observe. And be careful."

Taylor saluted formally and rode off, the grin breaking across his face just as he turned. Lee turned and began heading back toward the road. Now Heth was back.

"Sir, Rodes is heavily engaged. Shall I attack?"

Lee shook his head, then said loudly, "No." He rode on, then he said over his shoulder, "We are not yet prepared for a full engagement. Longstreet is not up."

Heth said, "There aren't that many of the enemy, sir."

"What are your casualties?"

"Moderate, sir. There's been some fighting. But Pender is in position. Together, sir, we could sweep them."

Lee waited. It did not feel right. There was something heavy and dark and tight about the day, riding stiffly in the broad barren field, in harsh sunlight. The firing in the north was mounting. Batteries of artillery had opened up.

"Who is commanding there?" Lee pointed to the hills beyond the town.

Heth blinked, suddenly remembering. "Sir, I'd forgotten. We have word that General Reynolds was killed."

Lee turned. "John Reynolds?"

"Yes, sir. Prisoners state he was killed this morning. I believe Doubleday has succeeded him."

"Are you sure?"

"The news seems reliable."

"I'm sorry," Lee said. His mind flashed a vision of Reynolds. A neat trim man. A gentleman, a friend. Lee shook his head. It was queer to be so strange and tight in the mind. He seemed unable to think clearly. Reynolds dead. Gone.

Doubleday behind him. Doubleday an unknown quantity, but certainly nothing spectacular. But Reynolds' First Corps was solid. What to do?

"I can support Rodes, sir," Heth said.

Lee looked at him. He knows he has brought this on; he wants to fight now to retrieve it. His answer is to fight, not to think; to fight, pure and simple. Lee rode slowly forward, nearing the trees ahead alongside the road. You can depend on the troops, but can you count on the generals? Why has Rodes attacked? Will Hill fight well, or Rodes either? What I need is Longstreet and he is not here. A mistake to bring him up last.

Another courier. "General Early has arrived, begs to report that he is attacking to the north of General Rodes."

Lee stopped, looked north. It was working almost like a plan. It was possible to see Intention in it. The Union formed to face him and fought well and now was being flanked from the north, simply because Lee's men had orders to come to Gettysburg, and they were coming in almost behind the Union defenses. Lee felt a sharpness in the air. His blood was rising. He had tried to be discreet, but it was all happening without him, without one decision; it was all in God's hands. And yet he could leave it alone himself no longer. Rodes and Early were attacking; Heth and Pender were waiting here in front of him. Lee's instinct sensed opportunity. Let us all go in together, as God has decreed a fight here.

He swung to Heth. "General, you may attack."

To Pender he said the same. He gave no further directions. The generals would know what to do now. With that word it was out of his hands. It had never really been in his hands at all. And yet his was the responsibility.

He rode forward to the rise ahead, across the small creek. Now he had a clearer view. Pender's Division was on the move; he heard the great scream of the massed Rebel yells. Now batteries were in position behind him, beginning to open up on the woods near the cupola. Lee ducked his head as the shot whickered over him. He did not like to stand in front of artillery. Some of the artillery was moving forward. Rifle fire was breaking out. The wind shifted; he was enveloped in smoke. Marshall's face appeared, an incoherent message. Lee tried to find some place to watch the assault. Pender's whole force was streaming forward across the fields, into the woods. Lee saw flags floating through white smoke, disembodied, like walking sticks. Shell bursts were appearing in the air, white flakes, round puffs. One blossomed near. There was Marshall again. Lee heard fragments split the air near him. He moved into a grove of trees: oak, chestnut. There was a white house nearby, a white rail fence, a dead horse lying in a black mound in the sun.

He waited in the grove, listening to the enormous sound of war. Eventually he sat, resting himself against the bole of a tree. It was dark and cool back in here out of the sun. Men were dying up ahead. He took off his hat, ran his fingers through his hair, felt his life beating in his chest. The fight went on. Lee thought for the first time that day of his son, Rooney, wounded, lying not far from here. He closed his eyes, prayed for his boy, for all of them. He put his hand down on black dirt, was reminded: Pennsylvania. I am the invader.

Once more the Rebel yell—inhuman screaming of the onrushing dead. Another unit was going. He rose and went forward, trying to see, but no point in that. There was too much smoke. Yet it might help if he was seen. He moved up out of the grove of trees, onto the road. The road ahead was crowded with wounded. There were men lying under wagons, out of the sun, most of them semi-naked, covered with bandages, blood. He saw another dead horse, a splintered wagon; the severed forefoot of a horse lay near him in gray dust. Smoke was pouring down the road as from a great furnace. He moved forward; his staff followed him. Here was A. P. Hill.

Hill said, white-faced, "Very hard going. Heth is down."

Lee looked at him, waiting.

"Wounded in the head. I don't know how serious. But the Division is moving. Pender is on the flank. But the Yankees are fighting well. I don't recall them fighting this well before."

Hill seemed peculiarly calm, vacant, as if he was not wholly present. He was a handsome man who had a great deal of money but was not "society" and was overly aware of it and very touchy about it.

Lee said, "Let me know General Heth's condition as soon as possible."

Lee sat down against a rail fence. A band came by, playing an incoherent song, fifes and bugles. The sky was overcast with blowing white smoke, the smell of hot guns, of blasted earth, the sweet smell of splintery trees. Lee was in the way, in the road; men were gathering around him, calling to him. He saw a house, an empty front porch. He moved toward that way and stared down toward the smoke. Firing was intense. He sent couriers to Early and Rodes to advise them of his new headquarters and to ask for progress. He had no idea of the whereabouts of Ewell, who was supposed to be in command over there and who probably knew less of what was happening than Lee did. Longstreet was right: command was too loose. But no time for that now.

A courier from Early: The enemy was falling back. Lee could hear an officer near him erupt in a high scream. "They're runnin', Great God Amighty, they're runnin'!"

Lee looked down the smoky street, saw a man helping another man along the road, saw masses of men moving vaguely through a field, saw flashes of artillery. The fire seemed to be slowing down. There were many men yelling.

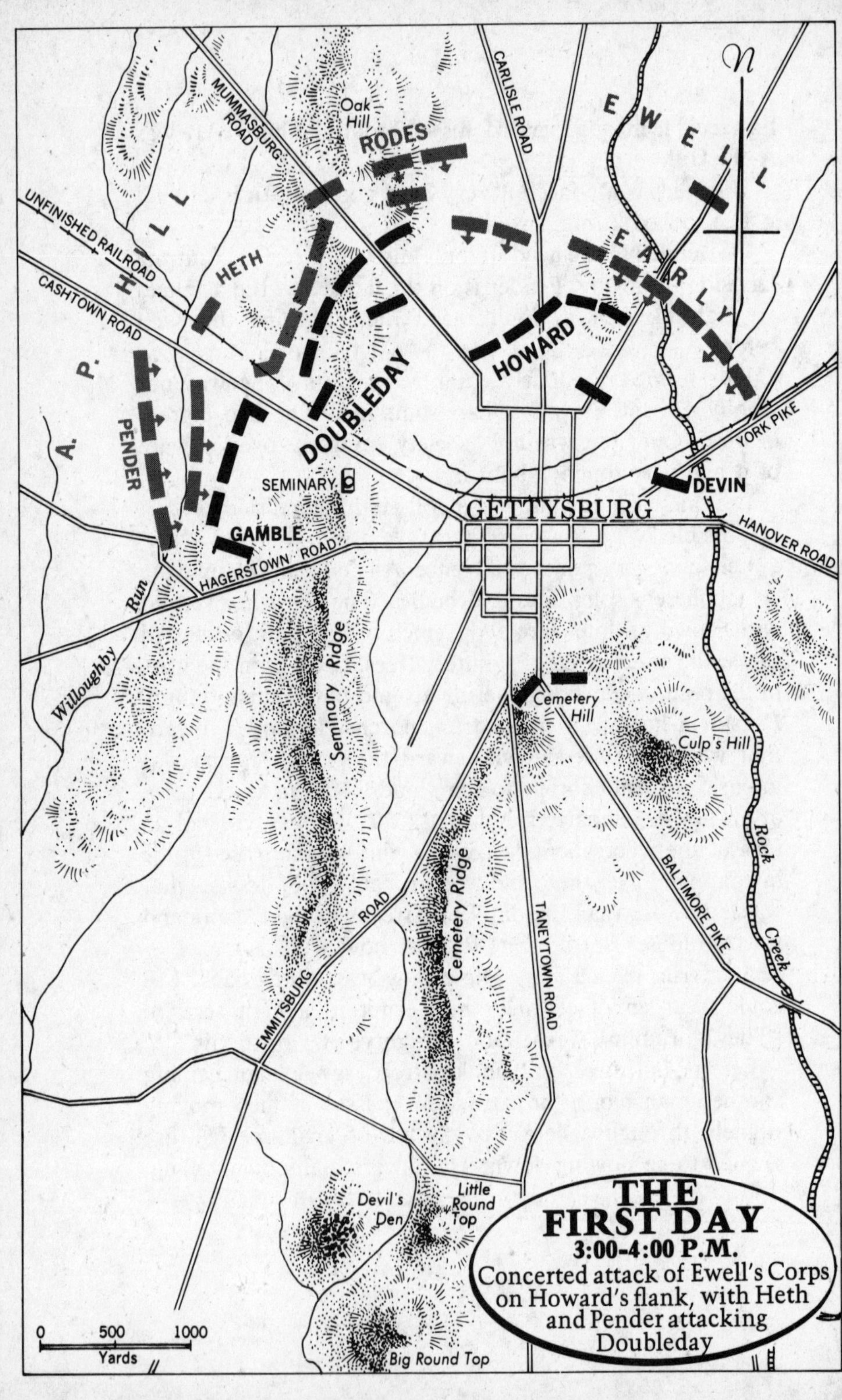

N
MUMMASBURG ROAD
Oak Hill
CARLISLE ROAD
E W E L L
RODES
UNFINISHED RAILROAD
A. P. HILL
HETH
CASHTOWN ROAD
EARLY
HOWARD
DOUBLEDAY
PENDER
YORK PIKE
SEMINARY
DEVIN
GETTYSBURG
GAMBLE
HAGERSTOWN ROAD
HANOVER ROAD
Willoughby Run
Seminary Ridge
Cemetery Hill
Culp's Hill
Rock Creek
BALTIMORE PIKE
TANEYTOWN ROAD
Cemetery Ridge
EMMITSBURG ROAD
Devil's Den
Little Round Top
Big Round Top
0 500 1000
Yards
THE FIRST DAY
3:00-4:00 P.M.
Concerted attack of Ewell's Corps on Howard's flank, with Heth and Pender attacking Doubleday

A lieutenant came down the road, pointing back toward the smoke, yelling wildly that someone was hurt.

A. P. Hill said, at Lee's elbow, "General Heth's surgeon has examined him, sir. He says he ought to be all right, but he will be out of action for a while."

"Where is he?"

"In a house over this way." Hill pointed.

"You will take good care of him, of course. And, General, see to yourself. You can do no more good now. I want you to rest."

Hill said softly, calmly, vacantly, "I'm fine, General, just fine."

But he looked as if he were about to faint. Lee was thinking: if Longstreet were only here. How many in the Union Army? If the First Corps is here and the Eleventh, the rest must not be far behind. He heard more men yelling. In the street he saw officers waving their hats, grinning enormous grins. Victory? A rider came up, from Pender. A young man with a marvelous wide mustache said, "General Pender begs to report the enemy is falling back." Officers threw hats in the air. Lee smiled, could not be heard. One man touched him, another patted his back. He raised his glasses and looked to the clearing smoke.

He turned to Marshall. "I'll go forward."

Traveler was at the rail outside. Lee mounted and rode. Men were cheering him now, touching the horse as he went by. He tried to control his face. The wounded were everywhere. Some of them were Union boys, looking at him insensibly as he went by. A courier from Early: a rout on the left flank. The Union Eleventh Corps was running. More cheers. Lee closed his eyes once briefly. God's will. *My trust in Thee. Oh Lord, bless You and thank You.*

He moved forward to the rise ahead, across a small creek. Taylor said, "This must be Willoughby Run." Lee halted at the crest. Now he could see; the land lay before him wreathed in smoky ridges. Half a mile away lay the town, white board buildings, dirt roads. Beyond it was a high hill that rose above a series of ridges running off to the east. Blue troops were pouring back through the town, moving up the sides of the hill. The couriers were right: they were retreating. Victory. Lee put his glasses to his eyes, felt his hands tremble, focused, saw: Union artillery forming on the high hill, men digging. The fight was not over. Must not let those men occupy the high ground. Lee turned. To Taylor he said, "Find Hill's chief of artillery, tell him I want fire placed on that hill. I don't want it occupied. What word do you have from Ewell? And send General Hill to me."

Taylor moved off. Lee was thinking: we must continue the assault. The blue troops are on the move; now we must keep them moving. But Heth is down. He looked for Pender's courier, informed him to tell General Pender to continue the assault. But Early and Rodes were closer, on the left. If they only kept moving. The guns on the high hill were beginning to fire.

Here was Powell Hill, looking worse. He said, "The men have done all they can do. Heth's division is exhausted. Pender says he has had the hardest fighting of the war."

Lee studied him, looked away, back to the hill above Gettysburg. Hill may be sick but Pender was trustworthy. If Pender had doubts . . .

Taylor arrived. "General Ewell is with General Early, sir. We are in communication."

"Good," Lee said. "Deliver this message in person. Tell General Ewell the Federal troops are retreating in confusion. It is only necessary to push those people to get possession of those heights. Of course, I do not know his situation, and I do not want him to engage a superior force, but I do want him to take that hill, if he thinks practicable, as soon as possible. Remind him that Longstreet is not yet up."

Taylor repeated the message, rode off. Beyond that hill Lee could begin to feel the weight of the Union Army, the massive blue force pouring his way. What kind of a soldier would Meade turn out to be? We must not give him the high ground. Lee looked southeast, saw two rounded hills. We might swing around that way. They have marched quicker than I expected. Thank the Lord for Longstreet's spy.

He heard more cheering, to the rear, looked, saw Longstreet. Moving forward slowly, calmly, like a black rock, grinning hungrily through the black beard. Lee flushed with pleasure. Longstreet dismounted, extended a hand.

"Congratulations, General. Wish I could have been here."

Lee took the hand warmly. "Come here, I want you to see this." He waved toward the field ahead, the hill beyond Gettysburg.

An officer near him said, "General Lee, it's Second Manassas all over again!"

"Not quite," Lee said cheerily, "not quite." He was delighted to have Longstreet here. Now through the streets Johnson's Division was moving, Longstreet's people could not be far behind. With every step of a soldier, with every tick of the clock, the army was gaining safety, closer to victory, closer to the dream of independence.

Longstreet studied the field. After a moment he said, "We were lucky."

"It couldn't have worked better if we had planned it."

Longstreet nodded. Lee explained the position that Ewell had orders to move to the left and take that hill. Longstreet studied the hill* while Lee spoke. After a moment he said, "Fine. But this is fine. This is almost perfect." He turned to Lee. "They're right where we want them. All we have to do is swing around that way—" he pointed toward Washington

*Cemetery Hill.

—"and get between them and Lincoln and find some good high ground, and they'll have to hit us, they'll have to, and we'll have them, General, we'll have them!"

His eyes were flashing; he was as excited as Lee had ever seen him. Lee said, amazed, "You mean you want me to *disengage?*"

"Of course." Longstreet seemed surprised. "You certainly don't mean—sir, I have been under the impression that it would be our strategy to conduct a defensive campaign, wherever possible, in order to keep this army intact."

"Granted. But the situation has changed."

"In what way?"

"We cannot disengage. We have already pushed them back. How can we move off in the face of the enemy?"

Longstreet pointed. "Very simply. Around to the right. He will occupy those heights and wait to see what we are going to do. He always has. Meade is new to the command. He will not move quickly."

Lee put his hand to his face. He looked toward the hill and saw the broken Union corps falling back up the slope. He felt only one urge: to press on and get it done. He said nothing, turning away. There was a messenger from General Ewell. Lee recognized the man, Captain James Power Smith, Ewell's aide. The Captain was delighted to see the Commanding General.

Ewell's message was cautious: "General Ewell says he will direct Early and Rodes to move forward, but he requests support of General Hill on his right. He says that there is a strong Union position south of the town which should be taken at once."

Lee asked which position Ewell meant. He handed Smith the glasses. Smith said the position was beyond the one in front, at the top of which there was a cemetery.

Lee looked at his watch. It was almost five o'clock. Still

two hours of daylight. He said to Longstreet, "General, how far away is your lead division?"

"McLaws. About six miles. He is beyond Johnson's train of wagons."

Lee shook his head. To Smith he said, "I have no force to attack the hill. General Hill's Corps has had hard fighting. Tell General Ewell to take that hill if at all possible. Have you seen Major Taylor?"

"No, sir."

"You must just have passed him."

Lee sent Smith away. He remembered: he had ordered artillery to fire on the hill, but none was firing. He sent to find out why. He began to realize he was really very tired. But if a strong Union force was on a hill to the south . . . but without Longstreet's Corps a general assault was impossible. Where was the artillery? Where was Hill? Why had Early and Rodes stopped their attacks? He could see the town below choked with soldiers, horses, but there was no advance.

He turned, saw Longstreet watching him. He had the look of a man surpressing his thoughts. Lee said, "Say it, General."

"We shouldn't have attacked here, General. Heth had his orders."

Lee waved a hand. "I know that. But we have pushed them back."

"In the morning we will be outnumbered."

Lee shrugged. Numbers were meaningless. "Had I paid attention to numbers, General . . ." Lee left the rest unsaid.

Longstreet said, "If we moved south, toward Washington, we could fight on ground of our choosing."

"The enemy is *here,* General. We did not want the fight, but the fight is here. What if I ask this army to retreat?"

"They will do as you order."

Lee shook his head again. He was growing weary of this. Why didn't Ewell's assault begin? A cautious commander, new to his command. And A. P. Hill is sick. Yet we won. The soldiers won. Lee pointed toward the hill.

"They will probably retreat. Or Ewell will push them off. But if Meade is there tomorrow, I will attack him."

"If Meade is there," Longstreet said implacably, "it is because he wants you to attack him."

That was enough. Lee thought: docile men do not make good soldiers. He said nothing. Longstreet could see the conversation was at an end. He said, "I'll bring my boys up as soon as I can."

Lee nodded. As Longstreet was going, Lee said, "General."

"Yes, sir?"

"Your spy was correct in his reports. Had it not been for that report, this army might have been destroyed in detail. I thank you."

Longstreet nodded. If the compliment pleased him, he did not show it. He moved off.

Lee stood alone, troubled. He had had enough of defensive war. The King of Spades. Let us attack, and let it be done. I am extraordinarily tired. You are an old man. And if something happens to you?

He picked up the glasses, waiting for Ewell's attack. No attack began.

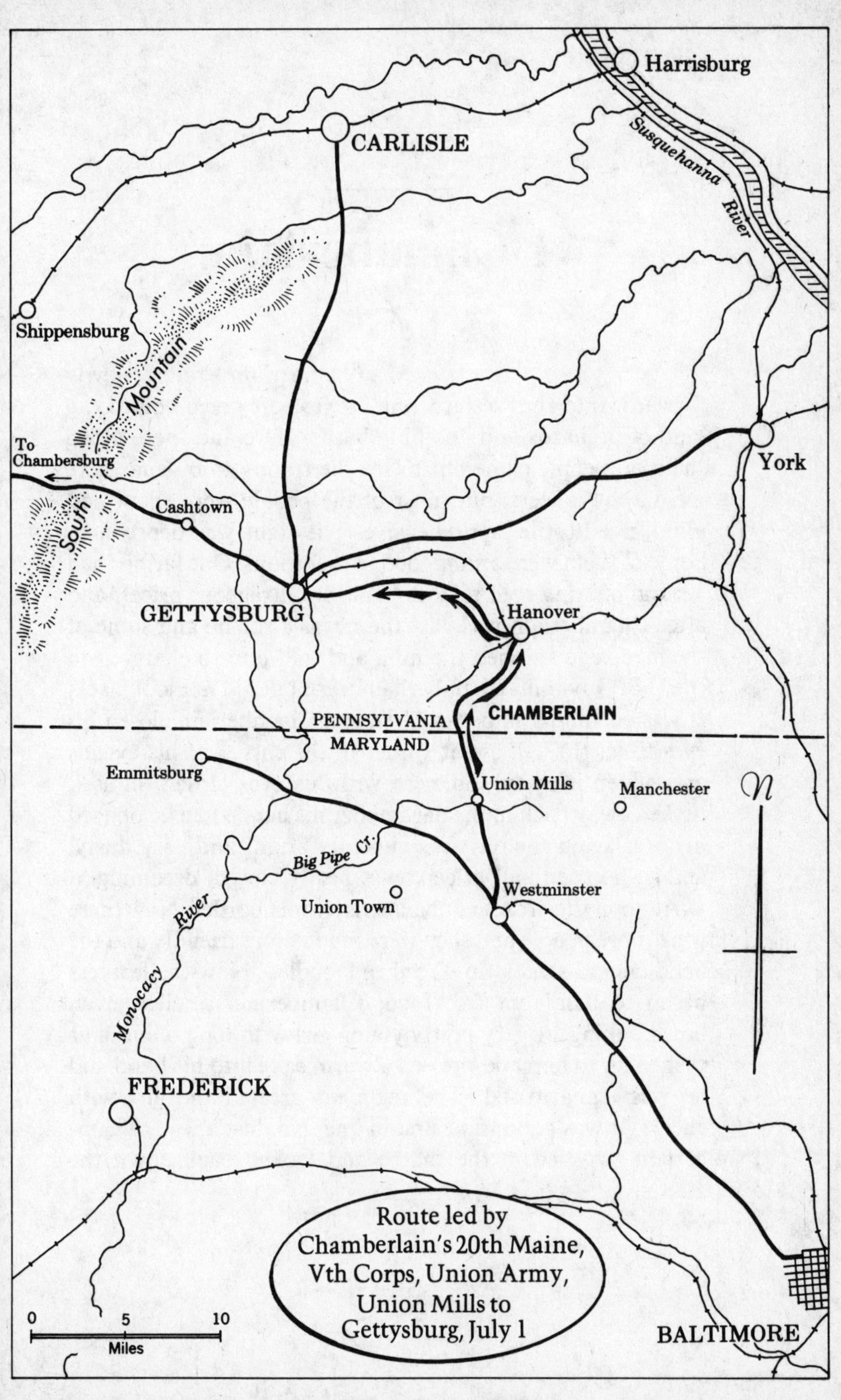
Harrisburg
CARLISLE
Susquehanna River
Shippensburg
South Mountain
To Chambersburg
Cashtown
York
GETTYSBURG
Hanover
CHAMBERLAIN
PENNSYLVANIA
MARYLAND
Emmitsburg
Union Mills
Manchester
N
Big Pipe Cr.
Westminster
Union Town
Monocacy River
FREDERICK
Route led by Chamberlain's 20th Maine, Vth Corps, Union Army, Union Mills to Gettysburg, July 1
0 5 10
Miles
BALTIMORE

4. Chamberlain

Chamberlain rode slowly forward, into the western sun. It was soft green country, a land of orchards and good big barns. Here and there along the road people came out to see the troops go by and there were a few cheers, but most of the people were silent and glum, not hostile, apprehensive. The sight was depressing. Some of them were selling food to the troops. One farmer had a stand offering cold milk for sale, at outrageous prices, and after Chamberlain was past there was a scuffle and some of the men requisitioned the milk and told him to charge it to the U.S. Guvmint. Chamberlain heard but did not look back. It was beginning to be very hot, and Chamberlain closed his eyes to let the salt sweat gather in the corner of his eyelids and wiped it away and rode with his eyes closed, himself tucked away back in the dark under his hat. When he opened his eyes again the day was violently bright and very dusty, and so he rode half asleep, eyes partly closed, dreaming.

At noon they reached the Pennsylvania border. Now there were more people and they were much more friendly and the band behind struck up "Yankee Doodle." Now the farmers began to hand out free food; Chamberlain smelled fresh bread baking. A very pretty young girl with long blond hair rushed up to him and pressed a warm cake into his hand and he was embarrassed. The regiment greeted the girl with cheers. It was good to be first in line. No dust ahead. Chamberlain swiveled in the saddle and looked back down the road, and there down in the dust like a huge blue snake came the whole Fifth Corps along the winding road, some men on horses riding high in black hats, among the tilting flags. More bands were playing. Chamberlain wiped sweat from his eyes.

It was time to dismount. A good officer rode as little as possible. He got down from the horse and began to march along in the dust, in the heat. Near him he could hear Tom Chamberlain talking to one of the new men from the Second Maine, explaining the ways of this regiment. Tom was proud but not too proud. The Second Maine had seen more action. Chamberlain thought of Tom and his mind wandered back to Maine: young Tom lost, in the dark of the winter, a long search, Mother crying, we never found him, he survived out there and came back himself, a grinning kid with a bright red nose, never once afraid . . .

"One of the things you get to know," Tom Chamberlain was saying, "is that this here brigade has got its own special bugle call. You ever hear tell of Dan Butterfield?"

"General Butterfield what was with Hooker?"

"Right. Same man. Well, he used to be our brigade commander."

"They say he was a pistol. No man like him for having a good time." He gave a lewd wink, suggestion of coarseness.

"Well, I don't know about that, but he liked to write bugle calls. Trouble with this army is too many bugle calls. Call for artillery and infantry and get up and eat and retreat and all that, and it got a mite confusin', so Ole Dan Butterfield wrote a call for this here Brigade, special. If there is an order for this Brigade, well, somebody else would be blowing his blame bugle and we'd think it was for us only it wasn't, but we would follow the order anyway, and next thing you know we'd be in trouble."

"That happened to us once," the Maine man said. "Half

the Regiment charged and the other half retreated. You had your choice." He chuckled. "Seems a good system, come to think on it."

"Well, in this Brigade we got a special call. You hear that call and you know the next call is for you. Goes like this:

"We call it 'Dan Butterfield,' just like this: 'Dan, Dan, Dan, Butterfield, Butterfield.' "

The Maine man said glumly, "In the middle of a fight I'm supposed to remember *that?*"

"It's easy if you remember." He sang it again: "Dan, Dan, Dan, Butterfield."

"Um," the Maine man said.

"Ole Butterfield wrote a lot of bugle calls. You know Butterfield's Lullaby?"

"Butterfield's what?"

Tom hummed a few bars of what was still known as Butterfield's Lullaby but which the army would later know as "Taps" and which now had no connotation of death, which simply meant rest for the night, rest after a long day in the dust and the sun, with the bugles blaring, and Joshua Chamberlain, listening, thought of the sound of Butterfield's Lullaby coming out of the dark, through a tent flap, with the campfires burning warm and red in the night, and Chamberlain thought: you can grow to love it.

Amazing. Chamberlain let his eyes close down to the slits, retreating within himself. He had learned that you could sleep on your feet on the long marches. You set your feet to going and after a while they went by themselves and you sort of turned your attention away and your feet went on walking painlessly, almost without feeling, and gradually you closed down your eyes so that all you could see were the heels of the man in front of you, one heel, other heel, one heel, other heel, and so you moved on dreamily in the heat and the dust, closing your eyes against the sweat, head down and gradually darkening, so you actually slept with the sight of the heels in front of you, one heel, other heel, and often when the man in front of you stopped you bumped into him. There were no heels today, but there was the horse he led by the reins. He did not know the name of this horse. He did not bother any more; the horses were all dead too soon. Yet you learn to love it.

Isn't that amazing? Long marches and no rest, up very early in the morning and asleep late in the rain, and there's a marvelous excitement to it, a joy to wake in the morning and feel the army all around you and see the campfires in the morning and smell the coffee . . .

. . . awake all night in front of Fredericksburg. We attacked in the afternoon, just at dusk, and the stone wall was aflame from one end to the other, too much smoke, couldn't see, the attack failed, couldn't withdraw, lay there all night in the dark, in the cold among the wounded and dying. Piled-up bodies in front of you to catch the bullets, using the dead for a shield; remember the sound? Of bullets in dead bodies? Like a shot into a rotten leg, a wet thick leg. All a man is: wet leg of blood. Remember the flap of a torn curtain in a blasted window, fragment whispering in that awful breeze: *never, forever, never, forever.*

You have a professor's mind. But that is the way it sounded.

Never. Forever.

Love that too?

Not love it. Not quite. And yet, I was never so alive.

Maine . . . is silent and cold.

Maine in the winter: air is darker, the sky is a deeper dark. A darkness comes with winter that these Southern people don't know. Snow falls so much earlier and in the winter you can walk in a snowfield among bushes, and visitors don't know that the bushes are the tops of tall pines, and you're standing in thirty feet of snow. Visitors. Once long ago visitors in the dead of winter: a preacher preaching hell-fire. Scared the fool out of me. And I resented it and Pa said I was right.

Pa.

When he thought of the old man he could see him suddenly in a field in the spring, trying to move a gray boulder. He always knew instinctively the ones you could move, even though the greater part was buried in the earth, and he expected you to move the rock and not discuss it. A hard and silent man, an honest man, a noble man. Little humor but sometimes the door opened and you saw the warmth within a long way off, a certain sadness, a slow, remote, unfathomable quality as if the man wanted to be closer to the world but did not know how. Once Chamberlain had a speech memorized from Shakespeare and gave it proudly, the old man listening but not looking, and Chamberlain remembered it still: "What a piece of work is man . . . in action how like an angel!" And the old man, grinning, had scratched his head and then said stiffly, "Well, boy, if he's an angel, he's sure a murderin' angel." And Chamberlain had gone on to school to make an oration on the subject: Man, the Killer Angel. And when the old man heard about it he was very proud, and Chamberlain felt very good remembering it. The old man was proud of his son, the Colonel. Of infantry. What would he have thought of the speech this morning? Home and Mother. Mother wanted me to be a parson. Vincent picked me, *me,* to lead the Regiment. Folks back home will know by now. Commander of the Regiment. Why *me?* What did Vincent see?

He turned his mind away from that. Think on it when the time comes. You think too much beforehand and you get too self-conscious and tight and you don't function well. He knew that he was an instinctive man, not a planner, and he did best when he fell back on instinct. Think of music now and singing. Pass the time with a bit of harmony. Hum songs, and rest.

But it was very hot.

Could use some Maine cool now.

Home. One place is just like another, really. Maybe not. But truth is it's all just rock and dirt and people are roughly the same. I was born up there but I'm no stranger here. Have always felt at home everywhere, even in Virginia, where they hate me. Everywhere you go there's nothing but the same rock and dirt and houses and people and deer and birds. They give it all names, but I'm at home everywhere. Odd thing: unpatriotic. I was at home in England. I would be at home in the desert. In Afghanistan or far Typee. All mine, it all belongs to me. My world.

Tom Chamberlain was saying, "You should have seen the *last* commander, Old Ames. He was the worst, I mean to tell you, the triple-toed half-wound, spotted mule *worst.*"

"Where was you boys at Chancellorsville?"

"Well now." A painful subject. Joshua Chamberlain opened his eyes.

"The fact is," Tom said gloomily, "we was not engaged."

"Well now, a lot us wa'n't engaged. That there Hooker, I hear he froze right up like a pond in the dark."

"Well, we had us a misfortune." Tom turned eyes sad as a trout. He was a lean, happy, excitable man who had turned out to be calm and serene in combat. Soldiering was beginning to intrigue him.

"The thing was, damn, we had these here 'noculations. You ever been 'noculated?"

The man swore earnestly. Tom nodded. "Well, then, you know. Only thing was, we wound up sick, half the dang regiment. And come time for the fight at Chancellorsville our Surgeon Major—that's a stumble-fingered man named

Wormy Monroe—he up and reported us unfit for combat. So they went ahead and sent us back to mind the dang telegraph wires. We wasn't allowed to 'sociate with nobody. Old Lawrence there he went on up and argued, but wouldn't nobody come near us. It was like he was carrying the plague. Lawrence said hang it, we ought to be the first ones in, we'd probably give the Rebs a disease and be more useful than any other outfit in the whole army. Matter of fact, way things turned, we probably would've been more use than most of them people. Anyway we wasn't in it."

The Maine man was chuckling. Chamberlain thought: would have thought mountain men were tougher than city boys. But mountain men get all the diseases. City boys get immune as they grow up. We were a thousand strong when we left Maine.

Gallant six hundred . . . Half a league, half a league . . .

It was quieter now. No one was talking. Sound of troops at route step, shuffle in the dust, dull clink of mess kits, a band in the distance, tinny, forlorn, raw call of a cow in the sunlight. A voice in his ear, a hand on his arm.

"Colonel, sir—" exasperated—"beg the Colonel's pardon, but would the Colonel do us all a favor and get back on that damned horse?"

Colonel opened his eyes into the glare, saw: Tozier. Color Sergeant Tozier. A huge man with a huge nose, sweat bubbling all over his face. "I tell you, Sir, be a damn site easier handlin' these here new recruits if the officers would act like they got sense, sir."

Chamberlain blinked, wiped at his sweat. Some of the men were watching with that odd soft look on their faces that still surprised Chamberlain. He started to say something, shook his head. Tozier was right. He mounted the horse.

Tozier said, "How are you, sir?"

Chamberlain nodded, grinned weakly.

"We don't need no more new commanding officers," Tozier said. "Here you, Lieutenant, keep an eye on the Colonel."

Tom said, "Yes, sir." Tozier departed. Chamberlain thought: good thing old Ames didn't see him. My boys. Ames shaped them. But they're mine. Year ago they held meetings to decide what to do; if they disagreed with an officer, they stopped and argued. Can't conduct an army as a town meeting.

They were coming into Hanover. Out in a field dead bodies lay in untidy rows. The arms were up above the heads, the clothes were scattered, shoes were missing. The hair of some was flickering in the wind and they looked alive. Chamberlain learned: Stuart had been through here and there'd been a brush. The sight of dead men awakened them all.

A clear day, very hot. Wind swinging to the south. Buzzards ahead. As they rode ladies waved handkerchiefs, a band played the "Star-Spangled Banner." Chamberlain wondered: will the people here let the buzzards have them? Or will they bury them, Stuart's men?

The people of Hanover were delighted to see them. Now as they got closer to the Rebels people seemed much happier everywhere. Happiness seemed to increase in direct proportion to how close you were. When we actually get there, Chamberlain thought, it will be easy to tell: the men will be kissing you.

Chamberlain rode upright through town. On the far side he slumped again. For a short while General Vincent came up to ride with him. Vincent was the new brigade commander—a very handsome man with thick sideburns, from the 83rd Pennsylvania. He had a good reputation and he had the air of a man who knew what he was doing. But Chamberlain had seen that air before. Hooker had it. And if ever there was a man who did not know what he was doing . . .

Vincent had heard about the 114 volunteers. He was impressed. He thought that things were looking up. The army was ready for a fight. That in itself was an impressive fact, after all that had happened. He showed Chamberlain the new brigade flag: triangular, white, with a blue border, a red Maltese Cross in the center. The man looked at it without interest. It meant nothing much, as yet. Vincent rode back. The man from the Second Maine said sadly, "You ever hear about *our* flag? It cost twelve hundred dollars."

But the men were tired. There was silence again. Chamberlain saw a rider going to the rear, a blue courier. Then there was the first wagon, then another. There was fighting at Gettysburg. Off against the horizon he could see a haze, a dark haze, as of dirt stirred into the air.

Nothing to do now but rest on the march. The troops became very still. It was darker now. The land around them was hilly and green, turning slowly gold, then hazy purple. It was a beautiful afternoon. At dark, word came forward to go into bivouac. Vincent came up and stopped the column, and the men moved gratefully out into a field, carrying the rails of the fences with them for evening fires. They had marched more than twenty miles again; it was now a hundred miles in five days. Now for the first time the new Maine men heard the call: Dan, Dan, Dan, Butterfield! Butterfield!

And then down the road came more riders, rushing to the rear on lathered horses. Chamberlain looked up to watch them go, sensing alarm. He could feel the Gray army beyond the hills. A moment later there came the bugle call: Dan, Dan, Dan, Butterfield, Butterfield, then forward.

A universal groan. No rest now. The rattle of the rails being dropped, a general cursing. Chamberlain reformed the regiment out in the road. Dispatch from Vincent: Move out.

Word of what had happened moved slowly down the column, but it was a long while before word came down to Chamberlain. By that time it was well after dark and the moon was rising, yellow in hazy air, huge in the trees, gazing like one single vacant eye, and Vincent rode up.

Two Corps had been engaged at Gettysburg and had been driven off. The First Corps had done well, but the Eleventh, those damn Dutchmen, had run again, as they did at Chancellorsville. Now the First was holding and screaming back for reinforcements. John Reynolds was hurt, possibly killed. Proceed with all possible speed.

Chamberlain did not protest. In the darkness he could feel his strength rising, coming over him in the cooler air of evening. Not far to Gettysburg now. He could hear no guns. But now along the roadway there were people rushing out, people lining the rail fences, anxious, overjoyed. From houses back off away from the road there was a waving of flags, a fluttering of white handkerchiefs; women lifted lamps at the windows. There were many healthy-looking young men lining the road and some of the men from Maine grumbled. But the rest were too tired. Chamberlain saw some staggering, then one fell out. He collapsed in a clatter of falling rifle, of mess tins rattling in the dust. He was pulled aside. Chamberlain arranged a detail to pick up fallen men.

On and on. Now it was much darker and the moon was high, and then ahead there was an officer, a staff officer, sitting on a black horse. He rode out to meet Chamberlain as he passed.

"Colonel, tell your men. General McClellan has assumed command of the army."

Chamberlain did not have to spread the word. It went down the ranks like a wind in wheat. Some of the men cheered hoarsely. One man fired a rifle, and then Tozier talked to him. For a long moment Chamberlain believed it. McClellan was back. God bless old Lincoln. The only general of the whole mess who knew what he was doing. But then the troops moved on and the moon went behind a cloud and Chamberlain knew that it could not be true.

But the men marched believing they were behind McClellan. He was the only general Chamberlain had ever seen who was truly loved. The Rebs loved Lee, no doubt of that. And we loved Mac. Chamberlain thought: two things an officer must do, to lead men. This from old Ames, who never cared about love: *You must care for your men's welfare. You must show physical courage.*

Well, Chamberlain thought, there's no McClellan. There's only Meade, whom none of these people know, let alone like, and he'll be cautious. So I've taken care, as best I can, of their welfare. Now tomorrow we'll see about the courage.

Now there were the wounded, the stragglers. Men limped back, sat out in the fields making fires, sulked along eastward, out in the dark. Now there were rumors: a terrible defeat, someone had blundered, two hundred thousand Rebs, the Eleventh Corps had deserted. Chamberlain ordered his men to close up and keep moving and not to talk. Damn the rumors. You never knew what was true until days or weeks or even months afterward. He called close up, close up, first order he had given since morning, and then shortly after that the order came to stop, at last.

It was almost midnight. There were clouds again and it was very dark, but Chamberlain could see a hill in front of him and masses of troops and tents ahead. The Twentieth Maine went off the road and most went to sleep without fires, some without pitching tents, for the night was warm and without a wind. Chamberlain asked a passing courier: how far to Gettysburg? and the man pointed back over his shoulder. You're there, Colonel, you're there.

Chamberlain lay down to rest. It was just after midnight. He wondered if McClellan would really be back. He prayed for a leader. For his boys.

5. Longstreet

He rode out of Gettysburg just after dark. His headquarters were back on the Cashtown Road, and so he rode back over the battlefield of the day. His staff recognized his mood and left him discreetly alone. He was riding slumped forward, head down, hat over his eyes. One by one they left him, moving ahead, cheering up when they were out of his company. He passed a hospital wagon, saw mounded limbs glowing whitely in the dark, a pile of legs, another of arms. It looked like masses of fat white spiders. He stopped in the road and lighted a cigar, looking around him at the tents and the wagons, listening to the rumble and music of the army in the night. There were a few groans, dead sounds from dying earth, most of them soft and low. There was a fire far off, a large fire in a grove of trees, men outlined against a great glare; a band was playing something discordant, unrecognizable. A dog passed him, trotted through the light of an open tent flap, paused, looked, inspected the ground, padded silently into the dark. Fragments of cloth, trees, chewed bits of paper littered the road. Longstreet took it all in, began to move on. He passed a black mound which seemed strange in the dark: lumpy, misshapen. He rode over and saw: dead horses. He rode away from the field, toward higher ground.

Lee would attack in the morning. Clear enough. Time and place not yet set. But he will attack. Fixed and unturnable, a runaway horse. Longstreet felt a depression so profound it deadened him. Gazing back on that black hill above Gettysburg, that high lighted hill already speckled with fires among the gravestones, he smelled disaster like distant rain.

It was Longstreet's curse to see the thing clearly. He was a brilliant man who was slow in speech and slow to move and silent-faced as stone. He had not the power to convince. He sat on the horse, turning his mind away, willing it away as a gun barrel swivels, and then he thought of his children, powerless to stop that vision. It blossomed: a black picture. She stood in the doorway: *the boy is dead.* She didn't even say his name. She didn't even cry.

Longstreet took a long deep breath. In the winter the fever had come to Richmond. In a week they were dead. All within a week, all three. He saw the sweet faces: moment of enormous pain. The thing had pushed him out of his mind, insane, but no one knew it. They looked at the plain blunt stubborn face and saw nothing but dull Dutch eyes, the great darkness, the silence. He had not thought God would do a thing like that. He went to church and asked and there was no answer. He got down on his knees and pleaded but there was no answer. She kept standing in the door: *the boy is dead.* And he could not even help her, could say nothing, could not move, could not even take her into his arms. Nothing to give. One strength he did not have. Oh God: *my boy is dead.*

He had tears in his eyes. Turn away from that. He mastered it. What he had left was the army. The boys were here. He even had the father, in place of God: old Robert Lee. Rest with that, abide with that.

His aides were all gone, all but two. Goree hung back from him in the growing dark. He rode on alone, silently, Goree trailing like a hunting dog, and met one of his surgeons coming up from camp: J. S. D. Cullen, delighted, having heard of the great victory, and Longstreet succeeded in depressing him, and Cullen departed. Longstreet lectured himself: depression is contagious; keep it to yourself. He needed something to cheer him, turned to two men behind him, found there was only one, not an aide, the Englishman: Fremantle. Exactly what he needed. Longstreet drew up to wait.

The Englishman came pleasantly, slowly forward. He was the kind of breezy, cheery man who brings humor with his presence. He was wearing the same tall gray hat and the remarkable coat. He said cheerily, tapping the great hat, "Don't mean to intrude upon your thoughts, General."

"Not 't'all." Longstreet said.

"Really, sir, if you'd rather ride alone . . ."

"Good to see you," Longstreet said.

The Englishman rode up grinning broadly through widely spaced teeth. He had entered the country by way of Mexico, riding in a wagon drawn by a tobacco-chewing man who had turned out to be, in his spare time, the local judge. Fremantle had seen many interesting things: a casual hanging, raw floods, great fires. He was continually amazed at the combination of raw earth and rough people, white columned houses and traces of English manner. He had not gotten used to the crude habit of shaking hands which was common among these people, but he forced himself. He was enjoying himself hugely. He had not changed his clothes in some days and he looked delightfully disreputable, yet mannered and cool and light in the saddle. Longstreet grinned again.

"Did you get a chance to see anything?"

"Well, as a matter of fact I *did.* I found rather a large tree and Lawley and I sat out in the open and there was quite a show. Lovely, oh lovely."

"You didn't happen to see a cavalry charge?" Stuart: not yet returned.

"Not a one," Fremantle gloomed. "Nor a hollow square. You know, sir, we really ought to discuss that at length on some occasion. Provided this war lasts long enough, which most people seem to think it won't. You fellows seem to do well enough without it, I must say. But still, one likes to feel a certain *security* in these matters, which the square gives, do you see? One likes to know, that is, where everyone is, at given moments. Ah, but then—" he took a deep breath, tapped his chest—"there's always tomorrow. I gather you expect a bit of an adventure tomorrow."

Longstreet nodded.

"Well, I shall try to find a position of advantage. I will appreciate your advice, although of course if I'm ever in the way at all, you must feel free, I mean, one must not hamper operations. Don't spare my feelings, sir. But if you'll tell me where to stand."

"I will."

Fremantle whacked a mosquito. "Another victory today. When I am clear about it all I shall write it down. Expect you chaps are getting rather used to victory, what? Damn!" He swatted another bug. "Must say, enormously impressive, this army. Yet the Federal fellas just keep on coming. Curious. I have a bit of difficulty, you know, understanding exactly *why.* Some time when there's time . . . but the war is ending, of course. I can feel that myself. That is the message I shall transmit to my people. No doubt of it."

He eyed Longstreet. Longstreet said nothing.

"Your General Lee is a wonder."

"Yes," Longstreet said.

"A thing one rarely sees." Fremantle paused. "Remarkable," he said. He was about to say something else but changed his mind.

"He holds this army together," Longstreet said.

"Strordnry dignity."

"Strordnry."

"I mean, one does not expect it. No offense, sir? But your General Lee is an *English* general, sir. Strordnry. He has gained some reputation, sir, as of course you know, but there is a tendency in Europe to, ah, think of Americans as, ah, somewhat behind the times, sometimes what, ah, how do I say this? One is on tricky ground here, but, sir, of course you understand, there are these cultural differences, a new land and all that. Yet, what I mean to say is, one did not expect General Lee."

"To be a gentleman," Longstreet said.

Fremantle squinted. After a moment he nodded. Longstreet was not offended. Fremantle said wonderingly, "Sir, you cannot imagine the surprise. One hears all these stories of Indians and massacres and lean backwoodsmen with ten-foot rifles and rain dances and what not, and yet here, your officers . . ." He shook his head. "Strordnry. Why, do you know, your General Lee is even a member of the Church of England?"

"True."

"He has great forbears."

"Yes," Longstreet said.

"I have noticed, sir, that you are always in camp near him. I must say, sir, that I am touched."

"Well," Longstreet said.

"Ah." Fremantle sighed. "We have so many things in common, your country and mine. I earnestly hope we shall become allies. Yet I feel you do not need us. But I must say, I am increasingly indebted to you for your hospitality."

"Our pleasure."

"Ah. Um." Fremantle cocked his head again. "One thing I'm very glad to see. Your General Lee is a moralist, as are all true gentlemen, of course, but he respects minor vice, harmless vice, when he finds it in others. Now that's the mark of the true gentleman. That is what distinguishes the man so to me, aside from his military prowess, of course. The *true* gentleman has no vices, but he allows you your own. Ah." He patted a saddlebag. "By which I mean, sir, to get to the heart of the matter, that I have a flagon of brandy at your disposal, should the occasion arise."

"It undoubtedly will." Longstreet bowed. "Thank you."

"You may call on me, sir."

Longstreet smiled.

"A small weakness," Fremantle went on cheerily, "of which I am not proud, you understand. But one sees so little whisky in this army. Amazing."

"Lee's example. Jackson didn't drink either. Nor does Stuart."

Fremantle shook his head in wonder. "Oh, by the way, there's a story going around, do you know? They say that General Lee was asleep, and the army was marching by, and fifteen thousand men went by on tiptoe so as not to wake him. Is that true?"

"Might have been." Longstreet chuckled. "I know one that I heard myself. While ago we sat around a fire, talked on Darwin. Evolution. You read about it?"

"Ah?"

"Charles Darwin. Theory of Evolution."

"Can't say that I have. There are so many of these things rattling about."

"Theory that claims that men are descended from apes."

"Oh *that.* Oh yes. Well, I've heard—distastefully—of that."

"Well, we were talking on that. Finally agreed that Darwin was probably right. Then one fella said, with great dignity he said, 'Well, maybe *you* are come from an ape, and maybe *I* am come from an ape, but General Lee, *he* didn't come from no ape.' "

"Well, of course." Fremantle did not quite see the humor. Longstreet grinned into the dark.

"It is a Christian army," Longstreet said. "You did not know Jackson."

"No. It was my great misfortune to arrive after his death. They tell great things of him."

"He was colorful," Longstreet said. "He was Christian."

"His reputation exceeds that of Lee."

"Well, pay no attention to that. But he was a good soldier. He could move troops. He knew how to hate." Longstreet thought: a good Christian. He remembered suddenly the day Jackson had come upon some of his troops letting a valiant Yankee color sergeant withdraw after a great fight. The men refused to fire at him, that man had been brave, he deserved to live. Jackson said, *"I don't want them brave, I want them dead."*

"They tell many stories of the man. I regret not having known him."

"He loved to chew lemons," Longstreet said.

"Lemons?"

"Don't know where he got them. He loved them. I remember him that way, sitting on a fence, chewing a lemon, his finger in the air."

Fremantle stared.

"He had a finger shot away," Longstreet explained. "When he held it down the blood would get into it and hurt him, so he would hold it up in the air and ride or talk with his arm held up, not noticing it. It was a sight, until you got used to it. Dick Ewell thought he was crazy. Ewell is rather odd himself. He told me Jackson told him that he never ate pepper because it weakened his left leg."

Fremantle's mouth was open.

"I'm serious," Longstreet said amiably. "A little eccentricity is a help to a general. It helps with the newspapers. The women love it too. Southern women like their men religious and a little mad. That's why they fall in love with preachers."

Fremantle was not following. Longstreet said, "He knew how to fight, Jackson did. A. P. Hill is good too. He wears a red shirt when he's going into battle. It's an interesting army. You've met George Pickett?"

"Oh yes."

"Perfume and all." Longstreet chuckled. "It's a hell of an

army." But thinking of Pickett, last in line, reminded him of Pickett's two brigade commanders: Garnett and Armistead. Old Armistead, torn by the war away from his beloved friend Win Hancock, who was undoubtedly waiting ahead on that black hill beyond Gettysburg. Armistead would be thinking of that tonight. And then there was Dick Garnett.

"Pickett's men are extraordinary men," Fremantle said. "The Virginians seem different, quite, from the Texans, or the soldiers from Mississippi. Is that true, do you think, sir?"

"Yes. Have you met Dick Garnett?"

"Ah, yes. Tall fella, rather dark. Wounded leg. Odd that . . ."

"Jackson tried to court-martial him. For cowardice in the face of the enemy. I've known Garnett for twenty years. No coward. But his honor is gone. You will hear bad things from people who know nothing. I want you to know the truth. Jackson was . . . a hard man."

Fremantle nodded silently.

"He also court-martialed A. P. Hill once. And Lee simply overlooked it. Well, come to think of it, I had some trouble with old Powell myself once; he wanted to fight me a duel. Matter of honor. I ignored him. It's an interesting army. Only Lee could hold it together. But the thing about Garnett troubles me. He thinks his honor is gone."

"A tragic thing," Fremantle said. There was tact there, a tone of caution.

"The papers, of course, all side with Jackson." Longstreet blew out a breath. "And Jackson is dead. So now Garnett will have to die bravely to erase the stain."

And he saw that Fremantle agreed. Only thing for a gentleman to do. Longstreet shook his head. A weary bitterness fogged his brain. He knew Garnett would die, no help for it now, unturnable, ridiculous, doomed with a festering, unseen wound.

Fremantle said, "You are not, ah, Virginia born, sir?"

"South Carolina," Longstreet said.

"Ah. That's in the far south isn't it, sir?"

"True," Longstreet said. He was weary of talk. "Honor," he said. "Honor without intelligence is a disaster. Honor could lose the war."

Fremantle was vaguely shocked.

"Sir?"

"Listen. Let me tell you something. I appreciate honor and bravery and courage. Before God . . . but the point of the war is not to show how brave you are and how you can die in a manly fashion, face to the enemy. God knows it's easy to die. Anybody can die."

In the darkness he could not see Fremantle's face. He talked to darkness.

"Let me explain this. Try to see this. When we were all young, they fought in a simple way. They faced each other out in the open, usually across a field. One side came running. The other got one shot in, from a close distance, because the rifle wasn't very good at a distance, because it wasn't a rifle. Then after that one shot they hit together hand to hand, or sword to sword, and the cavalry would ride in from one angle or another. That's the truth, isn't it? In the old days they fought from a distance with bows and arrows and ran at each other, man to man, with swords. But now, listen, now it's quite a bit different, and quite a few people don't seem to know that yet. But we're learning. Look. Right now, take a man with a good rifle, a good man with a good rifle which has a good range and may even be a repeater. He can kill at, oh, conservatively, two, three hundred yards shooting into the crowd attacking him. Forget the cannon. Just put one man behind a tree. You can hardly see him from two hundred yards away, but he can see you. And shoot. And shoot again. How many men do you think it will take to get to that man behind a tree, in a ditch, defended by cannon, if you have to cross an open field to get him? How many men? Well, I've figured it. At least three. And he'll kill at least two. The way you do it is this: one man fires while one man is moving, and the other is loading and getting ready to move. That's how the three men attack. There's always one moving and one firing. That way you can do it. If you forget the cannon. But you'll lose one man most probably on the way across the field, at least one, probably two, against a cannon you'll lose all three, no matter what you do, and that's across the field. Now. If you are attacking uphill . . ."

He broke it off. No point in talking this way to a foreigner. Might have to fight him sometime. But the man would not see. Longstreet had spoken to his own officers. They found what he said vaguely shameful. Defense? When Lee dug trenches around Richmond they called him, derisively, the King of Spades. Longstreet took a deep breath and let it go, remembering again that damned black hill, fires like eyes.

Fremantle said, bewildered, "But, sir, there is the example of Solferino. And of course the Charge of the Light Brigade."

"Yes," Longstreet said. Like all Englishmen, and most Southerners, Fremantle would rather lose the war than his dignity. Dick Garnett would die and die smiling. "Had he his hurts before?" Aye, then he died like a man. Longstreet, who had invented a transverse trench which no one would use, filed the matter forcefully in the dark cavern of his swelling brain and rode into camp.

That night, at supper, someone remarked casually that since the army needed ammunition, wouldn't it be proper for the ammunition factories to stay open on Sunday? Most of the officers agreed that it had not yet come to *that.*

Longstreet stayed up talking, as long as there was company, as long as there was a fire. Because when the fire was gone and the dark had truly come there was no way he could avoid the dead faces of his children.

6. Lee

Lee rode north through the town and out the Heidlersburg Road. There was a joy in the night all around him. The men yelled and whooped as he passed by. Many stopped and just smiled and some took off their hats. They had won again. The joy on their faces, the look of incredible pride, the way so many of them looked at him going by as if waiting for some sign of his approval of a job well done, another fight so nobly fought, lights in all the starry young eyes, and beyond that the way some of them had tears in their eyes as he went by, tears for him, for the cause, for the dead of the day; the sight of it was something very nearly unbearable, and he set his face and rode through saying nothing, nodding, touching his hat. Then he was out the other side of town, and there were piles of stacked Union muskets, blankets and canteens and wagons, the abandoned implements of war.

Ewell had made his headquarters in a farmhouse. He was there, along with Early and Rodes. They were all standing at a white gate as Lee rode up at the beginning of the night, enough light still in the sky so that the black mass of the hill to the east, the untaken hill, could still be seen against the evening sky. Lee thought: why did you not attack? Why? But he said nothing.

Ewell had the look of a great-beaked, hopping bird. He was bald and scrawny; his voice piped and squeaked like cracking eggshells. He had lost a leg at Manassas and had just recently returned to the army, and he was standing awkwardly balancing himself against the unfamiliar leg and scratching his head and swaying nervously, clutching a fence-post. Early stood beside him, dark, formal, composed. Rodes off to the side bowed formally at Lee's approach.

"Good evening, sir, God bless you, did you see them run? Did you see them? We whipped them again, by God, yes, sir, we did, sir." Ewell chattered. Lee sensed a strange thin quality in his voice, a wavery exuberance. He escorted Lee through the house, hobbling awkwardly on the wooden leg, talking about the bullet that had hit him there that afternoon while he was mounted on his horse. They went out into an arbor and sat in the warm evening under the grapevines and the soft sky and Ewell sat on the ground and hiked up his pants to show Lee where the bullet had hit, a Minnie ball just below the jointed knee, a vast gash of splintered white wood. Ewell was giggling, grinning, cocking his head off to the side like a huge parrot, chortling.

Lee asked the condition of the corps, the number of wounded. Early spoke up. Ewell deferred. Early stood with his legs wide apart, his hands clasped behind his back, heavy in the jaw, his face bleak and grim, black beard dirty and untrimmed. He had been a West Pointer, had left the army to become a lawyer, a prosecutor. He was utterly sure of himself. Lee watched and listened. Early explained the situation coolly and logically. Behind him, Ewell nodded in punctuation, his head twitching, his fingers fluttering. Lee felt a strangeness in the air, a coolness. Ewell should speak for himself. Rodes sat silently leaning forward, his hands on his knees, looking at the ground. There was a pause.

Lee said, "I had hoped you would move on through the town and take that hill."

Ewell blinked, rubbed his nose, looked at Early, looked at Rodes, patted his thigh. Lee, watching, felt a sudden acute depression.

Ewell said, "I didn't think it was, ah, practical. We were

waiting, ah, for many reasons. We had marched all day, and fought, and your orders were a caution against bringing on a general engagement." He jabbered, rambling, moving about in his chair. Early walked over and sat on the railing of the arbor. Ewell turned to him for confirmation.

Early said calmly, silently, bored, "There were reports of Federal troops in the north. We couldn't bring artillery to bear, and no word came from Hill, as you know. We decided it would be best to wait for Johnson." Yes, yes, Ewell nodded vigorously, thumping the wooden leg. "But he did not arrive until dark, just a while ago. He's out now, looking over the terrain."

Ewell went on nodding. Lee looked at Rodes, who said nothing. After a moment Early said, "You may remember, sir, that I passed over this ground a few days ago and am familiar with it. The hill is named Cemetery Hill. It has another hill beyond it, also occupied. It will be a very strong position."

Lee closed his eyes for a moment, was very tired. Think of all of it later. An aide brought a cup of hot boiled coffee, thick with sugar. Lee drank, revived, abruptly saw the face of Jackson in his mind, a flare of cold blue eyes. He looked up, blinked. Could almost see him. Jackson was here. Jackson was looking on.

Ewell was drinking coffee. Early had folded his arms. Rodes still gazed at the ground, plucking at one of his fingers. Lee said, "Can you attack on this flank, in the morning?"

Ewell sat up. Early did not move. Lee felt the depression, cold and slow and steady like a wind in his brain, shook his head to blow it away.

Early said, "That hill will be a very strong position. Once it is fortified. Which they are doing right now."

"Very strong." Ewell nodded violently.

"Have you looked over the ground, sir?" Early asked.

"From a distance."

Early leaned back into the dark. He spoke slowly, deliberately. "I do not think we should attack this point. This will be the strong point. Our troops have marched hard today and fought hard today. I suggest we hold here while the rest of the army makes an attack on the other flank."

"You think an attack here would succeed?"

"I think it would be very costly."

Ewell nodded. Lee turned.

"General Rodes?"

Rodes looked up, glanced away, shrugged.

"We'll attack, of course. But the men have had a good fight. And it will be a strong position." He looked up at Ewell, then quickly away. "I'm sorry we did not take it today."

"Well," Lee said. "Today is done."

"General Longstreet has not been engaged." Early said. "His Corps has not been fought for some time." He was referring to Chancellorsville, where Longstreet's men had been detached. "If he were to attack on the right he would draw the enemy from this position and we could then attempt the assault. Supported, of course, by General Hill."

Lee thought: Longstreet cannot stand the man. I wonder why? Something too cold here, something disagreeable in the silence of the eyes, the tilt of the head. Jubal. Strange name. Old Jubilee. Nothing happy about the man. And yet, unmistakable competence. Lee said, "Longstreet proposes that we move our army to the right around the enemy flank and interpose between Meade and Washington."

"And vacate this position?" Ewell popped his eyes, slapped the splintered wood again. "Leave this town, which we have just captured?"

Lee said, with some irritation, "The town is of no importance."

Ewell looked to Early. Early said slowly, "To move this entire Corps, in the face of a fortified enemy?" He smiled slightly, with a touch of the disdain for which he was rapidly becoming notorious.

"Hardly fitting," Ewell piped. "Hardly. Troops fought so hard for this town, do we move them out and march them off into the woods, in sight of the enemy? Morale will suffer, General. The boys are ready. Our boys are ready."

"Longstreet is on the defensive again." Early grinned. "I suppose that's to be expected. But really, sir, it seems to me, we are here and the enemy is there, and Hill and General Ewell have engaged and Longstreet has not. If Longstreet can be induced to attack on the right, we can give you this hill tomorrow by sundown."

Ewell was nodding again, pointing at Early, wagging a bony finger. They talked. Lee made no decision. Must not judge Ewell now. The man has been a good soldier for too long. First day in command of the Corps. Jackson's old Corps.

Hill is sick. Ewell indecisive. The hill untaken. Longstreet broods on defensive war. Lee said, "Would you gentlemen retreat?"

"Retreat? Retreat?" Ewell sat with his mouth open. Rodes looked up.

"Would you suggest that we fall back behind South Mountain?"

"Retreat?" Ewell was amazed. "But why?"

Lee said, "If we do not withdraw, and if we do not maneuver in the face of the enemy, then we must attack. There is no other alternative." He rose, not waiting for an answer. They accompanied him to the door. He saw a vase filled with flowers on a small wooden table. A picture of an old man frowned down out of an old round frame. Lee was thinking: very dangerous to withdraw. To pull this army with all its trains back through that pass. Without cavalry, it cannot be done. Stuart. I have waited long enough.

He thanked the men for their day's work, told them to get

a good night's rest. Once again he saw Jackson's blue eyes, probing, reproachful. He thought: General, we miss you.

He rode off into the dark. Taylor was there with messages. Lee answered them, one to Imboden, one to Chilton, sent Taylor off to find the raider, Harry Gilmore, who was with Johnson. He rode off with Venable and then, moving in out of the night to greet him, saw old Isaac Trimble, astride a pale horse, fiery old Isaac. Lee smiled a greeting. General Trimble was almost sixty. Not much older than *you,* old man. But he looks ancient. Do I look that old? I was tired before, but I am not tired now. No pain now. God's blessing. What will I do about Ewell?

Trimble said, "Sir, I beg your pardon, but I will not serve the man." He was furious. He raised one huge hand like a vast claw and made a gesture as if pushing a disgusting thing away from him, into the black air. "I will not serve the man. I am a volunteer aide with the man, sir, as you know. I most respectfully request another assignment." He shook his head violently, almost displacing his hat. "The man is a disgrace. Have you heard it all, sir? What they have been telling you? Ask the aides, sir, or General Gordon, or Johnson."

He went on. He was a marvelous old man who had sworn to be a Major General or a corpse. Lee gathered that he was talking about Ewell. Lee calmed him, but he wanted to hear.

Trimble said, "We should have taken that hill. God in His wisdom knows we could have taken that hill. Beyond Cemetery Hill there is another hill and it was totally unoccupied. There was no one there at all, and it commanded the town. Gordon saw it, sir, he was with us, me and Gordon and Ewell, all standing there in the flaming dark like great fat idiots with that bloody damned hill empty, begging your pardon, General, but that bloody damned hill was as bare as his bloody damned great head and it commands the town. We all saw it, General, as God is my witness, ask anyone here. McKim was there, Smith was there, they were all there.

I said, 'General Ewell, we have got to take that hill. General Jackson would not have stopped like this with the bluebellies on the run and plenty of light left and a hill like that empty as, oh God help us, I don't know what.' But nobody there at all. And the Federals running, no guns set up, nothing but one battery and one regiment in line."

He was running out of breath. Lee had stopped to listen. He sensed, among the anger, the bitter breath of truth. Trimble took off his hat and wiped it across his brow, and his white hair gleamed in the moonlight like wadded cotton. Lee said, "Go on."

"Yes, sir. Sir, I told him, General Ewell, I said to him, 'Sir, give me one division and I will take that hill.' And he said nothing at all. He stood there! He stared at me! I said, 'General Ewell, give me one *brigade,* and I will take that hill.' I was becoming disturbed, sir. And General Ewell put his arms behind him and blinked. So I said, 'General, give me one *regiment* and I will take that hill.' And he said nothing; he just shook his head, and I threw my sword down." Trimble gestured helplessly, actually close to tears. "Down on the ground in front of him." He raised both arms. "We could have done it, sir. A blind man should have seen it. Now they are working, up there, you can hear the axes. Now in the morning many a good boy will die."

He wiped his face. It was all out of him. The fire died. He slumped forward in the saddle.

"General, sir, I request another assignment."

Lee said softly, "Thank you, General. You will be of great service, thank you."

Now that Trimble was quieter Lee could question him. Dick Ewell had frozen; he had deferred to Early. Lee thought: I must look into this. He told Trimble to rest and he rode back to his headquarters in the dark. He was becoming increasingly tired, but there was much to do. Food. Get some fuel. The ancient body had no reserve. His chest was stuffed, a feeling of cool bleakness there, no strength in him. He thought of that and of Stuart off somewhere, possibly dead, and of Ewell's weakness and Hill's illness and the Union Army growing now in the night on that hill, blossoming darkly across the field like a fungus, a bristly fungus.

The headquarters was in a small stone house on Seminary Ridge. An elderly woman, the resident, was cooking for him. Lee chatted with her politely, his mind on other things, while aides came and went, Generals pushed in and out, reporters and artists and the Prussian and the Austrian passed in and out. There was a rocking chair for Lee; it received him like an enfolding arm. Taylor appeared with a squad of men, led by a man named Watters, a Marylander. Now late at night it was becoming difficult to recognize people, to remember their names. Lee prepared sealed orders to be given to each of Watters' men; they were to scatter out over the countryside and find Stuart and get him back to Gettysburg with all possible speed. When that was done Lee looked for Longstreet, but the stubborn face was not there. Lee closed his eyes. The uproar of jokes and joy went on around him. Must see Ewell *now,* without Early. He motioned to Marshall, sent for Ewell. The room gradually cleared. Lee signed orders. I do too much myself. He was thinking: retreat is not even an option; we must assault or maneuver. If we assault, Longstreet must bear the load.

Lee took a quick nap. He was awakened by the arrival of Ewell. He rose and went out into the night. The strange beaked figure waited with deference. Lee said, "How are you, sir?"

"I am fine, sir. The leg troubles me a bit."

Lee suggested a doctor. Ewell shook his head. "Drugs injure a man's thinking. The leg is minor. Sir?

"Johnson's men are in position now. He is very optimistic, much more than Early. I believe we ought to attack *there,* sir."

"Attack the hill?"

"Yes, sir. Culp's Hill or Cemetery Hill, or both, sir."

There was a new certainty in his voice. Lee was very glad to hear it. A small relief blossomed like a flower. Lee said only, "I have made no decision yet. But in your opinion, we should attack on your flank."

"Yes, sir."

Lee nodded. "I will consider it. I am glad to hear you are well."

"General," Ewell said. His face was not clear in the evening light, the lamplight from inside, the moon from the heavens, but there was a sadness in his voice, regret apparent in the motion of his head, the beak above the wild mustache bobbing. "I think I was too slow today, sir. I regret that very much. I was trying to be . . . careful. I may have been too careful."

Lee was moved. My good old soldier. He was embarrassed. He said quickly, "You won a victory, General." Ewell looked up. His eyes were strained. "It was not a large victory, it might have been larger, we might have pushed harder. But it was a victory. I am satisfied. The men fought well. This was your first day. It is not as easy as it sometimes appears."

"No, sir," Ewell said.

"Now get some rest." Lee sent him off. He went back into the stone house feeling much better. The old man had been a good soldier for too long; you cannot worry about Ewell. And then Lee thought: but sometimes I have seen it happen. A man loses part of himself, an arm, a leg, and though he has been a fine soldier he is never quite the same again; he has lost nothing else visible, but there is a certain softness in the man thereafter, a slowness, a caution. I did not expect it with Ewell. I do not understand it. Very little of a man is in a hand or a leg. A man is in his spirit and he has that in full no matter what part of his body dies, or all of it. But, Lee thought, you may not understand. It has not happened to you, so you don't understand. So don't judge. He was a good soldier. He is not Jackson. Jackson is gone—not entirely gone; Jackson was there today watching, and Ewell sees *his* eyes—but you cannot blame him for not being Jackson. You must make do with the tools God has given for the job. Richard Ewell, old Baldy . . . and his ridiculous horse.

Lee went back to the rocker. Midnight came, and he had not yet slept. Headquarters grew steadily more still. Lee thought again of Rooney Lee, wounded, and prayed for him. There was no time for a letter to his wife, that troubled woman. He closed his eyes and thought of Meade, out there, gathering the army. John Reynolds was dead. He prayed for the soul of Reynolds. And in the morning?

This is the great battle. Tomorrow or the next day. This will determine the war. Virginia is here, all the South is here. What will you do tomorrow?

No orders were out. Now he was alone. It was cooler. Taylor came and tucked a blanket around his knees and Lee did not argue. He was drifting off. Longstreet would be up in the morning. Pickett would be up by late afternoon. In the afternoon all the army will be here. And we will hit them. We will hit them with everything and drive them right off that hill and send them running back down the road to Washington. If Stuart's cavalry . . .

He woke briefly. Without cavalry in the rear no victory would be complete. Should we attack before Stuart comes? And if he comes with tired horses and weary men? If he comes at all . . .

Don't think on that. Lee closed his eyes. And let himself fall into the bright dark. For Thine be the Kingdom, and the Power . . .

7. Buford

He came back at last to the cemetery on the hill. All down the ridge they were digging in, all around the crest of the hill. He sat on the horse and watched the picks swinging in the moonlight, listened to the sound of shovels in the earth. The army was still coming in, marching by moonlight. It was almost two o'clock in the morning.

He rode slowly along the ridge, looking for headquarters. He had been hit once in the left arm and the bleeding had stopped but the genuine pain was just beginning. They had wrapped the arm and put his coat back on and he did not show the injury. He rode stiffly, dizzily, looking for someone to give him orders for what was left of his cavalry.

He found a small farmhouse, center of many lights, many horses tethered outside. The musk of cigar smoke was heavy in the warm air. He remembered an old Indian joke: follow cigar smoke; fat men *there.* Bright moonlight, a warm and cloudless night. They were posting cannon along the ridge by moonlight: pleasant looming shapes, rolling caissons. Buford thought: I need a drink. Whisky stiffens. He rode to the farmhouse and stopped in a crowd of horses and sat there. Rather not get down. Men were passing in and out, much conversation. A cloud of officers had clustered by the small lighted door, looking in. One glanced up, saw him, noted the star, turned, saluted quickly. Buford wiggled a finger; the man came forward: a major. Other men were turning. Buford rode the horse almost to the door.

Buford said, "Who's in command, and where do I find him?"

"Good evening, sir," the Major said. A very high voice. A lisp? "The officer in command is General Howard, sir. He may be found—"

"Don't be a damn fool, Edgar," another man said. He saluted Buford. "Begging your pardon, sir, but the truth is that General Hancock is in command, and if you'll—"

Another major, skinny, grinning. The first major said angrily, "I must remind you, sir, that General Howard is the *senior* officer on the field."

"But General Hancock has orders from General Meade himself."

They argued, ignoring Buford. He looked down in wonder. Other officers voiced opinions. Oliver Howard was the commander of the Eleventh Corps. He had arrived this morning with Reynolds. He had fought on the right and been broken, just as he had been broken at Chancellorsville. He was a one-armed man for whom Buford had no admiration. The majors confronted like wispy chickens; it was very strange. Behind them Buford saw suddenly a familiar face: John Gibbon, of Hancock's corps. Infantry. A cold, silent man. His brothers fought for the other side. Buford nodded. Gibbon nodded. A major was giving a lecture on military precedence: Howard could not be relieved except by written order or by Meade in person. Gibbon came up and took the reins.

"Evenin', John."

Buford bowed.

"A hard day?"

"Long," Buford admitted.

"Hancock's inside, if you want to see him." Gibbon led the horse out of the crowd. The argument went on behind them.

Buford watched it with awe. Never get used to it, the mind of headquarters, not if I live a thousand years.

Gibbon said, "That's been going on all night."

"I gather Meade's not here yet. Who's in command?"

"Take your choice." Gibbon grinned. But he was one of Hancock's fanatics. Good soldier.

"I have to refit my outfit," Buford said. "I need orders."

"Hancock got here late this afternoon, just as Howard's Corps was falling apart. They ran, them Dutchmen, just like they did at Chancellorsville. Hancock took command and reformed them on this hill, along with the First, and ever since then everybody's been coming to him for orders, and not Howard, and he's hopping mad. Kind of funny. He claims he's senior officer." Gibbon chuckled. "But Hancock has a verbal order from Meade. It's all very funny. Thing is, when Hancock's on the field the men naturally turn that way. Old Howard's really steamed."

"I just want orders," Buford said. "I'm kind of weary." He was thinking: need the long quiet again, want to get away from here. He dismounted, held briefly to the horse.

Gibbon called a man to take the reins. He said, "I'll get your orders. Why don't you wait out here?"

Buford sat on a rail. The arm was alive with pain. He said, "Is the army here?"

"Just about. All but Sedgewick. We've got Sykes and Geary and Sickles, along with Hancock. And Howard. Sedgewick will be here tomorrow, but he has a long march."

"Good," Buford said. He nodded, closed his eyes. Can relax now. He felt the beginning of sleep, even among the pain, the quiet dark coming, the soft rolling dreamless rest.

Gibbon said, "They're all inside."

Buford stirred, began to head toward the door. Gibbon said casually, "Why don't you stay out here?"

Buford moved sleepily toward the door. Need one last order, then a good long sleep. The aides near the door were parting, but something in Gibbon's voice caught him. He stopped, turned. Gibbon was there.

"Howard has made a complaint against you, John. He says you should have supported him on the right."

Buford nodded dumbly, then blinked. He raised the pained arm. Gibbon said, "He lost half his strength. Most of them got taken prisoner. He's mad as a hornet, lookin' for somebody to blame it on. I think he's picked you."

Buford felt nothing for a moment, a sort of sodden silence all through his brain, then the anger began to rise like a metal wave, like a hot tide in the dark. Buford could say nothing. No words came. Gibbon said softly, "Stay out here, John. I'll tell Hancock you're here."

He moved past Buford into the room. Buford blinked and blinked again and then began moving, pushing his way into the light, the smoke of the room. It was jammed with officers, all the brass. The anger made Buford dizzy. He tried to push his way through and the pain went all the way up his arm and into his chest and shocked him stiff. He could see faces: Sickles, the bully boy, the bright politician, a fat cigar clamped in a fat mouth, the man who was famous for having shot his wife's lover. Geary and Sykes were sitting, brooding; that damned Howard was making a speech. And there was Hancock against a wall, writing a note, talking to aides, issuing orders. Buford's vision blurred. The room was very hot and there was too much smoke. He had to push his way back out of the room into the open air. He kept saying aloud, God damn him, God damn him. He sat on a rail. In a moment he looked up and there was Hancock.

"How are you, John?"

Handsome face, watching. Buford focused. Hancock looked down with bright dark eyes. Buford said, "I'm all right."

"Heard you were with John Reynolds when he died."

"I was."

"Tell me."

Buford told him. Hancock would write the letter. Good, very good. Hancock was older since last time Buford saw him. Calm and cocky, damned good-looking man. Buford felt suddenly better. Cool, clean air.

Hancock said, "I'm sending the body back to his folks in Lancaster. They might appreciate a note from you."

"I'll send it."

"How's your division?"

Buford told him. Hancock was surprised. He hadn't known Buford was that involved. Buford said, "We were involved."

"Well, get yourself refitted. May need you in the morning."

There was commotion behind him. A mass of aides were riding up. Somebody blew a discordant bugle. Hancock stood up, grinned. Buford noted: why, Hancock's wearing a clean white shirt. Isn't that amazing. Clean as a whistle. Hancock said, "Here's Meade."

They all came out to meet him, the angry man with the squeaky voice. They gathered around him as he dismounted. Buford was pushed to the side. He heard Meade greet Hancock.

"Damn dark. I can't see a damn thing."

Hancock said he was very glad to see the General. Meade said, with great disgust, "Well, I hope to God this is good ground, General. Is it good ground?"

"Very good ground, General."

"Well, by God it better be, because we're going to have to fight here sure enough in the morning."

Buford was pushed too far away. Meade went on into the house. Flocks of officers gathered at the windows. Buford had enough; he had his orders. He got back on his horse and rode slowly back toward the cemetery. He had not much strength left. He called for one of his aides, but the buck-toothed boy was dead, and the yellow-haired boy was dead, and the Sergeant was down and would never recover. Buford stopped in the cemetery. He could not find the white angel. But he looked out across the town and he could see a great ocean of Rebel campfires, flooding the town, with fire burning all over those ridges to the west, flooding fire right up to the base of the hill. Buford took off his hat, looked up to the stars. He said to John Reynolds, "Well, John, we held the ground." He wiped his eyes. He thought: *have to get some more lieutenants.* Then he rode off down the hill into the black beneath the trees.

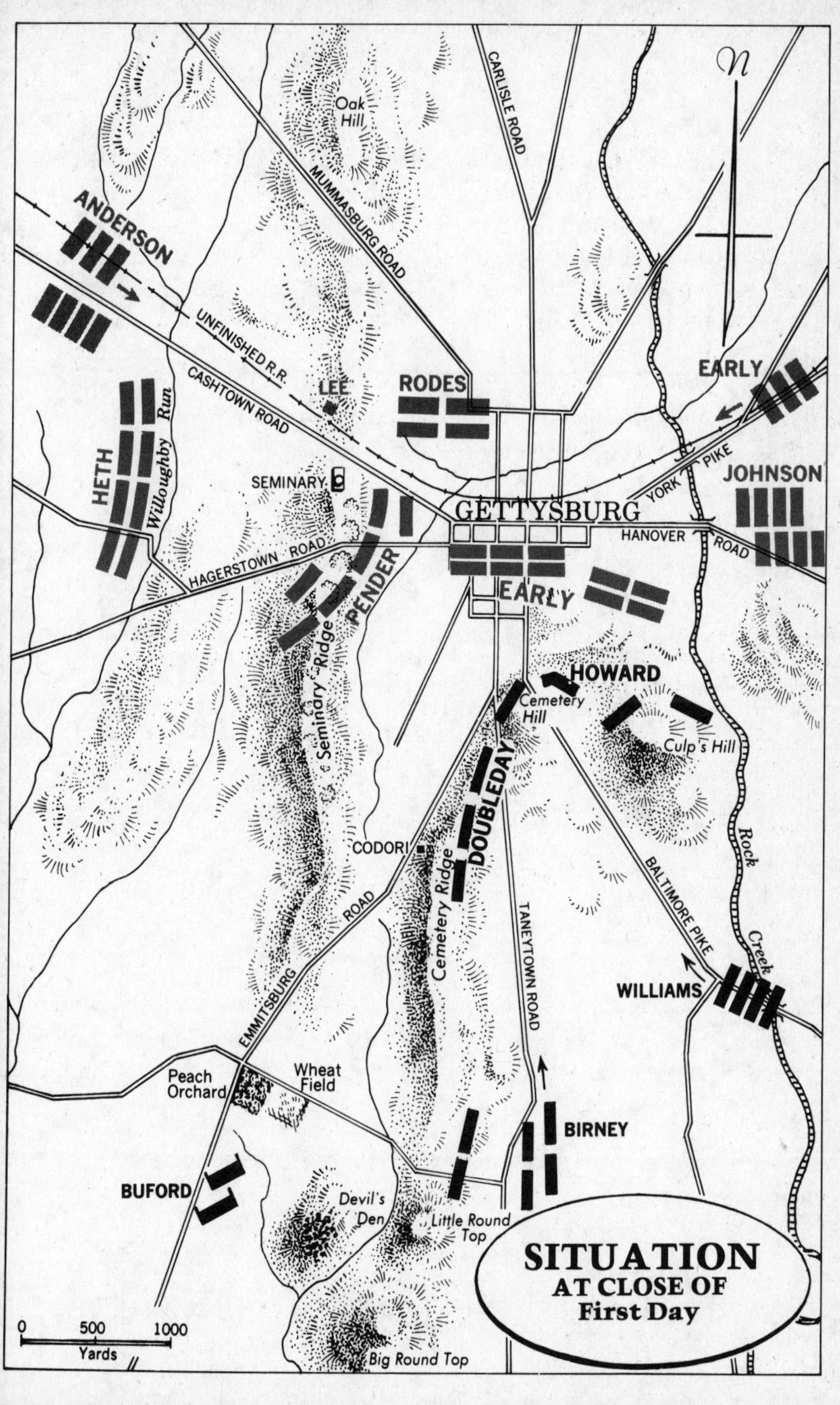
SITUATION
AT CLOSE OF
First Day
ANDERSON
HETH
LEE
RODES
EARLY
JOHNSON
PENDER
EARLY
HOWARD
DOUBLEDAY
WILLIAMS
BIRNEY
BUFORD
GETTYSBURG
Oak Hill
CARLISLE ROAD
MUMMASBURG ROAD
UNFINISHED R.R.
CASHTOWN ROAD
Willoughby Run
SEMINARY
HAGERSTOWN ROAD
YORK PIKE
HANOVER ROAD
Seminary Ridge
Cemetery Hill
Culp's Hill
CODORI
Cemetery Ridge
EMMITSBURG ROAD
TANEYTOWN ROAD
BALTIMORE PIKE
Rock Creek
Peach Orchard
Wheat Field
Devil's Den
Little Round Top
Big Round Top
0 500 1000
Yards
N

THURSDAY, JULY 2, 1863

THE SECOND DAY

He hath loosed the fateful lightning . . .

1. Fremantle

Awake in the dark, the stars still brightly shining. Fremantle, a slow riser, staggered into the dawn not quite knowing where he was. These people might conduct these things at a civilized hour. Three in the morning. Incredible. He washed in dirty water. Came vaguely awake. War!

The army awakened around him. He could sense the red battle forming today, coming like the sun. His senses shocked him awake. He expected cannon at any moment. He saw the first light of dawn a dusky rose in the east, the sun coming up from the direction of the enemy. He felt sleepily marvelous. He bid a cheery hello to Sorrel, Longstreet's aide.

"Major Sorrel, sir, good morning! I say, could you direct me to the battle?"

Sorrel, a neat and natty person, smiled and bowed. "Would you care for a bite to eat before the assault? We can serve Yankees done to order, before or after breakfast."

Fremantle could not suppress a yawn, smothered it politely with his hand. "I suppose there is time for a bun or two. How's General Longstreet this morning? My compliments, and I trust he slept well."

"Doubt if he slept at all. He's gone over to speak with General Lee."

"Does the man ever sleep? Amazing. He rarely even sits *down.*"

Sorrel smiled. A bird, annoyed at being awakened early, began chattering in the tree above him. Other officers began stepping out into the dark of the morning. There was Ross, the fat Austrian with the Scotch name. He was all aglow in the powder-blue uniform of the Austrian Hussars, complete with shining silver chamberpot for the head, waving a blue plume. As he came closer Fremantle observed with alarm that the man was spotlessly groomed; even his mustache was waxed, the ends slim and sharp like wiggly rapiers.

Ross boomed happily, patting himself fat-handedly across the stomach. "*C'est le sanglant appel de Mars,* eh, old chap?" He popped the slender Fremantle on the arm, unsettling him.

Fremantle said with distaste, "Early in the morning for that, old friend. Could you wait until after tea?"

The others were gathering around the breakfast table. Scheibert, the beardless Prussian, moody, prim, was dressed all in white, white coat, floppy white hat, the inevitable glittering monocle. While most of the officers of the army could speak French, few could speak German, and Scheibert's pride was continually offended, but he went on stubbornly using German military terms in conversation, was not understood, would not explain, sat fatly, whitely to the side, a rare sight, oddly comical in that company. Lawley, the correspondent, seemed ill again and had not made up his mind whether or not to ride today. There were the three medical people—Maury, Cullen, Barksdale—and others of Longstreet's staff: Latrobe, Goree, and the charming little Jew, Major Moses. They sat down to a splendid breakfast, and although Fremantle continued to wake up slowly, coming alive as the day came alive, warmly, brightly, with no clouds anywhere, the wind beginning to pick up and rustle the trees, the light beginning to sift down through the cool leaves, the dark branches, still Fremantle remained vaguely asleep.

The morning at war. Marvelous. Good men around a table. What a joy to be with the winners! All these men had nothing but contempt for the Yankees, whom they had beaten so often. There was even an air of regret at the table, a sense of seize the day, as if these bright moments of good fellowship before battle were numbered, that the war would soon be over, and all this would end, and we would all go back to the duller pursuits of peace. Fremantle enjoyed himself enormously. Southerners! They were *Englishmen,* by George. Fremantle was at home.

He ate hot eggs, warm bread, reveled in steaming tea, although the water from which the tea was made left an aftertaste in the mouth, afterthoughts in the brain: from what nearby barn? The men all chatted, joked. Fremantle was sorry to see breakfast end. But the sun was fully up. Now once more he could expect the big thunder of cannon. Must not miss it today. Sorrel promised to keep him informed. They rode together toward the lines, hoping for a good view.

So Fremantle came to Gettysburg, saw the bodies unburied in the fields, beginning to become offensive in the heat of the morning, poor chaps. They turned off to the right and rode up through a grove of trees to higher ground, and through the trees Fremantle could already see the blue ridge to the east, soft in the morning haze, where the Yankees were camped. But he could see no troops, no movement. He felt his stomach tighten, his breath grow sharp. In the presence of the enemy! In range of the guns! He passed a battery of Southern artillery, mixed Napoleons and Parrots, served by wagons stamped USA.

Sorrel said, "We get most of our wagons from the enemy. Many of the guns. Their artillery is very good. But ours will get better."

The Austrian, Ross, had ridden up beside them. One of the

gunners, a lean, barefoot man in dusty brown, stared at him unbelievingly as he passed, then bawled in a piercing voice that carried all along the line, "Hey, mister. You in blue. What you do, man, you look like you swallowed some mice."

Sorrel put his hand over his mouth. Ross stared back, uncomprehending.

Fremantle said cheerily, "The fellow is referring to the waxed mustache, old friend."

Ross grumbled, twitched the mustache, stroked the ends lovingly, glowered. They rode to Lee's headquarters, then beyond, up the ridge to where the Generals were meeting.

There was a gathering of officers, too many men. Sorrel suggested that if Fremantle wanted a good view, he should find a convenient tree. Fremantle wandered forward, with Lawley, through the cool green woods, to the same commanding position he had the day before, climbed the same wide oak. There below him, not fifty feet away, he recognized Longstreet, then Lee. The officers were in consultation.

Lee was standing with his back to the group, bareheaded, the white hair flicking in the breeze. He was gazing out toward the Union lines, which were clearly visible in the east. He put his field glasses to his eyes, looked, put them down, walked two or three paces south, turned, looked again, slowly walked back and forth. Longstreet was sitting on a camp stool, whittling slowly on a stick, making a point, sharpening the point, sharpening, sharpening. A. P. Hill, looking much healthier than the day before, was chatting with another officer, unidentified. Sitting next to Longstreet, on a stump, also whittling, was a tall slim man with an extraordinary face, eyes with a cold glint in them, erect in posture even as he sat, cutting a stick. Fremantle asked, impressed, "Who is that?"

Lawley: "That's Hood. John Bell Hood. They call him 'Sam,' I think. He commands one of Longstreet's divisions. From Texas, I believe."

"Does his behavior in battle match his appearance?"

"He does his job," Lawley said laconically.

"An interesting army," Fremantle said. "Most interesting."

Lee had turned, was saying something to Longstreet. Longstreet shook his head. Hill came closer.

Lawley said, "The Yankees have dug in. But I don't see any trenches anywhere here. That means we'll attack."

The "we" was inevitable, but Fremantle noticed it. He felt a part, almost a member, of this marvelous group of outnumbered men. Englishmen. They called themselves Americans, but they were transplanted Englishmen. Look at the names: Lee, Hill, Longstreet, Jackson, Stuart. And Lee was Church of England. Most of them were. All gentlemen. No finer gentlemen in England than Lee. Well, of course, here and there, possibly one exception. Or two.

Nevertheless, they are *our* people. Proud to have them. And perhaps they will rejoin the Queen and it will be as it was, as it always should have been.

They had talked of that the evening before. Every one of the officers had insisted that the South would be happier under the Queen than under the Union. Of course, hard to say what they meant. But if England came to help now, would it not be possible? That this soil would once again be English soil?

He had borrowed glasses from Sorrel, was looking at the Union lines. He could see the cannon now, rolled out in front of the trees. He could see men moving among the caissons, men on horseback moving in the trees; here and there a pennant blew. He saw a flash of gold. Breastworks were going up, twisted sticks, small, very far away. There was an open valley below him, partly cultivated, then a long bare rise to the Union line. To the left was the high hill, Cemetery Hill, that Ewell had failed to take the day before, the hill that had worried Longstreet. To the center was a wooded ridge.

To the right were two round hills, one rocky, the other wooded. The Union position was approximately three miles in length, or so it seemed from here. All this Fremantle saw with continually rising excitement.

He looked down, saw Longstreet rise, move off, shoulders bowed, wandering head down and lumbering, like a bearded stump, to stare out at the lines. Hood joined him. Once more Longstreet shook his head. Lee came back to a small table, stared at a map, looked up, back toward the Union lines, keeping his hand on the map. Fremantle had a good look at that extraordinary face. Lee looked weary, more pale then before. The sun was climbing; it was noticeably hotter. Fremantle felt a familiar rumble in his own stomach. Oh God, not the soldier's disease. Those damned cherries.

There seemed no point in remaining in the tree. Soldiers had observed him, hanging in the air like a plump gray fruit, were beginning to point and grin. Fremantle descended with dignity, joined the other foreigners. He heard, for the first time that day, music: a polka. He listened with surprise. He could not identify the sound but he knew the beat. It was followed by a march.

Ross said, "They play even during an attack. Not very good. But inspiring. Have you heard the Rebel yell?"

Fremantle nodded. "Godawful sound. I expect they learned it from Indians."

Ross opened wide his eyes. "Never thought of *that,*" he said. His silver helmet shifted. Sweat was all over his brow.

"I say, old friend, you really aren't going to wear that thing all day, are you? In this charming climate?"

"Well," Ross said. He tweaked his mustache. "One must be properly dressed. Teach these fellas respect."

Fremantle nodded. Understandable. One tried to be neat. But that *helmet.* And Ross did tend to look a bit ridiculous. Like some sort of fat plumed duck. These chaps all looked so natural, so . . . *earthy.* Not the officers. But the troops.

Hardly any uniform at all. Brown and yellow. Americans. Odd. So near, yet so far.

He saw Moxley Sorrel, walking briskly off on a mission, "corralled him," as the Americans would put it.

Sorrel said, "We've sent out engineers to inspect the ground to our right. We'll be attacking later in the day. Don't know where yet, so you can relax, I should say, for two hours or so at least."

"Have you heard from General Stuart?"

"Not a word. General Lee has sent out scouts to find him." Sorrel chuckled. "Cheer up, you may have your charge."

"I hope to have a good position today."

"We'll do all we can. I suggest you stay close to Longstreet. There'll be action where he is."

Sorrel moved off. Through the trees Fremantle saw Longstreet mounting his horse. Fremantle led his own horse that way. Longstreet had Goree with him, the aide from Texas. The greeting was friendly, even warm. Fremantle thought, startled, he *likes* me, and flushed with unexpected pride. He asked if he could ride with the General; Longstreet nodded. They rode down to the right, along the spine of the ridge, in under the trees. Most of Longstreet's staff had joined them.

Longstreet said to Hood, "I'll do what I can. His mind seems set on it."

Hood shrugged. He seemed smaller now when you were close. He had extraordinary eyes. The eyebrows were shaggy and tilted and the eyes were dark as coal so that he seemed very sad. Fremantle had a sudden numbing thought: by evening this man could be dead. Fremantle stared at him, transfixed, trying to sense a premonition. He had never had a premonition, but he had heard of them happening, particularly on the battlefield. Men often knew when their time had come. He stared at Hood, but truthfully, except for the sadness in the eyes, which may have been only weariness, for Hood had marched all night, there was no extra sensation, nothing at all but a certain delicious air of impending combat which was with them all, Longstreet most of all, sitting round and immobile on the black horse, gazing eastward.

Hood said, "Well, if he's right, then the war is over by sundown."

Longstreet nodded.

"We'll see. But going in without Pickett is like going in with one boot off. I'll wait as long as I can."

Hood cocked his head toward the Union lines. "Do you have any idea of the force?"

Longstreet ticked off the corps so far identified: five, counting the two involved in the first day's action. He thought there would be more very soon, that perhaps even now the entire army was up. Lee did not think so. But yesterday he had not thought the Yankees would be there at all, and they were there in force, and now today the Yankees were on the high ground and with Stuart gone there was no way of knowing just how many corps lay in wait beyond the haze of that far ridge.

Fremantle rode along politely, silently, listening. He had developed a confidence that was almost absolute. He knew that Longstreet was tense and that there was a certain gloom in the set of his face, but Fremantle knew with the certainty of youth and faith that he could not possibly lose this day, not with these troops, not with Englishmen, the gentlemen against the rabble. He rode along with delight blossoming in him like a roseate flower, listening. Longstreet looked at him vacantly, saw him, then looked at him.

"Colonel," he said abruptly, "how are you?"

"By George, sir, I am fine, I must say."

"You slept well?"

Fremantle thought: everyone seems concerned that I sleep well.

"Oh, very well." He paused. "Not *long,* mind you, but well."

Longstreet smiled. There seemed to be something about Fremantle that amused him. Fremantle was oddly flattered; he did not know why.

"I would like someday to meet the Queen," Longstreet said.

"I'm sure that could be arranged. Sir, you would be considered most welcome in my country, a most distinguished visitor."

There was firing below, a sharp popping, a scattering of shots, a bunch, another bunch, then silence. Longstreet put on his glasses, looked down into the valley. "Pickets," he said.

Fremantle, who did not know what to expect, started, gulped, stared. But he was delighted. He saw puffs of white smoke start up down in the valley, like vents in the earth, blow slowly lazily to his left, to the north. He looked up at the ridge, but he could see only a few black cannon, a single flag. He said abruptly, "I say, sir, you say you won't be attacking for a bit?"

Longstreet shook his head.

"Then, ah, if I may be so bold, what's to prevent the Yankees from attacking *you?*"

Longstreet looked at Hood.

"I mean, ah, I don't see that you have bothered to entrench," Fremantle went on.

Longstreet grinned. Hood grinned.

"An interesting thought." Longstreet smiled. "I confess, it had not occurred to me."

"Me neither," Hood said.

"But I suppose it's *possible,*" Longstreet said.

"You really think so?"

"Well." Longstreet hedged. He grinned, reached up along the edge of his hat, scratched his head. "I guess not." More soberly, he turned to Fremantle. "It would be most unlike General Meade to attack. For one thing, he is General

Meade. For another, he has just arrived on the field and it will take him some time to understand the position, like perhaps a week. Also, he has not yet managed to gather the entire Army of the Potomac, all two hundred thousand men, and he will be reluctant to move without his full force. Then again, he will think of reasons." Longstreet shook his head, and Fremantle saw that he had again lost his humor. "No, Meade will not do us the favor, the great favor. We will have to *make* him attack. We will have to occupy dangerous ground between him and Washington and let the politicians push him to the assault. Which they will most certainly do. Given time. We need time."

He paused, shook his head. They rode on in silence. Fremantle began to realize how remarkably still it was. Down in the valley the fields were open and still, the breeze had slowed, there was no movement of smoke. A few cows grazed in the shade, rested in dark pools of shade under the trees. Fremantle could feel the presence of that vast army; he knew it was there, thousands of men, thousands of horses, miles of cannon, miles of steel. And spread out beyond him and around him Lee's whole army in the dark shade, moving, settling, lining up for the assault, and yet from this point on the ridge under the tree he could look out across the whole valley and see nothing, hear nothing, feel nothing, not even a trembling of the earth, not even one small slow rumble of all those feet and wheels moving against the earth, moving in together like two waves meeting in a great ocean, like two avalanches coming down together down facing sides of a green mountain. The day had dawned clear, but now there were clouds beginning to patch the sky with hazy blots of cottony white, and not even any motion there, just the white silence against the blue. It was beginning to be very hot, hotter even then before, and Fremantle noticed perspiration on all the faces. He had not slept well, and suddenly the silence and the heat began to get to him. He was a man from a northern clime and England did not have this sort of weather, and when you have not slept . . .

He was most anxious to move on with Longstreet, but he saw Lawley and Ross pull off into an open field and sit down, and so he bade Longstreet goodbye and rode off to join his fellow Europeans. He let his horse roam with the others in a fenced field and found himself a grassy place under a charming tree and lay flat on his back, gazing up serenely into the blue, watching those curious flecks that you can see if you stare upward against the vacant blue, the defects of your own eye.

They chatted, telling stories of other wars. They discussed the strategy of Napoleon, the theories of Jomini, the women of Richmond. Fremantle was not that impressed by Napoleon. But he was impressed by the women of Richmond. He lay dreamily remembering certain ladies, a ball, a rose garden . . .

This land was huge. England had a sense of compactness, like a garden, a lovely garden, but this country was without borders. There was this refreshing sense of *space,* of blowing winds, too hot, too cold, too huge, raw in a way raw meat is raw—and yet there were the neat farms, the green country, so much like Home. The people so much like Home. Southern Home. Couldn't grow flowers, these people. No gardens. Great weakness. And yet. They are *Englishmen.* Should I tell Longstreet? Would it annoy him?

He thinks, after all, that he is an American.

Um. The great experiment. In democracy. The equality of rabble. In not much more than a generation they have come back to *class.* As the French have done. What a tragic thing, that Revolution. Bloody George was a bloody fool. But no matter. The experiment doesn't work. Give them fifty years, and all that equality rot is gone. Here they have that same love of the land and of tradition, of the right form, of breeding, in their horses, their women. Of course slavery is a bit embarrassing, but that, of course, will go. But the point is they do it all exactly as we do in Europe. And the North does not. *That's* what the war is really about. The North has those huge bloody cities and a thousand religions, and the only aristocracy is the aristocracy of wealth. The Northerner doesn't give a damn for tradition, or breeding, or the Old Country. He hates the Old Country. Odd. You very rarely hear a Southerner refer to "the Old Country." In that pained way a German does. Or an Italian. Well, of course, the South *is* the Old Country. They haven't left Europe. They've merely transplanted it. And *that's* what the war is about.

Fremantle opened an eye. It occurred to him that he might have come across something rather profound, something to take back to England. The more he thought about it, the more clear it seemed. In the South there was one religion, as in England, one way of life. They even allowed the occasional Jew—like Longstreet's Major Moses, or Judah Benjamin, back in Richmond—but by and large they were all the same nationality, same religion, same customs. A little rougher, perhaps, but . . . my word.

Fremantle sat up. Major Clarke was resting, back against a tree. Fremantle said, "I say, Major, Longstreet is an English name, I should imagine."

Clarke blinked.

"No, as a matter of fact, I don't think it is." He pondered. "Dutch, I think. Yes, come to think of it. Dutch all right. Comes from New Jersey, the old Dutch settlements up there."

"Oh." Fremantle's theory had taken a jolt. Well. But Longstreet was an exception. He was not a Virginian.

Fremantle again relaxed. He even began to feel hungry.

The morning moved toward noon.

2. Chamberlain

The Regiment sat in an open field studded with boulders like half-sunken balls. Small fires burned under a steam-gray sky. Chamberlain wandered, watching, listening. He did not talk; he moved silently among them, hands clasped behind his back, wandering, nodding, soaking in the sounds of voices, tabulating the light in men's eyes, moving like a forester through a treasured grove, noting the condition of the trees. All his life he had been a detached man, but he was not detached any more. He had grown up in the cold New England woods, the iron dark, grown in contained silence like a lone house on a mountain, and now he was no longer alone; he had joined not only the army but the race, not only the country but mankind. His mother had wanted him to join the church. Now he had his call. He wandered, sensing. Tired men. But ready. Please, God, do not withdraw them now. He saw illness in one face, told the man to report to sick call. One man complained. "Colonel, it keeps raining, these damn Enfields gonna clog on us. Whyn't we trade 'em for Springfields first chance we get?" Chamberlain agreed. He saw Bucklin, together with a cold-eyed group from the old Second Maine, nodded good morning, did not stop to talk. A young private asked him, "Sir, is it true that General McClellan is in command again?" Chamberlain had to say no. The private swore. Chamberlain finished the walk, went back alone to sit under a tree.

He had dreamed of her in the night, dreamed of his wife in a scarlet robe, turning witchlike to love him. Now when he closed his eyes she was suddenly there, hot candy presence. Away from her, you loved her more. The only need was her; she the only vacancy in the steamy morning. He remembered her letter, the misspelled words: "I lie here dreamyly." Even the misspelling is lovely.

A mass of men was coming down the road, unarmed, unspiked, no rifles visible: prisoners. They stopped near a long rock ledge which walled the road. Some of his own troops began drifting over that way, to stare, to chat. They were usually polite to prisoners. The accents fascinated them. Although some of the Regiment were sailing men, most of them had never been out of Maine. Chamberlain thought vaguely of the South. *She* had loved it. *She* had been at home. Heat and Spanish moss. Strange hot land of courtly manners and sudden violence, elegance and anger. A curious mixture: the white-columned houses high on the green hills, the shacks down in the dark valleys. Land of black and white, no grays. The South was a well-bred, well-mannered, highly educated man challenging you to a duel. *She* loved it. Dreamyly. She had liked being a professor's wife. She had been outraged when he went off to war.

Square-headed Kilrain: "Is the Colonel awake?"

Chamberlain nodded, looking up.

"I have found me a John Henry, sir."

"John who?"

"A John Henry, sir. A black man. A darky. He's over thataway."

Kilrain gestured. Chamberlain started to rise.

"I heard him a-groanin'," Kilrain said, "just before dawn. Would the Colonel care to see him?"

"Lead on."

Kilrain walked down a grassy slope away from the road, across the soft field, marshy with heavy rain, up a rise of granite to a gathering of boulders along the edge of a grove of dark trees. Chamberlain saw two men standing on a rock ledge, men of the Regiment. Kilrain sprang lightly up the rock. The two men—one was the newcomer, Bucklin—touched their caps and wished him "morning" and grinned and pointed.

The black man lay in the shadow between two round rocks. He was very big and very black. His head was shaved and round and resting on mossy granite. He was breathing slowly and deeply, audibly; his eyes were blinking. He wore a faded red shirt, ragged, dusty, and dark pants ragged around his legs. There were no sleeves in the shirt, and his arms had muscles like black cannonballs. His right arm was cupped across his belly. Chamberlain saw a dark stain, a tear, realized that the man had been bleeding. Bucklin was bending over him with a tin cup of coffee in his hand. The black man took a drink. He opened his eyes and the whites of his eyes were red-stained and ugly.

Chamberlain pointed to the wound.

"How bad is that?"

"Oh, not bad," Kilrain said. "I think he's bled a lot, but you know, you can't really tell."

Bucklin chuckled. "That's a fact."

"Bullet wound," Kilrain said. "Just under the ribs."

Chamberlain knelt. The black man's face was empty, inscrutable. The red eyes looked up out of a vast darkness. Then the man blinked and Chamberlain realized that there was nothing inscrutable here; the man was exhausted. Chamberlain had rarely seen black men; he was fascinated.

"We'll get him something to eat, then we'll get him to a surgeon. Is the bullet still in?"

Don't know. Don't think so. Haven't really looked." Kilrain paused. "He sure is black, and that's a fact."

"Did you get his name?"

"He said something I couldn't understand. Hell, Colonel, I can't even understand them Johnnies, and I've been a long time in this army." The black man drank more of the coffee, put out both hands and took the cup, drank, nodded, said something incomprehensible.

"Guess he was a servant on the march, took a chance to run away. Guess they shot at him."

Chamberlain looked at the bald head, the ragged dress. Impossible to tell the age. A young man, at least. No lines around the eyes. Thick-lipped, huge jaw. Look of animal strength. Chamberlain shook his head.

"He wouldn't be a house servant. Look at his hands. Field hands." Chamberlain tried to communicate. The man said something weakly, softly. Chamberlain, who could speak seven languages, recognized nothing. The man said a word that sounded like *Baatu, Baatu,* and closed his eyes.

"God," Kilrain said. "He can't even speak English."

Bucklin grunted. "Maybe he's just bad wounded."

Chamberlain shook his head. "No. I think you're right. I don't think he knows the language."

The man opened his eyes again, looked directly at Chamberlain, nodded his head, grimaced, said again, *Baatu, Baatu.* Chamberlain said, "Do you suppose that could be 'thank you'?"

The black man nodded strongly. "Tang oo, tang oo, baas."

"That's it," Chamberlain reached out, patted the man happily on the arm. "Don't worry, fella, you'll be all right." He gestured to Kilrain. "Here, let's get him up."

They carried the man down out of the rocks, lay him on open grass. A knot of soldiers gathered. The man pulled himself desperately up on one elbow, looked round in fear. Kilrain brought some hardtack and bacon and he ate with obvious hunger, but his teeth were bad; he had trouble chewing the hardtack. The soldiers squatted around him curiously. You saw very few black men in New England. Chamberlain knew one to speak to: a silent roundheaded man with a white wife, a farmer, living far out of town, without friends.

You saw black men in the cities but they kept to themselves. Chamberlain's curiosity was natural and friendly, but there was a reserve in it, an unexpected caution. The man was really very black. Chamberlain felt an oddness, a crawly hesitation, not wanting to touch him. He shook his head, amazed at himself. He saw: palm of the hand almost white; blood dries normally, skin seems dusty. But he could not tell whether it was truly dust or only a natural sheen of light on hair above black skin. But he felt it again: a flutter of unmistakable revulsion. Fat lips, brute jaw, red-veined eyeballs. Chamberlain stood up. He had not expected this feeling. He had not even known this feeling was there. He remembered suddenly a conversation with a Southerner a long time ago, before the war, a Baptist minister. White complacent face, sense of bland enormous superiority: *my dear man, you have to live among them, you simply don't understand.*

Kilrain said, "And this is what it's all about."

A soldier said softly, "Poor bastard."

"Hey, Sarge. How much you figure he's worth, this one, on the hoof?"

"Funny. Very funny. But they'd give a thousand dollars for him, I bet. Nine hundred for sure."

"Really? Hell." It was Bucklin, grinning. "Whyn't we sell him back and buy outen this army."

Chamberlain said to Kilrain, "He can't have been long in this country."

"No. A recent import, you might say."

"I wonder how much he knows of what's happening."

Kilrain shrugged. A crowd was gathering. Chamberlain said, "Get a surgeon to look at that wound."

He backed off. He stared at the palm of his own hand. A matter of thin skin. A matter of color. The reaction is instinctive. Any alien thing. And yet Chamberlain was ashamed; he had not known it was there. He thought: If I feel this way, even I, an educated man . . . what was in God's mind?

He remembered the minister: and what if it is *you* who are wrong, after all?

Tom came bubbling up with a message from Vincent: the Corps would move soon, on further orders. Tom was chuckling.

"Lawrence, you want to hear a funny thing? We were talking to these three Reb prisoners, trying to be sociable, you know? But mainly trying to figure 'em out. They were farm-type fellers. We asked them why they were fighting this war, thinkin' on slavery and all, and one fella said they was fightin' for their 'rats.' Hee. That's what he said." Tom giggled, grinned. "We all thought they was crazy, but we hadn't heard a-right. They kept on insistin' they wasn't fightin' for no slaves, they were fightin for their 'rats.' It finally dawned on me that what the feller meant was their 'rights,' only, the way they talk, it came out 'rats.' Hee. Then after that I asked this fella what rights he had that we were offendin', and he said, well, he didn't know, but he must have some rights he didn't know nothin' about. Now, aint that something?"

"Button your shirt," Chamberlain said.

"Yassuh, boss. Hey, what we got here?" He moved to see the surrounded black. The surgeon had bent over the man and the red eyes had gone wild with new fear, rolling horse-like, terrified. Chamberlain went away, went back to the coffeepot. He felt a slow deep flow of sympathy. To be alien and alone, among white lords and glittering machines, uprooted by brute force and threat of death from the familiar earth of what he did not even know was Africa, to be shipped in black stinking darkness across an ocean he had not dreamed existed, forced then to work on alien soil, strange beyond belief, by men with guns whose words he could not even comprehend. What could the black man know of what was happening? Chamberlain tried to imagine it. He had seen ignorance, but this was more than that. What could this man know of borders and states' rights and the Constitution and Dred Scott? What did he know of the war? And yet he was truly what it was all about. It simplified to that. Seen in the flesh, the cause of the war was brutally clear.

He thought of writing Fanny a quick letter. Dreamyly. He wanted to tell her about the black man. He wanted time to think. But the 83rd Pennsylvania was up and forming. Ellis Spear was coming along the line. It came to Chamberlain suddenly that they might move from here to battle. Under his command. He took a deep breath. Bloody lonely feeling.

He moved back to the cluster around the black man. The shirt was off and Nolan was attending him. The light was stronger; the sun was a blood red ball just over the hills. Chamberlain saw a glistening black chest, massive muscles. The black man was in pain.

Nolan said, "He'll be all right, Colonel. Bullet glanced off a rib. Cut the skin. Looks just like anybody else inside." Nolan clucked in surprise. "Never treated a Negro before. This one's a tough one. They all got muscles like this one, Colonel?"

"We'll have to leave him," Chamberlain said. "Let him have some rations, try to give him directions. Buster, can you talk to him?"

"A little. Found out who shot him. It was some woman in that town there, Gettysburg."

"A woman?"

"He came into town looking for directions and a woman came out on a porch and shot at him. He don't understand. I guess she didn't want to take a chance on being caught with him. But *shoot* him? Christ. He crawled out here figurin' on dyin'."

Chamberlain shook his head slowly.

Kilrain said, "He's only been in this country a few weeks. He says he'd like to go home. Since now he's free."

Bugles were blowing. The men were moving out into formation. Tom came up with the black mare.

"I don't know what I can do," Chamberlain said. "Give him some food. Bind him up. Make a good bandage. But I don't know what else."

"Which way is home, Colonel?"

"Let's go, Buster."

"Do I point him generally east?"

Chamberlain shrugged. He started to move off, and then he turned, and to the black face looking up, to the red eyes, he looked down and bowed slightly, touching his cap. "Goodbye, friend. Good luck. God bless you."

He rode off feeling foolish and angry, placed himself in front of the Regiment.

The Division was forming on level ground, down the road—great square blocks of blue. The colors were unfurled, the lines were dressed. A stillness came over the corps. They were expecting a review, possibly Meade himself. But no one came. Chamberlain sat on his horse, alone in the sun before the ranks of the Twentieth Maine. He heard Tozier behind him: "Dress it up, dress it up," a muffled complaint, whispers, the far sound of hoofs pawing the ground. His own horse stood quietly, neck down, nibbling Pennsylvania grass. Chamberlain let the mare feed. The day was very hot. He saw a buzzard floating along in the pale blue above, drifting and floating, and he thought of the smell of dead men and chicken hawks swooping down and the only eagle he'd ever seen, in captivity, back in Brewer, a vast wingspread, a murderous eye.

Colonel Vincent came down the line, trailing aides like blue clouds. Chamberlain saluted. Vincent looked very happy.

"We'll be moving up soon. No action this morning. I expect we'll be in reserve."

"Yes, sir."

"Reserve is the best duty. That means they'll use us where we're needed. 'Once more into the breach.'" He grinned brightly, showing teeth almost womanly white. "How does that go, Professor?"

Chamberlain smiled politely.

"You spell breach with an 'a,' am I right? Thought so. I'm a Harvard man myself." Vincent grinned, looked thoughtfully at the Regiment. "Glad you got those extra men. You may need 'em. How they getting along?"

"Fine."

Vincent nodded, reached out cheerily, patted Chamberlain on the arm. "You'll be all right, Colonel. Glad to have you with us. I'm having some beef driven up. If there's time, we'll have a good feed tonight in this brigade."

He was interrupted by bugles, and there it was: *Dan, Dan, Dan, Butterfield, Butterfield.* He swung his horse to listen, saw riders approaching, began to move that way. Over his shoulder he said, "Anything you need, Colonel," and he rode off.

The call came to advance. Chamberlain turned to face the Regiment. He ordered right shoulder arms; the rifles went up. He drew his sword, turned. Down the line the order came: advance. He gave the long order to Tozier, guide on the next regiment, the 118th Pennsylvania. He raised his sword. They began to move, the whole Corps in mass, at slow march forward through a flat farm, a peach orchard. He ordered route step. Looking far off down the line, he saw the men moving in a long blue wave, the heart-stopping sight of thousands of men walking silently forward, rifles shouldered and gleaming in the sun, colors bobbing, the officers in front on high-stepping horses. Chamberlain sucked in his breath: marvelous, marvelous. Behind him he could hear men joking, but he could not hear the jokes. Details of men, in front, were removing white rail fences. He rode past a house, slowed to let the men flow round it, saw a fat woman in a bonnet, a gray dress, standing on the porch, her hands in her apron. She extracted one hand, waved slowly, silently. Chamberlain bowed. Some of the men wished her good morning. A sergeant apologized for marching through her farm. The Regiment moved on across the open place and through a cornfield and some low bushes. Then there was high ground to the right. The front of the Corps swung to face south, rolled forward down a slope through more cornfields. The corn was high and the men tried not to trample it, but that was not possible. It was becoming a long walk, up and down in the heat, but Chamberlain was not tired. They came to a brook, cold water already very dirty from many men moving upstream. Chamberlain sent back word that no one was to fall out to fill a canteen; canteen bearers would be appointed. On the far side of the brook they came upon a broad road and the rear of the army. He saw a long line of dark wagons, a band of Provost guards, men gathered in groups around stacked rifles, small fires. To the right there was an artillery park, dozens of guns and caissons and horses. Beyond the road there was a rise of ground, and at that moment, looking upward toward a broad tree on a knoll just above, a tree with huge branches spread wide in the shape of a cup, full and green against a blue sky, Chamberlain heard the first gun, a cannon, a long soft boom of a gun firing a long way off.

A short while later the Corps was stopped. They were told to stop where they were and rest. The men sat in a flat field, an orchard to the left, trees and men everywhere, higher ground in front of them. They waited. Nothing happened. There was the sound of an occasional cannon. But even the crows nearby were silent. Some of the men began to lie back, to rest. Chamberlain rode briefly off to find out what would happen, but no one knew. When he returned he found himself a place under a tree. It was very hot. He had just closed his eyes when a courier arrived with a message from Meade to read to the troops. Chamberlain gathered them around him in the field, in the sunlight, and read the order.

Hour of decision, enemy on soil. When he came to the part about men who failed to do their duty being punished by instant death, it embarrassed him. The men looked up at him with empty faces. Chamberlain read the order and added nothing, went off by himself to sit down. Damn fool order. Mind of West Point at work.

No time to threaten a man. Not now. Men cannot be threatened into the kind of fight they will have to put up to win. They will have to be led. By *you,* Joshuway, by you. Well. Let's get on with it.

He looked out across the field. The men were sleeping, writing letters. Some of them had staked their rifles bayonet first into the ground and rigged tent cloth across to shade them from the sun. One man had built a small fire and was popping corn. No one was singing.

Kilrain came and sat with him, took off his cap, wiped a sweating red face.

"John Henry's still with us." He indicated the woods to the east. Chamberlain looked, did not see the dark head.

"We ought to offer him a rifle," Kilrain said.

There was a silence. Chamberlain said, "Don't know what to do for him. Don't think there's anything we can do."

"Don't guess he'll ever get home."

"Guess not."

"Suppose he'll wander to a city. Pittsburgh. Maybe New York. Fella can always get lost in a city."

A cannon thumped far off. A soldier came in from foraging, held a white chicken aloft, grinning.

Kilrain said, "God damn all gentlemen."

Chamberlain looked: square head, white hair, a battered face, scarred around the eyes like an old fighter. In battle he moved with a crouch, a fanged white ape, grinning. Chamberlain had come to depend on him. In battle men often seemed to melt away, reappearing afterward with tight mirthless grins. But Kilrain was always there, eyes that saw through smoke, eyes that could read the ground.

Chamberlain said suddenly, "Buster, tell me something. What do you think of Negroes?"

Kilrain brooded.

"There are some who are unpopular," he concluded.

Chamberlain waited.

"Well, if you mean the race, well, I don't really know." He hunched his shoulders. "I have reservations, I will admit. As many a man does. As you well know. This is not a thing to be ashamed of. But the thing is, you cannot judge a race. Any man who judges by the group is a peawit. You take men one at a time, and I've seen a few blacks that earned my respect. A few. Not many, but a few."

Chamberlain said, "To me there was never any difference."

"None at all?"

"None. Of course, I didn't know that many. But those I knew . . . well, you looked in the eye and there was a *man.* There was the divine spark, as my mother used to say. That was all there was to it . . . all there *is* to it."

"Um."

"We used to have visitors from the South before the war. It was always very polite. I never understood them, but we stayed off the question of slavery until near the end, out of courtesy. But toward the end there was no staying away from it, and there was one time I'll never forget. There was this minister, a Southern Baptist, and this professor from the University of Virginia. The professor was a famous man, but more than that, he was a good man, and he had a brain."

"Rare combination."

"True. Well, we sat drinking tea. Ladies were present. I'll never forget. He held the tea like this." Chamberlain extended a delicate finger. "I kept trying to be courteous, but this minister was so damned *wrong* and moral and arrogant all at the same time that he began to get under my skin. And finally he said, like this: 'Look here, my good man, you don't understand.' There was this tone of voice as if he was speaking to a stupid dull child and he was being patient but running out of patience. Then he said, 'You don't understand. You have to live with the Negro to understand. Let me put it this way. Suppose I kept a fine stallion in one of my fields. and suddenly one of your Northern abolitionists came up and insisted I should free it. Well, sir, I would not be more astonished. I feel exactly that way about my blacks, and I resent your lack of knowledge, sir.' "

Kilrain grunted. Chamberlain said, "I remember him sitting there, sipping tea. I tried to point out that a man is not a horse, and he replied, very patiently, that *that* was the thing I did not understand, that a Negro was not a man. Then I left the room."

Kilrain smiled. Chamberlain said slowly, "I don't really understand it. Never have. The more I think on it the more it horrifies me. How can they look in the eyes of a man and make a slave of him and then quote the Bible? But then right after that, after I left the room, the other one came to see me, the professor. I could see he was concerned, and I respected him, and he apologized for having offended me in my own home."

"Oh yes." Kilrain nodded. "He would definitely do that."

"But then he pointed out that he could not apologize for his views, because they were honestly held. And I had to see he was right there. Then he talked to me for a while, and he was trying to get through to *me,* just as I had tried with the minister. The difference was that this was a brilliant man. He explained that the minister was a moral man, kind to his children, and that the minister believed every word he said, just as I did, and then he said, 'My young friend, what if it is you who are wrong?' I had one of those moments when you feel that if the rest of the world is right, then you yourself have gone mad. Because I was really thinking of killing him, wiping him off the earth, and it was then I realized for the first time that if it was necessary to kill them, then I would kill them, and something at the time said: you cannot be utterly right. And there is still something every now and then which says, 'Yes, but what if you are wrong?' " Chamberlain stopped. A shell burst dimly a long way off, a dull and distant thumping.

They sat for a long while in silence. Then Kilrain said, softly smiling, "Colonel, you're a lovely man." He shook his head. "I see at last a great difference between us, and yet I admire ye, lad. You're an idealist, praise be."

Kilrain rubbed his nose, brooding. Then he said, "The truth is, Colonel, that there's no divine spark, bless you. There's many a man alive no more value than a dead dog. Believe me, when you've seen them hang each other . . . Equality? Christ in Heaven. What I'm fighting for is the right to prove I'm a better man than many. Where have you seen this divine spark in operation, Colonel? Where have you noted this magnificent equality? The Great White Joker in the Sky dooms us all to stupidity or poverty from birth. No two things on earth are equal or have an equal chance, not a leaf nor a tree. There's many a man worse than me, and some better, but I don't think race or country matters a damn. What matters is justice. 'Tis why I'm here. I'll be treated as I deserve, not as my father deserved. I'm Kilrain, and I God damn all gentlemen. I don't know who me father was and I don't give a damn. There's only one aristocracy, and that's right here—" he tapped his white skull with a thick finger—"and *you,* Colonel laddie, are a member of it and don't even know it. You are damned good at everything I've seen you do, a lovely soldier, an honest man, and you got a good heart on you too, which is rare in clever men. Strange thing, I'm not a clever man meself, but I know it when I run across it. The strange and marvelous thing about you, Colonel darlin', is that you believe in mankind, even preachers, whereas when you've got my great experience of the world you will have learned that good men are rare, much rarer than you think. Ah—" he raised his hands, smiling—"don't you worry about ministers. The more you kill, the more you do the world a service." He chuckled, rubbing his face. His nose was fat and soft, rippling under his fingers.

Chamberlain said, "What has been done to the black is a terrible thing."

"True. From any point of view. But your freed black will turn out no better than many the white that's fighting to free him. The point is that we have a country here where the past cannot keep a good man in chains, and that's the nature of the war. It's the aristocracy I'm after. All that lovely, plumed, stinking chivalry. The people who look at you like a piece of filth, a cockroach, ah." His face twitched to stark bitterness. "I tell you, Colonel, we got to win this war." He brooded. "What will happen, do you think, if we lose? Do you think the country will ever get back together again?"

"Doubt it. Wound is too deep. The differences . . . If they win there'll be two countries, like France and Germany in Europe, and the border will be armed. Then there'll be a third country in the West, and that one will be the balance of power."

Kilrain sat moodily munching on a blade of grass. More cannon thumped; the dull sound rolled among the hills. Kilrain said, "They used to have signs on tavern doors: Dogs and Irishmen keep out. You ever see them signs, Colonel?"

Chamberlain nodded.

"They burned a Catholic church up your way not long ago. With some nuns in it."

"Yes"

"*There* was a divine spark."

Chamberlain grinned, shook his head. Kilrain turned away. Chamberlain sat for a while silently and then took out a copy of *Harper's Weekly* he'd carried up with him and began to look through it. There was an article by a general from Argentina concerning the use of Negro troops. He said that they fought very well, with training.

Chamberlain's nose wrinkled. The world around him grew silent; there was something in the air. The odor of dead meat came down on the wind, drifting through the trees. Soft and sour, the smell of distant death. It passed like an invisible cloud. Kilrain said, "Make you a little wager, Colonel. We'll sit here all day and in the evening we'll march away again." He lay back. "So I might's well get some rest."

Chamberlain moved back against a tree. He was not tired. He closed his eyes, saw a sudden shocking memory of death, torn flaps of skin, the black rotted meat of muscle.

Kilrain said sleepily, "I bet nothing happens today."

But Chamberlain knew. He was certain. He looked toward the odor of death. Still early in the day. Long time until nightfall. They'll come. He could not relax. But what if it is *you* who are wrong? But I am not wrong. Thank God for that. If I were an officer for *them,* on the other side, what would I be feeling now?

The cannon had stilled. The old soldier was popping corn: pop pop poppity pop.

Chamberlain put down the paper, folded his arms. Waited.

3. Longstreet

They had taken a door from its hinges at the Thompson house and placed it across fence rails to serve as a map table. Lee stood above it with his arms folded behind him, staring down. Although the morning was warm and humid his coat was buttoned at the throat, his face pale. He put one hand down, drummed on the map, shook his head, then turned abruptly and walked off to the edge of the trees to look toward Cemetery Hill.

Longstreet sat gazing at the map, fixing it in his mind. Johnston and Clarke had scouted the Union position and it was drawn now on the map in blue ink. Longstreet looked down at the map and then up at the hazy blue ridge in the east, trying to orient himself.

There were two hills beyond Gettysburg: first Cemetery Hill and beyond that Culp's Hill. The Union army had dug in along the crest of both hills, in a crescent. From the two hills ran a long ridge, like the shaft of a fishhook, Cemetery Ridge, sloping gradually down to the south to two more hills, one rocky and bare, the other high and thickly wooded. Meade had put troops along the ridge so that his position was shaped like the fishhook, but there were no troops yet on the rocky hills.

Longstreet sat alone, a forbidding figure. He was thinking: Lee has made up his mind; there's nothing you can do. Well. Then there will be a scrap. He took a deep breath. Ought to get something to eat.

"General?"

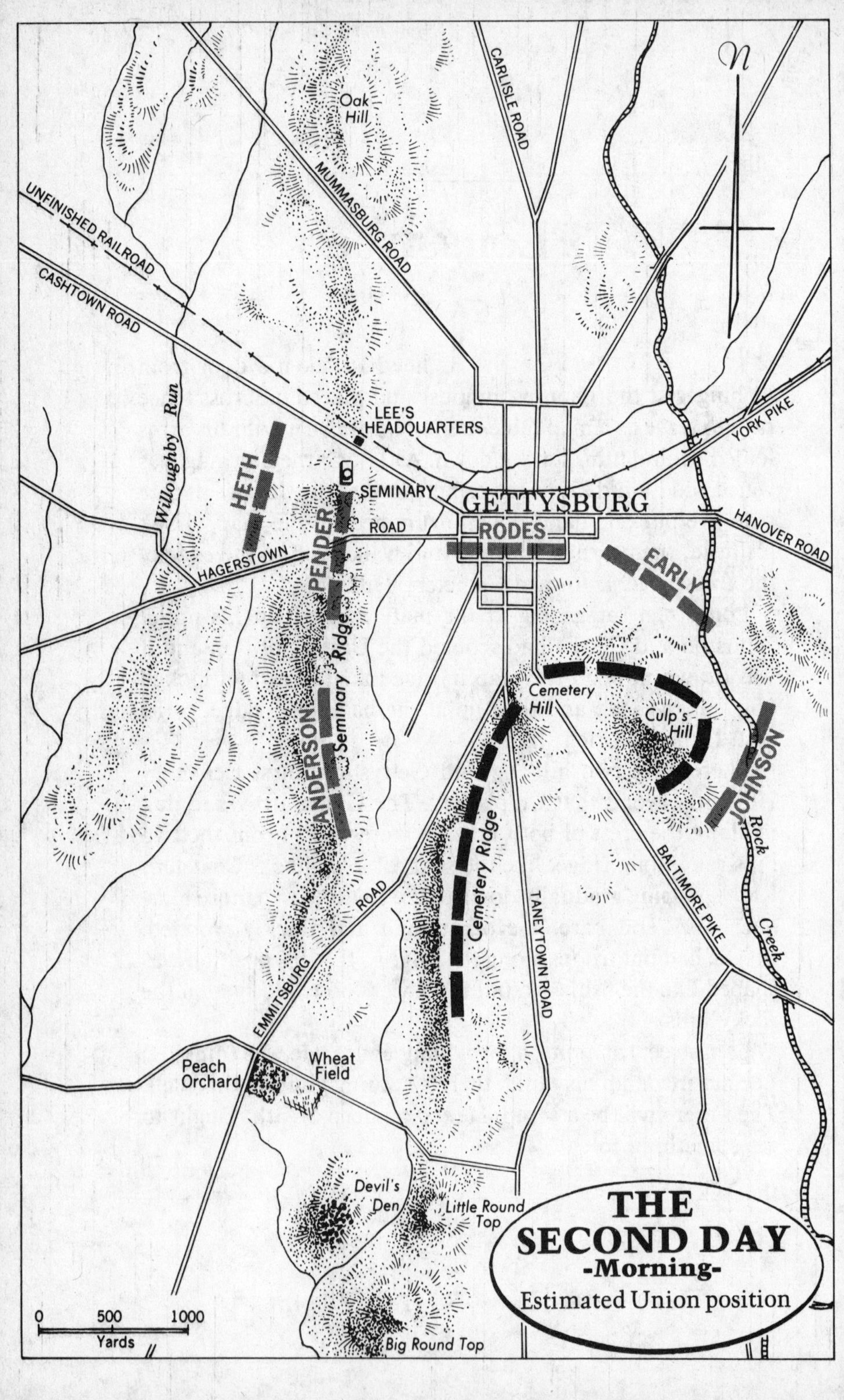

THE SECOND DAY
-Morning-
Estimated Union position

He looked down, saw the handsome face of Taylor, Lee's aide.

"General Lee wishes to speak to you, sir."

Lee was up on the rise by the Seminary, walking back and forth under the shade trees. Officers sat quietly by, joking softly, respectfully with each other, keeping an eye on the old man walking back and forth, back and forth, stopping to stare at the eastern hills, the eastern haze. Longstreet came up.

"General," Lee said.

Longstreet grunted. There was bright heat in Lee's eyes, like fever. Longstreet felt a shudder of alarm.

Lee said, "I like to go into battle with the agreement of my commanders, as far as possible, as you know. We are all members of this army, in a common cause."

Longstreet waited.

"I understand your position," Lee said. "I did not want this fight, but I think it was forced upon us. As the war was." He added, "As the war was." He stopped and frowned, put up his fingers and rubbed the bridge of his nose. "Well," he said. He gestured toward the north, toward Ewell. "General Ewell has changed his mind about attacking to the left. He insists the enemy is too firmly entrenched and has been heavily reinforced in the night. I've been over there personally. I tend to agree with him. There are elements of at least three Union corps occupying those hills."

Longstreet waited. Lee had been over to the left, through Gettysburg, to inspect Ewell's position, but he had not been to the right to check on Longstreet. It was a measure of his trust, and Longstreet knew it.

"I spoke to Ewell of your suggestion that he move around to the right. Both he and Early were opposed."

"*Early.*" Longstreet grimaced, spat.

"Yes." Lee nodded. "Both Generals were of the opinion that an attack on the right would draw off Union forces and that they would then be able to take the hills. They insist that withdrawing from Gettysburg, giving it back to the enemy, would be bad for morale, is unnecessary, and might be dangerous."

Lee looked at him, the deep-set eyes still bright, still hot, still questing. Longstreet said nothing.

"You disagree," Lee said.

Longstreet shrugged. He had disagreed last night, had argued all morning, but now he was setting his mind to it. The attack would come.

"We must attack," General Lee said forcefully. "We *must* attack. I would rather not have done it upon this ground, but every moment we delay the enemy uses to reinforce himself. We cannot support ourselves in this country. We cannot let him work around behind us and cut us off from home. We must hit him now. We pushed him yesterday; he will remember it. The men are ready. I see no alternative."

"Yes, sir," Longstreet said. He wants me to agree. But I cannot agree. Let's get on with it.

Lee waited for a moment, but Longstreet said nothing, and the silence lengthened until at last Lee said, "You will attack on the right with the First Corps."

Longstreet nodded. He took off his hat and wiped the sweat from his brow. He was beginning to relax inside, like an unclenching fist. Now that you knew for sure it was coming a man could rest a bit.

"I want you to attack *en echelon,* to take Cemetery Hill in reverse. Hill will support you with Pender and Anderson. Heth's Division will be in reserve. It had a hard day yesterday. Ewell's people will demonstrate, to keep them from reinforcing against you."

"All right," Longstreet said. "But I don't have Pickett. I have only Hood and McLaws."

Lee said, "You will have to go in without him."

Longstreet said stubbornly, "Law's Brigade is still coming up. I must have Law."

"How long will that take?"

"At least another hour."

"All right." Lee nodded. His head bobbed tightly; he was blinking.

"It will take time to position the men, the artillery."

"At your discretion, General."

"Sir." Longstreet bowed slightly.

"Let us go to the map." Lee turned back toward the table. "I am suspicious of written orders since that affair at Sharpsburg."

Back at the map table men waited for them expectantly. Someone told a joke; there was a ripple of laughter. Lee did not seem to notice.

McLaws and Hood were at the table, along with A. P. Hill. Hill had looked well in the morning, but he did not look well now. Lee bent down over the map. He said, "You will attack up the Emmitsburg Road, up Cemetery Ridge, passing in front of the Rocky Hill. Your objective will be to get in the rear of the Union Army."

McLaws bent over the map. He was a patient man, stubborn and slow, not brilliant, but a dependable soldier. He had a deep streak of sloppy sentimentality to him and he loved to sit around fires singing sad songs of home. He tended to be a bit pompous at times, but he was reliable.

Lee said to McLaws, "Well, General, do you think you can carry this line?"

McLaws shrugged, glanced briefly at Longstreet. He was well aware of Longstreet's theory of defensive tactics. He said pontifically, "Well, sir, I know of nothing to *prevent* my taking that line, but then, of course, I haven't seen it myself. I wouldn't mind taking out a line of skirmishers to reconnoiter the position."

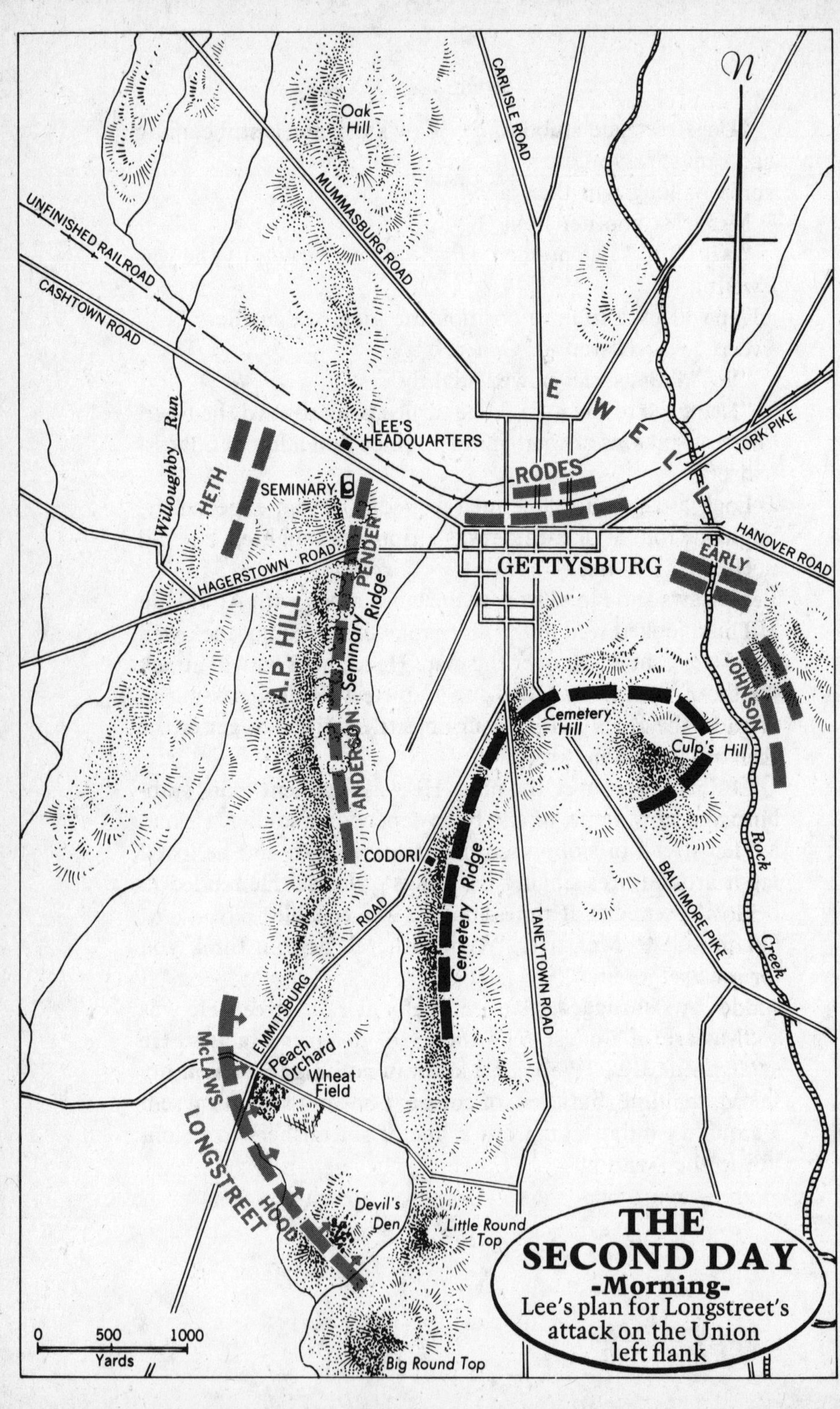
THE SECOND DAY
-Morning-
Lee's plan for Longstreet's attack on the Union left flank
n
Oak Hill
CARLISLE ROAD
MUMMASBURG ROAD
UNFINISHED RAILROAD
CASHTOWN ROAD
Willoughby Run
E W E L L
LEE'S HEADQUARTERS
YORK PIKE
RODES
HETH
SEMINARY
HANOVER ROAD
HAGERSTOWN ROAD
GETTYSBURG
EARLY
PENDER
Seminary Ridge
A.P. HILL
JOHNSON
Cemetery Hill
Culp's Hill
ANDERSON
CODORI
Cemetery Ridge
Rock Creek
BALTIMORE PIKE
TANEYTOWN ROAD
EMMITSBURG ROAD
McLAWS
Peach Orchard
Wheat Field
LONGSTREET
HOOD
Devil's Den
Little Round Top
Big Round Top
0 500 1000
Yards

"Unnecessary," Longstreet said. "Waste of time. We've had scouts out all morning. Let's get on with it, General. I don't want you to leave your Division."

McLaws looked to Lee. Lee nodded.

"Yes. Well, we will step off in echelon, from right to left. Ewell will wait until he hears your artillery. The left of your advance will be on the Emmitsburg Road. Your right will sweep under those rocky heights."

"We'll have enfilade fire coming down on us."

"Not for long," Lee said. "You'll be up over the ridge and take them in the rear. When you are heavily engaged, Ewell will take them in the front."

Longstreet nodded. It might work. Heavy loss, but it might work.

Hood, who had been silent, said suddenly, softly, "General Lee?"

They turned to face him. Lee considered him a fine tactician, and more than that, Hood was a man you listened to. He said, in that soft voice, "General, I'd like to send one brigade around those rocky heights. I think I can get into their wagon trains back there."

Lee shook his head quickly, raised a hand as if warding him off.

"Let's concentrate, General, concentrate. I can't risk losing a brigade."

Hood said nothing, glanced at Longstreet. McLaws was not quite sure where to post his Division. They discussed that for a while, and then explained it to Hill. Longstreet turned suddenly to Sorrel, who was standing by.

"Major, I need something to eat."

"To eat, sir? Of course, sir. What would you like, sir?"

"Marching food," Longstreet said. "I don't give a damn what."

Sorrel moved off. Longstreet looked up and saw Harry Heth, a white bandage on his head, standing weakly by a tree, looking down vacantly to the map table, trying to comprehend.

"How are you, Harry?" Longstreet said.

Heth turned, squinted, blinked. "I'm fine," he said. "What's happening? Are you going to attack? Where's my Division?"

Lee said, "Your Division will not fight today, General. I want you to rest." There was that tone in his voice, that marvelous warmth, that made them all look not at Heth but at Lee, the graybeard, the dark-eyed, the old man, the fighter.

"Sir, I'm fine," Heth said. But he could not even stand without the hand on the tree.

Lee smiled. "Of course, sir. But I would rather you rested. We will soon be needing you." He turned back to the table. "Gentleman?" he said.

They moved out. Alexander was off to place the artillery. McLaws moved out to join his Division. Hood walked for a moment at Longstreet's side.

"We marched all night," Hood said. "Took a two-hour break, from two A.M. to four, then marched again to get here."

"I know," Longstreet said.

"Law's people will come even farther, with no rest. It's twenty-four miles to Guilford. He left at three A.M. When he gets here he'll be pretty tired." Hood squinted at the sun. "Not that it makes much difference, I guess. But one thing, General. Everybody here's had first crack at the water. I want to round some up for Law's boys when they arrive. They'll be thirsty, wells may be dry."

"See to it," Longstreet said. "Any way you can." He paused, watched the men around him moving into motion, men mounting horses, cannon moving past and swinging into position, the artillery people beginning to dig trenches alongside the guns. He said, "Your idea of moving to the right was sound, but his mind was set. Well, we'll do what we can." He turned. At moments like this it was difficult to look a man in the eye. He put out his hand.

"Well, Sam, let's go to it. Take care of yourself."

Hood took the hand, held it for a moment. Sometimes you touched a man like this and it was the last time, and the next time you saw him he was cold and white and bloodless, and the warmth was gone forever.

Hood said, "And you, Pete." He walked away, thin, awkward, long bony strides. Longstreet thought: Best soldier in the army. If it can be done, *he* will do it. He and Pickett. My two. Oh God, there's not enough of them. We have to spend them like gold, in single pieces. Once they're gone, there will be no more.

Sorrel appeared with a tin plate, a steaming slab of meat.

"What's that?" Longstreet sniffed.

"Bit of steak, sir. Compliments of Major Moses."

Longstreet picked it up in his fingers, too hot, sucked the ends of his fingers: delicious.

"Major Moses thought you wanted fighting food, sir."

Longstreet ate with slow delight. Hot food for a hot day. Will be much hotter later on.

Longstreet moved toward his command. The corps was to be led into position by Lee's engineer, Captain Johnston, who had scouted the area this morning. Lee had gone off to see Ewell, to explain the attack to him. Longstreet told Johnston, "Time doesn't matter here. What matters is surprise. We *must* go on unobserved. We're hitting them on the flank. If they see us coming they'll have time to swing round their artillery and it'll be a damn slaughter. So you take your time, Captain, but I don't want us observed."

Johnston saluted, his face strained. "Sir," he said, "may I make a point?"

"Make away."

"General Lee has ordered me to conduct you to the field. But, sir, I scouted the Union position this morning, not the roads leading to it. I don't know much more about how to get there than you do."

Longstreet sighed. Stuart's fault. If there were cavalry here, the roads and routes would be known. Longstreet said, "All right, Captain. But anything you know is more than I know."

"But, sir, General Lee is giving me responsibility for an entire corps." Johnston sweated.

"I know, Captain. It's a weight, isn't it? Well. You lead on as best you can. If you get nervous, call. But I don't want us observed."

"Yes, sir, very good, sir." He rode off.

Longstreet took out a treasured cigar, lighted it, chomped it. Stuart. He ought to be court-martialed.

Would you do it? Court-martial Stuart?

Yes, I would.

Seriously? Or are you just talking?

Longstreet thought a moment. Lee wouldn't. Lee won't.

But I would.

The long march began at around noon, the sun high in a cloudless sea of burning haze. A messenger came in from Law: he had joined Hood's column back at Willoughby Run. A superb march. Longstreet sent his compliments, hoped Hood got him the water. On little things like that—a cup of water—battles were decided. Generalship? How much of a factor is it, really?

He rode in the dust of a blazing road, brooding in his saddle. The hot meat had fired him. He rode alone, and then there was cheering behind him, raw, hoarse cheering from dusty throats, and there was Lee—the old man with the slight smile, the eyes bright with new vigor, revived, the fight coming up to warm him like sunrise.

"General." Longstreet touched his cap.

"You don't mind if I accompany you?" Lee said in the gravely formal gentleman's way.

Longstreet bowed. "Glad to have you with us." There was a peculiar hilarity in Longstreet's breast, the mulish foolish hungry feeling you get just before an assault. There was a certain wild independence in the air, blowing like a hot wind inside his head. He felt an absurd impulse to josh old Lee, to pat him on the back and ruffle the white hair and tell immoral stories. He felt foolish, fond and hungry. Lee looked at him and abruptly smiled, almost a grin, a sudden light blazing in black round eyes.

"Heat reminds me of Mexico," Longstreet said. Visions of those days rolled and boiled: white smoke blowing through broken white buildings, wild-haired Pickett going over the wall, man's face with pools of dirt in the eyes, sky wheeling in black blotches, silver blotches, after the wound. *Lieutenant Longstreet: for distinguished service on the field of battle* . . .

"Yes, but there it was very dry." Lee squinted upward. "And I believe it was warmer. Yes, it was undoubtedly warmer."

"That was a good outfit. There were some very good men in that outfit."

"Yes," Lee said.

"Some of them are up ahead now, waiting for us."

And the past flared again in Longstreet's mind, and the world tilted, and for a moment they were all one army again, riding with old friends through the white dust toward Chapultepec. And then it was past. He blinked, grimaced, looked at Lee. The old man was gazing silently ahead into the rising dust.

"It troubles me sometimes," Longstreet said. His mind rang a warning, but he went on grimly, as you ride over rocks. "They're never quite the enemy, those boys in blue."

"I know," Lee said.

"I used to command those boys," Longstreet said. "Difficult thing to fight men you used to command."

Lee said nothing.

"Swore an oath too," Longstreet said. He shook his head violently. Strange thought to have, at this moment. "I must say, there are times when I'm troubled. But . . . couldn't fight against home. Not against your own family. And yet . . . we broke the vow."

Lee said, "Let's not think on this today."

"Yes," Longstreet said. There was a moment of dusty silence. He grumbled to himself: why did you start that? Why talk about that now? Damn fool.

Then Lee said, "There was a higher duty to Virginia. That was the first duty. There was never any doubt about that."

"Guess not," Longstreet said. But we broke the vow.

Lee said, "The issue is in God's hands. We will live with His decision, whichever way it goes."

Longstreet glanced at the dusty face, saw a shadow cross the eyes like a passing wing. Lee said, "I pray it will be over soon."

"Amen," Longstreet said.

They rode for a while in silence, a tiny island in the smoky stream of marching men. Then Lee said slowly, in a strange, soft, slow tone of voice, "Soldiering has one great trap."

Longstreet turned to see his face. Lee was riding slowly ahead, without expression. He spoke in that same slow voice.

"To be a good soldier you must love the army. But to be a good officer you must be willing to order the death of the thing you love. That is . . . a very hard thing to do. No other profession requires it. That is one reason why there are so very few good officers. Although there are many good men."

Lee rarely lectured. Longstreet sensed a message beyond it. He waited. Lee said, "We don't fear our own deaths, you and I." He smiled slightly, then glanced away. "We protect ourselves out of military necessity, not fear. You, sir, do not protect yourself enough and must give thought to it. I need you. But the point is, we are not afraid to die. We are prepared for our own deaths and for the deaths of comrades. We learn that at the Point. But I have seen this happen: We are not prepared for as many deaths as we have to face, inevitably as the war goes on. There comes a time . . ."

He paused. He had been gazing straight ahead, away from Longstreet. Now, black-eyed, he turned back, glanced once quickly into Longstreet's eyes, then looked away.

"We are never prepared for so many to die. Do you understand? No one is. We expect some chosen few. We expect an occasional empty chair, a toast to dear departed comrades. Victory celebrations for most of us, a hallowed death for a few. But the war goes on. And the men die. The price gets ever higher. Some officers . . . can pay no longer. We are prepared to lose some of us." He paused again. "But never *all* of us. Surely not all of us. But . . . that is the trap. You can hold nothing back when you attack. You must commit yourself totally. And yet, if they all die, a man must ask himself, will it have been worth it?"

Longstreet felt a coldness down his spine. He had never heard Lee speak this way. He had not known Lee thought of this kind of thing. He said, "You think I feel too much for the men."

"Oh no." Lee shook his head quickly. "Not too much. I did not say 'too much.' But I . . . was just speaking."

Longstreet thought: Possible? But his mind said: *No.* It is not that. That's the trap all right, but it's not my trap. Not yet. But he thinks I love the men too much. He thinks that's where all the talk of defense comes from. My God . . . But there's no time.

Lee said, "General, you know, I've not been well lately."

That was so unlike him that Longstreet turned to stare. But the face was calm, composed, watchful. Longstreet felt a rumble of unexpected affection. Lee said, "I hope my illness has not affected my judgment. I rely on you always to tell me the truth as you see it."

"Of course."

"No matter how much I disagree."

Longstreet shrugged.

"I want this to be the last battle," Lee said. He took a deep breath. He leaned forward slightly and lowered his voice, as if to confide something terribly important. "You know, General, under this beard I'm not a young man."

Longstreet chuckled, grumbled, rubbed his nose.

A courier came toiling down the dusty lane, pushing his horse through the crowded troops. The man rode to Lee. In this army Lee was always easy to find. The courier, whom Longstreet did not recognize, saluted, then for some unaccountable reason took off his hat, stood bareheaded in the sun, yellow hair plastered wetly all over his scalp.

"Message from General Hood, sir."

"Yes." Politely, Lee waited.

"The General says to tell you that the Yankees are moving troops up on the high Rocky Hill, the one to the right. And there's a signal team up there."*

Lee nodded, gave his compliments.

"That was to be expected. Tell General Hood that General Meade might have saved himself the trouble. We'll have that hill before night."

The courier put his hat back on and rode off. They rode on for a while in silence. Then Lee halted abruptly in the center of the road. He said, "I suppose I should be getting back. I'll only be in your way."

"Not at all," Longstreet said. But it was Lee's practice to back off, once the fight had begun, and let the commanders handle it. He could see that Lee was reluctant to go. Gradually it dawned on him that Lee was worried for *him*.

*The Confederates did not know that the local name for that hill was "Little Round Top." During the battle their most common name for it was simply "The Rocky Hill."

"You know," Lee said slowly, looking eastward again, toward the heights, "when I awoke this morning I half thought he'd be gone, General Meade, that he would not want to fight here. When I woke up I thought, yes, Meade will be gone, and Longstreet will be happy, and then I can please Old Pete, my warhorse."

"We'll make him sorry he stayed." Longstreet grinned.

"They fought well yesterday. Meredith's brigade put up a fine fight. They will fight well again today."

Longstreet smiled. "We'll see," he said.

Lee put out a hand. Longstreet took it. The grip no longer quite so firm, the hand no longer quite so large.

"God go with you," Lee said. It was like a blessing from a minister. Longstreet nodded. Lee rode off.

Now Longstreet was alone. And now he felt a cold depression. He did not know why. He chewed another cigar. The army ahead halted. He rode past waiting men, gradually began to become annoyed. He looked up and saw Captain Johnston riding back, his face flushed and worried.

"General," Johnston said, "I'm sorry, but if we go on down this road the enemy will view us."

Longstreet swore. He began to ride ahead, saw Joe Kershaw ahead, on horseback, waiting with his South Carolina Brigade. Longstreet said, "Come on, Joe, let's see what's up."

They rode together, Johnston following, across a road crossing from east to west. On the north corner there was a tavern, deserted, the door open into a black interior. Beyond the tavern was a rise—Herr Ridge, Johnston said, a continuation of the ridge leading out from town, facing Seminary Ridge about a mile away, not two miles from the Rocky Hill. Longstreet rode up from under a clump of trees into the open. In front of him was a broad green field at least half a mile wide, spreading eastward. To the south loomed the Rocky Hill, gray boulders clearly visible along the top, and beyond it the higher eminence of the Round Hill. Any march along here would be clearly visible to troops on that hill. Longstreet swore again.

"Damn!" he roared, then abruptly shut his mouth.

Johnston said worriedly, "General, I'm sorry."

Longstreet said, "But you're dead right. We'll have to find another road." He turned to Kershaw. "Joe, we're turning around. I'm taking over as guide. Send somebody for my staff."

Sorrel and Goree were coming up, then Osmun Latrobe. Longstreet outlined the change: both Divisions would have to stop where they were and turn around. Longstreet rode gloomily back along the line. God, how long a delay would there be? It was after one now. Lee's attack was *en echelon.* That took a long time. Well, we'll get this right in a hurry. He sent Sorrel to Lee with word of the change of direction. Then he scouted for a new path. He rode all the way back to the Cashtown Road, getting madder and madder as he rode. If Stuart had appeared at that moment Longstreet would have arrested him.

To save time, he ordered the brigades to double the line of march. But time was passing. There was a flurry over near the center. Longstreet sent Goree to find out what was happening and it turned out to be nothing much—a skirmish of pickets in Anderson's front.

They marched, seventeen thousand men, their wagons, their artillery. Captain Johnston was shattered; it was all his fault. Longstreet propped him up. If it was anybody's fault, it was Stuart's. But it was maddening. He found a new route along Willoughby Run, followed it down through the dark woods. At least it was out of the sun. Most of these men had marched all the day before and all the night and they were fading visibly, lean men, hollow-eyed, falling out to stare whitely at nothing as you passed, and they were expected to march now again and fight at the end of it. He moved finally

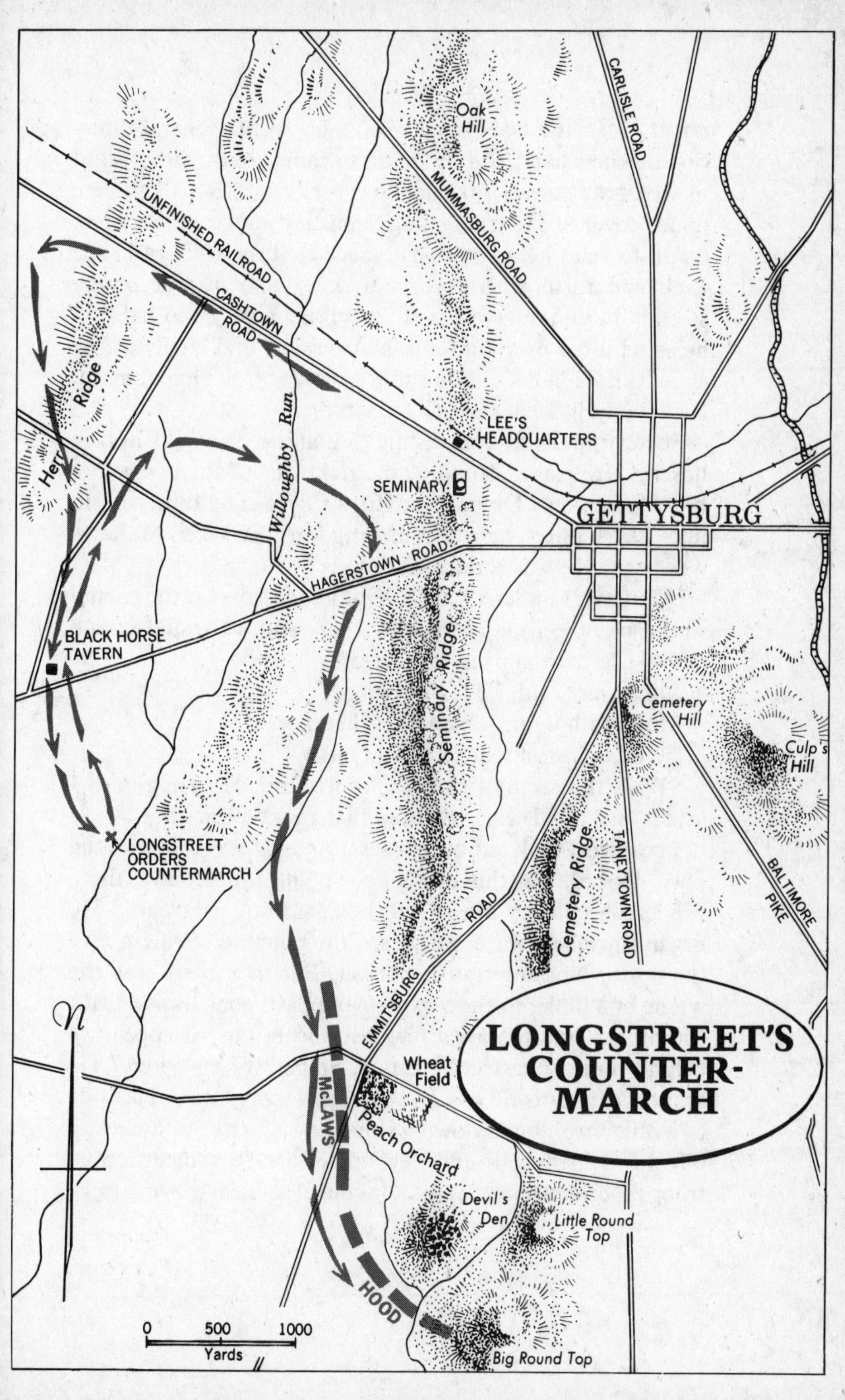

LONGSTREET'S COUNTER-MARCH
Oak Hill
CARLISLE ROAD
MUMMASBURG ROAD
UNFINISHED RAILROAD
CASHTOWN ROAD
Herr Ridge
Willoughby Run
LEE'S HEADQUARTERS
SEMINARY
GETTYSBURG
HAGERSTOWN ROAD
BLACK HORSE TAVERN
Seminary Ridge
Cemetery Hill
Culp's Hill
LONGSTREET ORDERS COUNTERMARCH
Cemetery Ridge
TANEYTOWN ROAD
BALTIMORE PIKE
EMMITSBURG ROAD
Wheat Field
McLAWS
Peach Orchard
Devil's Den
Little Round Top
HOOD
Big Round Top
0 500 1000
Yards

out through the woods across country in the general direction he knew had to be right and so came at last within sight of that gray tower, that damned rocky hill, but they were under cover of the trees along Seminary Ridge and so there ought to be at least some semblance of surprise. Sorrel rode back and forth with reports to Lee, who was becoming steadily more unnerved, and Sorrel had a very bad habit of being a bit too presumptuous on occasion, and finally Longstreet turned in his saddle and roared, "Sorrel, God damn it! Everybody has his pace. This is mine."

Sorrel retreated to a distance. Longstreet would not be hurried. He placed Hood to the right, then McLaws before him. Anderson's Division of Hill's Corps should be next in line. The soldiers were still moving into line when McLaws was back. He was mildly confused.

"General, I understood General Lee to say that the enemy would be up on the ridge back there and we would attack across the road and up the ridge."

Longstreet said, "That's correct."

McLaws hummed, scratched his face.

"Well?" Longstreet said ominously.

"Well, the enemy's right in front of me. He's dug in just across that road. He's all over that peach orchard."

Longstreet took out his glasses, rode that way, out into the open, looked. But this was a poor point, low ground; there was brush country ahead and he could not see clearly. He began to ride forward. He heard the popping of rifle fire to the north. Nothing much, not yet. But then there was the whine of a bullet in the air, here and past, gone away, death sliding through the air a few feet above him, disappearing behind him. Longstreet grunted. Sniper? From where? He scanned the brush. God knows. Can't worry now. He rode to a rail fence, stared down a slope, saw a battery a long way off, down in flat ground beyond the peach orchard. Blue troops speckled a long fence. He could see them moving rails.

Behind him, McLaws said, "Lot of them."

Longstreet looked up toward the ridge. But he could make out nothing at all. You don't suppose . . . they moved down here? Forward, off the ridge? How many? You don't suppose a whole Corps?"

He looked around, spied Fairfax, sent him off with word to Lee.

McLaws said, "What now?"

"Same plan. You hit them. Hood goes first. You key on his last Brigade. That will be G. T. Anderson."

"Right."

Longstreet was running low on aides. He found Goree, sent him off to Hood, telling him to send vedettes ahead to scout the ground. There was not a cavalryman near, not one horse. Longstreet swore. But he was feeling better. Any minute now it would all begin. All hell would break loose and then no more worrying and fretting and fuming; he'd hit straight up that road with everything he had. Never been afraid of that. Never been afraid to lose it all if necessary. Longstreet knew himself. There was no fear there. The only fear was not of death, was not of the war, was of blind stupid human frailty, of blind proud foolishness that could lose it all. He was thinking very clearly now. Mind seemed to uncloud like washed glass. Everything cool and crystal. He glanced at his watch. Getting on toward four o'clock. Good God. Lee's echelon plan would never work. Send messenger to Lee. Let's all go in together. The hell with a plan.

But no messenger was available A moment later one of Hood's boys found him, riding slowly forward, watching McLaws moving into position.

"Sir, message from General Hood. He says his scouts have moved to the right, says there's nothing there. Nothing between us and the Federal train. He suggests most urgently we move around the big hill there and take them from the rear."

Longstreet sighed. "Sonny boy," he said patiently, disgustedly, "you go back and tell Sam that I ben telling General Lee that same damn thing for two days, move to the right, and there aint no point in bringing it up again. Tell him to attack as ordered."

The young scout saluted and was gone. Longstreet sat alone. And there was happy-eyed Fremantle, dirty and cheery on a ragged horse. He seemed never to change his clothes.

"General, are things about to commence?"

"They are indeed." Longstreet grinned. "I suggest you find a convenient tree."

"I will, oh, I will indeed." He turned, pulling the horse away, then turned back. "Oh, sir, I say, best of luck."

"Charming," Longstreet said.

Barksdale's Brigade, Mississippians, was passing him, moving into line. He watched them place all extra baggage, all blankets, all kitbags, and post one lone guard—a frail young man who looked genuinely ill, who sagged against the fence. Longstreet approached and saw that the cornsilk hair was not young, not young at all. The frail young man was a gaunt man with white hair. And he was ill. He opened red eyes, stared vaguely upward.

"Howdy, General," he said. He smiled feebly.

Longstreet said, "Can I get you anything?"

The old man shook his head. He gasped, "Aint nothin' serious. Damn green apples. Damn Yankee apples." He clutched his stomach. Longstreet grinned, moved on.

He saw Barksdale from a long way off. The famous politician had his hat off and was waving it wildly and his white hair was flowing and bobbing, conspicuous, distinguished. Longstreet was fond of this Brigade. Privately he thought it the best in McLaws' whole Division, but of course he couldn't say so. But everybody knew Mississippi was tough. What was it that old man said back in Chambersburg? "You men of Virginia are gentlemen. But those people from *Missippi.*" Longstreet grinned. Another fella had said the same thing about Hood's Texans. The joke about breastworks. Oh God, let's go.

The same officer, back from Hood. The face was wary, the voice was firm. "General Hood begs to report, sir, that the enemy has his left flank in the air. He requests your presence, sir, or that of General Lee. He begs to inform you that in his opinion it would be most unwise to attack up the Emmitsburg Road. The ground is very bad and heavily defended. Whereas if we move to the rear, sir, there is no defense at all. The enemy has uncovered the Rocky Hill."

Longstreet said, "Tell General Hood . . ." Then he thought: they uncovered the Rocky Hill. McLaws has troops in front of him. Good God. They aren't back on the ridge at all; they've moved forward. He took out the map he had drawn of the position, tried to visualize it.

The Union Army was supposed to be up on the ridge. But it wasn't. It was down in the peach orchard.

He stared at the map again.

So Hood had found an opening to the right. Of course.

Longstreet stared again at his watch. Almost four. Lee was miles away. If I go to him now . . . He saw again the grave gray face, the dark reproachful eyes. Too late.

Well, Longstreet thought, Lee wants a frontal assault. I guess he'll have one. He turned to the messenger.

"Tell General Hood to attack as ordered."

McLaws and Barksdale came up together. Barksdale was breathing deeply, face pale, ready for the fight. He said, "When do we go in?"

"In a while, in a while."

There was a cannon to the right. The beginning? No. Hood was probing with his batteries. Longstreet extracted another cigar. The supply was low. Calmly he told Goree to go get some more. He looked up to see Harry Sellars, Hood's AG.

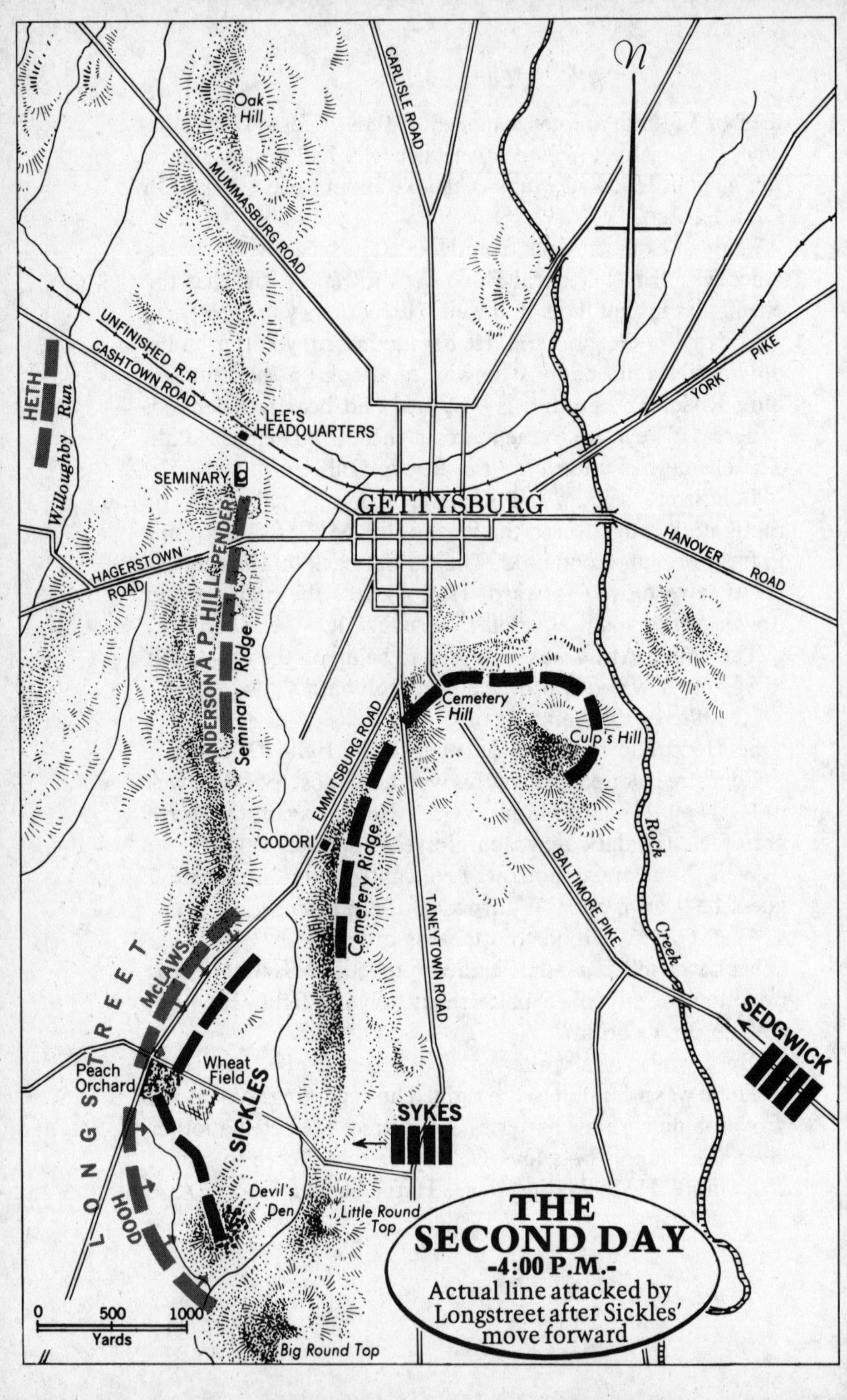
THE SECOND DAY
-4:00 P.M.-
Actual line attacked by Longstreet after Sickles' move forward
N
Oak Hill
CARLISLE ROAD
MUMMASBURG ROAD
UNFINISHED R.R.
CASHTOWN ROAD
HETH
Willoughby Run
LEE'S HEADQUARTERS
SEMINARY
GETTYSBURG
YORK PIKE
HANOVER ROAD
HAGERSTOWN ROAD
PENDER
A. P. HILL
ANDERSON
Seminary Ridge
Cemetery Hill
Culp's Hill
EMMITSBURG ROAD
CODORI
Cemetery Ridge
TANEYTOWN ROAD
BALTIMORE PIKE
Rock Creek
SEDGWICK
McLAWS
LONGSTREET
Peach Orchard
Wheat Field
SICKLES
SYKES
HOOD
Devil's Den
Little Round Top
Big Round Top
0
500
1000
Yards

Longstreet thought: Sellars is a good man, the best he has. Hood's trying to impress me. The cannon boomed. Sellars started talking. Longstreet said gently, "Harry, I'm sorry."

Sellars said, his voice touched with desperation, "General, will you *look* at the ground? We can't even mount artillery."

"All right." Longstreet decided to ride with him. Time was running out. Even now, if Lee attacked *en echelon,* some of the brigades could not attack before dark, unless everything went very smoothly, and it would not go smoothly, not today. Longstreet rode, listening to Sellars, thinking: when you study war it's all so clear. Everybody knows all the movements. General So and So should have done such and such. God knows we all try. We none of us lose battles on purpose. But now on this field what can we do that's undone?

He came on Hood, preparing to move out. There was something rare in his face; a light was shining from his eyes. Longstreet had heard men talk of Hood's face in a fight, but he had not seen it; the fight had not yet begun. But Hood's eyes, normally so soft and sad, were wide and black as round coals, shining with a black heat.

Hood said, "General, the ground is strewn with boulders. They are dug in all over the ground and there are guns in the rocks above. Every move I make is observed. If I attack as ordered I will lose half my Division, and they will still be looking down our throats from that hill. We *must* move to the right."

Longstreet said nothing. He looked down; through thick woods he could begin to see the boulders, great boulders tall as houses, piled one upon another like the wreckage of a vast explosion.

Hood said, "How can you mount cannon in that?"

Longstreet: "Sam . . ." He shook his head. He thought of it again. No. Too late. I cannot go against Lee. Not again. He said, "Sam, the Commanding General will not approve a move to the right. I argued it yesterday. I argued it all morning. Hell, I've been arguing against any attack at all. How can I call this one off? We have our orders. Go on in. We're waiting on you."

Hood stared at him with the black round eyes. Longstreet felt an overwhelming wave of sadness. They're all going in to die. But he could say nothing. Hood stared at him.

Hood: "Let me move to the right, up the Round Hill. If I could get a battery up there . . ."

Longstreet shook his head. "Not enough time. You'd have to cut trees; it would be dark before you were in action."

But he was staring upward at the top of the Rocky Hill. Everywhere you went, that damned hill looked down on you. The key to the position. Once they got a battery up there. Longstreet said, "You're going to have to take that hill."

He pointed.

Hood said, "They don't even need rifles to defend that. All they need to do is roll rocks down on you."

Longstreet said, "But you're going to have to take it."

"General, I do this under protest."

Longstreet nodded. Hood turned. His staff was waiting. He began issuing orders in a low voice. Longstreet backed away. Hood saluted and rode off. Longstreet rode back toward McLaws.

Goodbye, Sam. You're right. You're the best I've got. If I lose you, I don't know what I'll do. God bless you, Sam.

Longstreet was rattled. Never been this rattled in a fight. But the guns began and the sound livened him. We'll brood later. We'll count the dead and brood later. With any luck at all . . . but did you see those rocks?

He rode out into the open. That damned rocky hill stood off to his right, overlooking the field. That they should leave it uncovered was incredible. He saw motion: signal flags? Something was up there. Not a battery, not yet. The fire of Hood was spreading. The first brigade had hit. There was no wind now, the air all dead around him. Hood's smoke stayed where it was, then slowly, very slowly, like a huge ghost, the white cloud came drifting gracefully up the ridge, clinging to the trees, drifting and tearing. The second brigade was following. The fire grew. Longstreet moved to where McLaws and Barksdale were standing together. Wofford had come up.

They all stood together, waiting. The old man who was guarding the clothing of that one Mississippi regiment was asleep against the rail fence, his mouth open. Longstreet rode forward with Barksdale. The man was eager to go in. McLaws moved back and forth, checking the line.

There were woods in front of them, to the left a gray farmhouse. The men were scattered all through the trees, red pennants dipped down, rifles bristling like black sticks. Longstreet saw a shell burst in the woods ahead, another, another. The Yanks knew they were there, knew they were coming. God, did Meade have the whole Union army here? Against my two divisions?

McLaws came up. Even McLaws was getting nervous.

"Well, sir? When do I go in?"

"Calmly," Longstreet said, "calmly." He stared through his glasses. He could see through the trees a Union battery firing from an orchard on the far side of the road. He said, "We'll all go in directly." Something in Longstreet was savage now; he enjoyed holding them back, the savage power. He could feel the fire building in McLaws, in Barksdale, as water builds behind a damn.

But it was the point of an echelon attack. You begin on one side. The enemy is pressed and begins to move troops there. At the right moment your attack opens in another place. The enemy does not know where to move troops now, or to move any at all. He delays. He is upset where he is, not quite so definite. With luck, you catch him on the move. He does not realize the attack is *en echelon* for a while; he thinks perhaps it is a diversion, and he will be hit on another flank.

So he waits, and then gradually he is enveloped where he is, and if his line was thin to begin with, you have not allowed him to concentrate, and if he gambled and concentrated, then he is very weak somewhere, and somewhere you break through. So restraint was necessary now, and Longstreet got down off the horse and sat astride the fence for a while, chatting, the fire growing all around him, shells coming down in the woods ahead, beginning to fall in the field around him, and McLaws stood there blinking and Barksdale running fingers through his hair.

"Not yet, not yet," Longstreet said cheerily, but he got back on his horse and began riding slowly forward into the trees. In the dark of the trees he could smell splintered wood and see white upturned faces like wide white dirty flowers and he looked out to see a battery working steadily, firing into the woods. He heard the first moans but saw no dead. Almost time now. At his elbow, Barksdale was saying something, pleading. The Mississippi boys were staring not at Barksdale but at Longstreet. Longstreet looked down.

"Well," he said, "I guess it's time. If you're ready, sir, why don't you go take that battery, that battery right there?"

He pointed. Barksdale screamed, waved his hat. The men rose. Barksdale formed them in line, the shells zipping the leaves above him. They stepped out of the woods, Barksdale in front, on foot, forbidden to ride, and Longstreet saw them go off across the field and saw the enemy fire open up, a whole fence suddenly puff into white smoke, and the bullets whirred by and clipped among the leaves and thunked the trees, and Longstreet rode out into the open and took off his hat. Barksdale was going straight for the guns, running, screaming, far out in front, alone, as if in a race with all the world, hair streaming like a white torch. Longstreet rode behind him, his hat off, waving, screaming, Go! Go you Mississippi! Go!

4. Chamberlain

. . . heard the cannon begin. Sat up. Kilrain sat up. Tom Chamberlain went on sleeping, mouth open, saintly young, at peace.

Chamberlain said, "That's mostly in the west."

Kilrain cocked his head, listening. "I thought the Rebs were all up at Gettysburg." He looked at Chamberlain, eyes dark. 'You don't suppose they're flanking us again."

The cannons were blossoming, filling the air with thunder, far enough away to soften and roll, not angry yet, but growing.

"At Chancellorsville they came in on the right. This time they could be on the left."

"Do you think they'll ever learn, our goddamn generals?"

Chamberlain shook his head. "Wait."

The men in the field were stirring. Some of the newer men were pulling the tent halves down, but the others, professionals, had rolled over and were staring in the direction of the firing. The corn popper remained asleep.

Chamberlain thought: Alert the men? Some of them were looking to him. One stood up, yawned, stretched, glanced unconcernedly in his direction. Not yet. Chamberlain put the novel away.

Kilrain said, "That's a whole division."

Chamberlain nodded.

"Good thing their artillery aint very good."

A rider had come over the crest of the hill, was loping

down through the tall grass among the boulders. Chamberlain stood up. The courier saluted.

"Colonel Vincent's compliments, sir. You are instructed to form your regiment."

Chamberlain did not ask what was going on. He felt a coolness spreading all the way through him. He began buttoning his shirt as the courier rode off—no hurry, why hurry?—and began slipping on the belt and saber. When he was done with that he began smoothing his hair, yawned, grinned, turned to Tozier.

"Sergeant, have the Regiment fall in."

He looked down on Tom, sleeping Tom. Mom's favorite. He'll be all right. Did not want to wake him. Delayed a moment, buttoned his collar. Hot day for that. Shadows growing longer. Cool soon. He nudged Tom with his foot. Tom groaned, licked his lips, groaned again, opened his eyes.

"Hey, Lawrence." He blinked and sat up, heard the thunder. "What's happening?"

"Let's go," Chamberlain said.

"Right." He jumped to his feet. Chamberlain walked out into the sun. Some of the men were in line, forming by companies. The Regiment was bigger now; Chamberlain was glad of the new men. Ellis Spear had come sleepily up, disarranged, eyes wide. Chamberlain told him to bring everybody, cooks and prisoners, sick-call people. Chamberlain took a deep breath, smelled wet grass, hay, felt his heart beating, looked up into God's broad sky, shivered as a thrill passed through him. He looked down through the woods. The whole Brigade was forming.

And nothing happened. The guns thundered beyond the hill. They were in line, waiting. Chamberlain looked at his watch. Not quite four. The men were remarkably quiet, most of them still sleepy. Sergeant Ruel Thomas, an orderly, reported from sick call. Chamberlain nodded formally. Meade had ordered every soldier to action, even the Provost

Guards. This was it, the last great effort. Don't think now: rest.

Here, at last, was Vincent, riding at a gallop down the long slope. He reined up, the horse rising and kicking the air. All the faces watched him.

"Colonel, column of fours. Follow me."

Chamberlain gave the order, mounted, feeling weak. No strength in his arms. Vincent gave orders to aides; they galloped away. Vincent said, "They're attacking the left flank. Sickles has got us in one hell of a jam."

They began moving up the slope. The Twentieth Maine came after them, four abreast. Vincent was shaking his handsome head.

"Damn fool. Unbelievable. But I must say, remarkably beautiful thing to see."

They moved up between rocks. The artillery fire was growing, becoming massive. They found a narrow road leading upward: high ground ahead. Vincent spurred his horse, waved to Chamberlain to come on. They galloped across a wooden bridge, a dark creek, then up a narrow farm road. The firing was louder. A shell tore through the trees ahead, smashed a limb, blasted rock. Fragments spattered the air.

Chamberlain turned, saw Tom's white grinning face, saw him flick rock dust from his uniform, blinking it out of his eyes, grinning bleakly. Chamberlain grimaced, gestured. Tom said, "Whee."

Chamberlain said, "Listen, another one a bit closer and it will be a hard day for Mother. You get back to the rear and watch for stragglers. Keep your distance from me."

"Right, fine." Tom touched his cap, a thing he rarely did, and moved off thoughtfully. Chamberlain felt an easing in his chest, a small weight lifted. Vincent trotted coolly into the open, reined his horse. Chamberlain saw through a break in the trees, blue hills very far away, hazy ridges miles to the west, not ridges, mountains; he was on high ground. Vincent paused, looked back, saw the Regiment coming up the road, shook his head violently.

"That damn fool Sickles, you know him?"

"Know of him."

Another shell passed close, fifty yards to the left, clipped a limb, ricocheted up through the leaves. Vincent glanced that way, then back, went on.

"The Bully Boy. You know the one. The politician from New York. Fella shot his wife's lover. The Barton Key affair. You've heard of it?"

Chamberlain nodded.

"Well, the damn fool was supposed to fall in on the left of Hancock, right *there.*" Vincent pointed up the ridge to the right. "He should be right here, as a matter of fact, where we're standing. But he didn't like the ground." Vincent shook his head, amazed. "He didn't like the ground. So he just up and moved his whole Corps forward, hour or so ago. I saw them go. Amazing. Beautiful. Full marching line forward, as if they were going to pass in review. Moved right on out to the road down there. Leaving this hill uncovered. Isn't that amazing?" Vincent grimaced. "Politicians. Well, let's go."

The road turned upward, into dark woods. Shells were falling up there. Chamberlain heard the wicked hum of shrapnel in leaves.

Vincent said, "Don't mean to rush you people, but perhaps we better double-time."

The men began to move, running upward into the dark. Chamberlain followed Vincent up the rise. The artillery was firing at nothing; there was no one ahead at all. They passed massive boulders, the stumps of newly sawed trees, splinters of shattered ones. Chamberlain could begin to see out across the valley: mass of milky smoke below, yellow flashes. Vincent said, raising his voice to be heard, "Whole damn Rebel army hitting Sickles down there, coming up around his flank. Be here any minute. Got to hold this place. This way."

He pointed. They crossed the crown of the hill, had a brief glimpse all the way out across Pennsylvania, woods far away, a line of batteries massed and firing, men moving in the smoke and rocks below. Chamberlain thought: Bet you could see Gettysburg from here. Look at those rocks, marvelous position.

But they moved down off the hill, down into dark woods. Shells were passing over them, exploding in the dark far away. Vincent led them down and to the left, stopped in the middle of nowhere, rocks and small trees, said to Chamberlain, "All right, I place you here." Chamberlain looked saw a dark slope before him, rock behind him, ridges of rock to both sides. Vincent said, "You'll hold here. The rest of the Brigade will form on your right. Look's like you're the flank, Colonel."

"Right," Chamberlain said. He looked left and right, taking it all in. A quiet place in the woods. Strange place to fight. Can't see very far. The Regiment was moving up. Chamberlain called in the company commanders, gave them the position. Right by file into line. Vincent walked down into the woods, came back up. An aide found him with a message. He sent to the rest of the Brigade to form around the hill to the right, below the crown. Too much artillery on the crown. Rebs liked to shoot high. Chamberlain strode back and forth, watching the Regiment form along the ridge in the dark. The sun was behind the hill, on the other side of the mountain. Here it was dark, but he had no sense of temperature; he felt neither hot nor cold. He heard Vincent say, "Colonel?"

"Yes." Chamberlain was busy.

Vincent said, "You are the extreme left of the Union line. Do you understand that?"

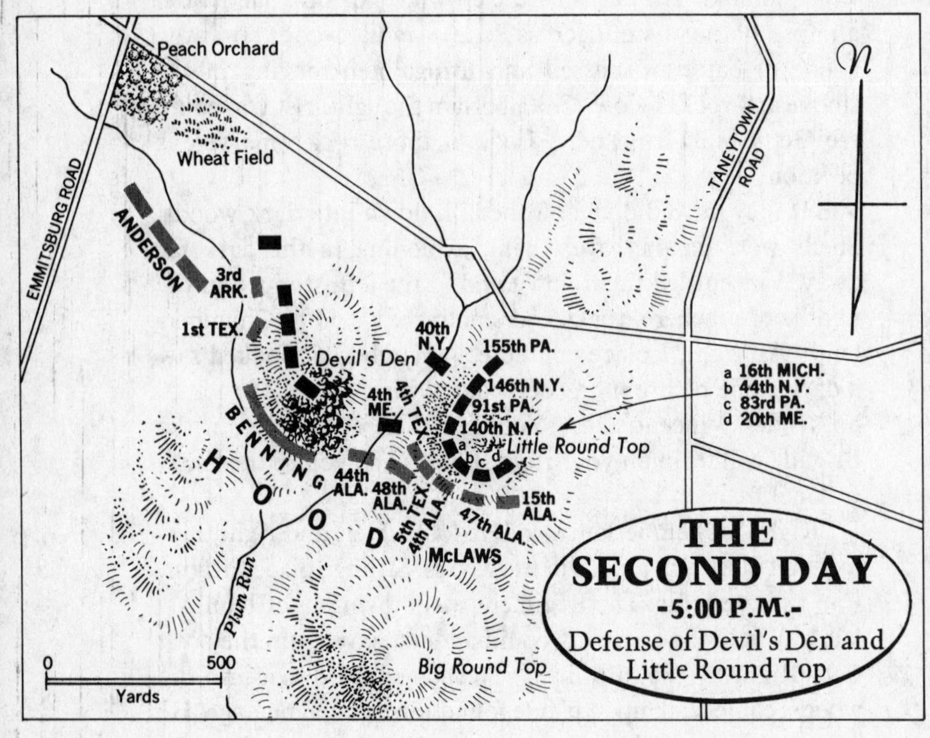

Peach Orchard
Wheat Field
EMMITSBURG ROAD
TANEYTOWN ROAD
ANDERSON
3rd ARK.
1st TEX.
Devil's Den
40th N.Y.
155th PA.
146th N.Y.
91st PA.
140th N.Y.
4th ME.
4th TEX.
a 16th MICH.
b 44th N.Y.
c 83rd PA.
d 20th ME.
Little Round Top
BENNING
HOOD
44th ALA.
48th ALA.
5th TEX.
4th ALA.
47th ALA.
15th ALA.
McLAWS
Plum Run
Big Round Top
0
500
Yards
THE SECOND DAY
-5:00 P.M.-
Defense of Devil's Den and Little Round Top

"Yes," Chamberlain said.

"The line runs from here all the way back to Gettysburg. But it stops here. You know what that means."

"Of course."

"You cannot withdraw. Under any conditions. If you go, the line is flanked. If you go, they'll go right up the hilltop and take us in the rear. You must defend this place to the last."

"Yes," Chamberlain said absently.

Vincent was staring at him.

"I've got to go now."

"Right," Chamberlain said, wishing him gone.

"Now we'll see how professors fight," Vincent said. "I'm a Harvard man myself."

Chamberlain nodded patiently, noting that the artillery fire had slackened. Could mean troops coming this way. Vincent's hand was out. Chamberlain took it, did not notice Vincent's departure. He turned, saw Ruel Thomas standing there with his horse. Chamberlain said, "Take that animal back and tie it some place, Sergeant, then come back."

"You mean leave it, sir?"

"I mean leave it."

Chamberlain turned back. The men were digging in, piling rocks to make a stone wall. The position was more than a hundred yards long, Chamberlain could see the end of it, saw the 83rd Pennsylvania forming on his right. On his left there was nothing, nothing at all. Chamberlain called Kilrain, told him to check the flank, to see that the joint between Regiments was secure. Chamberlain took a short walk. Hold to the last. To the last what? Exercise in rhetoric. Last man? Last shell? Last foot of ground? Last Reb?

The hill was shaped like a comma, large and round with a spur leading out and down:

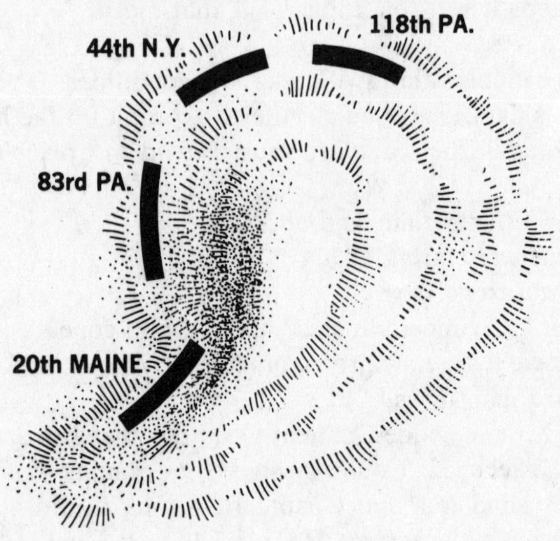

The Twentieth Maine was positioned along the spur, the other regiments curved around to the right. At the end of the spur was a massive boulder. Chamberlain placed the colors there, backed off. To the left of his line there was nothing. Empty ground. Bare rocks. He peered off into the darkness. He was used to fighting with men on each side of him. He felt the emptiness to his left like a pressure, a coolness, the coming of winter. He did not like it.

He moved out in front of his line. Through the trees to his right he could see the dark bulk of a larger hill. If the Rebs get a battery there. What a mess. This could be messy indeed. He kept turning to look to the vacant left, the dark emptiness. No good at all. Morrill's B Company was moving up. Chamberlain signaled. Morrill came up. He was a stocky man with an angular mustache, like a messy inverted U. Sleepy-eyed, he saluted.

"Captain, I want you to take your company out there." Chamberlain pointed to the left. "Go out a ways, but stay within supporting distance. Build up a wall, dig in. I want you there in case somebody tries to flank us. If I hear you fire I'll know the Rebs are trying to get round. Go out a good distance. I have no idea what's out there. Keep me informed."

Company B was fifty men. Alone out in the woods. Chamberlain was sorry. They'd all rather be with the Regiment. Messy detail. Well, he thought philosophically, so it goes. He moved on back up the hill, saw Morrill's men melt into the trees. Have I done all I can? Not yet, not yet.

Artillery was coming in again behind him. All down the line, in front of him, the men were digging, piling rocks. He thought of the stone wall at Fredericksburg. *Never, forever.* This could be a good place to fight. Spirits rose. Left flank of the whole line. Something to tell the grandchildren.

Nothing happening here. He hopped up the rocks, drawn toward the summit for a better look, saw an officer: Colonel Rice of the 44th New York, with the same idea.

Rice grinned happily. "What a view!"

He gestured. Chamberlain moved forward. Now he could see: masses of gray rock wreathed in smoke, gray men moving. If Sickles had a line down there it had already been flanked. He saw a Union battery firing to the south, saw sprays of men rush out of the woods, the smoke, and envelop it, dying, and then the smoke drifted over it. But now more masses were coming, in clots, broken lines, red battle flags plowing through the smoke, moving this way, drifting to the left, toward the base of the hill.

Rice said, glasses to his eyes, "My God, I can see all of it. Sickles is being overrun." He put the glasses down and smiled a foolish smile. "You know, there are an awful lot of people headin' this way."

Chamberlain saw gleams in the woods to the south. Bayonets? Must get back to the Regiment. Rice moved off, calling a thoughtful "good luck." Chamberlain walked down back into the dark. Awful lot of people coming this way. Sixty rounds per man. Ought to be enough.

"Colonel?"

At his elbow: Glazier Estabrook. Incapable of standing up straight; he *listed,* like a sinking ship. He was chewing a huge plug of tobacco. Chamberlain grinned, happy to see him.

"Colonel, what about these here prisoners?"

Chamberlain looked: six dark forms squatting in the rocks. The hard cases from the Second Maine. He had completely forgotten them.

Glazier said slowly, around the wet plug, "Now I wouldn't complain normal, Colonel, only if there's goin' to be a fight I got to keep an eye on my cousin. You understand, Colonel."

What he meant was that he would under no circumstances tend these prisoners during the coming engagement, and he was saying it as politely as possible. Chamberlain nodded. He strode to the prisoners.

"Any of you fellas care to join us?"

"The Rebs really coming?" The man said it wistfully, cautiously, not quite convinced.

"They're really comin'."

One man, bearded, stretched and yawned. "Well, be kind of dull sittin' up here just a-watchin'."

He stood. The others watched. At that moment a solid shot passed through the trees above them, tore through the leaves, ripped away a branch, caromed out into the dark over the line. A shower of granite dust drifted down. The ball must have grazed a ledge above. Granite dust had salt in it. Or perhaps the salt was from your own lips.

Chamberlain said, "Any man that joins us now, there'll be no charges."

"Well," another one said. He was the youngest; his beard was only a fuzz. "No man will call me a coward," he said. He rose. Then a third, a man with fat on him. The other three sat mute. Two looked away from his eyes; the last looked back in hate. Chamberlain turned away. He did not understand a man who would pass by this chance. He did not want to be with him. He turned back.

"I'll waste no man to guard you. I'll expect to find you here when this is over."

He walked down the hill with the three men, forgetting the incomprehensible three who would not come. He gave the three volunteers to Ruel Thomas, to post along the line. There were no rifles available. Chamberlain said, "You men wait just a bit. Rifles will be available after a while."

And now the softer roar of musketry began opening up behind him; the popping wave of an infantry volley came down from above, from the other side of the hill. The Rebs were pressing the front, against Rice's New York boys, the rest of the brigade. Now there was sharper fire, closer to home; the 83rd was opening up. The battle moved this way, like a wall of rain moving through the trees. Chamberlain strode down along the line. Tom came up behind him, Kilrain above. Private Foss was on his knees, praying. Chamberlain asked that he put in a kind word. Amos Long was sweating.

" 'Tis a hell of a spot to be in, Colonel. I cannot see fifty yards."

Chamberlain laid a hand on his shoulder. "Amos, they'll be a lot closer than that."

Jim and Bill Merrill, two brothers, were standing next to a sapling. Chamberlain frowned.

"Boys, why aren't you dug in?"

Jim, the older, grinned widely, tightly, scared but proud.

"Sir, I can't shoot worth a damn lying down. Never could. Nor Bill either. Like to fight standin', with the Colonel's permission."

"Then I suggest you find a thicker tree."

He moved on. Private George Washington Buck, former sergeant, had a place to himself, wedged between two rocks. His face was cold and gray. Chamberlain asked him how it was going. Buck said, "Keep an eye on me, sir. I'm about to get them stripes back."

A weird sound, a wail, a ghost, high and thin. For a vague second he thought it was the sound of a man in awful pain, many men. Then he knew: the Rebel yell. Here they come.

He drifted back to the center. To Tom he said, "You stay by me. But get down, keep down." Kilrain was sitting calmly, chewing away. He was carrying a cavalry carbine. A great roar of musketry from behind the hill. Full battle now. They must be swarming Sickles under. Kilrain was right. Flank attack. Whole Reb army coming right this way. Wonder who? Longstreet? He it was behind the stone wall at Fredericksburg. Now we have our own stone wall. Chamberlain hopped down along the line, telling men to keep good cover, pile rocks higher, fire slowly and carefully, take their time. Have to keep your eye on some of them; they loaded and loaded and never fired, just went on loading, and some of them came out of a fight with seven or eight bullets rammed home in a barrel, unfired. He looked again to the left, saw the bleak silence, felt a crawling uneasiness. Into his mind came the delayed knowledge: You are the left of the Union. The Army of the Potomac ends here.

He stopped, sat down on a rock.

A flank attack.

Never to withdraw.

He took a deep breath, smelled more granite dust. Never to withdraw. Had never heard the order, nor thought. Never really thought it possible. He looked around at the dark trees, the boulders, the men hunched before him in blue mounds, waiting. Don't like to wait. Let's get on, get on. But his mind said cheerily, coldly: Be patient, friend, be patient. You are not leaving here. Possibly not forever, except, as they say, trailing clouds of glory, if that theory really is true after all and they do send some sort of chariot, possibly presently you will be on it. My, how the mind does chatter at times like this. Stop thinking. Depart in a chariot of fire. I suppose it's possible. That He is waiting. Well. May well find out.

The 83rd engaged. Chamberlain moved to the right. He had been hoping to face a solid charge, unleash a full volley, but the Rebs seemed to be coming on like a lapping wave, rolling up the beach. He told the right to fire at will. He remained on the right while the firing began. A man down in E Company began it, but there was nothing there; he had fired at a falling branch, and Chamberlain heard a sergeant swearing, then a flurry of fire broke out to the right and spread down the line and the white smoke bloomed in his eyes. Bullets zipped in the leaves, cracked the rocks. Chamberlain moved down closer to the line. Far to the left he could see Tozier standing by the great boulder, with the colors.

Then he saw the Rebs.

Gray-green-yellow uniforms, rolling up in a mass. His heart seized him. Several companies. More and more. At least a hundred men. More. Coming up out of the green, out of the dark. They seemed to be rising out of the ground. Suddenly the terrible scream, the ripply crawly sound in your skull. A whole regiment. Dissolving in smoke and thunder. They came on. Chamberlain could see nothing but smoke, the blue mounds bobbing in front of him, clang of ramrods, grunts, a high gaunt wail. A bullet thunked into a tree near him. Chamberlain turned, saw white splintered wood. He ducked suddenly, then stood up, moved forward, crouched behind a boulder, looking.

A new wave of firing. A hole in the smoke. Chamberlain

saw a man on his knees before him, facing the enemy, arms clutching his stomach. A man was yelling an obscene word. Chamberlain looked, could not see who it was. But the fire from his boys was steady and heavy and they were behind trees and under rocks and pouring it in, and Chamberlain saw gray-yellow forms go down, saw a man come bounding up a rock waving his arms wide like a crazy Indian and take a bullet that doubled him right over so that he fell forward over the rocks and out of sight, and then a whole flood to the right, ten or twelve in a pack, suddenly stopping to kneel and fire, one man in fringed clothes, like buckskin, stopping to prop his rifle against a tree, and then to go down, punched backward, coming all loose and to rubbery pieces and flipping back so one bare foot stood up above a bloody rock. A blast of fire at Chamberlain's ear. He turned: Kilrain reloading the carbine. Said something. Noise too great to hear. Screams and yells of joy and pain and rage. He saw bloodstains spatter against a tree. Turned. Fire slowing. They were moving back. Thought: we've stopped 'em. By God and by Mary, we've stopped 'em.

The firing went on, much slower. Smoke was drifting away. But the din from the right was unceasing; the noise from the other side of the hill was one long huge roar, like the ground opening. Kilrain looked that way.

"Half expect 'em to come in from behind."

Chamberlain said, "Did you hear Morrill's Company?"

"No, sir. Couldn't hear nothing in that mess."

"Tom?"

Tom shook his head. He had the look of a man who has just heard a very loud noise and has not yet regained his hearing. Chamberlain felt a sudden moment of wonderful delight. He put out a hand and touched his brother's cheek.

"You stay down, boy."

Tom nodded, wide-eyed. "Damn right," he said.

Chamberlain looked out into the smoke. Morrill might

have run into them already, might already be wiped out. He saw: a red flag, down in the smoke and dark. Battle flag. A new burst of firing. He moved down the line, Kilrain following, crouched. Men were down. He saw the first dead: Willard Buxton of K. Neat hole in the forehead. Instantaneous. Merciful. First Sergeant Noyes was with him. Chamberlain touched the dead hand, moved on. He was thinking: with Morrill gone, I have perhaps three hundred men. Few more, few less. What do I do if they flank me?

The emptiness to the left was a vacuum, drawing him back that way. Men were drinking water. He warned them to save it. The new attack broke before he could get to the left.

The attack came all down the line, a full, wild, leaping charge. Three men came inside the low stone wall the boys had built. Two died; the other lay badly wounded, unable to speak. Chamberlain called for a surgeon to treat him. A few feet away he saw a man lying dead, half his face shot away. Vaguely familiar. He turned away, turned back. Half the right jawbone visible, above the bloody leer: face of the one of the Second Maine prisoners who had volunteered just a few moments past—the fat one. Never had time to know his name. He turned to Kilrain. "That was one of the Maine prisoners. Don't let me forget."

Kilrain nodded. Odd look on his face. Chamberlain felt a cool wind. He put a hand out.

"Buster? You all right?"

Bleak gray look. Holding his side.

"Fine, Colonel. Hardly touched me."

He turned, showed his side. Tear just under the right shoulder, blood filling the armpit. Kilrain stuffed white cloth into the hole. "Be fine in a moment. But plays hell with me target practice. Would you care for the carbine?"

He sat down abruptly. Weak from loss of blood. But not a bad wound, surely not a bad wound.

"You stay there," Chamberlain said. Another attack was

coming. New firing blossomed around them. Chamberlain knelt.

Kilrain grinned widely. "Hell, Colonel, I feel saintly."

"Tom'll get a surgeon."

"Just a bit of bandage is all I'll be needin'. And a few minutes off me feet. Me brogans are killin' me." Lapse into brogue.

Tom moved off into the smoke. Chamberlain lost him. He stood. Whine of bullets, whisking murder. Leaves were falling around him. Face in the smoke. Chamberlain stepped forward.

Jim Nichols, K Company: "Colonel, something goin' on in our front. Better come see."

Nichols a good man. Chamberlain hopped forward, slipped on a rock, nearly fell, hopped to another boulder, felt an explosion under his right foot, blow knocked his leg away, twirled, fell, caught by Nichols. Damned undignified. Hurt? Damn!

How are you, sir?

Looked at his foot. Hole in the boot? Blood? No. Numb. Oh my, begins to hurt now. But no hole, thank God. He stood up.

Nichols pointed. Chamberlain clambered up on a high boulder. Going to get killed, give 'em a good high target. Saw: they were coming in groups, from rock to rock, tree to tree, not charging wildly as before, firing as they came, going down, killing us. But there, back there: masses of men, flags, two flags, flanking, moving down the line. They're going to turn us. They're going to that hole in the left . . .

He was knocked clean off the rock. Blow in the side like lightning bolt. Must be what it feels like. Dirt and leaves in his mouth. Rolling over. This is ridiculous. Hands pulled him up. He looked down. His scabbard rippled like a spider's leg, stuck out at a ridiculous angle. Blood? No. But the hip, oh my. Damn, damn. He stood up. Becoming quite a target.

What was that now? He steadied his mind. Remembered: they're flanking us.

He moved back behind the boulder from which he had just been knocked. His hands were skinned; he was licking blood out of his mouth. His mind, temporarily sidetracked, oiled itself and ticked and turned and woke up, functioning. To Nichols: "Find my brother. Send all company commanders. Hold your positions."

Extend the line? No.

He brooded. Stood up. Stared to the left, then mounted the rock again, aware of pain but concentrating. To the left the Regiment ended, a high boulder there. Chamberlain thought: What was the phrase in the manual? Muddled brain. Oh yes: refuse the line.

The commanders were arriving. Chamberlain, for the first time, raised his voice. "You men! MOVE!"

The other commanders came in a hurry. Chamberlain said, "We're about to be flanked. Now here's what we do. Keep up a good hot masking fire, you understand? Now let's just make sure the Rebs keep their heads down. And let's keep a tight hold on the Eighty-third, on old Pennsylvania over there. I want no breaks in the line. That's *you* Captain Clark, understand? No breaks."

Clark nodded. Bullets chipped the tree above him.

"Now here's the move. Keeping up the fire, and keeping a tight hold on the Eighty-third, we *refuse* the line. Men will sidestep to the left, thinning out to twice the present distance. See that boulder? When we reach that point we'll refuse the line, form a new line at right angles. That boulder will be the salient. Let's place the colors there, right? Fine. Now you go on back and move your men in sidestep and form a new line to the boulder, and then back from the boulder like a swinging door. I assume that, ah, F Company will take the point. Clear? Any questions?"

They moved. It was very well done. Chamberlain limped

to the boulder, to stand at the colors with Tozier. He grinned at Tozier.

"How are you, Andrew?"

"Fine, sir. And you?"

"Worn." Chamberlain grinned. "A bit worn."

"I tell you this, Colonel. The boys are making a hell of a fight."

"They are indeed."

The fire increased. The Rebs moved up close and began aimed fire, trying to mask their own movement. In a few moments several men died near where Chamberlain was standing. One boy was hit in the head and the wound seemed so bloody it had to be fatal, but the boy sat up and shook his head and bound up the wound himself with a handkerchief and went back to firing. Chamberlain noted: most of our wounds are in the head or hands, bodies protected. Bless the stone wall. Pleasure to be behind it. Pity the men out there. Very good men. Here they come. Whose?

The next charge struck the angle at the boulder, at the colors, lapped around it, ran into the new line, was enfiladed, collapsed. Chamberlain saw Tom come up, whirling through smoke, saw a rip in his coat, thought: no good to have a brother here. Weakens a man. He sent to the 83rd to tell them of his move to the left, asking if perhaps they couldn't come a little this way and help him out. He sent Ruel Thomas back up the hill to find out how things were going there, to find Vincent, to tell him that life was getting difficult and we need a little help.

He looked for Kilrain. The old Buster was sitting among some rocks, aiming the carbine, looking chipper. Hat was off. An old man, really. No business here. Kilrain said, "I'm not much good to you, Colonel."

There was a momentary calm. Chamberlain sat.

"Buster, how are you?"

Grin. Stained crooked teeth. All the pores remarkably

clear, red bulbous nose. Eyes of an old man. How old? I've never asked.

"How's the ammunition?" Kilrain asked.

"I've sent back."

"They're in a mess on the other side." He frowned, grinned, wiped his mouth with the good hand, the right arm folded across his chest, a bloody rag tucked in his armpit. "Half expect Rebs comin' right over the top of the hill. Nothing much to do then. Be Jesus. Fight makes a thirst. And I've brought nothin' a-tall, would you believe that? Not even my emergency ration against snakebite and bad dreams. Not even a spoonful of Save the Baby."

Aimed fire now. He heard a man crying with pain. He looked down the hill. Darker down there. He saw a boy behind a thick tree, tears running down his face, ramming home a ball, crying, whimpering, aiming fire, jolted shoulders, ball of smoke, then turning back, crying aloud, sobbing, biting the paper cartridge, tears all over his face, wiping his nose with a wet sleeve, ramming home another ball.

Kilrain said, "I can stand now, I think."

Darker down the hill. Sunset soon. How long had this been going on? Longer pause than usual. But . . . the Rebel yell. A rush on the left. He stood up. Pain in the right foot, unmistakable squish of blood in the boot. Didn't know it was bleeding. See them come, bounding up the rocks, hitting the left flank. Kilrain moved by him on the right, knelt, fired. Chamberlain pulled out the pistol. No damn good except at very close range. You couldn't hit anything. He moved to the left flank. Much smoke. Smoke changing now, blowing this way, blinding. He was caught in it, a smothering shroud, hot, white, the bitter smell of burned powder. It broke. He saw a man swinging a black rifle, grunts and yells and weird thick sounds unlike anything he had ever heard before. A Reb came over a rock, bayonet fixed, black thin point forward and poised, face seemed blinded, head twitched. Chamberlain aimed the pistol, fired, hit the man dead center, down he went, folding; smoke swallowed him. Chamberlain moved forward. He expected them to be everywhere, flood of brown bodies, gray bodies. But the smoke cleared and the line was firm. Only a few Rebs had come up, a few come over the stones, all were down. He ran forward to a boulder, ducked, looked out: dead men, ten, fifteen, lumps of gray, blood spattering everywhere, dirty white skin, a clawlike hand, black sightless eyes. Burst of white smoke, again, again. Tom at his shoulder: "Lawrence?"

Chamberlain turned. All right? Boyish face. He smiled.

"They can't send us no help from the Eighty-third." Woodward said they have got their troubles, but they can extend the line a little and help us out."

"Good. Go tell Clarke to shift a bit, strengthen the center."

Kilrain, on hands and knees, squinting: "They keep coming in on the flank."

Chamberlain, grateful for the presence: "What do you think?"

"We've been shooting a lot of rounds."

Chamberlain looked toward the crest of the hill. No Thomas anywhere. Looked down again toward the dark. Motion. They're forming again. Must have made five or six tries already. To Kilrain: "Don't know what else to do."

Looked down the line. Every few feet, a man down. Men sitting facing numbly to the rear. He thought: let's pull back a ways. He gave the order to Spear. The Regiment bent back from the colors, from the boulder, swung back to a new line, tighter, almost a U. The next assault came against both flanks and the center all at once, worst of all. Chamberlain dizzy in the smoke began to lose track of events, saw only blurred images of smoke and death, Tozier with the flag, great black gaps in the line, the left flank giving again, falling back, tightening. Now there was only a few yards between the line on the right and the line on the left, and Chamberlain walked the narrow corridor between, Kilrain at his side, always at a crouch.

Ruel Thomas came back. "Sir? Colonel Vincent is dead."

Chamberlain swung to look him in the face. Thomas nodded jerkily.

"Yes, sir. Got hit a few moments after fight started. We've already been reinforced by Weed's Brigade, up front, but now Weed is dead, and they moved Hazlett's battery in up top and Hazlett's dead."

Chamberlain listened, nodded, took a moment to let it come to focus.

"Can't get no ammunition, sir. Everything's a mess up there. But they're holdin' pretty good. Rebs having trouble coming up the hill. Pretty steep."

"Got to have bullets," Chamberlain said.

Spear came up from the left. "Colonel, half the men are down. If they come again . . ." He shrugged, annoyed, baffled, as if by a problem he could not quite solve, yet ought to, certainly, easily. "Don't know if we can stop 'em."

"Send out word," Chamberlain said. "Take ammunition from the wounded. Make every round count." Tom went off, along with Ruel Thomas. Reports began coming in. Spear was right. But the right flank was better, not so many casualties there. Chamberlain moved, shifting men. And heard the assault coming, up the rocks, clawing up through the bushes, through the shattered trees, the pocked stone, the ripped and bloody earth. It struck the left flank. Chamberlain shot another man, an officer. He fell inside the new rock wall, face a bloody rag. On the left two Maine men went down, side by side, at the same moment, and along that spot there was no one left, no one at all, and yet no Rebs coming, just one moment of emptiness in all the battle, as if in that spot the end had come and there were not enough men left now to fill the earth, that final death was beginning there and spreading like a stain. Chamberlain saw movement below, troops drawn toward the gap as toward a cool place in all the heat, and looking down, saw Tom's face and yelled, but not being heard, pointed and pushed, but his hand stopped in mid-air, not my own brother, but Tom understood, hopped across to the vacant place and plugged it with his body so that there was no longer a hole but one terribly mortal exposed boy, and smoke cut him off, so that Chamberlain could no longer see, moving forward himself, had to shoot another man, shot him twice, the first ball taking him in the shoulder, and the man was trying to fire a musket with one hand when Chamberlain got him again, taking careful aim this time. Fought off this assault, thinking all the while coldly, calmly, perhaps now we are approaching the end. They can't keep coming. We can't keep stopping them.

Firing faded. Darker now. Old Tom. Where?

Familiar form in familiar position, aiming downhill, firing again. All right. God be praised.

Chamberlain thought: not right, not right at all. If he was hit, I sent him there. What would I tell Mother? What do I feel myself? His duty to go. No, no. Chamberlain blinked. He was becoming tired. Think on all that later, the theology of it.

He limped along the line. Signs of exhaustion. Men down, everywhere. He thought: we cannot hold.

Looked up toward the crest. Fire still hot there, still hot everywhere. Down into the dark. They are damned good men, those Rebs. Rebs, I salute you. I don't think we can hold you.

He gathered with Spear and Kilrain back behind the line. He saw another long gap, sent Ruel Thomas to this one. Spear made a count.

"We've lost a third of the men, Colonel. Over a hundred down. The left is too thin."

"How's the ammunition?"

"I'm checking."

A new face, dirt-stained, bloody: Homan Melcher, Lieutenant, Company F, a gaunt boy with buck teeth.

"Colonel? Request permission to go pick up some of our wounded. We left a few boys out there."

"Wait," Chamberlain said.

Spear came back, shaking his head. "We're out." Alarm stained his face, a grayness in his cheeks.

"Some of the boys have nothing at all."

"Nothing," Chamberlain said.

Officers were coming from the right. Down to a round or two per man. And now there was a silence around him. No man spoke. They stood and looked at him, and then looked down into the dark and then looked back at Chamberlain. One man said, "Sir, I guess we ought to pull out."

Chamberlain said, "Can't do that."

Spear: "We won't hold 'em again. Colonel, you know we can't hold 'em again."

Chamberlain: "If we don't hold, they go right on by and over the hill and the whole flank caves in."

He looked from face to face. The enormity of it, the weight of the line, was a mass too great to express. But he could see it as clearly as in a broad wide vision, a Biblical dream: If the line broke here, then the hill was gone, all these boys from Pennsylvania, New York, hit from behind, above. Once the hill went, the flank of the army went. Good God! He could see troops running; he could see the blue flood, the bloody tide.

Kilrain: "Colonel, they're coming."

Chamberlain marveled. But we're not so bad ourselves. One recourse: Can't go back. Can't stay where we are. Result: inevitable.

The idea formed.

"Let's fix bayonets," Chamberlain said.

For a moment no one moved.

"We'll have the advantage of moving downhill," he said.

Spear understood. His eyes saw; he nodded automatically. The men coming up the hill stopped to volley; weak fire came in return. Chamberlain said, "They've got to be tired, those Rebs. They've got to be close to the end. Fix bayonets. Wait. Ellis, you take the left wing. I want a right wheel forward of the whole Regiment."

Lieutenant Melcher said, perplexed, "Sir, excuse me, but what's a 'right wheel forward'?"

Ellis Spear said, "He means 'charge,' Lieutenant, 'charge.' "

Chamberlain nodded. "Not quite. We charge, swinging down to the right. We straighten out our line. Clarke hangs onto the Eighty-third, and we swing like a door, sweeping them down the hill. Understand? Everybody understand? Ellis, you take the wing, and when I yell you go to it, the whole Regiment goes forward, swinging to the right."

"Well," Ellis Spear said. He shook his head. "Well."

"Let's go." Chamberlain raised his saber, bawled at the top of his voice, "Fix bayonets!"

He was thinking: We don't have two hundred men left. Not two hundred. More than that coming at us. He saw Melcher bounding away toward his company, yelling, waving. Bayonets were coming out, clinking, clattering. He heard men beginning to shout, Maine men, strange shouts, hoarse, wordless, animal. He limped to the front, toward the great boulder where Tozier stood with the colors, Kilrain at his side. The Rebs were in plain view, moving, firing. Chamberlain saw clearly a tall man aiming a rifle at him. At *me.* Saw the smoke, the flash, but did not hear the bullet go by. Missed. Ha! He stepped out into the open, balanced on the gray rock. Tozier had lifted the colors into the clear. The Rebs were thirty yards off. Chamberlain raised his saber, let loose the shout that was the greatest sound he could make, boiling the yell up from his chest: *Fix bayonets! Charge! Fix bayonets! Charge! Fix bayonets! Charge!* He leaped down from the boulder, still screaming, his voice beginning to crack and give, and all around him his men were roaring animal screams, and he saw the whole Regiment rising and pouring over the wall and beginning to bound down through the dark bushes, over the dead and dying and wounded, hats coming off, hair flying, mouths making sounds, one man firing as he ran, the last bullet, last round. Chamberlain saw gray men below stop, freeze, crouch, then quickly turn. The move was so quick he could not believe it. Men were turning and running. Some were stopping to fire. There was the yellow flash and then they turned. Chamberlain saw a man drop a rifle and run. Another. A bullet plucked at Chamberlain's coat, a hard pluck so that he thought he had caught a thorn but looked down and saw the huge gash. But he was not hit. He saw an officer: handsome full-bearded man in gray, sword and revolver. Chamberlain ran toward him, stumbled, cursed the bad foot, looked up and aimed and fired and missed, then held aloft the saber. The officer turned, saw him coming, raised a pistol, and Chamberlain ran toward it downhill, unable to stop, stumbling downhill seeing the black hole of the pistol turning toward him, not anything else but the small hole yards away, feet away, the officer's face a blur behind it and no thought, a moment of gray suspension rushing silently, soundlessly toward the black hole . . . and the gun did not fire; the hammer clicked down on an empty shell, and Chamberlain was at the man's throat with the saber and the man was handing him his sword, all in one motion, and Chamberlain stopped.

"The pistol too," he said.

The officer handed him the gun: a cavalry revolver, Colt. "Your prisoner, sir." The face of the officer was very white, like old paper. Chamberlain nodded.

He looked up to see an open space. The Rebs had begun to fall back; now they were running. He had never seen them run; he stared, began limping forward to see. Great cries, incredible sounds, firing and yelling. The Regiment was driving in a line, swinging to the fight, into the dark valley. Men were surrendering. He saw masses of gray coats, a hundred or more, moving back up the slope to his front, in good order, the only ones not running, and thought: If they form again we're in trouble, desperate trouble, and he began moving that way, ignoring the officer he had just captured. At that moment a new wave of firing broke out on the other side of the gray mass. He saw a line of white smoke erupt, the gray troops waver and move back this way, stop, rifles begin to fall, men begin to run to the right, trying to get away. Another line of fire—Morrill. B Company. Chamberlain moved that way. A soldier grabbed his Reb officer, grinning, by the arm. Chamberlain passed a man sitting on a rock, holding his stomach. He had been bayoneted. Blood coming from his mouth. Stepped on a dead body, wedged between rocks. Came upon Ellis Spear, grinning crazily, foolishly, face stretched and glowing with a wondrous light.

"By God, Colonel, by God, by God," Spear said. He pointed. Men were running off down the valley. The Regiment was moving across the front of the 83rd Pennsylvania. He looked up the hill and saw them waving and cheering. Chamberlain said, aloud, "I'll be damned."

The Regiment had not stopped, was chasing the Rebs down the long valley between the hills. Rebs had stopped everywhere, surrendering. Chamberlain said to Spear, "Go on up and stop the boys. They've gone far enough."

"Yes, sir. But they're on their way to Richmond."

"Not today," Chamberlain said. "They've done enough today."

He stopped, took a deep breath, stood still, then turned to look for Tom. Saw Morrill, of Company B, wandering toward him through thick brush.

"Hey, Colonel, glad to see you. I was beginning to wonder."

Chamberlain stared. "*You* were beginning to wonder?"

"I tell you, Colonel, I keep thinking I better come back and help you, but you said stay out there and guard that flank, so I did, and I guess it come out all right, thank the Lord. Nobody came nowhere near me until just a few minutes ago. Then they come *backin'* my way, which I didn't expect. So we opened up, and they all turned around and quit, just like that. Damnedest thing you ever saw." He shook his head, amazed. "Easiest fight I was ever in."

Chamberlain sighed. "Captain," he said, "next time I tell you to go out a ways, please don't go quite so far."

"Well, Colonel, we looked around, and there was this here stone wall, and it was *comfortin',* you know?"

Tom was here, well, untouched. Chamberlain opened up into a smile. Tom had a Reb officer in tow, a weary gentleman with a face of grime and sadness, of exhausted despair.

"Hey, Lawrence, want you to meet this fella from Alabama. Cap'n Hawkins, want you to meet my brother. This here's Colonel Chamberlain."

Chamberlain put out a hand. "Sir," he said. The Alabama man nodded slightly. His voice was so low Chamberlain could hardly hear it. "Do you have some water?"

"Certainly." Chamberlain offered his own canteen. Off to the right a huge mass of prisoners: two hundred, maybe more. Most of them sitting, exhausted, heads down. Only a few men of the Regiment here, mostly Morrill's Company. Ironic. Chamberlain thought: well, he's the only one with ammunition.

Firing was slacking beyond the hill. The charge of the 20th Maine had cleared the ground in front of the 83rd Pennsylvania; they were beginning to move down the hill, rounding up prisoners. As the Reb flank on this side fell apart and running men began to appear on the other side of the hill the attack there would break up. Yes, firing was less. He heard whoops and hollers, felt a grin break out as if stepping into lovely sunshine. We did it, by God.

The Alabama man was sitting down. Chamberlain let him alone. Kilrain. Looked. Where? He moved painfully back up the rocks toward the position from which they had charged. Hip stiffening badly. Old Kilrain. Unhurtable.

He saw Kilrain from a distance. He was sitting on a rock, head back against a tree, arm black with streaked blood. But all right, all right, head bobbing bareheaded like a lively mossy white rock. Ruel Thomas was with him, and Tozier, working on the arm. Chamberlain bounded and slipped on wet rocks, forgetting his hurts, his throat stuffed. He knelt. They had peeled back the shirt and the arm was whitely soft where they had cleaned it and there was a mess around the shoulder. Great round muscle: strong old man. Chamberlain grinned, giggled, wiped his face.

"Buster? How you doin'? You old mick."

Kilrain peered at him vaguely cheerily. His face had a linen softness.

"They couldn't seem hardly to miss," he said regretfully, apologizing. "Twice, would you believe. For the love of Mary. *Twicet.*"

He snorted, gloomed, looked up into Chamberlain's eyes and blinked.

"And how are *you,* Colonel darlin'? This fine day?"

Chamberlain nodded, grinning foolishly. There was a tight long silent moment. Chamberlain felt a thickness all through his chest. It was like coming back to your father, having done something fine, and your father knows it, and you can see the knowledge in his eyes, and you are both too proud to speak of it. But he knows. Kilrain looked away. He tried to move bloody fingers.

"In the armpit," he gloomed forlornly. "For the love of

God. He died of his wounds. In the bloody bleedin' *armpit.* Ak."

To Tozier, Chamberlain said, "How is that?"

Tozier shrugged. "It's an arm."

"By God," Chamberlain said. "I think you'll live."

Kilrain blinked hazily. "Only an arm. Got to lose something, might's well be an arm. Can part with that easier than the other mechanics of nature, an thass the truth." He was blurring; he stretched his eyes. "Used to worry about that, you know? Only thing ever worried, really. Losing wrong part." His eyes closed; his voice was plaintive. "I could do with a nip right now."

"I'll see what I can do."

"You do pretty good." Kilrain blinked, peered, looking for him.

"Colonel?"

"Right here."

"The army was blessed . . ." But he ran out of breath, closed his eyes.

"You take it easy."

"Want you to know. Just in case. That I have never served . . ." He paused to breathe, put out the bloody hand, looked into Chamberlain's eyes. "Never served under a better man. Want you to know. Want to thank you, sir."

Chamberlain nodded. Kilrain closed his eyes. His face began to relax; his skin was very pale. Chamberlain held the great cold hand. Chamberlain said, "Let me go round up something medicinal."

"I'd be eternal grateful."

"You rest." Chamberlain was feeling alarm.

Tozier said, "I've sent off."

"Well I've seen them run," Kilrain said dreamily. "Glory be. Thanks to you, Colonel darlin'. Lived long enough to see the Rebs run. Come the Millennium. Did you see them run, Colonel darlin'?"

"I did."

"I got one fella. Raggedy fella. Beautiful offhand shot, if I say so mesel'."

"I've got to go, Buster."

"He was drawin' a bead on you, Colonel. I got him with one quick shot offhand. Oh lovely." Kilrain sighed. "Loveliest shot I ever made."

"You stay with him, Sergeant," Chamberlain said.

Thomas nodded.

"Be back in a while, Buster."

Kilrain opened his eyes, but he was drifting off toward sleep, and he nodded but did not see. Chamberlain backed away. There were some men around him from the old Second Maine and he talked to them automatically, not knowing what he was saying, thanking them for the fight, looking on strange young bloody faces. He moved back down the slope.

He went back along the low stone wall. The dead were mostly covered now with blankets and shelter halves, but some of them were still dying and there were groups of men clustered here and there. There were dead bodies and wounded bodies all down the wall and all down through the trees and blood was streaked on the trees and rocks and rich wet wood splinters were everywhere. He patted shoulders, noted faces. It was very quiet and dark down among the trees. Night was coming. He began to feel tired. He went on talking. A boy was dying. He had made a good fight and he wanted to be promoted before he died and Chamberlain promoted him. He spoke to a man who had been clubbed over the head with a musket and who could not seem to say what he wanted to say, and another man who was crying because both of the Merrill boys were dead, both brothers, and he would be the one who would have to tell their mother. Chamberlain reached the foot of the hill and came out into the last light.

Ellis Spear came up. There were tears in the corners of his

eyes. He nodded jerkily, a habit of Maine men, a greeting.

"Well," he said. He did not know what to say. After a moment he pulled out an impressively ornamented silver flask, dented, lustrous.

"Colonel? Ah, I have a beverage here which I have been saving for an, ah, appropriate moment. I think this is—well, would the Colonel honor me by joining me in a, ah, swallow?"

Chamberlain thought: Kilrain. But he could not hurt Spear's feelings. And his mouth was gritty and dry. Spear handed it over solemnly, gravely, with the air of a man taking part in a ceremony. Chamberlain drank. Oh, good. Very, very good. He saw one small flicker of sadness pass over Spear's face, took the bottle from his lips.

"Sorry, Ellis. 'Swallow' is a flighty word. An indiscriminate word. But thank you. Very much. And now."

Spear bowed formally. "Colonel, it has been my pleasure."

Here through the rocks was a grinning Tom. Young Tom. Only a boy. Chamberlain felt a shattering rush of emotion, restrained it. Behind Tom were troops of the 83rd Pennsylvania: Captain Woodward, Colonel Rice of the 44th New York. Chamberlain thought: Rice must be the new commander of the whole brigade.

Tom said with vast delight, ticking them off, "Lawrence, we got prisoners from the Fifteenth Alabama, the Forty-seventh Alabama, the Fourth and Fifth Texas. Man, we fought four Reb regiments!"

Four regiments would be perhaps two thousand men. Chamberlain was impressed.

"We got five hundred prisoners," Tom insisted.

The figure seemed high. Chamberlain: "What are our casualties?"

Tom's face lost its light. "Well, I'll go check."

Colonel Rice came up. Much darker now. He put out a hand.

"Colonel Chamberlain, may I shake your hand?"

"Sir."

"Colonel, I watched that from above. Colonel, that was the damnedest thing I ever saw."

"Well," Chamberlain said. A private popped up, saluted, whispered in Chamberlain's ear: "Colonel, sir, I'm guardin' these here Rebs with a empty rifle."

Chamberlain grinned. "Not so loud. Colonel Rice, we sure could use some ammunition."

Rice was clucking like a chicken. "Amazing. They ran like sheep."

Woodward said, "It was getting a bit tight there, Colonel, I'll say."

Rice wandered about, stared at the prisoners, wandered back, hands behind him, peered at Chamberlain, shook his head.

"You're not Regular Army?"

"No, sir."

"Oh yes. You're the professor. Um. What did you teach?"

"Rhetoric, sir."

"Really?" Rice grimaced. "Amazing." After a moment: "Where'd you get the idea to charge?"

Chamberlain said, "We were out of ammunition."

Rice nodded. "So. You fixed bayonets."

Chamberlain nodded. It seemed logical enough. It was beginning to dawn on him that what he had done might be considered unusual. He said, "There didn't seem to be any alternative."

Rice shook his head, chuckled, grunted.

Chamberlain said, "I heard about Colonel Vincent."

"Yes. Damn shame. They think he won't make it."

"He's still alive?"

"Not by much."

"Well. But there's always hope."

Rice looked at him. "Of course," Rice said.

Chamberlain wandered among his men. Ought to put them in some kind of order. He was beginning to feel an elation in him, like a bubble blowing up in his chest. A few moments later, Rice was back.

"Colonel, I have to ask your help. You see the big hill there, the wooded hill? There's nobody there. I think. General Warren wants that hill occupied. Could you do that?"

"Well," Chamberlain said. "If we had some ammunition."

"I'll move a train up. That hill's been unoccupied all day. If the Rebs get a battery there . . . it's the extreme flank of the Union line. Highest ground. Warren sends you his compliments and says to tell you he would prefer to have your regiment there."

Chamberlain said, "Well of course, sir. But the boys are tired. May take a while. And I sure need that ammunition."

"Right. I'll tell the General you'll be up soon as possible."

Chamberlain squinted. A wall of trees, thick brush. He sighed.

Tom was back. "I count about one hundred and thirty men, Lawrence. Forty to fifty already dead, about ninety wounded. Lot of boys walking around with minor stuff, one hundred thirty for the hospital."

Chamberlain thought: one hundred thirty down. We had three hundred in line. Almost half the Regiment. Kilrain is gone.

He told Spear of the move. He was becoming very tired. But along with the weariness he felt spasms of pure joy. Spear formed the Company, Rice took over the prisoners. Rice came by to watch them go.

"Colonel," Chamberlain said. "One thing. What's the name of this place? This hill. Has it got a name?"

"Little Round Top," Rice said. "Name of the hill you defended. The one you're going to is Big Round Top."

Little Round Top. Battle of Little Round Top. Well. I guess we'll remember it.

"Move'em out, Ellis."

He went back to say goodbye to Kilrain. The white head was visible from a long way off, sitting stumplike, motionless in the dark of the trees. He had leaned back and was staring at the sky, his eyes closed. He had welcomed Chamberlain to the Regiment and there had never been a day without him. He would be going back to the hospital now, and Chamberlain did not know what to say, did not know how to express it. Blue eyes opened in a weary face. Kilrain smiled.

"I'll be going, Buster," Chamberlain said.

Kilrain grumbled, looked sourly, accusingly at his bloody wound.

"Damn."

"Well, you take care. I'll send Tom back with word."

"Sure."

"We'll miss you. Probably get into all kinds of trouble without you."

"No," Kilrain said. "You'll do all right."

"Well, I have to go."

"Right. Goodbye, Colonel."

He put out a hand, formally. Chamberlain took it.

"It was a hell of a day, wasn't it, Buster?"

Kilrain grinned, his eyes glistened.

"I'll come down and see you tomorrow." Chamberlain backed off.

"Sure." Kilrain was blinking, trying to keep his eyes open. Chamberlain walked away, stopped, looked back, saw the eyes already closed, turned his back for the last time, moved off into the gathering dark.

He moved forward and began to climb the big hill in the dark. As he walked he forgot his pain; his heart began to beat quickly, and he felt an incredible joy. He looked at himself, wonderingly, at the beloved men around him, and he said to himself: Lawrence, old son, treasure this moment. Because you feel as good as a man can feel.

5. Longstreet

The hospital was an open field just back of the line. There were small white tents all over the field and bigger tents where the surgeons did the cutting. Hood was there, in a big tent, on a litter. Longstreet came in out of the dark, bowing under a canopy, saw the face like cold marble in yellow candlelight, eyes black and soft like old polished stones. Cullen and Maury were working together on the arm. Longstreet saw: not much left of the hand. Exposed bone. He thought of Jackson hit in the arm at Chancellorsville: died a slow death. *Let us cross over the river.* Hood's black eyes stared unseeing. Longstreet said softly, "Sam?"

Cullen looked up; Maury was tying a knot, went on working. Troops had gathered outside the canopy. A sergeant bawled: move on, move on. Hood stared at Longstreet, not seeing. There was dirt streaked in tear stains on his cheeks, but he was not crying now. His head twitched, cheek jerked. He said suddenly, in a light, strange, feathery voice, "Should have let me move to ri—" He breathed. "To the right."

Longstreet nodded. To Cullen, he said, "Can I talk to him?"

"Rather not. We've drugged him. Sir. Better let him sleep."

Hood raised the other arm, twitched fingers, let the hand fall. "Din see much. Boys went in an' hit the rocks. I got hit."

Longstreet, no good at talking, nodded.

"Should have moved right, Pete." Hood was staring at him, bright, drugged, eerie eyes. "How did it go, Pete?"

"Fine, Sam."

"We took those rocks?"

"Most of 'em."

"Took the rocks. Really did."

"Yes," Longstreet lied.

Hood's eyes blinked slowly, blearily. He put the good hand up to shade his eyes.

"Devil's Den. Good name for it."

"Yep."

"Worst ground I ever saw, you know that?" Hood laid the back of his hand across his eyes. His voice trembled. "Got to give my boys credit."

Longstreet said to Cullen, "Can you save the arm?"

"We're trying. But if we do, it won't be much use to him."

Hood said, "Casualties? Was casualties?"

"Don't know yet," Longstreet said. And then: "Not bad." Another lie.

Cullen said gloomily, plaintively, "He ought to go to sleep. Now don't fight it, General. Let it work. You just drift right on off."

Longstreet said softly, "You go to sleep now, Sam. Tell you all about it tomorrow."

"Shame not to see it." Hood took the hand away. His eyes were dreaming, closing like small doors over a dim light. "Should have gone to the right." He looked hazily at the hand. "You fellas try to save that now, you hear?"

"Yes, sir, General. Now why don't you . . . ?"

"Sure will miss it." Hood's eyes closed again; his face began smoothing toward sleep. Longstreet thought: he won't die. Not like Jackson. There was a blackness around Jackson's eyes. Longstreet reached down, touched Hood on the shoulder, then turned and went out into the moonlight.

Sorrel was there, with the silent staff. Longstreet mounted, rising up into the moonlight, looking out across the pale tents at the small fires, the black silence. He heard a boy crying, pitiful childish sobs, a deeper voice beyond, soothing. Longstreet shook his head to clear the sound, closed his eyes, saw Barksdale go streaming to his death against a flaming fence in the brilliant afternoon, hair blazing out behind him like white fire. Longstreet rode up the ridge toward the darker ground under the trees. Barksdale lies under a sheet. They have not covered his face; there is a flag over him. Semmes is dead. How many others? Longstreet cleared the brain, blew away bloody images, the brilliant fence in the bright gleaming air of the afternoon, tried to catalogue the dead. Must have figures. But he was not thinking clearly. There was a rage in his brain, a bloody cloudy area like mud stirred in a pool. He was like a fighter who has been down once and is up again, hurt and in rage, looking to return the blow, looking for the opening. But it was a silent rage, a crafty rage; he was learning war. He rode purposefully, slowly off into the dark feeling the swelling inside his chest like an unexploded bomb and in the back of his mind a vision of that gray rocky hill* all spiked with guns, massed with blue troops at the top, and he knew as certainly as he had ever known anything as a soldier that the hill could not be taken, not any more, and a cold, metal, emotionless voice told him that coldly, calmly, speaking into his ear as if he had a companion with him utterly untouched by the rage, the war, a machine inside wholly unhurt, a metal mind that did not feel at all.

"Sir?"

Longstreet swiveled in the saddle: Sorrel. The man said warily, "Captain Goree is here, sir. Ah, you sent for him."

Longstreet looked, saw the skinny Texan, gestured. Sorrel backed off. Longstreet said, "T. J. Want you to get out to the right and scout the position. No more damn fool counter-

*Little Round Top.

marches in the morning. Take most of the night but get it clear, get it clear. I've got Hood's Division posted on our right flank. Or what's left of it. I've put Law in command. You need any help, you get it from Law, all right?"

The Texan, a silent man, nodded but did not move. Longstreet said, "What's the matter?"

"They're blaming us," Goree said. His voice was squeaky, like a dry wagon wheel. He radiated anger. Longstreet stared.

"What?"

"I been talking to Hood's officers. Do you know they blame us? They blame *you*. For today."

Longstreet could not see the bony face clearly, in the dark, but the voice was tight and very high, and Longstreet thought: he could be a dangerous man, out of control.

Goree said, "You may hear of it, General. I had to hit this fella. They all said the attack was your fault and if General Lee knowed he wouldn't have ordered it and I just couldn't just stand there and I couldn't say right out what I felt, so I had to hit this one fella. Pretty hard. Had to do it. Ain' goin' to apologize neither. No time. But. Thought you ought to know."

"Is he dead?"

"I don't think so."

"Well, that's good." Longstreet meditated. "Well, don't worry on it. Probably won't hear another thing if you didn't kill him. Probably forgotten in the morning. One thing: I want no duels. No silly damn duels."

"Yes, sir. Thing is, if anything bad happens now, they all blame it on you. I seen it comin'. They can't blame General Lee. Not no more. So they all take it out on you. You got to watch yourself, General."

"Well," Longstreet said. "Let it go."

"Yes, sir. But it aint easy. After I saw you take all morning trying to get General Lee to move to the right."

"Let it go, T. J. We'll talk on it after the fight."

Goree moved out. There goes a damn good man. Longstreet felt the warmth of unexpected gratitude. He swung the black horse toward Lee's headquarters back on the road to Cashtown. Time now to talk. Good long talk. Watch the anger. Careful. But it is true. The men shied from blaming Lee. The Old Man is becoming untouchable. Now more than anything else he needs the truth. But . . . well, it's not his fault, not the Old Man. Longstreet jerked the horse, almost ran into Sorrel. They came out into a patch of bright moonlight. Longstreet saw: the man was hurt.

"Major," Longstreet said harshly. "How are you?"

"Sir? Oh, I'm fine, sir. Juss minor problem."

"That's a godawful piece of horse you've got there."

"Yes, sir. Lost the other one, sir. They shot it out from under me. It lost both legs. I was with Dearing's Battery. Hot time, sir." Sorrel bobbed his head apologetically.

Longstreet pointed. "What's the trouble with the arm?"

Sorrel shrugged, embarrassed. "Nothing much, sir. Bit painful, can't move it. Shrapnel, sir. Hardly broke the skin. Ah, Osmun Latrobe got hit too."

"How bad?"

"Just got knocked off the horse, I believe. This fighting is very hard on the horses, sir. I was hoping we could get a new supply up here, but these Yankee horses are just farm stock —too big, too slow. Man would look ridiculous on a plow horse."

"Well," Longstreet grumbled vaguely. "Take care of yourself, Major. You aint the most likable man I ever met, but you sure are useful."

Sorrel bowed. "I appreciate your sentiments, sir. The General is a man of truth."

"Have you got the casualty figures yet?"

"No, sir. I regret to say. Just preliminary reports. Indications are that losses will exceed one third."

Longstreet jerked his head, acknowledging.

Sorrel said carefully, "Possibly more. The figures could go . . ."

"Don't play it down," Longstreet said.

"No, sir. I think that casualties were much worse in Hood's Division. Won't have an exact count for some time. But . . . it appears that the Yankees put up a fight. My guess is Hood's losses will approach fifty percent."

Longstreet took a deep breath, turned away. Eight thousand men? Down in two hours. His mind flicked on. Not enough left now for a major assault. No way in the world. Lee will see. Now: the facts.

"I need a hard count, Major. As quickly as possible."

"Yes, sir. But, well, it's not easy. The men tend to suppress the truth. I hear, for example, that Harry Heth's Division was badly hurt yesterday, but his officers did not report all the losses to General Lee because they did not want General Heth to get into trouble."

"I want the truth. However black. But hard facts. Soon as you can. I rely on you. Also, I want an account of artillery available, rounds remaining, type of rounds, et cetera. Got that? Get out a note to Alexander."

Up the road at a gallop: a handsome horseman, waving a plumed hat in the night. He reined up grandly, waved the hat in one long slow swoop, bowed halfway down off the horse —a bored sweeping cavalier's gesture. Fairfax, another of Longstreet's aides.

"General Pickett's compliments, sir. He wishes to announce his presence upon the field."

Longstreet stared, grunted, gave an involuntary chuckle. "Oh grand," Longstreet said. "That's just grand." He turned to Sorrel. "Isn't that grand, Major? Now, let the battle commence." He grimaced, grunted. "Tell General Pickett I'm glad to have him here. At last."

Fairfax had a wide mouth: teeth gleamed in moonlight.

"General Pickett is gravely concerned, sir. He wishes to inquire if there are any Yankees left. He says to tell you that he personally is bored and his men are very lonely."

Longstreet shook his head. Fairfax went on cheerily: "General Pickett reported earlier today to General Lee, while General Longstreet was engaged in the entertainment on the right flank, but General Lee said that General Pickett's men would not be necessary in the day's action. General Pickett instructs me to inform you that his is a sensitive nature and that his feelings are wounded and that he and his Division of pale Virginians awaits you in yon field, hoping you will come tuck them in for the night and console them."

"Well," Longstreet mused. "Fairfax, are you drunk?"

"No, sir. I am quoting General Pickett's exact words, sir. With fine accuracy, sir."

"Well." Longstreet smiled once slightly, shrugged. "You can tell General Pickett I'll be along directly."

Fairfax saluted, bowed, departed. Longstreet rode on into the dark. Pickett's Division: five thousand fresh men. Damn fine men. It was like being handed a bright new shiny gun. He felt stronger. Now talk to Lee. He spurred the horse and began to canter toward the lights on the Cashtown Road.

Headquarters could be seen from a long way off, like a small city at night. The glow of it rose above the trees and shone reflected in the haze of the sky. He could begin to hear singing. Different bands sang different songs: a melody of wind. He began to pass clusters of men laughing off in the dark. They did not recognize him. He smelled whisky, tobacco, roasting meat. He came out into the open just below the Seminary and he could see Headquarters field filled with smoke and light, hundreds of men, dozens of fires. He passed a circle of men watching a tall thin black boy dressed in a flowing red dress, dancing, kicking heels. There was a sutler's store, a white wagon, a man selling a strange elixir with the high blessed chant of a preacher. He began to see civilians:

important people in very good clothes, some sleek carriages, many slaves. People come up from home to see how the army was doing, to deliver a package to a son, a brother. He rode out into the light and heads began to turn and fix on him and he felt the awkward flush come over his face as eyes looked at him and knew him and fingers began to point. He rode looking straight ahead, a crowd beginning to trail out after him like the tail of a comet. A reporter yelled a question. One of the foreigners, the one with the silver helmet like an ornate chamber pot, waved an intoxicated greeting. Longstreet rode on toward the little house across the road. Music and laughter and motion everywhere: a celebration. All the faces were happy. Teeth glittered through black beards. He saw pearl stickpins, silky, satiny clothing. And there against a fence: Jeb Stuart.

Longstreet pulled up.

The cavalier, a beautiful man, was lounging against a fence, a white rail fence, in a circle of light, a circle of admirers. Reporters were taking notes. Stuart was dressed in soft gray with butternut braid along the arms and around the collar and lace at his throat, and the feathered hat was swept back to hang happily, boyishly from the back of the head, and curls peeked out across the wide handsome forehead. Full-bearded, to hide a weak chin, but a lovely boy, carefree, mud-spattered, obviously tired, languid, cheery, confident. He looked up at Longstreet, waved a languid hello. He gave the impression of having been up for days, in the saddle for days, and not minding it. Longstreet jerked a nod, unsmiling. He thought: we have small use for you now. But you are Lee's problem. Longstreet slowed, not wanting to speak to Stuart. The crowd was beginning to press in around his horse, shouting congratulations. Longstreet looked from face to breathless face, amazed. Congratulations? For what? The crowd had moved in between him and Stuart. He pressed stubbornly forward toward Lee's cottage. It was impossible to answer questions: too much noise. He wished he had not come. Ride back later, when it's quiet. But too late to go now. One of Lee's people, Venable, had taken the reins of his horse. Someone was yelling in an eerie wail, "Way for General Longstreet, way for the General!" And there across the crowd he saw an open space by the door of the little house, and there in the light was Lee.

Quiet spread out from Lee. The old man stepped out into the light, came forward. Stuart swung to look. Longstreet saw men beginning to take off their hats in the old man's presence. Lee came up to Longstreet's horse, put out his hand, said something very soft. Longstreet took the hand. There was no strength in it. Lee was saying that he was glad to see him well, and there was that extraordinary flame in the dark eyes, concern of a loving father, that flicked all Longstreet's defenses aside and penetrated to the lonely man within like a bright hot spear, and Longstreet nodded, grumbled, and got down from the horse. Lee said accusingly that he had heard that Longstreet had been in the front line again and that he had promised not to do that, and Longstreet, flustered by too many people staring at him, too many strangers, said, well, he'd just come by for orders.

Lee said watchfully, smiling, "General Stuart is back."

The crowd opened for Jeb. He came forward with extended hand. Longstreet took it, mumbled, could not meet the younger eyes. Jeb was grinning a brilliant grin; hands were patting him on the back. Longstreet felt mulish. Damn fool. But he said nothing. Lee said that General Stuart ought to know how worried they had all been about him, and Stuart grinned like a proud child, but there was something wary in his eyes, looking at Lee, some small bit of question, and Longstreet wondered what the old man had said. Stuart said something about having seen a lot of Yankee countryside lately, and it was getting kind of dull, and slowly the noise began to grow up around them again. They moved toward the house, Lee taking Longstreet by the arm. They moved in a lane through hundreds of people, like Moses at the parting of the Sea. Somebody began a cheer, a formal cheer, a *university* cheer. A band struck up, oh Lord, "Bonny Blue Flag," again. Hands were touching Longstreet. He went up into the small house and into a small room, the roof closing in over him like the lid on a jar, but even here it was jammed with people, a tiny room no bigger than your kitchen, and all Lee's officers and aides, working, rushing in and out, and even here some people from Richmond. A place cleared for Lee and he sat down in a rocking chair and Longstreet saw him in the light and saw that he was tired. Lee rested a moment, closing his eyes. There was no place for Longstreet to sit except on the edge of the table, and so he sat there. Taylor pushed by, begging Longstreet's pardon, needing a signature on a letter to someone.

Lee raised a hand. "We'll rest for a moment."

Longstreet saw the old man sag, breathe deeply, his mouth open. Lines of pain around the eyes. He put the gray head down for a moment, then looked up quickly at Longstreet, shook his head slightly.

"A bit tired."

He never said anything like that. Lee never complained. Longstreet said, "Can I get you something?"

Lee shook his head. Aides were talking loudly about artillery, a message to Richmond. Longstreet thought: no rest here. Lee said, reading his mind, "I'll clear them out in a minute or two." He took another deep breath, almost a gasp, put a hand to his chest, shook his head with regret. His face was gray and still. He looked up with a vagueness in his eyes.

"It was very close this afternoon."

"Sir?"

"They almost broke. I could feel them breaking. I thought for a moment . . . I saw our flags go up the hill . . . I almost thought . . ."

Longstreet said, "It wasn't that close." But Lee's eyes were gazing by him at a vision of victory. Longstreet said nothing. He rubbed his mouth. Lee eyes strange: so dark and soft. Longstreet could say nothing. In the presence of the Commander the right words would not come.

Lee said, "The attacks were not coordinated. I don't know why. We shall see. But we almost did it, this day. I could see . . . an open road to Washington." He closed his eyes, rubbed them. Longstreet felt an extraordinary confusion. He had a moment without confidence, windblown and blasted, vacant as an exploded shell. There was a grandness in Lee that shadowed him, silenced him. You could not preach caution here, not to that face. And then the moment passed and a small rage bloomed, not at Lee but at Longstreet himself. He started to try to speak, but Lee said, "It was reported that General Barksdale was killed."

"Yes, sir."

"And General Semmes."

"Sir."

"And how is it with General Hood?"

"I think he'll live. I've just come from him."

"Praise God. We could not spare General Hood." He was gazing again into nowhere. After a moment he said, almost plaintively, "I've lost Dorsey Pender."

"Yes," Longstreet said. One by one: down the dark road. Don't think on that now.

Lee said, "He would have made a Corps commander, I think." The old man sat looking half asleep.

Longstreet said stiffly, "Sir, there are three Union corps dug in on the high ground in front of me."

Lee nodded. After a moment he said, "So very close. I believe one more push . . ."

A burst of shouting outside. The band had come closer. Longstreet said, "Today I lost almost half my strength." And felt like a traitor for saying it, the truth, the granite truth, felt a smallness, a rage. Lee nodded but did not seem to hear. Longstreet pushed on.

"The way to the right is still open, sir."

Lee looked up slowly, focused, slowly smiled, put out a hand, touched Longstreet's arm.

"Let me think, General."

"We have enough artillery for one more good fight. One more."

"I know." Lee took a breath, sat up. "Let me think on it. But, General, I am very glad to see you well."

Taylor pushed in again. Longstreet reached out, gripped the young man in a metal clasp.

"General Lee needs his rest. I want you to keep some of these people away."

Taylor drew back in frosty reproach, as if Longstreet's hand smelled badly of fish. Longstreet felt the coming of a serious rage. But Lee smiled, reached out for the papers in Taylor's hand.

"A few more moments, General. Then I'll send them off. Now, what have we here?"

Longstreet backed off. The white head bent down over the papers. Longstreet stood there. All his life he had taken orders and he knew the necessity for command and the old man in front of him was the finest commander he had ever known. Longstreet looked around at the faces. The gentlemen were chatting, telling lively funny stories. Out in the smoky night a band was mounting another song. Too many people, too much noise. He backed out the door. Come back later. In the night, later, when the old man is alone, we will have to talk.

He moved out into the crowd, head down, mounted his horse. Someone pulled his arm. He glared: Marshall, red-faced, waving papers, cheeks hot with rage.

"General Longstreet! Sir. Will you talk to him?"

"Who? What about?"

"I've prepared court-martial papers for General Stuart. General Lee will not sign them."

Longstreet grimaced. Of course not. But not my problem. Marshall held the reins. He was standing close by and the men nearby were backed off in deference and had not heard him. Longstreet said, "When did he finally get back?"

"This evening." Marshall, with effort, was keeping his voice down. "He was joyriding. For the fun of it. He captured about a hundred enemy wagons. And left us blind in enemy country. Criminal, absolutely criminal. Several of us have agreed to ask for court-martial, but General Lee says he will not discuss it at this time."

Longstreet shrugged.

"General. If there is not some discipline in this army . . . there are good men *dead,* sir." Marshall struggled. Longstreet saw a man closing in. Fat man with a full beard. Familiar face: a Richmond reporter. Yes, a theorist on war. A man with a silvery vest and many opinions. He came, notebook in hand. Longstreet itched to move, but Marshall held.

"I'd like your opinion, sir. You are the second-ranking officer in this army. Do you believe that these court-martial papers should be signed?"

Longstreet paused. Men were closing in, yelling more congratulations. Longstreet nodded once, deliberately.

"I do," he said.

"Will you talk to General Lee?"

"I will." Longstreet gathered the reins. Men were close enough now to hear, were staring up at him. "But you know, Marshall, it won't do any good."

"We can try, sir."

"Right." Longstreet touched his cap. "We can at least do that."

He spurred toward the cool dark. They opened to let him pass. Hats were off; they were cheering. He rode head down toward the silent road. He was amazed at the air of victory. He thought: got so that whenever they fight they assume there's victory that night. Face of Goree. They can't blame General Lee, not no more. But there was no victory today. So very close, the old man said. And yet it was not a loss. And Longstreet knew that Lee would attack in the morning. He would never quit the field. Not with the Union Army holding the field. Three Union corps on the hills above. Lee will attack.

Longstreet stopped, in darkness, looked back toward the light. A voice was calling. Longstreet turned to ride on, and then the voice registered and he looked back: a grinning Fremantle, hat held high like cloth on the arm of a scarecrow, bony, ridiculous. He looked like an illustration Longstreet had once seen of Ichabod Crane.

"Good evening, sir! My compliments, sir! Marvelous evening, what? Extraordinary! May I say, sir, that I observed your charge this afternoon, and I was inspired, sir, *inspired.* Strordnry, sir, a general officer at the front of the line. One's heart leaps. One's hat is off to you, sir." He executed a vast swirling bow, nearly falling from the horse, arose grinning, mouth a half moon of cheery teeth. Longstreet smiled.

"Will you take my hand, sir, in honor of your great victory?"

Longstreet took the limp palm, knowing the effort it cost the Englishman, who thought handshaking unnatural. "Victory?" Longstreet said.

"General Lee is the soldier of the age, the soldier of the age." Fremantle radiated approval like a tattered star, but he did it with such cool and delicate grace that there was nothing unnatural about it, nothing fawning or flattering. He babbled a charming hero-worship, one gentleman to another. Longstreet, who had never learned the art of compliment, admired it.

"May I ride along with you, sir?"

"Course."

"I do not wish to intrude upon your thoughts and schemes."

"No problem."

"I observed you with General Lee. I would imagine that there are weighty technical matters that occupy your mind."

Longstreet shrugged. Fremantle rode along beamily chatting. He remarked that he had watched General Lee during much of the engagement that day and that the General rarely sent messages. Longstreet explained that Lee usually gave the orders and then let his boys alone to do the job. Fremantle returned to awe. "The soldier of the age," he said again, and Longstreet thought: should have spoken to Lee. Must go back tonight. But . . . let the old man sleep. Never saw his face that weary. Soul of the army. *He's* in command. You are only the hand. Silence. Like a soldier.

He will attack.

Well. They love him. They do not blame him. They do impossible things for him. They may even take that hill.

". . . have no doubt," Fremantle was saying, "that General Lee shall become the world's foremost authority on military matters when this war is over, which would appear now to be only a matter of days, or at most a few weeks. I suspect all Europe will be turning to him for lessons."

Lessons?

"I have been thinking, I must confess, of setting some brief thoughts to paper," Fremantle announced gravely. "Some brief remarks of my own, appended to an account of this battle, and perhaps others this army has fought. Some notes as to the tactics."

Tactics?

"General Lee's various stratagems will be most instructive, most illuminating. I wonder, sir, if I might enlist your aid in this, ah, endeavor. As one most closely concerned? That is, to be brief, may I come to you when in need?"

"Sure," Longstreet said. Tactics? He chuckled. The tactics are simple: find the enemy, fight him. He shook his head, snorting. Fremantle spoke softly, in tones of awe.

"One would not think of General Lee, now that one has met him, now that one has looked him, so to speak, in the *eye,* as it were, one would not think him, you know, to be such a *devious* man."

"Devious?" Longstreet swung to stare at him, aghast.

"Oh my word," Fremantle went on devoutly, "but he's a tricky one. The Old Gray Fox, as they say. Charming phrase. American to the hilt."

"Devious?" Longstreet stopped dead in the road. "Devious." He laughed aloud. Fremantle stared an owlish stare.

"Why, Colonel, bless your soul, there aint a devious bone in Robert Lee's body, don't you know that?"

"My dear sir."

"By damn, man, if there is one human being in the world *less* devious than Robert Lee, I aint yet met him. By God and fire, Colonel, but you amuse me." And yet Longstreet was not amused. He leaned forward blackly across the pommel of the saddle. "Colonel, let me explain something. The secret of General Lee is that men love him and follow him with faith in him. That's one secret. The next secret is that General Lee makes a decision and he *moves,* with guts, and he's been up against a lot of sickly generals who don't know how to make decisions, although some of them have guts but whose men don't love them. That's why we win, mostly. Because we move with speed, and faith, and because we usually have the good ground. Tactics? God, man, we don't win because of tricks. What were the tactics at Malvern Hill? What were the tactics at Fredericksburg, where we got down behind a bloody stone wall and shot the bloody hell out of them as they came up, wave after wave, bravest thing you ever saw, because, listen, there are some damn good boys across the way, make no mistake on that. I've fought with those boys, and they know how to fight when they've got the ground, but tactics? Tactics?" He was stumbling for words, but it was pouring out of him in hot clumps out of the back of the brain, the words like falling coals, and Fremantle stared openmouthed.

"God in Heaven," Longstreet said, and repeated it, "there's no strategy to this bloody war. What it is is old Napoleon and a hell of a lot of chivalry. That's all it is. What were the tactics at Chancellorsville, where we divided the army, *divided* it, so help me God, in the face of the enemy, and got away with it because Joe Hooker froze cold in his stomach? What were the tactics yesterday? What were they today? And what will be the blessed tactics tomorrow? I'll tell you the tactics tomorrow. Devious? Christ in Heaven. Tomorrow we will attack an enemy that outnumbers us, an enemy that outguns us, an enemy dug in on the high ground, and let me tell you, if we win that one it will not be because of the tactics or because we are great strategists or because there is anything even remotely intelligent about the war at all. It will be a bloody miracle, a bloody miracle."

And then he saw what he was saying.

He cut it off. Fremantle's mouth was still open. Longstreet thought: very bad things to say. Disloyal. Fool. Bloody damned fool.

And then he began truly to understand what he had said.

It surfaced, like something long sunken rising up out of black water. It opened up there in the dark of his mind and he turned from Fremantle.

The Englishman said something. Longstreet nodded. The truth kept coming. Longstreet waited. He had known all this for a long time but he had never said it, except in fragments. He had banked it and gone on with the job, a soldier all his life. In his mind he could see Lee's beautiful face and suddenly it was not the same face. Longstreet felt stuffed and thick and very strange. He did not want to think about it.

He spurred the horse. Hero reared. Longstreet thought: you always know the truth; wait long enough and the mind will tell you. He rode beneath a low tree; leaves brushed his hat. He stopped. A voice at his elbow: Fremantle.

"Yes," Longstreet said. Damn fool things to say. To a guest.

"If I have disturbed you, sir . . ."

"Not at all. Things on my mind. If you don't mind, Colonel . . ."

Fremantle apologized. Longstreet said good night. He sat alone on his horse in the dark. There was a fire in a field. A boy was playing a harmonica, frail and lovely sound. Longstreet thought of Barksdale as he had gone to die, streaming off to death, white hair trailing him like white fire. Hood's eyes were accusing. Should have moved to the right. He thought: tactics are old Napoleon and a lot of chivalry.

He shuddered. He remembered that day in church when he prayed from the soul and listened and knew in that moment that there was no one there, no one to listen.

Don't think on these things. Keep an orderly mind. This stuff is like heresy.

It was quieter now and very warm and wet, a softness in the air, a mountain peace. His mind went silent for a time and he rode down the long road between the fires in the fields and men passed him in the night unknowing, and soldiers chased each other across the road. A happy camp, behind the line. There was music and faith. And pride. We have always had pride.

He thought suddenly of Stonewall Jackson, old Thomas, old Blue Light. *He* could move men. Yes. But you remember, he ordered *pikes* for his men, *spears,* for the love of God. And the pikes sit by the thousands, rusting now in a Richmond warehouse because Jackson is dead and gone to glory. But he would have used them. Pikes. Against cannon in black rows. Against that hill in the morning.

They come from another age. The Age of Virginia.

Must talk to Lee in the morning.

He's tired. Never saw him that tired. And sick. But he'll listen.

They all come from another age.

General Lee, I have three Union corps in front of me. They have the high ground, and they are dug in, and I am down to half my strength.

He will smile and pat you on the arm and say: go do it.

And perhaps we will do it.

He was approaching his own camp. He could hear laughter ahead, and there were many bright fires. He slowed, let Hero crop grass. He felt a great sense of shame. A man should not think these things. But he could not control it. He rode into camp, back to work. He came in silently and sat back under a dark tree and Sorrel came to him with the figures. The figures were bad. Longstreet sat with his back against a tree and out in the open there was a party, sounds of joy: George Pickett was telling a story.

He was standing by a fire, wild-haired, gorgeous, stabbing with an invisible sword. He could tell a story. A circle of men was watching him; Longstreet could see the grins, flash of a dark bottle going round. Off in the dark there was a voice of a young man singing: clear Irish tenor. Longstreet felt a long way off, a long, long way. Pickett finished with one mighty stab, then put both hands on his knees and crouched and howled with laughter, enjoying himself enormously. Longstreet wanted a drink. No. Not now. Later. In a few days. Perhaps a long bottle and a long sleep. He looked across the firelight and saw one face in the ring not smiling, not even listening, one still face staring unseeing into the yellow blaze: Dick Garnett. The man Jackson had court-martialed for cowardice. Longstreet saw Lo Armistead nudge him, concerned, whisper in his ear. Garnett smiled, shook his head, turned back to the fire. Armistead went on watching him, worried. Longstreet bowed his head.

Saw the face of Robert Lee. Incredible eyes. An honest man, a simple man. Out of date. They all ride to glory, all the plumed knights. Saw the eyes of Sam Hood, accusing eyes. He'll not go and die. Did not have the black look they get, the dying ones, around the eyes. But Barksdale is gone, and Semmes, and half of Hood's Division . . .

"Evening, Pete."

Longstreet squinted upward. Tall man holding a tall glass, youthful grin under steel-gray hair: Lo Armistead.

"How goes it, Pete?"

"Passing well, passing well."

"Come on and join us, why don't you? We liberated some Pennsylvania whiskey; ain't much left."

Longstreet shook his head.

"Mind if I set a spell?" Armistead squatted, perched on the ground sitting on his heels, resting the glass on his thigh. "What do you hear from Sam Hood?"

"May lose an arm."

Armistead asked about the rest. Longstreet gave him the list. There was a moment of silence. Armistead took a drink, let the names register. After a moment he said, "Dick Garnett is sick. He can't hardly walk."

"I'll get somebody to look after him."

"Would you do that, Pete? He'll have to take it, coming from you."

"Sure."

"Thing is, if there's any action, he can't stand to be out of it. But if you ordered him."

Longstreet said nothing.

"Don't suppose you could do that," Armistead said wistfully.

Longstreet shook his head.

"I keep trying to tell him he don't have to prove a thing,

not to us," Armistead brooded. "Well, what the hell." He sipped from the glass. "A pleasant brew. The Dutchmen make good whisky. Oh. Beg your pardon."

Longstreet looked out into the firelight. He recognized Fremantle, popeyed and grinning, rising awkwardly to his feet, tin cup raised for a toast. Longstreet could not hear. Armistead said, "I been talking to that Englishman. He isn't too bright, is he?"

Longstreet smiled. He thought: devious Lee.

Armistead said, "We put it to him, how come the limeys didn't come help us. In their own interest and all. Hell, perfectly obvious they ought to help. You know what he said? He said the problem was *slavery.* Now what do you think of that?"

Longstreet shook his head. That was another thing he did not think about. Armistead said disgustedly, "They think we're fighting to keep the slaves. He says that's what most of Europe thinks the war is all about. Now, what we supposed to do about that?"

Longstreet said nothing. The war was about slavery, all right. That was not why Longstreet fought but that was what the war was about, and there was no point in talking about it, never had been.

Armistead said, "Ole Fremantle said one thing that was interestin'. He said, whole time he's been in this country, he never heard the word 'slave.' He said we always call them 'servants.' Now you know, that's true. I never thought of it before, but it's true."

Longstreet remembered a speech: *In a land where all slaves are servants, all servants are slaves, and thus ends democracy.* A good line. But it didn't pay to think on it. Armistead was saying, "That Fremantle is kind of funny. He said that we Southerners were the most polite people he'd ever met, but then he noticed we all of us carry guns all the time, wherever we went, and he figured that maybe that was why. Hee."

Armistead chuckled. "But we don't really need the limeys, do we, Pete, you think? Not so long as we have old Bobby Lee to lead the way."

Pickett's party was quieting. The faces were turning to the moon. It was a moment before Longstreet, slightly deaf, realized they had turned to the sound of the tenor singing. An Irish song. He listened.

> . . . oh hast thou forgotten
> how soon we must sever?
> Oh hast thou forgotten
> how soon we must part?
> It may be for years,
> it may be forever . . .

"That boy can sing," Longstreet said. "That's 'Kathleen Mavourneen,' am I right?" He turned to Armistead.

The handsome face had gone all to softness. Longstreet thought he was crying, just for a moment, but there were no tears, only the look of pain. Armistead was gazing toward the sound of the voice and then his eyes shifted suddenly and he looked straight down. He knelt there unmoving while the whole camp grew slowly still and in the dark silence the voice sang the next verse, softer, with great feeling, with great beauty, very far off to Longstreet's dull ear, far off and strange, from another time, an older softer time, and Longstreet could see tears on faces around the fire, and men beginning to drop their eyes, and he dropped his own, feeling a sudden spasm of irrational love. Then the voice was done.

Armistead looked up. He looked at Longstreet and then quickly away. Out in the glade they were sitting motionless, and then Pickett got up suddenly and stalked, face wet with tears, rubbing his cheeks, grumbling, then he said stiffly, "Good cheer, boys, good cheer tonight." The faces looked up at him. Pickett moved to the rail fence and sat there and said, "Let me tell you the story of old Tangent, which is Dick

Ewell's horse, which as God is my final judge is not only the slowest and orneriest piece of horseflesh in all this here army, but possibly also the slowest horse in this hemisphere, or even in the history of all slow horses."

The faces began to lighten. A bottle began to move. Pickett sat on the rail fence like old Baldy Ewell riding the horse. The laughter began again, and in the background they played something fast and light and the tenor did not sing. In a few moments Pickett was doing a hornpipe with Fremantle, and the momentary sadness had passed like a small mist. Longstreet wanted to move over there and sit down. But he did not belong there.

Armistead said, "You hear anything of Win Hancock?"

"Ran in to him today." Longstreet gestured. "He's over that way, mile or so."

"That a fact?" Armistead grinned. "Bet he was tough."

"He was."

"Ha," Armistead chuckled. "He's the best they've got, and that's a fact."

"Yep."

"Like to go on over and see him, soon's I can, if it's all right."

"Sure. Maybe tomorrow."

"Well, that'll be fine." Armistead looked up at the moon. "That song there, 'Kathleen Mavourneen'?" He shrugged. Longstreet looked at him. He was rubbing his face. Armistead said slowly, "Last time I saw old Win, we played that, 'round the piano." He glanced at Longstreet, grinned vaguely, glanced away. "We went over there for the last dinner together, night before we all broke up. Spring of sixty-one." He paused, looked into the past, nodded to himself.

"Mira Hancock had us over. One more evening together. You remember Mira. Beautiful woman. Sweet woman. They were a beautiful couple, you know that? Most beautiful couple I ever saw. He sure looks like a soldier, now, and that's a fact."

Longstreet waited. Something was coming.

"Garnett was there, that last night. And Sydney Johnston. Lot of fellas from the old outfit. We were leaving the next day, some goin' North, some comin' South. Splitting up. God! You remember."

Longstreet remembered: a bright cold day. A cold cold day. A soldier's farewell: goodbye, good luck, and see you in Hell. Armistead said, "We sat around the piano, toward the end of the evening. You know how it was. Mary was playing. We sang all the good songs. That was one of them, 'Kathleen Mavourneen,' and there was 'Mary of Argyle,' and . . . ah. *It may be for years, and it may be forever.* Never forget that."

He stopped, paused, looked down into the whisky glass, looked up at Longstreet. "You know how it was, Pete."

Longstreet nodded.

"Well, the man was a brother to me. You remember. Toward the end of the evening . . . it got rough. We all began, well, you know, there were a lot of tears." Armistead's voice wavered; he took a deep breath. "Well, I was crying, and I went up to Win and I took him by the shoulder and I said, 'Win, so help me, if I ever lift a hand against you, may God strike me dead.' "

Longstreet felt a cold shudder. He looked down at the ground. There was nothing to say. Armistead said, shaken, "I've not seen him since. I haven't been on the same field with him, thank God. It . . . troubles me to think on it."

Longstreet wanted to reach out and touch him. But he went on looking at the dark ground.

"Can't leave the fight, of course," Armistead said. "But I think about it. I meant it as a vow, you see. You understand, Pete?"

"Sure."

"I thought about sitting this one out. But . . . I don't think I can do that. I don't think that would be right either."

"Guess not."

Armistead sighed. He drank the last of the whisky in a swift single motion. He took off the soft black hat and held it in his hand and the gray hair glistened wetly, and the band of white skin at the forehead shone in the light. With the hat off he was older, much older, old courtly Lo. Had been a fiery young man. Lothario grown old.

"Thank you, Pete." Armistead's voice was steady. "Had to talk about that."

"Course."

"I sent Mira Hancock a package to be opened in the event of my death. I . . . you'll drop by and see her, after this is done?"

Longstreet nodded. He said, "I was just thinking. Of the time you hit Early with the plate."

Armistead grinned. "Didn't hit him hard enough."

Longstreet smiled. Then was able to reach out and touch him. He just tapped him once lightly, one touch, on the shoulder, and pulled back his hand.

Out in the camp in the light of the fire Pickett was winding down. He was telling the story about the time during a cannonade when there was only one tree to hide behind and how the men kept forming behind the tree, a long thin line which grew like a pigtail, and swayed to one side or the other every time a ball came close, and as Pickett acted it out daintily, gracefully, it was very funny.

Armistead said, "Wonder if these cherry trees will grow at home. You think they'll grow at home?"

In a moment Armistead said, "Let's go join the party. Pete? Why not? Before they drink up all the whisky."

"No thanks. You go on."

"Pete, tomorrow could be a long day."

"Work to do." But Longstreet felt himself yielding, softening, bending like a young tree in the wind.

"Come on, Pete. One time. Do you good."

Longstreet looked out at all the bright apple faces. He saw again in his mind the steady face of Lee. He thought: I don't belong. But he wanted to join them. Not even to say anything. Just to sit there and listen to the jokes up close, sit inside the warm ring, because off here at this distance with the deafness you never heard what they said; you were out of it. But . . . if he joined there would be a stiffness. He did not want to spoil their night. And yet suddenly, terribly, he wanted it again, the way it used to be, arms linked together, all drunk and singing beautifully into the night, with visions of death from the afternoon, and dreams of death in the coming dawn, the night filled with a monstrous and temporary glittering joy, fat moments, thick seconds dropping like warm rain, jewel after jewel.

"Pete?"

Longstreet stood up. He let go the reins of command. He thought of the three Union corps, one of them Hancock, dug in on the hill, and he let them all go. He did not want to lead any more. He wanted to sit and drink and listen to stories. He said, "I guess one drink, if it's all right."

Armistead took him by the arm with a broad grin, and it was genuine; he took Longstreet by the arm and pulled him toward the circle.

"Hey, fellas," Armistead bawled, "look what I got. Make way for the Old Man."

They all stood to greet him. He sat down and took a drink and he did not think any more about the war.

6. Lee

He worked all that night. The noise went on around him until long after midnight. His staff was too small: must do something about that. But he could handle the work and there were many decisions that could be made only by the commanding officer, and the commanding officer should know as much as possible about the logistics of the situation, the condition of the army down to the last detail. He found that he could work right through the pain, that there came a second wind. If you sat quietly in a rocking chair you could work all night long. The trouble came when you tried to move. So he worked from the chair, not rising, and every now and then he rested his head in his hands and closed his eyes and blanked the brain, and so rested. The noise did not bother him. But he did not like people crowding too close. After a while he knew it was time to be alone. He told Taylor to ask the people outside to disperse. In a few moments it was very quiet. He rose up out of the chair and stepped out into the night. Time to make a plan now, time to make a decision.

The night air was soft and warm. Across the road there were still many fires in the field but no more bands, no more singing. Men sat in quiet groups, talking the long slow talk of night in camp at war; many had gone to sleep. There were stars in the sky and a gorgeous white moon. The moon shone on the white cupola of the seminary across the road—lovely view, good place to see the fight. He had tried to climb the ladder but it turned out not to be possible. Yet there was little pain now. Move slowly, slowly. He said to Taylor, "What day is it now?"

Taylor extracted a large round watch.

"Sir, it's long after midnight. It's already Friday."

"Friday, July third."

"Yes, sir, I believe that is correct."

"And tomorrow will be the Fourth of July."

"Sir?"

"Independence Day."

Taylor grunted, surprised. "I'd quite forgotten."

Curious coincidence, Lee thought. Perhaps an omen?

Taylor said, "The good Lord has a sense of humor."

"Wouldn't it be ironic—" Lee could not resist the thought —"if we should gain our independence from them, on their own Independence Day?" He shook his head, wondering. He believed in a Purpose as surely as he believed that the stars above him were really there. He thought himself too dull to read God's plan, thought he was not meant to know God's plan, a servant only. And yet sometimes there were glimpses. To Taylor he said, "I'll go sit with Traveler awhile and think. You will keep these people away."

"Yes, sir."

"I am sorry to keep you so late."

"My pleasure, sir."

"We should have a larger staff."

"Sir, I shall be offended."

"Well, I want to think for a while, alone."

"Sir."

Lee moved off into the dark pasture. Now in motion he was aware of stiffness, of weakness, of a suspended fear. He moved as if his body was filled with cold cement that was slowly hardening, and yet there was something inside bright and hot and fearful, as if something somewhere could break at any moment, as if a rock in his chest was teetering and could come crashing down. He found the dark horse in the night and stood caressing the warm skin, thick bristly mane, feeding sugar, talking.

Two alternatives. We move away to better ground, as Longstreet suggests. Or we stay. To the end.

He sat on a rail fence. *And so we broke the vow.* Longstreet's bitter phrase. It stuck in the mind like one of those spiny sticker burrs they had in the South, in Florida, small hooked seeds that lurk in the grass. Honest and stubborn man, Longstreet. We broke the vow. No point in thinking.

He remembered the night in Arlington when the news came: secession. He remembered a paneled wall and firelight. When we heard the news we went into mourning. But outside there was cheering in the streets, bonfires of joy. They had their war at last. But where was there ever any choice? The sight of fire against wood paneling, a bonfire seen far off at night through a window, soft and sparky glows always to remind him of that embedded night when he found that he had no choice. The war had come. He was a member of the army that would march against his home, his sons. He was not only to serve in it but actually to lead it, to make the plans and issue the orders to kill and burn and ruin. He could not do that. Each man would make his own decision, but Lee could not raise his hand against his own. And so what then? To stand by and watch, observer at the death? To do nothing? To wait until the war was over? And if so, from what vantage point and what distance? How far do you stand from the attack on your home, whatever the cause, so that you can bear it? It had nothing to do with causes; it was no longer a matter of vows.

When Virginia left the Union she bore his home away as surely as if she were a ship setting out to sea, and what was left behind on the shore was not his any more. So it was no cause and no country he fought for, no ideal and no justice. He fought for his people, for the children and the kin, and not even the land, because not even the land was worth the war, but the people were, wrong as they were, insane even as many of them were, they were his own, he belonged with his own. And so he took up arms wilfully, knowingly, in perhaps the wrong cause against his own sacred oath and stood now upon alien ground he had once sworn to defend, sworn in honor, and he had arrived there really in the hands of God, without any choice at all; there had never been an alternative except to run away, and he could not do that. But Longstreet was right, of course: he had broken the vow. And he would pay. He knew that and accepted it. He had already paid. He closed his eyes. Dear God, let it end soon.

Now he must focus his mind on the war.

Alternatives? Any real choice here?

Move on, to higher ground in another place.

Or stay and fight.

Well, if we stay, we must fight. No waiting. We will never be stronger. They will be gaining men from all directions. Most of the men will be militia and not the match of our boys, but they will come in thousands, bringing fresh guns. Supplies will come to them in rivers, but nothing will come to us. Richmond has nothing to send. So if we stay, we fight soon. No more chance of surprise. No more need for speed or mobility. But no more delay. We cannot sit and wait. Bad effect on the troops.

And if we pull out?

He saw that in his mind's eye: his boys backing off, pulling out, looking up in wonder and rage at the Yankee troops still in possession of the high ground. If we fall back, we will have fought here for two days and we will leave knowing that we did not drive them off, and if it was no defeat, surely it was no victory. And we have never yet left the enemy in command of the field.

I never saw soldiers fight well after a retreat.

We have always been outgunned. Our strength is in our pride.

But they have good ground. And they have fought well. On home ground.

He saw a man coming toward him, easy gait, rolling and serene, instantly recognizable: Jeb Stuart. Lee stood up. This must be done. Stuart came up, saluted pleasantly, took off the plumed hat and bowed.

"You wish to see me, sir?"

"I asked to see you alone," Lee said quietly. "I wished to speak with you alone, away from other officers. That has not been possible until now. I am sorry to keep you up so late."

"Sir, I was not asleep," Stuart drawled, smiled, gave the sunny impression that sleep held no importance, none at all.

Lee thought: here's one with faith in himself. Must protect that. And yet, there's a lesson to be learned. He said, "Are you aware, General, that there are officers on my staff who have requested your court-martial?"

Stuart froze. His mouth hung open. He shook his head once quickly, then cocked it to one side.

Lee said, "I have not concurred. But it is the opinion of some excellent officers that you have let us all down."

"General Lee," Stuart was struggling. Lee thought: now there will be anger. "Sir," Stuart said tightly, "if you will tell me who these *gentlemen* . . ."

"There will be none of that." Lee's voice was cold and sharp. He spoke as you speak to a child, a small child, from a great height. "There is no time for that."

"I only ask that I be allowed—"

Lee cut him off. "There is no time," Lee said. He was not a man to speak this way to a brother officer, a fellow Virginian; he shocked Stuart to silence with the iciness of his voice. Stuart stood like a beggar, his hat in his hands.

"General Stuart," Lee said slowly, "you were the eyes of this army." He paused.

Stuart said softly, a pathetic voice, "General Lee, if you please . . ." But Lee went on.

"You were my eyes. Your mission was to screen this army from the enemy cavalry and to report any movement by the enemy's main body. That mission was not fulfilled."

Stuart stood motionless.

Lee said, "You left this army without word of your movements, or of the movements of the enemy, for several days. We were forced into battle without adequate knowledge of the enemy's position, or strength, without knowledge of the ground. It is only by God's grace that we have escaped disaster."

"General Lee." Stuart was in pain, and the old man felt pity, but this was necessary; it had to be done as a bad tooth has to be pulled, and there was no turning away. Yet even now he felt the pity rise, and he wanted to say, it's all right, boy, it's all right; this is only a lesson, just one painful quick moment of learning, over in a moment, hold on, it'll be all right. His voice began to soften. He could not help it.

"It is possible that you misunderstood my orders. It is possible I did not make myself clear. Yet this must be clear: you with your cavalry are the eyes of the army. Without your cavalry we are blind, and that has happened once but must never happen again."

There was a moment of silence. It was done. Lee wanted to reassure him, but he waited, giving it time to sink in, to take effect, like medicine. Stuart stood breathing audibly. After a moment he reached down and unbuckled his sword, theatrically, and handed it over with high drama in his face. Lee grimaced, annoyed, put his hands behind his back, half turned his face. Stuart was saying that since he no longer held the General's trust, but Lee interrupted with acid vigor.

"I have told you that there is no time for that. There is a fight tomorrow, and we need you. We need every man, God knows. You must take what I have told you and learn from it, as a man does. There has been a mistake. It will not happen again. I know your quality. You are a good soldier. You are as good a cavalry officer as I have known, and your service to this army has been invaluable. I have learned to rely on your information; all your reports are always accurate. But no report is useful if it does not reach us. And that is what I wanted you to know. Now." He lifted a hand. "Let us talk no more of this."

Stuart stood there, sword in hand. Lee felt a vast pity, yet at the same time he could feel the coming of a smile. Good thing it was dark. He said formally, "General, this matter is concluded. There will be no further discussion of it. Good night."

He turned away. Stuart stood holding the sword, but he had too much respect for Lee to speak. He began to move slowly away. Lee saw him stop before going back out into the night and put the sword back on. A good boy. If he is a man, he will learn. But now he will be reckless, to prove himself. Must beware of that. Longstreet would not approve. But court-martial would have destroyed him. And he is spirited, and that is a great part of his value. Keep him on rein, but on a loose rein. He has to be checked now and then. But he's a fine boy. And I am sorry to have had to do that. Yet it was necessary.

He sat back on the fence. Another figure was coming. He sighed, wanting silence. But the man was Venable, back from Ewell's camp. Like all of Lee's aides he had too much to do and had slept little in the last two days and he was nearing exhaustion. He reported, speech blurred.

"Sir, I think I've, ah, pieced it together. I've been studying General Ewell's, ah, operation. Regret to say, very strange. There is much confusion in that camp."

"Is General Ewell in firm command?"

They had discussed it. Venable, who was fond of Dick Ewell, paused before answering. Then he said slowly, "Sir,

I think General Ewell defers too much to General Early. He is . . . uncertain. I regret the necessity for speaking, sir. I would have preferred not . . ."

"I know." Lee bowed his head. So. The choice of Dick Ewell had been a mistake. But how was one to know? Honest Old Baldy. Had been a fine soldier. But cannot command a corps. Could I have known? Who else was there? Dorsey Pender . . . is wounded.

Venable said, "General Ewell could not get his corps in position for the attack this afternoon until some hours after Longstreet had already begun. General Rodes got his men bottled up in the streets of Gettysburg and never attacked at all."

"Not at *all?*"

"No, sir. General Early attacked at dusk—"

"At dusk. But that was hours late."

"Yes, sir. Longstreet's attack was virtually over before Early got into action. But Early made no progress and called off the attack very soon. General Johnson managed to capture some trenches. Casualties were, ah, light."

Lee said nothing. He thought: Jackson would have *moved* . . . no time for that. He stared at the bold moon.

"You gave General Ewell my orders for the morning?"

"Yes, sir. He understands he is to be in position to attack at first light."

"He understands that."

"Yes, sir."

"He will have all night to prepare. That should be nearly ample time." There was in Lee's voice a rare touch of bitterness.

Venable paused warily, then said, "Are there further orders, sir?"

"Not just yet." Lee rested against the rail fence. Cannot depend on Ewell. Nor on Hill. There is only Longstreet. Pickett is fresh. Longstreet has fresh men. Virginians. For whom we broke the vow. Lee shook his head. Well, one thing is sure, if we attack tomorrow, it will be with Longstreet. He meditated a moment, weariness flowing through him like a bleak slow wind. Think *now,* before you get too tired. He dismissed Venable and turned back to the night.

He sat down once more against the rail fence. The horse moved in over him; he had to move to keep from being stepped on. He sat on the far side of the fence and reviewed the facts and made the decision.

It did not take him very long. He was by nature a decisive man, and although this was one of the great decisions of his life and he knew it, he made it quickly and did not agonize over it. He did not think of the men who would die; he had learned long ago not to do that. The men came here ready to die for what they believed in, for their homes and their honor, and although it was often a terrible death it was always an honorable death, and no matter how bad the pain it was only temporary, and after death there was the reward.

The decision was clear. It had been there in the back of his mind all that night, as he worked, remembering every moment the sight of his blue Virginia flags going up that long slope to the top, almost to victory, so close he could feel the world over there beginning to give like a rotten brick wall. He could not retreat now. It might be the clever thing to do, but cleverness did not win victories; the bright combinations rarely worked. You won because the men thought they would win, attacked with courage, attacked with faith, and it was the faith more than anything else you had to protect; that was one thing that was in your hands, and so you could not ask them to leave the field to the enemy. And even if you could do that, cleverly, there was no certainty they would find better ground anywhere else, not even any certainty that they could extricate themselves without trouble, and so he had known all along that retreat was simply no longer an alternative, the way a man of honor knows that when he has faced an enemy and exchanged one round of blows and stands there bleeding, and sees the blood of the enemy, a man of honor can no longer turn away.

So he would stay. And therefore, he would attack. The rest was clear as an engraving, so natural there seemed no alternative. There would be no surprise now; speed no longer mattered. So motion meant nothing. The enemy had been attacked on both wings; he had reinforced there and would be strongest there. So the weak point was the center.

The enemy had high ground on each wing, but in the center there was a long slope. So he would be softest there, and if you hit him there with everything you had, all the artillery firing to prepare the way in a *pont au feu,* if you sent Pickett's fresh Virginians straight up the center with Longstreet's hand the guiding force, the dominant force, you would drive a split in the center and cut Meade's army in two, break the rotten wall and send the broken pieces flying in all directions, so that if you sent Stuart's cavalry around to the rear he could complete the rout, in among the wagons to finish the wreckage, yes, Stuart raw with wounded pride and so anxious to redeem himself that he would let nothing stop him, and neither would Pickett, who had come in that day so desperately eager for battle.

Lee knelt and began to pray. His engineer's mind went on thinking while he prayed. He could find no flaw: we will go up the center and split them in two, on the defense no longer, attacking at last, Pickett and Hood and McLaws. By the end of the prayer he was certain: he felt a releasing thrill. This was the way, as God would have it. Face to face with the enemy, on grounds of his own choosing. End with honor.

The weight of it was gone. He felt a grave drowsiness. The horse nuzzled his ear; he smiled and rubbed the delicate nostrils. Then he began to drift off. He should go into bed now, but he was not comfortable lying down; he could not breathe. It was far better to sit in the night alone with the beautiful horse standing guard above him. It was not so bad to be an old man, drifting. Soon to see the Light. He wondered what it would be like to enter the Presence. They said there would be a fierce blinding light. How could they know, any of them? He wondered: Do you see all the old friends? At what age will they be? Will I see my father?

But it was all beyond him, and he accepted it. He had done his best: the Lord knew it. The heart thumped twice, a grave reminder. Lee nodded, as if at a summons, and prayed to the Lord for a little more time. After a while, he slept. He dreamed of little girls, dancing a cotillion. Then he dreamed of horses, herds of great horses, thundering by through black canyons of cloud. Beyond his tree, as he slept, the first blood light of dawn was rising up the sky.

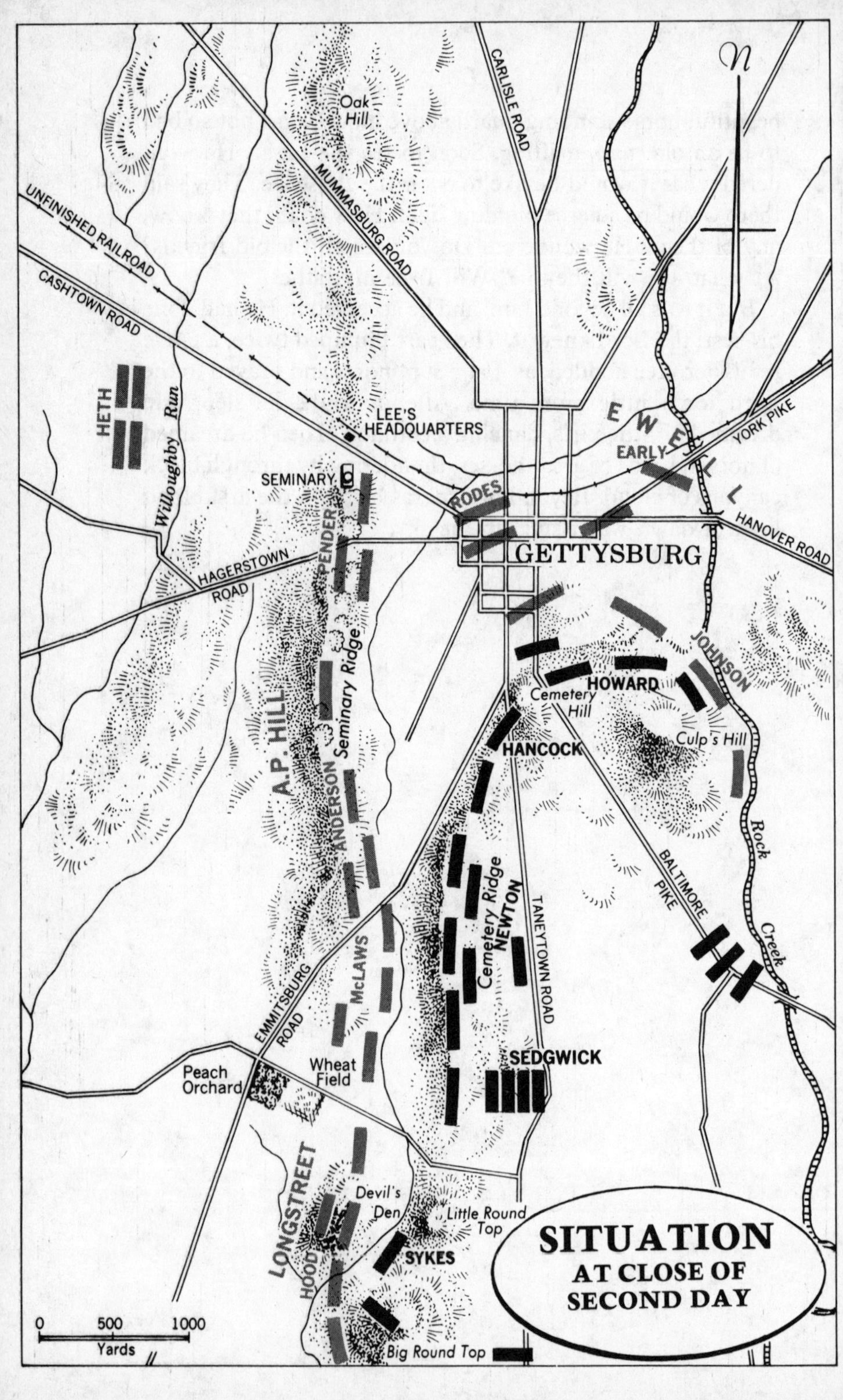
SITUATION
AT CLOSE OF
SECOND DAY
N
Oak Hill
CARLISLE ROAD
MUMMASBURG ROAD
UNFINISHED RAILROAD
CASHTOWN ROAD
HETH
Willoughby Run
LEE'S HEADQUARTERS
SEMINARY
EWELL
EARLY
YORK PIKE
RODES
HANOVER ROAD
GETTYSBURG
HAGERSTOWN ROAD
PENDER
Seminary Ridge
JOHNSON
HOWARD
Cemetery Hill
Culp's Hill
A.P. HILL
ANDERSON
HANCOCK
Rock Creek
BALTIMORE PIKE
Cemetery Ridge
NEWTON
TANEYTOWN ROAD
McLAWS
EMMITSBURG ROAD
SEDGWICK
Peach Orchard
Wheat Field
LONGSTREET
Devil's Den
Little Round Top
HOOD
SYKES
Big Round Top
0
500
1000
Yards

FRIDAY, JULY 3, 1863

Of His terrible swift sword . . .

1. Chamberlain

At dawn he climbed a tree and watched the day come. He was high on the summit of Round Top, higher than any man in either army. The sky was thick and gray, smelling of heat and rain; long mists drifted down between the ridges, lay in pools in the woods, rose toward the sun like white steam. He could see campfires burning in groups and clusters, like little cities sparkling in the mist, far, far off toward the blue hills to the east. He could look directly down on the gray crest of Little Round Top, saw the gunners there rising and stretching and heating coffee near black cannon. There were lights all down the Union line, a few horses moving, here and there a bugle, lights in the cemetery, a spattering of lights in Gettysburg. Here at the summit of Round Top the air was cool, there was no wind, the odor of death was very slight, just that one pale yellow scent, a memory in the silent air. The odor of coffee was stronger. Chamberlain sniffed and hoped, but he had none. All rations were gone. He lay back and watched the morning come.

The men lay below him in a line below the crest, receding down into the trees, the dark. In the night they had built a stone wall, had set out pickets, had taken prisoners. They had been joined at last by the 83rd Pennsylvania and the 44th New York, but they were still the extreme end of the Union line, the highest point on the field. Chamberlain kept pickets out all night, changing them every two hours, making them report every half hour. He did not sleep. As long as he kept moving the pain in the leg did not trouble him, but the foot kept bleeding and annoying him. No one had any rations. They had left Union Mills with three days' worth, but the troops had philosophically eaten most of that first chance they got. Chamberlain searched for coffee, which he badly needed. Just before sunup he began to get very, very tired, and so he climbed the tree and rested his legs. Dawn was always the worst time. Almost impossible to keep the eyes open. Close them and he thought of her, the red robe. This morning, oddly, he thought of her and of his two children. He could see them clearly, when he closed his eyes, playing at her feet like cubs, she looking up at him smiling calmly, waiting, pouting—but they would not even be up yet. Too early for them. They will sleep two more hours, at least. And here I sit on a hill in Pennsylvania. High on a hill, perched in a tree, watching the dawn come. A year ago I was in Maine, a teacher of languages. Amazing. The ways of God. Who would have thought? Well. It will be hard to go home again after this. Yesterday was . . . he closed his eyes. Saw the men behind the rocks, Tozier with the flag, the smoke, white faces, a scream for bayonets. Yesterday was . . . a dream.

He almost dozed. Came awake. Need someone to talk to. Sky all thick and gray. Rain? I hope so. But no, another scorcher. They don't even know about this kind of weather back in Maine.

"Colonel?" At the foot of the tree: Tom. Chamberlain smiled.

"Hey, Colonel, I got you some coffee."

He held aloft a steaming cup. Chamberlain's stomach twinged in anticipation. Tom clambered up, reaching.

Chamberlain took the hot cup, held it lovingly. "Oh, that's fine. Where did you find that?"

"Well . . ." Tom grinned. "Gee, you sure can see a ways from up here." He squinted. "Golly, that's the whole damn Reb army."

"Don't swear," Chamberlain said automatically. He thought of yesterday. I used him to plug a hole. My brother. Did it automatically, as if he was expendable. Reached out and put him there, as you move a chess piece.

"We sent out a detail," Tom said cheerily, yawning, "and found some poor departed souls down there and they were carrying coffee for which they had no more use, so we took it."

Chamberlain grimaced. "Ghoul," he said. But he drank, and the coffee was sweet with brown sugar, and strength boiled into him.

"How you feel, Colonel, sir? You notice I don't say 'Lawrence'."

"I feel fine."

"You know, I bet we're higher than anybody in the whole army. In *both* blame armies." Tom was pleased. "Now there's a thing to tell your children. My, what a view."

Chamberlain drank. After a moment he said, without thinking, "I miss old Buster."

"Kilrain? Yep. But he'll be all right."

The vacancy was there, a hole in the air, a special kind of loneliness. You wanted to have Buster to talk to when it was all over, to go over it, to learn, to understand, to see what you should have done.

Tom said, "You know, Lawrence? I close my eyes, I fall asleep."

"Better get down off the tree."

"You know what?"

"What?"

"I don't like bayonets." He squinted at Chamberlain, shrugged foolishly, blinked and yawned. "One thing about war I just don't like. Different, you know? Not like guns and cannon. Other men feel same way. You know what I mean?"

Chamberlain nodded.

"I couldn't use mine," Tom said ashamedly. "Yesterday. Just couldn't. Ran down the hill, yelling, screamed my head off. Hit one man with the rifle barrel. Bent the rifle all to hell, pardon me. But couldn't stick nobody. Didn't see much of that, either. Am glad to say. Most men won't stick people. When I was going back and looking at the dead, weren't many killed by bayonet."

Chamberlain said, "Nothing to be ashamed of."

"Lawrence?"

Chamberlain turned. Tom was gazing at him, owl-eyed.

"You weren't afraid, much, yesterday."

"Too busy," Chamberlain said.

"No." Tom shook his head. "I shoot and run around and all the time I'm scared green. But you weren't scared at all. Not at all. But at Fredericksburg you were scared."

Chamberlain said, "I was too busy. Had things to do. Couldn't think about getting hurt." But he remembered: There was more to it than that. There was an exultation, a huge delight: *I was alive.*

"Well," Tom said stubbornly, "you did real good." It was the old family expression, used by one brother to another, down the years. Did I do good? You did real good. Chamberlain grinned.

"You know what?" Tom said. He grabbed a branch, swung himself into a better position. "I think we're going to win this war." He looked to Chamberlain for confirmation. Chamberlain nodded, but he was too tired to think about it, all those noble ideals, all true, all high and golden in the mind, but he was just too tired, and he had no need to talk about it. He would hang onto these rocks, all right, of that he was certain. But he didn't know about another charge. He looked down on the men, the line running down the hill. A little ammunition, a little food. We'll hang onto these rocks, all right. Now if I could just get a little sleep . . .

"Lawrence? The way them Rebs kept coming yesterday . . . You got to admire 'em."

"Um," Chamberlain said.

"You think they'll come again today?"

Chamberlain looked out across the open air, gazed at the miles of campfires.

"Doesn't look like they're planning to depart."

"You think they'll come again."

"They'll come again," he said. He stirred himself on the branch. They'll come again, for sure. Must get more ammunition up here. What in God's name is keeping Rice?

"We only got about two hundred men," Tom said thoughtfully. Not with worry but with calculation, a new realist, assessing the cold truth.

"But the position is very good," Chamberlain said.

"I guess so," Tom admitted. Rumble of cannon. At first he thought it was thunder, out of the dark sky to the north. But he saw the flashes sparkle on Cemetery Hill and knew it was too early for thunder, and as he looked northward he could see sunlight breaking through the overcast, to the north and west, and shells falling on the far side of the cemetery. He put his glasses to his eyes and looked, but all he could see was smoke and mist, an occasional yellow flash. Below him, on the hilltop, the heads of the men turned north. Chamberlain thought: diversion. To Tom he said, "You go down and alert the pickets. May be a diversion on that flank. They may be coming this way again. Send Ruel Thomas to me, tell him to send another call to Rice for ammunition."

Tom started down the tree. He scratched himself, swore feebly.

"Lawrence, we're going to need another runner, sir, old brother. I go up and down this hill much more my legs going to fall off."

Chamberlain said, "Yes. Tell Ellis Spear to pick a man, send him to me."

Tom moved down into the dark. Chamberlain waited in the tree. It was a very good position. The hill was flat across the top, about thirty yards of flat rock, an occasional tree, but the ascent on all sides was steep. The ground facing the enemy was rocky and steep and heavy with trees, and the ground behind him fell away abruptly, a sheer drop of at least a hundred feet, no worry about assault from that side. The men had built another rock wall, and now, with enough ammunition, he could hold here for a long time. The end of the line. Overlooking all the world. They'll come again. Let 'em come.

He half expected another assault. But there was no sound from below. The sky was brighter now, breaks in the overcast; light streamed down in blinding rays. He shaded sleep-filled eyes, gazed out across the Southern lines to the blue hills to the east. Lovely country. If I close my eyes, you know, I'll go to sleep. If they come again, could use some rest first.

He heard a man snoring loudly just below his tree. He saw a round face, bearded, mouth open, flat on his back on a rock ledge, hands folded on his chest. Chamberlain smiled in envy. He thought: guess I better get down from here, look around.

But now he had sat for a long time and his leg had stiffened, there was a brutal pain in his foot. He limped along the rock, trying to work out the stiffness. Thirty-four years old, laddie, not the man you used to be. He walked painfully past the sleeping man. A tall thin boy grinned happily upward, touched his cap. Chamberlain said, "Good morning."

"Colonel, sir."

"How you getting along?"

"Hungry, sir." The boy started to get up. Chamberlain held out a hand.

"Never mind that. Take it easy." He looked down on the round-faced sleeper, smiled.

"Jonas can sleep anywhere," the boy said proudly.

Chamberlain moved on down the line. The battle in the north was growing. No diversion. Well. He felt oddly disappointed. Then a trace of pride. They tried this flank yesterday and couldn't move us. Now they're trying the other flank. He wondered who his opposite number was, the colonel on the far right, the last man on the right of the Union line. What troops did he lead? What was he thinking now? Good luck to you, Colonel, Chamberlain said silently, saluting in his mind. But you don't have soldiers like these.

He limped among the men, passing each one like a warming fire. He shared with them all the memory of yesterday. He had been with them to that other world; they were in it now, the high clear world of the last man in line, and all the enemy coming, Tozier on the rock with the flag in his hand, Tom plugging the gap, bayonets lifted, that last wild charge. He looked down smiling as he passed, patting shoulders, concerned with small wounds. One boy lay behind a rock. He had been shot through the cheek yesterday but had not gone to the rear, had charged, had come all this way to the top of the hill. Now he was down with a fever, and the wound in the face was inflamed. Chamberlain ordered him to the field hospital. There were several signs of sickness, one possible case of typhoid. Nothing to do but detail the men down the hill. But none of them wanted to go, some deathly afraid of the hospital itself, some not wanting to be away from men they knew, men they could trust, the Regiment of Home.

Chamberlain began to grow restless for food. He thought: we're forgotten up here. Nobody knows what these men did yesterday. They saved the whole line, God knows, and now I can't even feed them. He was becoming angry. He clambered back up the hill and tore open the wound inside his boot, which began again to bleed. He sat down at the top of the hill, listening to the cannon fire and musketry raging in the north, momentarily grateful that it was over *there,* and took off the boot, bound the foot, wished he could get something to wash it down with, but what water there was was dirty and bloody. There was a creek down below: Plum Run. Choked with yesterday's dead. Good to be high, up here; the smells of death don't seem to be rising. Wind still from the south, blowing it away. You know, the Regiment is weary.

That thought had taken a while to form, had formed slowly as he moved up and down the line. Just so far you can push a man.

He thought: a little food. A little rest. They'll be right again in a bit. Fewer than two hundred now. And there on the rock, sitting staring down at the long line of dark men shapeless under dark trees, he felt for the first time the sense of the coming end. They were dwindling away like sands in a glass. How long does it go on? Each one becoming more precious. What's left now is the best, each man a rock. But now there are so few. We began with a thousand and so whittled down, polishing, pruning, until what we had yesterday was superb, absolutely superb, and now only about two hundred, and, God, had it not been for those boys from the Second Maine . . . but the end is in sight. Another day like yesterday . . . and the Regiment will be gone. In the Union Army that was the way it was: they fought a unit until it bled to death. There were no replacements.

He shook his head, trying to shake away the thought. He could not imagine them gone. He would go with them. But if the war went on much longer . . . if there was one more fight like yesterday . . .

The sound of the battle in the north grew steadily in intensity. Chamberlain, alone, wished he knew anything at all about what was happening. He could not even talk to Ellis Spear, who was down in the woods with the other flank of the Regiment, where it joined the 83rd. He waited, alone, staying awake, listening. After a while there was a courier from Rice. He saw a puffing lieutenant staggering up among the rocks.

"Colonel Chamberlain? Sir, that's some climb." The lieutenant paused to gasp for air, leaned upon a tree.

"My men need rations, Lieutenant," Chamberlain said. He stood up on his bloody foot, boot in hand.

"Sir, Colonel Rice instructs me to tell you that you are relieved, sir."

"Relieved?" Men were gathering around him. Sergeant Tozier had come up, that big-nosed man, towered over the lieutenant, gloomed down at him.

"Colonel Fisher's people are coming up, sir, and will take over here. Colonel Rice informs me that he wishes to compliment you on a job well done and give your people a rest, so he wants you to fall back, and I'm to show you the way."

"Fall back." Chamberlain turned, looked around the hilltop. He did not want to go. You could defend this place against an army. Well. He looked at his tree, from which he had watched the dawn.

He gave the word to Tozier. The Twentieth Maine would stay in position until Fisher's brigade came up, but in a few moments he heard them coming—extraordinary, he had not expected anything quick to happen in this army. The lieutenant sat against a tree while Chamberlain moved among the troops, getting them ready to move. Chamberlain came back for one last look around. For a moment, at least, we were the flank of the army. From this point you could see the whole battlefield. Now they were going down, to blend into the mass below. He looked around. He would remember the spot. He would be back here, some day, after the war.

The men were in line, all down the hill. Tom and Ellis Spear were waiting down below.

"You'll guide us, Lieutenant."

"Yes, sir."

The lieutenant moved off, downward into the dark. Chamberlain said, "I'll be wanting to go back to Little Round Top as soon as possible. The Regiment will bury it's own dead."

"Yes, sir, but I'm to lead you to your new position first, sir, if you don't mind."

Chamberlain said, "Where are we going?"

"Oh, sir—" the lieutenant grinned—" a lovely spot. Safest place on the battlefield. Right smack dab in the center of the line. Very quiet there."

---

2. Longstreet

Goree was back in the gray dawn. The move to the south was still possible; the road to Washington was still open. But Union cavalry was closing in around Longstreet's flank. He sent orders to extend Hood's division. He sat in the gray light studying Goree's map, smelling rain, thinking that a little rain now would be marvelous, cool them, cool the battle fever, settle the dust. Wet mist flowed softly by; dew dripped from the leaves, pattered in the woods, but the morning was already warm. The heat would come again.

He drank coffee alone, dreaming. Scheibert, the Prussian, chatted with him about the Battle of Solferino. Longstreet could hear the laughter from Pickett's boys; some of them had been up all night. They were moving into line in the fields behind Seminary Ridge, out of sight of the Union guns. He was curt with Scheibert. The Prussian was not a fool; he bowed, departed. Longstreet studied the map. Rain would be a great blessing. Rain would screen our movements.

Lee came out of the mists. He was tall and gray on that marvelous horse, riding majestically forward in the gray light of morning outlined against the sky, the staff all around him and behind him, Lee alone in the center, larger than them all, erect, soldierly, gazing eastward toward the enemy line. He rode up, saluted grandly. Longstreet rose. Lee rested both hands on the pommel of his saddle. The mist thickened and blew between them; there was a ghostly quality in the look of him, of all his staff, ghost riders out of the past, sabers clanking, horses breathing thick and heavy in thick dank air.

Lee said, "General, good morning."

Longstreet offered him coffee. Lee declined. He said, "If you will mount up, General, I would like to ride over in that direction—" he gestured eastward—"some little way."

Longstreet called for his horse, mounted. He said, "I've had scouts out all night, General. I know the terrain now."

Lee said nothing. They rode toward the high ground, an opening in the trees. Longstreet looked out across a flat field of mist, fence posts, a ridge of stone black against the soft white flow of mist, then across the road and up the long rise toward the Union defenses, high out of the mist, fires burning, black cannon in plain view.

Longstreet said again, "Sir, I've discovered a way south that seems promising. If we would move—"

"General, the enemy is *there*—" Lee lifted his arm, pointed up the ridge in a massive gesture—"and there's where I'm going to strike him."

He turned and looked back at Longstreet for one long moment, straight into his eyes, fixing Longstreet with the black stare, the eyes of the General, and then turned away. Longstreet drew his head in, like a turtle.

Lee said slowly, face to the east, "The situation is basically unchanged. But you have Pickett now, and he is fresh. I want you to move your corps forward and take those heights, in the center, and split the Union line."

Longstreet took a deep breath. Lee said, "I have sent word to Ewell. He is to attack when you do, keeping the enemy pinned on that flank. Yours will be the main effort. Hill will be the reserve. You will have all our artillery preceding you, fixed on that one point. A *pont au feu.*"

He was watching Longstreet's face, gazing at him without expression, the eyes set far back under white brows, dark, touched with the cool light of the morning. Longstreet said, "Sir." He shook his head, groping for words. Lee waited.

"Sir, there are some things I must say."

Lee nodded, again without expression, immobile. The staff had moved back; the two Generals were alone. Longstreet said, "Sir. My two divisions, Hood and McLaws, lost almost half their strength yesterday. Do you expect me to attack again that same high ground which they could not take yesterday at full strength? With so many officers lost? Including Sam Hood?"

Lee was expressionless. The eyes were black and still.

Longstreet said, "Sir, there are now three Union corps on those rocky hills, on our flank. If I move my people forward we'll have no flank at all; they'll simply swing around and crush us. There are thirty thousand men on those heights to our right. Cavalry is moving out on my flank now. If I move Hood and McLaws, the whole rear of this army is open."

Lee's head shifted slightly, imperceptibly; his eyes shifted. He had been set, now he turned, looked away, looked down at the ground, then east again.

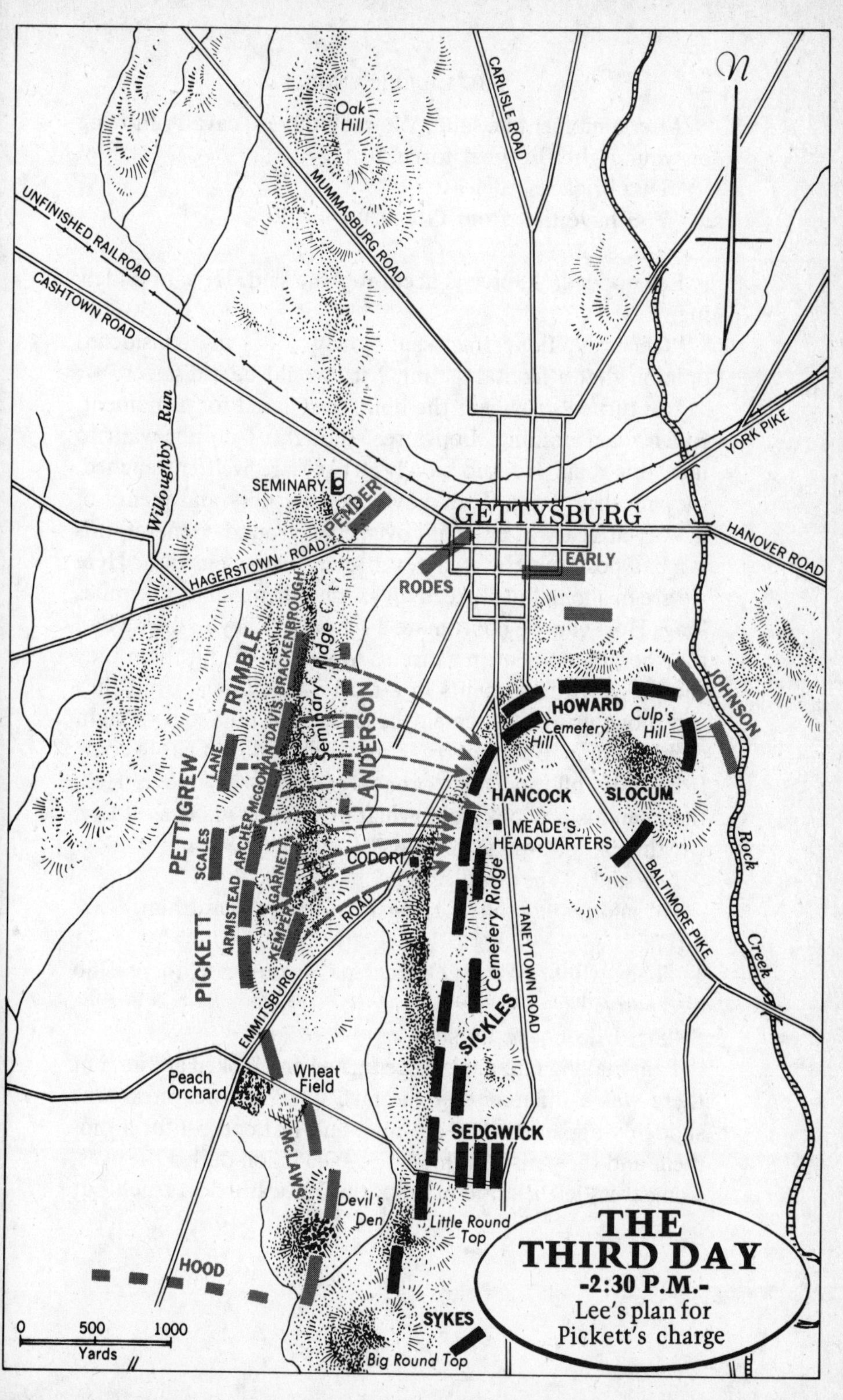
THE THIRD DAY
-2:30 P.M.-
Lee's plan for Pickett's charge
Oak Hill
CARLISLE ROAD
MUMMASBURG ROAD
UNFINISHED RAILROAD
CASHTOWN ROAD
Willoughby Run
SEMINARY
PENDER
GETTYSBURG
YORK PIKE
HANOVER ROAD
HAGERSTOWN ROAD
RODES
EARLY
TRIMBLE
BRACKENBROUGH
DAVIS
McGOWAN
Seminary Ridge
ANDERSON
LANE
PETTIGREW
ARCHER
SCALES
GARNETT
ARMISTEAD
KEMPER
PICKETT
CODORI
ROAD
EMMITSBURG
HOWARD
Cemetery Hill
Culp's Hill
JOHNSON
HANCOCK
SLOCUM
MEADE'S HEADQUARTERS
Cemetery Ridge
TANEYTOWN ROAD
BALTIMORE PIKE
Rock Creek
SICKLES
Peach Orchard
Wheat Field
McLAWS
SEDGWICK
Devil's Den
Little Round Top
HOOD
SYKES
Big Round Top
0 500 1000
Yards

After a moment he said, "You say there is cavalry moving on your right? In what force?"

"Two brigades, at least."

"You have that from Goree?"

"Yes, sir."

Lee nodded. "Goree is accurate," he said. He sat pondering.

"General," Longstreet said slowly, "it is my considered opinion that a frontal assault here would be a disaster."

Lee turned, frowned; the dark eyes flared for a moment. But he said nothing. Longstreet thought: I do not want to hurt this man. He said slowly, "They are well entrenched, they mean to fight. They have good artillery and plenty of it. Any attack will be uphill over open ground. General, this is a bad position. Have you ever seen a worse position? Here we are in a long line, spread all around them, a line five miles long. How can we coordinate an attack? They're massed all together, damn near in a circle. Anywhere we hit them they can bring reinforcements in a matter of minutes. And they can move up reinforcement behind those hills, out of sight of our cannon. But if *we* try to move in support it has to come from miles off, and their cannon can see every move. Hell, their cannon are looking down at us right now. General Lee, sir, this is not a good position."

Lee said, "They will break."

He said it very softly. Longstreet barely heard him. "Sir? Sir?"

"They will break," Lee repeated. "In any case, there is no alternative."

"Sir, I do not think so."

I am making him angry. Lee turned and looked at him, but there was a difference in the face now; the weariness was suddenly apparent. The old man had lost control for a moment and the pain was there; the exhaustion dulled the eyes. Longstreet felt a surge of emotion. He wanted to reach out and touch the old man, but that was impossible. You could not show affection here, no place for it here, too many men will die, must think clearly, but all the while he felt an icy despair, a cold dead place like dead skin. And then the guns began, cannon booming off to the left, where Ewell was. Longstreet swung in his saddle, saw A. P. Hill coming up, chatting with Pickett, and heads all turning at the sound of the guns. And now Lee's face was aflame. An anger Longstreet had never seen before contorted the old man's face. He pulled his horse savagely, almost snarled.

"What is Ewell up to? In God's name, can he follow no order at all?"

Lee galloped off to the left. Longstreet remained behind. Pickett came up, good cheer in his eye, babbling that his boys had been up for hours, and what was the plan? Longstreet said: nothing, and they recognized the mood and left him alone. Fits of weariness began to pass over Longstreet, as clouds pass over and dull the heat.

Colonel Marshall came back, from Lee. The word was that the Federals had opened an attack on Ewell, just as he was getting set. So. At least Ewell hadn't gone off half cocked. No. But what does Lee expect? How can we coordinate across all these miles? And now Meade is attacking. Good, very good. Meade begins to stir himself. Now that's excellent indeed. Given a bit of luck now, we can lure him down out of those damned bloody rocks. He's moving on my flank now. Good, very good. Let him come, let him come, and then when his arm is out far enough, when his nose is extended, I will chop it off with a chop they'll feel in London.

Lee was coming back. The sun was beginning to break through, the mist was rising. Lee rode slowly up, slouched a bit, no longer quite so trim. He smiled a haggard smile. Longstreet thought: He got mad at Ewell, now he's embarrassed.

Lee said, "No need for hurry now. General Ewell is engaged. General Meade has made a move. I must confess, I did not expect it." He pointed. "We'll ride forward."

They moved out toward the lines. Lee was thinking; Longstreet kept silent. The heat came slowly, steadily. They rode down to the Emmitsburg Road, in clear view of the Union lines. There were smells flowing up from the hospital. Out in the fields the dead lay everywhere in the litter of war. Here and there surgeons were moving, burial parties. Above them, on the Union lines, a cannon thumped, the ball passed overhead, exploded in an open field among dead bodies. Two of Lee's aides rode up, insisted that the Union gunners could see them much too clearly. They dismounted. Lee walked forward across the road into the peach orchard, where Barksdale had streamed to his death the day before. Lee cautioned Longstreet to keep his distance so that if a shot came down it would not get both of them at once. They were nearing the lines now; men began rising out of the ground, ragged apparitions. The aides quieted cheering, which would draw Union fire. The men stood awe-stricken, hats in their hands, whispering kind words, words of hope, words of joy. Longstreet looked into lean young grinning faces, bloodstained clothes, saw bodies bloated in the fields, dead horses everywhere. Ewell's fight in the north was stiffer, but down here the sound was softened; the wind was in the south, blowing toward the battle, blowing up between the lines. They were walking now in Wofford's line. Wofford came out to greet General Lee.

Wofford's Brigade had pushed up the ridge almost to the top the day before. Lee listened to him tell of it, then Lee said, "General, you went up there yesterday. Surely you can do it again."

"No, General, I think not," Wofford said. He seemed embarrassed to say it.

Lee said, "Why not?"

"Because yesterday we were chasing a broken enemy.

They've been heavily reinforced. They've had all night to entrench. And my boys . . . lost many friends yesterday."

Lee said nothing. Longstreet saw him clamp his jaw. He was walking slowly, hands clasped behind him. He said suddenly, "Well, but Pickett is here. And Stuart. Don't forget Stuart."

A sharpshooter's bullet shirred by overhead. Longstreet looked for it curiously. Shooting downhill, snipers always overshoot. They were moving into the front of the line, the bloody wheat field. Longstreet saw a battery being moved, guns being pulled back. He saw young Porter Alexander, his chief of artillery, in personal supervision. Good, he thought absently, very good, Alexander is seeing to it himself. The technical commander was Parson Pendleton, but Pendleton was a fool. There was high ground at the peach orchard. Alexander was posting some Napoleons there, waved as he rode by. Lee saw, approved wordlessly. He took his hat off, gazing upward at the long rise toward Cemetery Ridge. The sun gleamed on his white hair, the dark ridge along the brow line where the hat had pressed the hair down. Longstreet thought: he was not all that white-haired a year ago. He remembered yesterday: "I'll tell you a secret: I'm an old man."

I wish we could take the hill. Could flood right on over it and end the war, wipe them all away in one great motion. But we can't. No matter how much I wish . . . or trust in God . . .

Lee turned back. His face was again composed; he put the soft black hat back on his head. He called an aide: Venable, then Taylor. Longstreet waited to the side. Soldiers were drifting up to stand happily by, gazing with paternal affection at Lee, at Longstreet.

"Mornin' to ya, General. You look pert this mornin', sir."

"General, beggin' yer pardon, sir, I'd like to complain about the food, sir."

"We's back in the Union now, General."

They were ready. That superb morale. Lee touched his hat to the men. They moved away from the line. The sun broke through at last and poured heat on the roadway; the mist was gone. A rider came up from Hood's division, commanded now by General Law. Law reported Union cavalry moving in force across his flank, suggested strengthening his line with Robertson's Brigade. Longstreet agreed, Lee listening silently. Then they rode back toward the ridge where Pickett's men waited.

Ewell's fight was going on. They could see smoke blowing now across the top of the hill. Ewell reported that Johnson was being compelled to fall back from the trenches he had won the night before. Lee sat alone for a while, Longstreet a small way away. A slowly growing swarm of aides and other officers, reporters, foreigners, musicians, began gathering a respectful distance away. A band began playing "That Bonny Blue Flag," in Lee's honor. Skirmish firing broke out in the fields below Seminary Ridge; musketry popped in patches of white smoke as the lines felt and probed.

At last Lee turned, summoned Longstreet. Longstreet came up. Lee said, "General, we will attack the center."

He paused. Longstreet took a long breath, let it go.

"You will have Pickett's Division. But I think you are right about the flank. Leave Hood and McLaws where they are. I will give you Heth's Division. It was not engaged yesterday. And Pender's."

Longstreet nodded.

"You will have three divisions. Your objective will be that clump of trees . . . there."

He pointed. The center of the Union line, the center of the ridge. The clump of trees was clear, isolated. In the center of the clump was one large tree shaped like an umbrella.

Unmistakable. Longstreet nodded, listened, tried not to think.

"Your attack will be preceded by massed artillery fire. *A feu d'enfer.* We will concentrate all our guns on that small area. When the artillery has had its effect, your charge will break the line. The rest of Hill's people will be waiting. Stuart has already gone round to the rear."

Lee turned. Now the excitement was in his eyes. He leaned forward, gazing at Longstreet, hoping to strike fire, but Longstreet said nothing, stood listening, head bowed.

Lee said, "Those three divisions . . . will give you fifteen thousand men."

Longstreet said, "Yes, sir." He stared at the ridge. He said suddenly, "Hancock is up there."

Lee nodded. "Yes, that's the Second Corps."

Longstreet said, "Hard on Armistead."

Lee said, "You can begin at any time. But plan it well, plan it well. We stake everything on this."

"Sir?" Longstreet thought: I can't. "Sir," Longstreet said, "you are giving me two of Hill's divisions, only one of mine. Most of the troops will be Hill's. Wouldn't it be better to give the attack to Hill?"

Lee shook his head. He said, "General, I want *you* to make this attack." Longstreet took another deep breath. Lee said, "General, I need you."

Longstreet said, "Sir, with your permission."

Lee waited. Longstreet spoke and did not want to look him in the face, but did, spoke looking at the weary face, the ancient eyes, the old man who was more than father of the army, symbol of war. "Sir, I have been a soldier all my life. I have served from the ranks on up. You know my service. I have to tell you now, sir, that I believe this attack will fail. I believe that no fifteen thousand men ever set for battle could take that hill, sir."

Lee raised a hand. Longstreet had seen the anger before,

had never seen it turned toward him. It was as if Longstreet was betraying him. But Longstreet went on: "It is a distance of more than a mile. Over open ground. As soon as we leave the trees we will be under the fire of their artillery. From all over the field. At the top of the hill are Hancock's boys—"

Lee said, "That's enough."

He turned away. He called Taylor. For a long moment Longstreet thought: he is relieving me. But Lee was sending for someone. Longstreet thought: he should relieve me. He should give it to A. P. Hill. But he knew Hill could not take it, no one could take it; there was no one else Lee could rely on, nothing else to do. It was all set and fated like the coming of the bloody heat, the damned rising of the damned sun, and nothing to do, no way to prevent it, my weary old man, God help us, what are you doing?

Not thinking clearly any more, Longstreet composed himself. Lee came back. Lee said calmly, "General, do you have any question?"

Longstreet shook his head. Lee came to him, touched his arm.

"General, we all do our duty. We do what we have to do."

"Yes, sir," Longstreet said, not looking at him.

"Alexander is handling the artillery. He is very good. We will rely on him to break them up before Pickett gets there."

"Yes, sir."

"Heth is still too ill for action. I am giving his division to Johnston Pettigrew. Is that satisfactory to you?"

Longstreet nodded.

"Pender is out of action, too. Who would you suggest for the command there?"

Longstreet could not think. He said, "Anyone you choose."

"Well," Lee meditated. "How about Isaac Trimble? No one in the army has more fight in him than Trimble."

"Yes," Longstreet said.

"Good. Then that's agreed. Pettigrew, Pickett, and Trimble. The new commanders won't really matter, in an attack of this kind. The men will know where to go."

He went over the plan again. He wanted to be certain, this day, that it all went well, laying it all out like the tracks of a railroad. He was confident, excited, the blood was up. He thought the army could do anything. Longstreet felt the weariness, the heat of the day. The objective was clear. All fifteen thousand men would concentrate, finally, on a small stone wall perhaps a hundred yards wide. They might break through. It was possible.

Lee said, "The line there is not strong. Meade has strengthened both his flanks; he must be weak in the center. I estimate his strength in the center at not much more than five thousand men. The artillery barrage will upset them."

"Yes, sir."

"Is there anything you need? Take whatever time you need."

"I have always been slow," Longstreet said.

"There is no one I trust more."

"If the line can be broken . . ." Longstreet said.

"It can. It will." Lee paused, smiled.

"If it can be done, those boys will do it." Longstreet moved back formally, saluted.

Lee returned the salute, tall, erect, radiating faith and confidence. He said slowly, the voice of the father, "General Longstreet, God go with you."

Longstreet rode off to summon his staff.

What was needed now was control, absolute control. Lee was right about that: a man who could not control himself had no right to command an army. They must not know my doubts, *they must not.* So I will send them all forward and say nothing, absolutely nothing, except what must be said. But he looked down at his hands. They were trembling. Control took a few moments. He was not sure he could do it. There had never been anything like this in his life before. But here was Pickett, wide-eyed, curious, long hair ringed and combed, mounted on a black horse, under a great tree.

Longstreet told him the orders. Pickett whooped with joy. Longstreet let him go off to form his troops. He looked at his watch: not yet noon. It would be some time yet. He sent for the other officers, for Porter Alexander. The fight on the far left was dying; Ewell was done. There would be no support there. He felt a moment of curious suspension, as when you have been awake for a long time you have certain moments of unreality, of numbness, of the beginning of sleep. It passed. He heard cannon fire to the left, closer. A. P. Hill was shooting at something. Alexander rode up: a young man, nondescript face but very capable. He was excited, hatless. He apologized for the loss of the hat.

"Sir, ah, we seem to have upset Colonel Walton. He has just reminded me that he is the senior artillery officer in this Corps."

Longstreet moved out to the edge of the trees. He indicated the limits of the attack, where the fire should converge. He explained it slowly, methodically, with great care. The Union cannon up on the Rocky Hill would cause trouble. Alexander should assign guns to keep them quiet. He should have more guns ready to move forward with the attack, keeping the flanks clear. It occurred to Longstreet that this was a grave responsibility. He interrupted himself, said suddenly, "How old are you, son?"

"Sir? Ah, twenty-six, sir."

Longstreet nodded, looked into the unlined face, the bright, dark, anxious eyes. Best gunner in the corps. We make do with what we have. He said, "Can you clean those guns off that hill, son?"

"Sir? Well, sir, I don't know about that, sir."

"Well," Longstreet said. He thought: I'm seeking reassurance. Let it go. He said, "I am relying on you, son."

"Yes, sir." Alexander bobbed his head several times, kicked the turf. "I'll sure keep 'em shootin', sir."

"Don't open fire until I give you the word, until everything's in position. Then fire with everything you have. Get yourself a good observation point so you can see the damage we're doing. We've got to drive some of those people off that hill. If we don't do that . . . I'll rely on your judgment."

A great weight to put upon him. But nothing else to do. Alexander saluted, moved off. Here came Sorrel, bringing with him, on horseback, Generals Pettigrew and Trimble. Longstreet greeted them, sent for Pickett. He got down from his horse and walked over to the open space on the ground where the staff had spread the camp stools, and asked for coffee. They sat in a circle, lesser officers at a distance, almost in files, by rank. Longstreet wore the expressionless face, drank the coffee, said nothing at all, looked at them.

Johnston Pettigrew: handsome, fine-featured. An intellectual. Very few intellectuals in this army. He had attended the University of North Carolina and they talked of his grades there with reverence and awe. Curious thing, Longstreet thought. He smiled slightly. Here's our intellectual, Pettigrew, going into battle side by side with old Pickett, last in his class. He chuckled. The men were watching him, sensing his mood. They seemed happy to see him grin. Longstreet looked at Pettigrew.

"They tell me you've written a book."

"Sir? Oh, yes, sir." Firm sound to the voice, clear calm eye. Lee thinks the world of him. He will do all right.

"What was it about?"

"Oh, it was only a minor work, sir."

"I'll have to read it."

"You will have a copy, sir, with my compliments." To Longstreet's surprise, Pettigrew rose, summoned an aide, dispatched the man for the book.

Longstreet grinned again. He said, "General, I doubt if I'll have time today."

"At your leisure, sir." Pettigrew bowed formally.

Longstreet looked at Isaac Trimble. He was breathing hard, face red and puffy, a bewildered look to him. He had a reputation as a fire-breather. He did not look like it. His beard was fully white, his hair puffed and frizzled. Well, Longstreet thought, we shall see.

Pickett came up, joined the circle. Introductions were unnecessary. Longstreet ordered coffee all around, but Trimble would not take any; his stomach was troubling him. Sorrel was the only other officer to hear the orders. Longstreet explained it all slowly, watching them. Pickett was excited, could not sit still, sat rubbing his thighs with both hands, nodding, patting himself on the knees. Pettigrew was calm and pale and still. Trimble breathed deeply, rubbed his nose. His face grew more and more crimson. Longstreet began to understand that the old man was deeply moved. When he was done with the orders Longstreet drew the alignment in the dirt:

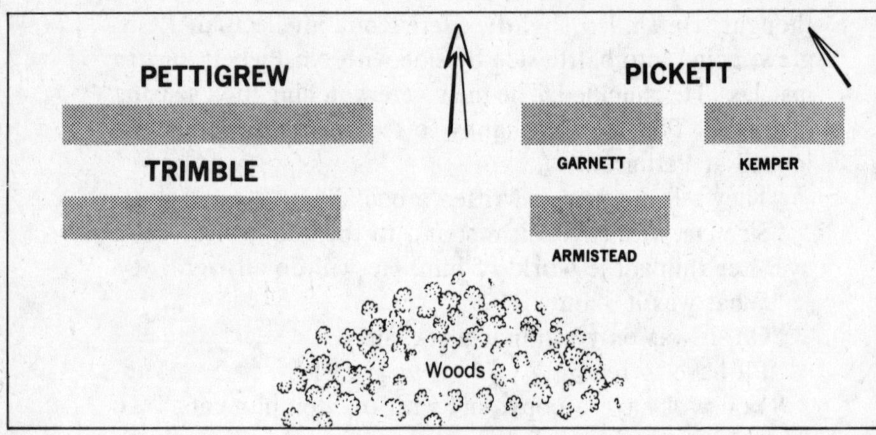

They all understood. Then Longstreet rose and walked out to the edge of the trees, out into the open, for a look at the Union line. He pointed to the clump of trees. There were a few minor questions. Longstreet told them to keep that clump in sight as they moved back to their troops, to make sure that there was no confusion. The attack would guide on Pickett. More minor questions, then silence. They stood together, the four men, looking up at the Union line. The mist had burned away; there were a few clouds, a slight haze. Hill's guns had stopped; there was a general silence.

Longstreet said, "Gentlemen, the fate of your country rests on this attack."

All eyes were on his face. He put out his hand.

"Gentlemen, return to your troops."

Pettigrew took his hand. "Sir, I want to say, it is an honor to serve under your command."

He moved off. Trimble took the hand. He was crying. He said huskily, tears all down the red glistening cheeks, "I want to thank you, sir, for the opportunity you have given me, sir, to serve here. I have prayed, sir." He stopped, choked. Longstreet pressed his hand. Trimble said, "I will take that wall, sir."

Pickett stayed. Longstreet said, "George, can you take that hill?"

Pickett grinned. My curly boy. He rushed off, hair flying. Here was Alexander, galloping up through the trees, exasperated.

"Sir, General Hill's artillery is dueling the Union people for some damned barn, sir, excuse me, but it's a tragic waste of ammunition. We don't have a limitless supply."

Longstreet said, "Give General Hill my compliments and tell him I suggest he reserve his ammunition for the assault."

Alexander rode off.

And so it's in motion.

Seminary Ridge was thick with trees, but the fields on both

sides were bare. Pickett's troops were beginning to form in the fields to the west, out of sight of the Union line. Longstreet rode to watch them, then back out through the trees to face east, looking up toward the Union line. His staff was with him: gaunt Goree asleep in his saddle, refusing to lie down. Longstreet saw a familiar figure standing some distance out in the field, alone, looking toward the Union line. He rode that way: Armistead. Looking up toward Hancock's wall. Longstreet stopped, nodded, let the man alone, rode away. Poor old Lo. Well. All over soon. One way or the other.

Lee was coming back down the line, aides preceding him, to keep the men from cheering. Alexander's guns were moving, realigning; horses were pulling caissons into position, stirring the dust. Lee was trim and calm, all business. He suggested they ride the lines again. Longstreet agreed silently. Pickett rode up, asked to accompany them. All the attack would guide on Pickett; it was necessary there be no mistake at all. The three men rode together along the front of the dark woods, in front of the cannon, the troops, the woods behind them a dark wall, and the long flat green rise in front of them, spreading upward and outward to the Emmitsburg Road, the rise beyond that, the visible breastworks, the stone wall near the crest, well named, Cemetery Ridge. Lee discussed the attack with Pickett; Longstreet was silent. There was a dip in the ground near the center; they rode down out of sight of the Union line. Lee was telling Pickett how to maneuver his troops sideways when he reached the road so that they would converge on that clump of trees toward the center. He had many suggestions as to how to use the ground. Longstreet dropped slightly behind them. They came out into the open again, in front of the point of woods from which Lee would watch the assault. Longstreet looked up the long rise.

He could begin to see it. When the troops came out of the woods the artillery would open up. Long-range artillery, percussion and solid shot, every gun on the hill. The guns to the right, on the Rocky Hill, would enfilade the line. The troops would be under fire with more than a mile to walk. And so they would go. A few hundred yards out, still in the open field, they would come within range of skirmish, aimed rifles. Losses would steadily increase. When they reached the road they would be slowed by the fence there, and the formation, if it still held, would begin to come apart. Then they would be within range of the rifles on the crest. When they crossed the road, they would begin to take canister fire and thousands of balls of shrapnel wiping huge holes in the lines. As they got closer, there would be double canister. If they reached the wall without breaking, there would not be many left. It was a mathematical equation. But maybe the artillery would break up the defense. There was that hope. But that was Hancock up there. And Hancock would not run. So it is mathematical after all. If they reach the road and get beyond it, they will suffer fifty percent casualties. I do not think they will even reach the wall.

Lee asked his advice on artillery support. Longstreet gave it quietly. They rode back down the line. A quietness was beginning to settle over the field. The sun was rising toward noon. They came back toward Longstreet's line. Lee said, "Well, we have left nothing undone. It is all in the hands of God."

Longstreet thought: it isn't God that is sending those men up that hill. But he said nothing. Lee rode away.

Pickett said earnestly, "Sir, how much time do we have?"

Terrible question. But he did not know what he was asking. Longstreet said, "Plenty of time. The guns will fire for at least an hour."

Pickett slapped his thighs.

"It's the waiting, sir, you know? Well, sir, I think I'll have the troops lie down. Then I'll write to Sallie. You'll see it's delivered, sir?"

Longstreet nodded.

Pickett rode off.

Nothing to do now but wait. The guns were in line, the caissons were stacking shot, the gunners digging their small trenches. One hundred and forty guns. And the Union boys will reply. It will be the greatest concentration of artillery ever fired.

Longstreet got down from his horse. He was very, very tired. He walked toward a cool grove of trees. Sorrel and Goree followed, but Longstreet waved them away. He sat with his back against a tree, put his head in his hands.

There is one thing you can do. You can resign now. You can refuse to lead it.

But I cannot even do that. Cannot leave the man alone. Cannot leave him with that attack in the hands of Hill. Cannot leave because I disagree, because, as he says, it's all in the hands of God. And maybe God really wants it this way. But they will mostly all die. We will lose it here. Even if they get to the hill, what will they have left, what will we have left, all ammunition gone, our best men gone? And the thing is, I cannot even refuse, I cannot even back away, I cannot leave him to fight it alone, they're my people, my boys. God help me, I can't even quit.

He closed his eyes. From a tree close by Colonel Fremantle saw him, thought he was resting before the great battle, could not help but wonder at the enormous calm of the man. What an incredible time to go to sleep!

3. Chamberlain

Past Little Round Top the ground dipped down into a saddle but the line ran straight, unbroken, along the saddle and up the ridge, rising toward the trees and the cemetery, that northern hill. The line was a marvelous thing to see: thousands of men and horses and the gleaming Napoleons, row on row, and miles of wagons and shells. Marching along the crest, they could see back to the Taneytown Road and the rows of tents, the hospitals, the endless black rows of more cannon, wagon trains. The sun was hot along the ridge, and men had stuck bayonets in the ground and rigged shelter halves, and here and there through scarred trees they could see down into the rocks below, bodies there in black clumps, soft among the gray boulders. Back in the woods of Little Round Top, up on the summit of the hill, they had been alone, but now they were in the midst of the army, the great army, a moving fragment of this unending line of men and guns lined along the spine of that ridge going out of sight to the north. Chamberlain gathered strength, limping along the ridge, tucking himself in under his soft black hat, out of the sun.

The lieutenant who was their guide was a dapper young man named Pitzer, who liked to gossip, to show that he was privy to great secrets. He had a runny nose and he sneezed repeatedly but seemed to be enjoying himself. He pointed out the place where the First Minnesota had made the charge that had the whole army talking. Three hundred men had charged, under Hancock's direction; only forty had come back. But they had broken a Reb assault, giving reserves time to get up. Chamberlain thought: their casualties much worse than mine. In a fight, it always seems that your fight is the hardest. Must remember that. What happened to them was much worse than what happened to us.

Pitzer said conversationally, "We very nearly retreated this morning."

"Retreated? *Why?*" Chamberlain was aghast.

"Meade wanted to pull the whole army out. Had a meeting of corps commanders last night. He really did." Pitzer sneezed emphatically. "Damn ragweed. Happens every sum—" He exploded again, plucked out a bright red handkerchief, wiped his nose, his wheezy eye, grinned. "Meade wrote an order for the whole army to withdraw, then held a meeting of corps commanders and asked for a vote. This army is great for meetings, Colonel. Old Sedgewick did the right thing. He fell asleep." Pitzer chuckled. "Old Uncle John, you can count on him. He voted, then he fell asleep."

"What was the vote?"

"Well, hell, *all* the corps commanders voted to stay. I mean the *only* one felt like pulling out was Meade. *General* Meade," he added thoughtfully, eying Chamberlain. Never knew how to take these civilian colonels. "It was unanimous. Meade had 'em write it out, so it's all on record. I was watching through a window, saw the whole thing, even old Sedgewick asleep. Now *there's* an officer. Him and Hancock." Pitzer shook his head admiringly, wheezing. "Hancock was something to behold. He says they'll come again one more time and we ought to be right here waiting."

"He says they'll come again? Hancock?"

"Yep."

"Where did he say they'd come?"

Pitzer grinned, pointed, wheezed. "Why, Colonel, right about here."

They were moving higher up the crest of the hill. They

were coming out on a long space of open ground along the crest before a grove of trees, the Cemetery. Down across the field there was a small farmhouse surrounded by horses, flags, many soldiers. Chamberlain could see, even at this distance: the high brass. To the left was a clump of trees, a stone fence, two batteries of artillery, the long line of troops lying in the sun, in the shade of the trees, dug in, waiting.

Pitzer said, pointing, "That's Meade's headquarters, over there. Position of your regiment will be back there, down near the road. You'll be in reserve behind the crest. Don't have to dig in, but don't go way." Pitzer led them down the grass, pointed to a flat space just above the road, the masses of guns and wagons, in plain sight of the headquarters. "Here it is, Colonel. I'm to place you here. Colonel Rice will be by in a bit. Says you are to report to General Sykes later on." He saluted, sneezed, wandered off, in no great hurry, wiping his nose.

Chamberlain placed the regiment. They sat in the field, in the sun. There were questions about rations. Chamberlain thought: All those wagons down there, there ought to be something. He sent Ruel Thomas out to scrounge. Brother Tom went off to find the hospital, to see how the boys were, to see how Buster Kilrain was getting along. Chamberlain smelled coffee, the lovely smell of cooking chicken. He tried to follow his nose, was interrupted by another odor. He climbed a stone fence, knee high, saw a shallow depression filled with dead horses, dragged there to get them off the crest, legs and guts and glaring teeth, beginning to smell. Wind still luckily from the south. Chamberlain went back across the stone fence, looked up toward the crest. Couldn't see much from here. Could sure use some food. Felt incredibly lonesome, no one to talk to anymore. Sat by himself. The men around him were rigging shade, collapsing. Ellis Spear came up, sat down, said hello, fell asleep. The sun was too much. The men were moving with slow, drugged movements. Chamberlain thought: Any minute now I will go to sleep. Dreamyly. He smiled. Did not want to sleep. Food. Get some fuel. Mustn't sleep.

A rider. Man stopped before him. Chamberlain squinted upward. Message from General Sykes. Would like the pleasure of Colonel Chamberlain's company.

Chamberlain squinted. "Where is he?"

The rider indicated the crest, trees at the far end. Chamberlain said, "Haven't got a horse, but I guess I can make that."

He staggered to his feet. The rider, solicitous, hopped down, offered him the horse, led the animal by the bridle, making Chamberlain feel boyish and ridiculous. Chamberlain took the reins, woke Ellis Spear, told him to take over. Spear agreed blearily. The messenger led Chamberlain up the crest.

Past a clump of trees to his left the view opened. He could see a long way down across open fields to a road, a farmhouse, a long sweep of wheat rising up to green woods on the far ridge, at least a mile off. Lovely country. Heat shimmered on the road. Chamberlain thought: must be ninety. Hope my next war is in Maine. Where I will fight dreamyly. Owe her a letter. Soon. Kids be playing now. Sitting down to lunch. Eating—cold, cold milk, thick white bread, cheese and cream, ah.

He rode up into the shade of the trees. Sitting there ahead . . . was Hancock.

Chamberlain perked up, straightened his uniform. He had seen Hancock only a few times, but the man was memorable. Picture-book soldier: tall and calm, handsome, magnetic. Clean white shirt, even here, white cuffs, hat cocked forward slightly jauntily, shading his eyes. He was sitting on a camp stool, gazing westward intently. He moved; his arm came up. He was eating a piece of chicken.

He was surrounded by Generals. Some of them Chamberlain recognized: Gibbon, of Hancock's Corps, the cold man with the icy reputation. He had three brothers with the South. How many out there today, across that silent field? There was Pleasanton, of the cavalry, and Newton, new commander of the First Corps. Chamberlain saw a vast pot of stewed chicken, a pot of hot tea, a disappearing loaf of battered bread, some pickles. His mouth opened, watered, gulped. The Generals went on eating mercilessly. The messenger took Chamberlain on past the food to a dark spot near a white barn. General Sykes was sitting there, smoking a cigar, staring down at some papers, dictating an order. The messenger introduced him as he dismounted, then departed with the horse. Sykes stood up, extended a hand, looked him over as you look over a horse you are contemplating buying.

"Chamberlain. Yes. Heard about you. Want to hear more. Want you to write a report. Rice says you did a good job."

Chamberlain nodded and said thank you and went on smelling chicken. Sykes was a small, thin, grouchy man, had the reputation of a gentleman, though somewhat bad-tempered. Chamberlain thought: There are no good-tempered generals.

Sykes said, observing Chamberlain with the same look one gives a new rifle, "Rice says you're a schoolteacher."

"Well," Chamberlain said, "not quite."

"You aren't Regular Army."

"No, sir. I taught at Bowdoin."

"Bowdin? *Oh,* you mean Bow-doyn. Yes. Heard of it. Amazing." He shook his head. "Tell me you ordered a bayonet charge, drove those people halfway to Richmond."

Chamberlain shifted his feet idiotically.

"Well, I'm going to look into it, Colonel, and let me tell you this, we need fightin' men in this army, any way we can get em, Regular Army or no, and one damn thing is sure, we can use some Brigade commanders. I'm going to look into it. Meantime, well done, well done. Now you go rest up. Nothing going to happen today."

He was finished, turned back to his work. Chamberlain asked about rations. Sykes told a lieutenant to see to it. Chamberlain saluted, backed off, out into the sun. No horse now, have to walk. Right foot on fire. Damn. He limped along the crest, not paying much attention to the view. He was a picturesque figure. He had not changed clothes nor washed nor shaved in a week. His blue pants were torn in several places and splotched with dried blood; his right boot was torn, his jacket was ripped at the shoulder, his sword was without a scabbard, was stuck into his belt. He hobbled along painfully, sleepily, detouring around the front of a Napoleon, didn't notice it until he opened his eyes and looked straight into the black maw, the hole of the barrel, and he blinked and came awake, momentarily, remembering Shakespeare's line: "the bubble reputation in the cannon's mouth." Doesn't look like a mouth. Looks like a damn dangerous hole. Stay away from that.

He was passing the group with Hancock and the chickens. He sighed wistfully, smelling fresh coffee, looked that way, was too proud to ask, saw a familiar figure: Meade himself. The crusty old stork, munching on a chicken leg. Chamberlain paused. Never saw much of Meade, didn't quite know what to think of him. But if he wants to retreat, he's a damn fool. Chamberlain had stopped; a number of the group of officers noticed him. Chamberlain looked down, saw blood coming out of his boot. That keeps up, I'm in trouble. Foot wounds always slow to heal. Wonder why?

An officer had detached himself from the group. Chamberlain had started to move on, but the officer came up, saluted. He was older than Chamberlain, but he was only a lieutenant. Sitting with all the generals. Chamberlain could feel the massed power; it was like being near great barrels of gunpowder. The lieutenant asked if he could be of service. Chamberlain said no thanks, wondering how to conquer pride and if a general would part with some chicken, and then felt ashamed, because his boys had none and would be guilty to eat something up here, but on the other hand, don't get something soon, and keep losing blood, might pass out, in all this damned heat, like you did the other time, and be no good to anybody.

The lieutenant introduced himself: Frank Haskell, aide to General Gibbon. He recognized Chamberlain's name. His eyes showed respect; now *that* was pleasant. Chamberlain explained that he'd been to see General Sykes and had no horse, and the foot was bothering him, and did the lieutenant think they might spare one scrawny leg, or even a neck? The lieutenant bowed, came back with *three* pieces of chicken, hot and greasy, wrapped in a dirty white cloth. Chamberlain took them with gratitude, staggered off down the hill. He ate one piece, preserved the other two. It was awful but marvelous. When he got back to the company he gave the two surviving pieces to Ellis Spear and told him to figure out a way to share them with somebody, that rations would be here soon, Sykes had promised.

He rested and took off his boot. Nothing to wrap it with. He tore off a bit of his shirt, was working away diligently, saw Tom coming.

Tom was losing the chipper edge. Chamberlain thought: Be all right in a bit. The young recover quickly. Must think on the theology of that: plugging a hole in the line with a brother. Except for that, it would all have been fine. An almost perfect fight, but the memory of that is a jar, is wrong. Some things a man cannot be asked to do. Killing of brothers. This whole war is concerned with the killing of brothers. Not my family. He thought of Gibbon. Praise be to God.

Must send Tom somewhere else. In that moment, Chamberlain made up his mind: Tom would have to go. Tell him soon. Not now.

Tom sat. Lines in the face. Something wrong. Chamberlain saw: Kilrain?

"Lawrence, I been down to the hospital. Godawful mess. No shade, no room. They lying everywhere, out in the sun. They cuttin' off arms and legs right out in the open, front of everybody, like they did at Fredericksburg. God, they ought to know better, they ought not do that in public. Some of them people *die.* Man ought to have privacy at a time like that. You got to yell sometimes, you know? Lord . . ."

"Did you see Kilrain?"

Tom nodded. He sat with his back against the wall, the small stone wall this side of the dead horses, plucking grass. He sighed.

Chamberlain said, "How is he?"

"Well, Lawrence, he died."

"Oh," Chamberlain said. He blinked. The world came into focus. He could see leaves of the trees dark and sharp against the blue sky. He could smell the dead horses.

"He died this morning, 'fore I got there. Couple of the boys was with him. He said to tell you goodbye and that he was sorry."

Chamberlain nodded.

"It wasn't the wounds. They say his heart give out."

Chamberlain had stopped wrapping his bloody foot. Now he went on. But he could see the weary Irish face, the red-nosed leprechaun. Just one small drink, one wee pint of the cruel . . .

Tom said, "I tell you, Lawrence, I sure was fond of the man."

"Yes," Chamberlain said.

Tom said nothing more. He sat plucking grass. Chamberlain wrapped the foot. The moment was very quiet. He sat looking down at his bloody leg, feeling the gentle wind, the heat from the south, seeing Kilrain dead on a litter, no more the steady presence. Sometimes he believed in a Heaven, mostly he believed in a Heaven; there ought to be a Heaven for young soldiers, especially young soldiers, but just as surely for the old soldier; there ought to be more than just that metallic end, and then silence, then the worms, and sometimes he believed, mostly he believed, but just this moment he did not believe at all, knew Kilrain was dead and gone forever, that the grin had died and would not reappear, never, there was nothing beyond the sound of the guns but the vast dark, the huge nothing, not even silence, just an end . . .

One sharp report, one single cannon. His head turned unconsciously to listen. A long flutter; the ball passed over, exploded on the far side of the road, along the edge of the hospitals there. He saw white smoke, splintered wood. He sat up.

Another gun. One single shot. And then the long roar as of the whole vast rumbling earth beginning to open. Chamberlain twitched around to see shells beginning to come over, falling first on the left, then almost instantly on the center, then to the right, then overhead, air bursts and ground bursts and solid shot. There was a blaze in the air obliterating his sight, hot breath of death, huge noise. He was rolled over in dirt, came out on his knees, face down. Very, very close. He looked down, around, amazed. Tom was near, flat on the ground. All right, all right. He saw other troops behind boulders, molded into depressions in the earth. The world was blowing up. Had been under artillery fire before but never like this. Am I all right? Sat up to probe, found self intact. Looked out over the wall, saw no one moving anywhere. Moment ago there had been men moving all along the crest, men sitting and wandering and riding horses, artillery moving here and there, a wagon, a caisson. Now they were all gone, as men vanish from a busy street when rain comes. There was burst after burst in the dirty air, yellow lightning shattering the ground, splintering rock, ripping limbs off the great trees and sending them twisting swirling dancing along the ground, along the ridge. But no man anywhere, no man at all, as if the whole army had suddenly sunk into the earth. There was a horse moving riderless; another came out of the smoke. Blowing smoke was . . . another shell very close shook the ground, shook his vision. He hid behind the stone wall, stared very hard for a moment at a circle of greenish dried moss, the fine gray grain of the rock the most vivid thing he had ever seen, what marvelous eyesight one has now, and he thought: must tell the men to keep down, but of course that's stupid, they're down, any fool knows that. Peeked up along the rock, saw down to where shells were bursting along the road, saw cooks and bakers scrambling to escape, horses and wagons wobbling away down the road. A shell hit a caisson; it blew up in a great black tower of smoke, small black fragments whirling up into the air, fine dust sifting down everywhere, settling on the lips, into the eyes. More sound now. Chamberlain turned, saw the Union guns beginning to open up, to give it back, saw forms moving in the smoke, saw a whole line fire at once, wondered if an attack was coming, thought: how can you form to repel an attack? You can't even stand. But it went on and on, all the guns in all the world firing, and the dust drifted down and the smoke began to envelop him, and he lay finally face down against the dust, the grass, thinking, well, I'll just wait a bit and look out again, and then gradually the world softened and the sound was a great lullaby, thunderous, madly, liquidly soothing, and he fell asleep.

Slept, but did not know how long. Woke to the sound of the continuing guns. No difference. Looked out across the rock, smoke everywhere, Union guns firing, men moving among the guns, hunched, a bloody horse running eerily by, three-legged, horrible sight, running toward the road. Another horse down with no head, like a broken toy. Man nearby, lying on his back, one hand groping upward, oddly reaching for the sky. Chamberlain closed his eyes, slept again. Opened them and lost all sense of time, had been sleeping since Noah in the sound of the guns, had slept through the mud and the ooze and thousands of days since Creation, the guns going on forever, like the endless rains of dawn. The earth was actually shuddering. It was as if you were a baby and your mother was shuddering with cold. More of the shells seemed to be passing overhead. He looked: there was a rider moving along in the smoke. Unbelievable. Familiar: Hancock. Chamberlain rose for a better look. It was Hancock all right. General Hancock had mounted his horse and was riding slowly along that ripped and thundering crest, chatting through puffs of smoke and showers of dirt to the men behind the wall, the men crouched in holes. There was an orderly behind him, carrying the flag of the Corps. The two horses moved slowly, unconcernedly along, an incredible sight, a dreamlike sight. They moved on up the line, ethereal, untouched. But the shells were definitely beginning to pass overhead. The Rebs were lengthening their aim, beginning to fire high, too long. Chamberlain saw a solid shot furrow the earth, an instant hole, almost a tunnel, black, spitting, and the shot rebounded a hundred feet into the air, spinning off across the road. Another caisson went; the hospital was pooled in smoke, as in the morning mist. Chamberlain rolled over onto his back and lay for a while longer, hands clasped on his chest, gazing at the sky, trying to see the balls as they passed. He became aware for the first time of the incredible variety of sound. The great roar was composed of a thousand different rips and whispers, most incredible noise he had ever heard or imagined, like a great orchestra of death, all the sounds of myriad death: the *whicker whicker* of certain shells, the weird thin scream of others, the truly frightful sound made by one strange species that came every few moments, an indescribable keening, like old Death as a woman gone mad and a-hunting you, screaming, that would be the Whitworth, new English cannon the Rebs had. Then there were the sounds of the bursts, flat splats in the air, deeper bursts in ground, brutal smash and crack of shot into rock, shot splattering dirt and whining off, whispers of rock fragments and dirt fragments and small bits of metal and horse and man rippling the air, spraying the ground, humming the air, and the Union cannon braying away one after another, and an occasional scream, sometimes even joy, some of the cannoneers screaming with joy at hitting something as when they saw a caisson blow up across the way. They could see the explosion from here, above the smoke, but not much else, too much smoke; possibly that's why the Reb shells were going overhead. Reb artillery never very accurate. Thank the Lord. Elevation too high now. And *we* ought to conserve our long-range stuff. They'll be coming now in a few moments, once the guns stop. God knows how many of them will come this time. Right in the path, Joshuway, aren't you? Well, we ought to save our artillery then, damn it, and let them get out in the open. But they'll be coming again. Please God, let's stop 'em. I have this one small regiment . . .

He thought: must form the regiment, face the crest. Enough ammunition? Send Tom to the rear. Poor old Kilrain. We'll miss you. We're right in the path. Would not have missed this for anything, not anything in the world. Will rest now. Dreamyly.

He put his face down. The shells fell all down the line, all over the crest, down in the road and back in the woods and on the hospital and in the artillery park. Chamberlain went to sleep.

4. Armistead

. . . saw it all begin, saw the guns go off one by one, each one a split second after the last, so that there was one long continuing blossoming explosion beginning on the right, erupting down through the grove and up the ridge to the left like one gigantic fuse sputtering up the ridge. Armistead looked at his watch: 1:07. He could see shells bursting on top of the ridge, on the Union lines, saw a caisson blow up in a fireball of yellow smoke, heard wild cheering amid the great sound of the cannon, but then the smoke came boiling up the ridge and he began to lose sight. Pickett was in front of him, out in the open, waving his hat and yelling wildly. Longstreet sat on a fence rail, motionless, crouched forward. There was too much smoke to see anything at all, just Longstreet's back, black, unmoving, and Pickett turning back through the smoke with joy in his face, and then the Union artillery opened up. The first shells came down in the trees beyond them. Longstreet turned slowly and looked. Then they began coming down in the field back there, where the Division was. Armistead turned and ran back through the trees across the ridge.

The Division lay in the open fields beyond the ridge. They had been there all morning, out in the open, through the growing heat. There was no protection: knee-high grass, low stone walls, off to the left a low field of rye. The shells began to come in on them and there was nothing to do but lie flat and hold the ground. Armistead walked out into the open, saw the men lying in long clumped rows, as if plowed up out of the earth, here and there an officer standing, a color sergeant, the flags erect in the earth and limp, no wind at all, and the shells bursting in sharp puffs everywhere, all down the line. Armstead walked among them. There was nothing he could do, no order to give. He saw the first bloody dead, heard the first agony. Men were telling him angrily to get down, get down, but he went on wandering. Off in the distance he could see Garnett doing the same, on horseback. After a while it was not really so bad. The shells were not so thick. They came down, and here and there a shock and a scream, but the masses of men lay in rows in the grass, and in the distance a band was playing. Armistead walked slowly back toward the trees, hoping to find out what was going on. His chest was very tight. He looked at his watch: 1:35.

He wanted some moments to himself. The firing would stop and then they would line up for the assault. Between that time and this there ought to be a private moment. He came in under the trees and saw Longstreet writing a note, sending it with a galloping aide. There was Pickett, writing too, sitting on a camp stool lost in thought, pen to his lips and staring off into space, as if composing a poem. Armistead smiled. He was closer to the guns now and the sound of the cannonade was enormous, like a beating of great wings, and all around him the air was fluttering and leaves were falling and the ground was shaking, and there was Pickett writing a poem, face furrowed with mighty thought, old George, never much of a thinker, and all that while in the back of Armistead's mind he could see Mary at the spinet: *it may be for years, it may be forever.* He could see the lips move, see tears on all the faces, but he could not hear that sound, the sound of the cannon was too great. He moved up closer to Pickett. Abruptly, not knowing beforehand that he would do it, he plucked the small ring from his little finger. Pickett looked up; his eyes glazed with concentration, focused, blinked.

"Here, George, send her this. My compliments." He handed Pickett the ring. Pickett took it, looked at it, a sentimental man; he reached out and took Armistead's hand and pumped it wordlessly, then flung an arm wildly out toward the guns, the noise, the hill to the east.

"Oh God, Lo, isn't it something? Isn't it marvelous? How does a man find words? Tell me something to say, Lo, you're good at that. Lord, I thought we'd missed it all. But do you know, this may be the last great fight of the war? Do you realize that? Isn't that marvelous?"

There was a long series of explosions; a tree limb burst. Armistead could hardly hear. But Pickett was profoundly moved. He was one of those, like Stuart, who looked on war as God's greatest game. At this moment Armistead seemed to be looking down from a long way away, from a long, sleepy, hazy distance. George was grinning, clapping him on the arm. He said something about Sallie having the ring mounted. Armistead moved away.

He saw Longstreet sitting alone in the same place, on the same rail, drew comfort from the solid presence. Some officers had that gift. He did not. Hancock had it. Superb soldier. *It may be for years, it may be forever . . .* don't think on that. He looked at his watch: 1:47. Cannot go on much longer.

But he did not want to think about the attack right now. All the plans were laid, the thing was set, the others had planned it, Longstreet and Lee and Pickett, now he would carry it out, but for these last few moments at least, the old soldier knows enough not to think about it. Shut the mind off and think on better days, remember things to be grateful for. Perhaps, like Pickett, you should write a letter. No. Would say the wrong things.

He went back toward his men, sat with his back against a tree, facing the open. He closed his eyes for a moment and he could see her again, Mary, *it may be for years, it may be forever,* and Hancock's face in tears, may God strike me dead. He opened his eyes, looked a question at Heaven, felt himself in the grip of these great forces, powerless, sliding down the long afternoon toward the end, as if it was all arranged somewhere, nothing he could have done to avoid it, not he or any Virginian. And he had said it and meant it: "If I lift a hand against you, friend, may God strike me dead." Well, it is all in His hands. Armistead took off his black hat and ran his hands through the gray hair, his forehead wet with perspiration, the hair wet and glistening in the light.

He was a grave and courtly man, a soldier all his life. He had a martial bearing and the kind of a face on which emotion rarely showed, a calm, almost regal quality. It had hindered him in the army because men thought he was not aggressive enough, but he was a good soldier, a dependable soldier, and all his life he had felt things more deeply than anyone knew—except *her,* so very briefly, before she died, as she was dying . . .

Don't think on that. But I loved her.

And loved much else. Always loved music. And good friends, and some moments together. Had much joy in the weather. So very rarely shared. I should have shared more. The way Pickett does, the way so many do. It's a liquid thing with them; it flows. But I . . . move on impulse. I gave him the ring. Premonition? Well, many will die. I'm a bit old for war. Will do my duty. I come from a line . . . no more of that. No need of that now. An Armistead does his duty, so do we all. But I wish, I wish it was not Hancock atop that hill. I wish this was Virginia again, my own green country, my own black soil. I wish . . . the war was over.

Quieter now. The fire was definitely slackening.

2:10

He sat patiently, his back to a tree. The attack would be soon enough. When he thought of that his mind closed down like a blank gray wall, not letting him see. No point in thinking of that. He sat quietly, silently, suspended, breathing the good warm air, the smoke, the dust. Mustn't look ahead at all. One tends to look ahead with imagination. Must not look backward either. But it is so easy to see her, there at the spinet, and all of us gathered round, and all of us crying, my dear old friend . . . Hancock has no time for painting now. He was rather good at it. Always meant to ask him for one of his works. Never enough time. Wonder how it has touched him? Two years of war. Point of pride: My old friend is the best soldier they have. My old friend is up on that ridge.

Here was Garnett, dressed beautifully, new gray uniform, slender, trim, riding that great black mare with the smoky nose. Armistead stood.

Garnett touched his cap. A certain sleepiness seemed to precede the battle, a quality of haze, of unreality, of dust in the air, dust in the haze. Garnett had the eyes of a man who has just awakened.

Garnett said, "How are you, Lo?"

Armistead said, "I'm fine, Dick."

"Well, that's good." Garnett nodded, smiling faintly. They stood under the trees, waiting, not knowing what to say. The fire seemed to be slackening.

Armistead said, "How's the leg?"

"Oh, all right, thank you. Bit hard to walk. Guess I'll have to ride."

"Pickett's orders, nobody rides."

Garnett smiled.

"Dick," Armistead said, "you're not going to ride."

Garnett turned, looked away.

"You can't do that," Armistead insisted, the cold alarm

growing. "You'll stand out like . . . you'll be a perfect target."

"Well," Garnett said, grinning faintly, "well, I tell you, Lo. I can't walk."

And cannot stay behind. Honor at stake. He could not let the attack go without him; he had to prove once and for all his honor, because there was Jackson's charge, never answered, still in the air wherever Garnett moved, the word on men's lips, watching him as he went by, for Jackson was gone and Jackson was a great soldier . . . there was nothing Armistead could say. He could feel tears coming to his eyes but he could not even do that. Must not let Garnett see. There was always a chance. Perhaps the horse would be hit early. Armistead put out a hand, touched the horse, sorry to wish death on anyone, anything.

Garnett said, "Just heard a funny thing. Thought you'd appreciate it."

"Oh?" Armistead did not look him in the face. A shot took off the limb of a tree nearby, clipped it off cleanly, so that it fell all at once, making a sound like a whole tree falling. Garnett did not turn.

"We have some educated troops, you know, gentlemen privates. Well, I was riding along the line and I heard one of these fellas, ex-professor type, declaiming this poem, you know the one: 'Backward, turn backward, oh Time, in your flight, and make me a child again, just for this fight.' And then there's a pause, and a voice says, in a slow drawl, 'Yep. A *gal* child.' "

Garnett chuckled. "Harrison and I found us some Pennsylvania whisky, and experimented, and found that it goes well with Pennsylvania water. Wa'nt bad a-tall. Tried to save you some, but first thing you know . . ." He shrugged helplessly.

Their eyes never quite met, like two lights moving, never quite touching. There was an awkward silence. Garnett said, "Well, I better get back." He moved back immediately, not attempting to shake hands. "I'll see you in a little bit," he said, and galloped off along the ridge.

Armistead closed his eyes, prayed silently. God protect him. Let him have justice. Thy will be done.

Armistead opened his eyes. Had not prayed for himself. Not yet. It was all out of his hands, all of it; there was nothing he could do about anything anywhere in the whole world. Now he would move forward and lead the men up the ridge to whatever end awaited, whatever plan was foreordained, and he felt a certain mild detachment, a curious sense of dull calm, as on those long, long Sunday afternoons when you were a boy and had to stay dressed and neat and clean with nothing to do, absolutely nothing, waiting for the grownups to let you go, to give you the blessed release to run out in the open and play. So he did not even pray. Not yet. It was all in God's hands.

Pickett rode toward him, staff trailing behind. The fire was definitely slower now; the air of the woods was clearing. Pickett's face was bright red. He reined up, but was hopping around in the saddle, patting the horse, slapping his own thigh, gesturing wildly, pointing, grinning.

"Lewis, how's everything, any questions?"

Armistead shook his head.

"Good, good. As soon as the guns cease fire, we step off. Garnett and Kemper the first line, you're in the second. Route step, no halting, no stopping to fire, want to get up there as fast as you can. I'll keep toward the right flank, to cover that side. Do you need anything?"

"Nothing."

"Good, fine." Pickett nodded violently. "How are you feeling?"

"I'm fine."

"That's good. One other point. All officers are ordered to walk. No officer takes his horse. Utterly foolish." Pickett's horse, catching the General's excitement, reared and wheeled; Pickett soothed him. "So you go on foot, no exceptions."

"Yes," Armistead said. "But what about Garnett?"

"What about . . . oh." Pickett grimaced. "That leg."

"I don't think he can walk."

Pickett said slowly, "*Damn* it."

"George, order him not to make the charge."

"I can't do that."

"He's in no condition."

But Pickett shook his head. "You know I can't do that."

"A man on a horse, in front of that line. George, he'll be the only rider in a line a mile wide. They'll have every gun on that hill on him."

Pickett rubbed the back of his neck, slammed his thigh. "He can't walk at all?"

"He might get fifty yards."

"Damn," Pickett said, caught himself guiltily. Not a good time to be swearing. "But you know how he feels. It's a matter of honor." Pickett threw up his hands abruptly, helplessly.

"Order him not to go, George."

Pickett shook his head reprovingly.

Armistead said, "All right. I understand. Yes. But I think . . . I'm getting a bit old for this business."

His voice was low and Pickett did not hear it, was not even listening. Armistead rode with him back into the woods along Seminary Ridge. The woods were dark and blessedly cool. He saw Longstreet sitting on a rail fence, gazing out into the glittering fields toward the enemy line. Pickett rode toward him and Longstreet turned slowly, swiveling his head, stared, said nothing. Pickett asked him about the guns. Longstreet did not seem to hear. His face was dark and still; he looked wordlessly at Pickett, then at Armistead, then turned back to the light. Pickett backed off. There was a savagery in Longstreet they all knew well. It showed rarely but it was always there and it was an impressive thing. Suddenly, in the dark grove, for no reason at all, Armistead looked at the dark face, the broad back, felt a bolt of almost stunning affection. It embarrassed him. But he thought: Before we go, I ought to say something.

Longstreet had moved suddenly, turning away from the rail. Armistead saw Pickett running up through the trees, a note in his hand, his face flushed. Longstreet stopped, turned to look at him, turned slowly, like an old man, looked at him with a strange face, a look tight and old that Armistead had never seen. Pickett was saying, "Alexander says if we're going at all, now's the time."

Longstreet stopped still in the dark of the woods. The huge glare behind him made it difficult to see. Armistead moved that way, feeling his heart roll over and thump once. Pickett said, pointing, "Alexander says we've silenced some Yankee artillery. They're withdrawing from the cemetery. What do you say, sir? Do we go in now?"

And Longstreet said nothing, staring at him, staring, and Armistead felt an eerie turning, like a sickness, watching Longstreet's face, and then he saw that Longstreet was crying. He moved closer. The General was crying. Something he never saw or ever expected to see, and the tears came to Armistead's eyes as he watched, saw Pickett beginning to lift his hands, holding out the note, asking again, and then Longstreet took a deep breath, his shoulders lifted, and then he nodded, dropping his head, taking his eyes away from Pickett's face, and in the same motion turned away, and Pickett let out a whoop and clenched a fist and shook it. Then he pulled a letter from his pocket and wrote something on it and handed it to Longstreet and Longstreet nodded again, and then Pickett was coming this way, face alight, look on his face of pure joy. And tears too, eyes flashing and watery, but with joy, with joy. He said something about being chosen for glory, for the glory of Virginia. He said, "Gentlemen, form your brigades."

Armistead moved out, called the brigade to its feet. He felt curiously heavy, slow, very tired, oddly sleepy. The heat was stuffy; one had trouble breathing.

The brigade dressed in a line. The fire had slackened all down the line; now for the first time there were long seconds of silence, long moments of stillness, and you could hear again the voices of the men, the movements of feet in grass and the clink of sabers, muskets, and that band was still piping, a polka this time, tinny and bumpy, joyous, out of tune. The men dressed right, line after line. Armistead moved silently back and forth. Down to the left he saw Garnett still on the horse. A mounted man in front of that line would not live five minutes. Every rifle on the crest would be aiming for him.

The orders came, bawled by a bull sergeant. The line began to move forward into the woods, forward toward the great yellow light of the open fields on the other side. They moved through the woods in good order, past the silent guns. Almost all the guns were quiet now. Armistead thought: Give the Yankees time to get set. Give Win Hancock time to get set. Move up reinforcements to the weak spots. Win, I'm sorry. Remember the old vow: May God strike me dead. And so the words came. I wish I could call them back. But Win understands. I have to come now. All in God's hands. Father, into your hands . . .

To the left of the line a rabbit broke from heavy brush, darted frantically out into the tall grass. A soldier said, close by, "That's right, ol' hare, you run, you run. If I'se an ol' hare, I'd run too."

A murmur, a laugh. They came out of the woods into the open ground.

The ground fell away from the woods into a shallow dip.

They were out of sight of the Union line. To the left there was a finger of woods between them and Pettigrew's men. They would not see Pettigrew until they had moved out a way. The day was lovely and hot and still, not a bird anywhere. Armistead searched the sky. Marvelous day, but very hot. He blinked. Would love to swim now. Cool clear water, lake water, cool and dark at the bottom, out of the light.

The Division was forming. Garnett was in front, Kemper to the right; Armistead's line lay across the rear. It was a matchless sight, the Division drawn up as if for review. He looked down the line at the rows of guns, the soft blue flags of Virginia; he began to look at the faces, the tight faces, the eyes wide and dark and open, and he could hear more bands striking up far off to the right. No hurry now, a stillness everywhere, that same dusty, sleepy pause, the men not talking, no guns firing. Armistead moved forward through the ranks, saw Garnett on the horse, went over to say goodbye. Garnett no longer looked well; his coat was buttoned at the throat. Armistead said, "Dick, for God's sake and mine, get down off the horse."

Garnett said, "I'll see you at the top, Lo."

He put out his hand. Armistead took it.

Armistead said, "My old friend."

It was the first time in Armistead's life he had ever really known a man would die. Always before there was at least a chance, but here no chance at all, and now the man was his oldest friend.

Armistead said, "I ought to ride too."

Garnett said, "Against orders."

Armistead looked down the long line. "Have you ever seen anything so beautiful?"

Garnett smiled.

Armistead said, "They never looked better, on any parade ground."

"They never did."

Armistead heard once more that sweet female voice, unbearable beauty of the unbearable past: *it may be for years, it may be forever. Then why art thou silent* . . . He still held Garnett's hand. He squeezed once more. Nothing more to say now. Careful now. He let the hand go.

He said, "Goodbye, Dick. God bless you."

Garnett nodded.

Armistead turned away, walked back to his brigade. Now for the first time, at just the wrong time, the acute depression hit him a blow to the brain. Out of the sleepiness the face of despair. He remembered Longstreet's tears. He thought: *a desperate thing.* But he formed the brigade. Out front, George Pickett had ridden out before the whole Division, was making a speech, but he was too far away and none of the men could hear. Then Pickett raised his sword. The order came down the line. Armistead, his voice never strong, bawled hoarsely, with all his force, "All right now, boys, for your wives, your sweethearts, for Virginia! At route step, forward, *ho!*"

He drew his sword, pointed it toward the ridge.

The brigade began to move.

He heard a chattering begin in the ranks. Someone seemed to be trying to tell a story. A man said, "Save your breath, boy." They moved in the tall grass, Garnett's whole line in front of them. The grass was trampled now, here and there a part in the line as men stepped aside to avoid a dead body, lost the day before. Armistead could still see nothing, nothing but the backs of the troops before him. He saw one man falter, looking to the right, gray-faced, to the sergeant who was watching him, had evidently been warned against him, now lifted a rifle and pointed it that way and the man got back into line.

The Northern artillery opened up, as if it had been asleep, or pulled back to lure them in. Massive wave of fire rolled over from the left. Pettigrew was getting it, then on the right batteries on the Rocky Hill were firing on Kemper. Garnett not yet really touched. Nothing much coming this way. But we didn't drive off any Yankee guns. Win's doing. He made them cease fire, knowing soon we'd be in the open. Guns to the left and right, nothing much in the center. Garnett's doing well.

He began to see. They were coming out into the open, up to where the ground dipped toward the Emmitsburg Road. Now to the left he could see the great mass of Pettigrew's Division, with Trimble coming up behind him, advancing in superb order, line after line, a stunning sight, red battle flags, row on row. Could not see Pettigrew, nor Trimble. The line must be a mile long. A mile of men, armed and coming, the earth shuddering with their movement, with the sound of the guns. A shell exploded in Garnett's line, another; gaps began to appear. Armistead heard the sergeants' hoarse "Close it up, close it up," and behind him he heard his own men coming and a voice saying calmly, cheerily, "Steady, boys, steady, there now, you can see the enemy, now you aint blind any more, now you know exactly where's to go, aint that fine?" A voice said hollowly, "That's just fine."

But the artillery sound was blossoming. A whole new set of batteries opened up; he could see smoke rolling across the top of the hill, and no counterfire from behind, no Southern batteries. God, he thought, they're out of ammunition. But no, of course not; they just don't like firing over our heads. And even as he thought of that he saw a battery moving out of the woods to his left, being rushed up to support the line. And then the first shell struck near him, percussion, killing a mass of men to his right rear, his own men, and from then on the shells came down increasingly, as the first fat drops of an advancing storm, but it was not truly bad. Close it up, close it up. Gaps in front, the newly dead, piles of red meat. One man down holding his stomach, blood pouring out of him like a butchered pig, young face, only a boy, the man bending over him trying to help, a sergeant screaming, "Damn it, I said close it up."

Kemper's Brigade, ahead and to the right, was getting it. The batteries on the Rocky Hill were enfilading him, shooting right down his line, sometimes with solid shot, and you could see the damn black balls bouncing along like bowling balls, and here and there, in the air, tumbling over and over like a blood-spouting cartwheel, a piece of a man.

Armistead turned to look back. Solid line behind him, God bless them, coming on. Not so bad, now, is it? We'll do it, with God's help. Coming, they are, to a man. All good men here. He turned back to the front. Garnett's men were nearing the road. He could see old Dick, still there, on the great black horse. And then the first storm of musketry: the line of skirmishers. He winced. Could not see, but knew. Long line of men in blue, lined, waiting, their sights set, waiting, and now the first line of gray is near, clear, nearer, unmissable, an officer screams, if they're soldiers at all they cannot miss, and they're Hancock's men. Armistead saw a visible waver pass through the ranks in front of him. Close it up, close it up. The line seemed to have drifted slightly to the left. Heavy roll of musket fire now. The march slowing. He saw Garnett move down, thought for a moment, but no, he was moving down into that one swale, the protected area Pickett had spoken of. Armistead halted the men. Stood incredibly still in the open field with the artillery coming down like hail, great bloody hail. To the left, two hundred yards away, Pettigrew's men were slowing. Some of the men in front had stopped to fire. No point in that, too soon, too soon. Pickett's left oblique began. The whole line shifted left, moving to join with Pettigrew's flank, to close the gap. It was beautifully done, superbly done, under fire, in the face of the enemy. Armistead felt enormous pride, his chest filled and stuffed with a furious love. He peered left, could not see Trimble. But they were closing in, the great mass converging.

Now he moved up and he could see the clump of trees, the one tree like an umbrella, Lee's objective, and then it was gone in smoke.

Garnett's boys had reached the road. They were slowing, taking down rails. Musket fire was beginning to reach them. The great noise increased, beating of wings in the air. More dead men: a long neat line of dead, like a shattered fence. And now the canister, *oh God,* he shuddered, millions of metal balls whirring through the air like startled quail, murderous quail, and now for the first time there was screaming, very bad sounds to hear. He began to move past wounded struggling to the rear, men falling out to help, heard the sergeants ordering the men back into line, saw gray faces as he passed, eyes sick with fear, But the line moved on. Dress it up, close it up. He looked back for a moment and walked backward up the long rise, looking backward at his line, coming steadily, slowly, heads down as if into the wind, then he turned back to face the front.

To the right the line was breaking. He saw the line falter, the men beginning to clump together. Massed fire from there. In the smoke he could see a blue line. Kemper's boys were shifting this way, slowing. Armistead was closing in. He saw a horse coming down through the smoke: Kemper. Riding. Because Garnett rode. Still alive, even on the horse. But there was blood on his shoulder, blood on his face, his arm hung limp, he had no sword. He rode to Armistead, face streaked and gray, screaming something Armistead could not hear, then came up closer and turned, waving the bloody arm.

"Got to come up, come up, help me, in God's name. They're flanking me, they're coming down on the right and firing right into us, the line's breaking, we've got to have help."

Armistead yelled encouragement; Kemper tried to explain. They could not hear each other. A shell blew very close, on the far side of the horse, and Armistead, partially shielded, saw black fragments rush by, saw Kemper nearly fall. He grabbed Kemper's hand, screaming, "I'll double-time." Kemper said, "Come quick, come quick, for God's sake," and reined the horse up and turned back to the right. And beyond him Armistead saw a long blue line, Union boys out in the open, kneeling and firing from the right, and beyond that violent light of rows of cannon, and another flight of canister passed over. Kemper's men had stopped to fire, were drifting left. Too much smoke to see. Armistead turned, called his aides, took off the old black felt and put it on the tip of his sword and raised it high in the air. He called for double-time, double-time; the cry went down the line. The men began to run. He saw the line waver, ragged now, long legs beginning to eat up the ground, shorter legs falling behind, gaps appearing, men actually seeming to disappear, just to vanish out of the line, leaving a stunned vacancy, and the line slowly closing again, close it up, close it up, beginning to ripple and fold but still a line, still moving forward in the smoke and the beating noise.

They came to the road. It was sunken into the field, choked like the bed of a stream with mounded men. Armistead jumped down, saw a boy in front of him, kneeling, crying, a row of men crouched under the far bank, an officer yelling, pounding with the flat of his sword. There was a house to the right, smoke pouring from the roof, a great clog of men jammed behind the house, but men were moving across the road and up toward the ridge. There was a boy on his knees on the road edge, staring upward toward the ridge, unmoving. Armistead touched him on the shoulder, said, "Come on, boy, come on." The boy looked up with sick eyes, eyes soft and black like pieces of coal. Armistead said, "Come on, boy. What will you think of yourself tomorrow?"

The boy did not move. Armistead told an officer nearby; "Move these people out." He climbed up the roadbank, over the gray rails on the far side, between two dead bodies, one a sergeant, face vaguely familiar, eyes open, very blue. Armistead stood high, trying to see.

Kemper's men had come apart, drifting left. There was a mass ahead but it did not seem to be moving. Up there the wall was a terrible thing, flame and smoke. He had to squint to look at it, kept his head down, looked left, saw Pettigrew's men still moving, but the neat lines were gone, growing confusion, the flags dropping, no Rebel yell now, no more screams of victory, the men falling here and there like trees before an invisible ax you could see them go one by one and in clumps, suddenly, in among the columns of smoke from the shell. Far to the left he saw: Pettigrew's men were running. He saw red flags streaming back to the rear. One of Pettigrew's brigades had broken on the far left. Armistead raised his sword, saw that the sword had gone through the hat and the hat was now down near his hand. He put the hat up again, the sword point on a new place, started screaming, follow me, follow me, and began the long last walk toward the ridge. No need for hurry now, too tired to run, expecting to be hit at any moment. Over on the right no horse. Kemper was down, impossible to live up there. Armistead moved on, expecting to die, but was not hit. He moved closer to the wall up there, past mounds of bodies, no line any more, just men moving forward at different speeds, stopping to fire, stopping to die, drifting back like leaves blown from the fire ahead. Armistead thought: we won't make it. He lifted the sword again, screaming, and moved on, closer, closer, but it was all coming apart; the whole world was dying. Armistead felt a blow in the thigh, stopped, looked down at blood on his right leg. But no pain. He could walk. He moved on. There was a horse coming down the ridge: great black horse with blood all over the chest, blood streaming through bubbly holes, blood on the saddle, dying eyes, smoke-gray at the muzzle: Garnett's horse.

Armistead held to watch the horse go by, tried to touch it. He looked for Garnett ahead; he might be afoot, might still be alive. But vision was mistier. Much, much smoke. Closer now. He could see separate heads; he could see men firing over the wall. The charge had come to a halt; the attack had stopped. The men ahead were kneeling to fire at the blue men on the far side of the wall, firing at the gunners of the terrible cannon. Canister came down in floods, wiping bloody holes. A few flags tilted forward, but there was no motion; the men had stalled, unable to go on, still thirty yards from the wall and no visible halt, unable to advance, unwilling to run, a deadly paralysis.

Armistead stopped, looked. Pettigrew's men were coming up on the left: not many, not enough. Here he had a few hundred. To the right Kemper's brigade had broken, but some of the men still fired. Armistead paused for one long second. It's impossible now, cannot be done; we have failed and it's all done, all those boys are dead, it's all done, and then he began to move forward automatically, instinctively, raising the black hat on the sword again, beginning to scream, "Virginians! With me! With me!" and he moved forward the last yards toward the wall, drawn by the pluck of that great force from within, for home, for country, and now the ground went by slowly, inexorably, like a great slow river, and the moment went by black and slow, close to the wall, closer, walking now on the backs of dead men, troops around beginning to move, yelling at last the wild Rebel yell, and the blue troops began to break from the fence. Armistead came up to the stone wall, and the blue boys were falling back. He felt a moment of incredible joy. A hot slap of air brushed his face, but he was not hit; to the right a great blast of canister and all the troops to his right were down, but then there was another rush, and Armistead leaped to the top of the wall, balanced high on the stones, seeing the blue troops running up the slope into the guns, and then he came down on the other side, had done it, had gotten inside the wall, and men moved in around him, screaming. And then he was hit, finally, in the side, doubling him. No pain at all, merely a nuisance. He moved toward a cannon the boys had just taken. Some blue troops had stopped near the trees above and were kneeling and firing; he saw the rifles aimed at him. Too weary now. He had made it all this way; this way was enough. He put an arm on the cannon to steady himself. But now there was a rush from the right. Blue troops were closing in. Armistead's vision blurred; the world turned soft and still. He saw again: a bloody tangle, men fighting hand to hand. An officer was riding toward him; there was a violent blow. He saw the sky, swirling round and round, thank God no pain. A sense of vast release, of great peace. I came all the way up, I came over the wall . . .

He sat against something. The fight went on. He looked down at his chest, saw the blood. Tried to breathe, experimentally, but now he could feel the end coming, now for the first time he sensed the sliding toward the dark, a weakening, a closing, all things ending now slowly and steadily and peacefully. He closed his eyes, opened them. A voice said, "I was riding toward you, sir, trying to knock you down. You didn't have a chance."

He looked up: a Union officer. I am not captured, I am dying. He tried to see: help me, help me. He was lifted slightly.

Everywhere the dead. All his boys. Blue soldiers stood around him. Down the hill he could see the gray boys moving back, a few flags fluttering. He closed his eyes on the sight, sank down in the dark, ready for death, knew it was coming, but it did not come. Not quite yet. Death comes at its own speed. He looked into the blue sky, at the shattered trees. *It may be for years, it may be forever* . . . The officer was speaking. Armistead said, "Is General Hancock . . . would like to see General Hancock."

A man said, "I'm sorry, sir. General Hancock has been hit."

"No," Armistead said. He closed his eyes. Not both of us. Not all of us. Sent to Mira Hancock, to be opened in the event of my death. But not both of us, please dear God . . .

He opened his eyes. Closer now. The long slow fall begins.

"Will you tell General Hancock . . . Can you hear me, son?"

"I can hear you, sir."

"Will you tell General Hancock, please, that General Armistead sends his regrets. Will you tell him . . . how very sorry I am . . ."

The energy failed. He felt himself flicker. But it was a long slow falling, very quiet, very peaceful, rather still, but always the motion, the darkness closing in, and so he fell out of the light and away, far away, and was gone.

---

5. Longstreet

Longstreet sat on a rail fence, hugging his chest with both arms. He suspended thinking; his mind was a bloody vacancy, like a room in which there has been a butchering. He tried once formally to pray, but there was no one there and no words came, and over and over he said to himself, Heavenly Father, Heavenly Father. He watched the battle dissolve to nightmare: the neat military lines beginning to come apart as they crossed the road and no order beyond that but black struggling clots and a few flags in the smoke, tilting like sails above a white sea, going down one by one. A shell burst near Longstreet and he felt the hot brutal breath, and then the sounds of battle were softer, the smoke began to blanket the field. But there were still a few flags moving toward the top of the hill. Longstreet put glasses to his eyes, saw ghost figures stumbling in white smoke, yellow blaze of cannon, black flakes of men spattering upward into a white sky, and then the smoke was too thick and he could not see anything and it was like going blind. A paralysis came over him. He sat staring off into the white sea where the guns still flashed and boomed softly, at a great distance, until he saw the first men beginning to come back out of the smoke. They came slowly up the long green slope, a ragged crowd of men. No one was running. They were moving with slow set stubborn unstoppable looks on their faces, eyes down, guns dragging the ground, and they were moving slowly but steadily, even though the Union guns had elevated and shells were still falling on them as they came back up the field. The smoke parted for a vision: the green field dirtied a vast mile with lumped bodies, white and red, and far across the field the whole army falling back in a speckled flood across the road to the safety of the woods, and there at the top of the hill one flag erect near the center of the Union line. Then that flag was down in the smoke, and Longstreet could no longer see, and the retreat began to flood by him.

The men parted as they passed him, not looking at him. He sat on an island in the stream of retreating men. He made no attempt to stop them. A man rode up on a black horse, a frantic man with blood on his face: Harry Bright, Pickett's staff. He was screaming. Longstreet stared at him. The man went on screaming. Longstreet made out: Pickett was asking for support. Longstreet shook his head, wordlessly, pointed down at the field. Bright did not yet understand. Longstreet said patiently, "Nine brigades went in. That's all we have." There was nothing to send now, no further help to give, and even if Lee on the other side would send support now it would be too late. Longstreet hugged his chest. He got down off the fence. A black horse rode up out of the smoke: familiar spot on a smoky forehead, blood bubbling from a foaming chest: Garnett's mount. Longstreet nodded. He told Bright to instruct Pickett to fall back. He sent word for a battery to move down the slope in front of him, to fire uphill and protect Pickett as he retreated.

The wind had changed. The smoke was blowing back across the field against his face. The guns were easing off. The men streamed by: nightmare army, faces gray and cold, sick. Longstreet felt a cold wind blowing in his brain. He stood up. He had sat long enough. He looked up to see Fremantle. A moment ago the man had been cheering wildly, not understanding what was happening. Now he was holding out a silver flask. Longstreet shook his head. It was all done. Along with all the horror of loss, and the weariness, and all the sick helpless rage, there was coming now a monstrous disgust. He was through. They had all died for nothing and he had sent them. He thought: a man is asked to bear too much. And he refused. He began slowly to walk forward. He was all done. He would find a gun somewhere and take a walk forward. He walked down the long slope in front of him toward that one battery that was still firing toward the blue line. He saw a rifle by a dead man, the man missing a leg and the leg nearby, bent and chewed at the knee, and the rifle clean and new and cold. He bent down to pick it up, and when he looked up he saw Lee.

The old man was riding the gray horse across the open ground in front of the trees. He had taken his hat off and the white hair and the unmistakable white head were visible from a long way off. He was walking the horse slowly along the ground among the first rows of dead where the cannon had begun to take them as they stepped out of the trees, and the retreating men were slowed at the sight of him. Longstreet stopped. The old man reined up and stood for a moment immobile, head turned eastward toward the enemy, the gray hat on the horn of the saddle. He sat there motionless as a statue and the men coming back began to turn toward him. He sat looking down, talking to them. Longstreet stood watching him. He knew that he would never forgive the old man, never. He stood paralyzed holding the rifle and tears were running down his cheeks. The old man saw him and began riding toward him. Longstreet could hear him: "It is all my fault, it is all my fault," and men were already arguing with him and shaking their heads in rage and shame, but Lee said, "We shall rest and try it again another day. Now you must show good order. Never let them see you run."

There were men all around him, some of them crying. A tall man in a gray beard was pleading with Lee to let them attack again. A bony boy in a ripped and bloody shirt had hold of the halter of his horse and was insisting that the General move to the rear. Lee said again, "It is all my fault," but they were shaking their heads. Lee saw Longstreet.

Longstreet waited, the rifle in his hand. Lee rode slowly forward. A crowd of men was gathering now, a hundred or more. The stream to the rear had slowed. Now it was quieter and the nearby cannon were no longer firing and Lee came forward out of the smoke and the nightmare. His face was hard and red, his eyes bright and hot; he had a stiff, set look to him and both hands held hard to the saddle horn and when he looked at Longstreet his eyes had nothing in them. The old man stopped the horse and pointed east. He said in a soft, feathery voice, "I think they are forming over there, General. I think they may attack."

Longstreet nodded. The old man's voice was very soft; Longstreet could hardly hear. Lee looked down on him from a long way away. Longstreet nodded again. There was motion in front of him and suddenly he saw George Pickett, bloodstained. His hat was gone; his hair streamed like a blasted flower. His face was pale; he moved his head like a man who has heard too loud a sound. He rode slowly forward. Lee turned to meet him. Longstreet was vaguely amazed that Pickett was still alive. He heard Pickett say something to Lee. George turned and pointed back down the hill. His face was oddly wrinkled.

Lee raised a hand. "General Pickett, I want you to reform your Division in the rear of this hill."

Pickett's eyes lighted as if a sudden pain had shot through him. He started to cry. Lee said again with absolute calm, "General, you must look to your Division."

Pickett said tearfully, voice of a bewildered angry boy, "General Lee, I have no Division." He pointed back down the hill, jabbing at the blowing smoke, the valley of wrecked men, turned and shuddered, waving, then saying, "Sir? What about my men?" as if even now there was still something Lee could do to fix it. "What about my men? Armistead is gone. Garnett is gone. Kemper is gone. All my colonels are gone. General, *every one.* Most of my men are gone. Good God, sir, what about my men?"

Longstreet turned away. Enough of this. He looked for his horse, beckoned. The groom came up. Longstreet could look down across the way and see blue skirmishers forming across his front. The land sloped to where the one battery was still firing uphill into the smoke. Longstreet nodded. I'm coming. He felt a tug at his leg, looked down: Sorrel. Let me go, Major. The staff was around him, someone had the reins of the horse. Longstreet felt the gathering of the last great rage. He looked down slowly and pulled at the reins slowly and said carefully, "Major, you better let this damned horse go."

And then he pointed.

"They're coming, do you see? I'm going to meet them. I want you to put fire down on them and form to hold right here. I'm going down to meet them."

He rode off down the hill. He moved very quickly and the horse spurred and it was magnificent to feel the clean air blow across your face, and he was aware suddenly of the cold tears blurring his eyes and tried to wipe them away, Old Hero shying among all the dead bodies. He leaped a fence and became aware of a horse following and swung and saw the face of Goree, the frail Texan trailing him like the wind. Ahead of him the guns were firing into a line of blue soldiers and Longstreet spurred that way and Goree pulled alongside, screaming, "What are your orders, General? Where you want me to go?"

A shell blew up in front of him. He swerved to the right. Goree was down and Longstreet reined up. The bony man was scrambling, trying to get to his feet. Rifle fire was beginning to pluck at the air around them. Longstreet saw some of the staff riding toward him, trying to catch up. He rode to Goree and looked down but he couldn't say anything more, no words would come, and he couldn't even stop the damn tears, and Goree's eyes looking up, filled with pain and sorrow and pity, was another thing he would remember as long as he lived, and he closed his eyes.

The staff was around him, looking at him with wild eyes. Someone again had the bridle of his horse. Bullets still plucked the air: song of the dark guitar. He wanted to sleep. Someone was yelling, "Got to pull back," and he shook his head violently, clearing it, and turned back to the guns, letting the mind begin to function. "Place the guns," he bawled, "bring down some guns." He began directing fire. He took another shell burst close by and again the great drone filled his ears and after that came a cottony murmury rush, like a waterfall, and he moved in a black dream, directing the fire, waiting for them to come, trying to see through the smoke where the shells were falling. But the firing began to stop. The storm was ending. He looked out through the smoke and saw no more blue troops; they had pulled back. He thought, to God: if there is any mercy in you at all you will finish it now.

But the blue troops pulled back, and there was no attack.

After a while Longstreet sat on a fence. He noticed the rifle still in his hand. He had never used it. Carefully, gently, he placed it on the ground. He stared at it for a while. Then he began to feel nothing at all. He saw the dirt-streaked face of T. J. Goree, watching him.

"How are you?" Longstreet said.

"Tolerable."

Longstreet pointed uphill. "They aren't coming."

Goree shook his head.

"Too bad," Longstreet said.

"Yes, sir."

"Too bad," Longstreet said again.

"Yes, sir. We got plenty canister left. If they hit us now we could sure make it hot for them."

Longstreet nodded. After a moment Goree said, "General, I tell you plain. There are times when you worry me."

"Well," Longstreet said.

"It's no good trying to get yourself killed, General. The Lord will come for you in His own time."

Longstreet leaned back against a fencepost and stared up into the sky. For a moment he saw nothing but the clean and wondrous sky. He sat for a moment, coming back to himself. He thought of Lee as he had looked riding that hill, his hat off so that the retreating men could see him and recognize him. When they saw him they actually stopped running. From Death itself.

It was darker now. Late afternoon. If Meade was coming he would have to come soon. But there was no sign of it. A few guns were still firing a long way off; heartbroken men would not let it end. But the fire was dying; the guns ended like sparks. Suddenly it was still, enormously still, a long pause in the air, a waiting, a fall. And then there was a different silence. Men began to turn to look out across the smoldering field. The wind had died; there was no motion anywhere but the slow smoke drifting and far off one tiny flame of a burning tree. The men stood immobile across the field. The knowledge began to pass among them, passing without words, that it was over. The sun was already beginning to set beyond new black clouds which were rising in the west, and men came out into the open to watch the last sunlight flame across the fields. The sun died gold and red, and the final light across the smoke was red, and then the slow darkness came out of the trees and flowed up the field to the stone wall, moving along above the dead and the dying like the shadowing wing of an enormous bird, but still far off beyond the cemtery there was golden light in the trees on the hill, a golden glow over the rocks and the men in the last high places, and then it was done, and the field was gray.

Longstreet sat looking out across the ground to the green rise of the Union line and he saw a blue officer come riding along the crest surrounded by flags and a cloud of men, and he saw troops rising to greet him.

"They're cheering," Goree said bitterly, but Longstreet could not hear. He saw a man raise a captured battle flag, blue flag of Virginia, and he turned from the sight. He was done. Sorrel was by his side, asking for orders. Longstreet shook his head. He would go somewhere now and sleep. He thought: couldn't even quit. Even that is not to be allowed. He mounted the black horse and rode back toward the camp and the evening.

With the evening came a new stillness. There were no guns, no music. Men sat alone under ripped branchless trees. A great black wall of cloud was gathering in the west, and as the evening advanced and the sky grew darker they could begin to see the lightning although they could not yet hear the thunder. Longstreet functioned mechanically, placing his troops in a defensive line. Then he sat alone by the fire drinking coffee. Sorrel brought the first figures from Pickett's command.

Armistead and Garnett were dead; Kemper was dying. Of the thirteen colonels in Pickett's Division seven were dead and six were wounded. Longstreet did not look at the rest. He held up a hand and Sorrel went away.

But the facts stayed with him. The facts rose up like shattered fenceposts in the mist. The army would not recover from this day. He was a professional and he knew that as a good doctor knows it, bending down for perhaps the last time over a doomed beloved patient. Longstreet did not know what he would do now. He looked out at the burial parties and the lights beginning to come on across the field like clusters of carrion fireflies. All that was left now was more dying. It was final defeat. They had all died and it had accomplished nothing, the wall was unbroken, the blue line was sound. He shook his head suddenly, violently, and remembered the old man again, coming bareheaded along the hill, stemming the retreat.

After a while Lee came. Longstreet did not want to see him. But the old man came in a cluster of men, outlined under that dark and ominous sky, the lightning blazing beyond his head. Men were again holding the bridle of the horse, talking to him, pleading; there was something oddly biblical about it, and yet even here in the dusk of defeat there was something else in the air around him; the man brought strength with his presence: doomed and defeated, he brought nonetheless a certain majesty. And Longstreet, knowing that he would never quite forgive him, stood to meet him.

Lee dismounted. Longstreet looked once into his face and then dropped his eyes. The face was set and cold, stonelike. Men were speaking. Lee said, "I would like a few moments alone with General Longstreet." The men withdrew. Lee sat in a camp chair near the fire and Longstreet sat and they were alone together. Lee did not speak. Longstreet sat staring at the ground, into the firelight. Lightning flared; a cool wind was blowing. After a while Lee said, "We will withdraw tonight."

His voice was husky and raw, as if he had been shouting. Longstreet did not answer. Lee said, "We can withdraw under cover of the weather. If we can reach the river, there will be no more danger."

Longstreet sat waiting, his mind vacant and cold. Gradually he realized that the old man was expecting advice, an opinion. But he said nothing. Then he looked up. The old man had his hand over his eyes. He looked vaguely different. Longstreet felt a chill. The old man said slowly, "Peter, I'm going to need your help."

He kept his hand over his eyes, shading himself as if from bright sunlight. Longstreet saw him take a deep breath and let it go. Then he realized that Lee had called him by his nickname. Lee said, "I'm really very tired."

Longstreet said quickly, "What can I do?"

Lee shook his head. Longstreet had never seen the old man lose control. He had not lost it now, but he sat there with his hand over his eyes and Longstreet felt shut away from his mind and in that same moment felt a shudder of enormous pity. He said, "General?"

Lee nodded. He dropped the hand and glanced up once quickly at Longstreet, eyes bright and black and burning. He shook his head again. He raised both palms, a gesture almost of surrender, palms facing Longstreet, tried to say something, shook his head for the last time. Longstreet said, "I will take care of it, General. We'll pull out tonight."

"I thought . . ." Lee said huskily.

Longstreet said, "Never mind."

"Well," Lee said. He took a long deep breath, faced the firelight. "Well, now we must withdraw."

"Yes."

They sat for a while in silence. Lee recovered. He crossed his legs and sat looking into the fire and the strength came back, the face smoothed calm again and grave, the eyes silent and dark. He said, "We must look to our own deportment. The spirit of the Army is still very good."

Longstreet nodded.

"We will do better another time."

Longstreet shook his head instinctively. He said, "I don't think so."

Lee looked up. The eyes were clearer now. The moment of weakness had come and passed. What was left was a permanent weariness. A voice in Longstreet said: let the old man alone. But there had been too much death; it was time for reality. He said slowly, "I don't think we can win it now."

After a moment Lee nodded, as if it were not really important. He said, "Perhaps."

"I don't think—" Longstreet raised his hands—"I don't know if I can go on leading them. To die. For nothing."

Lee nodded. He sat for a long while with his hands folded in his lap, staring at the fire, and the firelight on his face was soft and warm. Then he said slowly, "They do not die for us. Not for us. That at least is a blessing." He spoke staring at the fire. "Each man has his own reason to die. But if they go on, I will go on." He paused. "It is only another defeat." He looked up at Longstreet, lifted his hands, palms out, folded them softly, slowly. "If the war goes on—and it will, it will—what else can we do but go on? It is the same question forever, what else can we do? If they fight, we will fight with them. And does it matter after all who wins? Was that ever really the question? Will God ask that question, in the end?" He put his hands on his thighs, started painfully to rise.

He got to his feet, laboring. Longstreet reached forward instinctively to help him. Lee said, embarrassed, "Thank you," and then where Longstreet held his arm he reached up and covered Longstreet's hand. He looked into Longstreet's eyes. Then he said, "You were right. And I was wrong. And now you must help me see what must be done. Help us to *see.* I become . . . very tired."

"Yes," Longstreet said.

They stood a moment longer in the growing dark. The first wind of the coming storm had begun to break over the hills and the trees, cold and heavy and smelling of rain. Lee said, "I lectured you yesterday, on war."

Longstreet nodded. His mind was too full to think.

"I was trying to warn you. But . . . you have no Cause. You and I, we have no Cause. We have only the army. But if a soldier fights only for soldiers, he cannot ever win. It is only the soldiers who die."

Lee mounted the gray horse. Longstreet watched the old man clear his face and stiffen his back and place the hat carefully, formally on his head. Then he rode off into the dark. Longstreet stood watching him out of sight. Then he turned and went out into the field to say goodbye, and when that was done he gave the order to retreat.

---

6. Chamberlain

In the evening he left the Regiment and went off by himself to be alone while the night came over the field. He moved out across the blasted stone wall and down the long littered slope until he found a bare rock where he could sit and look out across the battlefield at dusk. It was like the gray floor of hell. Parties moved with yellow lights through blowing smoke under a low gray sky, moving from black lump to black lump while papers fluttered and blew and fragments of cloth and cartridge and canteen tumbled and floated across the gray and steaming ground. He remembered with awe the clean green fields of morning, the splendid yellow wheat. This was another world. His own mind was blasted and clean, windblown; he was still slightly in shock from the bombardment and he sat not thinking of anything but watching the last light of the enormous day, treasuring the last gray moment. He knew he had been present at one of the great moments in history. He had seen them come out of the trees and begin the march up the slope and when he closed his eyes he could still see them coming. It was a sight few men were privileged to see and many who had seen it best had not lived through it. He knew that he would carry it with him as long as he lived, and he could see himself as an old man trying to describe it to his grandchildren, the way the men had looked as they came out into the open and formed for the assault, the way they stood there shining and immobile, all the flags high and tilting and glittering in the sun, and then the way they all kicked to motion, suddenly, all beginning to move at once, too far away for the separate feet to be visible so that there seemed to be a silvery rippling all down the line, and that was the moment when he first felt the real fear of them coming: when he saw them begin to move.

Chamberlain closed his eyes and saw it again. It was the most beautiful thing he had ever seen. No book or music would have that beauty. He did not understand it: a mile of men flowing slowly, steadily, inevitably up the long green ground, dying all the while, coming to kill you, and the shell bursts appearing above them like instant white flowers, and the flags all tipping and fluttering, and dimly you could hear the music and the drums, and then you could hear the officers screaming, and yet even above your own fear came the sensation of unspeakable beauty. He shook his head, opened his eyes. Professor's mind. But he thought of Aristotle: pity and terror. So this is tragedy. Yes. He nodded. In the presence of real tragedy you feel neither pain nor joy nor hatred, only a sense of enormous space and time suspended, the great doors open to black eternity, the rising across the terrible field of that last enormous, unanswerable question.

It was dark around him. There was one small gray area of the sky still aglow in the west; the rest was blackness, and flashes of lightning. At that moment a fine rain began to fall and he heard it come toward him, seeking him in a light patter up the slope. He had dust all over him, a fine pulverized powder from the shelling, dust in his hair and eyes and dust gritty in his teeth, and now he lifted his face to the rain and licked his lips and could taste the dirt on his face and knew that he would remember that too, the last moment at Gettysburg, the taste of raw earth in the cold and blowing dark, the touch of cold rain, the blaze of lightning.

After a while brother Tom found him, sitting in the rain, and sat with him and shared the darkness and the rain. Chamberlain remembered using the boy to plug a hole in the line, stopping the hole with his own brother's body like a warm bloody cork, and Chamberlain looked at himself. It was so natural and clear, the right thing to do: fill the gap with the body of my brother. Therefore Tom would have to go, and Chamberlain told himself: Run the boy away from you, because if he stays with you he'll die. He stared at the boy in the darkness, felt an incredible love, reached out to touch him, stopped himself.

Tom was saying, "I guess you got to hand it to them, the way they came up that hill."

Chamberlain nodded. He was beginning to feel very strange, stuffed and strange.

"But we stood up to them. They couldn't break us," Tom said.

"No."

"Well, nobody ever said they wasn't good soldiers. Well, they're Americans anyway, even if they are Rebs."

"Yes," Chamberlain said.

"Thing I cannot understand. Thing I never will understand. How can they fight so hard, them Johnnies, and all for slavery?"

Chamberlain raised his head. He had forgotten the Cause. When the guns began firing he had forgotten it completely. It seemed very strange now to think of morality, or that minister long ago, or the poor runaway black. He looked out across the dark field, could see nothing but the yellow lights and outlines of black bodies stark in the lightning.

Tom said, "When you ask them prisoners, they never talk about slavery. But, Lawrence, how do you explain that? What else is the war about?"

Chamberlain shook his head.

"If it weren't for the slaves, there'd never have been no war, now would there?"

"No," Chamberlain said.

"Well then, I don't care how much political fast-talking you hear, that's what it's all about and that's what them fellers died for, and I tell you, Lawrence, I don't understand it at all."

"No," Chamberlain said. He was thinking of Kilrain: *no divine spark.* Animal meat: the Killer Angels.

Out in the field nearby they were laying out bodies, row after row, the feet all even and the toes pointing upward like rows of black leaves on the border of a garden. He saw again the bitter face of Kilrain, but Chamberlain did not hate the gentlemen, could not think of them as gentlemen. He felt instead an extraordinary admiration. It was as if they were his own men who had come up the hill and he had been with them as they came, and he had made it across the stone wall to victory, but they had died. He felt a violent pity. He said slowly, in memory of Kilrain, "Well, they're all equal now."

"In the sight of God, anyways."

"Yes," Chamberlain said. "In the sight of God."

Tom stood up. "Better get moving, Lawrence, there's a big rain coming."

Chamberlain rose, but he was not yet ready to go.

Tom said, "Do you think they'll attack again?"

Chamberlain nodded. They were not yet done. He felt an appalling thrill. They would fight again, and when they came he would be behind another stone wall waiting for them, and he would stay there until he died or until it ended, and he was looking forward to it with an incredible eagerness, as you wait for the great music to begin again after the silence. He shook his head, amazed at himself. He thought: have to come back to this place when the war is over. Maybe then I'll understand it.

The rain was much heavier now. He put on the stolen cavalry hat and blinked upward into the black sky. He thought: it was my privilege to be here today. He thanked God for the honor. Then he went back to his men.

The light rain went on falling on the hills above Gettysburg, but it was only the overture to the great storm to come. Out of the black night it came at last, cold and wild and flooded with lightning. The true rain came in a monster wind, and the storm broke in blackness over the hills and the bloody valley; the sky opened along the ridge and the vast water thundered down, drowning the fires, flooding the red creeks, washing the rocks and the grass and the white bones of the dead, cleansing the earth and soaking it thick and rich with water and wet again with clean cold rainwater, driving the blood deep into the earth, to grow again with the roots toward Heaven.

It rained all that night. The next day was Saturday, the Fourth of July.

"Thus ended the great American Civil War, which must upon the whole be considered the noblest and least avoidable of all the great mass conflicts of which till then there was record."

—Winston Churchill,
A History of the English-Speaking Peoples

AFTERWORD

ROBERT EDWARD LEE

In August he asks to be relieved of command. Of the battle he says:

> No blame can be attached to the army for its failure to accomplish what was projected by me. . . . I alone am to blame, in perhaps expecting too much of its prowess and valor . . . could I have forseen that the attack on the last day would fail, I should certainly have tried some other course . . . but I do not know what better course I could have pursued.

His request is not accepted, although he cites his poor health, and he serves until the end of the war. He never again attempts a Napoleonic assault. When the war is over, he believes that the issue has been settled by combat, that God has passed judgment. He lays down arms, asks his men to do the same. His great prestige brings a peace which might not otherwise have been possible. He asks Congress for pardon; it is never given. Dies of heart disease in 1870, perhaps the most beloved General in the history of American war.

JAMES LONGSTREET

That winter he requests relief from command, on the ground that he no longer believes the South can win the war. Lee prevails upon him to stay. He is wounded severely in the Wilderness, 1864, but returns to be Lee's most dependable soldier, his right hand until the end at Appomattox.

After the war he makes two great mistakes. First, he becomes a Republican, attempts to join with old comrade Grant in rebuilding the South. For this he is branded a turncoat, within two years of the end of the war is being referred to by Southern newspapers as "the most hated man in the South."

Second, as time passes and it becomes slowly apparent that the war was lost at Gettysburg, Longstreet gives as his opinion what he believes to be true: that the battle was lost by Robert E. Lee. This occurs long after Lee's death, when Lee has become the symbol of all that is fine and noble in the Southern cause. The South does not forgive Longstreet the insult to Lee's name. At the great reunion, years later, of the Army of Northern Virginia, Longstreet is not even invited, but he comes anyway, stubborn to the end, walks down the aisle in his old gray uniform, stars of a general on his collar, and is received by an enormous ovation by the men, with tears and an embrace from Jefferson Davis.

His theories on defensive warfare are generations ahead of his time. The generals of Europe are still ordering massed assaults against fortified positions long years after his death, in 1904, at the age of eighty-three.

RICHARD EWELL

Serves with courage until the end, but as a corps commander he is fated never to achieve distinction. Of the Battle of Gettysburg he is later to remark: "It took a great many mistakes to lose that battle. And I myself made most of them."

AMBROSE POWELL HILL

Never to take his place in the Richmond society he so dearly loved, so richly deserved. Five days before Appomattox, at the Battle of Five Forks, he is killed by a sniper's bullet.

JOHN BELL HOOD

Loses not the arm but the use of it; it remains withered within his pinned sleeve for the rest of his days. Complains bitterly about the handling of the army at Gettysburg, is later given a command of his own: the Army of Tennessee. Defeated in Atlanta by Sherman, he spends much of the rest of his life justifying his actions in the field.

DORSEY PENDER

His wound grows steadily worse. An operation is performed within the month, at Staunton, but he begins to hemorrhage. The leg is amputated. He dies within the month. His wife attributes his death to the judgment of God.

ISAAC TRIMBLE

Wounded, is left behind to be captured by the enemy. Loses his leg, survives the war. Of the charge at Gettysburg he says: "If the men I had the honor to command that day could not take that position, all Hell couldn't take it."

JOHNSTON PETTIGREW

Survives the charge at Gettysburg with only a minor wound in the hand. Is shot to death ten days later in a delaying action guarding the retreat across the Potomac.

GEORGE PICKETT

His Division is virtually destroyed. No field officer is unhurt. Of the thirteen colonels in his command that day seven are dead, six are wounded. His casualties exceed 60 percent. The famous Charge of the Light Brigade, in comparison, suffered casualties of approximately 40 percent. Pickett survives to great glory, but he broods on the loss. When the war is over he happens one day on John Singleton Mosby, on the way to see Robert Lee, and together they visit the old man. The meeting is, in Mosby's words, "singularly cold." After it is over, Pickett comes outside and says bitterly: "That man destroyed my Division."

JUBAL EARLY

Serves until near the end of the war, when Lee finds it necessary to relieve him because of complaints against him by citizens he has offended. His conduct after the war is notable for two episodes: he becomes the Southern officer most involved in trying to prove that Longstreet was responsible for the loss at Gettysburg, and he becomes the central figure in the infamous Louisiana lottery, which cost thousands of Southerners thousands of dollars.

ARTHUR FREMANTLE

Returns to England after three months in the Confederacy and writes a book on his experience, which is published in the South three months before the end of the war. It is a very readable and entertaining book, which predicts a certain Southern victory.

HARRISON

He vanishes from Longstreet's records. Years after the war Moxley Sorrel attends a play, notices something vaguely familiar about one of the actors, recognizes Harrison. He goes backstage for a moment, they speak for a moment, but Sorrel is a gentleman and Harrison is a player, and there is no further connection. Nothing else of Harrison is known.

JOHN BUFORD

Never to receive recognition for his part in choosing the ground and holding it, and in so doing saving not only the battle but perhaps the war, he survives the summer but is weakened by wounds. In December of that year he goes down with pneumonia, and dies of it.

WINFIELD SCOTT HANCOCK

Survives the wound at Gettysburg. When the war ends it is found that his Second Corps captured more prisoners, more colors, and suffered more casualties than the entire rest of the Army of the Potomac. An enormously popular man all his life, in 1880 he runs for the Presidency on the Democratic ticket, against Garfield, but the country has had two terms of Grant and is weary of Generals in high office, and so he is defeated, retires from public life. The package Lew Armistead sent Almira Hancock was Armistead's personal Bible.

JOSHUA LAWRENCE CHAMBERLAIN

In August he is given a brigade. Shortly thereafter he is so badly wounded, shot through both hips, that he is not expected to live. But he returns to become one of the most remarkable soldiers in American history. Wounded six times. Cited for bravery in action four times. Promoted to Brigadier General by special order of Ulysses Grant for heroism at Petersburg. Breveted Major General for heroism at Five Forks. He is the officer chosen by Grant from all other Northern officers to have the honor of receiving the Southern surrender at Appomattox, where he startles the world by calling his troops to attention to salute the defeated South. He is given first place in the last Grand Review in Washington. For his day at Little Round Top he is to receive the Congressional Medal of Honor.

In Maine he is elected Governor by the largest majority in the history of the state and returned to office three times, where he alienates political friends by refusing to agree to the impeachment of Andrew Johnson.

In 1876, elected President of Bowdoin University, where he attempts to modernize the school, introducing courses in science, de-emphasizing religion, and becomes involved in student demonstrations over the question of ROTC. Receives medal of honor from France for distinguished efforts in international education. When he retires from Bowdoin he has taught every subject in the curriculum except mathematics.

Dies of his wounds, June 1914, at the age of eighty-three.

About the Author

Michael Shaara was born in 1928 in Jersey City, New Jersey. After graduating from Rutgers University in 1951, he served as a paratrooper in the 82nd Airborne Division, was an amateur boxer, and a police officer. In 1960 he became a professor of creative writing at Florida State University, where he won a faculty-wide award for excellence in teaching. His writing career included the publication of some seventy short stories, beginning in the early 1950s in the heyday of science-fiction publications such as *Astounding* and *Galaxy*. Subsequent stories were published through the early 1970s in *The Saturday Evening Post, Playboy, Redbook, Cosmopolitan,* and others. His first novel, *The Broken Place* was published in 1968. Other novels include *The Herald* and *For Love of the Game* (published after his death).

Michael Shaara died in 1988 at the age of fifty-nine.